DEAN
KOONTZ
3 COMPLETE NOVELS

DEAN KOONTZ

3 COMPLETE NOVELS

THE HOUSE
OF THUNDER

SHADOWFIRES

MIDNIGHT

G. P. PUTNAM'S SONS NEW YORK

G. P. PUTNAM'S SONS
Publishers Since 1838
Published by the Penguin Group
Penguin Group (USA) Inc., 375 Hudson Street, New York, New York 10014, USA
Penguin Group (Canada), 90 Eglinton Avenue East, Suite 700, Toronto, Ontario M4P 2Y3, Canada
(a division of Pearson Penguin Canada Inc.)
Penguin Books Ltd, 80 Strand, London WC2R 0RL, England
Penguin Ireland, 25 St Stephen's Green, Dublin 2, Ireland (a division of Penguin Books Ltd)
Penguin Group (Australia), 250 Camberwell Road, Camberwell, Victoria 3124, Australia
(a division of Pearson Australia Group Pty Ltd)
Penguin Books India Pvt Ltd, 11 Community Centre, Panchsheel Park, New Delhi–110 017, India
Penguin Group (NZ), 67 Apollo Drive, Rosedale, North Shore 0632, New Zealand
(a division of Pearson New Zealand Ltd)
Penguin Books (South Africa) (Pty) Ltd, 24 Sturdee Avenue, Rosebank, Johannesburg 2196, South Africa

Penguin Books Ltd, Registered Offices: 80 Strand, London WC2R 0RL, England

The House of Thunder copyright © 1982 by Nkui, Inc.
Shadowfires copyright © 1987 by Nkui, Inc.
Midnight copyright © 1989 by Nkui, Inc.
The House of Thunder and *Shadowfires* were originally published under the pseudonym Leigh Nichols.

Library of Congress Cataloging-in-Publication Data

Koontz, Dean R. (Dean Ray), date.
  [Novels. Selections.]
  Three complete novels / Dean Koontz.
    p.   cm.
  Contents: The house of thunder—Shadowfires—Midnight.
  ISBN 0-399-14125-1
  1. Horror tales, America.   I. Title.
  PS3561.O55A6   1996   95-38315 CIP
  813'.54—dc20

Printed in the United States of America
10 9 8 7 6 5 4 3 2 1

Book design by Patrice Sheridan

This is a work of fiction. Names, characters, places, and incidents either are the product of the author's imagination
or are used fictitiously, and any resemblance to actual persons, living or dead, businesses, companies, events, or
locales is entirely coincidental.

While the author has made every effort to provide accurate telephone numbers and Internet addresses at the time
of publication, neither the publisher nor the author assumes any responsibility for errors, or for changes that occur
after publication. Further, the publisher does not have any control over and does not assume any responsibility for
author or third-party websites or their content.

CONTENTS

THE HOUSE
OF THUNDER

This book is for Gerda,
as it surely should have been
from the start.

FEAR COMES QUIETLY . . .

The year was 1980—an ancient time,

so long ago and far away. . . .

1

WHEN SHE WOKE, SHE THOUGHT SHE WAS BLIND. SHE OPEN-
ed her eyes and could see only purple darkness, ominous and shapeless shadows
stirring within other shadows. Before she could panic, that gloom gave way to a
pale haze, and the haze resolved into a white, acoustic-tile ceiling.

She smelled fresh bed linens. Antiseptics. Disinfectants. Rubbing alcohol.

She turned her head, and pain flashed the length of her forehead, as if an electric
shock had snapped through her skull from temple to temple. Her eyes immediately
swam out of focus. When her vision cleared again, she saw that she was in a
hospital room.

She could not remember being admitted to a hospital. She didn't even know
the name of it or in what city it was located.

What's wrong with me?

She raised one dismayingly weak arm, put a hand to her brow, and discovered
a bandage over half of her forehead. Her hair was quite short, too. Hadn't she
worn it long and full?

She had insufficient strength to keep her arm raised; she let it drop back to the
mattress.

She couldn't raise her left arm at all, for it was taped to a heavy board and
pierced by a needle. She was being fed intravenously: the chrome IV rack, with
its dangling bottle of glucose, stood beside the bed.

For a moment she closed her eyes, certain that she was only dreaming. When
she looked again, however, the room was still there, unchanged: white ceiling,
white walls, a green tile floor, pale yellow drapes drawn back at the sides of the
large window. Beyond the glass, there were tall evergreens of some kind and a
cloudy sky with only a few small patches of blue. There was another bed, but it
was empty; she had no roommate.

The side rails on her own bed were raised to prevent her from falling to the
floor. She felt as helpless as a baby in a crib.

She realized she didn't know her name. Or her age. Or anything else about herself.

She strained against the blank wall in her mind, attempting to topple it and release the memories imprisoned on the other side, but she had no success; the wall stood, inviolate. Like a blossom of frost, fear opened icy petals in the pit of her stomach. She tried harder to remember, but she had no success.

Amnesia. Brain damage.

Those dreaded words landed with the force of hammer blows in her mind. Evidently, she had been in an accident and had sustained a serious head injury. She considered the grim prospect of permanent mental disorientation, and she shuddered.

Suddenly, however, unexpected and unsought, her name came to her. Susan. Susan Thorton. She was thirty-two years old.

The anticipated flood of recollections turned out to be just a trickle. She could recall nothing more than her name and age. Although she probed insistently at the darkness in her mind, she couldn't remember where she lived. How did she earn her living? Was she married? Did she have any children? Where had she been born? Where had she gone to school? What foods did she like? What was her favorite kind of music? She could find no answers to either important or trivial questions.

Amnesia. Brain damage.

Fear quickened her heartbeat. Then, mercifully, she remembered that she had been on vacation in Oregon. She didn't know where she had come from; she didn't know what job she would return to once her vacation came to an end; but at least she knew where she was. Somewhere in Oregon. The last thing she could recall was a beautiful mountain highway. An image of that landscape came to her in vivid detail. She had been driving through a pine forest, not far from the sea, listening to the radio, enjoying a clear blue morning. She drove through a sleepy village of stone and clapboard houses, then passed a couple of slow-moving logging trucks, then had the road all to herself for a few miles, and then . . . then . . .

Nothing. After that, she had awakened, confused and blurry-eyed, in the hospital.

"Well, well. Hello there."

Susan turned her head, searching for the person who had spoken. Her eyes slipped out of focus again, and a new dull pain pulsed at the base of her skull.

"How are you feeling? You *do* look pale, but after what you've been through, that's certainly to be expected, isn't it? Of course it is. Of course."

The voice belonged to a nurse who was approaching the bed from the direction of the open door. She was a pleasantly plump, gray-haired woman with warm brown eyes and a wide smile. She wore a pair of white-framed glasses on a beaded chain around her neck; at the moment, the glasses hung unused on her matronly bosom.

Susan tried to speak. Couldn't.

Even the meager effort of straining for words made her so light-headed that she thought she might pass out. Her extreme weakness scared her.

The nurse reached the bed and smiled reassuringly. "I knew you'd come out of of it, honey. I just knew it. Some people around here weren't so sure as I was. But I knew you had moxie." She pushed the call button on the headboard of the bed.

Susan tried to speak again, and this time she managed to make a sound, though it was only a low and meaningless gurgle in the back of her throat. Suddenly she wondered if she would ever speak again. Perhaps she would be condemned to making grunting, gibbering animal noises for the rest of her life. Sometimes, brain damage resulted in a loss of speech, didn't it? *Didn't it?*

A drum was booming loudly and relentlessly in her head. She seemed to be turning on a carousel, faster and faster, and she wished she could put a stop to the room's nauseating movement.

The nurse must have seen the panic in Susan's eyes, for she said, "Easy now. Easy, kid. Everything'll be all right." She checked the IV drip, then lifted Susan's right wrist to time her pulse.

My God, Susan thought, if I can't speak, maybe I can't *walk*, either.

She tried to move her legs under the sheets. She didn't seem to have any feeling in them; they were even more numb and leaden than her arms.

The nurse let go of her wrist, but Susan clutched at the sleeve of the woman's white uniform and tried desperately to speak.

"Take your time," the nurse said gently.

But Susan knew she didn't have much time. She was teetering on the edge of unconsciousness again. The pounding pain in her head was accompanied by a steadily encroaching ring of darkness that spread inward from the edges of her vision.

A doctor in a white lab coat entered the room, apparently in answer to the call button that the nurse had pushed. He was a husky, dour-faced man, about fifty, with thick black hair combed straight back from his deeply lined face.

Susan looked beseechingly at him as he approached the bed, and she said, *Are my legs paralyzed?*

For an instant she thought she had actually spoken those words aloud, but then she realized she still hadn't regained her voice. Before she could try again, the rapidly expanding darkness reduced her vision to a small spot, a mere dot, then a pinpoint.

Darkness.

She dreamed. It was a bad dream, very bad, a nightmare.

For at least the two-hundredth time, she dreamed that she was in the House of Thunder again, lying in a pool of warm blood.

2

WHEN SUSAN WOKE AGAIN, HER HEADACHE WAS GONE. Her vision was clear, and she was no longer dizzy.

Night had fallen. Her room was softly lighted, but only featureless blackness lay beyond the window.

The IV rack had been taken away. Her needle-marked, discolored arm looked pathetically thin against the white sheet.

She turned her head and saw the husky, dour-faced man in the white lab coat. He was standing beside the bed, staring down at her. His brown eyes possessed a peculiar, disturbing power; they seemed to be looking *into* her rather than at her, as if he were carefully examining her innermost secrets, yet they were eyes that revealed nothing whatsoever of his own feelings; they were as flat as painted glass.

"What's . . . happened . . . to me?" Susan asked.

She could speak. Her voice was faint, raspy, and rather difficult to understand, but she was not reduced to a mute existence by a stroke or by some other severe brain injury, which was what she had feared at first.

She was still weak, however. Her meager resources were noticeably depleted even by the act of speaking a few words at a whisper.

"Where . . . am I?" she asked, voice cracking. Her throat burned with the passage of each rough syllable.

The doctor didn't respond to her questions right away. He picked up the bed's power control, which dangled on a cord that was wrapped around the side rail, and he pushed one of the four buttons. The upper end of the bed rose, tilting Susan into a sitting position. He put down the controls and half filled a glass with cold water from a metal carafe that stood on a yellow plastic tray on the nightstand.

"Sip it slowly," he said. "It's been a while since you've taken any food or liquid orally."

She accepted the water. It was indescribably delicious. It soothed her irritated throat.

When she had finished drinking, he took the glass from her and returned it to the nightstand. He unclipped a penlight from the breast pocket of his lab coat, leaned close, and examined her eyes. His own eyes remained flat and unreadable beneath bushy eyebrows that were knit together in what seemed to be a perpetual frown.

While she waited for him to finish the examination, she tried to move her legs under the covers. They were weak and rubbery and still somewhat numb, but they moved at her command. She wasn't paralyzed after all.

When the doctor finished examining her eyes, he held his right hand in front of her face, just a few inches away from her. "Can you see my hand?"

"Sure," she said. Her voice was faint and quavery, but at least it was no longer raspy or difficult to understand.

His voice was deep, colored by a vague guttural accent that Susan could not quite identify. He said, "How many fingers am I holding up?"

"Three," she said, aware that he was testing her for signs of a concussion.

"And now—how many?"

"Two."

"And now?"

"Four."

He nodded approval, and the sharp creases in his forehead softened a bit. His eyes still probed at her with an intensity that made her uncomfortable. "Do you know your name?"

"Yes. I'm Susan Thorton."

"That's right. Middle name?"

"Kathleen."

"Good. How old are you?"

"Thirty-two."

"Good. Very good. You seem clear-headed."

Her voice had become dry and scratchy again. She cleared her throat and said, "But that's just about *all* I'm able to remember."

He hadn't entirely relinquished his frown, and the lines in his broad, square face became sharply etched once more. "What do you mean?"

"Well, I can't remember where I live . . . or what kind of work I do . . . or whether I'm married . . . "

He studied her for a moment, then said, "You live in Newport Beach, California."

As soon as he mentioned the town, she could see her house: a cozy Spanish-style place with a red tile roof, white stucco walls, mullioned windows, tucked in among several tall palms. But no matter how hard she thought about it, the name of the street and the number of the house eluded her.

"You work for the Milestone Corporation in Newport," the doctor said.

"Milestone?" Susan said. She sensed a distant glimmer of memory in her mental fog.

The doctor looked down at her intensely.

"What's wrong?" she asked shakily. "Why are you staring like that?"

He blinked in surprise, then smiled somewhat sheepishly. Clearly, smiles did not come easily to him, and this one was strained. "Well . . . I'm concerned about you, of course. And I want to know what we're up against here. Temporary amnesia is to be expected in a case like this, and it can be easily treated. But if you're suffering from more than temporary amnesia, we'll have to change our entire approach. So you see, it's important for me to know whether the name Milestone means anything to you."

"Milestone," she said thoughtfully. "Yes, it's familiar. *Vaguely* familiar."

"You're a physicist at Milestone. You earned your doctorate at UCLA a few years ago, and you went to work at Milestone immediately thereafter."

"Ah," she said as the glimmer of memory grew brighter.

"We've learned a few things about you from the people at Milestone," he said. "You have no children. You aren't married; you never have been." He watched her as she tried to assimilate what he'd told her. "Is it starting to fall into place now?"

Susan sighed with relief. "Yes. To an extent, it is. Some of it's coming back to me . . . but not everything. Just random bits and pieces."

"It'll take time," he assured her. "After an injury like yours, you can't expect to recuperate overnight."

She had a lot of questions to ask him, but her curiosity was equaled by her bone-deep weariness and exceeded by her thirst. She slumped back against the pillows to catch her breath, and she asked for more water.

He poured only a third of a glass this time. As before, he warned her to take small sips.

She didn't need to be warned. Already, after having consumed nothing more than a few ounces of water, she felt slightly bloated, as if she'd eaten a full-course dinner.

When she had finished drinking, she said, "I don't know your name."

"Oh. I'm sorry. It's Viteski. Dr. Leon Viteski."

"I've been wondering about your accent," she said. "I do detect one, don't I? Viteski . . . Is your heritage Polish?"

He looked uncomfortable, and his gaze slid away from hers. "Yes. I was a war orphan. I came to this country in 1946, when I was seventeen. My uncle took me in." The spontaneity had gone out of his voice; he sounded as if he were reciting a carefully memorized speech. "I've lost most of my Polish accent, but I suppose I'll never shake it entirely."

Apparently, she had touched a sore spot. The mere mention of his accent made him strangely defensive.

He hurried on, speaking faster than he had spoken before, as if he were eager to change the subject. "I'm chief physician here, head of the medical staff. By the way . . . do you have any idea where 'here' is?"

"Well, I remember that I was on vacation in Oregon, though I can't remember exactly where I was going. So this must be somewhere in Oregon, right?"

"Yes. The town's Willawauk. About eight thousand people live here. It's the county seat. Willawauk County is mostly rural, and this is its only hospital. Not a huge facility. It's just four floors, two hundred and twenty beds. But we're good. In fact I like to think we're better than a lot of more sophisticated big-city hospitals because we're able to give more personal attention to patients here. And personal attention often makes an enormous difference in the rate of recovery."

His voice contained no trace of pride or enthusiasm, as it ought to have, considering what he was saying. It was almost as flat and monotonous as the voice of a machine.

Or is it just me? she wondered. Is it just that my perceptions are out of whack?

In spite of her weariness and in spite of the hammering that had just started up again inside her skull, she raised her head from the pillow and said, "Doctor, why am I here? What happened to me?"

"You don't recall anything about the accident?"

"No."

"Your car's brakes failed. It was on an extremely twisty stretch of road, two miles south of the Viewtop turnoff."

"Viewtop?"

"That's where you were headed. You had a confirmation of your reservation in your purse."

"It's a hotel?"

"Yes. The Viewtop Inn. A resort. A big, rambling old place. It was built fifty or sixty years ago, and I'd guess it's more popular now than it was then. A real get-away-from-it-all hotel."

As Dr. Viteski spoke, Susan slowly remembered. She closed her eyes and could see the resort in a series of colorful photographs that had illustrated an article in *Travel* magazine last February. She'd booked a room for part of her vacation as soon as she'd read about the place, for she had been charmed by the pictures of the inn's wide verandas, many-gabled roofline, pillared lobby, and extensive gardens.

"Anyway," Viteski said, "your brakes failed, and you lost control of your car. You went over the edge of a steep embankment, rolled twice, and slammed up against a couple of trees."

"Good God!"

"Your car was a mess." He shook his head. "It's a miracle you weren't killed."

She gingerly touched the bandage that covered half her forehead. "How bad is this?"

Viteski's thick, dark eyebrows drew together again, and it suddenly seemed to Susan that his expression was theatrical, not genuine.

"It isn't too serious," he said. "A wide gash. You bled heavily, and it healed rather slowly at first. But the stitches are scheduled to come out tomorrow or the day after, and I really don't believe there'll be any permanent scarring. We took considerable care to make sure the wound was neatly sewn."

"Concussion?" she asked.

"Yes. But only a mild one, certainly nothing severe enough to explain why you were in a coma."

She had been growing more tired and headachy by the minute. Now she was abruptly alert again. "Coma?"

Viteski nodded. "We did a brain scan, of course, but we didn't find any indication of an embolism. There wasn't any swelling of brain tissue, either. And there was no buildup of fluid in the skull, no signs whatsoever of cranial pressure. You did take a hard knock on the head, which surely had *something* to do with the coma, but we can't be much more specific than that, I'm afraid. Contrary to what the television medical dramas would have you believe, modern medicine doesn't always have an answer for everything. What's important is that you've come out of the coma with no apparent long-term effects. I know those holes in your memory are frustrating, even frightening, but I'm confident that, given sufficient time, they'll heal over, too."

He still sounds as if he's reciting well-rehearsed lines from a script, Susan thought uneasily.

But she didn't dwell on that thought, for this time Viteski's odd manner of speech was less interesting than what he had said. *Coma.* That word chilled her. *Coma.*

"How long was I unconscious?" she asked.

"Twenty-two days."

She stared at him, *gaped* at him in disbelief.

"It's true," he said.

She shook her head. "No. It can't be true."

She had always been firmly in control of her life. She was a meticulous planner who tried to prepare for every eventuality. Her private life was conducted with much the same scientific methodology that had made it possible for her to earn her doctorate in particle physics more than a year ahead of other students who were her age. She disliked surprises, and she disliked having to depend on anyone but herself, and she was virtually terrified of being helpless. Now Viteski was telling her that she had spent twenty-two days in a state of utter helplessness, totally dependent on others, and that realization deeply disturbed her.

What if she had never come out of the coma?

Or worse yet—what if she had awakened to find herself paralyzed from the neck down, condemned to a life of utter dependency? What if she'd had to be fed and dressed and taken to the bathroom by paid attendants for the rest of her life?

She shivered.

"No," she told Viteski. "I can't have lost that much time. I *can't* have. There must be some mistake."

"Surely you've noticed how thin you are," Viteski said. "You've dropped fifteen pounds or more."

She held up her arms. Like two sticks. Earlier, she had realized how frightfully thin they looked, but she hadn't wanted to think about what that meant.

"You've been getting fluids intravenously, of course," Dr. Viteski said. "Otherwise, you'd have died of dehydration long ago. There's been some nourishment in the fluids you've gotten, primarily glucose. But you've had no real food—no solid food, that is—in more than three weeks."

Susan was five-foot-five, and her ideal weight (considering her delicate bone structure) was about a hundred and ten pounds. At the moment she weighed between ninety and ninety-five, and the effect of the loss was dramatic. She put her hands on the blanket, and even through the covers she could feel how sharp and bony her hips were.

"Twenty-two days," she said wonderingly.

At last, reluctantly, she accepted the unacceptable.

When she stopped resisting the truth, her headache and her extreme weariness returned. As limp as a bundle of wet straw, she fell back against the pillows.

"That's enough for now," Viteski said. "I think I've let you talk too much. You've tired yourself unnecessarily. Right now you need plenty of rest."

"Rest?" she said. "No. For God's sake, I've *been* resting for twenty-two days!"

"There's no genuine rest when you're in a coma," Viteski said. "It isn't the same thing as normal sleep. Rebuilding your strength and stamina is going to take a while."

He picked up the control switch, pushed one of the four buttons, and lowered the head of the bed.

"No," Susan said, suddenly panicky. "Wait. Please, wait a minute."

He ignored her protests and put the bed all the way down.

She hooked her hands around the rails and tried to pull herself into a sitting position, but for the moment she was too exhausted to lift herself.

"You don't expect me to go to sleep, do you?" she asked, although she couldn't deny that she needed sleep. Her eyes were grainy, hot, and tired. Her eyelids felt as heavy as lead.

"Sleep is precisely what you need most," he assured her.

"But I *can't.*"

"You look as if you can," he said. "You're plainly worn out. And no wonder."

"No, no. I mean, I don't *dare* go to sleep. What if I don't wake up?"

"Of course you will."

"What if I slip into another coma?"

"You won't."

Frustrated by his inability to understand her fear, Susan gritted her teeth and said, "But what if I *do*?"

"Listen, you can't go through life being afraid to sleep," Viteski said slowly, patiently, as if he were reasoning with a small child. "Just relax. You're out of the coma. You're going to be fine. Now, it's quite late, and I need a bite of dinner and some sleep myself. Just relax. All right? Relax."

If this is his best bedside manner, Susan thought, then what is he like when he isn't *trying* to be nice?

He went to the door.

She wanted to cry out: *Don't leave me alone!* But her strong streak of self-reliance would not permit her to behave like a frightened child. She didn't want to lean on Dr. Viteski or on anyone else.

"Get your rest," he said. "Everything'll look better in the morning."

He turned out the overhead light.

Shadows sprang up as if they were living creatures that had been hiding under the furniture and behind the baseboard. Although Susan couldn't remember ever having been afraid of the dark, she was uneasy now; her heartbeat accelerated.

The only illumination was the cold, shimmering fluorescence that came through the open door from the hospital corridor, and the soft glow from a small lamp that stood on a table in one corner of the room.

Standing in the doorway, Viteski was starkly silhouetted by the hall light. His face was no longer visible; he looked like a black paper cutout. "Good night," he said.

He closed the door behind him, shutting out the corridor light altogether.

There was only one lamp now, no more than a single fifteen-watt bulb. The darkness crowded closer to Susan, laid long fingers across the bed.

She was alone.

She looked at the other bed, which was shrouded in shadows like banners of black crepe; it reminded her of a funeral bier. She wished ardently for a roommate.

This isn't right, she thought. I shouldn't be left alone like this. Not after I've just come out of a coma. Surely there ought to be somebody in attendance—a nurse, an orderly, *somebody*.

Her eyes were heavy, incredibly heavy.

No, she told herself angrily. I mustn't fall asleep. Not until I'm absolutely sure that my nice little nap won't turn into another twenty-two-day coma.

For a few minutes Susan struggled against the ever-tightening embrace of sleep, clenching her fists so that her fingernails dug painfully into her palms. But her eyes burned and ached, and at last she decided that it wouldn't hurt to close them for just a minute, just long enough to rest them. She was sure she could close her eyes without going to sleep. Of course she could. No problem.

She fell over the edge of sleep as if she were a stone dropping into a bottomless well.

She dreamed.

In the dream, she was lying on a hard, damp floor in a vast, dark, cold place.

She wasn't alone. *They* were with her. She ran, staggering blindly across the light-less room, down narrow corridors of stone, fleeing from a nightmare that was, in fact, a memory of a real place, a real time, a real horror that she had lived through when she was nineteen.

The House of Thunder.

3

THE FOLLOWING MORNING, A FEW MINUTES AFTER SUSAN woke, the plump, gray-haired nurse appeared. As before, her glasses were sus-pended from a beaded chain around her neck, and they bobbled on her motherly bosom with each step she took. She slipped a thermometer under Susan's tongue, took hold of Susan's wrist, timed the pulse, then put on her glasses to read the thermometer. As she worked, she kept up a steady line of chatter. Her name was Thelma Baker. She said she'd always known that Susan would pull through even-tually. She had been a nurse for thirty-five years, first in San Francisco and then here in Oregon, and she had seldom been wrong about a patient's prospects for recovery. She said she was such a natural-born nurse that she sometimes won-dered if she was the reincarnation of a woman who had been a first-rate nurse in a previous life. "Of course, I'm not much good at anything *else*," she said with a hearty laugh. "I'm sure as the devil not much of a housekeeper!" She said she wasn't very good at managing money, either; to hear her tell it, just balancing the checkbook every month was a Herculean task. Wasn't much good at marriage, she said. Two husbands, two divorces, no children. Couldn't cook very well, either. Hated to sew; *loathed* it. "But I'm a darned good nurse and proud of it," she said emphatically, more than once, always with that charming smile that involved her brown eyes as well as her mouth, a smile that showed how much she truly did enjoy her work.

Susan liked the woman. Ordinarily, she had little or no patience with nonstop talkers. But Mrs. Baker's chatter was amusing, frequently self-deprecating, and oddly soothing.

"Hungry?" Mrs. Baker asked.

"Starved." She had awakened with a ravenous appetite.

"You'll start taking solid food today," Mrs. Baker said. "A soft diet, of course."

Even as the nurse spoke, a young, blond, male orderly arrived with breakfast: cherry-flavored Jell-O, unbuttered toast with a single spoonful of grape jelly, and a thin, chalky-looking tapioca. To Susan, no other meal had ever been so ap-pealing. But she was disappointed by the size of the portions, and she said as much.

"It doesn't look like a lot," Mrs. Baker said, "but believe me, honey, you'll be stuffed before you've eaten half of it. Remember, you haven't taken solid food in three weeks. Your stomach's all shrunk up. It'll be a while before you'll have a normal appetite."

Mrs. Baker left to attend to other patients, and before long Susan realized that the nurse was right. Although there wasn't a great deal of food on the tray, and although even this simple fare tasted like ambrosia, it was more than she could eat.

As she ate, she thought about Dr. Viteski. She still felt that he had been wrong to let her alone, unattended. In spite of Mrs. Baker's sprightly manner, the hospital still seemed cold, unfriendly.

When she could eat no more, she wiped her mouth with the paper napkin, pushed the rolling bed table out of her way—and suddenly had the feeling she was being watched. She glanced up.

He was standing in the open door: a tall, elegant man of about thirty-eight. He was wearing dark shoes, dark trousers, a white lab coat, a white shirt, and a green tie, and he was holding a clipboard in his left hand. His face was arresting, sensitive; his superbly balanced features looked as if they had been carefully chiseled from stone by a gifted sculptor. His blue eyes were as bright as polished gems, and they provided an intriguing contrast to his lustrous black hair, which he wore full and combed straight back from his face and forehead.

"Miss Thorton," he said, "I'm delighted to see you sitting up, awake and aware." He came to the bed. His smile was even nicer than Thelma Baker's. "I'm your physician. Doctor McGee. Jeffrey McGee."

He extended his hand to her, and she took it. It was a dry, hard, strong hand, but his touch was light and gentle.

"I thought Dr. Viteski was my physician."

"He's chief of the hospital medical staff," McGee said, "but I'm in charge of your case." His voice had a reassuringly masculine timbre, yet it was pleasingly soft and soothing. "I was the admitting physician when you were brought into the emergency room."

"But yesterday, Dr. Viteski—"

"Yesterday was my day off," McGee said. "I take two days off from my private practice every week, but only one day off from my hospital rounds—only *one* day, mind you—so of course you chose that day. After you laid there like a stone for twenty-two days, after you worried me sick for twenty-two days, you had to come out of your coma when I wasn't here." He shook his head, pretending to be both astonished and hurt. "I didn't even find out about it until this morning." He frowned at her with mock disapproval. "Now, Miss Thorton," he teased, "if there are going to be any medical miracles involving my patients, I insist on being present when they occur, so that I can take the credit and bask in the glory. Understood?"

Susan smiled up at him, surprised by his lighthearted manner. "Yes, Dr. McGee. I understand."

"Good. Very good. I'm glad we got that straightened out." He grinned. "How are you feeling this morning?"

"Better," she said.

"Ready for an evening of dancing and bar-hopping?"

"Maybe tomorrow."

"It's a date." He glanced at her breakfast tray. "I see you've got an appetite."

"I tried to eat everything, but I couldn't."

"That's what Orson Welles said."

Susan laughed.

"You did pretty well," he said, indicating the tray. "You've got to start off with small, frequent meals. That's to be expected. Don't worry too much about regaining your strength. Before you know it, you'll be making a pig of yourself, and you'll be well along the road to recovery. Feeling headachy this morning? Drowsy?"

"No. Neither."

"Let me take your pulse," he said, reaching for her hand.

"Mrs. Baker took it just before breakfast."

"I know. This is just an excuse to hold hands with you."

Susan laughed again. "You're different from most doctors."

"Do you think a physician should be businesslike, distant, somber, humorless?"

"Not necessarily."

"Do you think I should try to be more like Dr. Viteski?"

"Definitely not."

"He iz an *egg*-cellent doktor," McGee said, doing a perfect imitation of Viteski's accented voice.

"I'm sure he is. But I suspect you're even better."

"Thank you. The compliment is duly noted and has earned you a small discount off my final bill."

He was still holding her hand. He finally looked at his watch and took her pulse.

"Will I live?" she asked when he finished.

"No doubt about it. You're bouncing back fast." He continued to hold her hand as he said, "Seriously now, I think a little humor between doctor and patient is a good thing. I believe it helps the patient maintain a positive attitude, and a positive attitude speeds healing. But some people don't *want* a cheerful doctor. They want someone who acts as if the weight of the world is on his shoulders. It makes them feel more secure. So if my joking bothers you, I can tone it down or turn it off. The important thing is that you feel comfortable and confident about the care you're getting."

"You go right ahead and be as cheerful as you want," Susan said. "My spirits need lifting."

"There's no reason to be glum. The worst is behind you now."

He squeezed her hand gently before finally letting go of it.

To her surprise, Susan felt a tug of regret that he had released her hand so soon.

"Dr. Viteski tells me there are lapses in your memory," he said.

She frowned. "Fewer than there were yesterday. I guess it'll all come back to me sooner or later. But there are still a lot of holes."

"I want to talk with you about that. But first I've got to make my rounds. I'll come back in a couple of hours, and I'll help you prod your memory—if that's all right with you."

"Sure," she said.

"You rest."

"What else is there to do?"

"No tennis until further notice."

"Darn! I had a match scheduled with Mrs. Baker."

"You'll just have to cancel it."

"Yes, Dr. McGee."

Smiling, she watched him leave. He moved with self-assurance and with considerable natural grace.

He'd already had a positive influence on her. A simmering paranoia had been heating up slowly within her, but now she realized that her uneasiness had been entirely subjective in origin, a result of her weakness and disorientation; there was no rational justification for it. Dr. Viteski's odd behavior no longer seemed important, and the hospital no longer seemed the least bit threatening.

■ Half an hour later, when Mrs. Baker looked in on her again, Susan asked for a mirror then wished she hadn't. Her reflection revealed a pale, gaunt face. Her gray-green eyes were bloodshot and circled by dark, puffy flesh. In order to facilitate the treatment and bandaging of her gashed forehead, an emergency room orderly had clipped her long blond hair; he had hacked at it with no regard for her appearance. The result was a shaggy mess. Furthermore, after twenty-two days of neglect, her hair was greasy and tangled.

"My God, I look terrible!" she said.

"Of course you don't," Mrs. Baker said. "Just a bit washed out. There's no permanent damage. As soon as you gain back the weight you lost, your cheeks will fill in, and those bags under your eyes will go away."

"I've got to wash my hair."

"You wouldn't be able to walk into the bathroom and stand at the sink. Your legs would feel like rubber. Besides, you can't wash your hair until the bandages come off your head, and that won't be until at least tomorrow."

"No. Today. Now. My hair's oily, and my head itches. It's making me miserable, and that's not conducive to recuperation."

"This isn't a debate, honey. You can't win, so save your breath. All I can do is see that you get a dry wash."

"Dry wash? What's that?"

"Sprinkle some powder in your hair, let it soak up some of the oil, then brush it out," Mrs. Baker said. "That's what we did for you twice a week while you were in a coma."

Susan put one hand to her lank hair. "Will it help?"

"A little."

"Okay, I'll do it."

Mrs. Baker brought a can of powder and a brush.

"The luggage I had with me in the car," Susan said. "Did any of it survive the crash?"

"Sure. It's right over there, in the closet."

"Would you bring me my makeup case?"

Mrs. Baker grinned. "He *is* a handsome devil, isn't he? And so nice, too." She winked as she said, "He isn't married, either."

Susan blushed. "I don't know what you mean."

Mrs. Baker laughed gently and patted Susan's hand. "Don't be embarrassed, kid. I've never seen one of Dr. McGee's female patients who *didn't* try to look her best. Teenage girls get all fluttery when he's around. Young ladies like you get a certain unmistakable glint in their eyes. Even white-haired grannies, half crippled

with arthritis, twenty years older than me—*forty* years older than the doctor—
they all make themselves look nice for him, and looking nice makes them feel
better, so it's all sort of therapeutic."

■ Shortly before noon, Dr. McGee returned, pushing a stainless-steel cafeteria
cart that held two trays. "I thought we'd have lunch together while we talk
about your memory problems."

"A doctor having lunch with his patient?" she asked, amazed.

"We tend to be less formal here than in your city hospitals."

"Who pays for lunch?"

"You do, of course. We aren't *that* informal."

She grinned. "What's for lunch?"

"For me, a chicken-salad sandwich and apple pie. For you, unbuttered toast
and tapioca and—"

"Already, this is getting monotonous."

"Ah, but this time there's something more exotic than cherry Jell-O," he said.
"*Lime* Jell-O."

"I don't think my heart can stand it."

"And a small dish of canned peaches. Truly a gourmet spread." He pulled up
a chair, then lowered her bed as far as it would go, so they could talk comfortably
while they ate.

As he put her tray on the bed table and lifted the plastic cover from it, he blinked
at her and said, "You look nice and fresh."

"I look like death warmed over," she said.

"Not at all."

"Yes, I do."

"Your *tapioca* looks like death warmed over, but *you* look nice and fresh.
Remember, I'm the doctor, and you're the patient, and the patient must never,
never, never disagree with the doctor. Don't you know your medical etiquette? If
I say you look nice and fresh, then, by God, you look nice and fresh!"

Susan smiled and played along with him. "I see. How could I have been so
gauche?"

"You look nice and fresh, Susan."

"Why, thank you, Dr. McGee."

"That's much better."

She had "washed" her hair with talcum powder, had lightly applied some
makeup, and had put on lipstick. Thanks to a few drops of Murine, her eyes were
no longer bloodshot, though a yellowish tint of sickness colored the whites of
them. She had also changed from her hospital gown into a pair of blue silk pajamas
that had been in her luggage. She knew she looked far less than her best; however,
she looked at least a little better, and looking a little better made her feel a *lot*
better, just as Mrs. Baker had said it would.

While they ate lunch, they talked about the blank spots in Susan's memory,
trying to fill in the holes, which had been numerous and huge only yesterday, but
which were fewer and far smaller today. Upon waking this morning, she had found
that she could remember most things without effort.

She had been born and raised in suburban Philadelphia, in a pleasant, white,
two-story house on a maple-lined street of similar houses. Green lawns. Porch

swings. A block party every Fourth of July. Carolers at Christmas. An Ozzie and Harriet neighborhood.

"Sounds like an ideal childhood," McGee said.

Susan swallowed a bit of lime Jell-O, then said, "It was an ideal *setting* for an ideal childhood, but unfortunately it didn't turn out that way. I was a very lonely kid."

"When you were first admitted here," McGee said, "we tried to contact your family, but we couldn't find anyone to contact."

She told him about her parents, partly because she wanted to be absolutely sure that there were no holes in those memories, and partly because McGee was easy to talk to, and partly because she felt a strong need to talk after twenty-two days of silence and darkness. Her mother, Regina, had been killed in a traffic accident when Susan was only seven years old. The driver of a beer delivery truck had suffered a heart attack at the wheel, and the truck had run a red light, and Regina's Chevy had been in the middle of the intersection. Susan couldn't remember a great deal about her mother, but that lapse had nothing whatsoever to do with her own recent accident and amnesia. After all, she had known her mother for only seven years, and twenty-five years had passed since the beer truck had flattened the Chevy; sadly but inevitably, Regina had faded from Susan's memory in much the same way that an image fades from an old photograph that has been left too long in bright sunlight. However, she could remember her father clearly. Frank Thorton had been a tall, somewhat portly man who had owned a moderately successful men's clothing store, and Susan had loved him. She always knew that he loved her, too, even though he never told her that he did. He was quiet, soft-spoken, rather shy, a completely self-contained man who was happiest when he was alone in his den with just a good book and his pipe. Perhaps he would have been more forthcoming with a son than he had been with his daughter. He always was more at ease with men than with women, and raising a girl was undoubtedly an awkward proposition for him. He died of cancer ten years after Regina's passing, the summer after Susan graduated from high school. And so she had entered adulthood even more alone than she had been before.

Dr. McGee finished his chicken-salad sandwich, wiped his mouth with a paper napkin, and said, "No aunts, no uncles?"

"One aunt, one uncle. But both of them were strangers to me. No living grandparents. But you know something—having such a lonely childhood wasn't *entirely* a bad thing. I learned to be *very* self-reliant, and that's paid off over the years."

As McGee ate his apple pie, and as Susan nibbled at her canned peaches, they talked about her university years. She had done her undergraduate work at Briarstead College in Pennsylvania, then had gone to California and had earned both her master's and doctorate at UCLA. She recalled those years with perfect clarity, although she actually would have preferred to forget some of what had happened during her sophomore year at Briarstead.

"Is something wrong?" McGee asked, putting down a forkful of apple pie that had been halfway to his mouth.

She blinked. "Huh?"

"Your expression . . . " He frowned. "For a moment there, you looked as if you'd seen a ghost."

"Yeah. In a way I did." Suddenly she was not hungry any more. She put down her spoon and pushed the bed table aside.

"Want to talk about it?"

"It was just a bad memory," she said. "Something I wish to God I *could* forget."

McGee put his own tray aside, leaving the pie unfinished. "Tell me about it."

"Oh, it's nothing I should burden you with."

"Burden me."

"It's a dreary story."

"If it's bothering you, tell me about it. Now and then, I like a good, dreary story."

She didn't smile. Not even McGee could make the House of Thunder amusing. "Well . . . in my sophomore year at Briarstead, I was dating a guy named Jerry Stein. He was sweet. I liked him. I liked him a lot. In fact, we were even beginning to talk about getting married after we graduated. Then he was killed."

"I'm sorry," McGee said. "How did it happen?"

"He was pledging a fraternity."

"Oh, Christ!" McGee said, anticipating her.

"The hazing . . . got out of hand."

"That's such a rotten, stupid way to die."

"Jerry had so much potential," she said softly. "He was bright, sensitive, a hard worker . . . "

"One night, when I was an intern on emergency-room duty, they brought in a kid who'd been severely burned in a college hazing ritual. They told us it was a test by fire, some macho thing like that, some *childish* damned thing like that, and it got out of hand. He was burned over eighty percent of his body. He died two days later."

"It wasn't fire that killed Jerry Stein," Susan said. "It was hate."

She shuddered, remembering.

"Hate?" McGee asked. "What do you mean?"

She was silent for a moment, her thoughts turning back thirteen years. Although the hospital room was comfortably warm, Susan felt cold, as bitterly cold as she had been in the House of Thunder.

McGee waited patiently, leaning forward slightly in his chair.

At last she shook her head and said, "I don't feel like going into the details. It's just too depressing."

"There were an unusual number of deaths in your life before you were even twenty-one."

"Yeah. At times it seemed as if I were cursed or something. Everyone I really cared about died on me."

"Your mother, your father, then your fiancé."

"Well, he wasn't actually my fiancé. Not quite."

"But he was the next thing to it."

"Everything but the ring," Susan said.

"All right. So maybe you need to talk about his death in order to finally get it out of your system."

"No," she said.

"Don't dismiss it so quickly. I mean, if he's still haunting you thirteen years later—"

She interrupted him. "But you see, no matter how much I talk about it, I'll *never* get it out of my system. It was just too awful to be forgotten. Besides, you told me that a positive mental attitude will speed up the healing process. Remember?"

He smiled. "I remember."

"So I shouldn't talk about things that just depress me."

He stared at her for a long moment. His eyes were incredibly blue, and they were so expressive that she had no doubt about the depth of his concern for her well-being.

He sighed and said, "Okay. Let's get back to the matter at hand—your amnesia. It seems like you remember nearly everything. What holes haven't filled in yet?"

Before she answered him, she reached for the bed controls and raised the upper end of the mattress a bit more, forcing herself to sit straighter than she had been sitting. Her back ached dully, not from an injury but from being immobilized in bed for more than three weeks. When she felt more comfortable, she put down the controls and said, "I still can't recall the accident. I remember driving along a twisty section of two-lane blacktop. I was about two miles south of the turnoff to the Viewtop Inn. I was looking forward to getting there and having dinner. Then, well, it's as if somebody just turned the lights out."

"It wouldn't be unusual if you *never* regained any memory of the accident itself," McGee assured her. "In cases like this, even when the patient eventually recalls all the other details of his life, he seldom remembers the incident or the impact that was the cause of the amnesia. That's the one blank spot that often remains."

"I suspected as much," she said. "And I'm not really upset about that. But there's one other thing I can't recall, and *that's* driving me nuts. My job. Dammit, I can't remember even the most minor thing about it, not even one little detail. I mean, I know I'm a physicist. I remember getting the degrees at UCLA, and all that sophisticated, specialized knowledge is still intact. I could start to work today without having to take a refresher course. But *who* was I working for? And what was I doing—*exactly?* Who was my boss? Who were my co-workers? Did I have an office? a laboratory? I must have worked in a lab, don't you think? But I can't remember what it looked like, how it was equipped, or where on earth it was!"

"You're employed by the Milestone Corporation in Newport Beach, California," McGee said.

"That's what Dr. Viteski told me. But the name doesn't mean a thing to me."

"All the rest of it has come back to you. This will, too. Just give it time."

"No," she said, shaking her head. "This is different somehow. The other blank spots were like mists . . . like banks of heavy fog. Even when I couldn't remember something, I could at least sense that there *were* memories stirring in the mist. And eventually the mist evaporated; everything cleared up. But when I try to recall what my job was, it's not like those misty blank spots. Instead, it's dark . . . very dark . . . black, just a perfectly black and empty hole that goes down and down and down forever. There's something . . . frightening about it."

McGee slid forward, sitting on the edge of his chair. His brow was knitted. "You were carrying a Milestone ID card in your wallet when you were brought into the emergency room," he said. "Maybe that'll refresh your memory."

"Maybe," she said doubtfully. "I'd sure like to see it."

Her wallet was in the bottom drawer of the nightstand. He got it for her.

She opened the wallet and found the card. It was laminated and bore a small photograph of her. At the top of the card, in blue letters against a white background, were three words: THE MILESTONE CORPORATION. Under that heading, her name was printed in bold black letters, and below her name was a physical description of her, including information about her age, height, weight, hair color, and eye color. At the bottom of the card, an employee identification number was printed in red ink. Nothing else.

Dr. McGee stood beside the bed, looking down at her as she examined the card. "Does it help?"

"No," she said.

"Not just a little bit?"

"I can't remember seeing this before."

She turned the card over and over in her hands, straining to make a connection, trying hard to switch on the current of memory. She couldn't possibly have been more amazed by the card if it had been an artifact from a nonhuman civilization and had just that very minute been brought back from the planet Mars; it could not have been more *alien*.

"It's all so weird," she said. "I've tried to remember back to when I last went to work, the day before I started my vacation. I can recall some of it. Parts of the day are crystal clear. I remember getting up that morning, having breakfast, glancing at the newspaper. That's all as fresh in my mind as the memory of the lunch I just ate. I recall going into the garage that morning, getting in the car, starting the engine . . . " She let her voice trail off as she stared down at the card. She fingered that small rectangle as if she were a clairvoyant feeling for some sort of psychic residue on the plastic. "I remember backing the car out of my driveway that morning . . . and the next thing I remember is . . . coming home again at the end of the day. In between, there's nothing but blackness, emptiness. And that's the way it is with *all* my memories of work, not just that day but *every* day. No matter how I try to sneak up on them, they elude me. They aren't there in the mist. Those memories simply don't exist any more."

Still standing beside the bed, McGee spoke to her in a soft, encouraging voice. "Of course they exist, Susan. Nudge your subconscious a little bit. Think about sitting behind the wheel of your car that morning."

"I have thought about it."

"Think about it again."

She closed her eyes.

"It was probably a typical August day in Southern California," he said, helping her set the scene in her mind. "Hot, blue, maybe a little smoggy."

"Hot and blue," she said, "but there wasn't any smog that day. Not even a single cloud, either."

"You got in the car and backed out of the driveway. Now think about the route you drove to work."

She was silent for almost a minute. Then she said, "It's no use. I can't remember."

He persisted gently. "What were the names of the streets you used?"

"I don't know."

"Sure you do. Give me the name of just one street. Just *one* to start the ball rolling."

She tried hard to snatch at least a single meager scrap of memory out of the void—a face, a room, a voice, *anything*—but she failed.

"Sorry," she said. "I can't come up with the name of even one street."

"You told me that you remembered backing down your driveway that morning. All right. If you remember that, then surely you remember which way you went when you pulled *out* of your driveway. Did you turn left, or did you turn right?"

Her eyes still closed, Susan considered his question until her head began to ache. Finally she opened her eyes, looked up at McGee, and shrugged. "I just don't know."

"Philip Gomez," McGee said.

"What?"

"Philip Gomez."

"Who's that? Somebody I should know?"

"The name doesn't mean anything to you?"

"No."

"He's your boss at Milestone."

"Really?" She tried to picture Philip Gomez. She couldn't summon up an image of his face. She couldn't recall anything whatsoever about the man. "My boss? Philip Gomez? Are you sure about that?"

McGee put his hands in the pockets of his lab coat. "After you were admitted to the hospital, we tried to locate your family. Of course, we discovered you didn't *have* a family, no close relatives at all. So we called your employer. I've talked to Phil Gomez myself. According to him, you've worked at Milestone for more than four years. He was extremely concerned about you. In fact he's called here, asking about you, four or five times since the accident."

"Can we call him now?" Susan asked. "If I hear his voice, maybe something will click into place for me. It might help me remember."

"Well, I don't have his home number," McGee said, "and we can't call him at work until tomorrow."

"Why not?"

"Today's Sunday."

"Oh," she said.

She hadn't even known what day of the week it was, and that realization left her feeling somewhat disoriented again.

"We'll definitely call tomorrow," McGee said.

"What if I talk to him and still can't remember anything about my work?"

"You will."

"No, listen, please don't be glib. Be straight with me. Okay? There's a chance I'll never remember anything about my job, isn't there?"

"That's not likely."

"But possible?"

"Well . . . anything's possible."

She slumped back against her pillows, suddenly exhausted, depressed, and worried.

"Listen," McGee said, "even if you never remember anything about Milestone, that doesn't mean you can't go back to work there. After all, you haven't forgotten what you know about physics; you're still a competent scientist. You've lost none of your education, none of your knowledge. Now, if you were suffering from global amnesia,which is the worst kind, you'd have forgotten nearly everything you ever learned, including how to read and write. But you don't have global amnesia, and that's *something* to be thankful for. Anyway, given time, you'll remember all of it. I'm sure of that."

Susan hoped he was correct. Her carefully structured, orderly life was in temporary disarray, and she found her condition to be enormously distressing. If that disarray were to become a permanent feature of her existence, she would find life almost unbearable. She had always been in control of her life; she *needed* to be in control.

McGee took his hands out of his pockets and looked at his watch. "I've got to be going. I'll stop by again for a couple of minutes before I go home for the day. Meanwhile, you relax, eat more of your lunch if you can, and don't worry. You'll remember all about Milestone when the time is right."

Suddenly, as she listened to McGee, Susan sensed—without understanding why or how she sensed it—that she would be better off if she never remembered anything about Milestone. She was seized by an arctic-cold, iron-hard fear for which she could find no explanation.

■ She slept for two hours. She didn't dream this time—or if she did dream, she didn't remember it.

When she woke, she was slightly clammy. Her hair was tangled; she combed it, wincing as she pulled out the knots.

Susan was just putting the comb back on the nightstand when Mrs. Baker entered the room, pushing a wheelchair ahead of her. "It's time for you to do a bit of traveling, kid."

"Where are we going?"

"Oh, we'll explore the hallways and byways of the exotic second floor of mysterious, romantic, colorful Willawauk County Hospital," Mrs. Baker said. "The trip of a lifetime. It'll be loads of fun. Besides, the doctor wants you to start getting some exercise."

"It's not going to be much exercise if I'm sitting in a wheelchair."

"You'll be surprised. Just sitting up, holding on, and gawking at the other patients will be enough to tire you out. You're not exactly in the same physical condition as an Olympic track and field star, you know."

"But I'm sure I can walk," Susan said. "I might need a little assistance, but if I could just lean on your arm at first, then I'm positive I could"—

"Tomorrow, you can try walking a few steps," Mrs. Baker said as she put down the side rail on the bed. "But today you're going to ride, and I'm going to play chauffeur."

Susan frowned. "I hate being an invalid."

"Oh, for heaven's sake, you're not an invalid. You're just temporarily incapacitated."

"I hate that, too."

Mrs. Baker positioned the wheelchair beside the bed. "First, I want you to sit up on the edge of the bed and swing your legs back and forth for a minute or two."

"Why?"

"It flexes the muscles."

Sitting up, without the bed raised to support her back, Susan felt woozy and weak. She clutched the edge of the mattress because she thought she was going to tumble off the bed.

"Are you all right?" Mrs. Baker asked.

"Perfect," Susan lied, and forced a smile.

"Swing your legs, kid."

Susan moved her legs back and forth from the knees down. They felt as if they were made of lead.

Finally, Mrs. Baker said, "Okay. That's enough."

Susan was dismayed to find that she was already perspiring. She was shaky, too.

Nevertheless, she said, "I *know* I can walk."

"Tomorrow," Mrs. Baker said.

"Really, I feel fine."

Mrs. Baker went to the closet and got the robe that matched Susan's blue pajamas. While Susan put on the robe, the nurse located a pair of slippers in one of the suitcases and put them on Susan's dangling feet.

"Okay, honey. Now, just slide off the bed nice and easy, lean your weight against me, and I'll help lower you into the chair."

As she came off the bed, Susan intended to disobey the nurse, intended to stand up straight all by herself and prove that she wasn't an invalid. However, as her feet touched the floor, she knew instantly that her legs would not support her if she dared to put all of her weight on them; a moment ago, they seemed to be made of lead, but now they were composed of knotted rags. Rather than collapse in a heap and be humiliated, she clutched Mrs. Baker and allowed herself to be settled into the wheelchair almost as if she were a baby being put into a stroller.

Mrs. Baker winked at her. "Still think you can run the mile?"

Susan was both amused and embarrassed by her own stubbornness. Smiling, blushing, she said, "Tomorrow. I'll do so much walking tomorrow that I'll wear big holes in my slippers. You just wait and see."

"Well, kid, I don't know if you have a whole lot of common sense or not, but you've sure as the devil got more than your share of spunk, and I've always admired spunkiness."

Mrs. Baker stepped behind the wheelchair and pushed it out of the room. Initially, the rolling motion caused Susan's stomach to flop and twist, but after several seconds she got control of herself.

The hospital was T-shaped, and Susan's room was at the end of the short, right-hand wing at the top of the T. Mrs. Baker took her out to the junction of the corridors and wheeled her into the longest wing, heading toward the bottom of the T.

Just being out of bed and out of her room made Susan feel better, fresher. The halls had dark green vinyl-tile floors, and the walls were painted a matching shade up to the height of three feet, after which they were a pale yellow, as was the pebbly, acoustic-tile ceiling; the effect of this–darkness below, light above—was to lift one's eyes upward, giving the hall a soaring, airy quality. The corridors were as spotlessly clean as Susan's room. She remembered the big Philadelphia hospital in which her father had finally succumbed to cancer; that place had been ancient, dreary, in need of paint, with dust thick on the windowsills, with years of grime pressed deep into its cracked tile floors. She supposed she ought to be thankful that she had wound up in Willawauk County Hospital.

The doctors, nurses, and orderlies here were also different from those in the hospital where her father had died. All of these people smiled at her. And they seemed genuinely concerned about the patients. As Susan was wheeled through the halls, many staff members paused in their tasks to have a word with her; every one of them expressed pleasure at seeing her awake, alert, and on the way to a full recovery.

Mrs. Baker pushed her to the end of the long main hallway, then turned and started back. Although Susan was already beginning to tire, she was nevertheless in relatively high spirits. She felt better today than she had felt yesterday, better this afternoon than this morning. The future seemed sure to grow brighter almost by the hour.

When the mood changed, it changed with the frightening abruptness of a shotgun blast.

As they passed between the elevators and the nurses' station—which faced each other midpoint in the corridor—one set of elevator doors opened, and a man stepped out directly in front of the wheelchair. He was a patient in blue- and white-striped pajamas, a dark brown robe, and brown slippers. Mrs. Baker stopped the wheelchair in order to let him pass. When Susan saw who he was, she nearly screamed. She *wanted* to scream but couldn't. Chest-tightening, throat-constricting fear had stricken her dumb.

His name was Ernest Harch. He was a squarely built man with a square face, squared-off features, and gray eyes the shade of dirty ice.

When she had testified against him in court, he had fixed her with those chilling eyes and hadn't glanced away from her for even the briefest moment. She had clearly read the message in his intimidating stare: *You're going to be sorry you ever took the witness stand.*

But that had been thirteen years ago. In the meantime, she had taken precautions to be sure he would not find her when he got out of prison. She had long ago stopped looking over her shoulder.

And now here he was.

He looked down at her as she sat helpless in the wheelchair, and she saw recognition flicker in his wintry eyes. In spite of the years that had passed, in spite of the emaciation that had altered her appearance in the last three weeks, he knew who she was.

She wanted to bolt out of the chair and run. She was rigid with fear; she couldn't move.

Only a second or two had passed since the elevator doors had opened, yet it seemed as if she had been confronting Harch for at least a quarter of an hour. The usual flow of time had slowed to a sludgelike crawl.

Harch smiled at her. To anyone but Susan, that smile might have appeared innocent, even friendly. But she saw hatred and menace in it.

Ernest Harch had been the pledge master in the fraternity that Jerry Stein had wanted to join. Ernest Harch had killed Jerry. Not by accident. Deliberately. In cold blood. In the House of Thunder.

Now, still smiling, he winked at Susan.

The fear-induced paralysis relaxed its tight grip on her, and somehow she found the strength to push up from the wheelchair, onto her feet. She took one step, trying to turn away from Harch, trying desperately to run, and she heard Mrs. Baker call out in surprise. She took a second step, feeling as if she were walking underwater, and then her legs buckled, and she started to fall, and someone caught her just in time.

As everything began to spin and wobble and grow dark, she realized that Ernest Harch was the one who had caught her. She was in his arms. She looked up into his face, which was as big as the moon.

Then for a while there was only darkness.

4

"IN DANGER?" McGEE SAID, LOOKING PUZZLED.

At the foot of the bed, Mrs. Baker frowned.

Susan was trying hard to remain calm and convincing. She possessed sufficient presence of mind to know that a hysterical woman was never taken seriously—especially not a hysterical woman recuperating from a head injury. There was a very real danger that she would appear to be confused or suffering from delusions. It was vital that Jeffrey McGee believe what she was going to tell him.

She had awakened in bed, in her hospital room, only a few minutes after fainting in the corridor. When she came to, McGee was taking her blood pressure. She had patiently allowed him to examine her before she had told him that she was in danger.

Now he stood beside the bed, one hand on the side rail, leaning forward a bit, a stethoscope dangling from his neck. "In danger from what?"

"That man," Susan said.

"What man?"

"The man who stepped out of the elevator."

McGee glanced at Mrs. Baker.

The nurse said, "He's a patient here."

"And you think he's somehow dangerous?" McGee asked Susan, still clearly perplexed.

Nervously fingering the collar of her pajama top, Susan said, "Dr. McGee, do you remember what I told you about an old boyfriend of mine named Jerry Stein?"

"Of course I remember. He was the one you were almost engaged to."

Susan nodded.

"The one who died in a fraternity hazing," McGee said.

"Ah, no," Mrs. Baker said sympathetically. This was the first that she had heard about Jerry. "That's a terrible thing."

Susan's mouth was dry. She swallowed a few times, then said, "It was what the fraternity called a 'humiliation ritual.' The pledge had to withstand intense humiliation in front of a girl, preferably his steady date, without responding to his tormentors. They took Jerry and me to a limestone cavern a couple of miles from the Briarstead campus. It was a favorite place for hazing rituals; they were fond of dramatic settings for their damned silly games. Anyway, I didn't want to go. Right from the start, I didn't want to be a part of it. Not that there was anything threatening about it. The mood was light-hearted at first, playful. Jerry was actually looking forward to it. But I suppose, on some deep subliminal level, I sensed an undercurrent of . . . malice. Besides, I suspected the fraternity brothers in charge of the hazing had been drinking. They had two cars, and I didn't want to get into either one, not if a drunk was driving. But they reassured me, and finally I went with them because Jerry wanted in the fraternity so badly. I didn't want to be a spoiler."

She looked out the window at the lowering September sky. A wind had risen, stirring the branches of the tall pines.

She hated talking about Jerry's death. But she had to tell McGee and Mrs. Baker everything, so that they would understand why Ernest Harch posed a very real, very serious threat to her.

She said, "The limestone caverns near Briarstead College are extensive. Eight or ten underground rooms. Maybe more. Some of them are huge. It's a damp, musty, moldy place, though I suppose it's paradise to a spelunker."

Gently urging her on, McGee said, "Caverns that large must be a tourist attraction, but I don't think I've ever heard of them."

"Oh, no, they haven't been developed for tourism," Susan said. "They're not like the Carlsbad Caverns or the Luray Caverns or anything like that. They're not pretty. They're all gray limestone, dreary as Hell. They're big, that's all. The largest cave is about the size of a cathedral. The Shawnee Indians gave that one a name: 'House of Thunder.'"

"Thunder?" McGee asked. "Why?"

"A subterranean stream enters the cave high in one corner and tumbles down a series of ledges. The sound of the falling water echoes off the limestone, so there's a continuous rumbling in the place."

The memory was still far too vivid for her to speak of it without feeling the cold, clammy air of the cavern. She shivered and pulled the blankets across her outstretched legs.

McGee's gaze met hers. In his eyes there was understanding and compassion. She could see that he knew how painful it was for her to talk about Jerry Stein.

The same expression was in Mrs. Baker's eyes. The nurse looked as if she might rush around to the side of the bed and give Susan a motherly hug.

Again, McGee gently encouraged her to continue her story. "The humiliation ritual was held in the House of Thunder?"

"Yeah. It was night. We were led into the cavern with flashlights, and then several candles were lit and placed on the rocks around us. There were just Jerry, me, and four of the fraternity brothers. I'll never forget their names or what they looked like. Never. Carl Jellicoe, Herbert Parker, Randy Lee Quince . . . and Ernest Harch. Harch was the fraternity's pledge master that year."

Outside, the day was rapidly growing darker under a shroud of thunderheads. Inside, the blue-gray shadows crawled out of the corners and threatened to take full possession of the hospital room.

As Susan talked, Dr. McGee switched on the bedside lamp.

"As soon as we were in the caverns, as soon as the candles had been lit, Harch and the other three guys pulled out flasks of whiskey. They *had* been drinking earlier. I was right about that. And they continued to drink all through the hazing. The more they drank, the uglier the whole scene got. At first they subjected Jerry to some funny, pretty much innocent teasing. In fact, everyone was laughing at first, even Jerry and me. Gradually, however, their taunting became nastier . . . meaner. A lot of it was obscene, too. Worse than obscene. *Filthy.* I was embarrassed and uneasy. I wanted to leave, and Jerry wanted me to get out of there, too, but Harch and the others refused to let me have a flashlight or a candle. I couldn't find my way out of the caverns in pitch blackness, so I had to stay. When they started needling Jerry about his being Jewish, there wasn't any humor in them at all, and that was when I knew for sure there was going to be trouble, bad trouble. They were all obviously drunk by then. But it wasn't just the whiskey talking. Oh, no. Not the whiskey alone. You could see that the prejudice—the *hatred*—wasn't just an act. Harch and the others—but especially Ernest Harch— had a streak of anti-Semitism as thick as sludge in a sewer.

"Briarstead wasn't a particularly sophisticated place," Susan continued. "There wasn't the usual cultural mix. There weren't many Jews on campus, and there weren't any in the fraternity that Jerry wanted to join. Not that the fraternity had a policy against admitting Jews or anyone else. There had been a couple of Jewish members in the past, though none for the last several years. Most of the brothers wanted Jerry in. It was only Harch and his three cronies who were determined to keep him out. They planned to make Hazing Month so rough for him, so utterly intolerable, that he would withdraw his application before the month was over. The humiliation ritual in the House of Thunder was to be the start of it. They didn't really intend to kill Jerry. Not in the beginning, not when they took us to the cavern, not when they were at least half sober. They just wanted to make him feel like dirt. They wanted to rough him up a little bit, scare him, let him know in no uncertain terms that he wasn't welcome. The verbal abuse escalated to physical abuse. They stood in a circle around him, shoving him back and forth, keeping him off balance. Jerry wasn't a fool. He realized this wasn't any ordinary hazing ritual. He wasn't a wimp, either. He couldn't be intimidated easily. When they shoved him too hard, he shoved back—which only made them more aggressive, of course. When they wouldn't stop shoving, Jerry hit Harch in the mouth and split the bastard's lip."

"And that was the trigger," McGee said.

"Yes. Then all hell broke loose."

Thunder grumbled again, and the hospital lights flickered briefly, and Susan had the strange, disquieting notion that some supernatural force was trying to carry her back in time, back to the waterfall roar and the darkness of the cavern.

She said, "Something about the mood of that place—the bone-deep chill, the dampness, the darkness, the steady roar of the waterfall, the sense of isolation— made it easier for the savage in them to come out. They beat Jerry . . . beat him to the floor and kept on beating him."

She trembled. The trembling became a more violent quivering; the quivering grew into a shudder of revulsion and of remembered terror.

"It was as if they were wild dogs, turning on an interloper from a strange pack," she said shakily. "I . . . I screamed at them . . . but I couldn't stop them. Finally, Carl Jellicoe seemed to realize that he'd gone too far, and he backed away. Then

Quince, then Parker. Harch was the last to get control of himself, and he was the first to realize they were all going to wind up in prison. Jerry was unconscious. He was . . . "

Her voice cracked, faltered.

It didn't seem like thirteen years; it seemed almost like yesterday.

"Go on," McGee said quietly.

"He was . . . bleeding from the nose . . . the mouth . . . and from one ear. He'd been very badly hurt. Although he was unconscious, he kept twitching uncontrollably. It looked like there might have been nerve or brain damage. I tried to . . . "

"Go on, Susan."

"I tried to get to Jerry, but Harch pushed me out of the way, knocked me down. He told the others that they were all going to go to prison if they didn't do something drastic to save themselves. He said that their futures had been destroyed, that they had no real future at all . . . unless they covered up what they'd done. He tried to convince them that they had to finish Jerry off and then kill me, too, and dump our bodies down one of the deep holes in the cavern floor. Jellicoe, Parker, and Quince were half sobered up by the shock of what they'd done, but they were still half drunk, too, and confused and scared. At first they argued with Harch, then agreed with him, then had second thoughts and argued again. They were afraid to commit murder, yet they were afraid *not* to. Harch was furious with them for being so wishy-washy, and he suddenly decided to *force* them to do what he wanted by simply giving them no other choice. He turned to Jerry and he . . . he . . . . "

She felt sick, remembering.

McGee held her hand.

Susan said, "He kicked Jerry . . . in the head . . . three times . . . and caved in one side of his skull."

Mrs. Baker gasped.

"Killed him," Susan said.

Outside, lightning slashed open the sky, and thunder roared through the resultant wound. The first fat droplets of rain struck the window.

McGee squeezed Susan's hand.

"I grabbed one of the flashlights and ran," she said. "Their attention was focused so completely on Jerry's body that I managed to get a bit of a head start on them. Not much but enough. They expected me to try to leave the caverns, but I didn't head toward the exit because I knew they'd catch me if I went that way, so I gained a few more seconds before they realized where I'd gone. I went deeper into the caves, through a twisty stone corridor, down a slope of loose rocks, into another underground room, then into another beyond that one. Eventually, I switched off the flashlight, so they wouldn't be able to follow the glow of it, and I went on as far as I could in complete darkness, feeling my way, inch by inch, stumbling, until I found a niche in the wall, a crawl hole, nothing more than that, hidden behind a limestone stalagmite. I slithered into it, as far back into it as I could possibly go, and then I was very, very quiet. Harch and the others spent hours searching for me before they finally decided I'd somehow gotten out of the caverns. I waited another six or eight hours, afraid to come out of hiding. I finally left the caverns when I couldn't deal with my thirst and claustrophobia any longer."

Rain pattered on the window, blurring the wind-tossed trees and the black-bellied clouds.

"Jesus," Mrs. Baker said, her face ashen. "You poor kid."

"They were put on trial?" McGee asked.

"Yes. The district attorney didn't think he could win if he charged them with first- or second-degree murder. Too many extenuating circumstances, including the whiskey and the fact that Jerry had actually struck the first blow when he'd busted Harch's lip. Anyway, Harch was convicted of manslaughter and got a five-year term in the state penitentiary."

"Just five years?" Mrs. Baker asked.

"I thought he should have been put away forever," Susan said, as bitter now as she had been the day she'd heard the judge hand down the sentence.

"What about the other three?" McGee asked.

"They were convicted of assault and of being accomplices to Harch, but because they'd had no previous run-ins with the law and were from good families, and because none of them actually struck the killing blows, they were all given suspended sentences and put on probation."

"Outrageous!" Mrs. Baker said.

McGee continued to hold Susan's hand, and she was glad that he did.

"Of course," she said, "all four of them were immediately expelled from Briarstead. And in a strange way, fate took a hand in punishing Parker and Jellicoe. They were taking the pre-med course at Briarstead, and they managed to finish their last year at another university, but after that they quickly discovered that no top-of-the-line medical school would accept students with serious criminal records. They hustled for another year, submitting applications everywhere, and they finally managed to squeeze into the medical program at a distinctly second-rate university. The night they were notified of their acceptance, they went drinking to celebrate, got stinking drunk, and were both killed when Parker lost control of the car and rolled it over twice. Maybe I should be ashamed to say this, but I was relieved and grateful when I heard what had happened to them."

"Of course you were," Mrs. Baker said. "That's only natural. Nothing to be ashamed of at all."

"What about Randy Lee Quince?" McGee asked.

"I never heard what happened to him," Susan said. "And I don't care . . . just as long as he suffered."

Two closely spaced explosions of lightning and thunder shook the world outside, and for a moment Susan and McGee and Mrs. Baker stared at the window, where the rain struck with greater force than before.

Then Mrs. Baker said, "It's a horrible story, just horrible. But I'm not sure I understand exactly what it has to do with your fainting spell in the hall a while ago."

Before Susan could respond, McGee said, "Apparently, the man who stepped out of the elevator, in front of Susan's wheelchair, was one of those fraternity brothers from Briarstead."

"Yes," Susan said.

"Either Harch or Quince."

"Ernest Harch," Susan said.

"An incredible coincidence," McGee said, giving her hand one last, gentle squeeze before letting go of it. "Thirteen years after the fact—and a whole continent away from where the two of you last saw each other."

Mrs. Baker frowned. "But you must be mistaken."

"Oh, no," Susan said, shaking her head vigorously. "I'll never forget that face. Never."

"But his name's not Harch," Mrs. Baker said.

"Yes, it is."

"No. It's Richmond. Bill Richmond."

"Then he's changed his name since I knew him."

"I wouldn't think a convicted criminal would be allowed to change his name," Mrs. Baker said.

"I didn't mean he changed it legally, in court, or anything like that," Susan said, frustrated by the nurse's reluctance to accept the truth. The man *was* Harch.

"What's he here for?" McGee asked Thelma Baker.

"He's having surgery tomorrow," the nurse said. "Dr. Viteski's going to remove two rather large cysts from his lower back."

"Not spinal cysts?"

"No. Fatty tissue cysts. But they're large ones."

"Benign?" McGee asked.

"Yes. But I guess they're deeply rooted, and they're causing him some discomfort."

"Admitted this morning?"

"That's right."

"And his name's Richmond. You're sure of that?"

"Yes."

"But it used to be *Harch*," Susan insisted.

Mrs. Baker took off her glasses and let them dangle on the beaded chain around her neck. She scratched the bridge of her nose, looked quizzically at Susan, and said, "How old was this Harch when he killed Jerry Stein?"

"He was a senior at Briarstead that year," Susan said. "Twenty-one years old."

"That settles it, then," the nurse said.

"Why?" McGee asked.

Mrs. Baker put her glasses on again and said, "Bill Richmond is only in his early twenties."

"He can't be," Susan said.

"In fact I'm pretty sure he's just twenty-one himself. He'd have been about eight years old when Jerry Stein was killed."

"He's not twenty-one," Susan said anxiously. "He's thirty-four by now."

"Well, he certainly doesn't *look* any older than twenty-one," Mrs. Baker said. "In fact he looks younger than that. A good deal younger than that. He's hardly more than a kid. If he was lying about it one way or the other, I'd think he was actually adding on a few years, not taking them off."

As the lights flickered again, and as thunder rolled across the hollow, sheet-metal sky, Dr. McGee looked at Susan and said, "How old did he look to you when he stepped out of the elevator?"

She thought about it for a moment, and she got a sinking feeling in her stomach. "Well . . . he looked *exactly* like Ernest Harch."

"Exactly like Harch looked back then?"

"Uh . . . yeah."

"Like a twenty-one-year-old college man?"

Susan nodded reluctantly.

McGee pressed the point. "Then you mean that he didn't look thirty-four to you?"

"No. But maybe he's aged well. Some thirty-four-year-olds could pass for ten years younger." She was confused about the apparent age discrepancy, but she was not the least bit confused about the man's identity: "He *is* Harch."

"Perhaps it's just a strong resemblance," Mrs. Baker said.

"No," Susan insisted. "It's him, all right. I recognized him, and I saw him recognize me, too. And I don't feel safe. It was my testimony that sent him to prison. If you'd have seen the way he glared at me in that courtroom . . . "

McGee and Mrs. Baker stared at her, and there was something in their eyes that made her feel as if this were a courtroom, too, as if she were standing before a jury, awaiting judgment. She stared back at them for a moment, but then she lowered her eyes because she was made miserable by the doubt she saw in theirs.

"Listen," McGee said, "I'll go take a look at this guy's records. Maybe I'll even have a word or two with him. We'll see if we can straighten this out."

"Sure," Susan said, knowing it was hopeless.

"If he's really Harch, we'll make sure he doesn't get anywhere near you. And if he *isn't* Harch, you'll be able to rest easy."

It's him, dammit!

But she didn't say anything; she merely nodded.

"I'll be back in a few minutes," McGee said.

Susan stared down at her pale, interlocked hands.

"Will you be okay?" McGee asked.

"Yeah. Sure."

She sensed a meaningful look and an unspoken message passing between the doctor and the nurse. But she didn't look up.

McGee left the room.

"We'll get this straightened out real quick, honey," Mrs. Baker assured her.

Outside, thunder fell out of the sky with the sound of an avalanche.

Night would come early. Already, the storm had torn apart the autumn afternoon and had blown it away. The twilight had been swept in ahead of schedule.

"His name's definitely Bill Richmond," McGee said when he returned a few minutes later.

Susan sat stiffly in bed, still disbelieving.

The two of them were alone in the room. The nurses had changed shifts, and Mrs. Baker had gone home for the day.

McGee toyed with the stethoscope around his neck. "And he's definitely just twenty-one years old."

"But you weren't gone nearly long enough to've checked out his background," Susan said. "If all you did was read through his medical records, then nothing has really been proved. He could have lied to his doctor, you know."

"Well, it turns out that Leon—Dr. Viteski, that is—has known Bill's parents, Grace and Harry Richmond, for twenty-five years. Viteski says he delivered all three of the Richmond babies himself, right here in this very hospital."

Doubt nibbled at Susan's solid conviction.

McGee said, "Leon treated all of Bill Richmond's childhood illnesses and injuries. He knows for an absolute fact that the kid was only eight years old, living in Pine Wells, just doing what eight-year-olds do, when Ernest Harch killed Jerry Stein, thirteen years ago, back there in Pennsylvania."

"Three thousand miles away."

"Exactly."

Susan sagged under a heavy burden of weariness and anxiety. "But he looked just like Harch. When he stepped out of the elevator this afternoon, when I looked up and saw that face, those damned gray eyes, I could have sworn . . . "

"Oh, I'm certain you didn't panic without good reason," he said placatingly. "I'm sure there's a resemblance."

Although she had come to like McGee a lot in just one day, Susan was angry with him for letting even a vaguely patronizing tone enter his voice. Her anger rejuvenated her a bit, and she sat up straighter in bed, her hands fisted at her sides. "Not just a resemblance," she said sharply. "He looked *exactly* like Harch."

"Well, of course, you've got to keep in mind that it's been a long time since you've seen Harch."

"So?"

"You may not remember him quite as well as you think you do," McGee said.

"Oh, I remember. Perfectly. This Richmond is the same height as Harch, the same weight, the same build."

"It's a fairly common body type."

"He has the same blond hair, the same square features, the same *eyes*. Such light gray eyes, almost transparent. How many people have eyes like that? Not very many. Feature by feature, this Bill Richmond and Ernest Harch are duplicates. It's not just a simple resemblance. It's a lot stranger than that. It's downright uncanny."

"Okay, okay," McGee said, holding up one hand to stop her. "Perhaps they are remarkably alike, virtually identical. If that's the case, then it's an incredible coincidence that you've encountered both of them, thirteen years apart, at opposite ends of the country; but that's all it is—a coincidence."

Her hands were cold. Freezing. She rubbed them together, trying to generate heat.

She said, "When it comes to the subject of coincidences, I agree with Philip Marlowe."

"Who?"

"Marlowe. He's a private detective in those novels by Raymond Chandler. *The Lady in the Lake, The Big Sleep, The Long Goodbye* . . . "

"Of course. Marlowe. Okay, so what did he have to say about coincidences?"

"He said, 'Show me a coincidence, and when I open it up for you, I'll show you at least two people inside, plotting some sort of mischief.' "

McGee frowned and shook his head. "That philosophy might be suitable for a character in a detective story. But out here in the real world, it's a little paranoid, don't you think?"

He was right, and she couldn't sustain her anger with him. As her fury faded, so did her strength, and she sank back against the pillows once more. "Could two people really look so much alike?"

"I've heard it said that everyone has an unrelated twin somewhere in the world, what some people call a 'doppelgänger.' "

"Maybe," Susan said, unconvinced. "But this was . . . different. It was weird. I'd swear he recognized me, too. He smiled so strangely. And he—*winked* at me!"

For the first time since he had returned to her room, McGee smiled. "Winked at you? Well, there's certainly nothing strange or uncanny about that, dear lady." His intensely blue eyes sparkled with amusement. "In case you didn't know it, men frequently wink at attractive women. Now don't tell me you've never been winked at before. Don't tell me you've spent your life in a nunnery or on a desert island." He grinned.

"There's nothing attractive about me at the moment," she insisted.

"Nonsense."

"My hair needs a real washing, not just brushed with powder. I'm emaciated, and I've got bags under my eyes. I hardly think I inspire romantic thoughts in my present condition."

"You're being too hard on yourself. Emaciated? No. You've just got a haunting Audrey Hepburn quality."

Susan resisted his charm, which wasn't easy. But she was determined to say everything that was on her mind. "Besides, it wasn't that kind of wink."

"Ahhhh," he said. "So now you admit you've been winked at in the past. Suddenly you're an *expert* on winking."

She refused to be coaxed and kidded into forgetting the man who had stepped out of the elevator.

"What kind of wink was it, exactly?" he asked, a teasing tone still in his voice.

"It was a smartass wink. Smug. There wasn't anything at all flirtatious about it, either. It wasn't warm and friendly, like a wink ought to be. It was cold. Cold and smug and nasty and . . . somehow threatening," she said, but even as she spoke she realized how ludicrous it sounded to give such an exhaustively detailed interpretation to something as simple as a wink.

"It's a good thing I didn't ask you to interpret his entire facial expression," McGee said. "We'd have been here until tomorrow morning!"

Susan finally succumbed. She smiled. "I guess it does sound pretty silly, huh?"

"Especially since we know for a fact that his name's Bill Richmond and that he's only twenty-one."

"So the wink was just a wink, and the threat was all in my head?"

"Don't you figure that's probably the case?" he asked diplomatically.

She sighed. "Yeah, I guess I do. And I suppose I should apologize for causing so much trouble about this."

"It wasn't any trouble," he said graciously.

"I'm awfully tired, weak, and my perceptions aren't as sharp as they should be. Last night, I dreamed about Harch, and when I saw that man step out of the elevator, looking so much like Harch, I just . . . lost my head. I panicked."

That was a difficult admission for her to make. Other people might act like Chicken Little at the slightest provocation, but Susan Kathleen Thorton expected herself to remain—and previously always *had* remained—calm and collected through any crisis that fate threw at her. She had been that way since she was just a little girl, for the circumstances of her lonely childhood had required her to be totally self-reliant. She hadn't even panicked in the House of Thunder, when Ernest Harch had kicked in Jerry's skull; she had run, had hidden, had survived—all because she had kept her wits about her at a time when most people, if thrust into the same situation, would surely have lost theirs. But now she had panicked; worse, she had let others see her lose control. She felt embarrassed and humbled by her behavior.

"I'll be a model patient from now on," she told Dr. McGee. "I'll take my medicine without argument. I'll eat real well, so I'll regain my strength just as quickly as possible. I'll exercise when I'm told to and only as much as I'm told to. By the time I'm ready to be discharged, you'll have forgotten all about the scene I caused today. In fact you'll wish that all of your patients were like me. That's a promise."

"I *already* wish all of my patients were exactly like you," he said. "Believe me, it's much more pleasant treating a pretty young woman than it is treating cranky old men with heart conditions."

After McGee had gone for the day, Susan arranged with one of the orderlies to have a rental television installed in her room. As afternoon faded into evening, she watched the last half of an old episode of "The Rockford Files," then the umpteenth rerun of an episode of "The Mary Tyler Moore Show." In spite of frequent bursts of storm-caused static, she watched the five o'clock news on a Seattle station, and she was dismayed to discover that the current international crises were pretty much the same as the international crises that had been at the top of the news reports more than three weeks ago, before she had fallen into a coma.

Later, she ate all the food on her dinner tray. Later still, she rang for one of the second-shift nurses and asked for a snack. A pert blonde named Marcia Edmonds brought her a dish of sherbet with sliced peaches. Susan ate all of that, too.

She tried not to think about Bill Richmond, the Harch look-alike. She tried not to think about the House of Thunder, or about the precious days she had lost in a coma, or about the remaining gaps in her memory, or about her current state of helplessness, or about anything else that might upset her. She concentrated on being a good patient and developing a positive attitude, for she was eager to get well again.

Nevertheless, an unspecific but chilling presentiment of danger disturbed her thoughts from time to time. A shapeless portent of evil.

Each time that her thoughts turned into that dark pathway, she forced herself to think only of pleasing things. Mostly, she thought about Dr. Jeffrey McGee: the grace with which he moved; the ear-pleasing timbre of his voice; the sensitivity and the intriguing scintillation of his exceptionally blue eyes; his strong, well-formed, long-fingered hands.

Near bedtime, after she had taken the sedative that McGee had prescribed for her, but before she had begun to get drowsy, the rain stopped falling. The wind, however, did not die down. It continued to press insistently against the window. It murmured, growled, hissed. It sniffed all around the window frame and thumped its paws of air against the glass, as if it were a big dog searching diligently for a way to get inside.

Perhaps because of the sound of the wind, Susan dreamed of dogs that night.

Dogs and then jackals. Jackals and then wolves. Werewolves. They changed fluidly from lupine to human form, then into wolves again, then back into men, always pursuing her or leaping at her or waiting in the darkness ahead to pounce on her. When they took the form of men, she recognized them: Jellicoe, Parker, Quince, and Harch. Once, as she was fleeing through a dark forest, she came upon a moonlit clearing in which the four beasts, in wolf form, were crouched over the corpse of Jerry Stein, tearing the flesh from its bones. They looked up at her and grinned malevolently. Blood and ragged pieces of raw flesh drooled from their white teeth and vicious jowls. Sometimes she dreamed they were chasing her through the caverns, between thrusting limestone stalagmites and stalactites, along narrow corridors of rock and earth. Sometimes they chased her across a vast field of delicate black flowers; sometimes they prowled deserted city streets, following her scent, forcing her to flee from a series of hiding places, snapping relentlessly at her heels. Once, she even dreamed that one of the creatures had slunk into her hospital room; it was a crouching wolf-thing, swathed in shadows, visible only in murky silhouette, watching her from the foot of the bed, one wild eye gleaming. Then it moved into the weak amber glow of the night light, and she saw that it had undergone another metamorphosis, changing from wolf to man this time. It was Ernest Harch. He was wearing pajamas and a bathrobe—

(*This isn't part of the dream!* she thought as icy shards of fear thrilled through her.)

—and he came around to the side of the bed. He bent down to look more closely at her. She tried to cry out; couldn't. She could not move, either. His face began to blur in front of her, and she struggled to keep it in focus, but she sensed that she was slipping back to the field of black flowers—

(*I've got to shake this off. Wake up. All the way. It was supposed to be a mild sedative. Just a mild one, dammit!*)

—and Harch's features ran together in one gray smear. The hospital room dissolved completely, and again she was plunging across a field of strange black flowers, with a pack of wolves baying behind her. The moon was full; oddly, however, it provided little light. She couldn't see where she was going, and she tripped over something, fell into the flowers, and discovered that she had stumbled over Jerry Stein's mutilated, half-eaten cadaver. The wolf appeared, loomed over her, snarling, leering, pushing its slavering muzzle down at her, down and down, until its cold nose touched her cheek. The beast's hateful face blurred and re-formed into an even more hateful countenance: that of Ernest Harch. It wasn't a wolf's nose touching her cheek any longer; it was now Harch's blunt finger. She flinched, and her heart began pounding so forcefully that she wondered why it didn't tear loose of her. Harch pulled his hand away from her and smiled. The field of black flowers was gone. She was dreaming that she was in her hospital room again—

(*Except it's not a dream. It's real. Harch is here, and he's going to kill me.*)

—and she tried to sit up in bed but was unable to move. She reached for the call button that would summon a nurse or an orderly, and although the button was only a few inches away, it suddenly seemed light-years beyond her reach. She strained toward it, and her arm appeared to stretch and stretch magically, until it was bizarrely elongated; her flesh and bones seemed to be possessed of an impossible elasticity. Still, her questing finger fell short of the button. She felt as if she were Alice, as if she had just stepped through the looking glass. She was now in that part of Wonderland in which the usual laws of perspective did not apply. Here, little was big, and big was little; near was far; far was near; there was no difference whatsoever between up and down, in and out, over and under. This sleep-induced, drug-induced confusion made her nauseous; she tasted bile in the back of her throat. Could she taste something like that if she were dreaming? She wasn't sure. She wished fervently that she could at least be certain whether she was awake or still fast asleep. "Long time no see," Harch said. Susan blinked at him, trying to keep him in focus, but he kept fading in and out. Sometimes, for just a second or two, he had the shining eyes of a wolf. "Did you think you could hide from me forever?" he asked, speaking in a whisper, leaning even closer, until his face was nearly touching hers. His breath was foul, and she wondered if her ability to smell was an indication that she was awake, that Harch was real. "Did you think you could hide from me forever?" Harch demanded again. She could not respond to him; her voice was frozen in her throat, a cold lump that she could neither spit out nor swallow. "You rotten bitch," Harch said, and his smile became a broad grin. "You stinking, rotten, smug little bitch. How do you feel now? Huh? Are you sorry you testified against me? Hmmm? Yeah. I'll bet you're real sorry now." He laughed softly, and for a moment the laughter became the low growling of a wolf, but then it turned into laughter again. "You know what I'm going to do to you?" he asked. His face began to blur. "Do you know what I'm going to do to you?" She was in a cavern. There were black flowers growing out of the stone floor. She was running from baying wolves. She turned a corner, and the cavern opened onto a shadowy city street. A wolf stood on the sidewalk, under a lamp-post, and it said, "Do you know what I'm going to do to you?" Susan ran and kept on running through a long, frightening, amorphous night.

Monday, shortly after dawn, she woke, groggy and damp with sweat. She remembered dreaming about wolves and about Ernest Harch. In the flat, hard, gray light of the cloudy morning, it seemed ridiculous for her to entertain the thought that Harch actually had been in her room last night. She was still alive, uninjured, utterly unmarked. It had all been a nightmare. All of it. Just a terrible nightmare.

5

NOT LONG AFTER SUSAN WOKE, SHE TOOK A SPONGE BATH WITH the help of a nurse. Refreshed, she changed into her spare pajamas, a green pair with yellow piping. A nurse's aide took the soiled blue silk pajamas into the bathroom, rinsed them in the sink, and hung them to dry on a hook behind the door.

Breakfast was larger this morning than it had been yesterday. Susan ate every bite of it and was still hungry.

A few minutes after Mrs. Baker came on duty with the morning shift, she came to Susan's room with Dr. McGee, who was making his morning rounds before attending to his private practice at his offices in Willawauk. Together, McGee and Mrs. Baker removed the bandages from Susan's forehead. There was no pain, just a prickle or two when the sutures were snipped and tugged loose.

McGee cupped her chin in his hand and turned her head from side to side, studying the healed wound. "It's a neat bit of tailoring, even if I do say so myself."

Mrs. Baker got the long-handled mirror from the nightstand and gave it to Susan.

She was pleasantly surprised to find that the scar was not nearly as bad as she had feared it would be. It was four inches long, an unexpectedly narrow line of pink, shiny, somewhat swollen skin, bracketed by small red spots where the stitches had been.

"The suture marks will fade away completely in ten days or so," McGee assured her.

"I thought it was a huge, bloody gash," Susan said, raising one hand to touch the new, smooth skin.

"Not huge," McGee said. "But it bled like a faucet gushing water when you were first brought in here. And it resisted healing for a while, probably because you frowned a lot while you were comatose, and the frowning wrinkled your forehead. There wasn't much we could do about that. Blue Cross wouldn't pay for an around-the-clock comedian in your room." He smiled. "Anyway, after the suture marks have faded, the scar itself will just about vanish, too. It won't look as wide as it looks now, and, of course, it won't be discolored. When it's fully healed, if you think it's still too prominent, a good plastic surgeon can use derm-abrasion techniques to scour away some of the scar tissue."

"Oh, I'm sure that won't be necessary," Susan said. "I'm sure it'll be almost invisible. I'm just relieved that I don't look like Frankenstein's monster."

Mrs. Baker laughed. "As if that were ever a possibility, what with your good looks. Goodness gracious, kid, it's a crime the way you underrate yourself!"

Susan blushed.

McGee was amused.

Shaking her head, Mrs. Baker picked up the scissors and the used bandages, and she left the room.

"Now," McGee said, "ready to talk to your boss at Milestone?"

"Phil Gomez," she said, repeating the name McGee had given her yesterday. "I still can't remember a thing about him."

"You will." McGee looked at his wristwatch. "It's a bit early, but not much. He might be in his office now."

He used the phone on the nightstand and asked the hospital operator to dial the Milestone number in Newport Beach, California. Gomez was already at work, and he took the call.

For a couple of minutes, Susan listened to one side of the conversation. McGee told Phil Gomez that she was out of her coma, and he explained about the tem-porary spottiness of her memory, always stressing the word "temporary." Finally, he passed the receiver to her.

Susan took it as if she were being handed a snake. She wasn't sure how she felt about making contact with Milestone. On one hand, she didn't want to go through the rest of her life with a gaping hole in her memory. On the other hand, however, she remembered how she had felt yesterday when the subject of Mile-stone had come up during her talk with McGee: She'd had the disquieting feeling that she might be better off if she never found out what her job had been. A worm of fear had coiled up inside of her yesterday. Now, again, she felt that same inexplicable fear, squirming.

"Hello?"

"Susan? Is that really you?"

"Yes. It's me."

Gomez had a high, quick, puppy-friendly voice. His words bumped into one another. "Susan, thank God, how good to hear from you, how very good indeed, really, I mean it, but of course you know I mean it. We've all been so concerned about you, worried half to death. Even Breckenridge was worried sick about you, and who would ever have thought *he* had any human compassion? So how are you? How are you feeling?"

The sound of his voice kindled no memories in Susan. It was the voice of an utter stranger.

They talked for about ten minutes, and Gomez tried hard to help her recall her work. He said that the Milestone Corporation was an independent, private-industry think tank working on contracts with ITT, IBM, Exxon, and other major corporations. That meant nothing to Susan; she had no idea what an independent, private-industry think tank *was*. Gomez told her that she was—or, rather, *had been*–working on a wide variety of laser applications for the communications industry. She couldn't remember a thing about that. He described her office at Milestone; it sounded like no place she had ever been. He talked about her friends and co-workers there: Eddie Gilroy, Ella Haversby, Tom Kavinsky, Anson Breckenridge, and others. Not one of the names was even slightly familiar to her. By the end of the conversation, Gomez's disappointment and concern were evident in his voice. He urged her to call him again, any time, if she thought it would help, and he suggested that she call some of the others at Milestone, too.

"And listen," he said, "no matter how long it takes you to recuperate, your job will be waiting for you here."

"Thank you," she said, touched by his generous spirit and by the depth of his concern for her.

"No need to thank me," he said. "You're one of the best we have here, and we don't want to lose you. If you weren't nearly a thousand miles away, we'd be there, camping out in your hospital room, doing our best to cheer you up and speed along the healing process."

A minute later, when Susan finally said goodbye to Gomez and hung up, McGee said, "Well? Any luck?"

"None. I still can't remember a thing about my job. But Phil Gomez seemed like a sweet man."

In fact Gomez seemed so nice, seemed to care about her so much, that she wondered how she could have forgotten him so completely.

And then she wondered why a dark dread had grown in her like a malignant tumor during the entire conversation. In spite of Phil Gomez, even the thought of the Milestone Corporation made her uneasy. Worse than uneasy. She was . . . afraid of Milestone. But she didn't know *why*.

■   Later Monday morning, she sat up on the edge of her bed and swung her legs back and forth for a while, exercising them.

Mrs. Baker helped her into a wheelchair and said, "This time I think you ought to make the trip yourself. Once around the entire second floor. If your arms get too tired, just ask any nurse to bring you back here."

"I feel great," Susan said. "I won't get tired. Actually I think maybe I'll try to make at least two trips around the halls."

"I knew that's what you'd say," Mrs. Baker told her. "You just set your mind to getting around once, and that'll be enough for now. Don't try to make a marathon out of it. After lunch and a nap, *then* you can do the second lap."

"You're pampering me too much. I'm a lot stronger than you think I am."

"I knew you'd say that, too. Kiddo, you're incorrigible."

Remembering yesterday's humiliation—when she had insisted she could walk but then hadn't even been able to lower herself into the wheelchair without Mrs. Baker's assistance—Susan blushed. "Okay. Once around. But after lunch and a nap, I'm going to make two *more* laps. And yesterday you said I might try walking a few steps today, and I intend to hold you to that, too."

"Incorrigible," Mrs. Baker repeated, but she was smiling.

"First," Susan said, "I want to have a better look out of this window."

She wheeled herself away from her own bed, past the other bed, which was still empty, and she stopped alongside the window through which she had been able to see (from her bed) only the sky and the upper portions of a few trees. The windowsill was high, and from the wheelchair she had to crane her neck to peer outside.

She discovered that the hospital stood atop a hill, one of a circle of hills that ringed a small valley. Some of the slopes were heavily forested with pines, fir, spruce, and a variety of other trees, while some slopes were covered with emerald-green meadows. A town occupied the floor of the valley and extended some of its neighborhoods into the lower reaches of the hills. Its brick, stone, and wood-sided buildings were tucked in among other trees, facing out on neatly squared-off streets. Although the day was drab and gray, and although ugly storm clouds churned across the sky, threatening rain, the town nonetheless looked serene and quite beautiful.

"It's lovely," Susan said.

"Isn't it?" Mrs. Baker said. "I'll never regret moving out of the city." She sighed. "Well, I've got work to do. Once you've made your circuit of the halls, call me so that I can help you get back into bed." She shook one plump finger at Susan. "And don't you dare try climbing out of that chair and into bed yourself. Regardless of what you think, you're still weak and shaky. You call for me."

"I will," Susan said, although she thought she might just carefully try getting into bed under her own steam, depending on how she felt after taking her wheelchair constitutional.

Mrs. Baker left the room, and Susan sat by the window for a while, enjoying the view.

After a couple of minutes, however, she realized that it was not the view that was delaying her. She hesitated to leave the room because she was afraid. Afraid of meeting Bill Richmond, the Harch look-alike. Afraid that he would smile that hard smile, turn those moonlight-pale eyes on her, wink slyly at her, and perhaps ask her how good old Jerry Stein was getting along these days.

Hell's bells, that's just plain ridiculous! she thought, angry with herself.

She shook herself, as if trying to throw off the irrational fear that clung to her.

He's not Ernest Harch. He's not the boogeyman, for God's sake, she told herself severely. He's thirteen years too young to be Harch. His name's Richmond, Bill

Richmond, and he comes from Pine Wells, and he doesn't know me. So why the devil am I sitting here, immobilized by the fear of encountering him out there in the corridor? What's *wrong* with me?

She shamed herself into motion. She put her hands to the chair's wheels and rolled out of the room, into the hallway.

She was surprised when her arms began to ache before she had gone even a fifth of the distance that she had planned to cover. By the time she traveled both of the short halls, across the top of the hospital's T-shaped floor plan, her muscles began to throb. She stopped the chair for a moment and massaged her arms and shoulders. Her fingers told her what she had wanted to forget: that she was terribly thin, wasted, far from being her old self.

She gritted her teeth and went on, turning the wheelchair into the long main hall. The effort to move and maneuver the chair was sufficiently demanding to require concentration on the task; therefore, it was amazing that she even saw the man at the nurses' station. But she *did* see him, and she stopped her wheelchair only fifteen feet from him. She gaped at him, stunned. Then she closed her eyes, counted slowly to three, opened them—and he was still there, leaning against the counter, chatting with a nurse.

He was tall, about six feet two, with brown hair and brown eyes. His face was long, and so were his features, as if someone had accidentally stretched the putty he was made from before God had had an opportunity to pop him into the kiln to dry. He had a long forehead, a long nose with long, narrow nostrils, and a chin that came to a sharp point. He was wearing white pajamas and a wine-red robe, just as if he were an ordinary patient. But as far as Susan was concerned, there wasn't anything ordinary about him.

She had half expected to encounter Bill Richmond, the Harch look-alike, somewhere in the halls. She had prepared herself for that, had steeled herself for it. But she hadn't expected *this*.

The man was Randy Lee Quince.

Another of the four fraternity men.

She stared at him in shock, in disbelief, in fear, willing him to vanish, praying that he was nothing more than an apparition or a figment of her fevered imagination. But he refused to do the gentlemanly thing and disappear; he remained— unwavering, solid, real.

As she was deciding whether to confront him or flee, he left the nurses' station, turning his back on Susan without glancing at her. He walked away and entered the fifth room past the elevators, on the left side of the hall.

Susan realized she'd been holding her breath. She gasped, and the air she drew into her lungs seemed as sharp and cold as a February night in the High Sierras, where she sometimes went skiing.

For a moment she didn't think she'd ever move again. She felt brittle, icy, as if she had crystallized.

A nurse walked by, her rubber-soled shoes squeaking slightly on the highly polished floor.

The squeak made Susan think of bats.

Her skin broke out in gooseflesh.

There had been bats in the House of Thunder. Bats rustling secretly, disturbed by the flashlights and the candles. Bats chittering nervously during the beating that the fraternity men had administered to poor Jerry. Bats cartwheeling through the pitch blackness, fluttering frantically against her as she doused her stolen flashlight and fled from Harch and the others.

The nurse at the counter, the one to whom Quince had been talking, noticed Susan and must have seen the fright in her face. "Are you all right?"

Susan breathed out. The expelled air was warm on her teeth and lips. Thawed, she nodded at the nurse.

The sound of squealing bats became distant, then swooped away into silence.

She rolled her wheelchair to the counter and looked up at the nurse, a thin brunette whose name she didn't know. "The man you were just talking to . . . "

The nurse leaned over the counter, looked down at her, and said, "The fellow who went into two-sixteen?"

"Yes, him."

"What about him?"

"I think I know him. Or *knew* him. A long time ago." She glanced nervously toward the room into which Quince had gone, then back at the nurse again. "But if he isn't who I think he is, I don't want to burst in on him and make a fool of myself. Do you know his name?"

"Yes, of course. He's Peter Johnson. Nice enough guy, if a little bit on the talky side. He's always coming out here to chat, and I'm beginning to fall behind on my record-keeping because of it."

Susan blinked. "Peter Johnson? Are you sure of that? Are you sure his name's not Randy Lee Quince?"

The nurse frowned. "Quince? No. It's Peter Johnson, all right. I'm sure of that."

Talking to herself as much as to the nurse, Susan said, "Thirteen years ago . . . back in Pennsylvania . . . I knew a young man who looked exactly like that."

"Thirteen years ago?" the nurse said. "Well, then for sure it wasn't this guy. Peter's only nineteen or twenty. Thirteen years ago, he'd have been a little boy."

Startled, but only for a moment, Susan quickly realized that this man *had* been young. Hardly more than a kid. He looked just like Randy Quince *had* looked, but not as Quince would look today. The only way he could be Randy Lee Quince was if Quince had spent the past thirteen years in suspended animation.

■ For lunch, she was given fewer soft foods than before, more solid fare. It was a welcome change of diet, and she cleaned her plate. She was eager to regain her strength and get out of the hospital.

To please Mrs. Baker, Susan lowered her bed, curled on her side, and pretended to nap. Of course, sleep was impossible. She couldn't stop thinking about Bill Richmond and Peter Johnson.

Two look-alikes? Dead ringers, both showing up in the same place, within one day of each other?

What were the odds on that? Astronomical. It wasn't merely unlikely; it was impossible.

Yet not impossible. Because they were here, dammit. She had seen them.

Rather than the chance arrival of two dead ringers, it seemed at least marginally more likely that the real Harch and the real Quince had, by chance, checked into the same hospital that she had checked into. She spent some time considering the possibility that they weren't merely look-alikes, that they were the genuine articles, but she couldn't make much of a case for that notion. They might both have changed their names and assumed entirely new identities after their individual periods of probation had expired, after they could quietly slip away without alerting probation officers. They might have stayed in touch during the years Harch was in prison, and later on they might have moved together to the same town in Oregon. There wasn't really any coincidence involved in that part of the scenario; after all, they had been close friends. They might even both have become ill at the same time and might have gone to the hospital on the same day; that *would* be a coincidence, all right, but not a particularly incredible one. Where it didn't hold up, where the whole house of cards collapsed, was when you considered their miraculously youthful appearance. Perhaps one of them might have passed thirteen years without noticeably aging; perhaps *one* of them might have been fortunate enough to inherit Methuselah's genes. But surely *both* men wouldn't have remained utterly untouched by the passing of so many years. No, that was simply too much to accept.

So where does that leave me? she wondered. With two look-alikes? The old doppelgänger theory again? If they are just a couple of doubles for Harch and Quince, were they cast up here by chance? Or is there a purpose to their arrival in this place, at this particular time? What sort of purpose? Is someone out to get me? And isn't *that* a crazy thought, for God's sake!

She opened her eyes and stared through the bed railing, across the adjacent bed, at the iron-gray sky beyond the window. Chilled, she pulled the covers tighter around her.

She considered other explanations.

Maybe they didn't look as much like Harch and Quince as she thought they did. McGee had suggested that her memory-pictures of their faces were certain to have grown cloudy over the years, whether or not she recognized that fact. He could be right. If you rounded up the real Harch and the real Quince, and if you stood them beside Richmond and Johnson, there might be only a mild resemblance. This dead ringer stuff could be mostly in her head.

But she didn't think so.

Was there a chance that the two men here in the hospital were the sons of Harch and Quince? No. That was a ridiculous theory. While they were too young to be Harch and Quince, these look-alikes were too old to be the children of those men. Neither Harch nor Quince would even have reached puberty by the year in which Richmond and Johnson were born; they couldn't possibly have sired children that long ago.

But now that the concept of blood relationships had arisen, she wondered if these two might be brothers of Harch and Quince. She didn't know if Harch had a brother or not. At the trial, his family had been there to offer him their support. However, there had only been his parents and a younger sister, no brother. Susan vaguely recalled that Randy Quince's brother had shown up at the trial. In fact, now that she thought hard about it, she remembered that the two Quince brothers had looked somewhat alike. But not *exactly* alike. Besides, the brother had been several years *older* than Randy. Of course, there might have been a younger Quince brother at home, one who had been too young to come to the trial. Brothers . . . She couldn't rule it out altogether. These men *could* conceivably be brothers to those who had terrorized her in the House of Thunder.

But, again, she didn't think so.

That left only one explanation: insanity. Maybe she was losing her mind. Suffering from delusions. Hallucinations. Perhaps she was taking the most innocent ingredients and cooking up bizarre paranoid fantasies.

No. She refused to give much consideration to that possibility. Oh, maybe she was too serious about life; *that* was an accusation she would be willing to consider. Sometimes she thought that she was almost too well balanced, too much in control of herself; she envied other people the ability to do silly, spur-of-the-moment, irrational, *exciting* things. If she were more able to let herself go now and then, more able to let her hair down, she wouldn't have missed out on quite so much fun over the years. Too sober, too serious, too much of an ant and not enough of a grasshopper? Yes. But insane, out of her mind? Definitely not.

And now she had run out of answers to the doppelgänger puzzle. Those were the only solutions that had thus far presented themselves, but none of them satisfied her.

She decided not to mention Peter Johnson to either Mrs. Baker or Dr. McGee. She was afraid she'd sound . . . flighty.

She huddled under the covers, watching the churning, sooty sky, wondering if she should simply shrug off the look-alikes, just forget all about them. Wondering if she should merely be amazed by them—or frightened of them. Wondering . . .

That afternoon, without asking for help, she got out of bed and into the wheelchair. Her legs almost failed to support her even for the two or three seconds she needed to stand on them; they felt as if the bones had been extracted from them. She became dizzy, and sweat popped out on her brow, but she made it into the chair all by herself.

Mrs. Baker entered the room only a moment later and scowled at her. "Did you get out of bed alone?"

"Yep. I told you I was stronger than you thought."

"That was a reckless thing to do."

"Oh, no. It was easy."

"Is that so?"

"Easy as cake."

"Then why did you break out in a sweat?"

Susan sheepishly wiped a hand across her damp brow. "I must be going through the change of life."

"Now don't you try to make me laugh," Mrs. Baker said. "You deserve to be scolded, and I'm just the grouch to do it. You're a stubborn one, aren't you?"

"Me? Stubborn?" Susan asked, pretending to be amazed by the very notion. "Not at all. I just know my own mind, if that's what you mean."

Mrs. Baker grimaced. "Stubborn is what I said, and stubborn is what I mean. Why, for heaven's sake, you might have slipped and fallen."

"But I didn't."

"You might have broken an arm or fractured a hip or something, and that would've set your recovery back *weeks!* I swear, if you were twenty years younger, I'd turn you over my knee and give you a good spanking."

Susan burst out laughing.

After a moment in which she was startled by her own statement, Mrs. Baker laughed, too. She leaned against the foot of the bed, shaking with laughter.

Just when Susan thought she had control of herself, her eyes met the nurse's eyes, and they grinned at each other, and then the laughter started all over again.

At last, as her laughing subsided to giggling, Mrs. Baker wiped tears from her eyes and said, "I can't believe I really said that!"

"Turn me over your knee, would you?"

"I guess you must bring out the mothering instincts in me."

"Well, it sure doesn't sound like standard nursing procedure," Susan said.

"I'm just glad you weren't insulted."

"And *I'm* just glad I'm not twenty years younger," Susan said, and they both started laughing again.

A couple of minutes later, when Susan wheeled herself into the hall to get some exercise, she felt in better spirits than she had been at any time since waking from the coma. The spontaneous, uncontrollable fit of laughter with Mrs. Baker had been wonderfully therapeutic. That shared moment, that unexpected but welcome intimacy, made Susan feel less alone and made the hospital seem considerably less cold and less gloomy than it had seemed only a short while ago.

Her arms still ached from the morning's tour in the wheelchair, but in spite of the soreness in her muscles, she was determined to make at least one more circuit of the second floor.

She wasn't worried about encountering Richmond and Johnson. She felt that she could handle such an encounter now. In fact she rather hoped she did meet them again. If she talked with them and took a closer look at them, their amazing resemblance to Harch and Quince might prove to be less remarkable than she had first thought. She didn't believe that would be the case, but she was willing to keep an open mind. And once she'd taken a second look at them, if they were *still* dead ringers for Harch and Quince, perhaps talking to them and getting to know them a bit would make them seem less threatening. In spite of what Philip Marlowe, that inimitable detective, had said, Susan very much wanted to believe that this was all just an incredible coincidence, for the alternatives to coincidence were bizarre and frightening.

By the time she had wheeled around the halls to room 216, she hadn't seen either of the look-alikes. She paused outside Peter Johnson's open door, finally worked up sufficient courage for the task at hand, and propelled herself inside. Going through the doorway, she put an unfelt smile on her face. She had a care-fully rehearsed line ready: *I saw you in the hall this morning, and you look so much like an old friend of mine that I just had to stop by and find out if . . .*

But Peter Johnson wasn't there.

It was a semiprivate room, like her own, and the man in the other bed said, "Pete? He's downstairs in radiology. They had some tests they wanted to put him through."

"Oh," she said. "Well, maybe I'll stop by later."

"Any message for him?"

"No. It wasn't anything important."

In the hall again, she considered asking one of the nurses for Bill Richmond's room number. Then she remembered that he'd just had surgery today and prob-ably wouldn't be feeling too well. This was the wrong time to pay him a visit.

When Susan got back to her own room, Mrs. Baker was pulling shut the privacy curtain that completely enclosed the second bed. "Brought you a roommate," she said, turning away from the closed curtain.

"Oh, good," Susan said. "A little company will make the time go a lot faster."

"Unfortunately, she won't be much company," Mrs. Baker said. "She'll probably spend most of her time sleeping. She's sedated right now, in fact."

"What's her name?"

"Jessica Seiffert."

"Is she very ill?"

Mrs. Baker sighed and nodded. "Terminal cancer, I'm afraid."

"Oh, I'm sorry."

"Well, I don't suppose she's got many regrets. Jessie's seventy-eight years old, after all, and she's led a pretty full life," Mrs. Baker said.

"You know her?"

"She lives here in Willawauk. And now, what about you? Do you feel up to taking a couple of steps, exercising those legs a little?"

"Absolutely."

The nurse pushed the wheelchair close to Susan's bed. "When you get up, hold on to the railing with your right hand, and hold on to me with your left hand. I'll walk you around nice and slow to the other side."

Susan was shaky and hesitant at first, but with each step, she gained self-assurance and moved faster. She wasn't ready to challenge anyone to a footrace—not even poor Jessica Seiffert—but she could feel the muscles flexing in her legs, and she had a pleasant, animal sense of being whole and functional. She was confident that she would spring back to health faster than McGee thought and would be discharged from the hospital well ahead of schedule.

When they reached the other side of the bed, Mrs. Baker said, "Okay, now up and in with you."

"Wait. Let me rest a second, and then let's go back around to the other side."

"Don't tax yourself."

"I can handle it. It's no strain."

"You're sure?"

"I wouldn't lie to you, would I? You might spank me."

The nurse grinned. "Keep that in mind."

As they stood there between the beds, letting Susan gather her strength for the return trip, both of them let their gazes travel to the curtain that was drawn tightly around the second bed, only two or three feet away.

"Does she have any family?" Susan asked.

"Not really. Nobody close."

"That would be awful," Susan whispered.

"What?"

"To die alone."

"No need to whisper," Mrs. Baker said. "She can't hear you. Anyway, Jessie's dealing with it damned well. Except that it's been quite a blow to her vanity. She was a beautiful woman when she was younger. And even in her later years, she was handsome. But she's lost an awful lot of weight, and the cancer's eaten at her until she looks haggard. She was always a tad vain about her appearance, so the disfiguring part of the disease is a lot worse for her than the knowledge that she's dying. She has a great many friends in town, but she specifically asked them not to come visit her in the hospital this time. She wants them to remember her as the woman she was. Doesn't want anyone but doctors and nurses to see her. That's why I drew the curtain around her bed. She's sedated, but if she woke up even for a few seconds and saw the curtain wasn't drawn, she'd be terribly upset."

"Poor soul," Susan said.

"Yes," Mrs. Baker said, "but don't feel too badly about it. That time comes for all of us, sooner or later, and she's held it off longer than a lot of folks."

They retraced their path around the bed, and then Susan got up into it and leaned back gratefully against the pillows.

"Hungry?" Mrs. Baker asked.

"Now that you mention it, yes. Famished."

"Good. You've got to put some flesh on your bones. I'll bring you a snack."

Raising her bed into a sitting position, Susan said, "Do you think it would bother Mrs. Seiffert if I switched on the television?"

"Not at all. She won't even know it's on. And if she does wake up and hear it, maybe she'll want to watch, too. Maybe it'll draw her out of her shell."

As Mrs. Baker left the room, Susan used the remote-control box to turn on the TV. She checked several channels until she found an old movie that was just beginning: *Adam's Rib*, with Spencer Tracy and Katharine Hepburn. She had seen it before, but it was one of those sophisticated, witty films that you could see again and again without becoming bored. She put the remote-control box aside and settled back to enjoy herself.

However, she found it difficult to pay attention to the opening scenes of the movie. Her eyes repeatedly drifted to the other bed. The drawn curtain made her uneasy.

It was no different from the privacy curtain that could be drawn around her own bed. It was hooked into a U-shaped metal track in the ceiling, and it fell to within a foot of the floor, blocking all but the wheels of the bed from view. Her own curtain had been pulled shut on a couple of occasions during the past two days—when it had been necessary for her to use a bedpan, and when she had changed pajamas.

Nevertheless, Jessica Seiffert's closed curtain disturbed Susan.

It's really nothing to do with the curtain itself, she thought. It's just being in the same room with someone who's dying. That's bound to make anyone feel a bit strange.

She stared at the curtain.

No. No, it wasn't the presence of death that bothered her. Something else. Something that she couldn't put her finger on.

The curtain hung straight, white, as perfectly still as if it were only a painting of a curtain.

The movie was interrupted for a commercial break, and Susan used the remote-control box to turn the sound all the way down.

Like a fly in amber, the room was suspended in silence.

The curtain was motionless; not even the slightest draft disturbed it.

Susan said, "Mrs. Seiffert?"

Nothing.

Mrs. Baker came in with a large dish of vanilla ice cream covered with canned blueberries. "How's *that* look?" she asked as she put it down on the bed table and swung the table in front of Susan.

"Enormous," Susan said, pulling her eyes away from the curtain. "I'll never finish all of it."

"Oh, yes, you will. You're on the road back now. That's plain to see. You'll be surprised what an appetite you'll have for the next week or two." She patted her gray hair and said, "Well, my shift just ended. Got to get home and make myself especially pretty. I've got a big date tonight—if you can call bowling, a hamburger dinner, and drinks a 'big date.' But you should get a gander at the guy I've been dating lately. He's a fine specimen of a man. If I was thirty years younger, I'd say he was a real hunk. He's been a lumberman all his life. He's got shoulders to measure a doorway. And you should see his hands! He's got the biggest, hardest, most calloused hands you've ever seen, but he's as gentle as a lamb."

Susan smiled. "Sounds like you might have a memorable night ahead of you."

"It's virtually guaranteed," Mrs. Baker said, turning toward the door.

"Uh . . . before you go."

The nurse turned to her. "Yes, honey, what do you need?"

"Would you . . . uh . . . check on Mrs. Seiffert?"

Mrs. Baker looked puzzled.

"Well," Susan said uneasily, "it's just . . . she's been so silent . . . and even though she's sleeping, it seems as if she's *too* silent . . . and I wondered if maybe . . . "

Mrs. Baker went straight to the second bed, pulled back the end of the curtain, and slipped behind it.

Susan tried to see beyond the curtain before it fell back into place, but she wasn't able to get a glimpse of Jessica Seiffert or of anything else other than the nurse's back.

She looked up at Tracy and Hepburn gesticulating and arguing in silence on the TV screen. She ate a spoonful of the ice cream, which tasted wonderful and hurt her teeth. She looked at the curtain again.

Mrs. Baker reappeared, and the curtain shimmered into place behind her, and again Susan didn't have a chance to see anything beyond.

"Relax," Mrs. Baker said. "She hasn't passed away. She's sleeping like a baby."

"Oh."

"Listen, kid, don't let it prey on your mind. Okay? She's not going to die in this room. She'll be here for a couple of days, maybe a week, until her condition's deteriorated enough for her to be transferred to the intensive care unit. That's where it'll happen, there among all the beeping and clicking life support machines that finally won't be able to support her worth a damn. Okay?"

Susan nodded. "Okay."

"Good girl. Now eat your ice cream, and I'll see you in the morning."

After Thelma Baker left, Susan turned up the sound on the TV set and ate all of her ice cream and tried not to look at Mrs. Seiffert's shrouded bed.

The exercise and the large serving of ice cream eventually conspired to make her drowsy. She fell asleep watching *Adam's Rib*.

In the dream, she was on a TV game show, in an audience of people who were wearing funny costumes. She herself was dressed as a hospital patient, wearing pajamas and a bandage around her head. She realized she was on "Let's Make a

Deal." The host of the show, Monty Hall, was standing beside her. "All right,
Susan!" he said with syrupy enthusiasm. "Do you want to keep the thousand
dollars you've already won, or do you want to trade it for whatever's behind
curtain number one!" Susan looked at the stage and saw that there were not three
curtains, as usual; there were, instead, three hospital beds concealed by privacy
curtains. "I'll keep the thousand dollars," she said. And Monty Hall said, "Oh,
Susan, do you *really* think that's wise? Are you *really* sure you're making the right
decision?" And she said, "I'll keep the thousand dollars, Monty." And Monty Hall
looked around at the studio audience, flashing his white-white teeth in a big smile.
"What do you think, audience? Should she keep the thousand, considering how
little a thousand dollars will buy in these times of high inflation, or should she
trade it for what's behind curtain number one?" The audience roared in unison:
"*Trade it! Trade it!*" Susan shook her head adamantly and said, "I don't want what's
behind the curtain. Please, I don't want it." Monty Hall—who had ceased to look
anything like Monty Hall and now looked distinctly satanic, with arched eyebrows
and terrible dark eyes and a wicked mouth—snatched the thousand dollars out
of her hand and said, "You'll take the curtain, Susan, because it's really what you
deserve. You have it coming to you, Susan. The curtain! Let's see what's behind
curtain number one!" On the stage, the curtain encircling the first hospital bed
was whisked aside, and two men dressed as patients were sitting on the edge of
the bed: Harch and Quince. They were both holding scalpels, and the stage lights
glinted on the razor-sharp cutting edges of the instruments. Harch and Quince
rose off the bed and started across the stage, heading toward the audience, toward
Susan, their scalpels held out in front of them. The audience roared with delight
and applauded.

■   A few minutes after Susan woke from her nap, the bedside phone rang. She
    picked up the receiver. "Hello?"
"Susan?"
"Yes."
"My God, I was so relieved to hear you were out of the coma. Burt and I have
been worried half to death!"
"I'm sorry. Uh . . . I . . . I'm not really sure who this is."
"It's *me*. Franny."
"Franny?"
"Franny Pascarelli, your next-door neighbor."
"Oh, Franny. Sure. I'm sorry."
Franny hesitated, then said, "You . . . uh . . . you do remember me, don't you?"
"Of course. I just didn't recognize your voice at first."
"I heard there was some . . . amnesia."
"I've gotten over most of that."
"Thank God."
"How are you, Franny?"
"Never mind about me. I waddle along from day to day, fighting the dreaded
double chin and the insidious, ever-expanding waistline, but nothing ever really
gets me down. You know me. But my God, what you've been through! How are
you?"

"Getting better by the hour."

"The people where you work . . . they said you might not come out of the coma. We were worried *sick*. Then this morning Mr. Gomez called and said you were going to be okay. I was so happy that I sat down and ate a whole Sara Lee coffee cake."

Susan laughed.

"Listen," Franny said, "don't worry about your house or anything like that. We're taking care of things for you."

"I'm sure you are. It's a relief having you for a neighbor, Franny."

"Well, you'd do the same for us."

They talked for a couple of minutes, not about anything important, just catching up on neighborhood gossip.

When Susan hung up, she felt as if she had at last established contact with the past that she had almost lost forever. She hadn't felt that way when she had spoken with Phil Gomez, for he had been merely a voice without a face, a cipher. But she remembered pudgy Franny Pascarelli, and remembering made all the difference. She and Franny were not really close friends; nevertheless, just talking to the woman made Susan feel that there truly was another world beyond Willawauk County Hospital and that she would eventually return to it. Curiously, talking to Franny also made Susan feel more isolated and alone than ever before.

Dr. McGee made his evening rounds shortly before dinnertime. He was wearing blue slacks, a red plaid shirt, a blue vee-neck sweater, and an open lab coat. Chest hairs, as black as those on his head, curled out of the open neck of his shirt. He was so slim and handsome that he looked as if he had stepped out of a men's fashion advertisement in a slick magazine.

He brought her a large, prettily wrapped box of chocolates and a few paperback books.

"You shouldn't have done this," Susan said, reluctantly accepting the gifts.

"It's not much. I wanted to."

"Well . . . thank you."

"Besides, it's all therapeutic. The candy will help you put on the weight you need. And the books will keep your mind off your troubles. I wasn't sure what kind of thing you liked to read, but since you mentioned Philip Marlowe and Raymond Chandler yesterday, I thought you might like mysteries."

"These are perfect," she said.

He pulled up a chair beside her bed, and they talked for almost twenty minutes, partly about her exercise sessions, partly about her appetite, partly about the remaining blank spots in her memory, but mostly about personal things like favorite books, favorite foods, favorite movies.

They *didn't* talk about Peter Johnson, the Quince look-alike she had seen this morning. She was afraid of sounding hysterical or even irrational. *Two* dead ringers? McGee would have to wonder if the problem wasn't in her own perceptions. She didn't want him to think she was at all . . . unbalanced.

Besides, in truth, she wasn't entirely sure that her perceptions *weren't* affected by her head injury. Her doubts about herself were small, niggling, but they were doubts nonetheless.

Finally, as McGee was getting up to leave, she said, "I don't see how you have any time for a private life, considering how much time you spend with your patients."

"Well, I don't spend as much time with other patients as I spend with you. You're special."

"I guess you don't often get a chance to treat an amnesiac," she said.

He smiled, and the smile was not conveyed solely by the curve of his finely formed lips; his eyes were a part of it, too—so clear, so blue, filled with what seemed to be affection. "It's not your amnesia that makes you so special. And I'm sure you're very well aware of that."

She wasn't quite sure of him. She didn't know if he was just being nice, just trying to lift her spirits, or whether he really found her attractive. But how could he find her appealing in her current condition? Every time she looked in the mirror, she thought of a drowned rat. Surely, his flirting was just a standard part of his professional bedside manner.

"How's your roommate been behaving?" he asked in a very soft, conspiratorial voice.

Susan glanced at the curtain. "Quiet as a mouse," she whispered.

"Good. That means she's not in pain. There isn't much I can do for her, but at least I can make her last days relatively painless."

"Oh, is she your patient?"

"Yes. Delightful woman. It's a shame that dying has to be such a long, slow process for her. She deserved a much better, cleaner exit."

He went to the other bed and stepped behind the curtain.

Yet again, Susan failed to get a glimpse of Mrs. Seiffert.

Behind the curtain, McGee said, "Hello, Jessie. How are you feeling today?"

There was a murmured response, nearly inaudible, a dry and brittle rasp, too low for Susan to make out any of the woman's words, even too low to be positively identifiable as a human voice.

She listened to McGee's side of the conversation for a minute or two, and then there was a minute of silence. When he came out from behind the curtain, she craned her neck, trying to see the old woman. But the curtain was drawn aside just enough for McGee to pass, not an inch more, and he let it fall shut immediately in his wake.

"She's a tough lady," he said with obvious admiration. Then he blinked at Susan and said, "In fact she's more than a little bit like you."

"Nonsense," Susan said. "I'm not tough. For heaven's sake, you should have seen me hobbling around this bed today, leaning on poor Mrs. Baker so hard that it's a miracle I didn't drag both of us down."

"I mean tough inside," McGee said.

"I'm a marshmallow." She was embarrassed by his compliments because she still couldn't decide in what spirit they were offered. Was he courting her? Or merely being nice? She changed the subject: "If you drew back the curtain, Mrs. Seiffert could watch some TV with me this evening."

"She's asleep," McGee said. "Fell asleep while I was talking to her. She'll probably sleep sixteen hours a day or more from here on out."

"Well, she might wake up later," Susan persisted.

"Thing is—she doesn't *want* the curtain left open. She's somewhat vain about her appearance."

"Mrs. Baker told me about that. But I'm sure I could make her feel at ease. She might be self-conscious at first, but I know I could make her feel comfortable."

"I'm sure you could," he said, "but I—"

"It can be excruciatingly boring just lying in bed all day. Some TV might make the time pass more quickly for her."

McGee took her hand. "Susan, I know you mean well, but I think it's best we leave the curtain closed, as Jessie prefers. You forget she's *dying*. She might not *want* the time to pass more quickly. Or she may find quiet contemplation infinitely preferable to watching an episode of 'Dallas' or 'The Jeffersons.' "

Although he hadn't spoken sharply, Susan was stung by what he had said. Because he was right, of course. No TV sitcom was going to cheer up a dying woman who was teetering between drug-heavy sleep and intolerable pain.

"I didn't mean to be insensitive," she said.

"Of course you didn't. And you weren't. Just let Jessie sleep, and stop worrying about her." He squeezed Susan's hand, patted it, and finally let it go. "I'll see you in the morning for a few minutes."

She sensed that he was trying to decide whether or not to bend down and kiss her on the cheek. He started to do it, then drew back, as if he were as unsure of her feelings as she was of his. Or maybe she was only imagining those intentions and reactions; she couldn't make up her mind which it had been.

"Sleep well."

"I will," she said.

He went to the door, stopped, turned to her again. "By the way, I've scheduled some therapy for you in the morning."

"What kind of therapy?"

"PT—physical therapy. Exercise, muscle training. For your legs, mostly. And a session in the whirlpool. An orderly will be around to take you downstairs to the PT unit sometime after breakfast."

■ Mrs. Seiffert couldn't feed herself, so a nurse fed dinner to her. Even that task was performed with the curtain drawn.

Susan ate dinner and read a mystery novel, which she enjoyed because it kept her mind off the Harch and Quince look-alikes.

Later, after a snack of milk and cookies, she shuffled to the bathroom, supporting herself against the wall, then shuffled back. The return trip seemed twice as long as the original journey.

When the night nurse brought a sedative, Susan knew she didn't need it, but she took it anyway, and in a short time she was sound asleep—

"*Susan . . . Susan . . . Susan . . .*"

—until a voice softly calling her name penetrated her sleep and caused her to sit suddenly upright in bed.

"*Susan . . .*"

Her heart was hammering because, even as groggy as she was, she detected something sinister in that voice.

The night lamp provided little light, but the room was not entirely dark. As far as she could see, no one was there.

She waited to hear her name again.

The night remained silent.

"Who's there?" she asked at last, squinting into the purple-black shadows in the corners of the room.

No one answered.

Shaking off the last clinging threads of sleep, she realized that the voice had come from her left, from the curtained bed. And it had been a man's voice.

The curtain still encircled the bed. In spite of the gloom, she could see it. The white material reflected and seemed even to amplify the meager glow of the night light. The curtain appeared to shimmer like a cloud of phosphorus.

"Is someone there?" she asked.

Silence.

"Mrs. Seiffert?"

The curtain didn't move.

Nothing moved.

According to the radiant face of the nightstand clock, it was 3:42 in the morning.

Susan hesitated, then snapped on the bedside lamp. The bright light stung her eyes, and she left it on only long enough to be sure there was no one lurking where the shadows had been. Jessica Seiffert's shrouded bed looked far less threatening in full light than it had in darkness.

She clicked off the lamp.

The shadows scurried back to their nests, and their nests were everywhere.

Maybe I was dreaming, she thought. Maybe it was only a voice calling to me in a dream.

But she was pretty sure that tonight had provided the first dreamless sleep she'd had since coming out of her coma.

She fumbled for the bed controls and raised herself halfway up into a sitting position. For a while she listened to the darkness, waited.

She didn't think she would be able to get back to sleep. The strange voice had reminded her of the Harch and Quince look-alikes, and that seemed like a perfect prescription for insomnia. But the sedative she had been given was evidently still doing its work, for in time she dozed.

6

ALL DAY YESTERDAY A STORM HAD BEEN PENDING. THE SKY had looked beaten, bruised, and swollen.

Now, Tuesday morning, the storm broke with no warning other than a single clap of thunder so loud that it seemed to shake the entire hospital. Rain fell suddenly and heavily like a giant tent collapsing with a *whoosh* and a roar.

Susan couldn't see the storm because the curtain around the other bed blocked her view of the window. But she could hear the thunder and see the brilliant flashes of lightning. The fat raindrops pounded on the unseen windowpane with the force of drumbeats.

She ate a filling breakfast of hot cereal, toast, juice, and a sweet roll, shuffled to and from the bathroom with more assurance and with less pain than she'd had last evening, then settled down in bed with another mystery novel.

She had read only a few pages when two orderlies arrived with a wheeled stretcher. The first one through the door said, "We're here to take you down to the physical therapy department, Miss Thorton."

She put her book aside, looked up—and felt as if February had just breathed down the back of her neck.

They were dressed in hospital whites, and the blue stitched lettering on their shirt pockets said *Willawauk County Hospital*, but they weren't merely two orderlies. They weren't anything as simple as that, nothing as ordinary as that.

The first man, the one who had spoken, was about five feet seven, pudgy, with dirty blond hair, a round face, dimpled chin, pug nose, and the small quick eyes of a pig. The other was taller, perhaps six feet, with red hair, hazel eyes, and a fair complexion spattered with freckles under the eyes and across the bridge of the nose; he was not handsome, but certainly good looking, and his open face, his soft-edged features, were distinctly Irish.

The pudgy one was Carl Jellicoe.

The redhead was Herbert Parker.

They were the last of the four fraternity brothers from the House of Thunder, friends of Harch and Quince.

Impossible. Nightmare creatures. They were meant to inhabit only the land of sleep.

But she was awake. And they were here. Real.

"Some storm, isn't it?" Jellicoe asked conversationally as a cannonade of thunder shot through the sky.

Parker pushed the wheeled stretcher all the way into the room and parked it parallel to Susan's bed.

Both men were smiling.

She realized that they were young, twenty or twenty-one. Like the others, they had been utterly untouched by the passing of thirteen years.

Two *more* look-alikes? Showing up here at the same time? Both of them employed as orderlies by the Willawauk County Hospital? No. Ridiculous. Preposterous. The odds against such an incredible coincidence were astronomical.

They had to be the real thing, Jellicoe and Parker themselves, not dead ringers.

But then, with stomach-wrenching suddenness, she remembered that Jellicoe and Parker were dead.

Dammit, they were *dead*.

Yet they were here, too, smiling at her.

Madness.

"No," Susan said, shrinking back from them, moving to the opposite edge of the bed, tight up against the tubular metal railing, which burned coldly through her thin pajamas. "No, I'm not going downstairs with you. Not me."

Jellicoe feigned puzzlement. Pretending not to see that she was terrified, pretending not to understand what she really meant, he glanced at Parker and said, "Have we fouled up? I thought we were supposed to bring down Thorton in two fifty-eight."

Parker fished in his shirt pocket, pulled out a folded slip of paper, opened it, read it. "Says right here. Thorton in two-five-eight."

Susan wouldn't have thought she'd known Jellicoe and Parker well enough to recognize their voices after thirteen years. She had met both of them for the first time on the night that they and the two others had beaten and murdered Jerry Stein. At the trial, Jellicoe had not spoken a word on the witness stand, had never even taken the stand, for he had exercised his rights under the Fifth Amendment to avoid incriminating himself; Parker had testified but not at length. Indeed, she *didn't* recognize Carl Jellicoe's voice. But when Herbert Parker spoke, reading from the slip of paper he had taken from his shirt pocket, Susan jerked in surprise, for he spoke with a Boston accent, which was something she had nearly forgotten.

He looked like Parker. He spoke like Parker. He had to *be* Parker.

But Herbert Parker was dead, buried, and rotting away in a grave somewhere!

They were both looking at her strangely.

She wanted to look at the nightstand, behind her, to see if there was anything she could conceivably use as a weapon, but she didn't dare take her eyes off them.

Jellicoe said, "Didn't your doctor tell you we'd be taking you downstairs for therapy this morning?"

"Get out of here," she said, her voice strained, tremulous. "Go away."

The two men glanced at each other.

A series of preternaturally brilliant lightning bolts pierced the cloud-dark day, shimmered on the rain-washed windowpane, and cast stroboscopic patterns of light and shadow on the wall opposite the foot of Susan's bed. The eerie light briefly transformed Carl Jellicoe's face, distorted it, so that for an instant his eyes were sunken caverns with a bead of hot white light far down at the bottom of each.

To Susan, Parker said, "Hey, listen, there's really nothing to worry about. It's only therapy, you know. It's not painful or anything like that."

"Yeah," Jellicoe said, now that the incredible barrage of lightning was over. He wrinkled his piggish face in an unnaturally broad smile. "You'll really like it down in the PT department, Miss Thorton." He stepped up to the bed and started to put down the railing on that side. "You'll *love* the whirlpool."

"I said, get out!" Susan screamed. "Get out! Get the *hell* out of here!"

Jellicoe flinched, stepped back.

Susan shook violently. Each beat of her heart was like the concrete-busting impact of a triphammer.

If she got on the stretcher and let them take her downstairs, she would never be brought back again. That would be the end of her. She knew it. She *knew* it.

"I'll claw your eyes out if you try to take me from this room," she said, struggling to keep the tremor out of her voice. "I mean it."

Jellicoe looked at Parker. "Better get a nurse."

Parker hurried out of the room.

The hospital's lights dimmed, went off, and for a moment there was only the funereal light of the storm-gray day, and then the power came on again.

Jellicoe turned his small, close-set eyes on Susan and favored her with an utterly empty smile that made her chilled blood even colder. "Just take it easy, huh? Look, lady, just relax. Will you do that for me?"

"Stay away."

"Nobody's going to come near you. So just stay calm," he said in a soft, singsong voice, making a placating gesture with his hands. "Nobody wants to hurt you. We're all your friends here."

"Dammit, don't pretend that you think I'm crazy," she said. She was both terrified and furious. "You know damned well I'm not nuts. You know what's going on here. *I* don't know, but *you* sure as hell do."

He stared at her, saying nothing. But there was mockery in his eyes and in the smug half-smile that turned up only one corner of his mouth.

"Get back," Susan said. "Get away from the bed. *Now!*"

Jellicoe retreated to the open door, but he didn't leave the room.

The sound of Susan's own heartbeat was so loud in her ears that it challenged the rain-wind-thunder-lightning chorus of the autumn storm.

Each breath caught in her dry, jagged throat and had to be torn loose with conscious effort.

Jellicoe watched her.

This can't be happening, she told herself frantically. I'm a rational woman. I'm a scientist. I don't believe in miraculous coincidences, and as sure as the sun will rise tomorrow, I don't believe in the supernatural. There aren't such things as ghosts. Dead men don't come back. *They don't!*

Jellicoe watched her.

Susan cursed her weak, emaciated body. Even if she had a chance to run, she wouldn't get more than a few steps. And if they forced her to fight for her life, she wouldn't last very long.

Finally, Herbert Parker returned with a nurse, a severe looking blonde who was a stranger to Susan.

"What's wrong here?" the nurse asked. "Miss Thorton, why are you upset?"

"These men," she said.

"What about them?" the nurse asked, coming to the bed.

"They want to hurt me," Susan said.

"No, they only want to take you down to the physical therapy department on the first floor," the nurse said. She was at the bed now, at the side where Carl Jellicoe had lowered the safety railing.

"You don't understand," Susan said, wondering how in the name of God she could explain the situation to this woman without sounding like a raving lunatic.

Parker was standing at the open door. He said, "She threatened to claw our eyes out."

Jellicoe had drifted closer and was near the foot of the bed; too near.

"Back off, you bastard," Susan said, virtually spitting the words at him.

He ignored her.

To the nurse, Susan said, "Tell him to back off. You don't understand. I've got good reason to be afraid of him. Tell him!"

"Now, there's no reason on earth for you to be upset," the nurse said.

"We're all your friends here," Jellicoe said.

"Susan, do you know where you are?" the nurse asked in a tone of voice usually reserved for very young children, very old people, and the mentally disturbed.

Frustrated, angry, Susan shouted at her. "Hell, yes, I know where I am. I'm in the Willawauk County Hospital. I suffered a head injury, and I was in a coma for three weeks, but I'm not suffering any kind of relapse. I'm not having hallucinations or delusions. I'm not hysterical. These men are—"

"Susan, would you do something for me?" the nurse asked, still using that excessively reasonable, syrupy, patronizing tone of voice. "Would you not shout? Would you please lower your voice? If you would just lower your voice and take a minute to catch your breath, I'm sure you'll feel calmer. Just take a few deep breaths and try to relax. Nothing can be accomplished until we're all relaxed and at ease with one another, until we're all polite to one another."

"Christ!" Susan said, burning with frustration.

"Susan, I want to give you this," the nurse said. She raised one hand; she was holding a damp cotton pad and a hypodermic syringe that she had already filled with an amber fluid.

"No," Susan said, shaking her head.

"It'll help you relax."

"No."

"Don't you want to relax?"

"I want to keep my guard up."

"It won't hurt, Susan."

"Get away from me."

The nurse leaned across the bed toward her.

Susan snatched up the paperback book that she'd been reading and threw it in the woman's face.

The nurse took a step backwards, but she was unhurt. She looked at Jellicoe. "Can you help me?"

"Sure," he said.

"Stay away," Susan warned him.

Jellicoe started around the side of the bed.

She twisted to her left, scooped a drinking glass off the nightstand, and pitched it at Jellicoe's head.

He ducked, and the glass missed, shattering explosively against the wall beyond him.

Susan looked for something else to throw.

He moved in fast, and she tried to claw his face, and he seized her wrists in his viselike hands. He was stronger than he looked. She couldn't have wrenched free of him even if she'd been in better condition.

"Don't struggle," the nurse said.

"We're all your friends here," Carl Jellicoe said for the third time.

Susan fought back but without effect. Jellicoe forced her back against the mattress. She slid down on the bed until she was stretched out flat, helpless.

Jellicoe pinned her arms at her sides.

The nurse pushed up the sleeve of her green pajamas.

Susan thrashed and drummed her feet on the bed and cried out for help.

"Hold her still," the nurse said.

"Not easy," Jellicoe said. "She's got a lot of fire in her."

What he said was true. She was surprised that she could resist at all. Panic had brought new energy with it.

The nurse said, "Well, at least, the way she's straining, I can see the vein. It's popped up real nice."

Susan screamed.

The nurse quickly swabbed her arm with the cotton pad. It was wet and cold.

Susan smelled alcohol and screamed again.

A freight train of thunder roared in and derailed with a hard, sharp crash. The hospital lights flickered out, on, out, on.

"Susan, if you don't hold perfectly still, I might accidentally break off the needle in your arm. Now, you don't want that to happen, do you?"

She refused to go peacefully. She writhed and twisted and tried to snake her way out of Jellicoe's grip.

Then a familiar voice said, "What in heaven's name is going on here? What're you doing to her?"

The blond nurse drew the needle back just as it was about to prick Susan's bare skin.

Jellicoe's grip relaxed as he turned to see who had spoken.

Susan strained to lift her head from the mattress.

Mrs. Baker was at the foot of the bed.

"Hysteria," the blond nurse said.

"She was violent," Jellicoe said.

"Violent?" Mrs. Baker said, clearly not believing it. She looked at Susan. "Honey, what's the matter?"

Susan looked up at Carl Jellicoe, who was still holding her. His gaze cut into her. He subtly increased the pressure he was applying with his fingers, and for the first time she realized that his flesh was warm, not cold and clammy like the flesh of the dead. She looked back at Mrs. Baker, and in a calm voice she said, "Do you remember what happened to me thirteen years ago? Yesterday, I told you and Dr. McGee all about it."

"Yes," Mrs. Baker said, lifting her chain-hung glasses off her bosom and putting them on her face. "Of course I remember. A terrible thing."

"Well, I was just having a nightmare about it when these two orderlies came into the room."

"All this is just because of a nightmare?" Mrs. Baker asked.

"Yes," Susan lied. She just wanted to get Jellicoe, Parker, and the blond nurse out of the room. When they were gone, perhaps then she could explain the true situation to Thelma Baker. If she tried to explain it now, Mrs. Baker might well agree with the blond nurse's diagnosis: hysteria.

"Let her go," Mrs. Baker said. "I'll handle this."

"She was violent," Jellicoe said.

"She was having a nightmare," Mrs. Baker said. "She's fully awake now. Let her go."

"Thelma," the blond nurse said, "it didn't seem like she was asleep when she threw that book at me."

"She's had a tough time, poor kid," Mrs. Baker said, pushing in to the side of the bed, nudging the other nurse away. "Go on, the rest of you, go on. Susan and I will talk this out."

"In my judgment—" the blond nurse began.

"Millie," Mrs. Baker said, "you know I trust your judgment implicitly. But this is a special case. I can handle it. I really can."

Reluctantly, Jellicoe let go of Susan.

Susan went limp with relief, then sat up in bed. She massaged one wrist, then the other. She could still feel where Jellicoe's fingers had dug into her.

The two orderlies drifted out of the room, taking the wheeled stretcher with them.

The blond nurse hesitated, biting her thin lower lip, but at last she left, too, still carrying the damp cotton pad and the syringe.

Mrs. Baker walked around the bed, being careful not to step on any shards of the broken drinking glass. She looked in on Mrs. Seiffert, came back to Susan, and said, "The old dear slept right through all the ruckus." She got another tumbler out of the nightstand and filled it with water from the dew-beaded metal pitcher that stood on a plastic tray atop the stand.

"Thank you," Susan said, accepting the water. She drank thirstily. Her throat was slightly sore from screaming, and the water soothed it.

"More?"

"No, that was enough," she said, putting the glass on the nightstand.

"Now," Mrs. Baker said, "for Pete's sake, what was all that about?"

Susan's relief quickly gave way to tension, to dread, for she realized that the terror wasn't over yet. In fact it had probably just begun.

OPENING THE CURTAIN

7

THE LIGHTNING AND THUNDER HAD MOVED OFF TOWARD THE next county, but the gray rain continued to fall, an ocean of it, and the day was dreary, still.

Susan sat in bed, feeling small and washed out, as if the rain, though never touching her, were nonetheless somehow sluicing away her very substance.

Standing beside the bed, hands thrust into the pockets of his lab coat, Jeffrey McGee said, "So now you're saying that look-alikes for *three* of those fraternity men have shown up here."

"Four."

"What?"

"I didn't tell you about the one I saw yesterday."

"That would be . . . Quince?"

"Yes."

"You saw him here? Or someone who looked like him?"

"In the hall, while I was in the wheelchair. He's a patient, just like Harch. Room two-sixteen. His name's supposed to be Peter Johnson." She hesitated, then said, "He looks nineteen."

McGee studied her in silence for a moment.

Although he had not yet been judgmental, although he seemed to be trying hard to find a way to believe her story, she could not meet his eyes. The things she had told him were so outlandish that the scientist in her was embarrassed merely by the need to speak of them. She looked down at her hands, which were knotted together in her lap.

McGee said, "Is that how old Randy Lee Quince was when he helped kill Jerry Stein? Was he just nineteen?"

"Yes. He was the youngest of the four."

And I know what's going through your mind right now, she thought. You're thinking about my head injury, about the coma, about the possibility of minor brain damage that didn't show up on any of your X rays or other tests, a tiny embolism, or perhaps an exceedingly small hemorrhage in a threadlike cerebral capillary. You're wondering if I've received a brain injury that just, by sheerest chance, happens to affect that infinitesimal lump of gray tissue in which the memories of the House of Thunder are stored; you're wondering if such an injury—a sand-grain blood clot or a minuscule, ruptured vessel—could cause those memories to become excessively vivid, resulting in my preoccupation with that one event in my life. Am I fixated on Jerry's murder for the simple reason that some abnormal pressure in my brain is focusing my attention relentlessly upon the House of Thunder? Is that pressure causing me to fantasize new developments in that old nightmare? Is that nearly microscopic rotten spot in my head altering my perceptions so that I believe I see dead ringers for Harch and the others, when, in reality, neither Bill Richmond nor Peter Johnson nor the two orderlies bear any resemblance whatsoever to the quartet of fraternity brothers? Well, maybe that *is* what's happening to me. But then again, maybe not. One minute, I think that is the explanation. The next minute, I know it must be something else altogether. They're *not* dead ringers. They *are* dead ringers. They're *not* the real Harch, Quince, Jellicoe, and Parker. They *are* the real Harch, Quince, Jellicoe, and Parker. I just don't know. God help me, I just don't know what's happening to me, so dear Dr. McGee, I can't blame you for your confusion and your doubts.

"So now there are four of them," he said. "Four dead ringers, all here in the hospital."

"Well . . . I don't know exactly."

"But didn't you just tell me—"

"I mean, yes, they look identical to the men who killed Jerry. But I don't know if they're nothing more than dead ringers or if they're . . . "

"Yes?"

"Well, maybe they're . . . something else."

"Such as?"

"In the case of Parker and Jellicoe . . . "

"Go on," he urged.

Susan simply couldn't bring herself to speculate aloud on the existence of ghosts. When Carl Jellicoe had been holding her down against the mattress, his hands clamped tightly on her arms, supernatural explanations had not been beyond consideration. But now it seemed like sheer lunacy to talk seriously about dead men returning from their graves to extract bloody vengeance from the living.

"Susan?"

She met his eyes at last.

"Go on," he urged again. "If the two orderlies aren't just look-alikes for Jellicoe and Parker, if they're something else, as you say, then what did you have in mind?"

Wearily, she said, "Oh, Jeez, I just don't know. I don't know what to say to you, how to explain it to you—or to myself, as far as that goes. I don't know what to think about it. I can only tell you what I saw with my own eyes—or what I thought I saw."

"Listen, I didn't mean to pressure you," he said quickly. "I know this can't be easy for you."

She saw pity in his lovely blue eyes, and she immediately looked away from him. She didn't want to be an object of pity to anyone, especially not to Jeffrey McGee. She loathed the very thought of it.

He was silent for a while, staring at the floor, apparently lost in thought.

She wiped her damp palms on the sheets and leaned back against the pillow. She closed her eyes.

Outside, the marching *tramp-tramp-tramp* of the rain transformed the entire Willawauk Valley into a parade ground.

He said, "Suggestion."

"I'm sure ready for one."

"You might not like it."

She opened her eyes. "Try me."

"Let me bring Bradley and O'Hara in here right now."

"Jellicoe and Parker."

"Their names are really Bradley and O'Hara."

"So Mrs. Baker told me."

"Let me bring them in here. I'll ask each of them to tell you a little something about himself: where he was born and raised, where he went to school, how he came to be working at this hospital. Then you can ask them any questions you want, anything at all. Maybe if you talk to them for a while, maybe if you get to know them a bit . . . "

"Maybe then I'll decide they don't look so much like Parker and Jellicoe after all," she said, completing the thought for him.

He moved closer, putting a hand on her shoulder, leaving her no choice but to look up at him and see the pity again. "Isn't it at least a *possibility* that, once you know them, you might see them differently?"

"Oh, yes," she said. "It's not only possible or probable. It's almost a certainty."

Clearly, her awareness and her objectivity surprised him.

She said, "I'm fully aware that my problem is most likely either psychological or the result of some organically rooted brain dysfunction related to the auto accident, or possibly not to the accident directly but to the effects of spending three weeks in a coma."

McGee shook his head and smiled; it was his turn to look embarrassed. "I keep forgetting you're a scientist."

"You don't have to coddle me, Dr. McGee."

Virtually glowing with relief, he put his hands behind him, palms flat on the mattress, and boosted himself up; he sat on the edge of the bed, beside her. That casual and unaffected act, such a spontaneous physical expression of the pleasure he took from her no-nonsense response, made him seem ten years younger than he was—and even more appealing than he had been. "You know, I was going crazy trying to think of some nice, gentle way to tell you that this whole look-alike business was probably in your head, and here you knew it all the time. Which means we can probably rule out one of the two diagnoses that you just outlined; I mean, it's probably *not* a psychological boogeyman that's riding you. You're too stable for that. You're amazing!"

"So my best hope is brain dysfunction," Susan said with heavy irony.

He sobered. "Well, listen, it can't be anything really life-threatening. It's certainly not a major hemorrhage or anything like that. If it was, you wouldn't be as fit and aware as you are. Besides, it wasn't serious enough to show up on the brain scan that we did while you were in the coma. It's something small, Susan, something treatable."

She nodded.

"But you're still scared of Bradley and O'Hara and the other two," he said.

"Yes."

"Even though you know it's most likely all in your head."

"The operative words are 'most likely.' "

"I'd go so far as to say it's *definitely* a perceptual problem resulting from brain dysfunction."

"I imagine you're right."

"But you're still scared of them."

"Very."

"Your recovery mustn't be set back by stress or depression," he said, frowning.

"I can cope, I guess. My middle name is Pollyanna."

He smiled again. "Good. That's the spirit."

Except that, in my heart, Susan thought, I don't for a minute believe that I've got either a psychological problem or any kind of brain dysfunction. Those answers just don't *feel* right. Intellectually, I can accept them, but on a gut level they seem wrong. What *feels* right is the answer that is no answer, the answer that makes no sense: These men *are* dead ringers for Harch, Quince, Jellicoe, and Parker, not just in my eyes but in reality; and they want something from me—probably my life.

Wiping one hand across her face as if she could slough off her weariness and cast it aside, Susan said, "Well . . . let's get this over with. Bring in Jellicoe and Parker, and let's see what happens."

"Bradley and O'Hara."

"Yeah, them."

"Listen, if you *think* of them as Jellicoe and Parker, then you're bound to *see* them as Jellicoe and Parker. You're playing right into your perceptual problem. Think of them as Denny Bradley and Pat O'Hara, and that might help you keep your perceptions clear; it might help you see them as they *are*."

"Okay. I'll think of them as Bradley and O'Hara. But if they *still* look like Jellicoe and Parker, I might want to see an exorcist instead of a neurologist."

He laughed.

She didn't.

■ McGee had briefly explained the situation to Bradley and O'Hara before he had brought them back to her room. They appeared to be concerned about Susan's condition, and they seemed eager to help in any way they could.

She tried not to let them see how much their presence still disturbed her. Although her stomach was clenched and although her heart was racing, she forced a smile for their benefit and tried to appear relaxed. She wanted to give McGee a fair chance to prove that these two men, on closer inspection, would turn out to be nothing but a pair of ordinary, innocuous young fellows without an ounce of meanness between them.

McGee stood beside the bed, one hand on the rail, occasionally touching her shoulder, offering moral support.

The orderlies stood at the foot of the bed. Initially, they were stiff, like a couple of schoolboys reciting a lesson in front of a stern teacher. But gradually they loosened up.

Dennis Bradley spoke first. He was the one who had held her down on the bed while the nurse had prepared to give her an injection.

"First of all," Bradley said, "I want to apologize if I was maybe a little too rough with you. I didn't mean to be. It's just that I was kind of scared, you know." He shifted his weight awkwardly from one foot to the other. "I mean, considering what you said . . . you know . . . about what you'd do . . . well, what you'd do to our *eyes* . . . "

"It's all right," Susan said, though she could still feel his fierce grip, his fingers pressing cruelly into her thin arms. "I was scared, too. Actually, I guess I owe *you* an apology. Both of you."

At McGee's urging, Bradley talked about himself. He had been born in Tucson, Arizona, twenty years ago last July. His parents had moved to Portland, Oregon, when he was nine. He had no brothers, one older sister. He had attended a two-year junior college and had taken special courses to prepare for a career as a paramedic. One year ago, he had accepted this job in Willawauk as a combination orderly and ambulance superintendent. He answered all of Susan's questions. He was unfailingly candid, outgoing, and helpful.

So was Patrick O'Hara, the redhead. He had been born and raised, he said, in Boston. His family was Irish Catholic. No, he'd never known anyone named Herbert Parker. In fact he'd never known anybody in Boston named Parker, Herbert or otherwise. Yes, he had an older brother, but, no, his brother didn't really look much like him. No, he'd never been to Briarstead College in Pennsylvania; never even heard of it before this minute. He had come West when he was eighteen, three years ago. He'd been in Willawauk for, let's see, sixteen, no, more like seventeen months.

Susan had to admit that both Dennis Bradley and Pat O'Hara were friendly. Now that she had gotten to know a little about them, she could cite no logical reason why she should any longer regard them as a threat to herself.

Neither of them appeared to be lying.

Neither of them seemed to be hiding anything.

Yet to her eyes, confused perception or not, Bradley still looked exactly like Carl Jellicoe.

Exactly.

O'Hara was still a dead ringer for Herbert Parker.

And Susan had the feeling, unsupported by anything that the two young men had just said or done, that they were not what they presented themselves to be, that they *were* lying and *were* hiding something. Intuitively, in spite of all the solid evidence to the contrary, she sensed that this show-and-tell had been nothing more than a well-wrought performance, an act which they had brought off with consummate skill.

Of course maybe I'm just a raving paranoid, completely starkers, she thought grimly.

When the two orderlies had left the room, McGee said, "Well?"

"It didn't work. I thought of them as Bradley and O'Hara, but they still looked like Jellicoe and Parker."

"You realize that doesn't prove or disprove the theory that you've got brain-injury-related perceptual problems."

"I know."

"We'll begin another series of tests first thing tomorrow, starting with new X rays."

She nodded.

He sighed. "Damn, I was hoping that a talk with Bradley and O'Hara would set your mind at ease, make you feel more comfortable and less anxious until we can pinpoint the cause of your condition and correct this perceptual confusion."

"I'm about as comfortable as a cat on a hot stove."

"I don't want you to be overwhelmed with stress or anxiety. That's going to slow your recuperation. I guess it wouldn't help to reason with you?"

"No. As I said, intellectually, I accept your explanation. But emotionally, instinctually, on a gut level, I still feel that the four fraternity men are coming back . . . ganging up on me."

She was cold. She put her hands and arms under the covers.

"Look," McGee said, deciding to attempt to reason with her even though she'd said it was no use. "Look, maybe you have good cause to be suspicious of Richmond and Johnson. It's not probable, but it is possible, *remotely* possible, that they're Harch and Quince living under new names."

"Hey, you're supposed to be making me feel more comfortable, less anxious. Remember?"

"My point is that you have absolutely *no* cause to be suspicious of Bradley and O'Hara. They can't be Jellicoe and Parker because those men are dead."

"I know. Dead."

"So you should feel better about Bradley and O'Hara."

"But I don't."

"Furthermore, Bradley and O'Hara can't have been brought here as part of some complicated, nefarious plot to get even with you for your testimony in that trial. They were here long before you ever arrived, before you even planned to take your vacation in Oregon, before you'd ever even heard of the Viewtop Inn. Are you saying someone knew—in some fantastic, magical, clairvoyant fashion—that you would have an accident here one day and wind up in Willawauk Hospital? Are you saying someone foresaw this and that he then set out to plant O'Hara here seventeen months ago—and then Dennis Bradley, a year ago?"

Her face was hot, for he was making her feel ridiculous. "Of course I don't believe that."

"Good."

"It's silly."

"Yes, it is. So you should feel perfectly safe with Bradley and O'Hara."

She could only speak the truth: "But I *don't* feel safe with them."

"But you *should*."

The building pressure in her passed the critical point. She exploded: "Dammit, do you think I *like* being a prisoner of my emotions, the helpless victim of fear? I *hate* it. It's not like me. I'm not this way. I feel . . . out of control. Never in my life, *never* have I made decisions or in any other way operated primarily on emotion. I'm a *scientist*, for Christ's sake. I've been a woman of science, a woman of reason, all of my adult life. And I've been proud of that. In a world that sometimes seems like a madhouse, I've been proud of my rationality, my unfailing stability. Don't you see? Don't you see what this is doing to me? I had a scientific, mathematical mind even as a child. I wasn't given to tantrums even back then, not even as a little girl. Sometimes, it seems as if I never really had a childhood."

Suddenly, to her surprise, a torrent of regrets, frustrations, and private pains, long held, long hidden, came pouring out of her, a deluge greater than that which had been released by the storm outside.

In a voice she hardly recognized as her own, a voice distorted by anguish, she said, "There've been times—usually late at night when I'm alone, which is most nights, most *days*, most always, God help me—times when I've thought there's something missing in me, some tiny piece that's an essential part of being human. I've felt different from other people, almost as if I'm a member of another species. I mean, God, the rest of the world seems driven at least as much by emotion as by intellect, as much by sentiment as by truth. I see others giving in to their emotions, abandoning reason, doing absurd things just for the hell of it. *Just for the hell of it!* I've never done anything in my life just for the hell of it. And the thing is, when I see friends or acquaintances just giving themselves over to their emotions, just *flowing* with their emotions . . . the thing of it is, they seem to *enjoy* it. And I can't. Never could. Too uptight. Too controlled. Always controlled. The iron maiden. I mean, I never cried over my mother's death. Okay, so maybe at seven I was too young to understand that I should cry. But I didn't cry at my father's funeral, either. I dealt with the mortician and ordered flowers and arranged for the grave to be dug and handled all the details with commendable efficiency, but I didn't *cry* for him. I loved him, in spite of his standoffish manner, and I missed him—God, how I missed him—but I didn't cry. *Shit.* I didn't *cry* for him. And so I told myself that it was good that I was different from other people. I told myself I was a better person than they were, superior to most of the rabble. I took tremendous pride in my unshakable self-control, and I built a life on that pride." She was shaking. Violently. She hugged herself. She looked at McGee. He seemed shocked. And she couldn't stop talking. "I built a life on that pride, dammit. Maybe not a very exciting life by most standards. But a life. I was at peace with myself. And now *this* has to happen to me. I *know* it isn't rational to fear Richmond, Johnson, Bradley, O'Hara . . . But I *do* fear them. I can't help myself. I have this intellectually stupid but emotionally powerful conviction that something extraordinary, something indescribably bizarre, maybe even something occult is happening here. I've lost control. I've given in to my emotions. I've become what I thought I wasn't. I've thrown over what I was, tipped it over and rolled it down a long hill. I'm no longer the Susan Thorton I was . . . and . . . it's . . . tearing . . . me . . . apart."

She shuddered, choked, doubled over on the bed, sitting with her head to her knees, and gasped for breath, and wept, wept.

McGee was speechless at first. Then he got her some Kleenex. Then some more Kleenex.

He said, "Susan, I'm sorry."

He said, "Are you all right?"

He got her a glass of water.

Which she didn't want.

He put it back on the nightstand.

He seemed confused.

He said, "What can I do?"

He said, "Jesus."

He touched her.

He held her.

That was what he could do.

She put her head against his shoulder and sobbed convulsively. Gradually, she became aware that her tears did not make her feel even more miserable, as she had expected they would when she had been trying so hard to repress them. Instead, they made her feel cleaner and better, as if they were flushing out the pain and misery that had caused them.

He said, "It's all right, Susan."

He said, "You're going to be fine."

He said, "You're not alone."

He comforted her, and that was something that no one had ever done for her before—perhaps because she had never allowed it.

■   A few minutes later.

"More Kleenex?" he asked.

"No, thank you."

"How do you feel?"

"Wrung out."

"I'm sorry."

"It wasn't anything you did."

"I kept browbeating you about Bradley and O'Hara."

"No, you didn't. You were only trying to help."

"Some help."

"You *did* help. You forced me to face up to something that I didn't want to face up to, something I desperately needed to face up to. I'm not as tough as I thought I was. I'm a different person than I thought I was. And maybe that's a good thing."

"All those things you said about yourself, all that stuff about how you thought you were different from other people—did you really believe that?"

"Yes."

"All those years?"

"Yes."

"But everyone has a breaking point."

"I know that now."

"And there's nothing wrong with being unable to cope now and then," he said.

"I've sure been unable recently. In spades."

He put one hand under her chin, lifted her head, and looked at her. His marvelous eyes were the bluest that she had yet seen them.

He said, "Whatever's wrong with you, no matter how subtle it might be, no matter how difficult it is to uncover the root of the problem, I'll find it. And I'll make you well again. Do you believe me, Susan?"

"Yes," she said, realizing that for the first time in her life she was, at least to some extent, willingly placing her fate in the hands of another person.

"We will discover what's causing this perceptual confusion, this quirky fixation on the House of Thunder, and we'll correct it. You won't have to go through the rest of your life seeing Ernest Harch and those other three men in the faces of total strangers."

"If that's what's happening."

"That *is* what's happening," he said.

"Okay. Until you've found the cause of my condition, until you've made me well, I'll try to cope with this craziness, with dead men who suddenly come back to life as hospital orderlies. I'll do my best to handle it."

"You can. I know it."

"But that doesn't mean I won't be scared."

"You're allowed to be scared now," he said. "You're no longer the iron maiden."

She smiled and blew her nose.

He sat there on the edge of the bed for a minute, thinking, and then he finally said, "The next time you think you see Harch or Jellicoe or Quince or Parker, there's something you can do to keep from panicking."

"I'd like to hear it."

"Well, when I was completing my residency at a hospital in Seattle—more years ago than I like to remember—we had a lot of cases of drug overdose. People were always coming into the emergency ward—or being brought in by police— suffering from bad drug trips, uncontrollable hallucinations that had them either climbing walls or shooting at phantoms with a real shotgun. No matter whether it was LSD, PCP, or some other substance, we didn't treat the patient with just counteractive drugs. We also talked him down. Encouraged him to loosen up. We held his hand and soothed him. Told him the big bad boogeymen he was seeing weren't real. And you know something? Usually, the talk did the trick, had a tremendous calming effect. I mean, frequently the talking down seemed more effective than the counteractive drugs that we administered."

"And that's what you want me to do when I see Harch or one of the others. You want me to talk myself down."

"Yes."

"Just tell myself they aren't real?"

"Yes. Tell yourself they're not real and they can't hurt you."

"Like saying a prayer to ward off vampires."

"In fact if you feel that praying would ward them off, don't hesitate. Don't be embarrassed to pray."

"I've never been a particularly religious person."

"Doesn't matter. If you want to pray, do it. Do whatever works for you. Do whatever you need to do to keep yourself calm until I've had a chance to come up with a permanent, medical solution for your condition."

"All right. Whatever you say."

"Ah, I'm pleased to see that you've finally got the proper subservient attitude toward your doctor."

She smiled.

He glanced at his wristwatch.

Susan said, "I've made you late to the office."

"Only a few minutes."

"I'm sorry."

"Don't worry about it. The only patients who had appointments this morning were all just hypochondriacs anyway."

She laughed, surprised that she still *could* laugh.

He kissed her cheek. It was just a peck, a quick buss, and it was over before she realized it was happening. Yesterday, she had thought that he was going to kiss her on the cheek, but he had backed off at the last second. Now he had done it—and she still didn't know what it meant. Was it merely an expression of sympathy, pity? Was it just affection? Just friendship? Or was it something more than that?

As soon as he had kissed her, he stood up, straightened his rumpled lab coat. "Spend the rest of the morning relaxing as best you can. Read, watch TV, anything to keep your mind off the House of Thunder."

"I'll call in the four look-alikes and get a poker game going," she said.

McGee blinked, then shook his head and grinned. "You sure spring back fast."

"Just obeying doctor's orders. He wants me to keep a positive attitude, no matter what."

"Mrs. Baker's right."

"About what?"

"About you. She says you've got plenty of moxie."

"She's too easily impressed."

"Mrs. Baker? She wouldn't be impressed if the Pope and the President walked through that door arm-in-arm."

Self-conscious, feeling that she didn't really deserve this praise after having broken down and wept, Susan straightened the blanket and the sheets around her and avoided responding to his compliment.

"Eat everything they give you for lunch," McGee said. "Then this afternoon, I want you to take the physical therapy you were scheduled for this morning."

Susan stiffened.

McGee must have seen the sudden change in her, for he said, "It's important, Susan. You need to have physical therapy. It'll get you back on your feet considerably faster. And if we discover some physical cause for your perceptual problems, something that necessitates major surgery, you'll withstand the stress and strain of the operation a great deal better if you're in good physical condition."

Resigned, she said, "All right."

"Excellent."

"But please . . . "

"What is it?"

"Don't send Jelli—" She cleared her throat. "Don't send Bradley and O'Hara to take me downstairs."

"No problem. We've got plenty of other orderlies."

"Thank you."

"And remember—chin up."

Susan put one fist under her chin, as if propping up her head, and she assumed a theatrical expression of heroic, iron-hard determination.

"That's the spirit," he said. "Think of yourself as Sylvester Stallone in *Rocky*."

"You think I look like Sylvester Stallone?"

"Well . . . more than you look like Marlon Brando."

"Gee, you sure know how to flatter a girl, Dr. McGee."

"Yeah. I'm a regular lady-killer." He winked at her, and it was the right kind of wink, very different from that which Bill Richmond had given her in the hall yesterday. "I'll see you later, when I make my evening rounds."

And then he was gone.

She was alone. Except for Jessica Seiffert. Which was the same as being alone. She still hadn't seen the woman.

Susan looked at the curtained bed. There was not even the slightest movement or noise from behind it.

At the moment, she did not want to be alone, so she said, "Mrs. Seiffert?"

There was no response.

She considered getting out of bed, going over there, and seeing if Mrs. Seiffert was all right. For reasons she could not explain, however, she was afraid to open that curtain.

8

SUSAN TRIED TO FOLLOW DOCTOR'S ORDERS. SHE PICKED UP A book and read for a few minutes, but she couldn't get interested in the story. She switched on the TV, but she couldn't find a program that held her attention. The only thing that engaged her interest was the mystery of the four look-alikes, the puzzle of their purpose. What did they intend to do to her? In spite of McGee's advice, she spent a large part of the morning thinking about Harch and the other three, worrying.

Clear evidence of an unnatural fixation, obsession, psychological illness or brain dysfunction, she thought. I say I don't believe in elaborate fantasies. I say I don't believe in the occult. And yet I believe these four are real, including the two who are dead. It makes no sense.

But she worried anyway, and she looked forward with unalloyed dread to the prospect of being taken from her room for therapy. Not that she felt safe in her room. She didn't. But at least her room was known territory. She didn't want to go downstairs. She recalled the way Jellicoe . . . the way *Dennis Bradley* had said it: "*We're here to take you downstairs.*" It had an ominous sound.

Downstairs.

Feeling guilty about ignoring much of McGee's advice, Susan made a point of eating everything she was served for lunch, which was what he had told her to do.

The condemned woman ate a hearty last meal, she thought with gallows humor. Then, angry with herself, she thought: Dammit, stop this! Get your act together, Thorton.

Just as she finished eating, the phone rang. It was a call from a couple of her fellow workers at Milestone. She didn't remember them, but she tried to be pleasant, tried to think of them as friends. It was nevertheless an awkward and disturbing conversation, and she was relieved when they finally hung up.

An hour after lunch, two orderlies came with a wheeled stretcher. Neither of them even faintly resembled any of the four fraternity men.

The first was a burly, fiftyish man with a beer gut. He had thick graying hair and a gray mustache. "Hi ya, gorgeous. You ordered a taxi?"

The second man was about thirty-five. He was bald and had a smooth, open, almost childlike face. He said, "We're here to take you away from all this."

"I was expecting a limousine," she said.

"Hey, sweetheart, what d'ya think *this* is?" the older one asked. He swept his open hand across the wheeled stretcher as if he were presenting an elegant motor coach. "Look at those classic lines!" He slapped the stretcher's three-inch foam mattress. "Look at that upholstery. Nothing but the best, the finest."

The bald one said, "Is there any other mode of transportation, other than a limousine, in which you could ride lying down?"

"With a chauffeur," said the older one, putting down the rail on her bed.

"With *two* chauffeurs," the bald one said, pushing the stretcher against the side of her bed. "I'm Phil. The other gent is Elmer Murphy."

"They call me Murf."

"They call him worse than that."

Although she was still afraid of being taken downstairs, into unknown territory, Susan was amused by their patter. Their friendliness, their efforts to make her feel at ease, and her determination not to disappoint McGee gave her sufficient courage to slide off the bed and onto the stretcher. Looking up at them, she said, "Are you two always like this?"

"Like what?" Murf asked.

"She means charming," Phil said, slipping a small, somewhat hard pillow under her head.

"Oh, yeah," Murf said. "We're always charming."

"Cary Grant has nothing on us."

"It's just something we were born with."

Phil said, "If you look under 'charm' in the dictionary—"

"—you'll see our faces," Murf finished for him.

They put a thin blanket over her, put one strap across her to keep the blanket in place, and wheeled her into the hall.

Downstairs.

To keep from thinking about where she was going, Susan said, "Why this contraption? Why not a wheelchair?"

"We can't deal with patients in wheelchairs," Phil said.

"They're too mobile," Murf said.

"Americans love mobility."

"They hate to sit still."

Phil said, "If we leave a patient alone in a wheelchair for just ten seconds—"

"—he's halfway to Mesopotamia by the time we get back," Murf finished.

They were at the elevators. Murf pushed the white button labeled *Down.*

"Lovely place," Phil said as the doors opened wide.

"What?" Murf said. "This elevator? Lovely?"

"No," Phil said. "Mesopotamia."

"You been there, huh?"

"That's where I spend my winters."

"Ya know, I don't think there *is* a Mesopotamia any more."

"Better not let the Mesopotamians hear you say that," Phil warned him.

They kept up their chatter in the elevator and all the way along the first-floor hall into the Physical Therapy Department, which was in one of the building's short wings. There, they turned her over to Mrs. Florence Atkinson, the specially trained therapist who was in charge of the hospital's PT program.

Florence Atkinson was a small, dark, birdlike woman, brimming with energy and enthusiasm. She guided Susan through half an hour of exercises, using a variety of machines and modified gym equipment that gave a workout to every muscle group. There was nothing in the least strenuous about it; a healthy person would have found it all laughably easy. "For your first couple of visits," Mrs. Atkinson said, "we'll concentrate primarily on passive exercise." But at the end of the half hour, Susan was exhausted and achy. Following the exercise period, she was given a massage that made her feel as if she were a loose collection of disjointed bones and ligaments that God had neglected to assemble into human form. After the massage, there was a session in the whirlpool. The hot, swirling water leached the remaining tension out of her, so that she felt not just loose but *liquid*. Best of all, she was allowed to take a shower in a stall that was equipped with a seat and handrails for invalids. The glorious feeling and scent of soap, hot water, and steam was so wonderful, so *exquisite*, that merely taking a bath seemed deliciously sinful.

Florence Atkinson dried Susan's shaggy blond hair with an electric blower while she sat in front of a dressing table mirror. It was the first time she had looked in a mirror in more than a day, and she was delighted to see that the bags under her eyes were entirely gone. The skin around her eyes was still a bit on the bluish side, but not much, and she actually had a touch of rosy color in her cheeks. The thin scar on her forehead was less red and swollen than it had been yesterday morning, when the bandages had come off, and she had no difficulty believing that it really would be all but invisible when it was entirely healed.

In her green pajamas again, she got onto the wheeled stretcher, and Mrs. Atkinson pushed her into the PT Department's waiting room. "Phil and Murf will be around for you in a few minutes."

"They can take their time. I feel like I'm floating on a warm, blue ocean. I could lay here forever," she said, wondering how on earth she could ever have been so afraid of being brought downstairs to PT.

She stared at the acoustic-tile ceiling for a minute or two, finding outlines of objects in the pattern of dots: a giraffe, a sailboat, a palm tree. Drowsy, she closed her eyes and yawned.

"She looks too satisfied, Phil."

"Yes, she does, Murf."

She opened her eyes and smiled up at them.

"Got to be careful about pampering the patients too much," Phil said.

"Massages, whirlpools, chauffeurs . . ."

"Pretty soon, she'll be wanting breakfast in bed."

"What is this, Phil, a hospital or a country club?"

"Sometimes I wonder, Murf."

"Well, if it isn't the Laurel and Hardy of Willawauk Hospital," Susan said.

They wheeled her out of the PT waiting room.

Murf said, "Laurel and Hardy? No, we think of ourselves more as the Bob and Ray of Willawauk."

They turned the corner into the long main hall. The hard pillow raised Susan's head just enough so she could see that the corridor was deserted. It was the first time she'd seen an empty hallway in the bustling hospital.

"Bob and Ray?" Phil said to Murf. "Speak for yourself. Me, I think I'm the Robert Redford of Willawauk."

"Robert Redford doesn't need a toupee."

"Neither do I."

"Right. You need an entire bearskin rug to cover that dome."

They had reached the elevators.

"You're being cruel, Murf."

"Just helping you face reality, Phil."

Murf pushed the white button labeled *Up.*

Phil said, "Well, Miss Thorton, I hope you've enjoyed your little trip."

"Immensely," she said.

"Good," Murf said. "And we guarantee you that the next part of it will be interesting."

"Very interesting," Phil agreed.

The elevator doors opened behind her.

They pushed her inside but didn't follow.

There were other people already in there. Four of them. Harch, Quince, Jellicoe, Parker. Harch and Quince were wearing pajamas and robes; they were standing at her left side. Jellicoe and Parker, in hospital whites, were at her right.

Shocked, disbelieving, she raised her head, looked out at Murf and Phil, who were standing in the elevator alcove on the first floor, staring in at her, smiling. They waved goodbye.

The doors closed. The lift started up.

Ernest Harch punched a button on the control panel, and they stopped between floors. He looked down at her. His frosty gray eyes were like circles of dirty ice, and they transmitted a chill to the heart of her.

Harch said, "Hello, bitch. Imagine meeting you here."

Jellicoe giggled. It was a burbling, chortling, piggish sound that matched his piggish face.

"No," she said numbly.

"Not going to scream?" Parker asked, grinning like a naughty, freckle-faced altar boy.

"We *had* hoped for a scream," Quince said, his long face looking even longer from her perspective.

"Too surprised to scream," Jellicoe said, and he giggled again.

She closed her eyes and did what Jeffrey McGee had suggested. She told herself that they were not real. She told herself that they couldn't hurt her. She told herself that they were just phantoms, the stuff of daydreams or, rather, daymares. *Not real.*

Someone put a hand on her throat.

Heart pounding, she opened her eyes.

It was Harch. He squeezed lightly, and the feel of her flesh in his grip apparently pleased him, for he laughed softly.

Susan put both of her hands on his, tried to pull it away. Couldn't. He was strong.

"Don't worry, bitch," he said. "I won't kill you."

He sounded *exactly* like Harch had sounded at the trial and in the House of Thunder. That was one voice she would never forget. It was deep, with a gravelly edge to it, a cold and merciless voice.

"No, we won't kill you yet," Quince said. "Not yet."

"When the time is right," Harch said.

She dropped her hands. She felt increasingly numb in her extremities. Her feet and hands were cold. She was shaking like an old car whose engine was badly out of tune; her rattling, banging heart was shaking her to pieces.

Harch stroked her throat softly, tenderly, as if he were admiring the graceful curve of it.

She shuddered with revulsion and turned her head away from him, looked at Jellicoe.

His pig eyes glinted. "How did you like our little song and dance in your room this morning?"

"Your name's Bradley," she said, willing it to be so, willing reality to return.

"No," he said. "Jellicoe."

"And I'm Parker, not O'Hara," the redhead said.

"You're both dead," she said shakily.

"All four of us are dead," Quince said.

She looked at the hawk-faced man, bewildered by his statement.

He said, "After I was kicked out of Briarstead, I went home to Virginia. My family wasn't very supportive. In fact they didn't want much contact with me at all. Very proper, very old-line Virginia hunt-country family, you understand. No breath of scandal must ever sully the family name." His face grew dark with anger. "I was given a modest income to tide me over until I could find work, and I was sent away. *Sent away!* My father—the self-righteous, sanctimonious, fucking *bastard*—cut me off as if I was a dead limb on a tree. What work was I to find that wasn't beneath me? I mean, I was from a privileged family. I wasn't bred to be a common laborer." He was virtually speaking through clenched teeth now. "I didn't get a chance to go to law school, as I'd wanted. Because of you, your testimony at the trial. Jesus, I hate your guts. It was because of you that I ended up in that dismal motel in Newport News. It was because of you that I slashed my wrists in that grubby little bathroom."

She closed her eyes. She thought: They aren't real. They can't hurt me.

"I was killed in prison," Harch said.

She kept her eyes tightly closed.

"Thirty-two days before I was scheduled to be paroled," he said. "Christ, I'd served almost *five* years, and with one month to go, I had the bad luck to cross a nigger who'd had a knife smuggled into his cell."

They're not real. They can't hurt me.

"And now I've finally come after you," Harch said. "I swore I would. In prison, a thousand times, ten thousand times, I swore I'd come after you some day. And you know what this Friday is, bitch? It's the anniversary of my death, that's what it is. This Friday makes seven years since that nigger shoved me up against the wall and cut my throat. Friday. That's when we're going to do it to you. Friday night. You've got about three days left, bitch. Just wanted to let you know. Just wanted you to sweat for a while first. Friday. We've got something really special planned for you on Friday."

"We're all dead because of you," Jellicoe said.

They're not real.

Their voices slashed at her.

"—if we could have found where she was hiding—"

"—would've kicked her head in, too—"

"—cut her pretty throat—"

"—hell, cut her heart out—"

"—bitch doesn't have a heart—"

They can't hurt me.

"—nothing but a stinking Jew-lover anyway—"

"—not bad looking—"

"—ought to screw her before we kill her—"

"—little on the scrawny side—"

"—she'll fatten up a bit by Friday—"

"—ever been screwed by a dead man?—"

She refused to open her eyes.

They're not real.

"—we'll all get on you—"

"—get *in* you—"

They can't hurt me.

"—all of that dead meat—"

"shoved up in you—"

They can't hurt me, can't hurt me, can't hurt . . .

"—Friday—"

"—Friday—"

A hand touched her breasts, and another hand clamped over her eyes.

She screamed.

Someone put a hard, rough hand over her mouth.

Harch said, "Bitch." And it must have been Harch who pinched her right arm; hard; harder still.

And then she passed out.

9

THE DARK DISSOLVED. IT WAS REPLACED BY MILKY FLUORESCENT light, waltzing shadows that spun lazily in time to some unheard music, and blurred shapes that bobbled above her and spoke to her in fuzzy but familiar voices.

"Look who we've got here, Murf."

"Who's that, Phil?"

"Sleeping Beauty."

Her vision cleared. She was lying on the stretcher. She blinked at the two orderlies who were looking down at her.

"And you think you're the handsome prince?" Murf said to Phil.

"Well, *you're* certainly no prince," Phil said.

Susan saw an acoustic-tile ceiling above the two men.

"He thinks he's a prince," Murf said to Susan. "Actually, he's one of the dwarfs."

"Dwarfs?" Phil said.

"Dwarfs," Murf said. "Either Ugly or Grumpy."

"There wasn't one named Ugly."

"Then Grumpy."

Susan turned her head left and right, bewildered. She was in the Physical Therapy Department's waiting room.

"Besides," Phil said, "Sleeping Beauty wasn't mixed up with any dwarfs. That was Snow White."

"Snow White?"

"Snow White," Phil said, gripping the bar at the foot of the stretcher and pushing as Murf guided from the other end.

They started moving toward the double doors that opened onto the first-floor corridor.

Her bewilderment was suddenly overlaid with fear. She tried to sit up, but she was restrained by the single strap across her middle. She said, "No, wait. Wait. Wait a minute, dammit!"

They stopped moving. Both men appeared to be startled by her outburst. Murf's bushy gray eyebrows were drawn together in a frown. Phil's round, childlike face was a definition of puzzlement.

"Where are you taking me?" she demanded.

"Well . . . back to your room," Murf said.

"What's wrong?" Phil asked.

She ran her hands over the fabric belt that held her down, felt desperately for the means by which it could be released. She found the buckle, but before she could tug at it, Murf put his hand on hers and gently moved it away from the strap.

"Wait," he said. "Just calm down, Miss Thorton. What's wrong?"

She glared up at them. "You already took me out of here once, took me as far as the elevators—"

"We didn't—"

"—then just pushed me in there with *them*, just abandoned me to them. I'm not going to let you do anything like that again."

"Miss Thorton, we—"

"How could you do that to me? Why in the name of God would you *want* to do that to me? What could you possibly have against me? You don't know me, really. I've never done anything to either of you."

Murf glanced at Phil.

Phil shrugged.

To Susan, Murf said, "Who's *them?*"

"You know," she said bitterly, angrily. "Don't pretend with me. Don't treat me like a fool."

"No, really," Murf said. "I really don't know who you're talking about."

"Me either," Phil said.

"Them!" she said exasperatedly. "Harch and the others. The four dead men, dammit!"

"Dead men?" Phil said.

Murf looked down at her as if she had lost her mind; then he abruptly broke into a smile. "Ah, I understand. You must've been dreaming."

She looked from one man to the other, and they appeared to be genuinely perplexed by her accusations.

Murf said to Phil, "I guess she dreamed that we took her out of here and put her in the elevator with some other patients who were . . . deceased." He looked down at Susan. "Is that it? Is that what you dreamed?"

"I can't have been dreaming. I wasn't even asleep," she said sharply.

"Of course you were asleep," Phil said, his voice every bit as patient and understanding as hers was sharp and angry. "We just now watched you wake up."

"A regular Sleeping Beauty," Murf said.

She shook her head violently, side to side. "No, no, no. I mean, I wasn't sleeping the *first* time you came in," she said, trying to explain but realizing that she sounded irrational. "I . . . I just closed my eyes for a second or two after Mrs. Atkinson left me here, and before I could possibly have had a chance to doze off, you came and took me out to the elevator and—"

"But that was all a dream, don't you see?" Murf said gently, smiling encouragingly.

"Sure," Phil said. "It had to be a dream because we don't ever move the deceased patients to the morgue by way of the public elevators."

"Not ever," Murf said.

"The deceased are transported in the service elevators," Phil explained.

"That's more discreet," Murf said.

"Discreet," Phil agreed.

She wanted to scream at them: *That's not the kind of dead men I'm talking about, you conniving bastards! I mean the dead men who've come back from the grave, the ones who walk and talk and somehow manage to pass for the living, the ones who want to kill me.*

But she didn't scream a word of that because she knew it would sound like the ravings of a lunatic.

"A dream," Murf said placatingly.

Phil said, "Just a bad dream."

She studied their faces, which loomed over her and appeared disproportionately huge from her awkward perspective. The gray-haired, fatherly Murf had kind eyes. And could Phil's smooth, round, childlike countenance successfully conceal vicious, hateful thoughts? No, she didn't believe that it could. His wide-eyed innocence was surely as genuine as her own fear and confusion.

"But how could it have been a dream?" she asked. "It was so real . . . so vivid."

"I've had a couple of dreams so vivid that they hung on for a minute or so after I woke up," Phil said.

"Yeah," Murf said. "Me, too."

She thought of Quince's speech about his suicide. She thought of the hand on her breasts, the other hand over her eyes, the third hand sealing shut her mouth when she tried to scream for help.

"But this was . . . *real,*" she said, though she was increasingly coming to doubt that. "At least . . . it *seemed* real . . . frighteningly real . . . "

"I swear to you, it wasn't more than five minutes ago that we got the call from Mrs. Atkinson, asking us to come and pick you up," Murf said.

"And we came straight down," Phil said.

"And here we are. But we weren't here before."

She licked her dry lips. "I guess . . . "

"A dream," Murf said.

"Had to've been a bad dream," Phil said.

At last, grudgingly, Susan nodded. "Yeah. I suppose so. Listen . . . I'm sorry."

"Oh, don't worry your pretty head," Murf told her. "There's no need for you to be sorry."

"I shouldn't have snapped at you the way I did," she said.

"Did she hurt your feelings, Phil?"

"Not in the least. Did she hurt your feelings, Murf?"

"Not one bit."

"There, you see," Phil said to Susan. "Absolutely no reason for you to apologize."

"No reason at all," Murf concurred.

"Now, do you feel up to traveling?" Phil asked her.

"We'll make it a nice, gentle ride," Murf promised.

Phil said, "We'll take the scenic route."

"First-class accommodations all the way," Murf said.

"Gourmet meals at the captain's table."

"Dancing in the ship's ballroom every night."

"Free deck chairs and shuffleboard, plus a complimentary happy-hour cocktail," Murf said.

She wished they would stop their bantering; it no longer amused her. She was somewhat dizzy, queasy, still considerably confused, as if she had drunk too much or had been drugged. Their swift patter was like a ball bouncing frenetically back and forth inside her head; it made her dizzier by the minute. But she didn't know how to tell them to be quiet without hurting their feelings; and if the terror in the elevator *had* been just a dream, she had already been unjustifiably rude.

She said, "Well . . . okay. Let's pull up anchor and get this ship out of the harbor."

"Bon voyage," Phil said.

"Lifeboat drill at sixteen hundred hours," Murf said.

They rolled the stretcher through the swing-hinged double doors, into the first-floor hallway.

"You're *sure* Sleeping Beauty wasn't mixed up with a bunch of dwarfs?" Murf asked Phil.

"I told you, it was Snow White. Murf, I'm beginning to think you're a hopeless illiterate."

"What a vile thing to say, Phil. I'm an educated man."

They turned into the long main hall and wheeled Susan toward the elevators.

Murf said, "It's just that I don't read children's fairy tales any more. I'm sure such stuff is adequate for you, but I prefer more complex literature."

"You mean the *Racing Form*?" Phil asked.

"Charles Dickens is more like it, Phil."

"And the *National Enquirer*?"

They reached the elevators.

Susan felt watchspring tense.

"I'll have you know that I've read all the published works of Louis L'Amour," Murf said, pressing the white button that was marked *Up*.

"Dickens to L'Amour," Phil said. "That's quite a spread, Murf."

"I'm a man of wide interests," Murf said.

Susan held her breath, waiting for the doors to open. A scream crouched in her chest, ready to leap up into her throat and out.

Please, God, she thought, not again.

"And what about you, Phil? Have you read any good cereal boxes lately?"

The elevator doors opened with a soft hum. They were behind Susan's head; she couldn't see into the cab.

Murf and Phil rolled her inside and came with her this time. There were no dead men waiting.

She let out her breath in a rush and closed her eyes. Relief brought with it a headache.

The trip back to her room was uneventful, but when she was transferring herself from the stretcher to her bed, she felt a twinge of pain in her right arm, just above the inner crook of the elbow. She abruptly remembered that Harch—or maybe one of the others—had pinched that arm hard, very hard, just before she had passed out in the elevator.

After the two orderlies left, Susan sat for a while with her hands in her lap, afraid to look at her arm. At last, however, she pushed up the right sleeve of her green pajamas. There was a bruise on her frail biceps, a darker oval on the pale skin, two inches above the elbow joint. It was a light bruise, but it was getting darker. About the size of a nickel. The color of a strawberry birthmark. Quite sore to the touch. A *fresh* bruise: no doubt about that.

But what did it mean? Was it proof that the encounter with Harch and the other three men had actually taken place, proof that it had not been merely a bad dream during a short nap? Or had she acquired the bruise while exercising in the PT Department, and—not consciously but subconsciously aware of it—had she then cleverly incorporated the injury into the dream about the dead men in the elevator?

She tried to remember if she had bumped her arm at any time during the therapy session. She couldn't be sure. She thought back to the shower that she had taken in the PT Department. Had her arm shown any discoloration then? Had there been a small spot of tenderness on the biceps? She didn't recall that there had been either a mark or any soreness whatsoever. However, it might have been so slight that it had escaped her notice then; after all, most bruises developed slowly.

I *must* have gotten it when I was exercising, she told herself. That's the only explanation that isn't . . . insane. Ernest Harch and the other fraternity brothers aren't real. They can't hurt me. They're only phantoms generated by some peculiar form of brain dysfunction. If I regain my strength, if McGee finds out what's wrong with me, if I get well again, that will be the last I'll ever see of these walking, talking dead men. In the meantime, they simply cannot hurt me.

■   Jeff McGee showed up for his evening rounds at half past five, dressed as if he were going to a fancy dinner party. He was wearing a dark blue suit that was well-tailored to his tall, trim frame, a pearl-gray shirt, a blue- and gray-striped necktie, and a sky-blue display handkerchief in the breast pocket of his suit jacket.

He looked so elegant and moved with such exceptional grace that Susan found herself suddenly responding to him sexually. From the moment she had seen him Sunday morning, she thought he was an extremely attractive man, but this was the very first time since waking from her long coma that she had experienced the warm, welcome, delicious fluttering-tingling-melting of sexual desire.

My God, she thought with amusement, I *must* be getting well: I'm horny!

McGee came directly to her bedside, and without hesitation this time, he leaned down and kissed her on the cheek, near the corner of her mouth. He was wearing a subtle after-shave lotion that smelled vaguely of lemons and even more vaguely of several unidentifiable herbs, but beneath that crisp fragrance, Susan detected the even more appealing, freshly scrubbed scent of his own skin.

She wanted to throw her arms around his neck and hold on to him, cling to him; she wanted to draw him close and take strength from him, strength she needed, strength he seemed to possess in such abundance. But however far their personal relationship had come in these past few days, it most certainly had not come *that* far. McGee felt considerable affection for her; she was sure of that. But given the natural restraints of the doctor-patient relationship, to which any romantic feelings had to remain strictly secondary, she could not cast aside all reserve. And given the fact that she couldn't entirely trust her perceptions—which told her that Jeff McGee felt a great deal more than mere affection for her—she dared risk nothing other than a swift, chaste kiss planted lightly on his cheek in return for the kiss that he had bestowed upon her.

"I'm in a bit of a hurry tonight," he said, drawing away from her too soon. "Let me have a quick look at Jessie Seiffert, see how's she's coming along, and then I'll be back for a few minutes."

He went to the other bed and slipped behind the curtain.

A whip of jealousy lashed through Susan. She wondered for whom he had put on his best suit. With whom was he having dinner tonight? A woman? Well, of course it would be a woman, and a pretty woman, too. A man didn't dress up like that, pocket handkerchief and all, just to grab a bite and have a few beers with the boys. Jeffrey McGee was a most desirable man, and there was never any shortage of women for desirable men. And he certainly didn't have the air of a celibate; good heavens, no! He had enjoyed a private life, a romantic life—all right, face up to it, a *sex* life—long before one Susan Kathleen Thorton had arrived on the scene. She could claim absolutely no right to be jealous of his relations with other women. Absolutely no right whatsoever. There was nothing serious between her and him; he was under no obligation to remain faithful to her. The very idea of that was patently ridiculous. Still, she *was* jealous; terribly, surprisingly jealous.

He stepped out from behind the curtain and returned to Susan's bedside. He took her hand and smiled at her; his hand was strong and warm, and his teeth were very white and even. "So tell me how it went down in PT. Did you have a good afternoon with Flo Atkinson?"

Susan had intended to recount the terror of that strikingly vivid dream in which she had been trapped in the elevator with Ernest Harch and the other fraternity men. But now she decided against telling McGee anything about it. She didn't want him to see her as just a weak, frightened, dependent woman. She didn't want him to pity her.

"It was a terrific afternoon in every detail," she lied.

"That's great. I'm glad to hear it."

"Yeah. The physical therapy is exactly what I need," she said, and at least that much was true.

"You've got some color in your face now."

"Washed my hair, too."

"Yes, it looks very nice."

"You're a terrible liar, Dr. McGee. It won't look nice for another six weeks or two months, thanks to your emergency room hairdresser, who apparently trims the incoming patients with a chain saw. At least now it's clean."

"I think it looks clean *and* nice," he insisted. "It's cute. Shaggy like that, it reminds me of . . . Peter Pan."

"Thanks a lot. Peter Pan was a boy."

"Well, you certainly can't be mistaken for a boy. Forget I said Peter Pan. It makes you look like . . . "

"An English sheepdog?"

"Are you determined to fend off any compliment I give you?"

"Come on, admit it. English sheepdog, right?"

He pretended to scrutinize her for canine qualities. "Well, now that you mention it . . . Do you know how to fetch a pair of slippers?"

"Arf, arf," she said.

"Seriously," he said, "you look good. I think your cheeks are already starting to fill out a bit."

"*You're* the one who's looking good. Sharp outfit."

"Thanks," he said, but he didn't tell her why he was wearing his best suit, which was the information she had been probing for when she'd complimented him. "See Harch or the others today?"

"Not a glimpse," she lied.

"That's a positive sign. I've scheduled tests for tomorrow morning. Blood samples, urinalysis, X rays . . . a spinal tap if necessary."

"Ouch."

"It won't be too bad."

"Easy for you to say. It's not *your* spine they'll be tapping."

"True. But if a tap is necessary, I'll do it myself, and I'm known for my gentle touch." He glanced at his watch. "I've got to run, I'm afraid."

"Heavy date?"

"I wish it were! Unfortunately, it's only the monthly meeting of the Tri-County Medical Association. I'm the dinner speaker tonight, and I've got stage fright."

She almost sighed aloud with relief. "Stage fright?" she said, hoping he wouldn't see how much she had feared the possibility of a hot romance in his life. "Not you. I can't imagine you being afraid of anything."

"Among other things," he said, "I'm afraid of snakes, and I have a mild case of claustrophobia, and I dread public speaking."

"What about English sheepdogs?"

"I adore English sheepdogs," he said, and he kissed her on the cheek again.

"They'll love your speech," she assured him.

"Well, anyway, it won't be the worst part of the evening," he said. "No matter how bad the speech is, it's sure to be better than the banquet food at the Holiday Inn."

She smiled. "See you in the morning."

He hesitated. "Are you sure you're all right?"

"I'm fine."

"Remember, if you see any of them again, just tell yourself they aren't real and—"

"—they can't hurt me."

"Remember that."

"I will."

"And listen, all the nurses on this floor have been apprised of your condition. If you have any attacks . . . hallucinations, just call for a nurse, and she'll help you. She'll talk you down."

"That's good to know."

"You aren't alone."

"I'm aware of that—and I'm grateful."

He left, turning at the door to smile and wave.

He had been gone for several minutes before Susan's sweet, warm, liquid feeling of sexual arousal faded, before her body heat subsided to a mere 98.6 degrees.

God, she thought wonderingly, he makes me feel like a young girl. A sex-crazy teenager.

She laughed softly at herself.

Then, although she wasn't alone, she *felt* alone.

Later, as she was eating dinner, she remembered what McGee had said about her inability to accept any of his compliments graciously. It was true. And odd. She thought about it for a while. She had never wanted compliments from a man half as much as she wanted them from Jeff McGee. Maybe she repeatedly turned aside his compliments as a means of forcing him to repeat them and elaborate upon them. No . . . The more she thought about it, the more she suspected that she ducked any praise from him because, deep down inside, she was afraid of the strong pull that he exerted on her, was afraid of the tremendous attraction she felt for him. Over the years, she'd had a few lovers, not many, but a few, and in every case she had been very much in control of the relationship. With each man, when the time had finally come to say goodbye, she had broken off the romance with regret but always without serious emotional trauma. She had been as thoroughly in command of her heart as she had been in command of her career as a physicist. But she sensed that it couldn't be like that with Jeff McGee. This would be a more intense relationship, more emotional, more entangling. Maybe it scared her a bit—even as she longed for it.

She knew she wanted Jeff McGee. His effect on her was undeniable. But aside from wanting him, did she also *love* him? That was a question which she had never needed to ask herself before.

Love?

It's impossible, dammit, she told herself. I can't be in love with a man I met only three short days ago. I hardly know anything about him. I haven't even given him a *real* kiss. Or received one from him. Just pecks on the cheek. For God's sake, I can't say for sure that his feelings for me are even remotely passionate. No one falls in love overnight. It simply doesn't happen that way.

Yet she knew it *had* happened to her. Just like in the movies.

All right, she thought, if it *is* love, then *why* is it? Have I fallen in love with him only because I'm sick and weak and helpless, only because I'm grateful to have a strong, reliable man on my side? If that's it, then it could hardly be called love; it's merely gratitude and a shameless, headlong flight from responsibility for my own life.

However, the more she thought about it, the more she came to feel that the love had been there first. Or at the very least, the love and the desperate need for McGee's strength had come to her simultaneously.

Which came first, she thought, the chicken or the egg? And does it matter anyway? What matters is how I feel about him—and I really want him.

Since, for the time being, romance had to take second place to recuperation, she tried to put the subject out of her mind. After dinner, she read several chapters of a good mystery novel and ate three or four chocolates. The night nurse, a perky brunette named Tina Scolari, brought Susan some ginger ale. She read more of the mystery, and it got even better. Outside, the rain stopped falling, and the irritatingly monotonous drumming of water on the windowpane ceased at last. She asked for and was given a second glass of ginger ale. The evening was relatively pleasant. For a while.

10

NURSE SCOLARI CAME IN AT 9:15. "YOU'VE GOT AN EARLY DAY tomorrow. Lots of tests." She gave Susan a small pill cup that contained a single pink tablet, the mild sedative that McGee had prescribed for her. While Susan washed the pill down with the last of her second glass of ginger ale, Nurse Scolari checked on Jessica Seiffert in the next bed, drawing back the curtain just far enough to ease behind it. When she reappeared, she said to Susan, "Lights out as soon as you feel drowsy."

"Sooner than that, even. I just want to finish this chapter," Susan said, indicating the book she had been reading. "Just two more paragraphs."

"Want me to help you to the bathroom, then?"

"Oh, no. I can make it on my own."

"You're sure?"

"Yes, positive."

The nurse stopped by the door and flipped up the switch that turned on the small night light at the far end of the room, so that Susan wouldn't have to cross the room to do it later. The swinging door had been propped open all day; on her way out, Nurse Scolari pushed up the rubber-tipped prop that was fixed to the base of the door, and she pulled the door shut behind her.

After Susan had read two more paragraphs, she got out of bed and went into the bathroom, trailing one hand lightly along the wall, so she could lean on it for support if that were suddenly necessary. After she brushed her teeth, she returned to bed. Her legs were weak and sore, especially the calves and the backs of her thighs, but she was no longer dangerously shaky. She walked without fear of falling, even though she was not yet entirely sure-footed, and even though she knew she still couldn't travel any great distance under her own steam.

In bed, she fluffed her pillows and used the power controls to lower the upper end of the mattress. She switched off the lamp that stood on her nightstand.

The moon-soft beams of the night light fell upon the curtain that enclosed Jessica Seiffert's bed and, as it had done last night, the white fabric seemed to absorb the light, magnify it, and cast back a phosphoric glow all of its own, making it by far the most prominent object in the shadowy room. Susan stared at it for a minute or two and felt a renewal of the curiosity and uneasiness that had plagued her ever since the unseen Seiffert woman had been brought into the room.

"Susan . . . "

She nearly exploded off the bed in surprise, sat straight up, quivering, the covers thrown back, her breath quick-frozen in her lungs, her heart briefly stilled.

"Susan . . . "

The voice was thin, dry, brittle, a voice of dust and ashes and time-ravaged vocal cords. It possessed a disturbing, bone-chilling quality that seemed, to Susan, to be inexplicably yet undeniably sinister.

"Susan . . . Susan . . . "

Even as low as it was, even as raspy and tortured as it was, that ruined voice was nevertheless clearly, indisputably masculine. And it was coming from behind the luminous curtain, from Jessica Seiffert's shrouded bed.

Susan finally managed to draw a breath, with a shudder and a gasp. Her heart started again with a *thud.*

"Susan . . . "

Last night, waking in the dead and lonely hours of the morning, she had thought she'd heard a voice calling to her from behind the curtain, but she had convinced herself that it had been only part of a dream, and she had gone back to sleep. Her senses had been dulled by sedatives, and she had not been sufficiently clear-headed to recognize that the voice was, indeed, real. Tonight, however, she was not asleep nor even sleepy yet; the sedative hadn't begun to take effect. Wide-eyed, not the least bit drowsy, she had no doubt whatsoever that the voice was real.

"Susan . . . "

It was the pleading cry of some grim and grisly siren, and it exerted an emotional, visceral pull that was almost physical in its intensity. Although she was afraid of the bizarre voice and was afraid, too, of whatever man—whatever *creature*—owned that voice, she had the urge to get up and go to Mrs. Seiffert's bed; she felt strangely compelled to draw back the white curtain and confront the being who was summoning her. She gripped a wad of sheets in one hand, seized the cold bed rail with the other hand, and resisted that crazy urge with all her might.

"Susan . . . "

She fumbled for the switch on the bedside lamp, found it after too many seconds had ticked by in darkness, clicked it. Light drove back the shadows, which seemed to retreat only with the greatest reluctance, as if they were hungry wolves that were slinking grudgingly away from prey that had at first appeared to be easy pickings.

Susan stared at the curtained bed. Waited.

There wasn't a sound.

Ten seconds passed. Twenty. Half a minute.

Nothing. Silence.

At last she said, "Who's there?"

No response.

More than twenty-four hours had passed since Susan had returned from her wheelchair constitutional to discover that a roommate had been installed in the other bed. Mrs. Baker had told her that it was Jessica Seiffert; otherwise, she wouldn't have known with whom she was sharing her room. More than twenty-four hours, and *still* she hadn't gotten a glimpse of Mrs. Seiffert. Nor had she heard the old woman speak a single word: she'd heard only that vague, wordless murmur that had answered Jeff McGee's questions, that soft mumbled response to the various nurses who had gone behind the curtain. People had come and gone and come again, attending to Mrs. Seiffert with commendable concern and diligence— emptying the old woman's bedpan, taking her temperature and her blood pressure, timing her pulse, feeding her meals, giving her medicine, changing her bed linens, offering her encouragement—but in spite of all that activity, Susan had not gotten even one brief peek at the mysterious occupant of the other bed.

And now she was troubled by the unsettling notion that Jessie Seiffert had never been in that bed to begin with. It was someone else. Ernest Harch? One of the other three fraternity men? Or something even worse than that?

This is insane.

It *had* to be Jessica Seiffert in that bed, for if it was not her, then everyone in the hospital was involved in some grotesque conspiracy. Which was impossible. Thoughts like those—paranoid fantasies of complicated conspiracies—were only additional proof of her brain dysfunction. Mrs. Baker hadn't lied to her. She knew that as surely as she knew her own name. Yet she couldn't stop considering the possibility that Jessica Seiffert didn't exist, that the unseen roommate was someone far less innocent and far less harmless than an old woman dying of cancer.

"Who's there?" she demanded again.

Again, there was no reply.

"Dammit," she said, "I know I didn't just imagine you!"

Or *did* I?

"I heard you call me," she said.

Or did I only *think* I heard it?

"Who are you? What are you doing here? What do you want from me?"

"*Susan . . .*"

She jerked as if she had been slapped, for the voice was even eerier in bright light than it had been in darkness. It belonged to darkness; it seemed impossible, twice as monstrous, when heard in the light.

Stay calm, she told herself. Stay cool. Stay collected. If I've got a brain injury that causes me to see things that are not really there, then it's entirely logical that it also causes me to hear sounds that were never made. Auditory hallucinations. There are such things.

"*Susan . . .*"

She had to regain control of herself before this episode progressed any further; she had to quickly squelch this incipient hysteria. She had to prove to herself that there was no voice coming from behind the curtain, that it was only an imagined voice. The best way to prove it was to go straight over there and draw back the curtain. The only thing she would find in Jessica Seiffert's bed was an old woman who was dying of cancer.

"*Susan . . .* "

"Shut up," she said.

Her hands were cold and damp. She wiped the icy sweat on the sheets. She took a deep breath, as if she thought that courage was merely a vapor that could be siphoned out of the air.

"*Susan . . . Susan . . .* "

Stop procrastinating, she told herself. Get up, get moving, get it over with.

She put down the safety rail and pushed back the covers and sat on the edge of the bed, legs dangling. She stood up, holding on to the mattress. She had gotten out of the bed on the side nearest Jessica Seiffert. Her slippers were on the other side, out of reach, and the green tile floor was cold against her bare feet. The distance between the two beds was only nine or ten feet. She could cover it in three shuffling steps, four at most. She took the first one.

"*Sssuuuuusssaaaaannn . . .* "

The thing in the bed—and in spite of her brave and oh-so-rational thoughts about auditory hallucinations, she could only think of it now as a *thing*—seemed to sense both her approach and her timidity. Its voice became even more hoarse, even more insistent and sinister than it had been; it did not speak her name so much as moan it.

"*Sssuuuuusssaaaaannn . . .* "

She considered returning to the bed and pushing the call button that would summon a nurse. But what if the nurse came and heard nothing? What if the nurse pulled back the curtain and found only an old, pathetic, dying woman who was murmuring senselessly in a drug-induced stupor? Which was almost certainly what she *would* find, of course. What then?

She took a second step toward the other bed, and the cold floor seemed to be getting colder.

The curtain fluttered as if something had brushed against the other side of it.

Susan's ice-water blood grew colder and moved sluggishly through her veins in spite of the rapid beating of her heart.

"*Sssuuuuusssaaaaannn . . .* "

She retreated one step.

The curtain fluttered again, and she saw a dark shape behind it.

The voice called her again, and this time there was definitely a threatening tone to it.

The curtain rustled, then flapped violently. It rattled the hooks by which it was suspended from the ceiling track. A dark form, shapeless but surely much too large to be a cancer-withered woman, groped clumsily against the far side of the white fabric, as if searching for a place to part it.

Susan was stricken by a premonition of death. Perhaps that was a sure sign of her mental imbalance; perhaps it was irrefutable proof that she was irrational and was imagining everything, yet the premonition was too powerful to be ignored. *Death.* Death was very near. Suddenly, the last thing on earth she wanted was to see what lay beyond the curtain.

She turned and fled. She stumbled around the foot of her own bed, then glanced back.

The curtain appeared to be caught in a turbulent whirlpool of crossdrafts—though she could feel no air moving in the room. It trembled and fluttered and rustled and billowed. And it was beginning to slide open.

She shuffled quickly into the bathroom—the door to the hall seemed too far away—and her legs protested at the speed that she demanded from them. In the bathroom, she closed the door and leaned against it, breathless.

It isn't real. It can't hurt me.

The bathroom was dark, and she could not tolerate being alone in the dark now. She felt for the switch and finally located it; the white walls, the white sink and commode, and the white ceramic-tile floor all gleamed brightly.

It can't hurt me.

She was still holding the doorknob. It moved in her hand. Someone was turning it from the other side.

She twisted the latch. It was loose, broken.

"No," she said. "No."

She held the knob as tightly as she could, and she put her shoulder to the door, digging her heels into the tile floor of the bathroom. For interminably long seconds, seconds that seemed like minutes, the person on the other side continued to try the knob, working it back and forth; it strained against Susan's hand, but she gritted her teeth and tensed her wasted muscles and refused to let herself be budged. After a while the knob stopped moving. She thought the surrender might be only a trick, so she maintained a firm grip.

Something scratched on the other side of the door. The sound, so near her face, startled her. It was a stealthy noise at first, but it quickly grew louder. Fingernails. Clawing at the wood.

"Who's there?"

She received no answer.

The nails scratched furiously for perhaps half a minute. Then paused. Then scratched again, but languidly this time. Now—steadily and relentlessly. Now—desultorily.

"What do you want?"

The only response was a new fit of scratching.

"Listen, if you'll just please tell me who you are, I'll open the door."

That promise accomplished nothing, either.

She listened worriedly to the fingernails that picked determinedly along the edges of the door, exploring the cracks between the door and the frame, as if purchase and leverage might be found there, sufficient to tear the door open or rip it from its hinges with one mighty heave.

Finally, after two or three more minutes of fruitless but busy scraping and probing, the noise stopped abruptly.

Susan tensed herself and prepared to recommence the struggle with the doorknob, but, much to her surprise and relief, the battle did not begin again.

She waited hopefully, hardly daring to breathe.

The bathroom gleamed in the hard fluorescent light, and a drop of water made a soft, soft *tink* as it fell from the faucet onto the metal stopper in the sink.

Gradually, Susan's panic subsided. A trickle of doubt found its way into her mind; the trickle became a stream, a flood. Slowly, reason reasserted itself. She began to consider, once more, the possibility that she had been hallucinating. After all, if there really had been a man—or something else—behind the curtain, and if he really had wanted to get his hands on her, she would not have been able to hold the door against him. Not in her enfeebled condition. If someone actually *had* been twisting the doorknob—and now she was virtually awash in doubt, floundering in it—then the person on the other side had been markedly weaker than she was. And no one in such poor health could have posed a serious threat to her.

She waited. Leaned hard against the door.

Her breath came to her more easily now.

Time passed at a measured, plodding pace, and her heart slowed, and the silence continued without interruption.

But as yet she was unable to relax her grip on the doorknob. She stared at her hand. Her knuckles were sharp and bloodless. Her fingers looked like talons curled around the metal knob.

She realized that Mrs. Seiffert was the only one around who was weaker than she herself. Had Mrs. Seiffert tried to get out of bed on her own? Is that what all the thrashing behind the curtain had been about? And had the old woman somehow crossed the room in drugged confusion or in desperate pain? Had it been Mrs. Seiffert clawing at the door, unable to speak, seeking help, scratching and scratching at the wood in a frantic bid to gain attention?

Good God, Susan thought, was I defending the door against a dying woman who was seeking nothing but my help?

But she didn't open the door. Couldn't. Not yet.

Eventually, she thought: No. No, Mrs. Seiffert, *if* she exists, is too debilitated to get out of bed and cross the room all by herself. She's an invalid, a limp bag of flesh and bones. It couldn't possibly have been Mrs. Seiffert. Besides, the threatening form that had risen up behind the curtain couldn't have been Mrs. Seiffert, either. It was too big.

In the sink, a drop of water fell.

On the other hand, maybe there hadn't been a rising form behind the curtain to begin with. Maybe the curtain had never really moved, either. Maybe there had been no mysterious voice, no hand turning the knob, no persistent scratching at the door. All in her head.

Brain dysfunction.

A sand-grain blood clot.

A tiny cerebral capillary with an even tinier hemorrhage.

A chemicoelectrical imbalance of some kind.

The more she thought about it, the easier it was to rule out supernatural and conspiratorial explanations. After a lot of consideration, she seemed to be left with only two possibilities: either she had imagined the entire thing . . . or Mrs. Seiffert now lay dead just the other side of the bathroom door, a victim of Susan's mental problems.

In either case, there was no one after her, no reason to continue to guard the door. At last she leaned away from it; her shoulder ached, and her entire left side was stiff. She relaxed her iron-tight grip on the knob, which was now slick and shiny with her sour sweat.

She opened the door. Just a crack.

No one tried to force his way into the bathroom.

Still frightened, prepared to slam the door shut at the slightest sign of movement, she opened it wider: two inches, three. She looked down, expecting the worst, but there was no elderly dead woman sprawled on the floor, no gray face contorted in an eternal expression of contempt and accusation.

The hospital room looked normal. The lamp burned beside her bed, and her covers were heaped in a tangled mess, as she had left them. The night light was still on, too. The curtain around Jessica Seiffert's bed was in place, hanging straight from the ceiling to the floor, stirred neither by a draft nor by a malevolent hand.

Susan slowly opened the door all the way.

No one leaped at her.

No dust-choked, half-human voice called to her.

So . . . every bit of it was the product of my imagination, she thought dismally. My runaway imagination, galloping merrily off on another journey through temporary madness. My damned, sick, *traitorous* brain.

All of her life, Susan had limited her drinking to infrequent social occasions, and even then she had allowed herself no more than two cocktails in one evening, for she had always hated being drunk. She had been booze-blasted once, just once, when she was a senior in high school, and that had been a memorable and extremely nasty experience. No artificially induced high, no matter how pleasant it might be, had ever seemed worth the loss of control that went along with it.

Now, without taking a single sip of alcohol, she could lose control in an instant and not even be aware that she had lost it. At least when you got drunk, you relinquished the reins of reason slowly, in stages, and you knew that you were no longer in the driver's seat. Drunk, you knew that your senses could not be trusted. But brain dysfunction was more insidious than that.

It scared her.

What if Jeff McGee couldn't find the problem?

What if there was no cure?

What if she was forced to spend the rest of her life teetering on the razor-edge of insanity, frequently toppling over the brink for short but devastating travels in the shadowy land of Never-Was?

She knew she couldn't live that way. Death would be far preferable to such a tortured existence.

She snapped off the bathroom light and fancied that she could feel the weight of the darkness on her back.

She followed the wall to her bed, wincing at the pain in the backs of her legs.

When she reached the bed, she used the power controls to lower it, and she put down the safety railing as she had done on the other side when she'd gotten out, and she started to sit down on the mattress, but then she hesitated. She raised up again and stood for a long while, staring at the curtain. Eventually, she accepted the fact that she could not simply go to sleep now; not yet. She had to find the courage to do what she had been unable to do earlier. She had to go over there, pull back the curtain, and prove to herself that her roommate was only an old, sick woman. Because if she did not do it now, the hallucinations might start again the moment that she turned out the light and put her head down on her pillow. Because if she didn't fight this sickness every step of the way, it would probably overwhelm her much sooner than if she resisted. Because she was Susan Kathleen Thorton, and Susan Kathleen Thorton never ran away from trouble.

She was standing beside her slippers. She put her cold feet in them.

She moved creakily around the bottom of her bed, holding on to it as she went. She shuffled across the space between the two beds and, standing in the open with nothing to hold on to, she raised one hand and touched the curtain.

The room seemed extraordinarily quiet—as if she were not the only one holding her breath.

The air was as still as the air in a crypt.

She closed her hand, clenching a wad of drapery material in her fist.

Open it, for heaven's sake! she told herself when she realized that she had been hesitating for almost a minute. There's nothing threatening behind here, nothing but one old lady who's sleeping through the last few days of her life.

Susan pulled the curtain aside. Overhead, the dozens of small metal hooks rattle-clattered along the stainless-steel track in the ceiling.

As she swept the curtain out of the way, Susan stepped closer to the bed, right up to the safety railing, and she looked down. In that gut-wrenching moment, she knew that there was a Hell and that she was trapped in it.

Mrs. Seiffert wasn't in the bed, as she should have been. Something else. Something hideous. A corpse. Jerry Stein's corpse.

No. It was just imagination.

Confused perceptions.

Brain dysfunction.

A minuscule hemorrhage in a tiny capillary.

And . . . oh yes . . . the well-known, oft-discussed, mischievous, sand-grain blood clot.

Susan went through the entire litany of medical explanations, but the corpse did not vanish or magically metamorphose into Mrs. Seiffert.

Nevertheless, Susan did not scream. She did not run. She was determined to sweat this one out; she would *force* herself back to reality. She clung to the safety railing to keep from collapsing.

She closed her eyes.

Counted to ten.

It isn't real.

She opened her eyes.

The corpse was still there.

The dead man was lying on his back, the covers drawn up to the middle of his chest, as if merely sleeping. One side of his skull had a crumpled look; it was indented, matted with dark, dry blood, where Ernest Harch had kicked him three times. The body's bare arms were atop the covers, stretched straight out at its sides; the hands were turned palms-up, and the fingers were bent into rigid curves, as if the dead man had made one last, futile grasp at life.

The corpse didn't look *exactly* like Jerry Stein, but that was only because it wasn't in very good condition; death had corrupted it somewhat. The skin was gray with greenish-black patches around the sunken eyes and at the corners of the purple, swollen, suppurating lips. The eyelids were mottled and crusty. Dark, peeling, oozing blisters extended out of the nostrils and across the upper lip. On both sides of the bloated, misshapen nose, other blisters glistened with some foul, brown fluid. In spite of the swelling and the discoloration and the disgusting disfigurement, the dead man was clearly Jerry Stein.

But Jerry had been dead for thirteen years. In that time, death would have visited upon him considerably more corruption than this. His flesh should have completely decomposed years ago. By now he should have been little more than a skeleton with a few strands of brittle hair clinging to its fleshless skull, the bleached bones bound together loosely by scraps of mummified skin and leathery ligaments. Yet he appeared to have been dead for only about ten days or a week, perhaps less.

Which is proof that this is a hallucination, Susan told herself, squeezing the bed's safety railing so hard that she wondered why it didn't bend in her hands. Only a hallucination. It doesn't conform to reality, to the laws of nature, or to logic; not in any detail. So it's only a vision, a horror that exists nowhere else but in my mind.

More proof of the corpse's nonexistence was the fact that Susan couldn't detect even the mildest odor of decay. If the dead man actually were here, even in this inexplicably early stage of decomposition, the stench would be overpowering. But the air, while not exactly sweet, was hospital clean, tainted only by Lysol.

Touch it, she told herself. That would dispel it. No one can touch and feel a mirage. Embracing a mirage is like embracing empty air: your arms come together around yourself. Go ahead. Touch it and prove it isn't really there.

She couldn't do it. She tried hard to pry her hand off the railing in order to reach out to the dead man's cold gray arm, but she didn't have the courage.

Instead, she said aloud, as if chanting magical words that would banish the vision: "It's not here. It's not real. It's all in my mind."

The crusted eyelids of the corpse fluttered.

No!

They opened.

No, she thought desperately. No, no, no, this is not happening to me.

Even open, these were not the eyes of a living man: they were rolled far back in the head, so that only the whites were visible; however, the whites were not white at all, but yellow and smeared with streaks of red-brown blood. Then those terrible eyes moved, rolled, *bulged,* and the brown irises were visible, though coated by milky cataracts. The eyes jittered for a moment, seeing nothing, and then they focused on Susan.

She screamed but didn't make a sound. The noise of the scream fell back inside of her, like a rubber ball bouncing down a long, long set of dark cellar stairs, until it came to the bottom and was still. She shook her head violently, and she gagged with revulsion, choked on her own sour saliva.

The corpse raised one stiff, gray hand. The rigormortised fingers gradually uncurled. It reached toward her.

She tore her hands off the bed's safety railing as if the metal had suddenly become red hot.

The corpse opened its filthy, oozing mouth. With rotting tongue and lips, it formed her name: *"Sssuuuuusssaaaaannn . . ."*

She stumbled backwards one step.

It isn't real, it isn't real, it isn't, isn't . . .

Jerkily, as if animated by a sputtering electrical current, the dead man sat up in bed.

It's all in my mind, she told herself, trying very hard to talk herself down, as McGee had advised.

The dead man called her name again and smiled.

Susan swung away from the apparition and bolted for the door to the hall, her slippered feet slapping flatly against the tile floor, and she (*I'm out of control*) reached the door after what seemed like hours, grabbed the big handle, tugged on it, but the door (*I've got to stop, get calm*) seemed to weigh a thousand tons, and she cursed her weakness, which was costing her precious seconds, and she heard a wet gurgling noise behind her (*Imagination!*), and she grunted and put her back into the should-have-been-simple task of opening the damned door, and finally she did drag it open, and she (*I'm running from a mirage*) plunged into the corridor, not daring to glance behind her to see if the corpse was in pursuit (*Just a mirage*), then she staggered, nearly fell, turned left, weaved down the hall, unable to progress in a straight line, her leg muscles afire, her knees and ankles melting more rapidly with each step she took, and she careened into the wall, put her hand against it, gasping, and shuffled forward, didn't think she could go on, then felt (*Imagined!*) the dead man's bitterly cold breath against the bare nape of her neck, and somehow she *did* go on, and she reached the main corridor, saw the nurses' station down by the elevators, tried to cry out, still couldn't produce a sound, and pushed away from the wall, hurrying as best she could along the dark green floor, beneath the pale yellow ceiling, hurrying toward the nurses' station. Toward help. Safety.

Nurse Scolari and a chunky, red-faced nurse named Beth Howe both did for Susan what she had been unable to do for herself: They talked her down, just as Jeff McGee had talked down the raving, hallucinating acid freaks in that Seattle hospital where he had served his residency. They brought her around behind the counter at the nurses' station and settled her into a spring-backed office chair. They gave her a glass of water. They reasoned with her, soothed her, listened to her, cajoled her, calmed her.

But they couldn't entirely convince her that it was safe to go back to room 258. She wanted another bed for the night, a different room.

"That's not possible, I'm afraid," Tina Scolari said. "You see, there's been an upturn in admissions the last day or so. The hospital's nearly full tonight. Besides, there's really nothing wrong with two fifty-eight. It's just a room like any other room. You know that's true, don't you, Susan? You know that what happened to you was just another of your attacks. It was just another dysfunctional episode."

Susan nodded, although she wasn't sure what she believed any more. "I still . . . I . . . don't want . . . to go back there," she said, her teeth chattering.

While Tina Scolari continued to talk to Susan, Beth Howe went to have a look in 258. She was gone only a couple of minutes, and upon her return, she reported that all was well.

"Mrs. Seiffert?" Susan asked.

"She's in bed where she belongs," Beth said.

"You're sure it's her?"

"Positive. Sleeping like a rock."

"And you didn't find . . . ?"

"Nothing else," Beth assured her.

"You looked where it might have hidden?"

"Not many places to hide in that room."

"But you did look?"

"Yes. Nothing was there."

They coaxed Susan into a wheelchair, and both of them took her back to 258. The closer they got to the room, the more violently Susan shivered.

The curtain was drawn tightly shut around the second bed.

They pushed her wheelchair past the first bed and kept going.

"Wait!" Susan said, sensing their intention.

"I want you to have a look for yourself," said Beth Howe.

"No, I shouldn't."

"Of course you should," Beth said.

"You must," Tina Scolari said.

"But . . . I don't think . . . I can."

"I'm sure you can," Tina Scolari said encouragingly.

They wheeled her right up to Jessica Seiffert's bed.

Beth Howe pulled the curtain aside.

Susan snapped her eyes shut.

Clutched the arms of the wheelchair.

"Susan, look," Tina said.

"Look," Beth said. "It's only Jessie."

"You see?"

"Only Jessie."

With her eyes closed, Susan could see the dead man—a man she had perhaps loved a long time ago, a man she now feared because the quick were meant to fear the dead—could see him on the inside of her eyelids as he sat up in the bed and smiled at her with soft lips that were like bursting pieces of spoiled fruit. The horror show behind her eyes was worse than what might lie in front of them, so she blinked; she looked.

An old woman lay in the bed, so small, so shrunken, so badly withered by disease that she looked, ironically, like a wrinkle-faced baby mistakenly placed in an adult's bed. Except—her skin was waxy and mottled, not smooth like a baby's skin, and her complexion was yellow, not newborn-pink. Her hair was yellow-gray. Her wrinkled mouth resembled a drawstring purse that had been pulled as tight as only a miser could pull it. An IV drip seeped into her through a gleaming needle that punctured her left arm, an arm that was far skinnier than Susan's.

"So that's Jessica Seiffert," Susan said, greatly relieved that such a person actually existed, but shocked that her befuddled brain could so easily—and more to the point, so *convincingly*—transform the old woman into a supernaturally animated male corpse.

"The poor old dear," said Beth.

"She's been the most popular citizen of Willawauk since I was a toddler," Tina said.

"Since before you were even around to toddle," Beth said.

"Everybody loves her," Tina said.

Jessica continued to sleep, her nostrils flaring almost imperceptibly with each shallow breath.

"I know two hundred people who'd be here to visit if Jessie would accept visitors," Beth said.

"But she doesn't want anyone seeing her like this," Tina said. "As if anyone would think less of her just because of what the cancer's done to her."

"It's always been the *inner* Jessie that Willawauk loves," Beth said.

"Exactly," Tina said.

"Feel better now?" Beth asked Susan.

"I guess so."

Beth closed the curtain.

Susan said, "You looked in the bathroom?"

"Oh, yes," Beth said. "It's empty."

"I'd like to have a look myself, if you don't mind," Susan said. She felt like a fool, but she was still a prisoner of her fear.

"Sure," Beth said obligingly. "Let's have a look and set your mind at ease."

Tina pushed the wheelchair to the open bathroom door, and Beth switched on the light in there.

No dead man waited in the white-on-white room.

"I feel like a perfect idiot," Susan said, feeling a blush creep into her cheeks.

"It's not your fault," Beth said.

Tina Scolari said, "Dr. McGee circulated a fairly long memo about your condition. He made it perfectly clear."

"We're all on your side," Beth said.

"We're all pulling for you," Tina agreed.

"You'll be well in no time. Really you will. McGee's a whiz. The best doctor we've got."

They helped Susan get into bed.

"Now," Tina Scolari said, "at the discretion of the night nurse, you are permitted to have a second sedative if the first one doesn't do the trick. They're mild enough. And in my judgment, you sure do need another one."

"I'll never get to sleep without it," Susan said. "And I was wondering . . . could you . . . "

"What is it?"

"Do you think . . . could someone stay with me . . . just until I fall asleep?"

Susan felt like a child for making that pathetic request: a dependent, emotionally immature, thumb-sucking, goblin-fearing, thirty-two-year-old child. She was disgusted with herself. But she couldn't help it. No matter how often she told herself about the bizarre effects of temporal-lobe brain lesions and sand-grain blood clots, regardless of how earnestly she argued to convince herself that one of those—or perhaps one of a dozen other—medical maladies was the cause of her *imaginary,* entirely imaginary, encounters with dead men, she was nonetheless terrified of being awake and alone in room 258—or anywhere else, in fact.

Tina Scolari looked at Beth Howe and raised her eyebrows inquiringly.

Beth considered it for a moment, then said, "Well, we aren't short-handed tonight, are we?"

"Nope," Tina said. "Everyone who was scheduled for duty showed up this evening. And so far there haven't been any big crises."

Beth smiled at Susan. "Slow night. No three-car crashes or barroom brawls or anything. I think one of us can spare an hour to sit with you until the sedative works."

"It probably won't even take an hour," Tina said. "You've overtaxed yourself, Susan. It'll catch up with you in a few minutes, and you'll go out like a light."

"I'll stay here," Beth said.

"I'd really appreciate it," Susan said, loathing herself for her inability to face the night alone.

Tina left but returned shortly with the second sedative in a pill cup.

When Susan took the pink tablet, she poured only a half-measure of water for herself because her hands were shaking too badly to safely manage a full tumbler. When she drank, the glass rattled against her teeth, and for a moment the pill stuck in her throat.

"I'm sure you'll have a good night now," Nurse Scolari said before she left.

Beth pulled up a chair beside the bed, smoothed her uniform skirt over her round knees, and sat quietly, reading a magazine.

Susan stared at the ceiling for a while, then glanced at Jessica Seiffert's curtained bed.

She looked the other way, too, at the darkness beyond the half-opened bathroom door.

She thought of the corpse scratching insistently at the closed bathroom door against which she had been leaning. She remembered the *click-snickety-click* of his fingernails as he probed the cracks around the door frame.

Of course that had never happened. Purely imaginary.

She closed her eyes.

Jerry, she thought, I loved you once. At least it was as close to love as an inexperienced, nineteen-year-old girl could ever get. And you said that you loved me. So why in the name of God would you come back now to terrorize me?

Of course it had never happened. Purely imaginary.

Please, Jerry, stay in the cemetery there in Philadelphia, where we put you so long ago. Please stay there. Don't come back here again. Please stay there. Please.

Without realizing that she was approaching sleep, she stepped over the rim of it and was gone.

11

A NURSE WOKE SUSAN AT SIX O'CLOCK WEDNESDAY MORNING. It was another gray day, but no rain was falling.

Jeffrey McGee arrived before six-thirty. He kissed her on the cheek again, but his lips lingered there for a couple of seconds longer than they had before.

"I didn't realize you'd be here so early," Susan said.

"I want to personally oversee most of the tests."

"But weren't you up late last night?"

"Nope. I inflicted my after-dinner speech on the Medical Association, and then I quickly slipped away before they had time to organize a lynching party."

"Seriously, how did it go?"

"Well, no one threw his dessert at me."

"I *told* you that you'd be a big success."

"Of course, maybe no one threw his dessert at me because it was the only edible part of the meal, and no one wanted to give it up."

"I'm sure you were wonderful."

"Well, I don't think I should plan to have a career on the lecture circuit. Anyway, enough about me. I understand there was some excitement here last night."

"Jeez, did they have to tell you about that?"

"Of course. And so do you. In detail."

"Why?"

"Because I said so."

"And the doctor must be obeyed."

"Right. So tell me."

Embarrassed, she told him everything about the corpse behind the curtain. Now, after a good night's sleep, the whole affair sounded ludicrous, and she wondered how she could ever have been convinced that any part of it was real.

When Susan finished talking, McGee said, "God, that's a hair-raising little tale!"

"You should've been there."

"But now that you've had time to think, you do realize it was just another episode."

"Of the Susan Thorton Soap Opera?"

"I mean, another attack, another hallucination," he said. "You do see that now?"

"Yes," she said miserably.

He blinked at her. "What's wrong?"

"Nothing."

He scowled at her and put his hand against her forehead to see if she was running a noticeable temperature. "Do you feel all right?"

"As right as I can feel under the circumstances," she said morosely.

"Cold?"

"No."

"You're shaking."

"A little."

"A lot."

She hugged herself and said nothing.

"What's wrong?" he asked again.

"I'm . . . scared."

"Don't be scared."

"Jesus, what's wrong with me?"

"We'll find out."

She couldn't stop shaking.

Yesterday morning, after she had broken down in front of McGee, after she wept against his shoulder, she had thought that she'd reached the bottom for sure. She had been ready and eager to believe that the future could only be brighter. For the first time in her life, she had admitted that she needed other people; she had confronted and accepted the unpleasant truth of her own vulnerability. That had been a shocking discovery for a woman who had built her life upon the erroneous but fiercely held assumption that she was strictly a creature of intellect, immune to emotional excess. But now she faced another realization that was even more shocking than the one whose impact she had already, somehow, absorbed: Having placed her fate in the hands of McGee and the Willawauk County Hospital's medical staff, having relinquished to them the responsibility for her survival, she now realized that the people upon whom she depended might fail her. Not intentionally, of course. But they were only human, too. *They* couldn't always control events, either. And if they failed to make her well, it wouldn't matter whether their failure was intentional or accidental or inevitable; in any case, she would be condemned to a chaotic existence, unable to distinguish reality from fantasy, and in time she would be driven completely mad.

And so she couldn't stop shaking.

"What's going to happen to me?"

"You'll be all right," McGee said.

"But . . . it's getting worse," she said, her voice quavering in spite of her determination to keep it steady.

"No. No, it isn't getting worse."

"Much worse," she insisted.

"Listen, Susan, last night's hallucination might have been more gruesome than the others—"

"*Might* have been?"

"Okay, it *was* more gruesome than the others—"

"And more vivid, more *real.*"

"—and more real. But it was the first one you've had since early yesterday morning, when you thought the two orderlies were Jellicoe and Parker. You're not in a *constant* state of flux between reality and—"

Susan shook her head and interrupted him. "No. The business with the orderlies . . . and the apparition later, here in the room . . . they weren't the only things I saw yesterday. There was an . . . an attack in between those two."

He frowned. "When?"

"Yesterday afternoon."

"You were with Mrs. Atkinson, downstairs in PT, yesterday afternoon."

"That's right. It happened shortly after I'd completed the therapy session, before I was brought back up here."

She told him how Murf and Phil had shoved her into the elevator with the four fraternity men.

"Why didn't you report all of this last evening when I was here?" McGee asked, a reprimanding tone to his voice.

"You were in such a hurry . . . "

"Not *that* much of a hurry. Am I a good doctor? I think I am. And a good doctor always has time for a patient in distress."

"I wasn't *in* distress by the time you made your evening rounds," she protested.

"Like hell you weren't. You had it all bottled up inside of you, but you were in distress sure enough."

"I didn't want to make you late for the Medical Association meeting."

"Susan, that's no excuse. I'm your *doctor.* You've got to level with your doctor at all times."

"I'm sorry," she said, looking down at her hands, unable to meet his forthright, blue-blue eyes. She couldn't bring herself to explain why she hadn't told him about the elevator vision. She had been worried that she would appear hysterical, that he would think less of her because she had panicked yet again. Worse, she had been afraid that he would pity her. And now that she was beginning to think that she was falling in love with him, the very *last* thing she wanted was for him to pity her.

"You don't dare hide things from me. You've got to tell me everything that happens, everything you feel. And I mean *everything*. If you *don't* tell me everything, then I might not be aware of an important symptom that would explain the root cause of all your troubles. I need every piece of information I can gather in order to make an informed diagnosis."

She nodded. "You're right. From now on, I won't hide anything from you."

"Promise?"

"Promise."

"Good."

"But you see," she said, still staring at her hands, which she was flexing and unflexing in nervous agitation, "it *is* getting a lot worse."

He put a hand against the side of her face, caressed her cheek.

She looked up at him.

"Listen," he said softly, reassuringly, "even if you *are* having more frequent attacks, at least you come out of them. And when one of these episodes passes, you're able to see it for what it was. After the fact, you're always aware that you were only hallucinating. Now, if you still believed that a dead man had come to get you last night, if you still thought that it had *really happened*, then you'd be in very deep trouble. If that's the way it was, then maybe I'd be sweating. But I'm not sweating yet. Am I? Do you see rivers of sweat streaming down my face? Are there dark, damp circles under my arms? Do I look as if I belong in a TV ad for Right Guard? Huh? Do I?"

She smiled. "You look as dry as toast."

"As dry as a sandbox," he said. "As dry as a stick of chalk. As dry as chicken cordon bleu when I try to cook it myself. Can you cook chicken cordon bleu, by the way?"

"I've made it a few times," she said.

"Does yours come out dry?"

She smiled again. "No."

"Good. I was *hoping* you could cook."

And what does he mean by that? she thought. His blue eyes seemed to say that he meant just what she thought he meant: He was as interested in her as she was in him. But still she couldn't trust her perceptions; she couldn't be positive of his intentions.

"Now," he said, "will you *please* think positive?"

"I'll try," she said.

But she couldn't stop shaking.

"Do more than try. Keep your chin up. That's doctor's orders. Now, I'll go find a couple of orderlies and a stretcher, and we'll go downstairs to diagnostic and get these tests out of the way. Are you ready to go?"

"I'm ready," she said.

"Smile?"

She did.

So did he. And he said, "Okay, now keep it on your face until further notice."
He headed toward the door, and over his shoulder he said, "I'll be right back."

He left, and her smile slipped off.

She glanced at the curtained bed.

She wished it wasn't there.

She longed for a glimpse of the sky, even if it was as gray and somber as it had
been yesterday. Perhaps if she could see the sky, she wouldn't feel quite so
trapped.

She had never before been this miserable; she felt wrung out and useless, even
though her physical recuperation was coming along well. Depression. That was
the enemy now. She was depressed not merely because other people had taken
some control of her life, but because they had taken over *all* control of it. She was
helpless. She could do absolutely nothing to shake off her illness. She could only
lie on an examining table as if she were a mindless hunk of meat, letting them
poke and prod her in their search for answers.

She looked at Mrs. Seiffert's bed again. The white curtain hung straight and still.

Last night, she had not merely opened a privacy curtain that had enclosed a
hospital bed. She had opened another curtain, too, a curtain beyond which lay
madness. For a few nightmarish minutes, she had stepped beyond the veil of
sanity, into a shadowy and moldering place from which few people ever returned.

She wondered what would have happened if she hadn't run away from her
hallucination last night. What would have happened if she had bravely and fool-
ishly refused to back off from Jerry Stein's decomposing corpse? She was afraid
she knew the answer. If she had held her ground, and if her long-dead lover had
clambered out of his bed and had touched her, if he had embraced her, if he had
pressed his rotting lips against her lips, stealing a warm kiss and giving her a cold
one in return, she would have snapped. Real or not, hallucination or not, she
would have snapped like a taut rubber band, and after that she would have been
forever beyond repair. They would have found her curled up on the floor, gibbering and chuckling, lost far down inside herself, and they would have transferred
her from Willawauk County Hospital to some quiet sanitarium, where she would
have been assigned to a nice room with soft, quilted walls.

She couldn't take much more of this. Not even for McGee. Not even for whatever future they might have together if she got well again. She was stretched taut.

Please, God, she thought, let the tests reveal something. Let McGee find the
problem. *Please.*

■ The walls and ceiling were the same shade of robin's-egg blue. Lying flat on
her back on the wheeled stretcher, her head raised just a few inches by a
firm little pillow, looking up, Susan almost felt as if she were suspended in the
middle of a summer sky.

Jeff McGee appeared beside her. "We're going to start with an EEG."

"Electroencephalogram," she said. "I never had one of those."

"Yes, you did," he said. "While you were in the coma. But of course you weren't
aware of it. You wouldn't remember it. Now, don't be afraid. It doesn't hurt at all."

"I know."

"It'll give us a look at the pattern of your brain waves. If you've got abnormal
brain function of any kind, it's almost sure to show up on an EEG."

"Almost?"

"It's not perfect."

A nurse rolled the EEG machine out of the corner where it had been standing, and she positioned it beside Susan.

"This works best if you're relaxed," McGee told Susan.

"I'm relaxed."

"It won't be very reliable at all or easily interpreted if you're in an emotional turmoil."

"I'm relaxed," she assured him.

"Let's see your hand."

She lifted her right hand off the stretcher's three-inch-thick mattress.

"Hold it straight out in front of you, keeping the fingers together. Okay. Now spread the fingers wide apart." He watched closely for a few seconds, then nodded with satisfaction. "Good. You're not trying to fake me out. You *are* calmer. You aren't trembling any more."

As soon as they had brought her downstairs, Susan became relatively calm, for she felt that progress, however limited, was finally being made. After all, as a first-rate physicist, she could understand, appreciate, and approve of what was happening now: tests, laboratories, the scientific method, a carefully planned search for answers conducted by eliminating possibilities until the solution stood alone, exposed. She was comfortable with that process and trusted it.

She trusted Jeffrey McGee, too. She had a lot of faith in his medical abilities and confidence in his intellect. He would know what to look for, and, more importantly, he would know how to recognize it when he saw it.

The tests would provide an answer, perhaps not quickly but eventually. McGee was now taking the first tentative steps toward putting an end to her ordeal.

She was sure of it.

"Calm as a clam," she said.

"Oyster," he said.

"Why oyster?"

"It seems to fit you better."

"Oh, you think I look more like an oyster than like a clam?"

"No. *Pearls* are found in oysters."

She laughed. "I'll bet you're a shameless come-on artist in a singles' bar."

"I'm a shark," he said.

McGee attached eight saline-coated electrodes to Susan's scalp, four on each side of her head.

"We'll take readings from both the left and the right side of the brain," he said, "then compare them. That'll be the first step in pinpointing the trauma."

The nurse switched on the EEG apparatus.

"Keep your head just as you have it," McGee told Susan. "Any sudden movement will interfere."

She stared at the ceiling.

McGee watched the green, fluorescent screen of the EEG monitor, which was not in Susan's line of sight.

"Looks good," he said, sounding somewhat disappointed. "No spikes. No flats. A nice, steady pattern. All within normal parameters."

Susan kept very still.

"Negative," he said, more to himself than to either her or the nurse.

Susan heard him click a switch.

"Now I'm taking a look at the comparative readings," McGee told her.

He was silent for a while.

The nurse moved off to another corner, readying another piece of equipment either for Susan or for a patient who had not yet been brought into the room.

After a while, McGee shut off the machine.

"Well?" Susan asked.

"Nothing."

"Nothing at all?"

"Well, the electroencephalograph is a useful device, but the data it provides aren't one hundred percent definitive. Some patients with serious intracranial diseases have been known to exhibit normal patterns during an EEG. And some people with no demonstrable disease have abnormal EEGs. It's a helpful diagnostic tool, but it isn't where we stop. It's where we begin."

Disappointed, but still certain that one or more of these tests would pinpoint her malady, Susan said, "What's next?"

As McGee removed the electrodes from Susan's scalp, he said, "Well, radiology's right next door. I want new X rays taken of your skull."

"Sounds like fun."

"Oh, it's a genuine laugh riot."

■   The radiology lab was an off-white room filled with lots of cumbersome, shiny, black and white equipment that looked somewhat dated to Susan. Of course she wasn't an expert on X-ray technology. Besides, she couldn't expect a hospital in rural Oregon to have all the very latest diagnostic tools. Though they might be a bit dated, Willawauk's machines looked more than adequate.

The radiologist was a young man named Ken Piper. He developed the plates while they waited, then pinned the sheets of X-ray film to a pair of light boxes. He and McGee studied the pictures, murmuring to each other, pointing at shadows and areas of brightness on the film.

Susan watched from the wheeled stretcher to which she had returned from the X-ray table.

They took down the first X rays, pinned up others, murmured and pointed again.

Eventually, McGee turned away from the light boxes, looking thoughtful.

Susan said, "What'd you find?"

He sighed and said, "What we *didn't* find are signs of brain lesions."

"We couldn't detect any collections of fluid, either," Ken Piper said.

"And there's been no shifting of the pineal gland, which you sometimes find in cases where the patient suffers from really vivid hallucinations," McGee said. "No depressions in the skull; not the slightest indication of intracranial pressure."

"It's just a perfectly clean set of pictures," Ken Piper said brightly, smiling down at her. "You've got nothing to worry about, Miss Thorton."

Susan looked at McGee and saw her own feelings mirrored in his eyes. Unfortunately, Ken Piper was wrong; she had *plenty* to worry about.

"Now what?" she asked.

"I want to do an LP," McGee said.

"What's that?"

"A lumbar puncture."

"Spinal tap?"

"Yeah. We might have missed something with the EEG and the X rays, something that'll show up in the spinal. And there are some conditions that can be identified only through spinal fluid analysis."

McGee used radiology's phone to ring the hospital's lab. He told the answering technician to get set up for a complete spinal workup on the samples he was about to take from Susan.

When he put the phone down, she said, "Let's get this over with."

In spite of the fact that McGee anesthetized Susan's lower spinal area with Novocaine, the lumbar puncture wasn't painless, but neither was it remotely as bad as she had expected it to be. It brought quick, sharp tears to her eyes, and she winced and bit her lip; but the worst part was having to remain perfectly still, worrying about the needle breaking off in her if she twitched or jerked suddenly.

McGee kept one eye on the manometer as he extracted the fluid, and he said, "Normal pressure."

A couple of minutes later, when the final sample had been taken, Susan whimpered with relief and wiped at the stinging tears that had beaded on her eyelashes.

McGee held up one glass tube full of spinal fluid and stared at it against the light. "Well, at least it's clear," he said.

"How long until we get the results?" Susan asked.

"It'll take a little while," McGee said. "In the meantime, we've still got a few minor tests to run. Feel up to giving some blood?"

"Anything for the cause."

Shortly before ten o'clock, while McGee went to the lab to see how the spinal workup was coming along, Murf and Phil arrived in diagnostic to escort Susan back to room 258. Although she knew that yesterday's terror in the elevator had not been real, although she knew that the orderlies were innocent of the malicious behavior that she had attributed to them in her hallucinations, she felt somewhat ill at ease with them.

"Everyone's missed you up on the second floor," Phil told Susan as they wheeled her stretcher into the hall.

"Lots of glum faces up there," Murf said.

"Oh, I'll bet," she said.

"It's true," Phil said.

"The place seems so grim without you," Murf said.

"Like a dungeon," Phil said.

"Like a cemetery," said Murf.

"Like a hospital," said Phil.

"It *is* a hospital," she said, playing along with them in an effort to keep her spirits up as they approached the elevators.

"You're absolutely right," Murf told her.

"It is a hospital, of course," Phil said.

"But with you around, fair lady—"

"—it seems warmer, brighter—"

"—like a resort hotel—"

"—in some country where it's always sunny—"

"—someplace exciting, exotic—"

"—like Mesopotamia."

They reached the elevators, and Susan held her breath.

"Phil, I told you yesterday—there isn't a Mesopotamia any more."

One of them pushed the elevator call button.

"Then where have I been going every winter, Murf? My travel agent always told me it was Mesopotamia."

"I'm afraid you've got a crooked travel agent, Phil. You've probably been going to New Jersey."

The elevator doors opened, and Susan stiffened, but there were no dead men waiting.

"No, I'm sure I've never been to New Jersey, Murf."

"Lucky for New Jersey, Phil."

Dammit, I can't live like this! Susan thought grimly as they rolled her out of the elevator and into the second-floor corridor. I just can't go through life being suspicious and frightened of everyone I meet. I can't cope with this constant expectation that one horror or another will pop out at me from behind every door and from around every corner.

How could *anyone* possibly get through an entire life that was like a continuous, exhausting ride through an especially nasty, gruesome, carnival funhouse?

Why would anyone *want* to get through such a life?

■ Jessica Seiffert was gone.

The curtain was open.

An orderly was stripping off the last of the soiled sheets and dropping them into a laundry cart. In answer to Susan's question, he said, "Mrs. Seiffert took a turn for the worse. They had to rush her down to intensive care."

"I'm sorry to hear that."

"Well, everyone expected it," the orderly said. "But it's still a shame. She's such a nice lady."

Susan *was* sorry for Jessica Seiffert, but she was also relieved that her roommate was gone.

It was nice to be able to see the window, even though the day was gray and misty and teetering on the edge of another storm.

■ Ten minutes after Susan had been delivered to her room by Phil and Murf, as she was sitting in bed, adjusting the covers around her, Mrs. Baker came in with a tray of food.

"You missed breakfast this morning. And honey, you just can't afford to skip a single meal. You're not well padded like I am. I could afford to skip a whole week of meals!"

"I'm starved."

"I don't doubt it for a minute," the nurse said, putting the tray down on the bed table. "How do you feel, kid?"

"Like a pincushion," Susan said, aware of a dull pain in her back, a souvenir of the spinal tap.

"Did Dr. McGee handle most things himself?"

"Yes."

"Then it could have been worse," Mrs. Baker said, removing the lid from the tray. "There are some around here who're not as gentle as McGee."

"Yes, but I'm afraid he's going to be late to his office."

"He doesn't have office hours Wednesday mornings," the nurse said. "Just five hours in the afternoon."

"Oh, and by the way," Susan said, "I saw so little of you yesterday that I forgot to ask you how everything went on Monday night."

Mrs. Baker blinked, and her forehead creased in perplexity. "Monday night?"

"How was your date? You know—the bowling and the hamburger dinner?"

For a couple of seconds, the nurse appeared to have no idea what Susan was talking about. Then her eyes suddenly brightened. "Oh! The date. Of course. My jolly big lumberman."

"The one with the shoulders to measure a doorway," Susan said, quoting what Mrs. Baker herself had said on Monday when describing her beau.

"And those big, hard, *gentle* hands," the nurse said rather wistfully.

Susan grinned. "That's better. I didn't think you could've forgotten *him*."

"It was a night to remember."

"I'm glad to hear it."

A mischievous expression came over Mrs. Baker's face. She said, "We knocked down all the pins. And I don't just mean at the bowling alley, either."

Susan laughed. "Why, Mrs. Baker, you've got a randy streak in you wider than I'd have thought."

The nurse's merry eyes gleamed behind her white-framed glasses. "Life's not very tasty if you don't add just a dash of spice now and then."

Unfolding her paper napkin and tucking it into the collar of her pajamas—she had changed into her recently laundered blue pair after returning from downstairs—Susan said, "I suspect you flavor it with more than just a *dash* of spice."

"Whole tablespoons sometimes."

"I knew it. Mrs. Baker, you're a regular Sybarite."

"No. I'm a Methodist, but Methodists know how to have fun, too. Now, you eat everything on that tray, honey. It's really good to see you starting to fill out in the face a little. We don't want any backsliding."

For the next half hour, Susan ate her late breakfast and watched the turbulent sky that roiled beyond the window. Masses of clouds, painted a dozen shades of gray, raced from horizon to horizon.

A few minutes after eleven o'clock, Jeff McGee came by. "Sorry I've been so long. We had the lab results some time ago, but I've been up in the intensive-care ward with Jessie Seiffert."

"How's she doing?"

"Fading fast."

"That's a shame."

"Yeah. It's a shame she has to die. But since there wasn't anything we could do for her, I'm glad she's finally going downhill in a hurry. She was always an active woman, and it was hard on her to be bedridden, harder than it might have been on a lot of other people. I hated to see her lingering and suffering these past few weeks." He shook his head sadly, then snapped his fingers as a thought struck him. "Say, something occurred to me when I was with Jessie, upstairs in intensive care. You know why you might have hallucinated Jerry Stein's corpse when you were actually looking at Jessie? I think there was a trigger that did it for you, that set you off."

"Trigger?"

"Yes. Initials."

"Initials," Susan echoed, not sure what he was talking about.

"That's right. Don't you see? Jerry Stein and Jessica Seiffert—both JS."

"Oh. I hadn't noticed that."

"Maybe you didn't notice it on a *conscious* level. But nothing escapes the sub-conscious; it's too damned observant. I'll bet you were aware of it subconsciously. It might have been the coincidence of their initials that fixated you on the curtain and made you so afraid of it. If that's the case, then perhaps none of your attacks is merely a random, spontaneous event. Maybe all of them were triggered by one thing or another, unimportant little events and observations that harkened back to some memory connected with the House of Thunder. And once that connection was made on an unconscious level, maybe the hallucinatory episode followed like clockwork."

He was visibly excited by the theory, and Susan said, "If what you say is true, what difference does it make?"

"I'm not entirely sure. I haven't had much time to think about all the ramifica-tions. But I suspect it could be important in helping me decide whether or not the official diagnosis should come down on the side of a physical cause."

She didn't like what she was hearing.

Frowning, she said, "If my hallucinations aren't merely random, spontaneous sparks thrown off by an injured brain, then perhaps the root cause of them isn't physical at all. Is that what you're saying? If the visions are triggered by some subtle psychological mechanism, then possibly the entire problem is best left to a psychiatrist."

"No, no, no," McGee said quickly, making a placating gesture with his hands. "We don't have enough data to leap to conclusions like that. We still have to pursue a physical explanation because that seems by far the most likely possibility, considering that you *did* suffer a head injury and were in a coma for more than three weeks."

Susan wanted very much to believe that her problem was entirely physical, nothing more than the expected consequences of vital tissue damage. If it was a tiny blood clot in the brain, a lesion, or some other malady of the flesh, medical science would take care of it posthaste. She trusted medical science precisely because it *was* a science. She *dis*trusted psychiatry because, to her way of thinking, which had been shaped by her education as a physicist, psychiatry was not really a science at all; she thought of it as little more than voodoo.

She shook her head adamantly. "You're wrong about the trigger effect of the initials. JS. It wasn't that. This isn't a psychological condition."

"I tend to agree with you," he said. "But we can't rule out any possibilities at this stage."

"*I* can. I've ruled it out."

"But I *can't*. I'm a doctor. And a doctor's got to remain objective."

For the first time since entering the room, he took her hand, and his touch was wonderfully soothing.

Squeezing his hand, she said, "What were the results of the spinal?"

With his free hand, McGee pulled thoughtfully on his ear. "The protein analysis showed no abnormalities. Then we did a blood count. If there had been too many red cells, that would've told us that there was bleeding either inside the skull, at the base of the brain, or somewhere along the spine."

"But the red count was normal," Susan said, anticipating him.

"Yes. Now, if there was an abundance of white cells, we'd know there was a cerebral or spinal infection."

"But the white count was normal, too."

"Yes."

Susan felt as if she were being backed into a corner by an advancing army of cold, hard facts. *You're as healthy as a teenager, the facts seemed to be shouting at her. Your body hasn't betrayed you. Your brain hasn't betrayed you, either. It's your mind that has gone rotten. You're not physically ill, Susan. There's no organic problem. You're just plain crazy; that's all. Nuts. You're as nutty as a jumbo-size can of Planter's Party Mix.*

She tried very hard not to listen to those invidious inner voices, tried to tune out the increasingly loud chorus of self-doubt, self-loathing, and confusion.

Plaintively, she said, "Didn't the spinal show *anything* out of the ordinary?"

"Not a thing. We even analyzed the sugar content of your spinal fluid. There are some diseases in which bacteria eat that particular sugar, so a low count would have set off alarms. But your spinal sugar is two-thirds the level of your blood sugar, and that's also normal."

"Sounds as if I'm a textbook example of a thirty-two-year-old woman in perfect health," she said with heavy irony.

McGee was clearly troubled by the difficulty he was having in pinpointing her illness. "No. *Something* is wrong somewhere."

"What?"

"I don't know."

"That's not terribly reassuring."

"We'll just keep looking."

"I have a feeling I'm going to be here a long time."

"No. We'll find it soon. We have to."

"But how?"

"Well, first of all, I'm taking the EEG printouts, the X rays, and all the lab data home with me. I'm going to go over everything one more time, with a magnifying glass if I have to. Maybe we didn't look carefully this morning. Maybe the answer was there and we just failed to spot it. Some little thing that was easily over-looked . . . some subtle anomaly . . . "

"And what if you still don't find anything?"

He hesitated, and he looked worried as he finally said, "Well, then . . . there's another test we can run."

"Tell me," she said.

"It's not a simple procedure."

"I could figure that much just by taking a look at your face," she said.

"A cerebral angiogram. It's a diagnostic technique that we usually reserve for functionally impaired stroke victims who've got to undergo brain surgery for clot removal or for the repair of a hemorrhaged blood vessel."

"What's it entail?"

"We'd inject a radiopaque substance into your bloodstream, into an artery between the heart and the brain, which means in the neck, and that isn't pleasant."

"I guess not."

"There's pain involved."

Susan put one hand to the side of her neck and rubbed the tender flesh uneasily.

McGee said, "And the procedure isn't entirely risk-free. A small percentage of patients suffer complications leading to death subsequent to an angiogram. Notice that I didn't say it was a 'tiny' percentage or an 'infinitesimal' percentage."

"You said it was a 'small' percentage, and I gather that means it's not large, but that it's also not small enough to be considered insignificant."

"Exactly."

"What we're talking about is a more sophisticated series of cranial X rays," she said. "Is that right?"

"Yes. As soon as the radiopaque tracer reaches the blood vessels in the brain, we take a long, rapid sequence of X rays, following its dispersal. That gives us the most detailed look at your cerebral circulatory system that we could hope to get. We're able to clearly define the size and shape of all the veins and arteries. We can pinpoint a clot, a hemorrhage, a bulge in an arterial wall, virtually anything, no matter how small it might be."

"Sounds like just the thing for getting to the bottom of my problem," Susan said.

"Ordinarily, I wouldn't even resort to an angiogram unless the patient had serious functional impairment—loss of speech, loss of motor control, partial paralysis—or was suffering from apoplectic stroke-related mental confusion of such severity that not even a hope of leading a normal life existed."

"Sounds like me," she said glumly.

"Oh, no. Not at all. There's an enormous difference between stroke-related mental disorientation and the kind of hallucinations you've been having. Believe it or not, your condition is the less life-disrupting of the two."

For a long moment, neither of them said anything. McGee stood beside the bed, and Susan sat there in it, feeling small and weak, and they just held hands in silence.

Then she said, "Suppose you still don't find anything when you look over the X rays and lab reports again this evening."

"Suppose."

"Would you order an angiogram for me then?"

He closed his eyes and thought about it for a moment.

Susan saw that there was a nervous tic in his left eyelid.

Finally he said, "I just don't know. It depends on so many things. I'd have to consider the old physician's credo: 'If you can't do any good, at least don't do any harm.' I mean, if there's not the slightest indication that your problem is physical, then scheduling an angiogram would be—"

"It *is* physical," Susan insisted.

"Even if there was evidence of a physical cause, sufficient evidence to justify putting you through an angiogram, I'd want to wait a few days until you were a little stronger."

She licked her lips, which felt dry and rough. "And if we did go through with an angiogram, and if it didn't reveal any physical damage to the brain, and if the hallucinations continued anyway—what then?" she asked.

"We'd have exhaused every avenue offered by traditional medicine."

"Surely not."

"We'd have to rule out a diagnosis of physical cause and start looking elsewhere."

"No."

"Susan, we'd simply have to."

"No."

"Consulting a psychiatrist is nothing that you should be ashamed of. It's only an—"

"I'm not ashamed of it," she said. "I just don't believe it would do any good."

"Modern psychiatry has achieved—"

"No," she said, cutting him off, afraid even to consider the possibility of submitting to years of therapy, years and years of continuing hallucinations. "No. There must be something wrong that you can locate, something you can *do*. There must be. There *has* to be."

He dropped the subject of psychiatry. "I'll do my best."

"That's all I'm asking."

"I'm not licked yet."

"Didn't think you were."

Apparently he saw that her lips were dry, for he said, "Like a drink of water?"

"Yes, please."

He poured it for her, and she drank all of it in several long, greedy swallows; then he returned the empty glass to the tray on the nightstand.

"Have you remembered anything at all about your job?" McGee asked.

His question startled her. The last time she had given a thought to the Milestone Corporation or to her job there was when she had telephoned Philip Gomez in Newport Beach on Monday morning. More than two days ago. Since then, she had pushed the entire subject to the back of her mind, had thrown a dark cloth over it—as if she were frightened of it. And she *was* frightened. Now, the mere mention of Milestone sent a chill through her. Furthermore, she was suddenly stricken by the strange and unnerving conviction that her bizarre hallucinations— the encounters with dead men—were all somehow directly related to her work at Milestone.

McGee evidently sensed her fear, for he leaned closer to her and said, "Susan? What's wrong?"

She told him what she had been thinking: that there was a link between the Milestone Corporation and her hallucinations.

"Link?" McGee asked. He was clearly perplexed. "What sort of link?"

"I haven't the faintest idea. But I *feel* it."

"Are you suggesting that you were having similar hallucinations *prior* to your auto accident?"

"No, no. How could that be?"

"You mean that you aren't sure if you were or weren't having them prior to the accident."

"I wasn't. Definitely not."

"You don't sound certain enough to please me."

So she thought about it for a minute.

He watched her with keen anticipation.

At last she said, "Yes. Yes, I'm sure. These attacks have come only since the accident. If I'd had them before, I wouldn't have forgotten them. Not something like this."

McGee cocked his head and regarded her at an angle. "If there's a physical cause of your condition—which is what both you and I want very much to believe—then it must be an injury arising out of the car crash."

"I know."

"It can't be something that was sparked by your work at Milestone. Because if it's caused by the pressure of your work or something like that—"

"—then we'd be talking about a psychological condition," she finished for him. "A nervous breakdown."

"Yes."

"Which it isn't."

"Then how can there be a link to Milestone?"

She frowned. "I don't know."

"So you must be wrong."

"I guess so. But I still . . . "

"Feel frightened?"

"Yes."

"That's easily explained," McGee said. "You're afraid of the Milestone Corporation for pretty much the same reason that you were afraid of the drawn curtain around Jessie's bed. You couldn't see what was on the other side of that curtain, which gave your imagination a chance to run wild. And your job has that same quality of the unknown about it. There's a curtain drawn around that part of your life, and because you can't see what lies beyond it, your imagination is given an opportunity to supply you with frightening possibilities. Perhaps because of an almost immeasurably small amount of brain damage, you're fixated on the House of Thunder and on what happened to you in that cavern; so it follows that your imagination, whenever it *does* have a chance to run wild, invariably harkens back to those events of thirteen years ago. Your hallucinations have nothing to do with your job, they can't have anything to do with it, because Milestone has nothing to do with the House of Thunder. You're just trying to tie them all together because . . . well, that's what it means to be psychologically *obsessed* with a single event in your life. Do you understand?"

"Yes."

"Yet the Milestone Corporation still frightens you."

"Every time you mention the name, a cold wave passes through me," she admitted.

She could see goose bumps on her arm where the sleeve of her pajamas had slid back.

McGee had been leaning against the bed all this time. Now he boosted himself up and sat on the edge of it, still holding her hand.

"I know it scares you," he said sympathetically. "Your hand is freezing. It wasn't cold at all when I first took hold of it, but the moment we started talking about your job, it just turned to ice."

"You see?"

"Yes, but those cold waves, those feelings of suspicion directed toward Milestone, all of those things are just facets of your obsession. This fear is like a miniature episode, a very small version of the kind of attack in which you thought you saw Jerry Stein's corpse. You have no logical reason to be afraid of Milestone or of anyone who works there."

She nodded, dismayed by the ever-complicating nature of her condition. "I guess I don't."

"You *know* you don't."

Susan sighed. "You know what I wish? I wish there were such things as ghosts. I wish this *were* a case of dead men returning from the grave to take revenge on me, like something out of one of those EC Horror Comics. I mean, Jeez, how much *easier* it would be to deal with *that*. No spinal taps. No angiograms. No sharply clawed little self-doubts tearing me apart from inside. All I'd have to do is call up a priest and ask him, please, to come over here and chase these nasty demonic spirits all the way back to Hell, where they belong."

McGee frowned at her, and there was a troubled expression in his eyes when he said, "Hey, I don't think I like to hear you talking that way."

"Oh, don't worry," Susan quickly assured him, "I'm not going to go mystical on you. I'm perfectly aware that there ain't no such things as ghosts. Besides, if there were ghosts, and if that's what these things were that've been bothering me lately, then they'd be transparent, wouldn't they? Or they'd look like a bunch of bed sheets with eye holes cut out of them. *That's* a ghost. They wouldn't be warm-skinned and solid like the things I've been running into and away from lately." She smiled at him. "Hey, I know why you're so worried all of a sudden! You're afraid that if it *did* turn out to be ghosts, then I wouldn't need you any more. Doctors don't perform exorcisms, right?"

He smiled, too. "Right."

"You're afraid that I'd cast you aside, just throw you over in favor of some priest with a prayer book in one hand and a golden crucifix in the other."

"Would you do that to me?" he asked.

"Never. For heaven's sake, too many things could go wrong if I relied on a priest. Like . . . what if I entrusted myself to a priest who'd lost his faith? Or what if I went to a Catholic priest for help—and then the ghosts all turned out to be Protestants? What good would an exorcism do me then?"

She was certain that McGee hadn't been conned by her forced good humor; he knew that she was still depressed and scared. But he played along with her anyway, for he apparently sensed, as she had done, that she'd dwelt on her problems far too much this morning and that chewing them over any longer would be harmful to her. She needed a change of subject, needed to kid around for a while, and McGee obliged.

"Well," he said, "as I understand it, the exorcism is supposed to work regardless of the spirit's religious affiliation in any prior life it might have lived. After all, what kind of mess would the supernatural world be in if it had to take logic into account? I mean, if Catholic exorcisms didn't work against Protestant ghosts, then a crucifix wouldn't repel a Jewish vampire."

"In that case, how *would* you repel a Jewish vampire?"

"You'd probably have to brandish a mezuzah at him instead of a crucifix."

"Or maybe you could just offer him a ham dinner," Susan said.

"That would only repel him if he was a devout, practicing Jewish vampire. And then what about Moslem vampires?"

"See?" she said. "It's all too complicated. I can't possibly fire you and hire a priest."

"Ah, it's so nice to know I'm needed."

"Oh, you're definitely needed," she assured him. "I need you. I *do* need you." She heard her voice change abruptly as she was speaking, heard the bantering tone evaporate in the intense heat of her true feelings for him. "There's no doubt about *that*." She was as startled by her own boldness as McGee appeared to be, but she couldn't stop herself. She could only plunge ahead recklessly, speaking too fast, in too much of a rush to express what had been on her mind and in her heart for the past day or two. "I need you, Jeff McGee. And if you want me to, I'll sit here all day, saying it over and over again, until my voice wears out."

He stared at her, his beautiful blue eyes a darker and more intense blue than she had ever seen them before.

She tried to read those eyes, but she couldn't tell a thing about the thoughts behind them.

As she waited for him to respond to her, Susan wondered if she had done something stupid. Had she misinterpreted his treatment of her and his reactions to her during the past few days? Where she had thought she'd seen romantic interest—was there really only doctorly concern? If she had mistaken his usual bedside manner for special interest, the next few minutes were going to be among the most socially awkward in her life.

She wished desperately that she could call back the words she had spoken, roll back the clock just one minute.

Then McGee kissed her.

It was not like any of the kisses that he had planted on her cheek or on the corner of her mouth during the past couple of days. There was nothing chaste or timid about it this time. He kissed her full upon the lips, tenderly yet forcefully, both giving and taking, seeking and demanding. She responded to him with an instancy and with a heat that were not at all like her; this time, there was no trace of the ice maiden in her, nothing whatsoever held in reserve, no part of her that stopped to think about keeping control of the situation and of the relationship that might follow. This would be different from all other love affairs she'd ever known. This time she, too, was being swept away. This kiss involved not only lips and tongues, but passion, hunger, need. He put his hands on her face, one on each side of her face, holding her gently but firmly, as if he was afraid that she would reconsider her commitment and would pull back from him—as if he could not bear the thought of her doing so.

When at last the kiss ended and they drew apart a few inches to look at each other, to decide how the kiss had changed them, Susan saw a mixture of emotions in McGee's face: happiness, surprise, awe, confusion, embarrassment.

His breathing was fast.

Hers was faster.

For a moment she thought she saw something else in his eyes, too; something . . . darker. For only a second or two, she thought she saw fear in his eyes, just a flicker of it, a fluttering bat-wing apprehension.

Fear?

Before she could decide what that might mean, before she could even be sure that she had actually seen fear in his eyes, the silence was broken, and the spell, too.

"You surprised me," Jeff said. "I didn't . . . "

"I was afraid I'd offended you or . . . "

"No, no. I just . . . didn't realize . . . "

" . . . that both of us . . . "

" . . . the feeling was mutual."

"I thought I understood and . . . Well, the signals you were sending out seemed . . . "

" . . . the kiss put an end to any doubts that you . . . "

"God, yes!"

"What a kiss," he said.

"Some kiss."

He kissed her again, but only briefly, glancing at the door with evident uneasiness. She couldn't blame him for holding back. He was a doctor, after all, and she was a patient; and necking with the patients was a couple of thousand miles below the level of decorum that was expected of a physician. She wanted to throw her arms around him and draw him tight against her; she wanted to possess him and be possessed by him. But she knew this was neither the right time nor the right place, and she let him draw back from her.

She said, "How long have you . . . "

"I don't know. Maybe even before you came out of the coma."

"Before that? Loved me . . . ?"

"You were so beautiful."

"But you didn't even know me then."

"So it probably really wasn't love at that point. But something. Even then, I felt *something*."

"I'm glad."

"And after you came out of the coma . . . "

"You found out what a charmer I am, and you were hooked."

He smiled. "Exactly. And I found out that you had what Mrs. Baker calls 'moxie.' I like a woman with moxie."

For a few seconds they were silent again, just staring at each other.

Then she said, "Can it really happen this fast?"

"It has."

"There's so much to talk about."

"A million things," he said.

"A billion," she said. "I hardly know a thing about your background."

"It's shady."

"I want to know everything there is to know about you," she said, holding one of his hands in both of hers. "Everything. But I guess . . . here, in this place . . . "

"It's too awkward here."

"Yes. It's hardly the right place for new lovers to become better acquainted with each other."

"I think we ought to keep our relationship on a strictly doctor-patient basis as long as you've got to be here. Later, when you're feeling better, when you've been discharged and our time together isn't so public . . . "

"That's probably wise," she said, although she wanted to touch him and to be touched by him in ways that doctors and patients didn't touch each other. "But does it have to be *strictly* doctor-patient? Can't we bend a little? Can't you at least kiss me on the cheek now and then?"

Jeff smiled and pretended to think hard about it. "Well . . . uh . . . let's see now . . . so far as I remember, the Hippocratic Oath doesn't contain any admonishment against kissing patients on the cheek."

"So how about right now?"

He kissed her on the cheek.

"Seriously," he said, "I think the most important thing now is for both of us to concentrate our energies on getting you well. If we can make you well again, then everything else—everything else there might be between us—will follow."

"You've given me a new motivation for beating this thing," Susan said.

"And you *will* beat it, too," he said in a tone of voice that admitted to no doubt. "*We'll* beat it. Together."

Looking at him now, Susan realized that she *had* seen fear in his eyes a couple of minutes ago. Although he would not express any pessimistic thoughts to her, there had to be a part of him that wondered if they really could find a way to put an end to her terrifying hallucinations. He wasn't a fool; he knew that failure was a lurking possibility. Fear? Yes. Yes, he had every right to be afraid. He was afraid that he had fallen in love with a woman who was on a fast train to a nervous breakdown or, worse, to the madhouse at the end of the line.

"Don't worry," she said.

"I'm not worried."

"I'm strong."

"I know."

"Strong enough to make it—with your help."

He kissed her on the cheek again.

Susan thought of what she'd said earlier about ghosts. She really did wish there were such things. If only her problem were that simple. Just ghosts. Just walking dead men who could be harried back to their graves by the recital of the proper prayers and by the liberal sprinkling of holy water. How nice it would be to discover that the problem was not within her, that the source lay outside of her. Knowing it was impossible, she nonetheless wished that they would find proof that the phantom Harch and the other phantoms were all real, that ghosts were real, and that she had never been sick at all.

A short while later, she got her wish—or something rather like it.

12

LUNCH CAME SO SOON AFTER HER LATE BREAKFAST THAT SUSAN couldn't finish everything, but she ate enough to win Mrs. Baker's approval.

An hour and a half later, she was taken downstairs for her second physical therapy session with Mrs. Atkinson. A new pair of orderlies came for her, but, happily, neither of them had a face from out of her past.

At the elevators, she expected the worst. Nothing happened.

She had not hallucinated since last night, when she had seen Jerry Stein's corpse in Jessica Seiffert's bed. As the orderlies wheeled her along the first-floor corridor toward the PT Department, she counted up the hours since that attack: almost sixteen.

Almost sixteen hours of peace.

Maybe there would never be another attack. Maybe the visions would stop as suddenly as they had begun.

The therapy session with Florence Atkinson was slightly more strenuous than the one Susan had been through yesterday, but the massage felt even better this time, and the shower was no less of a treat than it had been yesterday.

At the elevators once more, on the way back upstairs, Susan held her breath.

Again, nothing bad happened to her.

More than seventeen hours had passed now.

She had the feeling that she would be forever free of the hallucinations if she could only get through one entire day without them; one ghost-free day might be all she needed to cleanse her mind and her soul.

Less than seven hours to go.

When she got back to her room from the PT Department, two bouquets of fresh flowers were waiting for her; crysanthemums, carnations, roses, and sprays of baby's breath. There were cards attached to both arrangements. The first card urged her to get well soon, and it was signed, "As ever, Phil Gomez." The second one said, "We all miss you here at the slave pit." It was signed by a number of people. Susan recognized some of their names, but only because Phil Gomez had mentioned them on the telephone Monday morning. She stared at the list: Ella Haversby, Eddie Gilroy, Anson Breckenridge, Tom Kavinsky . . . Nine names altogether. She couldn't summon up a face to go with any one of them.

As on every other occasion when the Milestone Corporation had come to mind, the mere thought of it was sufficient to send a chill through her.

And she didn't know why.

She was determined to keep a positive attitude and let nothing disturb her, so she turned her mind away from Milestone. At least the flowers were pretty. She could enjoy them without thinking about where they had come from.

In bed again, she tried to read a book but discovered that the therapy session and the hot shower had made her sleepy. She napped. She didn't dream.

When she awoke, the room was playing host to a large party of shadows. Outside, the sun had just touched the mountains; although true sunset was still some time away, the cloud-darkened day was already slouching toward evening. She yawned, sat up, wiped at her matted eyes with the back of one hand.

The second bed was still empty.

According to the nightstand clock, it was four-thirty. Now nineteen hours since her most recent attack.

She wondered if the blossoming of her relationship with Jeff McGee was responsible for keeping the ghosts at bay. Having someone to love and *being* loved: that couldn't hurt. She hadn't wanted to believe that her problem was psychological, but now that it looked as if her troubles might be behind her, she was more willing to consider psychological explanations. Perhaps Jeff's love was all the medicine she had needed.

She got out of bed, stepped into her slippers, and made her way to the bathroom. Snapped on the light.

Jerry Stein's decapitated head was resting on the closed commode seat.

Susan stood on the white ceramic tiles, in the harsh white fluorescent light, her face equally as white as anything in the snow-white bathroom. She didn't want to believe her eyes.

It's not real.

The head was in the same terrible state of decomposition that it had been in last night, when Jerry had risen out of Jessie Seiffert's bed, moaning Susan's name through lips that glistened with corruption. The skin was still gray and gray-green. Both corners of the mouth were clotted with thick suppuration. Hideous blisters on the upper lip. And around the swollen nose. Dark, bubbled spots of decay at the corners of the eyes. Eyes open wide. Bulging from their sockets. They were opaque, sheathed in pearly cataracts, as they had been last night, and the whites of them were badly discolored, yellowish and streaked with blood. But at least these were unseeing eyes, as the eyes of a dead man ought to be: inanimate, blind. The head had been severed from the rest of the corpse with savage glee; a ragged mantle of flesh lay like a rumpled, frilly collar at the termination of the neck. Something small and bright lay twisted in a fold of that gray neck-skin, something that caught the light and gleamed. A pendant. A religious pendant. It was the small, gold-plated mezuzah that Jerry Stein had always worn.

It's not real, it's not real, it's not real . . .

That three-word charm seemed even less effective than usual; if anything, the grisly head became more vivid, more *real*, the longer that she stared at it.

Rigid with horror, yet determined to dispel the vision, Susan shuffled one step closer to the commode.

The dead eyes stared through her, unaware of her, fixed on something in another world.

It isn't real.

She reached out to touch the gray face. Hesitated.

What if the face came alive just as she put her hand against it? What if those graveyard eyes rolled and focused on her? What if that gaping, ruined mouth suddenly snapped at her, bit her fingers, and wouldn't let go? What if—

Stop it! she told herself angrily.

She heard a strange wheezing noise—and realized that it was the sound of her own labored breathing.

Relax, she said to herself. Dammit, Susan Kathleen Thorton, you're too old to believe in this nonsense.

But the head didn't fade away like a mirage.

Finally she pushed her trembling hand forward, through air that seemed as thick and resistant as water. She touched the dead man's cheek.

It felt solid.

It felt real.

Cold and greasy.

She jerked her hand back, shuddering and gagging.

The cataract-sheathed eyes didn't move.

Susan looked at the fingertips with which she had touched the head, and she saw that they were wet with a silvery slime. The scum of decomposition.

Sickened almost to the point of vomiting, Susan frantically wiped her sticky fingers on one leg of her blue pajamas, and she saw that the disgusting slime was staining the fabric.

It isn't real, isn't real, isn't, isn't . . .

Although she dutifully repeated that incantation, which was supposed to summon sanity, she had lost the courage required to continue with this confrontation. She wanted only to get the hell out of the bathroom, into the hospital room, into the corridor, down to the nurses' station by the elevators, where there was help. She turned—

—and froze.

Ernest Harch was standing in the open bathroom doorway, blocking her escape.

"No," she said thickly.

Harch grinned. He stepped into the bathroom with her and closed the door behind him.

He isn't real.

"Surprise," he said in that familiar, low, gravelly voice.

He can't hurt me.

"Bitch," he said.

Harch was no longer masquerading as William Richmond, the hospital patient. The pajamas and bathrobe had been discarded. Now he was wearing the clothes that he had worn in the House of Thunder on the night he had murdered Jerry Stein, thirteen years ago. Black shoes, black socks. Black jeans. A very dark blue shirt, almost black. She remembered that outfit because, in the House of Thunder, in the sputtering candlelight and the glow of the flashlights, he had reminded her of a Nazi in an old war movie. An SS man. Gestapo. Whatever the ones were who dressed all in black. His square face, his perfectly square features, pale yellow hair, ice-colored eyes—all of those things contributed to the image of a cold-blooded storm trooper, an image which, in life, he had always seemed to cultivate not only consciously but with care, with attention to detail, with a certain perverse pleasure.

"Do you like my little gift?" Harch asked, pointing to the head on the commode seat.

She couldn't speak.

"I know how much you loved your Jewboy," Harch said, his cold voice filled with an ice-hard hate. "So I thought I'd bring a piece of him back to you. Something for you to remember him by. Wasn't that thoughtful of me?" He laughed softly.

The power of speech returned to Susan with a jolt, and words burst from her: "You're dead, damn you, dead! You told me so yourself. You're dead."

Don't play along with this, she told herself desperately. For God's sake, listen to what you just said. Don't step into the hallucination willingly; back away from it.

"Yes," he said. "Of course I'm dead."

She shook her head. "I won't listen to this. You're not here. You're not real."

He stepped forward, farther into the small room.

She was backed against the wall, with the sink on her left side, the commode on her right. Nowhere to run.

Jerry Stein's dead eyes stared into space, oblivious of Harch's arrival.

One of Harch's strong hands snapped out, quick as a lashing whip, and seized Susan's left wrist before she knew what he was doing.

She tried to pull loose; couldn't.

Her mouth had gone as dry as ashes. Her tongue cleaved to the roof of her burned-out mouth.

Harch held her hand in a viciously tight grip. Grinning down at her, he dragged her to him—her slippers scraping on the tile—and he pressed her captive hand firmly against his slab-solid, rock-muscled chest.

"Do I *feel* real enough to suit you?" he demanded.

She sucked air. The weight of the indrawn breath seemed tremendous, sufficient to bring her crashing to the floor and on down, down into darkness.

No! she thought, terrified of surrendering to unconsciousness, afraid that she would wake up a madwoman. Mustn't pass out, for God's sake. Got to fight this. Got to fight it with all my heart.

"Do I *feel* real, you bitch? Do I? How do you like the way I feel?"

In the fluorescent light, his gray eyes, usually the color of dirty ice, looked almost white now, bright and utterly alien—just as they had looked that night in the House of Thunder, in the glow of the candles.

He rubbed Susan's hand back and forth across his big chest. The fabric had a coarse feel, and the buttons on the shirt were cold against Susan's skin.

Buttons? Would she actually imagine that she could feel the buttons—a tiny detail of that kind—in a *vision?* Would hallucinatory images be this vivid, this concrete, this thoroughly detailed?

"*Now* do you think I'm here?" Harch asked, grinning broadly but mirthlessly.

Somehow she found the strength to speak and to deny him one more time. Her dry tongue peeled off the powdery roof of her mouth with a sound she could almost hear, and she said, "No. Not here. Not here."

"*No?*"

"You aren't real."

"What a complete bitch!"

"You can't hurt me."

"We'll see about that, you little bitch. Oh, yeah, we'll sure see about *that.*"

Still gripping her left hand, he slid it over his chest, up to his shoulder, down his arm, made her feel his hard, flexed biceps.

Again, she tried to pull loose. And again, she failed. He was hurting her; his hand was like a steel pincer clenched around her fragile wrist.

He moved her captive hand back to his chest, then down to his flat, muscular belly.

"Am I real? Huh? What do you think? What's your considered opinion, Susan? Am I real?"

Susan felt something crumbling inside of her. Hope. Or maybe the last vestiges of her self-control. Or both.

It's only a vision, a sick fantasy generated by a damaged brain. Just an evil vision. Just a vision. It'll be over soon. Very soon. After all, how long can a vision last?

She thought of a frightening answer to her own question: *It could last forever; it could last for the rest of her life, until she drew her last breath in some padded room. Why not?*

Harch forced her hand onto his crotch.

He was very aroused. Even through his jeans, she could feel the great heat of him. The stiff, thick, pulsing shape of his maleness.

But he's dead.

"Feel *that?*" he demanded lasciviously, with a little laugh, a sneer. "Is *that* real?"

In the dark turmoil that whirled within her, a mad hilarity began to rise like a feeding shark in a night sea, streaking up toward the precious fragments of her sanity that still bobbled on the surface.

"Friday night, I'll shove this old poker right into you. Do you know what Friday night is? Seventh anniversary of my untimely demise. Seven years ago Friday, that nigger shoved a knife in my throat. So *this* Friday, I'll shove my poker all the way up into you, and then I'll use a knife on *you.*"

A high, silvery giggle tinkled deep within her, and she knew that she dared not let it escape. It was the whooping, bell-clear sickly sweet laughter of madness. If she gave voice to it just once, there would never be an end to it; she would pass the years in a corner, cackling to herself.

Harch let go of her hand.

She snatched it away from his crotch.

He slammed her back against the wall, jarring her bones. Pressed his body against hers. Ground his hips against her. And grinned.

She tried to squirm free of him. She was pinned by his weight, trapped.

"Should've banged that pretty little ass of yours thirteen years ago," Harch said. "A nice little gangbang right there in the goddamned cave. Then we should've slit your throat and dumped you into a sinkhole with the Jewboy."

He's not real, he can't hurt me, he's not—

No. It wasn't doing a bit of good to chant that stupid litany. He was real, all right. He was *here.*

And, of course, that was impossible.

He was real; he was here; he could hurt her; and he *would* hurt her.

She gave up the struggle to control the situation. She threw her head back and screamed.

Harch leaned away from her, taking his weight off her. He tilted his head, watching her with unconcealed amusement. He was enjoying this, as if her screams were music to him.

No one came to find out why she was screaming.

Where were the nurses? The orderlies, the doctors? Why couldn't they hear her? Even with the bathroom door shut, they should be able to hear her screaming.

Harch bent toward her, bringing his face close to hers. His gray eyes were shining like a wild animal's eyes in the beams of a car's headlights.

"Give me a little sample of what I'm going to get from you Friday night," he said in a sandpapery, wheedling voice. "Just a kiss. Give me a nice little kiss. Huh? Give your old Uncle Ernie a little kiss."

Whether or not this was really happening to her, she could not surrender entirely. She couldn't bring herself to kiss him even if it was all a dream. She twisted her head violently to one side, avoiding his lips, then to the other side, as he pursued her mouth with his own.

"You stinking bitch," he said angrily, finally giving up. "Saving all your kisses for your Jewboy?" He stepped back from her. He glanced at the head that rested on the commode; he looked at Susan again; at the head; at Susan. His smile was unholy. His voice became sarcastic, tinged with a black glee. "Saving your kisses for poor old Jerry Stein, are you? Isn't that touching? Such lovely, old-fashioned constancy. Oh, such admirable fidelity. I'm deeply moved. I truly, truly am. Oh, yes, by all means, you must give your virgin kisses only to Jerry."

Harch turned theatrically toward the moldering head, which was facing partly away from Susan.

No.

He reached for the head.

Susan thought of that rotting countenance, and tasted bile in the back of her mouth.

Still yammering about Susan's fidelity, Harch gripped a handful of the lank, brown hair on the grisly head.

Shaking with dread, Susan knew he was going to force her to kiss those cold, oozing lips.

Heart exploding, she saw an opportunity to escape, a slim chance, and she took it without hesitation; screamed; bolted. Harch was turned away from her, lifting the head off the commode. She pushed past him, squeezed between him and the sink, fumbled with the doorknob, expecting a hand to fall upon her neck, tore the door open, and burst into the hospital room, from the bright fluorescent light into the dim grayness of late-afternoon, throwing the bathroom door shut behind her.

At first she headed for the bed, for the call button that would summon a nurse, but she realized that she wouldn't reach it before Harch was upon her, so she whirled the other way, her legs rubbery, almost buckling beneath her, and she stumbled toward the outer door, which was standing open, and beyond which lay the corridor.

Screaming, she reached the doorway just as Mrs. Baker came in from the hall at a trot. They collided; Susan nearly fell; the nurse steadied her.

"Honey, what's wrong?"

"In the bathroom."

"You're soaked with sweat."

"*In the bathroom!*"

Mrs. Baker slipped a supportive arm around her.

Susan sagged against the generously padded woman, welcoming her strength.

"What's in the bathroom, kid?"

"Him."

"Who?"

"That b-b-bastard."

Susan shuddered.

"Who?" Mrs. Baker asked again.

"Harch."

"Oh, no, no, no."

"Yes."

"Honey, you're only having a—"

"He's *there*."

"He isn't real."

"He *is*."

"Come on."

"Where—?"

"Come with me," Mrs. Baker said.

"Oh, no."

"Come along."

"Let's get out of here."

"Come along with me."

She half coaxed, half carried Susan back into the room.

"But Jerry's head—"

"Jesus, you poor kid."

"—his decapitated head—"

"Nothing's really there."

"It *is*."

"This was a bad one, huh?"

"He was going to m-make me k-k-kiss that thing."

"Here now."

They were at the closed bathroom door.

"What are you doing?" Susan asked, panicky.

"Let's take a look."

"*For Christ's sake, what're you doing?*"

Mrs. Baker reached for the doorknob.

"Just showing you there's nothing to be afraid of."

Susan grabbed the woman's hand. "No!"

"Nothing to be afraid of," the nurse repeated soothingly.

"If it was just an hallucination—"

"It was."

"—then would I have been able to feel the goddamned buttons on his goddamned *shirt*?"

"Susan—"

"And would his disgusting erection have felt so big, so hot, so *real*?"

Mrs. Baker looked baffled.

I'm not making sense to her, Susan thought. To her, I sound and look like a
babbling lunatic. For that matter, am I making any sense to *me*?

Suddenly she felt foolish. Defeated.

"Have a look, Susan."

"Please don't do this to me."

"It's for your own good."

"Please don't."

"You'll see it's okay."

Whimpering now: "Please . . ."

Mrs. Baker started to open the door.

Susan snapped her eyes shut.

"Look, Susan."

She squeezed her eyes tightly shut.

"Susan, it's all right."

"He's still there."

"No."

"I can *feel* him."

"There's no one here but you and me."

"But . . ."

"Would I lie to you, honey?"

A drop of cold sweat trickled down the back of Susan's neck and slithered like a centipede along her spine.

"Susan, look."

Afraid to look but equally afraid to keep her eyes closed, she finally did as Mrs. Baker asked.

She looked.

She was standing at the threshold of the bathroom. Bleak fluorescent light. White walls. White sink. White ceramic tile. No sign of Ernest Harch. No staring, rotting head perched on the white commode.

"You see?" Mrs. Baker said cheerily.

"Nothing."

"Never was."

"Oh."

"Now do you feel better?"

She felt numb. And very cold.

"Susan?"

"Yeah. Better."

"You poor kid."

Depression settled over Susan, as if someone had draped a cloak of lead upon her shoulders.

"Good heavens," Mrs. Baker said, "your pajamas are *soaked* with sweat."

"Cold."

"I imagine you are."

"No. The head. Cold and greasy."

"There was no head."

"On the commode."

"No, Susan. There wasn't a head on the commode. That was part of the hallucination."

"Oh."

"You *do* realize that?"

"Yeah. Of course."

"Susan?"

"Hmmm?"

"Are you all right, honey?"

"Sure. I'll be all right. I'll be fine."

She allowed herself to be led away from the bathroom and back to her bed.

Mrs. Baker switched on the nightstand lamp. The huddling, late-afternoon shadows crept into the corners.

"First of all," Mrs. Baker said, "we've got to get you into something dry."

Susan's spare pajamas, the green pair, had been washed just that morning and were not yet ready to be worn. Mrs. Baker helped her strip out of the damp blue pair—they really were heavy with perspiration; you could almost wring them out as you would a washcloth—and helped her into a standard-issue hospital gown that laced up the back.

"Isn't that better?" Mrs. Baker asked.

"Isn't it?"

"Susan?"

"Hmmm?"

"I'm worried about you, honey."

"Don't worry. I just want to rest. I just want to go away for a while."

"Go away?"

"Just for a little while. Away."

13

"SUSAN?"

She opened her eyes and saw Jeff McGee looking down at her, his brow lined with concern.

She smiled and said, "Hi."

He smiled, too.

It was funny. The slow reshaping of his face from a frown into a smile seemed to take an incredibly long time. She watched the lines in his flesh rearrange themselves as if she were viewing a slow-motion film.

"How are you feeling?"

His voice was funny, too. It sounded distant, heavy, deeper than it had been before. Each word was drawn out as if she were listening to a phonograph record played at the wrong speed: too slow.

"I'm not feeling too bad," she said.

"I hear you had another episode."

"Yeah."

"Want to tell me about it?"

"No. Boring."

"I'm sure I wouldn't be bored."

"Maybe not. But *I* would."

"It'll help to talk about it."

"Sleep is what helps."

"You've been sleeping?"

"A little . . . on and off."

Jeff turned to someone on the other side of the bed and said, "Has she been sleeping ever since?"

It was a nurse. Mrs. Baker. She said, "Dozing. And kind of disassociated like you see."

"Just tired," Susan assured them.

Jeff McGee looked down at her again, frowning again.

She smiled at him and closed her eyes.

"Susan," he said.

"Hmmm?"

"I don't want you to sleep right now."

"Just for a while."

She felt as if she were adrift on a warm sea. It was so nice to be relaxed again; lazy.

"No," Jeff said. "I want you to talk to me. Don't sleep. Talk to me."

He touched her shoulder, shook her gently.

She opened her eyes, smiled.

"This isn't good," he said. "You mustn't try to escape like this. You know it isn't good."

She was perplexed. "Sleep isn't good?"

"Not right now."

"'Sleep ravels up the knitted sleeve of care,'" she misquoted in a thick voice. And closed her eyes.

"Susan?"

"In a while," she murmured. "In a while . . . "

■   "Susan?"

"Hmmm?"

"I'm going to give you an injection."

"Okay."

Something clinked softly.

"To make you feel better."

"I feel okay," she said drowsily.

"To make you more alert."

"Okay."

Coolness on her arm. The odor of alcohol.

"It'll sting but only for a second."

"Okay," she said.

The needle pierced her skin. She flinched.

"There you go, all finished."

"Okay," she said.

"You'll feel better soon."

"Okay."

■   Susan was sitting up in bed.

Her eyes were grainy, hot, and itchy. She rubbed at them with the back of one hand. Jeff McGee rang for a nurse and ordered some Murine, which he applied to Susan's eyes himself. The drops were cool and soothing.

She had a sour, metallic taste in her mouth. Jeff poured a glass of water for her. She drank all of it, but that didn't do much good.

Drowsiness still clung to her, but she was shaking it off minute by minute. She felt a bit cross at Jeff for spoiling her nice sleep.

"What did you give me?" she asked, rubbing one finger over the spot where he had administered the injection into her arm.

"Methylphenidate," he said.

"What's that?"

"A stimulant. It's good for bringing someone out of a severe depression."

She scowled. "I wasn't depressed. Just sleepy."

"Susan, you were heading toward total withdrawal."

"Just sleepy," she said querulously.

"Extreme, narcoleptic-phase depression," he insisted. He sat on the edge of the bed. "Now, I want you to tell me what happened to you in the bathroom."

She sighed. "Do I have to?"

"Yes."

"All of it?"

"All of it."

She was almost completely awake. If she had been suffering from a form of depression that caused her to seek escape in sleep, she certainly wasn't suffering from it any longer. If anything, she felt unnaturally energetic, even a bit edgy.

She thought about Ernest Harch in the bathroom. The severed head on the commode.

She shivered. She looked at Jeff and was warmed by his encouraging smile.

She forced a thin smile of her own. Trying hard to make light of what she'd been through, she said, "Gather 'round the old campfire, children, and I'll tell you a scary story."

■ She had dinner an hour later than usual. She didn't want anything; she wasn't hungry. However, Jeff insisted that she eat, and he sat with her, making sure that she finished most of the food on her tray.

They talked for more than an hour. His presence calmed her.

She didn't want him to leave, but he couldn't stay all night, of course. For one thing, he intended to go home and spend a couple of hours with her EEG printouts, her cranial X rays, and the lab reports on the spinal workup.

At last the time came for him to go. He said, "You'll be all right."

Wanting to be brave for him, braver than she felt, Susan said, "I know. Don't worry about me. Hey, I've got a lot of moxie, remember?"

He smiled. "The methylphenidate will start wearing off just about by bedtime. Then you'll get a sedative, a stronger one than you've been getting."

"I thought you didn't want me to sleep."

"That was different. That was unnatural sleep, psychological withdrawal. Tonight, I want you to sleep soundly."

Because when I'm sleeping soundly, Susan thought, I can't have one of my hallucinations, one of my little expeditions into the jungle of insanity. And if I have one more of them . . . one more safari into madness . . . I very likely won't come back. Just be swallowed up by the lions and tigers. One gulp. Gone.

"The nurses will stop in and out all evening," Jeff said. "About every fifteen minutes or so. Just to say hello and to let you know you aren't alone."

"All right."

"Don't just sit here in silence."

"I won't."

"Turn on your TV. Keep your mind active."

"I will," she promised.

He kissed her. It was a very nice kiss, tender and sweet. That helped, too.

Then he left, glancing back as he went out the door.

And she was alone.

■ She was tense for the rest of the evening, but the time passed without incident. She watched television. She even ate two pieces of candy from the box of chocolates that Jeff had brought her a couple of days ago. Two nightshift nurses—Tina Scolari and Beth Howe—took turns checking on her, and Susan found that she was even able to joke with them a little.

Later, just after she took the sedative that Jeff had prescribed for her, she felt the need to go to the bathroom. She looked at the closed door with trepidation and considered ringing the nurse to ask for a bedpan. She hesitated for a few minutes, but she grew increasingly ashamed of her timidity. What had happened to the stiff backbone on which she had always prided herself? Where was the famous Thorton pluck? She reached for the call button. Stopped herself. Finally, reluctantly, driven more by her protesting bladder than by her humiliation, she threw back the covers, got out of bed, and went to the bathroom.

Opened the door.

Turned on the light.

No dead men. No severed heads.

"Thank God," she said, her breath whooshing out of her in relief.

She went inside, closed the door, and went about her business. By the time she had finished and was washing her hands, her heart had slowed to a normal beat.

Nothing was going to happen.

She pulled a paper towel from the wall dispenser and started to dry her hands.

Her eye was suddenly caught by something gleaming on the bathroom floor. It was in the corner, against the wall. Something small and shiny.

She dropped the paper towel in the waste can.

She stepped away from the sink. Bent down. Picked up the glittering object.

She stared at it in disbelief.

Earlier, she had wished that ghosts were real. And now it appeared as if she'd been granted her wish.

She held the proof in her hand. The thing she had picked up from the floor. A thin gold chain and a gold-plated pendant. Jerry Stein's mezuzah. The same one that she had seen tangled around the ruined throat of his severed head.

GOING INTO TOWN

14

SUSAN WENT TO BED THAT NIGHT WITHOUT SHOWING THE gold mezuzah to anyone.

When she had found it on the bathroom floor, her first impulse had been to run with it straight to the nurses' station. She wanted to show it to as many people as she could find, for initially it seemed to be proof that she wasn't merely a victim of brain injury, and that the dead men's visitations were something considerably stranger than hallucinations.

On second thought, however, she decided to be cautious. If she clutched the mezuzah and ran breathlessly to show it to someone else, was it possible that she would open her hand in revelation—only to discover that she wasn't really clutching a mezuzah? She couldn't be sure that her brain was properly interpreting the images that her senses were transmitting to it. She might be having another attack right now, a miniepisode of brain dysfunction; when the fit passed, she might find that the gold mezuzah was only a small ball of scrap paper or a bent nail or a screw that had popped loose from the wall-mounted towel dispenser—or any of a hundred other mundane items. Better to wait, put the mezuzah aside, give herself time to recover from this attack—if it *was* another attack—and look at the object again, later, to see if it then appeared to be what it *now* appeared to be.

Furthermore, she suddenly wasn't very eager to consider the existence of walking dead men and the possibility of vengeance being taken from beyond the grave. When she'd been talking with Jeff McGee, she had jokingly wished that there really were such things as ghosts, so that her problems could be blamed on an external cause, rather than on her own loss of mental control. But she had not given any thought to what it would mean to her if her wish were granted. What it meant, she now saw with chilling clarity, was an even deeper descent into the cellars of insanity. She simply wasn't prepared to believe that dead men could come back from their tombs. She was a scientist, a woman of logic and reason. Whenever she saw gross superstition at work in other people, she was either amused or appalled by it. There wasn't room for the supernatural in her philosophy or, more importantly, in her self-image. This far, she had retained possession of her sanity primarily because a small part of her had clung tenaciously to the knowledge that her tormentors were only figments of her sick mind, nothing but imaginary creatures, phantoms. But if they were *real* . . .

What then?

What next?

She looked at her face in the mirror and could see the stark, haunted look in her own gray-green eyes.

Now there were new insanities, new terrors, new horrors to contemplate.

What next?

She didn't want to think about that. Indeed, there was no point in thinking about it until she knew whether the mezuzah was real or not.

Besides, the strong sedative she'd been given was beginning to take effect. Her eyes were rapidly becoming heavy, and her thoughts were getting fuzzy at the edges.

She carefully wrapped the gold pendant in a strip of toilet paper. She made a small, square, tidy bundle of it.

She left the bathroom, turning off the overhead fluorescents as she went. She got into bed and put the wad of toilet tissue in the top drawer of the nightstand, beside her wallet; closed the drawer; her little secret.

The sedative was like a great wave in the sea, rolling inexorably over her, pulling her down, down.

She reached out to snap off the bedside lamp, but she noticed that no one had turned on the night light. If she switched off her lamp, she would be in total darkness, except for what little indirect illumination the hall lights provided. She didn't like the prospect of lying alone in darkness, not even for the few minutes she would need to fall soundly asleep. She pulled her hand back from the lamp.

Staring at the ceiling, trying not to think, she lay in light—until, a minute later, she herself went out with the suddenness of a clicking switch.

■ Thursday morning. Clouds again. Also some torn strips of blue sky, like bright banners in the gloom.

Susan lay motionless for a minute or two, blinking at the window, before she remembered the treasure that she had secreted in the nightstand.

She raised the bed, sat up, quickly combed her shaggy hair with her fingers, then opened the nightstand drawer. The toilet tissue was there, where she remembered having put it. At least that much was real. She took it out and held it in the palm of her hand for a while, just staring at it. Finally, she opened it with as much care as she had employed in the wrapping of it.

The religious pendant lay in the center of the tissue. Its gold chain was tangled; it gleamed.

Susan picked it up, fingered it wonderingly. The mezuzah was real; there was no doubt about that.

As impossible as it seemed, it must follow that the dead men were real, too.

Ghosts?

She turned the pendant over and over in her fingers, the chain trailing out of her hand and along her arm, while she tried to make up her mind whether or not she wanted to believe in ghosts. And even if she wanted to believe in them, *could* she? Her ingrained level-headedness, her lifelong skepticism in such matters, and her preference for neatly packaged scientific answers made it difficult for her to turn abruptly away from logic and just blithely embrace superstition.

Even if she had been predisposed to supernatural explanations, there was one thing that would nevertheless have made it hard for her to accept the ghost theory. That one hitch was the mezuzah. If the dead men were malevolent spirits who were capable of vanishing in the blink of an eye—as Harch had seemed to vanish from the bathroom yesterday afternoon, taking Jerry Stein's severed head with him—then the mezuzah should have vanished, too. After all, if it was a part of the apparition, it couldn't also be a part of the real world. Yet here it was, in her hand.

Last night when her mind had been clouded by a sedative, it had seemed to her that the mezuzah was proof that there *were* such things as ghosts. However, now she realized that the pendant's existence proved only that the dead men were not merely hallucinations. In fact it didn't even prove that much; it only *indicated* that such was the case.

Ghosts? That seemed unlikely.

And with the mezuzah in her hand, blaming everything on brain dysfunction seemed too simplistic.

She couldn't completely forget about either of those theories, of course. But for the time being, she could relegate them to a back room in her mind.

So what explanations were left?

She stared at the mezuzah, frowning.

She seemed to have come full circle, back to the look-alike theory. But that was no good to her, either, because she had never been able to explain why four perfect look-alikes for the four fraternity brothers would show up in Willawauk County Hospital—of all places—intent upon tormenting and perhaps killing her. If a theory made absolutely no sense, then it was a worthless theory.

Besides, even the conspiracy theory didn't explain how Harch had disappeared from the windowless bathroom yesterday. It didn't explain how he could have recovered so completely and so quickly from the back surgery that he'd undergone on Monday. Or how Jerry Stein's corpse could have turned up in Jessica Seiffert's sickbed. Or why the corpse was not completely decomposed, reduced by now to a mere collection of bones.

Ghosts?

Brain dysfunction?

Bizarre conspiracies?

None of the available theories answered all of the questions—or even most of them. Every avenue of inquiry seemed to lead only to further confusion.

Susan felt light-headed.

She clenched her hand tightly around the mezuzah, as if she could squeeze the truth from it.

A nurse entered the room from the hall. It was Millie, the thin, fox-faced blonde. On Tuesday morning, when Susan had become hysterical at the appearance of the Jellicoe and Parker duplicates—the orderlies named Bradley and O'Hara—it had been Millie who had attempted to give Susan an injection against her will, while Carl Jellicoe held her down on the bed.

"The breakfast cart's just right down the hall," Millie said as she passed the bed, heading toward the bathroom. "Ought to be here in a minute," she added, slipping into the bathroom before Susan had an opportunity to respond.

Through the half-open door, Susan saw the nurse crouch down and peer behind the commode; first, around one side of it; then, around the other side. She squinted at the shadowy spots back there, where the overhead fluorescent lights didn't reach.

After the nurse had carefully inspected all around the toilet, she turned her back to it, still hunkering down. She swung her head left, right, keeping her eyes down toward the baseboard. She peeked behind the door. Under the sink.

Susan's eyes turned inexorably down to her own hand. The mezuzah, now hidden in her fist, seemed to grow icy, leaching the warmth from the flesh that encircled it.

The gold chain trailed from between her clenched fingers. Without fully understanding why she did it, operating solely on a hunch, Susan opened her fingers just long enough to quickly, surreptitiously push the chain in to keep company with the pendant. She made a fist again. Put the fist in her lap. Covered it with her other, open hand. Tried to look relaxed. Just sitting there in bed, yawning, blinking at the morning light, hands folded oh-so-casually in her lap.

Millie came out of the bathroom and over to the side of the bed. She hesitated for only a second or two, then said, "Say, did you find any jewelry in there yesterday?"

"Jewelry?"

"Yeah."

"In where?" Susan asked, feigning surprise, yawning. "You mean in the bathroom?"

"Yeah."

"You mean like pearl necklaces and diamond brooches?" Susan asked lightly, as if she thought the nurse was leading up to a joke.

"No. Nothing like that. It's mine. I lost it somewhere yesterday, and I can't find it."

"What kind of jewelry?"

Millie hesitated only an instant, then said, "A mezuzah. It was on a gold chain."

Susan could see the tension, the lies, the deception in the nurse's foxlike face and in her hard, watchful eyes.

It isn't yours, Susan thought. You didn't leave it here. You're a damned liar.

The mezuzah had been left behind by mistake. Obviously, it had dropped unnoticed from the severed head. And now they were trying to cover up and keep the charade going.

"Sorry," Susan said. "I didn't find anything."

The nurse stared at her.

Susan could see what they wanted her to believe. They wanted her to think that she had seen Millie's mezuzah on the bathroom floor and had linked it subconsciously to Jerry Stein's mezuzah, and thereby triggered another attack of nasty hallucinations.

But Millie's behavior had made Susan suspicious. And now she was sure that her problem was not merely psychological. They were running her through some kind of . . . test or program . . . a charade, the purpose of which she could not begin to understand. She was sure of that now.

But who were *they?*

"I hope you find it," she said to Millie, smiling sweetly.

"The chain must have broke," Millie said. "It could have fallen off anywhere, I guess."

The nurse wasn't a good liar. Neither her eyes nor her voice contained any conviction.

An orderly entered, pushing a cafeteria cart. Millie put Susan's breakfast tray on the bed table. Then both she and the orderly left.

Alone again, Susan opened her hand. The mezuzah was damp with perspiration.

■ Susan went into the bathroom, snapped on the fluorescent lights, and closed the door, leaving her untouched breakfast to get cold on the tray.

She began to examine the walls, starting behind the commode. It was drywall construction, not plaster; it was a pebbly surface, white, freshly painted, without a visible crack. At the corner, she examined the drywall joint with special care, but she didn't find anything out of the ordinary. The second wall bore no cracks, either, and the second corner was as smooth and seamless as the first one had been. The sink stood in the middle of the third wall; above the sink, the mirror filled in from the backsplash to the ceiling. On both sides of the sink and the mirror, the wall was perfectly even in texture, unmarked, normal.

Three-quarters of the way around the small room, in the third corner, behind the door, she found what she was looking for. The drywall joint was marred by an unnaturally straight hairline crack that extended all the way from the mitered junction of the three-inch-high base molding to the ceiling.

This is madness.

She raised her hands to her face, rubbed her eyes gently with her fingertips, blinked, looked at the corner again. The crack was still there, a knife-edge line that clearly had not been caused by the settling of the building over the years. It was a deliberate feature of the wall.

She went to the sink again, stared at the mirror, looking at the surface of it, not at her own reflection. It was a single sheet of glass; there was no division down the middle of it, nothing as obvious as that. Apparently, it served as an unconnected flange; it was probably fixed to the wall only on the left side, neatly concealing the pivot point behind it.

She knelt on the cold tile floor and peered beneath the sink. All of the plumbing, both the drain and the two water lines, came up out of the floor; nothing came out of the wall. She squirmed under the sink as far as she could and peered at the shadowed drywall back there. It was scarred by another crack that evidently came down from the ceiling, for the most part hidden by the mirror and the sink, appearing here and running all the way to the baseboard; this crack was as straight as a plumb line, just as the one in the corner was. The base molding had been cut through; the cut aligned with the crack in the wall. Susan was able to insert a fingernail into the crevice where the two sections of molding met; it had never been filled with putty.

She could feel a faint, cold draft puffing through that narrow gap, a vague but icy breath against her fingertips.

She retreated from beneath the sink and stood up, brushing her dusty hands together.

She stared thoughtfully at the six-foot-wide expanse of drywall between the corner by the door and the middle of the sink. Apparently, that entire section of the wall swung inward, away from the bathroom.

This was how Ernest Harch had exited, the severed head tucked under his arm, unaware that the mezuzah had fallen to the floor behind him.

What lay on the other side?

Madness.

■ Behind the second bed, the one in which Jessica Seiffert had lain until yesterday afternoon, Susan inspected the wall. It was marked by another hairline, ruler-straight crack that extended from the floor to the ceiling. From a distance of more than six or eight feet, the line was invisible. A similar seam was hidden in the corner.

Susan put one hand flat against the wall and pressed hard at several points on both sides of both cracks, hoping that the hidden doorway was operated by a pressure latch of some kind. But the wall remained in place in spite of her careful prodding.

She knelt down and squinted at the baseboard. Felt along it with one hand.

Again, there was a draft coming out of the gaps; faint but detectable, and cold.

Near the left-hand crack, she found a trace of grease. Lubricant for the swinging partition's secret hinges?

She pressed every couple of inches along the molding, but she could find no pressure latch there, either.

Secret doors? It seemed too bizarre to be true.

Shadowy conspirators moving clandestinely through the walls? That was a classic paranoid fantasy.

But what about the seams in the drywall?

Imagination.

And the drafts seeping through from hidden rooms?

Perceptual confusion.

And the grease?

Misinterpretation of visual and tactile stimuli due to brain dysfunction. A tiny cerebral hemorrhage. Or a sand-grain blood clot. Or a brain lesion. Or a—

"Like hell it is," she muttered.

■ Her oatmeal had gotten cold and gummy. She ate it anyway; more than ever, she needed to keep up her strength.

While she ate, she tried to figure out what the hell was going on. She seemed stuck with the conspiracy theory, though it made no sense at all.

Who could possibly have the resources and the determination to organize such an elaborate plot, such an incredible masquerade, involving four dead ringers that must have been located with only the most titanic effort? And for what purpose? Why all this expenditure of time and money and energy? What could be gained? Was some relative of one of the dead fraternity men—a father, mother, sister, brother—seeking revenge on Susan for her testimony at the trial, even though she had told only the truth? Seeking revenge—after thirteen years? By trying to drive her out of her mind? No. Good heavens, that was absurd! That was a scenario straight out of a comic book. People didn't seek revenge by means of such complicated—and *expensive*—conspiracies. If you were dead set on getting revenge for something like this, then you did it with a knife or a gun or poison. And you didn't wait thirteen years, either. Surely, a raging hatred—a hatred sufficiently powerful to inspire a vengeance killing—could not be sustained for thirteen years.

But what kind of hospital had hidden rooms and secret doors in its walls?

In a madhouse clinic, in a sanitarium for the hopelessly insane, there might be such secret doors—but only in the fevered minds of the most severely disturbed patients. Yet these doors were not merely figments of her demented imagination; she wasn't just a disassociated schizophrenic sitting in a padded cell, fantasizing that she was in some ordinary hospital in a town called Willawauk. She was *here*, damn it all. This was really happening. The secret doors *did* exist.

As she thought back over the past four days, she remembered a few strange incidents that hadn't seemed important at the time but which seemed vitally important now. They were incidents that should have alerted her to the fact that this place and the people in it were not what they pretended to be.

Viteski. The first indication that something was amiss had come from him.

Saturday night, when Susan had awakened from her coma, Dr. Viteski had been stiff, ill at ease, noticeably uncomfortable with her. When he had told her about her accident and about Willawauk County Hospital, his voice had been so stilted, so wooden, that each word had seemed like a cast-off splinter. At times he had sounded as if he were reciting lines from a well-memorized script. Perhaps that was precisely what he *had* been doing.

Mrs. Baker had made a mistake, too. On Monday, as the nurse was finishing up her shift and preparing to go home for the day, she had spoken of having a hot date that night with a man whose shoulders were big enough "to measure a doorway." Two days later, when Susan had asked belatedly whether the date was a success or not, Mrs. Baker had been lost for a moment, utterly baffled. For a *long* moment. Too long. Now, it seemed perfectly clear to Susan that the story about the lumberman and the bowling date and the hamburger dinner had been nothing but a spur-of-the-moment ad lib, the kind of sharp and colorful detail that a good actor frequently invents in order to contribute to the verisimilitude of a role. In actuality, there had been no aging, virile lumberman. No bowling date. Poor pudgy, graying Thelma Baker had not enjoyed a wild night of unrestrained passion, after all. The nurse merely improvised that romantic tale to flesh out her characterization, then later forgot what she had improvised—until Susan reminded her.

Susan finished eating the cold, gummy oatmeal. She started on the hardened whole-wheat toast, upon which the butter had congealed in milky-looking swirls, and she washed it down with swigs of orange juice.

The bruise, she thought as she continued to eat.

The bruise was another thing that should have made her suspicious. On Tuesday afternoon, when she had been trapped in the elevator with the four dead fraternity men, Harch had pinched her arm very hard. Later, there had been a small bruise on her biceps, two inches above the crook of her arm. She had told herself that she had unwittingly sustained the bruise during the exercise period in the therapy room, and that her subconscious mind had incorporated that injury into the hallucination. But that had not been the case. The bruise had been proof that Harch and the others were real; it had been like the mezuzah in the sense that both the bruise and the religious pendant were fragments of supposed hallucinations that had survived the dissipation of the rest of those nightmares.

Suddenly, Susan thought she knew *why* Harch had pinched her. He hadn't just been delighting in the opportunity to torture her. He had pinched her a moment or two before she had grown dizzy, seconds before she had swooned and passed out on the wheeled stretcher. She now understood that the cruel pinch was intended to cover the sting of a hypodermic needle. Harch had pinched her hard enough to make her cry, and then one of the other three men had quickly administered an injection before the first pain subsided, before she could distinguish the second pain as a separate event. Once the four men had thoroughly terrorized her, there had been, of course, no way for them to bring a dramatic and credible conclusion to the scene, unless she conveniently passed out—*because they were neither ghosts who could simply vanish in a puff of supernatural light and smoke, nor hallucinated images that would fade away as she finally regained her senses.* When she had failed to oblige them by fainting, they had been forced to knock her unconscious with a drug. And they had covered the injection with a pinch because, after all, no self-respecting ghost would require the assistance of sodium pentathol or some like substance in order to effect a suitably mysterious exit.

Susan paused as she was about to start eating a sweet roll with lemon icing, and she pushed up the sleeve of her hospital gown. The bruise was still there on her biceps, yellowing now. She peered closely at it, but too much time had elapsed for her to be able to find the tiny point at which the needle had pierced her skin.

Undoubtedly, her tormentors had made other mistakes which she had failed to notice. Indeed, she wouldn't have made anything of the mistakes that she *had* noticed, not if the Harch look-alike hadn't accidentally left the mezuzah behind in the bathroom, for the mezuzah had set her imagination ablaze and had cast a bright light of healthy suspicion upon her memories of other curious incidents.

All things considered, the conspirators had brought it off exceptionally well thus far; brilliantly, in fact.

But who *were* these people? Who had put so much money and energy and time into the painstakingly detailed creation of this three-dimensional drama? And for what purpose?

What in God's name do they want from me?

More than vengeance. No question about that. Something more than vengeance; something infinitely stranger—and worse.

In spite of the quiver of fear that shimmered through her and caused her stomach to yaw and pitch, Susan took a bite of the sweet roll. Fuel for the engine. Vital energy for the fight that lay ahead.

Reluctantly, she considered the role of Jeff McGee in all of this, and the pastry turned chalky and bitter in her mouth. She swallowed only with considerable effort, and that first bite of pastry went down as if it were a wet lump of clay. She nearly choked on it.

There was no chance whatsoever that Jeff was unaware of what was being done to her.

He was a part of it.

He was one of *them*—whoever they were.

Although she knew that she ought to eat to keep her strength, especially now that illness was not her only or even her primary enemy, Susan was unable to take another bite. The very thought of food was repellent. With the sweet roll still tasting like clay in her mouth, she pushed her breakfast tray aside.

She had trusted McGee.

He had betrayed her.

She had loved him.

He had taken advantage of her love.

Worst of all, she had willingly relinquished control to him, had given to him the responsibility for her life, for her *survival*, something she had never given to anyone before, something she would never even have considered doing with anyone else she had ever known—except, perhaps, for her father, who had never *wanted* responsibility for her, anyway. And now that she had forsaken her lifelong principle of self-reliance, now that she had allowed Jeff McGee to bring her out of her shell, now that she had allowed him to take control with his warm assurances of concern and his tender statements of devotion, *now* he had failed her. Intentionally.

Like all the others, he was playing his part in a conspiracy that seemed to have no other goal but to drive her out of her mind.

She felt used.

She felt like a fool.

She hated him.

■ The Milestone Corporation.

Somehow, the events of the past few days were directly related to the Milestone Corporation.

For several minutes she concentrated very hard on pushing back the black veil of amnesia that obscured all recollections of Milestone, but she found, as before, that the barrier was not a veil but a formidable shield, a veritable wall of lead, impenetrable.

The harder she struggled to remember, the greater and darker her fear became. Intuitively, she knew that she dared not remember what work she had done at Milestone. To remember was to die. She felt the truth of that in her bones, but she didn't understand it. For God's sake, what was so evil about Milestone?

■ She wondered about the automobile accident. Had it actually happened? Or was it a lie, too?

She closed her eyes and tried to relive the few minutes on the highway immediately prior to the crash that (supposedly) had taken place four weeks ago. The curve in the road . . . rounding it . . . slowly . . . slowly around . . . then blackness. She strained against the unyielding amnesia, but she could not seize the memory. She was reasonably sure that it had never happened.

Something frightening had transpired on that mountain road, just around that blind curve, but it hadn't been an accident. They had been waiting for her there—whoever *they* were—and they had taken her by force, and they had brought her to this place. *That* was how she had acquired her head injury. She had no proof of it, no memory of the kidnapping, but she also had no doubt, either.

■ Twenty minutes after Susan finished her cold breakfast, Jeff McGee stopped by on his morning rounds.

He kissed her on the cheek, and she returned the kiss, although she would have preferred not to be touched by him. She smiled and pretended to be glad to see him because she didn't want him to know that she suspected anything.

"How do you feel this morning?" he asked, leaning casually against the bed, smiling, supremely confident about his ability to keep her bamboozled.

"I feel marvelous," she said, wanting to hit him in the face with all her might. "Invigorated."

"Sleep soundly?"

"Like a hibernating bear. That was some sedative."

"I'm glad it worked. Speaking of medication, I've scheduled you for a tablet of methylphenidate at nine o'clock and another one at five this afternoon."

"I don't need it."

"Oh? Diagnosing yourself now? Did you sneak out and acquire a medical degree during the night?"

"Didn't have to. I just sent for it in the mail."

"How much did it cost?"

"Fifty bucks."

"Cheaper than mine," he said.

"God, I *hope* so," she said and smiled a smile she didn't feel. "Look, I don't need methylphenidate for the simple reason that I'm not suffering from depression any more."

"Not right at this moment, maybe. But another wave of deep narcoleptic depression might come at any time, especially if you have another one of your hallucinations. I believe in preventive medicine."

And I believe that you're a goddamned fraud, Dr. McGee, she thought.

She said, "But I don't need any pills. Really. I tell you, I'm *up!*"

"And I tell you, *I'm* the doctor."

"Who must be obeyed."

"Always."

"Okay, okay. One pill at nine and one at five."

"Good girl."

Why don't you just pat me on the head and scratch me behind the ears like you would a favorite dog? she thought bitterly, even as she kept her true emotions hidden.

She said, "Did you have a chance to look over my tests again last night?"

"Yeah. I spent almost five hours with them."

You damned liar, she thought. You didn't spend ten lousy minutes with them because you know I don't have a medical problem of any kind.

She said, "Five hours? That was above and beyond the call of duty. Thank you. Did you find anything?"

"I'm afraid not. The EEG graphs didn't turn up anything more than what I saw on the CRT readout yesterday. And your X rays are like a set of textbook illustrations labeled 'full cranial sequence of a healthy human female.'"

"I'm glad to know I'm human, anyway."

"Perfect specimen."

"And female."

"*Perfect* specimen," he said, grinning.

"What about the spinal tests?" Susan asked, playing along with him, softening her voice and permitting a trace of nervous strain to color it, carefully projecting exactly the proper amount of worry and self-concern. She beetled her brow to a carefully calculated degree, letting McGee read fear and doubt in the furrows of her creased forehead.

"I couldn't find any mistakes in the lab's procedures," McGee said. "There wasn't anything the pathologist overlooked, nothing he misread in the data."

Susan sighed wearily and let her shoulders sag.

McGee responded to the sigh, took her hand in his in an effort to comfort her. She resisted the powerful urge to pull loose of him and to slap his face.

She said, "Well . . . now what? Do we move on to the cerebral angiogram you talked about yesterday?"

"No, no. Not yet. I still need to do a lot of thinking about the advisability of that. And you need to regain more of your strength before we can give it serious consideration. For the next couple of days, I guess we're just in a holding pattern. I'm sorry, Susan. I know this is frustrating for you."

They talked for another five minutes, mostly about personal things, and McGee never appeared to realize that she was looking at him from a different and considerably less flattering perspective than that from which she had viewed him previously. She was surprised by her own acting ability and even rather pleased by it; she was as good as Mrs. Baker.

I'll beat these bastards at their own game, if I can only find out what the devil it *is,* she thought with more than a little satisfaction.

But no one in this vicious charade was half as good an actor as McGee. He had style and control and panache. Although Susan knew he was a fraud, just five minutes of personal chitchat with him was nearly sufficient to convince her of his sincerity. He was so kind and considerate. His blue eyes were achingly sensitive and utterly unclouded by any sign of deception. His concern for her well-being seemed genuine. He was charming, always charming. His laugh was natural, never forced.

But the most impressive thing about McGee's act was the love that he radiated. In his company, Susan felt as if she were cradled in love, swathed in it, afloat in a sea of it, protected by it. Over the years, there had been at least two other men who had loved her—men for whom she had felt only affection—but in neither case had she been so intensely aware of the love given to her. McGee's love was almost a visible radiance.

Yet it was fake.

It *had* to be fake.

He had to know what was going on here.

But when McGee left her room to continue his morning rounds, Susan was filled with doubt again. The possibility of her own madness rose in her mind for reconsideration. Hidden rooms, secret doors, a hospital full of conspirators? For what purpose? Seeking what gain? It seemed almost easier to believe herself insane than to believe that Jeff McGee was a liar and a fraud.

She even put her head down on the pillow and wept quietly for a few minutes, shaken, not sure whether she was weeping about his perfidy or about her lack of faith in him. She was miserable. She'd had within her grasp the kind of relationship with a man that she had long desired, with the kind of man she had always dreamed about. Now it was slipping away, or perhaps she was throwing it away. Confused, she didn't know which it was, didn't know what she ought to believe or exactly what she ought to feel.

Eventually, she reached under the pillow and pulled out the gold mezuzah.

She stared at it.

She turned it over and over again in her hand.

Gradually, the solidity of that object, the stark reality of it, brought her to her senses. Doubt evaporated.

She was not losing her mind. She wasn't mad—but she was very angry.

■   At nine o'clock, Millie brought the day's first dose of methylphenidate.

Susan took the capsule out of the small paper pill cup and said, "Where's Mrs. Baker this morning?"

"Thursday's her day off," Millie said, pouring a glass of water from the metal carafe. "She said something about washing and waxing her car this morning, then going on a last autumn picnic with some friends this afternoon. But wouldn't you know it: They say we're going to get a pretty good rain later this afternoon."

Oh, very nice. Very nice detail, Susan thought with a combination of sarcasm and genuine admiration for the planning that had gone into this production. *Thursday's her day off*. My, what a thoughtful, realistic touch that is! Even though this isn't an ordinary hospital, and even though Mrs. Baker isn't an ordinary nurse, and even though we're all involved in some unimaginably bizarre charade, she gets a day off for the sake of realism. Washing and waxing her car. A late autumn picnic. Oh, very nice indeed. A splendid bit of detail for authenticity's sake. My compliments to the scenarist.

Millie put down the metal carafe and handed the glass to Susan.

Susan pretended to put the capsule of methylphenidate in her mouth, palmed it instead, and drank two long swallows of ice water.

Henceforth, she wasn't going to take any of the medications that she was given. For all she knew, these people were slowly poisoning her.

■   Because she was a scientist, it naturally occurred to her that she might be the subject of an experiment. She might even have willingly agreed to take part in it. An experiment having to do with sensory manipulation or with mind control.

There was sufficient precedent to inspire such a theory. In the 1960s and 1970s, some scientists had voluntarily subjected themselves to sensory deprivation experiments, settling into dark, warm, watery SD tanks for such extended lengths of time that they temporarily lost all touch with reality and began to hallucinate.

Susan was sure she wasn't hallucinating, but she wondered if the second floor of the hospital had been adapted for an experiment in mind control or brainwashing techniques. Brainwashing sounded like a good bet. Was that the kind of research the Milestone Corporation was engaged in?

She considered the possibility very seriously for a while, but at last she discarded it. She couldn't believe that she would have permitted herself to be used and abused in this fashion, not even to further the cause of science, not even if it was a requirement of her job. She would have quit any job that demanded her to test her sanity to the breaking point.

Who would engage upon that sort of immoral research, anyway? It sounded like something that the Nazis might have done with their prisoners of war. But no reputable scientist would become involved with it.

Furthermore, she was a physicist, and her field in no way touched upon the behavioral sciences. Brainwashing was so far outside her field that she could imagine no circumstances under which she would have become associated with such an experiment.

No, she hadn't walked into this with her eyes open; she hadn't come to this place willingly.

■ McGee had scheduled Susan for a physical therapy session at ten o'clock Thursday morning.

Murf and Phil came for her at a few minutes before ten. As usual, they kept up a steady line of amusing patter all the way downstairs to the PT Department. Susan wanted to tell them that, in her humble opinion, they were definitely Academy Award material, but she didn't break her cover. She only smiled and laughed and responded when it seemed appropriate.

During the first part of the therapy session, Susan did all of the exercises that Florence Atkinson suggested, but at the halfway point, she complained of painful muscle cramps in her legs. She winced and groaned convincingly, though she actually had no cramps. She just didn't want to exhaust herself in a therapy session. She was saving her strength now, for she would have desperate need of it later.

She intended to escape tonight.

Mrs. Atkinson seemed genuinely concerned about the cramps. She cut short the exercise part of the session and gave Susan a longer massage than usual, plus ten extra minutes in the whirlpool. By the time Susan had taken a hot shower and had dried her hair, she felt much better than she had felt at any time since she had come out of her coma.

On the way back to her room, in the care of Phil and Murf once more, Susan grew tense at the elevators, wondering if another "hallucination" was planned for this moment. But the elevator was empty; the ride upstairs was uneventful.

She hadn't decided exactly how she should handle the next apparition.

She knew how she *wanted* to handle it. She wanted to respond with blind rage, with a furious assault that would drive them back in surprise. She wanted to claw their faces and draw their blood, lots of blood, which would be more proof that they weren't ghosts or hallucinations. She wanted to hurt them, and then she wanted to defiantly accuse them.

But she knew she couldn't do what she wanted. As long as they weren't aware that she was wise to their games, she had the advantage. But the moment she revealed her knowledge, she would lose what little freedom to maneuver that she now had. The charade would end abruptly. They would stop trying to drive her insane—which seemed to be their single-minded intention—and they would do something even worse than that to her. She was sure of it.

■   She ate every bite of her lunch.
        When Millie came to take the tray away, Susan yawned and said, "Boy, am I ready for a nap."

"I'll close the door so the hall noise won't bother you," the sharp-faced blonde said.

As soon as the nurse had gone, pulling the door shut behind her, Susan got out of bed and went to the closet, slid the door open. Blankets and pillows for the room's other bed were stored on the closet shelf. On the floor were Susan's battered suitcases, which supposedly had been salvaged from her wrecked car.

She dragged the suitcases into the room and opened them on the floor, praying that no one would walk in on her during the next few minutes. She rummaged quickly through the contents of the bags, putting together an outfit that was suitable for a jailbreak. A pair of jeans. A dark blue sweater. Thick, white athletic socks and a pair of Adidas running shoes. She shoved that bundle to the back of the shallow closet, then stood the suitcases in front to conceal it.

She shut the closet door and hurried back to the bed, got in, put up the safety railing, lowered the mattress, put her head down on her pillow, and closed her eyes.

She felt good. She felt as if she were in charge of her life again.

Then she had another unsettling thought; lately, she seemed to have an endless supply of them, and this one was especially unsettling. She wondered if she was being watched by concealed, closed-circuit television cameras. After all, if they went to the trouble of hidden rooms and secret doors, wouldn't they also put her under twenty-four-hour observation? And wouldn't they now know that she had found the mezuzah and that she was preparing to escape?

She opened her eyes and looked around the room, seeking places where cameras might be concealed. The heating vents in the walls, up near the ceiling, offered the only logical hiding places. There were two vents in two different walls. If cameras were placed in the heating ducts—a few inches behind the vent grilles in order to avoid detection from the glint of light on their lenses—and if they were properly positioned, fully motor-driven for the widest possible lateral view, aimed downward, and equipped with remote-control zoom lenses, then they would be able to cover most if not all of the hospital room.

For a few minutes Susan was sick with despair. She hugged herself and shuddered.

Gradually, however, her spirits rose somewhat, for she decided that there mustn't be any cameras. If there *were* cameras, she would have been observed handling the mezuzah this morning. It wouldn't have been necessary for Millie to question her about lost jewelry. If they had seen her with the mezuzah, they would have been afraid that she was aware of their charade, and they would have called a halt to it.

Wouldn't they?

Probably. There didn't seem to be any point to staging more "hallucinations" if she could no longer be fooled by them.

Yet, although she was pretty sure they wouldn't go on toying with her this way, she couldn't be absolutely positive about it, for she didn't know what motivated them.

She would just have to wait and see.

If she managed to get out of the hospital tonight, she would know that there hadn't been any TV cameras in her room.

On the other hand, if she started to sneak out of the place and got as far as the stairs and discovered the four dead men waiting for her there, smiling . . .

Although she now knew they *weren't* dead men, she nevertheless shuddered again.

She would just have to wait.

And see.

15

LATER THURSDAY AFTERNOON, A FAST-WEAVING LOOM OF WIND brought new gray cloth for the rents in the clouds, patching over every last glimpse of blue September sky. The hospital room darkened early again.

A crash, a roll, and an echo of thunder preceded a violent fall of rain. For a while, fat droplets of water snapped bullet-hard against the window in great profusion and with the sound of a dozen submachine guns. The wind hummed, then moaned, then howled like a wild thing in pain, then roared. In time, the storm abated somewhat, but only temporarily; it settled into a rhythmic pattern that alternated between fury and docility, between a torrential downpour and a pleasant drizzle. Cloudbursts were followed by the soothing pitter-patter of light autumn showers.

Although the storm waxed and waned, the day grew steadily darker, not brightening for even a moment, and Susan looked forward to the coming nightfall with barely containable excitement—and with fear, too.

For nearly an hour, she pretended to nap, her back turned to the closed door, while she watched the raging storm. She need not have continued with the ruse, for during that time no one came around to check on her.

Later, she sat up in bed and switched on the television set, in front of which she passed the rest of the afternoon. She didn't pay much attention to the programs that flickered across the screen. Her mind was elsewhere, preoccupied with plans and schemes and dreams of escape.

At five o'clock sharp, Nurse Scolari, who had come on duty at four, brought another dose of methylphenidate and a fresh carafe of ice water. Susan faked the taking of the capsule, palmed it as she had done with the first dose that morning.

At suppertime, McGee came in with two trays and announced that he was having dinner with her. "No candles. No champagne," he said. "But there are some delicious-looking stuffed pork chops and apple-nut cake for dessert."

"Sounds terrific to me," she said. "I never liked the taste of candles, anyway."

He also brought several magazines and two more paperback novels. "I thought maybe you might be running out of reading material."

He stayed for more than two hours, and they talked of many things. Eventually, the strain of playing the innocent, the stress of pretending to love him when she actually despised him—it all became almost too much for Susan to bear. She had found that she was a pretty good actress, but she had also learned that deception exacted a high toll from her. She was relieved and exhausted when McGee finally kissed her good night and left.

She was relieved, yes, but she was also curiously sorry to see him go. Until he was walking out of the door, she wouldn't have believed that she could be sorry to see him go; but when he crossed that threshold and disappeared into the corridor, Susan felt a sudden and unexpected loss, an emptiness. She knew she might never see him again—except in a court of law, where he would stand trial for his part in her kidnapping and peculiar torture. In spite of the fact that she knew him to be a fraud, she still found him to be good company. He was as charming as he had ever been. He was still a good conversationalist. He still had an excellent sense of humor and an appealing, infectious laugh. Worst of all, he still seemed to glow with love for her. She had tried hard to see through him, to discern the duplicitous bastard beneath the surface saint, and she had tried with all her might to hear the lies in his love talk, but she had failed.

If you know what's good for you, forget him, she told herself angrily. Just put him out of your mind. All the way out. Think about getting out of here. *That's* what's important. Getting out.

She looked at the bedside clock.

8:03.

Outside, lightning briefly drove back the darkness.

Rain fell and fell.

At nine o'clock, Tina Scolari brought the sedative that McGee had prescribed. Putting her cupped hand to her mouth, she pantomimed taking the sedative; she quickly washed down the nonexistent pill with a swallow of the water that the nurse offered her.

"Have a good night," Tina Scolari said.

"I'm sure I will."

A few minutes after the nurse had gone, Susan switched off the bedside lamp. The night light cast its phosphoric luminescence across the room, leaching all color from the chamber, so that everything appeared to be either ash-gray or the ghost-white of moonglow. The night light was no threat to the crowd of shadows, but it was good enough for what Susan had to do.

She waited another few minutes, lying in bed, staring at the dark ceiling, which flickered now and then with the reflected flash of lightning that bounced off the water-filmed window. She wanted to be certain that the nurse wasn't going to come back with some forgotten medication or with a warning about an early wake-up call for new tests.

At last she got up and went to the closet. She took two pillows and two blankets from the top shelf, carried them back to the bed. She arranged them under the covers in a series of lumps that she hoped would pass for a huddled, sleeping woman. The dummy was crude, but she didn't waste any more time with it; there were no awards for art and craftsmanship.

She returned to the closet. She reached behind the suitcases and located the bundle of clothes that she had put together earlier in the day. By the time she had pulled off her pajamas and had dressed in the jeans, sweater, heavy socks, and running shoes, and by the time she had retrieved her wallet from the nightstand, the bedside clock read 9:34.

She tucked the mezuzah in a pocket of her jeans, even though it was proof of nothing to anyone except her.

She went to the door and put her head against it, listening. She couldn't hear anything from the other side.

After a moment of nervous hesitation, after she wiped her sweaty palms on her jeans, she pushed the door open. Just a crack. Peered into the well-lighted hallway. Opened the door a few inches farther. Stuck her head out. Looked right. Looked left. There was no one in sight.

The corridor was silent. It was so silent, in fact, that in spite of the highly polished tile floor and the spotless yellow walls and the dust-free fluorescent ceiling lights, it seemed as if the building had been abandoned and had not known the sound of human activity for ages.

Susan left the room, easing the door shut behind her. She stood for a breathless moment with her back pressed flat against the door, afraid to step away from it, prepared to turn and scurry inside again, into her bed and under the covers, dispossessing the crudely formed dummy, at the slightest sound of an approaching nurse.

To her left lay the junction of the corridors, where the two short wings connected with the long main hall. If there was going to be any trouble, it would most likely come from that direction, for the nurses' station was around the corner and halfway down the longest corridor.

The silence continued, however, disturbed only by the low, distant rumble of the storm.

Convinced that further hesitation was more dangerous than any action she could take, Susan moved cautiously to the right, away from the confluence of corridors, directly toward the large fire door at the end of the short wing, where there was a red EXIT sign. She stayed close to the wall and kept glancing back toward the center of the building.

She was acutely aware of the squeaking noise made by her rubber-soled shoes on the highly polished tile floor. It wasn't really a loud sound, but it had the same nerve-grating quality as did the sound of fingernails scraped across a chalkboard.

She reached the metal fire door without incident and opened it. She winced as the push-bar handle rattled under her hand and as the big hinges rasped, creaked. Quickly, she stepped across the threshold, onto a stairwell landing, and shut the heavy door behind her as quietly as possible, which wasn't nearly quietly enough to suit her.

The stairs were bare concrete and were dimly lighted. There was only one small bulb on each landing. Here and there between the landings, the concrete walls were draped with shadows like webs of dust and soot.

Susan stood perfectly still and listened. The stairwell was even more silent than the second-floor hallway had been. Of course she had made so much noise with the door that any guard who might have been stationed on the stairs would now be frozen, listening, just as she was.

Nevertheless, she was sure that she was alone. They probably hadn't posted guards because they didn't expect her to try to escape; they didn't know that she was aware of their trickery. And the hospital staff—or the staff of *whatever* kind of institution this was—most likely used only the public and the service elevators, leaving the stairs for emergencies when the power failed.

She stepped to the black iron railing and leaned over it, looked up, then down. Four more flights of steps and four more landings lay above her. Two flights, one landing, and the bottom of the stairwell lay below.

She went down to the bottom, where there were two fire doors, one set in the inner wall of the stairwell and apparently opening onto a first-floor corridor, the other set in the outer wall. Susan put her hands on the push-bar and cracked open the outer door two or three inches.

Cold wind forced its way into the rough concrete vestibule and capered around Susan's legs. It seemed to be sniffing at her as if it were a large, excited dog trying to make up its mind whether to wag its tail or bite.

Beyond the door, a small rain-swept parking lot lay in the yellowish glow of a pair of tall sodium-vapor lamps, each of which bore two globes like luminescent fruit. It didn't look nearly large enough to be the public parking area. But if it was the staff's lot, where were all the cars? Now that visiting hours were over, the public lot would be virtually deserted, but there should still be quite a few cars in the staff's parking area, even at night. There were only four vehicles: a Pontiac, a Ford, and two other makes with which she was not familiar.

There was no one in the parking lot, so she stepped outside and let the fire door close behind her.

The rain had nearly stopped falling now, as the storm entered one of its quieter moments. Only a thin mist floated down from the night sky.

The wind, however, was fierce. It stood Susan's shaggy blond hair on end, made her eyes water, and forced her to squint. When it gusted, howling banshee-like, Susan had to stand with her head tucked down and her shoulders drawn up. It was surprisingly cold, too; it stung her exposed face and cut through the sweater she was wearing. She wished she had a jacket. She thought it seemed much *too* cold for September in Oregon. It was more like a late-November wind. Or even December.

Had they lied to her about the date? Why on earth would they have lied about that, too? But then again —why not? It made no less sense than anything else they had done.

She moved away from the emergency exit, into the shadows by a bristling evergreen shrub, where she crouched for a minute while she decided which way to go from here. She could head toward the front of the hospital and follow the road that led directly downhill into Willawauk. Or she could go overland and into town by a more cautious, circuitous route, to avoid being spotted by anyone at the hospital.

Lightning pulsed softly, and thunder crashed like a train derailing in the darkness.

No matter which way she went, she was going to get very wet. Already, the light mist had begun to paste her hair to her skull. Soon, the rain would be coming down hard again, and she would be soaked to the skin.

Then a frighteningly bold course of action occurred to her, and she launched herself upon it before she had time to think about it and lose her nerve. She ran out into the parking lot, toward the nearest car, the green Pontiac.

There were four cars in the lot, four chances that someone had left a set of keys in an ignition or under a seat or tucked up behind a sun visor. In rural towns like Willawauk, where almost everyone knew everyone else, people weren't worried about car thieves nearly so much as were people in the cities and suburbs. Trust thy neighbor: That was still a rule that people lived by in a few favored places. Four cars; four chances. She probably wouldn't have any luck, but it was worth taking a look.

She reached the Pontiac and tried the door on the driver's side. It was unlocked.

When she pulled the door open, the ceiling light came on inside the car. It seemed as bright as a lighthouse beacon, and she was sure that she had given herself away and that alarms would begin ringing at any moment.

"Damn!"

She slipped into the car, behind the steering wheel, and quickly closed the door, not concerned about the sound it made, just worried about shutting off that damned light.

"Stupid," she said, cursing herself.

She scanned the parking lot through the blurry, water-spotted windshield. She saw no one. She looked at the lighted windows of the four-story hospital; there was no one standing in any of them, no one watching her.

She sighed with relief and took a deep breath. The car reeked of stale tobacco smoke. Susan wasn't a smoker herself and was usually offended and sometimes even sickened by such odors. But this time the stench seemed like a sweet perfume to her, for at least it was not a *hospital* odor.

Increasingly confident that she was going to make good her escape, Susan leaned forward, thrusting one hand under the seat, feeling along the floor for the car keys—

—and froze.

The keys were in the ignition.

They glinted in the yellowish sodium-vapor glow that came through the car windows.

The sight of them rocked Susan. She stared at them with a mixture of elation and apprehension, and she found herself arguing with herself.

—*Something's wrong.*

—*No, things are just finally going my way for a change.*

—*It's too easy.*

—*This is what I hoped to find.*

—*And it's too easy.*

—*In small towns, some people do leave keys in their cars.*

—*In the very first car you checked?*

—*What's it matter whether it's the first or the fourth or the three hundredth car?*

—*It matters because it's too easy.*

—*Just luck. I'm overdue for some good luck.*

—*It's too easy.*

Sharp ax blades of lightning chopped up the pitch-black sky, and there was a bellow of thunder. Rain fell in spurts at first, then in a sudden, terrible flood.

Susan listened to the rain pounding on the car, watched it streaming down the windshield in rippling ribbons of sodium light, watched it as it continuously shattered the mirrored surfaces of the puddles on the pavement, and she knew that she wasn't going to walk all the way into town, which was as much as a mile away, longer if she went in a roundabout fashion. Why struggle through a cloudburst when she had a perfectly good automobile at her disposal? Okay, so maybe it was a little too easy—all right, so there wasn't any "maybe" about it; too easy by far—but there wasn't any law against things going smoothly and easily now and then. It was easy, this finding a key straight off, but it was also just a stroke of good fortune, nothing more than that.

What else *could* it be?

She twisted the key in the ignition. The engine came to life instantly.

She switched on the headlights and the windshield wipers, put the car in gear, and released the emergency brake. She drove out of the parking lot and around to the front of the hospital. She came to a one-lane, one-way drive, and turned the wrong way into it because the right way out would first take her beneath the brightly lit portico, where someone at the front doors might spot her. She reached the end of the short accessway without encountering any oncoming traffic, and she paused where the drive intersected the two-lane county road.

Glancing back at the four-story building from which she had just escaped, she saw a large sign on the well-manicured, rolling lawn. It was eight feet long and four or five feet high, set on a stone base, flanked by low shrubbery. Four small floodlights were evenly spaced along the top of the sign, their beams directed down upon the bold white lettering, which was set against a royal-blue background. Even through the heavy, wind-driven rain, Susan could read that sign without any difficulty:

THE MILESTONE CORPORATION

Susan stared at those three words in disbelief.

Then she raised her eyes to the building again, regarding it with confusion, cold fear, and anger. It wasn't a hospital at all.

But what in God's name was it?

And wasn't the Milestone Corporation supposed to be located in Newport Beach, California? That was where she lived. That was where she was supposed to work.

Get the hell out of here, she told herself urgently.

She turned left and drove downhill, away from the Milestone Corporation.

Through the rain and through the thin fog that blanketed the lowlands, Willawauk was visible as a collection of soft, fuzzy lights, none of which had clear points of origin, many of which bled together into yellow and white and pale pink blobs.

Susan remembered that Dr. Viteski had said the town boasted a population of eight thousand. It had to be exactly that: a boast. It just didn't look that big. At best, it appeared to be half that size.

Past the midpoint of the long hill, leaning over the steering wheel while she drove, squinting between the thumping windshield wipers, Susan watched a change come over the lights of Willawauk. Now they seemed to shimmer and wink and ripple and blink as if the entire town was an enormous, intricate neon sign. Of course that was only an effect of the weather.

One thing that did not change was the impression of size that the lights imparted. The town still appeared to be considerably smaller than eight thousand souls. Maybe even smaller than four thousand.

The county road took a hard turn to the right and descended a last slope, past the first houses in town. In some of them, lights shone at the windows; others were dark; all were obscured by the rain and by the eddying fog.

The county road became Main Street. They couldn't have picked a more bland or more apt name for their primary avenue. The heart of Willawauk was like ten thousand other towns scattered across the country. There was a pocket-size park with a war memorial statue at the entrance of it. There was a bar and grill named the Dew Drop Inn; its sign was fashioned out of orange neon, and the *D* in *Drop* was flickering on the edge of burnout; the windows were decorated with other neon advertisements, all for various brands of beer. The town supported a lot of small businesses, some local enterprises, some minor outlets of major national chains: Jenkin's Hardware; Laura Lee's Flowers; a Sears storefront that dealt solely in catalogue orders; the Plenty Good Coffee Shop, where Susan could see about a dozen customers seated in booths beyond the huge plate-glass windows; two dress shops; a men's store; the First National Bank of Willawauk; the Main Street Cinema, which was currently playing a double feature comprised of two of last summer's comedies, *Arthur* and *Continental Divide*; Thrift Savings and Loan, with its big electronic time-and-temperature sign; an intersection with three service stations—Arco, Union 76, and Mobil—and with a computer games arcade, Rock-etblast, on the fourth corner; Giullini Brothers, TV and Appliances; a small bookstore and another bar and grill on the left; a drugstore and a G.C. Murphy's five-and-dime on the right; a funeral home, Hathaway and Sons, set back from the street on a big chunk of property; an empty storefront, a hamburger joint, a furniture store . . .

Although Willawauk was like ten thousand other towns in so many details, a couple of things seemed . . . *wrong*. It seemed to Susan that everything in town was too neat. Every one of the stores looked as if it had been painted within the last month. Even the Arco, Union 76, and Mobil stations sparkled pristinely in the rain, gasoline pumps gleaming, service bay doors raised to proudly reveal brightly lighted, neatly ordered garages. There was not a single piece of litter in the gutters. Trees were planted in regularly spaced cutouts in the sidewalks on both sides of the street, and these were not merely well pruned, but meticulously shaped into two long lines of perfect clones. In all of the many street lamps, not one bulb was burned out. Not one. The only advertising sign with a fluttering neon letter was the one at the Dew Drop Inn, and that seemed to be the town's worst example of blight.

Perhaps Willawauk had an exceptionally strong and widely shared civic pride and an especially energetic citizenry. Or perhaps the rain and the thin veil of fog were softening the scene, concealing the frayed and tattered edges of everything. Except that rain usually made a town look drearier and shabbier than it actually was, not better. And could civic pride really explain a town that looked almost as if robots inhabited it?

Another strange thing was the small number of cars in view. In three blocks, she had passed only three cars and a camper van parked at the curb. In the lot beside the Main Street Cinema, there had been only two cars, and at the Dew Drop Inn, there had been only one other and one pickup truck. So far, she hadn't passed another car in motion; she was the only one driving tonight.

Well, the weather *was* wretched. People were wise to stay home on a night like this.

On the other hand, how many people did she know who usually did the wise thing?

Not very damned many.

Not *this* many.

The Dew Drop Inn was the kind of place that did good business in the middle of a blizzard. A simple rain wouldn't stop the serious drinkers from making their way to their favorite hangout, and most of them would come in cars, the better to kill each other as they weaved blearily home at two o'clock in the morning.

Keep driving, Susan told herself. Drive all the way through this burg and keep on going. Don't stop here. Something is wrong with this place.

But she didn't have a map, and she wasn't familiar with the countryside around these parts, and she didn't know how far it was to the nearest town, and she was also afraid that what had happened to her in the hospital—in *Milestone*—was turning her into a paranoid after all. Then, at the beginning of the fourth block, she saw a place where she was sure to find help, and she pulled her car into the parking lot.

Willawauk County Sheriff Headquarters

WILLAWAUK, OREGON

It was a squat, stone building with a slate roof and all-glass front doors, just south of the considerably more stately county courthouse.

Susan parked the stolen Pontiac near the entrance. She was glad to be getting out of the car; already, the odor of stale tobacco smoke had ceased to be the least bit appealing, even if it didn't remind her of the hospital.

She ran through the hammering rain. She ducked under a mammoth spruce tree, through which the cold wind soughed in an enormous chorus of whispers. From there she dashed to the shelter of a white aluminum awning, and thus to the glass doors, through which she pushed.

She found herself in a typically drab, institutional room with gray walls, fluorescent lights and a speckled, multicolored Armstrong tile floor designed to conceal wear. A U-shaped counter separated the largest part of the main room from a waiting area just inside the doors. Susan walked past several uncomfortable-looking metal chairs, past two small tables on which were stacked a variety of public service pamphlets, and went straight to the counter.

On the other side, there were several desks, file cabinets, a large work table, a bottled-water dispenser, a photocopier, a giant wall map of the county, and a huge bulletin board that was covered with tacked-on bulletins and photographs and wanted notices and odd scraps of paper.

In an adjacent alcove, out of sight, a woman dispatcher was talking to a patrol officer on a shortwave radio. The storm was throwing in bursts of static.

In the main room, there was only one man. He was sitting at a desk, typing on an IBM Selectric, his back turned to the counter and to Susan.

"Excuse me," Susan said, brushing at her rain-beaded eyelashes with the back of one hand. "Can you help me?"

He swung around on his swivel chair, smiled, and said, "I'm Officer Whitlock. What can I do for you?"

He was young, perhaps twenty or twenty-one.

He was a bit on the pudgy side.

He had dirty blond hair, a round face, a dimpled chin, a pug nose, and the small quick eyes of a pig.

He had a twisted, nasty smile.

He was Carl Jellicoe.

Susan sucked in a breath that seemed to pierce her lungs as if it were a nail, and she wasn't able to expel it.

When he had been wearing a hospital orderly's uniform, he had called himself Dennis Bradley. Now he was wearing a brown uniform with the County Sheriff's Department seal stitched to his left sleeve and to the breast pocket of his shirt, and he carried a .45-caliber revolver in a black leather holster on his hip, and he called himself Officer Whitlock.

Susan couldn't speak. Shock had seared her vocal cords as thoroughly as a gas flame could have; her throat was parched, cracking; her mouth was suddenly hot, dry, and filled with a burnt-out taste.

She couldn't move.

She finally let out her breath with a sob, and she gasped for more air, but she still couldn't move.

"Surprise, surprise," Jellicoe said, giggling, getting up from his swivel chair.

Susan shook her head, slowly at first, then vehemently, trying to deny his existence.

"Did you really think you could get away from us that easily? Did you really?" he asked, standing with his legs spread, hitching up his holster.

Susan stared at him, transfixed, her feet fused to the floor. Her hands were clenched tightly around the edge of the wooden counter, as if that were her only grip on reality.

Not taking his piggish little eyes off Susan, Jellicoe called out to someone in an adjoining room. "Hey, come look at what we've got here!"

Another deputy appeared. He was twenty or twenty-one, tall, with red hair and hazel eyes and a fair complexion that was spattered with freckles. In his hospital orderly's uniform, he had called himself Patrick O'Hara. Susan didn't know what he called himself now, but she knew what he had called himself thirteen years ago, when he had been a student at Briarstead College, when he had helped kill Jerry Stein in the House of Thunder: Herbert Parker.

"My, my," Parker said. "The lady looks distressed."

"Well, you see, the poor thing thought she'd gotten away from us," Jellicoe said.

"Did she really?" Parker said.

"Really."

"Doesn't she know she can never get away from us? Doesn't she know we're dead?"

Jellicoe grinned at her. "Don't you know we're dead, you silly little bitch?"

"You read about it in the newspapers," Parker reminded her. "Don't you recall?"

"The car accident?" Jellicoe prodded.

"About eleven years ago, it was."

In the communications alcove, the unseen dispatcher continued to talk with cruising patrol officers over the shortwave radio, as if nothing unusual were happening out here in the main room. But the woman *must* know.

"We rolled that damned car over like it was just a little toy," Jellicoe said.

"Rolled it twice," Parker said.

"What a mess it was."

"What a mess *we* were."

"All because of this slut."

They both started toward the counter, neither of them in a hurry, ambling between the desks, smiling.

"And now she thinks it'll be easy to run away from us," Carl Jellicoe said.

Parker said, "We're dead, you stupid bitch. Don't you understand what that means? You can't *hide* from dead men."

"Because we can be anywhere—"

"—everywhere—"

"—all at the same time."

"That's one of the advantages of being dead."

"Which doesn't *have* many advantages."

Jellicoe giggled again.

They were almost to the counter.

Susan was gasping now, breathing as frantically as a pumping bellows in a blazing forge.

"You aren't dead, damn you," she said, abruptly finding her voice.

"Oh, yes. We're dead—"

"—and buried—"

"—and gone to Hell—"

"—and come back again."

"And now this place is Hell."

"For you, it is, Susan. For you, for a little while, this is Hell."

Jellicoe was moving around to the gate, where a section of the countertop lifted to allow passage between the waiting area and the bullpen.

A heavy glass ashtray was on the counter, within Susan's reach. She finally moved, snatched up the ashtray, and threw it at Jellicoe's head.

He didn't just stand there and let the missile pass magically through his body to prove that he was, indeed, a ghost. For a dead man, Jellicoe exhibited a surprisingly healthy fear of being hurt. He ducked behind the counter.

The ashtray missed him, struck the metal desk, cracked apart, and clattered in pieces to the floor.

A long-handled, police-issue flashlight also stood on the counter, and Susan seized that, too. She swung it back over her shoulder, prepared to let it fly at Jellicoe, but out of the corner of her eye, she saw that Herbert Parker was drawing his revolver, so she fled across the waiting area, through the glass doors, into the night.

The boughs of the giant spruce flailed at one another, and the tree's tens of thousands of green needles were briefly colored silver by a flash of lightning.

Susan ran to the stolen Pontiac and jerked open the door. She got in and reached for the keys, which she had left dangling in the ignition.

The keys were gone.

For you, for a little while, this is Hell.

She glanced toward the glass doors.

Jellicoe and Parker were just coming out of the slumpstone building. They weren't in a hurry.

Susan slid across the seat, frantically pushed open the door on the passenger's side, and got out of the car, putting it between her and the two men.

She looked around, determining the best route of escape, hoping that her legs would hold up. Thank God for those physical therapy sessions with Mrs. Atkinson! Otherwise, she wouldn't have gotten this far. But four days of exercise and good food didn't mean she was back to full power. Eventually, she would collapse, and that moment would come for her long before it would come for either Jellicoe or Parker.

Above the roar of the rain, above the trumpeting of the wind, Jellicoe called to her. "There's no use running, Susan."

"There's no place to hide!" Parker shouted.

"Fuck you," she said, and she ran.

16

THE HOUSE HAD A WELCOMING LOOK TO IT. THERE WAS a white picket fence, a shrub-bordered walkway, and a wide front porch with an ornate wooden railing and an old-fashioned porch swing suspended from the rafters. Warm yellow light shone through the lace curtains that covered the downstairs windows.

For a few minutes, Susan stood at the gate in the fence, studying the house, wondering if it was a safe place. She was cold, thoroughly wet, and miserable, and the rain was still coming down hard. She was eager to get inside where it was warm and dry, but she didn't intend to walk into another trap if she could avoid it; she wanted to feel *right* about the house before she went up to the door, rang the bell, and asked for help.

Go on, she urged herself. Do it. Don't just stand here. The whole damned town can't be part of the conspiracy, for God's sake!

Everyone at the hospital was a part of it, of course, but then it wasn't a *real* hospital. It was the Milestone Corporation, whatever the hell *that* was.

The police were involved, too, which was outrageous and scary, constituting a stunning setback for her, but she understood how such a thing was possible. Sometimes, in a small town like Willawauk, if one major company totally dominated the economic life of the community—through the jobs it provided and the taxes it paid—then it wielded tremendous power over the local authorities, even to the extent of being able to use the police as a sub rosa enforcement arm for the company's own purposes and protection. Susan didn't know for sure that Milestone was *the* employer of note in town, but it clearly had used its influence and a lot of money to corrupt the sheriff's department. The situation was outlandish, although not unbelievable.

But that was where the conspiracy ended, surely. Milestone, all of its employees, and the police were part of it; all right, she could accept that much. Already, however, the size of the conspiracy was unwieldy. It couldn't possibly encompass anyone else without starting to unravel at the seams. By their very nature, conspiracies could not include *thousands* of people.

Nevertheless, she stood in the rain by the gate, studying the house, envying the people who were warm and dry inside—and fearing them, too.

She was three blocks from the sheriff's offices. She had gotten away from Jellicoe and Parker with little trouble, running down alleyways, staying in the shadows, darting from tree to tree across several lawns.

In fact, now that she thought about it, avoiding Jellicoe and Parker had been too easy. Like finding the keys in the Pontiac when she needed a car. With good reason, she had come to distrust easy escapes.

An exceptionally brilliant flash of lightning briefly transformed the night into day. Rain began falling harder than ever, and it seemed colder, too.

That was enough to propel Susan through the gate and up the walk to the front porch. She rang the bell.

She didn't see what else she could do. She had nowhere else to go, no one to turn to except strangers chosen at random from all the houses full of strangers on all these strange, rain-scoured streets.

The porch light came on.

Susan smiled and tried to appear harmless. She knew that she must look wild: waterlogged, her hair curled into tight ringlets and tangled in knots by the rain and the wind, her face still somewhat emaciated, her eyes stark and haunted. She was afraid of presenting such a bad image that people would be discouraged from opening their doors to her. A tremulous smile was not enough to make her look like the Welcome Wagon lady, but it was all she could offer.

Happily, the door opened, and a woman peered out, blinking in surprise. She was in her middle or late forties, a cherub-faced brunette with a pixie-style haircut. She didn't even wait for Susan to speak, but said, "Good gracious, whatever are you doing out on a night like this, without an umbrella or a raincoat? Is something wrong?"

"I've had some trouble," Susan said. "I was—"

"Car trouble?" the brunette asked, but she didn't wait for an answer. She was a bubbly, outgoing woman, and she seemed to have been waiting for someone who had an ear that needed talking off. "Oh, don't they just always break down in weather like this! Never on a sunny day in June. Always at night and always in a storm. And never when you can find a mechanic or when you have change for a pay phone. You'll be wanting to know if you can use our phone. That's it, isn't it? Well, of course, of course. Come in here where it's warm, call whoever you want. And I think I'll make you some hot coffee. By the look of you, you'll need something hot if you're going to stave off pneumonia." She stepped aside so that Susan could enter.

Startled by the woman's unreserved hospitality and by her nonstop chatter, Susan said, "Well . . . uh . . . I'm dripping."

"Won't hurt a thing. We've got a dark carpet—have to with the kids. Just imagine what they'd do to a *white* carpet—and it's an Antron Plus fiber, which means it just *won't* take a stain no matter how hard the little devils try. Besides, you're only dripping rainwater, not spaghetti sauce or chocolate syrup. A little rain isn't going to hurt it. Come in, come in."

Susan went inside, and the woman closed the door.

They were standing in a cozy foyer. The flower-patterned wallpaper was too busy for Susan's taste, but it wasn't unattractive. A small table stood against one wall of the foyer; a brass-framed mirror hung above the table; an arrangement of dried flowers stood on the table, in front of the mirror.

A television set was playing in another room. It was tuned to an action show; tires squealed; people shouted; guns blazed; dramatic music swelled.

"My name's Enid," the brunette said. "Enid Shipstat."

"I'm Susan Thorton."

"You know, Susan, you should always carry an umbrella in your car, even when it doesn't look like it's going to rain, just in case something like this happens. An umbrella and a flashlight and a first-aid kit. Ed—that's my hubby—he also keeps a little tire pump in the trunk, a little electric model that plugs right into the cigarette lighter, so if you get a flat that's caused by a slow leak or a puncture, then you can reinflate it long enough to get to a gas station. That way you don't have to change the tire yourself, out on the road, in bad weather, maybe in the middle of a storm like this. But good heavens, this isn't the time to talk about being a good girl scout, is it? What in the world is wrong with me? Here I am offering you all sorts of unsolicited advice, when you're standing there shaking like a leaf. Sometimes I think my mouth isn't wired up to my brain. Come on back to the kitchen. That's probably the warmest room in the house, and I can brew you up some good hot coffee. There's a phone in the kitchen, too."

Susan decided to wait until she'd had a few sips of coffee before explaining that her plight didn't involve car trouble. She followed Enid Shipstat into a narrow hall, where the only light was that spilling in from the foyer and a bluish TV glow that came from the living room, on the right.

As they passed the living-room archway, Susan almost stopped and gaped in surprise at the sight beyond the arch. It was a relatively normal American living room, arranged around the TV as most American living rooms were, but it was overfurnished with chairs and sofas—and with children. A dozen kids ringed the television, sitting on the furniture and on the floor, all intently watching the softly glowing screen, which provided, along with one small lamp, the only light in the room. A dozen heads turned as if they were all part of a single organism, and a dozen young faces looked expressionlessly at Susan for a moment, eyes shining with reflected TV light, then turned to the screen again when their attention was drawn by a burst of gunfire and the wail of a police siren. Their rapt silence and their blank expressions were eerie.

"I only have Hills Brothers," Enid said as she led Susan down the hall toward the kitchen. "That's the only kind of coffee Ed will drink. Personally, I like Folger's just as well, but Ed thinks it's not as mellow as Hills Brothers, and he just can't *stand* that Mrs. Olsen on the commercials. He says she reminds him of a busybody old schoolteacher he once had."

"Anything you've got is fine," Susan said.

"Well, like I told you, all we have is just Hills Brothers, I'm afraid, so I hope you like Hills Brothers."

"That'll be fine."

Susan wondered how the Shipstats managed to raise a dozen children in this simple, two-story house. It was a fairly large place, but not *that* large. The bedrooms would have to be organized like army barracks, with sets of bunk beds, at least four kids to a room.

As Enid Shipstat pushed open the swinging kitchen door, Susan said, "You've got quite a family."

"You *see* why we don't have a white carpet?" Enid said, and she laughed.

They stepped into the kitchen, a brightly lit room with clean yellow ceramic-tile counters and white cabinets with yellow porcelain knobs on the doors and drawers.

A young man was sitting sideways to the door, his elbows propped on the kitchen table, his head buried in his hands, bent over a large textbook.

"That's Tom, my oldest boy," Enid said with pride. "He's in his senior year at college, always studying. He's going to be a rich lawyer some day, and then he's going to support his poor old mom and dad in luxury. Isn't that right, Tom?" She winked at Susan to show that she was only kidding.

Tom took his hands down from his face, raised his head, and looked at Susan.

It was Ernest Harch.

Madness, Susan thought, her heart lurching into high gear. *Sheer madness*.

"This lady's had some trouble with her car," Enid told her son. "She needs to use our phone."

Harch smiled and said, "Hello, Susan."

Enid blinked. "Oh, you *know* each other."

"Yeah," Harch said. "We know each other real well."

The room seemed to tilt beneath Susan's feet.

Harch stood up.

Susan backed up, bumped against the refrigerator.

"Mom," Harch said to Enid, "I can help Susan, if you want to get back to your TV show."

"Well," Enid said, looking back and forth between Susan and Harch, "I was going to make some coffee . . . "

"I've already brewed up a pot," Harch said. "I always need coffee when I've got a long night of studying ahead of me. You know that, Mom."

"Well," Enid said to Susan, pretending not to notice the sudden tension in the room, "you see, it *is* one of my favorite shows, and I hate to miss it even one week because the story kind of continues episode to episode—"

"*Shut up, shut up, shut up!*" Susan said in a voice that was half whimper, half snarl. "Just cut the crap."

Enid's mouth fell open, and she blinked stupidly, as if she was genuinely amazed by Susan's outburst and was utterly unable to imagine the reason for it.

Harch laughed.

Susan took a step toward the swinging door through which she and Enid had entered the kitchen. "Don't try to stop me. I swear to God, I'll claw your eyes and I'll try my damnedest to bite your jugular open. I *swear* I will."

"Are you *crazy?*" Enid Shipstat said.

Still laughing, Harch started around the table.

Enid said, "Tom, is your friend joking, or what?"

"Don't try to stop me," Susan warned him as she edged away from the refrigerator.

"If this is a joke, it doesn't seem the least bit funny to me," Enid said.

Harch said, "Susan, Susan, it's no use. Don't you know that by now?"

Susan turned, slammed through the kitchen door, bolted into the hall. She half expected to find the children blocking her exit, but the hallway was deserted. The kids were still sitting in the living room when she ran past the archway. Bathed in blue light and the flickering reflections of the images on the screen, they appeared to be oblivious to the shouting in the kitchen.

What kind of house *is* this? Susan wondered desperately as she hurried down the shadowy hall. What kind of kids *are* they? Little zombies in front of that TV.

She reached the front door, tried it, and found that it was locked.

Harch entered the hall from the kitchen. He was pursuing her but without urgency, just as Jellicoe and Parker had done. "Listen, you stupid bitch, we'll get you whether you run or not."

Susan twisted the doorknob back and forth.

Harch approached leisurely along the shadowy hall. "Tomorrow night you'll pay for what you did to us. Tomorrow night, I'll have been dead for seven years, and you'll pay for that. We'll screw you, all four of us, every which way we can, turn you inside out and upside down, screw your damned brains out—"

The door shuddered as she pulled frantically on it, but it would not open.

"—screw you like we should have that night in the cave, and then we'll slit you wide open, all the way up the middle, and cut your pretty head off, just exactly the way we should have handled you, just like I *wanted* to do thirteen years ago."

Susan wished that she had the courage to spin around and face him, strike him, and go for his throat with her teeth. She could do something like that if she were sure it would hurt him; it wouldn't turn her stomach. She had the nerve and the rage to feel his blood bubbling in her mouth without gagging on it. But she was afraid that she would cut him and find that he *didn't* bleed, that he was dead, after all. She knew that was impossible. But now that she had encountered Harch again, now that she had seen those peculiar gray eyes once more, had seen them filled with an arctic hatred, she could no longer hold on to her carefully reasoned refutation of the supernatural. Her faith in the scientific method and in logic was crumbling again; she was being reduced to babbling fear once more, losing control, hating it, despising herself, but losing control nevertheless.

Jellicoe's words came back to her: *For you, for a little while, this is Hell.*

She wrenched at the door in blind panic, and it opened with a scraping sound. It hadn't been locked, just warped by the damp weather.

"You're wasting your energy, baby," Harch called after her. "Save it for Friday. I'd be angry if you were too worn out to be any fun on Friday."

She stumbled through the door, onto the porch, and down the three steps to the walk. She ran to the gate in the picket fence, into the rain and wind.

As she pelted along the dark street, splashing through deep puddles that came over the tops of her shoes, she heard Harch calling to her from back at the house.

" . . . pointless . . . no use . . . nowhere to hide . . . "

■ Susan approached the Main Street Cinema by way of alleys and parking lots. Before rounding the corner of the theater, onto the well-lighted Main Street sidewalk, she looked both ways, studying the rain-slashed night for signs of the police.

The ticket booth was closed. The last show for the night was already underway; no more tickets could be sold.

She pushed through the outer doors, into the lobby. It was deserted.

But it was warm, gloriously warm.

The lights had been turned off behind the refreshment counter, which seemed odd. Since theaters made more money from selling food and beverages than they did from their share of the ticket sales, they usually kept the refreshment stand open until the last patron had gone home after seeing the last scene of the final show of the night.

From inside the theater auditorium, music swelled, and Dudley Moore's voice was raised in drunken laughter. Obviously, the movie currently unreeling was *Arthur.*

She had come to the theater because she needed to get warm and dry; but more than that, she had to have a chance to sit and think, think, think—before she lost her mind altogether. From the moment she had walked into the sheriff's offices and had encountered Jellicoe, she had been *re*acting rather than acting, and she knew she must stop drifting wherever they pushed her. She had to regain control of events.

She had considered going up the street to the Plenty Good Coffee Shop instead of to the theater, but she had worried about the police cruising by and spotting her through the restaurant's big plate-glass windows. By contrast, the movie theater was a dark and private sanctuary.

She crossed the clean, plushly carpeted lobby to the padded inner doors, opened one of them just far enough to slip through, and closed it quickly behind her.

On the big screen, Arthur had just awakened in bed after a night of debauchery. It was John Gielgud's first scene. Susan had seen the film when it had first been released, early last summer. In fact she had liked it so much that she had gone to see it twice. She knew that the scene now playing was fairly early in the movie. There must be at least an hour to go before the end credits, an hour of dry, warm time during which she could attempt to make some sense of what had happened to her tonight.

Susan's eyes hadn't yet adjusted to the pitch-black theater. She couldn't see if there was a crowd or only a few patrons. Then she remembered that there were only two cars in the parking lot. Mustn't be a crowd; not many people would *walk* to the theater on a night like this.

She was standing beside the left-hand aisle seat in the last row, which was the only seat she could see clearly, and it was empty. She took it, rather than search for something more private and risk drawing attention to herself. Her wet clothes squished as she sat down, and they clung to her, cold and sticky.

She tuned the movie out.

She thought about ghosts.

Demons.

Walking dead men.

Again, she decided that she couldn't accept a supernatural explanation. At least not for the time being. For one thing, there wasn't anything to be gained by dwelling on the occult possibilities, for if that *was* the explanation, there was absolutely nothing she could do to save herself. If all the forces of Hell were aligned against her, then she was lost for sure, so she might just as well rule out the very possibility of it.

She ruled out madness, too. She might actually *be* mad, but there was nothing whatsoever she could do to change that if it were the case, so it was better not even to think about it.

Which left her with the conspiracy theory.

That wasn't much of a theory, either. She didn't have the slightest idea who, how, or why.

As she puzzled over those three essential questions, her thoughts were briefly disturbed by a wave of laughter that swept the theater. Although it came in reaction to a very funny scene in *Arthur* and wasn't at all out of place, there was something about the laughter which seemed distinctly *odd* to Susan.

Of course, the volume of laughter indicated that there were quite a few people in the theater, at least a hundred, maybe more, and that was certainly a surprise, considering the fact that there were only two cars in the parking lot. But that wasn't what was odd about it.

Something else.

Something about the sound of it.

The laughter subsided, and Susan's thoughts returned to her escape plans.

When had it begun to go wrong?

As soon as she had left the hospital—or, rather, as soon as she'd left Milestone— *that* was when it had begun to go wrong. The keys in the Pontiac. Too easy. Which meant they had known she would try to escape, and they had actually *wanted* her to try. The Pontiac had been left there expressly for her use.

But how had they known that she would think to look in the car for the keys? And how could they have been so certain that she would stop at the sheriff's station?

How could they have known she would go to the Shipstat house for help? Willawauk contained hundreds of other houses, other people to whom she might have turned. Why had the Harch look-alike been waiting with such perfect confidence at the Shipstat place?

She knew the most likely answer to her own question, but she didn't want to believe it. Didn't even want to consider it. Maybe they always knew where she was going to go next because they had *programmed* her to go there. Maybe they had planted a few crucial directives in her subconscious while she'd been in the coma. That would explain why they never seriously pursued her when she ran from them; they knew she would walk into their arms later, at a prearranged place.

Maybe she had no free will whatsoever. That possibility made her feel sick to her stomach—and in her soul, as well.

Who *were* these shadowy manipulators with godlike power over her?

Her train of thought was derailed by another wave of loud laughter that rolled through the theater, and this time she realized what was odd about the sound. It was the laughter of young people: higher pitched than that of a general audience, quicker and more eager and more shrill than the laughter of adults.

Her eyes had adapted somewhat to the darkness in the theater, and she raised her head, looked around. At least two hundred people were present. No, it was

more like three hundred. Of those nearest to Susan, of those she could see, all
appeared to be kids. Not young children. Teenagers. Thirteen to eighteen, or
thereabouts. High school and junior high kids. As far as she could tell, she was
the only adult in the crowd.

Why had three hundred kids walked through a fierce storm to see a movie that
was almost six months old? And what kind of uncaring parents would have permitted them to risk pneumonia and possibly even electrocution by lightning just
to come to a movie?

She thought of the dozen children at the Shipstat house, their faces glazed by
the bluish light from the TV.

Willawauk seemed to have more than its share of children.

And what the devil did all these children have to do with her own situation?

Something. There was some connection, but she couldn't figure it out.

While Susan was puzzling over the oddity of Willawauk's youthful population,
she saw a door open at the front of the theater, to the left of the screen. A pale
blue light shone in a room beyond the door. A tall man came out into the auditorium and closed the door behind him. He switched on a flashlight, one with a
very narrow beam, and pointed it at the floor immediately in front of him.

An usher?

He started up the aisle.

Toward Susan.

The theater was fairly large, three times longer than it was wide. The usher
took at least half a dozen steps up the sloping aisle before Susan became aware,
through some sixth sense, that he was a threat to her.

She stood up. Her wet clothes stuck to her. She had been in the theater only
fifteen minutes, not nearly long enough to dry out, and she was reluctant to leave.

The usher kept coming.

The narrow flashlight beam bobbled up and down a bit with each step the man
took.

Susan edged away from her seat, into the aisle. She squinted into the gloom
ahead, trying to perceive the usher's face.

He was forty feet away, coming slowly toward her, invisible behind his flashlight, suddenly silhouetted but unrevealed by a bright scene on the movie screen.

Dudley Moore said something funny.

The audience laughed.

Susan began to shake.

John Gielgud said something funny, and Liza Minnelli said something funny
right back at him, and the audience laughed again.

If I was programmed to steal the Pontiac, Susan thought, and if I was programmed to go to the sheriff's station and to the Shipstat house, then perhaps I
was also programmed to come here instead of going up the street to the Plenty
Good Coffee Shop or somewhere else.

The usher was no more than thirty feet away now.

Susan took three sliding steps backwards to the padded doors that opened onto
the lobby. She reached behind her and put one hand against the door.

The usher raised the flashlight, no longer directing it toward the sloping floor
in front of him, and shone it straight into Susan's face.

The beam wasn't terribly bright, but it blinded her because her eyes had adjusted to the darkness.

He's one of *them*, she thought. One of the dead men. Probably Quince because Quince hasn't yet put in an appearance tonight.

Or maybe it was Jerry Stein, his face rotting away from his bones, pus oozing from his swollen, purple lips. Jerry Stein, all dressed up in a neat usher's uniform, coming to say hello, coming to get a kiss.

There's nothing supernatural about this, she told herself in a desperate attempt to stave off panic.

But maybe it *was* Jerry, his face gray, a little green around the eyes, with brown-black blisters of corruption extending from his nostrils. Maybe it was Jerry, coming to give her a hug, coming to take her in his arms. Maybe he would lower his face to hers and put his lips to hers and thrust his cold, slimy tongue into her mouth in a grotesque kiss of graveyard passion.

For you, for a little while, this is Hell.

Susan flung open the door and raced out of the theater, into the lobby, across the plush carpeting, through the outer doors, not daring to look back. She turned right at the corner of the building, into the parking lot, and headed toward the dark alley. She sucked the humid air deep into her heaving lungs, and she felt as if she were breathing wet cotton.

In seconds, her clothes were as thoroughly soaked as they had been when she'd gone into the theater.

Hot flashes of pain shot through her legs, but she tried to ignore them. She told herself she could run all night if that was necessary.

But she knew she was lying to herself. She was quickly using up what little strength she had managed to store away during the past five days. Not much was left. Dregs.

■ The Arco Service Station was closed for the night. Rain lashed the gasoline pumps and rattled against the big windows and drummed on the metal garage doors.

Beside the station, a public telephone booth stood in shadows. Susan stepped into it but didn't close the door because closing it would turn on the booth light.

She had gotten change for a dollar from a change machine in a coin-operated laundromat. She dropped a dime in the phone and dialed the operator.

She was shivering uncontrollably now, miserably cold and exhausted.

"Operator."

"Operator, I'd like to place a long-distance call and charge it to my home number."

"And what is the number you're calling, please?"

Susan gave her Sam Walker's number in Newport Beach. She had dated Sam for over a year, and he had been more serious about their relationship than she had been. They had broken off last spring, not without pain, but they were still friends; they talked once in a while on the phone, and they occasionally encountered each other by accident at restaurants they both favored, in which case they weren't so estranged that they couldn't have dinner together.

It was perhaps a condemnation of her excessively solitary, self-reliant, go-it-alone nature that she had no really close girl friends from whom she could seek help. She had no one closer than Sam, and she had last seen him nearly five weeks before she had left on her vacation to Oregon.

"What is the number to which you wish to bill the call?" the operator asked.

Susan recited her home number in Newport Beach.

After fleeing from the Main Street Cinema, she had decided that she couldn't be sure of escaping from Willawauk unless she had help from someone outside of town. She didn't know if she could convince Sam that she was in danger and that the Willawauk police couldn't be trusted. Even though he knew she didn't take drugs or drink to excess, he'd have to wonder if she was stoned. She could not possibly tell him the whole story or even most of it; for sure, he'd think she had slipped a mental gear. The trick was to tell him only enough to make him come running or to convince him to call the FBI for her.

The FBI, for God's sake! It all sounded so ludicrous. But who else did you call when you couldn't trust the local police? Who else did you turn to? Besides, there was kidnapping involved here, and that was a federal offense, within the FBI's jurisdiction.

She would have called the Bureau's Oregon office herself, except she didn't think she'd be able to convince a total stranger that she was really in trouble. She wasn't even certain that she could convince Sam, who knew her very well.

Down in Newport Beach, Sam's phone began to ring.

Please be there, please, she thought.

A gust of icy wind rammed through the open door of the phone booth. It pummeled her back with hard-driven rain.

Sam's phone rang three times.

Four times.

Please, please, please . . .

A fifth time.

Then someone picked it up. "Hello?"

"Sam?"

"Hello?"

There was a lot of static on the line.

"Sam?"

"Yeah. Who's this?"

His voice was faint.

"Sam, it's me, Susan."

A hesitation. Then: "Suzie?"

"Yes."

"Suzie Thorton?"

"Yes," she said, relieved that at last she had touched someone beyond Willawauk.

"Where are you?" he asked.

"Willawauk, Oregon."

"Will *who* walk to Oregon?"

"No, no. Willawauk." She spelled it.

"Sounds like you're calling from Tahiti or something," he said as the static temporarily abated.

Listening to him, Susan felt a terrible suspicion uncoiling like a snake in her mind. A new chill slithered through her, tongue of ice flickering on her spine.

She said, "I can hardly hear you."

"I said, it sounds like you're calling from Tahiti or something."

Susan pressed the receiver tightly to her ear, put her hand over her other ear, and said, "Sam, you don't . . . "

"What? Suzie, are you there?"

"Sam . . . you don't . . . sound like yourself."

"Suzie, what's this all about?"

She opened her mouth, but she couldn't bring herself to speak the dreadful truth.

"Suzie?"

Even the goddamned *telephone company* couldn't be trusted in Willawauk.

"Suzie, are you there?"

Her voice cracked with fury and anger, but she spat out the unthinkable thought: "You aren't Sam Walker."

Static.

Silence.

More static.

At last he giggled and said, "Of course I'm not Walker, you stupid bitch."

It was Carl Jellicoe's giggle.

Susan felt a thousand years old, older than that, ancient, wasted, shriveled, hollow.

The wind changed direction, slammed against the side of the phone booth, rattled the glass.

Jellicoe said, "Why do you insist on thinking it's going to be easy to get away from us?"

Susan said nothing.

"There's no place to hide. Nowhere to run."

"Bastard," she said.

"You're finished. You're through," Jellicoe said. "Welcome to Hell, you dumb slut."

She slammed the phone down.

Susan stepped out of the booth and looked around at the rain-drenched service station and at the street beyond. Nothing moved. There was no one in sight. No one was coming after her. Yet.

She was still free.

No, not free. She was still on a very long leash, but she was not free. On a leash—and she had the strong feeling that they were about to begin reeling it in.

For a little while, she walked, hardly aware of the rain and the cold wind any more, stubbornly disregarding the pain in her legs, unable to formulate any new escape plans. She was merely passing time now, waiting for them to come for her.

She paused in front of St. John's Lutheran Church.

There was a light inside. It filtered out through the large, arched, stained-glass windows; it colored the rain red, blue, green, and yellow for a distance of three or four feet, and it imparted a rainbow glow to the thin veil of wind-whirled fog.

A parsonage was attached to the church, a Victorian-style structure: two full stories plus a gabled attic, bay windows on the second floor. The neatly tended lawn was illuminated by an ornate iron lamppost at the outer end of the walk, and two smaller, matching iron lamps on the porch posts, one on each side of the steps. A sign on the gate read, REV. POTTER B. KINFIELD.

Susan stood in front of Reverend Kinfield's house for a couple of minutes, one hand on the gate, leaning against it. She was too weary to go on, but she was too proud to lie down in the street and just give up as if she were a whipped dog.

Without hope, but also without anything else to do and without anywhere else to go, she finally went up the walk and climbed the steps to the parsonage porch. You were supposed to be able to count on clergymen. You were supposed to be able to go to them with any kind of problem and get help. Would that be true of clergymen in Willawauk? Probably not.

She rang the bell.

Although the outside lights were burning brightly, the house itself was dark. That didn't necessarily mean the preacher wasn't home. He might have gone to bed. It was late, after all. She didn't know exactly how late it was; she had lost track of time. But it must be somewhere between eleven o'clock and midnight.

She rang the bell again.

And again.

No lights came on inside. No one answered.

In anticipation of the minister's response to the bell, Susan had summoned up images of warmth and comfort: a toasty parlor; a big, soft easy chair; pajamas, a heavy robe, and slippers borrowed from the preacher's wife; maybe some nice buttered toast and hot chocolate; sympathy; outrage at what had been done to her; promises of protection and assistance; a bed with a firm mattress; crisp, clean sheets and heavy woolen blankets; two pillows; and a lovely, lovely feeling of being safe.

Now, when no one answered the door, Susan couldn't get those images out of her mind. She simply could not forget them and just walk away. The loss hurt too much, even though it was the loss of something she'd never really possessed in the first place. She stood on the porch, quivering on the verge of tears, desperately wanting those damned dry pajamas and that hot chocolate, wanting them with such fierce intensity that the wanting drove out all other emotions, including all fear of Ernest Harch and the walking dead men and the people behind Milestone.

She tried the door. It was locked.

She moved along the porch, trying the sash-hung windows. The three to the left of the door were all locked. The first one to the right was also locked, but the second one was not. It was swollen by the damp air, and it didn't move easily, but finally she raised it far enough to squeeze through, into the parsonage.

She had just committed an illegal act. But she was a desperate woman, and the Reverend Kinfield would surely understand once he heard all the facts. Besides, this was Willawauk, Oregon, where the normal rules of society didn't apply.

The interior of the house was utterly black. She couldn't see more than two or three inches in front of her face.

Curiously, the house wasn't warm, either. It seemed almost as cold as the night outside.

Susan felt her way along the wall, moving left, past the first window on that side of the door, then to the door itself. She located the switch on the wall, flicked it.

She blinked at the sudden flood of light—then blinked in surprise when she saw that the Lutheran parsonage was not what it appeared to be from the outside. It wasn't a gracious old Victorian house. It was a *ware*house: one room as large as a barn, more than two stories high, with no partitions, and a bare concrete floor. Life-size papier-mâché figures for a nativity scene, plus a large red sleigh complete with reindeer were suspended from the ceiling on wires, stored away until the holidays. The room itself was filled with cardboard cartons, hundreds upon hundreds of them stacked four and five high; there were also trunks, chests, enormous wooden crates, and a couple of dozen metal cabinets each about seven feet high, four feet deep and eight feet long. Everything was arranged in neat rows that extended the length of the building, with access aisles in between.

Baffled, Susan ventured away from the wall and went exploring through the stacks. In the first couple of cabinets, she found black choir robes hanging from metal bars, each robe sealed tightly in a clear plastic bag. In the third cabinet, she uncovered several Santa Claus outfits, two Easter Bunny costumes, and four sets of Pilgrims' clothes that apparently were used in Thanksgiving celebrations. The first of the cardboard cartons—according to the labels on them—contained religious pamphlets, Bibles, and church songbooks.

All of those things, including the Christmas figures that were suspended from the ceiling, were objects that any church might wish to store. Not, of course, in a fake parsonage; that part of it didn't make any sense at all. But those goods were perfectly legitimate.

Then she found other things that seemed out of place and more than a little strange.

Three entire, sixty-foot-long walls of boxes and crates—as many as two or three thousand containers—were filled with clothes. The labels told a curious story. The first hundred or so were all marked the same:

U.S. FASHIONS
WOMEN'S DRESSES
1960–1964
(KENNEDY ERA)

A smaller number of containers were labeled:

U.S. FASHIONS
MEN'S SUITS AND TIES
1960–1964
(KENNEDY ERA)

There were a lot of women's clothes, some men's clothes, and a few boxes of children's clothes from every subsequent fashion era through the late Seventies. There were even clusters of boxes in which the clothing of various subcultures was stored.

U.S. FASHIONS
MALE ATTIRE—MIXED
HIPPIE SUBCULTURE

All of this was not simply evidence of an ambitious clothing drive to benefit the church's overseas missions. It was clearly a long-term storage program.

Susan was also convinced that it wasn't merely some ambitious historical preservation project. These weren't museum samples of American clothing styles; these were entire wardrobes, sufficient to clothe hundreds upon hundreds of people in virtually any fashion period from the past twenty years.

It appeared as if the people of Willawauk were so extraordinarily thrifty—every man, woman and child of them—that they had joined en masse to preserve their out-of-date clothing, just in case old styles came back into fashion some day and could be used again. It was wise and admirable to attempt to circumvent the expensive tyranny of fashion designers. But in a throwaway culture like America's, where virtually everything was designed to be disposable, what kind of people, what kind of community, could organize and so perfectly execute an enormous storage program like this one?

A community of robots, perhaps.

A community of ants.

Susan continued to prowl through the stacks, her confusion increasing. She found scores of boxes labeled INFORMAL HOLIDAYS: HALLOWEEN. She peeled the tape off one of those boxes and opened it. It was crammed full of masks: goblins, witches, gnomes, vampires, the Frankenstein monster, werewolves, alien creatures, and assorted ghouls. She opened another box and found Halloween party decorations: orange and black paper streamers, plastic jack-o'-lanterns, bundles of real Indian corn, black paper cutouts of cats and ghosts. This huge collection of Halloween gear was not just for parties at St. John's Church; there was enough stuff here to decorate the entire town and to costume all of its children.

She moved along the aisles, reading labels on some of the hundreds of other containers:

INFORMAL HOLIDAYS: VALENTINE'S DAY
FORMAL HOLIDAYS: CHRISTMAS
FORMAL HOLIDAYS: NEW YEAR'S EVE
FORMAL HOLIDAYS: INDEPENDENCE DAY
FORMAL HOLIDAYS: THANKSGIVING
PRIVATE PARTIES: BABY SHOWER
PRIVATE PARTIES: BIRTHDAY
PRIVATE PARTIES: WEDDING ANNIVERSARY
PRIVATE PARTIES: BAR MITZVAH
PRIVATE PARTIES: BACHELOR/STAG

Susan finally stopped examining the boxes and the cabinets because she realized there were no answers to be found among them. They only raised new questions about Willawauk. In fact, the more she probed through this place, the more confused and disoriented and depressed she became. She felt as if she had chased a white rabbit and had fallen down a hole into a bizarre and considerably less than friendly Wonderland. Why were bar mitzvah decorations stored in St. John's Lutheran Church? And wasn't it strange for a church to store supplies for a stag party? Dirty movies, posters of naked women, party napkins bearing obscene cartoons—that sort of stuff kept in a *church?* Why wasn't the parsonage really a parsonage? Was there a Reverend Potter B. Kinfield, or was he only a fictitious character, a name on a gate plaque? If he existed, where did he live, if not in the parsonage? Was Willawauk inhabited by four thousand or more pack rats who never threw *anything* away? What was going on in this town? At a glance, everything appeared to be normal. But on closer inspection, there hadn't been a single thing about Willawauk that hadn't turned out to be strange.

How many other buildings in town were not what they appeared to be?

She walked wearily out of the storage aisles and returned to the front door. She was growing increasingly shaky. She wondered if there was any chance at all that she would eventually be able to climb out of the rabbit hole, back into the real world.

Probably not.

Outside again, she could barely stay on her feet. Her rain-sodden clothes felt as if they weighed a couple of thousand pounds. The impact of the raindrops was incredible, and the wind struck with sledgehammer blows that threatened to drive her to her knees.

She knew that Harch and the others would come for her, sooner or later, and until they did, she just wanted to sit where it was warm. All hope of escape had left her.

The church might be warm. At least it would be dry, and she would be out of the cold wind. That is—if the church was real. If it wasn't just a facade, like a false-front set on a Hollywood backlot.

There was light in the church, anyway. Maybe that was a good sign; maybe there would be heat, too.

She climbed the dozen brick steps toward the heavy, hand-carved oak doors, hoping they were unlocked.

The doors of a church were supposed to remain unlocked at all times, twenty-four hours a day, every day, so that you could go inside to pray or to be comforted whenever you needed to escape from the pain of life. That's the way it was *supposed* to be, but you could never be sure of anything in good old Willawauk, Oregon.

She reached the doors. There were four doors, two sets of two. She tried the one on the extreme right. It was unlocked.

At least *something* in Willawauk was as it should be.

Pulling open the door, about to step into the building, she heard an engine in the street behind her. The hiss of tires on the wet pavement. The squeal of brakes.

She turned and looked down the steps.

An ambulance had drawn up to the curb in front of the church. Three words were painted on the side of it: WILLAWAUK COUNTY HOSPITAL.

"There is no such goddamned thing," Susan said, surprised to find a drop of anger remaining in her vast pool of resignation and depression.

Jellicoe and Parker got out of the ambulance and looked up at her. They were no longer dressed as sheriff's deputies. They were wearing white raincoats and white rain hats, black boots. They were playing hospital orderlies again.

Susan didn't intend to run from them. She couldn't. Her strength and her will power were gone, used up.

On the other hand, she wasn't going to walk down the steps and into their arms, either. They would have to come and get her and carry her back to the ambulance.

Meanwhile, she would go inside where it was warm, go as far toward the front of the church as her legs would take her, so that Jellicoe and Parker would have to carry her that much farther when they took her out to the ambulance. It was a small, perhaps meaningless protest. Pathetic, really. But passive resistance was the only kind of which she was still capable.

The church *was* warm. It felt wonderful.

She shuffled through the vestibule. Into the church proper. Down the center aisle. Toward the altar.

It was a pretty church. Lots of wood, marble, and brass. During the day, when light was coming in through the stained-glass windows, painting everything in bright hues, it would be beautiful.

She heard Carl Jellicoe and Herbert Parker enter the church behind her.

Her aching, quivering legs supported her all the way to the front pew, but she knew they would crumple under her if she took another step.

"Hey, slut," Jellicoe said from the back of the church.

She refused to turn and face them, refused to acknowledge her fear of them.

She sat down on the first, highly polished pew.

"Hey, bitch."

Susan faced forward, staring at the large brass cross behind the altar. She wished she were a religious woman, wished she were able to take comfort from the sight of the cross.

At the front of the church, to the left of the altar, the door to the sacristy opened. Two men came out.

Ernest Harch.

Randy Lee Quince.

The extent to which she had been manipulated was clear now. Her escape hadn't been her own idea. It had been *their* idea, part of *their* game. They had been teasing her the way a cat will sometimes tease a captured mouse: letting it think there's a real hope of freedom, letting it squirm away, letting it run a few steps, then snatching it back again, brutally. The mezuzah hadn't been dropped accidentally in the bathroom. It had been left there on purpose, to nudge her toward an escape again, so that the cats could have their bit of fun.

She'd never really had a chance.

Harch and Quince descended the altar steps and moved to the communion railing.

Jellicoe and Parker appeared in the aisle at her side. They were both grinning.

She was limp. She couldn't even raise a hand to protect herself let alone to strike out against them.

"Has it been as much fun for you as it's been for us?" Carl Jellicoe asked her.

Parker laughed.

Susan said nothing. Stared straight ahead.

Harch and Quince opened a gate in the communion railing and walked up to the first pew, where Susan sat. They stared down at her, smiling. All of them smiling.

She stared between Quince and Harch, trying to keep her eyes fixed steadily on the cross. She didn't want them to see her quaking with fear; she was determined to deny them that pleasure, at least this one time.

Harch stooped down, squarely in front of her, forcing her to look at him.

"Poor baby," he said, his raspy voice making a mockery of any attempt at sympathy. "Is our poor little bitch tired? Did she run her little butt off tonight?"

Susan wanted to close her eyes and fall back into the darkness that waited within her. She wanted to go away inside herself for a long, long time.

But she fought that urge. She met Harch's hateful, frost-gray eyes, and her stomach churned, but she didn't look away.

"Cat got your tongue?"

"I hope not," Quince said. "I wanted to cut her tongue out myself!"

Jellicoe giggled.

To Susan, Harch said, "You want to know what's going on?"

She didn't respond.

"Do you want to know what this is all about, Susan?"

She glared at him.

"Oh, you're so tough," he said mockingly. "The strong, silent type. I *love* the strong, silent type."

The other three men laughed.

Harch said, "I'm sure you want to know what's going on, Susan. In fact I'm sure you're *dying* to know."

"Dying," Jellicoe said, giggling.

The others laughed, sharing a secret joke.

"The car accident you had," Harch said. "Two miles south of the turnoff to the Viewtop Inn. That part was true."

She refused to be prodded into speaking.

"You rolled the car over an embankment," Harch said. "Slammed it into a couple of big trees. We weren't lying about that. The rest of it, of course, was all untrue."

"We're all shameless fibbers," Jellicoe said, giggling.

"You didn't spend three weeks in a coma," Harch told her. "And the hospital was a fake, of course. All of it was lies, deceptions, a clever little game, a chance to have some fun with you."

She waited, continuing to meet his cold gaze.

"You didn't have a chance to languish in a coma," Harch said. "You died instantly in the crash."

Oh, shit, she thought wearily. What are they up to now?

"Instantly," Parker said.

"Massive brain damage," Jellicoe said.

"Not just a little cut on the forehead," Quince said.

"You're dead, Susan," Harch said.

"You're here with us now," Jellicoe said.

No, no, no, she thought. This is crazy. This is madness.

"You're in Hell," Harch said.

"With us," Jellicoe said.

"And we've been assigned to entertain you," Quince said.

"Which we're looking forward to," Parker said.

Quince said, "Very much."

No!

"Never thought you'd wind up here," Jellicoe said.

"Not a goody-goody bitch like you," Parker said.

"Must have all sorts of secret vices," Jellicoe said.

"We're really glad you could make it," Quince said.

Harch just stared at her, stared hard, his cold eyes freezing her to the core.

"We'll have a party," Jellicoe said.

Quince said, "An endless party."

"Just the five of us," Jellicoe said.

"Old friends," Parker said.

Susan closed her eyes. She knew it wasn't true. It *couldn't* be true. There wasn't such a place as Hell. No Hell or Heaven. That was what she had always believed.

And didn't nonbelievers go to Hell?

"Let's fuck her now, right here," Jellicoe said.

"Yeah," Quince said.

She opened her eyes.

Jellicoe was unzipping his pants.

Harch said, "No. Tomorrow night. The seventh anniversary of my death. I want it to have that significance for her."

Jellicoe hesitated, his fly half undone.

"Besides," Parker said, "we want to do it to her in the right place. This isn't the right place."

"Exactly," Harch said.

Please, God, please, Susan thought, let me find my way back up the rabbit hole . . . or let me just go to sleep. I could just lay back here against the pew . . . and go to sleep . . . forever.

"Let's get the bitch out of here," Harch said. He stood, reached down, seized Susan by her sweater, dragged her to her feet. "I've waited a long time for this," he said, his face close to hers.

She tried to pull away from him.

He slapped her face.

Her teeth rattled; her vision blurred. She sagged, and other hands grabbed her.

They carried her out of the church. They weren't gentle about it.

In the ambulance, they strapped her down, and Harch began to prepare a syringe for her.

Finally, she rose out of her lethargy far enough to speak. "If this is Hell, why do you need to give me an injection to knock me out? Why don't you just cast a spell on me?"

"Because *this* is so much more fun," Harch said, grinning, and with savage glee he rammed the hypodermic needle into her arm.

She cried out in pain.

Then she slept.

17

FLICKERING LIGHT.

Dancing shadows.

A high, dark ceiling.

Susan was in bed. The hospital bed.

Her arm hurt where Harch had stabbed her viciously with the needle. Her entire body ached.

This wasn't her old room. This place was cool, too cool for a hospital room. Her body was warm underneath the blankets, but her shoulders and neck and face were quite cool. This place was damp, too, and musty. Very musty.

And familiar.

Her vision was blurry. She squinted, but she still couldn't see anything.

Squinting made her dizzy. She felt as if she were on a merry-go-round instead of a bed; she spun around, around, and down into sleep again.

Later.

Before she opened her eyes, she lay for a moment, listening to the roar of falling water. Was it still raining outside? It sounded like a deluge, like Armageddon, another Great Flood.

She opened her eyes, and she was immediately dizzy again, although not as dizzy as before. There was flickering light, dancing shadows, as there had been the first time. But now she realized that it was candlelight, disturbed by crossdrafts.

She turned her head on the pillow and saw the candles. Ten thick cylinders of wax were arranged on the rocks and on the nearest limestone ledges and formations.

No!

She turned her head the other way, toward the roaring water, but she couldn't see anything. The candlelight drove the darkness back only a distance of about fifteen feet. The waterfall was much farther away than that, at least eighty or a hundred feet away, but there was no doubt that it was out there, tumbling and frothing in the blackest corner of the cave.

She was in the House of Thunder.

No, no, no, she told herself. No, this must be a dream. Or I'm delirious.

She closed her eyes, shutting out the candlelight. But she couldn't shut out the musty smell of the cavern or the thunderous noise of the underground waterfall.

She was three thousand miles away from the House of Thunder, dammit. She was in Oregon, not Pennsylvania.

Madness.

Or Hell.

Someone jerked the blankets off her, and she opened her eyes with a snap, gasping, crying out.

It was Ernest Harch. He put one hand on her leg, and she realized that she was naked. He slid his hand along her bare thigh, across her bristling pubic thatch, across her belly, to her breasts.

She went rigid at his touch.

He smiled. "No, not yet. Not yet, you sweet bitch. Not for a while yet. Tonight. That's when I want it. Right at the hour I died in prison. Right at the minute that damned nigger stuck a knife in my throat, *that's* when I'm going to stick a knife in your throat, and I'm going to be up inside you at the same time, screwing you, spurting inside you just as I push the knife deep into your pretty neck. Tonight, not now."

He took his hand off her breasts. He raised the other hand, and she saw that he was holding a hypodermic syringe.

She tried to sit up.

Jellicoe appeared and pushed her down.

"I want you to rest for a while," Harch said. "Rest up for the party tonight."

Again, he was vicious with the needle.

As he finished administering the injection, he said, "Carl, you know what I'm going to like most about killing her?"

"What's that?" Jellicoe asked.

"It's not the end. It's just the beginning. I get to kill her again and again."

Jellicoe giggled.

Harch said, "That's your fate, bitch. That's the way you're going to spend eternity. We're going to use you every night, and every night we're going to kill you. We'll do it a different way each time. There are thousands of ways, an infinite number of ways to die. You're going to experience all of them."

Madness.

She sank down into a drugged sleep.

■ Underwater. She was underwater and drowning.

She opened her eyes, gasping for breath, and realized that she was only under the *sound* of water. The waterfall.

She was still in bed. She tried to sit up, and the covers slid off her; but she hadn't the strength to stay sitting up, and she collapsed back against the pillows, heart pounding.

She closed her eyes.

For just a minute.

Oh, maybe for an hour.

No way to tell for sure.

"*Susan . . .*"

She opened her eyes, and she was filled with dread. Her vision was smeary, but she saw a face in the flickering light.

"*Susan . . .*"

He drew nearer, and she saw him clearly. It was Jerry. The awful, rotting face. His lips were riper, more swollen than before, bursting with pus.

"*Susan . . .*"

She screamed. The harder she screamed, the faster the bed seemed to spin. She whirled off into deepest space.

■ And woke again.

The effects of the drug had almost worn off. She lay with her eyes closed, afraid to open them.

She wished she had not awakened. She didn't want to be awake ever again. She wanted to die.

"Susan?"

She lay perfectly still.

Harch thumbed one of her eyelids open, and she twitched in surprise.

He grinned. "Don't try to fool me, you dumb bitch. I know you're there."

She felt numb. Afraid but numb. Maybe, if she was lucky, the numbness would grow and grow until that was the *only* thing she could feel.

"It's almost time," Harch said. "Did you know that? In an hour or so, the party starts. In three hours, I'll cut your throat wide open. See, that gives us two hours for the party. Wouldn't want to disappoint the other guys, would we? Two hours ought to satisfy them, don't you think? You'll wear them out fast, a sexy girl like you."

None of it seemed real. It was too crazy, too senseless, too fuzzy at the edges to be real. A hospital bed in the middle of a cave? Not real at all. The terror, the violence, the implied violence, the purity of Harch's evil . . . all of that had the quality of a dream.

Yet she could feel the two separate pains of the two needles that he had jammed in her arms. *That* felt real enough.

Harch threw the covers aside, exposing her again.

"Bastard," she said weakly, so weakly that she could barely hear her own voice.

"Just getting a preview," Harch said. "Say, baby, aren't you looking forward to it as much as I am? Hmmmmm?"

She closed her eyes, seeking oblivion, and she—

"*Harch!*"

—heard McGee shout her tormentor's name.

She opened her eyes and saw Harch turning away from her with a startled look on his face. He said, "What are *you* doing here?"

Lacking the strength to sit all the way up in bed, Susan lifted her head as far off the pillow as she could, which wasn't very far, and she saw Jeff McGee. He was only a few feet from the end of the bed. The draft-blown candle flames cast wavering shadows over him, so that he appeared to be wearing a rippling black cape. He was holding a long-barreled pistol, and it was pointed at Harch.

Harch said, "What in the hell are you—"

McGee shot him in the face. Harch pitched backwards, out of sight, and hit the floor with a sickening thud.

The pistol had made only a whispering sound, and Susan realized that part of the long barrel was a silencer.

That soft hiss, the sight of Harch's face exploding, the deadweight sound of him hitting the floor—all of that had the unmistakably gritty feeling of reality. It wasn't the stylized, exaggerated, endlessly extended, surreal violence to which she had been subjected during the last few days; there wasn't anything remotely dreamlike about this. It was death: cold, hard, quick.

McGee came around to the side of the bed.

Susan blinked at the pistol. She was no less confused by this strange turn of events. She felt herself teetering on the edge of a chasm. "Am I next?"

He shoved the gun in a pocket of his overcoat.

He was carrying a bag in his other hand, and he dropped that on the bed beside her. No, not a bag. It was a pillowcase, stuffed full of something.

"We're getting out of here," he said.

He began pulling clothes out of the pillowcase. Her clothes. Panties. A pair of dark slacks. A white sweater. A pair of penny loafers.

There was still a large, round object in the bottom of the pillowcase, and she regarded it with growing fear. The dreamlike feeling overtook her again; reality faded; and she was suddenly sure that the last thing in that pillowcase was Jerry Stein's severed, rotting head.

"No," she said. "Stop!"

He pulled out the last object. It was only her corduroy blazer, which had been rolled into a ball.

Not a dead man's head.

But she didn't feel any better. She was still adrift, unable to grab at the edge of reality and stabilize herself.

"No," she said. "No. I can't go through any more of this. Let's just get it over with."

McGee looked at her oddly for a moment, then understanding came into his blue eyes. "You think this is just a setup for another series of nasty little scenes."

"I'm very, very tired," she said.

"It's not," he said. "It's not a setup."

"I just want to be finished with this."

"Listen, half of your weariness is because of the drug they've been pumping into you. You'll perk up a bit in a little while."

"Go away."

She couldn't hold her head up any longer. She fell back on the pillow.

She didn't even care that she was naked before him. She didn't reach for the blankets. She wasn't sure she could pull them up, anyway. Besides, any attempt at modesty was ludicrous after what they had already done to her, after what they had seen of her.

She was cold. That didn't matter, either. Nothing mattered.

"Look," McGee said, "I don't expect you to understand what's going on. I'll explain later. Just trust me for now."

"I did," Susan said softly. "I trusted you."

"And here I am."

"Yes. And here you are."

"Here I am, *rescuing* you, dummy." He said it with what seemed to be very real frustration and affection.

"Rescuing me from what?"

"From Hell," he said. "Wasn't that the latest line they were feeding you? Hell. That's what the program called for."

"Program?"

He sighed and shook his head. "We don't have time for this now. You've got to trust me."

"Go away."

He slipped an arm under her shoulders and lifted her into a sitting position. He snatched up the white sweater and tried to get her arms into the sleeves.

She resisted him as best she could. "No more," she said. "No more sick games."

"Christ!" he said. He dropped the sweater and eased her back onto the pillow. "Stay here and listen. Can you *listen*?"

Before she could respond, he withdrew a penlight from his overcoat pocket, switched it on, and hurried away, into the darkness. The sound of the waterfall, toward which he was headed, soon masked the *tap-tap-tap* of his footsteps.

Maybe he would leave her alone now. Or finish her off. One or the other.

She closed her eyes.

The roar of the waterfall stopped abruptly.

In an instant, the House of Thunder became the House of Silence.

She opened her eyes, frowning. For a second, she thought she had gone deaf.

McGee shouted to her from the darkness. "Hear that? Nothing but a tape recording of a waterfall." He was drawing nearer as he spoke; there was no sound to mask his footsteps now. "It was a tape recording, blasting through four big quadraphonic speakers." He stepped into the glow of the candles and switched off his penlight. "Driest waterfall you'll ever see. And this cave? It's a bunch of hollowed-out rocks, papier mâché, cardboard and spit. A stage setting. That's why there're only a few candles; if you could see only a few feet farther, you'd know it was just a hoax. It's set in the middle of the high school gymnasium, so that you get a feeling of open space beyond the darkness. I'd turn the lights on and show you, except I don't dare draw any attention. The windows are blacked out, but even if a little light escaped, someone might notice—and come running. And that musty smell, in case you're wondering, is *canned* odor, guaranteed to make a spelunker feel right at home. Some of our people whipped it up in the lab. Aren't they handy?"

"What *is* Willawauk?" she asked, getting interested in spite of herself and in spite of her fear that she was being set up once more.

"I'll explain in the car," McGee said. "There isn't time now. You'll just *have* to trust me."

She hesitated, head spinning.

He said, "If you don't trust me, you might *never* find out what Willawauk is."

She let her breath out slowly. "All right."

"I *knew* you had moxie," he said, smiling.

"I'll need help."

"I know."

She let him dress her. She felt like a little girl as he put her sweater on for her, pulled her panties and then her jeans up her legs, and slipped her shoes on her feet.

"I don't think I can walk," she said.

"I didn't intend to ask you to walk. Can you at least hold the flashlight?"

"I think I can do that."

He picked her up. "Light as a feather. A *big* feather. Hold tight to my neck with your free arm."

She directed the light where he told her, and he carried her out of the phony cavern, across the floor of the gymnasium. The beam of the small flash bounced off the highly polished wood floor, and in that pale glow, she was aware that they passed under a basketball hoop. Then they went down a set of concrete steps, through a door that McGee had left ajar, and into a locker room.

The lights were on here, and three dead men were sprawled in the area between the coach's office and the lockers. Jellicoe and Parker were on the floor. Half of Jellicoe's face was gone. Parker had two holes in his chest. Quince was draped over a bench, still dripping blood onto the floor from a wound in his neck.

Beginning to huff a bit, McGee carried her between two rows of tall lockers, past the shower room, to another door that had been left ajar. He shouldered through it, into a well-lighted hallway.

Another dead man lay on the floor here.

"Who's he?" she asked.

"Guard," McGee said.

They went a short distance down the hall, turned the corner into another hall, and went to a set of metal doors, beside which lay another corpse, apparently another guard.

"Kill the flash," McGee said.

She switched it off, and he leaned against the pushbar handle on the metal doors, and then they were outside.

It was a clear, cool night. Almost an entire day had passed while she had slid in and out of a drugged stupor.

Two cars waited in the school lot. Breathing hard now, McGee took her to a blue Chevrolet and put her down beside it. She leaned against the car, for her legs were too limp to support her even for the few seconds he took to open the door and help her inside.

They drove boldly out of Willawauk by way of Main Street, which eventually turned into a county road. They were not only headed away from Willawauk, but also away from the building in which she had been hospitalized. Neither of them spoke until the last lights of town were out of sight, until only wild, green countryside lay around them.

Huddled in the passenger's seat, Susan looked over at McGee. His face was strange in the green luminescence of the dashboard gauges. Strange—but not threatening.

She still didn't entirely trust him. She didn't know what to believe.

"Tell me," she said.

"It's hard to know where to begin."

"Anywhere, dammit. Just begin."

"The Milestone Corporation," he said.

"Back there on the hill."

"No, no. That sign you saw on the hospital lawn when you escaped in the Pontiac—that was just put up to confuse you, to add to your disorientation."

"Then the place is really a hospital."

"A hospital—and other things. The real Milestone Corporation is in Newport Beach."

"And I work for them?"

"Oh, yes. That's all true. Although it wasn't Phil Gomez you spoke with on the phone. That was someone in Willawauk, pretending to be Gomez."

"What do I *do* at Milestone?"

"It's a think tank, just like I told you. But it doesn't work with private industry. Milestone's a front for a super-secret U.S. military think tank that functions under the direct control of the Secretary of Defense and the President. Congress doesn't even know it exists; its appropriations are obtained in a *very* roundabout fashion.

At Milestone, two dozen of the finest scientific minds in the country have been brought together with perhaps the most sophisticated data library and computer system in the world. Every man and woman at Milestone is a brilliant specialist in his or her field, and every science is covered."

"I'm one of the experts?" she asked, still not able to recall a thing about Milestone, still not even convinced that it actually existed.

"You're one of two particle physicists they have there."

"I can't remember."

"I know."

As he drove through the dark, forested countryside, McGee told her everything he knew about Milestone—or at least, everything he *professed* to know.

Milestone (according to McGee) had one primary goal: to develop an ultimate weapon—a particle beam, some new kind of laser, a new biological weapon, *anything*—which would in one way or another render nuclear weaponry not just obsolete but useless. The U.S. government had for some time been convinced that the Soviet Union was seeking nuclear superiority with the express intention of launching a first-strike attack the moment that such a monstrous tactic was likely to result in a clean, painless Soviet victory. But it hadn't been possible, until recently, to sell the American public on the idea that rearmament was a desperate necessity. Therefore, in the middle Seventies, the President and the Secretary of Defense could see no hope except a miracle; a miracle weapon that would cancel out the Soviet arsenal and free mankind from the specter of an atomic holocaust. While it wasn't possible to launch a massive arms buildup costing hundreds of billions of dollars, it *was* possible to secretly establish a new research facility, better funded than any had ever been before, and hope that American ingenuity would pull the country's ass out of the fire. In a sense, Milestone became America's last best hope.

"But surely that kind of research was already being done," Susan said. "Why was there a need to establish a new program?"

"Anti-war elements within the research community—primarily student lab assistants—were stealing information and leaking it to anyone who would listen and who would join the battle against the Pentagon war machine. In the mid-Seventies, the university-based weapons research establishment was crumbling. The President wanted that kind of research to go forward strictly in the shadows, so that any breakthroughs would remain the exclusive property of the United States.

"For years, the very existence of Milestone was unknown to Soviet Intelligence. When agents of the KGB finally learned of it, they were afraid that the U.S. might be nearing—or might already have achieved—its goal of rendering the Soviet war machine impotent. They knew they had to get their hands on one of Milestone's scientists and engage in weeks of unrestrained interrogation."

The Chevy began to accelerate too rapidly down a long, steep hill, and McGee tapped the brakes.

"The scientists at Milestone are encouraged to familiarize themselves with one another's fields of interest, in order to search for areas of overlap and to benefit from cross-fertilization of ideas. *Every one of the twenty-four department chiefs at Milestone knows a great deal about the workable ideas that have come out of the place so far.* It means that many of the Pentagon's future plans could be compromised by any *one* of the Milestone people."

"So the Soviets decided to snatch me," Susan said, gradually beginning to believe him, but still filled with doubts.

"Yeah. The KGB managed to find out who worked at Milestone, and it investigated everyone's background. You seemed the most likely target, for you were having serious doubts about the morality of weapons research. You had started on that road immediately after earning your doctorate, when you were only twenty-six, before you were really old enough to have developed a sophisticated system of values. As you grew older, you also grew concerned about your work and its impact on future generations. Doubts surfaced. You expressed them to your fellow workers, and you even took a month-long leave of absence to consider your position, during which time you apparently reached no conclusions, because you returned to work, still doubting."

"As far as I'm concerned, you might as well be talking about a total stranger," Susan said, regarding him suspiciously. "Why can't I remember any of this now that you're telling me about it?"

"I'll explain in a moment," he said. "We're about to be stopped."

They reached the bottom of the long hill and turned a bend. There was a mile-long straightaway ahead, and there seemed to be a roadblock straddling the center of it.

"What's that?" Susan asked anxiously.

"A security checkpoint."

"Is this where you turn me over to them? Is this where the game gets nasty again?" she asked, still having trouble believing that he was on her side.

He glanced at her, frowning. "Give me a chance, okay? Just give me a chance. We're leaving a highly restricted military zone, and we have to pass through security." He fished two sets of papers out of a coat pocket while he drove with one hand. "Slouch down and pretend to be asleep."

She did as he said, watching the brightly lighted checkpoint—two huts, a gate between them—through slitted eyes. Then she closed her eyes and let her mouth sag open as if she were sleeping deeply.

"Not a word out of you."

"All right," she said.

"No matter what happens—not a word."

McGee slowed the car, stopped, and wound down the windows.

Susan heard booted feet approaching.

The guard spoke, and McGee answered. Not in English.

Susan was so startled to hear them speaking in a foreign language that she almost opened her eyes. It hadn't occurred to her to ask him why she must feign sleep when he possessed papers that would get them through the checkpoint. He hadn't wanted her to be required to talk to the guards; one word of English, and they would both be finished.

The wait was interminable, but at last she heard the power-operated gate rolling out of the way. The car moved.

She opened her eyes but didn't dare glance back. "Where are we?" she asked McGee.

"You didn't recognize the language?"

"I'm afraid maybe I did."

"Russian," he said.

She was speechless. She shook her head: *no, no*.

"Thirty-some miles from the Black Sea," he said. "That's where we're headed. To the sea."

"*Inside the Soviet Union?* That's not possible. That's just crazy!"

"It's true."

"No," she said, huddling against the passenger door. "It can't be true. This *is* another setup."

"No," he said. "Hear me out."

She had no choice but to hear him out. She wasn't going to throw herself from a speeding car. And even if she could get out of the car without killing herself, she wouldn't be able to run. She wouldn't even be able to walk very far. The effect of the drugs had begun to fade, and she felt strength returning to her legs again, but she was nevertheless exhausted, virtually helpless.

Besides, maybe McGee was telling the truth this time. She wouldn't want to bet her life on it. But maybe.

He said, "KGB agents kidnapped you while you were on your vacation in Oregon."

"There never was a car accident, then?"

"No. That was just part of the program we designed to support the Willawauk charade. In reality, you were snatched in Oregon and smuggled out of the U.S. on a diplomatic flight."

She frowned. "Why can't I remember that?"

"You were sedated throughout the trip to Moscow."

"But I should at least remember being kidnapped," she insisted.

"All memories of that event were carefully scrubbed from your mind with certain chemical and hypnotic techniques—"

"Brainwashing."

"Yes. It was necessary to remove the memory of the kidnapping in order that the Willawauk program would seem like reality to you."

She had dozens of questions about Willawauk and about this "program" to which he repeatedly referred, but she restrained herself and allowed him to tell it in his own way.

"In Moscow, you were first taken to a KGB detention facility, a truly nasty place at Lubyianka Prison. When you failed to respond to questioning and to the standard array of psychological trickery, they got rougher with you. They didn't beat you or anything like that. No thumbscrews. But in some ways, it was worse than physical torture. They used a variety of unpleasant drugs on you, stuff with extremely dangerous side effects, very physically and mentally debilitating crap that should *never* be used on a human being for *any* reason. Of course, it was all just standard KGB procedure for extracting information from a stubborn source. But as soon as they employed those methods, as soon as they tried to *force* answers from you, a strange thing happened. You lost all conscious memory of your work at Milestone, every last scrap of it, and only a gaping hole was left where those memories had been."

"There's still a gaping hole," she said.

"Yes. Even drugged, even perfectly docile, you were unable to tell the KGB anything. They worked on you for five days, five very intense days, before they finally discovered what had happened."

McGee stopped talking and cut the car's speed in half as they approached a small village of about a hundred houses. This tiny village didn't resemble Willa-wauk in any way whatsoever. It was very obviously not an American place. Except for a few scattered electric lights, it appeared as if it belonged in another century. Some of the houses had stone roofs, others had board and thatched roofs. All the structures were squat, with very small windows, drab and somber places. It looked medieval.

When they had passed through the town and were on the open road again, McGee put his foot down hard on the accelerator once more.

"You were about to tell me why I lost all my memories of Milestone," Susan said.

"Yeah. Well, as it turns out, when anyone goes to work for the Milestone project, he must agree to undergo a series of highly sophisticated behavioral modification treatments that make it impossible for him to talk about his work with anyone outside of Milestone. If he won't agree to undergo the treatment, then he doesn't get the job. In addition, deep in their subconscious minds, all the employees of Milestone are fitted with cunningly engineered psychological mechanisms that can trigger memory blockages, memory blockages that prevent foreign agents from *forcing* vital information out of them. When someone tries to pry secret data out of a Milestone employee by means of torture or drugs or hypnosis, *all* of that employee's conscious knowledge of his work drops instantly far, far down into his deep subconscious mind, behind an impenetrable block, where it cannot be squeezed out."

Now she knew why she couldn't even recall what her laboratory at Milestone had looked like. "All the memories *are* still there, inside me, somewhere."

"Yes. When and if you get out of Russia, when you get back to the States, Milestone undoubtedly has some procedure for dissolving the block and bringing back your memory. And it's probably a procedure that can *only* be carried out at Milestone, something involving you and the computer, perhaps a series of block-releasing code words that the computer will reveal only to you, and only after you've been positively identified to it by letting it scan your fingerprints. Of course, this is merely conjecture. We don't really know *how* Milestone would restore your memory; if we knew, we'd have used the same technique. Instead, we had to resort to the Willawauk program in hopes of shattering the block with a brutal series of psychological shocks."

The night flashed by them. The land was much flatter now than it had been around Willawauk. There were fewer trees. A moon had risen, providing a ghostly radiance.

Susan slouched in her seat, both weary and tense, watching McGee's face as he spoke, trying hard to detect any sign of deception, desperately hoping that he wasn't just setting her up for *another* brutal psychological shock.

"A memory block can be based on any emotion—love, hate, fear—but the most effective is fear," McGee said. "That was the inhibitor that Milestone used when creating your block. *Fear.* On a deep subconscious level, you are terrified of revealing anything whatsoever about Milestone, for they have used hypnotic suggestion and drugs to convince you that you will die horribly and painfully the moment that you make even the smallest revelation to foreign agents. A fear block is by far the most difficult to break; usually, getting through it is utterly impossible—especially when it's as well implanted as your block is."

"But you found a way."

"Not me, personally. The KGB employs hordes of scientists who specialize in behavioral modification techniques—brainwashing and so forth—and a few of them think that a fear block *can* be demolished if the subject—that's you, in this case—is confronted with a fear far greater than the one upon which the block is based. Now, it isn't easy to find a fear that's greater than the fear of death. With most of us, that's numero uno. But the KGB had very thoroughly researched your life before they'd decided to snatch you, and when they looked through your dossier, they thought they saw your weak spot. They were looking for an event in your past that could be resurrected and reshaped into a living, breathing nightmare, into something you would fear more than death."

"The House of Thunder," she said numbly. "Ernest Harch."

"Yes," McGee said. "That was the key to the plan they put together. After studying you for some time, the KGB determined that you were an unusually well-ordered, efficient, rational person; they knew you abhorred disorder and sloppy thinking. In fact you seemed to be almost compulsively, obsessively ordered in every aspect of your life."

"Obsessive? Yes," she said, "I guess maybe I am. Or I *was.*"

"To the KGB, it appeared that the best way to make you come apart at the seams was to plunge you into a nightmare world in which *everything* gradually became more and more irrational, a world in which the dead could come back to life, in which nothing and no one was what it seemed to be. So they brought you to Willawauk, and they sealed off one wing of the behavioral research hospital located there, turned it into a stage for their elaborate charades. They intended to push you slowly toward a mental and/or an emotional collapse, culminating in a scene in the phony House of Thunder. They had a very nasty bit of business planned. Rape. Repeated rape and torture at the hands of the four 'dead' men."

Susan shook her head, bewildered. "But forcing me into a mental and emotional collapse . . . What good would that do them? Even if the fear block was broken in the process, I wouldn't have been in any condition to provide them with the information they wanted. I'd have been a babbling fool . . . or catatonic."

"Not forever. A mental and emotional breakdown brought on by extreme *short-term* pressure is the easiest form of mental illness to cure," McGee said. "As soon as they'd broken you, they would have removed your memory block by promising relief from terror in return for your total submission and cooperation. Then they'd have immediately begun to rehabilitate you, nursing you back to sanity, or at least to a semblance of it, to a state in which you could be questioned and in which you could be relied upon to provide accurate information."

"But wait," she said. "Wait a minute. Getting together the look-alikes, writing the script for the whole damned thing, working out all the contingencies, converting the wing of the hospital . . . all of that must have taken a lot of time. I was only kidnapped a few weeks ago . . . wasn't I?"

He didn't answer right away.

"*Wasn't I?*" she demanded.

"You've been inside the Soviet Union for more than a year," McGee said.

"No. Oh, no. No, no, I can't have been."

"You have. Most of the time, you were on ice in Lubyianka, just sitting in a cell, waiting for something to happen. But you don't remember that part of it. They erased all of that before bringing you to Willawauk."

Her confusion gave way to white-hot anger. "*Erased?*" She sat up straight in her seat, her hands squeezed into fists. "You say it so casually. Erased. You talk as if I'm a goddamned tape recorder! Jesus Christ, I spent a year in a stinking prison, and then they stole that year from me, and then they put me through this thing with Harch and the others . . . " Rage choked off her voice.

But she realized that she now believed him. Almost. She had almost no doubt at all that *this* was the truth.

"You have a right to be furious," McGee said, glancing at her, his eyes unreadable in the glow from the dashboard. "But please don't be angry with me. I didn't have anything to do with what happened to you then. I didn't have anything to do with you until they finally brought you to Willawauk, and then I had to bide my time until there was a chance of breaking you out of there."

They rode in silence for a minute, while Susan's anger cooled from a boil to a simmer.

They came to the edge of the moonlit sea and turned south on a highway where, at last, there was other traffic, though not much. The other vehicles were mostly trucks.

Susan said, "Who the hell *are* you? How do you fit into this whole thing?"

"To understand that," he said, "you'll have to understand about Willawauk first."

Confusion and suspicion roiled in her again. "Even in a year, they couldn't possibly have built that entire town. Besides, don't tell me they'd go to all *that* trouble just to pump me about the work being done at Milestone."

"You're right," he said. "Willawauk was built in the early 1950s. It was designed to be a perfect model of an average, American small town, and it's constantly being modernized and refined."

"But why? Why a model American town here in the middle of the USSR?"

"Willawauk is a training facility," McGee said. "It's where Soviet deep-cover agents are trained to think like Americans, to *be* Americans."

"What's a . . . deep-cover agent?" she asked as McGee swung the Chevy into the outer lane and passed a lumbering, exhaust-belching truck of stolid Soviet make.

"Every year," McGee said, "between three and four hundred children, exceptionally bright three- and four-year-olds, are chosen to come to Willawauk. They're taken from their parents, who are not told what the child has been chosen for and who will never see their child again. The kids are assigned new foster parents in Willawauk. From that moment on, two things happen to them. First, they go through intense, daily indoctrination sessions designed to turn them into fanatical Soviet Communists. And believe me, I don't use the word 'fanatical' lightly. Most of those kids are transformed into fanatics who make the Ayatollah Khomeini's followers seem like sober, reasonable Oxford professors. There's a two-hour indoctrination session every morning of their lives; worse, subliminal indoctrination tapes are played during the night, while they sleep."

"Sounds like they're creating a small army of child robots," Susan said.

"That's precisely what they're doing. Child robots, spy robots. Anyway, secondly, the kids are taught to live like Americans, to think like Americans, and to *be* Americans—at least on the surface. They must be able to pass for patriotic Americans without ever revealing their underlying, fanatical devotion to the Soviet cause. Only American English is spoken in Willawauk. These children grow up without knowing a word of Russian. All books are in English. All the movies are American movies. Television shows are taped from the three American networks and from various independent stations—all kinds of shows, including entertainment, sports, news—and are then replayed to every house in Willawauk on a closed-circuit TV system. These kids grow up with the same media backgrounds, with the same experiences as real American kids. Each group of trainees shares social touchstones with its corresponding generation of true Americans. Finally, after many years of this, when the Willawauk children are saturated with U.S. culture, when the day-to-day minutiae of U.S. life is deeply ingrained in them, they are infiltrated into the U.S. with impeccable documents—usually between the ages of eighteen and twenty-one. Some of them are placed in colleges and universities with the aid of superbly forged family histories and high school records that, when supported by a network of Soviet sympathizers within the U.S., cannot be disputed. The infiltrators find jobs in a variety of industries, many of them in government, and they spend ten, fifteen, twenty, or more years slowly working up into positions of power and authority. Some of them will never be called upon to do any dirty work for their Soviet superiors; they will live and die as patriotic Americans—even though in their hearts, where they truly exist, they *know* they are good Russians. Others will be used for sabotage and espionage. *Are* used, all the time."

"My God," Susan said, "the expense of such a program! The maniacal effort it would take to establish and maintain it is almost beyond conception. Is it really worth the expenditures?"

"The Soviet government thinks so," McGee said. "And there have been some astonishing successes. They have people placed in sensitive positions within the U.S. aerospace industry. They have Willawauk graduates in the Army, the Navy, and the Air Force; not more than a few hundred, of course, but several of those have become high-ranking officers over the years. There are Willawauk graduates in the U.S. media establishment, which provides them with a perfect platform from which to sow disinformation. From the Soviet point of view, the best thing of all is that one U.S. senator, two congressmen, one state governor, and a score of other influential American political figures are Willawauk people."

"Good God!"

Her own anger and fear were temporarily forgotten as the enormity of the entire plot became clear to her.

"And it's rare that a Willawauk graduate can be turned into a double agent, serving the Americans. Willawauk people are just too well programmed, too fanatical to become turncoats. The hospital at Willawauk, where you were kept, serves the town as a fully equipped medical center, much better than hospitals in many other parts of the USSR, but it's also a center for research into behavioral modification and mind control. Its discoveries in those areas have helped to make the Willawauk kids into the most tightly controlled, most devoted and reliable espionage web in the world."

"And you. What about you, McGee? Where do you fit in? And is your name really McGee?"

"No," he said. "My name's Dimitri Nicolnikov. I was born a Russian, to parents in Kiev, thirty-seven years ago. Jeff McGee is my Willawauk name. You see, I was one of the first Willawauk kids, though that was in the early days of the program, when they took young teenagers and tried to make deep-cover agents out of them in three or four years of training. Before they started working solely with kids obtained at the age of three or four. And I'm one of the few who ever turned double agent on them. Although they don't know it as yet."

"They will when they find all the bodies you left behind."

"We'll be long gone by then."

"You're so confident."

"I've got to be," he said, giving her a thin smile. "The alternative is unthinkable."

Again, Susan was aware of the man's singular strength, which was one of the things that had made her fall in love with him.

Am I still in love with him? she wondered.

Yes.

No.

Maybe.

"How old were you when you underwent training in Willawauk?"

"Like I said, that was before they started taking them so young and spending so many years on them. The recruits then were twelve or thirteen. I was there from the age of thirteen to the age of eighteen."

"So you finished the training almost twenty years ago. Why weren't you seeded into the U.S.? Why were you still in Willawauk when I showed up?"

Before he could answer her, the traffic ahead began to slow down on the dark road. Brake lights flashed on the trucks as they lumbered to a halt.

McGee tapped the Chevy's brakes.

"What's going on?" Susan asked, suddenly wary.

"It's the Batum checkpoint."

"What's that?"

"A travel-pass inspection station just north of the city of Batum. That's where we're going to catch a boat out of the country."

"You make it sound as simple as just going away on a holiday," she said.

"It could turn out like that," he said, "if our luck holds just a little longer."

The traffic was inching ahead now, as each vehicle stopped at the checkpoint, each driver passing his papers to a uniformed guard. The guard was armed with a submachine gun that was slung over his left shoulder.

Another uniformed guard was opening the doors on the back of some of the trucks, shining a flashlight inside.

"What're they looking for?" Susan asked.

"I don't know. This isn't usually part of the procedure at the Batum checkpoint."

"Are they looking for us?"

"I doubt it. I don't expect them to find out we're gone from Willawauk until closer to midnight. At least an hour from now. Whatever these men are searching for, it doesn't seem to be all that important. They're being casual about it."

Another truck was passed. The line of traffic moved forward. There were now three trucks in front of the Chevy.

"They're probably just hoping to catch a black market operator with contraband goods," McGee said. "If it was *us* they were looking for, there'd be a hell of a lot more of them swarming around, and they'd be a lot more thorough with their searches."

"We're that important?"

"You better believe it," he said worriedly. "If they lose you, they lose one of the potentially biggest intelligence coups of all time."

Another truck was waved through the checkpoint.

McGee said, "If they could break you and pick your mind clean, they'd get enough information to tip the East-West balance of power permanently in the direction of the East. You're *very* important to them, dear lady. And as soon as they realize that I've gone double on them, they'll want me almost as bad as they'll want to get you back. Maybe they'll even want me worse, because they'll *have* to find out how many of their deep-cover agents in the U.S. have been compromised."

"And how many of them *have* you compromised?"

"All of them," he said, grinning.

Then it was their turn to face the checkpoint guard. McGee turned down the window and passed out two sets of papers. The inspection was perfunctory; the papers were coming back through the window almost as soon as they had been handed out.

McGee thanked the guard, whose attention was already turned to the truck behind them. Then they headed into Batum, and McGee rolled up his window as he drove.

"Black market sweep, like I thought," he said.

As they drove into the outskirts of the small port city, Susan said, "If you were a graduate of Willawauk at eighteen, why weren't you seeded into the U.S. nineteen years ago?"

"I was. I earned my college degrees there, a medical degree with a specialty in behavioral modification medicine. But by the time I had obtained an important job with connections to the U.S. defense establishment, I was no longer a faithful Russian. Remember, in those days, recruits were chosen at the age of thirteen. They weren't yet putting three-year-olds into the Willawauk program. I had lived twelve years of ordinary life in Russia, before my training was begun, so I had a basis for comparing the U.S. and the Soviet systems. I had no trouble changing sides. I acquired a love for freedom. I went to the FBI and told them all about myself and all about Willawauk. At first, for a couple of years, they used me as a conduit for phony data which helped screw up Soviet planning. Then, five years ago, it was decided that I would go back to the USSR as a double agent. I was 'arrested' by the FBI. There was a big trial, during which I refused to utter one word. The papers called me the 'Silent Spy.' "

"My God, I remember! It was a big story back then."

"It was widely advertised that, even though caught red-handed in the transmission of classified information, I refused even to state what country I was from. Everyone *knew* it was Russia, of course, but I played this impressively stoic role. Pleased the hell out of the KGB."

"Which was the idea."

"Of course. After the trial, I received a long prison sentence, but I didn't serve much time. Less than a month. I was quickly traded to the USSR for an American agent whom they were holding. When I was brought back to Moscow, I was welcomed as a hero for maintaining the secret of the Willawauk training program and the deep-cover network. I was the famous Silent Spy. I was eventually sent back to work at my old alma mater, which was what the CIA had hoped would happen."

"And ever since, you've been passing information the other way, to the U.S."

"Yes," he said. "I've got two contacts in Batum, two fishermen who have limited-profit deals with the government, so they own their own boats. They're Georgians, of course. This is Georgian SSR that we're traveling through, and a lot of Georgians despise the central government in Moscow. I pass information to my fishermen, and they pass it along to Turkish fishermen with whom they rendezvous in the middle of the Black Sea. And thereafter, it somehow winds up with the CIA. One of those fishermen is going to pass us along to the Turks the same way he passes classified documents. At least, I *hope* he'll do it."

■ Access to the Batum docks was restricted; all ships, including the fishing boats, could be reached only by passing through one of several checkpoints. There were guarded gates that accepted trucks loaded with cargo, and there was one gate that accepted only military vehicles and personnel, and there were gates to accommodate dock workers, sailors, and others who were obliged to approach on foot; Susan and McGee went to one of the latter.

At night the wharves were poorly lighted, gloomy, except around the security checkpoints, where floodlights simulated the glare of noon. The walk-through gate was overseen by two uniformed guards, both armed with Kalisnikovs; they were involved in an animated conversation that could be heard even outside the hut in which they sat. Neither guard bestirred himself from that small, warm place; neither wanted to bother conducting a close inspection. McGee passed both his and Susan's forged papers through the sliding window. The older of the two guards examined the documents perfunctorily and quickly passed them back, not once pausing in the discussion he was having with his compatriot.

The chainlike gate, crowned with wickedly pointed barbed wire, swung open automatically when one of the guards in the hut touched the proper button. McGee and Susan walked onto the docks, uncontested, and the gate swung shut behind them.

Susan held on to McGee's arm, and they walked into the gloom, toward rows of large dark buildings that blocked their view of the harbor.

"Now what?" Susan whispered.

"Now we go to the fishermen's wharf and look for a boat called the *Golden Net*," McGee said.

"It seems so easy," she said.

"Too easy," he said worriedly.

He glanced back at the checkpoint through which they had just passed, and his face was drawn with apprehension.

■ Leonid Golodkin was master of the *Golden Net*, a hundred-foot fishing trawler with immense cold-storage capacity. He was a ruddy, rough-hewn man with a hard-edged, leathery face and big hands.

Summoned by one of his crewmen, he came to the railing at the gangway, where McGee and Susan waited in the weak yellow glow of a dock lamp. Golodkin was scowling. He and Jeff McGee began to converse in rapid, emotional Russian.

Susan couldn't understand what they were saying, but she had no difficulty understanding Captain Golodkin's mood. The big man was angry and frightened.

Ordinarily, when McGee had information to pass to Golodkin for transfer to Turkish fishermen on the high sea, those documents were forwarded through a black market vodka dealer who operated in Batum, two blocks from the wharves. McGee and Golodkin rarely met face-to-face, and McGee *never* came to the boat. Until tonight.

Golodkin nervously scanned the docks, apparently searching for curious on-lookers, agents of the secret police. For a long, dreadful moment, Susan thought he was going to refuse to let them come aboard. Then, reluctantly, Golodkin swung back the hinged section of railing at the top of the gangway and hurried them through the open boarding gate. Now that he had grudgingly decided to take them in, he was clearly impatient to get them below-decks, out of sight.

They crossed the afterdeck to a spiral, metal staircase and went below. They followed Golodkin along a cold, musty, dimly lighted corridor, and Susan wondered if she would ever again be in a place that wasn't somehow alien and forbidding.

The captain's quarters at the end of the corridor were unquestionably foreign, even though the room was warm and well lighted by three lamps. There was a desk—on which stood a half-filled brandy snifter—a bookcase with glass doors, a liquor cabinet, and four chairs, including the one behind the desk. A sleeping alcove was separated from the main cabin by a drawn curtain.

Golodkin motioned them to two of the chairs, and McGee and Susan sat down.

Directing Susan's attention to the brandy, McGee said, "Would you like a glass of that?"

She was shivering. The mere thought of brandy warmed her. "Yeah," she said. "It would sure hit the spot right now."

In Russian, McGee asked Golodkin for brandy, but before the captain could respond, the curtains rustled in front of the alcove, drawing everyone's attention. Rustled . . . and parted. Dr. Leon Viteski stepped into the main cabin. He was holding a silencer-equipped pistol, and he was smiling.

A shockwave passed through Susan. Angry about being betrayed again, furious about being manipulated through yet another charade, Susan looked at McGee, hating herself for having trusted him.

But McGee appeared to be just as surprised as she was. At the sight of Viteski, Jeff started to rise from his chair, reaching into his coat pocket for his own pistol.

Captain Golodkin stopped him from drawing the weapon and took it away from him.

"Leonid," McGee said in an accusatory tone. Then he said something in Russian that Susan couldn't understand.

"Don't blame poor Leonid," Dr. Viteski said. "He had no choice but to play along with us. Now sit down, please."

McGee hesitated, then sat. He glanced at Susan, saw doubt in her eyes, and said, "I didn't know."

She wanted to believe him. His face was ashen, and there was fear in his eyes, and he looked like a man who had suddenly come eye-to-eye with Death. *But he's a good actor*, she reminded herself. For days, he had deceived her; he might *still* be deceiving her.

Viteski walked around the desk and sat in the captain's chair.

Golodkin stood by the door, his face unreadable.

"We've known about you for two and a half years," Viteski told McGee.

McGee's pale face reddened. His embarrassment appeared to be genuine.

"And we've known about your contact with Leonid almost as long as we've known about you," Viteski said. "The good captain has been working with us ever since we discovered that he was one of your couriers."

McGee looked at Golodkin.

The captain flushed and shuffled his feet.

"Leonid?" McGee said.

Golodkin frowned, shrugged, and said something in Russian.

Susan watched Jeff McGee as McGee watched the captain. He seemed truly abashed.

"Leonid had no choice but to betray you," Viteski told McGee. "We have a strong grip on him. His family, of course. He doesn't like the fact that we've turned him into a double agent, but he knows we hold his reins. He's been quite useful, and I'm sure he'll be useful unmasking other agents in the future."

McGee said, "For two years or more, every time I passed documents to Leonid—"

"—he passed them directly to us," Viteski said. "We tinkered with them, edited them, inserted false data to mislead the CIA, then returned your packages to Leonid. *Then* he passed them to the Turks."

"Shit," McGee said bitterly.

Viteski laughed. He picked up the brandy glass and sipped the amber liquid.

Susan watched both men, and she grew increasingly uneasy. She began to think this wasn't just another charade. She began to think that McGee really *had* meant to take her to safety and that he *had* been betrayed. Which meant that both of them had lost their last best chance of gaining freedom.

To Viteski, McGee said, "If you knew I was going to try to rescue Susan, why didn't you stop me before I took her out of that House of Thunder mock-up, before I shattered the illusion?"

Viteski tasted the brandy again. "We'd already decided that she couldn't be broken. She just wasn't responding satisfactorily to the program. *You* saw that."

"I was half out of my mind with fear," Susan said.

Viteski looked at her and nodded. "Yes. *Half* out of your mind. And that was as far as you were going to get, I believe. You weren't going to break down. You're too tough for that, my dear. At worst, you would have withdrawn into some semicatatonic state. But not a breakdown. Not *you*. So we decided to scrap the program and go with the contingency plan."

"*What* contingency plan?" McGee asked.

Viteski looked at Leonid Golodkin and spoke rapidly in Russian.

Golodkin nodded and left the room.

"What did you mean by that?" McGee asked.

Viteski didn't respond. He merely smiled and picked up the brandy snifter again.

To McGee, Susan said, "What's going on?"

"I don't know," McGee said.

He held out his hand, and after only a brief hesitation, Susan took it. He gave her a smile of encouragement, but it was tissue-thin, unconvincing. Behind the smile, she saw fear.

Viteski said, "This is excellent brandy. Must be black market stuff. You can't buy anything this good over the counter—unless you can get into one of the stores reserved for high Party officials. I'll have to ask the good captain for the name of his dealer."

The door opened, and Leonid Golodkin came in. Two people entered behind him.

One of the newcomers was Jeffrey McGee.

The other was Susan Thorton.

Two more look-alikes.

They were even dressed the same as Jeff and Susan.

Susan's veins seemed to crystallize into fragile tubes of ice as she stared at her own duplicate.

The fake Susan smiled. The resemblance was uncanny.

His face bloodless, his eyes haunted, the real Jeff McGee glared at Leon Viteski and said, "What the hell is this?"

"The contingency plan," Viteski said. "We had it in reserve right from the start, though we didn't tell *you*, of course."

The fake Susan spoke to the real Susan: "It's absolutely fascinating to be in the same room with you at last."

Shocked, Susan said, "She sounds exactly like me!"

The fake McGee said, "We've been working with tapes of your voices for nearly a year." He sounded exactly like the real McGee.

Viteski smiled at the doppelgängers with what appeared to be paternal pride. Then, to the real McGee, he said, "You'll be shot and dumped overboard in the middle of the Black Sea. These two will go back to the U.S. in your places. *Our* Susan will start working at Milestone again." He turned to Susan and said, "My dear, it would have been most helpful if we could have broken you. It would have given us a head start. Nevertheless, we'll still get most of what we wanted by placing your look-alike in your office at Milestone. It'll just take us a lot longer; that's all. In a year or so, we'll have found out everything you could've told us. And if our little ruse can last longer than a year, we'll wind up getting even more data than we could've gotten from you." He turned to Jeff. "We expect your double will find a place in the American intelligence community, perhaps in their behavioral control research, and that'll give us *another* well-placed mole."

"It won't work," McGee said. "They may sound like Susan and me. And your surgeons did a damned good job of making them look like us. But no surgeon can alter fingerprints."

"True," Viteski said. "But you see, for people with very high security clearances, the U.S. has a special system of filing and retrieving fingerprints. It's called SIDEPS, Security ID Protection System. It's part of a Defense Department computer to

which we've managed to gain access. We can simply pull the electronic represen-
tation of your fingerprints and replace them with electronic representations of the
fingerprints of your look-alikes. In this age of centralized computer data storage,
it isn't necessary to change the real prints; we need only change the computer's
memory of what the real prints look like."

"It'll work," Susan said softly, plagued by a mental image of her own body
being dumped over the side of the *Golden Net*, into the cold waters of the Black
Sea.

"Of course it'll work," Viteski said happily. "In fact, we would have sent the
duplicates back to the U.S. even if you had broken and had told us everything we
wanted to know." Viteski finished the brandy in his glass, sighed in appreciation
of it, and got to his feet, holding the pistol. "Captain, while I cover these two,
please tie their hands securely."

Golodkin already had the rope. He made McGee and Susan stand while he tied
their hands behind their backs.

"Now," Viteski said, "take them someplace very private and secure." To McGee
and Susan, he said, "Your twins will visit you later. They have a number of questions about your intimate habits, things that will help them perfect their imitations.
I suggest that you answer them truthfully because several of the questions are
meant to test your veracity; they already know the correct answers to those test
questions, and if you don't respond properly, they'll slowly cut you to pieces until
you're convinced that cooperation is in your best interests."

Susan glanced at the McGee look-alike. The man was smiling; it was not a nice
smile. He looked like McGee in every respect except one: He did not have McGee's
compassion and sensitivity. He appeared to be quite capable of torturing an adversary into bloody, agonized submission.

Susan shuddered.

"I'll say goodbye now," Viteski said. "I'll be leaving the ship before it gets
underway." He smiled smugly. "Bon voyage."

Golodkin ushered McGee and Susan into the corridor, while Viteski remained
behind in the captain's cabin with the look-alikes. In cold silence, refusing to reply
to anything that McGee said, Leonid Golodkin escorted them to another companionway and drove them down into the bowels of the trawler, to the bottom deck,
into the compartments that serviced the cargo holds. The place reeked of fish.

He took them into a small storage locker at the foot of the companionway; it
was no larger than four meters on a side. The walls were hung with spare coils of
rope; thicker hawsers were coiled and braided in stacks upon the deck. The walls
were also racked with tools, including gaffs and skewers. There were four block-
and-tackle sets of varying sizes, and crates of spare machine parts.

Golodkin made them sit on the bare deck, which was ice-cold. He tied their
feet together, then checked to be sure that the ropes on their hands were tightly
knotted. When he left, he turned off the lights and closed the door, plunging them
into unrelieved blackness.

"I'm scared," Susan said.

McGee didn't reply.

She heard him scuffling about, twisting, wrenching at something.

"Jeff?"

He grunted. He was straining against something in the darkness, beginning to breathe hard.

"What're you doing?" she asked.

"Ssshh!" he said sharply.

A moment later, hands groped over her, and she almost cried out in surprise before she realized it was McGee. He had freed himself, and now he was feeling for her bonds.

As he unknotted the ropes that bound her hands, he put his mouth against her ear and spoke in the softest whisper possible. "I doubt that anyone's listening in on us, but we can't be too careful. Golodkin didn't tighten my knots that last time; he *loosened* them just a bit."

Her hands came free of the ropes. She rubbed her chafed wrists. Putting her mouth to Jeff's ear in the darkness, she said, "How much more will he do to help us?"

"Probably nothing," McGee whispered. "He's already taken an enormous risk. From here on, we can count only on ourselves. We won't be given another chance."

He moved away from her as she got to her feet. He fumbled in the darkness for a while before he finally found the light switch and flipped it on.

Even before McGee moved away from the switch, Susan knew what he would go after, and she shivered with revulsion.

As she had anticipated, he went straight to the long-handled, fishermen's gaffs that hung on the wall and pulled two of them out of the spring-clips that held them. The slightly curved hooks at the ends of the gaffs were wickedly sharp; the light glinted on the pointed tips.

Susan took one of the weapons when Jeff handed it to her, but she whispered, "I can't."

"You've got to."

"Oh, God."

"Your life or theirs," he whispered urgently.

She nodded.

"You can do it," he said. "And if we're lucky, it'll be easy. They won't be expecting anything. I'm sure they aren't aware that Golodkin locked us in a room full of handy weapons."

She watched while he decided upon the best positions from which to launch a surprise attack, and then she stood where he told her.

He turned out the lights again.

It was the deepest darkness she had ever known.

■   McGee heard a furtive, rustling noise in the dark. He stiffened, cocked his head, listened attentively. Then he realized what it was, and he relaxed. He called softly to Susan, "Just a rat."

She didn't answer.

"Susan?"

"I'm okay," she said softly from her position on the other side of the small cabin. "Rats don't worry me."

In spite of their precarious situation, McGee smiled.

They waited for long, tiresome minutes.

The *Golden Net* suddenly shuddered, and the deck began to vibrate as the engines were started up. Later, bells clanged in other parts of the vessel. The quality of the deck vibrations changed when, at last, the boat's screws began to churn in the water.

More minutes. More waiting.

They had been underway at least ten minutes, perhaps for a quarter of an hour, long enough to be out of Batum harbor, before there was finally a sound at the door.

McGee tensed and raised the gaff.

The door swung inward, and light spilled through from the corridor. The doppelgängers entered, first the woman and then the man.

McGee was positioned to the left of the door, almost behind it. He stepped out, swung the gaff, and hooked the vicious point through the belly of his own twin, just as the man switched on the cabin lights. Revolted by the sudden gush of blood, sickened by what he had to do, nevertheless determined to do it, McGee wrenched the long-handled hook, twisted it inside his twin, trying to tear the man wide open. The gored McGee collapsed at the feet of the real McGee, flopping as if he were a fish, too shocked and too shattered by the flood of pain to scream.

The woman had a gun. It was the same silencer-equipped pistol that Viteski had been holding in the captain's cabin. She stumbled back in surprise and then fired a nearly silent shot at McGee.

Missed.

Fired again.

McGee felt the bullet tug at his sleeve, but he had been spared a second time.

Behind the fake Susan, the real Susan stepped out from behind a stack of crates and swung the other gaff.

Blood exploded from the look-alike's throat, and her eyes bulged, and the gun dropped from her hand.

McGee's heart twisted inside of him. Although he knew that he was witnessing the death of the look-alike, he was shaken by the terrible sight of Susan's slender throat being pierced by the iron hook . . . Susan's sweet mouth dribbling blood . . .

The fake Susan fell to her knees, then toppled onto her side, eyes glazed, mouth open in a cry that would never be given voice.

McGee turned and looked down at the other one, at the carbon copy of himself. The man was holding his ruined belly, trying to hold his intestines inside of him. His face was contorted in agony and, mercifully, the light of life abruptly went out of his eyes.

It's like seeing a preview of my own death, McGee thought as he stared down into the duplicate's face.

He felt cold and empty.

He had never enjoyed killing, though he had always been able to do it when it was necessary. He suspected he wouldn't be able to kill any more, regardless of the need.

Susan turned away from the bodies, stumbled into a corner, leaned against the wall, and retched violently.

McGee closed the door.

■ Later in the night, in a cabin that had been reserved for the fake Susan and the fake McGee, Susan sat on the lower of two bunk beds and said, "Does Golodkin know for sure which we are?"

Standing by the porthole, looking out at the dark sea, McGee said, "He knows."

"How can you be sure?"

"He didn't say a word to you—because he knows you couldn't answer him in Russian."

"So now we go back and start feeding tricked-up data to the Russians, but they think it's the real dope, coming from their two look-alikes."

"Yes," McGee said. "*If* we can figure out what channels they were supposed to use to get their information out." ·

They were both silent a while. McGee seemed fascinated with the ocean, even though he could see very little of it in the darkness.

Susan sat studying her hands, searching for any blood that she had failed to scrub away. After a while, she said, "Was that a bottle of brandy Golodkin left?"

"Yes."

"I need a shot."

"I'll pour you a double," McGee said.

■ At sea, shortly after dawn.

Susan woke, a scream caught in her throat, gasping, gagging.

McGee switched on the light.

For a moment Susan couldn't remember where she was. Then it came back to her.

Although she knew where she was, she couldn't stop gasping. Her dream was still with her, and it was a dream that, she thought, might just possibly be a reality, too. ·

McGee had jumped down from the upper bunk. He knelt beside her bed. "Susan, it's okay. It's really okay. We're at sea, and we're going to make it."

"No," she said.

"What do you mean?"

"The crew."

"What about the crew?"

"Harch, Quince, Jellicoe, and Parker. They're all members of the crew."

"No, no," he said. "You were dreaming."

"*They're here!*" she insisted, panicky.

"The charade is over," McGee assured her patiently. "It's not going to start again." ·

"They're *here*, dammit!"

He couldn't calm her. He had to take her through the entire boat as the crew began the day's trawling. He had to show her every room on board and let her see every crewman in order to prove to her, beyond all doubt, that Harch and the others were not aboard.

■ They had breakfast in their cabin, where they could talk without rubbing Golodkin's face in the fact that Susan couldn't speak Russian.

She said, "Where *did* they locate the look-alikes of Harch and the other three?"

"Soviet agents in the U.S. obtained photographs of Harch and the others from newspaper and college files," McGee said. "A search was made for Russians who even vaguely resembled the four fraternity men, and then perfection was achieved with the help of plastic surgery and the judicious use of makeup."

"Harch's eyes . . ."

"Special contact lenses."

"Like a Hollywood film."

"What?"

"Special effects."

"Yes, I guess they were worthy of Hollywood, all right."

"Jerry Stein's corpse."

"A hideous piece of work, wasn't it?"

She began to shake uncontrollably.

"Hey," he said. "Easy, easy."

She couldn't stop shaking.

He held her.

■ She felt better the next day on the Turkish boat after the transfer had been effected.

Their sleeping accommodations were more comfortable, cleaner, and the food was better, too.

Over a lunch of cold meats and cheeses, she said to McGee, "I *must* be important for the U.S. to sacrifice your cover to get me out of there."

He hesitated, then said, "Well . . . that wasn't the original plan."

"Huh?"

"I wasn't supposed to bring you out."

She didn't understand.

McGee said, "I was supposed to kill you before the Willawauk program had a chance to work on you. A bit of air in a hypodermic needle—*bang*, a lethal brain embolism. Something like that. Something that no one could trace to me. That way, I'd be kept in place, and there'd be no chance of the Soviets breaking you."

The blood had gone from her face. She had suddenly lost her appetite. "Why *didn't* you kill me?"

"Because I fell in love with you."

She stared at him, blinking.

"It's true," he said. "During the weeks we were setting you up for the program, working with you, planting the hypnotic suggestions that sent you to the sheriff's station and the Shipstat house, I was impressed by your strength, your strong will. It wasn't easy to set you up and manipulate you. You had . . . moxie."

"You fell in love with my moxie?"

He smiled. "Something like that."

"And couldn't kill me?"

"No."

"They'll be mad at you back in the States."

"To hell with them."

■ Two nights later, in a bedroom in the United States Ambassador's residence in Istanbul, Susan woke, screaming.

The maid came at a run. A security man. The ambassador and McGee.

"The house staff," Susan said, clutching at McGee. "We can't trust the house staff."

McGee said, "None of them looks like Harch."

"How do I know? I haven't seen them all," she said.

"Susan, it's three o'clock in the morning," the security man said.

"I *have* to see them," she said frantically.

The ambassador looked at her for a moment, glanced at McGee. Then, to the security man, he said, "Assemble the staff."

Neither Harch nor Quince nor Jellicoe nor Parker was employed by the United States Ambassador to Turkey.

"I'm sorry," Susan said.

"It's okay," McGee assured her.

"It's going to take a while," she said apologetically.

"Of course it will."

"Maybe the rest of my life," she said.

■ A week later, in Washington, D.C., in a hotel suite that was being paid for by the United States government, Susan went to bed with Jeff McGee for the first time. They were very good together. Their bodies fit together like pieces of a puzzle. They moved together fluidly, in perfect, silken rhythm. That night, for the first time since leaving Willawauk, sleeping naked with McGee, Susan did not dream.

■ The year was 1980—an ancient time, so long ago and far away. Humanity was divided into armed camps, millions lived in chains, freedom was in jeopardy, and a town like Willawauk actually existed. But there is a new world order, and the human heart has been purified. Has it not? A place like Willawauk is impossible now. Evil has been purged from the human soul. Has it not?

SHADOWFIRES

This book is dedicated to
Dick and Ann Laymon
who simply can't be as nice
as they seem.
And a special hello
to Kelly.

PART ONE

DARK

To know the darkness is to love the light,

to welcome dawn and fear the coming night

—THE BOOK OF COUNTED SORROWS

1 SHOCK

BRIGHTNESS FELL FROM THE AIR, NEARLY AS TANGIBLE AS rain. It rippled down windows, formed colorful puddles on the hoods and trunks of parked cars, and imparted a wet sheen to the leaves of trees and to the chrome on the bustling traffic that filled the street. Miniature images of the California sun shimmered in every reflective surface, and downtown Santa Ana was drenched in the clear light of a late-June morning.

When Rachael Leben exited the lobby doors of the office building and stepped onto the sidewalk, the summer sunshine felt like warm water on her bare arms. She closed her eyes and, for a moment, turned her face to the heavens, bathing in the radiance, relishing it.

"You stand there smiling as if nothing better has ever happened to you or ever will," Eric said sourly when he followed her out of the building and saw her luxuriating in the June heat.

"Please," she said, face still tilted to the sun, "let's not have a scene."

"You made a fool of me in there."

"I certainly did not."

"What the hell are you trying to prove, anyway?"

She did not respond; she was determined not to let him spoil the lovely day. She turned and started to walk away.

Eric stepped in front of her, blocking her way. His gray-blue eyes usually had an icy aspect, but now his gaze was hot.

"Let's not be childish," she said.

"You're not satisfied just to leave me. You've got to let the world know you don't need me or any damn thing I can give you."

"No, Eric. I don't care what the world thinks of you—one way or the other."

"You want to rub my face in it."

"That's not true, Eric."

"Oh, yes," he said. "Hell, yes. You're just reveling in my humiliation. Wallowing in it."

She saw him as she had never seen him before: a pathetic man. Previously he'd seemed strong to her: physically, emotionally, and mentally strong; strong-willed; strongly opinionated. He was aloof, too, and sometimes cold. He could be cruel. And there had been times during their seven years of marriage when he had been as distant as the moon. But until this moment, he'd never seemed weak or pitiable.

"Humiliation?" she said wonderingly. "Eric, I've done you an enormous favor. Any other man would buy a bottle of champagne to celebrate."

They had just left the offices of Eric's attorneys, where their divorce settlement had been negotiated with a speed that had surprised everyone but Rachael. She had startled them by arriving without an attorney of her own and by failing to press for everything to which she was entitled under California's community-property laws. When Eric's attorney presented a first offer, she had insisted it was too generous and had given them another set of figures that had seemed more reasonable to her.

"Champagne, huh? You're going to be telling everyone you took twelve and a half million less than you deserved just so you could get a quick divorce and be done with me fast, and I'm supposed to stand here grinning? Christ."

"Eric—"

"Couldn't *wait* to be done with me. Cut off a goddamn *arm* to be done with me. And I'm supposed to celebrate my humiliation?"

"It's a matter of principle with me not to take more than—"

"Principle, my ass."

"Eric, you know I wouldn't—"

"Everyone'll be looking at me and saying, 'Christ, just how insufferable must the guy have been if it was worth twelve and a half million to be rid of him!'"

"I'm not going to tell anyone what we settled for," Rachael said.

"Bullshit."

"If you think I'd ever talk against you or gossip about you, then you know even less about me than I'd thought."

Eric, twelve years her senior, had been thirty-five and worth four million when she'd married him. Now he was forty-two, and his fortune totaled more than thirty million, and by any interpretation of California law, she was entitled to thirteen million dollars in the divorce settlement—half the wealth accumulated during their marriage. Instead, she insisted on settling for her red Mercedes 560 SL sports car, five hundred thousand dollars, and no alimony—which was approximately one twenty-sixth of what she could have claimed. She had calculated that this nest egg would give her the time and resources to decide what to do with the rest of her life and to finance whatever plans she finally made.

Aware that passersby were staring as she and Eric confronted each other on the sun-splashed street, Rachael said quietly, "I didn't marry you for your money."

"I wonder," he said acidly and irrationally. His bold-featured face wasn't handsome at the moment. Anger had carved it into an ugly mask—all hard, deep, down-slashing lines.

Rachael spoke calmly, with no trace of bitterness, with no desire to put him in his place or to hurt him in any way. It was just over. She felt no rage. Only mild regret. "And now that it's finally over, I don't expect to be supported in high style and great luxury for the rest of my days. I don't want your millions. You earned them, not me. Your genius, your iron determination, your endless hours in the office and the lab. You built it all, you and you alone, and you alone deserve what you've built. You're an important man, maybe even a great man in your field, Eric, and I am only me, Rachael, and I'm not going to pretend I had anything to do with your triumphs."

The lines of anger in his face deepened as she complimented him. He was accustomed to occupying the dominant role in all relationships, professional and private. From his position of absolute dominance, he relentlessly forced submission to his wishes—or crushed anyone who would not submit. Friends, employees, and business associates always did things Eric Leben's way, or they were history. Submit or be rejected and destroyed—those were their only choices. He enjoyed the exercise of power, thrived on conquests as major as million-dollar deals and as minor as winning domestic arguments. Rachael had done as he wished for seven years, but she would not submit any longer.

The funny thing was that, by her docility and reasonableness, she had robbed him of the power on which he thrived. He had been looking forward to a protracted battle over the division of spoils, and she had walked away from it. He relished the prospect of acrimonious squabbling over alimony payments, but she thwarted him by rejecting all such assistance. He had pleasurably anticipated a court fight in which he would make her look like a gold-digging bitch and reduce her, at last, to a creature without dignity who would be willing to settle for far less than was her due. Then, although leaving her rich, he would have felt that the war had been won and he had beaten her into submission. But when she made it clear that his millions were of no importance to her, she had eliminated the one power he still had over her. She had cut him off at the knees, and his anger arose from his realization that, by her docility, she had somehow made herself his equal—if not his superior—in any further contact they might have.

She said, "Well, the way I see it, I've lost seven years, and all I want is reasonable compensation for that time. I'm twenty-nine, almost thirty, and in a way, I'm just beginning my life. Starting out later than other people. This settlement will give me a terrific start. If I lose the bundle, if someday I have reason to wish I'd gone for the whole thirteen million . . . well, then that's my tough luck, not yours. We've been through all this, Eric. It's finished."

She stepped around him, trying to walk away, but he grabbed her arm, halting her.

"Please let me go," she said evenly.

Glaring at her, he said, "How could I have been so wrong about you? I thought you were sweet, a bit shy, an unworldly little fluff of a girl. But you're a nasty little ball-buster, aren't you?"

"Really, this is an absolutely crazy attitude. And this crude behavior isn't worthy of you. Now let me go."

He gripped her even tighter. "Or is this all just a negotiating ploy? Huh? When the papers are drawn up, when we come back to sign everything on Friday, will you suddenly have a change of heart? Will you want more?"

"No, I'm not playing any games."

His grin was tight and mean. "I'll bet that's it. If we agree to such a ridiculously low settlement and draw up the papers, you'll refuse to sign them, but you'll use them in court to try to prove we were going to give you the shaft. You'll pretend the offer was *ours* and that we tried to strong-arm you into signing it. Make me look bad. Make me look as if I'm a real hard-hearted bastard. Huh? Is that the strategy? Is that the game?"

"I told you, there's no game. I'm sincere."

He dug his fingers into her upper arm. "The truth, Rachael."

"Stop it."

"Is that the strategy?"

"You're hurting me."

"And while you're at it, why don't you tell me all about Ben Shadway, too?"

She blinked in surprise, for she had never imagined that Eric knew about Benny.

His face seemed to harden in the hot sun, cracking with more deep lines of anger. "How long was he fucking you before you finally walked out on me?"

"You're disgusting," she said, immediately regretting the harsh words because she saw that he was pleased to have broken through her cool facade at last.

"How long?" he demanded, tightening his grip.

"I didn't meet Benny till six months after you and I separated," she said, striving to keep a neutral tone that would deny him the noisy confrontation he apparently desired.

"How long was he poaching on me, Rachael?"

"If you know about Benny, you've had me watched, something you've no right to do."

"Yeah, you want to keep your dirty little secrets."

"If you *have* hired someone to watch me, you know I've been seeing Benny for just five months. Now let go. You're still hurting me."

A young bearded guy, passing by, hesitated, stepped toward them, and said, "You need help, lady?"

Eric turned on the stranger in such a rage that he seemed to spit the words out rather than speak them: "Butt out, mister. This is my wife, and it's none of your goddamn business."

Rachael tried to wrench free of Eric's iron grip without success.

The bearded stranger said, "So she's your wife—that doesn't give you the right to hurt her."

Letting go of Rachael, Eric fisted his hands and turned more directly toward the intruder.

Rachael spoke quickly to her would-be Galahad, eager to defuse the situation. "Thank you, but it's all right. Really. I'm fine. Just a minor disagreement."

The young man shrugged and walked away, glancing back as he went.

The incident had at last made Eric aware that he was in danger of making a spectacle of himself, which a man of his high position and self-importance was loath to do. However, his temper had not cooled. His face was flushed, and his lips were bloodless. His eyes were the eyes of a dangerous man.

She said, "Be happy, Eric. You've saved millions of dollars and God knows how much more in attorneys' fees. You won. You didn't get to crush me or muddy my reputation in court the way you had hoped to, but you still won. Be happy with that."

With a seething hatred that shocked her, he said, "You stupid, rotten bitch. The day you walked out on me, I wanted to knock you down and kick your stupid face in. I should've done it. Wish I had. But I thought you'd come crawling back, so I didn't. I should've. Should've kicked your stupid face in." He raised his hand as if to slap her. But he checked himself even as she flinched from the expected blow. Furious, he turned and hurried away.

As she watched him go, Rachael suddenly understood that his sick desire to dominate everyone was a far more fundamental need than she'd realized. By stripping him of his power over her, by turning her back on both him and his money, she had not merely reduced him to an equal but had, in his eyes, *unmanned* him. That had to be the case, for nothing else explained the degree of his rage or his urge to commit violence, an urge he had barely controlled.

She had grown to dislike him intensely, if not hate him, and she had feared him a little, too. But until now, she had not been fully aware of the immensity and intensity of the rage within him. She had not realized how thoroughly dangerous he was.

Although the golden sunshine still dazzled her eyes and forced her to squint, although it still baked her skin, she felt a cold shiver pass through her, spawned by the realization that she'd been wise to leave Eric when she had—and perhaps fortunate to escape with no more physical damage than the bruises his fingers were certain to have left on her arm.

Watching him step off the sidewalk into the street, she was relieved to see him go. A moment later, relief turned to horror.

He was heading toward his black Mercedes, which was parked along the other side of the avenue. Perhaps he actually was blinded by his anger. Or maybe it was the brilliant June sunlight flashing on every shiny surface that interfered with his vision. Whatever the reason, he dashed across the southbound lanes of Main Street, which were at the moment without traffic, and kept on going into the northbound lanes, directly into the path of a city garbage truck that was doing forty miles an hour.

Too late, Rachael screamed a warning.

The driver tramped his brake pedal to the floorboards. But the shriek of the truck's locked wheels came almost simultaneously with the sickening sound of impact.

Eric was hurled into the air and thrown back into the southbound lanes as if by the concussion wave of a bomb blast. He crashed into the pavement and tumbled twenty feet, stiffly at first, then with a horrible looseness, as if he were constructed of string and old rags. He came to rest facedown, unmoving.

A southbound yellow Subaru braked with a banshee screech and a hard flat wail of its horn, halting only two feet from him. A Chevy, following too close, rammed into the back of the Subaru and pushed it within a few inches of the body.

Rachael was the first to reach Eric. Heart hammering, shouting his name, she dropped to her knees and, by instinct, put one hand to his neck to feel for a pulse. His skin was wet with blood, and her fingers slipped on the slick flesh as she searched desperately for the throbbing artery.

Then she saw the hideous depression that had reshaped his skull. His head had been staved in along the right side, above the torn ear, and all the way forward past the temple to the edge of his pale brow. His head was turned so she could see one eye, which was open wide, staring in shock, though sightless now. Many wickedly sharp fragments of bone must have been driven deep into his brain. Death had been instantaneous.

She stood up abruptly, tottering, nauseated. Dizzy, she might have fallen if the driver of the garbage truck had not grabbed hold of her, provided support, and escorted her around the side of the Subaru, where she could lean against the car.

"There was nothin' I could do," he said miserably.

"I know," she said.

"Nothin' at all. He run in front of me. Didn't look. Nothin' I could do."

At first Rachael had difficulty breathing. Then she realized she was absent-mindedly scrubbing her blood-covered hand on her sundress, and the sight of those damp rusty-scarlet stains on the pastel-blue cotton made her breath come quicker, too quick. Hyperventilating, she slumped against the Subaru, closed her eyes, hugged herself, and clenched her teeth. She was determined not to faint. She strove to hold in each shallow breath as long as possible, and the very process of changing the rhythm of her breathing was a calming influence.

Around her she heard the voices of motorists who had left their cars in the snarl of stalled traffic. Some of them asked her if she was all right, and she nodded; others asked if she needed medical attention, and she shook her head—no.

If she had ever loved Eric, that love had been ground to dust beneath his heel. It had been a long time since she'd even *liked* him. Moments before the accident, he'd revealed a pure and terrifying hatred of her, so she supposed she should have been utterly unmoved by his death. Yet she was badly shaken. As she hugged herself and shivered, she was aware of a cold emptiness within, a hollow sense of loss that she could not quite understand. Not grief. Just . . . loss.

She heard sirens in the distance.

Gradually she regained control of her breathing.

Her shivering grew less violent, though it did not stop entirely.

The sirens grew nearer, louder.

She opened her eyes. The bright June sunshine no longer seemed clean and fresh. The darkness of death had passed through the day, and in its wake, the morning light had acquired a sour yellow cast that reminded her more of sulfur than of honey.

Red lights flashing, sirens dying, a paramedic van and a police sedan approached along the northbound lanes.

"Rachael?"

She turned and saw Herbert Tuleman, Eric's personal attorney, with whom she had met only minutes ago. She had always liked Herb, and he had liked her as well. He was a grandfatherly man with bushy gray eyebrows that were now drawn together in a single bar.

"One of my associates . . . returning to the office . . . saw it happen," Herbert said, "hurried up to tell me. My God."

"Yes," she said numbly.

"My God, Rachael."

"Yes."

"It's too . . . crazy."

"Yes."

"But . . ."

"Yes," she said.

And she knew what Herbert was thinking. Within the past hour, she had told them she would not fight for a large share of Eric's fortune but would settle for, proportionately, a pittance. Now, by virtue of the fact that Eric had no family and no children from his first marriage, the entire thirty million plus his currently un-valued stock in the company would almost certainly, by default, come into her sole possession.

2   SPOOKED

THE HOT, DRY AIR WAS FILLED WITH THE CRACKLE OF POLICE radios, a metallic chorus of dispatchers' voices, and the smell of sun-softened asphalt.

The paramedics could do nothing for Eric Leben except convey his corpse to the city morgue, where it would lie in a refrigerated room until the medical ex-aminer had time to attend to it. Because Eric had been killed in an accident, the law required an autopsy.

"The body should be available for release in twenty-four hours," one of the policemen had told Rachael.

While they had filled out a brief report, she had sat in the back of one of the patrol cars. Now she was standing in the sun again.

She no longer felt sick. Just numb.

They loaded the draped cadaver into the van. In spots, the shroud was dark with blood.

Herbert Tuleman felt obliged to comfort Rachael and repeatedly suggested that she return with him to his law office. "You need to sit down, get a grip on yourself," he said, one hand on her shoulder, his kindly face wrinkled with concern.

"I'm all right, Herb. Really, I am. Just a little shaken."

"Some cognac. That's what you need. I've got a bottle of Remy Martin in the office bar."

"No, thank you. I guess it'll be up to me to handle the funeral, so I've got things to attend to."

The two paramedics closed the rear doors on the van and walked unhurriedly to the front of the vehicle. No need for sirens and flashing red emergency beacons. Speed would not help Eric now.

Herb said, "If you don't want brandy, then perhaps coffee. Or just come and sit with me for a while. I don't think you should get behind a wheel right away."

Rachael touched his leathery cheek affectionately. He was a weekend sailor, and his skin had been toughened and creased less by age than by his time upon the sea. "I appreciate your concern. I really do. But I'm fine. I'm almost ashamed of how well I'm taking it. I mean . . . I feel no grief at all."

He held her hand. "Don't be ashamed. He was my client, Rachael, so I'm aware that he was . . . a difficult man."

"Yes."

"He gave you no reason to grieve."

"It still seems wrong to feel . . . so little. Nothing."

"He wasn't just a difficult man, Rachael. He was also a fool for not recognizing what a jewel he had in you and for not doing whatever was necessary to make you want to stay with him."

"You're a dear."

"It's true. If it weren't *very* true, I wouldn't speak of a client like this, not even when he was . . . deceased."

The van, bearing the corpse, pulled away from the accident scene. Paradoxically, there was a cold, wintry quality to the way the summer sun glimmered in the white paint and in the polished chrome bumpers, making it appear as if Eric were being borne away in a vehicle carved from ice.

Herb walked with her, through the gathered onlookers, past his office building, to her red 560 SL. He said, "I could have someone drive Eric's car back to his house, put it in the garage, and leave the keys at your place."

"That would be helpful," she said.

When Rachael was behind the wheel, belted in, Herb leaned down to the window and said, "We'll have to talk soon about the estate."

"In a few days," she said.

"And the company."

"Things will run themselves for a few days, won't they?"

"Certainly. It's Monday, so shall we say you'll come see me Friday morning? That gives you four days to . . . adjust."

"All right."

"Ten o'clock?"

"Fine."

"You sure you're okay?"

"Yes," she said, and she drove home without incident, though she felt as though she were dreaming.

She lived in a quaint three-bedroom bungalow in Placentia. The neighborhood was solidly middle-class and friendly, and the house had loads of charm: French windows, window seats, coffered ceilings, a used-brick fireplace. She'd made the down payment and moved a year ago, when she left Eric. Her house was far different from the place in Villa Park, which was set on an acre of manicured grounds and which boasted every luxury; however, she liked her cozy bungalow better than his Spanish-modern mansion, not merely because the scale seemed more human here but also because the Placentia house was not tainted by countless bad memories as was the house in Villa Park.

She took off her bloodstained blue sundress. She washed her hands and face, brushed her hair, and reapplied what little makeup she wore. Gradually the mundane task of grooming herself had a calming effect. Her hands stopped trembling. Although a hollow coldness remained at the core of her, she stopped shivering.

After dressing in one of the few somber outfits she owned—a charcoal-gray suit with a pale gray blouse, slightly too heavy for a hot summer day—she called Attison Brothers, a firm of prestigious morticians. Having ascertained that they could see her immediately, she drove directly to their imposing colonial-style funeral home in Yorba Linda.

She had never made funeral arrangements before, and she had never imagined that there would be anything amusing about the experience. But when she sat down with Paul Attison in his softly lighted, darkly paneled, plushly carpeted, uncannily quiet office and listened to him call himself a "grief counselor," she saw dark humor in the situation. The atmosphere was so meticulously somber and so self-consciously reverent that it was stagy. His proffered sympathy was oily yet ponderous, relentless and calculated, but surprisingly she found herself playing along with him, responding to his condolences and platitudes with clichés of her own. She felt as if she were an actor trapped in a bad play by an incompetent playwright, forced to deliver her wooden lines of dialogue because it was less embarrassing to persevere to the end of the third act than to stalk off the stage in the middle of the performance. In addition to identifying himself as a grief counselor, Attison referred to a casket as an "eternal bower." A suit of burial clothes, in which the corpse would be dressed, was called "the final raiments." Attison said "preparations for preservation" instead of "embalming," and "resting place" instead of "grave."

Although the experience was riddled with macabre humor, Rachael was not able to laugh even when she left the funeral home after two and a half hours and was alone in her car again. Ordinarily she had a special fondness for black humor, for laughter that mocked the grim, dark aspects of life. Not today. It was neither grief nor any kind of sadness that kept her in a gray and humorless mood. Nor worry about widowhood. Nor shock. Nor the morbid recognition of Death's lurking presence in even the sunniest day. For a while, as she tended to other details of the funeral, and later, at home once more, as she called Eric's friends and business associates to convey the news, she could not quite understand the cause of her unremitting solemnity.

Then, late in the afternoon, she could no longer fool herself. She knew that her mental state resulted from fear. She tried to deny what was coming, tried not to think about it, and she had some success at not thinking, but in her heart she knew. She knew.

She went through the house, making sure that all the doors and windows were locked. She closed the blinds and drapes.

■   At five-thirty, Rachael put the telephone on the answering machine. Reporters had begun to call, wanting a few words with the widow of the Great Man, and she had no patience whatsoever for media types.

The house was a bit too cool, so she reset the air conditioner. But for the susurrant sound of cold air coming through the wall vents and the occasional single ring the telephone made before the machine answered it, the house was as silent as Paul Attison's gloom-shrouded office.

Today, deep silence was intolerable; it gave her the creeps. She switched on the stereo, tuned to an FM station playing easy-listening music. For a moment, she stood before the big speakers, eyes closed, swaying as she listened to Johnny Mathis singing "Chances Are." Then she turned up the volume so the music could be heard throughout the house.

In the kitchen, she cut a small piece of semisweet dark chocolate from a bar and put it on a white saucer. She opened a split of fine, dry champagne. She took the chocolate, the champagne, and a glass into the master bathroom.

On the radio, Sinatra was singing "Days of Wine and Roses."

Rachael drew a tub of water as hot as she could tolerate, added a drizzle of jasmine-scented oil, and undressed. Just as she was about to settle in to soak, the pulse of fear which had been beating quietly within her suddenly began to throb hard and fast. She tried to calm herself by closing her eyes and breathing deeply, tried telling herself that she was being childish, but nothing worked.

Naked, she went into the bedroom and got the .32-caliber pistol from the top drawer of the nightstand. She checked the magazine to be sure it was fully loaded. Switching off both safeties, she took the thirty-two into the bathroom and put it on the deep blue tile at the edge of the sunken tub, beside the champagne and chocolate.

Andy Williams was singing "Moon River."

Wincing, she stepped into the hot bath and settled down until the water had slipped most of the way up the slopes of her breasts. It stung at first. Then she became accustomed to the temperature, and the heat was good, penetrating to her bones and finally dispelling the chill that had plagued her ever since Eric had dashed in front of the truck almost seven and a half hours ago.

She nibbled at the candy, taking only a few shavings from the edge of the piece. She let them melt slowly on her tongue.

She tried not to think. She tried to concentrate on just the mindless pleasure of a good hot steep. Just drift. Just *be*.

She leaned back in the tub, savoring the taste of chocolate, relishing the scent of jasmine in the rising steam.

After a couple of minutes, she opened her eyes and poured a glass of champagne from the ice-cold bottle. The crisp taste was a perfect complement to the lingering trace of chocolate and to the voice of Sinatra crooning the nostalgic and sweetly melancholy lines of "It Was a Very Good Year."

For Rachael, this relaxing ritual was an important part of the day, perhaps the *most* important. Sometimes she nibbled at a small wedge of sharp cheese instead of chocolate and sipped a single glass of chardonnay instead of champagne. Sometimes it was an extremely cold bottle of dark beer—Heineken or Beck's— and a handful of the special plump peanuts that were sold by an expensive nut shop in Costa Mesa. Whatever her choice of the day, she consumed it with care and slow delight, in tiny bites and small sips, relishing every nuance of taste and scent and texture.

She was a "present-focused" person.

Benny Shadway, the man Eric had thought was Rachael's lover, said there were basically four types of people: past-, present-, future-, and omni-focused. Those focused primarily on the future had little interest in the past or present. They were often worriers, peering toward tomorrow to see what crisis or insoluble problem might be hurtling toward them—although some were shiftless dreamers rather than worriers, always looking ahead because they were unreasonably certain they were due for great good fortune of one kind or another. Some were also worka-holics, dedicated achievers who believed that the future and opportunity were the same thing.

Eric had been such a one, forever brooding about and eagerly anticipating new challenges and conquests. He had been utterly bored with the past and impatient with the snail's pace at which the present sometimes crept by.

A present-focused person, on the other hand, expended most of his energy and interest in the joys and tribulations of the moment. Some present-focused types were merely sluggards, too lazy to prepare for tomorrow or even to contemplate it. Strokes of bad luck often caught them unaware, for they had difficulty accepting the possibility that the pleasantness of the moment might not go on forever. And when they found themselves mired in misfortune, they usually fell into ruinous despair, for they were incapable of embarking upon a course of action that would, at some point in the future, free them from their troubles. However, another type of present-focused person was the hard worker who could involve himself in the task at hand with a single-mindedness that made for splendid efficiency and crafts-manship. A first-rate cabinetmaker, for example, had to be a present-focused per-son, one who did not look forward impatiently to the final assembly and completion of a piece of furniture but who directed his attention entirely and lovingly to the meticulous shaping and finishing of each rung and arm of a chair, to each drawer face and knob and doorframe of a china hutch, taking his greatest satisfaction in the *process* of creation rather than in the culmination of the process.

Present-focused people, according to Benny, are more likely to find obvious solutions to problems than are other people, for they are not preoccupied with either what was or what might come to pass but only with what *is*. They are also the people most sensuously connected with the physical realities of life—therefore the most perceptive in some ways—and they most likely have more sheer pleasure and fun than any dozen past- or future-oriented citizens.

"You're the best kind of present-oriented woman," Benny had once told her over a Chinese dinner at Peking Duck. "You prepare for the future but never at the expense of losing touch with *now*. And you're so admirably able to put the past behind you."

She had said, "Ah, shut up and eat your moo goo gai pan."

Essentially, what Benny said was true. Since leaving Eric, Rachael had taken five courses in business management at a Pepperdine extension, for she intended to launch a small business. Perhaps a clothing store for upscale women. A place that would be dramatic and fun, the kind of shop that people talked about as not only a source of well-made clothes but an experience. After all, she'd attended UCLA, majoring in dramatic arts, and had earned her bachelor's degree just before meeting Eric at a university function; and though she had no interest in acting, she had real talent for costume and set design, which might serve her well in creating an unusual decor for a clothing store and in acquiring merchandise for sale. How-ever, she had not yet gone so far as to commit herself to the acquisition of an M.B.A. degree nor to choosing a particular enterprise. Rooted in the present, she proceeded to gather knowledge and ideas, waiting patiently for the moment when her plans would simply . . . crystallize. As for the past—well, to dwell on yester-day's pleasures was to risk missing out on pleasures of the moment, and to dwell on past pains and tragedies was a pointless waste of energy and time.

Now, resting languorously in her steaming bath, Rachael drew a deep breath of the jasmine-scented air.

She hummed along softly with Johnny Mathis as he sang "I'll Be Seeing You."

She tasted the chocolate again. She sipped the champagne.

She tried to relax, to drift, to go with the flow and embrace the mellow mood in the best California tradition.

For a while she pretended to be completely at ease, and she did not entirely realize that her detachment was only pretense until the doorbell rang. The instant the bell sounded above the lulling music, she sat up in the water, heart hammering, and grabbed for the pistol with such panic that she knocked over her champagne glass.

When she had gotten out of the tub and put on her blue robe, she held the gun at her side, with the muzzle pointed at the floor, and walked slowly through the shadowy house to the front door. She was filled with dread at the prospect of answering the bell; at the same time, she was irresistibly drawn to the door as if in a trance, as if compelled by the mesmeric voice of a hypnotist.

She paused at the stereo to switch it off. The ensuing silence had an ominous quality.

In the foyer, with her hand upon the knob, she hesitated as the bell rang again. The front door had no window, no sidelights. She had been meaning to have a fish-eye security lens installed, through which she would be able to study the person on the doorstep, and now she ardently wished that she had not procrastinated. She stared at the dark oak before her, as if she might miraculously acquire the power to see through it and clearly identify the caller beyond. She was trembling.

She did not know why she faced the prospect of a visitor with such unmitigated dread.

Well, perhaps that was not exactly true. Deep down—or even not so deep—she knew why she was afraid. But she was reluctant to admit the source of her fear, as if admission would transform a horrible possibility into a deadly reality.

The bell rang again.

3 · JUST VANISHED

WHILE LISTENING TO NEWS ON THE RADIO DURING THE DRIVE home from his office in Tustin, Ben Shadway heard about Dr. Eric Leben's sudden death. He wasn't sure how he felt. Shocked, yes. But he wasn't saddened, even though the world had lost a potentially great man. Leben had been brilliant, indisputably a genius, but he had also been arrogant, self-important, perhaps even dangerous.

Ben mostly felt relieved. He had been afraid that Eric, finally aware that he could never regain his wife, would harm her. The man hated to lose. There was a dark rage in him usually relieved by his obsessive commitment to his work, but it might have found expression in violence if he had felt deeply humiliated by Rachael's rejection.

Ben kept a cellular phone in his car—a meticulously restored 1956 Thunderbird, white with blue interior—and he immediately called Rachael. She had her answering machine on, and she did not pick up the receiver when he identified himself.

At the traffic light at the corner of Seventeenth Street and Newport Avenue, he hesitated, then turned left instead of continuing on to his own house in Orange Park Acres. Rachael might not be home right now, but she would get there eventually, and she might need support. He headed for her place in Placentia.

The June sun dappled the Thunderbird's windshield and made bright rippling patterns when he passed through the inconstant shadows of overhanging trees. He switched off the news and put on a Glenn Miller tape. Speeding through the California sun, with "String of Pearls" filling the car, he found it hard to believe that anyone could die on such a golden day.

By his own system of personality classification, Benjamin Lee Shadway was primarily a past-focused man. He liked old movies better than new ones. De Niro, Streep, Gere, Field, Travolta, and Penn were of less interest to him than Bogart, Bacall, Gable, Lombard, Tracy, Hepburn, Cary Grant, William Powell, Myrna Loy. His favorite books were from the 1920s, 1930s, and 1940s: hard-boiled stuff by Chandler and Hammett and James M. Cain, and the early Nero Wolfe novels. His music of choice was from the swing era: Tommy and Jimmy Dorsey, Harry James, Duke Ellington, Glenn Miller, the incomparable Benny Goodman.

For relaxation, he built working models of locomotives from kits, and he collected all kinds of railroad memorabilia. There are no hobbies so reeking with nostalgia or more suited to a past-focused person than those dealing with trains.

He was not focused *entirely* on the past. At twenty-four, he had obtained a real-estate license, and by the time he was thirty-one, he had established his own brokerage. Now, at thirty-seven, he had six offices with thirty agents working under him. Part of the reason for his success was that he treated his employees and customers with a concern and courtesy that were old-fashioned and enormously appealing in the fast-paced, brusque, and plastic world of the present.

Lately, in addition to his work, there was one other thing that could distract Ben from railroads, old movies, swing music, and his general preoccupation with the past: Rachael Leben. Titian-haired, green-eyed, long-limbed, full-bodied Rachael Leben.

She was somehow both the girl next door and one of those elegant beauties to be found in any 1930s movie about high society, a cross between Grace Kelly and Carole Lombard. She was sweet-tempered. She was amusing. She was smart. She was everything Ben Shadway had ever dreamed about, and what he wanted to do was get in a time machine with her, travel back to 1940, take a private compartment on the Superchief, and cross the country by rail, making love for three thousand miles in time with the gently rocking rhythm of the train.

She'd come to his real-estate agency for help in finding a house, but the house had not been the end of it. They had been seeing each other frequently for five months. At first he had been fascinated by her in the same way any man might be fascinated by any exceptionally attractive woman, intrigued by the thought of what her lips would taste like and of how her body would fit against his, thrilled by the texture of her skin, the sleekness of her legs, the curve of hip and breast. However, soon after he got to know her, he found her sharp mind and generous heart as appealing as her appearance. Her intensely sensuous appreciation for the world around her was wondrous to behold; she could find as much pleasure in a red sunset or in a graceful configuration of shadows as in a hundred-dollar, seven-course dinner at the county's finest restaurant. Ben's lust had quickly turned to infatuation. And sometime within the past two months—he could not pinpoint the date—infatuation had turned to love.

Ben was relatively confident that Rachael loved him, too. They had not yet quite reached the stage where they could forthrightly and comfortably declare the true depth of their feelings for each other. But he felt love in the tenderness of her touch and in the weight of her gaze when he caught her looking secretly at him.

In love, they had not yet *made* love. Although she was a present-focused woman with the enviable ability to wring every last drop of pleasure from the moment, that did not mean she was promiscuous. She didn't speak bluntly of her feelings, but he sensed that she wanted to progress in small, easy steps. A leisurely romance provided plenty of time for her to explore and savor each new strand of affection in the steadily strengthening bond that bound them to each other, and when at last they succumbed to desire and surrendered to complete intimacy, sex would be all the sweeter for the delay.

He was willing to give her as much time as she required. For one thing, day by day he felt their need growing, and he derived a special thrill from contemplating the tremendous power and intensity of the lovemaking when they finally unleashed their desire. And through her, he had come to realize that they would be cheating themselves out of the more innocent pleasures of the moment if they rushed headlong through the early stages of courtship to satisfy a libidinal urge.

Also, as a man with an affinity for better and more genteel ages, Ben was old-fashioned about these matters and preferred not to jump straight into bed for quick and easy gratification. Neither he nor Rachael was a virgin, but he found it emotionally and spiritually satisfying—and erotic as hell—to wait until the many threads linking them had been woven tightly together, leaving sex for the last strand in the bond.

He parked the Thunderbird in Rachael's driveway, beside her red 560 SL, which she had not bothered to put in the garage.

Thick bougainvillea, ablaze with thousands of red blossoms, grew up one wall of the bungalow and over part of the roof. With the help of a latticework frame, it formed a living green-and-scarlet canopy above the front stoop.

Ben stood in cool bougainvillea shadows, with the warm sun at his back, and rang the bell half a dozen times, growing concerned when Rachael took so long to respond.

Inside, music was playing. Suddenly, it was cut off.

When at last Rachael opened the door, she had the security chain in place, and she looked warily through the narrow gap. She smiled when she saw him, though it seemed as much a smile of nervous relief as of pleasure. "Oh, Benny, I'm so glad it's you."

She slipped the brass chain and let him in. She was barefoot, wearing a tightly belted silky blue robe—and carrying a gun.

Disconcerted, he said, "What're you doing with that?"

"I didn't know who it might be," she said, switching on the two safeties and putting the pistol on the small foyer table. Then, seeing his frown and realizing that her explanation was inadequate, she said, "Oh, I don't know. I guess I'm just . . . shaky."

"I heard about Eric on the radio. Just minutes ago."

She came into his arms. Her hair was partially damp. Her skin was sweet with the fragrance of jasmine, and her breath smelled of chocolate. He knew she must have been taking one of her long lazy soaks in the tub.

Holding her close, he felt her trembling. He said, "According to the radio, you were there."

"Yes."

"I'm sorry."

"It was horrible, Benny." She clung to him. "I'll never forget the sound of the truck hitting him. Or the way he bounced and rolled along the pavement." She shuddered.

"Easy," he said, pressing his cheek against her damp hair. "You don't have to talk about it."

"Yes, I do," she said. "I've got to talk it out if I'm ever going to get it off my mind."

He put a hand under her chin and tilted her lovely face up to him. He kissed her once, gently. Her mouth tasted of chocolate.

"Okay," he said. "Let's go sit down, and you can tell me what happened."

"Lock the door," she said.

"It's okay," he said, leading her out of the foyer.

She stopped and refused to move. "Lock the door," she insisted.

Puzzled, he went back and locked it.

She took the pistol from the foyer and carried it with her.

Something was wrong, something more than Eric's death, but Ben did not understand what it was.

The living room was shrouded in deep shadows, for she had drawn all the drapes. That was distinctly odd. Ordinarily she loved the sun and reveled in its warm caress with the languid pleasure of a cat sunning on a windowsill. He had never seen the drapes drawn in this house until now.

"Leave them closed," Rachael said when Ben started to unveil the windows.

She switched on a single lamp and sat in its amber glow, in the corner of a peach-colored sofa. The room was very modern, all in shades of peach and white with dark blue accents, polished bronze lamps, and a bronze-and-glass coffee table. In her blue robe she was in harmony with the decor.

She put the pistol on the table beside the lamp. Near to hand.

Ben retrieved her champagne and chocolate from the bathroom and brought them to her. In the kitchen, he got another cold split of champagne and a glass for himself.

When he joined her on the living-room sofa, she said, "It doesn't seem right. The champagne and chocolate, I mean. It looks as if I'm celebrating his death."

"Considering what a bastard he was to you, perhaps a celebration would be justified."

She shook her head adamantly. "No. Death is never a cause for celebration, Benny. No matter what the circumstances. Never."

But she unconsciously ran her fingertips back and forth along the pale, pencil-thin, barely visible three-inch scar that followed the edge of her delicate jawline on the right side of her face. A year ago, in one of his nastier moods, Eric had thrown a glass of Scotch at her. It had missed, hitting the wall and shattering, but a sharp fragment had caught her on the rebound, slicing her cheek, requiring fifteen expertly sewn little stitches to avoid a prominent scar. That was the day she finally walked out on him. Eric would never hurt her again. She had to be relieved by his death even if only on a subconscious level.

Pausing now and then to sip champagne, she told Ben about this morning's meeting in the attorney's office and about the subsequent altercation on the sidewalk when Eric took her by the arm and seemed on the verge of violence. She recounted the accident and the hideous condition of the corpse in vivid detail, as if she had to put every terrible, bloody image into words in order to be free of it. She told him about making the funeral arrangements as well, and as she spoke, her shaky hands gradually grew steadier.

He sat close, turned sideways to face her, with one hand on her shoulder. Sometimes he moved his hand to gently massage her neck or to stroke her copper-brown hair.

"Thirty million dollars," he said when she had finished, shaking his head at the irony of her getting everything when she had been willing to settle for so little.

"I don't really want it," she said. "I've half a mind to give it away. A large part of it, anyway."

"It's yours to do with as you wish," he said. "But don't make any decisions now that you'd regret later."

She looked down into the champagne glass that she held in both hands. Frowning worriedly, she said, "Of course, he'd be furious if I gave it away."

"Who?"

"Eric," she said softly.

Ben thought it odd that she should be concerned about Eric's disapproval. Obviously she was still shaken by events and not yet quite herself. "Give yourself time to adjust to the circumstances."

She sighed and nodded. "What time is it?"

He looked at his watch. "Ten minutes till seven."

"I called a lot of people earlier this afternoon and told them what happened, let them know about the funeral. But there must be thirty or forty more to get in touch with. He had no close relatives—just a few cousins. And an aunt he loathed. Not many friends, either. He wasn't a man who cared much for friends, and he didn't have much talent for making them. But lots of business associates, you know. God, I'm not looking forward to the chore."

"I have my cellular phone in the car," Ben said. "I can help you call them. We'll get it done fast."

She smiled vaguely. "And just how would that look—the wife's boyfriend helping her contact the bereaved?"

"They don't have to know who I am. I'll just say I'm a friend of the family."

"Since I'm all that's left of the family," Rachael said, "I guess that wouldn't be a lie. You're my best friend in the world, Benny."

"More than just a friend."

"Oh, yes."

"Much more, I hope."

"I hope," she said.

She kissed him lightly and, for a moment, rested her head upon his shoulder.

■ They contacted all of Eric's friends and business associates by eight-thirty, at which time Rachael expressed surprise that she was hungry. "After a day like this and everything that I saw . . . isn't it sort of hard-boiled of me to have an appetite?"

"Not at all," Ben said gently. "Life goes on, babe. The living have got to live. Fact is, I read somewhere that witnesses to sudden and violent death usually experience a sharp increase in all their appetites during the days and weeks that follow."

"Proving to themselves that they're alive."

"Trumpeting it."

She said, "I can't offer much of a dinner, I'm afraid. I have the makings of a salad. And we could cook up a pot of rigatoni, open a jar of Ragú sauce."

"A veritable feast fit for a king."

She brought the pistol with her to the kitchen and put it down on the counter near the microwave oven.

She had closed the Levolor blinds. Tight. Ben liked the view from those rear windows—the lushly planted backyard with its azalea beds and leafy Indian laurels, the property wall that was completely covered by a riotously bright tangle of red and yellow bougainvillea—and he reached for the control rod to open the slats.

"Please don't," she said. "I want . . . the privacy."

"No one can see in from the yard. It's walled and gated."

"Please."

He left the blinds as she wanted them.

"What are you afraid of, Rachael?"

"Afraid? But I'm not."

"The gun?"

"I told you—I didn't know who was at the door, and since it's been such an upsetting day . . . "

"Now you know it was me at the door."

"Yes."

"And you don't need a gun to deal with me. Just the promise of another kiss or two will keep me in line."

She smiled. "I guess I should put it back in the bedroom where it belongs. Does it make you nervous?"

"No. But I—"

"I'll put it away as soon as we've got dinner cooking," she said, but there was a tone in her voice that made her statement seem less like a promise than a delaying tactic.

Intrigued and somewhat uneasy, he opted for diplomacy and said no more for the moment.

She put a big pot of water on the stove to boil while he emptied the jar of Ragú into a smaller pot. Together, they chopped lettuce, celery, tomatoes, onions, and black olives for the salad.

They talked as they worked, primarily about Italian food. Their conversation was not quite as fluid and natural as usual, perhaps because they were trying too hard to be lighthearted and to put all thoughts of death aside.

Rachael mostly kept her eyes on the vegetables as she prepared them, bringing her characteristically effortless concentration to the task, rendering each rib of celery into slices that were all precisely the same width, as if symmetry were a vital element in a successful salad and would enhance the taste.

Distracted by her beauty, Ben looked at her as much as at the culinary work before him. She was almost thirty, appeared to be twenty, yet had the elegance and poise of a grande dame who'd had a long lifetime in which to learn the angles and attitudes of perfect gracefulness. He never grew tired of looking at her. It wasn't just that she excited him. By some magic that he could not understand, the sight of her also relaxed him and made him feel that all was right with the world and that he, for the first time in his often lonely life, was a complete man with a hope of lasting happiness.

Impulsively he put down the knife with which he had been slicing a tomato, took the knife from her hand and set it aside, turned her toward him, pulled her against him, slipped his arms around her, and kissed her deeply. Now her soft mouth tasted of champagne instead of chocolate. She still smelled faintly of jasmine, though beneath that fragrance was her own clean and appealing scent. He moved his hands slowly down her back, tracing the concave arc to her bottom, feeling the firm and exquisitely sculpted contours of her body through the silky robe. She was wearing nothing underneath. His warm hands grew hot—then much hotter—as the heat of her was transmitted through the material to his own flesh.

She clung to him for a moment with what seemed like desperation, as if she were shipwrecked and he were a raft in a tossing sea. Her body was stiff. Her hands clutched tensely, fingers digging into him. Then, after a moment, she relaxed against him, and her hands began to move over his back and shoulders and upper arms, testing and kneading his muscles. Her mouth opened wider, and their kiss became hungrier. Her breathing quickened.

He could feel her full breasts pressing against his chest. As if with a will and intention of their own, his hands moved more urgently in exploration of her.

The phone rang.

Ben remembered at once that they had forgotten to put it on the answering machine again when they had finished contacting people with the news of Eric's death and funeral, and in confirmation it rang again, stridently.

"Damn," Rachael said, pulling back from him.

"I'll get it."

"Probably another reporter."

He took the call on the wall phone by the refrigerator, and it was not a reporter. It was Everett Kordell, chief medical examiner for the city of Santa Ana, phoning from the morgue. A serious problem had arisen, and he needed to speak to Mrs. Leben.

"I'm a family friend," Ben said. "I'm taking all calls for her."

"But I've got to speak to her personally," the medical examiner insisted. "It's urgent."

"Surely you can understand that Mrs. Leben has had a difficult day. I'm afraid you'll simply have to deal with me."

"But she's got to come downtown," Kordell said plaintively.

"Downtown? You mean to the morgue? Now?"

"Yes. Right away."

"Why?"

Kordell hesitated. Then: "This is embarrassing and frustrating, and I assure you that it'll all be straightened out sooner or later, probably very soon, but . . . well, Eric Leben's corpse is missing."

Certain that he'd misunderstood, Ben said, "Missing?"

"Well . . . perhaps misplaced," Everett Kordell said nervously.

"Perhaps?"

"Or perhaps . . . stolen."

Ben got a few more details, hung up, and turned to Rachael.

She was hugging herself, as if in the grip of a sudden chill. "The morgue, you said?"

He nodded. "The damn incompetent bureaucrats have apparently lost the body."

Rachael was very pale, and her eyes had a haunted look. But, curiously, she did not appear to be surprised by the startling news.

Ben had the strange feeling that she had been waiting for this call all evening.

 # 4 DOWN WHERE THEY KEEP THE DEAD

TO RACHAEL, THE CONDITION OF THE MEDICAL EXAMINER'S office was evidence that Everett Kordell was an obsessive-compulsive personality. No papers, books, or files cluttered his desk. The blotter was new, crisp, unmarked. The pen-and-pencil set, letter opener, letter tray, and silver-framed pictures of his family were precisely arranged. On the shelves behind his desk were two hundred or three hundred books in such pristine condition and so evenly placed that they almost appeared to be part of a painted backdrop. His diplomas and two anatomy charts were hung on the walls with an exactitude that made Rachael wonder if he checked their alignment every morning with ruler and plumb line.

Kordell's preoccupation with neatness and orderliness was also evident in his appearance. He was tall and almost excessively lean, about fifty, with a sharp-featured ascetic face and clear brown eyes. Not a strand of his graying, razor-cut hair was out of place. His long-fingered hands were singularly spare of flesh, almost skeletal. His white shirt looked as if it had been laundered only five minutes ago, and the straight creases in each leg of his dark brown trousers were so sharp they almost glinted in the fluorescent light.

When Rachael and Benny were settled in a pair of dark pine chairs with forest-green leather cushions, Kordell went around the desk to his own chair. "This is most distressing to me, Mrs. Leben—to add this burden to what you've already been through today. It's quite inexcusable. I apologize again and extend my deepest sympathies, though I know nothing I say can make the matter any less disturbing. Are you all right? Can I get you a glass of water or anything?"

"I'm okay," Rachael said, though she could not remember ever feeling worse.

Benny reached out and squeezed her shoulder reassuringly. Sweet, reliable Benny. She was so glad he was with her. At five eleven and a hundred fifty pounds, he was not physically imposing. With brown hair, brown eyes, and a pleasing but ordinary face, he seemed like a man who would vanish in a crowd and be virtually invisible at a party. But when he spoke in that soft voice of his, or moved with his uncanny grace, or just looked hard at you, his sensitivity and intelligence were instantly discernible. In his own quiet way, he had the impact of a lion's roar. Everything would be easier with Benny at her side, but she worried about getting him involved in this.

To the medical examiner, Rachael said, "I just want to understand what's happened."

But she was afraid that she understood more than Kordell.

"I'll be entirely candid, Mrs. Leben," Kordell said. "No point in being otherwise." He sighed and shook his head as if he still had difficulty believing such a screwup had happened. Then he blinked, frowned, and turned to Benny. "You're not Mrs. Leben's attorney, by any chance?"

"Just an old friend," Benny said.

"Really?"

"I'm here for moral support."

"Well, I'm hoping we can avoid attorneys," Kordell said.

"I've absolutely no intention of retaining legal counsel," Rachael assured him.

The medical examiner nodded glumly, clearly unconvinced of her sincerity. He said, "I'm not ordinarily in the office at this hour." It was nine-thirty Monday night. "When work unexpectedly backs up and it's necessary to schedule late autopsies, I leave them to one of the assistant medical examiners. The only exceptions are when the deceased is a prominent citizen or the victim of a particularly bizarre and complex homicide. In that case, when there's certain to be a lot of heat involved—the media and politicians, I mean—then I prefer not to put the burden on my subordinates, and if a night autopsy is unavoidable, I stay after hours. Your husband was, of course, a very prominent citizen."

As he seemed to expect a response, she nodded. She didn't trust herself to speak. Fear had risen and fallen in her ever since she had received the news of the body's disappearance, and at the moment it was at high tide.

"The body was delivered to the morgue and logged in at 12:14 this afternoon," Kordell continued. "Because we were already behind schedule and because I had a speaking engagement this afternoon, I ordered my assistants to proceed with the cadavers in the order of their log entries, and I arranged to handle your husband's body myself at 6:30 this evening." He put his fingertips to his temples, massaging lightly and wincing as if merely recounting these events had given him an excruciating headache. "At that time, when I'd prepared the autopsy chamber, I sent an assistant to bring Dr. Leben's body from the morgue . . . but the cadaver couldn't be found."

"Misplaced?" Benny asked.

"That's rarely happened during my tenure in this office," Kordell said with a brief flash of pride. "And on those few occasions when a cadaver has been misplaced—sent to a wrong autopsy table, stored in the wrong drawer, or left on a gurney with an improper ID tag—we've always located it within five minutes."

"But tonight you couldn't find it," Benny said.

"We looked for nearly an hour. Everywhere. Everywhere," Kordell said with evident distress. "It makes no sense. No sense whatsoever. Given our procedures, it's an impossibility."

Rachael realized that she was clutching the purse in her lap so tightly that her knuckles were sharp and white. She tried to relax her hands, folded them. Afraid that either Kordell or Benny would suddenly read a fragment of the monstrous truth in her unguarded eyes, she closed them and lowered her head, hoping the men would think she was simply reacting to the dreadful circumstances that had brought them here.

From within her private darkness, Rachael heard Benny say, "Dr. Kordell, is it possible that Dr. Leben's body was released in error to a private mortuary?"

"We'd been informed earlier today that the Attison Brothers' firm was handling funeral arrangements, so of course we called them when we couldn't find the body. We suspected they'd come for Dr. Leben and that a day employee of the morgue had mistakenly released the cadaver without authorization, prior to autopsy. But they tell us they never came to collect, were in fact waiting for a call from us, and don't have the deceased."

"What I meant," Benny said, "was that perhaps Dr. Leben's body was released in error to another mortician who had come to collect someone else."

"That, of course, was another possibility that we explored with, I assure you, considerable urgency. Subsequent to the arrival of Dr. Leben's body at 12:14 this afternoon, four other bodies were released to private mortuaries. We sent employees to all of those funeral homes to confirm the identity of the cadavers and to make sure none of them was Dr. Leben. None of them was."

"Then what do you suppose has happened to him?" Benny asked.

Eyes closed, Rachael listened to their macabre conversation in darkness, and gradually it began to seem as if she were asleep and as if their voices were the echoey phantom voices of characters in a nightmare.

Kordell said, "Insane as it seems, we were forced to conclude the body's been stolen."

In her self-imposed blackness, Rachael tried unsuccessfully to block out the gruesome images that her imagination began to supply.

"You've contacted the police?" Benny asked the medical examiner.

"Yes, we brought them into it as soon as we realized theft was the only remaining explanation. They're downstairs right now, in the morgue, and of course they want to speak with you, Mrs. Leben."

A soft rhythmic rasping noise was coming from Everett Kordell's direction. Rachael opened her eyes. The medical examiner was nervously sliding his letter opener in and out of its protective sheath. Rachael closed her eyes again.

Benny said, "But are your security measures so inadequate that someone could waltz right in off the street and steal a corpse?"

"Certainly not," Kordell said. "Nothing like this has happened before. I tell you, it's inexplicable. Oh, yes, a determined person might be clever enough to find a way through our security, but it wouldn't be an easy job. Not easy at all."

"But not impossible," Benny said.

The rasping noise stopped. From the new sounds that followed, Rachael figured that the medical examiner must be compulsively rearranging the silver-framed photographs on his desk.

She concentrated on that image to counteract the mad scenes that her darkly cunning imagination had conjured for her horrified consideration.

Everett Kordell said, "I'd like to suggest that both of you accompany me to the morgue downstairs, so you can see firsthand exactly how tight our security is and how very difficult it would be to breach it. Mrs. Leben? Do you feel strong enough to take a tour of the facility?"

Rachael opened her eyes. Both Benny and Kordell were watching her with concern. She nodded.

"Are you sure?" Kordell asked, rising and coming out from behind his desk. "Please understand that I'm not insisting on it. But it would make me feel ever so much better if you would let me show you how careful we are, how responsibly we fulfill our duties here."

"I'm okay," she said.

Picking at a tiny piece of dark lint that he had just spotted on his sleeve, the medical examiner headed toward the door.

As Rachael got up from her chair and turned to follow Kordell, she was swept by a wave of dizziness. She swayed.

Benny took her arm, steadied her. "This tour isn't necessary."

"Yes," she said grimly. "Yes, it is. I've got to see. I've got to know."

Benny looked at her strangely, and she couldn't meet his eyes. He knew something was wrong, something more than Eric's death and disappearance, but he didn't know what. He was unabashedly curious.

Rachael had intended to conceal her anxiety and keep him out of this hideous affair. But deceit was not one of her talents, and she knew he had been aware of her fear from the moment he'd stepped into her house. The dear man was both intrigued and concerned, staunchly determined to stay by her side, which was exactly what she didn't want, but she couldn't help that now. Later, she would have to find a way to get rid of Benny because, much as she needed him, it was not fair to drag him into this mess, not fair to put his life in jeopardy the way hers was.

Right now, however, she had to see where Eric's battered corpse had lain, for she hoped a better understanding of the circumstances surrounding the body's disappearance would allay her worst fears. She needed all her strength for the tour of the morgue.

They left the office and went down where the dead waited.

■ The broad, tile-floored, pale gray corridor ended at a heavy metal door. A white-uniformed attendant sat at a desk in an alcove to the right, this side of the door. When he saw Kordell approaching with Rachael and Benny, he got up and fished a set of bright jangling keys from the pocket of his uniform jacket.

"This is the only interior entrance to the morgue," Kordell said. "The door is always locked. Isn't that right, Walt?"

"Absolutely," the attendant said. "You did want to go in, Dr. Kordell?"

"Yes."

When Walt slid the key into the lock, Rachael saw a tiny spark of static electricity.

Kordell said, "There's an attendant—Walt or someone else—on duty at this desk twenty-four hours a day, seven days a week. No one can get in without his assistance. And he keeps a registry of all visitors."

The wide door was unlocked, and Walt was holding it open for them. They went inside, where the cool air smelled of antiseptics and of something un-identifiable that was less pungent and less clean. The door closed behind them with a faint creak of hinges that seemed to echo through Rachael's bones. The lock engaged automatically with a hollow thunk.

Two sets of double doors, both open, led to big rooms on both sides of the morgue corridor. A fourth windowless metal portal, like that through which they had just entered, lay at the far end of the chilly hallway.

"Now please let me show you the only exterior entrance, where the morgue wagons and the morticians' vehicles pull up," Kordell said, leading the way toward the distant barrier.

Rachael followed him, though just being in this repository of the dead, where Eric had so recently lain, made her knees weak and broke her out in a sweat along the back of her neck and all over her scalp.

"Wait a second," Benny said. He turned to the door through which they had come, pushed down on the bar handle, and opened it, startling Walt, who was just returning to his desk on the other side. Letting the heavy door fall shut again, Benny looked at Kordell and said, "Although it's always locked from the outside, it's always open from the inside?"

"That's right, of course," Kordell said. "It'd be too much trouble to have to summon the attendant to be let out as well as in. Besides, we can't risk having someone accidentally locked in here during an emergency. Fire or earthquake, for example."

Their footsteps echoed eerily off the highly polished tile floor as they continued along the corridor toward the exterior service door at the far end. When they passed the two large rooms, Rachael saw several people in the chamber on the left, standing and moving and talking softly in a glare of crisp, cold fluorescent light. Morgue workers wearing hospital whites. A fat man in beige slacks and a beige-yellow-red-green madras sports jacket. Two men in dark suits looked up as Rachael walked by.

She also saw three dead bodies: still, shrouded shapes lying on stainless-steel gurneys.

At the end of the hall, Everett Kordell pushed open the wide metal door. He stepped outside and beckoned them.

Rachael and Benny followed. She expected to find an alleyway beyond, but though they had left the building, they were not actually outside. The exterior morgue door opened onto one of the underground levels of an adjacent multistory parking garage. It was the same garage in which she'd parked her 560 SL just a short while ago, though she'd left it a few levels above this one.

The gray concrete floor, the blank walls, and the thick pillars holding up the gray concrete ceiling made the subterranean garage seem like an immense, starkly modernistic, Western version of a pharaoh's tomb. The sodium-vapor ceiling lights, widely spaced, provided a jaundice-yellow illumination that Rachael found fitting for a place that served as an antechamber to the hall of the dead.

The area around the morgue entrance was a no-parking zone. But a score of cars were scattered farther out in the vast room, half in the crepuscular bile-yellow light and half in purple-black shadows that had the velvet texture of a casket lining.

Looking at the cars, she had the extraordinary feeling that something was hiding among them, watching.

Watching her in particular.

Benny saw her shiver, and he put his arm around her shoulders.

Everett Kordell closed the heavy morgue door, then tried to open it, but the bar handle could not be depressed. "You see? It locks automatically. Ambulances, morgue wagons, and hearses drive down that ramp from the street and stop here. The only way to get in is to push this button." He pushed a white button in the wall beside the door. "And speak into this intercom." He brought his mouth close to a wire speaker set flush in the concrete. "Walt? This is Dr. Kordell at the outer door. Will you buzz us back in, please?"

Walt's voice came from the speaker. "Right away, sir."

A buzzer sounded, and Kordell was able to open the door again.

"I assume the attendant doesn't just open for anyone who asks to be let in," Benny said.

"Of course not," Kordell said, standing in the open doorway. "If he's sure he recognizes the voice and if he knows the person, he buzzes him through. If he doesn't recognize the voice, or if it's someone new from a private mortuary, or if there's any reason to be suspicious, the attendant walks through the corridor that we just walked, all the way from the front desk, and he inspects whoever's seeking admittance."

Rachael had lost all interest in these details and was concerned only about the gloom-mantled garage around them, which provided a hundred excellent hiding places.

Benny said, "At that point the attendant, not expecting violence, could be overpowered, and the intruder could force his way inside."

"Possibly," Kordell said, his thin face drawing into a sharp scowl. "But that's never happened."

"The attendants on duty today swear that they logged in everyone who came and went—and allowed only authorized personnel to enter?"

"They swear," Kordell said.

"And you trust them all?"

"Implicitly. Everyone who works here is aware that the bodies in our custody are the remains of other people's loved ones, and we know we have a solemn— even sacred—responsibility to protect those remains while we're in charge of them. I think that's evident in the security arrangements I've just shown you."

"Then," Benny said, "someone either had to pick the lock—"

"It's virtually unpickable."

"Or someone slipped into the morgue while the outer door was open for legitimate visitors, hid out, waited until he was the only living person inside, then spirited Dr. Leben's body away."

"Evidently yes. But it's so unlikely that—"

Rachael said, "Could we go back inside, please?"

"Certainly," Kordell said at once, eager to please. He stepped out of her way.

She returned to the morgue corridor, where the cold air carried a faint foul smell beneath the heavy scent of pine disinfectant.

5 UNANSWERED QUESTIONS

IN THE HOLDING ROOM WHERE THE CADAVERS AWAITED AUtopsy, the air was even colder than in the morgue's corridor. Glimmering strangely in all metal surfaces, the stark fluorescent light imparted a wintry sheen to the stainless-steel gurneys and to the bright stainless-steel handles and hinges on the cabinets along the walls. The glossy white enamel finish of the chests and cabinets, though surely no thicker than an eighth of an inch, had a curiously deep—even bottomless—appearance similar to the mysterious, lustrous depth of a landscape of moon-washed snow.

She tried not to look at the shrouded bodies and refused to think about what might lie in some of the enormous cabinet drawers.

The fat man in the madras jacket was Ronald Tescanet, an attorney representing the city's interests. He had been called away from dinner to be on hand when Rachael spoke with the police and, afterward, to discuss the disappearance of her husband's body. His voice was too mellifluous, almost greasy, and he was so effusively sympathetic that his condolences poured forth like warm oil from a bottle. While the police questioned Rachael, Tescanet paced in silence behind them, frequently smoothing his thick black hair with his plump white hands, each of which was brightened by two gold and diamond rings.

As she had suspected, the two men in dark suits were plainclothes police. They showed Rachael their ID cards and badges. Refreshingly, they did not burden her with unctuous sympathy.

The younger of the two, beetle-browed and burly, was Detective Hagerstrom. He said nothing at all, leaving the questioning entirely to his partner. He stood unmoving, like a rooted oak, in contrast to the attorney's ceaseless roaming. He watched with small brown eyes that gave Rachael the impression of stupidity at first; but after a while, on reconsideration, she realized that he possessed a higher than average intelligence which he kept carefully veiled.

She worried that somehow Hagerstrom, by virtue of a cop's almost magical sixth sense, would pierce her deception and see the knowledge that she was concealing. As inconspicuously as possible, she avoided meeting his gaze.

The older cop, Detective Julio Verdad, was a small man whose complexion was the shade of cinnamon and whose black eyes had a vague trace of purple like the skins of ripe plums. He was a sharp dresser: a well-tailored blue suit, dark but summerweight; a white shirt that might have been silk, with French cuffs held together by gold and pearl cuff links; a burgundy necktie with a gold tie chain instead of a clip or tack; dark burgundy Bally loafers.

Although Verdad spoke in clipped sentences and was almost curt, his voice was unfailingly quiet and gentle. The contrast between his lulling tone and his brisk manner was disconcerting. "You've seen their security, Mrs. Leben."

"Yes."

"And are satisfied?"

"I suppose."

To Benny, Verdad said, "You are?"

"Ben Shadway. An old friend of Mrs. Leben's."

"Old school friend?"

"No."

"A friend from work?"

"No. Just a friend."

The plum-dark eyes gleamed. "I see." To Rachael, Verdad said, "I have a few questions."

"About what?"

Instead of answering at once, Verdad said, "Like to sit down, Mrs. Leben?"

Everett Kordell said, "Yes, of course, a chair," and both he and the fat attorney, Ronald Tescanet, hurried to draw one away from a corner desk.

Seeing that no one else intended to sit, concerned about being placed in a position of inferiority with the others peering down at her, Rachael said, "No, thank you. I'll stand. I can't see why this should take very long. I'm certainly in no mood to linger here. What is it you want to ask me, anyway?"

Verdad said, "An unusual crime."

"Body snatching," she said, pretending to be both baffled and sickened by what had happened. The first emotion had to be feigned; the second was more or less genuine.

"Who might have done it?" Verdad asked.

"I've no idea."

"You know no one with a reason?"

"Someone with a motive for stealing Eric's body? No, of course not," she said.

"He had enemies?"

"In addition to being a genius in his field, he was a successful businessman. Geniuses often unwittingly arouse jealousy on the part of colleagues. And, inevitably, some people envied his wealth. And some felt he'd . . . wronged them on his climb up the ladder."

"*Had* he wronged people?"

"Yes. A few. He was a driven man. But I strongly doubt that any of his enemies are the type to take satisfaction from a revenge as pointless and macabre as this."

"He was not just driven," Verdad said.

"Oh?"

"He was ruthless."

"Why do you say that?"

"I've read about him," Verdad said. "Ruthless."

"All right, yes, perhaps. And difficult. I won't deny it."

"Ruthlessness makes passionate enemies."

"You mean so passionate that body snatching would make sense?"

"Perhaps. I'll need the names of his enemies, people who might have reason to hold a grudge."

"You can get that information from the people he worked with at Geneplan," she said.

"His company? But you're his wife."

"I knew very little about his business. He didn't want me to know. He had very strong opinions about . . . my proper place. Besides, for the past year I've been separated from him."

Verdad looked surprised, but somehow Rachael sensed that he had already done some background work and knew what she was telling him.

"Divorcing?" he asked.

"Yes."

"Bitter?"

"On his part, yes."

"So this explains it."

"Explains what?" she asked.

"Your utter lack of grief."

She had begun to suspect that Verdad was twice as dangerous as the silent, motionless, watchful Hagerstrom. Now she was sure of it.

"Dr. Leben treated her abominably," Benny said in her defense.

"I see," Verdad said.

"She had no reason to grieve for him," Benny said.

"I see."

Benny said, "You're acting as if this is a murder case, for God's sake."

"Am I?" Verdad said.

"You're treating her as if she's a suspect."

"Do you think so?" Verdad asked quietly.

"Dr. Leben was killed in a freak accident," Benny said, "and if anyone was at fault, it was Leben himself."

"So we understand."

"There were at least a dozen witnesses."

"Are you Mrs. Leben's attorney?" Verdad inquired.

"No, I told you—"

"Yes, the old friend," Verdad said, making his point subtly.

"If you were an attorney, Mr. Shadway," Ronald Tescanet said, stepping forward so quickly that his jowls trembled, "you'd understand why the police have no choice but to pursue this unpleasant line of questioning. They must, of course, consider the possibility that Dr. Leben's body was stolen to prevent an autopsy. To *hide* something."

"How melodramatic," Benny said scornfully.

"But conceivable. Which would mean that his death was not as cut-and-dried as it appeared to be," Tescanet said.

"Exactly," Verdad said.

"Nonsense," Benny said.

Rachael appreciated Benny's determination to protect her honor. He was unfailingly sweet and supportive. But she was willing to let Verdad and Hagerstrom regard her as a possible murderess or at least an accomplice to murder. She was incapable of killing anyone, and Eric's death was entirely accidental, and in time that would be clear to the most suspicious homicide detective. But while Hagerstrom and Verdad were busy satisfying themselves on those points, they would not be free to pursue other avenues of inquiry closer to the terrible truth. They were in the process of dragging their own red herring across the trail, and she would not take offense at their misdirected suspicion as long as it kept them baying after the wrong scent.

She said, "Lieutenant Verdad, surely the most logical explanation is that, in spite of Dr. Kordell's assertions, the body has simply been misplaced." Both the stork-thin medical examiner and Ronald Tescanet protested. She quietly but firmly cut them off. "Or maybe it was kids playing an elaborate joke. College kids. An initiation rite of some sort. They've been known to do worse."

"I think I already know the answer to this question," Benny said. "But is it possible that Eric Leben was not dead after all? Could his condition have been misjudged? Is it possible that he walked out of here in a daze?"

"No, no, no!" Tescanet said, blanching and suddenly sweating in spite of the cold air.

"Impossible," Kordell said simultaneously. "I saw him. Massive head injuries. No vital signs whatsoever."

But this off-the-wall theory seemed to intrigue Verdad. He said, "Didn't Dr. Leben receive medical attention immediately after the accident?"

"Paramedics," Kordell said.

"Highly trained, reliable men," Tescanet said, mopping his doughy face with a handkerchief. He had to be doing rapid mental arithmetic right now, calculating the difference between the financial settlement that might be necessitated by a morgue screwup and the far more major judgment that might be won against the city for the incompetence of its paramedics. "They would never, regardless of circumstances, *never* mistakenly pronounce a man dead when he wasn't."

"One—there was no heartbeat whatsoever," Kordell said, counting the proofs of death on fingers so long and supple that they would have served him equally well if he had been a concert pianist instead of a pathologist. "The paramedics had a perfectly flat line on the small EKG unit in their van. Two—no respiration. Three—steadily falling body temperature."

"Unquestionably dead," Tescanet murmured.

Lieutenant Verdad now regarded the attorney and the chief medical examiner with the same flat expression and hawkish eyes that he had turned on Rachael. He probably didn't think Tescanet and Kordell—or the paramedics—were covering up malpractice or malfeasance. But his nature and experience ensured his willingness to suspect anyone of anything at any time, given even the poorest reason for suspicion.

Scowling at Tescanet's interruption, Everett Kordell continued, "Four—there was absolutely no perceptible electrical activity in the brain. We have an EEG machine here in the morgue. We frequently use it in accident cases as a final test. That's a safety procedure I've instituted since taking this position. Dr. Leben was attached to the EEG the moment he was brought in, and we could find no perceptible brain waves. I was present. I saw the graph. Brain death. If there is any single, universally accepted standard for declaring a man dead, it's when the attending physician encounters a condition of full and irreversible cardiac arrest coupled with brain death. The pupils of Dr. Leben's eyes wouldn't dilate in bright light. And no respiration. With all due respect, Mrs. Leben, your husband was as dead as any man I've ever seen, and I will stake my reputation on that."

Rachael had no doubt that Eric had been dead. She had seen his sightless, unblinking eyes as he lay on the blood-spattered pavement. She had seen, too well, the deep concavity running from behind his ear all the way to the curve of his brow: the crushed and splintered bone. However, she was thankful that Benny had unwittingly confused things and had given the detectives yet another false trail to pursue.

She said, "I'm sure he was dead. I've no doubt of it. I saw him at the scene of the accident, and I know there could have been no mistaken diagnosis."

Kordell and Tescanet looked immeasurably relieved.

With a shrug, Verdad said, "Then we discard the hypothesis."

But Rachael knew that, once the possibility of misdiagnosis had been planted in the cops' minds, they would expend time and energy in the exploration of it, which was all that mattered. Delay. That was the name of the game. Delay, stall, confuse the issue. She needed time to confirm her own worst suspicions, time to decide what must be done to protect herself from various sources of danger.

Lieutenant Verdad led Rachael past the three draped bodies and stopped with her at an empty gurney that was bedecked with rumpled shrouds. On it lay a thick paper tag trailing two strands of plastic-coated wire. The tag was crumpled.

"That's all we've got to go on, I'm afraid. The cart that the corpse once occupied and the ID tag that was once tied to its foot." Only inches from Rachael, the detective looked hard at her, his intense dark eyes as flat and unreadable as his face. "Now, why do you suppose a body snatcher, whatever his motivation, would take the time to untie the tag from the dead man's toe?"

"I don't have the slightest idea," she said.

"The thief would be worried about getting caught. He'd be in a hurry. Untying the tag would take precious seconds."

"It's crazy," she said shakily.

"Yes, crazy," Verdad said.

"But then the whole thing's crazy."

"Yes."

She stared down at the wrinkled and vaguely stained shroud, thinking of how it had wrapped her husband's cold and naked cadaver, and she shuddered uncontrollably.

"Enough of this," Benny said, putting his arm around her for warmth and support. "I'm getting you the hell out of this place."

■ Everett Kordell and Ronald Tescanet accompanied Rachel and Benny to the elevator in the parking garage, continuing to make a case for the morgue's and the city's complete lack of culpability in the body's disappearance. They were not convinced by her repeated assurances that she did not intend to sue anyone. There were so many things for her to think and worry about that she had neither the energy nor the inclination to persuade them that her intentions were benign. She just wanted to be rid of them so she could get on with the urgent tasks that awaited her.

When the elevator doors closed, finally separating her and Benny from the lean pathologist and the corpulent attorney, Benny said, "If it was me, I think I *would* sue them."

"Lawsuits, countersuits, depositions, legal strategy meetings, courtrooms—boring, boring, boring," Rachael said. She opened her purse as the elevator rose.

"Verdad is a cool son of a bitch, isn't he?" Benny said.

"Just doing his job, I guess." Rachael took the thirty-two pistol out of her purse.

Benny, watching the light move on the board of numbers above the lift's doors, did not immediately see the gun. "Yeah, well, he could do his job with a little more compassion and a little less machinelike efficiency."

They had risen one and a half floors from the basement. On the indicator panel, the 2 was about to light. Her Mercedes was one level farther up.

Benny had wanted to bring his car, but Rachael had insisted on driving her own. As long as she was behind the wheel, her hands were occupied and her attention was partly on the road, so she couldn't become morbidly preoccupied with the frightening situation in which she found herself. If she had nothing to do but brood about recent developments, she would very likely lose the tenuous self-control she now possessed. She had to remain busy in order to hold terror at arm's length and stave off panic.

They reached the second floor and kept going up.

She said, "Benny, step away from the door."

"Huh?" He looked down from the lightboard, blinked in surprise when he saw the pistol. "Hey, where the hell did you get that?"

"Brought it from home."

"Why?"

"Please step back. Quickly now, Benny," she said shakily, aiming at the doors.

Still blinking, confused, he got out of the way. "What's going on? You're not going to shoot anybody."

Her thunderous heartbeat was so loud that it muffled his voice and made it sound as if he were speaking to her from a distance.

They arrived at the third floor.

The indicator board went *ping!* The 3 lighted. The elevator stopped with a slight bounce.

"Rachael, answer me. What is this?"

She did not respond. She had gotten the gun after leaving Eric. A woman alone ought to have a gun . . . especially after walking out on a man like him. As the doors rolled open, she tried to remember what her pistol instructor had said: Don't jerk the trigger; squeeze it slowly, or you'll pull the muzzle off target and miss.

But no one was waiting for them, at least not in front of the elevator. The gray concrete floor, walls, pillars, and ceiling looked like those in the basement from which they'd begun their ascent. The silence was the same, too: sepulchral and somehow threatening. The air was less dank and far warmer than it had been three levels below, though it was every bit as still. A few of the ceiling lights were burned out or broken, so a greater number of shadows populated the huge room than had darkened the basement, and they seemed deeper as well, better suited for the complete concealment of an attacker, though perhaps her imagination painted them blacker than they really were.

Following her out of the elevator, Benny said, "Rachael, who are you afraid of?"

"Later. Right now let's just get the hell out of here."

"But—"

"Later."

Their footsteps echoed and reechoed hollowly off the concrete, and she felt as if they were walking not through an ordinary parking garage in Santa Ana but through the chambers of an alien temple, under the eye of an unimaginably strange deity.

At that late hour, her red 560 SL was one of only three cars parked on the entire floor. It stood alone, gleaming, a hundred feet from the elevator. She walked directly toward it, circled it warily. No one crouched on the far side. Through the windows, she could see that no one was inside, either. She opened the door, got in quickly. As soon as Benny climbed in and closed his door, she hit the master lock switch, started the engine, threw the car in gear, popped the emergency brake, and drove too fast toward the exit ramp.

As she drove, she engaged the safeties on her pistol and, with one hand, returned it to her purse.

When they reached the street, Benny said, "Okay, now tell me what this cloak-and-dagger stuff is all about."

She hesitated, wishing she had not brought him this far into it. She should have come to the morgue alone. She'd been weak, needed to lean on him, but now if she didn't break her dependency on him, if she drew him further into it, she would without doubt be putting his life in jeopardy. She had no right to endanger him.

"Rachael?"

She stopped at a red traffic light at the intersection of Main Street and Fourth, where a hot summer wind blew a few scraps of litter into the center of the crossroads and spun them around for a moment before sweeping them away.

"Rachael?" Benny persisted.

A shabbily dressed derelict stood at the corner, only a few feet away. He was filthy, unshaven, and drunk. His nose was gnarled and hideous, half eaten away by melanoma. In his left hand he held a wine bottle imperfectly concealed in a paper bag. In his grubby right paw he gripped a broken alarm clock—no glass covering the face of it, the minute hand missing—as if he thought he possessed a great treasure. He stooped down, peered in at her. His eyes were fevered, blasted.

Ignoring the derelict, Benny said, "Don't withdraw from me, Rachael. What's wrong? Tell me. I can help."

"I don't want to get you involved," she said.

"I'm already involved."

"No. Right now you don't know anything. And I really think that's best."

"You promised—"

The traffic light changed, and she tramped the accelerator so suddenly that Benny was thrown against his seat belt and cut off in midsentence.

Behind them, the drunk with the clock shouted: *"I'm Father Time!"*

Rachael said, "Listen, Benny, I'll take you back to my place so you can get your car."

"Like hell."

"Please let me handle this myself."

"Handle *what*? What's going on?"

"Benny, don't interrogate me. Just please don't do that. I've got a lot to think about, a lot to do . . . "

"Sounds like you're going somewhere else tonight."

"It doesn't concern you," she said.

"Where are you going?"

"There're things I've got to . . . check out. Never mind."

Getting angry now, he said, "You going to shoot someone?"

"Of course not."

"Then why're you packing a gun?"

She didn't answer.

He said, "You got a permit for a concealed weapon?"

She shook her head. "A permit, but just for home use."

He glanced behind to see if anyone was near them, then leaned over from his seat, grabbed the steering wheel, and jerked it hard to the right.

The car whipped around with a screech of tires, and she hit the brakes, and they slid sideways six or eight yards, and when she tried to straighten the wheel he grabbed it again, and she shouted at him to stop it, and he let go of the wheel, which spun through her hands for a moment, but then she was firmly in control once more, pulled to the curb, stopped, looked at him, said, "What are you— crazy?"

"Just angry."

"Let it be," she said, staring out at the street.

"I want to help you."

"You can't."

"Try me. Where do you have to go?"

She sighed. "Just to Eric's place."

"His house? In Villa Park? Why?"

"I can't tell you."

"After his house, where?"

"Geneplan. His office."

"Why?"

"I can't tell you that, either."

"Why not?"

"Benny, it's dangerous. It could get violent."

"So what the fuck am I—porcelain? Crystal? Shit, woman, do you think I'm going to fly into a million goddamn pieces at the tap of a goddamn finger?"

She looked at him. The amber glow of the streetlamp came through only her half of the windshield, leaving him in darkness, but his eyes shone in the shadows. She said, "My God, you're furious. I've never heard you use that kind of language before."

He said, "Rachael, do we have something or not? I think we have something. Special, I mean."

"Yes."

"You really think so?"

"You know I do."

"Then you can't freeze me out of this. You can't keep me from helping you when you need help. Not if we're to go on from here."

She looked at him, feeling very tender toward him, wanting more than anything to bring him into her confidence, to have him as her ally, but involving him would be a rotten thing to do. He was right now thinking what kind of trouble she might be in, his mind churning furiously, listing possibilities, but nothing he could imagine would be half as dangerous as the truth. If he knew the truth, he might not be so eager to help, but she dared not tell him.

He said, "I mean, you know I'm a pretty old-fashioned guy. Not very with it by most standards. Staid in some ways. Hell, half the guys in California real estate wear white cords and pastel blazers when they go to work on a summer day like this, but I don't feel comfortable in less than a three-piece suit and wing tips. I may be the last guy in a real-estate office who even knows what a goddamn vest *is.* So when someone like me sees the woman he cares about in trouble, he has to help, it's the only thing he *can* do, the plain old-fashioned thing, the right thing, and if she won't let him help, then that's pretty much a slap in the face, an affront to all his values, a rejection of what he *is*, and no matter how much he likes her, he's got to walk, it's as simple as that."

She said, "I never heard you make a speech before."

"I never had to before."

Both touched and frustrated by his ultimatum, Rachael closed her eyes and leaned back in the seat, unable to decide what to do. She kept her hands on the steering wheel, gripping it tightly, for if she let go, Benny would be sure to see how badly her hands were shaking.

He said, "Who are you afraid of, Rachael?"

She didn't answer.

He said, "You know what happened to his body, don't you?"

"Maybe."

"You know who took it."

"Maybe."

"And you're afraid of them. Who are they, Rachael? For God's sake, who would do something like that—and why?"

She opened her eyes, put the car in gear, and pulled away from the curb. "Okay, you can come along with me."

"To Eric's house, the office? What're we looking for?"

"That," she said, "I'm not prepared to tell you."

He was silent for a moment. Then he said, "Okay. All right. One step at a time. I can live with that."

She drove north on Main Street to Katella Avenue, east on Katella to the expensive community of Villa Park, into the hills toward her dead husband's estate. In the upper reaches of Villa Park, the big houses, many priced well over a million dollars, were less than half visible beyond screens of shrubbery and the gathered cloaks of night. Eric's house, looming beyond a row of enormous Indian laurels, seemed darker than any other, a cold place even on a June night, the many windows like sheets of some strange obsidian that would not permit the passage of light in either direction.

6   THE TRUNK

THE LONG DRIVEWAY, MADE OF RUST-RED MEXICAN PAVING tiles, curved past Eric Leben's enormous Spanish-modern house before finally turning out of sight to the garages in back. Rachael parked in front.

Although Ben Shadway delighted in authentic Spanish buildings with their multiplicity of arches and angles and deep-set leaded windows, he was no fan of Spanish *modern.* The stark lines, smooth surfaces, big plate-glass windows, and total lack of ornamentation might seem stylish and satisfyingly clean to some, but he found such architecture boring, without character, and perilously close to the cheap-looking stucco boxes of so many southern California neighborhoods.

Nevertheless, as he got out of the car and followed Rachael down a dark Mex-ican-tile walkway, across an unlighted veranda where yellow-flowering succu-lents and bloom-laden white azaleas glowed palely in enormous clay pots, to the front door of the house, Ben was impressed by the place. It was massive—cer-tainly ten thousand square feet of living space—set on expansive, elaborately landscaped grounds. From the property, there was a view of most of Orange County to the west, a vast carpet of light stretching fifteen miles to the pitch-black ocean; in daylight, in clear weather, one could probably see all the way to Catalina. In spite of the spareness of the architecture, the Leben house reeked of wealth. To Ben, the crickets singing in the bushes even sounded different from those that chirruped in more modest neighborhoods, less shrill and more me-lodious, as if their minuscule brains encompassed awareness of—and respect for—their surroundings.

Ben had known that Eric Leben was a very rich man, but somehow that knowl-edge had had no impact until now. Suddenly he sensed what it meant to be worth tens of millions of dollars. Leben's wealth pressed on Ben, like a very real weight.

Until he was nineteen, Ben Shadway had never given much thought to money. His parents were neither rich enough to be preoccupied with investments nor poor enough to worry about paying next month's bills, nor had they much am-bition, so wealth—or lack of it—had not been a topic of conversation in the Shadway household. However, by the time Ben completed two years of military service, his primary interest was money: making it, investing it, accumulating ever-larger piles.

He did not love money for its own sake. He did not even care all that much for the finer things that money could buy; imported sports cars, pleasure boats, Rolex watches, and two-thousand-dollar suits held no great appeal for him. He was happier with his meticulously restored 1956 Thunderbird than Rachael was with her new Mercedes, and he bought his suits off the rack at Harris & Frank. Some men loved money for the power it gave them, but Ben was no more inter-ested in exercising power over others than he was in learning Swahili.

To him, money was primarily a time machine that would eventually allow him to do a lot of traveling back through the years to a more appealing age—the 1920s, 1930s, and 1940s, which held so much interest for him. Thus far, he had worked long hours with a few days off. But he intended to build the company into one of the top real-estate powerhouses in Orange County within the next five years, then sell out and take a capital gain large enough to support him comfortably for most—if not the rest—of his life. Thereafter, he could devote himself almost entirely to swing music, old movies, the hard-boiled detective fiction he loved, and his min-iature trains.

Although the Great Depression extended through more than a third of the period to which Ben was attracted, it seemed to him like a far better time than the present. During the twenties, thirties, and forties, there had been no terrorists, no end-of-the-world atomic threat, no street crime to speak of, no frustrating fifty-five-mile-per-hour speed limit, no polyester or lite beer. Television, the moron box that is the curse of modern life, was not a major social force by the end of the forties. Currently, the world seemed a cesspool of easy sex, pornography, illiterate fiction, witless and graceless music. The second, third, and fourth decades of the century were so fresh and innocent by comparison with the present that

Ben's nostalgia sometimes deepened into a melancholy longing, into a profound desire to have been born before his own time.

Now, as the respectful crickets offered trilling songs to the otherwise peaceful silence of the Leben estate, as a warm wind scented with star jasmine blew across the sea-facing hills and through the long veranda, Ben could almost believe that he had, in fact, been transported back in time to a more genteel, less hectic age. Only the architecture spoiled the halcyon illusion.

And Rachael's pistol.

That spoiled things, too.

She was an extraordinarily easygoing woman, quick to laugh and slow to anger, too self-confident to be easily frightened. Only a very real and very serious threat could compel her to arm herself.

Before getting out of the car, she had withdrawn the gun from her purse and had clicked off the safeties. She warned Ben to be alert and cautious, though she refused to say exactly what it was that he should be alert to and cautious of. Her dread was almost palpable, yet she declined to share her worry and thus relieve her mind; she jealously guarded her secret as she had done all evening.

He suppressed his impatience with her—not because he had the forbearance of a saint but simply because he had no choice but to let her proceed with her revelations at her own pace.

At the door of the house, she fumbled with her keys, trying to find the lock and keyhole in the gloom. When she had walked out a year ago, she'd kept her house key because she'd thought she would need to return later to collect some of her belongings, a task that had become unnecessary when Eric had everything packed and sent to her along with, she said, an infuriatingly smug note expressing his certainty that she would soon realize how foolish she had been and seek reconciliation.

The cold, hard scrape of key metal on lock metal gave rise to an unfortunate image in Ben's mind: a pair of murderously sharp and gleaming knives being stropped against each other.

He noticed a burglar-alarm box with indicator lights by the door, but the system was evidently not engaged because none of the bulbs on the panel was lit.

While Rachael continued to poke at the lock with the key, Ben said, "Maybe he had the locks changed after you moved out."

"I doubt it. He was *so* confident that I'd move back in with him sooner or later. Eric was a very confident man."

She found the keyhole. The key worked. She opened the door, nervously reached inside, snapped on the lights in the foyer, and went into the house with the pistol held out in front of her.

Ben followed, feeling as if the male and female roles had been wrongly reversed, feeling as if he ought to have the gun, feeling a bit foolish when you came right down to it.

The house was perfectly still.

"I think we're alone," Rachael said.

"Who did you expect to find?" he asked.

She did not answer.

Although she had just expressed the opinion that they were alone, she advanced with her pistol ready.

They went slowly from room to room, turning on every light, and each new revelation of the interior made the house more imposing. The rooms were large, high-ceilinged, white-walled, airy, with Mexican-tile floors and lots of big windows; some had massive fireplaces of either stone or ceramic tile; a few boasted oak cabinets of superb craftsmanship. A party for two hundred guests would not have strained the capacity of the living room and adjacent library.

The furniture was as starkly modern and functional as the rather forbidding architecture. The upholstered white sofas and chairs were utterly free of ornamentation. Coffee tables, end tables, and all the occasional tables were also quite plain, finished in mirror-bright high-gloss enamel, some black and some white.

The only color and drama were provided by an eclectic group of paintings, antiques, and objets d'art. The bland decor was intended to serve as an unobtrusive backdrop against which to display those items of surpassing quality and value, each of which was artfully illuminated by indirect lighting or tightly focused overhead minispots. Over one fireplace was a tile panel of birds by William de Morgan, which had been done (Rachael said) for Czar Nicholas I. Here, a blazing Jackson Pollock canvas. There, a Roman torso carved from marble, dating to the first century B.C. The ancient was intermixed with the new in wildly unconventional but striking arrangements. Here, a nineteenth-century Kirman panel recording the lives of the greatest shahs of Persia. Here, a bold Mark Rothko canvas featuring only broad bands of color. There, a pair of Lalique crystal-deer consoles, each holding an exquisite Ming vase. The effect was both breathtaking and jarring— and altogether more like a museum than a real home.

Although he had known Rachael was married to a wealthy man, and although he had known that she had become a very wealthy widow as of this morning, Ben had given no thought to what her wealth might mean to their relationship. Now her new status impinged upon him like an elbow in his side, making him uncomfortable. *Rich*. Rachael was very damn rich. For the first time, that thought had meaning for him.

He realized he'd need to sit down and think about it at length, and he would need to talk with her forthrightly about the influence of so much money, about the changes for better and worse that it might cause between them. However, this was neither the time nor the place to pursue the matter, and he decided to put it out of his mind for the moment. That was not easy. A fortune in tens of millions was a powerful magnet relentlessly drawing the mind regardless of how many other urgent matters required attention.

"You lived here six years?" he asked disbelievingly as they moved through the cool sterile rooms, past the precisely arranged displays.

"Yes," she said, relaxing slightly as they roamed deeper into the house without encountering a threat of any kind. "Six long years."

As they inspected the white vaulted chambers, the place began to seem less like a house and more like a great mass of ice in which some primeval catastrophe had embedded scores of gorgeous artifacts from another, earlier civilization.

He said, "It seems . . . forbidding."

"Eric didn't care about having a real home—a cozy, livable home, I mean. He never was much aware of his surroundings anyway. He lived in the future, not the present. All he wanted of his house was that it serve as a monument to his success, and that's what you see here."

"I'd expect to see your touch—your sensual style—everywhere, *somewhere,* but it's nowhere in sight."

"Eric allowed no changes in decor," she said.

"And you could live with that?"

"I did, yes."

"I can't picture you being happy in such a chilly place."

"Oh, it wasn't that bad. Really, it wasn't. There *are* many amazingly beautiful things here. Any one of them can occupy hours of study . . . contemplation . . . and provide great pleasure, even spiritual pleasure."

He always marveled at how Rachael routinely found the positive aspect of even difficult circumstances. She wrung every drop of enjoyment and delight from a situation and did her best to ignore the unpleasant aspects. Her present-focused, pleasure-oriented personality was an effective armor against the vicissitudes of life.

At the rear of the ground floor, in the billiards room that looked out upon the swimming pool, the largest object on display was an intricately carved, claw-footed, late-nineteenth-century billiards table that boasted teak rails inlaid with semiprecious stones.

"Eric never played," Rachael said. "Never held a cue stick in his hands. All he cared about was that the table is one of a kind and that it cost more than thirty thousand dollars. The overhead lights aren't positioned to facilitate play; they're aimed to present the table to its best advantage."

"The more I see of this place, the better I understand him," Ben said, "but the less able I am to grasp why you ever married him."

"I was young, unsure of myself, perhaps looking for the father figure that'd always been missing in my life. He was so calm. He had such tremendous self-assurance. In him, I saw a man of power, a man who could carve out a niche for himself, a ledge on the mountainside where I could find stability, safety. At the time, I thought that was all I wanted."

Implicit in those words was the admission that her childhood and adolescence had been difficult at best, confirming a suspicion Ben had harbored for months. She seldom spoke of her parents or of her school years, and Ben believed that those formative experiences had been so negative as to leave her with a loathing for the past, a distrust of the uncertain future, and a defensive ability to focus intently upon whatever great or meager joys the moment offered.

He wanted to pursue that subject now, but before he could say anything, the mood abruptly changed. A sense of imminent danger had hung heavy in the air upon their entrance, then had faded as they progressed from one deserted white room to another with the growing conviction that no intruder lurked within the house. Rachael had stopped pointing the pistol ahead of her and had been holding it at her side with the muzzle aimed at the floor. But now the threatening atmosphere clouded the air again when she spotted three distinct fingerprints and a portion of a palmprint on one arm of a sofa, etched into the snowy fabric in a burgundy-dark substance which, on closer inspection, looked as if it might be blood.

She crouched beside the sofa, peering closely at the prints, and Ben saw her shiver. In a tremulous whisper she said, "Been here, damn it. I was afraid of this. Oh, God. Something's happened here." She touched one finger to the ugly stain, instantly snatched her hand away, and shuddered. "Damp. My God, it's *damp*."

"*Who's* been here?" Ben asked. "What's happened?"

She stared at the tip of her finger, the one with which she had touched the stain, and her face was distorted with horror. Slowly she raised her eyes and looked at Ben, who had stooped beside her, and for a moment he thought her terror had reached such a peak that she was prepared, at last, to tell him everything and seek his help. But after a moment he could see the resolve and self-control flooding back into her gaze and into her lovely face.

She said, "Come on. Let's check out the rest of the house. And for God's sake, be careful."

He followed her as she resumed her search. Again she held the pistol in front of her.

In the huge kitchen, which was nearly as well equipped as that of a major restaurant, they found broken glass scattered across the floor. One pane had been smashed out of the French door that opened onto the patio.

"An alarm system's no good if you don't use it," Ben said. "Why would Eric go off and leave a house like this unprotected?"

She didn't answer.

He said, "And doesn't a man like him have servants in residence?"

"Yes. A nice live-in couple with an apartment over the garage."

"Where are they? Wouldn't they have heard a break-in?"

"They're off Monday and Tuesday," she said. "They often drive up to Santa Barbara to spend the time with their daughter's family."

"Forced entry," Ben said, lightly kicking a shard of glass across the tile floor. "Okay, now hadn't we better call the police?"

She merely said, "Let's look upstairs." As the sofa had been stained with blood, so her voice was stained with anxiety. But worse: there was a bleakness about her, a grim and sombrous air, that made it easy to believe she might never laugh again.

The thought of Rachael without laughter was unbearable.

They climbed the stairs with caution, entered the upstairs hall, and checked out the second-floor rooms with the wariness they might have shown if unraveling a mile of tangled rope with the knowledge that a poisonous serpent lay concealed in the snarled line.

At first nothing was out of order, and they discovered nothing untoward—until they entered the master bedroom, where all was chaos. The contents of the walk-in closet—shirts, slacks, sweaters, shoes, suits, ties, and more—lay in a torn and tangled mess. Sheets, a white quilted spread, and feather-leaking pillows were strewn across the floor. The mattress had been heaved off the springs, which had been knocked halfway off the frame. Two black ceramic lamps were smashed, the shades ripped and then apparently stomped. Enormously valuable paintings had been wrenched from the walls and slashed to ribbons, damaged beyond repair. Of a pair of graceful Klismos-style chairs, one was upended, and the other had been hammered against a wall until it had gouged out big chunks of plaster and was itself reduced to splintered rubble.

Ben felt the skin on his arms puckering with gooseflesh, and an icy current quivered along the back of his neck.

Initially he thought that the destruction had been perpetrated by someone engaged upon a methodical search for something of value, but on taking a second look, he realized that such was not the case. The guilty party had unquestionably been in a blind rage, violently trashing the bedroom with malevolent glee or in a frenzy of hatred. The intruder had been someone possessed of considerable strength and little sanity. Someone strange. Someone infinitely dangerous.

With a recklessness evidently born of fear, Rachael plunged into the adjacent bathroom, one of only two places in the house that they had not yet searched, but the intruder was not there, either. She stepped back into the bedroom and surveyed the ruins, shaky and pale.

"Breaking and entering, now vandalism," Ben said. "You want me to call the cops, or should you do it?"

She did not reply but entered the last of the unsearched places, the enormous walk-in closet, returning a moment later, scowling. "The wall safe's been opened and emptied."

"Burglary too. Now we've got to call the cops, Rachael."

"No," she said. The bleakness that had hung about her like a gray and sodden cloak now became a specific presence in her gaze, a dull sheen in those usually bright green eyes.

Ben was more alarmed by that dullness than he had been by her fear, for it implied fading hope. Rachael, *his* Rachael, had never seemed capable of despair, and he couldn't bear to see her in the grip of that emotion.

"No cops," she said.

"Why not?" Ben said.

"If I bring the cops into it, I'll be killed for sure."

He blinked. "What? Killed? By the police? What on earth do you mean?"

"No, not by the cops."

"Then who? Why?"

Nervously chewing on the thumbnail of her left hand, she said, "I should never have brought you here."

"You're stuck with me. Rachael, really now, isn't it time you told me more?"

Ignoring his plea, she said, "Let's check the garage, see if one of the cars is missing," and she dashed from the room, leaving him no choice but to hurry after her with feeble protests.

■ A white Rolls-Royce. A Jaguar sedan the same deep green as Rachael's eyes. Then two empty stalls. And in the last space, a dusty, well-used, ten-year-old Ford with a broken radio antenna.

Rachael said, "There should be a black Mercedes 560 SEL." Her voice echoed off the walls of the long garage. "Eric drove it to our meeting with the lawyers this morning. After the accident . . . after Eric was killed, Herb Tuleman—the attorney—said he'd have the car driven back here and left in the garage. Herb is reliable. He always does what he says. I'm sure it was returned. And now it's gone."

"Car theft," Ben said. "How long does the list of crimes have to get before you'll agree to calling the cops?"

She walked to the last stall, where the battered Ford was parked in the harsh bluish glare of a fluorescent ceiling strip. "And this one doesn't belong here at all. It's not Eric's."

"It's probably what the burglar arrived in," Ben said. "Decided to swap it for the Mercedes."

With obvious reluctance, with the pistol raised, she opened one of the Ford's front doors, which squeaked, and looked inside. "Nothing."

He said, "What did you expect?"

She opened one of the rear doors and peered into the back seat.

Again there was nothing to be found.

"Rachael, this silent sphinx act is irritating as hell."

She returned to the driver's door, which she had opened first. She opened it again, looked in past the wheel, saw the keys in the ignition, and removed them.

"Rachael, damn it."

Her face was not simply troubled. Her grim expression looked as if it had been carved in flesh that was really stone and would remain upon her visage from now until the end of time.

He followed her to the trunk. "What are you looking for now?"

At the back of the Ford, fumbling with the keys, she said, "The intruder wouldn't have left this here if it could be traced to him. A burglar wouldn't leave such an easy clue. No way. So maybe he came here in a stolen car that *couldn't* be traced to him."

Ben said, "You're probably right. But you're not going to find the registration slip in the trunk. Let's try the glove compartment."

Slipping a key into the trunk lock, she said, "I'm not looking for the registration slip."

"Then what?"

Turning the key, she said, "I don't really know. Except . . . "

The lock clicked. The trunk lid popped up an inch.

She opened it all the way.

Inside, blood was puddled thinly on the floor of the trunk.

Rachael made a faint mournful sound.

Ben looked closer and saw that a woman's blue high-heeled shoe was on its side in one corner of the shallow compartment. In another corner lay a woman's eyeglasses, the bridge of which was broken, one lens missing and the other lens cracked.

"Oh, God," Rachael said, "he not only stole the car. He killed the woman who was driving it. Killed her and stuffed the body in here until he had a chance to dispose of it. And now where will it end? Where will it end? Who will stop him?"

Badly shocked by what they'd found, Ben was nevertheless aware that when Rachael said "him," she was talking about someone other than an unidentified burglar. Her fear was more specific than that.

7   NASTY
LITTLE GAMES

TWO SNOWFLAKE MOTHS SWOOPED AROUND THE OVERHEAD fluorescent light, batting against the cool bulbs, as if in a frustrated suicidal urge to find the flame. Their shadows, greatly enlarged, darted back and forth across the walls, over the Ford, across the back of the hand that Rachael held to her face.

The metallic odor of blood rose out of the open trunk of the car. Ben took a step backward to avoid the noxious scent.

He said, "How did you know?"

"Know what?" Rachael asked, eyes still closed, head still bowed, coppery red-brown hair falling forward and half concealing her face.

"You knew what you might find in the trunk. How?"

"No. I didn't know. I was half afraid I'd find . . . something. Something else. But not this."

"Then what *did* you expect?"

"Maybe something worse."

"Like what?"

"Don't ask."

"I have asked."

The soft bodies of the moths tapped against the fire-filled tubes of glass above. *Tap-tap-tick-tap*.

Rachael opened her eyes, shook her head, started walking away from the battered Ford. "Let's get out of here."

He grabbed her by the arm. "We have to call the cops now. And you'll have to tell them whatever it is you know about what's going on here. So you might as well tell me first."

"No police," she said, either unwilling or unable to look at him.

"I was ready to go along with you on that. Until now."

"No police," she insisted.

"But someone's been killed!"

"There's no body."

"Christ, isn't the blood enough?"

She turned to him and finally met his eyes. "Benny, please, please, don't argue with me. There's no time to argue. If that poor woman's body were in the trunk, it might be different, and we might be able to call the cops, because with a body they'd have something to work on and they'd move a lot faster. But without a body to focus on, they'll ask a lot of questions, endless questions, and they won't believe the answers I could give them, so they'll waste a lot of time. But there's none to waste because soon there're going to be people looking for me . . . dangerous people."

"Who?"

"If they aren't already looking for me. I don't think they could've learned that Eric's body is missing, not yet, but if they have heard about it, they'll be coming here. We've got to go."

"Who?" he demanded exasperatedly. "Who are they? What are they after? What do they want? For God's sake, Rachael, let me in on it."

She shook her head. "Our agreement was that you could come with me but that I wasn't going to answer questions."

"I made no such promises."

"Benny, damn it, my *life* is on the line."

She was serious; she really meant it; she was desperately afraid for her life, and that was sufficient to break Ben's resolve and make him cooperate. Plaintively he said, "But the police could provide protection."

"Not from the people who may be coming after me."

"You make it sound as if you're being pursued by demons."

"At least."

She quickly embraced him, kissed him lightly on the mouth.

She felt good in his arms. He was badly shaken by the thought of a future without her.

Rachael said, "You're terrific. For wanting to stand by me. But go home now. Get out of it. Let me handle things myself."

"Not very damn likely."

"Then don't interfere. Now let's *go*."

Pulling away from him, she headed back across the five-car garage toward the door that led into the house.

A moth dropped from the light and fluttered against his face, as if his feelings for Rachael were, at the moment, brighter than the fluorescent bulbs. He batted it away.

He slammed the lid on the Ford's trunk, leaving the wet blood to congeal and the gruesome smell to thicken.

He followed Rachael.

At the far end of the garage, near the door that led into the house through the laundry room, she stopped, staring down at something on the floor. When Ben caught up with her, he saw some clothes that had been discarded in the corner, which neither he nor she had noticed when they had entered the garage. There were a pair of soft white vinyl shoes with white rubber soles and heels, wide white laces. A pair of baggy pale green cotton pants with a drawstring waist. And a loose short-sleeve shirt that matched the pants.

Looking up from the clothes, he saw that Rachael's face was no longer merely pale and waxen. She appeared to have been dusted with ashes. Gray. Seared.

Ben looked down at the suit of clothes again. He realized it was an outfit of the sort surgeons wore when they went into an operating theater, what they called hospital whites. Hospital whites had once actually been white, but these days they were usually this soft shade of green. However, not only surgeons wore them. Many other hospital employees preferred the same basic uniform. Furthermore, he had seen the assistant pathologists and attendants dressed in exactly the same kind of clothes at the morgue, only a short while ago.

Rachael drew a deep hissing breath through clenched teeth, shook herself, and went into the house.

Ben hesitated, staring intently at the discarded pair of shoes and rumpled clothes. Riveted by the soft green hue. Half mesmerized by the random patterns of gentle folds and creases in the material. His mind spinning. His heart pounding. Breathlessly considering the implications.

When at last he broke the spell and hurried after Rachael, Ben discovered that sweat had popped out all over his face.

■ Rachael drove much too fast to the Geneplan Building in Newport Beach. She handled the car with considerable skill, but Ben was glad to have a seat belt. Having ridden with her before, he knew she enjoyed driving even more than she enjoyed most other things in life; she was exhilarated by speed, delighted by the SL's maneuverability. But tonight she was in too much of a hurry to take any pleasure from her driving skill, and although she was not exactly reckless, she took some turns at such high speed and changed lanes so suddenly that she could not be accused of timidity.

He said, "Are you in some kind of trouble that rules out turning to the police? Is that it?"

"Do you mean—am I afraid the cops would get something on me?"

"Are you?"

"No," she said without hesitation, in a tone that seemed devoid of deception.

"'Cause if somehow you've gotten in deep with the wrong kind of people, it's never too late to turn back."

"Nothing like that."

"Good. I'm glad to hear it."

The backsplash of dim light from the dashboard meters and gauges was just bright enough to softly illuminate her face but not bright enough to reveal the tension in her or the unhealthy grayness that fear had brought to her complexion. She looked now as Ben always thought of her when they were separated: breathtaking.

In different circumstances, with a different destination, the moment would have been like something from a perfect dream or from one of those great old movies. After all, what could be more thrilling or exquisitely erotic than being with a gorgeous woman in a sleek sports car, barreling through the night toward some romantic destination, where they could forsake the snug contours of bucket seats for cool sheets, the excitement of high-speed travel having primed them for fiercely passionate lovemaking.

She said, "I've done nothing wrong, Benny."

"I didn't really think you had."

"You implied . . . "

"I had to ask."

"Do I look like a villain to you?"

"You look like an angel."

"There's no danger I'll land in jail. The worst that can happen to me is that I'll wind up a victim."

"Damned if I'll let that happen."

"You're really very sweet," she said. She glanced away from the road and managed a thin smile. "Very sweet."

The smile was confined to her lips and did not chase the fear from the rest of her face, did not even touch her troubled eyes. And no matter how sweet she thought he was, she was still not prepared to share any of her secrets with him.

■ They reached Geneplan at eleven-thirty.

Dr. Eric Leben's corporate headquarters was a four-story, glass-walled building in an expensive business park off Jamboree Road in Newport Beach, stylishly irregular in design with six sides that were not all of equal length, and with a modernistic polished marble and glass porte cochere. Ben usually despised such architecture, but he grudgingly had to admit that the Geneplan headquarters had a certain appealing boldness. The parking lot was divided into sections by long planters overflowing with vine geraniums heavily laden with wine-red and white blooms. The building was surrounded by an impressive amount of green space as well, with artfully arranged palm trees. Even at this late hour, the trees, grounds, and building were lit by cunningly placed spotlights that imparted a sense of drama and importance to the place.

Rachael pulled her Mercedes around to the rear of the building, where a short driveway sloped down to a large bronze-tinted door that evidently rolled up to admit delivery trucks to an interior loading bay on the basement level. She drove to the bottom and parked at the door, below ground level, with concrete walls rising on both sides. She said, "If anyone gets the idea I might come to Geneplan, and if they drive by looking for my car, they won't spot it down here."

Getting out of the car, Ben noticed how much cooler and more pleasant the night was in Newport Beach, closer to the sea, than it had been in either Santa Ana or Villa Park. They were much too far from the ocean—a couple of miles— to hear the waves or to smell the salt and seaweed, but the Pacific air nevertheless had an effect.

A smaller, man-size door was set in the wall beside the larger entrance and also opened into the basement level. It had two locks.

Living with Eric, Rachael had run errands to and from Geneplan when he hadn't the time himself and when, for whatever reason, he did not trust a subordinate with the task, so she'd once possessed keys. But the day she walked out on him, she put the keys on a small table in the foyer of the Villa Park house. Tonight, she had found them exactly where she'd left them a year ago, on the table beside a tall nineteenth-century Japanese cloisonné vase, dust-filmed. Evidently Eric had instructed the maid not to move the keys even an inch. He must have intended that their undisturbed presence should be a subtle humiliation for Rachael when she came crawling back to him. Happily, she had denied him that sick satisfaction.

Clearly, Eric Leben had been a supremely arrogant bastard, and Ben was glad that he had never met the man.

Now Rachael opened the steel door, stepped into the building, and switched on the lights in the small underground shipping bay. An alarm box was set in the concrete wall. She tapped a series of numbers on its keyboard. The pair of glowing red lights winked out, and a green bulb lit up, indicating that the system was deactivated.

Ben followed her to the end of the chamber, which was sealed off from the rest of the subterranean level for security reasons. At the next door there was another alarm box for another system independent of that which had guarded the exterior door. Ben watched her switch it off with another number code.

She said, "The first one is based on Eric's birthday, this one on mine. There're more ahead."

They proceeded by the beam of the flashlight that Rachael had brought from the house in Villa Park, for she did not want to turn on any lights that might be spotted from outside.

"But you've a perfect right to be here," Ben said. "You're his widow, and you've almost certainly inherited everything."

"Yes, but if the wrong people drive by and see lights on, they'll figure it's me, and they'll come in to get me."

He wished to God she'd tell him who these "wrong people" were, but he knew better than to ask. Rachael was moving fast, eager to put her hands on whatever had drawn her to this place, then get out. She would have no more patience for his questions here than she'd had in the house in Villa Park.

As he accompanied her through the rest of the basement to the elevator, up to the second floor, Ben was increasingly intrigued by the extraordinary security system in operation after normal business hours. There was a third alarm to be penetrated before the elevator could be summoned to the basement. On the second floor, they debarked from the elevator into a reception lounge also designed with security in mind. In the searching beam of Rachael's flashlight, Ben saw a sculpted beige carpet, a striking desk of brown marble and brass for the receptionist, half a dozen brass and leather chairs for visitors, glass and brass coffee tables, and three large and ethereal paintings that might have been by Martin Green, but even if the flashlight had been switched off, he would have seen the blood-red alarm lights in the darkness. Three burnished brass doors—probably solid-core and virtually impenetrable—led out of the lounge, and alarm lights glowed beside each of them.

"This is nothing compared to the precautions taken on the third and fourth levels," Rachael said.

"What's up there?"

"The computers and duplicate research data banks. Every inch is covered by infrared, sonic, and visual-motion detectors."

"We going up there?"

"Fortunately, we don't have to. And we don't have to go out to Riverside County, either, thank God."

"What's in Riverside?"

"The actual research labs. The entire facility is underground, not just for biological isolation but for better security against industrial espionage, too."

Ben was aware that Geneplan was a leader in the most fiercely competitive and rapidly developing industry in the world. The frantic race to be first with a new product, when coupled with the natural competitiveness of the kind of men drawn into the industry, made it necessary to guard trade secrets and product development with a care that was explicitly paranoid. Still, he was not quite prepared for the obvious siege mentality that lay behind the design of Geneplan's electronic security.

Dr. Eric Leben had been a specialist in recombinant DNA, one of the most brilliant figures in the rapidly expanding science of gene splicing. And Geneplan was one of the companies on the cutting edge of the extremely profitable biobusiness that had grown out of this new science since the late 1970s.

Eric Leben and Geneplan held valuable patents on a variety of genetically engineered microorganisms and new strains of plant life, including but not limited to: a microbe that produced an extremely effective hepatitis vaccine, which was currently undergoing the process of acquiring the FDA seal but was now only a year away from certain approval and marketing; another man-made microbe "factory" that produced a supervaccine against all types of herpes; a new variety of corn that could flourish even if irrigated with salt water, making it possible for farmers to cultivate abundant crops in arid lands within pumping distance of the seacoast, where nothing had previously grown; a new family of slightly altered oranges and lemons genetically modified to be impervious to fruit flies, citrus canker, and other diseases, thus eliminating the need for pesticides in a large portion of the citrus-fruit industry. Any one such patent might be worth tens or even hundreds of millions of dollars, and Ben supposed it was only prudent for Geneplan to be paranoid and to spend a small fortune to guard the research data that led to the creation of each of these living gold mines.

Rachael went to the middle of the three doors, deactivated the alarm, and used another key to disengage the lock.

When Ben went through the door behind her and eased it shut, he discovered that it was enormously heavy and would have been immovable if it had not been hung in perfect balance on cunningly designed ball-bearing hinges.

She led him along a series of dark and silent corridors, through additional doors to Eric's private suite. There she required one more code for a final alarm box.

Inside the sanctum sanctorum at last, she quickly crossed a vast expanse of antique Chinese carpet in rose and beige to Eric's massive desk. It was as ultra-modern as that of the company's front-lounge receptionist but even more stunning and expensive, constructed of rare gold-veined marble and polished malachite.

The bright but narrowly focused lance of the flashlight beam revealed only the middle of the big room as Rachael advanced through it, so Ben had only glimpses and shadowy impressions of the decor. It seemed even more determinedly modern than Eric Leben's other haunts, downright futuristic.

She put her purse and pistol on the desk as she passed it, went to the wall behind, where Ben joined her. She played the flashlight over a four-foot-square painting: broad bands of sombrous yellow and a particularly depressing gray separated by a thin swath of blood-dark maroon.

"Another Rothko?" Ben asked.

"Yeah. And with an important function besides just being a piece of art."

She slipped her fingers under the burnished steel frame, feeling along the bottom. A latch clicked, and the big painting swung away from the wall, to which it had been firmly fixed rather than hung on wire. Behind the hinged Rothko was a large wall safe with a circular door about two feet in diameter. The steel face, dial, and handle gleamed.

"Trite," Ben said.

"Not really. Not your ordinary wall safe. Four-inch-thick steel casing, six-inch face and door. Not just set in the wall but actually welded to the steel beams of the building itself. Requires not one but two combinations, the first forward, the second reverse. Fireproof and virtually blastproof, too."

"What's he keep in there—the meaning of life?"

"Some money, I guess, like in the safe at the house," she said, handing Ben the flashlight. She turned the dial and began to put in the first combination. "Important papers."

He aimed the light at the safe door. "Okay, so what're we after exactly? The cash?"

"No. A file folder. Maybe a ring-binder notebook."

"What's in it?"

"The essentials of an important research project. More or less an abstract of the developments to date, including copies of Morgan Lewis's regular reports to Eric. Lewis is the project head. And with any luck, Eric's personal project diary is in here, too. All of his practical and philosophical thoughts on the subject."

Ben was surprised that she had answered. Was she finally prepared to let him in on at least some of her secrets?

"What subject?" he asked. "What's this particular research project all about?"

She did not respond but blotted her sweat-damp fingers on her blouse before easing the safe's dial backward toward the first number of the second combination.

"Concerning what?" he pressed.

"I have to concentrate, Benny," she said. "If I overshoot one of these numbers, then I'll have to start all over and put the first set in again."

He had gotten all he was going to get, the one little scrap about the file. But, not caring to stand idly by, having nothing else to do but pressure her, he said, "There must be hundreds of research files on scores of projects, so if he keeps just one of them here, it's got to involve the most important thing Geneplan's currently working on."

Squinting, and with her tongue poked out between her teeth, she brought all of her attention to bear on the dial.

"Something big," he said.

She said nothing.

He said, "Or it's research they're doing for the government, the military. Something extremely sensitive."

Rachael put in the final number, twisted the handle, opened the small steel door, and said, "Oh, damn."

The safe was empty.

"They got here before us," she said.

"Who?" Ben demanded.

"They must've suspected that I knew."

"Who suspected?"

"Otherwise, they wouldn't have been so quick to get rid of the file," she said.

"Who?" Ben said.

"Surprise," said a man behind them.

As Rachael gasped, Ben was already turning, seeking the intruder. The flashlight beam caught a tall, bald man in a tan leisure suit and a green-and-white-striped shirt. His head was so completely hairless that he must have shaved it. He had a square face, wide mouth, proud nose, Slavic cheekbones, and gray eyes the shade of dirty ice. He was standing on the other side of the desk. He resembled the late Otto Preminger, the film director. Sophisticated in spite of his leisure suit. Obviously intelligent. Potentially dangerous. He had confiscated the pistol that Rachael had put down with her purse when she had come into the office.

Worse, the guy was holding a Smith & Wesson Model 19 Combat Magnum. Ben was familiar with—and deeply respected—that revolver. Meticulously constructed, it had a four-inch barrel, was chambered for the .357 Magnum cartridge, weighed a moderate thirty-five ounces, and was so accurate and so powerful that it could even be used for deer hunting. Loaded with hollow-point expanding cartridges or with armor-piercing rounds, it was as deadly a handgun as any in the world, deadlier than most.

In the beam of the Eveready, the intruder's gray eyes glistened strangely.

"Lights on," the bald man said, raising his voice slightly, and immediately the room's overhead lights blinked to life, evidently engaged by a voice-activated switch, a trick that suited Eric Leben's preference for ultramodern design.

Rachael said, "Vincent, put the gun away."

"Not possible, I'm afraid," the bald man said. Though his head was quite naked, the back of his big hand had plenty of hair, almost like a pelt, and it even bristled on his fingers between the knuckles.

"There's no need for violence," Rachael said.

Vincent's smile was sour, imparting a cold viciousness to his broad face. "Indeed? No need for violence? I suppose that's why you brought a pistol," he said, holding up the thirty-two that he had snatched off the desk.

Ben knew the S&W Combat Magnum had twice the recoil of a forty-five, which was why it featured large hand-filling stocks. In spite of the superb accuracy built into it, the weapon could be wildly inaccurate in the hands of an inexperienced shooter unprepared for the hard kick it delivered. If the bald man did not appreciate the tremendous power of the gun, if he were inexperienced, he would almost certainly fire the first couple of shots high into the wall, over their heads, which might give Ben time to reach him and take him out.

"We didn't really believe Eric would've been reckless enough to tell you about Wildcard," Vincent said. "But apparently he did, the poor damn fool, or you wouldn't be here, rummaging in his office safe. No matter how badly he treated you, Rachael, he still had a weakness for you."

"He was too proud," she said. "Always was. He liked to brag about his accomplishments."

"Ninety-five percent of Geneplan's staff is in the dark about the Wildcard Project," Vincent said. "It's that sensitive. Believe me, no matter how much you may have hated him, he thought you were special, and he wouldn't have bragged about it to anyone else."

"I didn't hate him," she said. "I pity him. Especially now. Vincent, did you know he'd broken the cardinal rule?"

Vincent shook his head. "Not until . . . tonight. It was a mad thing to do."

Intently watching the bald man, Ben reluctantly decided that the guy was experienced with the Combat Magnum and would not be startled by its recoil. His grip on it was not at all casual; his right hand was clenched tightly. His aim was not casual, either; his right arm was extended, stiff and straight, elbow locked, with the muzzle lined up between Rachael and Ben. He would only have to swing it a couple of inches in either direction to blow one or both of them away.

Unaware that Ben could be of more use in such a situation than he'd ever given her reason to believe, Rachael said, "Forget the damn gun, Vincent. We don't need guns. We're all in this together now."

"No," Vincent said. "No, as far as the rest of us are concerned, you're not in this. Never should've been. We simply don't trust you, Rachael. And this friend of yours . . ."

The dirty-gray eyes shifted focus from Rachael to Ben. His gaze was piercing, disconcerting. Although his eyes lingered on Ben only a second or two, there was an iciness in them that was transmitted to Ben, sending a chill along his spine.

Then, having failed to detect that he was dealing with someone far less innocent than appearances indicated, Vincent looked away from Ben, back at Rachael, and said, "He's a complete outsider. If we don't want you in this, then we certainly aren't about to make room for *him*."

To Ben, that statement sounded ominously like a death sentence, and at last he moved with a sinuosity and lightning speed worthy of a striking snake. Taking a big chance that the second command to the voice-activated switch would be as simple as the first, he said, "Lights *off!*" The room instantly went dark as he simultaneously threw the flashlight at Vincent's head, but, Jesus, the guy was already turning to fire at him, and Rachael was screaming—Ben hoped she was diving for the floor—and the sudden darkness was cast into confusion by the whipping beam of the tumbling Eveready, which he hoped would be enough to give him the edge, an edge he badly needed because, just a fraction of a second after the lights went out and the flashlight left his hand, he was already pitching forward, onto the malachite desk in a sliding belly flop that ought to carry him across and into Vincent, committed to action, no turning back now, all of this like a film run at twice its normal speed, yet with an eerie objective time sense so slowed down that each second seemed like a minute, which was just the old program taking control of his brain, the fighting animal taking charge of the body. In the next single second a hell of a lot happened all at once: Rachael was still screaming shrilly, and Ben was sliding, and the flashlight was tumbling, and the muzzle of the Magnum flashed blue-white, and Ben sensed a slug passing over him so close it might have singed his hair, heard the whine of its passage even above the thunderous roar of the shot itself—*skeeeeeeeen*—felt the coldness of the polished malachite through his shirt, and the flashlight struck Vincent as the shot exploded and as Ben was crossing the desk, Vincent grunted from the blow, the flash rebounded and fell to the floor, its lance of light coming to rest on a six-foot piece of abstract bronze sculpture, and Ben was off the desk by then, colliding with his adversary, both of them going down hard. The gun fired again. The shot went into the ceiling. Ben was sprawled on top of Vincent in the darkness, but with a perfect intuitive sense of the relationship of their bodies, which made it possible for him to bring a knee up between the man's thighs, smashing it into the unprotected crotch, and Vincent screamed louder than Rachael, so Ben rammed his knee up again, showing no mercy, daring no mercy, chopped him in the throat, too, which cut off the scream, then hit him along the right temple, hit him again, hard, harder, and a third shot rang out, deafening, so Ben chopped him once more, harder still, then the gun fell out of Vincent's suddenly limp hand, and gaspingly Ben said, "Lights on!"

Instantly the room brightened.

Vincent was out cold, making a slight wet rattling noise as slow inhalations and exhalations passed through his injured throat.

The air stank of gunpowder and hot metal.

Ben rolled off the unconscious man and crawled to the Combat Magnum, taking possession of it with more than a little relief.

Rachael had ventured from behind the desk. Stooping, she picked up her thirty-two pistol, which Vincent had also dropped. The look she gave Ben was part shock, part astonishment, part disbelief.

He crawled back to Vincent and examined him. Thumbed up one eyelid and then the other, checking for the uneven dilation that might indicate a severe concussion or other brain injury. Gently inspected the man's right temple, where two edge-of-the-hand chops had landed. Felt his throat. Made sure his breathing, though hampered, was not too badly obstructed. Took his wrist, located his pulse, timed it.

He sighed and said, "He won't die, thank God. Sometimes it's hard to judge how much force is enough . . . or too much. But he won't die. He'll be out for a while, and when he comes around he'll need medical attention, but he'll be able to get to a doctor on his own."

Speechless, Rachael stared at him.

He took a cushion from a chair and used it to prop up Vincent's head, which would help keep the trachea open if there was some bleeding in the throat.

He quickly searched Vincent but did not find the Wildcard file. "He must have come here with others. They opened the safe, took the contents, while he stayed behind to wait for us."

She put a hand on his shoulder, and he raised his head to meet her eyes. She said, "Benny, for God's sake, you're just a real-estate salesman."

"Yeah," he said, as if he didn't understand the implied question, "and I'm a damn good one, too."

"But . . . the way you handled him . . . the way you . . . so fast . . . violent . . . so sure of yourself . . . "

With satisfaction so intense it almost hurt, he watched her as she grappled with the realization that she was not the only one with secrets.

Showing her no more mercy than she'd thus far shown him, letting her stew in her curiosity, he said, "Come on. Let's get the hell out of here before someone else shows up. I'm good at these nasty little games, but I don't particularly enjoy them."

8   DUMPSTER

WHEN AN OLD WINO IN SOILED PANTS AND A RAGGED Hawaiian shirt wandered into the alley, stacked some crates, and climbed up to search in the garbage dumpster for God knows what treasures, two rats had leaped from the bin, startling him. He had fallen off his makeshift ladder—just as he'd caught a glimpse of the dead woman sprawled in the garbage. She wore a cream-colored summer dress with a blue belt.

The wino's name was Percy. He couldn't remember his last name. "Not really sure I ever had one," he said when Verdad and Hagerstrom questioned him in the alley a short while later. "For a fact, I ain't used a last name since I can remember. Guess maybe I did have one sometime, but my memory ain't what it used to be on account of the damn cheap wine, barf brew, which is the only rot I can pay for."

"You think this slimeball killed her?" Hagerstrom asked Verdad, as if the alky couldn't hear them unless they spoke directly to him.

Studying Percy with extreme distaste, Verdad replied in the same tone of voice. "Not likely."

"Yeah. And even if he saw anything important, he wouldn't know what it meant, and he won't remember it anyway."

Lieutenant Verdad said nothing. As an immigrant born and raised in a far less fortunate and less just country than that to which he now willingly pledged his allegiance, he had little patience and no understanding for lost cases like Percy. Born with the priceless advantage of United States citizenship, how could a man turn from all the opportunities around him and *choose* degradation and squalor? Julio knew he ought to have more compassion for self-made outcasts like Percy. He knew this ruined man might have suffered, might have endured tragedy, been broken by fate or by cruel parents. A graduate of the police department's aware-ness programs, Julio was well versed in the psychology and sociology of the outcast-as-victim philosophy. But he would have had less trouble understanding the alien thought processes of a man from Mars than he had trying to get a handle on wasted men like this one. He just sighed wearily, tugged on the cuffs of his white silk shirt, and adjusted his pearl cuff links, first the right one, then the left.

Hagerstrom said, "You know, sometimes it seems like a law of nature that any potential witness to a homicide in this town has got to be drunk and about three weeks away from his last bath."

"If the job was easy," Verdad said, "we wouldn't like it so much, would we?"

"I would. Jesus, this guy stinks."

As they talked about him, Percy did, in fact, seem oblivious. He picked at an unidentifiable piece of crud that had crusted to one of the sleeves of his Hawaiian shirt, and after a deep rumbling burp, he returned to the subject of his burnt-out cerebellum. "Cheap hooch fuzzies up your brain. I swear Christ, I think my brain's shrinkin' a little bit more every day, and the empty spaces is fillin' up with hairballs and old wet newspapers. I think a cat sneaks up on me and spits the hairballs in my ears when I'm asleep." He sounded entirely serious, even a bit afraid of such a bold and invasive feline.

Although he wasn't able to remember his last name or much of anything else, Percy had enough brain tissue left—in there among the hairballs and old wet newspapers—to know that the proper thing to do upon finding a corpse was to call the police. And though he was not exactly a pillar of the community with much respect for the law or any sense of common decency, he had hurried im-mediately in search of the authorities. He thought that reporting the body in the dumpster might earn him a reward.

Now, after arriving with the technicians from the Scientific Investigation Divi-sion more than an hour ago, and after fruitlessly questioning Percy while the SID men strung their cables and switched on their lights, Lieutenant Verdad saw an-other rat explode in panic from the garbage as the coroner's men, having overseen the extensive photographing of the corpse in situ, began to haul the dead woman out of the dumpster. Pelt matted with filth, tail long and pink and moist, the disgusting rodent scurried along the wall of the building toward the mouth of the alley. Julio required every bit of his self-control to keep from drawing his gun and firing wildly at the creature. It dashed to a storm drain with a broken grating and vanished into the depths.

Julio hated rats. The mere sight of a rat robbed him of the self-image he had painstakingly constructed during more than nineteen years as an American citizen and police officer. When he glimpsed a rat, he was instantly stripped of all that he had accomplished and become in nearly two decades, was transformed into pathetic little Julio Verdad of the Tijuana slums, where he had been born in a one-room shack made of scrap lumber and rusting barrels and tar paper. If the right of tenancy had been predicated upon mere numbers, the rats would have owned that shack, for the seven members of the Verdad clan were far outnumbered by vermin.

Watching *this* rat scramble out of the portable floodlights and into shadows and down the alley drain, Julio felt as if his good suit and custom-made shirt and Bally loafers were sorcerously transformed into thirdhand jeans, a tattered shirt, and badly worn sandals. A shudder passed through him, and for a moment he was five years old again, standing in that stifling shack on a blistering August day in Tijuana, staring down in paralyzed horror at the two rats that were chewing busily at the throat of the four-month-old baby, Ernesto. Everyone else was outside, sitting in patches of shade along the dusty street, fanning themselves, the children playing at quiet games and sipping at water, the adults cooling off with the beer they'd purchased cheap from two young *ladrones* who had successfully broken into a brewery warehouse the night before. Little Julio tried to scream, tried to call for help, but no sound would escape him, as if words and cries could not rise because of the heavy, humid August air. The rats, aware of him, turned boldly upon him, hissing, and even when he lunged forward, swatting furiously at them, they backed off only with great reluctance and only after one of them had tested his mettle by biting the meatiest part of his left hand. He screamed and struck out in even greater fury, routing the rats at last, and he was still screaming when his mother and his oldest sister, Evalina, rushed in from the sun-scorched day to find him weeping blood from his hand as if from stigmata—and his baby brother dead.

Reese Hagerstrom—having been partners with Julio long enough to know about his dread of rats, but too considerate ever to mention that fear directly or even indirectly—put one of his enormous hands on Julio's slender shoulder and said, by way of distraction, "I think I'll give Percy five bucks and tell him to get lost. He had nothing to do with this, and we're not going to get anything more out of him, and I'm sick of the stink of him."

"Go ahead," Julio said. "I'm in for two-fifty of it."

While Reese dealt with the wino, Julio watched the dead woman being hauled out of the dumpster. He tried to distance himself from the victim. He tried to tell himself she didn't look real, looked more like a big rag doll, and maybe even was a doll, or a mannequin, just a mannequin. But it was a lie. She looked real enough. Hell, she looked *too* real. They deposited her on a tarp that had been spread on the pavement for that purpose.

In the glare of the portable lights, the photographer took a few more pictures, and Julio moved in for a closer look. The dead woman was young, in her early twenties, a black-haired and brown-eyed Latino. In spite of what the killer had done to her, and in spite of the garbage and the industrious rats, there was reason to believe that she had been at least attractive and perhaps beautiful. She had gone to her death in a summery cream-colored dress with blue piping on the collar and sleeves, a blue belt, and blue high-heeled shoes.

She was only wearing one shoe. No doubt the other was in the dumpster.

There was something unbearably sad about her gay dress and her one bare foot with its meticulously painted toenails.

At Julio's direction, two uniformed men donned rubber boots, put on scented surgical masks, and climbed into the dumpster to go through every piece of rubbish. They were searching for the other shoe, the murder weapon, and anything else that might pertain to the case.

They found the dead woman's purse. She had not been robbed, for her wallet contained forty-three dollars. According to her driver's license, she was Ernestina Hernandez, twenty-four, of Santa Ana.

Ernestina.

Julio shivered. The similarity between her name and that of his long-dead little brother, Ernesto, gave him a chill. Both the child and the woman had been left for the rats, and though Julio had not known Ernestina, he felt an instant, profound, and only partially explicable obligation to her the moment he learned her name.

I will find your killer, he promised her silently. You were so lovely, and you died before your time, and if there is any justice in the world, any hope of making sense out of life, then your murderer cannot go unpunished. I swear to you, even if I have to go to the ends of the earth, I will find your killer.

Two minutes later, they found a blood-spattered lab coat of the kind doctors wore. Four words were stitched on the breast pocket: SANTA ANA CITY MORGUE.

"What the hell?" Reese Hagerstrom said. "You think someone from the morgue cut her throat?"

Frowning at the lab coat, Julio Verdad said nothing.

A lab man carefully folded the coat, trying not to shake loose any hairs or fibers that might be clinging to it. He put it into a plastic bag, which he sealed tightly.

Ten minutes later, the officers in the dumpster found a sharp scalpel with traces of blood on the blade. An expensive, finely crafted instrument of surgical quality. Similar to those used in hospital operating rooms. Or in a medical examiner's pathology lab.

The scalpel, too, was put in a plastic bag, then laid beside the lab coat, which lay beside the now-draped body.

By midnight, they had not found the dead woman's other blue shoe. But there was still about sixteen inches of garbage in the dumpster, and the missing item was almost certain to turn up in that last layer of refuse.

9   SUDDEN DEATH

BULLETING THROUGH THE HOT JUNE NIGHT, FROM THE Riverside Freeway to I-15 East, then east on I-10, past Beaumont and Banning, skirting the Morongo Indian Reservation, to Cabazon and beyond, Rachael had plenty of time to think. Mile by mile, the metropolitan sprawl of southern California fell behind; the lights of civilization grew sparser, dimmer. They headed deeper into the desert, where vast stretches of empty darkness opened on all sides, and where often the only things to be seen on the plains and hills were a few toothy rock formations and scattered Joshua trees limned by frost-pale moonlight that waxed and waned as it was screened by the thin and curling clouds that filigreed the night sky. The barren landscape said all that could be said about solitude, and it encouraged introspection, as did the lulling hum of the Mercedes's engine and the whisper of its spinning tires on the pavement.

Slumped in the passenger's seat, Benny was stubbornly silent for long periods, staring at the black ribbon of highway revealed in the headlights. A few times, they engaged in short conversations, though the topic was always so light and inconsequential that, under the circumstances, it seemed surreal. They discussed Chinese food for a while, subsided into a deep and mutual silence, then talked of Clint Eastwood movies, followed by another and longer silence.

She was aware that Benny was paying her back for her refusal to share her secrets with him. He surely knew that she was stunned by the ease with which he had disposed of Vincent Baresco in Eric's office and that she was dying to know where he had learned to handle himself so well. By turning cool on her, by letting the brooding silences draw out, he was telling her that she was going to have to give him some information in order to get some in return.

But she could not give. Not yet. She was afraid he had already been drawn too far into this deadly business, and she was angry with herself for letting him get involved. She was determined not to drag him deeper into the nightmare—unless his survival depended upon a complete understanding of what was happening and of what was at stake.

As she turned off Interstate 10 onto State Highway 111, now only eleven miles from Palm Springs, she wondered if she could have done more to dissuade him from coming with her to the desert. But upon leaving Geneplan's offices in Newport Beach, he had been quietly adamant, and attempting to change his mind had seemed as fruitless as standing on the shore of the Pacific and commanding an incoming tide to reverse itself immediately.

Rachael deeply regretted the awkwardness between them. In the five months since they had met, this was the first time they had been uneasy with each other, the first time that their relationship had been touched by even a hint of anger or had been in any way less than entirely harmonious.

Having departed Newport Beach at midnight, they arrived in Palm Springs and drove through the heart of town on Palm Canyon Drive at one-fifteen Tuesday morning. That was ninety-nine miles in only an hour and fifteen minutes, for an average speed of eighty miles an hour, which should have given Rachael a sense of speed. But she continued to feel that she was creeping snail-slow, falling farther and farther behind events, losing ground by the minute.

Summer, with its blazing desert heat, was a somewhat less busy tourist season in Palm Springs than other times of the year, and at one-fifteen in the morning the main street was virtually deserted. In the hot and windless June night, the palm trees stood as still as images painted on canvas, illuminated and slightly silvered by the streetlights. The many shops were dark. The sidewalks were empty. The traffic signals still cycled from green to yellow to red to green again, although hers was the only car passing through most of the intersections.

She almost felt as if she were driving through a post-Armageddon world, depopulated by disease. For a moment she was half convinced that if she switched on the radio, there would be no music—only the cold empty hiss of static all the way across the dial.

Since receiving the news of Eric's missing corpse, she had known that something terrible had come into the world, and hour by hour she had grown more bleak. Now even an empty street, which would have looked peaceful to anyone else, stirred ominous thoughts in her. She knew she was overreacting. No matter what happened in the next few days, this was not the end of the world.

On the other hand, she thought, it might be the end of *me,* the end of *my* world.

Driving from the commercial district into residential areas, from neighborhoods of modest means into wealthier streets, she encountered even fewer signs of life, until at last she pulled into a Futura Stone driveway and parked in front of a low, sleek, flat-roofed stucco house that was the epitome of clean-lined desert architecture. The lush landscaping was distinctly not of the desert—ficus trees, benjamina, impatiens, begonias, beds of marigolds and Gerber daisies—green and thick and flower-laden in the soft glow of a series of Malibu lights. Those were the only lights burning; all the front windows were dark.

She had told Benny that this was another of Eric's houses—though she had been closemouthed about the reason she had come. Now, as she switched off the headlights, he said, "Nice little vacation retreat."

She said, "No. This is where he kept his mistress."

Enough soft light fell from the Malibu fixtures, rebounded from the lawn and from the edge of the driveway, penetrated the windows of the car, and touched Benny's face to reveal his look of surprise. "How did you know?"

"A little over a year ago, just a week before I left him, she—Cindy Wasloff was her name—she called the house in Villa Park. Eric had told her never to phone there except in the direst emergency, and if she spoke with anyone but him, she was supposed to say she was the secretary of some business associate. But she was furious with him because, the night before, he'd beaten her pretty badly, and she was leaving him. First, however, she wanted to let me know he'd been keeping her."

"Had you suspected?"

"That he had a mistress? No. But it didn't matter. By then I'd already decided to call it quits. I listened to her and commiserated, got the address of the house, because I thought maybe the day would come when I might be able to use the fact of Eric's adultery to pry myself loose from him if he wouldn't cooperate in the divorce. Even as ugly as it got, it never got quite *that* tawdry, thank God. And it would have been exceedingly tawdry indeed if I'd had to go public with it . . . because the girl was only sixteen."

"What? The mistress?"

"Yes. Sixteen. A runaway. One of those lost kids, from the sound of her. You know the type. They start doing drugs in junior high and just seem to . . . burn away too many gray cells. No, that's not right, either. The drugs don't destroy brain cells so much as they . . . eat away at their souls, leave them empty and purposeless. They're pathetic."

"Some are," he said. "And some are scary. Bored and listless kids who've tried everything. They either become amoral sociopaths as dangerous as rattlesnakes— or they become easy prey. I gather you're telling me that Cindy Wasloff was easy prey and that Eric swept her in out of the gutter for some fun and games."

"And apparently she wasn't the first."

"He had a thing for teenage girls, huh?"

Rachael said, "What he had a thing about was getting old. It terrified him. He was only forty-one when I left him, still a young man, but every year when his birthday rolled around he was crazier about it than the year before, as if at any moment he'd blink and find himself in a nursing home, decrepit and senile. He had an irrational fear of growing old and dying, and the fear expressed itself in all sorts of ways. For one thing, year by year, *newness* in everything became increasingly important to him: new cars every year, as if a twelve-month-old Mercedes was ready for the scrap heap; a constant change of wardrobe, out with the old and in with the new . . . "

"And the modern art, modern architecture, all the ultramodern furniture."

"Yes. And the latest electronic gadgetry. And I guess teenage girls were just another part of his obsession with staying young and . . . cheating death. I guess, in his twisted mind, being with young girls kept him young, too. When I learned about Cindy Wasloff and this house in Palm Springs, I realized that one of the main reasons he'd married me was because I was twelve years younger than him, twenty-three to his thirty-five. I was just one more means of slowing down the flow of time for him, and when I started to get into my late twenties, when he could see me getting a little older, then I no longer served that purpose quite as well for him, so he needed younger flesh like Cindy."

She opened her door and got out of the car, and Benny got out on his side. He said, "So exactly what're we looking for here? Not just his current mistress; you wouldn't have rocketed out here like a race-car driver just to get a peek at his latest bimbo."

Closing her door, withdrawing the thirty-two pistol from her purse, and heading toward the house, Rachael did not—could not—answer.

The night was warm and dry. The vault of the clear desert sky was spangled with an incredibility of stars. The air was still, and all was silent but for crickets singing in the shrubbery.

Too much shrubbery. She looked around nervously at all the looming dark forms and black spaces beyond the glow of the Malibu lights. Lots of hiding places. She shivered.

The door was ajar, which seemed an ominous sign. She rang the bell, waited, rang again, waited, rang and rang, but no one responded.

At her side, Benny said, "It's probably your house now. You inherited it with everything else, so I don't think you need an invitation to go in."

The door, ajar as it was, provided more invitation than she would have liked. It looked as if it were the open door on a trap. If she went inside in search of the bait, the trap might be sprung, and the door might slam behind her.

Rachael took a step back, kicked out with one foot, knocking the door inward. It swung back hard against the wall of the foyer with a shuddering crash.

"So you don't expect to be welcomed with open arms," Benny said.

The exterior light above the door shed pale beams a few feet into the foyer, though not as far as she had hoped. She could see that no one lurked in the first six or eight feet, but beyond lay darkness that might shelter an assailant.

Because he didn't know everything she knew and therefore didn't appreciate the true extent of the danger, because he expected nothing worse than another Vincent Baresco with another revolver, Benny was bolder than Rachael. He stepped past her into the house, found the wall switch in the foyer, and snapped on the lights.

Rachael went inside and moved past him. "Damn it, Benny, don't be so quick to step through a doorway. Let's be slow and careful."

"Believe it or not, I can handle just about any teenage girl who wants to throw a punch at me."

"It's not the mistress I'm worried about," she said sharply.

"Then who?"

Tight-lipped, holding her pistol at the ready, she led the way through the house, turning on lights as they went.

The uncluttered ultramodern decor—more futuristic than in any of Eric's other habitats—bordered on starkness and sterility. A highly polished terrazzo floor that looked as cold as ice, no carpet anywhere. Levolor metal blinds instead of drapes. Hard-looking chairs. Sofas that, if moved to the depths of a forest, might have passed for giant fungi. Everything was in pale gray, white, black, and taupe, with no color except for scattered accent pieces all in shades of orange.

The kitchen had been wrecked. The white-lacquered breakfast table and two chairs were overturned. The other two chairs had been hammered to pieces against everything else in sight. The refrigerator was badly dented and scraped; the tempered glass in the oven door was shattered; the counters and cabinets were gouged and scratched, edges splintered. Dishes and drinking glasses had been pulled from the cupboards and thrown against the walls, and the floor was prickled and glinting with thousands of sharp shards. Food had been swept off the shelves of the refrigerator onto the floor: Pickles, milk, macaroni salad, mustard, chocolate pudding, maraschino cherries, a chunk of ham, and several unidentifiable substances were congealing in a disgusting pool. Beside the sink, above the cutting board, all six knives had been removed from their rack and, with tremendous force, had been driven into the wall; some of the blades were buried up to half their lengths in the drywall, while two had been driven in to their hilts.

"You think they were looking for something?" Benny asked.

"Maybe."

"No," he said, "I don't think so. It's got the same look as the bedroom in the Villa Park house. Weird. Creepy. This was done in a rage. Out of fierce hatred, in a frenzy, a fury. Or by someone who takes pure, unadulterated pleasure in destruction."

Rachael could not take her eyes off the knives embedded in the wall. A deep sick quivering filled her stomach. Her chest and throat tightened with fear.

The gun in her hand felt different from the way it had felt just a moment ago. Too light. Too small. Almost like a toy. If she had to use it, would it be effective? Against *this* adversary?

They continued through the silent house with considerably greater caution. Even Benny had been shaken by the psychopathic violence that had been unleashed here. He no longer taunted her with his boldness, but stayed close at her side, warier than he had been.

In the large master bedroom, there was more destruction, though it was not as extensive or as indicative of insane fury as the damage in the kitchen. Beside the king-size bed of black-lacquered wood and burnished stainless steel, a torn pillow leaked feathers. The bedsheets were strewn across the floor, and a chair was overturned. One of the two black ceramic lamps had been knocked off a nightstand and broken, and the shade had been crushed. The shade on the other lamp was cocked, and the paintings hung askew on the walls.

Benny stooped and carefully lifted a section of one of the sheets to have a closer look at it. Small reddish spots and a single reddish smear shone with almost preternatural brilliance on the white cotton.

"Blood," he said.

Rachael felt a cold sweat suddenly break out on her scalp and along the back of her neck.

"Not much," Benny said, standing again, his gaze traveling over the tangled sheets. "Not much, but definitely blood."

Rachael saw a bloody handprint on the wall beside the open door that led into the master bedroom. It was a man's print, and large—as if a butcher, exhausted from his hideous labors, had leaned there for a moment to catch his breath.

The lights were on in the large bathroom, the only chamber in the house that had not been dark when they'd reached it. Through the open door, Rachael could see virtually everything either directly or in the mirrors covering one wall: gray tile with a burnt-yellow border, big sunken tub, shower stall, toilet, one edge of the counter that held the sinks, bright brass towel racks and brass-rimmed recessed ceiling lamps. The bathroom appeared deserted. However, when she crossed the threshold, she heard someone's quick, panicked breathing, and her own heartbeat, already trotting, *raced*.

Close behind her, Benny said, "What's wrong?"

She pointed to the opaque shower stall. The glass was so heavily frosted that nothing could be seen of the person on the other side, not even a tenebrous form. "Somebody's in there."

Benny leaned forward, listening.

Rachael had backed against the wall, the muzzle of the thirty-two aimed at the shower door.

"Better come out of there," Benny said to the person in the stall.

No answer. Just quick, thin wheezing.

"Better come out right now," Benny said.

"Come out, damn you!" Rachael said, her raised voice echoing harshly off the gray tile and the bright mirrors.

From the stall came an unexpectedly woeful mewling that was the very essence of terror. It sounded like a child.

Shocked, concerned, but still wary, Rachael edged toward the frosted glass.

Benny stepped past her, took hold of the brass handle, and pulled the door open. "Oh, my God."

Rachael saw a nude girl huddled pathetically on the tile floor of the shadowy stall, her back pressed into the corner. She looked no older than fifteen or sixteen and must be the current mistress in residence, the latest—and last—of Eric's pitiable "conquests." Her slender arms were crossed over her breasts more in fear and self-defense than in modesty. She was trembling uncontrollably, and her eyes were wide with terror, and her face was pale, sickly, waxen.

She was probably quite pretty, but it was difficult to tell for sure, not because of the gloominess of the enclosed shower stall but because she had been badly beaten. Her right eye was blackened and beginning to swell. Another ugly bruise was forming on her right cheek, from the corner of the eye all the way down to the jaw. Her upper lip had been split; blood still oozed from it, and blood covered her chin. There were bruises on her arms as well, and a big one on her left thigh.

Benny turned away, clearly as embarrassed for the girl as he was alarmed by her condition.

Lowering her pistol, stooping at the shower door, Rachael said, "Who did this to you, honey? Who did this?" She already knew what the answer must be, dreaded hearing it, but was morbidly compelled to ask the question.

The girl could not respond. Her bleeding lips moved, and she tried to form words, but all that came out was that thin grievous whining, broken into chords by an especially violent siege of the shivers. Even if she had spoken, she would most likely not have answered the question, for she was obviously in shock and to some degree disassociated from reality. She seemed only partially aware of Rachael and Benny, with the larger part of her attention focused on some private horror. She met Rachael's eyes but didn't really seem to see her.

Rachael reached into the stall with one hand. "Honey, it's all right. Everything's all right. No one's going to hurt you anymore. You can come out now. We won't let anyone hurt you anymore."

The girl stared through Rachael, murmuring softly but urgently to herself, shaken by a wind of fear that blew through some grim inner landscape in which she seemed trapped.

Rachael handed her gun to Benny. She stepped into the big shower stall and knelt beside the girl, speaking softly and reassuringly to her, touching her gently on the face and arms, smoothing her tangled blond hair. At the first few touches, the girl flinched as if she'd been struck, though the contact briefly broke her trance. She looked *at* Rachael for a moment instead of through her, and she allowed herself to be coaxed to her feet and out of the shadowy stall, though by the time she crossed the sill of the shower into the bathroom, she was already retreating once more into her semicatatonic state, unable to answer questions or even to respond with a nod when spoken to, unable to meet Rachael's eyes.

"We've got to get her to a hospital," Rachael said, wincing when she got a better look at the poor child's injuries in the brighter light of the bathroom. Two finger-nails on the girl's right hand had been broken back almost to the cuticle and were bleeding; one finger appeared to be broken.

Rachael sat with her on the edge of the bed while Benny went through the closets and various dresser drawers, looking for clothes.

She listened for strange noises elsewhere in the house.

She heard none.

Still, she listened attentively.

In addition to panties, faded blue jeans, a blue-checkered blouse, peds, and a pair of New Balance running shoes, Benny found a trove of illegal drugs. The bottom drawer of one of the nightstands contained fifty or sixty hand-rolled joints, a plastic bag full of unidentified brightly colored capsules, and another plastic bag containing about two ounces of white powder. "Probably cocaine," Benny said.

Eric had not used drugs; he had disdained them. He had always said that drugs were for the weak, for the losers who could not cope with life on its own terms. But obviously he had not been averse to supplying all sorts of illicit substances to the young girls he kept, ensuring their docility and compliance at the expense of further corrupting them. Rachael had never loathed him as much as she did at that moment.

She found it necessary to dress the naked girl as she would have had to dress a very small child, although the teenager's helpless daze—marked by spells of shivers and occasional whimpering—was caused by shock and terror rather than by the illegal chemicals that Benny had found in the nightstand.

As Rachael quickly dressed the girl, chivalrous Benny kept his eyes discreetly averted. Having found her purse while searching for her clothes, he now went through it, seeking identification. "Her name's Sarah Kiel, and she turned sixteen just two months ago. Looks like she's come west from . . . Coffeyville, Kansas."

Another runaway, Rachael thought. Maybe fleeing an intolerable home life. Maybe just a rebellious type who chafed at discipline and entertained the illusion that life on her own, without restrictions, would be pure bliss. Off to L.A., the Big Orange, to take a shot at the movie business, dreaming of stardom. Or maybe just seeking some excitement, an escape from the boredom of the vast and slumbering Kansas plains.

Instead of the expected romance and glamour, Sarah Kiel had found what most girls like her found at the end of the California rainbow: a hard and homeless life on the streets—and eventually the solicitous attention of a pimp. Eric must have either bought her from a pimp or found her himself while on the prowl for the kind of fresh meat that would keep him feeling young. Ensconced in an expensive Palm Springs house, supplied with all the drugs she wanted, plaything of a very rich man, Sarah had surely begun to convince herself that she was, after all, des-tined for a fairy-tale life. The naive child could not have guessed the true extent of the danger into which she had stepped, could not have conceived of the horror that would one day pay a visit and leave her dazed and mute with terror.

"Help me get her out to the car," Rachael said as she finished dressing Sarah Kiel.

Benny put an arm around the girl from one side, and Rachael held her from the other side; and although Sarah shuffled along under her own power, she would have collapsed several times if they had not provided support. Her knees kept buckling.

The night smelled of star jasmine stirred by a breeze that also rustled shrubbery, causing Rachael to glance nervously at the shadows.

They put Sarah in the car and fastened her seat belt for her, whereupon she slumped against the restraining straps and let her head fall forward. It was possible for a third person to ride in the 560 SL, although it was necessary for the extra passenger to sit sideways in the open storage space behind the two bucket seats and endure a bit of squeezing. Benny was too big to fit, so Rachael got behind the seats, and he took the wheel for the trip to the hospital.

As they pulled out of the driveway, a car turned the corner, headlights washing over them, and when they entered the street, the other car suddenly surged forward, fast, coming straight at them.

Rachael's heart stuttered, and she said, "Oh, hell, it's *them!*"

The oncoming car angled across the narrow street, intending to block it. Benny wasted no time asking questions, immediately changed directions, pulling hard on the wheel, putting the other car behind them. He tramped the accelerator; tires squealed; the Mercedes leaped forward with dependable quickness, racing past the low dark houses. Ahead, the street ended in a cross street, forcing them to turn either left or right, so Benny had to slow down, and Rachael lowered her head and peered through the rear window against which she was crammed, and she saw that the other car—a Cadillac of some kind, maybe a Seville—was following close, very close, closer.

Benny took the corner wide, at a frightening slant, and Rachael would have been thrown by the sudden force of the turn if she hadn't been wedged tightly in the storage space behind the seats. There was nowhere for her to be thrown *to,* and she didn't even have to hold on to anything, but she did hold on to the back of Sarah Kiel's seat because she felt as if the world were about to fall out from under her, and she thought, *God, please, don't let the car roll over.*

The Mercedes didn't roll, hugged the road beautifully, came out into a straight stretch of residential street, and accelerated. But behind them, the Cadillac almost went over on its side, and the driver overcompensated, which made the Caddy swing so dangerously wide that it sideswiped a Corvette parked at the curb. Sparks showered into the air, cascaded along the pavement. The Caddy lurched away from the impact and looked like it would veer across the street and into the cars along the other curb, but then it recovered. It had lost some ground, but it came after them again, its driver undaunted.

Benny whipped the little 560 SL into another turn, around another corner, holding it tighter this time, then stood on the accelerator for a block and a half, so it seemed as if they were in a rocket ship instead of an automobile. Just when Rachael felt herself pressed back with a force of maybe 4.5 Gs, just when it seemed they would break the chains of gravity and explode straight into orbit, Benny manipulated the brakes with all the style of a great concert pianist executing "Moonlight Sonata," and as he came up on another stop sign with no intention of obeying it, he spun the wheel as hard as he dared, so from behind it must have looked as if the Mercedes had just *popped* off that street onto the street that intersected from the left.

He was as expert at evasive driving as he had proved to be at hand-to-hand combat, and Rachael wanted to say, *Who the hell are you, anyway, not just a placid real-estate salesman with a love of trains and swing music, damned if you are,* but she didn't say anything because she was afraid she would distract him, and if she distracted him at this speed, they would inevitably roll—or worse—and be killed for sure.

■   Ben knew that the 560 SL could easily win a speed contest with the Cadillac out on the open roads, but it was a different story on streets like these, which were narrow and occasionally bisected by speed bumps to prevent drag racing. Besides, there were traffic lights as they drew nearer the center of town, and even at this dead hour of the morning he had to slow for those main intersections, at least a little, or risk plowing broadside into a rare specimen of crosstown traffic. Fortunately, the Mercedes cornered about a thousand times better than the Cadillac, so he didn't have to slow down nearly as much as his pursuers, and every time he switched streets he gained a few yards that the Caddy could not entirely regain on the next stretch of straightaway. By the time he had zigzagged to within a block of Palm Canyon Drive, the main drag, the Caddy was more than a block and a half behind and losing ground, and he was finally confident that he would shake the bastards, whoever they were—

—and that was when he saw the police car.

It was parked at the front of a line of curbed cars, at the corner of Palm Canyon, a block away, and the cop must have seen him coming in the rearview mirror, coming like a bat out of hell, because the flashing red and blue beacons on the roof of the cruiser came on, bright and startling, ahead on the right.

"Hallelujah!" Ben said.

"No," Rachael said from her awkward seat in the open storage space behind him, shouting though her mouth was nearly at his ear. "No, you can't go to the cops! We're dead if you go to the cops."

Nevertheless, as he rocketed toward the cruiser, Ben started to brake because, damn it, she'd never told him *why* they couldn't rely on the police for protection, and he was not a man who believed in taking the law into his own hands, and surely the guys in the Cadillac would back off fast if the cops came into it.

But Rachael shouted, "No! Benny, for Christ's sake, trust me, why don't you? We're dead if you stop. They'll blow our brains out, sure as hell."

Being accused of not trusting her—that hurt, stung. He trusted her, by God, trusted her implicitly because he loved her. He didn't *understand* her worth shit, not tonight he didn't, but he did trust her, and it was like a knife twisting in his heart to hear that note of disappointment and accusation in her voice. He took his foot off the brake and put it back on the accelerator, swept right past the black-and-white so fast that the light from its swiveling emergency beacons flashed through the Mercedes only once and then were behind. When he'd glanced over, he'd seen two uniformed officers looking astonished. He figured they'd wait for the Caddy and then give chase to both cars, which would be fine, just fine, because the guys in the Caddy couldn't catch up with him and blow his brains out if they had the police on their tail.

But to Ben's surprise and dismay, the cops pulled out right after him, siren screaming. Maybe they had been so shocked by the sight of the Mercedes coming at them like a jet that they hadn't noticed the Cadillac farther back. Or maybe they'd seen the Caddy but had been so startled by the Mercedes that they hadn't realized the second car was approaching at almost the same high speed. Whatever their reasoning, they shot away from the curb and fell in behind him as he hung a right onto Palm Canyon Drive.

Ben made that turn with the reckless aplomb of a stunt driver who knows that his roll bars and special stabilizers and heavy duty hydraulic shock absorbers and other sophisticated equipment remove most of the danger from such risky maneuvers—except he didn't have roll bars and special stabilizers. He realized he'd miscalculated and was about to turn Rachael and Sarah and himself into canned meat, three lumps of imitation Spam encased in expensive German steel, Jesus, and the car tilted onto two tires, he smelled smoking rubber, it seemed an hour they teetered on edge, but by the grace of God and the brilliance of the Benz designers they came down again onto all fours with a jolt and crash that, by virtue of another miracle, did not blow out any tires, though Rachael hit her head on the ceiling and let out her breath in a whoosh that he felt on the back of his neck.

He saw the old man in the yellow Banlon shirt and the cocker spaniel even before the car stopped bouncing on its springs. They had been crossing the street in the middle of the block when he had come around the corner like a fugitive from a demolition derby. He was bearing down on them at a frightening speed, and they were frozen in surprise and fear, both dog and man, heads up, eyes wide. The guy looked ninety, and the dog seemed decrepit, too, so it didn't make sense for them to be out on the street at nearly two o'clock in the morning. They ought to have been home in bed, occupied with dreams of fire hydrants and well-fitted false teeth, but here they were.

"Benny!" Rachael shouted.

"I see, I see!"

He had no hope of stopping in time, so he not only jumped on the brakes but turned across Palm Canyon, a combination of forces that sent the Mercedes into a full spin combined with a slide, so they went around a full hundred and eighty degrees and wound up against the far curb. By the time he peeled rubber, roared back across the street, and was headed north again, the old man and the cocker had finally tottered for the safety of the sidewalk—and the police cruiser was no more than ten yards behind him.

In the mirror, he could see that the Caddy had also turned the corner and was still giving chase, undeterred by the presence of the police. Crazily the Caddy pulled out around the black-and-white, trying to pass it.

"They're lunatics," Ben said.

"Worse," Rachael said. "Far worse."

In the passenger seat, Sarah Kiel was making urgent noises, but she did not appear to be frightened by the current danger. Instead, it seemed as if the violence of the chase had stirred the sediment of memory, recalling for her the other—and worse—violence that she had endured earlier in the night.

Picking up speed as he headed north on Palm Canyon, Ben glanced again at the mirror and saw that the Cadillac had pulled alongside the police cruiser. They appeared to be drag racing back there, just a couple of carloads of guys out for some fun. It was . . . well, it was downright silly was what it was. Then suddenly it wasn't silly at all because the intentions of the men in the Caddy became horribly clear with the repeated winking of muzzle flashes and the *tat-tat-tat-tat-tat-tat* of automatic weapons fire. They had opened up on the cops with a submachine gun, as if this weren't Palm Springs but Chicago in the Roaring Twenties.

"They shot the cops!" he said, as astonished as he had ever been in his life.

The black-and-white went out of control, jumped the curb, crossed the sidewalk, and rammed through the plate-glass window of an elegant boutique, but still a guy in the back seat of the Cadillac continued to lean out the window, spraying bullets back at the cruiser until it was out of range.

In the seat beside Ben, Sarah said, "Uh, uh, uh, uh, uh, uh," and she twitched and spasmed as if someone were raining blows on her. She seemed to be reliving the beating she had taken, oblivious of the immediate danger.

"Benny, you're slowing down," Rachael said urgently.

Overcome by shock, he had relaxed his foot on the accelerator.

The Cadillac was closing on them as hungrily as any shark had ever closed on any swimmer.

Ben tried to press the gas pedal through the floorboards, and the Mercedes reacted as if it were a cat that had just been kicked in the butt. They exploded up Palm Canyon Drive, which was relatively straight for a long way, so he could even put some distance between them and the Cadillac before he made any turns. And he did make turns, one after the other, off into the west side of town now, up into the hills, back down, working steadily south, through older residential streets where trees arched overhead to form a tunnel, then through newer neighborhoods where the trees were small and the shrubbery too sparse to conceal the reality of the desert on which the town had been built. With every corner he rounded, he widened the gap between them and the killers in the Cadillac.

Stunned, Ben said, "They wasted two cops just because the poor bastards got in the way."

"They want us real bad," Rachael said. "That's what I've tried to tell you. They want us so very bad."

The Caddy was two blocks behind now, and within five or six more turns, Ben would lose them because they wouldn't have him in sight and wouldn't know which way he had gone.

Hearing a tremor in his voice that surprised him, a quavering note that he didn't like, he said, "But, damn it, they never really had much of a chance of catching us. Not with us in this little beauty and them in a lumbering Caddy. They had to see that. They had to. One chance in a hundred. At best. One chance in a hundred, but they still wasted the cops."

He half wheeled and half slid around another turn, onto a new street.

"Ohmygod, ohmygod, ohmygod," Sarah said softly, frantically, drawing down in the seat as far as the safety harness would allow, crossing her arms over her breasts as she had done in the shower stall when she had been naked.

Behind Ben, sounding as shaky as he did, Rachael said, "They probably figured the police had gotten our license number—and theirs, too—and were about to call them in for identification."

The Cadillac headlights turned the corner far back, losing ground more rapidly now. Ben took another turn and sped along another dark and slumbering street, past older houses that had gotten a bit seedy and no longer measured up to the Chamber of Commerce's fantasy image of Palm Springs.

"But you've implied that the guys in the Caddy would get their hands on you even quicker if you went to the police."

"Yes."

"So why wouldn't they want the police to nab us?"

Rachael said, "It's true that in police custody I'd be even easier to nail. I'd have no chance at all. But killing me then will be a lot messier, more public. The people in that Cadillac . . . and their associates . . . would prefer to keep this private if they can, even if that means they'll need more time to get their hands on me."

Before the Cadillac headlights could appear again, Ben executed yet another turn. In a minute he would finally slip away from their pursuers for good. He said, "What the hell do they want from you?"

"Two things. For one . . . a secret they think I have."

"But you don't have it?"

"No."

"What's the second thing?"

"Another secret that I *do* know. I share it with them. They already know it, and they want to stop me from telling anyone else."

"What is it?"

"If I told you, they'd have as much reason to kill you as me."

"I think they *already* want my butt," Ben said. "I'm in too deep already. So tell me."

"Keep your mind on your driving," she said.

"Tell me."

"Not now. You've got to concentrate on getting away from them."

"Don't worry about that, and don't try to use it as an excuse to clam up on me, damn it. We're already out of the woods. One more turn, and we'll have lost them for good."

The right front tire blew out.

10 NAILS

IT WAS A LONG NIGHT FOR JULIO AND REESE.

By 12:32, the last of the garbage in the dumpster had been inspected, but Ernestina Hernandez's blue shoe had not been found.

Once the trash had been searched and the corpse had been moved to the morgue, most detectives would have decided to go home to get some shut-eye and start fresh the next day—but not Lieutenant Julio Verdad. He was aware the trail was freshest in the twenty-four hours after the discovery of the body. Furthermore, for at least a day following assignment to a new case, he had difficulty sleeping, for then he was especially troubled by a sense of the horror of murder.

Besides, this time, he had a special obligation to the victim. For reasons which might have seemed inadequate to others but which were compelling to him, he felt a deep commitment to Ernestina. Bringing her killer to justice was not just his job but a point of honor with Julio.

His partner, Reese Hagerstrom, accompanied him without once commenting on the lateness of the hour. For Julio and for no one else, Reese would work around the clock, deny himself not only sleep but days off and regular meals, and make any sacrifice required. Julio knew, if it ever became necessary for Reese to step into the path of a bullet and *die* for Julio, the big man would make that ultimate sacrifice as well, and without the slightest hesitation. It was something which they both understood in their hearts, in their bones, but of which they had never spoken.

At 12:41 in the morning, they took the news of Ernestina's brutal death to her parents, with whom she had lived, a block east of Main Street in a modest house flanked by twin magnolias. The family had to be awakened, and at first they were disbelieving, certain that Ernestina had come home and gone to bed by now. But, of course, her bed was empty.

Though Juan and Maria Hernandez had six children, they took this blow as hard as parents with one precious child would have taken it. Maria sat on the rose-colored sofa in the living room, too weak to stand. Her two youngest sons—both teenagers—sat beside her, red-eyed and too shaken to maintain the macho front behind which Latino boys of their age usually hid. Maria held a framed photograph of Ernestina, alternately weeping and tremulously speaking of good times shared with the beloved daughter. Another daughter, nineteen-year-old Laurita, sat alone in the dining room, unapproachable, inconsolable, clutching a rosary. Juan Hernandez paced agitatedly, jaws clenched, blinking furiously to repress his tears. As patriarch, it was his duty to provide an example of strength to his family, to be unshaken and unbroken by this visitation of *muerta*. But it was too much for him to bear, and twice he retreated to the kitchen where, behind the closed door, he made soft strangled sounds of grief.

Julio could do nothing to relieve their anguish, but he inspired trust and hope for justice, perhaps because his special commitment to Ernestina was clear and convincing. Perhaps because, in his soft-spoken way, he conveyed a hound-dog perseverance that lent conviction to promises of swift justice. Or perhaps his smoldering fury at the very *existence* of death, all death, was painfully evident in his face and eyes and voice. After all, that fury had burned in him for many years now, since the afternoon when he had discovered rats chewing out the throat of his baby brother, and by now the fire within him must have grown bright enough to show through for all to see.

From Mr. Hernandez, Julio and Reese learned that Ernestina had gone out for an evening on the town with her best girlfriend, Becky Klienstad, with whom she worked at a local Mexican restaurant, where both were waitresses. They had gone in Ernestina's car: a powder-blue, ten-year-old Ford Fairlane.

"If this has happened to my Ernestina," Mr. Hernandez said, "then what's happened to poor Becky? Something must have happened to her, too. Something very terrible."

From the Hernandez kitchen, Julio telephoned the Klienstad family in Orange. Becky—actually Rebecca—was not yet home. Her parents had not been worried because she was, after all, a grown woman, and because some of the dance spots that she and Ernestina favored were open until two in the morning. But now they were very worried indeed.

■ 1:20 A.M.

In the unmarked sedan in front of the Hernandez house, Julio sat behind the wheel and stared bleakly out at the magnolia-scented night.

Through the open windows came the susurration of leaves stirring in the vague June breeze. A lonely, cold sound.

Reese used the console-mounted computer terminal to generate an APB and pickup order on Ernestina's powder-blue Ford. He'd obtained the license number from her parents.

"See if there're any messages on hold for us," Julio said.

At the moment he did not trust himself to operate the keyboard. He was full of anger and wanted to pound on something—anything—with both fists, and if the computer gave him any trouble or if he hit one wrong key by mistake, he might take out his frustration on the machine merely because it was a convenient target.

Reese accessed the police department's data banks at headquarters and requested on-file messages. Softly glowing green letters scrolled up on the video display. It was a report from the uniformed officers who'd gone to the morgue, at Julio's direction, to ascertain if the scalpel and bloodstained morgue coat found in the dumpster could be traced to a specific employee on the coroner's staff. Officials at the coroner's office were able to confirm that a scalpel, lab coat, set of hospital whites, surgical cap, and a pair of antistatic lab shoes were missing from the morgue's supplies closet. However, no specific employee could be linked with the theft of those items.

Looking up from the VDT, gazing at the night, Julio said, "This murder is somehow tied to the disappearance of Eric Leben's body."

"Could be coincidence," Reese said.

"You believe in coincidence?"

Reese sighed. "No."

A moth fluttered against the windshield.

"Maybe whoever stole the body also killed Ernestina," Julio said.

"But why?"

"That's what we must find out."

Julio drove away from the Hernandez house.

He drove away from the fluttering moth and the whispering leaves.

He turned north and drove away from downtown Santa Ana.

However, although he followed Main Street, where closely spaced streetlamps blazed, he could not drive away from the deep darkness, not even temporarily, for the darkness was within him.

■ 1:38 A.M.

They reached Eric Leben's Spanish-modern house quickly, for there was no traffic. Night in that wealthy neighborhood was respectfully still. Their footsteps clicked hollowly on the tile walkway, and when they rang the doorbell, it sounded as if it were echoing back to them from the bottom of a deep well.

Julio and Reese had no authority whatsoever in Villa Park, which was two towns removed from their own jurisdiction. However, in the vast urban sprawl of Orange County, which was essentially one great spread-out city divided into many communities, a lot of crimes were not conveniently restricted to a single jurisdiction, and a criminal could not be allowed to gain time or safety by simply crossing the artificial political boundary between one town and another. When it became necessary to pursue a lead into another jurisdiction, one was required to seek an escort from the local authorities or obtain their approval or even enlist them to make the inquiries themselves, and these requests were routinely honored.

But because time was wasted going through proper channels, Julio and Reese frequently skipped the protocol. They went where they needed to go, talked with whomever they needed to talk, and only informed local authorities when and if they found something pertinent to their case—or if a situation looked as if it might turn violent.

Few detectives operated that boldly. Failure to follow standard procedures might result in a reprimand. Repeated violations of the rules might be viewed as a dismal lack of respect for the command structure, resulting in disciplinary suspension. Too much of that, and even the finest cop could forget about further promotions—and might have to worry about hanging on to collect his pension.

The risks did not particularly concern Julio or Reese. They wanted promotions, of course. And they wanted their pensions. But more than career advancement and financial security, they wanted to solve cases and put murderers in prison. Being a cop was pointless if you weren't willing to put your life on the line for your ideals, and if you *were* willing to risk your life, then it made no sense to worry about small stuff like salary increases and retirement funds.

When no one responded to the bell, Julio tried the door, but it was locked. He didn't attempt to void the lock or force it. In the absence of a court order, what they needed to get them into the Leben house was probable cause to believe that criminal activity of some kind was under way on the premises, that innocent people might be harmed, and that there was nothing less than a public emergency.

When they circled to the back of the house, they found what they needed: a broken pane of glass in the French door that led from the patio into the kitchen. They would have been remiss if they had not assumed the worst: that an armed intruder had forced his way into the house to commit burglary or to harm whoever resided legally within.

Drawing their revolvers, they entered cautiously. Shards of broken glass crunched underfoot.

As they moved from room to room, they turned on lights and saw enough to justify intrusion. The bloody palmprint etched into the arm of the white sofa in the family room. The destruction in the master bedroom. And in the garage . . . Ernestina Hernandez's powder-blue Ford.

Inspecting the car, Reese found bloodstains on the back seat and floor mats. "Some of it's still a little sticky," he told Julio.

Julio tried the trunk of the car and found it unlocked. Inside, there was more blood, a pair of broken eyeglasses—and one blue shoe.

The shoe was Ernestina's, and the sight of it caused Julio's chest to tighten.

As far as Julio knew, the Hernandez girl had not worn glasses. In photographs he had seen at the Hernandez home, however, Becky Klienstad, friend and fellow waitress, had worn a pair like these. Evidently, both women had been killed and stuffed into the Ford's trunk. Later, Ernestina's corpse had been heaved into the dumpster. But what happened to the other body?

"Call the locals," Julio said. "It's time for protocol."

■ 1:52 A.M.

When Reese Hagerstrom returned from the sedan, he paused to put up the electric garage doors to air out the smell of blood that had risen from the open trunk of the Ford and reached into every corner of the long room. As the doors rolled up, he spotted a discarded set of hospital whites and a pair of antistatic shoes in one corner. "Julio? Come here and look at this."

Julio had been staring intently into the bloody trunk of the car, unable to touch anything lest he ruin precious evidence, but hoping to spot some small clue by sheer dint of intense study. He joined Reese at the discarded clothes.

Reese said, "What the hell is going on?"

Julio did not reply.

Reese said, "The evening started out with one missing corpse. Now two are missing—Leben and the Klienstad girl. And we've found a third we wish we hadn't. If someone's collecting dead bodies, why wouldn't they keep Ernestina Hernandez, too?"

Puzzling over these bizarre discoveries and the baffling link between the snatching of Leben's corpse and the murder of Ernestina, Julio unconsciously straightened his necktie, tugged on his shirt sleeves, and adjusted his cuff links. Even in summer heat, he would not forsake a tie and long-sleeve shirt, the way some detectives did. Like a priest, a detective held a sacred office, labored in the service of the gods of Justice and Law, and to dress any less formally would have seemed, to him, as disrespectful as a priest celebrating the Mass in jeans and a T-shirt.

"Are the locals coming?" he asked Reese.

"Yes. And as soon as we've had a chance to explain the situation to them, we've got to go up to Placentia."

Julio blinked. "Placentia? Why?"

"I checked messages when I got to the car. HQ had an important one for us. The Placentia police have found Becky Klienstad."

"Where? Alive?"

"Dead. In Rachael Leben's house."

Astonished, Julio repeated the question that Reese had asked only a few minutes ago: "What the hell is going on?"

■ 1:58 A.M.

To get to Placentia, they drove from Villa Park through part of Orange, across a portion of Anaheim, over the Tustin Avenue bridge of the Santa Ana River, which was only a river of dust during this dry season. They passed oil wells where the big pumps, like enormous praying mantises, worked up and down, a shade lighter than the night around them, identifiable and yet somehow mysterious shapes that added one more ominous note to the darkness.

Placentia was usually one of the quietest communities in the county, neither rich nor poor, just comfortable and content, with no terrible drawbacks, with no great advantages over other nearby towns except, perhaps, for the enormous and beautiful date palms which lined some of its streets. Palms of remarkable lushness and stature lined the street on which Rachael Leben lived, and their dense overhanging fronds appeared to be afire in the flickering reflection of the red emergency beacons on the clustered police cars parked under them.

Julio and Reese were met at the front door by a tall uniformed Placentia officer named Orin Mulveck. He was pale. His eyes looked strange, as if he had just seen something he would never choose to remember but would also never be able to forget. "Neighbor called us because she saw a man leaving the house in a hurry, and she thought there was something suspicious about him. When we came to check the place out, we found the front door standing wide open, lights on."

"Mrs. Leben wasn't here?"

"No."

"Any indication where she is?"

"No." Mulveck had taken off his cap and was compulsively combing his fingers through his hair. "Jesus," he said more to himself than to Julio or Reese. Then: "No, Mrs. Leben is gone. But we found the dead woman in Mrs. Leben's bedroom."

Entering the cozy house behind Mulveck, Julio said, "Rebecca Klienstad."

"Yeah."

Mulveck led Julio and Reese across a charming living room decorated in shades of peach and white with dark blue accents and brass lamps.

Julio said, "How'd you identify the deceased?"

"She was wearing one of those medical-alert medallions," Mulveck said. "Had several allergies, including one to penicillin. You seen those medallions? Name, address, medical condition on it. Then, how we got onto you so fast—we asked our computer to check the Klienstad woman through Data Net, and it spit out that you were looking for her in Santa Ana in connection with the Hernandez killing."

The Law Enforcement Data Net, through which the county's many police agencies shared information among their computers, was a new program, a natural outgrowth of the computerization of the sheriff's department and all local police. Hours, sometimes days, could be saved with the use of Data Net, and this was not the first time Julio found reason to be thankful that he was a cop in the Microchip Age.

"Was the woman killed here?" Julio asked as they circled around a burly lab technician who was dusting furniture for fingerprints.

"No," Mulveck said. "Not enough blood." He was still combing one hand through his hair as he walked. "Killed somewhere else and . . . and brought here."

"Why?"

"You'll see why. But damned if you'll *understand* why."

Puzzling over that cryptic statement, Julio trailed Mulveck down a hallway into the master bedroom. He gasped at the sight awaiting him and for a moment could not breathe.

Behind him, Reese said, "Holy shit."

Both bedside lamps were burning, and though there were still shadows around the edges of the room, Rebecca Klienstad's corpse was in the brightest spot, mouth open, eyes wide with a vision of death. She had been stripped naked and nailed to the wall, directly over the big bed. One nail through each hand. One nail just below each elbow joint. One in each foot. And a large spike through the hollow of the throat. It was not precisely the classic pose of crucifixion, for the legs were immodestly spread, but it was close.

A police photographer was still snapping the corpse from every angle. With each flash of his strobe unit, the dead woman seemed to move on the wall; it was only an illusion, but she appeared to twitch as if straining at the nails that held her.

Julio had never seen anything as savage as the crucifixion of the dead woman, yet it had obviously been done not in a white-hot madness but with cold calculation. Clearly, the woman had already been dead when brought here, for the nail holes weren't bleeding. Her slender throat had been slashed, and that was evidently the mortal wound. The killer—or killers—had expended considerable time and energy finding the nails and the hammer (which now lay on the floor in one corner of the room), hoisting the corpse against the wall, holding it in place, and precisely driving the impaling spikes through the cool dead flesh. Apparently the head had drooped down, chin to chest, and apparently the killer had wanted the dead woman to be staring at the bedroom door (a grisly surprise for Rachael Leben), so he had looped a wire under the chin and had tied it tautly to a nail driven into the wall above her skull, to keep her facing out. Finally he had taped her eyes open—so she would be staring sightlessly at whoever discovered her.

"I understand," Julio said.

"Yes," Reese Hagerstrom said shakily.

Mulveck blinked in surprise. Pearls of sweat glistened on his pale forehead, perhaps not because of the June heat. "You've got to be joking. You understand this . . . madness? You see a *reason* for it?"

Julio said, "Ernestina and this girl were murdered primarily because the killer needed a car, and they *had* a car. But when he saw what the Klienstad woman looked like, he dumped the other one and brought the second body here to leave this message."

Mulveck nervously combed one hand through his hair. "But if this psycho intended to kill Mrs. Leben, if she was his primary target, why not just come here and get her? Why just leave a . . . a message?"

"The killer must have had reason to suspect that she wouldn't be at home. Maybe he even called first," Julio said.

He was remembering Rachael Leben's extreme nervousness when he had questioned her at the morgue earlier this evening. He had sensed that she was hiding something and that she was very much afraid. Now he knew that, even then, she had realized her life was in danger.

But who was she afraid of, and why couldn't she turn to the police for help? What was she hiding?

The police photographer's camera click-flashed.

Julio continued: "The killer knew he wouldn't be able to get his hands on her right away, but he wanted her to know she could expect him later. He—or they—wanted to scare her witless. And when he took a good look at this Klienstad woman he had killed, he knew what he must do."

"Huh?" Mulveck said. "I don't follow."

"Rebecca Klienstad was voluptuous," Julio said, indicating the crucified woman. "So is Rachael Leben. Very similar body types."

"And Mrs. Leben has hair much the same as the Klienstad girl's," Reese said. "Coppery brown."

"Titian," Julio said. "And although this woman isn't nearly as lovely as Mrs. Leben, there's a vague resemblance, a similarity of facial structure."

The photographer paused to put new film in his camera.

Officer Mulveck shook his head. "Let me get this straight. The way it was supposed to work—Mrs. Leben would eventually come home and when she walked into this room she would see this woman crucified and know, by the similarities, that it was *her* this psycho really wanted to nail to the wall."

"Yes," Julio said, "I think so."

"Yes," Reese agreed.

"Good God," Mulveck said, "do you realize how black, how bitter, how deep this hatred must be? Whoever he is, what could Mrs. Leben possibly have done to make him hate her like that? What sort of enemies does she have?"

"Very dangerous enemies," Julio said. "That's all I know. And . . . if we don't find her quickly, we won't find her alive."

The photographer's camera flashed.

The corpse seemed to twitch.

Flash, twitch.

Flash, twitch.

11

GHOST STORY

WHEN THE RIGHT FRONT TIRE BLEW, BENNY HARDLY SLOWED. He wrestled with the wheel and drove another half block. The Mercedes thumped and shuddered and rocked along, crippled but cooperative.

No headlights appeared behind them. The pursuing Cadillac had not yet turned the corner two blocks back. But it would. Soon.

Benny kept looking desperately left and right.

Rachael wondered what sort of bolthole he was searching for.

Then he found it: a one-story stucco house with a FOR SALE sign in the front yard, set on a big half-acre lot, grass unmown, separated from its neighbors by an eight-foot-high concrete-block wall that was also finished in stucco and that afforded some privacy. There were lots of trees on the property as well, and overgrown shrubbery in need of a gardener's attention.

"Eureka," Benny said.

He swung into the driveway, then pulled across one corner of the lawn and around the side of the house. In back, he parked on a concrete deck, under a redwood patio cover. He switched off the headlights, the engine.

Darkness fell over them.

The car's hot metal made soft pinging sounds as it cooled.

The house was unoccupied, so no one came out to see what was happening. And because the place was screened from the neighbors on both sides by the wall and trees, no alarm was raised from those sources, either.

Benny said, "Give me your gun."

From her perch behind the seats, Rachael handed over the pistol.

Sarah Kiel was watching them, still trembling, still afraid, but no longer in a trance of terror. The violence of the chase seemed to have jolted her out of her preoccupation with her memories of other, earlier violence.

Benny opened his door and started to get out.

Rachael said, "Where are you going?"

"I want to make sure they go past and don't double back. Then I've got to find another car."

"We can change the tire—"

"No. This heap's too easy to spot. We need something ordinary."

"But where will you get another car?"

"Steal it," he said. "You just sit tight, and I'll be back as soon as I can."

He closed his door softly, sprinted back the way they had come, slipped around the corner of the house, and was gone.

■ Scuttling in a half crouch along the side of the house, Ben heard a chorus of distant sirens. Police cars and ambulances were probably still converging on Palm Canyon Drive, a mile or two away, where the bullet-riddled cops had ridden their cruiser through the windows of a boutique.

Ben reached the front of the house and saw the Cadillac coming along the street. He dove into a lush planting bed at the corner and cautiously peered between branches of the overgrown oleander bushes, which were heavily laden with pink flowers and poisonous berries.The Caddy cruised slowly by, giving him a chance to ascertain that there were three men inside. He could see only one clearly—the guy in the front passenger's seat, who had a receding hairline, a mustache, blunt features, and a mean slash of a mouth.

They were looking for the red Mercedes, of course, and they were smart enough to know that Ben might have tried to slip into a shadowy niche and wait until they had gone past. He hoped to God that he had not left obvious tire tracks across the short stretch of unmown lawn that he'd traversed between the driveway and the side of the house. It was dense Bermuda grass, highly resilient, and it hadn't been watered as regularly as it should have been, so it was badly blotched with brown patches, which provided a natural camouflage to further conceal the marks of the Mercedes's passage. But the men in the Caddy might be trained hunters who could spot the most subtle signs of their quarry's trail.

Hunkering in the bushy oleander, still wearing his thoroughly inappropriate suit trousers, vest, white shirt, and tie with the knot askew, Ben felt ridiculous. Worse, he felt hopelessly inadequate to meet the challenge confronting him. He'd been a real-estate salesman too long. He was not up to this sort of thing anymore, not for an extended length of time. He was thirty-seven, and he'd last been a man of action when he'd been twenty-one, which seemed a date lost in the mists of the Paleolithic era. Although he had kept in shape over the years, he was rusty. To Rachael, he had looked formidable when he'd gone after the man named Vincent Baresco in Eric Leben's Newport Beach office, and his handling of the car had no doubt impressed her, but he knew his reflexes weren't what they had once been. And he knew these people, his nameless enemies, were deadly serious.

He was scared.

They had blown away those two cops as if swatting a couple of annoying flies. Jesus.

What secret did they share with Rachael? What could be so damn important that they would kill anyone, even cops, to keep a lid on it?

If he lived through the next hour, he would get the truth out of her one way or another. Damned if he would let her keep stalling.

The Caddy's engine sort of purred and sort of rumbled, and the car moved past at a crawl, and the guy with the mustache looked right at Ben for a moment, or seemed to, stared right between the oleander branches that Ben was holding slightly apart. Ben wanted to let the branches close up, but he was afraid the movement would be seen, slight as it was, so he just looked back into the other man's eyes, expecting the Caddy to stop and the doors to fly open, expecting a submachine gun to start crackling, shredding the oleander leaves with a thousand bullets. But the car kept moving past the house and on down the street. Watching its taillights dwindle, Ben let out his breath with a shudder.

He crept free of the shrubbery, went out to the street, and stood in the shadows by a tall jacaranda growing near the curb. He stared after the Cadillac until it had traveled three blocks, climbed a small hill, and disappeared over the crest.

In the distance, there were still sirens, though fewer. They had sounded angry before. Now they sounded mournful.

Holding the thirty-two pistol at his side, he hurried off into the night-cloaked neighborhood in search of a car to steal.

■   In the 560 SL, Rachael had moved up front to the driver's seat. It was more comfortable than the cramped storage space, and it was a better position from which to talk with Sarah Kiel. She switched on the little overhead light provided for map reading, confident it would not be seen past the property's thick screen of trees. The moon-pale glow illuminated a portion of the dashboard, the console, Rachael's face, and Sarah's stricken countenance.

The battered girl, having been shaken from her catatonic state, was at last capable of responding to questions. She was holding her curled right hand protectively against her breast, which somehow gave her the look of a small, injured bird. Her torn fingernails had stopped bleeding, but her broken finger was grotesquely swollen. With her left hand, she tenderly explored her blackened eye, bruised cheek, and split lip, frequently wincing and making small, thin sounds of pain. She said nothing, but when her frightened eyes met Rachael's, awareness glimmered in them.

Rachael said, "Honey, we'll get you to a hospital in just a few minutes. Okay?"

The girl nodded.

"Sarah, do you have any idea who I am?"

The girl shook her head.

"I'm Rachael Leben, Eric's wife."

Fear seemed to darken the blue of Sarah's eyes.

"No, honey, it's all right. I'm on your side. Really. I was in the process of divorcing him. I knew about his young girls, but that has nothing to do with why I left him. The man was sick, honey. Twisted and arrogant and sick. I learned to despise and fear him. So you can speak freely with me. You've got a friend in me. You understand?"

Sarah nodded.

Pausing to look around at the darkness beyond the car, at the blank black windows and patio doors of the house on one side and the untended shrubbery and trees on the other, Rachael locked both doors with the master latch. It was getting warm inside the car. She knew she should open the windows, but she felt safer with them closed.

Returning her attention to the teenager, Rachael said, "Tell me what happened to you, honey. Tell me everything."

The girl tried to speak, but her voice broke. Violent shivers coursed through her.

"Take it easy," Rachael said. "You're safe now." She hoped that was true. "You're safe. Who did this to you?"

In the frosty glow of the map light, Sarah's skin looked as pallid as carved bone. She cleared her throat and whispered, "Eric. Eric b-beat me."

Rachael had known this would be the answer, yet it chilled her to the marrow and, for a moment, left her speechless. At last she said, "When? When did he do this to you?"

"He came . . . at half past midnight."

"Dear God, not even an hour before we got there! He must've left just before we arrived."

From the time she'd left the city morgue earlier this evening, she had hoped to catch up with Eric, and she should have been pleased to learn they were so close behind him. Instead, her heart broke into hard drumlike pounding and her chest tightened as she realized how closely they had passed by him in the warm desert night.

"He rang the bell, and I answered the door, and he just . . . he just . . . hit me." Sarah carefully touched her blackened eye, which was now almost swollen shut. "Hit me and knocked me down and kicked me twice, kicked my legs . . . "

Rachael remembered the ugly bruises on Sarah's thighs.

" . . . grabbed me by the hair . . . "

Rachael took the girl's left hand, held it.

" . . . dragged me into the bedroom . . . "

"Go on," Rachael said.

" . . . just *tore* my pajamas off, you know, and . . . and kept yanking on my hair and hitting me, hitting, punching me . . . "

"Has he ever beaten you before?"

"N-no. A few slaps. You know . . . a little roughhouse. That's all. But tonight . . . tonight he was wild . . . so full of *hatred*."

"Did he say anything?"

"Not much. Called me names. Awful names, you know. And his speech—it was funny, slurred."

"How did he look?" Rachael asked.

"Oh God . . . "

"Tell me."

"A couple teeth busted out. Bruised up. He looked bad."

"How bad?"

"*Gray*."

"What about his head, Sarah?"

The girl gripped Rachael's hand very tightly. "His face . . . all gray . . . like, you know, like ashes."

"What about his head?" Rachael repeated.

"He . . . he was wearing a knitted cap when he came in. He had it pulled way down, you know what I mean, like a toboggan cap. But when he was beating me . . . when I tried to fight back . . . the cap came off."

Rachael waited.

The air in the car was stuffy and tainted by the acid stink of the girl's sweat.

"His head was . . . it was all banged up," Sarah said, her voice thickening with terror, horror, and disgust.

"The side of his skull?" Rachael asked. "You saw that?"

"All broken, punched in . . . terrible, terrible."

"His eyes. What about his eyes?"

Sarah tried to speak, choked. She lowered her head and closed her eyes for a moment, struggling to regain control of herself.

Seized by the irrational but quite understandable feeling that someone—or some*thing*—was stealthily creeping up on the Mercedes, Rachael surveyed the night again. It seemed to pulse against the car, seeking entrance at the windows.

When the brutalized girl raised her head again, Rachael said, "Please, honey, tell me about his eyes."

"Strange. Hyper. Spaced out, you know? And . . . clouded . . . "

"Sort of muddy-looking?"

"Yeah."

"His movements. Was there anything odd about the way he moved?"

"Sometimes . . . he seemed jerky . . . you know, a little spastic. But most of the time he was quick, too quick for me."

"And you said his speech was slurred."

"Yeah. Sometimes it didn't make any sense at all. And a couple times he stopped hitting me and just stood there, swaying back and forth, and he seemed . . . confused, you know, as if he couldn't figure where he was or who he was, as if he'd forgotten all about me."

Rachael found that she was trembling as badly as Sarah—and that she was drawing as much strength from the contact with the girl's hand as the girl was drawing from her.

"His touch," Rachael said. "His skin. What did he *feel* like?"

"You don't even have to ask, do you? 'Cause you already know what he felt like. Huh?" the girl said. "Don't you? Somehow . . . you already know."

"But tell me anyway."

"Cold. He felt too cold."

"And moist?" Rachael asked.

"Yeah . . . but . . . not like sweat."

"Greasy," Rachael said.

The memory was so vivid that the girl gagged on it and nodded.

Ever so slightly greasy flesh, like the first stage—the very earliest stage—of putrefaction, Rachael thought, but she was too sick to her stomach and too sick at heart to speak that thought aloud.

Sarah said, "Tonight I watched the eleven o'clock news, and that's when I first heard he'd been killed, hit by a truck earlier in the day, yesterday morning, and I'm wondering how long I can stay in the house before someone comes to put me out, and I'm trying to figure what to do, where to go from here. But then little more than an hour after I see the story about him on the news, he shows up at the door, and at first I think the story must've been all wrong, but then . . . oh, Christ . . . then I knew it wasn't wrong. He . . . he really was killed. He *was*."

"Yes."

The girl tenderly licked her split lip. "But somehow . . . "

"Yes."

" . . . he came back."

"Yes," Rachael said. "He came back. In fact, he's still *coming* back. He's not made it all the way back yet and probably won't ever make it."

"But how—"

"Never mind how. You don't want to know."

"And who—"

"You don't want to *know* who! Believe me, you don't want to know, can't afford to know. Honey, you've got to listen closely now, and I want you to take to heart what I'm saying to you. You can't tell anyone what you've seen. Not anyone. Understand? If you do . . . you'll be in terrible danger. There're people who'd kill you in a minute to keep you from talking about Eric's resurrection. There's more involved here than you can ever know, and they'll kill as many people as necessary to keep their secrets."

A dark, ironic, and not entirely sane laugh escaped the girl. "Who could I tell that would believe me, anyway?"

"Exactly," Rachael said.

"They'd think I was crazy. It's nuts, the whole thing, just plain impossible."

Sarah's voice had a bleak edge, a haunted note, and it was clear that what she had seen tonight had changed her forever, perhaps for the better, perhaps for the worse. She would never be the same again. And for a long time, perhaps for the rest of her life, sleep would not be easily attained, for she would always fear what dreams might come.

Rachael said, "All right. Now, when we get you to a hospital, I'll pay all your bills. And I'm going to give you a check for ten thousand dollars as well, which I hope to God you won't throw away on drugs. And if you want me to, I'll call your parents out there in Kansas and ask them to come for you."

"I . . . I think I'd like that."

"Good. I think that's very good, honey. I'm sure they've been worried about you."

"You know . . . Eric would've killed me. I'm sure that's what he wanted. To kill me. Maybe not me in particular. Just someone. He just felt like he *had* to kill someone, like it was a *need* in him, in his blood. And I was there. You know? Convenient."

"How did you get away from him?"

"He . . . he sort of *phased out* for a couple of minutes. Like I told you, he seemed confused at times. And then at one point his eyes just sort of clouded up even worse, and he started making this funny little wheezing noise. He turned away from me and looked around, as if he was really mixed up . . . you know, bewildered. He seemed to get weak, too, because he leaned against the wall there by the bathroom door and hung his head down."

Rachael remembered the bloody palmprint on the bedroom wall, beside the bathroom door.

"And when he was like that," Sarah said, "when he was distracted, I was flat on the bathroom floor, hurt real bad, hardly able to move, and so the best I could do was crawl into the shower stall, and I was sure he'd come in after me when he got his senses back, you know, but he didn't. Like he forgot me. Came to his senses and either didn't remember I'd been there or couldn't figure out where I'd gone to. And then, after a while, I heard him farther back in the house, pounding things, breaking things."

"He pretty much wrecked the kitchen," Rachael said, and in a dark corner of her memory was the image of the knives driven deep into the kitchen wall.

Tears slid first from Sarah's good eye, then from the blackened and swollen one, and she said, "I can't figure . . . "

"What?" Rachael asked.

"Why he'd come after *me*."

"He probably didn't come after you specifically," Rachael said. "If there was a wall safe in the house, he would've wanted the money from it. But basically, I think he's just . . . looking for a place to go to ground for a while, until the process . . . runs its course. Then, when he blanked out for a moment and you hid from him, and when he came around again and didn't see you, he probably figured you'd gone for help, so he had to get out of there fast, go somewhere else."

"The cabin, I'll bet."

"What cabin?"

"You don't know about his cabin up at Lake Arrowhead?"

"No," Rachael said.

"It's not on the lake, really. Farther up there on the mountain. He took me up to it once. He owns a couple of acres of woods and this neat cabin—"

Someone tapped on the window.

Rachael and Sarah cried out in surprise.

It was only Benny. He pulled open Rachael's door and said, "Come on. I've got us a new set of wheels. It's a gray Subaru—one hell of a lot less conspicuous than this buggy."

Rachael hesitated, catching her breath, waiting for her drumming heartbeat to slow down. She felt as if she and Sarah were kids who'd been sitting at a camp fire, telling ghost stories, trying to spook each other and succeeding all too well. For an instant, crazily, she had been certain that the tapping at the window was the hard, bony *click-click-click* of a skeletal finger.

12   SHARP

FROM THE MOMENT JULIO MET ANSON SHARP, HE DISLIKED THE man. Minute by minute, his dislike intensified.

Sharp came into Rachael Leben's house in Placentia in more of a swagger than a walk, flashing his Defense Security Agency credentials as if ordinary policemen were expected to fall to their knees and venerate a federal agent of such high position. He looked at Becky Klienstad crucified on the wall, shook his head, and said, "Too bad. She was a nice-looking piece, wasn't she?" With an authoritarian briskness that seemed calculated to offend, he told them that the murders of the Hernandez and Klienstad women were now part of an extremely sensitive federal case, removed from the jurisdiction of local police agencies, for reasons that he could not—or would not—divulge. He asked questions and demanded answers, but he would give no answers of his own. He was a big man, even bigger than Reese, with chest and shoulders and arms that looked as if they had been hewn from immense timbers, and his neck was almost as thick as his head. Unlike Reese, he enjoyed using his size to intimidate others and had a habit of standing too close, intentionally violating your space, *looming* over you when he talked to you, looking down with a vague, barely perceptible, yet nevertheless infuriating smirk. He had a handsome face and seemed vain about his looks, and he had thick blond hair expensively razor-cut, and his jewel-bright green eyes said, *I'm better than you, smarter than you, more clever than you, and I always will be.*

Sharp told Orin Mulveck and the other Placentia police officers that they were to vacate the premises and immediately desist in their investigation. "All of the evidence you've collected, photographs you've taken, and paperwork you've generated will be turned over to my own team at once. You will leave one patrol car and two officers at the curb and assign them to assist us in any way we see fit."

Clearly, Orin Mulveck was no happier with Sharp than Julio and Reese were. Mulveck and his people had been reduced to the role of the federal agent's glorified messenger boys, and none of them liked it, though they would have been considerably less offended if Sharp had handled them with more tact—hell, with any tact at all.

"I'll have to check your orders with my chief," Mulveck said.

"By all means," Sharp said. "Meanwhile, please get all your people out of this house. And you are all under orders not to speak of anything you've seen here. Is that understood?"

"I'll check with my chief," Mulveck said. His face was red and the arteries were pounding in his temples when he stalked out.

Two men in dark suits had come with Sharp, neither as large as he, neither as imposing, but both of them cool and smug. They stood just inside the bedroom, one on each side of the door, like temple guards, watching Julio and Reese with unconcealed suspicion.

Julio had never encountered Defense Security Agency men before. They were far different from the FBI agents that he had sometimes worked with, less like policemen than FBI men were. They wore elitism as if it were a pungent cologne.

To Julio and Reese, Sharp said, "I know who you are, and I know a little bit about your reputations—two hound dogs. You bite into a case and you just never let go. Usually that's admirable. This time, however, you've got to unclench your teeth and let go. I can't make it clear enough. Understand me?"

"It's basically our case," Julio said tightly. "It started in our jurisdiction, and we caught the first call."

Sharp frowned. "I'm telling you it's over and you're out. As far as your department's concerned, there *is* no case for you to work on here. The files on Hernandez, Klienstad, and Leben have all been pulled from your records, as if they never existed, and from now on *we* handle everything. I've got my own forensics team driving in from L.A. right now. We don't need or want anything you can provide.

Comprende, amigo? Listen, Lieutenant Verdad, you're *gone*. Check with your superiors if you don't believe me."

"I don't like it," Julio said.

"You don't have to like it," Sharp said.

■ Julio drove only two blocks from Rachael Leben's house before he had to pull over to the curb and stop. He threw the car into park with a violent swipe at the gearshift and said, "Damn! Sharp's so sold on himself he probably thinks someone ought to bottle his piss and sell it as perfume."

During the ten years Reese had worked with Julio, he had never seen his partner this angry. Furious. His eyes looked hard and hot. A tic in his right cheek made half his face twitch. The muscles in his jaws clenched and unclenched, and the cords in his neck were taut. He looked like he wanted to break something in half. Reese was struck by the weird thought that if Julio had been a cartoon character, steam would have been pouring from his ears.

Reese said, "He's an asshole, sure, but he's an asshole with a lot of authority and connections."

"Acts like a damn storm trooper."

"I suppose he's got his job to do."

"Yeah, but it's *our* job he's doing."

"Let it go," Reese said.

"I can't."

"Let it go."

Julio shook his head. "No. This is a special case. I feel a special obligation to that Hernandez girl. Don't ask me to explain it. You'd think I was getting sentimental in my old age. Anyway, if it was just an ordinary case, just the usual homicide, I'd let it go in a minute, I would, I really would, but this one is special."

Reese sighed.

To Julio, nearly every case was special. He was a small man, especially for a detective, but he was *committed,* damned if he wasn't, and one way or another he found an excuse for persevering in a case when any other cop would have given up, when common sense said there was no point in continuing, and when the law of diminishing returns made it perfectly clear that the time had come to move on to something else. Sometimes he said, "Reese, I feel a special commitment to this victim 'cause he was so young, never had a chance to know life, and it isn't fair, it *eats* at me." And sometimes he said, "Reese, this case is personal and special to me because the victim was so old, so old and defenseless, and if we don't go an extra mile to protect our elderly citizens, then we're a very sick society; this *eats* at me, Reese." Sometimes the case was special to Julio because the victim was pretty, and it seemed such a tragedy for any beauty to be lost to the world that it just *ate* at him. But he could be equally eaten because the victim was ugly, therefore already disadvantaged in life, which made the additional curse of death too unfair to be borne. This time, Reese suspected that Julio had formed a special attachment to Ernestina because her name was similar to that of his long-dead little brother. It didn't take much to elicit a fierce commitment from Julio Verdad. Almost any little thing would do. The problem was that Julio had such a deep reservoir of compassion and empathy that he was always in danger of drowning in it.

Sitting rigidly behind the steering wheel, lightly but repeatedly thumping one fist against his thigh, Julio said, "Obviously, the snatching of Eric Leben's corpse and the murders of these two women are connected. But how? Did the people who stole his body kill Ernestina and Becky? And why? And why nail her to the wall in Mrs. Leben's bedroom? That's so grotesque!"

Reese said, "Let it go."

"And where's Mrs. Leben? What's she know about this? Something. When I questioned her, I sensed she was holding something back."

"Let it go."

"And why would this be a national security matter requiring Anson Sharp and his damn Defense Security Agency?"

"Let it go," Reese said, sounding like a broken record, aware that it was useless to attempt to divert Julio, but making the effort anyway. It was their usual litany; he would have felt incomplete if he had not upheld his end of it.

Less angry now than thoughtful, Julio said, "It must have something to do with work Leben's company is doing for the government. A defense contract of some kind."

"You're going to keep poking around, aren't you?"

"I told you, Reese, I feel a special connection with that poor Hernandez girl."

"Don't worry; they'll find her killer."

"Sharp? We're supposed to rely on *him?* He's a jackass. You see the way he dresses?" Julio, of course, was always impeccably dressed. "The sleeves on his suit jacket were about an inch too short, and it needed to be let out along the back seam. And he doesn't polish his shoes often enough; they looked like he'd just been hiking in them. How can he find Ernestina's killer if he can't even keep his shoes properly polished?"

"I have a feeling of my own about this one, Julio. I think they'll have our scalps if we don't just let it go."

"I can't walk away," Julio said adamantly. "I'm still in. I'm in for the duration. You can opt out if you want."

"I'll stay."

"I'm putting no pressure on you."

"I'm in," Reese said.

"You don't have to do anything you don't want to do."

"I said I was in, and I'm in."

Five years ago, in an act of unparalleled bravery, Julio Verdad had saved the life of Esther Susanne Hagerstrom, Reese's daughter and only child, who had then been just four years old and achingly small and very helpless. In the world according to Reese Hagerstrom, the seasons changed and the sun rose and the sun set and the sea rose and the sea fell all for one reason: to please Esther Susanne. She was the center, the middle, the ends, and the circumference of his life, and he had almost lost her, but Julio had saved her, had killed one man and nearly killed two others in order to rescue her, so now Reese would have walked away from a million-dollar inheritance sooner than he would have walked away from his partner.

"I can handle everything on my own," Julio said. "Really."

"Didn't you hear me say I was in?"

"We're liable to screw ourselves into disciplinary suspensions."

"I'm in."

"Could be kissing good-bye to any more promotions."

"I'm in."

"You're in, then?"

"I'm in."

"You're sure?"

"I'm sure."

Julio put the car in gear, pulled away from the curb, and headed out of Placentia. "All right, we're both a little whacked out, need some rest. I'll drop you off at your place, let you get a few hours in the sack, and pick you up at ten in the morning."

"And where will you be going while I'm sleeping?"

"Might try to get a few winks myself," Julio said.

Reese and his sister, Agnes, lived with Esther Susanne on East Adams Avenue in the town of Orange, in a pleasant house that Reese had rather substantially remodeled himself during his days off. Julio had an apartment in an attractive Spanish-style complex just a block off Fourth Street, way out at the east end of Santa Ana.

Both of them would be going home to cold and lonely beds. Julio's wife had died of cancer seven years ago. Reese's wife, Esther's mother, had been shot and killed during the same incident in which he had almost lost his little girl, so he had been a widower five years, only two less than Julio.

On the 57 Freeway, shooting south toward Orange and Santa Ana, Reese said, "And if you can't sleep?"

"I'll go into the office, nose around, try to see if anyone knows anything about this Sharp and why he's so damned hot to run the show. Maybe ask around here and there about Dr. Eric Leben, too."

"What're we going to do exactly when you pick me up at ten in the morning?"

"I don't know yet," Julio said. "But I'll have figured out something by then."

13   REVELATIONS

THEY TOOK SARAH KIEL TO THE HOSPITAL IN THE STOLEN gray Subaru. Rachael arranged to pay the hospital bills, left a ten-thousand-dollar check with Sarah, called the girl's parents in Kansas, then left the hospital with Ben and went looking for a suitable place to hole up for the rest of the night.

By 3:35 Tuesday morning, grainy-eyed and exhausted, they found a large motel on Palm Canyon Drive with an all-night desk clerk. Their room had orange and white drapes that almost made Ben's eyes bleed, and Rachael said the bedspread pattern looked like yak puke, but the shower and air-conditioning worked, and the two queen-size beds had firm mattresses, and the unit was at the back of the complex, away from the street, where they could expect quiet even after the town came alive in the morning, so it wasn't exactly hell on earth.

Leaving Rachael alone for ten minutes, Ben drove the stolen Subaru out the motel's rear exit, left it in a supermarket parking lot several blocks away, and returned on foot. Both going and coming, he avoided passing the windows of the motel office and therefore did not stir the curiosity of the night clerk. Tomorrow, with the need for wheels less urgent, they could take time to rent a car.

In his absence, Rachael had visited the ice-maker and the soda-vending machine. A plastic bucket brimming with ice cubes stood on the small table by the window, plus cans of Diet Coke and regular Coke and A&W Root Beer and Orange Crush.

She said, "I thought you might be thirsty."

He was suddenly aware that they were smack in the middle of the desert and that they had been moving in a sweat for hours. Standing, he drank an Orange Crush in two swallows, finished a root beer nearly as fast, then sat down and popped the tab on a Diet Coke. "Even with the hump, how do camels do it?"

As if dropping under an immense weight, she sat down on the other side of the table, opened a Coke, and said, "Well?"

"Well what?"

"Aren't you going to ask?"

He yawned, not out of perversity, and not because he wanted to irritate her, but because at that moment the prospect of sleep was more appealing than finally learning the truth of her circumstances. He said, "Ask what?"

"The same questions you've been asking all night."

"You made it clear you wouldn't give answers."

"Well, now I will. Now there's no keeping you out of it."

She looked so sad that Ben felt a cold premonition of death in his bones and wondered if he had, indeed, been foolish to involve himself even to help the woman he loved. She was looking at him as if he were already dead—as if they were *both* dead.

"So if you're ready to tell me," he said, "then I don't need to ask questions."

"You're going to have to keep an open mind. What I'm about to tell you might seem unbelievable . . . damn strange."

He sipped the Diet Coke and said, "You mean about Eric dying and coming back from the dead?"

She jerked in surprise and gaped at him. She tried to speak but couldn't get any words out.

He had never in his life elicited such a rewarding reaction from anyone else, and he took enormous pleasure in it.

At last she said, "But . . . but how . . . when . . . what . . . "

He said, "How do I know what I know? When did I figure it out? What clued me in?"

She nodded.

He said, "Hell, if someone had stolen Eric's body, they'd surely have come with a car of their own to haul it away. They wouldn't have had to kill a woman and steal *her* car. And there were those discarded hospital whites in the garage in Villa Park. Besides, you were scared witless from the moment I showed up at your door last evening, and you aren't easily spooked. You're a very competent and self-sufficient woman, not the type to get the willies. In fact, I've never seen you scared of anything except maybe . . . Eric."

"He really was killed by that truck, you know. It isn't just that they misdiagnosed his condition."

The desire for sleep retreated a bit, and Ben said, "His business—and genius—

was genetic engineering. And the man was obsessed with staying young. So I figure he found a way to edit out the genes linked to aging and death. Or maybe he edited *in* an artificially constructed gene for swift healing, tissue stasis . . . immortality."

"You endlessly amaze me," she said.

"I'm quite a guy."

Her own weariness gave way to nervous energy. She could not keep still. She got up and paced.

He remained seated, sipping his Diet Coke. He had been badly rattled all night; now it was her turn.

Her bleak voice was tinted by dread, resignation. "When Geneplan patented its first highly profitable artificial microorganisms, Eric could've taken the company public, could've sold thirty percent of his stock and made a hundred million overnight."

"A hundred? Jesus!"

"His two partners and three of the research associates, who also had pieces of the company, half wanted him to do just that because they'd have made a killing, too. Everyone else but Vincent Baresco was leaning toward going for the gold. Eric refused."

"Baresco," Ben said. "The guy who pulled the Magnum on us, the guy I trashed in Eric's office tonight—is he a partner?"

"It's *Dr.* Vincent Baresco. He's on Eric's handpicked research staff—one of the few who know about the Wildcard Project. In fact, only the six of them knew everything. Six plus me. Eric loved to brag to me. Anyway, Baresco sided with Eric, didn't want Geneplan to go public, and he convinced the others. If it remained a privately held company, they didn't have to please stockholders. They could spend money on unlikely projects without defending their decisions."

"Such as a search for immortality or its equivalent."

"They didn't expect to achieve full immortality—but longevity, regeneration. It took a *lot* of funds, money that stockholders would've wanted to see paid out in dividends. Eric and the others were getting rich, anyway, from the modest percentage of corporate profits they distributed to themselves, so they didn't desperately need the capital they'd get by going public."

"Regeneration," Ben said thoughtfully.

At the window, Rachael stopped pacing, cautiously drew back the drape, and peered out at the night-cloaked motel parking lot.

She said, "God knows, I'm no expert in recombinant DNA. But . . . well, they hoped to develop a benign virus that'd function as a 'carrier' to convey new genetic material into the body's cells and precisely place the new bits on the chains of chromosomes. Think of the virus as a sort of living scalpel that does genetic surgery. Because it's microscopic, it can perform minute operations no real scalpel ever could. It can be designed to seek out—and attach itself to—a certain portion of a chromosomal chain, either destroying the gene already there or inserting a new one."

"And they *did* develop it?"

"Yes. Then they needed to positively identify genes associated with aging and edit them out—*and* develop artificial genetic material for the virus to carry into the cells. Those new genes would be designed to halt the aging process and tremendously boost the natural immune system by cuing the body to produce vastly larger quantities of interferon and other healing substances. Follow me?"

"Mostly."

"They even believed they could give the human body the ability to regenerate ruined tissue, bone, and vital organs."

She still stared out at the night, and she appeared to have gone pale—not at something she had seen but at the consideration of what she was slowly revealing to him.

Finally she continued: "Their patents were bringing in a river of money, a flood. So they spent God knows how many tens of millions, farming out pieces of the research puzzle to geneticists not in the company, keeping the work fragmented so no one was likely to realize the true intent of their efforts. It was like a privately financed equivalent of the Manhattan Project—and maybe even more secret than the development of the atomic bomb."

"Secret . . . because if they succeeded, they wanted to keep the blessing of an extended life span for themselves?"

"Partly, yes." Letting the drape fall in place, she turned from the window. "And by holding the secret, by dispensing the blessing only to whomever they chose— just imagine the *power* they'd wield. They could essentially create a long-lived elite master race that owed its existence to them. And the threat of withholding the gift would be a bludgeon that could make virtually anyone cooperate with them. I used to listen to Eric talk about it, and it sounded like nonsense, pipe dreams, even though I knew he was a genius in his field."

"Those men in the Cadillac who pursued us and shot the cops—"

"From Geneplan," she said, still full of nervous energy, pacing again. "I recognized the car. It belongs to Rupert Knowls. Knowls supplied the initial venture capital that got Eric started. After Eric, he's the chief partner."

"A rich man . . . yet he's willing to risk his reputation and his freedom by gunning down two cops?"

"To protect this secret, yeah, I guess he is. He's not exactly a scrupulous man to begin with. And confronted with *this* opportunity, I suppose he'll stretch his scruples even further than usual."

"Okay. So they developed the technique to prolong life and promote incredibly rapid healing. Then what?"

Her lovely face had been pale. Now it darkened as if a shadow had fallen across it, though there was no shadow. "Then . . . they began experiments on lab animals. Primarily white mice."

Ben sat up straighter in his chair and put the can of Diet Coke aside, because from Rachael's demeanor he sensed that she was reaching the crux of the story.

She paused for a moment to check the dead bolt on the room door, which opened onto a covered breezeway that flanked the parking lot. The lock was securely engaged, but after a moment's hesitation she took one of the straight-backed chairs from the table, tipped it onto two legs, and braced it under the doorknob for extra protection.

He was sure she was being overly cautious, treading the edge of paranoia. On the other hand, he didn't object.

She returned to the edge of the bed. "They injected the mice, *changed* the mice, working with mouse genes instead of human genes, of course, but applying the same theories and techniques they intended to use to promote human longevity. And the mice, a short-lived variety, survived longer . . . twice as long as usual and still kicking. Then three times as long . . . four times . . . and still young. Some mice were subjected to injuries of various kinds—everything from contusions and abrasions to punctures, broken bones, serious burns—and they healed at a remarkable rate. They recovered and flourished after their kidneys were virtually destroyed. Lungs eaten half away by acid fumes were regenerated. They actually regained their vision after being blinded. And then . . . "

Her voice trailed away, and she glanced at the fortified door, then at the window, lowered her head, closed her eyes.

Ben waited.

Eyes still closed, she said, "Following standard procedure, they killed some mice and put them aside for dissection and for thorough tissue tests. Some were killed with injections of air—embolisms. Killed others with lethal injections of formaldehyde. And there was no question they were dead. Very dead. But those that weren't yet dissected . . . they came back. Within a few hours. Lying there in the lab trays . . . they just . . . started twitching, squirming. Bleary-eyed, weak at first . . . *but they came back*. Soon they were on their feet, scurrying about their cages, eating—fully alive. Which no one had anticipated, not at all. Oh, sure, before the mice were killed, they'd had tremendously enhanced immune systems, truly astonishing capacity to heal, and life spans that had been dramatically increased, but . . . " Rachael raised her head, opened her eyes, looked at Ben. "But once the line of death is crossed . . . who'd imagine it could be *re*crossed?"

Ben's hands started shaking, and a wintry shiver followed the track of his spine, and he realized that the true meaning and power of these events had only now begun to sink in.

"Yes," Rachael said, as if she knew what thoughts and emotions were racing through his mind and heart.

He was overcome by a strange mixture of terror, awe, and wild joy: terror at the idea of anything, mouse or man, returning from the land of the dead; awe at the thought that humankind's genius had perhaps shattered nature's dreadful chains of mortality; joy at the prospect of humanity freed forever from the loss of loved ones, freed forever from the great fears of sickness and death.

And as if reading his mind, Rachael said, "Maybe one day . . . maybe even one day soon, the threat of the grave will pass away. But not yet. Not quite yet. Because the Wildcard Project's breakthrough is not entirely successful. The mice that came back were . . . strange."

"Strange?"

Instead of elaborating on that freighted word, she said, "At first the researchers thought the mice's odd behavior resulted from some sort of brain damage—maybe not to cerebral tissues but to the fundamental *chemistry* of the brain—that couldn't be repaired even by the mice's enhanced healing abilities. But that wasn't the case. They could still run difficult mazes and repeat other complex tricks they'd been taught before they'd died—"

"So somehow the memories, knowledge, probably even personality survives the brief period of lifelessness between death and rebirth."

She nodded. "Which would indicate that some small current still exists in the brain for a time after death, enough to keep memory intact until . . . resurrection. Like a computer during a power failure, barely holding on to material in its short-term memory by using the meager flow of current from a standby battery."

Ben wasn't sleepy anymore. "Okay, so the mice could run mazes, but there was something strange about them. What? How strange?"

"Sometimes they became confused—more frequently at first than after they'd been back with the living awhile—and they repeatedly rammed themselves against their cages or ran in circles chasing their tails. That kind of abnormal behavior slowly passed. But another, more frightening behavior emerged . . . and endured."

Outside a car pulled into the motel parking lot and stopped.

Rachael glanced worriedly at the barricaded door.

In the still desert air, a car door opened, closed.

Ben sat up straighter in his chair, tense.

Footsteps echoed softly through the empty night. They were heading away from Rachael's and Ben's room. In another part of the motel, the door to another room opened and closed.

With visible relief Rachael let her shoulders sag. "Mice are natural-born cowards, of course. They never fight their enemies. They're not equipped to. They survive by running, dodging, hiding. They don't even fight among themselves for supremacy or territory. They're meek, timid. But the mice who came back weren't meek at all. They fought one another, and they attacked mice that had *not* been resurrected—and they even tried to nip at the researchers handling them, though a mouse has no hope of hurting a man and is ordinarily acutely aware of that. They flew into rages, clawing at the floors of their cages, pawing at the air as if fighting imaginary enemies, sometimes even clawing at themselves. Occasionally these fits lasted less than a minute, but more often went on until the mouse collapsed in exhaustion."

For a moment, neither spoke.

The silence in the motel room was sepulchral, profound.

At last Ben said, "In spite of this strangeness in the mice, Eric and his researchers must've been electrified. Dear God, they'd hoped to extend the life span—and instead they defeated death altogether! So they were eager to move on to development of similar methods of genetic alteration for human beings."

"Yes."

"In spite of the mice's unexplained tendency to frenzies, rages, random violence."

"Yes."

"Figuring that problem might never arise in a human subject . . . or could be dealt with somewhere along the way."

"Yes."

Ben said, "So . . . slowly the work progressed, but too slowly for Eric. Youth-oriented, youth-*obsessed,* and inordinately afraid of dying, he decided not to wait for a safe and proven process."

"Yes."

"That's what you meant in Eric's office tonight, when you asked Baresco if he knew Eric had broken the cardinal rule. To a genetics researcher or other specialist in biological sciences, the cardinal rule would be—what?—that he should never experiment with human beings until all encountered problems and unanswered questions are dealt with at the test-animal level or below."

"Exactly," she said. She had folded her hands in her lap to keep them from shaking, but her fingers kept picking at one another. "And Vincent didn't know Eric had broken the cardinal rule. *I* knew, but it must've come as a nasty shock to them when they heard Eric's body was missing. The moment they heard, they knew he'd done the craziest, most reckless, most unforgivable thing he possibly could've done."

"And now what?" Ben asked. "They want to help him?"

"No. They want to kill him. Again."

"Why?"

"Because he won't come back all the way, won't ever be exactly like he was. This stuff wasn't *perfected* yet."

"He'll be like the lab animals?"

"Probably. Strangely violent, dangerous."

Ben thought of the mindless destruction in the Villa Park house, the blood in the trunk of the car.

Rachael said, "Remember—he was a ruthless man all his life and troubled by barely suppressed violent urges even before this. The mice started out meek, but Eric didn't, so what might he be like now? Look what he did to Sarah Kiel."

Ben remembered not only the beaten girl but the wrecked kitchen in the Palm Springs house, the knives driven into the wall.

"And if Eric murders someone in one of these rages," Rachael said, "the police are more likely to learn he's alive, and Wildcard will be blown wide open. So his partners want to kill him in some *very* final manner that'll rule out another resurrection. I wouldn't be surprised if they dismembered the corpse or burned it to ashes and then disposed of the remains in several locations."

Good God, Ben thought, is this reality or Chiller Theater?

He said, "They want to kill you because you know about Wildcard?"

"Yes, but that's not the only reason they'd like to get their hands on me. They've got two others at least. For one thing, they probably think I know where Eric will go to ground."

"But you don't?"

"I had some ideas. And Sarah Kiel gave me another one. But I don't know for sure."

"You said there's a third reason they'd want you?"

She nodded. "I'm first in line to inherit Geneplan, and they don't trust me to continue pumping enough money into Wildcard. By removing me, they stand a much better chance of retaining control of the corporation and of keeping Wildcard secret. If I could've gotten to Eric's safe ahead of them and could've put my hands on his project diary, I would've had solid proof that Wildcard exists, and then they wouldn't have dared touch me. Without proof, I'm vulnerable."

Ben rose and began to move restlessly around the room, thinking furiously.

Somewhere in the night, not far beyond the motel walls, a cat cried either in anger or in passion. It went on a long time, rising and falling, an eerie ululation.

Finally Ben said, "Rachael, why are *you* pursuing Eric? Why this desperate rush to reach him before the others? What'll you do if you find him?"

"Kill him," she said without hesitation, and the bleakness in her green eyes was now complemented by a Rachael-like determination and iron resolve. "Kill him for good. Because if I don't kill him, he's going to hide out until he's in better condition, until he's a bit more in control of himself, and then he's going to come kill me. He died furious with me, consumed by such hatred for me that he dashed blindly out into traffic, and I'm sure that same hatred was seething in him the moment awareness returned to him in the county morgue. In his clouded and twisted mind, I'm very likely his primary obsession, and I don't think he'll rest until I'm dead. Or until he's dead, really dead this time."

He knew she was right. He was deeply afraid for her.

His preference for the past was as strong in him now as it had ever been, and he longed for simpler times. How mad had the modern world become? Criminals owned the city streets at night. The whole planet could be utterly destroyed in an hour with the pressing of a few buttons. And now . . . *now* dead men could be reanimated. Ben wished for a time machine that could carry him back to a better age: say the early 1920s, when a sense of wonder was still alive and when faith in the human potential was unsullied and unsurpassed.

Yet . . . he remembered the joy that had surged in him when Rachael had first said that death had been beaten, before she had explained that those who came back from beyond were frighteningly changed. He had been *thrilled*. Hardly the response of a genuine stick-in-the-mud reactionary. He might peer back at the past and long for it with full-blown sentimentalism, but in his heart he was, like others of his age, undeniably attracted to science and its potential for creating a brighter future. Maybe he was not such a misfit in the modern world as he liked to pretend. Maybe this experience was teaching him something about himself that he would have preferred not to learn.

He said, "Could you really pull the trigger on Eric?"

"Yes."

"I'm not sure you could. I suspect you'd freeze up when you were really confronted with the moral implications of murder."

"This wouldn't be murder. He's no longer a human being. He's already dead. The living dead. The walking dead. He's not a man anymore. He's different. *Changed.* Just as those mice were changed. He's only a thing now, not a man, a dangerous *thing,* and I wouldn't have any qualms about blowing his head off. If the authorities ever found out, I don't think they'd even try to prosecute me. And I see no moral questions that would put me on trial in my own mind."

"You've obviously thought hard about this," he said. "But why not hide out, keep a low profile, let Eric's partners find him and kill him for you?"

She shook her head. "I can't bet everything on their success. They might fail. They might not get to him before he finds me. This is *my* life we're talking about, and by God I'm not trusting in anyone but me to protect it."

"And me," he said.

"And you, yes. And you, Benny."

He came to the bed and sat down on the edge of it, beside her. "So we're chasing a dead man."

"Yes."

"But we've got to get some rest now."

"I'm beat," she agreed.

"Then where will we go tomorrow?"

"Sarah told me about a cabin Eric has in the mountains near Lake Arrowhead. It sounded secluded. Just what he needs now, for the next few days, while the initial healing's going on."

Ben sighed. "Yeah, I think we might find him in a place like that."

"You don't have to come with me."

"I will."

"But you don't *have* to."

"I know. But I will."

She kissed him lightly on the cheek.

Though she was weary, sweaty, and rumpled, with lank hair and bloodshot eyes, she was beautiful.

He had never felt closer to her. Facing death together always forged a special bond between people, drew them even closer regardless of how very close they might have been before. He knew, for he had been to war in the Green Hell.

Tenderly she said, "Let's get some rest, Benny."

"Right," he said.

But before he could lie down and turn off the lights, he had to break out the magazine of the Smith & Wesson Combat Magnum that he had taken off Vincent Baresco several hours ago and count the remaining cartridges. Three. Half the magazine's load had been expended in Eric's office, when Baresco had fired wildly in the darkness as Ben attacked him. Three left. Not much. Not nearly enough to make Ben feel secure, even though Rachael had her own thirty-two pistol. How many bullets were required to stop a walking dead man? Ben put the Combat Magnum on the nightstand, where he could reach out and lay his hand on it in an instant if he needed it during what remained of the night.

In the morning, he would buy a box of ammunition. Two boxes.

14 LIKE A NIGHT BIRD

LEAVING TWO MEN BEHIND AT RACHAEL LEBEN'S HOUSE IN PLACentia—where the crucified corpse of Rebecca Klienstad had finally been taken down from the bedroom wall—and leaving other men at the Leben house in Villa Park and still others at the Geneplan offices, Anson Sharp of the Defense Security Agency choppered through the desert darkness with two more agents, flying low and fast, to Eric Leben's stylish yet squalid love nest in Palm Springs. The pilot put the helicopter down in a bank parking lot less than a block off Palm Canyon Drive, where a nondescript government car was waiting. The chuffling rotors of the aircraft sliced up the hot dry desert air and flung slabs of it at Sharp's back as he dashed to the sedan.

Five minutes later, they arrived at the house where Dr. Leben had kept his string of teenage girls. Sharp wasn't surprised to find the front door ajar. He rang the bell repeatedly, but no one answered. Drawing his service revolver, a Smith & Wesson Chief's Special, he led the way inside, in search of Sarah Kiel who, according to the most recent report on Leben, was the current piece of fluff in residence.

The Defense Security Agency knew about Leben's lechery because it knew *everything* about people engaged in top-secret contract work with the Pentagon. That was something civilians like Leben just could never seem to understand: Once they accepted the Pentagon's money and undertook highly sensitive research work, they had absolutely no privacy. Sharp knew all about Leben's fascination with modern art, modern design, and modern architecture. He knew about Eric Leben's marital problems in detail. He knew what foods Leben preferred, what music he liked, what brand of underwear he wore; so of course he also knew every little thing about the teenage girls because the potential for blackmail that they presented was related to national security.

When Sharp stepped into the kitchen and saw the destruction, especially the knives driven into the wall, he figured he would not find Sarah Kiel alive. She would be nailed up in another room, or maybe bolted to the ceiling, or maybe hacked to pieces and hung on wire to form a bloody mobile, maybe even worse. You couldn't guess what might happen next in this case. *Anything* could happen.

Weird.

Gosser and Peake, the two young agents with Sharp, were startled and made uneasy by the mess in the kitchen and by the psychopathic frenzy it implied. Their security clearance and need to know were as high as Sharp's, so they were aware that they were hunting for a walking dead man. They knew Eric Leben had risen from a morgue slab and escaped in stolen hospital whites, and they knew a half-alive and deranged Eric Leben had killed the Hernandez and Klienstad women to obtain their car, so Gosser and Peake held their service revolvers as tightly and cautiously as Sharp held his.

Of course, the DSA was fully aware of the nature of the work Geneplan was doing for the government: biological warfare research, the creation of deadly man-made viruses. But the agency also knew the details of other projects under way within the company, including the Wildcard Project, although Leben and his associates had labored under the delusion that the secret of Wildcard was theirs alone. They were unaware of the federal agents and stoolies among them. And they did not realize how quickly government computers had ascertained their intentions merely by surveying the research they farmed out to other companies and extrapolating the purpose of it all.

These civilian types just could not understand that when you bargained with Uncle Sam and eagerly took his money, you couldn't sell only a small piece of your soul. You had to sell it all.

Anson Sharp usually enjoyed bringing that bit of nasty news to people like Eric Leben. They thought they were such big fish, but they forgot that even big fish are eaten by bigger fish, and there was no bigger fish in the sea than the whale called Washington. Sharp loved to watch that realization sink in. He relished seeing the self-important hotshots break into a sweat and quiver. They usually tried to bribe him or reason with him, and sometimes they begged, but of course he could not let them off the hook. Even if he could have let them off, he would not have done it, because he liked nothing more than seeing them squirm before him.

Dr. Eric Leben and his six cronies had been permitted to proceed unhampered with their revolutionary research into longevity. But if they had solved all the problems and achieved a useful breakthrough, the government would have moved in on them and would have absorbed the project by one means or another, through the swift declaration of a national defense emergency.

Now Eric Leben had screwed up everything. He administered the faulty treatment to himself and then accidentally put it to the test by walking in front of a damn garbage truck. No one could have anticipated such a turn of events because the guy had seemed too smart to risk his own genetic integrity.

Looking at the broken china and the trampled food that littered the floor, Gosser wrinkled his choirboy face and said, "The guy's a real berserker."

"Looks like the work of an animal," Peake said, frowning.

Sharp led them out of the kitchen, through the rest of the house, finally to the master bedroom and bath, where more destruction had been wrought and where there was also some blood, including a bloody palmprint on the wall. It was probably Leben's print: proof that the dead man, in some strange fashion, lived.

No cadaver could be found in the house, neither Sarah Kiel's nor anybody else's, and Sharp was disappointed. The nude and crucified woman in Placentia had been unexpected and kinky, a welcome change from the corpses he usually saw. Victims of guns, knives, plastique, and the garroting wire were old news to Sharp; he had seen them in such plenitude over the years that he no longer got a kick out of them. But he had sure gotten a kick out of that bimbo nailed to the wall, and he was curious to see what Leben's deranged and rotting mind might come up with next.

Sharp checked the hidden safe in the floor of the bedroom closet and found that it had been emptied.

Leaving Gosser behind to house-sit in case Leben returned, Sharp took Peake along on a search of the garage, expecting to find Sarah Kiel's body, which they did not. Then he sent Peake into the backyard with a flashlight to examine the lawn and flower beds for signs of a freshly dug grave, though it seemed unlikely that Leben, in his current condition, would have the desire or the foresight to bury his victims and cover his tracks.

"If you don't find anything," Sharp told Peake, "then start checking the hospitals. In spite of the blood, maybe the Kiel girl wasn't killed. Maybe she managed to run away from him and get medical attention."

"If I find her at some hospital?"

"I'll need to know at once," Sharp said, for he would have to prevent Sarah Kiel from talking about Eric Leben's return. He would try to use reason, intimidation, and outright threats to ensure her silence. If that didn't work, she would be quietly removed.

Rachael Leben and Ben Shadway also had to be found soon and silenced.

As Peake set out on his assigned tasks—and while Gosser waited alertly inside the house—Sharp climbed into the unmarked sedan at the curb and had the driver return him to the bank parking lot off Palm Canyon Drive, where the helicopter was still waiting for him.

Airborne again, heading for the Geneplan labs in Riverside, Anson Sharp stared out at the night landscape as it rushed past below the chopper, his eyes narrowed as if he were a night bird seeking prey.

15 LOVING

BEN'S DREAMS WERE DARK AND FULL OF THUNDER, BLASTED BY strange lightning that illuminated nothing in a landscape without form, inhabited by an unseen but fearful creature that stalked him through the shadows, where all was vast and cold and lonely. It was—and yet was not—the Green Hell where he had spent more than three years of his youth, a familiar yet unfamiliar place, the same as it had been, yet changed as landscapes can be only in dreams.

Shortly after dawn, he came awake with bird-thin cries, full of dread, shuddering, and Rachael was with him. She had moved from the other bed and had drawn him to her, comforting him. Her warm tender touch dispelled the cold and lonely dream. The rhythmic thumping of her heart seemed like the steady throbbing of a bright lighthouse beacon along a fogbound coast, each pulse a reassurance.

He believed she had intended to offer nothing more than the comfort that a good friend could provide, though perhaps unconsciously she brought the greater gift of love and sought it in return. In the half-awake state following sleep, when his vision seemed filtered by a semitransparent cloth, when an invisible thinness of warm silk seemed to interpose itself between his hands and everything he touched, and while sounds were still dream-muffled, his perceptions were not sharp enough to determine how and when her offered comfort became offered— and accepted—love. He only knew that it happened and that, when he drew her unclothed body to his, he felt a *rightness* that he had never felt before in his thirty-seven years.

He was at last within her, and she was filled with him. It was fresh and wondrous, yet they did not have to search for the rhythms and patterns that pleased them, because they knew what was perfect for them as lovers of a decade might know.

Although the softly rumbling air conditioner kept the room cool, Ben had an almost psychic awareness of desert heat pressing at the windows. The cool chamber was a bubble suspended outside the reality of the harsh land, just as their special moment of tender coupling was a bubble drifting outside the normal flow of seconds and minutes.

Only one opaque window of frosted glass—high in the kitchenette wall—was not covered with a drape, and upon it the rising sun built a slowly growing fire. Outside, palm fronds, fanning lazily in a breeze, filtered the beams of the sun; feathery tropical shadows and frost-pale light fell on their nude bodies, rippling as they moved.

Ben saw her face clearly even in that inconstant light. Her eyes were shut, mouth open. She drew deep breaths at first, then breathed more quickly. Every line of her face was exquisitely sensuous—but also infinitely precious. His perception of her preciousness mattered more to him than the shatteringly sensuous vision she presented, for it was an emotional rather than physical response, a result of their months together and of his great affection for her. Because she was so special to him, their coupling was not merely an act of sex but an immeasurably more gratifying act of love.

Sensing his examination, she opened her eyes and looked into his, and he was electrified by that new degree of contact.

The palm-patterned morning light grew rapidly brighter, changing hue as well, from frost-pale to lemon-yellow to gold. It imparted those colors to Rachael's face, slender throat, full breasts. As the richness of the light increased, so did the pace of their lovemaking, till both were gasping, till she cried out and cried out again, at which moment the breeze outside became a sudden energetic wind that whipped the palm fronds, casting abruptly frantic shadows through the milky window, upon the bed. At precisely the moment when the wind-sculpted shadows leaped and shuddered, Ben thrust deep and shuddered too, emptying copious measures of himself into Rachael, and just when the last rush of his seed had streamed from him, the spill of wind was also depleted, flowing away to other corners of the world.

In time he withdrew from her, and they lay on their sides, facing each other, heads close, their breath mingling. Still, neither spoke nor needed to, and gradually they drifted toward sleep again.

He had never before felt as fulfilled and contented as this. Even in the good days of his youth, before the Green Hell, before Vietnam, he had never felt half this fine.

She slept before Ben did, and for a long pleasant moment he watched as a bubble of saliva slowly formed between her parted lips, and popped. His eyes grew heavy, and the last thing he saw before he closed them was the vague—almost invisible—scar along her jawline, where she had been cut when Eric had thrown a glass at her.

Drifting down into a restful darkness, Ben almost felt sorry for Eric Leben, because the scientist had never realized love was the closest thing to immortality that men would ever know and that the only—and best—answer to death was loving. Loving.

16   IN THE ZOMBIE ZONE

FOR PART OF THE NIGHT HE LAY FULLY CLOTHED ON THE BED in the cabin above Lake Arrowhead, in a condition deeper than sleep, deeper than coma, his body temperature steadily declining, his heart beating only twenty times a minute, blood barely circulating, drawing breath shallowly and only intermittently. Occasionally his respiration and heartbeat stopped entirely for periods as long as ten or fifteen minutes, during which the only life within him was at a cellular level, though even that was not life as much as stasis, a strange twilight existence that no other man on earth had ever known. During those periods of suspended animation, with cells only slowly renewing themselves and performing their functions at a greatly reduced pace, the body was gathering energy for the next period of wakefulness and accelerated healing.

He *was* healing, and at an astonishing rate. Hour by hour, almost visibly, his multitude of punctures and lacerations were scabbing over, closing up. Beneath the ugly bluish blackness of the bruises that he had suffered from the brutal impact with the garbage truck, there was already a visible yellow hue arising as the blood from crushed capillaries was leached from the tissues. When he was awake, he could feel fragments of his broken skull pressing insistently into his brain, even though medical wisdom held that tissue of the brain was without nerve endings and therefore insensate; it was not a pain as much as a pressure, like a Novocaine-numbed tooth registering the grinding bit of a dentist's drill. And he could sense, without understanding how, that his genetically improved body was methodically dealing with that head injury as surely as it was closing up its other wounds. For a week he would need much rest, but during that time the periods of stasis would grow shorter, less frequent, less frightening. That was what he wanted to believe. In two or three weeks, his physical condition would be no worse than that of a man leaving the hospital after major surgery. In a month he might be fully recovered, although he'd always have a slight—or even pronounced—depression along the right side of his skull.

But mental recovery was not keeping pace with the rapid physical regeneration of tissues. Even when awake, heartbeat and respiration close to normal, he was seldom fully alert. And during those brief periods when he possessed approximately the same intellectual capacity he had known before his death, he was acutely and dismally aware that for the most part he was functioning in a robotic state, with frequent lapses into a confused and, at times, virtually animalistic condition.

He had strange thoughts.

Sometimes he believed himself to be a young man again, recently graduated from college, but sometimes he recognized that he was actually past forty. Sometimes he did not know exactly where he was, especially when he was out on the road, driving, with no familiar reference points to his own past life; overcome by confusion, feeling lost and sensing that he would *forever* be lost, he had to pull over to the edge of the highway until the panic passed. He knew that he had a great goal, an important mission, though he was never quite able to define his purpose or destination. Sometimes he thought he was dead and making his way through the levels of hell on a Dantean journey. Sometimes he thought he had killed people, although he could not remember who, and then he *did* briefly remember and shrank from the memory, not only shrank from it but convinced himself that it was not a memory at all but a fantasy, for of course he was incapable of cold-blooded murder. Of course. Yet at other times he thought about how exciting and satisfying it would be to kill someone, anyone, everyone, because in his heart he knew they were after him, all of them, out to get him, the rotten bastards, as they had always been out to get him, though they were even more determined now than ever. Sometimes he thought urgently, *Remember the mice, the mice, the deranged mice bashing themselves to pieces against the walls of their cages,* and more than once he even said it aloud, "Remember the mice, the mice," but he had no idea what those words meant: what mice, where, when?

He saw strange things, too.

Sometimes he saw people who could not possibly be there: his long-dead mother, a hated uncle who had abused him when he had been a little boy, a neighborhood bully who had terrorized him in grade school. Now and then, as if suffering from the delirium tremens of a chronic alcoholic, he saw things crawling out of the walls, bugs and snakes and more frightening creatures that defied definition.

Several times, he was certain that he saw a path of perfectly black flagstones leading down into a terrible darkness in the earth. Always compelled to follow those stones, he repeatedly discovered the path was illusory, a figment of his morbid and fevered imagination.

Of all the apparitions and illusions that flickered past his eyes and through his damaged mind, the most unusual and the most disturbing were the shadow-fires. They leaped up unexpectedly and made a crackling sound that he not only heard but *felt* in his bones. He would be moving right along, walking with reasonable sure-footedness, passing among the living with some conviction, functioning better than he dared believe he could—when suddenly a fire would spring up in the shadowed corners of a room or in the shadows clustered beneath a tree, in any deep pocket of gloom, flames the shade of wet blood with hot silvery edges, startling him. And when he looked close, he could see that nothing was burning, that the flames had erupted out of thin air and were fed by nothing whatsoever, as if the shadows themselves were burning and made excellent fuel in spite of their lack of substance. When the fires faded and were extinguished, no signs of them remained—no ashes, charred fragments, or smoke stains.

Though he had never been afraid of fire before he died, had never entertained the pyrophobic idea that he was destined to die in flames, he was thoroughly terrified of these hungry phantom fires. When he peered into the flickering brightness, he felt that just beyond lay a mystery he must solve, though the solution would bring him unimaginable anguish.

In his few moments of relative lucidity, when his intellectual capacity was nearly what it once had been, he told himself that the illusions of flames merely resulted from misfiring synapses in his injured brain, electrical pulses shorting through the damaged tissues. And he told himself that the illusions frightened him because, above all else, he was an intellectual, a man whose life had been a life of the mind, so he had every *right* to be frightened by signs of brain deterioration. The tissues would heal, the shadowfires fade forever, and he would be all right. That was also what he told himself. But in his less lucid moments, when the world turned tenebrous and eerie, when he was gripped by confusion and animal fear, he looked upon the shadowfires with unalloyed horror and was sometimes reduced to paralysis by something he thought he glimpsed within—or beyond—the dancing flames.

Now, as dawn insistently pressed upon the resistant darkness of the mountains, Eric Leben ascended from stasis, groaned softly for a while, then louder, and finally woke. He sat up on the edge of the bed. His mouth was stale; he tasted ashes. His head was filled with pain. He touched his broken pate. It was no worse; his skull was not coming apart.

The meager glow of morning entered by two windows, and a small lamp was on—not sufficient illumination to dispel all the shadows in the bedroom, but enough to hurt his extremely sensitive eyes. Watery and hot, his eyes had been less able to adapt to brightness since he had risen from the cold steel gurney in the morgue, as if darkness were his natural habitat now, as if he did not belong in a world subject either to sun or to man-made light.

For a couple of minutes he concentrated on his breathing, for his rate of respiration was irregular, now too slow and deep, now too fast and shallow. Taking a stethoscope from the nightstand, he listened to his heart as well. It was beating fast enough to assure that he would not soon slip back into a state of suspended animation, though it was unsettlingly arrhythmic.

In addition to the stethoscope, he had brought other instruments with which to monitor his progress. A sphygmomanometer for measuring his blood pressure. An ophthalmoscope which, in conjunction with a mirror, he could use to study the condition of his retinas and the pupil response. He had a notebook, too, in which he had intended to record his observations of himself, for he was aware—sometimes only dimly aware but always aware—that he was the first man to die and come back from beyond, that he was making history, and that such a journal would be invaluable once he had fully recovered.

Remember the mice, the mice . . .

He shook his head irritably, as if that sudden baffling thought were a bothersome gnat buzzing around his face. *Remember the mice, the mice:* He had not the slightest idea what it meant, yet it was an annoyingly repetitive and peculiarly urgent thought that had assailed him frequently last night. He vaguely suspected that he did, in fact, know the meaning of the mice and that he was suppressing the knowledge because it frightened him. However, when he tried to focus on the subject and force an understanding, he had no success but became increasingly frustrated, agitated, and confused.

Returning the stethoscope to the nightstand, he did not pick up the sphygmomanometer because he did not have the patience or the dexterity required to roll up his shirt sleeve, bind the pressure cuff around his arm, operate the bulb-type pump, and simultaneously hold the gauge so he could read it. He had tried last night, and his clumsiness had finally driven him into a rage. He did not pick up the ophthalmoscope, either, for to examine his own eyes he would have to go into the bathroom and use the mirror. He could not bear to see himself as he now appeared: gray-faced, muddy-eyed, with a slackness in his facial muscles that made him look . . . half dead.

The pages of his small notebook were mostly blank, and now he did not attempt to add further observations to his recovery journal. For one thing, he had found that he was not capable of the intense and prolonged concentration required to write either intelligibly or legibly. Besides, the sight of his sloppily scrawled handwriting, which previously had been precise and neat, was yet another thing that had the power to excite a vicious rage in him.

Remember the mice, the mice bashing themselves against the walls of their cages, chasing their tails, the mice, the mice . . .

Putting both hands to his head as if to physically suppress that unwanted and mysterious thought, Eric Leben lurched out of bed, onto his feet. He needed to piss, and he was hungry. Those were two good signs, two indications that he was alive, at least more alive than dead, and he took heart from those simple biological needs.

He started toward the bathroom but stopped suddenly when fire leaped up in a corner of the room. Not real flames but shadowfire. Blood-red tongues with silver edges. Crackling hungrily, consuming the shadows from which they erupted yet in no way reducing that darkness. Squinting his light-stung eyes, Eric found that, as before, he was compelled to peer into the flames, and within them he thought he saw strange forms writhing and . . . and beckoning to him . . .

Though he was unaccountably terrified of these shadowfires, a part of him, perverse beyond his understanding, longed to go within the flames, pass through them as one might pass through a door, and learn what lay beyond.

No!

As he felt that longing grow into an acute need, he desperately turned away from the fire and stood swaying in fear and bewilderment, two feelings that, in his current fragile state, quickly metamorphosed into anger, the anger into rage. Everything seemed to lead to rage, as if it were the ultimate and inevitable distillate of all other emotions.

A brass-and-pewter floor lamp with a frosted crystal shade stood beside an easy chair, within his reach. He seized it with both hands, lifted it high above his head, and threw it across the room. The shade shattered against the wall, and gleaming shards of frosted crystal fell like cracking ice. The metal base and pole hit the edge of the white-lacquered dresser and rebounded with a clang, clattered to the floor.

The thrill of destruction that shivered through him was of a dark intensity akin to a sadistic sexual urge, and its power was nearly as great as orgasm. Before his death, he had been an obsessive achiever, a builder of empires, a compulsive acquirer of wealth, but following his death he had become an engine of destruction, as fully compelled to smash property as he had once been compelled to acquire it.

The cabin was decorated in ultramodern with accents of art deco—like the ruined floor lamp—not a style particularly well suited to a five-room mountain cabin but one which satisfied Eric's need for a sense of newness and modernity in all things. In a frenzy, he began to reduce the trendy decor to piles of bright rubble. He picked up the armchair as if it weighed only a pound or two and heaved it at the three-panel mirror on the wall behind the bed. The tripartite mirror exploded, and the armchair fell onto the bed in a rain of silvered glass. Breathing hard, Eric seized the damaged floor lamp, held it by the pole, swung it at a piece of bronze sculpture that stood on the dresser, using the heavy base of the lamp as a huge hammer—*bang!*—knocking the sculpture to the floor, swung the lamp-hammer twice at the dresser mirror—*bang, bang!*—smashing, smashing, swung it at a painting hanging on the wall near the door to the bathroom, brought the picture down, hammered the artwork where it lay on the floor. He felt good, so good, never better, *alive*. As he gave himself entirely and joyfully to his berserker rage, he snarled with animal ferocity or shrieked wordlessly, though he was able to form one special word with unmistakable clarity, "Rachael," spoke it with unadulterated hatred, spittle spraying, "Rachael, Rachael." He pounded the makeshift hammer into a white-lacquered occasional table that had stood beside the armchair, pounded and pounded until the table was reduced to splinters—"Rachael, Rachael"—struck the smaller lamp on the nightstand and knocked it to the floor. *Bang!* Arteries pounding furiously in his neck and temples, blood singing in his ears, he hammered the nightstand itself until he had broken the handles off the drawers, hammered the wall, "Rachael," hammered until the pole lamp was too bent to be of any further use, angrily tossed it aside, grabbed the drapes and ripped them from their rods, tore another painting from the wall and put his foot through the canvas, "Rachael, Rachael, Rachael." He staggered wildly now and flailed at the air with his big arms and turned in circles, a crazed bull, and he abruptly found it hard to breathe, felt the insane strength drain out of him, felt the mad destructive urge flowing away, away, and he dropped to the floor, onto his knees, stretched flat out on his chest, head turned to one side, face in the deep-pile carpet, gasping. His confused thoughts were even muddier than the strange and clouded eyes that he could not bear to look at in a mirror, but though he no longer possessed demonic energy, he had the strength to mutter that special name again and again while he lay on the floor: "Rachael . . . Rachael . . . Rachael . . . "

PART TWO

DARKER

Night has patterns that can be read

less by the living than by the dead

— THE BOOK OF COUNTED SORROWS

17 PEOPLE ON THE MOVE

CHOPPERING IN FROM PALM SPRINGS, ANSON SHARP HAD arrived before dawn at Geneplan's bacteriologically secure underground research laboratories near Riverside, where he had been greeted by a contingent of six Defense Security Agency operatives, four U.S. marshals, and eight of the marshals' deputies, who had arrived minutes before him. Under the pretense of a national defense emergency, fully supported by valid court orders and search warrants, they identified themselves to Geneplan's night security guards, entered the premises, applied seals to all research files and computers, and established an operations headquarters in the rather sumptuously appointed offices belonging to Dr. Vincent Baresco, chief of the research staff.

As dawn dispelled the night and as day took possession of the world above the subterranean laboratories, Anson Sharp slumped in Baresco's enormous leather chair, sipped black coffee, and received reports, by phone, from subordinates throughout southern California, to the effect that Eric Leben's coconspirators in the Wildcard Project were all under house arrest. In Orange County, Dr. Morgan Eugene Lewis, research coordinator of Wildcard, was being detained with his wife at his home in North Tustin. Dr. J. Felix Geffels was being held at his house right there in Riverside. Dr. Vincent Baresco, head of all research for Geneplan, had been found by DSA agents in Geneplan's Newport Beach headquarters, unconscious on the floor of Eric Leben's office, amidst indications of gunplay and a fierce struggle.

Rather than take Baresco to a public hospital and even partially relinquish control of him, Sharp's men transported the bald and burly scientist to the U.S. Marine Corps Air Station at El Toro, where he was seen by a Marine physician in the base infirmary. Having received two hard blows to the throat that made it impossible for him to speak, Baresco used a pen and notepad to tell DSA agents that he had been assaulted by Ben Shadway, Rachael Leben's lover, when he had caught them in the act of looting Eric's office safe. He was disgruntled when they refused to believe that was the whole story, and he was downright shocked to discover they knew about Wildcard and were aware of Eric Leben's return from the dead. Using pen and notepad again, Baresco had demanded to be transferred to a civilian hospital, demanded to know what possible charges they could lodge, demanded to see his lawyer. All three demands were, of course, ignored.

Rupert Knowls and Perry Seitz, the money men who had supplied the large amount of venture capital that had gotten Geneplan off the ground nearly a decade ago, were at Knowls's sprawling ten-acre estate, Havenhurst, in Palm Springs. Three Defense Security Agency operatives had arrived at the estate with arrest warrants for Knowls and Seitz and with a search warrant. They had found an illegally modified Uzi submachine gun, doubtless the weapon with which two Palm Springs policemen had been murdered only a couple of hours earlier.

Currently and indefinitely under detention at Havenhurst, neither Knowls nor Seitz was raising objections. They knew the score. They would receive an unattractive offer to convey to the government all research, rights, and title to the Wildcard enterprise, without a shred of compensation, and they would be required to remain forever silent about that undertaking and about Eric Leben's resurrection. They would also be required to sign murder confessions which could be used to keep them acquiescent the rest of their lives. Although the offer had no legal basis or force, although the DSA was violating every tenet of democracy and breaking innumerable laws, Knowls and Seitz would accept the terms. They were worldly men, and they knew that failure to cooperate—and especially any attempt to exercise their constitutional rights—would be the death of them.

Those five were sitting on a secret that was potentially the most powerful in history. The immortality process was currently imperfect, true, but eventually the problems would be solved. Then whoever controlled the secrets of Wildcard would control the world. With so much at stake, the government was not concerned about observing the thin line between moral and immoral behavior, and in this very special case, it had no interest whatsoever in the niceties of due process.

After receiving the report on Seitz and Knowls, Sharp put down the phone, got up from the leather chair, and paced the windowless subterranean office. He rolled his big shoulders, stretched, and tried to work a kink out of his thick, muscular neck.

He had begun with eight people to worry about, eight possible leaks to plug, and now five of those eight had been dealt with quickly and smoothly. He felt pretty good about things in general and about himself in particular. He was damned good at his job.

At times like this, he wished he had someone with whom to share his triumphs, an admiring assistant, but he could not afford to let anyone get close to him. He was the deputy director of the Defense Security Agency, the number two man in the whole outfit, and he was determined to become director by the time he was forty. He intended to secure that position by collecting sufficient damaging material about the current director—Jarrod McClain—to force him out *and* to blackmail McClain into writing a wholehearted recommendation that Anson Sharp replace him. McClain treated Sharp like a son, making him privy to every secret of the agency, and already Sharp possessed most of what he needed to destroy McClain. But, as he was a careful man, he would not move until there was no possibility whatsoever of his coup failing. And when he ascended to the director's chair, he would not make the mistake of taking a subordinate to his bosom, as McClain had embraced him. It would be lonely at the top, *must* be lonely if he were to survive up there a long time, so he made himself get used to loneliness now: though he had protégés, he did not have friends.

Having worked the stiffness out of his thick neck and immense shoulders, Sharp returned to the chair behind the desk, sat down, closed his eyes, and thought about the three people who remained on the loose and who must be apprehended. Eric Leben, Mrs. Leben, Ben Shadway. They would not be offered a deal, as the other five had been. If Leben could be taken "alive," he would be locked away and studied as if he were a lab animal. Mrs. Leben and Shadway would simply be terminated and their deaths made to look accidental.

He had several reasons for wanting them dead. For one thing, they were both independent-minded, tough, and honest—a dangerous mixture, volatile. They might blow the Wildcard story wide open for the pure hell of it or out of misguided idealism, thus dealing Sharp a major setback on his climb to the top. The others—Lewis, Geffels, Baresco, Knowls, and Seitz—would knuckle under out of sheer self-interest, but Rachael Leben and Ben Shadway could not be counted on to put their own best interests first. Besides, neither had committed a criminal act, and neither had sold his soul to the government as the men of Geneplan had done, so no swords hung over their heads; there were no credible threats by which they could be controlled.

But most important of all, Sharp wanted Rachael Leben dead simply because she was Shadway's lover, because Shadway cared for her. He wanted to kill her first, in front of Ben Shadway. And he wanted Shadway dead because he had hated the man for almost seventeen years.

Alone in that underground office, eyes closed, Sharp smiled. He wondered what Ben Shadway would do if he knew that his old nemesis, Anson Sharp, was hunting for him. Sharp was almost painfully eager for the inevitable confrontation, eager to see the astonishment on Shadway's face, eager to waste the son of a bitch.

■ Jerry Peake, the young DSA Agent assigned by Anson Sharp to find Sarah Kiel, carefully searched for a freshly dug grave on Eric Leben's walled property in Palm Springs. Using a high-intensity flashlight, being diligent and utterly thorough, Peake tramped through flower beds, struggled through shrubbery, getting his pant legs damp and his shoes muddy, but he found nothing suspicious.

He turned on the pool lights, half expecting to find a dead woman either floating there—or weighted to the blue bottom and peering up through chlorine-treated water. When the pool proved to be free of corpses, Peake decided he had been reading too many mystery novels; in mystery novels, swimming pools were always full of bodies, but never in real life.

A passionate fan of mystery fiction since he was twelve, Jerry Peake had never wanted to be anything other than a detective, and not just an ordinary detective but something special, like a CIA or FBI or DSA man, and not just an ordinary DSA man but an investigative genius of the sort that John Le Carré, William F. Buckley, or Frederick Forsythe might write about. Peake wanted to be a legend in his own time. He was only in his fifth year with the DSA, and his reputation as a whiz was nonexistent, but he was not worried. He had patience. No one became a legend in just five years. First, you had to spend a lot of hours doing dog's work—

like tramping through flower beds, snagging your best suits on thorny shrubbery, and peering hopefully into swimming pools in the dead of night.

When he did not turn up Sarah Kiel's body on the Leben property, Peake made the rounds of the hospitals, hoping to find her name on a patient roster or on a list of recently treated outpatients. He had no luck at his first two stops. Worse, even though he had his DSA credentials, complete with photograph, the nurses and physicians with whom he spoke seemed to regard him with skepticism. They cooperated, but guardedly, as if they thought he might be an imposter with hidden—and none too admirable—intentions.

He knew he looked too young to be a DSA agent; he was cursed with a frustratingly fresh, open face. And he was less aggressive in his questioning than he should be. But this time, he was sure the problem was not his baby face or slightly hesitant manner. Instead, he was greeted with doubt because of his muddy shoes, which he had cleaned with paper towels but which remained smeary-looking. And because of his trouser legs: Having gotten wet, the material had dried baggy and wrinkled. You could not be taken seriously, be respected, or become a legend if you looked as if you'd just slopped pigs.

An hour after dawn, at the third hospital, Desert General, he hit pay dirt in spite of his sartorial inadequacies. Sarah Kiel had been admitted for treatment during the night. She was still a patient.

The head nurse, Alma Dunn, was a sturdy white-haired woman of about fifty-five, unimpressed with Peake's credentials and incapable of being intimidated. After checking on Sarah Kiel, she returned to the nurses' station, where she'd made Peake wait, and she said, "The poor girl's still sleeping. She was . . . sedated only a few hours ago, so I don't expect she'll be awake for another few hours."

"Wake her, please. This is an urgent national security matter."

"I'll do no such thing," Nurse Dunn said. "The girl was hurt. She needs her rest. You'll have to wait."

"Then I'll wait in her room."

Nurse Dunn's jaw muscles bulged, and her merry blue eyes turned cold. "You certainly will not. You'll wait in the visitors' lounge."

Peake knew he would get nowhere with Alma Dunn because she looked like Jane Marple, Agatha Christie's indomitable amateur detective, and no one who looked like Miss Marple would be intimidated. "Listen, if you're going to be uncooperative, I'll have to talk to your superior."

"That's fine with me," she said, glancing down disapprovingly at his shoes. "I'll get Dr. Werfell."

■   Beneath the Earth in Riverside, Anson Sharp slept for one hour on the Ultrasuede sofa in Vincent Baresco's office, showered in the small adjacent bathroom, and changed into a fresh suit of clothes from the suitcase that he had kept with him on every leg of his zigzagging route through southern California the previous night. He was blessed with the ability to fall asleep at will in a minute or less, without fail, and to feel rested and alert after only a nap. He could sleep anywhere he chose, regardless of background noise. He believed this ability was just one more proof that he was destined to climb to the top, where he longed to be, proof that he was superior to other men.

Refreshed, he made a few calls, speaking with agents guarding the Geneplan partners and research chiefs at various points in three counties. He also received reports from other men at the Geneplan offices in Newport Beach, Eric Leben's house in Villa Park, and Mrs. Leben's place in Placentia.

From the agents guarding Baresco at the U.S. Marine Air Station in El Toro, Sharp learned that Ben Shadway had taken a Smith & Wesson .357 Magnum off the scientist in the Geneplan office last night, and that the revolver could not be located anywhere in that building. Shadway had not left it behind, had not disposed of it in a nearby trash container or hallway, but apparently had chosen to hold on to it. Furthermore, agents in Placentia reported that a .32-caliber semi-automatic pistol, registered to Rachael Leben, could be found nowhere in her house, and the assumption was that she was carrying it, though she did not possess a permit to carry.

Sharp was delighted to learn that both Shadway and the woman were armed, for that contributed to the justification of an arrest warrant. And when he cornered them, he could shoot them down and claim, with a measure of credibility, that they had opened fire on him first..

■ As Jerry Peake waited at the nurses' station for Alma Dunn to return with Dr. Werfell, the hospital came alive for the day. The empty halls grew busy with nurses conveying medicines to patients, with orderlies transporting patients in wheelchairs and on gurneys to various departments and operating theaters, and with a few doctors making very early rounds. The pervading scent of pine disinfectant was increasingly overlaid with others—alcohol, clove oil, urine, vomit— as if the busily scurrying staff had stirred stagnant odors out of every corner of the building.

In ten minutes, Nurse Dunn returned with a tall man in a white lab coat. He had handsome hawkish features, thick salt-and-pepper hair, and a neat mustache. He seemed familiar, though Peake was not sure why. Alma Dunn introduced him as Dr. Hans Werfell, supervising physician of the morning shift.

Looking down at Peake's muddy shoes and badly wrinkled trousers, Dr. Werfell said, "Miss Kiel's physical condition is not grave by any means, and I suppose she'll be out of here today or tomorrow. But she suffered severe emotional trauma, so she needs to be allowed to rest when she can. And right now she's resting, sound asleep."

Stop looking at my shoes, damn you, Peake thought. He said, "Doctor, I understand your concern for the patient, but this is an urgent matter of national security."

Finally raising his gaze from Peake's shoes, Werfell frowned skeptically and said, "What on earth could a sixteen-year-old girl have to do with national security?"

"That's classified, strictly classified," Peake said, trying to pull his baby face into a suitably serious and imposing expression that would convince Werfell of the gravity of the situation and gain his cooperation.

"No point waking her, anyway," Werfell said. "She'd still be under the influence of the sedative, not in any condition to give accurate answers to your questions."

"Couldn't you give her something to counteract the drug?"

With only a frown, Werfell registered severe disapproval. "Mr. Peake, this is a hospital. We exist to help people get well. We wouldn't be helping Miss Kiel to get well if we pumped her full of drugs for no other purpose than to counteract *other* drugs and please an impatient government agent."

Peake felt his face flush. "I wasn't suggesting you violate medical principles."

"Good." Werfell's patrician face and manner were not conducive to debate. "Then you'll wait until she wakes naturally."

Frustrated, still trying to think why Werfell looked familiar, Peake said, "But we think she can tell us where to find someone whom we desperately *must* find."

"Well, I'm sure she'll cooperate when she's awake and alert."

"And when will that be, Doctor?"

"Oh, I imagine . . . another four hours, maybe longer."

"What? Why that long?"

"The night physician gave her a very mild sedative, which didn't suit her, and when he refused to give her anything stronger, she took one of her own."

"One of her own?"

"We didn't realize until later that she had drugs in her purse: a few Benzedrine tablets wrapped in one small packet of foil—".

"Bennies, uppers?"

"Yes. And a few tranquilizers in another packet, and a couple of sedatives. Hers was much stronger than the one we gave her, so she's pretty deep under at the moment. We've confiscated her remaining drugs, of course."

Peake said, "I'll wait in her room."

"No," Werfell said.

"Then I'll wait just outside her room."

"I'm afraid not."

"Then I'll wait right here."

"You'll be in the way here," Werfell said. "You'll wait in the visitors' lounge, and we'll call you when Miss Kiel is awake."

"I'll wait here," Peake insisted, scrunching his baby face into the sternest, toughest, most hard-boiled look he could manage.

"The visitors' lounge," Werfell said ominously. "And if you do not proceed there immediately, I'll have hospital security men escort you."

Peake hesitated, wishing to God he could be more aggressive. "All right, but you damn well better call me the *minute* she wakes up."

Furious, he turned from Werfell and stalked down the hall in search of the visitors' lounge, too embarrassed to ask where it was. When he glanced back at Werfell, who was now in deep conversation with another physician, he realized the doctor was a dead ringer for Dashiell Hammett, the formidable Pinkerton detective and mystery novelist, which was why he had looked familiar to a dedicated reader like Peake. No wonder Werfell had such a tremendous air of authority. Dashiell Hammett, for God's sake. Peake felt a little better about having deferred to him.

■   They slept another two hours, woke within moments of each other, and made love again in the motel bed. For Rachael, it was even better this time than it had been before: slower, sweeter, with an even more graceful and fulfilling rhythm. She was sinewy, supple, taut, and she took enormous and intense pleasure in her superb physical condition, drew satisfaction from each flexing and gentle thrusting and soft lazy grinding of her body, not merely the usual pleasure of male and female organs mating, but the more subtle thrill of muscle and tendon and bone functioning with the perfect oiled smoothness that, like nothing else, made her feel young, healthy, *alive.*

With her special gift for fully experiencing the moment, she let her hands roam over Benny's body, marveling over his leanness, testing the rock-hard muscles of his shoulders and arms, kneading the bunched muscles of his back, glorying in the silken smoothness of his skin, the rocking motion of his hips against hers, pelvis to pelvis, the hot touch of his hands, the branding heat of his lips upon her cheeks, her mouth, her throat, her breasts.

Until this interlude with Benny, Rachael had not made love in almost fifteen months. And never in her life had she made love like this: never this good, this tender or exciting, never this satisfying. She felt as if she had been half dead heretofore and this was the hour of her resurrection.

Finally spent, they lay in each other's arms for a while, silent, at peace, but the soft afterglow of lovemaking slowly gave way to a curious disquiet. At first she was not certain what disturbed her, but soon she recognized it as that rare and peculiar feeling that someone had just walked over her grave, an irrational but convincingly instinctive sensation that brought a vague chill to her bare flesh and a colder shiver to her spine.

She looked at Benny's gentle smile, studied every much-loved line of his face, stared into his eyes—and had the shocking, unshakable feeling that she was going to lose him.

She tried to tell herself that her sudden apprehension was the understandable reaction of a thirty-year-old woman who, having made one bad marriage, had at last miraculously found the right man. Call it the I-don't-deserve-to-be-this-happy syndrome. When life finally hands us a beautiful bouquet of flowers, we usually peer cautiously among the petals in expectation of a bee. Superstition—evinced especially in a distrust of good fortune—was perhaps the very core of human nature, and it was natural for her to fear losing him.

That was what she tried to tell herself, but she knew her sudden terror was something more than superstition, something darker. The chill along her spine deepened until she felt as if each vertebra had been transformed into a lump of ice. The cool breath that had touched her skin now penetrated deeper, down toward her bones.

She turned from him, swung her legs out of the bed, stood up, naked and shivering.

Benny said, "Rachael?"

"Let's get moving," she said anxiously, heading toward the bathroom through the golden light and palm shadows that came through the single, undraped window.

"What's wrong?" he asked.

"We're sitting ducks here. Or might be. We've got to keep moving. We've got to keep on the offensive. We've got to find him before he finds us—or before anyone else finds us."

Benny got out of bed, stepped between her and the bathroom door, put his hands on her shoulders. "Everything's going to be all right."

"Don't say that."

"But it will."

"Don't tempt fate."

"We're strong together," he said. "Nothing's stronger."

"Don't," she insisted, putting a hand to his lips to silence him. "Please. I . . . I couldn't bear losing you."

"You won't lose me," he said.

But when she looked at him, she had the terrible feeling that he was already lost, that death was very near to him, inevitable.

The I-don't-deserve-to-be-this-happy syndrome.

Or maybe a genuine premonition.

She had no way of knowing which it was.

■   The search for Dr. Eric Leben was getting nowhere.

The grim possibility of failure was, for Anson Sharp, like a great pressure pushing in on the walls of Geneplan's underground labs in Riverside, compressing the windowless rooms, until he felt as if he were being slowly crushed. He could not abide failure; he was a winner, always a winner, superior to all other men, and that was the only way he cared to think of himself, the only way he could *bear* to think of himself, as the sole member of a superior species, for that image of himself justified anything he wished to do, anything at all, and he was a man who simply could not live with the moral and ethical limitations of ordinary men.

Yet field agents were filing negative reports from every place that the walking dead man might have been expected to show up, and Sharp was getting angrier and more nervous by the hour. Perhaps their knowledge of Eric Leben was not quite as thorough as they thought. In anticipation of these events, perhaps the geneticist had prepared a place where he could go to ground, and had managed to keep it secret even from the DSA. If that were the case, the failure to apprehend Leben would be seen as Sharp's personal failure, for he had identified himself too closely with the operation in expectation of taking full credit for its success.

Then he got a break. Jerry Peake called to report that Sarah Kiel, Eric Leben's underage mistress, had been located in a Palm Springs hospital. "But the damn medical staff," Peake explained in his earnest but frustratingly wimpy manner, "isn't cooperative."

Sometimes Anson Sharp wondered if the advantages of surrounding himself with weaker—and therefore unthreatening—young agents were outweighed by the disadvantage of their inefficiency. Certainly none of them would pose a danger to him once he had ascended to the director's chair, but neither were they likely to do anything on their own hook that would reflect positively on him as their mentor.

Sharp said, "I'll be there before she shakes off the sedative."

The investigation at the Geneplan labs could proceed without him for a while. The researchers and technicians had arrived for the day and had been sent home with orders not to report back until notified. Defense Security Agency computer mavens were seeking the Wildcard files hidden in the Geneplan data banks, but their work was so highly specialized that Sharp could neither supervise nor understand it.

He made a few telephone calls to several federal agencies in Washington, seeking—and obtaining—information about Desert General Hospital and Dr. Hans

Werfell that might give him leverage with them, then boarded his waiting chopper and flew back across the desert to Palm Springs, pleased to be on the move again.

■ Rachael and Benny taxied to the Palm Springs Airport, rented a clean new Ford from Hertz, and drove back into town in time to be the first customers· at a clothing store that opened at nine-thirty. She bought tan jeans, a pale yellow blouse, thick white tube socks, and Adidas jogging shoes. Benny chose blue jeans, a white shirt, tube socks, and similar shoes, and they changed out of their badly rumpled clothes in the public rest rooms of a service station at the north end of Palm Canyon Drive. Unwilling to waste time stopping for breakfast, partly because they were afraid of being spotted, they grabbed Egg McMuffins and coffee at McDonald's, and ate as they drove.

Rachael had infected Benny with her premonition of oncoming death and her sudden—almost clairvoyant—sense that time was running out, which had first struck her at the motel, just after they had made love for the second time. Benny had attempted to reassure her, calm her, but instead he had grown more uneasy by the minute. They were like two animals independently and instinctively perceiving the advance of a terrible storm.

Wishing they could have gone back for her red Mercedes, which would have made better time than the rental Ford, Rachael slumped in the passenger's seat and nibbled at her take-out breakfast without enthusiasm, while Benny drove north on State Route 111, then west on Interstate 10. Although he squeezed as much speed out of the Ford as anyone could have, handling it with that startling combination of recklessness and ease that was so out of character for a real-estate salesman, they would not reach Eric's cabin, above Lake Arrowhead, until almost one o'clock in the afternoon.

She hoped to God that would be soon enough.

And she tried not to think about what Eric might be like when—and if—they found him.

18 ZOMBIE BLUES

THE DARK RAGE PASSED, AND ERIC LEBEN REGAINED HIS SENSES— such as they were—in the debris-strewn bedroom of the cabin, where he had smashed nearly everything he could get his hands on. A hard, sharp pain pounded through his head, and a duller pain throbbed in all of his muscles. His joints felt swollen and stiff. His eyes were grainy, watery, hot. His teeth ached, and his mouth tasted of ashes.

Following each fit of mindless fury, Eric found himself, as now, in a gray mood, in a gray world, where colors were washed out, where sounds were muted, where the edges of objects were fuzzy, and where every light, regardless of the strength of its source, was murky and too thin to sufficiently illuminate anything. It was as if the fury had drained him, and as if he had been forced to power down until he could replenish his reserves of energy. He moved sluggishly, somewhat clumsily, and he had difficulty thinking clearly.

When he had finished healing, the periods of coma and the gray spells would surely cease. However, that knowledge did not lift his spirits, for his muddy thought processes made it difficult for him to think ahead to a better future. His condition was eerie, unpleasant, even frightening; he felt that he was not in control of his destiny and that, in fact, he was trapped within his own body, chained to this now-imperfect, half-dead flesh.

He staggered into the bathroom, slowly showered, brushed his teeth. He kept a complete wardrobe at the cabin, just as he did at the house in Palm Springs, so he would never need to pack a suitcase when visiting either place, and now he changed into khaki pants, a red plaid shirt, wool socks, and a pair of woodsman's boots. In his strange gray haze, that morning routine required more time than it should have: He had trouble adjusting the shower controls to get the right temperature; he kept dropping the toothbrush into the sink; he cursed his stiff fingers as they fumbled with the buttons on his shirt; when he tried to roll up his long sleeves, the material resisted him as if it possessed a will of its own; and he succeeded in lacing the boots only with monumental effort.

Eric was further distracted by the shadowfires.

Several times, at the periphery of his vision, ordinary shadows burst into flames. Just short-circuiting electrical impulses in his badly damaged—but healing—brain. Illusions born in sputtering cerebral synapses between neurons. Nothing more. However, when he turned to look directly at the fires, they never faded or winked out as mere mirages might have done, but grew even brighter.

Although they produced no smoke or heat, consumed no fuel, and had no real substance, he stared at those nonexistent flames with greater fear each time they appeared, partly because within them—or perhaps beyond them—he saw something mysterious, frightening; darkly shrouded and monstrous figures that beckoned through the leaping brightness. Although he knew the phantoms were only figments of his overwrought imagination, although he had no idea what they might represent to him or why he should be afraid of them, he *was* afraid. And at times, mesmerized by shadowfires, he heard himself whimpering as if he were a terrorized child.

Food. Although his genetically altered body was capable of miraculous regeneration and rapid recuperation, it still required proper nutrition—vitamins, minerals, carbohydrates, proteins—the building blocks with which to repair its damaged tissues. And for the first time since arising in the morgue, he was hungry.

He shuffled unsteadily into the kitchen, shambled to the big refrigerator.

He thought he saw something crawling out of the slots in a wall plug just at the edge of vision. Something long, thin. Insectile. Menacing. But he knew it was not real. He had seen things like it before. It was another symptom of his brain damage. He just had to ignore it, not let it frighten him, even though he heard its chitinous feet tap-tap-tapping on the floor. Tap-tap-tapping. He refused to look. *Go away.* He held on to the refrigerator. Tapping. He gritted his teeth. *Go away.* The sound faded. When he looked toward the wall plug, there was no strange insect, nothing out of the ordinary.

But now his uncle Barry, long dead, was sitting at the kitchen table, grinning at him. As a child, he had frequently been left with Uncle Barry Hampstead, who had abused him, and he had been too afraid to tell anyone. Hampstead had threatened to hurt him, to cut off his penis, if he told anyone, and those threats had been so vivid and hideous that Eric had not doubted them for a minute. Now Uncle Barry sat at the table, one hand in his lap, grinning, and said, "Come here, little sweetheart; let's have some fun," and Eric could *hear* the voice as clearly as he'd heard it thirty-five years ago, though he knew that neither the man nor the voice was real, and he was as terrified of Barry Hampstead as he had been long ago, though he knew he was now far beyond his hated uncle's reach.

He closed his eyes and willed the illusion to go away. He must have stood there, shaking, for a minute or more, not wanting to open his eyes until he was certain the apparition would be gone. But then he began to think that Barry *was* there and was slipping closer to him while his eyes were closed and was going to grab him by the privates any second now, grab him and squeeze—

His eyes snapped open.

The phantom Barry Hampstead was gone.

Breathing easier, Eric got a package of Farmer John sausage-and-biscuit sandwiches from the freezer compartment and heated them on a tray in the oven, concentrating intently on the task to avoid burning himself. Fumblingly, patiently, he brewed a pot of Maxwell House. Sitting at the table, shoulders hunched, head held low, he washed the food down with cup after cup of the hot black coffee.

He had an insatiable appetite for a while, and the very act of eating made him feel more truly alive than anything he'd done since he'd been reborn. Biting, chewing, tasting, swallowing—by those simple actions, he was brought further back among the living than at any point since he'd stepped in the way of the garbage truck on Main Street. For a while, his spirits began to rise.

Then he slowly became aware that the taste of the sausage was neither as strong nor as pleasing as when he had been fully alive and able to appreciate it; and though he put his nose close to the hot, greasy meat and drew deep breaths, he was unable to smell its spicy aroma. He stared at his cool, ash-gray, clammy hands, which held the biscuit-wrapped sausage, and the wad of steaming pork looked more alive than his own flesh.

Suddenly the situation seemed uproariously funny to Eric: a dead man sitting at breakfast, chomping stolidly on Farmer John sausages, pouring hot Maxwell House down his cold gullet, desperately pretending to be one of the living, as if death could be reversed by pretense, as if life could be regained merely by the performance of enough mundane activities—showering, brushing his teeth, eating, drinking, crapping—and by the consumption of enough homely products. He *must* be alive, because they wouldn't have Farmer John sausages and Maxwell House in either heaven or hell. Would they? He must be alive, because he had used his Mr. Coffee machine and his General Electric oven, and over in the corner his Westinghouse refrigerator was humming softly, and although those manufacturers' wares were widely distributed, surely none of them would be found on the far shores of the river Styx, so he *must* be alive.

Black humor certainly, very black indeed, but he laughed out loud, laughed and laughed—until he heard his laughter. It sounded hard, coarse, cold, not really laughter but a poor imitation, rough and harsh, as if he were choking, or as if he had swallowed stones that now rattled and clattered against one another in his throat. Dismayed by the sound, he shuddered and began to weep. He dropped the sausage-stuffed biscuit, swept the food and dishes to the floor, and collapsed forward, folding his arms upon the table and resting his head in his arms. Great gasping sobs of grief escaped him, and for a while he was immersed in a deep pool of self-pity.

The mice, the mice, remember the mice bashing against the walls of their cages . . .

He still did not know the meaning of that thought, could not recall any mice, though he felt that he was closer to understanding than ever before. A memory of mice, white mice, hovered tantalizingly just beyond his grasp.

His gray mood darkened.

His dulled senses grew even duller.

After a while, he realized he was sinking into another coma, one of those periods of suspended animation during which his heart slowed dramatically and his respiration fell to a fraction of the normal rate, giving his body an opportunity to continue with repairs and accumulate new reserves of energy. He slipped from his chair to the kitchen floor and curled fetally beside the refrigerator.

■   Benny turned off Interstate 10 at Redlands and followed State Route 30 to 330. Lake Arrowhead lay only twenty-eight miles away.

The two-lane blacktop cut a twisty trail into the San Bernardino Mountains. The pavement was hoved and rough in some spots, slightly potholed in others, and frequently the shoulder was only a few inches wide, with a steep drop beyond the flimsy guardrails, leaving little leeway for mistakes. They were forced to slow considerably, though Benny piloted the Ford much faster than Rachael could have done.

Last night Rachael had spilled her secrets to Benny—the details of Wildcard and of Eric's obsessions—and she had expected him to divulge his in return, but he had said nothing that would explain the way he had dealt with Vincent Baresco, the uncanny way he could handle a car, or his knowledge of guns. Though her curiosity was great, she did not press him. She sensed that his secrets were of a far more personal nature than hers and that he had spent a long time building barriers around them, barriers that could not easily be torn down. She knew he would tell her everything when he felt the time was right.

They traveled only a mile on Route 330 and were still twenty miles from Running Springs when he apparently decided that, in fact, the time had come. As the road wound higher into the sharply angled mountains, more trees rose up on all sides—birches and gnarled oaks at first, then pines of many varieties, tamarack, even a few spruce—and soon the pavement was more often than not cloaked in the velvety shadows of those overhanging boughs. Even in the air-conditioned car, you could feel that the desert heat was being left behind, and it was as if the escape from those oppressive temperatures buoyed Benny and encouraged him to talk. In a darkish tunnel of pine shadows, he began to speak in a soft yet distinct voice.

"When I was eighteen, I joined the Marines, volunteered to fight in Vietnam. I wasn't antiwar like so many were, but I wasn't prowar either. I was just for my country, right or wrong. As it turned out, I had certain aptitudes, natural abilities, that made me a candidate for the Corps' elite cadre: Marine Reconnaissance, which is sort of the equivalent of the Army Rangers or Navy Seals. I was spotted early, approached about recon training, volunteered, and eventually they honed me into as deadly a soldier as any in the world. Put any weapon in my hands, I knew how to use it. Leave me empty-handed, and I could still kill you so quick and easy you wouldn't know I was coming at you until you felt your own neck snap. I went to Nam in a recon unit, guaranteed to see plenty of action, which is what I wanted— plenty of action—and for a few months I was totally gung ho, delighted to be in the thick of it."

Benny still drove the car with consummate skill, but Rachael noticed that the speed began to drop slowly as his story took him deeper into the jungles of Southeast Asia.

He squinted as the sun found its way through holes in the tree shadows and as spangles of light cascaded across the windshield. "But if you spend several months knee-deep in blood, watching your buddies die, sidestepping death yourself again and again, seeing civilians caught repeatedly in the cross fire, villages burned, little children maimed . . . well, you're bound to start doubting. And I began to doubt."

"Benny, my God, I'm sorry. I never suspected you'd been through anything like that, such horror—"

"No point feeling sorry for me. I came back alive and got on with my life. That's better than what happened to a lot of others."

Oh, God, Rachael thought, what if you hadn't come back? I would have never met you, never loved you, never known what I'd missed.

"Anyway," he said softly, "doubts set in, and for the rest of that year, I was in turmoil. I was fighting to preserve the elected government of South Vietnam, yet that government seemed hopelessly corrupt. I was fighting to preserve the Vietnamese culture from obliteration under communism, yet that very same culture was being obliterated by the tens of thousands of U.S. troops who were diligently Americanizing it."

"We wanted freedom and peace for the Vietnamese," Rachael said. "At least that's how I understood it." She was not yet thirty, seven years younger than Benny; but those were seven crucial years, and it had not been *her* war. "There's nothing so wrong with fighting for freedom and peace."

"Yeah," he said, his voice haunted now, "but we seemed to be intent on creating that peace by killing everyone and leveling the whole damn country, leaving no one to enjoy whatever freedom might follow. I had to wonder . . . Was my country misguided? Downright wrong? Even possibly . . . evil? Or was I just too young and too naive, in spite of my Marine training, to understand?" He was silent for a moment, pulling the car through a sharp right-hand turn, then left just as sharply when the mountainside angled again. "By the time my tour of duty ended, I'd answered none of those questions to my satisfaction . . . and so I volunteered for another tour."

"You stayed in Nam when you could have gone home?" she asked, startled. "Even though you had such terrible doubts?"

"I had to work it out," he said. "I just had to. I mean, I'd killed people, a lot of people, in what I thought was a just cause, and I had to know whether I'd been right or wrong. I couldn't walk away, put it out of my mind, get on with my life, and just *forget* about it. Hell, no. I had to work it out, decide if I was a good man or a killer, and then figure what accommodation I could reach with life, with my own conscience. And there was no better place to work it out, to analyze the problem, than right there in the middle of it. Besides, to understand why I stayed on for a second tour, you've got to understand me, the me that existed then: very young, idealistic, with patriotism as much a part of me as the color of my eyes. I loved my country, *believed* in my country, totally believed, and I couldn't just shed that belief like . . . well, like a snake sheds skin."

They passed a road sign that said they were sixteen miles from Running Springs and twenty-three miles from Lake Arrowhead.

Rachael said, "So you stayed in Nam another whole year?"

He sighed wearily. "As it turned out . . . two years."

■ In his cabin high above Lake Arrowhead, for a time that he could not measure, Eric Leben drifted in a peculiar twilight state, neither awake nor asleep, neither alive nor dead, while his genetically altered cells increased production of enzymes, proteins, and other substances that would contribute to the healing process. Brief dark dreams and unassociated nightmare images flickered through his mind, like hideous shadows leaping in the bloody light of tallow candles.

When at last he rose from his trancelike condition, full of energy again, he was acutely aware that he had to arm himself and be prepared for action. His mind was still not entirely clear, his memory threadbare in places, so he did not know exactly who might be coming after him, but instinct told him that he was being stalked.

Sure as hell, someone'll find this place through Sarah Kiel, he told himself.

That thought jolted him because he could not remember who Sarah Kiel was. He stood with one hand on a kitchen counter, swaying, straining to recall the face and identity that went with that name.

Sarah Kiel . . .

Suddenly he remembered, and he cursed himself for having brought the damn girl here. The cabin was supposed to be his secret retreat. He should never have told anyone. One of his problems was that he needed young women in order to feel young himself, and he always tried to impress them. Sarah *had* been impressed by the five-room cabin, outfitted as it was with all conveniences, the acres of private woods, and the spectacular view of the lake far below. They'd had good sex outside, on a blanket, under the boughs of an enormous pine, and he had felt wonderfully young. But now Sarah knew about his secret retreat, and through her others—the stalkers whose identities he could not quite fix upon—might learn of the place and come after him.

With new urgency, Eric pushed away from the counter and headed toward the door that opened from the kitchen into the garage. He moved less stiffly than before, with more energy, and his eyes were less bothered by bright light, and no phantom uncles or insects crept out of the corners to frighten him; the period of coma had apparently done him some good. But when he put his hand on the doorknob, he stopped, jolted by another thought:

Sarah can't tell anyone about this place because Sarah is dead, I killed her only a few hours ago . . .

A wave of horror washed over Eric, and he held fast to the doorknob as if to anchor himself and prevent the wave from sweeping him away into permanent darkness, madness. Suddenly he recalled going to the house in Palm Springs, remembered beating the girl, the naked girl, mercilessly hammering her with his

fists. Images of her bruised and bleeding face, twisted in terror, flickered through
his damaged memory like slides through a broken stereopticon. But had he actually killed her? No, no, surely not. He enjoyed playing rough with women, yes,
he could admit that, enjoyed hitting them, liked nothing more than watching them
cower before him, but he would never *kill* anyone, never had and never would,
no, surely not, no, he was a law-abiding citizen, a social and economic winner,
not a thug or psychopath. Yet he was abruptly assaulted by another unclear but
fearful memory of nailing Sarah to the wall in Rachael's house in Placentia, nailing
her naked above the bed as a warning to Rachael, and he shuddered, then realized
it had not been Sarah but someone else nailed up on that wall, someone whose
name he did not even know, a stranger who had vaguely resembled Rachael, but
that was ridiculous, he had not killed *two* women, had not even killed one, but
now he also recalled a garbage dumpster, a filthy alleyway, and yet *another*
woman, a third woman, a pretty Latino, her throat slashed by a scalpel, and he
had shoved her corpse into the dumpster . . .

No. My God, what have I made of myself? he wondered, nausea twisting his
belly. I'm both researcher and subject, creator and creation, and that has to've
been a mistake, a terrible mistake. Could I have become . . . my own Frankenstein
monster?

For one dreadful moment, his thought processes cleared, and truth shone
through to him as brightly as the morning sun piercing a freshly washed window.

He shook his head violently, pretending that he wanted to be rid of the last
traces of the mist that had been clouding his mind, though in fact he was trying
desperately to rid himself of his unwelcome and unbearable clarity. His badly
injured brain and precarious physical condition made the rejection of the truth an
easy matter. The violent shaking of his head was enough to make him dizzy, blur
his vision, and bring the shrouding mists back to his memory, hindering his
thought processes, leaving him confused and somewhat disoriented.

The dead women were false memories, yes, of course, yes, they could not be
real, because he was incapable of cold-blooded murder. They were as unreal as
his uncle Barry and the strange insects that he sometimes thought he saw.

Remember the mice, the mice, the frenzied, biting, angry mice . . .

What mice? What do angry mice have to do with it?

Forget the damn mice.

The important thing was that he could not possibly have murdered even one
person, let alone three. Not him. Not Eric Leben. In the murkiness of his half-lit
and turbulent memory, these nightmare images were surely nothing but illusions,
just like the shadowfires that sprang from nowhere. They were merely the result
of short-circuiting electrical impulses in his shattered brain tissue, and they would
not stop plaguing him until that tissue was entirely healed. Meanwhile, he dared
not dwell on them, for he would begin to doubt himself and his perceptions, and
in his fragile mental condition, he did not have the energy for self-doubt.

Trembling, sweating, he pulled open the door, stepped into the garage, and
switched on the light. His black Mercedes 560 SEL was parked where he had left
it last night.

When he looked at the Mercedes, he was suddenly stricken by a memory of
another car, an older and less elegant one, in the trunk of which he had stashed
a dead woman—

No. False memories again. Illusions. Delusions.

He carefully placed one splayed hand against the wall, leaned for a moment, gathering strength and trying to clear his head. When at last he looked up, he could not recall why he was in the garage.

Gradually, however, he was once again filled with the instinctive sense that he was being stalked, that someone was coming to get him, and that he must arm himself. His muddied mind would not produce a clear picture of the people who might be pursuing him, but he *knew* he was in danger. He pushed away from the wall, moved past the car, and went to the workbench and tool rack at the front of the garage.

He wished that he'd had the foresight to keep a gun at the cabin. Now he had to settle for a wood ax, which he took down from the clips by which it was mounted on the wall, breaking a spider's web anchored to the handle. He had used the ax to split logs for the fireplace and to chop kindling. It was quite sharp, an excellent weapon.

Though he was incapable of cold-blooded murder, he knew he could kill in self-defense if necessary. No fault in protecting himself. Self-defense was far different from murder. It was justifiable.

He hefted the ax, testing its weight. Justifiable.

He took a practice swing with the weapon. It cut through the air with a whoosh. Justifiable.

■ Approximately nine miles from Running Springs and sixteen miles from Lake Arrowhead, Benny pulled off the road and parked on a scenic lay-by, which featured two picnic tables, a trash barrel, and lots of shade from several huge bristlecone pines. He switched off the engine and rolled down his window. The mountain air was forty degrees cooler than the air in the desert from which they had come; it was still warm but not stifling, and Rachael found the mild breeze refreshing as it washed through the car, scented by wildflowers and pine sap.

She did not ask why he was pulling off the road, for his reasons were obvious: It was vitally important to him that she understand the conclusions he had reached in Vietnam and that she have no illusions about the kind of man that the war had made of him, and he did not trust himself to convey all of those things adequately while also negotiating the twisty mountain lane.

He told her about his second year of combat. It had begun in confusion and despair, with the awful realization that he was not involved in a *clean* war the way World War II had been clean, with well-delineated moral choices. Month by month, his recon unit's missions took him deeper into the war zone. Frequently they crossed the line of battle, striking into enemy territory on clandestine missions. Their purpose was not only to engage and destroy the enemy, but also to engage civilians in a peaceful capacity in hope of winning hearts and minds. Through those varied contacts, he saw the special savagery of the enemy, and he finally reached the conclusion that this unclean war forced participants to choose between degrees of immorality: On one hand, it was immoral to stay and fight, to be a part of death dealing and destruction; on the other hand, it was an even greater moral wrong to walk away, for the political mass murder that would follow a collapse of South Vietnam and Cambodia was certain to be many times worse than the casualties of continued warfare.

In a voice that made Rachael think of the dark confessionals in which she had knelt as a youth, Benny said, "In a sense, I realized that, bad as we were for Vietnam, after us there would be only worse. After us, a bloodbath. Millions executed or worked to death in slave-labor camps. After us . . . the deluge."

He did not look at her but stared through the windshield at the forested slopes of the San Bernardino Mountains.

She waited.

At last he said, "No heroes. I wasn't yet even quite twenty-one years old, so it was a tough realization for me—that I was no hero, that I was essentially just the lesser of two evils. You're supposed to be an idealist at twenty-one, an optimist and an idealist, but I saw that maybe a lot of life was shaped by those kinds of choices, by choosing between evils and hoping always to choose the least of them."

Benny took a deep breath of the mountain air coming through the open window, expelled it forcefully, as though he felt sullied just by talking about the war and as though the clean air of the mountains would, if drawn in deeply enough, expunge old stains from his soul.

Rachael said nothing, partly because she did not want to break the spell before he told her everything. But she was also rendered speechless by the discovery that he had been a professional soldier, for that revelation forced her to reevaluate him completely.

She'd thought of him as a wonderfully uncomplicated man, as an ordinary real-estate broker; his very plainness had been attractive. God knew, she'd had more than enough color and flamboyance with Eric. The image of simplicity which Benny projected was soothing; it implied equanimity, reliability, dependability. He was like a deep, cool, and placid stream, slow-moving, soothing. Until now, Benny's interest in trains and old novels and forties music had seemed merely to confirm that his life had been free of serious trauma, for it did not seem possible that a life-battered and complicated man could take such unalloyed pleasure from those simple things. When he was occupied with those pastimes, he was wrapped in childlike wonder and innocence of such purity that it was hard to believe he'd ever known disillusionment or profound anguish.

"My buddies died," he said. "Not all of them but too damn many, blown away in firefights, cut down by snipers, hit by antipersonnel mines, and some got sent home crippled and maimed, faces disfigured, bodies *and* minds scarred forever. It was a high price to pay if we weren't fighting for a noble cause, if we were just fighting for the lesser of two evils, a *damn* high price. But it seemed to me the only alternative—just walking away—was an out only if you shut your eyes to the fact that there are degrees of evil, some worse than others."

"So you volunteered for a third tour of duty," Rachael said.

"Yes. Stayed, survived. Not happy, not proud. Just doing what had to be done. A lot of us made that commitment, which wasn't easy. And then . . . that was the year we pulled our troops out, which I'll never forgive or forget, because it wasn't just an abandonment of the Vietnamese, it was an abandonment of *me*. I understood the terms, and still I'd been willing to make the sacrifice. Then my country, in which I'd believed so deeply, forced me to walk away, to just let the greater evil win, as if I was supposed to find it easy to deny the complexity of the moral issues after I'd finally grasped the tangled nature of them, as if it had all been a fuckin' *game* or something!"

She had never before heard anger like this in his voice, anger as hard as steel and ice-cold, never imagined he had the capacity for it. It was a fully controlled, quiet rage—but profound and a little frightening.

He said, "It was a bad shock for a twenty-one-year-old kid to learn that life wasn't going to give him a chance to be a real pure hero, but it was even worse to learn that his own country could force him to do the *wrong* thing. After we left, the Cong and Khmer Rouge slaughtered three or four million in Cambodia and Vietnam, and another half million died trying to escape to the sea in pathetic, flimsy little boats. And . . . and in a way I can't quite convey, I feel those deaths are on my hands, on all our hands, and I feel the weight of them, sometimes so heavy I don't think I can hold up under it."

"You're being too hard on yourself."

"No. Never too hard."

"One man can't carry the world on his shoulders," she said.

But Benny would not allow that weight to be lifted from him, not even a fraction of it. "That's why I'm past-focused, I guess. I've learned that the worlds I have to live in—the present world and the world to come—aren't clean, never will be, and give us no choices between black and white. But there's always at least the illusion that things were a lot different in the past."

Rachael had always admired his sense of responsibility and his unwavering honesty, but now she saw that those qualities ran far deeper in him than she had realized—perhaps too deep. Even virtues like responsibility and honesty could become obsessions. But, oh, what lovely obsessions compared with those of other men she had known.

At last he looked at her, met her gaze, and his eyes were full of a sorrow— almost a melancholy—that she had never seen in them before. But other emotions were evident in his eyes as well, a special warmth and tenderness, great affection, love.

He said, "Last night and this morning . . . after we made love . . . Well, for the first time since before the war, I saw an important choice that was strictly black and white, no grays whatsoever, and in that choice there's a sort of . . . a sort of salvation that I thought I'd never find."

"What choice?" she asked.

"Whether to spend my life with you—or not," he said. "To spend it with you is the right choice, entirely right, no ambiguities. And to let you slip away is wrong, all wrong; I've no doubt about that."

For weeks, maybe months, Rachael had known she was in love with Benny. But she had reined in her emotions, had not spoken of the depth of her feelings for him, and had not permitted herself to think of a long-term commitment. Her childhood and adolescence had been colored by loneliness and shaped by the terrible perception that she was unloved, and those bleak years had engendered in her a craving for affection. That craving, that *need* to be wanted and loved, was what had made her such easy prey for Eric Leben and had led her into a bad marriage. Eric's obsession with youth in general and with her youth in particular had seemed like love to Rachael, for she had desperately wanted it to be love. She had spent the next seven years learning and accepting the grim and hurtful truth—that love had nothing to do with it. Now she was cautious, wary of being hurt again.

"I love you, Rachael."

Heart pounding, wanting to believe that she could be loved by a man as good and sweet as Benny, but afraid to believe it, she tried to look away from his eyes because the longer she stared into them the closer she came to losing the control and cool detachment with which she armored herself. But she could not look away. She tried not to say anything that would make her vulnerable, but with a curious mixture of dismay, delight, and wild exhilaration, she said, "Is this what I think it is?"

"What do you think it is?"

"A proposal."

"Hardly the time or place for a proposal, is it?" he said.

"Hardly."

"Yet . . . that's what it is. I wish the circumstances were more romantic."

"Well . . . "

"Champagne, candlelight, violins."

She smiled.

"But," he said, "when Baresco was holding that revolver on us, and when we were being chased down Palm Canyon Drive last night, the thing that scared me most wasn't that I might be killed . . . but that I might be killed *before I'd let you know how I felt about you.* So I'm letting you know. I want to be with you always, Rachael, always."

More easily than she would have believed possible, the words came to her own lips. "I want to spend my life with you, too, Benny."

He put a hand to her face.

She leaned forward and kissed him lightly.

"I love you," he said.

"God, I love you."

"If we get through this alive, you'll marry me?"

"Yes," she said, seized by a sudden chill. "But damn it, Benny, why'd you have to bring the *if* part into it?"

"Forget I said it."

But she could not forget. Earlier in the day, in the motel room in Palm Springs, just after they had made love the second time, she'd experienced a presentiment of death that had shaken her and had filled her with the need to *move,* as if a deadly weight would fall on them if they stayed in the same place any longer. That uncanny feeling returned. The mountain scenery, which had been fresh and alluring, acquired a somber and threatening aspect that chilled her even though she knew it was entirely a subjective change. The trees seemed to stretch into mutant shapes, their limbs bonier, their shadows darker.

"Let's go," she said.

He nodded, apparently understanding her thoughts and perceiving the same change of mood that she felt.

He started the car, pulled onto the road. When they had rounded the next bend, they saw another sign: LAKE ARROWHEAD—15 MILES.

■ Eric looked over the other tools in the garage, seeking another instrument for his arsenal. He saw nothing useful.

He returned to the house. In the kitchen, he put the ax on the table and pulled open a few drawers until he located a set of knives. He chose two—a butcher's knife and a smaller, pointier blade.

With an ax and two knives, he was prepared for both arm's-length combat and close-in fighting. He still wished he had a gun, but at least he was no longer defenseless. If someone came looking for him, he would be able to take care of himself. He would do them serious damage before they brought him down, a prospect that gave him some satisfaction and that, somewhat to his surprise, brought a sudden grin to his face.

The mice, the mice, the biting, frenzied mice . . .

Damn. He shook his head.

The mice, mice, mice, maniacal, clawing, spitting . . .

That crazy thought, like a fragment of a demented nursery rhyme, spun through his mind again, frightening him, and when he tried to focus on it, tried to understand it, his thoughts grew muddy once more, and he simply could not grasp the meaning of the mice.

The mice, mice, bloody-eyed, bashing against cage walls . . .

When he continued to strain for the elusive memory of the mice, a throbbing white pain filled his head from crown to temples and burned across the bridge of his nose, but when he stopped trying to remember and attempted, instead, to put the mice out of his mind, the pain grew even worse, a sledgehammer striking rhythmically behind his eyes. He had to grit his teeth to endure it, broke out in a sweat, and with the sweat came anger duller than the pain but growing even as the pain grew, unfocused anger at first but not for long. He said, "Rachael, Rachael," and clenched the butcher's knife. "Rachael . . . "

19   SHARP AND THE STONE

ON ARRIVING AT THE HOSPITAL IN PALM SPRINGS, ANSON SHARP had done easily what Jerry Peake had been unable to do with mighty striving. In ten minutes, he turned Nurse Alma Dunn's stonefaced implacability to dust, and he shattered Dr. Werfell's authoritarian calm, reducing both of them to nervous, uncertain, respectful, cooperative citizens. Theirs was grudging cooperation, but it was cooperation nonetheless, and Peake was deeply impressed. Though Sarah Kiel was still under the influence of the sedatives that she had taken in the middle of the night, Werfell agreed to wake her by whatever means necessary.

As always, Peake watched Sharp closely, trying to learn how the deputy director achieved his effects, much as a young magician might study a master prestidigitator's every move upon the stage. For one thing, Sharp used his formidable size to intimidate; he stood close, towering over his adversaries, staring down ominously, huge shoulders drawn up, full of pent-up violence, a volatile man. Yet the threat never became overt, and in fact Sharp frequently smiled. Of course, the smile was a weapon, too, for it was too wide, too full of teeth, utterly humorless, and strange.

More important than Sharp's size was his use of every trick available to a highly placed government agent. Before leaving the Geneplan labs in Riverside, he had employed his Defense Security Agency authority to make several telephone calls to various federal regulatory agencies in Washington, from whose computer files he had obtained what information he could on Desert General Hospital and Dr. Hans Werfell, information that could be used to strong-arm them.

Desert General's record was virtually spotless. The very highest standards for staff physicians, nurses, and technicians were strictly enforced; nine years had passed since a malpractice suit had been filed against the hospital, and no suit had ever been successful; the patient-recovery rate for every illness and surgical procedure was higher than the normal average. In twenty years, the only stain on Desert General had been the Case of the Purloined Pills. That was what Peake named the affair when Sharp quickly briefed him on arrival, before confronting Dunn and Werfell; it was a name Peake did not share with Sharp, since Sharp was not a reader of mysteries as Peake was and did not have Peake's sense of adventure. Anyway, just last year, three nurses at Desert General had been caught altering purchase and dispensation records in the pharmacy, and upon investigation it was discovered they had been stealing drugs for years. Out of spite, the three had falsely implicated six of their superiors, including Nurse Dunn, though the police had eventually cleared Dunn and the others. Desert General was put on the Drug Enforcement Agency's "watch list" of medical institutions, and Alma Dunn, though cleared, was shaken by the experience and still felt her reputation endangered.

Sharp took advantage of that weak spot. In a discreet session with Alma Dunn in the nurses' lounge, with only Peake as a witness, Sharp subtly threatened the woman with a very public reopening of the original investigation, this time at the federal level, and not only solicited her cooperation but brought her almost to tears, a feat that Peake—who likened Alma Dunn to Agatha Christie's indomitable Miss Jane Marple—had thought impossible.

At first, it appeared as if Dr. Werfell would be more difficult to crack. His record as a physician was unblemished. He was highly regarded in the medical community, possessed an AMA Physician of the Year Award, contributed six hours a week of his time to a free clinic for the disadvantaged, and from every angle appeared to be a saint. Well . . . from every angle but one: He had been charged with income-tax evasion five years ago and had lost in court on a technicality. He had failed to comply *precisely* with IRS standards of record keeping, and though his failure was unintentional, a simple ignorance of the law, ignorance of the law was not an acceptable defense.

Cornering Werfell in a two-bed room currently unoccupied by patients, Sharp used the threat of a new IRS investigation to bring the doctor to his knees in about five minutes flat. Werfell seemed certain that his records would be found acceptable now and that he would be cleared, but he also knew how expensive and time-consuming it was to defend himself against an IRS probe, and he knew that his reputation would be tarnished even when he was cleared. He looked to Peake for sympathy a few times, knowing he would get none from Sharp, but Peake did his best to imitate Anson Sharp's air of granite resolution and indifference to others.

Being an intelligent man, Werfell quickly determined that the prudent course would be to do as Sharp wished in order to avoid another tax-court nightmare, even if it meant bending his principles in the matter of Sarah Kiel.

"No reason to fault yourself or lose any sleep over a misguided concern about professional ethics, Doctor," Sharp said, clapping one beefy hand on the physician's shoulder in a gesture of reassurance, suddenly friendly and empathetic now that Werfell had broken. "The welfare of our country comes before anything else. No one would dispute that or think you'd made the wrong decision."

Dr. Werfell did not exactly recoil from Sharp's touch, but he looked sickened by it. His expression did not change when he looked from Sharp to Jerry Peake.

Peake winced.

Werfell led them out of the untenanted room, down the hospital corridor, past the nurses' station—where Alma Dunn watched them warily while pretending not to look—to the private room where Sarah Kiel remained sedated. As they went, Peake noticed that Werfell, who had previously seemed to resemble Dashiell Hammett and who had looked tremendously imposing, was now somewhat shrunken, diminished. His face was gray, and he seemed older than he had been just a short while ago.

Although Peake admired Anson Sharp's ability to command and to get things done, he did not see how he could adopt his boss's methods as his own. Peake wanted not only to be a successful agent but to be a legend, and you could be a legend only if you played fair and *still* got things done. Being infamous was not at all the same as being a legend, and in fact the two could not coexist. If he had learned nothing else from five thousand mystery novels, Peake had at least learned that much.

Sarah Kiel's room was silent except for her slow and slightly wheezy breathing, dark but for a single softly glowing lamp beside her bed and the few thin beams of bright desert sun that burned through at the edges of the heavy drapes drawn over the lone window.

The three men gathered around the bed, Dr. Werfell and Sharp on one side, Peake on the other.

"Sarah," Werfell said quietly. "Sarah?" When she didn't respond, the physician repeated her name and gently shook her shoulder.

She snorted, murmured, but did not wake.

Werfell lifted one of the girl's eyelids, studied her pupil, then held her wrist and timed her pulse. "She won't wake naturally for . . . oh, perhaps another hour."

"Then do what's necessary to wake her *now*," Anson Sharp said impatiently. "We've already discussed this."

"I'll administer an injection to counteract," Werfell said, heading toward the closed door.

"Stay here," Sharp said. He indicated the call button on the cord that was tied loosely to one of the bed rails. "Have a nurse bring what you need."

"This is questionable treatment," Werfell said. "I won't ask any nurse to be involved in it." He went out, and the door sighed slowly shut behind him.

Looking down at the sleeping girl, Sharp said, "Scrumptious."

Peake blinked in surprise.

"Tasty," Sharp said, without raising his eyes from the girl.

Peake looked down at the unconscious teenager and tried to see something scrumptious and tasty about her, but it wasn't easy. Her blond hair was tangled and oily because she was perspiring in her drugged sleep, her limp and matted tresses were unappealingly sweat-pasted to forehead, cheeks, and neck. Her right eye was blackened and swollen shut, with several lines of dried and crusted blood radiating from it where the skin had been cracked and torn. Her right cheek was covered by a bruise from the corner of her swollen eye all the way to her jaw, and her upper lip was split and puffy. Sheets covered her almost to the neck, except for her thin right arm, which had to be exposed because one broken finger was in a cast; two fingernails had been cracked off at the cuticle, and the hand looked less like a hand than like a bird's long-toed, bony claw.

"Fifteen when she first moved in with Leben," Sharp said softly. "Not much past sixteen now."

Turning his attention from the sleeping girl to his boss, Jerry Peake studied Sharp as Sharp studied Sarah Kiel, and he was not merely struck by an incredible insight but *whacked* by it so hard he almost reeled backward. Anson Sharp, deputy director of the DSA, was both a pedophile and a sadist.

Perverse hungers were apparent in the man's hard green eyes and predatory expression. Clearly, he thought Sarah was scrumptious and tasty not because she looked so great right now but because she was only sixteen and badly battered. His rapturous gaze moved lovingly over her blackened eye and bruises, which obviously had as great an erotic impact upon him as breasts and buttocks might have upon a normal man. He was a tightly controlled sadist, yes, and a pedophile who kept his sick libido in check, a pervert who had redirected his mutant needs into wholly acceptable channels, into the aggressiveness and ambition that had swiftly carried him almost to the top of the agency, but a sadist and a pedophile nonetheless.

Peake was as astonished as he was appalled. And his astonishment arose not only from this terrible insight into Sharp's character but from the very fact that he'd had such an insight in the first place. Although he wanted to be a legend, Jerry Peake knew that, even for twenty-seven, he was naive and—especially for a DSA man—woefully prone to look only at the surfaces of people and events rather than down into more profound levels. Sometimes, in spite of his training and his important job, he felt as if he were still a boy, or at least as if the boy in him were still too much a part of his character. Now, staring at Anson Sharp as Sharp hungered for Sarah Kiel, absolutely *walloped* by this insight, Jerry Peake was suddenly exhilarated. He wondered if it was possible to finally begin to grow up even as late as twenty-seven.

Anson Sharp was staring at the girl's torn and broken hand, his green eyes radiant, a vague smile playing at the corners of his mouth.

With a thump and swish that startled Peake, the door to the room opened, and Dr. Werfell returned. Sharp blinked and shook himself as if coming out of a mild trance, stepped back, and watched as Werfell raised the bed, bared Sarah's left arm, and administered an injection to counteract the effect of the two sedatives she had taken.

In a couple of minutes, the girl was awake, relatively aware, but confused. She could not remember where she was, how she had gotten there, or why she was so battered and in pain. She kept asking who Werfell, Sharp, and Peake were, and Werfell patiently answered all her questions, but mostly he monitored her pulse and listened to her heart and peered into her eyes with a lighted instrument.

Anson Sharp grew impatient with the girl's slow ascension from her drugged haze. "Did you give her a large enough dose to counteract the sedative or did you hedge it, Doctor?"

"This takes time," Werfell said coldly.

"We don't *have* time," Sharp said.

A moment later, Sarah Kiel stopped asking questions, gasped in shock at the sudden return of her memory, and said, "Eric!"

Peake would not have imagined that her face could go paler than it was already, but it did. She began to shiver.

Sharp returned swiftly to the bed. "That'll be all, Doctor."

Werfell frowned. "What do you mean?"

"I mean she's alert now, and we can question her, and you can get out and leave us to it. Clear?"

Dr. Werfell insisted he should stay with his patient in case she had a delayed reaction to the injection. Sharp became more adamant, invoking his federal authority. Werfell relented but moved toward the window to open the drapes first. Sharp told him to leave them closed, and Werfell went to the light switch for the overhead fluorescents, but Sharp told him to leave them off. "The bright light will hurt the poor girl's eyes," Sharp said, though his sudden concern for Sarah was transparently insincere.

Peake had the uncomfortable feeling that Sharp intended to be hard on the girl, frighten her half to death, whether or not that approach was necessary. Even if she told them everything they wanted to know, the deputy director was going to terrorize her for the sheer fun of it. He probably viewed mental and emotional abuse as being at least partially satisfying and socially acceptable alternatives to the things he really wanted to do: beat her and fuck her. The bastard wanted to keep the room as dark as possible because shadows would contribute to the mood of menace that he intended to create.

When Werfell left the room, Sharp went to the girl's bed. He put down the railing on one side and sat on the edge of the mattress. He took her uninjured left hand, held it in both his hands, gave it a reassuring squeeze, smiled down at her, and as he spoke he began to slide one of his huge hands up and down her slender arm, even all the way up under the short sleeve of her hospital gown, slowly up and down, which was not at all reassuring but provocative.

Peake stepped back into a corner of the room, where shadows sheltered him, partly because he knew he would not be expected to ask questions of the girl, but also because he did not want Sharp to see his face. Although he had achieved the first startling insight of his life and was gripped by the heady feeling that he was not going to be the same man in a year that he was now, he had not yet changed so much that he could control his expressions or conceal his disgust.

"I can't talk about it," Sarah Kiel told Sharp, watching him warily and shrinking back from him as far as she could. "Mrs. Leben told me not to tell anyone anything."

Still holding her good hand in his left, he raised his right hand, with which he had been stroking her arm, and he gently rubbed his thick knuckles over her smooth, unblemished left cheek. It almost seemed like a gesture of sympathy or affection, but it was not.

He said, "Mrs. Leben is a wanted criminal, Sarah. There's a warrant for her arrest. I had it issued myself. She's wanted for serious violations of the Defense Security Act. She may have stolen defense secrets, may even intend to pass them to the Soviets. Surely you've no desire to protect someone like that. Hmmmmm?"

"She was nice to me," Sarah said shakily.

Peake saw that the girl was trying to ease away from the hand that stroked her face but was plainly afraid of giving offense to Sharp. Evidently she was not yet certain that he was threatening her. She'd get the idea soon.

She continued: "Mrs. Leben's paying my hospital bills, gave me some money, called my folks. She . . . she was s-so nice, and she told me not to talk about this, so I won't break my promise to her."

"How interesting," Sharp said, putting his hand under her chin and lifting her head to make her look at him with her one good eye. "Interesting that even a little whore like you has some principles."

Shocked, she said, "I'm no whore. I never—"

"Oh, yes," Sharp said, gripping her chin now and preventing her from turning her head away. "Maybe you're too thickheaded to see the truth about yourself, or too drugged up, but that's what you are, a little whore, a slut in training, a piglet who's going to grow up to be a fine sweet pig."

"You can't talk to me like this."

"Honey, I talk to whores any way I want."

"You're a cop, some kind of cop, you're a public *servant*," she said, "you can't treat me—"

"Shut up, honey," Sharp said. The light from the only lamp fell across his face at an angle, weirdly exaggerating some features while leaving others entirely in shadow, giving his face a deformed look, a demonic aspect. He grinned, and the effect was even more unnerving. "You shut your dirty little mouth and open it only when you're ready to tell me what I want to know."

The girl gave out a thin, pathetic cry of pain, and tears burst from her eyes. Peake saw that Sharp was squeezing her left hand very hard and grinding the fingers together in his big mitt.

For a while, the girl talked to avoid the torture. She told them about Leben's visit last night, about the way his head was staved in, about how gray and cool his skin had felt.

But when Sharp wanted to know if she had any idea where Eric Leben had gone after leaving the house, she clammed up again, and he said, "Ah, you do have an idea," and he began to grind her hand again.

Peake felt sick, and he wanted to do something to help the girl, but there was nothing he could do.

Sharp eased up on her hand, and she said, "Please, that was the thing . . . the thing Mrs. Leben most wanted me not to tell anyone."

"Now, honey," Sharp said, "it's stupid for a little whore like you to pretend to have scruples. I don't believe you have any, and you *know* you don't have any, so cut the act. Save us some time and save yourself a lot of trouble." He started to grind her hand again, and his other hand slipped down to her throat and then to her breasts, which he touched through the thin material of her hospital gown.

In the shadowed corner, Peake was almost too shocked to breathe, and he wanted to be *out* of there. He certainly did not want to watch Sarah Kiel be abused and humiliated; however, he could not look away or close his eyes, because Sharp's unexpected behavior was the most morbidly, horrifyingly fascinating thing Peake had ever seen.

He was nowhere near coming to terms with his previous shattering insight, and already he was experiencing yet another major revelation. He'd always thought of policemen—which included DSA agents—as Good Guys with capital Gs, White Hats, Men on White Horses, valiant Knights of the Law, but that image of purity was suddenly unsustainable if a man like Sharp could be a highly regarded member in good standing of that noble fraternity. Oh, sure, Peake knew there were some bad cops, bad agents, but somehow he had always thought the bad ones were caught early in their careers and that they never had a chance of advancing to high positions, that they self-destructed, that slime like that got what was coming to them and got it pretty quickly, too. He believed only virtue was rewarded. Besides, he had always thought he'd be able to smell corruption in another cop, that it would be evident from the moment he laid eyes on the guy. And he had never imagined that a flat-out *pervert* could hide his sickness and have a successful career in law enforcement. Maybe most men were disabused of such naive ideas long before they were twenty-seven, but it was only now, watching the deputy director behave like a thug, like a regular damn barbarian, that Jerry Peake began to see that the world was painted more in shades of gray than in black and white, and this revelation was so powerful that he could no more have averted his eyes from Sharp's sick performance than he could have looked away from Jesus returning on a chariot of fire through an angel-bedecked sky.

Sharp continued to grind the girl's hand in his, which made her cry harder, and he had a hand on her breasts and was pushing her back hard against the bed, telling her to quiet down, so she was trying to please him now, choking back her tears, but still Sharp squeezed her hand, and Peake was on the verge of making a move, to hell with his career, to hell with his future in the DSA, he couldn't just stand by and watch this brutality, he even took a step toward the bed—

And that was when the door opened wide and The Stone entered the room as if borne on the shaft of light that speared in from the hospital corridor behind him. That was how Jerry Peake thought of the man from the moment he saw him: The Stone.

"What's goin' on here?" The Stone asked in a voice that was quiet, gentle, deep but not real deep, yet commanding.

The guy was not quite six feet tall, maybe five eleven, even five ten, which left him several inches shorter than Anson Sharp, and he was about a hundred and seventy pounds, a good fifty pounds lighter than Sharp. Yet when he stepped through the door, he seemed like the biggest man in the room, and he *still* seemed like the biggest even when Sharp let go of the girl and stood up from the edge of the bed and said, "Who the hell are you?"

The Stone switched on the overhead fluorescents and stepped farther into the room, letting the door swing shut behind him. Peake pegged the guy as about forty, though his face looked older because it was full of wisdom. He had close-cut dark hair, sun-weathered skin, and solid features that looked as if they had been jackhammered out of granite. His intense blue eyes were the same shade as those of the girl in the bed but clearer, direct, piercing. When he turned those eyes briefly toward Jerry Peake, Peake wanted to crawl under a bed and hide. The Stone was compact and powerful, and though he was really smaller than Sharp, he appeared infinitely stronger, more formidable, as if he actually weighed every ounce as much as Sharp but had compressed his tissues into an unnatural density.

"Please leave the room and wait for me in the hall," said The Stone quietly.

Astonished, Sharp took a couple of steps toward him, loomed over him, and said, "I asked you who the hell you are."

The Stone's hands and wrists were much too large for the rest of him: long, thick fingers; big knuckles; every tendon and vein and sinew stood out sharply, as if they were hands carved in marble by a sculptor with an exaggerated appreciation for detail. Peake sensed that they were not quite the hands that The Stone had been born with, that they had grown larger and stronger in response to day after day of long, hard, manual labor. The Stone looked as if he thrived on the kind of heavy work that was done in a foundry or quarry or, considering his sun-darkened skin, a farm. But not one of those big, easy, modern farms with a thousand machines and an abundant supply of cheap field hands. No, if he had a farm, he had started it with little money, with bad rocky land, and he had endured lousy weather and sundry catastrophes to bring fruit from the reluctant earth, building a successful enterprise by the expenditure of much sweat, blood, time, hopes, and dreams, because the strength of all those successfully waged struggles was in his face and hands.

"I'm her father, Felsen Kiel," The Stone told Sharp.

In a small voice devoid of fear and filled with wonder, Sarah Kiel said, "Daddy . . ."

The Stone started past Sharp, toward his daughter, who had sat up in bed and held out a hand toward him.

Sharp stepped in his way, leaned close to him, loomed over him, and said, "You can see her when we've finished the interrogation."

The Stone looked up at Sharp with a placid expression that was the essence of equanimity and imperturbability, and Peake was not only gladdened but *thrilled* to see that Sharp was not going to intimidate this man. "Interrogate? What right have you to interrogate?"

Sharp withdrew his wallet from his jacket, opened it to his DSA credentials. "I'm a federal agent, and I am in the middle of an urgent investigation concerning a matter of national security. Your daughter has information that I've got to obtain as soon as possible, and she is being less than cooperative."

"If you'll step into the hall," The Stone said quietly, "I'll speak with her. I'm sure she isn't obstructin' you on purpose. She's a troubled girl, yes, and she's allowed herself to be misguided, but she's never been bad at heart or spiteful. I'll speak to her, find out what you need to know, then convey the information to you."

"No," Sharp said. *"You'll* go into the hall and wait."

"Please move out of my way," The Stone said.

"Listen, mister," Sharp said, moving right up against The Stone, glaring down at him, "if you want trouble from me, you'll get it, more than you can deal with. You obstruct a federal agent, and you're just about giving him a license to come down on you as hard as he wants."

Having read the name on the DSA credentials, The Stone said, "Mr. Sharp, last night I was awakened by a call from a Mrs. Leben, who said my daughter needed me. That's a message I've been waitin' a long time to hear. It's the growin' season, a busy time—"

The guy *was* a farmer, by God, which gave Peake new confidence in his powers of observation. In spit-polished city shoes, polyester pants, and starched white shirt, The Stone had the uncomfortable look specific to a simple country man who has been forced by circumstances to exchange his work clothes for unfamiliar duds.

"—a very busy season. But I got dressed the moment I hung up the phone, drove the pickup a hundred miles to Kansas City in the heart of the night, got the dawn flight out to Los Angeles, then the connector flight here to Palm Springs, a taxi—"

"Your travel journal doesn't interest me one damn bit," Sharp said, still blocking The Stone.

"Mr. Sharp, I am plain bone-weary, which is the fact I'm tryin' to impress upon you, and I am most eager to see my girl, and from the looks of her she's been cryin', which upsets me mightily. Now, though I'm not an angry man by nature, or a trouble-makin' man, I don't know quite what I might do if you keep treatin' me high-handed and try to stop me from seein' what my girl's cryin' about."

Sharp's face tightened with anger. He stepped back far enough to give himself room to plant one big hand on The Stone's chest.

Peake was not sure whether Sharp intended to guide the man out of the room and into the corridor or give him one hell of a shove back against the wall. He never found out which it was because The Stone put his own hand on Sharp's wrist and bore down and, without seeming to make any effort whatsoever, he removed Sharp's hand from his chest. In fact, he must have put as much painful pressure on Sharp's wrist as Sharp had applied to Sarah's fingers, for the deputy director went pale, the redness of anger draining right out of him, and a queer look passed through his eyes.

Letting go of Sharp's hand, The Stone said, "I know you're a federal agent, and I have the greatest respect for the law. I know you can see this as obstruction, which would give you a good excuse to knock me on my can and clap me in handcuffs. But I'm of the opinion that it wouldn't do you or your agency the least bit of good if you roughed me up, 'specially since I've told you I'll encourage my daughter to cooperate. What do you think?"

Peake wanted to applaud. He didn't.

Sharp stood there, breathing heavily, trembling, and gradually his rage-clouded eyes cleared, and he shook himself the way a bull sometimes will shake itself back to its senses after unsuccessfully charging a matador's cape. "Okay. I just want to get my information *fast*. I don't care how. Maybe you'll get it faster than I can."

"Thank you, Mr. Sharp. Give me half an hour—"

"Five minutes!" Sharp said.

"Well, sir," The Stone said quietly, "you've got to give me time to say hello to my daughter, time to hug her. I haven't seen her in almost eighteen months. And I need time to get the whole story from her, to find out what sort of trouble she's in. That's got to come first, 'fore I start throwin' questions at her."

"Half an hour's too damn long," Sharp said. "We're in pursuit of a man, a dangerous man, and we—"

"If I was to call an attorney to advise my daughter, which is her right as a citizen, it'd take him hours to get here—"

"Half an hour," Sharp told The Stone, "and not one damn minute more. I'll be in the hall."

Previously, Peake had discovered that the deputy director was a sadist and a pedophile, which was an important thing to know. Now he had made another discovery about Sharp: The son of a bitch was, at heart, a coward; he might shoot you in the back or sneak up on you and slit your throat, yes, those things seemed within his character, but in a face-to-face confrontation, he would chicken out if the stakes got high enough. And that was an even *more* important thing to know.

Peake stood for a moment, unable to move, as Sharp went to the door. He could not take his eyes off The Stone.

"Peake!" Sharp said as he pulled the door open.

Finally Peake followed, but he kept glancing back at Felsen Kiel, The Stone. Now *there,* by God, was a legend.

20 COPS ON SICK LEAVE

DETECTIVE REESE HAGERSTROM WENT TO BED AT FOUR O'CLOCK Tuesday morning, after returning from Mrs. Leben's house in Placentia, and he woke at ten-thirty, unrested because the night had been full of terrible dreams. Glassy-eyed dead bodies in trash dumpsters. Dead women nailed to walls. Many of the nightmares had involved Janet, the wife Reese had lost. In the dreams, she was always clutching the door of the blue Chevy van, the infamous van, and crying, "They've got Esther, they've got Esther!" In every dream, one of the guys in the van shot her exactly as he had shot her in real life, point-blank, and the large-caliber slug pulverized her lovely face, blew it away . . .

Reese got out of bed and took a very hot shower. He wished that he could unhinge the top of his head and sluice out the hideous images that lingered from the nightmares.

Agnes, his sister, had taped a note on the refrigerator in the kitchen. She had taken Esther to the dentist for a scheduled checkup.

Standing by the sink, looking out the window at the big coral tree in the rear yard, Reese drank hot black coffee and ate a slightly stale doughnut. If Agnes could see the breakfast he made for himself, she would be upset. But his dreams had left him queasy, and he had no appetite for anything heavier. Even the doughnut was hard to swallow.

"Black coffee and greasy doughnuts," Agnes would say if she knew. "One'll give you ulcers, other'll clog your arteries with cholesterol. Two slow methods of suicide. You want to commit suicide, I can tell you a hundred quicker and less painful ways to go about it."

He thanked God for Agnes, in spite of her tendency, as his big sister, to nag him about everything from his eating habits to his taste in neckties. Without her, he might not have held himself together after Janet's death.

Agnes was unfortunately big-boned, stocky, plain-looking, with a deformed left hand, destined for spinsterhood, but she had a kind heart and a mothering instinct second to none. After Janet died, Agnes arrived with a suitcase and her favorite cookbook, announcing that she would take care of Reese and little Esther "just for the summer," until they were able to cope on their own. As a fifth-grade teacher in Anaheim, she had the summer off and could devote long hours to the patient rebuilding of the shattered Hagerstrom household. She had been with them five years now, and without her, they'd be lost.

Reese even liked her good-natured nagging. When she encouraged him to eat well-balanced meals, he felt cared for and loved.

As he poured another cup of black coffee, he decided to bring Agnes a dozen roses and a box of chocolates when he came home today. He was not, by nature, given to frequent expressions of his feelings, so he tried to compensate now and then by surprising those he cared for with gifts. The smallest surprises thrilled Agnes, even coming from a brother. Big-boned, stocky, plain-faced women were not used to getting gifts when there was no occasion requiring them.

Life was not only unfair but sometimes decidedly cruel. That was not a new thought to Reese. It was not even inspired by Janet's untimely and brutal death—or by the fact that Agnes's warm, loving, generous nature was trapped forever inside a body that most men, too focused on appearances, could never love. As a policeman, frequently confronted by the worst in humankind, he had learned a long time ago that cruelty was the way of the world—and that the only defense against it was the love of one's family and a few close friends.

His closest friend, Julio Verdad, arrived as Reese was pouring a third cup of black coffee. Reese got another cup from the cabinet and filled it for Julio, and they sat at the kitchen table.

Julio looked as if he'd had little sleep, and in fact Reese was probably the only person capable of detecting the subtle signs of overwork in the lieutenant. As usual, Julio was well dressed: smartly tailored dark blue suit, crisp white shirt, perfectly knotted maroon-and-blue tie with gold chain, maroon pocket handker-chief, and oxblood Bally loafers. He was as neat and precise and alert as always, but vague sooty smudges were visible under his eyes, and his soft voice was surely if immeasurably softer than usual.

"Up all night?" Reese asked.

"I slept."

"How long? An hour or two? That's what I thought. You worry me," Reese said. "You'll wear yourself down to bone someday."

"This is a special case."

"They're all special cases to you."

"I feel a special obligation to the victim, Ernestina."

"This is the *thousandth* victim you've felt a special obligation toward," Reese noted.

Julio shrugged and sipped his coffee. "Sharp wasn't bluffing."

"About what?"

"About pulling this out of our hands. The names of the victims—Ernestina Hernandez and Rebecca Klienstad—are still in the files, but *only* the names. Plus a memorandum indicating that federal authorities requested the case be remanded to their jurisdiction for 'reasons of national security.' This morning, when I pushed Folbeck about letting you and me assist the feds, he came down hard. Said, 'Holy fuckin' Christ, Julio, stay out of it. That's an order.' His very words."

Folbeck was chief of detectives, a devout Mormon who could hold his own with the most foulmouthed men in the department but who *never* took the Lord's name in vain. That was where he drew the line. In spite of his vivid and frequent use of four-letter words, Nicholas Folbeck was capable of angrily lecturing any detective heard to mutter a blasphemy. In fact, he'd once told Reese, "Hagerstrom, please don't say 'goddamn' or 'holy Christ' or anything like that in my presence ever again. I purely hate that shit, and I won't fuckin' tolerate it." If Nick Folbeck's warning to Julio had included blasphemy as well as mere trash talk, the pressure on the department to stay out of this case had come from higher authorities than Anson Sharp.

Reese said, "What about the file on the body-snatching case, Eric Leben's corpse?"

"Same thing," Julio said. "Removed from our jurisdiction."

Business talk had taken Reese's mind off last night's bloody dreams of Janet, and his appetite had returned a little. He got another doughnut from the breadbox. He offered one to Julio, but Julio declined. Reese said, "What else have you been up to?"

"For one thing . . . I went to the library when it opened and read everything I could find on Dr. Eric Leben."

"Rich, a scientific genius, a business genius, ruthless, cold, too stupid to know he had a great wife—we already know about him."

"He was also obsessed," Julio said.

"I guess geniuses usually are, with one thing or another."

"What obsessed him was immortality."

Reese frowned. "Say what?"

"As a graduate student, and in the years immediately following his acquisition of a doctorate, when he was one of the brightest young geneticists doing recombinant DNA research anywhere in the world, he wrote articles for a lot of journals and published research papers dealing with various aspects of the extension of the human life span. A *flood* of articles; the man is driven."

"Was driven. Remember that garbage truck," Reese said.

"Even the driest, most technical of those pieces have a . . . well, a *fire* in them, a passion that grips you," Julio said. He pulled a sheet of paper from one of his inside jacket pockets, unfolded it. "This is a line from an article that appeared in a popular science magazine, more colorful than the technical journal stuff: 'It may be possible, ultimately, for man to reshape himself genetically and thereby deny the claim of the grave, to live longer than Methuselah—and even to be both Jesus and Lazarus in one, raising *himself* up from the mortuary slab even as death lays him down upon it.'"

Reese blinked. "Funny, huh? His body's stolen from the morgue, which is sort of being 'raised up,' though not the way he meant it."

Julio's eyes were strange. "Maybe not funny. Maybe not stolen."

Reese felt a strangeness coming into his own eyes. He said, "You don't mean . . . no, of course not."

"He was a genius with unlimited resources, perhaps the brightest man ever to work in recombinant DNA research, and he was obsessed with staying young and avoiding death. So when he just seems to get up and walk away from a mortuary . . . is it so impossible to imagine that he did, in fact, get up and walk away?"

Reese felt his chest tightening, and he was surprised to feel a thrill of fear pass through him. "But is such a thing possible, after the injuries he suffered?"

"A few years ago, definitely impossible. But we're living in an age of miracles, or at least in an age of infinite possibilities."

"But how?"

"That's part of what we'll have to find out. I called UCI and got in touch with Dr. Easton Solberg, whose work on aging is mentioned in Leben's articles. Turns out Leben knew Solberg, looked up to him as a mentor, and for a while they were fairly close. Solberg has great praise for Leben, says he isn't the least surprised that Leben made a fortune out of DNA research, but Solberg also says there was a dark side to Eric Leben. And he's willing to talk about it."

"What dark side?"

"He wouldn't say on the phone. But we have an appointment with him at UCI at one o'clock."

As Julio pushed his chair back and got up, Reese said, "How can we keep digging into this and stay out of trouble with Nick Folbeck?"

"Sick leave," Julio said. "As long as I'm on sick leave, I'm not officially investigating anything. Call it personal curiosity."

"That won't hold up if we're caught at it. Cops aren't supposed to *have* personal curiosity in a situation like this."

"No, but if I'm on sick leave, Folbeck's not going to be worrying about what I'm doing. It's less likely that anyone'll be looking over my shoulder. In fact, I sort of implied that I wanted nothing to do with anything this hot. Told Folbeck that, given the heat on this, it might be best for me to get away for a few days, in case the media pick up on it and want me to answer questions. He agreed."

Reese got to his feet. "I better call in sick, too."

"I already did it for you," Julio said.

"Oh. Okay, then, let's go."

"I mean, I thought it would be all right. But if you don't want to get involved in this—"

"Julio, I'm in."

"Only if you're sure."

"I'm *in*," Reese said exasperatedly.

And he thought but did not say: You saved my Esther, my little girl, went right after those guys in the Chevy van and got her out of there alive, you were like a man possessed, they must've thought it was a demon on their tail, you put your own life on the line and saved Esther, and I loved you before that because you were my partner and a good one, but after that I *loved* you, you crazy little bastard, and as long as I live I'm going to be there when you need me, no matter what.

In spite of his natural difficulty expressing his most profound feelings, Reese wanted to say all of that to Julio, but he kept silent because Julio did not want effusive gratitude and would be embarrassed by it. All Julio wanted was the commitment of a friend and partner. Undying gratitude would, if openly expressed, impose a barrier between them by obviously placing Julio in a superior position, and ever afterward they would be awkward with each other.

In their daily working relationship, Julio always had been in the superior position, of course, deciding how to proceed at nearly every step of a homicide investigation, but his control was never blatant or obvious, which made all the difference. Reese would not have cared if Julio's dominance had been obvious; he did not mind deferring to Julio because in some ways Julio was the quicker and smarter of the two.

But Julio, having been born and raised in Mexico, having come to the States and made good, had a reverence and a passion for democracy, not only for democracy in the political arena but for democracy in all things, even in one-to-one relationships. He could assume the mantle of leadership and dominance if it were conveyed by mutual unspoken consent; but if his role were made overt, he would not be able to fulfill it, and the partnership would suffer.

"I'm in," Reese repeated, rinsing their coffee cups in the sink. "We're just two cops on sick leave. So let's go recuperate together."

21 ARROWHEAD

THE SPORTING-GOODS STORE WAS NEAR THE LAKE. IT WAS BUILT in the form of a large log cabin, and a rustic wooden sign advertised BAIT, TACKLE, BOAT RENTALS, SPORTING GOODS. A Coors sign was in one window, a Miller Lite sign in another. Three cars, two pickup trucks, and one Jeep stood in the sunny part of the parking lot, the early-afternoon sun glinting off their chrome and silvering their windows.

"Guns," Ben said when he saw the place. "They might sell guns."

"We have guns," Rachael said.

Ben drove to the back of the lot, off the macadamed area, onto gravel that crunched under the tires, then through a thick carpet of pine needles, finally parking in the concealing shade of one of the massive evergreens that encircled the property. He saw a slice of the lake beyond the trees, a few boats on the sun-dappled water, and a far shore rising up into steep wooded slopes.

"Your thirty-two isn't exactly a peashooter, but it's not particularly formidable, either," Ben told her as he switched off the engine. "The .357 I took off Baresco is better, next thing to a cannon, in fact, but a shotgun would be perfect."

"Shotgun? Sounds like overkill."

"I always prefer to go for overkill when I'm tracking down a walking dead man," Ben said, trying to make a joke of it but failing. Rachael's already haunted eyes were touched by a new bleak tint, and she shivered.

"Hey," he said, "it'll be all right."

They got out of the rental car and stood for a moment, breathing in the clean, sweet mountain air. The day was warm and undisturbed by even the mildest breeze. The trees stood motionless and silent, as if their boughs had turned to stone. No cars passed on the road, and no other people were in sight. No birds flew or sang. The stillness was deep, perfect, preternatural.

Ben sensed something ominous in the stillness. It almost seemed to be an omen, a warning to turn back from the high vastness of the mountains and retreat to more civilized places, where there were noise and movement and other people to turn to for help in an emergency.

Apparently stricken by the same uneasy feeling that gripped Ben, Rachael said, "Maybe this is nuts. Maybe we should just get out of here, go away somewhere."

"And wait for Eric to recover from his injuries?"

"Maybe he won't recover enough to function well."

"But if he does, he'll come looking for you."

She sighed, nodded.

They crossed the parking lot and went into the store, hoping to buy a shotgun and some ammunition.

Something strange was happening to Eric, stranger even than his return from the dead. It started as another headache, one of the many intense migraines that had come and gone since his resurrection, and he did not immediately realize there was a difference about this one, a weirdness. He just squinted his eyes to block out some of the light that irritated him, and refused to succumb to the unrelenting and debilitating throbbing that filled his skull.

He pulled an armchair in front of the living-room window and took up a vigil, looking down through the sloping forest, along the dirt road that led up from the more heavily populated foothills nearer the lake. If enemies came for him, they would follow the lane at least part of the way up the slope before sneaking into the woods. As soon as he saw where they left the road, he would slip out of the cabin by the back door, move around through the trees, creep in behind the intruders, and take them by surprise.

He had hoped that the pounding in his head would subside a bit when he sat down and leaned back in the big comfortable chair. But it was getting much worse than anything he had experienced previously. He felt almost as if his skull were . . . soft as clay . . . and as if it were being hammered into a new shape by every fierce throb. He clenched his jaws tighter, determined to weather this new adversity.

Perhaps the headache was made worse by the concentration required to study the tree-shadowed road for advancing enemies. If it became unbearable, he would have to lie down, though he was loath to leave his post. He sensed danger approaching.

He kept the ax and the two knives on the floor beside the chair. Each time he glanced down at those sharp blades, he felt not only reassured but strangely exultant. When he put his fingertips to the handle of the ax, a dark and almost erotic thrill coursed through him.

Let them come, he thought. I'll show them Eric Leben is still a man to be reckoned with. Let them come.

Though he still had difficulty understanding who might be seeking him, he somehow knew that his fear was not unreasonable. Then names popped into his mind: Baresco, Seitz, Geffels, Knowls, Lewis. Yes, of course, his partners in Geneplan. They would know what he'd done. They would decide that he had to be found quickly and terminated in order to protect the secret of Wildcard. But they were not the only men he had to fear. There were others . . . shadowy figures he could not recall, men with more power than the partners in Geneplan.

For a moment he felt that he was about to break through a wall of mist into a clear place. He was on the verge of achieving a clarity of thought and a fullness of memory that he had not known since rising from the gurney in the morgue. He held his breath and leaned forward in his chair with tremulous anticipation. He almost had it, all of it: the identity of the other pursuers, the meaning of the mice, the meaning of the hideous image of the crucified woman that kept recurring to him . . .

Then the unremitting pain in his head knocked him back from the brink of enlightenment, into the mist again. Muddy currents invaded the clearing stream of his thoughts, and in a moment all was clouded as before. He let out a thin cry of frustration.

Outside, in the forest, movement caught his attention. Squinting his hot watery eyes, Eric slid forward to the chair's edge, leaned toward the large window, peered intently at the tree-covered slope and the shadow-dappled dirt lane. No one there. The movement was simply the work of a sudden breeze that had finally broken the summer stillness. Bushes stirred, and the evergreen boughs lifted slightly, drooped, lifted, drooped, as if the trees were fanning themselves.

He was about to ease farther back in the chair when a scintillant blast of pain, shooting across his forehead, virtually *threw* him back. For a moment he was in such horrendous agony that he could not move or cry out or breathe. When at last breath could be drawn, he screamed, though by then it was a scream of anger rather than pain, for the pain went as abruptly as it had come.

Afraid that the bright explosion of pain had signified a sudden turn for the worse, perhaps even a coming apart of his broken skull, Eric raised one shaky hand to his head. First he touched his damaged right ear, which had nearly been torn off yesterday morning but which was now firmly attached, lumpish and un-usually gristly to the touch but no longer drooping and raw.

How could he heal so fast? The process was supposed to take a few weeks, not a few hours.

He slowly slipped his fingers upward and gingerly explored the deep depres-sion along the right side of his skull, where he had made contact with the garbage truck. The depression was still there. But not as deep as he remembered it. And the concavity was solid. It had been slightly mushy before. Like bruised and rotting fruit. But no longer. He felt no tenderness in the flesh, either. Emboldened, he pressed his fingers harder into the wound, massaged, probed from one end of the indentation to the other, and everywhere he encountered healthy flesh and a firm shell of bone. The cracked and splintered skull had already knit up in less than a day, and the holes had filled in with new bone, which was flat-out impossible, damn it, impossible, but that was what had happened. The wound was healed, and his brain tissue was once more protected by a casing of unbroken bone.

He sat stupefied, unable to comprehend. He remembered that his genes had been edited to enhance the healing process and to promote cell rejuvenation, but damned if he remembered that it was supposed to happen this fast. Grievous wounds closing in mere hours? Flesh, arteries, and veins reconstituted at an almost visible rate? Extensive bone re-formation completed in less than a day? Christ, not even the most malignant cancer cells in their most furious stages of unchecked reproduction could match that pace!

For a moment he was exhilarated, certain that his experiment had proved a far greater success than he had hoped. Then he realized that his thoughts were still confused, that his memory was still tattered, even though his brain tissue must have healed as thoroughly as his skull had done. Did that mean that his intellect and clarity of mind would never be fully restored, even if his tissues were repaired? That prospect frightened him, especially as he again saw his uncle Barry Hampstead, long dead, standing over in the corner, beside a crackling pillar of shadow-fire.

Perhaps, though he had come back from the land of the dead, he would always remain, in part, a dead man, regardless of his miraculous new genetic structure.

No. He did not want to believe that, for it would mean that all his labors, plans, and risks were for nothing.

In the corner, Uncle Barry grinned and said, "Come kiss me, Eric. Come show me that you love me."

Perhaps death was more than the cessation of physical and mental activity. Perhaps some other quality was lost . . . a quality of spirit that could not be reanimated as successfully as flesh and blood and brain activity.

Almost of its own volition, his questing hand moved tremblingly from the side of his head to his brow, where the recent explosion of pain had been centered. He felt something odd. Something *wrong*. His forehead was no longer a smooth plate of bone. It was lumpy, knotted. Strange excrescences had arisen in an apparently random pattern.

He heard a mewling sound of pure terror, and at first he did not realize that he had made the noise himself.

The bone over each eye was far thicker than it should have been.

And a smooth knot of bone, almost an inch high, had appeared at his right temple.

How? My God, how?

As he explored the upper portion of his face in the manner of a blind man seeking an impression of a stranger's appearance, crystals of icy dread formed in him.

A narrow gnarled ridge of bone had appeared down the center of his forehead, extending to the bridge of his nose.

He felt thick, pulsing arteries along his hairline, where there should have been no such vessels.

He could not stop mewling, and hot tears sprang to his eyes.

Even in his clouded mind, the terrifying truth of the situation was evident. Technically, his genetically modified body had been killed by his brutal encounter with the garbage truck, but life of a kind had been maintained on a cellular level, and his edited genes, functioning on a mere trickle of life force, had sent urgent signals through his cooling tissues to command the amazingly rapid production of all substances needed for regeneration and rejuvenation. And now that repairs had been made, his altered genes were not switching off the frantic growth. Something was wrong. The genetic switches were staying open. His body was frenetically adding bone and flesh and blood, and though the new tissues were probably perfectly healthy, the process had become something like a cancer, though the rate of growth far outstripped that of even the most virulent cancer cells.

His body was re-forming itself.

But into what?

His heart was hammering, and he had broken into a cold sweat.

He pushed up from the armchair. He had to get to a mirror. He had to see his face.

He did not want to see it, was repelled by the thought of what he would find, was scared of discovering a grotesquely alien reflection in the mirror, but at the same time he urgently had to know what he was becoming.

■ In the sporting-goods store by the lake, Ben chose a Remington semi-automatic 12-gauge shotgun with a five-round magazine. Properly handled, it could be a devastating weapon—and he knew how to handle it. He picked up two boxes of shells for the shotgun, plus one box of ammunition for the Smith & Wesson .357 Combat Magnum that he had taken off Baresco, and another box for Rachael's .32-caliber pistol.

They looked as if they were preparing for war.

Although no permit or waiting period was required when purchasing a shot-gun—as was the case with a handgun—Ben had to fill out a form, divulging his name, address, and Social Security number, then provide the clerk with proof of identity, preferably a California driver's license with a laminated photograph. While Ben stood at the yellow Formica counter with Rachael, completing the form, the clerk—"Call me Sam," he'd said, when he had shown them the shop's gun selection—excused himself and went to the north end of the room to assist a group of fishermen who had questions about several fly rods.

The second clerk was with another customer at the south end of the long room, carefully explaining the differences among types of sleeping bags.

Behind the counter, on a wall shelf, beside a large display of cellophane-wrapped packages of beef jerky, stood a radio tuned to a Los Angeles AM station. While Ben and Rachael had selected a shotgun and ammunition, only pop music and commercials had issued from the radio. But now the twelve-thirty news report was under way, and suddenly Ben heard his own name, and Rachael's, coming over the airwaves.

" . . . *Shadway and Rachael Leben on a federal warrant. Mrs. Leben is the wife of the wealthy entrepreneur Eric Leben, who was killed in a traffic accident yesterday. According to a Justice Department spokesman, Shadway and Mrs. Leben are wanted in connection with the theft of highly sensitive, top-secret research files from several Geneplan Corporation projects funded by the Department of Defense, as well as for suspicion of murder in the case of two Palm Springs police officers killed last night in a brutal machine-gun attack.*"

Rachael heard it too. "That's crazy!"

Putting one hand on her arm to quiet her, Ben glanced nervously at the two clerks, who were still busy elsewhere in the store, talking to other customers. The last thing Ben wanted was to draw their attention to the news report. The clerk named Sam had already seen Ben's driver's license before pulling a firearms information form from the file. He knew Ben's name, and if he heard it on the radio, he was almost certain to react to it.

Protestations of innocence would be of no use. Sam would call the cops. He might even have a gun behind the counter, under the cash register, and might try to use it to keep Ben and Rachael there until the police arrived, and Ben did not want to have to take a gun away from him and maybe hurt him in the process.

"Jarrod McClain, director of the Defense Security Agency, who is coordinating the investigation and the manhunt for Shadway and Mrs. Leben, issued a statement to the press in Washington within the past hour, calling the case 'a matter of grave concern that can reasonably be described as a national security crisis.' "

Sam, over in the fishing-gear department, laughed at something a customer said—and started back toward the cash register. One of the fishermen was coming with him. They were talking animatedly, so if the news report was registering with them, it was getting through, at best, on only a subconscious level. But if they stopped talking before the report concluded . . .

"Though asserting that Shadway and Mrs. Leben have seriously damaged their country's security, neither McClain nor the Justice Department spokesman would specify the nature of the research being done by Geneplan for the Pentagon."

The two approaching men were twenty feet away, still discussing the merits of various brands of fly rods and spinning reels.

Rachael was staring at them apprehensively, and Ben bumped lightly against her to distract her, lest her expression alert them to the significance of the news on the radio.

" . . . recombinant DNA as Geneplan's sole business . . . "

Sam rounded the end of the sales counter. The customer's course paralleled that of the clerk, and they continued talking across the yellow Formica as they approached Rachael and Ben.

"Photographs and descriptions of Benjamin Shadway and Rachael Leben have gone out to all police agencies in California and most of the Southwest, along with a federal advisory that the fugitives are armed and dangerous."

Sam and the fisherman reached the cash register, where Ben turned his attention back to the government form.

The newscaster had moved on to another story.

Ben was startled and delighted to hear Rachael launch smoothly into a line of bubbly patter, engaging the fisherman's attention. The guy was tall, burly, in his fifties, wearing a black T-shirt that exposed his beefy arms, both of which featured elaborate blue-and-red tattoos. Rachael professed to be simply fascinated by tattoos, and the angler, like most men, was flattered and pleased by the gushy attention of a beautiful young woman. Anyone listening to Rachael's charming and slightly witless chatter—for she assumed the attitude of a California beach girl airhead—would never have suspected that she had just listened to a radio reporter describe her as a fugitive wanted for murder.

The same slightly pompous-sounding reporter was currently talking about a terrorist bombing in the Mideast, and Sam, the clerk, clicked a knob on the radio, cutting him off in midsentence. "I'm plain sick of hearing about those damn 'A-rabs,' " he said to Ben.

"Who isn't?" Ben said, completing the last line of the form.

"Far as I'm concerned," Sam said, "if they give us any more grief, we should just nuke 'em and be done with it."

"Nuke 'em," Ben agreed. "Back to the Stone Age."

The radio was part of the tape deck, and Sam switched that on, popped in a cassette. "Have to be farther back than the Stone Age. They're *already* living in the damn Stone Age."

"Nuke 'em back to the Age of Dinosaurs," Ben said as a song by the Oak Ridge Boys issued from the cassette player.

Rachael was making astonished and squeamish sounds as the fisherman told her how the tattoo needles embedded the ink way down beneath all three layers of skin.

"Age of the Dinosaurs," Sam agreed. "Let 'em try their terrorist crap on a tyrannosaurus, huh?"

Ben laughed and handed over the completed form.

The purchases had already been charged to Ben's Visa card, so all Sam had to do was staple the charge slip and the cash-register tape to one copy of the firearms information form and put the paperwork in the bag that held the four boxes of ammunition. "Come see us again."

"I'll sure do that," Ben said.

Rachael said good-bye to the tattooed fisherman, and Ben said hello *and* good-bye to him, and they both said good-bye to Sam. Ben carried the box containing the shotgun, and Rachael carried the plastic sack that contained the boxes of ammunition, and they moved nonchalantly across the room toward the front door, past stacks of aluminum bait buckets with perforated Styrofoam liners, past furled minnow-seining nets and small landing nets that looked like tennis rackets with badly stretched strings, past ice chests and thermos bottles and colorful fishing hats.

Behind them, in a voice that he believed to be softer than it actually was, the tattooed fisherman said to Sam: "Quite a woman."

You don't know the half of it, Ben thought as he pushed open the door for Rachael and followed her outside.

Less than ten feet away, a San Bernardino County sheriff's deputy was getting out of a patrol car.

■   Fluorescent light bounced off the green and white ceramic tile, bright enough to reveal every hideous detail, too bright.

The bathroom mirror, framed in brass, was unmarred by spots or yellow streaks of age, and the reflections it presented were crisp and sharp and clear in every detail, too clear.

Eric Leben was not surprised by what he saw, for while sitting in the living-room armchair, he had already hesitantly used his hands to explore the startling changes in the upper portions of his face. But visual confirmation of what his disbelieving hands had told him was shocking, frightening, depressing—and more fascinating than anything else he'd seen in his entire life.

A year ago, he had subjected himself to the imperfect Wildcard program of genetic editing and augmentation. Since then, he had caught no colds, no flu, had been plagued by no mouth ulcers or headaches, not even acid indigestion. Week by week, he had gathered evidence supporting the contention that the treatment had wrought a desirable change in him without negative side effects.

Side effects.

He almost laughed. Almost.

Staring in horror at the mirror, as if it were a window onto hell, he raised one trembling hand to his forehead and touched, again, the narrow rippled ridge of bone that had risen from the bridge of his nose to his hairline.

The catastrophic injuries he had suffered yesterday had triggered his new healing abilities in a way and to a degree that invasive cold and flu viruses had not. Thrown into overdrive, his cells had begun to produce interferon, a wide spectrum of infection-fighting antibodies, and especially growth hormones and proteins, at an astonishing rate. For some reason, those substances were continuing to flood his system after the healing was complete, after the need for them was past. His body was no longer merely replacing damaged tissue but was adding new tissue at an alarming rate, tissue without apparent function.

"No," he said softly, "no," trying to deny what he saw before him. But it was true, and he felt its truth under his fingertips as he explored farther along the top of his head. The strange bony ridge was most prominent on his forehead, but it was on top of his head, as well, beneath his hair, and he even thought he could feel it growing as he traced its course toward the back of his skull.

His body was transforming itself either at random or to some purpose that he could not grasp, and there was no way of knowing when it would finally stop. It might never stop. He might go on growing, changing, reconstituting himself in myriad new images, endlessly. He was metamorphosing into a freak . . . or just possibly, ultimately, into something so utterly alien that it could no longer be called human.

The bony ridge tapered away at the back of his skull. He moved his hand forward again to the thickened shelf of bone above his eyes. It made him look vaguely like a Neanderthal, though Neanderthal man had not had a bony crest up the center of his head. Or a knob of bone at one temple. Nor had Neanderthals— or any other ancestors of humanity—ever featured the huge, swollen blood vessels where they shone darkly and pulsed disgustingly in his brow.

Even in his current degenerative mental condition, with every thought fuzzy at the edges and with his memory clouded, Eric grasped the full and horrible meaning of this development. He would never be able to reenter society in any acceptable capacity. Beyond a doubt, he was his own Frankenstein monster, and he had made—was continuously making—a hopeless and eternal outcast of himself.

His future was so bleak as to give new meaning to the word. He might be captured and survive in a laboratory somewhere, subjected to the stares and probes of countless fascinated scientists, who would surely devise endless tests that would seem like valid and justifiable experiments to them but would be pure and simple torture to him. Or he might flee into the wilderness and somehow make a pathetic life there, giving birth to legends of a new monster, until someday a hunter stumbled across him by accident and brought him down. But no matter which of many terrible fates awaited him, there would be two grim constants: unrelenting fear, not so much fear of what others would do to him, but fear of what his own body was doing to him; and loneliness, a profound and singular loneliness that no other man had ever known or ever would know, for he would be the only one of his kind on the face of the earth.

Yet his despair and terror were at least slightly ameliorated by curiosity, the same powerful curiosity that had made him a great scientist. Studying his hideous reflection, staring at this genetic catastrophe in the making, he was riveted, aware that he was seeing things no man had ever seen. Better yet: things that man had not been *meant* to see. That was an exhilarating feeling. It was what a man like him lived for. Every scientist, to some degree, seeks a glimpse of the great dark mysteries underlying life and hopes to understand what he sees if he is ever given that glimpse. This was more than a glimpse. This was a long, slow look into the enigma of human growth and development, as long a look as he cared to make it, its duration determined only by the extent of his courage.

The thought of suicide flickered only briefly through his mind and then was gone, for the opportunity presented to him was even more important than the certain physical, mental, and emotional anguish that he would endure henceforth. His future would be a strange landscape, shadowed by fear, lit by the lightning of pain, yet he was compelled to journey through it toward an unseen horizon. *He had to find out what he would become.*

Besides, his fear of death had by no means diminished due to these incredible developments. If anything, because he now seemed nearer the grave than at any time in his life, his necrophobia had an even tighter grip on him. No matter what form and quality of life lay ahead of him, he must go on; though his metamorphosis was deeply depressing and bloodcurdling, the alternative to life held even greater terror for him.

As he stared into the mirror, his headache returned.

He thought he saw something new in his eyes.

He leaned closer to the mirror.

Something about his eyes was definitely odd, different, but he could not quite identify the change.

The headache became rapidly more severe. The fluorescent lights bothered him, so he squinted to close out some of the white glare.

He looked away from his own eyes and let his gaze travel over the rest of his reflection. Suddenly he thought he perceived changes occurring along his right temple as well as in the zygomatic bone and zygomatic arch around and under his right eye.

Fear surged through him, purer than any fear he had known thus far, and his heart raced.

His headache now blazed throughout his skull and even down into a substantial portion of his face.

Abruptly he turned away from the mirror. It was difficult though possible to look upon the monstrous changes after they had occurred. But watching the flesh and bone transform itself before his eyes was a far more demanding task, and he possessed neither the fortitude nor the stomach for it.

Crazily he thought of Lon Chaney, Jr., in that old movie, *The Wolfman,* Chaney so appalled by the sight of his lupine metamorphosis that he was overcome by terror of—and pity for—himself. Eric looked at his own large hands, half expecting to see hair sprouting on them. That expectation made him laugh, though as before, his laugh was a harsh and cold and broken sound, utterly humorless, and it quickly turned into a series of wrenching sobs.

His entire head and face were filled with pain now—even his lips stung—and as he lurched out of the bathroom, bumping first into the sink, then colliding with the doorjamb, he made a thin high-pitched keening sound that was, in one note, a symphony of fear and suffering.

■   The San Bernardino County Sheriff's Deputy wore dark sunglasses that concealed his eyes and, therefore, his intentions. However, as the policeman got
out of the patrol car, Ben saw no telltale tension in his body, no indications that
he recognized them as the infamous betrayers of Truth, Justice, and the American
Way, of whom the radio newsman had recently spoken.

Ben took Rachael's arm, and they kept moving.

Within the past few hours, their descriptions and photographs had been wired
to all police agencies in California and the Southwest, but that did not mean they
were every lawman's first priority.

The deputy seemed to be staring at them.

But not all cops were sufficiently conscientious to study the latest bulletins
before hitting the road, and those who had gone on duty early this morning, as
this man might have done, would have left before Ben's and Rachael's photographs had been posted.

"Excuse me," the deputy said.

Ben stopped. Through the hand he had on Rachael's arm, he felt her stiffen.
He tried to stay loose, smile. "Yes, sir?"

"That your Chevy pickup?"

Ben blinked. "Uh . . . no. Not mine."

"Got a taillight busted out," the deputy said, taking off his sunglasses, revealing
eyes free of suspicion.

"We're driving that Ford," Ben said.

"You know who owns the truck?"

"Nope. Probably one of the other customers in there."

"Well, you folks have a nice day, enjoy our beautiful mountains," the deputy
said, moving past them and into the sporting-goods store.

Ben tried not to run straight to the car, and he sensed that Rachael was resisting
a similar urge. Their measured stroll was almost too nonchalant.

The eerie stillness, so complete when they had arrived, was gone, and the day
was full of movement. Out on the water, an outboard motor buzzed like a swarm
of hornets. A breeze had sprung up, coming in off the blue lake, rustling the trees,
stirring the grass and weeds and wildflowers. A few cars passed on the state route,
rock and roll blaring through the open windows of one of them.

They reached the rental Ford in the cool shadows of the pines.

Rachael pulled her door shut, winced at the loud *chunk* it made, as if the sound
would draw the deputy back. Her green eyes were wide with apprehension. "Let's
get out of here."

"You got it," he said, starting the engine.

"We can find another place, more private, where you can unpack the shotgun
and load it."

They pulled out onto the two-lane blacktop that encircled the lake, heading
north. Ben kept checking the rearview mirror. No one was following them; his
fear that their pursuers were right on their tail was irrational, paranoid. He kept
checking the mirror anyway.

The lake lay on their left and below them, glimmering, and the mountains rose
on their right. In some areas, houses stood on large plots of forested land. Some

were magnificent, almost country-style mansions, and others were neatly kept but humble summer cottages. In other places, the land was either government-owned or too steep to provide building sites, and the wilderness encroached in a weedy and brambled tangle of trees. A lot of dry brush had built up, too, and signs warned of the fire danger, an annual summer-autumn threat throughout southern California. The road snaked and rolled, climbed and fell, through alternating patches of shade and golden sunlight.

After a couple of minutes, Rachael said, "They can't really believe we stole defense secrets."

"No," Ben agreed.

"I mean, I didn't even know Geneplan *had* defense contracts."

"That's not what they're worried about. It's a cover story."

"Then why *are* they so eager to get their hands on us?"

"Because we know that Eric has . . . come back."

"And you think the government knows, too?" she asked.

"You said the Wildcard project was a closely held secret. The only people who knew were Eric, his partners in Geneplan, and you."

"That's right."

"But if Geneplan had its hand in the Pentagon's pocket on other projects, then you can bet the Pentagon knew everything worth knowing about the owners of Geneplan and what they were up to. You can't accept lucrative top-secret research work and at the same time hold on to your privacy."

"That makes sense," she said. "But Eric might not have realized it. Eric believed he could have the best of everyone, all the time."

A road sign warned of a dip in the pavement. Ben braked, and the Ford jolted over a rough patch, springs squeaking, frame rattling.

When they came through to smoother blacktop, he said, "So the Pentagon knew enough about Wildcard to realize what Eric had done to himself when his body disappeared from the morgue. And now they want to contain the story, keep the secret, because they see it as a weapon or, at least, as a source of tremendous power."

"Power?"

"If perfected, the Wildcard process might mean immortality to those who undergo treatment. So the people who control Wildcard will decide who lives forever and who doesn't. Can you imagine any better weapon, any better tool with which to establish political control of the whole damn world?"

Rachael was silent awhile. Then she said softly, "Jesus, I've been so focused on the personal aspects of this, so intent on what it means to *me*, that I haven't looked at it from a broader perspective."

"So they have to get hold of us," Ben said.

"They don't want us blowing the secret till Wildcard's perfected. If it were blown first, they couldn't continue research unhampered."

"Exactly. Since you're going to inherit the largest block of stock in Geneplan, the government might figure you can be persuaded to cooperate for the good of your country and for your own gain."

She shook her head. "I couldn't be persuaded. Not about this. For one thing, if there's any hope at all of dramatically extending the human life span and promoting healing through genetic engineering, then the research should be done publicly, and the benefits should be available to everyone. It's immoral to handle it any other way."

"I figured that's how you'd feel," he said, pulling the Ford through a sharp right-hand turn, then sharply to the left again.

"Besides, I couldn't be persuaded to continue research along the same avenue the Wildcard group has been following, because I'm sure it's the wrong route."

"I knew you'd say that," Ben said approvingly.

"Admittedly, I know very little about genetics, but I can see there's just too much danger involved in the approach they're taking. Remember the mice I told you about. And remember . . . the blood in the trunk of the car at the house in Villa Park."

He remembered, which was one reason he had wanted the shotgun.

She said, "If I took control of Geneplan, I might want to fund continued longevity research, but I'd insist on scrapping Wildcard and starting fresh from a new direction."

"I knew you'd say that, too," Ben told her, "and I figure the government also has a pretty good idea what you'd say. So I don't have much hope that they just want a chance to persuade you. If they know anything about you—and as Eric's wife, you've got to be in their files—then they know you couldn't be bribed or threatened into doing something you thought was really wrong, couldn't be corrupted. So they probably won't even bother trying."

"It's my Catholic upbringing," she said with a touch of irony. "A very stern, strict, religious family, you know."

He didn't know. This was the first she had ever spoken of it.

Softly she said, "And very early, I was sent to a boarding school for girls, administrated by nuns. I grew to hate it . . . the endless Masses . . . the humiliation of the confessional, revealing my pathetic little sins. But I guess it shaped me for the better, huh? Might not be so all-fired incorruptible if I hadn't spent all those years in the hands of the good sisters."

He sensed that these revelations were but a twig on an immense and perhaps ugly tree of grim experience.

He glanced away from the road for a second, wanting to see her expression. But he was foiled by the constantly, rapidly changing mosaic of tree shadows and sunlight that came through the windshield and dappled her countenance. There was an illusion of fire, and her face was only half revealed to him, half hidden beyond the shifting and shimmering curtain of those phantom flames.

Sighing, she said, "Okay, so if the government knows it can't persuade me, why's it issuing warrants on a bunch of trumped-up charges and putting so much manpower into the search for me?"

"They want to kill you," Ben said bluntly.

"*What?*"

"They'd rather get you out of the picture and deal with Eric's partners, Knowls and Seitz and the others, because they already know those men are corruptible."

She was shocked, and he was not surprised by her shock. She was not unworldly or terribly naive. But she was, by choice, a present-focused person who had given little thought to the complexities of the changing world around her, except when that world impinged upon her primary desire to wring as much pleasure as possible from the moment. She accepted a variety of myths as a matter of convenience, as a way of simplifying her life, and one myth was that her government would always have her best interests at heart, whether the issue was war, a reform of the justice system, increased taxation, or anything else. She was apolitical and saw no reason to be concerned about who might win—or usurp—the power flowing from the ballot box, for it was easy to believe in the benign intentions of those who so ardently desired to serve the public.

She gaped in astonishment at him. He did not even have to see that expression through the flickering light and shadow to know it held tenancy of her face, for he sensed it in the change in her breathing and in the greater tension that suddenly gripped her and caused her to sit up straighter.

"Kill me? No, no, Benny. The U.S. government just executing civilians as if this were some banana republic? No, surely not."

"Not necessarily the whole government, Rachael. The House, Senate, president, and cabinet secretaries haven't held meetings to discuss the obstacle you pose, haven't conspired by the hundreds to terminate you. But someone in the Pentagon or the DSA or the CIA has determined that you're standing in the way of the national interest, that you pose a threat to the welfare of millions of citizens. When they weigh the welfare of millions against one or two little murders, the choice is clear to them, as it always is to collectivist thinkers. One or two little murders—tens of *thousands* of murders—are always justifiable when the welfare of the masses is at stake. At least, that's how they see it, even if they do pretend to believe in the sanctity of the individual. So they can order one or two little murders and even feel righteous about it."

"Dear God," she said with feeling. "What have I dragged you into, Benny?"

"You didn't drag me into anything," he said. "I forced my way in. You couldn't keep me out of it. And I've no regrets."

She seemed unable to speak.

Ahead, on the left, a branch road led down to the lake. A sign announced: LAKE APPROACH—BOAT LAUNCHING FACILITIES.

Ben turned off the state route and followed the narrower gravel road down through a crowd of immense trees. In a quarter of a mile, he drove out of the trees, into a sixty-foot-wide, three-hundred-foot-long open area by the shore. Sequins of sunlight decorated the lake in some places, and serpentine streams of sunlight wriggled across the shifting surface in other places, and here and there brilliant shafts bounced off the waves and dazzled the eye.

More than a dozen cars, pickups, and campers were parked at the far end of the clearing, several with empty boat trailers behind them. A big recreational pickup—black with red and gray stripes, bedecked with gobs of sun-heated chrome—was backed up near the water's edge, and three men were launching a twenty-four-foot twin-engine Water King from their trailer. Several people were eating lunch at picnic tables near the shore, and an Irish setter was sniffing under a table in search of scraps, and two young boys were tossing a football back and forth, and eight or ten fishermen were tending their poles along the bank.

They all looked as if they were enjoying themselves. If any of them realized the world beyond this pleasant haven was turning dark and going mad, he was keeping it to himself.

Benny drove to the parking area but tucked the Ford in by the edge of the forest, as far from the other vehicles as he could get. He switched off the engine and rolled down his window. He put his seat back as far as it would go in order to give himself room to work, took the shotgun box on his lap, opened it, withdrew the gun, and threw the empty box into the back seat.

"Keep a watch out," he told Rachael. "You see anybody coming, let me know. I'll get out and meet him. Don't want anybody to see the shotgun and be spooked. It's sure as hell not hunting season."

"Benny, what're we going to do?"

"Just what we planned to do," he said, using one of the car keys to slit the shrink-wrapped plastic in which the shotgun was encased. "Follow the directions Sarah Kiel gave you, find Eric's cabin, and see if he's there."

"But the warrants for our arrest . . . people wanting to kill us . . . doesn't that change everything?"

"Not much." He discarded the shredded plastic and looked the gun over. It came fully assembled, a nice piece of work, and it felt good and reliable in his hands. "Originally we wanted to get to Eric and finish him before he healed entirely and came looking to finish *you*. Now maybe what we'll have to do is capture him instead of kill him—"

"Take him alive?" Rachael said, alarmed by that suggestion.

"Well, he's not exactly alive, is he? But I think we're going to have to take him in whatever condition he's in, tie him up, drive him someplace like . . . well, someplace like the offices of the *Los Angeles Times*. Then we can hold a real shocker of a press conference."

"Oh, Benny, no, no, we can't." She shook her head adamantly. "That's crazy. He's going to be violent, extremely violent. I told you about the mice. You saw the blood in the trunk of the car, for God's sake. The destruction everywhere he's been, the knives in the wall of the Palm Springs house, the beating he gave Sarah. We can't risk getting close to him. He won't respect the gun, if that's what you're thinking. He won't have any fear of it at all. You get close enough to try to capture him, and he'll take your head off in spite of the gun. He might even have a gun of his own. No, no, if we see him, we've got to finish him right away, shoot him without any hesitation, shoot him again and again, do so much damage to him that he won't be able to *come back* again."

A panicky note had entered her voice, and she had spoken faster and faster as she strove to convince Ben. Her skin was powder-white, and her lips had acquired a bluish tint. She was shivering.

Even considering their precarious situation and the admittedly hideous nature of their quarry, her fear seemed too great to Ben, and he wondered how much her reaction to Eric's resurrection was heightened by the ultrareligious childhood that had formed her. Without fully understanding her own feelings, perhaps she was afraid of Eric not merely because she knew his potential for violence, and not merely because he was a walking dead man, but because he had dared to seize the power of God by defeating death and thereby had become not simply a zombie but some hellborn creature returned from the realm of the damned.

Forgetting the shotgun for a moment, taking both her hands in his, he said, "Rachael, honey, I can handle him; I've handled worse than him, much worse—"

"Don't be so confident! That's what'll get you killed."

"I'm trained for war, well trained to take care of myself—"

"Please!"

"And I've kept in top shape all these years because Nam taught me that the world can turn dark and mean overnight and that you can't count on anything but yourself and your closest friends. That was a nasty lesson about the modern world that I didn't want to admit I'd learned, which is why I've spent so much time immersed in the past. But the very fact that I've kept in shape and kept practicing my fighting skills is proof of the lesson. Tip-top shape, Rachael. And I'm well armed." He hushed her when she tried to object. "We have no choice, Rachael. That's what it comes down to. No other choice. If we just kill him, blast the sucker with twenty or thirty rounds from the shotgun, kill him so bad he stays dead for good this time—then we have no proof of what he did to himself. We just have a corpse. Who could prove he'd been reanimated? It'd look as if we stole his body from the morgue, pumped it full of buckshot, and concocted this crazy story, maybe concocted it to cover the very crimes the government is accusing us of."

"Lab tests of his cell structure would prove something," Rachael said. "Examination of his genetic material—"

"That would take weeks. Before then, the government would've found a way to claim the body, eliminate us, and doctor the test results to show nothing out of the ordinary."

She started to speak, hesitated, and stopped because she was obviously beginning to realize that he was right. She looked more forlorn than any woman he had ever seen.

He said, "Our only hope of getting the government off our backs is to get proof of Wildcard and break the story to the press. The only reason they want to kill us is to keep the secret, so when the secret is blown, we'll be safe. Since we didn't get the Wildcard file from Eric's office safe, Eric himself is the only proof we have a chance of putting our hands on. And we need him alive. They need to see him breathing, functioning, in spite of his staved-in head. They need to *see* the change in him that you suspect there'll be—the irrational rages, the sullen quality of the living dead."

She swallowed hard. She nodded. "All right. Okay. But I'm so scared."

"You can be strong; you have it in you."

"I know I do. I know. But . . . "

He leaned forward and gave her a kiss.

Her lips were icy.

■   Eric groaned and opened his eyes.

Evidently he had descended once more into a short period of suspended animation, a minor but deep coma, for he slowly regained consciousness on the floor of the living room, sprawled among at least a hundred sheets of typing paper. His splitting headache was gone, although a peculiar burning sensation extended from the top of his skull downward to his chin, all across his face, and in most of his muscles and joints as well, in shoulders and arms and legs. It was not an unpleasant burning, and not pleasant either, just a neutral sensation unlike anything he had felt before.

I'm like a candy man, made of chocolate, sitting on a sun-washed table, melting, melting, but melting from the *inside.*

For a while he just lay there, wondering where the weird thought had come from. He was disoriented, dizzy. His mind was a swamp in which unconnected thoughts burst like stinking bubbles on the watery surface. Gradually the water cleared a bit and the soupy mud of the swamp grew somewhat firmer.

Pushing up to a sitting position, he looked at the papers strewn around him and could not remember what they were. He picked up a few and tried to read them. The blurry letters would not at first resolve into words; then the words would not form coherent sentences. When at last he could read a bit, he could understand only a fraction of what he read, but he could grasp enough to realize that this was the third paper copy of the Wildcard file.

In addition to the project data stored in the Geneplan computers, there had been one hard-copy file in Riverside, one in his office safe at the headquarters in Newport Beach, and a third here. The cabin was his secret retreat, known only to him, and it had seemed prudent to keep a fully updated file in the hidden basement safe, as insurance against the day when Seitz and Knowls—the money men behind his work—tried to take the corporation away from him through clever financial maneuvering. That anticipated treachery was unlikely because they needed him, needed his genius, and would most likely still need him when Wildcard was perfected. But he was not a man who took chances. (Other than the one big chance, when he had injected himself with the devil's brew that was turning his body into pliable clay.) He had not wanted to risk being booted out of Geneplan and finding himself cut off from data crucial to the production of the immortality serum.

Evidently, after stumbling out of the bathroom, he had gone down to the basement, had opened the safe, and had brought the file up here for perusal. What had he been seeking? An explanation for what was happening to him? A way to undo the changes that had occurred—that were *still* occurring—in him?

That was pointless. These monstrous developments had been unanticipated. Nothing in the file would refer to the possibility of runaway growth or point the way to salvation. He must have been seized by delirium, for only in such a state would he have bothered to pursue a magic cure in this pile of Xeroxes.

He knelt in the scattered papers for a minute or two, preoccupied by the strange though painless burning sensation that filled his body, trying to understand its source and meaning. In some places—along his spine, across the top of his head, at the base of his throat, in his testicles—the heat was accompanied by an eerie tingle. He almost felt as if a billion fire ants had made their home within him and were moving by the millions through his veins and arteries and through a maze of tunnels they had burrowed in his flesh and bone.

Finally he got to his feet, and a fierce anger rose in him for no specific reason, and with no particular target. He kicked out furiously, stirring up a briefly airborne, noisy cloud of papers.

A frightening rage seethed under the surface of the mindswamp, and he was just perceptive enough to realize that it was in some way quite different from the previous rages to which he had succumbed. This one was . . . even more primal, less focused, less of a *human* rage, more like the irrationally churning fury of an animal. He felt as if some deeply buried racial memory were asserting itself, something crawling up out of the genetic pit, up from ten million years ago, up from the faraway time when men were only apes, or from a time even farther removed than that, from an unthinkably ancient age when men were as yet only amphibian creatures crawling painfully onto a volcanic shore and breathing air for the first time. It was a cold rage instead of hot like the ones before it, as cold as the heart of the Arctic, a billion years of coldness . . . reptilian. Yes, that was the feel of it, an icy reptilian rage, and when he began to grasp its nature, he recoiled from further consideration of it and desperately hoped that he would be able to keep it under control.

The mirror.

He was certain that changes had taken place in him while he had been unconscious on the living-room floor, and he knew he should go into the bathroom and look at himself in the mirror. But suddenly he was shaken anew by fear of what he was becoming, and he could not find the courage to take even one step in that direction.

Instead, he decided to employ the Braille approach by which he had previously discovered the first alterations in his face. Feeling the differences before seeing them would prepare him somewhat for the shock of his appearance. Hesitantly he raised his hands to explore his face but did not get that far because he saw that his *hands* were changing, and he was arrested by the sight of them.

They were not radically different hands from what they had been, but they were unquestionably not his hands anymore, not the hands he had used all his life. The fingers were longer and thinner, perhaps a whole inch longer, with fleshier pads at the tips. The nails were different, too: thicker, harder, yellowish, more pointed than ordinary fingernails. They were nascent claws, damned if they weren't, and if the metamorphosis continued, they would probably develop into even more pointed, hooked, and razor-sharp talons. His knuckles were changing, too—larger, bonier, almost like arthritic knuckles.

He expected to find his hands stiff and less usable than they had been, but to his surprise the altered knuckles worked easily, fluidly, and proved superior to the knuckles out of which they had grown. He worked his hands experimentally and discovered that he was incredibly dexterous; his elongated fingers possessed a new suppleness and startling flexibility.

And he sensed that the changes were continuing unchecked, though not fast enough for him to actually see the bones growing and the flesh remaking itself. But by tomorrow his hands would surely be far more radically changed than they were now.

This was electrifyingly different from the apparent random, tumorlike excrescences of bone and tissue that had formed across his forehead. These hands were not just the result of an excess of growth hormones and proteins. This growth had purpose, direction. In fact, he suddenly noticed that on both hands, between thumb and forefinger, below the first knuckle of each digit, translucent webs had begun to fill in the empty space.

Reptilian. Like the cold rage that he knew would (if he let it) erupt in a frenzy of destruction. Reptilian.

He lowered his hands, afraid to look at them anymore.

He no longer had the courage to explore the contours of his face, not even by touch. The mere prospect of looking into a mirror filled him with dread.

His heart was hammering, and with each thunderous beat, it seemed to pound spikes of fear and loneliness into him.

For a moment he was utterly lost, confused, directionless. He turned left, then right, took a step in one direction, then in another, the Wildcard papers crunching like dead leaves under his feet. Not sure what to do or where to go, he stopped and stood with shoulders slumped, head hung low under a weight of despair—

—until suddenly the weird burning in his flesh and the eerie tingle along his spine were supplemented with a new sensation: hunger. His stomach growled, and his knees grew weak, and he started to shake with hunger. He began to work his mouth and to swallow continuously, involuntarily, hard swallows that almost hurt, as if his body were *demanding* to be fed. He headed toward the kitchen, his shakes getting worse with every step, his knees growing weaker. The sweat of need poured from him in streams, in rivers. A hunger unlike anything he had ever known before. Rabid hunger. Painful. Tearing at him. His vision clouded, and his thoughts funneled down toward one subject: food. The macabre changes taking place in him would require a great deal more fuel than usual, energy for tearing down old tissues, building blocks with which to construct new tissues—yes, of course—his metabolism was running wild, like a great furnace out of control, a raging fire, it had broken down and assimilated the Farmer John sausage-and-biscuit sandwiches that he had eaten earlier, and it needed more, much more, so by the time he opened the cupboard doors and began pulling cans of soup and stew from the shelves, he was wheezing and gasping, muttering wordlessly, grunting like a savage or a wild beast, sickened and repelled by his loss of control but too hungry to worry about it, frightened but hungry, despairing but so hungry, hungry, hungry . . .

■   Following the directions Sarah Kiel had given Rachael, Ben turned off the state route onto a narrow, poorly maintained macadam lane that climbed a steep slope. The lane led deeper into the forest, where the deciduous trees gave way entirely to evergreens, many of which were ancient and huge. They drove half a mile, passing widely separated driveways that served houses and summer cottages. A couple of structures were fully visible, though most could barely be seen between the trees or were entirely hidden by foliage and forest shadows.

The farther they went, the less the sun intruded upon the forest floor, and Rachael's mood darkened at the same rate as the landscape. She held the thirty-two pistol in her lap and peered anxiously ahead.

The pavement ended, but the road continued with a gravel surface for more than another quarter of a mile. They passed just two more driveways, plus two Dodge Chargers and a small motor home parked in a lay-by near one driveway, before coming to a closed gate. Made of steel pipe, painted sky blue, and padlocked, the gate was unattached to any fence and served only to limit vehicular access to the road beyond, which further declined in quality from gravel to dirt.

Wired securely to the center of the barrier, a black-and-red sign warned:

NO TRESPASSING
PRIVATE PROPERTY

"Just like Sarah told you," Ben said.

Beyond the gate lay Eric Leben's property, his secret retreat. The cabin was not visible, for it was another quarter of a mile up the mountainside, entirely screened by trees from this angle.

"It's still not too late to turn back," Rachael said.

"Yes, it is," Ben said.

She bit her lip and nodded grimly. She carefully switched off the double safeties on her pistol.

■ Eric used the electric opener to take the lid off a large can of Progresso minestrone, realized he needed a pot in which to heat it, but was shaking too badly to wait any longer, so he just drank the cold soup out of the can, threw the can aside, wiping absentmindedly at the broth that dripped off his chin. He kept no fresh food in the cabin, only a few frozen things, mostly canned goods, so he opened a family-size Dinty Moore beef stew, and he ate that cold, too, all of it, so fast he kept choking on it.

He chewed the beef with something akin to manic glee, taking a strangely intense pleasure from the tearing and rending of the meat between his teeth. It was a pleasure unlike any he had experienced before—primal, savage—and it both delighted and frightened him.

Although the stew was fully cooked, requiring only reheating, and although it was laden with spices and preservatives, Eric could smell the traces of blood remaining in the beef. Though the blood content was minuscule and thoroughly cooked, Eric perceived it not merely as a vague scent but as a strong, nearly overpowering odor, a thrilling and thoroughly delicious organic *incense*, which caused him to shudder with excitement. He breathed deeply and was dizzied by the blood fragrance, and on his tongue it was ambrosian.

When he finished the cold beef stew, which took only a couple of minutes, he opened a can of chili and ate that even more quickly, then another can of soup, chicken noodle this time, and finally he began to take the sharp edge off his hunger. He unscrewed the lid from a jar of peanut butter, scooped some out with his fingers, and ate it. He did not like it as well as he liked the meat, but he knew it was good for him, rich in the nutrients that his racing metabolism required. He consumed more, cleaned out most of the jar, then threw it aside and stood for a moment, gasping for breath, exhausted from eating.

The queer, painless fire continued to burn in him, but the hunger had substantially abated.

Out of the corner of his eye, he saw his uncle Barry Hampstead sitting in a chair at the small kitchen table, grinning at him. This time, instead of ignoring the phantom, Eric turned toward it, took a couple of steps closer, and said, "What do you want here, you son of a bitch?" His voice was gravelly, not at all like it had once been. "What're you grinning at, you goddamn pervert? You get the hell out of here."

Uncle Barry actually began to fade away, although that was not surprising: He was only an illusion born of degenerated brain cells.

Unreal flames, feeding on shadows, danced in the darkness beyond the cellar door, which Eric had evidently left open when he had come back upstairs with the Wildcard file. He watched the shadowfires. As before, he felt some mystery beckoning, and he was afraid. However, emboldened by his success in chasing away Barry Hampstead's shade, he started toward the flickering red and silver flames, figuring either to dispel them or to see, at last, what lay within them.

Then he remembered the armchair in the living room, the window, the lookout he had been keeping. He had been distracted from that important task by a chain of events: the unusually brutal headache, the changes he had felt in his face, the macabre reflection in the mirror, the Wildcard file, his sudden crippling hunger, Uncle Barry's apparition, and now the false fires beyond the cellar door. He could not concentrate on one thing for any length of time, and he cried out in frustration at this latest evidence of mental dysfunction.

He moved back across the kitchen, kicking aside an empty Dinty Moore beef stew can and a couple of soup cans, heading for the living room and his abandoned guardpost.

Reeeeee, reeeeee, reeeeee . . . the one-note songs of the cicadas, monotonous to the human ear but most likely rich in meaning to other insects, echoed shrilly yet hollowly through the high forest.

Standing beside the rental car, keeping a wary eye on the woods around them, Ben distributed four extra shotgun shells and eight extra rounds for the Combat Magnum in the pockets of his jeans.

Rachael emptied out her purse and filled it with three boxes of ammunition, one for each of their guns. That was surely an excessive supply—but Ben did not suggest that she take any less.

He carried the shotgun under one arm. Given the slightest provocation, he could swing it up and fire in a fraction of a second.

Rachael carried the thirty-two pistol and the Combat Magnum, one in each hand. She wanted Ben to carry both the Remington and the .357, but he could not handle both efficiently, and he preferred the shotgun.

They moved off into the brush just far enough to slip around the padlocked gate, returning to the dirt track on the other side.

Ahead, the road rose under a canopy of pine limbs, flanked by rock-lined drainage ditches bristling with dead dry weeds that had sprung up during the rainy season and withered during the arid spring and summer. About two hundred yards above them, the lane took a sharp turn to the right and disappeared. According to Sarah Kiel, the lane ran straight and true beyond the bend, directly to the cabin, which was approximately another two hundred yards from that point.

"Do you think it's safe to approach right out on the road like this?" Rachael whispered, even though they were still so far from the cabin that their normal speaking voices could not possibly have carried to Eric.

Ben found himself whispering, too. "It'll be okay at least until we reach the bend. As long as we can't see him, he can't see us."

She still looked worried.

He said, "*If* he's even up there."

"He's up there," she said.

"Maybe."

"He's up there," she insisted, pointing to vague tire tracks in the thin layer of dust that covered the hard-packed dirt road.

Ben nodded. He had seen the same thing.

"Waiting," Rachael said.

"Not necessarily."

"Waiting."

"He could be recuperating."

"No."

"Incapacitated."

"No. He's ready for us."

She was probably right about that as well. He sensed the same thing she did: oncoming trouble.

Curiously, though they stood in the shadows of the trees, the nearly invisible scar along her jawline, where Eric had once cut her with a broken glass, was visible, more visible than it usually was in ordinary light. In fact, to Ben, it seemed to glow softly, as if the scar responded to the nearness of the one who had inflicted it, much the way that a man's arthritic joints might alert him to an oncoming storm. Imagination, of course. The scar was no more prominent now than it had been an hour ago. The illusion of prominence was just an indication of how much he feared losing her.

In the car, on the drive up from the lake, he had tried his best to persuade her to remain behind and let him handle Eric alone. She was opposed to that idea—possibly because she feared losing Ben as much as he feared losing her.

They started up the lane.

Ben looked nervously left and right as they went, uncomfortably aware that the heavily forested mountainside, gloomy even at midday, provided countless hiding places—ambush points—very close to them on both sides.

The air was heavily laced with the odor of evergreen sap, the crisp and appealing fragrance of dry pine needles, and the musty scent of some rotting deadwood.

Reeeeee, reeeeee, reeeeee . . .

■ He had returned to the armchair with a pair of binoculars that he had remembered were in the bedroom closet. Only minutes after settling down at the window, before his dysfunctioning thought processes could take off on yet another tangent, he saw movement two hundred yards below, at the sharp bend in the road. He played with the focus knob, pulling the scene in clearer, and in spite of the depth of the shadows at that point along the lane, he saw the two people in perfect detail: Rachael and the bastard she had been sleeping with, Shadway.

He had not known whom he expected—other than Seitz, Knowls, and the men of Geneplan—but he had certainly not expected Rachael and Shadway. He was stunned and could not imagine how she had learned of this place, though he knew that the answer would be obvious to him if his mind had been functioning normally.

They were crouched along the bank that flanked the road down there, fairly well concealed. But they had to reveal a little of themselves in order to get a good look at the cabin, and what little they revealed was enough for Eric to identify them in the magnified field of the binoculars.

The sight of Rachael enraged him, for she had rejected him, the only woman in his adult life to reject him—the bitch, the ungrateful stinking *bitch!*—and she turned her back on his money, too. Even worse: in the miasmal swamp of his deranged mind, *she* was responsible for his death, had virtually killed him by angering him to distraction and then letting him rush out onto Main Street, into the path of the truck. He could believe she had actually planned his death in order to inherit the very fortune on which she'd claimed to have no designs. Yes, of course, why not? And now there she was with her lover, with the man she had been fucking behind his back, and she had clearly come to finish the job that the garbage truck had started.

They pulled back beyond the bend, but a few seconds later he saw movement in the brush, to the left of the road, and he caught a glimpse of them moving off into the trees. They were going to make a cautious indirect approach.

Eric dropped the binoculars and shoved up from the armchair, stood swaying, in the grip of a rage so great that he almost felt crushed by it. Steel bands tightened across his chest, and for a moment he could not draw his breath. Then the bands snapped, and he sucked in great lungsful of air. He said, "Oh, Rachael, Rachael," in a voice that sounded as if it were echoing up from hell. He liked the sound of it, so he said her name again: "Rachael, Rachael . . . "

From the floor beside the chair, he plucked up the ax.

He realized that he could not handle the ax and both knives, so he chose the butcher's knife and left the other blade behind.

He would go out the back way. Circle around. Slip up on them through the woods. He had the cunning to do it. He felt as if he had been born to stalk and kill.

Hurrying across the living room toward the kitchen, Eric saw an image of himself in his mind's eye: He was ramming the knife deep into her guts, then ripping it upward, tearing open her flat young belly. He made a shrill sound of eagerness and almost fell over the empty soup and stew cans in his haste to reach the back door. He would cut her, cut her, cut. And when she dropped to the ground with the knife in her belly, he would go at her with the ax, use the blunt edge of it first, smashing her bones to splinters, breaking her arms and legs, and then he would turn the wondrous shiny instrument over in his hands—his strange and powerful new hands!—and use the sharp edge.

By the time he reached the rear door and yanked it open and went out of the house, he was in the grip of that reptilian fury that he had feared only a short while ago, a cold and calculating fury, called forth out of genetic memories of inhuman ancestors. Having at last surrendered to that primeval rage, he was surprised to discover that it felt *good.*

22   WAITING FOR THE STONE

JERRY PEAKE SHOULD HAVE BEEN ASLEEP ON HIS FEET, FOR he had been up all night. But seeing Anson Sharp humiliated had revitalized him better than eight hours in the sheets could have. He felt marvelous.

He stood with Sharp in the corridor outside Sarah Kiel's hospital room, waiting for Felsen Kiel to come and tell them what they needed to know. Peake required considerable restraint to keep from laughing at his boss's vindictive grousing about the farmer from Kansas.

"If he wasn't a know-nothing shit-kicker, I'd come down so hard on him that his teeth would still be vibrating next Christmas," Sharp said. "But what's the point, huh? He's just a thick-headed Kansas plowboy who doesn't know any better. No point talking to a brick wall, Peake. No point getting angry with a brick wall."

"Right," Peake said.

Pacing back and forth in front of Sarah's closed door, glowering at the nurses who passed in the corridor, Sharp said, "You know, those farm families way out there on the plains, they get strange 'cause they breed too much among themselves, cousin to cousin, that sort of thing, which makes them more stupid generation by generation. But not only stupid, Peake. That inbreeding makes them stubborn as mules."

"Mr. Kiel sure does seem stubborn," Peake said.

"Just a dim-witted shit-kicker, so what's the point of wasting energy breaking his butt? He wouldn't learn his lesson anyway."

Peake could not risk an answer. He required almost superhuman determination to keep a grin off his face.

Six or eight times during the next half hour, Sharp said, "Besides, it's faster to let *him* get the information out of the girl. She's a dim bulb herself, a drugged-up little whore who's probably had syphilis and clap so often her brain's like oatmeal. I figured it'd take us hours to get anything out of her. But when that shit-kicker came into the room, and I heard the girl say 'Daddy' in that happy-shaky little voice, I knew he'd get out of her what we needed a lot faster than we could get it. Let him do our job for us, I thought."

Jerry Peake marveled at the deputy director's boldness in trying to reshape Peake's perception of what had actually happened in Sarah's room. Then again, maybe Sharp was beginning to believe that he had not backed down and had cleverly manipulated The Stone, getting the best of him. He was fruitcake enough to buy his own lies.

Once, Sharp put a hand on Peake's shoulder, not in a comradely manner but to be sure of his subordinate's attention. "Listen, Peake, don't you get the wrong idea about the way I came on with that little whore. The foul language I used, the threats, the little bit of hurt I caused her when I squeezed her hand . . . the way I touched her . . . didn't mean a thing. Just a technique, you know. A good method for getting quick answers. If this wasn't a national security crisis, I'd never have tried that stuff. But sometimes, in special situations like this, we have to do things for our country that maybe neither we nor our country would ordinarily approve of. We understand each other?"

"Yes, sir. Of course." Surprised by his own ability to fake naïveté and admiration, and to do it convincingly, Peake said, "I'm amazed you'd worry that I'd misunderstand. I'd never have thought of such an approach myself. But the moment you went to work on her . . . well, I knew what you were doing, and I admired your interrogation skills. I see this case as an opportunity, sir. I mean, the chance to work with you, which I figured would be a very valuable learning experience, which it has been—even more valuable than I'd hoped."

For a moment Sharp's marble-hard green eyes fixed on Peake with evident suspicion. Then the deputy director decided to take him at his word, for he relaxed a bit and said, "Good. I'm glad you feel that way, Peake. This is a nasty business sometimes. It can even make you feel dirty now and then, what you have to do, but it's for the country, and that's what we always have to keep in mind."

"Yes, sir. I always keep that in mind."

Sharp nodded and began to pace and grumble again.

But Peake knew that Sharp had enjoyed intimidating and hurting Sarah Kiel and had *immensely* enjoyed touching her. He knew that Sharp was a sadist and a pedophile, for he had seen those dark aspects of his boss surge clearly to the surface in that hospital room. No matter what lies Sharp told him, Jerry Peake was never going to forget what he had seen. Knowing these things about the deputy director gave Peake an enormous advantage—though, as yet, he had absolutely no idea how to benefit from what he had learned.

He had also learned that Sharp was, at heart, a coward. In spite of his bullying ways and impressive physical appearance, the deputy director would back down in a crunch, even against a smaller man like The Stone, as long as the smaller man stood up to him with conviction. Sharp had no compunctions about violence and would resort to it when he thought he was fully protected by his government position or when his adversary was sufficiently weak and unthreatening, but he would back off if he believed he faced the slightest chance of being hurt himself. Possessing that knowledge, Peake had another big advantage, but he did not yet see a way to use that one, either.

Nevertheless, he was confident he would eventually know how to apply the things he had learned. Making well-considered, fair, and effective use of such insights was precisely what a legend did best.

Unaware of having given Peake two good knives, Sharp paced back and forth with the impatience of a Caesar.

The Stone had demanded half an hour alone with his daughter. When thirty minutes had passed, Sharp began to look at his wristwatch more frequently.

After thirty-five minutes, he walked heavily to the door, put a hand against it, started to push inside, hesitated, and turned away. "Hell, give him another few minutes. Can't be easy getting anything coherent out of that spaced-out little whore."

Peake murmured agreement.

The looks that Sharp cast at the closed door became increasingly murderous. Finally, forty minutes after they had left the room at The Stone's insistence, Sharp tried to cover his fear of confrontation with the farmer by saying, "I have to make a few important calls. I'll be at the public phones in the lobby."

"Yes, sir."

Sharp started away, then looked back. "When the shit-kicker comes out of there, he's just going to have to wait for me no matter how long I take, and I don't give a damn how much that upsets him."

"Yes, sir."

"It'll do him good to cool his heels awhile," Sharp said, and he stalked off, head held high, rolling his big shoulders, looking like a very important man, evidently convinced that his dignity was intact.

Jerry Peake leaned against the wall of the corridor and watched the nurses go by, smiling at the pretty ones and engaging them in brief flirtatious conversation when they were not too busy.

Sharp stayed away for twenty minutes, giving The Stone a full hour with Sarah, but when he came back from making his important—probably nonexistent—phone calls, The Stone had still not appeared. Even a coward could explode if pushed too far, and Sharp was furious.

"That lousy dirt-humping hayseed. He can't come in here, reeking of pigshit, and screw up *my* investigation."

He turned away from Peake and started toward Sarah's room.

Before Sharp took two steps, The Stone came out.

Peake had wondered whether Felsen Kiel would look as imposing on second encounter as he had appeared when stepping dramatically into Sarah's room and interrupting Anson Sharp in an act of molestation. To Peake's great satisfaction, The Stone was even more imposing than on the previous occasion. That strong, seamed, weathered face. Those oversized hands, work-gnarled knuckles. An air of unshakable self-possession and serenity. Peake watched with a sort of awe as the man crossed the hallway, as if he were a slab of granite come to life.

"Gentlemen, I'm sorry to keep you waitin'. But, as I'm sure you understand, my daughter and I had a lot of catchin' up to do."

"And as *you* must understand, this is an urgent national security matter," Sharp said, though more quietly than he had spoken earlier.

Unperturbed, The Stone said, "My daughter says you want to know if maybe she has some idea where a fella named Leben is hidin' out."

"That's right," Sharp said tightly.

"She said somethin' about him bein' a livin' dead man, which I can't quite get clear with her, but maybe that was just the drugs talkin' through her. You think?"

"Just the drugs," Sharp said.

"Well, she knows of a certain place he might be," The Stone said. "The fella owns a cabin above Lake Arrowhead, she says. It's a sort of secret retreat for him." He took a folded paper from his shirt pocket. "I've written down these directions." He handed the paper to Peake. To Peake, not to Anson Sharp.

Peake glanced at The Stone's precise, clear handwriting, then passed the paper to Sharp.

"You know," The Stone said, "my Sarah was a good girl up until three years ago, a fine daughter in every way. Then she fell under the spell of a sick person who got her onto drugs, put twisted thoughts in her head. She was only thirteen then, impressionable, vulnerable, easy pickin'."

"Mr. Kiel, we don't have time—"

The Stone pretended not to hear Sharp, even though he was looking directly at him. "My wife and I tried our best to find out who it was that had her spellbound, figured it had to be an older boy at school, but we could never identify him. Then one day, after a year durin' which hell moved right into our home, Sarah up and disappeared, ran off to California to 'live the good life.' That's what she wrote in the note to us, said she wanted to live the good life and that we were unsophisticated country people who didn't know anythin' about the world, said we were full of funny ideas. Like honesty, sobriety, and self-respect, I suppose. These days, lots of folks think those are funny ideas."

"Mr. Kiel—"

"Anyway," The Stone continued, "not long after that, I finally learned who it was corrupted her. A teacher. Can you credit that? A *teacher*, who's supposed to be a figure of respect. New young history teacher. I demanded the school board investigate him. Most of the other teachers rallied round him to fight any investigation 'cause these days a lot of 'em seem to think we exist just to keep our mouths shut and pay their salaries no matter what garbage they want to pump into our children's heads. Two-thirds of the teachers—"

"Mr. Kiel," Sharp said more forcefully, "none of this is of any interest to us, and we—"

"Oh, it'll be of interest when you hear the whole story," The Stone said. "I can assure you."

Peake knew The Stone was not the kind of man who rambled, knew all of this had some purpose, and he was eager to see where it was going to wind up.

"As I was sayin'," The Stone continued, "two-thirds of the teachers and half the town were agin me, like *I* was the troublemaker. But in the end they turned up worse stuff about that history teacher, worse than givin' and sellin' drugs to some of his students, and by the time it was over, they were glad to be shed of him. Then, the day after he was canned, he showed up at the farm, wantin' to go man to man. He was a good-sized fella, but he was on somethin' even then, what you call pot-marijuana or maybe even stronger poison, and it wasn't so hard to handle him. I'm sorry to say I broke both his arms, which is worse than I intended."

Jesus, Peake thought.

"But even that wasn't the end of it, 'cause it turned out he had an uncle was president of the biggest bank in our county, the very same bank has my farm loans. Now, any man who allows personal grudges to interfere with his business judgment is an idiot, but this banker fella was an idiot 'cause he tried to pull a fast one to teach me a lesson, tried to reinterpret one of the clauses in my biggest loan, hopin' to call it due and put me at risk of my land. The wife and I been fightin' back for a year, filed a lawsuit and everythin', and just last week the bank had to back down and settle our suit out of court for enough to pay off half my loans."

The Stone was finished, and Peake understood the point, but Sharp said impatiently, "So? I still don't see what it has to do with me."

"Oh, I think you do," The Stone said quietly, and the eyes he turned on Sharp were so intense that the deputy director winced.

Sharp looked down at the directions on the piece of paper, read them, cleared his throat, looked up. "This is all we want. I don't believe we'll need to talk further with either you or your daughter."

"I'm certainly relieved to hear that," The Stone said. "We'll be goin' back to Kansas tomorrow, and I wouldn't want to think this will be followin' us there."

Then The Stone smiled. At Peake, not at Sharp.

The deputy director turned sharply away and stalked do⌐n the hall. Peake returned The Stone's smile, then followed his boss.

23   THE DARK OF THE WOODS

REEEEEE, REEEEEE, REEEEEE, REEEEEE . . . AT FIRST THE STEAM-whistle cries of the cicadas pleased Rachael because they were reminiscent of grade-school field trips to public parks, holiday picnics, and the hiking she had done while in college. However, she quickly grew irritated by the piercing noise. Neither the brush nor the heavy pine boughs softened the racket. Every molecule of the cool dry air seemed to reverberate with that grating sound, and soon her teeth and bones were reverberating with it, too.

Her reaction was, in part, a result of Benny's sudden conviction that he had heard something in the nearby brush that was not part of the ordinary background noises of a forest. She silently cursed the insects and willed them to shut up so she could hear any unnatural sounds—such as twigs snapping and underbrush rustling from the passage of something more substantial than the wind.

The Combat Magnum was in her purse, and she was holding only the thirty-two pistol. She had discovered she needed one hand to push aside tall weeds and to grab convenient branches to pull herself over steeper or more treacherous stretches of ground. She considered getting the .357 out of the bag, but the sound of the zipper would pinpoint their location to anyone who might be seeking them.

Anyone. That was a cowardly evasion. Surely, only one person might be seeking them out here. Eric.

She and Benny had been moving directly south across the face of the mountainside, catching brief glimpses of the cabin on the slope a couple of hundred yards above, being careful to interpose trees and brush and rock formations between themselves and the large picture windows that made her think of enormous, square eye sockets. When they had been about thirty yards past the cabin, they had turned east, which was upslope, and the way proved sufficiently steep that they had progressed at only half the speed they had been making previously. Benny's intention had been to circle the cabin and come in behind it. Then, when they had ascended only about a hundred yards—which put them still a hundred yards below and thirty south of the structure—Benny heard something, stopped, eased up against the protective cover of a spruce trunk that had a five-foot diameter, cocked his head, and raised the shotgun.

Reeeeee, reeeeee, reeeeee . . .

In addition to the ceaseless cicada chorus—which had not fallen silent because of their presence and, therefore, would not fall silent to reveal anyone else's presence, either—there was the annoyance of a noisy wind. The breeze that had sprung up when they had come out of the sporting-goods store down by the lake, less than three-quarters of an hour ago, had evidently grown stronger. Not much of it reached as far as the sheltered forest floor, barely a soft breath. But the upper reaches of the massive trees stirred restlessly, and a hollow mournful moaning settled down from above as the wind wove through the interstices of the highest branches.

Rachael stayed close to Benny and pressed against the trunk of the spruce. The rough bark prickled even through her blouse.

She felt as if they remained frozen there, listening alertly and peering intently into the woods, for at least a quarter of an hour, though she knew it must have been less than a minute. Then, warily, Benny started uphill again, angling slightly to the right to follow a shallow dry wash that was mostly free of brush. She stayed close behind him. Sparse brown grass, crisp as paper, lightly stroked their legs. They had to take care to avoid stepping on some loose stones deposited by last spring's runoff of melting snow, but they made somewhat better progress than they had outside the wash.

The flanking walls of brush presented the only drawback to the easier new route. The growth was thick, some dry and brown, some dark green, and it pressed in at both sides of the shallow wash, with only a few widely separated gaps through which Benny and Rachael could look into the woods beyond. She half expected Eric to leap through the bushes and set upon them. She was encouraged only by the brambles tangled through a lot of the brush and by the wicked thorns she saw on some of the bushes themselves, which might give a would-be attacker second thoughts about striking from that direction.

On the other hand, having already returned from the dead, would Eric be concerned about such minor obstacles as thorns?

They went only ten or fifteen yards, before Benny froze again, half crouching to present a smaller target, and raised the shotgun.

This time, Rachael heard it, too: a clatter of dislodged pebbles.

Reeeeee, reeeeee . . .

A soft scrape as of shoe leather on stone.

She looked left and right, then up the slope, then down, but she saw no movement associated with the noise.

A whisper of something moving through brush more purposeful than mere wind.

Nothing more.

Ten seconds passed uneventfully.

Twenty.

As Benny scanned the bushes around them, he no longer retained any vestige of that deceptive I'm-just-an-ordinary-everyday-real-estate-salesman look. His pleasant but unexceptional face was now an arresting sight: The intensity of his concentration brought a new sharpness to his brow, cheekbones, and jaws; an instinctive sense of danger and an animal determination to survive were evident in his squint, in the flaring of his nostrils, and in the way his lips pulled back in a humorless, feral grin. He was spring-tense, acutely aware of every nuance of the forest, and just by looking at him, Rachael could tell that he had hair-trigger reflexes. This was the work he had been trained for—hunting and being hunted. His claim to being largely a past-focused man seemed like pretense or self-delusion, for there was no doubt whatsoever that he possessed an uncanny ability to focus entirely and powerfully on the present, which he was doing now.

The cicadas.

The wind in the attic of the forest.

The occasional trilling of a distant bird.

Nothing else.

Thirty seconds.

In these woods, at least, they were supposed to be the hunters, but suddenly they seemed to be the prey, and this reversal of roles frustrated Rachael as much as it frightened her. The need to remain silent was nerve-shredding, for she wanted to curse out loud, shout at Eric, challenge him. She wanted to *scream*.

Forty seconds.

Cautiously Benny and Rachael began moving uphill again.

They circled the large cabin until they came to the edge of the forest at the rear of it, and every step of the way they were stalked—or believed themselves to be stalked. Six more times, even after they left the dry wash and turned north through the woods, they stopped in response to unnatural sounds. Sometimes the snap of a twig or a not-quite-identifiable scraping noise would be so close to them that it seemed as if their nemesis must be only a few feet away and easily seen, yet they saw nothing.

Finally, forty feet in back of the cabin, just inside the tree line where they were still partially concealed by purple shadows, they crouched behind upthrusting blocks of granite that poked out of the earth like worn and slightly rotted teeth. Benny whispered, "Must be a lot of animals in these woods. That must've been what we heard."

"What kind of animals?" she whispered.

In a voice so low that Rachael could barely hear it, Benny said, "Squirrels, foxes. This high up . . . maybe a wolf or two. Can't have been Eric. No way. He's not had the survival or combat training that'd make it possible to be that quiet or to stay hidden so well and so long. If it was Eric, we'd have spotted him. Besides, if it'd been Eric, and if he's as deranged as you think he might be, then he'd have tried to jump us somewhere along the way."

"Animals," she said doubtfully.

"Animals."

With her back against the granite teeth, she looked at the woods through which they had come, studying every pocket of darkness and every peculiar shape.

Animals. Not a single, purposeful stalker. Just the sounds of several animals whose paths they had crossed. Animals.

Then why did she still feel as if something were back there in the woods, watching her, hungering for her?

"Animals," Benny said. Satisfied with that explanation, he turned from the woods, got up from a squat to a crouch, and peered over the lichen-speckled granite formation, examining the rear of Eric's mountain retreat.

Rachael was not convinced that the only source of danger was the cabin, so she rose, leaned one hip and shoulder against the rock, and took a position that allowed her to shift her attention back and forth from the rustic building in front of them to the forest behind.

At the rear of the mountain house, which stood on a wide shelf of land between slopes, a forty-foot-wide area had been cleared to serve as a backyard, and the summer sun fell across the greater part of it. Rye grass had been planted but had grown only in patches, for the soil was stony. Besides, Eric apparently had not installed a sprinkler system, which meant even the patchy grass would be green only for a short while between the melting of the winter snow and the parching summer. Having died a couple of weeks ago, in fact, the grass was now mown to a short, brown, prickly stubble. But flower beds—evidently irrigated by a passive-drip system—ringed the wide stained-wood porch that extended the length of the house; a profusion of yellow, orange, fire-red, wine-red, pink, white, and blue blossoms trembled and swayed and dipped in the gusty breeze—zinnias, geraniums, daisies, baby chrysanthemums, and more.

The cabin was of notched-log-and-mortar construction, but it was not a cheap, unsophisticated structure. The workmanship looked first-rate; Eric must have spent a bundle on the place. It stood upon an elevated foundation of invisibly mortared stones, and it boasted large casement-style French windows, two of which were partway open to facilitate ventilation. A black slate roof discouraged dry-wood moths and the playful squirrels attracted to shake-shingle roofs, and there was even a satellite dish up there to assure good TV reception.

The back door was open even wider than the two casement windows, and, taken with the bright bobbing flowers, that should have given the place a welcoming look. Instead, to Rachael, the open door resembled the gaping lid of a trap, flung wide to disarm the sniffing prey that sought the scented bait.

Of course, they would go in anyway. That was why they had come here: to go in, to find Eric. But she didn't have to like it.

After studying the cabin, Benny whispered, "Can't sneak up on the place; there's no cover. Next-best thing is a fast approach, straight in at a run, and hunker down along the porch railing."

"Okay."

"Probably the smartest thing is for you to wait here, let me go first, and see if maybe he's got a gun and starts taking potshots at me. If there's no gunfire, you can come after me."

"Stay here alone?"

"I'll never be far away."

"Even ten feet is too far."

"And we'll be separated only for a minute."

"That's exactly sixty times longer than I could stand being alone here," she said, looking back into the woods, where every deep pool of shadow and every unidentifiable form appeared to have crept closer while her attention was diverted. "No way, José. We go together."

"I figured you'd say that."

A tempest of warm wind whirled across the yard, stirring up dust, whipping the flowers, and lashing far enough into the perimeter of the forest to buffet Rachael's face.

Benny edged to the end of the granite formation, the shotgun held in both hands, peered around the corner, taking one last look at each of the rear windows to be sure no one was looking out of them.

The cicadas had stopped singing.

What did their sudden silence mean?

Before she could call that new development to Benny's attention, he flung himself forward, out of the concealment of the woods. He bolted across the patchy, dead brown lawn.

Propelled by the electrifying feeling that something murderous was bounding through the shadowed forest behind her—was reaching for her hair, was going to seize her, was going to drag her away into the dark of the woods—Rachael plunged after Benny, past the rocks, out of the trees, into the sun. She reached the back porch even as he was hunkering down beside the steps.

Breathless, she stopped beside him and looked back toward the forest. Nothing was pursuing her. She could hardly believe it.

Fast and light on his feet, Benny sprang up the porch steps, to the wall beside the open door, where he put his back to the logs and listened for movement inside the house. Evidently he heard nothing, for he pulled open the screen door and went inside, staying low, the shotgun aimed in front of him.

Rachael went after him, into a kitchen that was larger and better equipped than she expected. On the table, a plate held the remnants of an unfinished breakfast of sausages and biscuits. Soup cans and an empty jar of peanut butter littered the floor.

The cellar door was open. Benny cautiously, quietly pushed it shut, closing off the sight of steps descending into the gloom beyond.

Without being told what to do, Rachael hooked a kitchen chair with one hand, brought it to the door, tilted it under the knob, and wedged it into place, creating an effective barricade. They could not go into the cellar until they had searched the main living quarters of the cabin; for if Eric was in one of the ground-floor rooms, he might slip into the kitchen as soon as they went down the steps, might close the door and lock them in the dark basement. Conversely, if he was in the windowless basement already, he might creep upstairs while they were searching for him and sneak in behind them, a possibility they had just precluded by wedging that door shut.

She saw that Benny was pleased by the perception she'd shown when she'd put that chair under the knob. They made a good team.

She braced another door, which probably opened onto the garage, used a chair on that one, too. If Eric was in there, he could escape by rolling up the big outer door, of course, but they would hear it no matter where they were in the cabin and would have him pinpointed.

They stood in the kitchen for a moment, listening. Rachael could hear only the gusty breeze humming in the fine-mesh screen of the open kitchen window, sighing through the deep eaves under the overhanging slate roof.

Staying low and moving fast, Benny rushed through the doorway between the kitchen and the living room, looking left and right as he crossed the threshold. He signaled to Rachael that the way was clear, and she went after him.

In the ultramodern living room, the cabin's front door was open, though not as wide as the back door had been. A couple of hundred loose sheets of paper, two small ring-bound notebooks with black vinyl covers, and several manila file folders were scattered across the floor, some rumpled and torn.

Also on the floor, beside an armchair near the big front window, lay a medium-size knife with a serrated blade and a point tip. A couple of sunbeams, having pierced the forest outside, struck through the window, and one touched the steel blade, making its polished surface gleam, rippling lambently along its cutting edge.

Benny stared worriedly at the knife, then turned toward one of the three doors that, in addition to the kitchen archway, opened off the living room.

Rachael was about to pick up some of the papers to see what they were, but when Benny moved, she followed.

Two of the doors were closed tight, but the one Benny had chosen was ajar an inch. He pushed it open all the way with the barrel of the shotgun and went through with his customary caution.

Guarding the rear, Rachael remained in the living room, where she could see the open front door, the two closed doors, the kitchen arch, but where she also had a view of the room into which Benny had gone. It was a bedroom, wrecked in the same way that the bedroom in the Villa Park mansion and the kitchen in the Palm Springs house had been wrecked, proof that Eric had been here and that he had been seized by another demented rage.

In the bedroom, Benny gingerly rolled aside one of the large mirrored doors on a closet, looked warily inside, apparently found nothing of interest. He moved across the bedroom to the adjoining bath, where he passed out of Rachael's sight.

She glanced nervously at the front door, at the porch beyond, at the kitchen archway, at each of the other two closed doors.

Outside, the gusty breeze moaned softly under the overhanging roof and made a low, eager whining noise. The rustle of wind-stirred trees carried through the open front door.

Inside the cabin, the deep silence grew even deeper. Curiously enough, that stillness had the same effect on Rachael as a crescendo in a symphony: while it built, she became tenser, more convinced that events were hurtling toward an explosive climax.

Eric, damn it, where are you? Where are you, Eric?

Benny seemed to have been gone an ominously long time. She was on the verge of calling to him in panic, but finally he reappeared, unharmed, shaking his head to indicate that he had found no sign of Eric and nothing else of interest.

They discovered that the two closed doors opened onto two more bedrooms that shared a second bath between them, although Eric had furnished neither chamber with beds. Benny explored both rooms, closets, and the connecting bath, while Rachael stood in the living room by one doorway and then by the other, watching. She could see that the first room was a study with several bookshelves laden with thick volumes, a desk, and a computer; the second was empty, unused.

When it became clear that Benny was not going to find Eric in that part of the cabin, either, Rachael bent down, plucked up a few sheets of paper—Xerox copies, she noted—from the floor, and quickly scanned them. By the time Benny returned, she knew what she had found, and her heart was racing. "It's the Wildcard file," she said sotto voce. "He must've kept another copy here."

She started to gather up more of the scattered pages, but Benny stopped her. "We've got to find Eric first," he whispered.

Nodding agreement, she reluctantly dropped the papers.

Benny went to the front door, eased open the creaky screen door with the least amount of noise he could manage, and satisfied himself that the plank-floored porch was deserted. Then Rachael followed him into the kitchen again.

She slipped the tilted chair out from under the knob of the basement door, pulled the door open, and backed quickly out of the way as Benny covered it with the shotgun.

Eric did not come roaring out of the darkness.

With tiny beads of sweat shimmering on his forehead, Benny went to the threshold, found the switch on the wall of the stairwell, and flicked on the lights below.

Rachael was also sweating. As was surely the case with Benny, her perspiration was not occasioned by the warm summer air.

It was still not advisable for Rachael to accompany Benny into the windowless chamber below. Eric might be outside, watching the house, and he might slip inside at the opportune moment; then, as they returned to the kitchen, they might be ambushed from above when they were in the middle of the stairs and most vulnerable. So she remained at the threshold, where she could look down the cellar steps and also have a clear view of the entire kitchen, including the archway to the living room and the open door to the rear porch.

Benny descended the plank stairs more quietly than seemed humanly possible, although some noise was unavoidable: a few creaks, a couple of scraping noises. At the bottom, he hesitated, then turned left, out of sight. For a moment Rachael saw his shadow on the wall down there, made large and twisted into an odd shape by the angle of the light, but as he moved farther into the cellar, the shadow dwindled and finally went with him.

She glanced at the archway. She could see a portion of the living room, which remained deserted and still.

In the opposite direction, at the porch door, a huge yellow butterfly clung to the screen, slowly working its wings.

A clatter sounded from below, nothing dramatic, as if Benny had bumped against something.

She looked down the steps. No Benny, no shadow.

The archway. Nothing.

The back door. Just the butterfly.

More noise below, quieter this time.

"Benny?" she said softly.

He did not answer her. Probably didn't hear her. She had spoken at barely more than a whisper, after all.

The archway, the back door . . .

The stairs: still no sign of Benny.

"Benny," she repeated, then saw a shadow below. For a moment her heart twisted because the shadow looked so strange, but Benny appeared and started up toward her, and she sighed with relief.

"Nothing down there but an open wall safe tucked behind the water heater," he said when he reached the kitchen. "It's empty, so maybe that's where he kept the files that're spread over the living room."

Rachael wanted to put down her gun and throw her arms around him and hug him tight and kiss him all over his face just because he had come back from the cellar alive. She wanted him to know how happy she was to see him, but the garage still had to be explored.

By unspoken agreement, she removed the tilted chair from under the knob and opened the door, and Benny covered it with the shotgun. Again, there was no sign of Eric.

Benny stood on the threshold, fumbled for the switch, found it, but the lights in the garage were dim. Even with a small window high in one wall, the place remained shadowy. He tried another switch, which operated the big electric door. It rolled up with much humming-rumbling-creaking, and bright brassy sunlight flooded inside.

"That's better," Benny said, stepping into the garage.

She followed him and saw the black Mercedes 560 SEL, additional proof that Eric had been there.

The rising door had stirred up some dust, motes of which drifted lazily through the in-slanting sunlight. Overhead in the rafters, spiders had been busy spinning ersatz silk.

Rachael and Benny circled the car warily, looked through the windows (saw the keys dangling in the ignition), and even peered underneath. But Eric was not to be found.

An elaborate workbench extended across the entire back of the garage. Above it was a peg board tool rack, and each tool hung in a painted outline of itself. Rachael noticed that no wood ax hung in the ax-shaped outline, but she did not even give the missing instrument a second thought because she was only looking for places where Eric could hide; she was not, after all, doing an inventory.

The garage provided no sheltered spaces large enough for a man to conceal himself, and when Benny spoke again, he no longer bothered to whisper. "I'm beginning to think maybe he's been here and gone."

"But that's his Mercedes."

"This is a two-car garage, so maybe he keeps a vehicle up here all the time, a Jeep or four-wheel-drive pickup good for scooting around these mountain roads. Maybe he knew there was a chance the feds would learn what he'd done to himself and would be after him, with an APB on the car, so he split in the Jeep or whatever it was."

Rachael stared at the black Mercedes, which stood like a great sleeping beast. She looked up at the webs in the rafters. She stared at the sun-splashed dirt road that led away from the garage. The stillness of the mountain redoubt seemed less ominous than it had since their arrival; not peaceful and serene by any means, certainly not welcoming, either, but it was somewhat less threatening.

"Where would he go?" she asked.

Benny shrugged. "I don't know. But if I do a thorough search of the cabin, maybe I'll find something that'll point me in the right direction."

"Do we have time for a search? I mean, when we left Sarah Kiel at the hospital last night, I didn't know the feds might be on this same trail. I told her not to talk about what had happened and not to tell anyone about this place. At worst, I thought maybe Eric's business partners would start sniffing around, trying to get something out of her, and I figured she'd be able to handle them. But she won't be able to stall the government. And if she believes we're traitors, she'll even think she's doing the right thing when she tells them about this place. So they'll be here sooner or later."

"I agree," Benny said, staring thoughtfully at the Mercedes.

"Then we've no time to worry about where Eric went. Besides, that's a copy of the Wildcard file in there on the living-room floor. All we have to do is pick it up and get out of here, and we'll have all the proof we need."

He shook his head. "Having the file is important, maybe even crucial, but I'm not so sure it's enough."

She paced agitatedly, the thirty-two pistol held with the muzzle pointed at the ceiling rather than down, for an accidentally triggered shot would ricochet off the concrete floor. "Listen, the whole story's right there in black and white. We just give it to the press—"

"For one thing," Benny said, "the file is, I assume, a lot of highly technical stuff—lab results, formulae—and no reporter's going to understand it. He'll have to take it to a first-rate geneticist for review, for *translation.*"

"So?"

"So maybe the geneticist will be incompetent or just conservative in his assumption of what's possible in his field, and in either case he might disbelieve the whole thing; he might tell the reporter it's a fraud, a hoax."

"We can deal with that kind of setback. We can keep looking until we find a geneticist who—"

Interrupting, Benny said, "Worse: Maybe the reporter will take it to a geneticist who does his own research for the government, for the Pentagon. And isn't it logical that federal agents have contacted a lot of scientists specializing in recombinant DNA research, warning them that media types might be bringing them certain stolen files of a highly classified nature, seeking analysis of the contents?"

"The feds can't know that's my intention."

"But if they've got a file on you—and they do—then they know you well enough to suspect that'd be your plan."

"All right, yes," she admitted unhappily.

"So any Pentagon-supported scientist is going to be real eager to please the government and keep his own fat research grants, and he's sure as hell going to alert them the moment such a file comes into his hands. Certainly he's not going to risk *losing* his grants or being prosecuted for compromising defense secrets, so at best he'll tell the reporter to take his damn file and get lost, and he'll keep his mouth shut. At best. Most likely he'll give the reporter to the feds, and the reporter will give *us* to the feds. The file will be destroyed, and very likely we'll be destroyed, too."

Rachael didn't want to believe what he said, but she knew there was truth in it.

Out in the woods, the cicadas were singing again.

"So what do we do now?" she asked.

Evidently Benny had been thinking hard about that question as they had gone through room after room of the cabin without finding Eric, for his answer was well prepared. "With both Eric and the file in our possession, we're in a lot stronger position. We wouldn't have just a bunch of cryptic research papers that only a handful of people could understand; we'd also have a walking dead man, his skull staved in, and by God, *that's* dramatic enough to guarantee that virtually any newspaper or television network will run an all-stops-pulled story before getting expert opinions on the file itself. Then there'll be no reason for the government or anyone else trying to shut us up. Once Eric's seen on TV news, his picture'll show up on the covers of *Time* and *Newsweek,* and the *National Enquirer* will have enough material for a decade, and David Letterman will be making zombie jokes every night, so silencing us won't achieve anything."

He took a deep breath, and she had a hunch that he was going to propose something she would not like in the least.

When he continued, he confirmed her hunch. "All right, like I said, I need to search this place thoroughly to see if I can come up with any clue that'll tell us where Eric's gone. But the authorities may show up here soon. Now that we've got a copy of the Wildcard file, we can't risk having it taken away from us, so you've got to leave with the file while I—"

"You mean, split up?" she said. "Oh, no."

"It's the only way, Rachael. We—"

"No."

The thought of leaving him alone here was chilling.

The thought of being alone herself was almost too much to bear, and she realized with terrible poignancy how tight the bonds between them had become in just the past twenty-four hours.

She loved him. God, how she loved him.

He fixed her with his gentle, reassuring brown eyes. In a voice neither patronizing nor abrasively commanding but nevertheless full of authority and reason, a voice which brooked no debate—probably the tone he had learned to use in Vietnam, in crises, with soldiers of inferior rank—he said, "You'll take the Wildcard file out of here, get copies made, send some off to friends in widely separated places, and secrete a few others where you can get your hands on them with short notice. Then we won't have to worry about losing our only copy or having it taken away from us. We'll have real good insurance. Meanwhile, I'll thoroughly search the cabin here, see what I can turn up. If I find something that points us toward Eric, I'll meet up with you at a prearranged place, and we'll go after him together. If I don't get a lead on him, we'll meet up and hide out together, until we can decide what to do next."

She did not want to split up and leave him alone here. Eric might still be around. Or the feds might show up. Either way Benny might be killed. But his arguments for splitting up were convincing; damn it, he was right.

Nevertheless, she said, "If I go alone and take the car, how will you get out of here?"

He glanced at his wristwatch not because he needed to know the time (she thought) but to impress upon her that time was running out. "You'll leave the rental Ford for me," he said. "That's got to be ditched soon, anyway, because the cops might be onto it. You'll take this Mercedes, and I'll take the Ford just far enough to swap it for something else."

"They'll be on the lookout for the Mercedes, too."

"Oh, sure. But the APB will specify a black 560 SEL with this particular license number, driven by a man fitting Eric's description. You'll be driving, not Eric, and we'll switch license plates with one of those cars parked along the gravel road farther down the mountain, which ought to take care of things."

"I'm not so sure."

"I am."

Hugging herself as if this were a day in November rather than a day in June, Rachael said, "But where would we meet up later?"

"Las Vegas," he said.

The answer startled her. "Why there?"

"Southern California's too hot for us. I'm not confident we can hide out here. But if we hop over to Vegas, I have a place."

"What place?"

"I own a motel on Tropicana Boulevard, west of the Strip."

"You're a Vegas wheeler-dealer? Old-fashioned, conservative Benny Shadway is a Vegas wheeler-dealer?"

"My real-estate development company's been in and out of Vegas property several times, but I'm hardly a wheeler-dealer. It's small stuff by Vegas standards. In this case, it's an older motel with just twenty-eight rooms and a pool. And it's not in the best repair. In fact, it's closed up at the moment. I finished the purchase two weeks ago, and we're going to tear it down next month, put up a new place: sixty units, a restaurant. There's still electrical service. The manager's suite is pretty shabby, but it has a working bathroom, furniture, telephone—so we can hide out there if we have to, make plans. Or just wait for Eric to show up someplace very public and cause a sensation that the feds can't put a lid on. Anyway, if we can't get a lead on him, hiding out is all we *can* do."

"I'm to drive to Vegas?" she asked.

"That'd be best. Depending on how badly the feds want us—and considering what's at stake, I think they want us real bad—they'll probably have men at the major airports. You can take the state route past Silverwood Lake, then pick up Interstate Fifteen, be in Vegas this evening. I'll follow in a couple of hours."

"But if the cops show up—"

"Alone, without you to worry about, I can slip away from them."

"You think they're going to be incompetent?" she asked sourly.

"No. I just know I'm *more* competent."

"Because you were trained for this. But that was more than one and a half decades ago."

He smiled thinly. "Seems like yesterday, that war."

And he had kept in shape. She could not dispute that. What was it he'd said— that Nam had taught him to be prepared because the world had a way of turning dark and mean when you least expected it?

"Rachael?" he asked, looking at his watch again.

She realized that their best chance of surviving, of having a future together, was for her to do what he wanted.

"All right," she said. "All right. We'll split. But it scares me, Benny. I guess I don't have the guts for this kind of thing, the right stuff. I'm sorry, but it really scares me."

He came to her, kissed her. "Being scared isn't anything to be ashamed of. Only madmen have no fear."

24

A SPECIAL FEAR
OF HELL

DR. EASTON SOLBERG HAD BEEN MORE THAN FIFTEEN MIN-utes late for his one o'clock meeting with Julio Verdad and Reese Hagerstrom. They had stood outside his locked office, and he had finally come hurrying along the wide hall, clutching an armload of books and manila folders, looking harried, more like a twenty-year-old student late to class than a sixty-year-old professor overdue for an appointment.

He was wearing a rumpled brown suit one size too large for him, a blue shirt, and a green-and-orange-striped tie that looked, to Julio, as if it had been sold exclusively in novelty shops as a joke gift. Even by a generous appraisal, Solberg was not an attractive man, not even plain. He was short and stocky. His moonish face featured a small flat nose that would have been called pug on some men but that was simply porcine on him, small close-set gray eyes that looked watery and myopic behind his smudged glasses, a mouth that was strangely wide considering the scale on which the rest of his visage was constructed, and a receding chin.

In the hall outside his office, apologizing effusively, he had insisted on shaking hands with the two detectives, in spite of the load in his arms; therefore, he kept dropping books, which Julio and Reese stooped to pick up.

Solberg's office was chaos. Books and scientific journals filled every shelf, spilled onto the floor, rose in teetering stacks in the corners, were piled every which way on top of furniture. On his big desk, file folders, index cards, and yellow legal-size tablets were heaped in apparent disorder. The professor shifted mounds of papers off two chairs to give Julio and Reese places to sit.

"Look at that lovely view!" Solberg said, stopping suddenly and gaping at the windows as he rounded his desk, as if noticing for the first time what lay beyond the walls of his office.

The Irvine campus of the University of California was blessed with many trees, rolling green lawns, and flower beds, for it sprawled over a large tract of prime Orange County land. Below Dr. Solberg's second-floor office, a walkway curved across manicured grass, past impatiens blazing with thousands of bright blos-soms—coral, red, pink, purple—and vanished under the branches of jacarandas and eucalyptus.

"Gentlemen, we are among the most fortunate people on earth: to be here, in this beautiful land, under these temperate skies, in a nation of plenty and toler-ance." He stepped to the window and opened his stubby arms, as if to embrace all of southern California. "And the trees, especially the trees. There are some wonderful specimens on this campus. I love trees, I really do. That's my hobby: trees, the study of trees, the cultivation of unusual specimens. It makes for a welcome change from human biology and genetics. Trees are so majestic, so *noble*. Trees give and give to us—fruit, nuts, beauty, shade, lumber, oxygen—and take nothing in return. If I believed in reincarnation, I'd pray to return as a tree." He glanced at Julio and Reese. "What about you? Don't you think it'd be grand to come back as a tree, living the long majestic life of an oak or giant spruce, giving of yourself the way orange and apple trees give, growing great strong limbs in which children could climb?" He blinked, surprised by his own monologue. "But of course you're not here to talk about trees and reincarnation, are you? You'll have to forgive me . . . but, well, that *view*, don't you know? Just captured me for a moment."

In spite of his unfortunate porcine face, disheveled appearance, apparent disorganization, and evident tendency to be late, Dr. Easton Solberg had at least three things to recommend him: keen intelligence, enthusiasm for life, and optimism. In a world of doomsayers, where half the intelligentsia waited almost wistfully for Armageddon, Julio found Solberg refreshing. He liked the professor almost at once.

As Solberg went behind his desk, sat in a large leather chair, and half disappeared from view beyond his paperwork, Julio said, "On the phone you said there was a dark side to Eric Leben that you could discuss only in person—"

"And in strictest confidence," Solberg said. "The information, if pertinent to your case, must go in a file somewhere, of course, but if it's not pertinent, I expect discretion."

"I assure you of that," Julio said. "But as I told you earlier, this is an extremely important investigation involving at least two murders and the possible leak of top-secret defense documents."

"Do you mean Eric's death might not have been accidental?"

"No," Julio said. "That was definitely an accident. But there are other deaths . . . the details of which I'm not at liberty to discuss. And more people may die before this case is closed. So Detective Hagerstrom and I hope you'll give us full and immediate cooperation."

"Oh, of course, of course," Easton Solberg said, waving one pudgy hand to dismiss the very idea that he might be uncooperative. "And although I don't know for a certainty that Eric's emotional problems are related to your case, I expect— and fear—that they may be. As I said . . . he had a dark side."

However, before Solberg got around to telling them of Leben's dark side, he spent a quarter of an hour praising the dead geneticist, apparently unable to speak ill of the man until he had first spoken highly of him. Eric was a genius. Eric was a hard worker. Eric was generous in support of colleagues. Eric had a fine sense of humor, an appreciation for art, good taste in most things, and he liked dogs.

Julio was beginning to think they ought to form a committee and solicit contributions to build a statue of Leben for display under a fittingly imposing rotunda in a major public building. He glanced at Reese and saw his partner was plainly amused by the bubbly Solberg.

Finally the professor said, "But he was a troubled man, I'm sorry to say. Deeply, deeply troubled. He had been my student for a while, though I quickly realized the student was going to outdistance the teacher. When we were no longer student-teacher but colleagues, we remained friendly. We weren't friends, just friendly, because Eric did not allow any relationship to become close enough to qualify as friendship. So, close as we were professionally, it was years before I learned about his . . . obsession with young girls."

"How young?" Reese asked.

Solberg hesitated. "I feel as if I'm . . . betraying him."

"We may already know much of what you've got to tell us," Julio said. "You'll probably only be confirming what we know."

"Really? Well . . . I knew of one girl who was fourteen. At the time, Eric was thirty-one."

"This was before Geneplan?"

"Yes. Eric was at UCLA then. Not rich yet, but we could all see he would one day leave academia and take the real world by storm."

"A respected professor wouldn't go around bragging about bedding fourteen-year-old girls," Julio said. "How'd you find out?"

"It happened on a weekend," Dr. Solberg said, "when his lawyer was out of town and he needed someone to post bail. He trusted no one but me to keep quiet about the ugly details of the arrest. I sort of resented that, too. He knew I'd feel a moral obligation to endorse any censure movement against a colleague involved in such sordid business, but he also knew I'd feel obligated to keep any confidences he imparted, and he counted on the second obligation being stronger than the first. Maybe, to my discredit, it was."

Easton Solberg gradually settled deeper in his chair while he talked, as if trying to hide behind the mounds of papers on his desk, embarrassed by the sleazy tale he had to tell. That Saturday, eleven years ago, after receiving Leben's call, Dr. Solberg had gone to a police precinct house in Hollywood, where he had found an Eric Leben far different from the man he knew: nervous, uncertain of himself, ashamed, lost. The previous night, Eric had been arrested in a vice-squad raid at a hot-bed motel where Hollywood streetwalkers, many of them young runaways with drug problems, took their johns. He was caught with a fourteen-year-old girl and charged with statutory rape, a mandatory count even when an underage girl admittedly solicits sex for pay.

Initially Leben told Easton Solberg that the girl had looked considerably older than fourteen, that he'd had no way of knowing she was a juvenile. Later, however, perhaps disarmed by Solberg's kindness and concern, Leben broke down and talked at length of his obsession with young girls. Solberg had not really wanted to know any of it, but he could not refuse Eric a sympathetic ear. He sensed that Eric—who was a distant and self-possessed loner, unlikely ever to have unburdened himself to anyone—desperately needed to confide his intimate feelings and fears to someone at that bleak, low point in his life. So Easton Solberg listened, filled with both disgust and pity.

"His was not just a lust for young girls," Solberg told Julio and Reese. "It was an obsession, a compulsion, a terrible gnawing *need*."

Only thirty-one then, Leben was nevertheless deeply frightened of growing old and dying. Already longevity research was the center of his career. But he did not approach the problem of aging *only* in a scientific spirit; privately, in his personal life, he dealt with it in an emotional and irrational manner. For one thing, he felt that he somehow absorbed the vital energies of youth from the girls he bedded. Although he knew that notion was ridiculous, almost superstitious, he was still compelled to pursue those girls. He was not really a child molester in the classic sense, did not force himself on mere children. He only went after those girls who were willing to cooperate, usually teenage runaways reduced to prostitution.

"And sometimes," Easton Solberg said with soft dismay, "he liked to . . . slap them around. Not really beat them but rough them up. When he explained it to me, I had the feeling that he was explaining it to himself for the first time. These girls were so young that they were full of the special arrogance of youth, that arrogance born of the certainty they'd live forever; and Eric felt that, by hurting them, he was knocking the arrogance out of them, teaching them the fear of death. He was, as he put it, 'stealing their innocence, the energy of their youthful innocence,' and he felt that somehow this made him younger, that the stolen innocence and youth became his own."

"A psychic vampire," Julio said uneasily.

"Yes!" Solberg said. "Exactly. A psychic vampire who could stay young forever by draining away the youth of these girls. Yet at the same time, he knew it was a fantasy, knew the girls could not keep him young, but knowing and acknowledging it did nothing to loosen the grip of the fantasy. And though he knew he was sick—even mocked himself, called himself a degenerate—he couldn't break free of his obsession."

"What happened to the charge of statutory rape?" Reese asked. "I'm not aware he was tried or convicted. He had no police record."

"The girl was remanded to juvenile authorities," Solberg said, "and put in a minimum-security facility. She slipped away, skipped town. She'd been carrying no identification, and the name she gave them proved false, so they had no way of tracking her. Without the girl, they had no case against Eric, and the charges were dropped."

"You urged him to seek psychiatric help?" Julio asked.

"Yes. But he wouldn't. He was an extremely intelligent man, introspective, and he had already analyzed himself. He knew—or at least believed that he knew—the cause of his mental condition."

Julio leaned forward in his chair. "And the cause as he saw it?"

Solberg cleared his throat, started to speak, shook his head as if to say that he needed a moment to decide how to proceed. He was obviously embarrassed by the conversation and was equally disturbed by his betrayal of Eric Leben's confidence even though Leben was now dead. The heaps of papers on the desk no longer provided adequate cover behind which to hide, so Solberg got up and went to the window because it afforded the opportunity to turn his back on Julio and Reese, thus concealing his face.

Solberg's dismay and self-reproach over revealing confidential information about a dead man—of whom he had been little more than an acquaintance— might have seemed excessive to some, yet Julio admired Solberg for it. In an age when few believed in moral absolutes, many would betray a friend without a qualm, and a moral dilemma of this nature would be beyond their understanding. Solberg's old-fashioned moral anguish seemed excessive only by current, decadent standards.

"Eric told me that, as a child, he was sexually molested by an uncle," Solberg said to the window glass. "Hampstead was the man's name. The abuse started when Eric was four and continued till he was nine. He was terrified of this uncle but too ashamed to tell anyone what was happening. Ashamed because his family was so religious. That's important, as you'll see. The Leben family was devoutly, ardently religious. Nazarenes. Very strict. No music. No dancing. That cold, narrow religion that makes life a bleakness. Of course, Eric felt like a sinner because of what he'd done with his uncle, even though he was forced into it, and he was afraid to tell his parents."

"It's a common pattern," Julio said, "even in families that aren't religious. The child blames himself for the adult's crime."

Solberg said, "His terror of Barry Hampstead—that was the first name, yes—grew greater month by month, week by week. And finally, when Eric was nine, he stabbed Hampstead to death."

"Nine?" Reese said, appalled. "Good heavens."

"Hampstead was asleep on the sofa," Solberg continued, "and Eric killed him with a butcher's knife."

Julio considered the effects of that trauma on a nine-year-old boy who was already emotionally disturbed from the ordeal of long-term physical abuse. In his mind's eye, he saw the knife clutched in the child's small hand, rising and falling, blood flying off the shining blade, and the boy's eyes fixed in horror upon his grisly handiwork, repelled by what he was doing, yet compelled to finish it.

Julio shivered.

"Though everyone then learned what had been going on," Solberg said, "Eric's parents somehow, in their twisted way, saw him as both a fornicator and a murderer, and they began a fevered and very psychologically damaging campaign to save his soul from hell, praying over him day and night, disciplining him, forcing him to read and reread passages of the Bible aloud until his throat cracked and his voice faded to a hoarse whisper. Even after he got out of that dark and hateful house and got through college by working part-time jobs and winning scholarships, even after he'd piled up a mountain of academic achievements and had become a respected man of science, Eric continued to half believe in hell and in his own certain damnation. Maybe he even more than *half* believed."

Suddenly Julio saw what was coming, and a chill as cold as any he had ever felt sneaked up the small of his back. He glanced at his partner and saw, in Reese's face, a look of horror that mirrored Julio's feelings.

Still staring out at the verdant campus, which was as thoroughly sun-splashed as before but which seemed to have grown darker, Easton Solberg said, "You already know of Eric's deep and abiding commitment to longevity research and his dream of immortality achieved through genetic engineering. But now perhaps you see why he was so obsessed with achieving that unrealistic—some would call it irrational and impossible—goal. In spite of all his education, in spite of his ability to reason, he was illogical about this one thing: in his heart he believed that he would go to hell when he died, not merely because he had sinned with his uncle but because he had killed his uncle as well, and was both a fornicator and a murderer. He told me once that he was afraid he'd meet his uncle again in hell and that eternity would be, for him, total submission to Barry Hampstead's lust."

"Dear God," Julio said shakily, and he unconsciously made the sign of the cross, something he had not done outside of church since he was a child.

Turning away from the window and facing the detectives at last, the professor said, "So for Eric Leben, immortality on earth was a goal sought not only out of a love of life but out of a special fear of hell. I imagine you can see how, with such motivation, he was destined to be a driven man, obsessed."

"Inevitably," Julio said.

"Driven to young girls, driven to seek ways to extend the human life span, driven to cheat the devil," Solberg said. "Year by year it became worse. We drifted apart after that weekend when he made his confessions, probably because he regretted that he'd told me his secrets. I doubt he even told his wife about his uncle and his childhood when he married her a few years later. I was probably the only one. But in spite of the growing distance between us, I heard from poor Eric often enough to know his fear of death and damnation became worse as he grew older. In fact, after forty, he was downright frantic. I'm sorry he died yesterday; he was a brilliant man, and he had the power to contribute so much to humanity. On the other hand, his was not a happy life. And perhaps his death was even a blessing in disguise because . . . "

"Yes?" Julio said.

Solberg sighed and wiped one hand over his moonish face, which had sagged somewhat with weariness. "Well, sometimes I worried about what Eric might do if he ever achieved a breakthrough in the kind of research he was pursuing. If he thought he had a means of editing his genetic structure to dramatically extend his life span, he might have been just foolish enough to experiment on himself with an unproven process. He would know the terrible risks of tampering with his own genetic makeup, but compared to his unrelenting dread of death and the afterlife, those risks might seem minor. And God knows what might have happened to him if he had used himself as a guinea pig."

What would you say if you knew that his body disappeared from the morgue last night? Julio wondered.

25   ALONE

THEY DID NOT ATTEMPT TO PUT THE XEROX OF THE WILD-card file in order, but scooped up all the loose papers from the cabin's living-room floor and dropped them in a plastic Hefty garbage bag that Benny got from a box in one of the kitchen drawers. He twisted the top of the bag and secured it with a plastic-coated wire tie, then placed it on the rear floor of the Mercedes, behind the driver's seat.

They drove down the dirt road to the gate, on the other side of which they had parked the Ford. As they had hoped, on the same ring with the car keys, they found a key that fit the padlock on the gate.

Benny brought the Ford inside, and as he edged past her, Rachael drove the Mercedes out through the gate and parked just beyond.

She waited nervously with the 560 SEL, her thirty-two in one hand and her gaze sweeping the surrounding forest.

Benny went down the road on foot, out of sight, to the three vehicles that were parked on the lay-by near one of the driveway entrances they had passed earlier on their way up the mountainside. He carried with him the two license plates from the Mercedes—plus a screwdriver and a pair of pliers. When he returned, he had the plates from one of the Dodge Chargers, which he attached to the Mercedes.

He got in the car with her and said, "When you get to Vegas, go to a public phone, look up the number for a guy named Whitney Gavis."

"Who's he?"

"An old friend. And he works for me. He's watching over that rundown motel

I told you about—the Golden Sand Inn. In fact, he found the property and turned me on to its potential. He's got keys. He can let you in. Tell him you need to stay in the manager's suite and that I'll be joining you tonight. Tell him as much as you want to tell him; he can keep his mouth shut, and if he's going to be dragged into it, he should know how serious this is."

"What if he's heard about us on the radio or TV?"

"Won't matter to Whitney. He won't believe we're killers or Russian agents. He's got a good head on him, an excellent bullshit detector, and nobody has a better sense of loyalty than Whit. You can trust him."

"If you say so."

"There's a two-car garage behind the motel office. Make sure you put the Mercedes in there, out of sight, soon as you arrive."

"I don't like this."

"I'm not crazy about it, either," Benny said. "But it's the right plan. We've already discussed it." He leaned over and put one hand against her face, then kissed her.

The kiss was sweet, and when it ended she said, "As soon as you've searched the cabin, you'll leave? Whether or not you've found any clue to where Eric might've gone?"

"Yes. I want to get out before the feds show up."

"And if you find a clue to where he's gone, you won't go after him alone?"

"What did I promise you?"

"I want to hear you say it again."

"I'll come for you first," Benny said. "I won't tackle Eric alone. We'll handle him together."

She looked into his eyes and was not sure if he was telling the truth or lying. But even if he was lying, she could do nothing about it because time was running out. They could delay no longer.

"I love you," he said.

"I love you, Benny. And if you get yourself killed, I'm never going to forgive you."

He smiled. "You're some woman, Rachael. You could rouse a heartbeat in a rock, and you're all the motivation I need to come back alive. Don't you worry about that. Now, lock the doors when I get out—okay?"

He kissed her again, lightly this time. He got out of the car, slammed the door, waited until he saw the power-lock buttons sinking into their mountings, then waved her on.

She drove down the gravel lane, glancing repeatedly in the rearview mirror to keep Benny in sight as long as possible, but eventually the road turned, and he disappeared beyond the trees.

■ Ben drove the rental Ford up the dirt lane, parked in front of the cabin. A few big white clouds had appeared in the sky, and the shadow of one of them rippled across the log structure.

Holding the twelve-gauge in one hand and the Combat Magnum in the other— Rachael had taken only the thirty-two—he climbed the steps to the porch, wondering if Eric was watching him.

Ben had told Rachael that Eric had left, gone to some other hiding place. Per-

haps that was true. Indeed, the odds were high that it was true. But a chance
remained, however slim, that the dead man was still here, perhaps observing from
some lookout in the forest.

Reeeeee, reeeeee . . .

He tucked the revolver into his belt, at his back, and entered the cabin cautiously by the front door, the shotgun ready. He went through the rooms again,
looking for something that might tell him where Eric had established another
hidey-hole comparable to the cabin.

He had not lied to Rachael; it really was necessary to conduct such a search,
but he did not require an hour to do it, as he'd claimed. If he did not find anything
useful in fifteen minutes, he would leave the cabin and prowl the perimeter of the
lawn for some sign of a place where Eric had entered the woods—trampled brush,
footprints in soft soil. If he found what he was looking for, he would pursue his
quarry into the forest.

He had not told Rachael about that part of his plan because, if he had, she
would never have gone to Vegas. But he could not enter those woods and track
down his man with Rachael at his side. He had realized as much on the way up
through the forest, on their first approach to the cabin. She was not as sure of
herself in the wilds as Ben was, not as quick. If she went with him, he would
worry about her, be distracted by her, which would give the advantage to Eric if
the dead man was, in fact, out there somewhere.

Earlier, he had told Rachael that the odd sounds they had heard in the woods
were caused by animals. Maybe. But when they had found the cabin abandoned,
he had let those forest noises sound again in his memory, and he had begun to
feel that he had been too quick to dismiss the possibility that Eric had been stalking
them through the shadows, trees, and brush.

■   All the way down the narrow lane, from gravel to blacktop, until she reached
the state route that rounded Lake Arrowhead, Rachael was more than half
convinced that Eric was going to rush the car from the surrounding woods and
fling himself at the door. With superhuman strength born of a demonic rage,
he might even be able to put a fist through the closed window. But he did not
appear.

On the state route, circling the lake, she worried less about Eric and more about
police and federal agents. Every vehicle she encountered looked, at first sight, like
a patrol car.

Las Vegas seemed a thousand miles away.

And she felt as if she had deserted Benny.

■   When Peake and Sharp had arrived at the Palm Springs Airport, directly from
their meeting with The Stone, they had discovered that the helicopter, a Bell
JetRanger, had developed engine trouble. The deputy director, full of pent-up
anger that he had been unable to vent on The Stone, nearly took off the chopper
pilot's head, as if the poor man not only flew the craft but was also responsible
for its design, construction, and maintenance.

Peake winked at the pilot behind Sharp's back.

No other helicopter had been for hire, and the two choppers belonging to the
county sheriff's substation had been engaged and unavailable for quick reas-

signment. Reluctantly Sharp had decided they had no choice but to drive from Palm Springs to Lake Arrowhead. The dark green government sedan came with a red emergency beacon that was usually kept in the trunk but which could be mounted to the roof beading with a thumbscrew clamp in less than a minute. They håd a siren, too. They had used both the flashing beacon and the siren to clear traffic out of their way, hurtling north on Highway 111, then virtually *flying* west on I-10 toward the Redland exit. They had topped ninety miles an hour nearly all the way, the Chevy's engine roaring, the frame shimmying under them. Jerry Peake, behind the wheel, had worried about a blowout because if a tire blew at that speed they were dead men.

Sharp seemed unconcerned about a blowout, but he complained about the lack of air-conditioning and about the warm wind blowing into his face through the open windows. It was as if, certain of his destiny, he were incapable of imagining himself dying now, here, in a rolling car; as if he believed he was entitled to every comfort regardless of the circumstances—like a crown prince. In fact, Peake realized that was probably *exactly* how Sharp looked at it.

Now they were in the San Bernardino Mountains, on State Route 330, a few miles from Running Springs, forced by the twisting road to travel at safer speeds. Sharp was silent, brooding, as he had been ever since they had turned off I-10 at the Redland exit. His anger had subsided. He was calculating now, scheming. Peake could almost hear the clicking, whirring, ticking, and humming of the Machiavellian mechanism that was Anson Sharp's mind.

Finally, as alternating bursts of sunlight and forest shadows slapped the windshield and filled the car with flickering ghostly movement, Sharp said, "Peake, you may be wondering why only the two of us have come here, why I haven't alerted the police or brought more backup of my own."

"Yes, sir. I was wondering," Peake said.

Sharp studied him for a while. "Jerry, are you ambitious?"

Watch your ass, Jerry! Peake thought as soon as Sharp called him by his first name, for Sharp was not a man who would ever be chummy with a subordinate.

He said, "Well, sir, I want to do well, be a good agent, if that's what you mean."

"I mean more than that. Do you hope for promotion, greater authority, the chance to be in charge of investigations?"

Peake suspected that Sharp would be suspicious of a junior agent with too much ambition, so he did not mention his dream of becoming a Defense Security Agency legend. Instead, he said disingenuously, "Well, I've always sort of dreamed of one day working my way up to assistant chief of the California office, where I could have some input on operations. But I've got a lot to learn first."

"That's all?" Sharp asked. "You strike me as a bright, capable young man. I'd expect you to've set your sights on something higher."

"Well, sir, thank you, but there are quite a few bright, capable guys in the agency about my age, and if I could make assistant chief of the district office with *that* competition, I'd be happy."

Sharp was silent for a minute, but Peake knew the conversation was not over. They had to slow to make a sharp rightward curve, and around the bend a raccoon was crossing the road, so Peake eased down on the brake and slowed even further, letting the animal scurry out of the way. At last the deputy director said, "Jerry, I've been watching you closely, and I like what I see. You have what it takes to go far in the company. If you've a desire to go to Washington, I'm convinced you'd be an asset in various posts at headquarters."

Jerry Peake was suddenly scared. Sharp's flattery was excessive, and his implied patronage too generous. The deputy director wanted something from Peake, and in return he wanted Peake to buy something from him, something with a high price tag, maybe a lot higher than Peake was willing to pay. But if he refused to accept the deal Sharp was leading to, he'd make a lifelong enemy of the deputy director.

Sharp said, "This is not public knowledge, Jerry, and I'd ask you to keep it to yourself, but within two years the director is going to retire and recommend that I take his place at the head of the agency."

Peake believed that Sharp was sincere, but he also had the queer feeling that Jarrod McClain, director of the DSA, would be surprised to hear about his own pending retirement.

Sharp continued: "When that happens, I'll be getting rid of many of the men Jarrod has installed in high positions. I don't mean to be disrespectful of the director, but he's too much of the old school, and the men he's promoted are less company agents than bureaucrats. I'll be bringing in younger and more aggressive men—like you."

"Sir, I don't know what to say," Peake told him, which was as true as it was evasive.

As intently as Peake watched the road ahead, Sharp watched Peake. "But the men I'll have around me must be totally reliable, totally committed to my vision for the agency. They must be willing to take any risks, make any sacrifices, give whatever is required to further the cause of the agency and, of course, the welfare of the country. At times, rarely but predictably, they'll be in situations where they must bend the law a little or even break it altogether for the good of country and agency. When you're up against the scum we've got to deal with—terrorists, Soviet agents—you can't always play strictly within the rules, not if you want to win, and our government has created the agency to *win*, Jerry. You're young, but I'm sure you've been around long enough to know what I'm talking about. I'm sure you've bent the law a few times yourself."

"Well, sir, yes, a little, maybe," Peake said carefully, beginning to sweat under the collar of his white shirt.

They passed a sign: LAKE ARROWHEAD—10 MILES.

"All right, Jerry, I'm going to level with you and hope you're the solid, reliable man I think you are. I haven't brought a lot of backup with us because the word's come down from Washington that Mrs. Leben and Benjamin Shadway have to go. And if we're going to take care of them, we need to keep the party small, quiet, discreet."

"Take care of them?"

"They're to be terminated, Jerry. If we find them at the cabin with Eric Leben, we try our best to take Leben prisoner so he can be studied under lab conditions, but Shadway and the woman have to be terminated, with prejudice. That would be difficult if not impossible with a lot of police present; we'd have to delay the terminations until we had Shadway and Mrs. Leben in our sole custody, then stage a fake escape attempt or something. And with too many of our own men present, there'd be a greater chance of the terminations leaking out to the media. In a way, it's sort of a blessing that you and I are getting a chance to handle this alone, because we'll be able to stage it just right before the police and media types are brought in."

Terminate? The agency had no license to terminate civilians. This was mad. But Peake said, "Why terminate Shadway and Mrs. Leben?"

"I'm afraid that's classified, Jerry."

"But the warrant that cites them for suspected espionage and for the police murders in Palm Springs . . . well, that's just a cover story, right? Just a way to get the local cops to help us in the search."

"Yes," Sharp said, "but there's a great deal about this case you don't know, Jerry. Information that's tightly held and that I can't share with you, not even though I'm asking you to assist me in what may appear, to you, to be a highly illegal and possibly even immoral undertaking. But as deputy director, I assure you, Shadway and Mrs. Leben *are* a mortal danger to this country, so dangerous that we dare not let them speak with the media or with local authorities."

Bullshit, Peake thought, but he said nothing, just drove onward under felt-green and blue-green trees that arched over the road.

Sharp said, "The decision to terminate is not mine alone. It comes from Washington, Jerry. And not just from Jarrod McClain. Much higher than that, Jerry. Much higher. The very highest."

Bullshit, Peake thought. Do you really expect me to believe the president ordered the cold-blooded killing of two hapless civilians who've gotten in over their heads by no real fault of their own?

Then he realized that, before the insights he had achieved at the hospital in Palm Springs a short while ago, he might well have been naive enough to believe every word of what Sharp was telling him. The new Jerry Peake, enlightened both by the way Sharp had treated Sarah Kiel and by the way he'd reacted to The Stone, was not quite so gullible as the old Jerry Peake, but Sharp had no way of knowing that.

"From the highest authority, Jerry."

Somehow, Peake knew that Anson Sharp had his own reasons for wanting Shadway and Rachael Leben dead, that Washington knew nothing about Sharp's plans. He could not cite the reason for his certainty in this matter, but he had no doubt. Call it a hunch. Legends—and would-be legends—had to trust their hunches.

"They're armed, Jerry—and dangerous, I assure you. Though they aren't guilty of the crimes we've specified on the warrant, they are guilty of other crimes of which I can't speak because you don't have a high enough security clearance. But you can rest assured that we won't exactly be gunning down a pair of upstanding citizens."

Peake was amazed by the tremendously increased sensitivity of his crap detector. Only yesterday, when he had been in awe of every superior agent, he might not have perceived the pure, unadulterated stink of Sharp's smooth line, but now the stench was overwhelming.

"But sir," Peake said, "if they surrender, give up their guns? We still terminate . . . with prejudice?"

"Yes."

"We're judge, jury, and executioner?"

A note of impatience entered Sharp's voice. "Jerry, damn it all, do you think I *like* this? I killed in the war, in Vietnam, when my country told me killing was necessary, and I didn't like that much, not even when it was a certifiable enemy, so I'm not exactly jumping with joy over the prospect of killing Shadway and Mrs. Leben, who on the surface would appear to deserve killing a whole hell of a lot less than the Vietcong did. However, I am privy to top-secret information that's convinced me they're a terrible threat to my country, and I am in receipt of orders *from the highest authority* to terminate them. If you want to know the truth, it makes me a little sick. Nobody likes to face the fact that sometimes an immoral act is the only right thing to be done, that the world is a place of moral grays, not just black and white. I don't like it, but I know my duty."

Oh, you like it well enough, Peake thought. You like it so much that the mere prospect of blowing them away has you so excited you're ready to piss in your pants.

"Jerry? Do you know your duty, too? Can I count on you?"

■ In the living room of the cabin, Ben found something that he and Rachael had not noticed before: a pair of binoculars on the far side of the armchair near the window. Putting them to his eyes and looking out the window, he could clearly see the bend in the dirt road where he and Rachael had crouched to study the cabin. Had Eric been in the chair, watching them with the binoculars?

In less than fifteen minutes, Ben finished searching the living room and the three bedrooms. It was at the window of the last of these chambers that he saw the broken brush at the far edge of the lawn, at a point well removed from that place where he and Rachael had come out of the forest on their initial approach to the cabin. That was, he suspected, where Eric had gone into the woods just after spotting them with the binoculars. Increasingly, it appeared that the noises they heard in the forest had been the sounds of Eric stalking them.

Very likely Leben was still out there, watching.

The time had come to go after him.

Benny left the bedroom, crossed the living room. In the kitchen, as he pushed open the rear screen door, he saw the ax out of the corner of his eye: It was leaning against the side of the refrigerator.

Ax?

Turning away from the door, frowning, puzzled, he looked down at the sharp blade. He was certain it had not been there when he and Rachael had entered the cabin through the same door.

Something cold crawled through the hollow of his spine.

After he and Rachael had made the first circuit of the house, they had wound up in the garage, where they had discussed what they must do next. Then they had come back inside and had gone straight through the kitchen to the living room to gather up the Wildcard file. That done, they had returned to the garage, gotten into the Mercedes, and driven down to the gate. Neither time had they passed *this* side of the refrigerator. Had the ax been here then?

The icy entity inside Ben's spine had crept all the way up to the base of his skull.

Ben saw two explanations for the ax—only two. First, perhaps Eric had been in the kitchen while they'd been in the adjacent garage planning their next move.

He could have been holding the weapon, waiting for them to return to the house, intending to catch them by surprise. They had been only feet away from Eric without realizing it, only moments away from the quick, biting agony of the ax. Then, for some reason, as Eric listened to them discuss strategy, he had decided against attacking, opted for some other course of action, and had put down the ax.

Or . . .

Or Eric had not been in the cabin then, had only entered later, after he saw them drive away in the Mercedes. He had discarded the ax, thinking they were gone for good, then had fled without it when he heard Benny returning in the Ford.

One or the other.

Which? The need to answer that question seemed urgent and all-important. Which?

If Eric had been here earlier, when Rachael and Ben were in the garage, why hadn't he attacked? What had changed his mind?

The cabin was almost as empty of sound as a vacuum. Listening, Ben tried to determine if the silence was one of expectation, shared by him and one other lurking presence, or a silence of solitude.

Solitude, he soon decided. The dead, hollow, empty stillness that you experienced only when you were utterly and unquestionably alone. Eric was not in the house.

Ben looked through the screen door at the woods that lay beyond the brown lawn. The forest appeared still, as well, and he had the unsettling feeling that Eric was not out there, either, that he would have the woods to himself if he searched for his prey among the trees.

"Eric?" he said softly but aloud, expecting and receiving no answer. "Where the hell have you gone, Eric?"

He lowered the shotgun, no longer bothering to hold it at the ready because he knew in his bones that he would not encounter Eric on this mountain.

More silence.

Heavy, oppressive, profound silence.

He sensed that he was teetering precariously on the edge of a horrible revelation. He had made a mistake. A deadly mistake. One that he could not correct. But what was it? What mistake? Where had he gone wrong? He looked hard at the discarded ax, desperately seeking understanding.

Then his breath caught in his throat.

"My God," he whispered. "Rachael."

■ Lake Arrowhead—3 miles.

Peake got behind a slow-moving camper in a no-passing zone, but Sharp did not seem bothered by the delay because he was busy seeking Peake's agreement to the double murder of Shadway and Mrs. Leben.

"Of course, Jerry, if you have the slightest qualms at all about participating, then you leave it to me. Naturally, I expect you to back me up in a pinch—that's part of your job, after all—but if we can disarm Shadway and the woman without trouble, then I'll handle the terminations myself."

I'll still be an accessory to murder, Peake thought.

But he said, "Well, sir, I don't want to let you down."

"I'm glad to hear you say that, Jerry. I would be disappointed if you didn't have the right stuff. I mean, I was so sure of your commitment and courage when I decided to bring you along on this assignment. And I can't stress strongly enough how grateful your country and the agency will be for your wholehearted cooperation."

You psycho creep, you lying sack of shit, Peake thought.

But he said, "Sir, I don't want to do anything that would be opposed to the best interests of my country—or that would leave a black mark of any kind on my agency record."

Sharp smiled, reading total capitulation in that statement.

■ Ben moved slowly around the kitchen, peering closely at the floor, where traces of broth from the discarded soup and stew cans glistened on the tile. He and Rachael had taken care to step over and around the spills when they had gone through the kitchen, and Ben had not previously noticed any of Eric's footprints in the mess, which was something he was certain he would have seen.

Now he found what had not been there earlier: almost a full footprint in a patch of thick gravy from the Dinty Moore can, and a heelprint in a gob of peanut butter. A man's boots, large ones, by the look of the tread.

Two more prints shone dully on the tile near the refrigerator, where Eric had tracked the gravy and peanut butter when he had gone over there to put down the ax and, of course, to hide. To hide. Jesus. When Ben and Rachael had entered the kitchen from the garage and had stepped into the living room to gather up the scattered pages of the Wildcard file, Eric had been crouched at the far side of the refrigerator, hiding.

Heart racing, Ben turned away from the prints and hurried to the door that connected with the garage.

■ Lake Arrowhead.
   They had arrived.

The slow-moving camper pulled into the parking lot of a sporting-goods store, getting out of their way, and Peake accelerated.

Having consulted the directions that The Stone had written on a slip of paper, Sharp said, "You're headed the right way. Just follow the state route north around the lake. In four miles or so, look for a branch road on the right, with a cluster of ten mailboxes, one of them with a big red-and-white iron rooster on top of it."

As Peake drove, he saw Sharp lift a black attaché case onto his lap and open it. Inside were two thirty-eight pistols. He put one on the seat between them.

Peake said, "What's that?"

"Your gun for this operation."

"I've got my service revolver."

"It's not hunting season. Can't have a lot of noisy gunfire, Jerry. That might bring neighbors poking around or even alert some sheriff's deputy who just happens to be in the area." Sharp withdrew a silencer from the attaché case and began to screw it onto his own pistol. "You can't use a silencer on a revolver, and we sure don't want anybody interrupting us until it's over and we've had plenty of time to adjust the bodies to fit our scenario."

What the hell am I going to do? Peake wondered as he piloted the sedan north along the lake, looking for a red-and-white iron rooster.

■ On another road, State Route 138, Rachael had left lake Arrowhead behind. She was approaching Silverwood Lake, where the scenery of the high San Bernardinos was even more breathtaking—though she had no eye for scenery in her current state of mind.

From Silverwood, 138 led out of the mountains and almost due west until it connected with Interstate 15. There, she intended to stop for gasoline, then follow 15 north and east, all the way across the desert to Las Vegas. That was a drive of more than two hundred miles over some of the most starkly beautiful and utterly desolate land on the continent, and even under the best of circumstances, it could be a lonely journey.

Benny, she thought, I wish you were here.

She passed a lightning-blasted tree that reached toward the sky with dead black limbs.

The white clouds that had recently appeared were getting thicker. A few of them were not white.

■ In the empty garage, Ben saw a two-inch-by-four-inch patch of boot-tread pattern imprinted on the concrete floor in some oily fluid that glistened in the beams of intruding sunlight. He knelt and put his nose to the spot. He was certain that the vague smell of beef gravy was not an imaginary scent.

The tread mark must have been here when he and Rachael returned to the car with the Wildcard pages, but he had not noticed it.

He got up and moved farther into the garage, studying the floor closely, and in only a few seconds he saw a small moist brown glob about half the size of a pea. He touched his finger to it, brought the finger to his nose. Peanut butter. Carried here on the sole or heel of one of Eric Leben's boots while Ben and Rachael were in the living room, busily stuffing the Wildcard file into the garbage bag.

Returning here with Rachael and the file, Ben had been in a hurry because it had seemed to him that the most important thing was to get her out of the cabin and off the mountain before either Eric or the authorities showed up. So he had not looked down and had not noticed the tread mark or the peanut butter. And, of course, he'd seen no reason to search for signs of Eric in places he had searched only minutes earlier. He could not have anticipated this cleverness from a man with devastating brain injuries—a walking dead man who, if he followed at all in the pattern of the lab mice, should be somewhat disoriented, deranged, mentally and emotionally unstable. Therefore, Ben could not blame himself; no, he had done the right thing when he had sent Rachael off in the Mercedes, thinking he was sending her away all by herself, never realizing that she was not alone in the car. How could he have realized? It was the *only* thing he could have done. It was not at all his fault, this unforeseeable development was not his fault, not his fault— but he cursed himself vehemently.

Waiting in the kitchen with the ax, listening to them plan their next moves as they stood in the garage, Eric must have realized that he had a chance of getting

Rachael alone, and evidently that prospect appealed to him so much that he was willing to forgo a whack at Ben. He'd hidden beside the refrigerator until they were in the living room, then crept into the garage, took the keys from the ignition, quietly opened the trunk, returned the keys to the ignition, climbed into the trunk, and pulled the lid shut behind himself.

If Rachael had a flat tire and opened the trunk . . .

Or if, on some quiet stretch of desert highway, Eric decided to kick the back seat of the car off its mountings and climb through from the trunk . . .

His heart pounding so hard that it shook him, Ben raced out of the garage toward the rental Ford in front of the cabin.

■   Jerry Peake spotted the red-and-white iron rooster mounted atop one mailbox of ten. He turned into a narrow branch road that led up a steep slope past widely separated driveways and past houses mostly hidden in the forest that encroached from both sides.

Sharp had finished screwing silencers on both thirty-eights. Now he took two fully loaded spare magazines from the attaché case, kept one for himself, and put the other beside the pistol that he had provided for Peake. "I'm glad you're with me on this one, Jerry."

Peake had not actually said that he was with Sharp on this one, and in fact he could not see any way he could participate in cold-blooded murder and still live with himself. For sure, his dream of being a legend would be shattered.

On the other hand, if he crossed Sharp, he would destroy his career in the DSA.

"The macadam should turn to gravel," Sharp said, consulting the directions The Stone had given him.

In spite of all his recent insights, in spite of the advantages those insights should have given him, Jerry Peake did not know what to do. He did not see a way out that would leave him with both his self-respect and his career. As he drove up the slope, deeper into the dark of the woods, a panic began to build in him, and for the first time in many hours he felt inadequate.

"Gravel," Anson Sharp noted as they left the pavement.

Suddenly Peake saw that his predicament was even worse than he had realized because Sharp was likely to kill him, too. If Peake tried to stop Sharp from killing Shadway and the Leben woman, then Sharp would simply shoot Peake first and set it up to look as if the two fugitives had done it. That would even give Sharp an excuse to kill Shadway and Mrs. Leben: "They wasted poor damn Peake, so there was nothing else I could do." Sharp might even come out of it a hero. On the other hand, Peake couldn't just step out of the way and let the deputy director cut them down, for that would not satisfy Sharp; if Peake did not participate in the killing with enthusiasm, Sharp would never really trust him and would most likely shoot him *after* Shadway and Mrs. Leben were dead, then claim one of them had done it. Jesus. To Peake (whose mind was working faster than it had ever worked in his life), it looked as if he had only two choices: join in the killing and thereby gain Sharp's total trust—or kill Sharp before Sharp could kill anyone else. But no, wait, that was no solution, either—

"Not much farther," Sharp said, leaning forward in his seat, peering intently through the windshield. "Slow it to a crawl."

—no solution at all, because if he shot Sharp, no one would ever believe that Sharp had intended to kill Shadway and Mrs. Leben—after all, what was the bastard's *motive?*—and Peake would wind up on trial for blowing away his superior. The courts were never ever easy on cop killers, even if the cop killer was another cop, so sure as hell he'd go to prison, where all those seven-foot-tall, no-neck criminal types would just *delight* in raping a former government agent. Which left—what?—one horrible choice and only one, which was to join in the killing, descend to Sharp's level, forget about being a legend and settle for being a goddamn Gestapo thug. This was crazy, being trapped in a situation with no right answers, only wrong answers, crazy and unfair, damn it, and Peake felt as if the top of his head were going to blow off from the strain of seeking a better answer.

"That's the gate she described," Sharp said. "And it's open! Park this side of it."

Jerry Peake stopped the car, switched off the engine.

Instead of the expected quietude of the forest, another sound came through the open windows the moment the sedan fell silent: a racing engine, another car, echoing through the trees.

"Someone's coming," Sharp said, grabbing his silencer-equipped pistol and throwing open his door just as a blue Ford roared into view on the road above them, bearing down at high speed.

■ While the service-station attendant filled the Mercedes with Arco unleaded, Rachael got candy and a can of Coke from the vending machines. She leaned against the trunk, alternately sipping Coke and munching on a Mr. Goodbar, hoping that a big dose of refined sugar would lift her spirits and make the long drive ahead seem less lonely.

"Going to Vegas?" the attendant asked.

"That's right."

"I 'spected so. I'm good at guessing where folks is headed. You got that Vegas look. Now listen, first thing you play when you get there is roulette. Number twenty-four, 'cause I have this hunch about it, just looking at you. Okay?"

"Okay. Twenty-four."

He held her Coke while she got the cash from her wallet to pay him. "You win a fortune, I'll expect half, of course. But if you lose, it'll be the devil's work, not mine."

He bent down and looked in her window just as she was about to drive away. "You be careful out there on the desert. It can be mean."

"I know," she said.

She drove onto I-15 and headed north-northeast toward distant Barstow, feeling very much alone.

26   A MAN GONE BAD

BEN SWUNG THE FORD AROUND THE BEND AND STARTED TO accelerate but saw the dark green sedan just beyond the open gate. He braked, and the Ford fishtailed on the dirt lane. The steering wheel jerked in his hands. But he did not lose control of the car, kept it out of the ditches on both sides, and slid to a halt in a roiling cloud of dust about fifty yards above the gate.

Below, two men in dark suits had already gotten out of the sedan. One of them was hanging back, although the other—and bigger—man was rushing straight up the hill, closing fast, like a too-eager marathon runner who had forgotten to change into his running shorts and shoes. The yellowish dust gave the illusion of marbled solidity as it whirled through veined patterns of shade and sunshine. But in spite of the dust and in spite of the thirty yards that separated Ben from the oncoming man, he could see the gun in the guy's hand. He could also see the silencer, which startled him.

No police or federal agents used silencers. And Eric's business partners had opened up with a submachine gun in the heart of Palm Springs, so it was unlikely they would suddenly turn discreet.

Then, only a fraction of a second after Ben saw the silencer, he got a good look at the grinning face of the oncoming man, and he was simultaneously astonished, confused, and afraid. Anson Sharp. It had been sixteen years since he had seen Anson Sharp in Nam, back in '72. Yet he had no doubt about the man's identity. Time had changed Sharp, but not much. During the spring and summer of '72, Ben had expected the big bastard to shoot him in the back or hire some Saigon hoodlum to do it—Sharp had been capable of anything—but Ben had been very careful, had not given Sharp the slightest opportunity. Now here was Sharp again, as if he'd stepped through a time warp.

What the hell had brought him here now, more than a decade and a half later? Ben had the crazy notion that Sharp had been looking for him all this time, anxious to settle the score, and just happened to track him down now, in the midst of all these other troubles. But of course that was unlikely—impossible—so somehow Sharp must be involved with the Wildcard mess.

Less than twenty yards away, Sharp took a shooter's spreadlegged stance on the road below and opened fire with the pistol. With a *whap* and a wet crackle of gummy safety glass, a slug punched through the windshield one foot to the right of Ben's face.

Throwing the car into reverse, he twisted around in his seat to see the road behind. Steering with one hand, he drove backward up the dirt lane as fast as he dared. He heard another bullet ricochet off the car, and it sounded very close. Then he was around the turn and out of Sharp's sight.

He reversed all the way to the cabin before he stopped. There he shifted the Ford into neutral, left the engine running, and engaged the handbrake, which was the only thing holding the car on the slope. He got out and quickly put the shotgun and the Combat Magnum on the dirt to one side. Leaning back in through the open door, he gripped the release lever for the handbrake and looked down the hill.

Two hundred yards below, the Chevy sedan came around the bend, moving fast, and started up toward him. They slowed when they saw him, but they did not stop, and he dared to wait a couple of seconds longer before he popped the handbrake and stepped back.

Succumbing to gravity, the Ford rolled down the lane, which was so narrow that the Chevy could not pull entirely out of the way. The Ford encountered a small bump, jolted over it, and veered toward one drainage ditch. For a moment Ben thought the car was going to run harmlessly off to the side, but it stuttered over other ruts that turned it back on course.

The driver of the Chevy stopped, began to reverse, but the Ford was picking up a lot of speed and was bearing down too fast to be avoided. The Ford hit another bump and angled somewhat toward the left again, so at the last second the Chevy swung hard to the right in an evasive maneuver, almost dropping into the ditch. Nevertheless, the two vehicles collided with a clang and crunch of metal, though the impact wasn't as direct or as devastating as Ben had hoped. The right front fender of the Ford hit the right front fender of the Chevy, then the Ford slid sideways to the left, as if it might come around a hundred and eighty degrees until it was sitting alongside the Chevy, both of them facing uphill. But when it had made only a quarter turn, the Ford's rear wheels slammed into the ditch, and it halted with a shudder, perpendicular to the road, effectively blocking it.

The stricken Chevy rolled erratically backward for maybe thirty feet, narrowly missing the other ditch, then came to a halt. Both front doors were flung open. Anson Sharp got out of one, and the driver got out of the other, and neither of them appeared to have been hurt, which was pretty much what Ben had expected when the Ford had not hit them head-on.

Ben grabbed the shotgun and the Combat Magnum, turned, and ran around the side of the cabin. He sprinted across the sun-browned backyard to the toothlike granite formations from which he and Rachael had observed the place earlier. He paused for a moment to scan the woods ahead, looking for the quickest cover, then moved off into the trees, toward the same brush-flanked dry wash that he and Rachael had used before.

Behind him, in the distance, Sharp was calling his name.

■ Still caught in the spiderweb of his moral dilemma, Jerry Peake hung back a little from Sharp and watched his boss warily.

The deputy director had lost his head the moment he had seen Shadway in the blue Ford. He had gone charging up the road, shooting from a disadvantageous position, when he had little or no chance of hitting his target. Besides, he could see that the woman was not in the car with Shadway, and if they did kill the man before asking questions, they might not be able to find out where she had gone. It was shockingly sloppy procedure, and Peake was appalled.

Now Sharp stalked the perimeter of the rear yard, breathing like an angry bull, in such a peculiar state of excitement and rage that he seemed oblivious of the danger of presenting such a high profile. At several places along the edge of the woods, he took a step or two into the knee-high weeds, peering down through the serried ranks of trees.

From three sides of the yard, the forested land fell away in a jumble of rocky slopes and narrow defiles that offered countless shadowed hiding places. They had lost Shadway for the moment. That much was obvious to Peake. They should call for backup now, because otherwise their man was going to slip entirely away from them through the wilderness.

But Sharp was determined to kill Shadway. He was not going to listen to reason. Peake just watched and waited and said nothing.

Looking down into the woods, Sharp shouted: "United States government, Shadway. Defense Security Agency. You hear me? DSA. We want to talk to you, Shadway."

An invocation of authority was not going to work, not now, not after Sharp had started shooting the moment he had seen Ben Shadway.

Peake wondered if the deputy director was undergoing a breakdown, which would explain his behavior with Sarah Kiel and his determination to kill Shadway and his ill-advised, irresponsible, blazing-gun charge up the road a couple of minutes ago.

Stomping along the edge of the woods, wading a few steps into the underbrush again, Sharp called out: "Shadway! Hey, it's me, Shadway. Anson Sharp. Do you remember me, Shadway? Do you remember?"

Jerry Peake took one step back and blinked as if someone had just slapped him in the face: Sharp and Shadway knew each other, for God's sake; *knew* each other, not merely in the abstract as the hunter and the hunted know each other, but personally. And it was clear—from Sharp's taunting manner, crimson face, bulging eyes, and stentorian breathing—that they were bitter adversaries. This was a grudge match of some kind, which eliminated any small doubt Peake might have had about the possibility that anyone above Sharp in the DSA had ordered Shadway and Mrs. Leben killed. Sharp had decided to terminate these fugitives, Sharp and no one else. Peake's instincts had been on the money. But it did not solve anything to know he had been right when he'd smelled deception in Sharp's story. Right or not, he was still left with the choice of either cooperating with the deputy director or pulling a gun on him, and neither course would leave him with both his career and his self-respect intact.

Sharp plunged deeper into the woods, started down a slope into the gloom beneath interlacing boughs of pine and spruce. He looked back, shouted at Peake to join in the chase, took several more steps into the brush, glanced back again and called out more insistently when he saw that Peake had not moved.

Reluctantly Peake followed. Some of the tall grass was so dry and brittle that it prickled through his socks. Burrs and bits of milkweed fluff adhered to his trousers. When he leaned against the trunk of a tree, his hand came away sticky with resin. Vines tried to trip him up. Brambles snagged his suit. His leather-soled shoes slipped treacherously on the stones, on patches of dry pine needles, on moss, on everything. Climbing over a fallen tree, he put his foot down in a teeming nest of ants; although he hurriedly moved out of their way and wiped them off his shoe, a few scaled his leg, and finally he had to pause, roll up his trousers, and brush the damn things off his badly bitten calf.

"We're not dressed for this," he told Sharp when he caught up with him.

"Quiet," Sharp said, easing under a low-hanging pine branch heavy with thorn-tipped cones.

Peake's feet almost skidded out from under him, and he grabbed desperately at a branch. Barely managing to stay on his feet, he said, "We're going to break our necks."

"Quiet!" Sharp whispered furiously. Over his shoulder, he looked back angrily at Peake. His face was unnerving: eyes wide and wild, skin flushed, nostrils flared, teeth bared, jaw muscles taut, the arteries throbbing in his temples. That savage expression confirmed Peake's suspicion that since spotting Shadway the deputy director had been out of control, driven by an almost maniacal hatred and by sheer blood lust.

They pushed through a narrow gap in a wall of dense and bristly brush decorated with poisonous-looking orange berries. They stumbled into a shallow dry wash—and saw Shadway. The fugitive was fifteen yards farther along the channel, following it down through the forest. He was moving low and fast, carrying a shotgun.

Peake crouched and sidled against the wall of the channel to make as difficult a target of himself as possible.

But Sharp stood in full view, as if he thought he was Superman, bellowed Shadway's name, pulled off several shots with the silencer-equipped pistol. With a silencer, you traded range and accuracy for the quiet you gained, so considering the distance between Sharp and Shadway, virtually every shot was wasted. Either Sharp did not know the effective range of his weapon—which seemed unlikely— or he was so completely a captive of his hatred that he was no longer capable of rational action. The first shot tore bark off a tree at the edge of the dry wash, two yards to Shadway's left, and with a high thin whine, the second slug ricocheted off a boulder. Then Shadway disappeared where the runoff channel curved to the right, but Sharp fired three more shots, in spite of being unable to see his target.

Even the finest silencer quickly deteriorates with use, and the soft *whump* of Sharp's pistol grew noticeably louder with each round he expended. The fifth and final shot sounded like a wooden mallet striking a hard but rubbery surface, not thunderous by any means but loud enough to echo for a moment through the woods.

When the echo faded, Sharp listened intently for a few seconds, then bounded back across the dry wash toward the same gap in the brush through which they had entered the channel. "Come on, Peake. We'll get the bastard now."

Following, Peake said, "But we can't chase him down in these woods. He's better dressed for it than we are."

"We're getting out of the woods, damn it," Sharp said, and indeed they were headed back the way they had come, up toward the yard behind the cabin. "All I wanted to do was make sure we got him moving, so he wouldn't just lie in here and wait us out. He's moving now, by God, and what he'll do is head straight down the mountain toward the lake road. He'll try to steal some transportation down there, and with any luck at all we'll nail the son of a bitch as he's trying to hot-wire some fisherman's car. Now *come on.*"

Sharp still had that savage, frenetic, half-sane look, but Peake realized that the deputy director was not, after all, as overwhelmed and as totally controlled by hatred as he had at first appeared. He was in a rage, yes, and not entirely rational, but he had not lost all of his cunning. He was still a dangerous man.

■ Ben was running for his own life, but he was in a panic about Rachael as well. She was heading to Nevada in the Mercedes, unaware that Eric was curled up in the trunk. Somehow Ben had to catch up with her, though minute by minute she was getting a greater lead on him, rapidly decreasing his hope of closing the gap. At the very least he had to find a telephone and get hold of Whitney Gavis, his man in Vegas, so when Rachael got there and called Whitney for the motel keys, he would be able to alert her to Eric's presence. Of course, Eric might break out of that trunk or be released from it long before Rachael arrived in Vegas, but that hideous possibility did not even bear contemplation.

Rachael alone on the darkening desert highway . . . a strange noise in the trunk . . . her cold dead husband suddenly kicking his way out of confinement, knocking the back seat off its hinge pins . . . clambering into the passenger compartment . . .

That monstrous picture shook Ben so badly that he dared not dwell on it. If he gave it too much thought, it would start to seem like an inevitable scenario, and he would be unable to go on.

So he resolutely refused to think the unthinkable, and he left the dry wash for a deer trail that offered a relatively easy descent for thirty yards before turning between two fir trees in a direction he did not wish to pursue. Thereafter, progress became considerably more difficult, the ground more treacherous: a wild blackberry patch, wickedly thorned, forced him to detour fifty yards out of his way; a long slope of rotten shale crumbled under his feet, obliging him to descend at an angle to avoid pitching headfirst to the bottom as the surface shifted beneath him; deadfalls of old trees and brush forced him either to go around or to climb over at the risk of a sprained ankle or broken leg. More than once, he wished that he were wearing a pair of woodsman's boots instead of Adidas running shoes, though his jeans and long-sleeve shirt provided some protection from burrs and scratchy branches. Regardless of the difficulty, he forged ahead because he knew that eventually he would reach the lower slopes where the houses below Eric Leben's cabin stood on less wild property; there he would find the going easier. Besides, he had no choice but to go on because he did not know if Anson Sharp was still on his tail.

Anson Sharp.

It was hard to believe.

During his second year in Nam, Ben had been a lieutenant in command of his own recon squad—serving under his platoon captain, Olin Ashborn—planning and executing a series of highly successful forays into enemy-held territory. His sergeant, George Mendoza, had been killed by machine-gun fire during a mission to free four U.S. prisoners of war being held at a temporary camp before transfer to Hanoi. Anson Sharp was the sergeant assigned to replace Mendoza.

From the moment he had met Sharp, Ben had not cared for him. It was just one of those instinctive reactions, for initially he had not seen anything seriously wrong with Sharp. The man was not a great sergeant, not Mendoza's equal, but he was competent, and he did not do either drugs or alcohol, which put him a notch above a lot of other soldiers in that miserable war. Perhaps he relished his authority a bit too much and came down too hard on the men under him. Perhaps his talk about women was colored by a disquieting disrespect for them, but at first it had seemed like the usual boring and only half-serious misogyny that you sometimes heard from a certain number of men in any large group; Ben had seen nothing evil about it—until later. And perhaps Sharp had been too quick to advise against contact when the enemy was sighted and too quick to encourage withdrawal once the enemy was engaged, but at first he could not have been accurately labeled a coward. Yet Ben had been wary of him and had felt somewhat guilty about it because he had no substantial reasons for distrusting his new sergeant.

One of the things he had disliked was Sharp's apparent lack of conviction in all things. Sharp seemed to have no opinions about politics, religion, capital punishment, abortion, or any of the other issues that interested his contemporaries. Sharp also had no strong feelings about the war, either pro or con. He didn't care who won, and he regarded the quasidemocratic South and the totalitarian North as moral equals—if he thought about it at all in moral terms. He had joined the Marines to avoid being drafted into the Army, and he felt none of that leatherneck pride or commitment that made the corps a home to most of the other men in it. He intended to have a military career, though what drew him to the service was not duty or pride but the hope of promotion to a position of real power, early retirement in just twenty years, and a generous pension; he could talk for hours about military pensions and benefits.

He had no special passion for music, art, books, sports, hunting, fishing, or anything else—except for himself. He himself was his own—and only—passion. Though not a hypochondriac, he was certainly obsessed with the state of his health and would talk at length about his digestion, his constipation or lack of it, and the appearance of his morning stool. Another man might simply say, "I have a splitting headache," but Anson Sharp, plagued by a similar condition, would expend two hundred words describing the degree and nature of the agony in excruciating detail and would use a finger to trace the precise line of the pain across his brow. He spent a lot of time combing his hair, always managed to be clean-shaven even under battle conditions, had a narcissistic attraction to mirrors and other reflective surfaces, and made a virtual crusade of obtaining as many creature comforts as a soldier could manage in a war zone.

It was difficult to like a man who liked nothing but himself.

But if Anson Sharp had been neither a good nor an evil man when he had gone to Nam—just bland and self-centered—the war had worked upon the unformed clay of his personality and had gradually sculpted a monster. When Ben became aware of detailed and convincing rumors of Sharp's involvement in the black market, an investigation had turned up proof of an astonishing criminal career. Sharp had been involved in the hijacking of goods in transit to post exchanges and canteens, and he had negotiated the sale of those stolen supplies to buyers in the Saigon underworld. Additional information indicated that, while not a user or direct seller of drugs, Sharp facilitated the commerce in illegal substances between the Vietnamese Mafia and U.S. soldiers. Most shocking of all, Ben's sleuthing led to the discovery that Sharp used some profits from criminal activity to keep a pied-àterre in Saigon's roughest nightclub district; there, with the assistance of an exceedingly vicious Vietnamese thug who served as a combination houseboy and dungeon master, Sharp maintained an eleven-year-old girl—Mai Van Trang—as a virtual slave, sexually abusing her whenever he had the opportunity, otherwise leaving her to the mercy of the thug.

The inevitable court-martial had not proceeded as predictably as Ben hoped.

He wanted to put Sharp away for twenty years in a military prison. But before the case came to trial, potential witnesses began to die or disappear at an alarming pace. Two Army noncoms—pushers who'd agreed to testify against Sharp in return for lenient treatment—were found dead in Saigon alleyways, throats cut. A lieutenant was fragged in his sleep, blown to bits. The weasel-faced houseboy and poor Mai Van Trang disappeared, and Ben was sure that the former was alive somewhere and that the latter was just as certainly dead and buried in an unmarked grave, not a difficult disposal problem in a nation torn by war and undermined by unmarked graves. In custody awaiting trial, Sharp could effectively plead innocence to involvement in this series of convenient deaths and vanishings, though it was surely his influence with the Vietnamese underworld that provided for such favorable developments. By the start of the court-martial, all of the witnesses against Sharp were gone, and the case was essentially reduced to Ben's word—and that of his investigators—against Sharp's smug protestations of innocence. There wasn't sufficient concrete evidence to ensure his imprisonment but far too much circumstantial evidence to get him off the hook entirely. Consequently he was stripped of his sergeant's stripes, demoted to private, and dishonorably discharged.

Even that comparatively light sentence had been a blow to Sharp, whose deep and abiding self-love had not permitted him to entertain the prospect of any punishment whatsoever. His personal comfort and well-being were his central—perhaps only—concern, and he seemed to take it for granted that, as a favored child of the universe, he would always be assured of unrelieved good fortune. Before shipping out of Vietnam in disgrace, Sharp had used all of his remaining contacts to arrange a short surprise visit to Ben, too short to do any harm, but just long enough to convey a threat: "Listen, asshole, when you get stateside again, just remember I'll be there, waiting for you. I'll know when you're coming home, and I'll have a greeting ready for you."

Ben had not taken the threat seriously. For one thing, well before the court-martial, Sharp's hesitancy on the battlefield had grown worse, so bad on some occasions that he had come perilously close to disobeying orders rather than risk his precious skin. If he had not been brought to court for theft, black-marketeering, drug dealing, and statutory rape, he very likely would have been arraigned on charges of desertion or other offenses related to his increasing cowardice. He might talk of stateside vengeance, but he would not have the guts for it. And for another thing, Ben was not worried about what would happen to him when he went home because, by then, for better or worse, he had committed himself to the war until the end of it; and that commitment gave him every reason to believe he would go home in a box, in no condition to give a damn whether or not Anson Sharp was waiting for him.

Now, descending through the shadowy forest and at last reaching the first of the half-cleared properties where houses were tucked in among the trees, Ben wondered how Anson Sharp, stripped of rank and dishonorably discharged, could have been accepted into training as a DSA agent. A man gone bad, like Sharp, usually continued skidding downward once his slide began. By now he should have been on his second or third term in prison for civilian crimes. At best, you could have expected to encounter him as a seedy grifter scratching out a dishonest living, so pathetically small-time that he did not draw the notice of the authorities.

Even if he had cleaned up his act, he could not have wiped a dishonorable discharge off his record. And with that discredit, he would have been summarily rejected by *any* law-enforcement agency, especially by an organization with standards as high as those of the Defense Security Agency.

So how the hell did he swing it? Ben wondered.

He chewed on that question as he climbed over a split-rail fence and cautiously skirted a two-story brick and weathered-pine chalet, dashing from tree to tree and bush to bush, staying out of sight as much as possible. If someone looked out a window and saw a man with a shotgun in one hand and a big revolver tucked into the waistband at his back, a call to the county sheriff would be inevitable.

Assuming that Sharp wasn't lying when he had identified himself as a Defense Security Agency operative—and there seemed no point in lying about it—the next thing Ben had to wonder about was how far Sharp had risen in the DSA. After all, it seemed far too coincidental for Sharp to have been assigned, by mere chance, to an investigation involving Ben. More likely Sharp had arranged his assignment when he had read the Leben file and discovered that Ben, his old and perhaps mostly forgotten nemesis, had a relationship with Rachael. He'd seen a long-delayed chance for revenge and had seized it. But surely an ordinary agent could not choose assignments, which meant Sharp must be in a sufficiently high position to set his own work schedule. Worse than that: Sharp was of such formidable rank that he could open fire on Ben without provocation and expect to be able to cover up a murder committed in the plain sight of one of his fellow DSA operatives.

With the threat of Anson Sharp layered on top of all the other threats that he and Rachael faced, Ben began to feel as if he were caught up in a war again. In war, incoming fire usually started up when you least expected it, and from the most unlikely source and direction. Which was exactly what Anson Sharp's appearance was: surprise fire from the most unlikely source.

At the third mountainside house, Ben nearly walked in among four young boys who were engaged in their own stealthy game of war, alerted at the last minute when one of them sprang from cover and opened fire on another with a cap-loaded machine gun. For the first time in his life, Ben experienced a vivid flashback to the war, one of those mental traumas that the media ascribed to every veteran. He fell and rolled behind several low-growing dogwoods, where he lay listening to his pounding heart, stifling a scream for half a minute until the flashback passed.

None of the boys had seen him, and when he set out again, he crawled and belly-crawled from one point of cover to another. From the leafy dogwood to a clump of wild azaleas. From the azaleas to a low limestone formation, where the desiccated corpse of a ground squirrel lay as if in warning. Then over a small hill, through rough weeds that scratched his face, under another split-rail fence.

Five minutes later, almost forty minutes after setting out from the cabin, he bulled his way down a brush-covered slope and into a dry drainage ditch alongside the state route that circled the lake.

Forty minutes, for God's sake.

How far into the lonely desert had Rachael gotten in forty minutes?

Don't think about that. Just keep moving.

He crouched in the tall weeds for a moment, catching his breath, then stood up and looked both ways. No one was in sight. No traffic was coming or going on the two-lane blacktop.

Considering that he had no intention of throwing away either the shotgun or the Combat Magnum, which made him frightfully conspicuous, he was lucky to find himself here on a Tuesday and at this hour. The state route would not have been as lightly used at any other time. During the early morning, the road would be busy with boaters, fishermen, and campers on their way to the lake, and later many of them would be returning. But in the middle of the afternoon—it was 2:55—they were comfortably settled for the day. He was also fortunate it was not a weekend, for then the road would have been heavily traveled regardless of the hour.

Deciding that he would be able to hear oncoming traffic before it drew into sight—and would, therefore, have time to conceal himself—he climbed out of the ditch and headed north on the pavement, hoping to find a car to steal.

27 ON THE ROAD AGAIN

BY 2:55, RACHAEL WAS THROUGH THE EL CAJON PASS, STILL TEN miles south of Victorville and almost forty-five miles from Barstow.

This was the last stretch of the interstate on which indications of civilization could be seen with any frequency. Even here, except for Victorville itself and the isolated houses and businesses strung between it and Hesperia and Apple Valley, there was mostly just a vast emptiness of white sand, striated rock, seared desert scrub, Joshua trees and other cactuses. During the hundred and sixty miles between Barstow and Las Vegas, there would be virtually only two outposts—Calico, the ghost town (with a cluster of attendant restaurants, service stations, and a motel or two), and Baker, which was the gateway to Death Valley National Monument and which was little more than a pit stop that flashed by in a few seconds, gone so quickly that it almost seemed like a mirage. Halloran Springs, Cal Neva, and Stateline were out there, too, but none of them really qualified as a town, and in one case the population was fewer than fifty souls. Here, where the great Mojave Desert began, humankind had tested the wasteland's dominion, but after Barstow its rule remained undisputed.

If Rachael had not been so worried about Benny, she would have enjoyed the endless vistas, the power and responsiveness of the big Mercedes, and the sense of escape and release that always buoyed her during a trip across the Mojave. But she could not stop thinking about him, and she wished she had not left him alone, even though he had made a good argument for his plan and had given her little choice. She considered turning around and going back, but he might have left by the time she reached the cabin. She might even drive straight into the arms of the police if she returned to Arrowhead, so she kept the Mercedes moving at a steady sixty miles an hour toward Barstow.

Five miles south of Victorville, she was startled by a strange hollow thumping that seemed to come from underneath the car: four or five sharp knocks, then silence. She swore under her breath at the prospect of a breakdown. Letting the speed fall to fifty and then slowly to forty, she listened closely to the Mercedes for more than half a mile.

The hum of the tires on the pavement.

The purr of the engine.

The soft whisper of the air-conditioning.

No knocking.

When the unsettling sound did not recur, she accelerated to sixty again and continued to listen expectantly, figuring that the unknown trouble was something that occurred only at higher speeds. But when, after another mile, there was no noise, she decided she must have run over potholes in the pavement. She had not seen any potholes, and she could not recall that the car had been jolted simultaneously with the thumping sound, but she could think of no other explanation. The Mercedes's suspension system and heavy-duty shocks were superb, which would have minimized the jolt of a few minor bumps, and perhaps the strange sound itself had distracted her from whatever little vibration there had been.

For a few miles, Rachael remained edgy, not exactly waiting for the entire drive train to drop out with a great crash or for the engine to explode, but half expecting some trouble that would delay her. However, when the car continued to perform with its usual quiet reliability, she relaxed, and her thoughts drifted back to Benny.

■   The green Chevy sedan had been damaged in the collision with the blue Ford—bent grille, smashed headlight, crumpled fender—but its function had not been impaired. Peake had driven down the dirt road to gravel to macadam to the state route that circled the lake, with Sharp sitting in the passenger seat, scanning the woods around them, the silencer-equipped pistol in his lap. Sharp had been confident (he said) that Shadway had gone in another direction, well away from the lake, but he had been vigilant nonetheless.

Peake had expected a shotgun blast to hit the side window and take him out at any moment. But he got down to the state route alive.

They had cruised back and forth on the main road until they had found a line of six cars and pickups parked along the berm. Those vehicles probably belonged to anglers who had gone down through the woods to the nearby lake, to a favorite but hard-to-reach fishing hole. Sharp had decided that Shadway would come off the mountain to the south of the cars and, perhaps recalling having passed them on his way to the cabin turnoff, would come north on the state route—maybe using one of the drainage ditches for cover or even staying in the forest parallel to the road—with the intention of hot-wiring new wheels for himself. Peake had slipped the sedan behind the last vehicle in the line of six, a dirty and battered Dodge station wagon, pulling over just a bit farther than the cars in front, so Shadway would not be able to see the Chevy clearly when he walked in from the south.

Now Peake and Sharp slumped low in the front seat, sitting just high enough to see through the windshield and through the windows of the station wagon in front of them. They were ready to move fast at the first sign of anyone messing with one of the cars. Or at least Sharp was ready. Peake was still in a quandary.

The trees rustled in the gusty breeze.

A wicked-looking dragonfly swooped past the windshield on softly thrumming, iridescent wings.

The dashboard clock ticked faintly, and Peake had the weird but perhaps explicable feeling that they were sitting on a time bomb.

"He'll show up in the next five minutes," Sharp said.

I hope not, Peake thought.

"We'll waste the bastard, all right," Sharp said.

Not me, Peake thought.

"He'll be expecting us to keep cruising the road, back and forth, looking for him. He won't expect us to anticipate him and be lying in wait here. He'll walk right into us."

God, I hope not, Peake thought. I hope he heads south instead of north. Or maybe goes over the top of the mountain and down the other side and never comes *near* this road. Or God, please, how about just letting him cross this road and go down to the lake and walk across the water and off onto the other shore?

Peake said, "Looks to me as if he's got more firepower than we do. I mean, I saw a shotgun. That's something to think about."

"He won't use it on us," Sharp said.

"Why not?"

"Because he's a prissy-assed moralist, that's why. A *sensitive* type. Worries about his goddamn soul too much. His type can justify killing only in the middle of a war—and only a war he believes in—or in some other situation where he has absolutely no other choice but to kill in order to save himself."

"Yeah, well, but if we start shooting at him, he won't have any choice except to shoot back. Right?"

"You just don't understand him. In a situation like this—which *isn't* a damn war—if there's any place to run, if he's not backed into a tight corner, then he'll always choose to run instead of fighting. It's the morally superior choice, you see, and he likes to think of himself as a morally superior guy. Out here in these woods, he's got plenty of places to run. So if we shoot and hit him, it's over. But if we miss, he won't shoot back—not that pussy-faced hypocrite—he'll run, and we'll have another chance to track him down and take another whack at him, and he'll keep giving us chances until, sooner or later, he either shakes loose of us for good or we blow him away. Just for God's sake don't ever back him into a corner; always leave him an out. When he's running, we have a chance of shooting him in the back, which is the wisest thing we could do, because the guy was in Marine Recon, and he was good, better than most, the best—I have to give him that much—the best. And he seems to've stayed in condition. So if he had to do it, he could take your head off with his bare hands."

Peake was unable to decide which of these new revelations was most appalling: that, to settle a grudge of Sharp's, they were going to kill not only an innocent man but a man with an unusually complex and faithfully observed moral code; or that they were going to shoot him in the back if they had the chance; or that their target would put his own life at extreme risk rather than casually waste them, though they were prepared to casually waste *him*; or that, if given no other choice, the guy had the ability to utterly destroy them without working up a sweat. Peake had last been to bed yesterday afternoon, almost twenty-two hours ago, and he badly needed sleep, but his grainy eyes were open wide and his mind was alert as he contemplated the wealth of bad news that he had just received.

Sharp leaned forward suddenly, as if he'd spotted Shadway coming up from the south, but it must have been nothing, for he leaned back in his seat again and let out his pent-up breath.

He's as scared as he is angry, Peake thought.

Peake steeled himself to ask a question that would most likely anger or at least irritate Sharp. "You know him, sir?"

"Yeah," Sharp said sourly, unwilling to elaborate.

"From where?"

"Another place."

"When?"

"Way back," Sharp said in a tone of voice that made it clear there were to be no more questions.

From the beginning of this investigation yesterday evening, Peake had been surprised that someone as high as the deputy director would plunge right into the fieldwork, shoulder to shoulder with junior agents, instead of coordinating things from an office. This was an important case. But Peake had been involved in other important cases, and he had never seen any of the agency's titled officers actually getting their hands dirty. Now he understood: Sharp had chosen to wade into the muddy center of this one because he had discovered that his old enemy, Shadway, was involved, and because only in the field would he have an opportunity to kill Shadway and stage the shooting to look legitimate.

"Way back," Sharp said, more to himself this time than to Jerry Peake. "Way back."

■   The roomy interior of the Mercedes-Benz trunk was warm because it was heated by the sun. But Eric Leben, curled on his side in the darkness, felt another and greater warmth: the peculiar and almost pleasant fire that burned in his blood, flesh, and bones, a fire that seemed to be melting him down into . . . something other than a man.

The inner and outer heat, the darkness, the motion of the car, and the hypnotic humming of the tires had lulled him into a trancelike state. For a time he had forgotten who he was, where he was, and why he had put himself in this place. Thoughts eddied lazily through his mind, like opalescent films of oil drifting, rippling, intertwining, and forming slow-motion whirlpools on the surface of a lake. At times his thoughts were light and pleasant: the sweet body curves and skin textures of Rachael, Sarah, and other women with whom he had made love; the favorite teddy bear he had slept with as a child; fragments of movies he had seen; lines of favorite songs. But sometimes the mental images grew dark and frightening: Uncle Barry grinning and beckoning; an unknown dead woman in a dumpster; another woman nailed to a wall—naked, dead, staring; the hooded figure of Death looming out of shadows; a deformed face in a mirror; strange and monstrous hands somehow attached to his own wrists . . .

Once, the car stopped, and the cessation of movement caused him to float up from the trance. He quickly reoriented himself, and that icy reptilian rage flooded back into him. He eagerly flexed and unflexed his strong, elongated, sharp-nailed hands in anticipation of choking the life out of Rachael—she who had denied him, she who had rejected him, she who had sent him into the path of death. He almost burst out of the trunk, then heard a man's voice, hesitated. Judging by the bits of inane conversation he was able to overhear, and because of the noise of a gas-pump nozzle being inserted into the fuel tank, Eric realized that Rachael had stopped at a service station, where there were sure to be a few—and perhaps a lot of—people. He had to wait for a better opportunity.

Earlier, back at the cabin, when he had opened the trunk, he had immediately noted that the rear wall was a solid metal panel, making it impossible for him to simply kick the car's rear seat off its pins and clamber through into the passenger compartment. Furthermore, the latch mechanism was unreachable from within the trunk because of a metal cover plate fastened in place by several Phillips-head screws. Fortunately, Rachael and Shadway had been so busy gathering up the copy of the Wildcard file that Eric had been able to snatch a Phillips screwdriver off the tool rack, remove the latch plate, climb into the trunk, and close the lid. Even in the dark, he could find the bared latch, slip the blade of the screwdriver into the mechanism, and pop it open with no difficulty.

If he heard no voices the next time they stopped, he could be out of the trunk in a couple of seconds, fast enough to get his hands on her before she realized what was happening.

At the service station, as he waited silently and patiently within the trunk, he brought his hands to his face and thought he detected additional changes from those he had seen and felt at the cabin. Likewise, when he explored his neck, shoulders, and most of his body, he did not seem to be formed quite as he should have been.

He thought he felt a patch of . . . scales.

Revulsion made his teeth chatter.

He quickly stopped examining himself.

He wanted to know what he was becoming.

Yet he didn't want to know.

He needed to know.

And he couldn't bear knowing.

Dimly he suspected that, having intentionally edited a small portion of his own genetic material, he had created an imbalance in unknown—perhaps unknowable—life chemistries and life forces. The imbalance had not been severe until, upon his death, his altered cells had begun to perform as they had never been meant to perform, healing at a rate and to an extent that was unnatural. That activity—the overwhelming flood of growth hormones and proteins it produced—in some manner released the bonds of genetic stability, threw off the biological governor that ensured a slow, slow, measured pace for evolution. Now he was evolving at an alarming rate. More accurately, perhaps, he was *de*volving, his body seeking to re-create ancient forms still stored within the tens of millions of years of racial experience in his genes. He knew that he was fluctuating mentally between the familiar modern intellect of Eric Leben and the alien consciousnesses of several primitive states of the human race, and he was afraid of devolving both mentally and physically to some bizarre form so remote from human experience that he would cease to exist as Eric Leben, his personality dissolved forever in a prehistoric simian or reptilian consciousness.

She had done this to him—had killed him, thereby triggering the runaway response of his genetically altered cells. He wanted vengeance, wanted it so much he ached, wanted to rip the bitch open and slash her steaming guts, wanted to pull out her eyes and break open her head, wanted to claw off that pretty face, that smug and hateful face, chew off her tongue, then put his mouth down against her spurting arteries and drink, drink . . .

He shuddered again, but this time it was a shudder of primal need, a quiver of inhuman pleasure and excitement.

After the fuel tank was filled, Rachael returned to the highway, and Eric was lulled into his trancelike state once more. This time his thoughts were stranger, dreamier than those that had occupied him previously. He saw himself loping across a mist-shrouded landscape, barely half erect; distant mountains smoked on the horizon, and the sky was a purer and darker blue than he had ever seen it before, yet it was familiar, just as the glossy vegetation was different from anything he had ever encountered as Eric Leben but was nevertheless known to some other being buried deep within him. Then, in his half-dreams, he was no longer even partially erect, not the same creature at all, slithering now on his belly over warm wet earth, drawing himself up onto a spongy rotting log, clawing at it with long-toed feet, shredding the bark and mushy wood to reveal a huge nest of squirming maggots, into which he hungrily thrust his face . . .

Transported by a dark savage thrill, he drummed his feet against the sidewall of the trunk, an action that briefly roused him from the tenebrous images and thoughts that filled his mind. He realized that his drumming feet would alert Rachael, and he stopped after—he hoped—only a few hard kicks.

The car slowed, and he fumbled in the dark for the screwdriver in case he had to pop the latch and get out fast. But then the car accelerated again—Rachael had not understood what she had heard—and he fell back into the ooze of primordial memories and desires.

Now, mentally drifting in some far place, he continued to change physically. The dark trunk was like a womb in which an unimaginable mutant child formed and re-formed and re-formed again. It was both something old and something new in the world. Its time had passed—and yet its time was still coming.

■ Ben figured they would expect him to remember the line of parked cars along the western shoulder of the state route and would be waiting for him to steal one. Furthermore, they would probably count on him making his way north on the road itself, using the ditch along the eastern berm for cover when he heard traffic coming. Or they might think he'd stay on the eastern slope, on the highland side of the road, cautiously following the blacktop north but using the trees and brush for cover. However, he did not think they would expect him to cross the road, enter the woods on the western side of it—the lake side—and then head north under the cover of *those* trees, eventually coming up on the parked cars from behind.

He figured correctly. When he had gone north some distance with the highway on his right and the lake on his left, he cut up the slope to the state route, cautiously crawled up the final embankment, peered over the top, and looked south toward the parked cars. He saw two men slumped in the front seat of the dark green Chevy sedan. They were tucked behind a Dodge station wagon, so he would not have been able to see them if he'd approached from the south instead of circling behind. They were looking the other way, watching geometrically framed slices of the two-lane highway through the windows of the cars parked in front of theirs.

Easing down from the top of the embankment, Ben lay on the slope for a minute, flat on his back. His mattress was composed of old pine needles, withered rye grass, and unfamiliar plants with variegated caladiumlike leaves that bruised under him and pressed their cool juice into the cloth of his shirt and jeans. He was so dirty and stained from the frantic descent of the mountainside below Eric's cabin that he had no concern about what additional mess these plants might make of him.

The Combat Magnum, tucked under his waistline, pressed painfully against the small of his back, so he shifted slightly onto one side to relieve that pressure. Uncomfortable though it was, the Magnum was also reassuring.

As he considered the two men waiting for him on the road above, he was tempted to head farther north until he found untended cars elsewhere. He might be able to steal a vehicle from another place and leave the area before they decided he was gone.

On the other hand, he might walk a mile or two or three without discovering other cars parked beyond the view of their owners.

And it was unlikely that Sharp and his fellow agent would wait here very long. If Ben did not show up soon, they would wonder if they had misjudged him. They would start cruising, perhaps stopping now and then to get out and scan the woods on both sides of the road, and though he was better at these games than they were, he could not be sure that they would not surprise him somewhere along the way.

Right now, he had the advantage of surprise, for he knew where they were, while they had no idea where he was. He decided to make good use of that advantage.

First, he looked around for a smooth fist-sized rock, located one, and tested its weight in his hand. It felt right—substantial. He unbuttoned his shirt part of the way, slipped the rock inside against his belly, and rebuttoned.

With the semiautomatic Remington twelve-gauge in his right hand, he stealthily traversed the embankment, moving south until he felt that he was just below the rear end of their Chevrolet. Edging up to the top of the slope again, he found that he had estimated the distance perfectly: The rear bumper of their sedan was inches from his face.

Sharp's window was open—standard government cars seldom boasted air-conditioning—and Ben knew he had to make the final approach in absolute silence. If Sharp heard anything suspicious and looked out his window, or if he even glanced at his side-view mirror, he would see Ben scurrying behind the Chevy.

A convenient noise, just loud enough to provide cover, would be welcome, and Ben wished the wind would pick up a bit. A good strong gust, shaking the trees, would mask his—

Better yet, the sound of a car engine rose, approaching from the north, from behind the sedan. Ben waited tensely, and a gray Pontiac Firebird appeared from that direction. As the Firebird drew nearer, the sound of rock music grew louder: a couple of kids on a pleasure ride, windows open, cassette player blaring, Bruce Springsteen singing enthusiastically about love and cars and foundry workers. Perfect.

Just as the supercharged Firebird was passing the Chevy, when the noise of engine and Springsteen were loudest, and when Sharp's attention was almost certainly turned in a direction exactly opposite that of his side-view mirror, Ben scrambled quickly over the top of the embankment and crept behind the sedan. He stayed low, under their back window, so he would not be seen in the rearview mirror if the other DSA agent checked the road behind.

As the Firebird and Springsteen faded, Ben duckwalked to the left rear corner of the Chevy, took a deep breath, leaped to his feet, and pumped a round from the shotgun into the back tire on that side. The blast shattered the still mountain air with such power that it scared Ben even though he knew it was coming, and both men inside cried out in alarm. One of them shouted, "Stay down!" The car sagged toward the driver's side. His hands stinging from the recoil of the first shot, Ben fired again, strictly to scare them this time, putting the load low over the top of the car, just low enough so some of the shot skipped across the roof, which to those inside must have sounded like pellets impacting in the interior. Both men were down on the front seat, trying to stay out of the line of fire, a position which also made it impossible for them either to see Ben or to shoot at him.

He fired another round into the dirt shoulder as he ran, paused to blow out the front tire on the driver's side, causing the car to sag further in that direction. He pumped one more load into the same tire solely for dramatic effect—the thunderous crash of the shotgun had unnerved even him, so it must have paralyzed Sharp and the other guy—then glanced at the windshield to be sure both of his adversaries were still below the line of fire. He saw no sign of them, and he put his sixth and final shot through the glass, confident that he would not seriously hurt either man but would scare them badly enough to ensure that they would continue to hug the car seat for another half minute or so.

Even as the shotgun pellets were lodging in the back seat of the Chevy and the safety glass was still falling out into the front seat, Ben took three running steps, dropped flat to the ground, and pulled himself under the Dodge station wagon. When they got the courage to lift their heads, they would figure he had run into the woods on one side of the road or the other, where he was reloading and waiting to make another pass at them when they showed themselves. They would never expect to find him lying prostrate on the ground beneath the very next car in line.

His lungs tried to draw breath in great noisy gulps, but he forced himself to breathe slowly, easily, rhythmically, *quietly.*

He wanted to rub his hands and arms, which stung from firing the shotgun so rapidly and from such unusual positions. But he rubbed nothing, just endured, knowing the stinging and numbness would subside unattended.

After a while, he heard them talking back there, and then he heard a door open.

"Damn it, Peake, come on!" Sharp said.

Footsteps.

Ben turned his head to the right, looking out from beneath the station wagon. He saw Sharp's black Freeman wing tips appear beside the car. Ben owned a pair just like them. These were scuffed, and several spiky burrs clung to the laces.

On the left, no shoes appeared.

"*Now,* Peake!" Sharp said in a hoarse whisper that was as good as a shout.

Another door opened back there, followed by hesitant footsteps, and then shoes came into view at the left side of the station wagon as well. Peake's cheaper black oxfords were in even worse shape than Anson Sharp's shoes: mud was smeared over the tops of them and caked along the soles and heels, and there were twice as many burrs clinging to his laces.

The two men stood on opposite sides of the station wagon, neither of them speaking, just listening and looking.

Ben had the crazy idea that they would hear his pounding heart, for to him it sounded like a timpani.

"Might be ahead, between two of these cars, waiting to sandbag us," Peake whispered.

"He's gone back into the woods," Sharp said in a voice as soft as Peake's, but with scorn. "Probably watching us from cover right now, trying not to laugh."

The smooth, fist-sized rock that Ben had tucked inside his shirt was pressing into his belly, but he did not shift his position for fear the slightest sound would give him away.

Finally Sharp and Peake moved together, paralleling each other, stepping out of sight. They were probably looking warily into all the cars and between them.

But they were not likely to get down on their knees and look underneath, because it was insane of Ben to hide there, flat on his belly, nearly helpless, with no quick way out, where he could be shot as easily as the proverbial fish in the barrel. If his risk paid off, he would throw them off his trail, send them sniffing in the wrong direction, and have a chance to boost one of these cars. However, if they thought he was dumb enough—or clever enough—to hide under the station wagon, he was a dead man.

Ben prayed that the owner of the wagon would not return at this inopportune moment and drive the heap away, leaving him exposed.

Sharp and Peake reached the front of the line of vehicles and, having found no enemy, returned, still walking on opposite sides of the cars. They spoke a bit louder now.

"You said he'd never shoot at us," Peake remarked sourly.

"He didn't."

"He shot at me, sure enough," Peake said, his voice rising.

"He shot at the car."

"What's the difference? We were *in* the car."

They stopped beside the station wagon once more.

Ben looked left and right at their shoes, hoping he would not have to sneeze, cough, or fart.

Sharp said, "He shot at the tires. You see? No point disabling our transportation if he was going to kill us."

"He shot out the windshield," Peake said.

"Yeah, but we were staying down, out of the way, and he knew he wouldn't hit us. I tell you, he's a damn pussy, a prissy moralist, sees himself as the guy in the white hat. He'd shoot at us only if he had no choice, and he'd never shoot at us *first*. We'll have to start the action. Listen, Peake, if he'd wanted to kill us, he could have poked the barrel of that piece through either one of our side windows, could've taken us both out in two seconds flat. Think about it."

They were both silent.

Peake was probably thinking about it.

Ben wondered what Sharp was thinking. He hoped Sharp wasn't thinking about Edgar Allan Poe's *The Purloined Letter*. He did not suppose there was much danger of that because he did not think Sharp had ever in his life read anything other than skin magazines.

"He's down in those woods," Sharp said at last, turning his back on the station wagon, showing Ben his heels. "Down toward the lake. He can see us now, I'll bet. Letting us make the next move."

"We have to get another car," Peake said.

"First you've got to go down in these woods, have a look around, see if you can flush him out."

"Me?"

"You," Sharp said.

"Sir, I'm not really dressed for that sort of thing. My shoes—"

"There's less underbrush here than there was up near Leben's cabin," Sharp said. "You'll manage."

Peake hesitated but finally said, "What'll you be doing while I'm poking around down there?"

"From here," Sharp said, "I can look almost straight down through the trees, into the brush. If you get near him down there on his own level, he might be able to move away from you under the cover of rocks and bushes, without you getting a glimpse of him. But see, from up above here, I'm almost sure to see him moving. And when I do, I'll go straight for the bastard."

Ben heard a peculiar noise, like a lid being unscrewed from a mayonnaise jar. For a moment he could not imagine what it was, then realized Sharp was taking the silencer off his pistol.

Sharp confirmed that suspicion. "Maybe the shotgun still gives him the advantage—"

"Maybe?" Peake said with amazement.

"—but there's two of us, two guns, and without silencers we'll get better range. Go on, Peake. Go down there and smoke him out for me."

Peake seemed on the point of rebellion, but he went.

Ben waited.

A couple of cars passed on the road.

Ben remained very still, watching Anson Sharp's shoes. After a while, Sharp moved one step away from the car, which was as far as he could go in that direction, for one step put him at the very brink of the embankment that sloped down into the woods.

When the next car rumbled along, Ben used the cover of its engine noise to slip out from under the Dodge wagon on the driver's side, where he crouched against the front door, below window level. Now the station wagon was between him and Sharp.

Holding the shotgun in one hand, he opened a few buttons on his shirt. He withdrew the rock that he had found in the forest.

On the other side of the Dodge, Sharp moved.

Ben froze, listened.

Evidently Sharp had only been sidestepping along the edge of the embankment to keep Peake in sight below.

Ben knew he had to act swiftly. If another car came by, he would present quite a spectacle to anyone in it: a guy in filthy clothes, holding a rock in one hand and a shotgun in the other, with a revolver tucked into his waistband. With one tap of the horn, any passing driver could warn Sharp of the wild man at his back.

Rising up from a crouch, Ben looked across the station wagon, directly at the back of Sharp's head. If Sharp turned around now, one of them would have to shoot the other.

Ben waited tensely until he was certain that Sharp's attention was directed down toward the northwest portion of the woods. Then he pitched the round fist-sized rock as hard as he could, across the top of the car, very high, very wide of Sharp's head, so the wind of its passage would not draw the man's attention. He hoped Sharp would not see the rock in flight, hoped it would not hit a tree too soon but would fall far into the forest before impacting.

He was doing a lot of earnest hoping and praying lately.

Without waiting to see what happened, he dropped down beside the car again and heard his missile shredding pine boughs or brush and finally impacting with a resonant thunk.

"Peake!" Sharp called out. "Back of you, back of you. Over that way. Movement over there in those bushes, by the drainage cut."

Ben heard a scrape and clatter and rustle that might have been Anson Sharp bolting off the top of the embankment and down into the forest. Suspecting that it was too good to be true, he rose warily.

Amazingly, Sharp was gone.

With the state route to himself, Ben hurried along the line of parked cars, trying doors. He found an unlocked four-year-old Chevette. It was a hideous bile-yellow heap with clashing green upholstery, but he was in no position to worry about style.

He got in, eased the door shut. He took the .357 Combat Magnum out of his waistband and put it on the seat, where he could reach it in a hurry. Using the stock of the shotgun, he hammered the ignition switch until he broke the key plate off the steering column.

He wondered if the noise carried beyond the car and down through the woods to Sharp and Peake.

Putting the Remington aside, he hastily pulled the ignition wires into view, crossed the two bare ends, and tramped on the accelerator. The engine sputtered, caught, raced.

Although Sharp probably had not heard the hammering, he surely heard the car starting, knew what it meant, and was without a doubt frantically climbing the embankment that he had just descended.

Ben disengaged the handbrake. He threw the Chevette in gear and pulled onto the road. He headed south because that was the way the car was facing, and he had no time to turn it around.

The hard, flat crack of a pistol sounded behind him.

He winced, pulled his head down on his shoulders, glanced in the rearview mirror, and saw Sharp lurching between the sedan and the Dodge station wagon out into the middle of the road, where he could line up a shot better.

"Too late, sucker," Ben said, ramming the accelerator all the way to the floor.

The Chevette coughed as if it were a tubercular, spavined old dray horse being asked to run the Kentucky Derby.

A bullet clipped the rear bumper or maybe a fender, and the high-pitched *skeeeeeeen* sounded like the Chevette's startled bleat of pain.

The car stopped coughing and shuddering, surged forward at last, spewing a cloud of blue smoke in its wake.

In the rearview mirror, Anson Sharp dwindled beyond the smoke as if he were a demon tumbling back into Hades. He might have fired again, but Ben did not hear the shot over the scream of the Chevette's straining engine.

The road topped a hill and sloped down, turned to the right, sloped some more, and Ben slowed a bit. He remembered the sheriff's deputy at the sporting-goods store. The lawman might still be in the area. Ben figured he had used up so much good luck in his escape from Sharp that he would be tempting fate if he exceeded the speed limit in his eagerness to get away from Arrowhead. After all, he was in filthy clothes, driving a stolen car, carrying a shotgun and a Combat Magnum, so if he was stopped for speeding, he could hardly expect to be let off with just a fine.

He was on the road again. That was the most important thing now—staying on the road until he had caught up with Rachael either out on I-15 or in Vegas.

Rachael was going to be all right.

He was sure that she would be all right.

White clouds had moved in low under the blue summer sky. They were growing thicker. The edges of some of them were gunmetal-gray.

On both sides of the road, the forest settled deeper into darkness.

28   DESERT HEAT

RACHAEL REACHED BARSTOW AT 3:40 TUESDAY AFTERNOON. SHE thought about pulling off I-15 to grab a sandwich; she had eaten only an Egg McMuffin this morning and two small candy bars purchased at the Arco service station before she'd gotten on the interstate. Besides, the morning's coffee and the recent can of Coke were working through her; she began to feel a vague need to use a rest room, but she decided to keep moving. Barstow was large enough to have a police department plus a California Highway Patrol substation. Though there was little chance that she would encounter police of any kind and be identified as the infamous traitor of whom the radio reporter had spoken, her hunger and bladder pressure were both too mild to justify the risk.

On the road between Barstow and Vegas, she would be relatively safe, for CHiPs were rarely assigned to that long stretch of lonely highway. In fact, the threat of being stopped for speeding was so small (and so well and widely understood) that the traffic moved at an average speed of seventy to eighty miles an hour. She pushed the Mercedes up to seventy, and other cars passed her, so she was confident that she would not be pulled over by a patrol car even in the unlikely event that one appeared.

She recalled a roadside rest stop with public facilities about thirty miles ahead.

She could wait to use that bathroom. As for food, she was not going to risk malnutrition merely by postponing dinner until she got to Vegas.

Since coming through the El Cajon Pass, she had noticed that the number and size of the clouds were increasing, and the farther she drove into the Mojave, the more somber the heavens became. Previously the clouds had been all white, then white with pale gray beards, and now they were primarily gray with slate-dark streaks. The desert enjoyed little precipitation, but during the summer the skies could sometimes open as if in reenactment of the biblical story of Noah, sending forth a deluge that the barren earth was unprepared to absorb. For the majority of its course, the interstate was built above the runoff line, but here and there road signs warned FLASH FLOODS. She was not particularly worried about being caught in a flood. However, she was concerned that a hard rain would slow her down considerably, and she was eager to make Vegas by six-fifteen or six-thirty.

She would not feel half safe until she was settled in Benny's shuttered motel. And she would not feel entirely safe until he was with her, the drapes drawn, the world locked out.

Minutes after leaving Barstow, she passed the exit for Calico. Once the service stations and motels and restaurants at that turnoff were behind her, virtually unpeopled emptiness lay ahead for the next sixty miles, until the tiny town of Baker. The interstate and the traffic upon it were the only proof that this was an inhabited planet rather than a sterile, lifeless hunk of rock orbiting silently in a sea of cold space.

As this was a Tuesday, traffic was light, more trucks than cars. Thursday through Monday, tens of thousands of people were on their way to and from Vegas. Frequently, Fridays and Sundays, the traffic was so heavy that it looked startlingly anachronistic in this wasteland—as if all the commuters from a great city had been simultaneously transported back in time to a barren era prior to the Mesozoic epoch. But now, on several occasions, Rachael's was the only vehicle in sight on her side of the divided highway.

She drove over a skeletal landscape of scalped hills and bony plains, where white and gray and umber rock poked up like exposed ribs—like clavicles and scapulae, radii and ulnae, here an ilium, there a femur, here two fibulae, and over there a cluster of tarsals and metatarsals—as if the land were a burial ground for giants of another age, the graves reopened by centuries of wind. The many-armed Joshua trees—like monuments to Shiva—and the other cactuses of the higher desert were not to be found in these lower and hotter regions. The vegetation was limited to some worthless scrub, here and there a patch of dry brown bunchgrass. Mostly the Mojave was sand, rock, alkaline plains, and solidified lava beds. In the distance, to the north, were the Calico mountains, and still farther north the Granite Mountains rose purple and majestic at the horizon, and far to the southeast were the Cady Mountains: all appeared to be stark, hard-edged monoliths of bare and forbidding stone.

At 4:10, she reached the roadside rest area that she had recalled when deciding not to stop in Barstow. She slowed, left the highway, and drove into a large empty parking lot. She stopped in front of a low concrete-block building that housed men's and women's rest rooms. To the right of the rest rooms, a piece of ground was shaded by sturdy metal latticework on four eight-foot metal poles, and under that sun-foiling shelter were three picnic tables. The scrub and bunchgrass were cleared away from the surrounding area, leaving clean bare sand, and blue garbage cans with hinged lids bore polite requests in white block letters—PLEASE DO NOT LITTER.

She got out of the Mercedes, taking only the keys and her purse, leaving the thirty-two and the boxes of ammunition hidden under the driver's seat, where she had put them when she stopped for gas at the entrance to I-15. She closed the door, locked it more from habit than out of necessity.

For a moment she looked up at the sky, which was ninety percent concealed behind steel-gray clouds, as if it were girdling itself in armor. The day remained very hot, between ninety and one hundred degrees, although two hours ago, before the cloud cover settled in, the temperature had surely been ten or even twenty degrees higher.

Out on the interstate, two enormous eighteen-wheelers roared by, heading east, ripping apart the desert's quiet fabric but laying down an even more seamless cloth of silence in their wake.

Walking to the door of the women's rest room, she passed a sign that warned travelers to watch out for rattlesnakes. She supposed they liked to slither in from the desert and stretch full-length on the sunbaked concrete sidewalks.

The rest room was hot, ventilated only by jalousie windows set high in the walls, but at least it had been cleaned recently. The place smelled of pine-scented disinfectant. She also detected the limey odor of concrete that had cooked too long in the fierce desert sun.

■   Eric ascended slowly from an intense and vivid dream—or perhaps an unthinkably ancient racial memory—in which he was something other than a man. He was crawling inside a rough-walled burrow, not his own but that of some other creature, creeping downward, following a musky scent with the sure knowledge that succulent eggs of some kind could be found and devoured in the gloom below. A pair of glowing amber eyes in the inkiness was the first indication he had of resistance to his plans. A warm-blooded furry beast, well armed with teeth and claws, rushed at him to protect its subterranean nest, and he was suddenly engaged in a fierce battle that was simultaneously terrifying and exhilarating. Cold, reptilian fury filled him, making him forget the hunger that had driven him in search of eggs. In the darkness, he and his adversary bit, tore, and lashed at each other. Eric hissed—the other squealed and spat—and he inflicted more ruinous wounds than he received, until the burrow filled with the exciting stink of blood and feces and urine . . .

Regaining human consciousness, Eric realized that the car was no longer moving. He had no idea how long it had been stopped—maybe only a minute or two, maybe hours. Struggling against the hypnotic pull of the dreamworld that he'd just left, wanting to retreat back into that thrillingly violent and reassuringly simple place of primal needs and pleasures, he bit down on his lower lip to clear his head and was startled—but, on consideration, not surprised—to find that his teeth seemed sharper than they had been previously. He listened for a moment, but he heard no voices or other noises outside. He wondered if they had gone all the way to Vegas and if the car was now parked in the motel garage where Shadway had told Rachael to put it.

The cold, inhuman rage that he had felt in his dream was in him still, although redirected now from an amber-eyed, burrow-dwelling little mammal to Rachael. His hatred of her was overwhelming, and his need to get his hands on her—tear out her throat, rip open her guts—was building toward a frenzy.

He fumbled in the pitch-black trunk for the screwdriver. Though there was no more light than before, he did not seem quite as blind as he had been. If he was not actually *seeing* the vague dimensions of his Stygian cell, then he was evidently apprehending them with some newfound sixth sense, for he possessed at least a threshold awareness of the position and features of each metal wall. He also perceived the screwdriver lying against the wall near his knees, and when he reached down to test the validity of that perception, he put his hand on the ribbed Lucite handle of the tool.

He popped the trunk lid.

Light speared in. For a moment his eyes stung, then adjusted.

He pushed the lid up.

He was surprised to see the desert.

He climbed out of the trunk.

■   Rachael washed her hands at the sink—there was hot water but no soap— and dried them in the blast of the hot-air blower that was provided in lieu of paper towels.

Outside, as the heavy door closed behind her, she saw that no rattlesnakes had taken up residence on the walkway. She went only three steps before she also saw that the trunk of the Mercedes was open wide.

She stopped, frowning. Even if the trunk had not been locked, the lid could not have slipped its catch spontaneously.

Suddenly she knew: *Eric.*

Even as his name flashed through her mind, he appeared at the corner of the building, fifteen feet away from her. He stopped and stared as if the sight of her riveted him as much as she was frozen by the sight of him.

It was Eric, yet it was not Eric.

She stared at him, horrified and disbelieving, not immediately able to comprehend his bizarre metamorphosis, yet sensing that the manipulation of his genetic structure had somehow resulted in these monstrous changes. His body appeared deformed; however, because of his clothing, it was hard to tell precisely what had happened to him. Something was different about his knee joints and his hips. And he was hunchbacked: his red plaid shirt was straining at the seams to contain the mound that had risen from shoulder to shoulder. His arms had grown two or three inches, which would have been obvious even if his knobby and strangely jointed wrists had not thrust out beyond his shirt cuffs. His hands looked fearfully powerful, deformed by human standards, yet with a suggestion of suppleness and dexterity; they were mottled yellow-brown-gray; the hugely knuckled and elongated fingers terminated in claws; in places, his skin seemed to have been supplanted by pebbly scales.

His strangely altered face was the worst thing about him. Every aspect of his once-handsome countenance was changed, yet just enough of his familiar features remained to leave him recognizable. Bones had re-formed, becoming broader and flatter in some places, narrower and more rounded in others, heavier over and

under his now-sunken eyes and through his jawline, which was prognathous. A
hideous serrated bony ridge had formed up the center of his lumpish brow and—
diminishing—trailed across the top of his scalp.

"Rachael," he said.

His voice was low, vibratory, and hoarse. She thought there was a mournful,
even melancholy, note in it.

On his thickened forehead were twin conical protrusions that appeared to be
half formed, although they seemed destined to be horns the size of Rachael's
thumb when they were finished growing. Horns would have made no sense at all
to her if the patches of scaly flesh on his hands had not been matched by patches
on his face and by wattles of dark leathery skin under his jaw and along his neck
in the manner of certain reptiles; a few lizards had horns, and perhaps at some
point in mankind's distant beginnings, evolution had included an amphibian stage
boasting such protuberances (though that seemed unlikely). Other elements of
his tortured visage were human, while still others were apelike. She dimly began
to perceive that tens of millions of years of genetic heritage had been unleashed
within him, that every stage of evolution was fighting for control of him at the
same time; long-abandoned forms—a multitude of possibilities—were struggling
to reassert themselves as if his tissues were just so much putty.

"Rachael," he repeated but still did not move. "I want . . . I want . . . " He could
not seem to find the words to finish the thought, or perhaps he simply did not
know what it was he wanted.

She could not move, either, partly because she was paralyzed by terror but
partly because she desperately wanted to understand what had happened to him.
If in fact he was being pulled in opposing directions by the many racial memories
within his genes, if he was devolving toward a subhuman state while his modern
form and intellect strove to retain dominance of its tissues, then it seemed every
change in him should be functional, with a purpose obviously connected to one
prehuman form or another. However, that did not appear to be the case. In his
face, pulsing arteries and gnarled veins and bony excrescences and random concavities seemed to exist without reason, with no connection to any known creature
on the evolutionary ladder. The same was true of the hump on his back. She
suspected that, in addition to the reassertion of various forms from human biological heritage, *mutated* genes were causing purposeless changes in him or, perhaps, were pushing him toward some alien life-form utterly different from the
human species.

"Rachael . . . "

His teeth were sharp.

"Rachael . . . "

The gray-blue irises of his eyes were no longer perfectly round but were tending
toward a vertical-oval shape like those in the eyes of serpents. Not all the way
there, yet. Apparently still in the middle of metamorphosis. But no longer quite
the eyes of a man.

"Rachael . . . "

His nose seemed to have collapsed part of the way into his face, and the nostrils
were more exposed than before.

"Rachael . . . please . . . please . . . " He held one monstrous hand toward her
in a pathetic gesture, and in his raspy voice was a note of misery and another of

self-pity. But there was an even more obvious and more affecting note of love and longing that seemed to surprise him every bit as much as it surprised her. "Please . . . please . . . I want . . . "

"Eric," she said, her own voice almost as strange as his, twisted by fear and weighted down with sadness. "What do you want?"

"I want . . . I . . . I want . . . not to be . . . "

"Yes?"

" . . . afraid . . . "

She did not know what to say.

He took one step toward her.

She immediately backed up.

He took another step, and she saw that he was having a little trouble with his feet, as if they had changed within his boots and were no longer comfortable in that confinement.

Again she retreated to match his advance.

Squeezing the words out as if it were agony to form and expel them, he said, "I want . . . you . . . "

"Eric," she said softly, pityingly.

" . . . you . . . you . . . "

He took three quick, lurching steps; she scampered four backward.

In that voice fit for a man trapped in hell, he said, "Don't . . . don't reject me . . . don't . . . Rachael, don't . . . "

"Eric, I can't help you."

"Don't reject me."

"You're beyond help, Eric."

"Don't reject me . . . *again.*"

She had no weapons, just her car keys in one hand and her purse in the other, and she cursed herself for leaving the pistol in the Mercedes. She backed farther away from him.

With a savage cry of rage that made Rachael go cold in the late-June heat, Eric came at her in a head-long rush.

She threw her purse at his head, turned, and sprinted into the desert behind the comfort station. The soft sand shifted under her feet, and a couple of times she almost twisted an ankle, almost fell, and the sparse scrub brush whipped at her legs and almost tripped her, but she did not fall, kept going, ran fast as the wind, tucked her head down, drew her elbows in to her sides, ran, ran for her life.

■ When confronting Rachael on the walk beside the rest rooms, Eric's initial reaction had surprised him. Seeing her beautiful face, her titian hair, and her lovely body beside which he had once lain, Eric was unexpectedly overcome with remorse for the way he had treated her and was filled with an unbearable sense of loss. The primal fury that had been churning in him abruptly subsided, and more human emotions held sway, though tenuously. Tears stung his eyes. He found it difficult to speak, not only because changes within his throat made speech more difficult, but because he was choked up with regret and grief and a sudden crippling loneliness.

But she rejected him again, confirming the worst suspicions he had of her and jolting him out of his anguish and self-pity. Like a wave of dark water filled with churning ice, the cold rage of an ancient consciousness surged into him again. The desire to stroke her hair, to gently touch her smooth skin, to take her in his arms—that vanished instantly and was replaced by something stronger than desire, by a profound need to kill her. He wanted to gut her, bury his mouth in her still-warm flesh, and finally proclaim his triumph by urinating on her lifeless remains. He threw himself at her, still wanting her but for different purposes.

She ran, and he pursued.

Instinct, racial memory of countless other pursuits—memories not only in the recesses of his mind but flowing in his blood—gave him an advantage. He would bring her down. It was only a matter of time.

She was fast, this arrogant animal, but they were always fast when propelled by terror and the survival instinct, fast for a while but not forever. And in their fear, the hunted were never as cunning as the hunter. Experience assured him of that.

He wished that he had taken off the boots, for they restricted him now. But his own adrenaline level was so high that he had blocked out the pain in his cramped toes and twisted heels; temporarily the discomfort did not register.

The prey fled south, though nothing in that direction offered the smallest hope of sanctuary. Between them and the faraway mountains, the inhospitable land was home only to things that crawled and crept and slithered, things that bit and stung and sometimes ate their own young to stay alive.

■ Having run only a few hundred yards, Rachael was already gasping for breath. Her legs felt leaden.

She was not out of shape; it was just that the desert heat was so fierce it virtually had substance, and running through it seemed almost as bad as trying to run through water. For the most part, the heat did not come down from above, because all but a sliver or two of sky was clouded over. Instead, the heat came *up*, rising from the scorching sand that had been baking in the now-hidden sun, storing that terrific heat since dawn, until the clouds had arrived within the last hour or so. The day was still warm, ninety degrees, but the air rising off the sand must have been well over a hundred. She felt as if she were running across a furnace grate.

She glanced back.

Eric was about twenty yards behind her.

She looked straight ahead and pushed harder, really pumping her legs, putting everything she had into it, crashing through that wall of heat, only to find endless other walls beyond it, sucking in hot air until her mouth went dry and her tongue cleaved to the roof of her mouth and her throat began to crack and her lungs began to burn. A natural hedge line of stunted mesquite lay ahead, extending twenty or thirty yards to the left, an equal distance to the right. She didn't want to detour around it, because she was afraid she'd lose ground to Eric. The mesquite was only knee high, and as far as she could see it was neither too solid nor too deep, so she plunged through the hedge, whereupon it proved to be deeper than it looked, fifteen or twenty feet across, and also somewhat more tightly grown than it appeared. The spiky, oily plant poked at her legs and snagged her jeans and delayed her with such tenacity that it seemed to be sentient and in league with Eric. Her racing heart began to pound harder, too hard, slamming against her breastbone. Then she was through the hedge, with hundreds of bits of mesquite bark and leaves stuck on her jeans and socks. She increased her pace again, gushing sweat, blinking salty streams of the same effluvient from her eyes before it could blur her vision too much, tasting it at the corners of her mouth. If she kept pouring at this rate, she'd dehydrate dangerously. Already she saw whirls of color at the periphery of her vision, felt a flutter of nausea in her stomach, and sensed incipient dizziness that might abruptly overwhelm her. But she kept pumping her legs, streaking across the barren land, because there was absolutely nothing else she could do.

She glanced back again.

Eric was closer. Only fifteen yards now.

At great cost, Rachael reached into herself and found a little more strength, a little more energy, an additional measure of stamina.

The ground, no longer treacherously soft, hardened into a wide flat sheet of exposed rock. The rock had been abraded by centuries of blowing sand that had carved hundreds of fine, elaborate whorls in its surface—the fingerprints of the wind. It provided good traction, and she picked up speed again. Soon, however, her reserves would be used up, and dehydration would set in—though she dared not think about that. Positive thinking was the key, so she thought positively for fifty more strides, confident of widening the gap between them.

The third time she glanced back, she loosed an involuntary cry of despair.

Eric was closer. Ten yards.

That was when she tripped and fell.

The rock ended, and sand replaced it. Because she had not been looking down and had not seen that the ground was going to change, she twisted her left ankle. She tried to stay up, tried to keep going, but the twist had destroyed her rhythm. The same ankle twisted again the very next time she put that foot down. She shouted—"No!"—and pitched to the left, rolled across a few weeds, stones, and clumps of crisp bunchgrass.

She wound up at the brink of a big arroyo—a naturally carved water channel through the desert, which was a roaring river during a flash flood but dry most of the time, dry now—about fifty feet across, thirty deep, with walls that sloped but only slightly. Even as she stopped rolling at the arroyo, she took in the situation, saw what she must do, did it: She threw herself over the brink, rolling again, down the steep wall this time, desperately hoping to avoid sharp rocks and rattlesnakes.

It was a bruising descent, and she hit bottom with enough force to knock half the wind out of her. Nevertheless, she scrambled to her feet, looked up, and saw Eric—or the thing that Eric had become—staring down at her from the top of the arroyo wall. He was just thirty or thirty-five feet above her, but thirty vertical feet seemed like more distance than thirty horizontally measured feet; it was as if she were standing in a city street, with him peering down from the roof of a three-story building. Her boldness and his hesitation had gained her some time. If he had rolled down right behind her, he very likely would have caught her by now.

She had won a brief reprieve, and she had to make the best of it. Turning right, she ran along the flat bed of the arroyo, favoring her twisted ankle. She did not know where the arroyo would lead her. But she stayed on the move and kept her eyes open for something that she could easily turn to her advantage, something that would save her, something . . .

Something.

Anything.

What she needed was a miracle.

She expected Eric to plunge down the wall of the gulch when she began to run, but he did not. Instead, he stayed up there at the edge of the channel, running alongside the brink, looking down at her, matching her progress step for step.

She supposed he was looking for an advantage of his own.

29   REMADE MEN

WITH THE HELP OF THE RIVERSIDE COUNTY SHERIFF'S DEPART-ment, which provided a patrol car and a deputy to drive it, Sharp and Peake were back in Palm Springs by four-thirty Tuesday afternoon. They took two rooms in a motel along Palm Canyon Drive.

Sharp called Nelson Gosser, the agent who had been left on duty at Eric Leben's Palm Springs house. Gosser bought bathrobes for Peake and Sharp, took their clothes to a one-hour laundry and dry cleaner, and brought them two buckets of Kentucky Fried Chicken with coleslaw, fries, and biscuits.

While Sharp and Peake had been at Lake Arrowhead, Rachael Leben's red Mercedes 560 SL had been found, with one flat tire, behind an empty house a few blocks west of Palm Canyon Drive. Also, the blue Ford that Shadway had been driving in Arrowhead was traced to an airport rental agency. Of course, neither car offered any hope of a lead.

Sharp called the airport and spoke with the pilot of the Bell JetRanger. Repairs on the chopper were nearly completed. It would be fully fueled and at the deputy director's disposal within an hour.

Avoiding the french fries because he believed that eating them was begging for heart disease, ignoring the coleslaw because it had turned sour last April, he peeled the crisp and greasy breading off the fried chicken and ate just the meat, no fatty skin, while he made a number of other calls to subordinates at the Geneplan labs in Riverside and at several places in Orange County. More than sixty agents were on the case. He could not speak to all of them, but by contacting six, he got a detailed picture of where the various aspects of the investigation were going.

Where they were going was nowhere.

Lots of questions, no answers. Where was Eric Leben? Where was Ben Shadway? Why hadn't Rachael Leben been with Shadway at the cabin above Lake Arrowhead? Where had she gone? Where was she now? Was there any danger of Shadway and Mrs. Leben putting their hands on the kind of proof that could blow Wildcard wide open?

Considering all of those urgent unanswered questions and the humiliating fail-ure of the expedition to Arrowhead, most other men would have had little appetite, but with gusto Anson Sharp worked through the last of the chicken and biscuits. And considering that he had put his entire future at risk by virtually subordinating the agency's goals in this case to his own personal vendetta against Ben Shadway, it seemed unlikely that he would be able to lie down and enjoy the deep and untroubled sleep of an innocent child. But as he turned back the covers on the queen-sized motel bed, he had no fear of insomnia. He was always able to sleep the moment he rested his head on the pillow, regardless of the circumstances.

He was, after all, a man whose only passion was himself, whose only commitment was to himself, whose only interests lay in those things which impinged directly upon him. Therefore, taking care of himself—eating well, sleeping, staying fit, and maintaining a good appearance—was of paramount importance. Besides, truly believing himself to be superior to other men and favored by fate, he could not be devastated by any setback, for he was certain that bad luck and disappointment were transitory conditions, insignificant anomalies in his otherwise smooth and ever-ascending path to greatness and acclaim.

Before slipping into bed, Sharp sent Nelson Gosser to deliver some instructions to Peake. Then he directed the motel switchboard to hold all calls, pulled the drapes shut, took off his robe, fluffed his pillow, and stretched out on the mattress.

Staring at the dark ceiling, he thought of Shadway and laughed.

Poor Shadway must be wondering how in the hell a man could be court-martialed and dismissed from the Marine Corps with a dishonorable discharge and still become a DSA agent. That was the primary problem with good old pure-hearted Ben: He labored under the misconception that some behavior was moral and some immoral, that good deeds were rewarded and that, ultimately at least, bad deeds brought misery down upon the heads of those committing them.

But Anson Sharp knew there was no justice in the abstract, that you had to fear retribution from others only if you *allowed* them to retaliate, and that altruism and fair play were not automatically rewarded. He knew that morality and immorality were meaningless concepts; your choices in life were not between good and evil but between those things that would benefit you and those things that would not. And only a fool would do anything that did not benefit him or that benefited someone else more than it did him. Looking out for number one was all that counted, and any decision or action that benefited number one was good, regardless of its effect on others.

With his actions limited only by that extremely accommodating philosophy, he'd found it relatively easy to erase the dishonorable discharge from his record. His respect for computers and knowledge of their capabilities were also invaluable.

In Vietnam, Sharp had been able to steal large quantities of PX and USO-canteen supplies with astonishing success because one of his coconspirators—Corporal Eugene Dalmet—was a computer operator in the division quartermaster's office. With the computer, he and Gene Dalmet were able to accurately track all supplies within the system and choose the perfect place and time at which to intercept them. Later, Dalmet often managed to erase all record of a stolen shipment from the computer; then, through computer-generated orders, he was able to direct unwitting supply clerks to destroy the paper files relating to that shipment—so no one could prove the theft had ever occurred because no one could prove there had been anything to steal in the first place. In this brave new world of bureaucrats and high technology, it seemed that nothing was actually real unless there were paperwork and extensive computer data to support its existence. The scheme worked wonderfully until Ben Shadway started nosing around.

Shipped back to the States in disgrace, Sharp was not despairing because he took with him the uplifting knowledge of the computer's wondrous talent for remaking records and rewriting history. He was sure he could use it to remake his reputation as well.

For six months he took courses in computer programming, worked at it day and night, to the exclusion of all else, until he was not only a first-rate operator-programmer but a hacker of singular skill and cleverness. And those were the days when the word *hacker* had not yet been invented.

He landed a job with Oxelbine Placement, an executive-employment agency large enough to require a computer programmer but small and low-profile enough to be unconcerned about the damage to its image that might result from hiring a man with a dishonorable discharge. All Oxelbine cared about was that he had no civilian criminal record and was highly qualified for his work in a day when the computer craze had not yet hit the public, leaving businesses hungry for people with advanced data-processing skills.

Oxelbine had a direct link with the main computer at TRW, the largest credit-investigating firm. The TRW files were the primary source for local and national credit-rating agencies. Oxelbine paid TRW for information about executives who applied to it for placement and, whenever possible, reduced costs by selling to TRW information that TRW did not process. In addition to his work for Oxelbine, Sharp secretly probed at TRW's computer, seeking the scheme of its data-encoding system. He used a tedious trial-and-error approach that would be familiar to any hacker a decade later, though in those days the process was slower because the computers were slower. In time, however, he learned how to access any credit files at TRW and, more important, discovered how to add and delete data. The process was easier then than it would be later because, in those days, the need for computer security had not yet been widely recognized. Accessing his own dossier, he changed his Marine discharge from dishonorable to honorable, even gave himself a few service commendations, promoted himself from sergeant to lieutenant, and cleaned up a number of less important negatives on his credit record. Then he instructed TRW's computer to order a destruction of the company's existing hard-copy file on him and to replace it with a file based on the new computer record.

No longer stigmatized by the dishonorable-discharge notation on his credit record, he was able to obtain a new job with a major defense contractor, General Dynamics. The position was clerical and did not require security clearance, so he avoided coming under the scrutiny of the FBI and the GAO, both of which had linkages with an array of Defense Department computers that would have turned up his true military history. Using the Hughes computer's links with those same Defense Department systems, Sharp was eventually able to access his service records at the Marine Corps Office of Personnel (MCOP) and change them as he had changed his file at TRW. Thereafter, it was a simple matter to have the MCOP computer issue an order for the destruction of the hard copy of Sharp's Marine records and replacement with the "updated, corrected, and amended" file.

The FBI maintained its own records of men involved in criminal activity while in military service. It used these for cross-checking suspects in civilian criminal cases—and when required to conduct an investigation of a federal job applicant who was in need of a security clearance. Having compromised the MCOP computer, Sharp directed it to send a copy of his new records to the FBI, along with a notation that his previous file contained "serious inaccuracies of libelous nature, requiring its immediate destruction." In those days, before anyone had heard of hackers or realized the vulnerability of electronic data, people believed what computers told them; even bureau agents, trained to be suspicious, believed computers. Sharp was relatively confident that his deception would succeed.

A few months later, he applied to the Defense Security Agency for a position in its training program, and waited to see if his campaign to remake his reputation had succeeded. It had. He was accepted into the DSA after passing an FBI investigation of his past and character. Thereafter, with the dedication of a true powermonger and the cunning of a natural-born Machiavelli, he had begun a lightning-fast ascent through the DSA. It didn't hurt that he was able to use *that* computer to improve his agency records by inserting forged commendations and exceptional service notations from senior officers after they were killed in the line of duty or died of natural causes and were unable to dispute those postdated tributes.

Sharp had decided that he could be tripped up only by a handful of men who'd served with him in Vietnam and had participated in his court-martial. Therefore, after joining the DSA, he began keeping track of those who posed a threat. Three had been killed in Nam after Sharp was shipped home. Another died years later in Jimmy Carter's ill-conceived attempt to rescue the Iranian hostages. Another died of natural causes. Another was shot in the head in Teaneck, New Jersey, where he'd opened an all-night convenience store after retiring from the Marines and where he'd had the misfortune to be clerking when a Benzedrine-crazed teenager tried to commit armed robbery. Three other men—each capable of revealing Sharp's true past and destroying him—returned to Washington after the war and began careers in the State Department, FBI, and Justice Department. With great care—but without delay, lest they discover Sharp at the DSA—he planned the murder of all three and executed those plans without a hitch.

Four others who knew the truth about him were still alive—including Shadway—but none of them was involved in government or seemed likely to discover him at the DSA. Of course, if he ascended to the director's chair, his name would more often appear in the news, and enemies like Shadway might be more likely to hear of him and try to bring him down. He had known for some time that those four must die sooner or later. When Shadway had gotten mixed up in the Leben case, Sharp had seen it as yet one more gift of fate, additional proof that he, Sharp, was destined to rise as far as he wished to go.

Given his own history, Sharp was not surprised to learn of Eric Leben's self-experimentation. Others professed amazement or shock at Leben's arrogance in attempting to break the laws of God and nature by cheating death. But long ago Sharp had learned that absolutes like Truth—or Right or Wrong or Justice or even Death—were no longer so absolute in this high-tech age. Sharp had remade his reputation by the manipulation of electrons, and Eric Leben had attempted to remake himself from a corpse into a living man by the manipulation of his own genes, and to Sharp it was all part of the same wondrous enchiridion to be found in the sorcerer's bag of twentieth-century science.

Now, sprawled comfortably in his motel bed, Anson Sharp enjoyed the sleep of the amoral, which is far deeper and more restful than the sleep of the just, the righteous, and the innocent.

■ Sleep eluded Jerry Peake for a while. He had not been to bed in twenty-four hours, had chased up and down mountains, had achieved two or three shattering insights, and had been exhausted when they got back to Palm Springs a short while ago, too exhausted to eat any of the Kentucky Fried Chicken that Nelson Gosser supplied. He was still exhausted, but he could not sleep.

For one thing, Gosser had brought a message from Sharp to the effect that Peake was to catch two hours of shut-eye and be ready for action by seven-thirty this evening, which gave him half an hour to shower and dress after he woke. Two hours! He needed ten. It hardly seemed worth lying down if he had to get up again so soon.

Besides, he was no nearer to finding a way out of the nasty moral dilemma that had plagued him all day: serve as an accomplice to murder at Sharp's demand and thereby further his career at the cost of his soul; or pull a gun on Sharp if that became necessary, thus ruining his career but saving his soul. The latter course seemed an obvious choice, except that if he pulled a gun on Sharp he might be shot and killed. Sharp was cleverer and quicker than Peake, and Peake knew it. He had hoped that his failure to shoot at Shadway would have put him in such disfavor with the deputy director that he would be booted off the case, dropped with disgust, which would not have been good for his career but would sure have solved this dilemma. But Sharp's talons were deep in Jerry Peake now, and Peake reluctantly acknowledged that there would be no easy way out.

What most bothered him was the certainty that a smarter man than he would already have found a way to use this situation to his great advantage. Having never known his mother, having been unloved by his sullen widowed father, having been unpopular in school because he was shy and introverted, Jerry Peake had long dreamed of remaking himself from a loser into a winner, from a nobody into a legend, and now his chance had come to start the climb, but he did not know what to do with the opportunity.

He tossed. He turned.

He planned and schemed and plotted against Sharp and for his own success, but his plans and schemes and plots repeatedly fell apart under the weight of their own poor conception and naïveté. He wanted so badly to be George Smiley or Sherlock Holmes or James Bond, but what he *felt* like was Sylvester the Cat witlessly plotting to capture and eat the infinitely clever Tweetie Bird.

His sleep was filled with nightmares of falling off ladders and off roofs and out of trees while pursuing a macabre canary that had Anson Sharp's face.

■ Ben had wasted time ditching the stolen Chevette at Silverwood Lake and finding another car to steal. It would be suicidal to keep the Chevette when Sharp had both its description and license number. He finally located a new black Merkur parked at the head of a long footpath that led down to the lake, out of sight of its fisherman owner. The doors were locked, but the windows were open a crack for ventilation. He had found a wire coat hanger in the trunk of the Chevette—along with an incredible collection of other junk—and he had brought it along for just this sort of emergency. He'd used it to reach through the open top of the window and pop the door latch, then had hot-wired the Merkur and headed for Interstate 15.

He did not reach Barstow until four forty-five. He had already arrived at the unnerving conclusion that he would never be able to catch up to Rachael on the road. Because of Sharp, he had lost too much time. When the lowering sky released a few fat drops of rain, he realized that a storm would slow the Merkur down even more than the reliably maneuverable Mercedes, widening the gap between him and Rachael. So he swung off the lightly trafficked interstate, into the heart of Barstow, and used a telephone booth at a Union 76 station to call Whitney Gavis in Las Vegas.

He would tell Whitney about Eric Leben hiding in the trunk of Rachael's car. With any luck at all, Rachael would not stop on the road, would not give Eric an easy opportunity to go after her, so the dead man would wait in his hidey-hole until they were all the way into Vegas. There, forewarned, Whit Gavis could fire about six rounds of heavy buckshot into the trunk as Eric opened it from the inside, and Rachael, never having realized she was in danger, would be safe.

Everything was going to be all right.

Whit would take care of everything.

Ben finished tapping in the number, using his AT&T card for the call, and in a moment Whit's phone began to ring a hundred and sixty miles away.

The storm was still having trouble breaking. Only a few big drops of rain spattered against the glass walls of the booth.

The phone rang, rang.

The previously milky clouds had curdled into immense gray-black thunderheads, which in turn had formed still-darker, knotted, more malignant masses that were moving at great speed toward the southeast.

The phone rang again and again and again.

Be there, damn it, Ben thought.

But Whit was not there, and wishing him home would not make it true. On the twentieth ring, Ben hung up.

For a moment he stood in the telephone booth, despairing, not sure what to do.

Once, he'd been a man of action, with never a doubt in a crisis. But in reaction to various unsettling discoveries about the world he lived in, he had tried to remake himself into a different man—student of the past, train fancier. He had failed in that remake, a failure that recent events had made eminently clear: He could not just stop being the man he had once been. He accepted that now. And he had thought that he had lost none of his edge. But he realized that all those years of pretending to be someone else had dulled him. His failure to look in the Mercedes's trunk before sending Rachael away, his current despair, his confusion, his sudden lack of direction were all proof that too much pretending had its deadly effect.

Lightning sizzled across the swollen black heavens, but even that scalpel of light did not split open the belly of the storm.

He decided there was nothing to be done but hit the road, head for Vegas, hope for the best, though hope seemed futile now. He could stop in Baker, sixty miles ahead, and try Whit's number again.

Maybe his luck would change.

It *had* to change.

He opened the door of the booth and ran to the stolen Merkur.

Again, lightning blasted the charred sky.

A cannonade of thunder volleyed back and forth between the sky and the waiting earth.

The air stank of ozone.

He got in the car, slammed the door, started the engine, and the storm finally broke, throwing a million tons of water down upon the desert in a sudden deluge.

30   RATTLESNAKES

RACHAEL HAD BEEN FOLLOWING THE BOTTOM OF THE WIDE ARroyo for what seemed miles but was probably only a few hundred yards. The illusion of greater distance resulted partly from the hot pain in her twisted ankle, which was subsiding but only slowly.

She felt trapped in a maze through which she might forever search futilely for a nonexistent exit. Narrower arroyos branched off the primary channel, all on the right-hand side. She considered pursuing another gulch, but each intersected the main run at an angle, so she couldn't see how far they extended. She was afraid of deviating into one, only to encounter a dead end within a short distance.

To her left, three stories above, Eric hurried along the brink of the arroyo, following her limping progress as if he were the mutant master of the maze in a Dungeons and Dragons game. If and when he started down the arroyo wall, she would have to turn and immediately climb the opposite wall, for she now knew she could not hold her own in a chase. Her only chance of survival was to get above him and find some rocks to hurl down on him as he ascended in her wake. She hoped he would not come after her for a few more minutes, because she needed time for the pain in her ankle to subside further before testing it in a climb.

Distant thunder sounded from Barstow in the west: one long peal, another, then a third that was louder than the first two. The sky over this part of the desert was gray and soot-black, as if heaven had caught fire, burned, and was now composed only of ashes and cold black coals. The burnt-out sky had settled lower as well, until it almost seemed to be a lid that was going to come down all the way and clamp tightly over the top of the arroyo. A warm wind whistled mournfully and moaned up there on the surface of the Mojave, and some gusts found their way down into the channel, flinging bits of sand in Rachael's face. The storm already under way in the west had not reached here yet, but it would arrive soon; a pre-storm scent was heavy in the air, and the atmosphere had the electrically charged feeling that preceded a hard rain.

She rounded a bend and was startled by a pile of dry tumbleweeds that had rolled into the gulch from the desert above. Stirred by a downdraft, they moved rapidly toward her with a scratchy sound, almost a hiss, as if they were living creatures. She tried to sidestep those bristly brown balls, stumbled, and fell full-length into the powdery silt that covered the floor of the channel. Falling, she feared for the ankle she had already hurt, but fortunately she did not twist it again.

Even as she fell, she heard more noise behind her. She thought for a moment that the sound was made by the tumbleweeds still rubbing against one another in their packlike progress along the arroyo, but a harder clatter alerted her to the true source of the noise. When she looked back and up, she saw that Eric had started down the wall of the gulch. He'd been waiting for her to fall or to encounter an obstacle; now that she was down, he was swiftly taking advantage of her bad luck. He had descended a third of the incline and was still on his feet, for the slope was not quite as steep here as it had been where Rachael had rolled over the edge. As he came, he dislodged a minor avalanche of dirt and stones, but the wall of the arroyo did not give way entirely. In a minute he would reach the bottom and then, in ten steps, would be on top of her.

Rachael pushed up from the ground, ran toward the other wall of the gulch, intending to climb it, but realized she had dropped her car keys. She might never find her way back to the car; in fact, she'd probably either be brought down by Eric or get lost in the wasteland, but if by some miracle she did reach the Mercedes, she had to have the keys.

Eric was almost halfway down the slope, descending through dust that rose from the slide he had started.

Frantically looking for the keys, she returned to the place where she'd fallen, and at first she couldn't see them. Then she glimpsed the shiny notched edges poking out of the powdery brown silt, almost entirely buried. Evidently she'd fallen atop the keys, pressing them into the soft soil. She snatched them up.

Eric was more than halfway to the arroyo floor.

He was making a strange sound: a thin, shrill cry—half stage whisper, half shriek.

Thunder pounded the sky, somewhat closer now.

Still pouring sweat, gasping for breath, her mouth seared by the hot air, her lungs aching, she ran to the far wall again, shoving the car keys into a pocket of her jeans. This embankment had the same degree of slope as the one Eric was descending, but Rachael discovered that ascending on her feet was not as easy as coming down that way; the angle worked against her as much as it would have worked for her if she'd been going the other direction. After three or four yards, she had to drop forward against the bank, desperately using hands and knees and feet to hold on and thrust herself steadily up the incline.

Eric's eerie whisper-shriek rose behind her, closer.

She dared not look back.

Fifteen feet farther to the top.

Her progress was maddeningly hampered every foot of the way by the softness of the earth face she was climbing. In spots, it tended to crumble under her as she tried to find or make handholds and footholds. She required all the tenacity of a spider to retain what ground she gained, and she was terrified of suddenly slipping back all the way to the bottom.

The top of the arroyo was less than twelve feet away, so she must be about two stories above the floor of it.

"*Rachael,*" the Eric-thing said behind her in a raspy voice like a rat-tail file drawn across her spine.

Don't look down, don't, don't, for God's sake, don't . . .

Vertical erosion channels cut the wall from top to bottom, some only a few inches wide and a few inches deep, others a foot wide and two feet deep. She had to stay away from those; for, where they scored the slope too close to one another, the earth was especially rotten and most prone to collapse under her.

Fortunately, in some places there were bands of striated stone—pink, gray, brown, with veins of what appeared to be white quartz. These were the outer edges of rock strata that the eroding arroyo had only recently begun to uncover, and they provided firmer footholds.

"Rachael. . . "

She grabbed a foot-deep rock ledge that thrust out of the soft earth above her, intending to pull and kick her way onto it, hoping that it would not break off, but before she could test it, something grabbed at the heel of her right shoe. She couldn't help it: she had to look down this time, and there he was, dear God, the Eric-thing, on the arroyo wall beneath her, holding himself in place with one hand, reaching up with the other, trying to get a grip on her shoe, coming up only an inch short of his goal.

With dismaying agility, more like an animal than a human being, he flung himself upward. His hands and knees and feet refastened to the earthen wall with frightening ease. He reached eagerly for her again. He was now close enough to clutch at her calf instead of at the bottom of her shoe.

But she was not exactly moving like a sloth. She was damn fast, too, responding even as he moved toward her. Reflexes goosed by a flood of adrenaline, she let go of the wall with her knees and feet, holding on only to the rock ledge an arm's length above her head, dangling, recklessly letting the untested stone support her entire weight. As he reached for her, she pulled her legs up, then kicked down with both feet, putting all the power of her thighs into it, striking his grasping hand, smashing his long bony, mutant fingers.

He loosed an inhuman wail.

She kicked again.

Instead of slipping back down the wall, as Rachael had hoped he would, Eric held on to it, surged upward another foot, shrieking in triumph, and took a swipe at her.

At the same moment she kicked out again, smashing one foot into his arm, stomping the other squarely into his face.

She heard her jeans tear, then felt a flash of pain and knew that he had hooked claws through the denim even as her kick had landed.

He bellowed in pain, finally lost his hold on the wall, and hung for an instant by the claws in her jeans. Then the claws snapped, and the cloth tore, and he fell away into the arroyo.

Rachael didn't wait long enough to watch him tumble two stories to the bottom of the gulch, but turned at once to the demanding task of heaving herself onto the narrow stone ledge from which she hung precariously. Pulsations of pain, throbbing in time with her wildly pounding heart, coursed through her arms from wrists to shoulders. Her straining muscles twitched and rebelled at her demands. Clenching her teeth, breathing through her nose so hard that she snorted like a horse, she struggled upward, digging at the wall beneath the ledge with her feet to provide what little thrust she could. By sheer perseverance and determination— spiced with a generous measure of motivating terror—she clambered onto the ledge at last.

Exhausted, suffering several pains, she nevertheless refused to pause. She dragged herself up the last eight feet of the arroyo wall, finding handholds in a few final outcroppings of rock and among the erosion-exposed roots of the mesquite bushes that grew at the brink. Then she was at the edge, over the top, pushing through a break in the mesquite, and she rolled onto the surface of the desert.

Lightning stepped down the sky as if providing a staircase for some descending god, and all around Rachael the low desert scrub threw short-lived, giant shadows.

Thunder followed, hard and flat, and she felt it reverberate in the ground against her back.

She dragged herself back to the brink of the arroyo, praying that she would see the Eric-thing still at the bottom, motionless, dead a second time. Maybe he'd fallen on a rock. There *were* a few rocks on the floor of the gulch. It was possible. Maybe he had landed on one of them and had snapped his spine.

She peered over the edge.

He was more than halfway up the wall again.

Lightning flashed, illuminating his deformed face, silvering his inhuman eyes, plating an electric gleam to his too-sharp teeth.

Leaping up, Rachael started kicking at the loose earth along the brink and at the brush that grew there, knocking it down on top of him. He hung from the quartz-veined ledge, keeping his head under it for protection, so the sandy earth and brush cascaded harmlessly over him. She stopped kicking dirt, looked around for some stones, found a few about the size of eggs, and hurled them down at his hands. When the stones connected with his grotesque fingers, he let go of the ledge and moved entirely under it, clinging to the earth in the shadow of that stone shelf, where she could not hit him.

She could wait for him to reappear, then pelt him again. She could keep him pinned there for hours. But nothing would be gained. It would be a tense, wearying, futile enterprise; when she exhausted the supply of stones within her reach and had only dirt to throw, he would ascend with animal quickness, undeterred by that pathetic bombardment, and he would finish her.

A white-hot celestial cauldron tipped, spilling forth a third molten streak of lightning. It made contact with the earth much closer than the two before it, no more than a quarter of a mile away, accompanied by a simultaneous crash worthy of Armageddon, and with a crackle-sizzle that was the voice of Death speaking in the language of electricity.

Below, unfazed by the lightning, emboldened by the cessation of the attack Rachael had been waging, the Eric-thing put one monstrous hand over the edge of the ledge.

She kicked more dirt down on him, lots of it. He withdrew his hand, taking shelter again, but she continued to stomp away at the rotten brink of the embankment. Suddenly an enormous chunk collapsed directly under her feet, and she nearly fell into the arroyo. As the ground began to shift, she threw herself backward just in time to avoid catastrophe, and landed hard on her buttocks.

With so much dirt pouring down over him, he might hesitate longer before making another attempt to pull himself across the overhanging ledge. His caution might give her an extra couple of minutes' lead time. She got up and sprinted off into the forbidding desert.

The overused muscles in her legs were repeatedly stabbed and split by cleaver-sharp pains. Her right ankle remained tender, and her right calf burned where the claws had cut through her jeans.

Her mouth was drier than ever, and her throat was cracking. Her lungs felt seared by her deep shuddering gasps of hot desert air.

She didn't succumb to the agony, couldn't afford to succumb, just kept on running, not as fast as before but as fast as she could.

Ahead, the land became less flat than it had been, began to roll in a series of low hills and hollows. She ran up a hill and down, up another, on and on, trying to put concealing barriers between herself and Eric before he crawled out of the arroyo. Eventually, deciding to stay in one of the hollows, she turned in a direction that she thought was north; though her sense of direction might have become totally fouled up during the chase, she believed she had to go north first, then east, if she hoped to circle around to the Mercedes, which was now at least a mile away, probably much farther.

Lightning . . . *lightning.*

This time, an incredibly long-lived bolt glimmered between the thunderheads and the ground below for at least ten seconds, racing-jigging south to north, like a gigantic needle trying to sew the storm tight to the land forever.

That flash and the empyrean blast that followed were sufficient to bring the rain, at last. It fell hard, pasting Rachael's hair to her skull, stinging her face. It was cool, blessedly cool. She licked her chapped lips, grateful for the moisture.

Several times she looked back, dreading what she would see, but Eric was never there.

She had lost him. And even if she'd left footprints to mark her flight, the rain would swiftly erase them. In his alien incarnation, he might somehow be able to track her by scent, but the rain would provide cover in that regard as well, scrubbing her odor from the land and air. Even if his strange eyes provided better vision than the human eyes they had once been, he would not be able to see far in this heavy rain and gloom.

You've escaped, she told herself as she hurried north. You're going to be safe.

It was probably true.

But she didn't believe it.

■ By the time Ben Shadway drove just a few miles east of Barstow, the rain not only filled the world but became the world. Except for the metronomic thump of the windshield wipers, all sounds were those of water in motion, drowning out everything else: a ceaseless drumming on the roof of the Merkur, the snap-snap-snap of droplets hitting the windshield at high speed, the slosh and hiss of wet pavement under the tires. Beyond the comfortable—though abruptly humid—confines of the car, most of the light had bled out of the bruised and wounded storm-dark sky, and little remained to be seen other than the omnipresent rain falling in millions of slanting gray lines. Sometimes the wind caught sheets of water the same way it might catch sheer curtains at an open window, blowing them across the vast desert floor in graceful, undulant patterns, one filmy layer after another, gray on gray. When the lightning flashed—which it did with unnerving frequency—billions of drops turned bright silver, and for a second or two, it appeared as if snow were falling on the Mojave; at other times, the lightning-transformed rain seemed more like glittery, streaming tinsel.

The downpour grew worse until the windshield wipers could not keep the glass clear. Hunching over the steering wheel, Ben squinted into the storm-lashed day. The highway ahead was barely visible. He had switched on the headlights, which did not improve visibility. But the headlights of oncoming cars—though few—were refracted by the film of water on the windshield, stinging his eyes.

He slowed to forty, then thirty. Finally, because the nearest rest area was over twenty miles ahead, he drove onto the narrow shoulder of the highway, stopped, left the engine running, and switched on the Merkur's emergency blinkers. Since he had failed to reach Whitney Gavis, his concern for Rachael was greater than ever, and he was more acutely aware of his inadequacies by the minute, but it would be foolhardy to do anything other than wait for the blinding storm to subside. He would be of no help whatsoever to Rachael if he lost control of the car on the rain-greased pavement, slid into one of the big eighteen-wheelers that constituted most of the sparse traffic, and got himself killed.

After Ben had waited through ten minutes of the hardest rain he had ever seen, as he was beginning to wonder if it would ever let up, he saw that a sluice of fast-moving dirty water had overflowed the drainage channel beside the road. Because the highway was elevated a few feet above the surrounding land, the water could not flow onto the pavement, but it did spill into the desert beyond. As he looked out the side window of the Merkur, he saw a sinuous dark form gliding smoothly across the surface of the racing yellow-brown torrent, then another similar form, then a third and a fourth. For a moment he stared uncomprehendingly before he realized they were rattlesnakes driven out of the ground when their dens flooded. There must have been several nests of rattlers in the immediate area, for in moments two score of them appeared. They made their way across the steadily widening spate to higher and drier ground, where they came together, coiling among one another—weaving, tangling, knotting their long bodies—forming a writhing and fluxuous mass, as if they were not individual creatures but parts of one entity that had become detached in the deluge and was now struggling to re-form itself.

Lightning flashed.

The squirming rattlers, like the mane of an otherwise buried Medusa, appeared to churn with greater fury as the stroboscopic storm light revealed them in stuttering flashes.

The sight sent a chill to the very marrow of Ben's bones. He looked away from the serpents and stared straight ahead through the rain-washed windshield. Minute by minute, his optimism was fading; his despair was growing; his fear for Rachael had attained such depth and intensity that it began to shake him, physically shake him, and he sat shivering in the stolen car, in the blinding rain, upon the somber storm-hammered desert.

■ The cloudburst erased whatever trail Rachael might have left, which was good, but the storm had drawbacks, too. Though the downpour had reduced the temperature only a few degrees, leaving the day still very warm, and although she was not even slightly chilled, she was nevertheless soaked to the skin. Worse, the drenching rain fell in cataracts which, combined with the midday gloom that the gray-black clouds had imposed upon the land, made it difficult to maintain a good sense of direction; even when she risked ascending from one of the hollows onto a hill, to get a fix on her position, the poor visibility left her less than certain that she was heading back toward the rest area and the Mercedes. Worse still, the lightning shattered through the malignant bellies of the thunderheads and crashed to the ground with such frequency that she figured it was only a matter of time until she was struck by one of those bolts and reduced to a charred and smoking corpse.

But worst of all, the loud and unrelenting noise of the rain—the hissing, chuckling, sizzling, crackling, gurgling, dripping, burbling, and hollow steady drumming—blotted out any warning sounds that the Eric-thing might have made in pursuit of her, so she was in greater danger of being set upon by surprise. She repeatedly looked behind her and glanced worriedly at the tops of the gentle slopes on both sides of the shallow little hollow through which she hurried. She slowed every time she approached a turn in the course of the hollow, fearing that he would be just around the bend, would loom out of the rain, strange eyes radiant in the gloom, and would seize her in his hideous hands.

When, without warning, she encountered him at last, he did not see her. She turned one of those bends that she found so frightening, and Eric was only twenty or thirty feet away, on his knees in the middle of the hollow, preoccupied with some task that Rachael could not at first understand. A wind-carved, flute-holed rock formation projected out from the slope in a wedge-shaped wing, and Rachael quickly took cover behind it before he saw her. She almost turned at once to creep back the way she had come, but his peculiar posture and attitude had intrigued her. Suddenly it seemed important to know what he was doing because, by secretly observing him, she might learn something that would guarantee her escape or even something that would give her an advantage over him in a confrontation at some later time. She eased along the rock formation, peering into several convexities and flute holes, until she found a wind-sculpted bore about three inches in diameter, through which she could see Eric.

He was still kneeling on the wet ground, his broad humped back bowed to the driving rain. He appeared to have . . . changed. He did not look quite the same as when he had confronted her outside the public rest rooms. He was still monstrously deformed, though in a vaguely different way from before. A subtle difference but important . . . What was it, exactly? Peering out of the flute hole in the stone, wind whistling softly through the eight- or ten-inch-deep bore and blowing in her face, Rachael strained her eyes to get a better view of him. The rain and murky light hampered her, but she thought he seemed more apelike. Hulking, slump-shouldered, slightly longer in the arms. Perhaps he was also less reptilian than he had been, yet still with those grotesque, bony, long, and wickedly taloned hands.

Surely any change she perceived must be imaginary, for the very structure of his bones and flesh couldn't have altered noticeably in less than a quarter of an hour. Could it? Then again . . . why not? If his genetic integrity had collapsed thoroughly since he had beaten Sarah Kiel last night—when he'd still been human in appearance—if his face and body and limbs had been altered so drastically in the twelve hours between then and now, the pace of his metamorphosis was obviously so frantic that, indeed, a difference might be noticeable in just a quarter of an hour.

The realization was unnerving.

It was followed by a worse realization: Eric was holding a thick, writhing snake—one hand gripping it near the tail, the other hand behind its head—and he was eating it alive. Rachael saw the snake's jaws unhinged and gaping, fangs like twin slivers of ivory in the flickering storm light, as it struggled unsuccessfully to curl its head back and bite the hand of the man-thing that held it. Eric was tearing at the middle of the serpent with his inhumanly sharp teeth, ripping hunks of meat loose and chewing enthusiastically. Because his jaws were heavier and longer than the jaws of any man, their obscenely eager movement—the crushing and grinding of the snake—could be seen even at this distance.

Shocked and nauseated, Rachael wanted to turn away from the spy-hole in the rock. However, she did not vomit, and she did not turn away, because her nausea and disgust were outweighed by her bafflement and her need to understand Eric.

Considering how much he wanted to get his hands on her, why had he abandoned the chase? Had he forgotten her? Had the snake bitten him and had he, in his savage rage, traded bite for bite?

But he was not merely striking back at the snake: he was *eating* it, eagerly consuming one solid mouthful after another. Once, when Eric looked up at the fulminous heavens, Rachael saw his storm-lit countenance twisted in a frightening expression of inhuman ecstasy. He shuddered with apparent delight as he tore at the serpent. His hunger seemed as urgent and insatiable as it was unspeakable.

Rain slashed, wind moaned, thunder crashed, lightning flashed, and she felt as if she were peering through a chink in the walls of hell, watching a demon devour the souls of the damned. Her heart hammered hard enough to compete with the sound of the rain drumming on the ground. She knew she should run, but she was mesmerized by the pure evil of the sight framed in the flute hole.

She saw a second snake—then a third, fourth, fifth—oozing out of the rain-pooled ground around Eric's knees. He was kneeling at the entrance to a den of the deadly creatures, a nest that was apparently flooding with the runoff from the storm. The rattlers wriggled forth and, finding the man-thing in their midst, immediately struck at his thighs and arms, biting him repeatedly. Though Eric neither cried out nor flinched, Rachael was filled with relief, knowing that he would soon collapse from the effects of the venom.

He threw aside the half-eaten snake and seized another. With no diminishment of his perverse hunger, he sank his pointed, razored teeth into the snake's living flesh and tore loose one dripping gobbet after another. Maybe his altered metabolism was capable of dealing with the potent venom of the rattlers—either breaking it down into an array of harmless chemicals, or repairing tissues as rapidly as the venom damaged them.

Chain lightning flashed back and forth across the malevolent sky, and in that incandescent flare, Eric's long sharp teeth gleamed like shards of a broken mirror. His strangely shining eyes cast back a cold reflection of the celestial fire. His wet, tangled hair streamed with short-lived silvery brightness; the rain glistered like molten silver on his face; and all around him the earth sizzled as if the lightning-lined water was actually melted fat bubbling and crackling in a frying pan.

At last, Rachael broke the mesmeric hold that the scene exerted, turned from the flute hole, and ran back the way she had come. She sought another hollow between other low hills, a different route that would lead her to the roadside comfort station and the Mercedes.

Leaving the hilly area and recrossing the sandy plains, she was frequently the tallest thing in sight, much taller than the desert scrub. Once more, she worried about being struck by lightning. In the eerie stroboscopic light, the bleak and barren land appeared to leap and fall and leap again, as if eons of geological activity were being compressed into a few frantic seconds.

She tried to enter an arroyo, where she might be safe from the lightning. But the deep gulch was two-thirds full of muddy, churning water. Flotillas of whirling tumbleweed boats and bobbing mesquite rafts were borne on the water's rolling back.

She was forced to find a route around the network of flooded arroyos. But in time she came to the rest area where she had first encountered Eric. Her purse was still where she had dropped it, and she picked it up. The Mercedes was also exactly where she'd left it.

A few steps from the car, she halted abruptly, for she saw that the trunk lid, previously open, was now closed. She had the dreadful feeling that Eric—or the thing that had once been Eric—had returned ahead of her, had climbed into the trunk again, and had pulled the lid shut behind him.

Shaking, indecisive, afraid, Rachael stood in the drenching rain, reluctant to go closer to the car. The parking lot, lacking adequate drainage, was being transformed into a shallow lake. She stood in water that came over the tops of her running shoes.

The thirty-two pistol was under the driver's seat. If she could reach it before Eric threw open the trunk lid and came out . . .

Behind her, the staccato plop-plop-plop of water dripping off the picnic-table cover sounded like scurrying rats. More water sheeted off the comfort-station roof, splashing on the sidewalk. All around, the falling rain slashed into the pools and puddles with a crackling-cellophane sound that seemed to grow louder by the second.

She took a step toward the car, another, halted again.

He might not be in the trunk but inside the car itself. He might have closed the trunk and slipped into the back seat or even into the front, where he could be lying now—silent, still, unseen—waiting for her to open the door. Waiting to sink his teeth into her the way he'd sunk them into the snakes . . .

Rain streamed off the roof of the Mercedes, rippled down the windows, blurring her view of the car's shadowy interior.

Scared to approach the car but equally afraid of turning back, Rachael at last took another step forward.

Lightning flashed. Looming large and ominous in the stuttering light, the black Mercedes suddenly reminded her of a hearse.

Out on the highway, a large truck passed, engine roaring, big tires making a slushy sound on the wet pavement.

Rachael reached the Mercedes, jerked open the driver's door, saw no one inside. She fumbled under the seat for the pistol. Found it. While she still had the courage to act, she went around to the back of the car, hesitated only a second, pushed on the latch button, and lifted the trunk lid, prepared to empty the clip of the thirty-two into the Eric-thing if it was crouching there.

The trunk was empty. The carpet was soaked, and a gray puddle of rain spread over the center of the compartment, so she figured it had remained open to the elements until an especially strong gust of wind had blown it shut.

She slammed the lid, used her keys to lock it, returned to the driver's door, and got in behind the wheel. She put the pistol on the passenger's seat, where she could grab it quickly.

The car started without hesitation. The windshield wipers flung the rain off the glass.

Outside, the desert beyond the concrete-block comfort station was rendered entirely in shades of slate: grays, blacks, browns, and rust. In that dreary sandscape, the only movement was the driving rain and the windblown tumbleweed.

Eric had not followed her.

Maybe the rattlesnakes had killed him, after all. Surely he could not have survived so many bites from so many snakes. Perhaps his genetically altered body, though capable of repairing massive tissue damage, was not able to counteract the toxic effects of such potent venom.

She drove out of the rest area, back onto the highway, heading east toward Las Vegas, grateful to be alive. The rain was falling too hard to permit safe travel above forty or fifty miles an hour, so she stayed in the extreme right lane, letting the more daring motorists pass her. Mile by mile she tried to convince herself that the worst was past—but she remained unconvinced.

■ Ben put the Merkur in gear and pulled onto the highway again.

The storm was moving rapidly eastward, toward Las Vegas. The rolling thunder was more distant than before, a deep rumble rather than a bone-jarring crash. The lightning, which had been striking perilously close on all sides, now flickered farther away, near the eastern horizon. Rain was still falling hard, but it no longer came down in blinding sheets, and driving was possible again.

The dashboard clock confirmed the time on Ben's watch: 5:15. Yet the summer day was darker than it should have been at that hour. The storm-blackened sky had brought an early dusk, and ahead the somber land was fading steadily in the embrace of a false twilight.

At his current speed, he would not reach Las Vegas until about eight-thirty tonight, probably two or three hours after Rachael had gotten there. He would have to stop in Baker, the only outpost in this part of the Mojave, and try to reach Whitney Gavis again. But he had the feeling he was not going to get hold of Whit. A feeling that maybe his and Rachael's luck had run out.

31 FEEDING FRENZY

ERIC REMEMBERED THE RATTLESNAKES ONLY VAGUELY. THEIR fangs had left puncture wounds in his hands, arms, and thighs, but those small holes had already healed, and the rain had washed the bloodstains from his sodden clothes. His mutating flesh burned with that peculiar painless fire of ongoing change, which completely masked the lesser sting of venom. Sometimes his knees grew weak, or his stomach churned with nausea, or his vision blurred, or a spell of dizziness seized him, but those symptoms of poisoning grew less noticeable minute by minute. As he moved across the storm-darkened desert, images of the serpents rose in his memory—writhing forms curling like smoke around him, whispering in a language that he could almost understand—but he had difficulty believing that they had been real. A few times, he recalled biting, chewing, and swallowing mouthfuls of rattler meat, gripped by a feeding frenzy. A part of him responded to those bloody memories with excitement and satisfaction. But another part of him—the part that was still Eric Leben—was disgusted and repelled, and he repressed those grim recollections, aware that he would lose his already tenuous grip on sanity if he dwelt on them.

He moved rapidly toward an unknown place, propelled by instinct. Mostly he ran fully erect, more or less like a man, but sometimes he loped and shambled, with his shoulders hunched forward and his body bent in an apelike posture. Occasionally he was overcome with the urge to drop forward on all fours and scuttle across the wet sand on his belly; however, that queer compulsion frightened him, and he successfully resisted it.

Shadowfires burned here and there upon the desert floor, but he was not drawn toward them as he had been before. They were not as mysterious and intriguing · as they had been previously, for he now suspected that they were gateways to hell. Previously, when he had seen those phantom flames, he had also seen his long-dead uncle Barry, which probably meant that Uncle Barry had come out of the fire. Eric was sure that Barry Hampstead resided in hell, so he figured the doors were portals to damnation. When Eric had died in Santa Ana yesterday, he had become Satan's property, doomed to spend eternity with Barry Hampstead, but at the penultimate moment he had thrown off the claims of the grave and had rescued his own soul from the pit. Now Satan was opening these doors around him, in hopes he would be impelled by curiosity to investigate one gate or another and, on stepping through, would deliver himself to the sulfurous cell reserved for him. His parents had warned him that he was in danger of going to hell, that his surrender to his uncle's desires—and, later, the murder of his tormentor—had damned his soul. Now he knew they were right. Hell was close. He dared not look into its flames, where something beckoned and smiled.

He raced on through the desert scrub. The storm, like clashing armies, blasted the day with bright bursts and rolling cannonades.

His unknown destination proved to be the comfort station at the roadside rest area where he had first confronted Rachael. Activated by solenoids that had misinterpreted the storm as nightfall, banks of fluorescent lights had blinked on at the front of the structure and over the doors on each side. In the parking lot, a few mercury-vapor arc lamps cast a bluish light on the puddled pavement.

When he saw the squat concrete-block building in the rain-swept murk ahead, Eric's muddy thoughts cleared, and suddenly he remembered everything Rachael had done to him. His encounter with the garbage truck on Main Street was *her* doing. And because the violent shock of death was what had triggered his malignant growth, he blamed his monstrous mutation on her as well. He'd almost gotten his hands on her, had almost torn her to pieces, but she'd slipped away from him when he'd been overcome by hunger, by a desperate need to provide fuel for his out-of-control metabolism. Now, thinking of her, he felt that cold reptilian rage well up in him again, and he loosed a thin bleat of fury that was lost in the noise of the storm.

Rounding the side of the building, he sensed someone near. A thrill coursed through him. He dropped to all fours and crouched against the block wall, in a pool of shadow just beyond the reach of the nearest fluorescent light.

He listened—head cocked, breath held. A jalousie window was open above his head, high in the men's-room wall. Movement inside. A man coughed. Then Eric heard soft, sweet whistling: "Memories," from the musical *Cats.* The scrape and click of footsteps on concrete. The door opened outward onto the walk, eight or ten feet from where Eric crouched, and a man appeared.

The guy was in his late twenties, solidly built, rugged-looking, wearing boots, jeans, cowboy shirt, and a tan Stetson. He stood for a moment beneath the sheltering overhang, looking out at the falling rain. Suddenly he became aware of Eric, turned, stopped whistling, and stared in disbelief and horror.

As the other turned toward him, Eric moved so fast he seemed to be a leaping reflection of the lightning that flashed along the eastern horizon. Tall and well-muscled, the cowboy would have been a dangerous adversary in a fight with an ordinary man, but Eric Leben was no longer an ordinary man—or even quite a man at all. And the cowboy's shock at his attacker's appearance was a grave disadvantage, for it paralyzed him. Eric slammed into his prey and drove all five talons of his right hand into the man's belly, very deep. At the same time, seizing his prey's throat with his other hand, he destroyed the windpipe, ripping out the voice box and vocal cords, ensuring instant silence. Blood spurted from severed carotid arteries. Death glazed the cowboy's eyes even before Eric tore open his belly. Steaming guts cascaded onto rain-wet concrete, and the dead man collapsed into his own hot entrails.

Feeling wild and free and powerful, Eric settled down atop the warm corpse. Strangely, killing no longer repulsed or frightened him. He was becoming a primal beast who took a savage delight in slaughter. However, even the part of him that remained civilized—the Eric Leben part—was undeniably exhilarated by the violence, as well as by the enormous power and catlike quickness of his mutant body. He knew he should have been shocked, nauseated, but he was not. All his life, he had needed to dominate others, to crush his adversaries, and now the need found expression in its purest form: cruel, merciless, violent murder.

He was also, for the first time, able to remember clearly the murder of the two young women whose car he had stolen in Santa Ana on Monday evening. He felt no burdensome responsibility for their deaths, no rush of guilt, only a sweet dark satisfaction and a fierce sort of glee. Indeed, the memory of their spilled blood, the memory of the naked woman whom he had nailed to the wall, only contributed to his exhilaration over the murder of the cowboy, and his heart pounded out a rhythm of icy joy.

Then, for a while, lowering himself onto the corpse by the men's-room door, he lost all conscious awareness of himself as a creature of intellect, as a creature with a past and a future. He descended into a dreamy state where the only sensations were the smell and taste of blood. The drumming and gurgling of rain continued to reach him, too, but it seemed now that it was an internal rather than external noise, perhaps the sound of change surging through his arteries, veins, bones, and tissues.

He was jolted out of his trance by a scream. He looked up from the ruined throat of his prey, where he'd buried his muzzle. A woman was standing at the corner of the building, wide-eyed, one arm held defensively across her breasts. Judging by her boots, jeans, and cowboy shirt, she was with the man whom Eric had just killed.

Eric realized that he had been feeding on his prey, and he was neither startled nor appalled by that realization. A lion would not be surprised or dismayed by its own savagery. His racing metabolism generated hunger unlike any he had ever known, and he needed rich nutrients to allay those pangs. In the meat of his prey, he found the food he required, just as the lion found what it needed in the flesh of the gazelle.

The woman tried to scream again but could not make a sound.

Eric rose from the corpse. He licked his blood-slicked lips.

The woman ran into the wind-driven rain. Her Stetson flew off, and her yellow hair streamed behind her, the only brightness in the storm-blackened day.

Eric pursued her. He found indescribable pleasure in the feel of his feet pounding on the hard concrete, then on waterlogged sand. He splashed across the flooded macadam parking lot, gaining on her by the second.

She was heading toward a dull red pickup truck. She glanced back and saw him drawing nearer. She must have realized that she would not reach the pickup in time to start it and drive away, so she turned toward the interstate, evidently hoping to get help from the driver of one of the infrequently passing cars or trucks.

The chase was short. He dragged her down before she had reached the end of the parking lot. They rolled through dirty ankle-deep water. She flailed at him, tried to claw him. He sank his razored talons into her arms, nailing them to her sides, and she let out a terrible cry of pain. Thrashing furiously, they rolled one last time, and then he had her pinned down in the storm runoff, which was chilly in spite of the warm air around them.

For a moment he was surprised to find his blood subsiding, replaced by carnal hunger as he looked down upon the helpless woman. But he merely surrendered to that need as he had surrendered to the urgent need for blood. Beneath him, sensing his intent, the woman tried desperately to throw him off. Her screams of pain gave way to shrill cries of pure terror. Ripping his talons loose of her arm, he shredded her blouse and put his dark, gnarled, inhuman hand upon her bare breasts.

Her screams faded. She stared up at him emptily—voiceless, shaking, paralyzed by dread.

A moment later, having torn open her pants, he eagerly withdrew his manhood from his own jeans. Even in his frenzy to couple with her, he realized that the erect organ in his hand was not human; it was large, strange, hideous. When the woman's gaze fell upon that monstrous staff, she began to weep and whimper. She must have thought that the gates of hell had opened and that demons had come forth. Her horror and abject fear further inflamed his lust.

The storm, which had been subsiding, grew worse for a while, as if in malevolent accompaniment to the brutal act that he was about to perpetrate.

He mounted her.

The rain beat upon them.

The water sloshed around them.

A few minutes later, he killed her.

Lightning blazed, and as its reflection played across the flooded parking lot, the woman's spreading blood looked like opalescent films of oil on the water.

After he had killed her, he fed.

When he was satiated, his primal urges grew less demanding, and the part of him that possessed an intellect gained dominance over the savage beast. Slowly he became aware of the danger of being seen. There was little traffic on the interstate, but if one of the passing cars or trucks pulled into the rest area, he would be spotted. He hurriedly dragged the dead woman across the macadam, around the side of the comfort station, and into the mesquite behind the building. He disposed of the dead man there as well.

He found the keys in the ignition of the pickup. The engine turned over on the second try.

He had taken the cowboy's hat. Now he jammed it on his head, pulling the brim down, hoping it would disguise the strangeness of his face. The pickup's fuel gauge indicated a full tank, so he would not need to stop between here and Vegas. But if a passing motorist glanced over and saw his face . . . He must remain alert, drive well, attract no notice—always resisting the retrograde evolution that steadily pulled him into the mindless perspective of the beast. He had to remember to avert his grotesque face from the vehicles he passed and from those that passed him. If he took those precautions, then the hat—in conjunction with the early dusk brought by the storm—might provide sufficient cover.

He looked into the rearview mirror and saw a pair of unmatched eyes. One was a luminous pale green with a vertical slit-shaped orange iris that gleamed like a hot coal. The other was larger, dark, and . . . multifaceted.

That jarred him as nothing had for a while, and he looked quickly away from the mirror. Multifaceted? That was far too alien to bear consideration. Nothing like that had featured in any stage of human evolution, not even in ancient eras when the first gasping amphibians had crawled out of the sea onto the shore. Here was proof that he was not merely devolving, that his body was not merely struggling to express all the potential in the genetic heritage of humankind; here was proof that his genetic structure had run amok and that it was conveying him toward a form and consciousness that had nothing to do with the human race. He was becoming something *else*, something beyond reptile or ape or Neanderthal or Cro-Magnon man or modern European man, something so strange that he did not have the courage or the curiosity to confront it.

Henceforth, when he glanced in the mirror, he would be certain that it provided a view only of the roadway behind and revealed no slightest aspect of his own altered countenance.

He switched on the headlights and drove away from the rest area onto the highway.

The steering wheel felt odd in his malformed, monstrous hands. Driving, which should have been as familiar to him as walking, seemed like a singularly exotic act—and difficult, too, almost beyond his capabilities. He clutched the wheel and concentrated on the rainy highway ahead.

The whispering tires and metronomic thump of the windshield wipers seemed to pull him on through the storm and the gathering darkness, toward a special destiny. Once, when his full intellect returned to him for a brief moment, he thought of William Butler Yeats and remembered a fitting scrap of the great man's poetry:

And what rough beast, its hour come round at last,
Slouches towards Bethlehem to be born?

32   FLAMINGO PINK

TUESDAY AFTERNOON, AFTER THEIR MEETING WITH DR. EASTON Solberg at UCI, Detectives Julio Verdad and Reese Hagerstrom, still on sick leave, had driven to Tustin, where the main offices of Shadway Realty were located in a suite on the ground floor of a three-story Spanish-style building with a blue tile roof. Julio had spotted the stakeout car on the first pass. It was an unmarked muck-green Ford, sitting at the curb half a block from Shadway Realty, where the occupants had a good view of those offices and of the driveway that serviced the parking lot alongside the building. Two men in blue suits were in the Ford: One was reading a newspaper and the other was keeping watch.

"Feds," Julio said as he cruised by the stakeout.

"Sharp's men? DSA?" Reese wondered.

"Must be."

"A little obvious, aren't they?"

"I guess they don't really expect Shadway to turn up here," Julio said. "But they have to go through the motions."

Julio parked half a block behind the stakeout, putting several cars between him and the DSA's Ford, so it was possible to watch the watchers without being seen.

Reese had participated in scores of stakeouts with Julio, and surveillance duty had never been the ordeal it might have been with another partner. Julio was a complex man whose conversation was interesting hour after hour. But when one or both of them did not feel up to conversation, they could sit through long silences in comfort, without awkwardness—one of the surest tests of friendship.

Tuesday afternoon, while they watched the watchers and also watched the offices of Shadway Realty, they talked about Eric Leben, genetic engineering, and the dream of immortality. That dream was by no means Leben's private obsession. A deep longing for immortality, for commutation of the death sentence, had surely filled humankind since the first members of the species had acquired self-awareness and a crude intelligence. The subject had a special poignancy for Reese and Julio because both had witnessed the deaths of much-loved wives and had never fully recovered from their losses.

Reese could sympathize with Leben's dream and even understand the scientist's reasons for subjecting himself to a dangerous genetic experiment. It had gone wrong, yes: the two murders and the hideous crucifixion of the one dead girl were proof that Leben had come back from the grave as something less than human, and he must be stopped. But the deadly result of his experiments—and the folly of them—did not entirely foreclose sympathy. Against the rapacious hunger of the grave, all men and women were united, brothers and sisters.

As the sunny summer day grew dreary under an incoming marine layer of ash-gray clouds, Reese felt a cloak of melancholy settle upon him. He might have been overwhelmed by it if he had not been on the job, but he *was* on the job in spite of also being on sick leave.

They—like the DSA stakeout team—were not expecting Shadway to arrive at his headquarters, but they were hoping to identify one of the real-estate agents operating out of the office. As the afternoon wore on they saw several people entering and leaving the premises, but one tall, thin woman with a Betty Boop cap of black hair was the most noticeable, her angular storklike frame emphasized by a clinging flamingo-pink dress. Not pale pink, not frilly pink, but bold flame-hot pink. She came and went twice, both times chauffeuring middle-aged couples who had arrived at the office in their own cars—evidently clients for whom she was tracking down suitable houses. Her own car, with its personalized license plate—REQUEEN, which most likely stood for Real Estate Queen—was a new canary-yellow Cadillac Seville with wire wheels, as memorable as the woman herself.

"That one," Julio said when she returned to the office with the second couple.

"Hard to lose in traffic," Reese agreed.

At 4:50, she had again come out of the Shadway Realty door and had hurried like a scurrying bird for her car. Julio and Reese had decided that she was probably going home for the day. Leaving the DSA stakeout to its fruitless wait for Benjamin Shadway, they followed the yellow Cadillac down First Street to Newport Avenue and north to Cowan Heights. She lived in a two-story stucco house with a shake-shingle roof and lots of redwood balconies and decking on one of the steeper streets in the Heights.

Julio parked in front as the pink lady's Caddy disappeared behind the closing garage door. He got out of the car to check the contents of the mailbox—a federal crime—in hope of discovering the woman's name. A moment later he got back into the car and said, "Theodora Bertlesman. Apparently goes by the name Teddy, because that was on one of the letters."

They waited a couple of minutes, then went to the house, where Reese rang the bell. Summer wind, warm in spite of the winter-gray sky from which it flowed, breathed through surrounding bougainvillea, red-flowered hibiscus, and fragrant star jasmine. The street was still, peaceful, the sounds of the outside world eliminated by the most effective filter known to man—money.

"Should've gotten into real estate, I think," Reese said. "Why on earth did I ever want to be a cop?"

"You were probably a cop in a previous life," Julio said dryly, "in another century when being a cop was a better scam than selling real estate. You just fell into the same pattern this time around, without realizing things had changed."

"Caught in a karma loop, huh?"

A moment later, the door opened. The stork-tall woman in the flamingo-pink dress looked down at Julio, then only slightly up at Reese, and she was less birdlike and more impressive close up than she had been from a distance. Earlier, watching her from the car, Reese had not been able to see the porcelain clarity of her skin, her startling gray eyes, or the sculpted refinement of her features. Her Betty Boop hair, which had looked lacquered—even ceramic—from fifty yards, now proved to be thick and soft. She was no less tall, no less thin, and no less flamboyant than she had seemed before, but her chest was certainly not flat, and her legs were lovely.

"May I help you?" Teddy Bertlesman asked. Her voice was low and silken. She radiated such an air of quiet self-assurance that if Julio and Reese had been two dangerous men instead of two cops, they might not have dared try anything with her.

Presenting his ID and badge, Julio introduced himself and said, "This is my partner, Detective Hagerstrom," and explained that they wanted to question her about Ben Shadway. "Maybe my information is out of date, but I believe you work as a sales agent in his firm."

"Of course, you know perfectly well that I do," she said without scorn, even with some amusement. "Please come in."

She led them into a living room as bold in its decor as she was in her dress but with undeniable style and taste. A massive white-marble coffee table. Contemporary sofas upholstered in a rich green fabric. Chairs in peach silk moiré, with elaborately carved arms and feet. Four-foot-tall emerald vases holding huge stalks of white-plumed pampas grass. Very large and dramatic modern art filled the high walls of the cathedral-ceilinged room, giving a comfortable human scale to what could have been a forbidding chamber. A wall of glass presented a panorama of Orange County. Teddy Bertlesman sat on a green sofa, the windows behind her, a pale nimbus of light around her head, and Reese and Julio sat on moiré chairs, separated from her by the enormous marble table that seemed like an altar.

Julio said, "Ms. Bertlesman—"

"No, please," she said, slipping off her shoes and drawing her long legs up under herself. "Either call me Teddy or, if you insist on remaining formal, it's *Miss* Bertlesman. I despise that ridiculous *Miz* business; it makes me think of the South before the Civil War—dainty ladies in crinolines, sipping mint juleps under magnolia trees while black mammies tend to them."

"Miss Bertlesman," Julio continued, "we are most eager to speak to Mr. Shadway, and we hope you might have an idea where he is. For instance, it occurs to us that, being a real-estate developer and investor as well as broker, he might own rental properties that are currently vacant, one of which he might now be using—"

"Excuse me, but I don't see how this falls in your jurisdiction. According to your ID, you're Santa Ana policemen. Ben has offices in Tustin, Costa Mesa, Orange, Newport Beach, Laguna Beach, and Laguna Niguel, but none in Santa Ana. And he lives in Orange Park Acres."

Julio assured her that part of the Shadway-Leben case fell into the jurisdiction of the Santa Ana Police Department, and he explained that cross-jurisdictional cooperation was not uncommon, but Teddy Bertlesman was politely skeptical and subtly uncooperative. Reese admired the diplomacy, finesse, and aplomb with which she fielded probing questions and answered without saying anything useful. Her respect for her boss and her determination to protect him became increasingly evident, yet she said nothing that made it possible to accuse her of lying or harboring a wanted man.

At last, recognizing the futility of the authoritarian approach, apparently hoping revelation of his true motives and a blatant bid for sympathy would work where authority had failed, Julio sighed, leaned back in his chair, and said, "Listen, Miss Bertlesman, we've lied to you. We aren't here in any official capacity. Not strictly speaking. In fact, we're both supposed to be on sick leave. Our captain would be furious if he knew we were still on this case, because federal agencies have taken charge and have told us to back off. But for a lot of reasons, we can't do that, not and keep our self-respect."

Teddy Bertlesman frowned—quite prettily, Reese thought—and said, "I don't understand—"

Julio held up one slim hand. "Wait. Just listen for a moment."

In a soft, sincere, and intimate voice far different from his official tone, he told her how Ernestina Hernandez and Becky Klienstad had been brutally murdered— one thrown in a dumpster, the other nailed to a wall. He told her about his own baby brother, Ernesto, who had been killed by rats a long time ago in a faraway place. He explained how that tragedy had contributed to his obsession with unjust death and how the similarity between the names Ernesto and Ernestina was one of the several things that had made the Hernandez girl's murder a special and very personal crusade for him.

"Though I'll admit," Julio said, "if the names weren't similar and if other factors weren't the same, then I'd simply have found different reasons to make a crusade of this. Because I almost *always* make a crusade of a case. It's a bad habit of mine."

"A wonderful habit," Reese said.

Julio shrugged.

Reese was surprised that Julio was so thoroughly aware of his own motivations. Listening to his partner, contemplating the degree of insight and self-awareness at which these statements hinted, Reese acquired an even greater respect for the man.

"The point is," Julio told Teddy Bertlesman, "I believe your boss and Rachael Leben are guilty of nothing, that they may be just pawns in a game they don't even fully understand. I think they're being used, that they might be killed as scapegoats to further the interests of others, perhaps even the interests of the government. They need help, and I guess what I'm trying to tell you is that they've sort of become another crusade of mine. Help me to help them, Teddy."

Julio's performance was astonishing, and from anyone else it might have looked like exactly that—a mere performance. But there was no mistaking his sincerity or the depth of his concern. Though his dark eyes were watchful, and though there was a shrewdness in his face, his commitment to justice and his great warmth were unmistakably genuine.

Teddy Bertlesman was smart enough to see that Julio was not shucking and jiving her, and she was won over. She swung her long legs off the sofa and slid forward to the edge of it in a whispery rustle of pink silk, a sound that seemed to pass like a breeze over Reese, raising the small hairs on the backs of his hands and sending a pleasant shiver through him. "I knew darn well Ben Shadway was no threat to national security," Teddy said. "Those federal agents came sniffing around with that line, and it was all I could do to keep from laughing in their faces. No, in fact, it was all I could do to keep from *spitting* in their faces."

"Where might Ben Shadway have gone, he and Rachael Leben?" Julio asked. "Sooner or later, the feds are going to find them, and I think that for their sake

Reese and I had better find them first. Do you have any idea where we should look?"

Rising from the sofa in a brilliant hot-pink whirl, stalking back and forth across the living room on stiltlike legs that ought to have been awkward but were the essence of grace, looking incredibly tall to Reese because he was still sitting on the moiré chair, pausing now and standing provocatively hip-shot in thought, then pacing again, Teddy Bertlesman considered the possibilities and enumerated them: "Well, okay, he owns property—mostly small houses—all over the county. Right now . . . the only ones not rented . . . let me see . . . One, there's a little bungalow in Orange, a place on Pine Street, but I don't figure he'd be there because he's having some work done on it—a new bathroom, improvements to the kitchen. He wouldn't hide where there're going to be workmen coming and going. Two, there's half of a duplex in Yorba Linda . . . "

Reese listened to her, but for the moment he did not care what she said; he left that part to Julio. All Reese had the capacity to care about was the way she looked and moved and sounded; she filled all his senses to capacity, leaving no room for anything else. At a distance she had seemed angular, birdlike, but up close she was a gazelle, lean and swift and not the least angular. Her size was less impressive than her fluidity, which was like that of a professional dancer, and her fluidity was less impressive than her suppleness, and her suppleness was less impressive than her beauty, and her beauty was less impressive than her intelligence and energy and flair.

Even when her pacing took her away from the window wall, she was surrounded by a nimbus of light. To Reese, she seemed to glow.

He had felt nothing like this in five years, since his Janet had been killed by the men in the van who'd tried to snatch little Esther that day in the park. He wondered if Teddy Bertlesman had taken special notice of him, too, or whether he was just another lump of a cop to her. He wondered how he could approach her without making a fool of himself and without giving offense. He wondered if there could ever be anything between a woman like her and a man like him. He wondered if he could live without her. He wondered when he was going to be able to breathe again. He wondered if his feelings showed. He didn't *care* if they showed.

" . . . the motel!" Teddy stopped pacing, looked startled for a moment, then grinned. An amazingly lovely grin. "Yes, of course, that would be the most likely place."

"He owns a motel?" Julio asked.

"A run-down place in Las Vegas," Teddy said. "He just bought it. Formed a new corporation to make the purchase. Might take the feds a while to tumble to the place because it's such a recent acquisition and in another state. Place is empty, out of business, but it was sold with furnishings. Even the manager's apartment was furnished, I think, so Ben and Rachael could squirrel away there in comfort."

Julio glanced at Reese and said, "What do you think?"

Reese had to look away from Teddy in order to breathe and speak. With a funny little wheeze, he said, "Sounds right."

Pacing again, flamingo-pink silk swirling around her knees, Teddy said, "I *know* it's right. Ben's in that project with Whitney Gavis, and Whitney is maybe the only man on earth Ben really, fully trusts."

"Who's this Gavis?" Julio asked.

"They were in Vietnam together," she said. "They're tight. As tight as brothers. Tighter, maybe. You know, Ben's a real nice guy, one of the best, and anyone'll tell you so. He's gentle, open, so darn honest and honorable that some people just plain don't believe him for a while, until they've gotten to know him better. But it's funny . . . in a way . . . he holds almost everybody at arm's length, never quite reveals himself completely. Except, I think, with Whit Gavis. It's as if things happened to him in the war that made him forever different from other people, that made it impossible for him to be truly close to anyone except those who went through the same thing he went through and came out with their minds in one piece. Like Whit."

"Is he close in the same way with Mrs. Leben?" Julio asked.

"Yes, I think so. I think he loves her," Teddy said, "which makes her about the luckiest woman I know."

Reese sensed jealousy in Teddy's voice, and his heart felt as if it broke loose and plummeted down through his chest.

Apparently Julio heard the same note, for he said, "Forgive me, Teddy, but I'm a cop, and I'm curious by nature, and you sounded as if you wouldn't mind if he'd fallen for you."

She blinked in surprise, then laughed. "Me and Ben? No, no. For one thing, I'm taller than he is, and in heels I positively tower over him. Besides, he's a home-body—a quiet, peaceful man who reads old mystery novels and collects trains. No, Ben's a great guy, but I'm far too flamboyant for him, and he's too low-key for me."

Reese's heart stopped plummeting.

Teddy said, "Oh, I'm just jealous of Rachael because she's found herself a good man, and I haven't. When you're my size, you know from the start that men aren't going to flock to you—except basketball players, and I hate jocks. Then, when you get to be thirty-two, you can't help feeling a bit sour every time you see someone catch a good one, can't help it even when you're happy for them."

Reese's heart *soared.*

After Julio had asked a few more questions about the motel in Las Vegas and had ascertained its location, he and Reese got up, and Teddy accompanied them to the door. Step by step, Reese wracked his mind for an approach, an opening line. As Julio opened the door, Reese looked back at Teddy and said, "Uh, excuse me, Miss Bertlesman, but I'm a cop, and asking questions is my business, you know, and I was wondering if you're . . . " He didn't know where to go with it. " . . . if you're maybe . . . uh . . . seeing anyone particular." Listening to himself, Reese was amazed and dismayed that Julio could sound so smooth while he, trying to imitate his partner's cool manner, could sound so rough and obvious.

Smiling up at him, she said, "Does this have bearing on the case you're investigating?"

"Well . . . I just thought . . . I mean . . . I wouldn't want you mentioning this conversation to anyone. I mean, it's not just that we could get in trouble with our captain . . . but if you mentioned the motel to anyone, you might jeopardize Mr. Shadway and Mrs. Leben and . . . well . . . "

He wanted to shoot himself, put an end to this humiliation.

She said, "I'm not seeing anyone special, not anyone I'd share secrets with."

Reese cleared his throat. "Well, uh, that's good. All right."

He started to turn toward the door, where Julio was giving him a strange look, and Teddy said, "You are a big one, aren't you?"

Reese faced her again. "Excuse me?"

"You're quite a big guy. Too bad there aren't more your size. A girl like me would almost seem petite to you."

What does she mean by that? he wondered. Anything? Just polite conversation? Is she giving me an opening? If it's an opening, how should I respond to it?

"It would be nice to be thought of as petite," she said.

He tried to speak. Could not.

He felt stupid, awkward, and shy as he'd been at sixteen.

Suddenly he *could* speak, but he blurted out the question as he might have done as a boy of sixteen: "Miss-Bertlesman-would-you-go-out-with-me-some-time?"

She smiled and said, "Yes."

"You would?"

"Yes."

"Saturday night? Dinner? Seven o'clock?"

"Sounds nice."

He stared at her, amazed. "Really?"

She laughed. "Really."

A minute later, in the car, Reese said, "Well, I'll be damned."

"I never realized you were such a smooth operator," Julio said kiddingly, affectionately.

Blushing, Reese said, "By God, life's funny, isn't it? You never know when it might take a whole new turn."

"Slow down," Julio said, starting the engine and driving away from the curb. "It's just a date."

"Yeah. Probably. But . . . I got a feeling it might turn out to be more than just that."

"A smooth operator *and* a romantic fool," Julio said as he steered the car down out of the Heights, toward Newport Avenue.

After some thought, Reese said, "You know what Eric Leben forgot? He was so obsessed with living forever, he forgot to enjoy the life he had. Life may be short, but there's a lot to be said for it. Leben was so busy planning for eternity, he forgot to enjoy the moment."

"Listen," Julio said, "if romance is going to make a philosopher out of you, I may have to get a new partner."

For a few minutes Reese was silent, submerged in memories of well-tanned legs and flamingo-pink silk. When he surfaced again, he realized that Julio was not driving aimlessly. "Where we going?"

"John Wayne Airport."

"Vegas?"

"Is that okay with you?" Julio asked.

"Seems like the only thing we can do."

"Have to pay for tickets out of our own pockets."

"I know."

"You want to stay here, that's all right."

"I'm in," Reese said.

"I can handle it alone."

"I'm in."

"Might get dangerous from here on, and you have Esther to think about," Julio said.

My little Esther and now maybe Theodora "Teddy" Bertlesman, Reese thought. And when you find someone to care about—when you *dare* to care—that's when life gets cruel; that's when they're taken from you; that's when you lose it all. A premonition of death made him shiver.

Nevertheless, he said, "I'm in. Didn't you hear me say I'm in? For God's sake, Julio, I'm *in.*"

33   VIVA LAS VEGAS

FOLLOWING THE STORM ACROSS THE DESERT, BEN SHADWAY reached Baker, California, gateway to Death Valley, at 6:20.

The wind was blowing much harder than it had been back toward Barstow. The driven rain snapped against the windshield with a sound like thousands of impacting bullets. Service-station, restaurant, and motel signs were swinging on their mountings, trying to tear loose and fly away. A stop sign twitched violently back and forth, caught in turbulent currents of air, and seemed about to screw itself out of the ground. At a Shell station, two attendants in yellow rain slickers moved with their heads bowed and shoulders hunched; the tails of their glistening vinyl coats flapped against their legs and whipped out behind them. A score of bristly tumbleweeds, some four or five feet in diameter, bounced-rolled-sailed across tiny Baker's only east-west street, swept in from the desolate landscape to the south.

Ben tried to call Whitney Gavis from a pay phone inside a small convenience store. He couldn't get through to Vegas. Three times, he listened to a recorded message to the effect that service had been temporarily interrupted. Wind moaned and shrieked against the store's plate-glass windows, and rain drummed furiously on the roof—which was all the explanation he required for AT&T's troubles.

He was scared. He had been badly worried ever since finding the ax propped against the refrigerator in the kitchen of Eric's mountain cabin. But now his fear was escalating by the moment because he began to feel that *everything* was going wrong for him, that luck had turned entirely against him. The encounter with Sharp, the disastrous change in the weather, his inability to reach Whit Gavis when the phones had been working, now the trouble with the lines to Vegas, made it seem as if the universe was, indeed, not accidental but was a machine with dark and frightful purpose, and that the gods in charge of it were conspiring to make certain he would never again see Rachael alive.

In spite of his fear, frustration, and eagerness to hit the road again, he paused long enough to grab a few things to eat in the car. He'd had nothing since breakfast in Palm Springs, and he was famished.

The clerk behind the counter—a blue-jeaned, middle-aged woman with sun-bleached hair, her brown skin toughened by too many years on the desert—sold him three candy bars, a few bags of peanuts, and a six-pack of Pepsi. When Ben asked her about the phones, she said, "I hear tell there's been flash flooding east of here, out near Cal Neva, and worse around Stateline. Undermined a few telephone poles, brought down the lines. Word is, it'll be repaired in a couple of hours."

"I never knew it rained this hard in the desert," he said as she gave him change.

"Don't rain—really rain, I mean—but maybe three times a year. Though when we do get a storm, it sometimes comes down like God is breaking his promise about the fire next time and figures to wipe us out with a great flood like before."

The stolen Merkur was parked half a dozen steps beyond the exit from the store, but Ben was soaked again during the few seconds needed to get to the car. Inside, he popped open a can of Pepsi, took a long swallow, braced the can between his thighs, peeled the wrapper off a candy bar, started the engine, and drove back toward the interstate.

Regardless of how terrible the weather got, he would have to push toward Vegas at the highest possible speed, seventy or eighty miles an hour, faster if he could manage it, even though the chances were very high that, sooner or later, he would lose control of the car on the rain-greased highway. His inability to reach Whit Gavis had left him with no alternative.

Ascending the entrance ramp to I-15, the car coughed once and shuddered, but then it surged ahead without further hesitation. For a minute, heading east-northeast toward Nevada, Ben listened intently to the engine and glanced repeatedly at the dashboard, expecting to see a warning light blink on. But the engine purred, and the warning lights remained off, and none of the dials or gauges indicated trouble, so he relaxed slightly. He munched on his candy bar and gradually put the Merkur up to seventy, carefully testing its responsiveness on the treacherously wet pavement.

■   Anson Sharp was awake and refreshed by 7:10 Tuesday evening. From his motel room in Palm Springs, with the background sound of hard rain on the roof and water gurgling through a downspout near his window, he called subordinates at several places throughout southern California.

From Dirk Cringer, an agent at the case-operation headquarters in Orange County, Sharp learned that Julio Verdad and Reese Hagerstrom had not dropped out of the Leben investigation as they were supposed to have done. Given their well-earned reputation as bulldog cops who were reluctant to quit even hopeless cases, Sharp had ordered both of their personal cars fitted with hidden transmitters last night and had assigned men to follow them electronically, at a distance from which Verdad and Hagerstrom would not spot a tail. That precaution had paid off, for this afternoon they had visited UCI to meet with Dr. Easton Solberg, a former associate of Leben's, and later they had spent a couple of hours on stakeout in front of Shadway Realty's main office in Tustin.

"They spotted our team and set up their own surveillance half a block back," Cringer said, "where they could watch both us and the realty office."

"Must've thought they were real cute," Sharp said, "when all the time we were watching them while they watched us."

"Then they followed one of the real-estate agents home, a woman named The-odora Bertlesman."

"We already interviewed her about Shadway, didn't we?"

"Yeah, everyone who works with him in that office. And this Bertlesman woman wasn't any more cooperative than the rest of them, maybe less."

"How long were Verdad and Hagerstrom at her place?"

"More than twenty minutes."

"Sounds like she might've been more open with them. Have any idea what she told them?"

"No," Cringer said. "She lives on a hillside, so it was hard to get a clear angle on any of the windows with a directional microphone. By the time we could've set it up, Verdad and Hagerstrom were leaving anyway. They went straight from her place to the airport."

"What?" Sharp said, surprised. "LAX?"

"No. John Wayne Airport here in Orange County. That's where they are now, waiting for a flight out."

"What flight? To where?"

"Vegas. They bought tickets on the first available flight to Vegas. It leaves at eight o'clock."

"Why Vegas?" Sharp said, more to himself than to Cringer.

"Maybe they finally decided to give up on the case like they were told. Maybe they're going off for a little holiday."

"You don't go off on a holiday without packing suitcases. You said they went straight to the airport, which I suppose means they didn't make a quick stop home to grab a change of clothes."

"Straight to the airport," Cringer confirmed.

"All right, good," Sharp said, suddenly excited. "Then they're probably trying to get to Shadway and Mrs. Leben before we do, and they've reason to believe the place to look is somewhere in Las Vegas." There was a chance he would get his hands on Shadway, after all. And this time, the bastard would not slip away. "If there're any seats left on that eight o'clock flight, I want you to put two of your men aboard."

"Yes, sir."

"I have men here in Palm Springs, and we'll head to Vegas, too, just as soon as we can. I want to be in place at the airport there and ready to track Verdad and Hagerstrom the moment they arrive."

Sharp hung up and immediately called Jerry Peake's room.

Outside, thunder roared in the north and faded to a soft rumble as it moved south through the Coachella Valley.

Peake sounded groggy when he answered.

"It's almost seven-thirty," Sharp told him. "Be ready to roll in fifteen minutes."

"What's happening?"

"We're going to Vegas after Shadway, and this time luck's on our side."

■ One of the many problems of driving a stolen car is that you can't be sure of its mechanical condition. You can't very well ask for a guarantee of reliability and a service history from the owner before you make off with his wheels.

The stolen Merkur failed Ben forty miles east of Baker. It began coughing, wheezing, and shuddering as it had done on the entrance ramp to the interstate a while ago, but this time it did not cease coughing until the engine died. He steered onto the berm and tried to restart the car, but it would not respond. All he was doing was draining the battery, so he sat for a moment, despairing, as the rain fell by the pound and by the hundred-weight upon the car.

But surrender to despair was not his style. After only a few seconds, he formulated a plan and put it into action, inadequate though it might be.

He tucked the .357 Combat Magnum under his belt, against the small of his back, and pulled his shirt out of his jeans to cover the gun. He would not be able to take the shotgun, and he deeply regretted the loss of it.

He switched on the Merkur's emergency flashers and got out into the pouring rain. Fortunately, the lightning had passed away to the east. Standing in the storm-gray twilight gloom beside the disabled car, he shielded his eyes with one hand and looked into the rain, toward the west, where distant headlights were approaching.

I-15 was still lightly traveled. A few determined gamblers were trekking toward their mecca and would probably have been undeterred by Armageddon, though there were more big trucks than anything else. He waved his arms, signaling for help, but two cars and three trucks passed him without slowing. As their tires cut through puddles on the pavement, they sent sheets of water pluming in their wake, some of which cascaded over Ben, adding to his misery.

About two minutes later, another eighteen-wheeler came into view. It was bearing so many lights that it appeared to be decorated for Christmas. To Ben's relief, it began to brake far back and came to a full stop on the berm behind the Merkur.

He ran back to the big rig and peered up at the open window where a craggy-faced man with a handlebar mustache squinted down at him from the warm, dry cab. "Broke down!" Ben shouted above the cacophony of wind and rain.

"Closest mechanic you're going to find is back in Baker," the driver called down to him. "Best cross over to the westbound lanes and try to catch a ride going that way."

"Don't have time to find a mechanic and get her fixed!" Ben shouted. "Got to make Vegas fast as I can." He had prepared the lie while waiting for someone to stop. "My wife's in the hospital there, hurt bad, maybe dying."

"Good Lord," the driver said, "you better come aboard, then."

Ben hurried around to the passenger's door, praying that his benefactor was a highballer who would keep the pedal to the metal in spite of the weather and rocket into Vegas in record time.

■   Driving across the rain-lashed Mojave on the last leg of the trip to Las Vegas, with the darkness of the storm slowly giving way to the deeper darkness of night, Rachael felt lonelier than she'd ever felt before—and she was no stranger to loneliness. The rain had not let up for the past couple of hours, largely because she was more than keeping pace with the storm as it moved eastward, driving deeper into the heart of it. The hollow beating of the windshield wipers and the droning of the tires on the wet road were like the shuttles of a loom that wove not cloth but isolation.

Much of her life had been lived in loneliness and in emotional—if not always physical—isolation. By the time Rachael was born, her mother and father had discovered that they could not abide each other, but for religious reasons they had been unwilling to consider divorce. Therefore, Rachael's earliest years passed in a loveless house, where her parents' resentment toward each other was inadequately concealed. Worse, each of them seemed to view her as the other's child—a reason to resent her, too. Neither was more than dutifully affectionate.

As soon as she was old enough, she was sent to Catholic boarding schools where, except for holidays, she remained for the next eleven years. In those institutions, all run by nuns, she made few friends, none close, partly because she had a very low opinion of herself and could not believe that anyone would *want* to be friends with her.

A few days after she graduated from prep school, the summer before she was to enter college, her parents were killed in a plane crash on their way home from a business trip. Rachael had been under the impression that her father had made a small fortune in the garment industry by investing money that her mother had inherited the year of their wedding. But when the will was probated and the estate was settled, Rachael discovered that the family business had been skirting bankruptcy for years and that their upper-class life-style had eaten up every dollar earned. Virtually penniless, she had to cancel her plans to attend Brown University and, instead, went to work as a waitress, living in a boarding-house and saving what she could toward a more modest education in California's tax-supported university system.

A year later, when she finally started school, she made no real friends because she had to keep waitressing and had no time for the extracurricular activities through which college relationships are formed. By the time she received her degree and launched herself upon a program of graduate study, she had known at least eight thousand nights of loneliness.

She was easy prey for Eric when, needing to feed on her youth as a vampire feeds on blood, he had determined to make her his wife. He was twelve years her senior, so he knew far more about charming and winning a young woman than men her own age knew; he made her feel wanted and special for the first time in her life. Considering the difference in their ages, perhaps she also saw in him a father figure capable of giving her not only the love of a husband but the parental love she had never known.

Of course, it had turned out less well than she expected. She learned that Eric didn't love her but loved, instead, the thing that she symbolized to him—vigorous, healthful, energetic youth. Their marriage soon proved to be as loveless as that of her parents.

Then she had found Benny. And for the first time in her life she had not been lonely.

But now Benny was gone, and she didn't know if she would ever see him again.

The Mercedes's windshield wipers beat out a monotonous rhythm, and the tires sang a one-note tune—a song of the void, of despair and loneliness.

She attempted to comfort herself with the thought that at least Eric posed no further threat to her or Ben. Surely he was dead from a score of rattlesnake bites. Even if his genetically altered body could safely metabolize those massive doses of virulent poison, even if Eric could return from the dead a second time, he was obviously degenerating, not merely physically but also mentally. (She had a vivid mental image of him kneeling on the rain-soaked earth, eating a living serpent, as frightening and elemental as the lightning that flashed above him.) If he survived the rattlesnakes, he would very likely remain on the desert, no longer a human being but a *thing*, loping hunchbacked or squirming on its belly through the hillocks of sand, slithering down into the arroyos, feeding greedily on other desert dwellers, a threat to any beast he encountered but no longer a threat to her. And even if some glimmer of human awareness and intelligence remained in him, and if he still felt the need to avenge himself on Rachael, he would find it difficult if not impossible to come out of the desert into civilization and move freely about. If he tried that, he would create a sensation—panic, terror—wherever he went, and would probably be chased down and captured or shot.

Yet . . . she was still afraid of him.

She remembered glancing up at him as he followed her from the top of the arroyo wall, remembered staring down at him later when she had been on top and he had been climbing after her, remembered the way he had looked when she had last seen him engaged in battle with the nest of rattlers. In all those memories there was something about him that . . . well . . . something that seemed almost mythic, that transcended nature, that seemed powerfully supernatural, undying and unstoppable.

She shuddered with a sudden chill that spread outward from the marrow of her bones.

A moment later, topping a rise in the highway, she saw that she was nearing the end of the current leg of her journey. In a broad dark valley directly ahead and below, Las Vegas glimmered like a miraculous vision in the rain. So many millions of lights shone in every hue that the city looked bigger than New York, though it was actually one-twentieth the size. Even from this distance, at least fifteen miles, she could make out the Strip with all its dazzling resort hotels and the downtown casino center that some called Glitter Gulch, for those areas blazed with by far the greatest concentrations of lights, all of which seemed to blink, pulse, and twinkle.

Less than twenty minutes later, she came out of the vast empty reaches of the bleak Mojave onto Las Vegas Boulevard South, where the neon shimmered across the rain-mirrored road in waves of purple, pink, red, green, and gold. Pulling up to the front doors of the Bally's Grand, she almost wept with relief when she saw the bellmen, valet-parking attendants, and a few hotel guests standing under the porte cochere. For hours on the interstate, the passing cars had seemed untenanted in the storm-obscured night, so it was wonderful to see people again, even if they were all strangers.

At first, Rachael hesitated to leave the Mercedes with a valet-parking attendant because the precious Wildcard file was in a garbage bag on the floor behind the driver's seat. But she decided that no one was likely to steal a garbage bag, especially not one full of creased and crumpled papers. Besides, it would be safer with the valet than parked in the public lot. She left the car in his care and took a claim check for it.

She had mostly recovered from the twist she'd given her ankle when running from Eric. The claw punctures in her calf throbbed and burned, although those wounds felt better, too. She entered the hotel with only a slight limp.

For a moment, she was almost thrown into shock by the contrast between the stormy night behind her and the excitement of the casino. It was a glittery world of crystal chandeliers, velvet, brocade, plush carpets, marble, polished brass, and green felt, where the sound of wind and rain could not be heard above the roar of voices exhorting Lady Luck, the ringing of slot machines, and the raucous music of a pop-rock band in the lounge.

Gradually Rachael became uncomfortably aware that her appearance made her an object of curiosity in these surroundings. Of course, not everyone—not even a majority of the clientele—dressed elegantly for a night of drinking, nightclub shows, and gambling. Women in cocktail dresses and men in fine suits were common, but others were dressed more casually: some in polyester leisure suits, some in jeans and sports shirts. However, none of them wore a torn and soiled blouse (as she did), and none of them wore jeans that looked as if they might have just been through a rodeo contest (as she did), and none of them boasted filthy sneakers with blackened laces and one sole half torn off from scrambling up and down arroyo walls (as she did), and none of them was dirty-faced and stringy-haired (as she was). She had to assume that, even in the escapist world of Vegas, people watched some TV news and might recognize her as the infamous traitor and fugitive wanted throughout the Southwest. The last thing she needed was to call attention to herself. Fortunately, gamblers are a single-minded group, more intent upon their wagering than upon the need to breathe, and few of them even glanced up from their games to look at her; none looked twice.

She hurried around the perimeter of the casino to the public telephones, which were in an alcove where the casino noise faded to a soft roar. She called information for Whitney Gavis's number. He answered on the first ring. Rather breathlessly she said, "I'm sorry, you don't know me, my name's Rachael—"

"Ben's Rachael?" he interrupted.

"Yes," she said, surprised.

"I know you, know all about you." He had a voice amazingly like Benny's: calm and measured and reassuring. "And I just heard the news an hour ago, that *ridiculous* damn story about defense secrets. What a crock. Anybody who knows Benny wouldn't believe it for a second. I don't know what's going on, but I figured you guys would be coming my way if you needed to go to ground for a while."

"He's not with me, but he sent me to you," Rachael explained.

"Say no more. Just tell me where you are."

"The Grand."

"It's eight o'clock. I'll be there by eight-ten. Don't go wandering around. They have so much surveillance in those casinos you're bound to be on a monitor somewhere if you go onto the floor, and maybe one of the security men on duty will have seen the evening news. Get my drift?"

"Can I go to the rest room? I'm a mess. I could use a quick washup."

"Sure. Just don't go onto the casino floor. And be back by the phones in ten minutes, 'cause that's where I'll meet you. There're no security cameras by the phones. Sit tight, kid."

"Wait!"

"What is it?" he asked.

"What do you look like? How will I recognize you?"

He said, "Don't worry, kid. I'll recognize you. Benny's shown me your picture so often that every detail of your gorgeous face is burned into my cerebral cortex. Remember, sit tight!"

The line went dead, and she hung up.

■ Jerry Peake was not sure he wanted to be a legend anymore. He was not even sure he wanted to be a DSA agent, legendary or otherwise. Too much had been happening too fast. He was unable to assimilate it properly. He felt as if he were trying to walk through one of those big rolling barrels that were sometimes used as the entrance to a carnival funhouse, except they were spinning this barrel about five times faster than even the most sadistic carny operator would dare, and it also seemed to be an endless tube from which he would never emerge. He wondered if he would ever get his feet under him and know stability again.

Anson Sharp's call had roused Peake from a sleep so deep that it almost required a headstone. Even a quick cold shower had not entirely awakened him. A ride through rain-washed streets to the Palm Springs airport, with siren wailing and emergency beacon flashing, had seemed like part of a bad dream. At the airfield, at 8:10, a light transport twin turbo-prop arrived from the Marine Corps Training Center at nearby Twentynine Palms, provided as an interservice courtesy to the Defense Security Agency on an emergency basis, little more than half an hour after Sharp had requested it. They boarded and immediately took off into the storm. The daredevil-steep ascent of the hotshot military pilot, combined with the howling wind and driving rain, finally blew away the lingering traces of sleep. Peake was wide awake, gripping the arms of his seat so hard that his white knuckles looked as if they would split through his skin.

"With any luck," Sharp told Peake and Nelson Gosser (the other man he'd brought along), "we'll land at McCarran International, in Vegas, about ten or fifteen minutes ahead of that flight from Orange County. When Verdad and Hagerstrom come waltzing into the terminal, we'll be ready to put them under tight surveillance."

■ At 8:10, the 8:00 P.M. flight to Vegas had not yet taken off from John Wayne Airport in Orange County, but the pilot assured the passengers that departure was imminent. Meanwhile, there were beverages, honey-roasted beer nuts, and mint wafers to make the minutes pass more pleasantly.

"I love these honey-roasted beer nuts," Reese said, "but I just remembered something I don't like at all."

"What's that?" Julio asked.

"Flying."

"It's a short flight."

"A man doesn't expect to have to fly all over the map when he chooses a career in law enforcement."

"Forty-five minutes, fifty at most," Julio said soothingly.

"I'm *in*," Reese said quickly before Julio could start to get the wrong idea about his objections to flying. "I'm in the case for the duration, but I just wish there was a boat to Vegas."

At 8:12, they taxied to the head of the runway and took off.

■ Driving east in the red pickup, Eric struggled mile by mile to retain sufficient human consciousness to operate the truck. Sometimes bizarre thoughts and feelings plagued him: a wishful longing to leave the truck and run naked across the dark desert plains, hair flying in the wind, the rain sluicing down his bare flesh; an unsettlingly urgent need to burrow, to squirm into a dark moist place and hide; a hot, fierce, demanding sexual urge, not human in any regard, more like an animal's rutting fever. He also experienced memories, clear images in his mind's eye, that were not his own but from some genetic storage bank of racial recollections: scavenging hungrily in a rotting log for grubs and wriggling insects; mating with some musk-drenched creature in a dank and lightless den . . . If he allowed any of these thoughts, urges, or memories to preoccupy him, he would slip away into that mindless subhuman state he had entered both times when he had killed back at the rest area, and in that condition he'd drive the pickup straight off the road. Therefore, he tried to repress those alluring images and urges, strove to focus his attention on the rainy highway ahead. He was largely successful—though at times his vision briefly clouded, and he began to breathe too fast, and the siren call of other states of consciousness became almost too much to bear.

For long stretches of time, he felt nothing physically unusual happening to him. But on several occasions he was aware of changes taking place, and then it was as if his body were a ball of tangled worms that, having recently lain dormant and still, suddenly began to squirm and writhe frantically. After having seen his in- human eyes in the rearview mirror back at the rest stop—one green and orange with a slit-shaped iris, the other multifaceted and even stranger—he had not dared to look at himself, for he knew that his sanity was already precarious. However, he could see his hands upon the steering wheel, and he was aware of ongoing alterations in them: For a while, his elongated fingers grew shorter, thicker, and the long hooked nails retracted somewhat, and the web between thumb and the first finger all but vanished; then the process reversed itself, and his hands grew larger again, the knuckles lumpier, the claws even sharper and more wickedly pointed than before. At the moment, his hands were so hideous—dark, mottled, with a backward-curving spur at the base of each monstrous nail, and with one extra joint in each finger—that he kept his gaze on the road ahead and tried not to look down.

His inability to confront his own appearance resulted not merely from fear of what he was becoming. He was afraid, yes, but he also took a sick, demented pleasure in his transformation. At least for the moment, he was immensely strong, lightning-quick, and deadly. Except for his inhuman appearance, he was the per- sonification of that macho dream of absolute power and unstoppable fury that every young boy entertained and that no man ever quite outgrew. He could not allow himself to dwell on this, for his power fantasies could trigger a descent into the animal state.

The peculiar and not unpleasant fire in his flesh, blood, and bones was with him now at all times, without pause, and in fact it grew hotter by the hour. Previously he had thought of himself as a man melting into new forms, but now he almost felt as if he were not melting but aflame, as if fire would leap from his fingertips at any moment. He had given it a name: the changefire.

Fortunately, the debilitating spasms of intense pain that had seized him early in his metamorphosis were no longer a part of the changes. Now and then an ache arose, or a brief stabbing agony, but nothing as intense as before and nothing that lasted longer than a minute or two. Apparently, during the past ten hours, amorphousness had become a genetically programmed condition of his body, as natural to him—and therefore as painless—as respiration, a regular heartbeat, digestion, and excretion.

Periodic attacks of cripplingly severe hunger were the only pains he suffered. However, those pangs could be excruciating, unlike any hunger he had ever known in his previous life. As his body destroyed old cells and manufactured new ones at a frantic pace, it required a lot of fuel to fire the process. He also found himself urinating far more frequently than usual, and each time he pulled off the road to relieve his bladder, his urine reeked ever more strongly of ammonia and other chemicals.

Now, as he drove the pickup over a rise in the highway and suddenly found himself looking down upon the sprawling, scintillant spectacle of Las Vegas, he was hit once more by a hunger that seized his stomach in a viselike grip and twisted hard. He began to sweat and shake uncontrollably.

He steered the pickup onto the berm and stopped. He fumbled for the handbrake, pulled it on.

He had begun to whimper when the first pangs struck him. Now he heard himself growling deep in his throat, and he sensed his self-control rapidly slipping away as his animal needs became more demanding, less resistible.

He was afraid of what he might do. Maybe leave the car and go hunting in the desert. He could get lost out there in those trackless barrens, even within a few miles of Vegas. Worse: all intellect fled, guided by pure instinct, he might go onto the highway and somehow stop a passing car, drag the screaming driver from the vehicle, and rip him to pieces. Others would see, and then there would be no hope of journeying secretly to the shuttered motel in Vegas where Rachael was hiding.

Nothing must stop him from reaching Rachael. The very thought of her brought a blood-red tinge to his vision and elicited an involuntary shriek of rage that rebounded shrilly off the rain-washed windows of the truck. Taking his revenge on her, killing her, was the one desire powerful enough to have given him the strength to resist devolution during the long drive across the desert. The possibility of revenge had kept him sane, had kept him going.

Desperately repressing the primal consciousness that acute hunger had unleashed within him, he turned eagerly to the Styrofoam cooler that was in the open storage compartment behind the pickup's front seat. He had seen it when he had gotten into the truck at the rest area, but he had not thus far explored its contents. He lifted the lid and saw, with some relief, that the cowboy and the girl had been making a sort of picnic of their trip to Vegas. The cooler contained half a dozen sandwiches in tightly sealed Ziploc bags, two apples, and a six-pack of beer.

With his dragon hands, Eric shredded the plastic bags and ate the sandwiches almost as fast as he could stuff them into his mouth. Several times he choked on the food, gagged on gummy wads of bread and meat, and had to concentrate on chewing them more thoroughly.

Four of the sandwiches were filled with thick slices of rare roast beef. The taste and smell of the half-cooked flesh excited him almost unbearably. He wished the beef had been raw and dripping. He wished he could have sunk his teeth into the living animal and could have torn loose throbbing chunks of its flesh.

The other two sandwiches were Swiss cheese and mustard, no meat, and he ate them, too, because he needed all the fuel he could get, but he did not like them, for they lacked the delicious and exhilarating flavor of blood. He remembered the taste of the cowboy's blood. Even better, the intensely coppery flavor of the woman's blood, taken from her throat and from her breast . . . He began to hiss and to twist back and forth in his seat, exhilarated by those memories. Ravenous, he ate the two apples as well, although his enlarged jaws, strangely reshaped tongue, and sharply pointed teeth had not been designed for the consumption of fruit.

He drank all of the beer, choking and spluttering on it as he poured it down. He had no fear of intoxication, for he knew that his racing metabolism would burn off the alcohol before he felt any effect from it.

For a while, having devoured every ounce of food in the cooler, he slumped back in the driver's seat, panting. He stared stupidly at the water-filmed windows, the beast within him temporarily subdued. Dreamy memories of murder and vaguer recollections of coupling with the cowboy's woman drifted like tendrils of smoke across the back of his mind.

Out on the night-clad desert, shadowfires burned.

Doorways to hell? Beckoning him to the damnation that had been his destiny but that he had escaped by beating death?

Or merely hallucinations? Perhaps his tortured subconscious mind, terrified of the changes taking place in the body it inhabited, was trying desperately to externalize the changefire to transfer the heat of metamorphosis out of his flesh and blood and into these vivid illusions.

That was the most intellectual train of thought he had ridden in many hours, and for a moment he felt a heartening resurgence of the cognitive powers that had earned him the reputation of a genius in his field. But only for a moment. Then the memory of blood returned, and a shiver of savage pleasure passed through him, and he made a thick guttural sound in the back of his throat.

A few cars and trucks passed on the highway to his left. Heading east. Heading to Vegas. Vegas . . .

Slowly he recalled that he was also bound for Vegas, for the Golden Sand Inn, for a rendezvous with revenge.

DARKEST

Night can be sweet as a kiss

though not a night like this

—THE BOOK OF COUNTED SORROWS

34 CONVERGENCE

AFTER WASHING HER FACE AND DOING WHAT LITTLE SHE COULD
with her lank and tangled hair, Rachael returned to the vicinity of the public
telephones and sat on a red leatherette bench nearby, where she could see everyone who approached from the front of the hotel lobby and from the stairs that led
out of the sunken casino. Most people remained down on the bright and noisy
gaming level, but the lobby concourse was filled with a steady stream of passersby.

She studied all the men as surreptitiously as possible. She was not trying to spot
Whitney Gavis, for she had no idea what he looked like. However, she was worried that someone might recognize her from photographs on television. She felt
that enemies were everywhere, all around her, closing in—and while that might
be paranoia, it might also be the truth.

If she had ever been wearier and more miserable, she could not remember the
time. The few hours of sleep she'd had last night in Palm Springs had not prepared
her for today's frantic activity. Her legs ached from all the running and climbing
she had done; her arms felt stiff, leaden. A dull pain extended from the back of
her neck to the base of her spine. Her eyes were bloodshot, grainy, and sore.
Although she had stopped in Baker for a pack of diet sodas and had emptied all
six cans during the drive to Vegas, her mouth was dry and sour.

"You look beat, kid," Whitney Gavis said, stepping up to the bench on which
she sat, startling her.

She'd seen him approaching from the front of the lobby, but she had turned
her attention to other men, certain that he could not be Whitney Gavis. He was
about five nine, an inch or two shorter than Benny, perhaps more solidly built
than Benny, with heavier shoulders, a broader chest. He was wearing baggy white
pants and a soft pastel-blue cotton-knit shirt, a modified *Miami Vice* look without
the white jacket. However, the left side of his face was disfigured by a web of red
and brown scars, as if he'd been deeply cut or burned—or both. His left ear was
lumpy, gnarled. He walked with a stiff and awkward gait, laboriously swinging
his left hip in a manner that indicated either that the leg was paralyzed or, more

likely, that it was an artificial limb. His left arm had been amputated midway between the elbow and the wrist, and the stump poked out of the short sleeve of his shirt.

Laughing at her surprise, he said, "Evidently Benny didn't warn you: as knight-errant riding to the rescue, I leave something to be desired."

Blinking up at him, she said, "No, no, I'm glad you're here, I'm glad to have a friend no matter . . . I mean, I didn't . . . I'm sure that you . . . Oh, hell, there's no reason to . . . " She started to get up, then realized he might be more comfortable sitting down, then realized *that* was a patronizing thought, and consequently found herself bobbing up and down in embarrassing indecision.

Laughing again, taking her by the arm with his one hand, Whitney said, "Relax, kid. I'm not offended. I've never known anyone who's less concerned about a person's appearance than Benny; he judges you by what you are and what you deliver, not by the way you look or by your physical limitations, so it's just exactly like him to forget to mention my . . . shall we say 'peculiarities'? I refuse to call them handicaps. Anyway, you've every reason to be disconcerted, kid."

"I guess he didn't have time to mention it, even if he'd given it a thought," she said, deciding to remain standing. "We parted in quite a hurry."

She'd been startled because she had known that Benny and Whitney had been in Vietnam together, and on first seeing this man's grievous infirmities, she couldn't understand how he could have been a soldier. Then, of course, she realized he had been a whole man when he had gone to Southeast Asia and that he'd lost his arm and leg in that conflict.

"Ben's all right?" Whitney asked.

"I don't know."

"Where is he?"

"Coming here to join me, I hope. But I don't know for sure."

Suddenly she was stricken by the awful realization that it might just as easily have been her Benny who had returned from the war with his face scarred, one hand gone, one leg blown off, and that thought was devastating. Since Monday night, when Benny had taken the .357 Magnum away from Vince Baresco, Rachael had more or less unconsciously thought of him as endlessly resourceful, indomitable, and virtually invincible. She had been afraid for him at times, and since she had left him alone on the mountain above Lake Arrowhead, she had worried about him constantly. But deep down she had wanted to believe that he was too tough and quick to come to any harm. Now, seeing how Whitney Gavis had returned from the war, and knowing that Benny had served at Whitney's side, Rachael abruptly knew and felt—and finally believed—that Benny was a mortal man, as fragile as any other, tethered to life by a thread as pitifully thin as those by which everyone else was suspended above the void.

"Hey, are you all right?" Whitney asked.

"I . . . I'll be okay," she said shakily. "I'm just exhausted . . . and worried."

"I want to know everything—the *real* story, not the one on the news."

"There's a lot to tell," she said. "But not here."

"No," he said, looking around at the passersby, "not here."

"Benny's going to meet me at the Golden Sand."

"The motel? Yeah, sure, that's a good place to hole up, I guess. Not exactly first-class accommodations."

"I'm in no position to be choosy."

He'd entrusted his car to the valet, too, and he presented both his claim check and Rachael's when they left the hotel.

Beyond the enormous, high-ceilinged porte cochere, wind-harried rain slashed the night. The lightning had abated, but the downpour was not gray and dreary and lightless, at least not in the vicinity of the hotel. Millions of droplets reflected the amber and yellow lights that surrounded the entrance to the Grand, so it looked as if a storm of molten gold were plating the Strip in an armor fit for angels.

Whitney's car, a like-new white Karmann Ghia, was delivered first, but the black Mercedes rolled up behind it. Although she knew that she was calling attention to herself in front of the valets, Rachael insisted on looking carefully in the back seat and in the trunk before she would get behind the wheel and drive away. The plastic garbage bag containing the Wildcard file was where she had left it, though that was not what she was looking for. She was being ridiculous, and she knew it. Eric was dead—or reduced to a subhuman form, creeping around in the desert more than a hundred miles from here. There was no way he could have trailed her to the Grand, no way he could have gotten into the car during the short time it had been parked in the hotel's underground valet garage. Nevertheless, she looked warily in the trunk and was relieved when she found it empty.

She followed Whitney's Karmann Ghia onto Flamingo Boulevard, drove east to Paradise Boulevard, then turned south toward Tropicana and the shelter of the shuttered Golden Sand Inn.

Even at night and in the cloaking rain, Eric dared not drive along Las Vegas Boulevard South, that garish and baroque street that the locals called the Strip. The night was set ablaze by eight- and ten-story signs of blinking-pulsing-flashing incandescent bulbs, and by hundreds upon hundreds of miles of glowing neon tubes folded upon themselves as if they were the luminous intestines of transparent deep-water fish. The blur of water on the pickup's windows and the cowboy hat, its brim turned down, were not sufficient to disguise his nightmarish face from passing motorists. Therefore, he turned off the Strip well before he reached the hotels, on the first eastbound street he encountered, just past the back of McCarran International Airport. That street boasted no hotels, no carnivalesque banks of lights, and the traffic was sparse. By a circuitous route, he made his way to Tropicana Boulevard.

He had overheard Shadway telling Rachael about the Golden Sand Inn, and he had no difficulty finding it on a relatively undeveloped and somewhat dreary stretch of Tropicana. The single-story, U-shaped building embraced a swimming pool, with the open end exposed to the street. Sun-weathered wood trim in need of paint. Stained, cracked, pockmarked stucco. A tar-and-crushed-rock roof of the type common in the desert, bald and in need of rerocking. A few windows broken and boarded over. Landscaping overrun by weeds. Dead leaves and paper litter drifted against one wall. A large neon sign, broken and unlit, hung between twenty-foot-tall steel posts near the entrance drive, swinging slightly on its pivots as the wind wailed in from the west.

Nothing but empty scrubland lay for two hundred yards on either side of the Golden Sand Inn. Across the boulevard was a new housing development currently under construction: a score of homes in various stages of framing, skeletal shapes in the night and rain. But for the few cars passing on Tropicana, the motel was relatively isolated here on the southeastern edge of the city.

And judging by the total lack of lights, Rachael had not yet arrived. Where was she? He had driven very fast, but he did not believe he could have passed her on the highway.

As he thought about her, his heart began to pound. His vision acquired a crimson tint. The memory of blood made his saliva flow. That familiar cold rage spread out in icy crystals through his entire body, but he clenched his shark-fierce teeth and strove to remain at least functionally rational.

He parked the pickup on the graveled shoulder of the road more than a hundred yards past the Golden Sand, easing the front end into a shallow drainage ditch to give the impression that it had slid off the road and had been abandoned until morning. He switched off the headlights, then the engine. The pounding of the rain was louder now that the competing sound of the engine was gone. He waited until the eastbound and westbound lanes of the boulevard were deserted, then threw open the passenger-side door and got out into the storm.

He sloshed through the drainage ditch, which was full of racing brown water, and made his way across the barren stretch of desert toward the motel. He ran, for if a car came along Tropicana, he had nothing behind which to hide except a few tumbleweeds still rooted in the sandy soil and shaking in the wind.

Exposed to the elements, he again wanted to strip off his clothes and succumb to a deep-seated desire to run free through the wind and night, away from the lights of the city, into wild places. But the greater need for vengeance kept him clothed and focused on his objective.

The motel's small office occupied the northeast corner of the U-shaped structure. Through the big plate-glass windows, he could see only a portion of the unlighted room: the dim shapes of a sofa, one chair, an empty postcard rack, an end table and lamp, and the check-in desk. The manager's apartment, where Shadway had told Rachael to take shelter, was probably reached through the office. Eric tried the door, the knob disappearing in his huge leathery hand; it was locked, as he had expected.

Abruptly he saw a vague reflection of himself in the wet glass, a horned demonic visage bristling with teeth and twisted by strange bony excrescences. He looked quickly away, choking back the whimper that tried to escape him.

He moved into the courtyard, where doors to motel rooms lay on three sides. There were no lights, but he could see a surprising amount of detail, including the dark blue shade of paint on the doors. Whatever he was becoming, it was perhaps a creature with better night vision than a man possessed.

A battered aluminum awning overhung the cracked walkway that served all three wings, forming a shabby promenade. Rain drizzled from the awning, splashed onto the edge of the concrete walk, and puddled in a strip of grass that had been almost entirely choked out by weeds. His boots made thick squelching sounds as he walked through the weeds onto the concrete pool apron.

The swimming pool had been drained, but the storm was beginning to fill it again. Down at the deeper end of the sloped bottom, at least a foot of water had already collected. Beneath the water, an elusive—and perhaps illusory—shadow-fire flickered crimson and silver, further distorted by the rippling of the fluid under which it burned.

Something about that shadowfire, more than any other before it, shot sparks of fear through him. Looking down into the black hole of the mostly empty pool, he was overcome by an instinctive urge to run, to put as much distance between himself and this place as possible.

He quickly turned away from the pool.

He stepped under the aluminum awning, where the tinny drumming of the rain made him feel claustrophobic, as if he were sealed inside a can. He went to room 15, near the center of the middle wing of the U, and tried the door. It was locked, too, but the lock looked old and flimsy. He stepped back and began kicking the door. By the third blow, he was so excited by the very act of destruction that he began to keen shrilly and uncontrollably. On the fourth kick, the lock snapped, and the door flew inward with a screech of tortured metal.

He went inside.

He remembered Shadway telling Rachael that electrical service had been maintained, but he did not switch on the lights. For one thing, he did not want to alert Rachael to his presence when, at last, she arrived. Besides, because of his drastically improved night vision, the dimensions of the lightless room and the contours of the furniture were revealed in sufficient detail to allow him to roam the chamber without falling over things.

Quietly he closed the door.

He moved to the window that looked out upon the courtyard, parted the musty, greasy drapes an inch or two, and peered into the lesser gloom of the blustery night. From here, he had a commanding view of the open end of the motel and of the door to the office.

When she came, he would see her.

Once she had settled in, he would go after her.

He shifted his weight impatiently from one foot to the other.

He made a thin, whispery, eager sound.

He longed for the blood.

Amos Zachariah Tate—the craggy-faced, squint-eyed trucker with the carefully tended handlebar mustache—looked as if he might be the reincarnation of an outlaw who had prowled these same solitary reaches of the Mojave in the days of the Old West, preying upon stagecoaches and pony-express riders. However, his manner was more that of an itinerant preacher from the same age: soft-spoken, most courteous, generous, yet hard-bitten, with firm convictions about the redemption of the soul that was possible through the love of Jesus.

He provided Ben not merely with a free ride to Las Vegas but with a wool blanket to ward off the chill that the truck's air conditioner threw upon his rain-sodden body, coffee from one of two large thermos bottles, a chewy granola bar, and spiritual advice. He was genuinely concerned about Ben's comfort and physical well-being, a natural-born Good Samaritan who was embarrassed by displays of gratitude and who was devoid of self-righteousness, which drained all of the potential offensiveness from his well-meant, low-key pitch for Jesus.

Besides, Amos believed Ben's lie about a desperately injured—perhaps dying—wife in the Sunrise Hospital in Vegas. Although Amos said he did not usually take the laws of the land lightly—even minor laws like speed limits—he made an exception in this case and pushed the big rig up to sixty-five and seventy miles an hour, which was as fast as he felt he dared go in this foul weather.

Huddled under the warm wool blanket, sipping coffee, chewing the sweet granola bar and thinking bitter thoughts of death and loss, Ben was grateful to Amos Tate, but he wished they could make even better speed. If love was the closest that human beings could hope to come to immortality—which was what he'd thought when in bed with Rachael—then he had been given a key to life everlasting when he had found her. Now, at the gates of that paradise, it seemed the key was being snatched out of his hand. When he considered the bleakness of life without her, he wanted to seize control of the truck from Amos, push the driver aside, get behind the wheel, and make the rig *fly* to Vegas.

But all he could do was pull the blanket a little tighter around himself and, with growing trepidation, watch the dark miles go by.

The manager's apartment at the Golden Sand Inn had been unused for a month or more, and it had a stale smell. Although the odor was not strong, Rachael repeatedly wrinkled her nose in distaste. There was a quality of putrescence in the smell which, over time, would probably leave her nauseated.

The living room was large, the bedroom small, the bathroom minuscule. The tiny kitchen was cramped and dreary but completely equipped. The walls did not look as if they had been painted in a decade. The carpets were threadbare, and the kitchen linoleum was cracked and discolored. The furniture was sagging and scarred and splitting at the seams, and the major kitchen appliances were dented and scraped and yellowing with age.

"Not a layout you're ever going to see in *Architectural Digest,*" Whitney Gavis said, bracing himself against the refrigerator with the stump of his left arm and reaching behind with his one good hand to insert the plug in the wall socket. The motor came on at once. "But the stuff works, pretty much, and it's unlikely anyone's going to look for you here."

As they had gone through the apartment, turning on lights, she had begun to tell him the real story behind the warrants for her and Benny's arrest. Now they pulled up chairs at the Formica-topped kitchen table, which was filmed with gray dust and ringed with a score of cigarette scars, and she told him the rest of it as succinctly as she could.

Outside, the moaning wind seemed like a sentient beast, pressing its featureless face to the windows as if it wanted to hear the tale she told or as if it had something of its own to add to the story.

Standing at the window of room 15, waiting for Rachael to arrive, Eric had felt the changefire growing hotter within him. He began to pour sweat; it streamed off his brow and down his face, gushed from every pore as if trying to match the rate at which the rain ran off the awning of the promenade beyond the window. He felt as if he were standing in a furnace, and every breath he drew seared through his lungs. All around him now, in every corner, the room was filled with the phantom flames of shadowfires, at which he dared not look. His bones felt molten, and his flesh was so hot that he would not have been surprised to see real flames spurt from his fingertips.

"Melting . . . " he said in a voice deep and guttural and thoroughly inhuman. " . . . the . . . melting man."

His face suddenly *shifted*. A terrible crunching-splintering noise filled his ears for a moment, issuing from within his skull, but it turned almost at once into a sickening, spluttering, oozing liquid sound. The process was accelerating insanely. Horrified, terrified—but also with a dark exhilaration and a wild demonic joy— he sensed his face changing shape. For a moment he was aware of a gnarled brow extending so far out over his eyes that it penetrated his peripheral vision, but then it was gone, subsiding, the new bone melting into his nose and mouth and jawline, pulling his nominally human countenance forward into a rudimentary, misshapen snout. His legs began to give way beneath him, so he turned reluctantly from the window, and with a crash he fell to his knees on the floor. Something snapped in his chest. To accommodate the snoutlike restructuring of his visage, his lips split farther back along his cheeks. He dragged himself onto the bed, rolled onto his back, giving himself entirely to the devastating yet not essentially unpleasant process of revolutionary change, and as from a great distance he heard himself making peculiar sounds: a doglike growl, a reptilian hiss, and the wordless but unmistakable exclamations of a man in the throes of sexual orgasm.

For a while, darkness claimed him.

When he came partially to his senses a few minutes later, he found that he had rolled off the bed and was lying beneath the window, where he had recently been keeping a watch for Rachael. Although the changefire had not grown cooler, although he still felt his tissues seeking new forms in every part of his body, he resolutely pushed aside the drapes and reached up toward the window. In the dim light, his hands looked enormous and chitinous, as if they belonged to a crab or lobster that had been gifted with fingers instead of pincers. He grabbed the sill and pulled himself off the floor, stood. He leaned against the glass, his breath coming in great hot gasps that steamed the pane.

Light shone in the windows of the motel office.

Rachael must have arrived.

Instantly he was seething with hatred. The motivating memory-smell of blood filled his nostrils.

But he also had an immense and strangely formed erection. He wanted to mount her, then kill her as he had taken and then slain the cowboy's woman. In his degenerate and mutant state, he was unsettled to discover that he was having trouble holding on to an understanding of her identity. Second by second he was ceasing to care who she was: the only thing that mattered now was that she was female—and prey.

He turned away from the window and tried to reach the door, but his metamorphosing legs collapsed beneath him. Again, for a time, he squirmed and writhed upon the motel floor, the changefire hotter than ever within him.

His genes and chromosomes, once the undisputed regulators—the masters— of his very form and function, had become plastic themselves. They were no longer primarily re-creating previous stages in human evolution but were exploring utterly alien forms that had nothing to do with the physiological history of the human species. They were mutating either randomly or in response to inexplicable forces and patterns he could not perceive. And as they mutated, they directed his body to produce the mad flood of hormones and proteins with which his flesh was molded.

He was becoming something that had never before walked the earth and that had never been meant to walk it.

■ The Marine Corps twin-engine turboprop transport from Twentynine Palms landed in driving rain at McCarren International Airport in Las Vegas at 9:03 P.M. Tuesday. It was only ten minutes ahead of the estimated time of arrival for the scheduled airline flight from Orange County on which Julio Verdad and Reese Hagerstrom were passengers.

Harold Ince, a DSA agent in the Nevada office, met Anson Sharp, Jerry Peake, and Nelson Gosser at the debarkation gate.

Gosser immediately headed for another gate, where the incoming flight from Orange County would unload. It would be his job to run a discreet tail on Verdad and Hagerstrom until they had left the terminal, whereupon they would become the responsibility of the surveillance team that would be waiting outside.

Ince said, "Mr. Sharp, sir, we're cutting it awful close."

"Tell me something I don't know," Sharp said, walking swiftly across the waiting area that served the gate, toward the long corridor that led to the front of the terminal.

Peake hurried after Sharp, and Ince—a much shorter man than Sharp—hustled to stay at his side. "Sir, the car's waiting for you out front, discreetly at the end of the taxi line, as you requested."

"Good. But what if they don't take a cab?"

"One rental-car desk is still open. If they stop to make those arrangements, I'll warn you at once."

"Good."

They reached the moving walkway and stepped onto the rubber belt. No other flights had landed recently or were about to take off, so the corridor was deserted. On the speaker system that served the long hall, taped messages from Vegas showroom performers—Joan Rivers, Paul Anka, Rodney Dangerfield, Tom Dreesen, Bill Cosby, and others—offered lame jokes and, mostly, advice about safety on the pedway: Please use the moving handrail, stay to the right, allow other passengers to pass on the left, and be careful not to trip at the end of the moving belt.

Dissatisfied with the leisurely speed of the walkway, striding along between the moving handrails, Sharp glanced down and slightly back at Ince and said, "How's your relationship with the Las Vegas police?"

"They're cooperative, sir."

"That's all?"

"Well, maybe better than that," Ince said. "They're good guys. They have a hell of a job to do in this city, what with all the hoods and transients, and they handle it well. Got to give them credit. They're not soft, and because they know how hard it is to keep the peace, they have a lot of respect for cops of all kinds."

"Like us?"

"Like us."

"If there's shooting," Sharp said, "and if someone reports it, and if the Vegas uniforms arrive before we've been able to mop up, can we count on them to conform their reports to our needs?"

Ince blinked in surprise. "Well, I . . . maybe."

"I see," Sharp said coldly. They reached the end of the moving walkway. As they strode into the main lobby of the terminal, he said, "Ince, in days to come, you better build a tighter relationship with the local agencies. Next time, I don't want to hear 'maybe.' "

"Yes, sir. But—"

"You stay here, maybe over by the newsstand. Make yourself as inconspicuous as possible."

"That's why I'm dressed this way," Ince said. He was wearing a green polyester leisure suit and an orange Banlon shirt.

Leaving Ince behind, Sharp pushed through a glass door and went outside, where rain was blowing under the overhanging roof.

Jerry Peake caught up with him at last.

"How long do we have, Jerry?"

Glancing at his watch, Peake said, "They land in five minutes."

The taxi line was short at this hour—only four cabs. Their car was parked at the curb marked ARRIVALS—UNLOADING ONLY, about fifty feet behind the last taxi. It was one of the agency's standard crap-brown Fords that might as well have had UNMARKED LAW-ENFORCEMENT SEDAN painted on the sides in foot-tall block letters. Fortunately, the rain would disguise the institutional nature of the car and would make it more difficult for Verdad and Hagerstrom to spot a tail.

Peake got behind the wheel, and Sharp sat in the passenger's seat, putting his attaché case on his lap. He said, "If they take a cab, get close enough to read its plates, then fall way back. Then if we lose it, we can get a quick fix on its destination from the taxi company."

Peake nodded.

Their car was half sheltered by the overhang and half exposed to the storm. Rain hammered only on Sharp's side, and only his windows were blurred by the sheeting water.

He opened the attaché case and removed the two pistols whose registration numbers could be traced neither to him nor to the DSA. One of the silencers was fresh, the other too well used when they had pursued Shadway at Lake Arrowhead. He fitted the fresh one to a pistol, keeping that weapon for himself. He gave the other gun to Peake, who seemed to accept it with reluctance.

"Something wrong?" Sharp asked.

Peake said, "Well . . . sir . . . do you still want to kill Shadway?"

Sharp gave him a narrow look. "It isn't what I want, Jerry. Those are my orders: terminate him. Orders from authorities so high up the ladder that *I* sure as hell am not going to buck them."

"But . . . "

"What is it?"

"If Verdad and Hagerstrom lead us to Shadway and Mrs. Leben, if they're right *there,* you can't terminate anyone in front of them. I mean, sir, those detectives won't keep their mouths shut. Not them."

"I'm pretty sure I can make Verdad and Hagerstrom back off," Sharp assured him. He pulled the clip out of the pistol to make sure it was fully loaded. "The bastards are supposed to stay out of this, and they know it. When I catch them red-handed in the middle of it, they're going to realize that their careers and pensions are in jeopardy. They'll back off. And when they're gone, we'll take out Shadway and the woman."

"If they don't back off?"

"Then we take them out, too," Sharp said. With the heel of his hand, he slammed the clip back into the pistol.

The refrigerator hummed noisily.

The damp air still smelled stale, with a hint of decay.

They hunched over the old kitchen table like two conspirators in one of those old war movies about the anti-Nazi underground in Europe. Rachael's thirty-two pistol lay on the cigarette-scarred Formica, within easy reach, though she did not really believe she would need it—at least not tonight.

Whitney Gavis had absorbed her story—in a condensed form—with remarkably little shock and without skepticism, which surprised her. He did not seem to be a gullible man. He would not believe just any crazy tale he was told. Yet he had believed her wild narrative. Maybe he trusted her implicitly because Benny loved her.

"Benny showed you pictures of me?" she had asked. And Whitney had said, "Yeah, kid, the last couple months, you're all he can talk about." So she said, "Then he knew that what we had together was special, knew it before I did." Whitney said, "No, he told me that you knew the relationship was special, too, but you were afraid to admit it just yet; he said you'd come around, and he was right." She said, "If he showed you pictures of me, why didn't he show me pictures of you or at least *talk* about you, since you're his best friend?" And Whitney had said, "Benny and me are committed to each other, have been ever since Nam, as good as brothers, better than brothers, so we share everything. But until recently, you hadn't committed to him, kid, and until you did, he wasn't going to share everything with you. Don't hold that against him. It's Nam that made him that way."

Vietnam was probably another reason that Whitney Gavis believed her incredible tale, even the part about being pursued by a mutant beast in the Mojave Desert. After a man had been through the madness of Vietnam, maybe nothing strained his credulity anymore.

Now Whitney said, "But you don't know for certain that those snakes killed him."

"No," Rachael admitted.

"If he came back from the dead after being hit by the truck, is it possible he could come back after dying of multiple snakebites?"

"Yes. I suppose so."

"And if he doesn't stay dead, you can't be certain he'll just degenerate into something that'll remain out there on the desert, living pretty much an animal's existence."

"No," she said, "of course, I can't guarantee that, either."

He frowned, and the scarred side of his otherwise handsome face puckered and creased as if it were paper.

Outside, the night was marked by ominous noises, though all were related to the storm: the fronds of a palm tree scraped against the roof; the motel sign, stirred by the wind, creaked on corroded hinges; a loose section of downspouting popped and rattled against its braces. Rachael listened for sounds that could not be explained by the wind and rain, heard none, but kept listening anyway.

Whitney said, "The really disturbing thing is that Eric must've overheard Benny telling you about this place."

"Maybe," Rachael said uneasily.

"Almost certainly, kid."

"All right. But considering his appearance when I last saw him, he won't be able to just stand out along the road and hitch a ride. Besides, he seemed to be devolving mentally and emotionally, not just physically. I mean . . . Whitney, if you could've seen him with those snakes, you'd realize how unlikely it is that he'd have the mental capacity to find a path out of the desert and somehow get all the way here to Vegas."

"Unlikely, but not impossible," he said. "Nothing's impossible, kid. After I had my run-in with an antipersonnel mine in Nam, they told my family I couldn't possibly live. But I did. So they told me I couldn't possibly regain enough muscle control of my damaged face to speak without impairment. But I did. Hell, they had a whole list of things that were impossible—but none of them turned out to be. And I didn't have your husband's advantage—this genetic business."

"If you can call it an advantage," she said, remembering the hideous notched ridge of bone on Eric's forehead, the nascent horns, the inhuman eyes, the fierce hands . . .

"I should arrange other accommodations for you."

"No," she said quickly. "This is where Benny's expecting to find me. If I'm not here—"

"Don't sweat it, kid. He'll find you through me."

"No. If he shows up, I want to be here."

"But—"

"I want to be here," she insisted sharply, determined not to be talked into another course of action. "As soon as he gets here, I want to . . . I have to . . . see him. I have to *see* him."

Whitney Gavis studied her for a moment. He had a discomfitingly intense gaze. Finally he said, "God, you really love him, don't you?"

"Yes," she said tremulously.

"I mean *really* love him."

"Yes," she repeated, trying to prevent her voice from cracking with emotion. "And I'm worried about him . . . so very worried."

"He'll be all right. He's a survivor."

"If anything happens to him—"

"Nothing will," Whitney said. "But I guess there's not much danger in you staying here tonight, at least. Even if your husband . . . even if Eric gets to Vegas, it sounds as if he's going to have to stay out of sight and make a slow and careful journey of it. Probably won't arrive for a few days—"

"If ever."

"—so we can wait until tomorrow to find another place for you. You can stay here and wait for Benny tonight. And he'll come. I know he will, Rachael."

Tears shimmered in her eyes. Not trusting herself to speak, she merely nodded.

With the good grace not to remark upon her tears and the good sense not to try to comfort her, Whitney pushed himself up from the kitchen table and said, "Yes, well, all right, then! If you're going to spend even one night in this dump, we've got to make the place more comfortable. For one thing, although there may be towels and some sheets in the linen closet, they're probably dusty, mildewed or even crawling with disease. So what I'll do is, I'll go buy a set of sheets, towels . . . and how about some food?"

"I'm starved," she said. "I only had an Egg McMuffin early this morning and a couple of candy bars later, but I've burned all that off half a dozen times over. I made a quick stop in Baker, but that was after my encounter with Eric, and I didn't have much appetite. Just picked up a six-pack of diet soda 'cause I was feeling so dehydrated."

"I'll bring back some grub, too. You want to give me a dinner order, or do you trust me?"

She stood up and wearily pushed a pale and trembling hand through her hair. "I'll eat almost anything except turnips and squid."

He smiled. "Lucky for you, this is Vegas. Any other town, the only store open at this hour would be the turnip and squid emporium. But hardly anything in Vegas ever closes. You want to come with me?"

"I shouldn't be showing my face."

He nodded. "You're right. Well, I ought to be back in an hour. You be okay here?"

"Really," she said, "I'm safer here than anywhere else I've been since yesterday morning."

■ In the velvety blackness of room 15, Eric crawled aimlessly across the floor, first one way and then another, twitching, kicking spasmodically, hitching and shuddering and squirming like a broken-backed cockroach.

"Rachael . . . "

He heard himself speak that word and only that word, each time with a different intonation, as if it constituted his entire vocabulary. Although his voice was thick as mud, those two syllables were always clear. Sometimes he knew what the word meant, remembered who she was, but at other times it had no meaning for him. However, regardless of whether or not he knew what it meant, the name predictably engendered precisely the same response in him each time he spoke it: mindless, icy fury.

"Rachael . . . "

Caught helplessly in the tides of change, he groaned, hissed, gagged, whimpered, and sometimes he laughed softly in the back of his throat. He coughed and choked and gasped for breath. He lay on his back, shaking and bucking as the changes surged through him, clawing at the air with hands twice as large as his hands had been in his previous life.

Buttons popped off his red plaid shirt. One of the shoulder seams split as his body swelled and bent into a grotesque new form.

"Rachael . . . "

During the past several hours, as his feet had grown larger and smaller and then larger again, his boots periodically pinched. Now they were painfully confining, crippling, and he could not bear them any longer. He literally tore them off, frenziedly ripped away the soles and heels, wrenched with his powerful hands until the sturdily stitched seams split, used his razored claws to puncture and shred the leather.

His unshod feet proved to have changed as completely as his hands had done. They were broader, flatter, with an exceptionally gnarled and bony bridge, the toes as long as fingers, terminating in claws as sharp as those on his hands.

"Rachael . . ."

Change *smashed* through him as if it were a bolt of lightning blasting through a tree, the current entering at the highest point of the highest limb and sizzling out through the hair-fine tips of the deepest roots.

He twitched and spasmed.

He drummed his heels against the floor.

Hot tears flooded from his eyes, and rivulets of thick saliva streamed from his mouth.

Sweating copiously, being burned alive by the change fire within him, he was nevertheless cold at the core. There was ice in both his heart and mind.

He squirmed into a corner and curled up, hugging himself. His breastbone cracked, shuddered, swelled larger, and sought a new shape. His spine creaked, and he felt it shifting within him to accommodate other alterations in his form.

Only seconds later, he skittered out of the corner in a crablike crawl. He stopped in the middle of the room and rose onto his knees. Gasping, moaning deep in his throat, he knelt for a moment with his head hung low, letting the dizziness flow out with his rancid sweat.

The changefire had finally cooled. For the moment, his form had stabilized.

He stood, swaying.

"Rachael . . ."

He opened his eyes and looked around the motel room, and he was not surprised to discover that his vision was nearly as good in the dark as it had ever been in full daylight. Furthermore, his field of vision had dramatically increased: when he looked straight ahead, objects on both his left and right sides were as clear and as sharply detailed as those things immediately in front of him.

He went to the door. Parts of his mutated body seemed ill formed and dysfunctional, forcing him to hitch along like some hard-shelled crustacean that had only recently developed the ability to stand upright like a man. Yet he was not crippled; he could move quickly and silently, and he had a sense of tremendous strength far greater than anything he had ever known before.

Making a soft hissing noise that was lost in the sounds of wind and drizzling rain, he opened the door and stepped into the night, which welcomed him.

35 SOMETHING THAT LOVES THE DARK

WHITNEY LEFT THE MANAGER'S APARTMENT AT THE GOLDEN Sand Inn by way of the rear door of the kitchen. It opened into a dusty garage where, earlier, they had put the black Mercedes. Now the 560 SEL stood in small puddles of rainwater that had dripped from it. His own car was outside, in the serviceway behind the motel.

Turning to Rachael, who stood on the threshold between kitchen and garage, Whitney said, "You lock this door behind me and sit tight. I'll be back as soon as I can."

"Don't worry. I'll be fine," she said. "I've got to get the Wildcard file in order. That'll keep me busy."

He had no trouble understanding why Ben had fallen so hard for her. Even as disheveled as she was, pale with exhaustion and worry, Rachael was gorgeous. But her beauty was not her only attribute. She was caring, perceptive, smart, and tough—not a common mix of qualities.

"Ben will probably show up before I do," he assured her.

She smiled thinly, grateful for his attempt to cheer her. She nodded, bit her lower lip, but could not speak because, obviously, she was still more than half convinced that she would never again see Ben alive.

Whitney motioned her back from the threshold and pulled the door shut between them. He waited until he heard her engage the dead-bolt lock. Then he crossed the grease- and oil-stained concrete floor, passing the front of the Mercedes, not bothering to put up the big rear door, but heading toward the side entrance.

The three-car garage, illuminated by a single bare bulb dangling on a cord from a crossbeam, was filthy and musty, a badly cluttered repository of old and poorly maintained maintenance equipment plus a lot of stuff that was just plain junk: rusting buckets; tattered brooms; ragged, motheaten mops; a broken outdoor vacuum cleaner; several motel-room chairs with broken legs or torn upholstery, which the previous owners had intended to repair and put back into service; scraps of lumber; coils of wire and coiled hoses; a bathroom sink; spare brass sprinkler heads spilling from an overturned cardboard box; one cotton gardening glove lying palm up like a severed hand; cans of paint and lacquer, their contents almost surely thickened and dried beyond usefulness. This trash was piled along the walls, scattered over portions of the floor, and stacked precariously in the loft.

Just as he unlocked the dead bolt on the side door of the garage, before he actually opened the door, Whitney heard a rattling in the garage behind him. The noise was short-lived; in fact, it stopped even as he turned to see what it was.

Frowning, he let his gaze travel over the piles of junk, the Mercedes, the gas furnace in the far corner, the sagging workbench, and the hot-water heater. He saw nothing out of the ordinary.

He listened.

The only sounds were the many voices of the wind in the eaves and the rain on the roof.

He turned away from the door, walked slowly to the car, circled it, but found nothing that could have caused the noise.

Maybe one of the piles of junk had shifted under its own weight—or had been disturbed by a rat. He would not be surprised to discover that the moldering old building was rat-infested, though he had not previously seen evidence of such an infestation. The trash was piled so haphazardly that he could not discern if it was all in the same position as it had been a moment ago.

He returned to the door again, took one last look around, then went out into the storm.

Even as the wind-harried rain slashed at him, he belatedly realized what he had heard in the garage: someone trying to pull open the big rear door from outside. But it was an electric door that could not be operated manually while in its automatic mode, and was therefore secure against prowlers. Whoever had tried it must have realized, at once, that he could not get in that way, which explained why the rattling had lasted only a moment.

Whitney limped warily toward the corner of the garage and the serviceway beyond it to see if anyone was still there. The rain was falling hard, making a crisp sound on the walk, a sloppier sound on the earth, spilling off the corner of the roof where the downspout was missing. All that wet noise effectively masked his own footsteps, as it would mask the activities of anyone behind the garage, and though he listened intently to the night, he did not at first hear anything unusual. He took six or eight steps, pausing twice to listen, before the patter and susurration of the rain was cut by a frightening noise. *Behind* him. It was partly a hiss like escaping steam, partly a thin catlike whine, partly a thick and menacing growl, and it put the hair up on the back of his neck.

He turned quickly, cried out, and stumbled backward when he saw the thing looming over him in the gloom. Incomprehensibly strange eyes looked down at him from a height of six and a half feet or more. They were bulging, mismatched eyes, each as large as an egg, one pale green and the other orange, iridescent like the eyes of some animals, one rather like the eye of a hyperthyroid cat, the other featuring a mean slit-shaped iris reminiscent of a serpent, both *beveled* and many-faceted, for God's sake, like the eyes of an insect.

For a moment Whit stood transfixed. Suddenly a powerful arm lashed out at him, backhanded him across the face, and knocked him down. He fell onto the concrete walk, hurting his tailbone, and rolled into mud and weeds.

The creature's arm—*Leben's* arm, Whit knew that it had to be Eric Leben transformed beyond understanding—had appeared not to be hinged like a human arm. It seemed to be segmented, equipped with three or four smaller, elbowlike joints that could lock in any combination and that gave it tremendous flexibility. Now, stunned by the vicious blow he had taken, half paralyzed by terror, looking up at the beast as it approached him, he saw that it was slump-shouldered and hunchbacked yet possessed a queer sort of grace, perhaps because its legs, mostly concealed by tattered jeans, were similar in design to the powerful, segmented arms.

Whit realized he was screaming. He had screamed—*really* screamed—only once before in his life, in Nam, when the antipersonnel mine had blown up beneath him, when he had lain on the jungle floor and had seen the bottom half of his own leg lying five yards away, the bloody mangled toes poking through burnt and blasted boot leather. Now he screamed again and could not stop.

Over his own screams, he heard a shrill keening sound from his adversary, what might have been a cry of triumph.

Its head rolled and bobbled strangely, and for a moment Whit had a glimpse of terrible hooked teeth.

He tried to scoot backward across the sodden earth, propelling himself with his good right arm and the stump of the other, but he was unable to move fast. He did not have time to get his legs under him. He managed to retreat only a couple of yards before Leben reached him and bent down and grabbed him by the foot of his left leg, fortunately the artificial leg, and began to drag him toward the open door of the garage.

Even in the night shadows and rain, Whit could see enough of the man-thing's hand to know that it was as thoroughly inhuman as the rest of the beast. And huge. And powerful.

Frantically Whit Gavis kicked out with his good foot, putting all the force he had into the blow, and connected solidly with Leben's leg. The man-thing shrieked, though apparently not in pain as much as in anger. In response, it wrenched his artificial leg so hard that the securing straps tore loose of their buckles. With a brief agony that robbed Whit of breath, the prosthetic limb came loose, leaving him at an even greater disadvantage.

■ In the cramped kitchen of the motel manager's apartment, Rachel had just opened the plastic garbage bag and had removed one handful of rumpled, soiled Xeroxes from the disorganized Wildcard file when she heard the first scream. She knew immediately that it was Whitney, and she also knew instinctively that there could be only one cause of it: Eric.

She threw the papers aside and plucked the thirty-two pistol off the table. She went to the rear door, hesitated, then unlocked it.

Stepping into the dank garage, she paused again, for there was movement on all sides of her. A strong draft swept in through the open side door from the raging night beyond, swinging the single dirty light bulb on its cord. The motion of the light made shadows leap up and fall back and leap up again in every corner. She looked around warily at the stacks of eerily illuminated trash and old furniture, all of which seemed alive amidst the animated shadows.

Whitney's screaming was coming from outside, so she figured that Eric was out there, too, rather than in the garage. She abandoned caution and hurried past the black Mercedes, stepping over a couple of paint cans and around a pile of coiled garden hoses.

A piercing, blood-freezing shriek cut through Whitney's screams, and Rachael knew without doubt that it was Eric, for that shrill cry was similar to the one he'd made while pursuing her across the desert earlier in the day. But it was more fierce and furious than she remembered, more powerful, and even less human and more alien than it had been before. Hearing that monstrous voice, she almost turned and ran. Almost. But, after all, she was not capable of abandoning Whitney Gavis.

She plunged through the open door, into the night and tempest, the pistol held out in front of her. The Eric-thing was only a few yards away, its back to her. She cried out in shock because she saw that it was holding Whitney's leg, which it seemed to have torn from him.

An instant later, she realized that it was the artificial leg, but by then she had drawn the beast's attention. It threw the fake limb aside and turned toward her, its impossible eyes gleaming.

Its appearance was so numbingly horrific that she, unlike Whitney, was unable to scream; she tried, but her voice failed her. The darkness and rain mercifully concealed many details of the mutant form, but she had an impression of a massive and misshapen head, jaws that resembled a cross between those of a wolf and a crocodile, and an abundance of deadly teeth. Shirtless and shoeless, clad only in jeans, it was a few inches taller than Eric had been, and its spine curved up into hunched and deformed shoulders. There was an immense expanse of breastbone that looked as if it might be covered with horns or spines of some sort, and with rounded knobby excrescences. Long and strangely jointed arms hung almost to its knees. The hands were surely just like the hands of demons who, in the fiery depths of hell, cracked open human souls and ate the meat of them.

"Rachael . . . Rachael . . . come for you . . . Rachael," the Eric-thing said in a vile and whispery voice, slowly forming each word with care, as if the knowledge and use of language were nearly forgotten. The creature's throat and mouth and tongue and lips were no longer designed for the production of human speech; the formation of each syllable obviously required tremendous effort and perhaps some pain. "Come . . . for . . . you . . . "

It took a step toward her, its arms swinging against its sides with a scraping, clicking, chitinous sound.

It.

She could no longer think of him as Eric, as her husband. Now, he was just a thing, an abomination, that by its very existence made a mockery of everything else in God's creation.

She fired point-blank at its chest.

It did not even flinch at the impact of the slug. It emitted a high-pitched squeal that seemed more an expression of eagerness than pain, and it took another step.

She fired again, then a third time, and a fourth.

The multiple impacts of the slugs made the beast stagger slightly to one side, but it did not go down.

"Rachael . . . Rachael . . . "

Whitney shouted, "Shoot it, kill it!"

The pistol's clip held ten rounds. She squeezed off the last six as fast as she could, certain that she hit the thing every time in the gut and chest and even in the face.

It finally roared in pain and collapsed onto its knees, then toppled facedown in the mud.

"Thank God," she said shakily, "thank God," and she was suddenly so weak that she had to lean against the outside wall of the garage.

The Eric-thing retched, gagged, twitched, and pushed up onto hands and knees.

"No," she said disbelievingly.

It raised its grisly head and stared fiercely at her with cold, mismatched lantern eyes. Slowly lids slid down over the eyes, then slowly up, and when revealed again, those radiant ovals seemed brighter than before.

Even if its altered genetic structure provided for incredibly rapid healing and for resurrection after death, surely it could not recover *this* fast. If it could repair and reanimate itself in seconds after succumbing to ten bullet wounds, it was not just a quick healer, and not just potentially immortal, but virtually invincible.

"Die, damn you," she said.

It shuddered and spat something into the mud, then lurched up from the ground, all the way to its feet.

"Run!" Whitney shouted. "For Christ's sake, Rachael, *run!*"

She had no hope of saving Whitney. There was no point in staying to be killed with him.

"Rachael," the creature said, and in its gravelly mucus-thick voice were anger and hunger and hatred and dark need.

No more bullets in the gun. There were boxes of ammunition in the Mercedes, but she could never reach them in time to reload. She dropped the pistol.

"Run!" Whit Gavis shouted again.

Heart hammering, Rachael sprinted back into the garage, leaping over the paint cans and garden hoses. A twinge of pain shot through the ankle she had twisted earlier in the day, and the claw punctures in her thigh began to burn as if they were fresh wounds.

The demon shrieked behind her.

As she went, Rachael toppled a set of freestanding metal shelves laden with tools and boxes of nails, hoping to delay the thing if it pursued her immediately instead of finishing Whitney Gavis first. The shelves went over with a resounding crash, and by the time she reached the open kitchen door, she heard the beast clambering through the debris. It had, indeed, left Whitney alive, for it was in a frenzy to put its hands upon her.

She bounded across the threshold, slammed the kitchen door, but before she could engage the dead-bolt latch, the door was thrown open with tremendous force. She was propelled across the kitchen, nearly fell, somehow stayed on her feet, but struck her hip against the edge of a counter and slammed backward into the refrigerator hard enough to send a brief though intense current of pain from the small of her back to the base of her neck.

It came in from the garage. In the kitchen light, it appeared immense and was more hideous than she had wanted to believe.

For a moment, it stood just inside the door, glaring across the small dusty kitchen. It lifted its head and expanded its chest as if giving her an opportunity to admire it. Its flesh was mottled brown-gray-green-black, with lighter patches that almost resembled human skin, though it was mostly pebbled like elephant hide and scaly in some places. The head was pear-shaped, set at a slant on the thick muscular neck, with the round end at the top and the slimmer end at the bottom of the face. The entire narrow part of the "pear" was composed of a snoutlike protrusion and jaws. When it opened its enormous mouth to hiss, the pointed teeth within were sharklike in their sharpness and profusion. The darting tongue was dark and quick and utterly inhuman. Its entire face was lumpy; in addition to a pair of hornlike knobs on its forehead, there were odd convexities and concavities that seemed to have no biological purpose, plus tumorous knots of bone or other tissue. On its brow and radiating downward from its eyes, throbbing arteries and swollen veins shone just beneath the skin.

In the Mojave, earlier in the day, she had thought that Eric was undergoing retrograde evolution, that his genetically altered body was becoming a sort of patchwork of ancient racial forms. But this thing owed nothing to human physiological history. This was the nightmare product of genetic chaos, a creature that went neither backward nor forward along the chain of human evolution. It was embarked upon a sidewise biological *re*volution—and had severed most if not all links with the human seed from which it sprang. Some of Eric's consciousness evidently still existed within the dreadful hulk, although Rachael suspected only the faintest trace of his personality and intellect remained and that soon even this spark of Eric would be extinguished forever.

"See . . . me . . . " it said, reinforcing her feeling that it was preening before her.

She edged away from the refrigerator, toward the open door between the kitchen and the living room.

It raised one murderous hand, palm out, as if to tell her she must stop retreating. The segmented arm appeared capable of bending backward or forward at four places, and each of those bizarre joints was protected by hard brown-black plates of tissue that seemed similar in substance to a beetle's carapace. The long, claw-tipped fingers were frightening, but something worse lay in the center of its palm: a round, sucker-shaped orifice as large as a half-dollar. As she stared in horror at this Dantean apparition, the orifice in its palm opened and closed slowly, opened and closed like a raw wound, opened and closed. The function of the mouth-in-hand was in part mysterious and in part too dreadfully clear; as she stared, it grew red and moist with an obscene hunger.

Panicked, she made a break for the nearby doorway and heard the beast's feet clicking like cloven hooves on the linoleum as it rushed after her. Five or six steps into the living room, heading toward the door that opened into the motel office, with eight or ten steps to go, she saw the beast looming at her right side.

It moved so *fast*!

Screaming, she threw herself to the floor and rolled to escape its grasp. She collided with an armchair, shot to her feet, and put the chair between her and the enemy.

When she changed directions, the creature had not immediately followed. It was standing in the center of the room, watching her, apparently aware that it had cut her off from her only route of escape and that it could take time to relish her terror before it closed in for the kill.

She began to back toward the bedroom.

It said, "Raysheeeel, Raysheeeel," no longer capable of speaking her name clearly.

The tumorous lumps across the beast's forehead rippled and re-formed. Right before her eyes, one of its small horns melted away entirely as another minor wave of change passed through the creature, and a new vein traced a path across its face much like a slow-moving fissure forming in the earth.

She continued to edge backward.

It moved toward her with slow, easy steps.

"Raysheeeel . . . "

■ Convinced that a dying wife lay in an intensive-care ward waiting for her husband, Amos Tate wanted to drive Ben all the way to Sunrise Hospital, which would have taken him too far away from the Golden Sand Inn. Ben had to insist strenuously on being dropped at the corner of Las Vegas Boulevard and Tropicana. And as there was no good reason to refuse Amos's generous offer, Ben was reduced to admitting that he had lied about the wife, though he offered no explanation. He flung off the blanket, threw open the cab door, jumped down to the street, and ran east on Tropicana, past the Tropicana Hotel, leaving the startled trucker staring after him in puzzlement.

The Golden Sand Inn was approximately a mile ahead, a distance he could ordinarily cover in six minutes or less. But in the heavy rain, he did not want to risk sprinting at top speed, for if he fell and broke an arm or leg, he would not be in any condition to help Rachael if, in fact, she needed help. (God, please, let her be warm and safe and sound and in need of no help at all!) He ran along the shoulder of the broad boulevard, the revolver digging into his flesh where it was tucked under his waistband. He splashed through puddles that filled every depression in the macadam. Only a few cars passed him; several of the drivers slowed to stare, but none offered him a lift. He did not bother trying to hitch a ride, for he sensed that he had no time to waste.

A mile was not a great distance, but tonight it seemed like a journey to the far end of the world.

■   Julio and Reese had been able to board the plane in Orange County with their service revolvers holstered under their coats because they had presented their police credentials to the attendant at the metal-detecting security gate. Now, having landed at McCarran International in Las Vegas, they used their ID again to obtain swift service from the clerk at the rental-car desk, an attractive brunette named Ruth. Instead of just handing them the keys and sending them out to the lot to locate their designated rental on their own, she telephoned a night-duty mechanic to pick it up and drive it around to the front entrance of the terminal.

Since they had not come dressed for rain, they stood inside the terminal at a set of glass doors until they saw the Dodge pull up at the curb, then went out into the storm. The mechanic, more suitably dressed for the foul weather in a vinyl raincoat with a vinyl hood, quickly checked their rental papers and turned the car over to them.

Although clouds had claimed the sky late in the day in Orange County, Reese had not realized things would be worse to the east and had not bargained for a landing in a rainstorm. Though their descent and touchdown had been as smooth as glass, he had gripped the arms of his seat so tightly that his hands were still slightly stiff and achy.

Safely on the ground, he should have been relieved, but he could not forget Teddy Bertlesman, the tall pink lady, and he could also not forget little Esther waiting at home for him. This morning, he'd had only his Esther to live for, just that one small blessing, which was not a sufficient abundance to tempt the cruelty of fate. But now there was also the glorious real-estate saleswoman, and Reese was acutely aware that when a man had more reason to live he was more likely to die.

Superstitious nonsense, perhaps.

But the rain, when he had expected a clear desert night, seemed like a bad omen, and he was uneasy.

As Julio drove away from the terminal, Reese wiped the rain off his face and said, "What about all those TV commercials for Vegas on the L.A. stations?"

"What about them?"

"Where's the sunshine? Where're all those girls in tiny little bikinis?"

"What do you care about girls in bikinis when you have a date with Teddy Bertlesman on Saturday?"

Don't talk about that, Reese thought superstitiously.

He said, "Hell, this doesn't look like Vegas. This looks more like Seattle."

■ Rachael slammed the bedroom door and thumbed in the button to engage the flimsy lock. She ran to the only window, pulled open the rotting drapes, found it had jalousie panes, and realized that, because of those metal cross-ribs, there was no easy exit.

Looking around for something that could be used as a weapon, she saw only the bed, two nightstands, one lamp, and a chair.

She expected the door to crash inward, but it did not.

She heard nothing from the creature in the living room, and its silence, while welcome, was also unnerving. What was it up to?

She ran to the closet, slid the door open, and looked inside. Nothing of use. Just a tier of empty shelves in one corner and then a rod and empty hangers. She could not fashion a weapon out of a few wire hangers.

The doorknob rattled.

"Raysheeeel," the thing hissed tauntingly.

A fragment of Eric's consciousness evidently did remain within the mutant, for it was that Eric-part that wanted to make her sweat and wanted her to have plenty of time to contemplate what he was going to do to her.

She would die here, and it would be a slow and terrible death.

In frustration, she started to turn away from the empty clothes rod and hangers, but noticed a trap in the closet ceiling, an access to the attic.

The creature thumped a heavy hand against the door, then again and again. "Raysheeeel . . . "

She slipped inside the closet and tugged on the shelves to test their sturdiness. To her relief, they were built in, screwed to the wall studs, so she was able to climb them as if they were a ladder. She stood on the fourth tier, her head only a foot below the ceiling. Holding the adjacent rod with one hand, she reached out and up to one side with her free hand, beyond the shelves, and quietly pushed up the hinged trap.

"Raysheeeel, Raysheeeel," it crooned, dragging its claws down the outside of the locked bedroom door, then throwing itself lightly—almost teasingly—against that barrier.

In the closet, Rachael climbed one more step, got a grip on two edges of the overhead opening, swung off the shelves, dangled for a moment with the rod against her breasts, then muscled herself up and into the attic. There was no flooring, just two-by-four beams sixteen inches apart, with sheathed pads of Fiberglas insulation laid between those supports. In the wan yellow light that rose through the open trap, she saw the attic ceiling was very low, providing only a four-foot-high space, with roofing nails poking through in a lot of places, and with larger exposed rafter nails lancing out here and there. To her surprise, the attic was not limited to the area over the office and the manager's apartment, but led off across the ceilings of all the rooms in that long wing.

Below, something crashed so hard that she felt the reverberation through the bedroom-ceiling beams on which she knelt. Another crash was accompanied by the dry splintering of wood and the hard sharp snap of breaking metal.

She quickly closed the trap, plunging the attic into perfect darkness. She crawled as silently as possible along a parallel pair of two-by-fours, one hand and one knee on each of them, until she was about eight feet from the trap. There she stopped and waited in the high lightless chamber.

Anxiously she listened for movement in the room below. With the trap closed, she could not easily hear what was happening down there, for the heavy rain was hammering on the motel's roof only inches above her head.

She prayed that, in his degenerate state, with an IQ closer to that of an animal than a man, the Eric-thing would be unable to puzzle out her route of escape.

■ With only one arm and one leg, Whitney Gavis had first dragged himself toward the garage in dogged pursuit of the departing creature that had torn off his artificial leg. But by the time he reached the open door, he knew that he was fooling himself: with his handicaps, he could do nothing to help Rachael. Handicaps—that's what they were. Earlier, he had jokingly called his amputations "peculiarities" and had told Rachael that he refused to use the word "handicaps." In the current situation, however, there was no room for self-delusion; the painful truth had to be faced. Handicaps. He was furious with himself for his limitations, furious with the long-ago war and the Vietcong and life in general, and for a moment he was almost overcome by tears.

But being angry did no good, and Whit Gavis did not waste time and energy on either fruitless activities or self-pity. "Put a lid on it, Whit," he said aloud. He turned away from the garage and began to haul himself laboriously along the muddy ground toward the paved alley, intending to crawl all the way out to Tropicana and into the middle of that boulevard, where the sight of him would surely stop even the most unsympathetic motorist.

He had gone only six or eight yards when his face, which had been numbed by a blow from the beast's club-hard hand, suddenly began to burn and sting. He flopped on his back, face turned up into the cold rain, raised his good hand, and felt his disfigured cheek. He found deep lacerations cutting through the scar tissue that was part of his Vietnam legacy.

He was sure that Leben had not clawed him, that the blow that knocked him down was delivered with the back of the immense, bony hand. But he was undeniably cut in four or five places, and he was bleeding freely, especially from one laceration that extended up into his left temple. Did that damn fugitive from a Halloween party have spurs on its knuckles or something? His probing fingers set off little detonations of pain in his face, and he immediately dropped his hand.

Rolling onto his belly again, he continued dragging himself toward the street.

"Doesn't matter," he said. "That side of your face is never going to win you any beauty contests, anyway."

He refused to think about the thick, swift stream of blood that he had felt flowing down from his temple.

■ Crouching in the lightless attic, Rachael began to believe that she had fooled the Eric-thing. Its degeneration was apparently mental as well as physical, just as she had suspected, and it did not possess sufficient intellectual capacity to figure out what had happened to her. Her heart continued to pound wildly, and she was still shaking, but she dared to hope.

Then the plyboard trapdoor in the closet ceiling swung upward, and light from below speared into the attic. The mutant's hideous hands reached through the opening. Then its head came into view, and it pulled itself into the upper chamber, turning its mad eyes upon her as it came.

She scuttled across the attic as fast as she dared go. She was acutely aware of the nails lancing down just inches above her head. She also knew that she must not put her weight down on the insulated hollows between the two-by-fours because there was no flooring; if she misstepped, shifting her weight off the beams for even a second, she would crash through the Sheetrock that formed the ceilings of the rooms below, tumbling into one of those chambers. Even if she did not tear loose electrical wires and fixtures in the fall—and thus escaped electrocution— she might break a leg or even snap her spine when she hit the floor below. Then she would be able only to lie immobile while the beast descended and took its sweet time with her.

She went about thirty feet, with at least another hundred and fifty feet of the motel attic ahead of her, before she glanced back. The thing had clambered all the way through the trap and was staring after her.

"Rayeeshuuuul," it said, the quality of its speech declining by the minute.

It slammed the trapdoor shut, plunging them into total darkness, where it had all the advantages.

■ Ben's soggy Adidas running shoes were so thoroughly saturated that they began to slip on his feet. He felt the mild irritation of an incipient blister on his left heel.

When at last he came within sight of the Golden Sand Inn, where lights shone in the office windows, he slowed down long enough to shove one hand under his rain-soaked shirt and pull the Combat Magnum out of the waistband at the hollow of his back.

He wished he had the Remington shotgun that he had left behind in the disabled Merkur.

As he reached the motel's entrance drive, he saw a man crawling away from the place, toward Tropicana. An instant later he realized it was Whit Gavis without the artificial leg and, apparently, injured.

■ He had become something that loved the dark. He did not know what he was, did not clearly remember what—or who—he had once been, did not know where he was ultimately bound or for what purpose he existed, but he knew that his rightful place was now in darkness, where he not only thrived but ruled.

Ahead, the prey made her way cautiously through the blackness, effectively blinded and moving too slowly to stay out of his reach much longer. Unlike her, he was not hampered by the lack of light. He could see her clearly, and he could see most details of the place through which they crept.

He was, however, slightly confused as to his whereabouts. He knew that he had climbed up into this long tunnel, and from the smell of it he also knew its walls were made of wood, yet he felt as if he should be deep under the earth. The place was similar to moist dark burrows which he vaguely remembered from another age and which he found appealing for reasons he did not entirely comprehend.

Around him, shadowfires sprang to life, flourished for a moment, then faded away. He knew that he had once been afraid of them, but he could not recall the reason for his fear. Now the phantom flames seemed of no consequence to him, harmless as long as he ignored them.

The prey's female scent was pungent, and it inflamed him. Lust made him reckless, and he had to struggle against the urge to rush forward and throw himself upon her. He sensed that the footing here was perilous, yet caution had far less appeal than the prospect of sexual release.

Somehow he knew that it was dangerous to stray off the beams and into the hollow spaces, though he did not know why. Keeping to those safe tracks was easier for him than for the prey, because in spite of his size he was more agile than she. Besides, he could see where he was going, and she could not.

Each time she started to look back, he squinted so she would not be able to pinpoint his position by spotting his radiant eyes. When she paused to listen, she could surely hear him coming, but her inability to get a visual fix had her obviously terrified.

The stink of her acute terror was as strong as her femaleness, though sour. The former scent sparked his blood lust as effectively as the latter incited his sexual desire. He longed to feel her blood spurting against his lips, to taste it on his tongue, to push his mouth within her slashed abdomen in search of the rich and satisfying flesh of her liver.

He was twenty feet behind her.

Fifteen.

Ten.

■ Ben helped Whit sit up against a four-foot-high retaining wall that enclosed a tangle of weeds where once had been a bed of flowers. Above them, the motel sign scraped and creaked in the wind.

"Don't worry about me," Whit said, pushing him away.

"Your face—"

"Help *her*. Help Rachael."

"You're bleeding."

"I'll live, I'll live. But it's after Rachael," Whit said with that unnervingly familiar note of purest horror and desperation that Ben had not heard in anyone's voice since Vietnam. "It left me, and it went after her."

"It?"

"You have a gun? Good. A Magnum. Good."

"It?" Ben repeated.

Abruptly the wind wailed louder, and the rain fell as if a dam had broken above them, and Whit raised his voice to be heard over the storm. "Leben. It's Leben, but he's changed. My God, he's changed. Not really Leben anymore. Genetic chaos, she calls it. Retrograde evolution, devolution, she says. Massive mutations. Hurry, Ben! The manager's apartment!"

Unable to understand what the hell Whit was talking about, but sensing that Rachael was in even graver danger than he had feared, Ben left his old friend propped against the retaining wall and ran toward the entrance to the motel office.

■ Blind, half deafened by the thunderous impact of the rain upon the roof, Rachael crawled through the mine-dark attic as fast as she dared. Though she was afraid that she was moving too slowly to escape the beast, she came to the end of the long chamber sooner than she'd expected, bumping up against the outer wall at the end of the motel's first wing.

Crazily, she had given no thought to what she would do when she reached a dead end. Her mind had been focused so intently upon the need to stay beyond the reach of the Eric-thing that she had proceeded as if the attic would go on forever.

She let out a whimper of despair when she discovered that she was cornered. She shuffled to her right, hoping that the attic made a turn and continued over the middle wing of the U-shaped building. In fact, it must have done just that, but she encountered a concrete-block partition between the two wings, perhaps a fire wall. Searching frantically in the darkness, she could feel the cool, rough surface of the blocks and the lines of mortar, and she knew there would be no pass-through in such a barrier.

Behind her, the Eric-thing issued a wordless cry of triumph and obscene hunger that pierced the curtain of rain noise and seemed to originate only inches from her ear.

She gasped and snapped her head around, shocked by the nearness of the demonic voice. She'd thought she had a minute to scheme, half a minute at least. But for the first time since the beast had cast the attic into absolute darkness by closing the trap door, Rachael saw its murderous eyes. The radiant pale green orb was undergoing changes that would no doubt make it more like the orange serpent's eye. She was so close that she could see the unspeakable hatred in that alien gaze. It . . . *it* was no more than six feet from her.

Its breath reeked.

She somehow knew that it could see her clearly.

And it was reaching for her in the darkness.

She sensed its grotesque hand straining toward her.

She pressed back against the concrete blocks.

Think, *think.*

Cornered, she could do nothing except embrace one of the very dangers that she had thus far been striving to avoid: Instead of clinging precariously to the beams, she threw herself to one side, into the insulated hollow between a pair of two-by-fours, and the old Sheetrock cracked and collapsed beneath her. She fell straight out of the attic, down through the ceiling of one of the motel rooms, praying that she would not land on the edge of a dresser or chair, would not break her back, praying that she would not become easy meat—

—and she dropped smack into the middle of a bed with broken springs and a mattress that had become a breeding ground for mold and fungus. Those cold and

slimy growths burst beneath her, spewing spores, oozing sticky fluids, and ex-
uding a noxious odor almost as bad as rotten eggs, though she breathed deeply
of it without complaint because she was alive and unhurt.

Above, the Eric-thing started down through the ceiling in a less radical fashion
than she had chosen, clinging to the ceiling beams and kicking out more Sheetrock
to make a wider passageway for itself.

She rolled off the bed and stumbled across the dark motel room in search of
the door.

■ In the manager's apartment, Ben found the shattered bedroom door, but the
bedroom itself was deserted, as were the living room and the kitchen. He
looked in the garage as well, but neither Rachael nor Eric was there. Finding
nothing was better than finding a lot of blood or her battered corpse, though not
much better.

With Whitney's urgent warnings still echoing in his mind, Ben quickly retraced
his path through the apartment to the motel office and out into the courtyard.
From the corner of his eye, he saw movement down at the end of the first wing.

Rachael. Even in the gloom, there was no mistaking her.

She came out of one of the motel rooms, moving fast, and with immense relief
Ben called her name. She looked up, then ran toward him along the awning-
covered promenade. At first he thought her attitude was one of ordinary excitement or perhaps joy at the sight of him, but almost at once he realized she was
propelled by terror.

"Benny, run!" she shouted as she approached. "Run, for God's sake, run!"

Of course, he would not run because he could not abandon Whit out there
against the wall of the weed-choked flower bed, and he could not carry Whit and
run at the same time, so he stood his ground. However, when he saw the thing
that came out of that motel room behind her, he *wanted* to run, no doubt of that;
all courage fled him in an instant, even though the darkness allowed him to see
only a fraction of the nightmare that pursued her.

Genetic chaos, Whit had said. Devolution. Moments ago, those words had
meant little or nothing to Ben. Now, on his first glimpse of the thing that Eric Leben
had become, he understood as much as he needed to understand for the moment.
Leben was both Dr. Frankenstein and the Frankenstein monster, both the exper-
imenter and the unlucky subject of the experiment, a genius and a damned soul.

Rachael reached Ben, grabbed him by the arm, and said, "Come on, come on,
hurry."

"I can't leave Whit," he said. "Stand back. Let me get a clear shot at it."

"No! That's no good, no good. Jesus, I shot it ten times, and it got right up
again."

"This is a hell of a lot more powerful weapon than yours," he insisted.

The hideous Grendelesque figure raced toward them—virtually galloped in
long graceful strides—along the canopied promenade, not in the awkward sham-
ble that Ben had expected when first catching sight of it, but with startling and
dismaying speed. Even in the weak gray light, parts of its body appeared to glisten
like polished obsidian armor, not unlike the shells of certain insects, while in other
places there was the scintillant silvery sheen of scales.

Ben barely had time to spread his legs in a shooter's stance, raise the Combat

Magnum in both hands, and squeeze off a shot. The revolver roared, and fire flashed from its muzzle.

Fifteen feet away, the creature was jolted by the impact of the slug, stumbled, but did not go down. Hell, it didn't even stop; it came forward with less speed but still too fast.

He squeezed off a second shot, a third.

The beast screamed—a sound like nothing Ben had ever heard, and like nothing he wanted to hear again—and was at last halted. It fell against one of the steel poles that held up the aluminum awning and clung to that support.

Ben fired again, hitting it in the throat this time.

The impact of the .357 Magnum blew it away from the awning post and sent it staggering backward.

The fifth shot knocked it down at last, although only to its knees. It put one shovel-size hand to the front of its throat, and its other arm bent in an impossible fashion until it had put its other hand against the back of its neck.

"Again, again!" Rachael urged.

He pumped the sixth and final shot into the kneeling creature, and it pitched backward on the concrete, flopped onto its side, lay silent, motionless.

The Combat Magnum had a roar only slightly less impressive than a cannon's. In the comparative stillness that followed the dwindling echo of the last gunshot, the drumming rain sounded hardly louder than a whisper.

"Do you have more bullets?" Rachael demanded, still in a state of acute terror.

"It's all right," Ben said shakily. "It's dead, it's dead."

"If you have more cartridges, *load them!*" she shouted.

He was not shocked by her tone or by the panic in her voice, but he *was* shocked when he realized that she was not really hysterical—scared, yes, damn scared, but not out of control. She knew what she was talking about; she was terrified but not irrational, and she believed he would need to reload quickly.

This morning—an eternity ago—on the way to Eric's cabin above Lake Arrowhead, Ben had stuffed some extra rounds into his pockets along with a few spare shells for the shotgun. He had discarded the shotgun ammo when he had left the 12-gauge in the Merkur along I-15. Now, checking his pockets, he turned up only two revolver cartridges where he had expected to find half a dozen, and he figured that the others had spilled out with the shotgun shells when he had discarded those.

But it was all right, everything was okay, nothing to fear: the creature on the promenade had not moved and was not going to move.

"Hurry," Rachael urged.

His hands were shaking. He broke out the revolver's cylinder and slipped one cartridge into a chamber.

"*Benny*," she said warningly.

He looked up and saw the beast moving. It had gotten its huge hands under itself and was trying to push up from the concrete.

"Holy shit," he said. He fumbled the second round into the gun, snapped the cylinder back into place.

Incredibly, the beast had already risen to its knees and reached out to another awning post.

Ben aimed carefully, squeezed the trigger. The Combat Magnum boomed again.

The thing was jolted as the slug tore into it, but it held fast to the post, emitting an ungodly screech. It turned luminous eyes on Ben, and in them he thought he saw a challenge and an indestructible hatred.

Ben's hands were shaking so bad that he was afraid he was going to miss with the next—and last—shot. He had not been this rattled since his first combat mission in Nam.

It clawed for handholds on the post and heaved onto its feet.

His confidence shattered, but unwilling to admit that a weapon as devastatingly powerful as the .357 Magnum was inadequate, Ben fired the final round.

Again the beast went down, but this time it was not still for even a few seconds. It writhed and squealed and kicked in agony, the carapace-hard portions of its body scraping and clicking against the concrete.

Ben would have liked to believe that it was in its death throes, but by now he knew no ordinary gun would cut it down; an Uzi rigged for fully automatic fire, perhaps, or a fully automatic AK-91 assault rifle, or the equivalent, but not an ordinary gun.

Rachael pulled at him, wanting him to run before the beast got onto its feet again, but there was still the problem of Whit Gavis. Ben could save himself and Rachael by running, but in order to save Whit, he had to stay and fight and go on fighting until either he or the mutant Leben was dead.

Perhaps because he felt as if he were in the midst of a war again, he thought of Vietnam and of the particularly cruel weapon that had been such a special and infamous part of that brutal conflict: napalm. Napalm was jellied gasoline, and for the most part it killed whatever it touched, eating through flesh all the way to the bone, scoring the bone all the way to the marrow. In Nam, the stuff had been dreaded because, once unleashed, it brought inescapable death. Given enough time, he possessed the knowledge to manufacture a serviceable homemade version of napalm; he did *not* have the time, of course, although he realized that he could put his hands on gasoline in its mundane liquid form. Though the jellied brand was preferable, the ordinary stuff was effective in its own right.

As the mutant stopped screeching and writhing, as it began to struggle onto its knees once more, Ben grabbed Rachael by the shoulder and said, "The Mercedes—where is it?"

"The garage."

He glanced toward the street and saw that Whit had presciently dragged himself around the corner of the retaining wall, where he was hidden from the motel. The wisdom of Nam: Help your buddies as much as possible, then cover your own ass as soon as you can. Initiates of that war never forgot the lessons it taught them. As long as Leben believed that Ben and Rachael were on the motel property, he was not likely to go out toward Tropicana and accidentally find the helpless man hiding against the wall. For a few more minutes, anyway, Whit was fairly safe where he was.

Casting aside the useless revolver, Ben grabbed Rachael's hand and said, "Come on!"

They ran around the side of the office toward the garage at the back of the motel, where the gusting wind was repeatedly banging the open door against the wall.

36 THE MANY FORMS OF FIRE

SLUMPED AGAINST THE RETAINING WALL, FACING OUT TOWARD Tropicana, Whitney Gavis felt that the rain was washing him away. He was a man made of mud, and the rain was dissolving him. Moment by moment, he grew weaker, too weak to raise a hand to check the bleeding from his cheek and temple, too weak to shout at the dishearteningly few cars that whisked by on the wide boulevard. He was lying in a shadowed area, thirty feet back from the roadway, where their headlights did not sweep across him, and he supposed none of the drivers noticed him.

He had watched Ben empty the Combat Magnum into Leben's mutated hulk, and he had seen the mutant rise up again. As there was nothing he could do to help, he had concentrated upon pulling himself around the corner of the four-foot-high wall of the flower bed, intending to make himself more visible to those passing on the boulevard, hoping someone would spot him and stop. He even dared to hope for a passing patrol car and a couple of well-armed cops, but merely hoping for help was not going to be good enough.

Behind him, he had heard Ben fire two more shots, heard him and Rachael talking frantically, then running footsteps. He knew that Ben would never bug out on him, so he figured they'd thought of something else that might stop Leben. The problem was that, weak as he felt, he did not know if he was going to last long enough to find out what new strategy they had devised.

He saw another car coming west on Tropicana. He tried to call out but failed; he tried to raise one arm from his lap so he could wave to attract attention, but the arm seemed nailed to his thigh.

Then he noticed this car was moving far slower than previous traffic, and it was approaching half in its lane and half on the shoulder of the road. The closer it got, the slower it moved.

Medevac, he thought, and that thought spooked him a little because this wasn't Nam, for God's sake, this was Vegas, and they didn't have Medevac units in Vegas. Besides, this was a car, not a helicopter.

He shook his head to clear it, and when he looked again the car was closer.

They're going to pull right into the motel, Whit thought, and he would have been excited except he suddenly didn't have sufficient energy for excitement. And the already deep black night seemed to be getting blacker.

■ As soon as Ben and Rachael had entered the garage, they'd closed and locked the outer door. She did not have the keys with her, and there was no thumb latch on this side of the kitchen door, so they had to leave that one standing open and just hope that Leben came at them from the other direction.

"No door will keep it out, anyway," Rachael said. "It'll get in if it knows we're here."

Ben had recalled garden hoses among the heaps of junk that the former owners had left behind: "Existing supplies, tools, materials, and sundry useful items," they had called the trash when trying to boost the sales price of the place. He found a pair of rusted hedge clippers, intending to use them to chop a length of hose that might work as a siphon, but then he saw a coil of narrow, flexible rubber tubing hanging from a hook on the wall, which was even more suitable.

He snatched the tubing off the hook and hastily stuffed one end into the Mercedes's fuel tank. He sucked on the other end and barely avoided getting a mouthful of gasoline.

Rachael had been busy searching through the junk for a container without a hole in the bottom. She slipped a galvanized bucket under the siphon only seconds before the gasoline began to flow.

"I never knew gas fumes could smell so sweet," he said as he watched the golden fluid streaming into the bucket.

"Even this might not stop it," she said worriedly.

"If we saturate it, the damage from fire will be much more extensive than—"

"You have matches?" Rachael interrupted.

He blinked. "No."

"Me neither."

"Damn."

Looking around the cluttered garage, she said, "Would there be any here?"

Before he could answer, the knob on the side door of the garage rattled violently. Evidently the Leben-thing had seen them go around the motel or had followed their trail by scent—only God knew what its capabilities were, and in this case maybe even God was in the dark—and already it had arrived.

"The kitchen," Ben said urgently. "They didn't bother taking anything or cleaning out the drawers. Maybe you'll find some matches there."

Rachael ran to the end of the garage and disappeared into the apartment.

The beast threw itself against the outside door, which was not a hollow-core model like the one it had easily smashed through in the bedroom. This more solid barrier would not immediately collapse, but it shuddered and clattered in its loosely fitted jamb. The mutant hit it again, and the door gave out a dry-wood splintering sound but still held, and then it was hit a third time.

Half a minute, Ben thought, glancing back and forth from the door to the gasoline collecting in the bucket. Please, God, let it hold just half a minute more.

The beast hit the door again.

■ Whit Gavis didn't know who the two men were. They had stopped their car along the boulevard and had run to him. The big man was taking his pulse, and the smaller guy—he looked Mexican—was using one of those detachable glove-compartment flashlights to examine the lacerations in Whitney's face and temple. Their dark suits had quickly gotten darker as the rain soaked them.

They might have been some of the federal agents who were after Ben and Rachael, but at this point Whitney didn't care if they were lieutenants in the devil's own army, because surely no one could pose a greater danger than the deadly creature that was stalking the motel grounds. Against that enemy, all men ought to be united in a common cause. Even federal agents, even DSA men, would be welcome allies in this battle. They would have to give up the idea of keeping the Wildcard Project a secret; they would see that there was no way this particular line of life-extension research could be safely carried on; and they would stop trying to silence Ben and Rachael, would help stop the thing that Leben had become, yes, that was certainly what they would do, so Whitney told them what was happening, urged them to help Ben and Rachael, alerted them to the nature of the danger that they faced . . .

"What's he saying?" the big one asked.

"I can't make it out exactly," the small, well-dressed, Mexican-looking man said. He had stopped examining the cuts and had fished Whitney's wallet out of his trousers.

The big man carefully felt Whitney's left leg. "This isn't a recent injury. He lost the leg a long time ago. The same time he lost the arm, I guess."

Whitney realized that his voice was no louder than a whisper and that it was mostly drowned out by the patter, splash, and gurgle of the rain. He tried again.

"I think he's delirious," the big man said.

I'm not delirious, damn it, just weak, Whitney tried to say. But no words came from him at all this time, which scared him.

"It's Gavis," the smaller man said, studying the driver's license in Whitney's wallet. "Shadway's friend. The man Teddy Bertlesman told us about."

"He's in a bad way, Julio."

"You've got to take him in the car and get him to a hospital."

"Me?" the bigger man said. "What about you?"

"I'll be all right here."

"You can't go in alone," the big man said, his face carved by lines of worry and bejeweled with rain.

"Reese, there's not going to be trouble here," the smaller man said. "It's only Shadway and Mrs. Leben. They're no danger to me."

"Bullshit," the bigger man said. "Julio, there's someone else. Neither Shadway nor Mrs. Leben did this to Gavis."

"*Leben!*" Whitney managed to expel the name loud enough for it to carry above the sound of the rain.

The two men looked at him, puzzled.

"Leben," he managed again.

"Eric Leben?" Julio asked.

"Yes," Whitney breathed. "Genetic . . . chaos . . . chaos, mutation . . . guns . . . guns . . . "

"What about guns?" the bigger man—Reese—asked.

" . . . won't . . . stop . . . him," Whitney finished, exhausted.

"Get him into the car, Reese," Julio said. "If he isn't in a hospital in ten or fifteen minutes, he's not going to make it."

"What's he mean that guns won't stop Leben?" Reese asked.

"He's delirious," Julio said. "Now *move!*"

Frowning, Reese scooped Whitney up as easily as a father might lift a small child.

The one named Julio hurried ahead, splashing through puddles of dirty water, and opened the back door of their car.

Reese maneuvered Whitney gently onto the seat, then turned to Julio. "I don't like this."

"Just go," Julio said.

"I swore I'd never cut and run on you, that I'd always be there when you needed me, any way you needed me, no matter what."

"Right now," Julio said sharply, "I need you to take this man to a hospital." He slammed the rear door.

A moment later, Reese opened the front door and got in behind the wheel. To Julio, he said, "I'll be back as soon as I can."

Lying on the rear seat, Whitney said, "Chaos . . . chaos . . . chaos . . . chaos." He was trying to say a lot of other things, convey a more specific warning, but only that one word would come out.

Then the car began to move.

■ Peake had pulled to the side of Tropicana Boulevard and had switched off the headlights when Hagerstrom and Verdad had coasted to a stop along the shoulder about a quarter of a mile ahead.

Leaning forward, squinting through the smeary windshield past the monotonously thumping wipers, Sharp twice rubbed a stubborn patch of condensation from the glass and at last said, "Looks like . . . they've found someone lying in front of that place. What *is* that place?"

"Seems like it's out of business, a deserted motel," Peake said. "Can't quite read that old sign from here. Golden . . . something."

"What're they doing here?" Sharp wondered.

What am I doing here? Peake wondered silently.

"Could this be where Shadway and the Leben bitch are hiding out?" Sharp wondered.

Dear God, I hope not, Peake thought. I hope we never find them. I hope they're on a beach in Tahiti.

"Whoever those bastards have found," Sharp said, "they're putting him in their car."

Peake had given up all hope of becoming a legend. He had also given up all hope of becoming one of Anson Sharp's favorite agents. All he wanted was to get through this night alive, to prevent whatever killing he could, and to avoid humiliating himself.

■ At the side of the garage, the battered door cracked again, from top to bottom this time, and the jamb splintered, too, and one hinge tore loose, and the lock finally exploded, and everything crashed inward, and there was Leben, the beast, coming through like something that had broken out of a bad dream into the real world.

Ben grabbed the bucket—which was more than half full—and headed toward the kitchen door, trying to move fast without spilling any of the precious gasoline.

The creature saw him and let loose a shriek of such intense hatred and rage that the sound seemed to penetrate deep into Ben's bones and vibrate there. It kicked aside an outdoor vacuum cleaner and clambered over the piles of trash— including a fallen set of metal shelves—with arachnoid grace, as if it were an immense spider.

Entering the kitchen, Ben heard the thing close behind him. He dared not look back.

Half the cupboard doors and drawers were open, and just as Ben entered,

Rachael pulled out another drawer. She cried—"There!"—and snatched up a box of matches.

"Run!" Ben said. "Outside!"

They absolutely had to put more distance between themselves and the beast, gain time and room to pull the trick they had in mind.

He followed her out of the kitchen into the living room, and some of the gasoline slopped over the edge of the pail, spattering the carpet and his shoes.

Behind them, the mutant crashed through the kitchen, slamming shut cupboard doors, heaving aside the small kitchen table and chairs even though that furniture wasn't in its way, snarling and shrieking, apparently in the grip of a destructive frenzy.

Ben felt as if he were moving in slow motion, fighting his way through air as thick as syrup. The living room seemed as long as a football field. Then, finally nearing the end of the room, he was suddenly afraid that the door to the motel office was going to be locked, that they were going to be halted here, with no time or room to set fire to the beast, at least not without serious risk of immolating themselves in the process. Then Rachael threw open the door, and Ben almost shouted with relief. They rushed into the motel office, through the swinging gate in one end of the check-in counter, across the small public area, through the outer glass door, into the night beneath the breezeway—and nearly collided with Detective Verdad, whom they had last seen on Monday evening, at the morgue in Santa Ana.

"What in the name of God?" Verdad said as the beast shrieked in the motel office behind them.

Ben saw that the rain-soaked policeman had a revolver in his hand. He said, "Back off and shoot it when it comes through the door. You can't kill it, but maybe you can slow it down."

■ It wanted the female prey, it wanted blood, it was full of a cold rage, it was burning with hot desire, and it would not be stopped, not by guns or doors, not by anything, not until it had taken the female, buried its aching member inside her, not until it had killed both of them and fed upon them, it wanted to chew out their soft sweet eyes, bury its muzzle in their torn and spurting throats, it wanted to feed on the bloody pulsing muscle of their hearts, wanted to burrow through their eviscerated corpses in search of their rich livers and kidneys, it felt that overwhelming hunger beginning to grow within it again, the changefire within it needed more fuel, a mild hunger now but soon to get worse, like before, an all-consuming hunger that could not be denied, it needed *meat,* and it pushed through the glass door, out into the night wind and blowing rain, and there was another male, a smaller one, and fire flashed from something in the smaller male's hand, and a brief sharp pain stung its chest, and fire flashed again, and another pain, so it roared a furious challenge at its pathetic assailant—

■ Just this morning, when he had been at the library doing research related to the unofficial investigation he intended to conduct with Reese, Julio had read several magazine and journal articles Eric Leben had written about genetic engineering and about the prospects for the success of life extension by means of genetic manipulation. Later, he had spoken with Dr. Easton Solberg at UCI,

had done a lot of thinking since then, and had just heard Whitney Gavis's disjointed ramblings about genetic chaos and mutation. He was not a stupid man,
so when he saw the nightmare creature that followed Shadway and Mrs. Leben
out of the motel office, he quickly determined that something had gone terribly
wrong with Eric Leben's experiment and that this monstrosity was, in fact, the
scientist himself.

As Julio unhesitatingly opened fire on the creature, Mrs. Leben and Shadway—
who, judging from the smell of it, was carrying a bucket full of gasoline—hurried
from beneath the cover of the breezeway into the rainy courtyard. The first two
rounds did not faze the mutant, though it stopped for a moment as if baffled by
Julio's sudden and unexpected appearance. To his astonishment, he saw that he
might not be able to bring it down with the revolver.

It lurched forward, hissing, and swung one multiple-jointed arm at him as if to
knock his head off his shoulders.

Julio barely ducked under the blow, felt the arm brush through his hair, and
fired up into the beast's chest, which bristled with spines and strangely shaped
lumps of tissue. If it embraced him, he would be impaled upon those breast spikes,
and that realization brought his finger to bear upon the trigger again and again.

Those three shots finally drove the thing backward until it collided with the
wall by the office door, where it stood for a moment, clawing at the air.

Julio fired the sixth and final round in the revolver, hitting his target again, but
still it remained standing—hurt and maybe even dazed, but standing. He always
carried a few extra cartridges in his jacket pocket, even though he had never before
needed spare rounds in all his years of police work, and now he fumbled for them.

The creature shoved away from the motel wall, apparently having already re-
cuperated from the six rounds it had just taken. It cut loose a cry so savage and
furious that Julio turned away from it at once and ran into the courtyard, where
Shadway and Mrs. Leben were standing at the far end of the swimming pool.

■ Peake had hoped that Sharp would send him off after Hagerstrom and the
unknown man that the cop had loaded into the back seat of the rental car.
Then, if shooting took place at the abandoned motel, it would be entirely Sharp's
responsibility.

But Sharp said, "Let Hagerstrom go. Looks to me like he's taking that guy to a
doctor. Anyway, Verdad is the real brains of the team. If Verdad's staying here,
then this is where the action is; this is where we'll find Shadway and the woman."

When Lieutenant Verdad headed back along the motel driveway toward the
lighted office, Sharp told Peake to pull down there and park in front of the place.
By the time they stopped again on the shoulder of the boulevard in front of the
dilapidated sign—GOLDEN SAND INN—they heard the first gunshots.

Oh, hell, Peake thought miserably.

■ Lieutenant Verdad stood on one side of Benny, hastily reloading his revolver.

Rachael stood on the other side, sheltering the box of wooden matches from
the relentless rain. She had withdrawn one match and had been holding it and
the box in her cupped hands, silently cursing the wind and water that would try
to extinguish the flame the moment it was struck.

From the front of the motel courtyard, backlit by the amber light spilling through the office windows, the Eric-thing approached in that frighteningly swift, darkly graceful stride that seemed entirely at odds with its size and with its cumbersome, gnarled appearance. It emitted a shrill, ululant cry as it raced toward them. Clearly, it had no fear.

Rachael was afraid that its reckless advance was justified, that the fire would do it no more damage than the bullets.

It was already halfway along the forty-foot length of the pool. When it reached the end, it would only have to turn the corner and come another fifteen feet before it would be upon them.

The lieutenant had not finished reloading his revolver, but he snapped the cylinder into place anyway, apparently deciding that he didn't have time to slip the last two cartridges into their chambers.

The beast reached the corner of the pool.

Benny gripped the bucket of gasoline with both hands, one on the rim and the other on the bottom. He swung it back at his side, brought it forward, and threw the contents all over the face and chest of the mutant as it leaped across the last fifteen feet of concrete decking.

■ At a run, Peake followed Sharp past the motel office and into the courtyard just in time to see Shadway throw a bucket full of something into the face of—

Of what? Christ, what *was* that thing?

Sharp, too, halted in amazement.

The creature screamed in fury and staggered back from Shadway. It wiped at its monstrous face—Peake saw eyes that glowed orange like a pair of hot coals—and pawed at its chest, trying to remove whatever Shadway had thrown on it.

"Leben," Sharp said. "Holy shit, it must be Leben."

Jerry Peake understood at once, even though he didn't *want* to understand, did not want to know, for this was a secret that it would be dangerous to know, dangerous not only to his physical well-being but to his sanity.

■ The gasoline seemed to have choked and temporarily blinded it, but Rachael
   knew that it would recover from this assault as quickly as it had recovered from being shot. So, as Benny dropped the empty bucket and stepped out of the way, she struck the match and only then realized she should have had a torch, something she could have set aflame and then thrown at the creature. Now she had no choice but to step in close with the short-stemmed match.

The Eric-thing had stopped shrieking and, temporarily overcome by the gasoline fumes, was hunched over, wheezing noisily, gasping for air.

She took only three steps toward it before the wind or the rain—or both—extinguished the match.

Making a strange terrified mewling that she could not control, she slid open the box, took out another match, and struck it. This time she had not even taken one step before the flame went out.

The demonic mutant seemed to be breathing easier, and it began to straighten up, raising its monstrous head again.

The rain, Rachael thought desperately, the rain is washing the gasoline off its body.

As she shakily withdrew a third match, Benny said, "Here," and he turned the empty bucket upright on the concrete at her feet.

She understood. She rasped the third match against the striking pad on the side of the box, couldn't get it to light.

The creature drew in a deep breath at last, another. Recovering, it shrieked at them.

She scraped the match against the box again and let out a cry of relief when the flame spurted up. The instant the match was lit, she dropped it straight into the bucket, and the residue of gasoline burst into flames.

Lieutenant Verdad, who had been waiting to do his part, stepped in fast and kicked the bucket at the Eric-thing.

The flaming pail struck one of the beast's jean-clad thighs, where some of the gasoline had landed when Benny had thrown it. The fire leaped out of the bucket onto the jeans and raced up over the creature's spiny chest, swiftly enveloped the misshapen head.

The fire did not stop it.

Screaming in pain, a pillar of flame, the thing nevertheless came forward faster than Rachael would have believed possible. In the red-orange light of the leaping fire, she saw its outreaching hands, saw what appeared to be *mouths* in the palms, and then it had its hands on her. Hell could be no worse than having those hands on her; she almost died right there from the horror of it. The thing seized her by one arm and by the neck, and she felt those orifices within its hands eating into her flesh, and she felt the fire reaching out for her, and she saw the spikes on the mutant's huge chest where she could be so quickly and easily impaled—a multitude of possible deaths—and now it lifted her, and she knew she was certainly dead, finished, but Verdad appeared and opened fire with his revolver, squeezing off two shots that hit the Eric-thing in the head, but even before he could pull off a third shot, Benny came in at a flying leap, in some crazy karate movement, airborne, driving both feet into the monster's shoulder, and Rachael felt it let go of her with one hand, so she wrenched and kicked at its flaming chest, and suddenly she was free, the creature was toppling into the shallow end of the empty swimming pool, she fell to the concrete decking, free, free—except that her shoes were on fire.

■ Ben delivered the kick and threw himself to the left, hit the decking, rolled, and came immediately onto his feet in time to see the creature falling into the shallow end of the empty pool. He also saw that Rachael's shoes were afire from gasoline, and he dove for her, threw himself upon her, and smothered the flames.

For a moment, she clung fiercely to him, and he held her tightly with an equal need of reassurance. He had never before felt anything half as good as her heart's frantic pounding, which was conveyed through her breast to his.

"Are you all right?"

"Good enough," she said shakily.

He hugged her again, then gave her a quick examination. There was a bleeding circlet on her arm and another on her neck, where the mouths in the mutant's hands had attached themselves to her, but neither wound looked serious.

In the pool, the creature was screaming in a way it had not screamed before, and Ben was sure that these must be its death cries—although he would not have taken any bets on it.

Together, with his arm around her waist and her arm encircling him, they went to the edge of the pool, where Lieutenant Verdad was already standing.

Burning as if it were made of the purest candle tallow, the beast staggered down the sloping floor of the pool, perhaps trying to reach the collected rainwater at the deep end. But the falling rain did nothing to quench the flames, and Ben suspected that the puddle below would be equally ineffective. The fire was inexplicably intense, as if the gasoline were not the only fuel, as if something in the mutant's body chemistry were also feeding the flames. At the halfway point, the creature collapsed onto its knees, clawing at the air and then at the wet concrete before it. It continued to the bottom, crawling, then slithering along on its belly, finally dragging itself laboriously toward hoped-for salvation.

■ The shadowfire burned within the water, down under the cooling surface, and he was drawn toward it, not merely to extinguish the flames that were consuming his body but to snuff out the changefire within him, too. The unbearable pain of immolation had jolted what remained of his human consciousness, had bestirred him from the trancelike state into which he had retreated when the savage alien part of him had gained dominance. For a moment he knew who he was, what he had become, and what was happening to him. But he also knew that the knowledge was tenuous, that awareness would fade, that the small remaining portion of his intellect and personality would eventually be completely destroyed in the process of growth and change, and that the only hope for him was death.

Death.

He had striven hard to avoid death, had taken insane risks to save himself from the grave, but now he welcomed Charon.

Eaten alive by fire, he dragged himself down, down toward the shadowfire beneath the water, the strange fire burning on a far shore.

He stopped screaming. He had traveled beyond pain and terror, into a great lonely calm.

He knew that the flaming gasoline would not kill him, not that alone. The changefire within him was worse than the external fire. The changefire was blazing very brightly now, burning in every cell, *raging,* and he was overwhelmed by a painful hunger a thousand times more demanding and excruciating than any he had known before. He was desperate for fuel, for carbohydrates and proteins and vitamins and minerals with which to support his uncontrolled metabolism. But because he was in no condition to stalk and kill and feed, he could not provide his system with the fuel it needed. Therefore, his body started to cannibalize itself; the changefire did not subside but began to burn up some of his tissues in order to obtain the enormous amounts of energy required to transform those tissues that it did *not* consume as fuel. Second by second, his body weight rapidly declined, not because the gasoline was feeding on it but because *he* was feeding on himself, devouring himself from within. He felt his head changing shape, felt his arms shrinking and a second pair of arms extruding from his lower rib cage. Each change consumed more of him, yet the fires of mutation did not subside.

At last he could not pull himself any closer to the shadowfire that burned beneath the water. He stopped and lay still, choking and twitching.

But to his surprise, he saw the shadowfire rise out of the water ahead. It moved toward him until it encircled him, until his world was all aflame, inside and out.

In his dying agony, Eric finally understood that the mysterious shadowfires had been neither gateways to hell nor merely meaningless illusions generated by misfiring synapses in the brain. They were illusions, yes. Or, more accurately, they were hallucinations cast off by his subconscious, meant to warn him of the terrible destiny toward which he had been plunging ever since he had arisen from that slab in the morgue. His damaged brain had functioned too poorly for him to grasp the logical progression of his fate, at least on a conscious level. But his subconscious mind had known the truth and had tried to provide clues by creating the phantom shadowfires: *fire* (his subconscious had been telling him), fire is your destiny, the insatiable inner fire of a superheated metabolism, and sooner or later it is going to burn you up alive.

His neck dwindled until his head sat almost directly upon his shoulders.

He felt his spine lengthening into a tail.

His eyes sank back under a suddenly more massive brow.

He sensed that he had more than two legs.

Then he sensed nothing at all as the changefire swept through him, consuming the last fuel it could find. He descended into the many kinds of fire.

■   Before Ben's eyes, in only a minute or less, the creature burned—the flames leaped high into the air, seethed, *roared*—until there was nothing left of the corpse but a small bubbling pool of sludge, a few little flickering flames down there in the darkness that reclaimed the empty swimming pool. Uncomprehending, Ben stood in silence, unable to speak. Lieutenant Verdad and Rachael seemed equally amazed, for they did not break the silence, either.

It was broken, at last, by Anson Sharp. He was coming slowly around the edge of the pool. He had a gun, and he looked as if he would use it. "What the hell happened to him? What the *hell*?"

Startled, not having seen the DSA agents until now, Ben stared at his old enemy and said, "Same thing that's going to happen to you, Sharp. He did to himself what you'll do to yourself sooner or later, though in a different way."

"What're you talking about?" Sharp demanded.

Holding Rachael and trying to ease his body between her and Sharp, Ben said, "He didn't like the world the way he found it, so he set out to make it conform to his own twisted expectations. But instead of making a paradise for himself, he made a living hell. It's what you'll make for yourself, given time."

"Shit," Anson Sharp said, "you've gone off the deep end, Shadway. Way off the deep end." To Verdad, he said, "Lieutenant, please put down your revolver."

Verdad said, "What? What're you talking about? I—"

Sharp shot Verdad, and the detective was flung off the concrete into the mud by the impact of the bullet.

■ Jerry Peake—a devoted reader of mysteries, given to dreams of legendary achievement—had a habit of thinking in melodramatic terms. Watching Eric Leben's monstrously mutated body burning away to nothing in the empty swimming pool, he was shocked, horrified, and frightened; but he was also thinking at an unusually furious pace for him. First, he made a mental list of the similarities between Eric Leben and Anson Sharp: They loved power, thrived on it; they were cold-blooded and capable of anything; they had a perverse taste for young girls . . . Then Jerry listened to what Ben Shadway said about how a man could make his own hell on earth, and he thought about that, too. Then he looked down at the smoldering remnants of the mutant Leben, and it seemed to him that he was at a crossroads between his own earthly paradise and hell: He could cooperate with Sharp, let murder be done, and live with the guilt forever, damned in this life as well as in the next; *or* he could resist Sharp, retain his integrity and self-respect, and feel good about himself no matter what happened to his career in the DSA. The choice was his. Which did he want to be—the thing down there in the pool or a *man?*

Sharp ordered Lieutenant Verdad to put down the gun, and Verdad began to question the order, and Sharp shot him, just shot him, with no argument or hesitation.

So Jerry Peake drew his own gun and shot Sharp. The slug hit the deputy director in the shoulder.

Sharp seemed to have sensed the impending betrayal, because he had started to turn toward Jerry even as Jerry shot him. He squeezed off a round of his own, and Jerry took the bullet in the leg, though he fired simultaneously. As he fell, he had the enormous pleasure of seeing Anson Sharp's head explode.

■ Rachael stripped the jacket and shirt off Lieutenant Verdad and examined the bullet wound in his shoulder.

"I'll live," he said. "It hurts like the devil, but I'll live."

In the distance, the mournful sound of sirens arose, drawing rapidly nearer.

"That'll be Reese's doing," Verdad said. "As soon as he got Gavis to the hospital, he'll have called the locals."

"There really isn't too much bleeding," she said, relieved to be able to confirm his own assessment of his condition.

"I told you," Verdad said. "Heck, I can't die. I intend to stay around long enough to see my partner marry the pink lady." He laughed at her puzzlement and said, "Don't worry, Mrs. Leben. I'm not out of my head."

■ Peake was flat on his back on the concrete decking, his head raised somewhat on the hard pillow of the pool coping.

With a wide strip of his own torn shirt, Ben had fashioned a tourniquet for Peake's leg. The only thing he could find to twist it with was the barrel of Anson Sharp's discarded, silencer-equipped pistol, which was perfect for the job.

"I don't think you really need a tourniquet," he told Peake as the sirens drew steadily nearer, gradually overwhelming the patter of the rain, "but better safe than sorry. There's a lot of blood, but I didn't see any spurting, no torn artery. Must hurt like the devil, though."

"Funny," Peake said, "but it doesn't hurt much at all."

"Shock," Ben said worriedly.

"No," Peake said, shaking his head. "No, I don't think I'm going into shock. I've got none of the symptoms—and I know them. You know what I think maybe it is?"

"What?"

"What I just did—shooting my own boss when he went bad—is going to make me a legend in the agency. Damned if it isn't. I didn't see it that way until he was dead. So, anyway, maybe a legend just doesn't feel pain as much as other people do." He grinned at Ben.

Ben returned a frown for the grin. "Relax. Just try to relax—"

Jerry Peake laughed. "I'm not delirious, Mr. Shadway. Really, I'm not. Don't you see? Not only am I a legend, but I can still laugh at myself! Which means that maybe I really do have what it takes. I mean, see, maybe I can make a big reputation for myself and not let it go to my head. Isn't that a nice thing to learn about yourself?"

"It's a nice thing," Ben agreed.

The night was filled with screaming sirens, then the bark of brakes, and then the sirens died as running footsteps sounded on the motel driveway.

■   Soon there would be questions—thousands of them—from police officers in Las Vegas, Palm Springs, Lake Arrowhead, Santa Ana, Placentia, and other places.

Following that ordeal, the media would have questions of their own. ("How do you *feel*, Mrs. Leben? Please? How do you *feel* about your husband's murderous spree, about nearly dying at his hands, how do you *feel*?") They would be even more persistent than the police—and far less courteous.

But now, as Jerry Peake and Julio Verdad were loaded into the paramedics' van and as the uniformed Las Vegas officers kept a watch on Sharp's corpse to make certain no one touched it before the police coroner arrived, Rachael and Ben had a moment together, just the two of them. Detective Hagerstrom had reported that Whitney Gavis had made it to the hospital in time and was going to pull through, and now he was getting into the emergency van with Julio Verdad. They were blessedly alone. They stood under the promenade awning, holding each other, neither of them speaking at first. Then they seemed to realize simultaneously that they would not be alone together again for long, frustrating hours, and they both tried to speak at once.

"You first," he said, holding her almost at arm's length, looking into her eyes.

"No, you. What were you going to say?"

"I was wondering . . . "

"What?"

" . . . if you remembered."

"Ah," she said because she knew instinctively what he meant.

"When we stopped along the road to Palm Springs," he said.

"I remember," she said.

"I proposed."

"Yes."

"Marriage."

"Yes."

"I've never done that before."

"I'm glad."

"It wasn't very romantic, was it?"

"You did just fine," she said. "Is the offer still open?"

"Yes. Is it still appealing?"

"Immensely appealing," she said.

He pulled her close again.

She put her arms around him, and she felt protected, yet suddenly a shiver passed through her.

"It's all right," he said. "It's over."

"Yeah, it's over," she said, putting her head against his chest. "We'll go back to Orange County, where it's always summer, and we'll get married, and I'll start collecting trains with you. I think I could get *into* trains, you know? We'll listen to old swing music, and we'll watch old movies on the VCR, and together we'll make a better world for ourselves, won't we?"

"We'll make a better world," he agreed softly. "But not that way. Not by hiding from the world as it really is. Together, we don't need to hide. Together, we've got the power, don't you think?"

"I don't think," she said. "I *know.*"

The rain had tailed off to a light drizzle. The storm was moving eastward, and the mad voice of the wind was stilled for now.

MIDNIGHT

To Ed and Pat Thomas
of the Book Carnival,
who are such nice people
that sometimes I suspect
they're not really human
but aliens from
another, better world

ALONG THE NIGHT COAST

Where eerie figures caper

to some midnight music

that only they can hear.

— THE BOOK OF COUNTED SORROWS

1

JANICE CAPSHAW LIKED TO RUN AT NIGHT.

Nearly every evening between ten and eleven o'clock, Janice put on her gray sweats with the reflective blue stripes across the back and chest, tucked her hair under a headband, laced up her New Balance shoes, and ran six miles. She was thirty-five but could have passed for twenty-five, and she attributed her glow of youth to her twenty-year-long commitment to running.

Sunday night, September 21, she left her house at ten o'clock and ran four blocks north to Ocean Avenue, the main street through Moonlight Cove, where she turned left and headed downhill toward the public beach. The shops were closed and dark. Aside from the faded-brass glow of the sodium-vapor streetlamps, the only lights were in some apartments above the stores, at Knight's Bridge Tavern, and at Our Lady of Mercy Catholic Church, which was open twenty-four hours a day. No cars were on the street, and not another person was in sight. Moonlight Cove always had been a quiet little town, shunning the tourist trade that other coastal communities so avidly pursued. Janice liked the slow, measured pace of life there, though sometimes lately the town seemed not merely sleepy but dead.

As she ran down the sloping main street, through pools of amber light, through layered night shadows cast by wind-sculpted cypresses and pines, she saw no movement other than her own—and the sluggish, serpentine advance of the thin fog through the windless air. The only sounds were the soft *slap-slap* of her rubber-soled running shoes on the sidewalk and her labored breathing. From all available evidence, she might have been the last person on earth, engaged upon a solitary post-Armageddon marathon.

She disliked getting up at dawn to run before work, and in the summer it was more pleasant to put in her six miles when the heat of the day had passed, though neither an abhorrence of early hours nor the heat was the real reason for her nocturnal preference; she ran on the same schedule in the winter. She exercised at that hour simply because she liked the night.

Even as a child, she had preferred night to day, had enjoyed sitting out in the yard after sunset, under the star-speckled sky, listening to frogs and crickets. Darkness soothed. It softened the sharp edges of the world, toned down the too-harsh colors. With the coming of twilight, the sky seemed to recede; the universe expanded. The night was *bigger* than the day, and in its realm, life seemed to have more possibilities.

Now she reached the Ocean Avenue loop at the foot of the hill, sprinted across the parking area and onto the beach. Above the thin fog, the sky held only scattered clouds, and the full moon's silver-yellow radiance penetrated the mist, providing sufficient illumination for her to see where she was going. Some nights the fog was too thick and the sky too overcast to permit running on the shore. But now the white foam of the incoming breakers surged out of the black sea in ghostly phosphorescent ranks, and the wide crescent of sand gleamed palely between the lapping tide and the coastal hills, and the mist itself was softly aglow with reflections of the autumn moonlight.

As she ran across the beach to the firmer, damp sand at the water's edge and turned south, intending to run a mile out to the point of the cove, Janice felt wonderfully alive.

Richard—her late husband, who had succumbed to cancer three years ago— had said that her circadian rhythms were so post-midnight focused that she was more than just a night person. "You'd probably love being a vampire, living between sunset and dawn," he'd said, and she'd said, "I vant to suck your blood." God, she had loved him. Initially she worried that the life of a Lutheran minister's wife would be boring, but it never was, not for a moment. Three years after his death, she still missed him every day—and even more at night. He had been—

Suddenly, as she was passing a pair of forty-foot, twisted cypresses that had grown in the middle of the beach, halfway between the hills and the waterline, Janice was sure that she was not alone in the night and fog. She saw no movement, and she was unaware of any sound other than her own footsteps, raspy breathing, and thudding heartbeat; only instinct told her that she had company.

She was not alarmed at first, for she thought another runner was sharing the beach. A few local fitness fanatics occasionally ran at night, not by choice, as was the case with her, but of necessity. Two or three times a month she encountered them along her route.

But when she stopped and turned and looked back the way she had come, she saw only a deserted expanse of moonlit sand, a curved ribbon of luminously foaming surf, and the dim but familiar shapes of rock formations and scattered trees that thrust up here and there along the strand. The only sound was the low rumble of the breakers.

Figuring that her instinct was unreliable and that she was alone, she headed south again, along the beach, quickly finding her rhythm. She went only fifty yards, however, before she saw movement from the corner of her eye, thirty feet to her left: a swift shape, cloaked by night and mist, darting from behind a sand-bound cypress to a weather-polished rock formation, where it slipped out of sight again.

Janice halted and, squinting toward the rock, wondered what she had glimpsed. It had seemed larger than a dog, perhaps as big as a man, but having seen it only peripherally, she had absorbed no details. The formation—twenty feet long, as low as four feet in some places and as high as ten feet in others—had been shaped by wind and rain until it resembled a mound of half-melted wax, more than large enough to conceal whatever she had seen.

"Someone there?" she asked.

She expected no answer and got none.

She was uneasy but not afraid. If she had seen something more than a trick of fog and moonlight, it surely had been an animal—and not a dog because a dog would have come straight to her and would not have been so secretive. As there were no natural predators along the coast worthy of her fear, she was curious rather than frightened.

Standing still, sheathed in a film of sweat, she began to feel the chill in the air. To maintain high body heat, she ran in place, watching the rocks, expecting to see an animal break from that cover and sprint either north or south along the beach.

Some people in the area kept horses, and the Fosters even ran a breeding and boarding facility near the sea about two and a half miles from there, beyond the northern flank of the cove. Perhaps one of their charges had gotten loose. The thing she'd seen from the corner of her eye had not been as big as a horse, though it might have been a pony. On the other hand, wouldn't she have heard a pony's thudding hoofbeats even in the soft sand? Of course, if it was one of the Fosters' horses—or someone else's—she ought to attempt to recover it or at least let them know where it could be found.

At last, when nothing moved, she ran to the rocks and circled them. Against the base of the formation and within the clefts in the stone were a few velvet-smooth shadows, but for the most part all was revealed in the milky, shimmering, lunar glow, and no animal was concealed there.

She never gave serious thought to the possibility that she had seen someone other than another runner or an animal, that she was in real danger. Aside from an occasional act of vandalism or burglary—which was always the work of one of a handful of disaffected teenagers—and traffic accidents, local police had little to occupy them. Crimes against person—rape, assault, murder—were rare in a town as small and tightly knit as Moonlight Cove; it was almost as if, in this pocket of the coast, they were living in a different and more benign age from that in which the rest of California dwelt.

Rounding the formation and returning to the firmer sand near the roiling surf, Janice decided that she had been snookered by moonlight and mist, two adept deceivers. The movement had been imaginary; she was alone on the shore.

She noted that the fog was rapidly thickening, but she continued along the crescent beach toward the cove's southern point. She was certain that she would get there and be able to return to the foot of Ocean Avenue before visibility declined too drastically.

A breeze sprang up from the sea and churned the incoming fog, which seemed to solidify from a gauzy vapor into a white sludge, as if it were milk being transformed into butter. By the time Janice reached the southern end of the dwindling strand, the breeze was stiffening and the surf was more agitated as well, casting up sheets of spray as each wave hit the piled rocks of the man-made breakwater that had been added to the natural point of the cove.

Someone stood on that twenty-foot-high wall of boulders, looking down at her. Janice glanced up just as a cloak of mist shifted and as moonlight silhouetted him.

Now fear seized her.

Though the stranger was directly in front of her, she could not see his face in the gloom. He seemed tall, well over six feet, though that could have been a trick of perspective.

Other than his outline, only his eyes were visible, and they were what ignited her fear. They were a softly radiant amber like the eyes of an animal revealed in headlight beams.

For a moment, peering directly up at him, she was transfixed by his gaze. Backlit by the moon, looming above her, standing tall and motionless upon ramparts of rock, with sea spray exploding to the right of him, he might have been a carved stone idol with luminous jewel eyes, erected by some demon-worshiping cult in a dark age long passed. Janice wanted to turn and run, but she could not move, was rooted to the sand, in the grip of that paralytic terror she had previously felt only in nightmares.

She wondered if she were awake. Perhaps her late-night run was indeed part of a nightmare, and perhaps she was actually asleep in bed, safe beneath warm blankets.

Then the man made a queer low growl, partly a snarl of anger but also a hiss, partly a hot and urgent cry of need but also cold, cold.

And he moved.

He dropped to all fours and began to descend the high breakwater, not as an ordinary man would climb down those jumbled rocks but with catlike swiftness and grace. In seconds he would be upon her.

Janice broke her paralysis, turned back on her own tracks, and ran toward the entrance to the public beach—a full mile away. Houses with lighted windows stood atop the steep-walled bluff that overlooked the cove, and some of them had steps leading down to the beach, but she was not confident of finding those stairs in the darkness. She did not waste any energy on a scream, for she doubted anyone would hear her. Besides, if screaming slowed her down, even only slightly, she might be overtaken and silenced before anyone from town could respond to her cries.

Her twenty-year commitment to running had never been more important than it was now; the issue was no longer good health but, she sensed, her very survival. She tucked her arms close to her sides, lowered her head, and sprinted, going for speed rather than endurance, because she felt that she only needed to get to the lower block of Ocean Avenue to be safe. She did not believe the man—or whatever the hell he was—would continue to pursue her into that lamplit and populated street.

High-altitude, striated clouds rushed across a portion of the lunar face. The moonlight dimmed, brightened, dimmed, and brightened in an irregular rhythm, pulsing through the rapidly clotting fog in such a way as to create a host of phantoms that repeatedly startled her and appeared to be keeping pace with her on all sides. The eerie, palpitant light contributed to the dreamlike quality of the chase, and she was half convinced that she was really in bed, fast asleep, but she did not halt or look over her shoulder because, dream or not, the man with the amber eyes was still behind her.

She had covered half the strand between the point of the cove and Ocean Avenue, her confidence growing with each step, when she realized that two of the phantoms in the fog were not phantoms after all. One was about twenty feet to her right and ran erect like a man; the other was on her left, less than fifteen feet away, splashing through the edge of the foam-laced sea, loping on all fours, the size of a man but certainly not a man, for no man could be so fleet and graceful in the posture of a dog. She had only a general impression of their shape and size, and she could not see their faces or any details of them other than their oddly luminous eyes.

Somehow she knew that neither of these pursuers was the man whom she had seen on the breakwater. He was behind her, either running erect or loping on all fours. She was nearly encircled.

Janice made no attempt to imagine who or what they might be. Analysis of this weird experience would have to wait for later; now she simply accepted the existence of the impossible, for as the widow of a preacher and a deeply spiritual woman, she had the flexibility to bend with the unknown and unearthly when confronted by it.

Powered by the fear that had formerly paralyzed her, she picked up her pace. But so did her pursuers.

She heard a peculiar whimpering and only slowly realized that she was listening to her own tortured voice.

Evidently excited by her terror, the phantom forms around her began to keen. Their voices rose and fell, fluctuating between a shrill, protracted bleat and a guttural gnarl. Worst of all, punctuating those ululant cries were bursts of words, too, spoken raspily, urgently: *"Get the bitch, get the bitch, get the bitch . . . "*

What in God's name *were* they? Not men, surely, yet they could stand like men and speak like men, so what else could they *be* but men?

Janice felt her heart swelling in her breast, pounding hard.

"Get the bitch . . . "

The mysterious figures flanking her began to draw closer, and she tried to put on more speed to pull ahead of them, but they could not be shaken. They continued to narrow the gap. She could see them peripherally but did not dare look at them directly because she was afraid that the sight of them would be so shocking that she would be paralyzed again and, frozen by horror, would be brought down.

She was brought down anyway. Something leaped upon her from behind. She fell, a great weight pinning her, and all three creatures swarmed over her, touching her, plucking and tugging at her clothes.

Clouds slipped across most of the moon this time, and shadows fell in as if they were swatches of a black cloth sky.

Janice's face was pressed hard into the damp sand, but her head was turned to one side, so her mouth was free, and she screamed at last, though it was not much of a scream because she was breathless. She thrashed, kicked, flailed with her hands, desperately trying to strike them, but hitting mostly air and sand.

She could see nothing now, for the moon was completely lost.

She heard fabric tearing. The man astride her tore off her Nike jacket, ripped it to pieces, gouging her flesh in the process. She felt the hot touch of a hand, which seemed rough but human.

His weight briefly lifted from her, and she wriggled forward, trying to get away, but they pounced and crushed her into the sand. This time she was at the surf line, her face in the water.

Alternately keening, panting like dogs, hissing and snarling, her attackers loosed frantic bursts of words as they grabbed at her:

" . . . *get her, get her, get, get, get . . .* "

" . . . *want, want, want it, want it . . .* "

" . . . *now, now, quick, now, quick, quick, quick . . .* "

They were pulling at her sweat pants, trying to strip her, but she wasn't sure if they wanted to rape or devour her; perhaps neither; what they wanted was, in fact, beyond her comprehension. She just knew they were overcome by some tremendously powerful urge, for the chilly air was as thick with their *need* as with fog and darkness.

One of them pushed her face deeper into the wet sand, and the water was all around her now, only inches deep but enough to drown her, and they wouldn't let her breathe. She knew she was going to die, she was pinned now and helpless, going to die, and all because she liked to run at night.

2

ON MONDAY, OCTOBER 13, TWENTY-TWO DAYS AFTER THE death of Janice Capshaw, Sam Booker drove his rental car from the San Francisco International Airport to Moonlight Cove. During the trip, he played a grim yet darkly amusing game with himself, making a mental list of reasons to go on living. Although he was on the road for more than an hour and a half, he could think of only four things: Guinness Stout, really good Mexican food, Goldie Hawn, and fear of death.

That thick, dark, Irish brew never failed to please him and to provide a brief surcease from the sorrows of the world. Restaurants consistently serving first-rate Mexican food were more difficult to locate than Guinness; its solace was therefore more elusive. Sam had long been in love with Goldie Hawn—or the screen image she projected—because she was beautiful *and* cute, earthy and intelligent, and seemed to find life so much damn fun. His chances of meeting Goldie Hawn were about a million times worse than finding a great Mexican restaurant in a northern California coastal town like Moonlight Cove, so he was glad that she was not the *only* reason he had for living.

As he drew near his destination, tall pines and cypresses crowded Highway 1, forming a gray-green tunnel, casting long shadows in the late-afternoon light. The day was cloudless yet strangely forbidding; the sky was pale blue, bleak in spite of its crystalline clarity, unlike the tropical blue to which he was accustomed in Los Angeles. Though the temperature was in the fifties, hard sunshine, like glare bouncing off a field of ice, seemed to freeze the colors of the landscape and dull them with a haze of imitation frost.

Fear of death. That was the best reason on his list. Though he was just forty-two years old—five feet eleven, a hundred and seventy pounds, and currently healthy—Sam Booker had skated along the edge of death six times, had peered into the waters below, and had not found the plunge inviting.

A road sign appeared on the right side of the highway: OCEAN AVENUE, MOON-LIGHT COVE, 2 MILES.

Sam was not afraid of the pain of dying, for that would pass in a flicker. Neither was he afraid of leaving his life unfinished; for several years he had harbored no goals or hopes or dreams, so there was nothing to finish, no purpose or meaning. But he *was* afraid of what lay beyond life.

Five years ago, more dead than alive on an operating-room table, he had undergone a near-death experience. While surgeons worked frantically to save him, he had risen out of his body and, from the ceiling, looked down on his carcass and the medical team surrounding it. Then suddenly he'd found himself rushing through a tunnel, toward dazzling light, toward the Other Side: the entire near-death cliché that was a staple of sensationalistic supermarket tabloids. At the penultimate moment, the skillful physicians had pulled him back into the land of the living, but not before he had been afforded a glimpse of what lay beyond the mouth of that tunnel. What he'd seen had scared the crap out of him. Life, though often cruel, was preferable to confronting what he now suspected lay beyond it.

He reached the Ocean Avenue exit. At the bottom of the ramp, as Ocean Avenue turned west, under Pacific Coast Highway, another sign read: MOONLIGHT COVE ½ MILE.

A few houses were tucked in the purple gloom among the trees on both sides of the two-lane blacktop; their windows glowed with soft yellow light even an hour before nightfall. Some were of that half-timbered, deep-eaved, Bavarian architecture that a few builders, in the 1940s and '50s, had mistakenly believed was in harmony with the northern California coast. Others were Monterey-style bungalows with white clapboard or shingle-covered walls, cedar-shingled roofs, and rich—if fairy-tale rococo—architectural details. Since Moonlight Cove had enjoyed much of its growth in the past ten years, a large number of houses were sleek, modern, many-windowed structures that looked like ships tossed up on some unimaginably high tide, stranded now on these hillsides above the sea.

When Sam followed Ocean Avenue into the six-block-long commercial district, a peculiar sense of *wrongness* immediately overcame him. Shops, restaurants, taverns, a market, two churches, the town library, a movie theater, and other unremarkable establishments lined the main drag, which sloped down toward the ocean, but to Sam's eyes there was an indefinable though powerful strangeness about the community that gave him a chill.

He could not identify the reasons for his instant negative reaction to the place, though perhaps it was related to the somber interplay of light and shadow. At this dying end of the autumn day, in the cheerless sunlight, the gray stone Catholic church looked like an alien edifice of steel, erected for no human purpose. A white stucco liquor store gleamed as if built from time-bleached bones. Many shop windows were cataracted with ice-white reflections of the sun as it sought the horizon, as if painted to conceal the activities of those who worked beyond them. The shadows cast by the buildings, by the pines and cypress, were stark, spiky, razor-edged.

Sam braked at a stoplight at the third intersection, halfway through the commercial district. With no traffic behind him, he paused to study the people on the sidewalks. Not many were in sight, eight or ten, and they also struck him as wrong, though his reasons for thinking ill of them were less definable than those that formed his impression of the town itself. They walked briskly, purposefully, heads up, with a peculiar air of urgency that seemed unsuited to a lazy, seaside community of only three thousand souls.

He sighed and continued down Ocean Avenue, telling himself that his imagination was running wild. Moonlight Cove and the people in it probably would not have seemed the least unusual if he had just been passing by on a long trip and turned off the coast highway only to have dinner at a local restaurant. Instead, he had arrived with the knowledge that something was rotten there, so of course he saw ominous signs in a perfectly innocent scene.

At least that was what he told himself. But he knew better.

He had come to Moonlight Cove because people had died there, because the official explanations for their deaths were suspicious, and he had a hunch that the truth, once uncovered, would be unusually disturbing. Over the years he had learned to trust his hunches; that trust had kept him alive.

He parked the rented Ford in front of a gift shop.

To the west, at the far end of a slate-gray sea, the anemic sun sank through a sky that was slowly turning muddy red. Serpentine tendrils of fog began to rise off the choppy water.

3

IN THE PANTRY OFF THE KITCHEN, SITTING ON THE FLOOR WITH her back against a shelf of canned goods, Chrissie Foster looked at her watch. In the harsh light of the single bare bulb in the ceiling socket, she saw that she had been locked in that small, windowless chamber for nearly nine hours. She had received the wristwatch on her eleventh birthday, more than four months ago, and she had been thrilled by it because it was not a kid's watch with cartoon characters on the face; it was delicate, ladylike, gold-plated, with roman numerals instead of digits, a real Timex like her mother wore. Studying it, Chrissie was overcome by sadness. The watch represented a time of happiness and family togetherness that was lost forever.

Besides feeling sad, lonely, and a little restless from hours of captivity, she was scared. Of course, she was not as scared as she had been that morning, when her father had carried her through the house and thrown her into the pantry. Then, kicking and screaming, she had been *terrified* because of what she had seen. Because of what her parents had become. But that white-hot terror could not be sustained; gradually it subsided to a low-grade fever of fear that made her feel flushed and chilled at the same time, queasy, headachy, almost as if she were in the early stages of flu.

She wondered what they were going to do to her when they finally let her out of the pantry. Well, no, she didn't worry about what they were going to do, for she was pretty sure she already knew the answer to that one: They were going to change her into one of them. What she wondered about, actually, was how the change would be effected—and what, exactly, she would become. She knew that her mother and father were no longer ordinary people, that they were something else, but she had no words to describe what they had become.

Her fear was sharpened by the fact that she lacked the words to explain to herself what was happening in her own home, for she had always been in love with words and had faith in their power. She liked to read just about anything: poetry, short stories, novels, the daily newspaper, magazines, the backs of cereal boxes if nothing else was at hand. She was in sixth grade at school, but her teacher, Mrs. Tokawa, said she read at a tenth-grade level. When she was not reading, she was often writing stories of her own. Within the past year she had decided she was going to grow up to write novels like those of Mr. Paul Zindel or the sublimely silly Mr. Daniel Pinkwater or, best of all, those of Ms. Andre Norton.

But now words failed; her life was going to be far different from what she had imagined. She was frightened as much by the loss of the comfortable, bookish future she had foreseen as she was by the changes that had taken place in her parents. Eight months shy of her twelfth birthday, Chrissie had become acutely aware of life's uncertainty, grim knowledge for which she was ill prepared.

Not that she had already given up. She intended to fight. She was not going to let them change her without resistance. Soon after she had been thrown into the pantry, once her tears had dried, she had looked over the contents of the shelves, searching for a weapon. The pantry contained mostly canned, bottled, and packaged food, but there were also laundry and first-aid and handyman supplies. She had found the perfect thing: a small aerosol-spray can of WD-40, an oil-based lubricant. It was a third the size of an ordinary spray can, easily concealed. If she could surprise them, spray it in their eyes and temporarily blind them, she could make a break for freedom.

As though reading a newspaper headline, she said, "Ingenious Young Girl Saves Self with Ordinary Household Lubricant."

She held the WD-40 in both hands, taking comfort from it.

Now and then a vivid and unsettling memory recurred: her father's face as it had looked when he had thrown her into the pantry—red and swollen with anger, his eyes darkly ringed, nostrils flared, lips drawn back from his teeth in a feral snarl, every feature contorted with rage. "I'll be back for you," he had said, spraying spittle as he spoke. "I'll be back."

He slammed the door and braced it shut with a straight-backed kitchen chair that he wedged under the knob. Later, when the house fell silent and her parents seemed to have gone away, Chrissie had tried the door, pushing on it with all her might, but the tilted chair was an immovable barricade.

I'll be back for you. I'll be back.

His twisted face and bloodshot eyes had made her think of Mr. Robert Louis Stevenson's description of the murderous Hyde in the story of Dr. Jekyll, which she had read a few months ago. There was madness in her father; he was not the same man that he once had been.

More unsettling was the memory of what she had seen in the upstairs hall when she had returned home after missing the school bus and had surprised her parents. No. They were not really her parents any more. They were . . . something else.

She shuddered.

She clutched the can of WD-40.

Suddenly, for the first time in hours, she heard noise in the kitchen. The back door of the house opened. Footsteps. At least two, maybe three or four people.

"She's in there," her father said.

Chrissie's heart stuttered, then found a new and faster beat.

"This isn't going to be quick," said another man. Chrissie did not recognize his deep, slightly raspy voice. "You see, it's more complicated with a child. Shaddack's not sure we're even ready for the children yet. It's risky."

"She's got to be converted, Tucker." That was Chrissie's mother, Sharon, though she did not sound like herself. It was her voice, all right, but without its usual softness, without the natural, musical quality that had made it such a perfect voice for reading fairy tales.

"Of course, yes, she's got to be done," said the stranger, whose name was evidently Tucker. "I know that. Shaddack knows it too. He sent me here, didn't he? I'm just saying it might take more time than usual. We need a place where we can restrain her and watch over her during the conversion."

"Right here. Her bedroom upstairs."

Conversion?

Trembling, Chrissie got to her feet and stood facing the door.

With a scrape and clatter, the tilted chair was removed from under the knob.

She held the spray can in her right hand, down at her side and half behind her, with her forefinger on top of the nozzle.

The door opened, and her father looked in at her.

Alex Foster. Chrissie tried to think of him as Alex Foster, not as her father, just Alex Foster, but it was difficult to deny that in some ways he was still her dad. Besides, "Alex Foster" was no more accurate than "father" because he was someone altogether new.

His face was no longer warped with rage. He appeared more like himself: thick blond hair; a broad, pleasant face with bold features; a smattering of freckles across his cheeks and nose. Nevertheless, she could see a terrible difference in his eyes. He seemed to be filled with a strange urgency, an edgy tension. Hungry. Yes, that was it: Daddy seemed hungry . . . consumed by hunger, frantic with hunger, *starving* . . . but for something other than food. She did not understand his hunger but she sensed it, a fierce *need* that engendered a constant tension in his muscles, a need of such tremendous power, so hot, that waves of it seemed to rise from him like steam from boiling water.

He said, "Come out of there, Christine."

Chrissie let her shoulders sag, blinked as if repressing tears, exaggerated the shivers that swept through her, and tried to look small, frightened, defeated. Reluctantly she edged forward.

"Come on, come on," he said impatiently, motioning her out of the pantry.

Chrissie stepped through the doorway and saw her mother, who was beside and slightly behind Alex. Sharon was pretty—auburn hair, green eyes—but there was no softness or motherliness about her any more. She was hard looking and changed and full of the same barely contained nervous energy that filled her husband.

By the kitchen table stood a stranger in jeans and plaid hunting jacket. He was evidently the Tucker to whom her mother had spoken: tall, lean, all sharp edges and angles. His close-cropped black hair bristled. His dark eyes were set under a deep, bony brow; his sharply ridged nose was like a stone wedge driven into the center of his face; his mouth was a thin slash, and his jaws were as prominent as those of a predator that preyed on small animals and snapped them in half with one bite. He was holding a physician's black leather bag.

Her father reached for Chrissie as she came out of the pantry, and she whipped up the can of WD-40, spraying him in the eyes from a distance of less than two feet. Even as her father howled in pain and surprise, Chrissie turned and sprayed her mother, too, straight in the face. Half-blinded, they fumbled for her, but she slipped away from them and dashed across the kitchen.

Tucker was startled but managed to grab her by the arm.

She spun toward him and kicked him in the crotch.

He did not let go of her, but the strength went out of his big hands. She tore herself away from him and sprinted into the downstairs hallway.

4

FROM THE EAST, TWILIGHT DRIFTED DOWN ON MOONLIGHT Cove, as if it were a mist not of water but of smoky purple light. When Sam Booker got out of his car, the air was chilly; he was glad that he was wearing a wool sweater under his corduroy sportcoat. As a photocell activated all the streetlamps simultaneously, he strolled along Ocean Avenue, looking in shop windows, getting a feel for the town.

He knew that Moonlight Cove was prosperous, that unemployment was virtually nonexistent—thanks to New Wave Microtechnology, which had headquartered there ten years ago—yet he saw signs of a faltering economy. Taylor's Fine Gifts and Saenger's Jewelry had vacated their shops; through their dusty, plate-glass windows, he saw bare shelves and empty display cases and deep, still shadows. New Attitudes, a trendy clothing store, was having a going-out-of-business sale, and judging by the dearth of shoppers, their merchandise was moving sluggishly even at fifty to seventy percent off the original prices.

By the time he had walked two blocks west, to the beach end of town, crossed the street, and returned three blocks along the other side of Ocean Avenue to Knight's Bridge Tavern, twilight was swiftly waning. A nacreous fog was moving in from the sea, and the air itself seemed iridescent, shimmering delicately; a plum-colored haze lay over everything, except where the streetlamps cast showers of mist-softened yellow light, and above it all was a heavy darkness coming down.

A single moving car was in sight, three blocks away, and at the moment Sam was the only pedestrian. The solitude combined with the queer light of the dying day to give him the feeling that this was a ghost town, inhabited only by the dead. As the gradually thickening fog seeped up the hill from the Pacific, it contributed to the illusion that *all* of the surrounding shops were vacant, that they offered no wares other than spider webs, silence, and dust.

You're a dour bastard, he told himself. Too grim by half.

Experience had made a pessimist of him. The traumatic course of his life to date precluded grinning optimism.

Tendrils of fog slipped around his legs. At the far edge of the darkening sea, the pallid sun was half extinguished. Sam shivered and went into the tavern to get a drink.

Of the three other customers, none was in a noticeably upbeat mood. In one of the black vinyl booths off to the left, a middle-aged man and woman were leaning toward each other, speaking in low voices. A gray-faced guy at the bar was hunched over his glass of draft beer, holding it in both hands, scowling as if he had just seen a bug swimming in the brew.

In keeping with its name, Knight's Bridge reeked ersatz British atmosphere. A different coat of arms, each no doubt copied from some official heraldic reference book, had been carved from wood and hand-painted and inset in the back of every barstool. A suit of armor stood in one corner. Fox-hunting scenes hung on the walls.

Sam slid onto a stool eight down from the gray-faced man. The bartender hurried to him, wiping a clean cotton rag over the already immaculate, highly polished oak counter.

"Yes, sir, what'll it be?" He was a round man from every aspect: a small round potbelly; meaty forearms with a thick thatching of black hair; a chubby face; a mouth too small to be in harmony with his other features; a puggish nose that ended in a round little ball; eyes round enough to give him a perpetual look of surprise.

"You have Guinness?" Sam asked.

"It's a fundamental of a *real* pub, I'd say. If we didn't have Guinness . . . why, we might as well convert to a tea shop." His was a mellifluous voice; every word he spoke sounded as smooth and round as he looked. He seemed unusually eager to please. "Would you like it cold or just slightly chilled? I keep it both ways."

"Very slightly chilled."

"Good man!" When he returned with a Guinness and a glass, the bartender said, "Name's Burt Peckham. I own the joint."

Carefully pouring the stout down the side of the glass to ensure the smallest possible head, Sam said, "Sam Booker. Nice place, Burt."

"Thanks. Maybe you could spread the word. I try to keep it cozy and well stocked, and we used to have quite a crowd, but lately it seems like most of the town either joined a temperance movement or started brewing their own in their basements, one or the other."

"Well, it's a Monday night."

"These last couple months, it's not been unusual to be half empty even on a Saturday night, which never used to happen." Burt Peckham's round face dimpled with worry. He slowly polished the bar while he talked. "What it is—I think maybe this health kick Californians have been on for so long has finally just gone too far. They're all staying home, doing aerobics in front of the VCR, eating wheat germ and egg whites or whatever the hell it is they eat, drinking nothing but bottled water and fruit juice and titmouse milk. Listen, a tipple or two a day is *good* for you."

Sam drank some of the Guinness, sighed with satisfaction, and said, "This sure tastes as if it ought to be good for you."

"It is. Helps your circulation. Keeps your bowels in shape. Ministers ought to be touting its virtues each Sunday, not preaching against it. *All* things in moderation—and that includes a couple of brews a day." Perhaps realizing that he was polishing the bar a bit obsessively, he hung the rag on a hook and stood with his arms folded across his chest. "You just passing through, Sam?"

"Actually," Sam lied, "I'm taking a long trip up the coast from L.A. to the Oregon line, loafing along, looking for a quiet place to semi-retire."

"Retire? You kidding?"

"*Semi*-retire."

"But you're only, what, forty, forty-one?"

"Forty-two."

"What are you—a bank robber?"

"Stockbroker. Made some good investments over the years. Now I think I can drop out of the rat race and get by well enough just managing my own portfolio. I want to settle down where it's quiet, no smog, no crime. I've had it with L.A."

"People really make money in stocks?" Peckham asked. "I thought it was about as good an investment as a craps table in Reno. Wasn't everybody wiped out when the market blew up a couple years ago?"

"It's a mug's game for the little guy, but you can do all right if you're a broker and if you don't get swept up in the euphoria of a bull market. No market goes up forever or down forever; you just have to guess right about when to start swimming against the current."

"Retiring at forty-two," Peckham said wonderingly. "And when I got into the bar business, I thought I was set for life. Told my wife—in good times, people drink to celebrate, in bad times they drink to forget, so there's no better business than a tavern. Now look." He indicated the nearly empty room with a sweeping gesture of his right hand. "I'd have done better selling condoms in a monastery."

"Get me another Guinness?" Sam asked.

"Hey, maybe this place will turn around yet!"

When Peckham returned with the second bottle of stout, Sam said, "Moonlight Cove might be what I've been looking for. I guess I'll stay a few days, get the feel of it. Can you recommend a motel?"

"There's only one left. Never been much of a tourist town. No one here really wanted that, I guess. Up until this summer, we had four motels. Now three are out of business. I don't know . . . even as pretty as it is, maybe this burg is dying. As far as I can see, we aren't losing population but . . . dammit, we're losing *something*." He snatched up the bar rag again and began to polish the oak. "Anyway, try Cove Lodge on Cypress Lane. That's the last cross street on Ocean Avenue; it runs along the bluff, so you'll probably have a room with an ocean view. Clean, quiet place."

5

AT THE END OF THE DOWNSTAIRS HALL, CHRISSIE FOSTER THREW open the front door. She raced across the wide porch and down the steps, stumbled, regained her balance, turned right, and fled across the yard, past a blue Honda that evidently belonged to Tucker, heading for the stables. The hard slap of her tennis shoes seemed to boom like cannon fire through the swiftly fading twilight. She wished that she could run silently—and faster. Even if her parents and Tucker didn't reach the front porch until she was swallowed by shadows, they would still be able to hear where she was going.

Most of the sky was a burnt-out black, though a deep red glow marked the western horizon, as if all the light of the October day had been boiled down to that intense crimson essence, which had settled at the bottom of the celestial cauldron. Wispy fog crept in from the nearby sea, and Chrissie hoped it would swiftly thicken, dense as pudding, because she was going to need more cover.

She reached the first of the two long stables and rolled aside the big door. The familiar and not unpleasant aroma—straw, hay, feed grain, horseflesh, liniment, saddle leather, and dry manure—wafted over her.

She snapped the night-light switch, and three low-wattage bulbs winked on, bright enough to dimly illuminate the building without disturbing the occupants. Ten generously proportioned stalls flanked each side of the dirt-floored main aisle, and curious horses peered out at her above several of the half-size doors. A few belonged to Chrissie's parents, but most were being boarded for people who lived in and around Moonlight Cove. The horses snuffled and snorted, and one whinnied softly, as Chrissie ran past them to the last box on the left, where a dapple-gray mare named Godiva was in residence.

Access to the stalls also could be had from outside the building, although in this cool season the exterior Dutch-style doors were kept bolted both top and bottom to prevent heat escaping from the barn. Godiva was a gentle mare and particularly amicable with Chrissie, but she was skittish about being approached in the dark; she might rear or bolt if surprised by the opening of her exterior stall door at this hour. Because Chrissie could not afford to lose even a few seconds in calming her mount, she had to reach the mare from inside the stable.

Godiva was ready for her. The mare shook her head, tossing the thick and lustrous white mane for which she had been named, and blew air through her nostrils in greeting.

Glancing back toward the stable entrance, expecting to see Tucker and her parents storm in at any moment, Chrissie unlatched the half-door. Godiva came out into the aisle between the rows of stalls.

"Be a lady, Godiva. Oh, please be sweet for me."

She could not take time to saddle the mare or slip a bit between her teeth. With a hand against Godiva's flank, she guided her mount past the tack room and feed shed that occupied the last quarter of the barn, startling a mouse that scurried across her path into a shadowy corner. She rolled open the door at that end, and cool air swept in.

Without a stirrup to give her a leg up, Chrissie was too small to mount Godiva.

A blacksmith's shoeing stool stood in the corner by the tack room. Keeping a hand against Godiva to gentle her, Chrissie hooked the stool with one foot and pulled it to the horse's side.

Behind her, from the other end of the barn, Tucker shouted, "Here she is! The stable!" He ran toward her.

The stool did not give her much height and was no substitute for a stirrup.

She could hear Tucker's pounding footsteps, close, closer, but she didn't look at him.

He cried, "I got her!"

Chrissie grabbed Godiva's magnificent white mane, threw herself against the big horse and up, up, swinging her leg high, scrabbling desperately against the mare's side, pulling hard on the mane. It must have hurt Godiva, but the old girl was stoic. She didn't rear or whinny in pain, as if some equine instinct told her that this little girl's life depended on equanimity. Then Chrissie was on Godiva's back, tilting precariously but aboard, holding tight with her knees, one hand full of mane, and she slapped the horse's side.

"Go!"

Tucker reached her as she shouted that single word, grabbed at her leg, snared her jeans. His deep-set eyes were wild with anger; his nostrils flared, and his thin lips pulled back from his teeth. She kicked him under the chin, and he lost his grip on her.

Simultaneously Godiva leaped forward, through the open door, into the night.

"She's got a horse!" Tucker shouted. "She's on a horse!"

The dapple-gray sprinted straight toward the meadowed slope that led to the sea a couple of hundred yards away, where the last muddy-red light of the sunset painted faint, speckled patterns on the black water. But Chrissie didn't want to go down to the shore because she was not sure how high the tide was. At some places along the coast, the beach was not broad even at low tide; if the tide were high now, deep water would meet rocks and bluffs at some points, making passage impossible. She could not risk riding into a dead end with her parents and Tucker in pursuit.

Even without the benefit of a saddle and at a full gallop, Chrissie managed to pull herself into a better position astride the mare, and as soon as she was no longer leaning to one side like a stunt rider, she buried both hands in the thick white mane, gripped fistful of that coarse hair, and tried to use it as a substitute for reins. She urged Godiva to turn left, away from the sea, away from the house as well, back along the stables, and out toward the half-mile driveway that led to the county road, where they were more likely to find help.

Instead of rebelling at this crude method of guidance, patient Godiva responded immediately, turning to the left as prettily as if she had a bit in her teeth and had felt the tug of a rein. The thunder of her hooves echoed off the barn walls as they raced past that structure.

"You're a great old girl!" Chrissie shouted to the horse. "I love you, girl."

They passed safely wide of the east end of the stable, where she had first entered to get the mare, and she spotted Tucker coming out of the door. He was clearly surprised to see her heading that way instead of down to the ocean. He sprinted toward her, and he was startlingly quick, but he was no match for Godiva.

They came to the driveway, and Chrissie kept Godiva on the soft verge, parallel to that hard-surfaced lane. She leaned forward, as tight against the horse as she could get, terrified of falling off, and every hard thud of hooves jarred through her bones. Her head was turned to the side, so she saw the house off to the left, the windows full of light but not welcoming. It was no longer her home; it was hell between four walls, so the light at the windows seemed, to her, to be demonic fires in the rooms of Hades.

Suddenly she saw something racing across the front lawn toward the driveway, toward her. It was low and fast, the size of a man but running on all fours—or nearly so—loping, about twenty yards away and closing. She saw another equally bizarre figure, almost the size of the first, running behind it. Though both creatures were backlit by the house lights, Chrissie could discern little more than their shapes, yet she knew what they were. No, correct that: She knew *who* they probably were, but she still didn't know *what* they were, though she had seen them in the upstairs hall this morning; she knew what they had been—people like her—but not what they were now.

"Go, Godiva, go!"

Even without the flap of reins to signal the need for greater speed, the mare increased the length of her stride, as if she shared a psychic link with Chrissie.

Then they were past the house, tearing flat-out across a grassy field, paralleling the macadam driveway, whizzing toward the county road less than half a mile to the east. The nimble-footed mare worked her great haunch muscles, and her powerful stride was so lullingly rhythmic and exhilarating that Chrissie soon was hardly aware of the rocking-jolting aspect of the ride; it seemed as if they were skimming across the earth, nearly flying.

She looked over her shoulder and did not see the two loping figures, although they were no doubt still pursuing her through the multilayered shadows. With the muddy-red candescence along the western horizon fading to deep purple, with the lights of the house rapidly dwindling, and with a crescent moon beginning to thrust one silver-bright point above the line of hills in the east, visibility was poor.

Though she could not see those pursuers who were on foot, she had no difficulty spotting the headlights of Tucker's blue Honda. In front of the house, a couple of hundred yards behind her now, Tucker swung the car around in the driveway and joined the chase.

Chrissie was fairly confident that Godiva could outrun any man or beast other than a better horse, but she knew that the mare was no match for a car. Tucker would catch them in seconds. The man's face was clear in her memory: the bony brow, sharp-ridged nose, deeply set eyes like a pair of hard, black marbles. He'd had about him that aura of unnatural vitality that Chrissie sometimes had seen in her parents—abundant nervous energy coupled with a queer look of hunger. She knew he would do anything to stop her, that he might even attempt to ram Godiva with the Honda.

He could not, of course, use the car to follow Godiva overland. Reluctantly Chrissie employed her knees and the mane in her right hand to turn the mare away from the driveway and the county road, where they were most likely to reach help quickly. Godiva responded without hesitation, and they headed toward the woods that lay at the far side of the meadow, five hundred yards to the south.

Chrissie could see the forest only as a black, bristly mass vaguely silhouetted against the marginally less dark sky. The details of the terrain she must cross appeared to her more in memory than in reality. She prayed that the horse's night vision was keener than hers.

"That's my girl, go, go, you good old girl, go!" she shouted encouragingly to the mare.

They made their own wind in the crisp, still air. Chrissie was aware of Godiva's hot breath streaming past her in crystallized plumes, and her own breath smoked from her open mouth. Her heart pounded in time with the frantic thumping of hooves, and she felt almost as if she and Godiva were not rider and horse but one being, sharing the same heart and blood and breath.

Though fleeing for her life, she was as pleasantly thrilled as she was terrified, and that realization startled her. Facing death—or in this case something perhaps worse than death—was peculiarly exciting, darkly attractive in a way and to an extent that she could never have imagined. She was almost as frightened of the unexpected thrill as of the people who were chasing her.

She clung tightly to the dapple-gray, sometimes bouncing on the horse's bare back, lifting dangerously high, but holding fast, flexing and contracting her own muscles in sympathy with those of the horse. With every ground-pummeling stride, Chrissie grew more confident that they would escape. The mare had heart and endurance. When they had traversed three-quarters of the field, with the woods looming, Chrissie decided to turn east again when they reached the trees, not straight toward the county road but in that general direction, and—

Godiva fell.

The mare had put a foot in some depression—a ground squirrel's burrow, the entrance to a rabbit's warren, perhaps a natural drainage ditch—stumbled, and lost her balance. She tried to recover, failed, and fell, bleating in terror.

Chrissie was afraid that her mount would crash down on her, that she would be crushed, or at least break a leg. But there were no stirrups to ensnare her feet, no saddle horn to snag her clothes, and because she instinctively let go of the dapple-gray's mane, she was thrown free at once, straight over the horse's head and high into the air. Though the ground was soft and further cushioned by a thick growth of wild grass, she met it with numbing impact, driving the air from her lungs and banging her teeth together so hard that her tongue would have been bitten off if it had been between them. But she was three yards away from the horse and safe in that regard.

Godiva was the first to rise, scrambling up an instant after crashing down. Eyes wide with fright, she cantered past Chrissie, favoring her right foreleg, which evidently was only sprained; if it had been broken, the horse would not have gotten up.

Chrissie called to the mare, afraid the horse would wander off. But her breath was coming in ragged gasps, and the name issued from her in a whisper: "Godiva!"

The horse kept going west, back toward the sea and the stables.

By the time Chrissie got up on her hands and knees, she realized that a lame horse was of no use to her, so she made no further effort to recall the mare. She was gasping for breath and mildly dizzy, but she knew she had to get moving because she was no doubt still being stalked. She could see the Honda, headlights on, parked along the lane more than three hundred yards to the north. With all the bloody glow of sunset having seeped out of the horizon, the meadow was black. She could not determine if low, swift-moving figures were out there, though she knew they must be approaching and that she would surely fall into their hands within a minute or two.

She got to her feet, turned south toward the woods, staggered ten or fifteen yards until her legs recovered from the shock of her fall, and finally broke into a run.

6

OVER THE YEARS SAM BOOKER HAD DISCOVERED THAT THE length of the California coast was graced by charming inns that featured master-quality stonework, weathered wood, cove ceilings, beveled glass, and lushly planted courtyards with used-brick walkways. In spite of the comfortable images its name evoked and the singularly scenic setting that it enjoyed, Cove Lodge was not one of those California jewels. It was just an ordinary stucco, two-story, forty-room, rectangular box, with a drab coffee shop at one end, no swimming pool. Amenities were limited to ice and soda machines on both floors. The sign above the motel office was neither garish nor in the artistic mode of some modern neon, just small and simple—and cheap.

The evening desk clerk gave him a second-floor room with an ocean view, though location didn't matter to Sam. Judging by the dearth of cars in the lot, however, rooms with a view were not in short supply. Each level of the motel had twenty units in banks of ten, serviced by an interior hall carpeted in short-nap orange nylon that seared his eyes. Rooms on the east overlooked Cypress Lane; those on the west faced the Pacific. His quarters were at the northwest corner: a queen-size bed with a sagging mattress and worn blue-green spread, cigarette-scarred nightstands, a television bolted to a stand, table, two straight-back chairs, cigarette-scarred bureau, phone, bathroom, and one big window framing the night-blanketed sea.

When disheartened salesmen, down on their luck and teetering on the edge of economic ruin, committed suicide on the road, they did the deed in rooms like this.

He unpacked his two suitcases, putting his clothes in the closet and bureau drawers. Then he sat on the edge of the bed and stared at the telephone on the nightstand.

He should call Scott, his son, who was back home in Los Angeles, but he couldn't do it from this phone. Later, if the local police became interested in him, they would visit Cove Lodge, examine his long-distance charges, investigate the numbers he had dialed, and try to piece together his real identity from the identities of those with whom he had spoken. To maintain his cover, he must use his room phone only to call his contact number at the Bureau office in L.A., a secure line that would be answered with "Birchfield Securities, may I help you?" Furthermore, in phone-company records that line *was* registered to Birchfield, the nonexistent firm with which Sam was supposedly a stockbroker; it could not be traced ultimately to the FBI. He had nothing to report yet, so he did not lift the receiver. When he went out to dinner, he could call Scott from a pay phone.

He did not want to talk to the boy. It would be purely a duty call. Sam dreaded it. Conversation with his son had ceased to be pleasurable at least three years ago, when Scott had been thirteen and, at that time, already motherless for a year. Sam wondered if the boy would have gone wrong quite as rapidly or so completely if Karen had lived. That avenue of thought led him, of course, to the contemplation of his own role in Scott's decline: Would the boy have turned bad regardless of the quality of the parental guidance that he received; was his fall inevitable, the weakness in him or in his stars? Or was Scott's descent a direct result of his father's failure to find a way to steer him to a better, brighter path?

If he kept brooding about it, he was going to pull a Willy Loman right there in Cove Lodge, even though he was not a salesman.

Guinness stout.

Good Mexican food.

Goldie Hawn.

Fear of death.

As a list of reasons for living, it was damned short and too pathetic to contemplate, but perhaps it was just long enough.

After he used the bathroom, he washed his hands and face in cold water. He still felt tired, not the least refreshed.

He took off his corduroy jacket and put on a thin, supple leather shoulder holster that he retrieved from a suitcase. He'd also packed a Smith & Wesson .38 Chief's Special, which he now loaded. He tucked it into the holster before slipping into his jacket again. His coats were tailored to conceal the weapon; it made no bulge, and the holster fit so far back against his side that the gun could not be seen easily even if he left the jacket unbuttoned.

For undercover assignments, Sam's body and face were as well tailored as his jackets. He was five eleven, neither tall nor short. He weighed one hundred and seventy pounds, mostly bone and muscle, little fat, yet he was not a thick-necked weightlifter type in such superb condition that he would draw attention. His face was nothing special: neither ugly nor handsome, neither too broad nor too narrow, marked neither by unusually sharp nor blunt features, unblemished and unscarred. His sandy-brown hair was barbered in a timelessly moderate length and style that would be unremarkable in an age of brush cuts or in an era of shoulder-length locks.

Of all the aspects of his appearance, only his eyes were truly arresting. They were gray-blue with darker blue striations. Women had often told him that his were the most beautiful eyes they had ever seen. At one time he had cared what women said of him.

He shrugged, making sure the holster was hanging properly.

He did not expect to need the gun that evening. He had not begun to nose around and draw attention to himself; and since he had not yet pushed anyone, no one was ready to push back.

Nevertheless, from now on he would carry the revolver. He could not leave it in the motel room or lock it in his rental car; if someone conducted a determined search, the gun would be found, and his cover would be blown. No middle-aged stockbroker, searching for a coastal haven in which to take early retirement, would go armed with a snub-nosed .38 of that make and model. It was a cop's piece.

Pocketing his room key, he went out to dinner.

7

AFTER SHE CHECKED IN, TESSA JANE LOCKLAND STOOD FOR A long time at the big window in her room at the Cove Lodge, with no lights on. She stared out at the vast, dark Pacific and down at the beach from which her sister, Janice, supposedly had ventured forth on a grimly determined mission of self-destruction.

The official story was that Janice had gone to the shore alone at night, in a state of acute depression. She had taken a massive overdose of Valium, swallowing the capsules with several swigs from a can of Diet Coke. Then she had stripped off her clothes and had swum out toward far Japan. Losing consciousness because of the drugs, she soon slipped into the cold embrace of the sea, and drowned.

"Bullshit," Tessa said softly, as if speaking to her own vague reflection in the cool glass.

Janice Lockland Capshaw had been a hopeful person, unfailingly optimistic—a trait so common in members of the Lockland clan as to be genetic. Not once in her life had Janice sat in a corner feeling sorry for herself; if she had tried it, within seconds she would have begun laughing at the foolishness of self-pity and would have gotten up and gone to a movie, or for a psychologically therapeutic run. Even when Richard died, Janice had not allowed grief to metastasize into depression, though she loved him greatly.

So what would have sent her into such a steep emotional spiral? Contemplating the story the police wanted her to believe, Tessa was driven to sarcasm. Maybe Janice had gone out to a restaurant, been served a bad dinner, and been so crushed by the experience that suicide had been her only possible response. Yeah. Or maybe her television went on the blink, and she missed her favorite soap opera, which plunged her into irreversible despair. Sure. Those scenarios were about as plausible as the nonsense that the Moonlight Cove police and coroner had put in their reports.

Suicide.

"Bullshit," Tessa repeated.

From the window of her motel room, she could see only a narrow band of the beach below, where it met the churning surf. The sand was dimly revealed in the wintry light of a newly risen quarter moon, a pale ribbon curving southwest and northwest around the cove.

Tessa was overcome by the desire to stand on the beach from which her sister had supposedly set out on that midnight swim to the graveyard, the same beach to which the tide had returned her bloated, ravaged corpse days later. She turned from the window and switched on a bedside lamp. She removed a brown leather jacket from a hanger in the closet, pulled it on, slung her purse over her shoulder, and left the room, locking the door behind her. She was certain—irrationally so—that merely by going to the beach and standing where Janice supposedly had stood, she would uncover a clue to the true story, through an amazing insight or flicker of intuition.

8

AS THE HAMMERED-SILVER MOON ROSE ABOVE THE DARK eastern hills, Chrissie raced along the tree line, looking for a way into the woods before her strange pursuers found her. She quickly arrived at Pyramid Rock, thus named because the formation, twice as tall as she was, had three sides and came to a weather-rounded point; when younger, she had fantasized that it had been constructed ages ago by a geographically displaced tribe of inch-high Egyptians. Having played in this meadow and forest for years, she was as familiar with the terrain as with the rooms of her own house, certainly more at home there than her parents or Tucker would be, which gave her an advantage. She slipped past Pyramid Rock, into the gloom beneath the trees, onto a narrow deer trail that led south.

She heard no one behind her and did not waste time squinting back into the darkness. But she suspected that, as predators, her parents and Tucker would be silent stalkers, revealing themselves only when they pounced.

The coastal woodlands were comprised mostly of a wide variety of pines, although a few sweet gums flourished, too, their leaves a scarlet blaze of autumn color in daylight but now as black as bits of funeral shrouds. Chrissie followed the winding trail as the land began to slope into a canyon. In more than half the forest, the trees grew far enough apart to allow the cold glow of the partial moon to penetrate to the underbrush and lay an icy crust of light upon the trail. The incoming fog was still too thin to filter out much of that wan radiance, but at other places the interlacing branches blocked the lunar light.

Even where moonlight revealed the way, Chrissie dared not run, for she would surely be tripped by the surface roots of the trees, which spread across the deer-beaten path. Here and there low-hanging branches presented another danger to a runner, but she hurried along.

As if reading from a book of her own adventures, a book like one of those she so much liked, she thought, *Young Chrissie was as surefooted as she was resourceful and quick-thinking, no more intimidated by the darkness than by the thought of her monstrous pursuers. What a girl she was!*

Soon she would reach the bottom of the slope, where she could turn west toward the sea or east toward the county route, which bridged the canyon. Few people lived in that area, more than two miles from the outskirts of Moonlight Cove; fewer still lived by the sea, since portions of the coastline were protected by state law and were closed to construction. Though she had little chance of finding help toward the Pacific, her prospects to the east were not noticeably better, because the county road was lightly traveled and few houses were built along it; besides, Tucker might be patrolling that route in his Honda, expecting her to head that way and flag down the first passing car she saw.

Frantically wondering where to go, she descended the last hundred feet. The trees flanking the trail gave way to low, impenetrable tangles of bristly scrub oaks called chaparral. A few immense ferns, ideally suited to the frequent coastal fogs, overgrew the path, and Chrissie shivered as she pushed through them, for she felt as if scores of small hands were grabbing at her.

A broad but shallow stream cut a course through the bottom of the canyon, and she paused by its bank to catch her breath. Most of the streambed was dry. At this time of year, only a couple of inches of water moved lazily through the center of the channel, glimmering darkly in the moonlight.

The night was windless.

Soundless.

Hugging herself, she realized how cold it was. In jeans and a blue-plaid flannel shirt, she was adequately dressed for a crisp October day, but not for the cold, damp air of an autumn night.

She was chilled, breathless, scared, and unsure of what her next move ought to be, but most of all she was angry with herself for those weaknesses of mind and body. Ms. Andre Norton's wonderful adventure stories were filled with dauntless young heroines who could endure far longer chases—and far greater cold and other hardships—than this, and always with wits intact, able to make quick decisions and, usually, right ones.

Spurred by comparing herself to a Norton girl, Chrissie stepped off the bank of the stream. She crossed ten feet of loamy soil eroded from the hills by last season's heavy rains and tried to jump across the shallow, purling band of water. She splashed down a few inches short of the other side, soaking her tennis shoes. Nevertheless she went on through more loam, which clumped to her wet shoes, ascended the far bank, and headed neither east nor west but south, up the other canyon wall toward the next arm of the forest.

Though she was entering new territory now, at the extremity of the section of the woods that had been her playground for years, she was not afraid of getting lost. She could tell east from west by the movement of the thin, incoming fog and by the position of the moon, and from those signs she could stay on a reliably southward course. She believed that within a mile she would come to a score of houses and to the sprawling grounds of New Wave Microtechnology, which lay between Foster Stables and the town of Moonlight Cove. There she would be able to find help.

Then, of course, her *real* problems would begin. She would have to convince someone that her parents were no longer her parents, that they had changed or been possessed or been somehow taken over by some spirit or . . . force. And that they wanted to turn her into one of them.

Yeah, she thought, good luck.

She was bright, articulate, responsible, but she was also just an eleven-year-old kid. She would have a hard time making anyone believe her. She had no illusions about that. They would listen and nod their heads and smile, and then they would call her parents, and her parents would sound more plausible than she did. . . .

But I've got to try, she told herself, as she began to ascend the sloped southern wall of the canyon. If I don't try to convince someone, what else can I do? Just surrender? No chance.

Behind her, a couple of hundred yards away, from high on the far canyon wall down which she had recently descended, something shrieked. It was not an entirely human cry—not that of any animal, either. The first shrill call was answered by a second, a third, and each shriek was clearly that of a different creature, for each was in a noticeably variant voice.

Chrissie halted on the steep trail, one hand against the deeply fissured bark of a pine, under a canopy of sweet-scented boughs. She looked back and listened as her pursuers simultaneously began to wail, an ululant cry reminiscent of the baying of a pack of coyotes . . . but stranger, more frightening. The sound was so cold, it penetrated her flesh and pierced like a needle to her marrow.

Their baying was probably a sign of their confidence: They were certain they would catch her, so they no longer needed to be quiet.

"What *are* you?" she whispered.

She suspected they could see as well as cats in the dark.

Could they smell her, as if they were dogs?

Her heart began to slam almost painfully within her breast.

Feeling vulnerable and alone, she turned from the puling hunters and scrambled up the trail toward the southern rim of the canyon.

9

AT THE FOOT OF OCEAN AVENUE, TESSA LOCKLAND WALKED through the empty parking lot and onto the public beach. The night breeze off the Pacific was just cranking up, faint but chilly enough that she was glad to be wearing slacks, a wool sweater, and her leather jacket.

She crossed the soft sand, toward the seaside shadows that lay beyond the radius of the glow from the last streetlamp, past a tall cypress growing on the beach and so radically shaped by ocean winds that it reminded her of an Erté sculpture, all curved lines and molten form. On the damp sand at the surf's edge, with the tide lapping at the strand inches from her shoes, Tessa stared westward. The partial moon was insufficient to light the vast, rolling main; all she could see were the nearest three lines of low, foam-crested breakers surging toward her from out of the gloom.

She tried to picture her sister standing on this deserted beach, washing down thirty or forty Valium capsules with a Diet Coke, then stripping naked and plunging into the cold sea. No. Not Janice.

With growing conviction that the authorities in Moonlight Cove were incompetent fools or liars, Tessa walked slowly south along the curving shoreline. In the pearly luminescence of the immature moon, she studied the sand, the widely separated cypresses farther back on the beach, and the time-worn formations of rock. She was not looking for physical clues that might tell her what had happened to Janice; those had been erased by wind and tide during the past three weeks. Instead, she was hoping that the very landscape itself and the elements of night—darkness, cool wind, and arabesques of pale but slowly thickening fog—would inspire her to develop a theory about what had *really* happened to Janice and an approach she might use to prove that theory.

She was a filmmaker specializing in industrials and documentaries of various kinds. When in doubt about the meaning and purpose of a project, she often found that immersion in a particular geographical locale could inspire narrative and thematic approaches to making a film about it. In the developmental stages of a new travel film, for instance, she often spent a couple of days casually strolling around a city like Singapore or Hong Kong or Rio, just absorbing details, which was more productive than thousands of hours of background reading and brainstorming, though of course the reading and brainstorming had to be a part of it too.

She had walked less than two hundred feet south along the beach, when she heard a shrill, haunting cry that halted her. The sound was distant, rising and falling, rising and falling, then fading.

Chilled more by that strange call than by the brisk October air, she wondered what she had heard. Although it had been partly a canine howl, she was certain it was not the voice of a dog. Though it was also marked by a feline whine and wail, she was equally certain it had not issued from a cat; no domestic cat could produce such volume, and to the best of her knowledge, no cougars roamed the coastal hills, certainly not in or near a town the size of Moonlight Cove.

Just as she was about to move on, the same uncanny cry cut the night again, and she was fairly sure it was coming from atop the bluff that overlooked the beach, farther south, where the lights of sea-facing houses were fewer than along the middle of the cove. This time the howl ended on a protracted and more guttural note, which might have been produced by a large dog, though she still felt it had to have come from some other creature. Someone living along the bluff must be keeping an exotic pet in a cage: a wolf, perhaps, or some big mountain cat not indigenous to the northern coast.

That explanation did not satisfy her, either, for there was some peculiarly familiar quality to the cry that she could not place, a quality not related to a wolf or mountain cat. She waited for another shriek, but it did not come.

Around her the darkness had deepened. The fog was clotting, and a lumpish cloud slid across half of the two-pointed moon.

She decided she could better absorb the details of the scene in the morning, and she turned back toward the mist-shrouded streetlamps at the bottom of Ocean Avenue. She didn't realize she was walking so fast—almost running—until she had left the shore, crossed the beach parking lot, and climbed half the first steep block of Ocean Avenue, at which point she became aware of her pace only because she suddenly heard her own labored breathing.

10

THOMAS SHADDACK DRIFTED IN A PERFECT BLACKNESS THAT was neither warm nor cool, where he seemed weightless, where he had ceased to feel any sensation against his skin, where he seemed limbless and without musculature or bones, where he seemed to have no physical substance whatsoever. A tenuous thread of thought linked him to his corporeal self, and in the dimmest reaches of his mind, he was still aware that he was a man—an Ichabod Crane of a man, six-feet-two, one hundred and sixty-five pounds, lean and bony, with a too-narrow face, a high brow, and brown eyes so light they were almost yellow.

He was also vaguely aware that he was nude and afloat in a state-of-the-art sensory-deprivation chamber, which looked somewhat like an old-fashioned iron lung but was four times larger. The single low-wattage bulb was not lit, and no light penetrated the shell of the tank. The pool in which Shaddack floated was a few feet deep, a ten-percent solution of magnesium sulfate in water for maximum buoyancy. Monitored by a computer—as was every element of that environment—the water cycled between ninety-three degrees Fahrenheit, the temperature at which a floating body was least affected by gravity, and ninety-eight degrees, at which the heat differential between human body temperature and surrounding fluid was marginal.

He suffered from no claustrophobia. A minute or two after he stepped into the tank and closed the hatch behind him, his sense of confinement entirely faded.

Deprived of sensory input—no sight, no sound, little or no taste, no olfactory stimulation, no sense of touch or weight or place or time—Shaddack let his mind break free of the dreary restraints of the flesh, soaring to previously unattainable heights of insight and exploring ideas of a complexity otherwise beyond his reach.

Even without the assistance of sensory deprivation, he was a genius. *Time* magazine had said he was, so it must be true. He had built New Wave Microtechnology from a struggling firm with initial capital of twenty thousand dollars to a three-hundred-million-a-year operation that conceived, researched, and developed cutting-edge microtechnology.

At the moment, however, Shaddack was making no effort to focus his mind on current research problems. He was using the tank strictly for recreational purposes, for the inducement of a specific vision that never failed to enthrall and excite him.

His vision:

Except for that thin thread of thought that tethered him to reality, he believed himself to be within a great, laboring machine, so immense that its dimensions could be ascertained no more easily than could those of the universe itself. It was the landscape of a dream but infinitely more textured and intense than a dream. Like an airborne mote within the eerily lit bowels of that colossal imaginary mechanism, he drifted past massive walls and interconnected columns of whirling drive shafts, rattling drive chains, myriad thrusting piston rods joined by sliding blocks to connecting rods that were in turn joined by crank wrists to well-greased cranks that turned flywheels of all dimensions. Servomotors hummed, compressors huffed, distributors sparked as electrical current flashed through millions of tangled wires to far reaches of the construct.

For Shaddack, the most exciting thing about this visionary world was the manner in which steel drive shafts and alloy pistons and hard rubber gaskets and aluminum cowlings were joined with organic parts to form a revolutionary entity possessed of two types of life: efficient mechanical animation and the throb of organic tissue. For pumps, the designer had employed glistening human hearts that pulsated tirelessly in that ancient lub-dub rhythm, joined by thick arteries to rubber tubing that snaked into the walls; some of them pumped blood to parts of the system that required organic lubrication, while others pumped high-viscosity oil. Incorporated into other sections of the infinite machine were tens of thousands of lung sacs functioning as bellows and filters; tendons and tumorlike excrescences of flesh were employed to join lengths of pipe and rubber hoses with more flexibility and surety of seal than could have been attained with ordinary nonorganic couplings.

Here was the best of organic and machine systems wedded in one perfect structure. As Thomas Shaddack imagined his way through the endless avenues of this dream place, he was enraptured even though he did not understand—or care—what ultimate function any of it had, what product or service it labored to bring forth. He was excited by the entity because it was clearly efficient at whatever it was doing, because its organic and inorganic parts were brilliantly integrated.

All of his life, for as many of his forty-one years as he could recall, Shaddack had struggled against the limitations of the human condition, striving with all his will and heart to rise above the destiny of his species. He wanted to be more than merely a man. He wanted to have the power of a god and to shape not only his own future but that of all mankind. In his private sensory-deprivation chamber, transported by this vision of a cybernetic organism, he was closer to that longed-for metamorphosis than he could be in the real world, and that was what invigorated him.

For him the vision was not simply intellectually stimulating and emotionally moving, but powerfully erotic too. As he floated through that imaginary semi-organic machine, watching it throb and pulsate, he surrendered to an orgasm that he felt not merely in his genitals but in every fiber; indeed he was unaware of his fierce erection, unaware of the forceful ejaculations around which his entire body contracted, for he perceived the pleasure to be diffused throughout him rather than focused in his penis. Milky threads of semen spread through the dark pool of magnesium-sulfate solution.

A few minutes later the sensory-deprivation chamber's automatic timer activated the interior light and sounded a soft alarm. Shaddack was called back from his dream to the real world of Moonlight Cove.

11

CHRISSIE FOSTER'S EYES ADJUSTED TO THE DARKNESS, AND SHE was able to find her way swiftly through even unfamiliar territory.

When she reached the rim of the canyon, she passed between a pair of Monterey cypresses and onto another mule-deer trail leading south through the forest. Protected from the wind by the surrounding trees, those enormous cypresses were lush and full, neither badly twisted nor marked by antlerlike branches as they were along the windswept shore. For a moment she considered climbing high into those leafy reaches, with the hope that her pursuers would pass beneath, unaware of her. But she dared not take that chance; if they smelled her or divined her presence by some other means, they would ascend, and she would be unable to retreat.

She hurried on and quickly reached a break in the trees. Beyond lay a meadow that sloped from east to west, as did most of the land thereabout. The breeze picked up and was strong enough to ruffle her blond hair continuously. The fog was not as thin as it had been when she'd left Foster Stables on horseback, but the moonlight was still unfiltered enough to frost the knee-high, dry grass that rippled when the wind blew.

As she ran across the field toward the next stand of woods, she saw a large truck, strung with lights as if it were a Christmas tree, heading south on the inter-state, nearly a mile east of her, along the crest of the second tier of coastal hills. She ruled out seeking help from anyone on the distant freeway, for they were all strangers headed to faraway places, therefore even less likely than locals to believe her. Besides, she read newspapers and watched TV, so she had heard all about the serial killers that roamed the interstates, and she had no trouble imagining tabloid headlines summing up her fate: YOUNG GIRL KILLED AND EATEN BY ROVING CANNIBALS IN DODGE VAN; SERVED WITH A SIDE OF BROCCOLI AND PARSLEY FOR GARNISH; BONES USED FOR SOUP.

The county road lay half a mile closer, along the tops of the first hills, but no traffic moved on it. In any case she already had rejected the idea of seeking help there, for fear of encountering Tucker in his Honda.

Of course she believed that she had heard three distinct voices among the eerie pulings of those who stalked her, which had to mean that Tucker had abandoned his car and was with her parents now. Maybe she could safely head toward the county highway, after all.

She thought about that as she sprinted across the meadow. But before she had made up her mind to change course, those dreadful cries rose behind her again, still in the woods but closer than before. Two or three voices yowled simultane-ously, as if a pack of baying hounds was at her heels, though stranger and more savage than ordinary dogs.

Abruptly Chrissie stepped into thin air and found herself falling into what, for an instant, seemed to be a terrible chasm. But it was only an eight-foot-wide, six-foot-deep drainage channel that cleaved the meadow, and she rolled to the bottom of it unharmed.

The angry shrieking of her pursuers grew louder, nearer, and now their voices had a more frenetic quality . . . a note of need, of hunger.

She scrambled to her feet and started to clamber up the six-foot wall of the channel, when she realized that to her left, upslope, the ditch terminated in a large culvert that bored away into the earth. She froze halfway up the arroyo and con-sidered this new option.

The pale concrete pipe offered the lambent moonlight just enough of a reflec-tive surface to be visible. When she saw it, she knew immediately that it was the main drainage line that carried rainwater off the interstate and county road far above and east of her. Judging by the shrill cries of the hunters, her lead was dwindling. She was increasingly afraid that she would not make the trees at the far side of the meadow before being brought down. Perhaps the culvert was a dead end and would provide her with a haven no more secure than the cypress that she had considered climbing, but she decided to risk it.

She slid to the floor of the arroyo again and scurried to the conduit. The pipe was four feet in diameter. By stooping slightly she was able to walk into it. She went only a few steps, however, before she was halted by a stench so foul that she gagged.

Something was dead and rotting in that lightless passage. She could not see what it was. But maybe she was better off not seeing; the carcass might look worse than it smelled. A wild animal, sick and dying, must have crawled into the pipe for shelter, where it perished from its disease.

She backed hastily out of the drain, drawing deep breaths of the fresh night air.

From the north came intermingled, ululant wails that literally put the hair up on the back of her neck.

They were closing fast, almost on top of her.

She had no choice but to hide deep in the culvert and hope they could not catch her scent. She suddenly realized that the decaying animal might be to her benefit, for if those stalking her *were* able to smell her as though they were hounds, the stench of decomposition might mask her own odor.

Entering the pitch-black culvert again, she followed the convex floor, which sloped gradually upward beneath the meadow. Within ten yards she put her foot in something soft and slippery. The horrid odor of decay burst upon her with even greater strength, and she knew she had stepped in the dead thing.

"Oh, yuck."

She gagged and felt her gorge rise, but she gritted her teeth and *refused* to throw up. When she was past the putrid mass, she paused to scrape her shoes on the concrete floor of the pipe.

Then she hurried farther into the drain. Scurrying with her knees bent, shoulders hunched, and head tucked down, she realized she must have looked like a troll scuttling into its secret burrow.

Fifty or sixty feet past the unidentified dead thing, Chrissie stopped, crouched, and turned to look back toward the mouth of the culvert. Through that circular aperture she had a view of the ditch in moonlight, and she could see more than she had expected because, by contrast with the darkness of the drain, the night beyond seemed brighter than when she had been out there.

All was silent.

A gentle breeze flowed down the pipe from drainage grilles in the highways above and to the east, pushing the odor of the decomposing animal away from her, so she could not detect even a trace of it. The air was tainted only by a mild dankness, a whiff of mildew.

Silence gripped the night.

She held her breath for a moment and listened intently.

Nothing.

Still crouching, she shifted her weight from foot to foot.

Silence.

She wondered if she should head deeper into the culvert. Then she wondered whether snakes were in the pipe. Wouldn't that be a perfect place for snakes to nest when the oncoming night's cool air drove them to shelter?

Silence.

Where were her parents? Tucker? A minute ago they had been close behind her, within striking distance.

Silence.

Rattlesnakes were common in the coastal hills, though not active at this time of year. If a nest of rattlers—

She was so unnerved by the continuing, unnatural silence that she had the urge to scream, just to break that eerie spell.

A shrill cry shattered the quietude outside. It echoed through the concrete tunnel, past Chrissie, and bounced from wall to wall along the passage behind her, as if the hunters were approaching her not only from outside but from the depths of the earth behind her.

Shadowy figures leaped into the arroyo beyond the culvert.

12

SAM FOUND A MEXICAN RESTAURANT ON SERRA STREET, TWO blocks from his motel. One sniff of the air inside the place was enough to assure him the food would be good. That mélange was the odiferous equivalent of a José Feliciano album: chili powder, bubbling hot *chorizo*, the sweet fragrance of tortillas made with *masa harina*, cilantro, bell peppers, the astringent tang of jalapeño chiles, onions. . . .

The Perez Family Restaurant was as unpretentious as its name, a single rectangular room with blue vinyl booths along the side walls, tables in the middle, kitchen at the rear. Unlike Burt Peckham at Knight's Bridge Tavern, the Perez family had as much business as they could handle. Except for a two-chair table at the back, to which Sam was led by the teenage hostess, the restaurant was filled to capacity.

The waiters and waitresses were dressed casually in jeans and sweaters, the only nod to a uniform being white half-aprons tied around their waists. Sam didn't even ask for Guinness, which he had never found in a Mexican restaurant, but they had Corona, which would be fine if the food was good.

The food was *very* good. Not truly, unequivocally great, but better than he had a right to expect in a northern coastal town of just three thousand people. The corn chips were homemade, the salsa thick and chunky, the albondigas soup rich and sufficiently peppery to break him out in a light sweat. By the time he received an order of crab enchiladas in tomatillo sauce, he was half convinced that he *should* move to Moonlight Cove as soon as possible, even if it meant robbing a bank to finance early retirement.

When he got over his surprise at the food's quality, he began to pay as much attention to his fellow diners as to the contents of his plate. Gradually he noted several odd things about them.

The room was unusually quiet, considering that it was occupied by eighty or ninety people. High-quality Mexican restaurants—with fine food, good beer, and potent margaritas—were festive places. At Perez's, however, diners were talking animatedly at only about a third of the tables. The other two-thirds of the customers ate in silence.

After he tilted his glass and poured from the fresh bottle of Corona that had just been served to him, Sam studied some of the silent eaters. Three middle-aged men sat in a booth on the right side of the room, scarfing up tacos and enchiladas and chimichangas, staring at their food or at the air in front of them, occasionally looking at each other but exchanging not a word. On the other side of the room, in another booth, two teenage couples industriously devoured a double platter of mixed appetizers, never punctuating the meal with the chatter and laughter one expected of kids their age. Their concentration was so intense that the longer Sam watched them, the odder they seemed.

Throughout the room, people of all ages, in groups of all kinds, were fixated on their food. Hearty eaters, they had appetizers, soup, salads, and side dishes as well as entrees; on finishing, some ordered "a couple more tacos" or "another burrito," before also asking for ice cream or flan. Their jaw muscles bulged as they chewed, and as soon as they swallowed, they quickly shoveled more into their mouths. A few ate with their mouths open. Some swallowed with such force that Sam could actually hear them. They were red-faced and perspiring, no doubt from jalapeño-spiced sauces, but not one offered a comment like, "Boy, this is hot," or "Pretty good grub," or even the most elementary conversational gambit to his companions.

To the third of the customers who were happily jabbering away at one another and progressing through their meals at an ordinary pace, the almost fevered eating of the majority apparently went unnoticed. Bad table manners were not rare, of course; at least a quarter of the diners in any town would give Miss Manners a stroke if she dared to eat with them. Nevertheless, the gluttony of many of the customers in the Perez Family Restaurant seemed astonishing to Sam. He supposed that the polite diners were inured to the behavior of the other patrons because they had witnessed it so many times before.

Could the cool sea air of the northern coast be *that* appetite-enhancing? Did some peculiar ethnic background or fractured social history in Moonlight Cove mitigate against the universal development of commonly accepted Western table manners?

What he saw in the Perez Family Restaurant seemed a puzzle for which any sociologist, desperately seeking a doctoral thesis subject, would be eager to find a solution. After a while, however, Sam had to turn his attention away from the more ravenous patrons because their behavior was killing his own appetite.

Later, when he was figuring the tip and putting money on the table to cover his bill, he surveyed the crowd again, and this time realized that none of the heavy eaters was drinking beer, margaritas, or anything alcoholic. They had ice water or Cokes, and some were drinking milk, glass after glass, but every last man and woman of these gourmands seemed to be a teetotaler. He might not have noticed their temperance if he had not been a cop—and a good one—trained not only to observe but to think about what he observed.

He remembered the scarcity of drinkers at Knight's Bridge Tavern.

What ethnic culture or religious group inculcated a disdain for alcohol while encouraging mannerlessness and gluttony?

He could think of none.

By the time Sam finished his beer and got up to leave, he was telling himself that he'd overreacted to a few crude people, that this queer fixation on food was limited to a handful of patrons and not as widespread as it seemed. After all, from his table in the back, he had not been able to see the entire room and every last one of the customers. But on his way out, he passed a table where three attractive and well-dressed young women were eating hungrily, none of them speaking, their eyes glazed; two of them had flecks of food on their chins, of which they seemed oblivious, and the third had so many corn-chip crumbs sprinkled across the front of her royal-blue sweater that she appeared to be breading herself with the intention of going into the kitchen, climbing into an oven, and *becoming* food.

He was glad to get out in the clean night air.

Sweating both from the chili-spiced dishes and the heat in the restaurant, he had wanted to take his jacket off, but he had not been able to do so because of the gun he was packing in a shoulder holster. Now he relished the chilling fog that was being harried eastward by a gentle but steady breeze.

13

CHRISSIE SAW THEM ENTER THE DRAINAGE CHANNEL, AND for a moment she thought they were all going to clamber up the far side of it and off across the meadow in the direction she had been heading. Then one of them turned toward the mouth of the culvert. The figure approached the drain on all fours, in a few stealthy and sinuous strides. Though Chrissie could see nothing more of it than a shadowy shape, she had trouble believing that this thing was either one of her parents or the man called Tucker. But who else could it be?

Entering the concrete tunnel, the predator peered forward into the gloom. Its eyes shone softly amber-green, not as bright here as in moonlight, dimmer than glow-in-the-dark paint, but vaguely radiant.

Chrissie wondered how well it could see in absolute darkness. Surely its gaze could not penetrate eighty or a hundred feet of lightless pipe to the place where she crouched. Vision of that caliber would be supernatural.

It stared straight at her.

Then again, who was to say that what she was dealing with here was not supernatural? Perhaps her parents had become . . . werewolves.

She was soaked in sour sweat. She hoped the stench of the dead animal would screen her body odor.

Rising from all fours into a crouch, blocking most of the silvery moonlight at the drain entrance, the stalker slowly came forward.

Its heavy breathing was amplified by the curved concrete walls of the culvert. Chrissie breathed shallowly through her open mouth lest she reveal her presence.

Suddenly, only ten feet into the tunnel, the stalker spoke in a raspy, whispery voice and with such urgency that the words were almost run together in a single long string of syllables: *"Chrissie, you there, you, you? Come me, Chrissie, come me, come, want you, want, want, need, my Chrissie, my Chrissie."*

That bizarre, frantic voice gave rise in Chrissie's mind to a terrifying image of a creature that was part lizard, part wolf, part human, part something unidentifiable. Yet she suspected that its actual appearance was even worse than anything she could imagine.

"Help you, want help you, help, now, come me, come, come. You there, there, you there?"

The worst thing about the voice was that, in spite of its cold hoarse note and whispery tone, in spite of its alienness, it was familiar. Chrissie recognized it as her mother's. Changed, yes, but her mother's voice just the same.

Chrissie's stomach was cramped with fear, but she was filled with another pain, too, that for a moment she could not identify. Then she realized that she ached with loss; she missed her mother, wanted her mother back, her *real* mother. If she'd had one of those ornate silver crucifixes like they always used in the fright films, she probably would have revealed herself, advanced on this hateful thing, and demanded that it surrender possession of her mother. A crucifix probably would not work because nothing in real life was as easy as in the movies; besides, whatever had happened to her parents was far stranger than vampires and were-wolves and demons jumped up from hell. But if she'd had a crucifix, she would have tried it anyway.

"Death, death, smell death, stink, death . . . "

The mother-thing quickly advanced into the tunnel until it came to the place where Chrissie had stepped in a slippery, putrefying mass. The brightness of the shining eyes was directly related to the nearness of moonlight, for now they dimmed. Then the creature lowered its gaze to the dead animal on the culvert floor.

From beyond the mouth of the drain came the sound of something descending into the ditch. Footfalls and the clatter of stones were followed by another voice, equally as fearsome as that of the stalker now hunched over the dead animal. Calling into the pipe, it said, *"She there, there, she? What found, what, what?"*

" . . . raccoon . . . "

"What, what it, what?"

"Dead raccoon, rotten, maggots, maggots," the first one said.

Chrissie was stricken by the macabre fear that she had left a tennis-shoe imprint in the rotting muck of the dead raccoon.

"Chrissie?" the second asked as it ventured into the culvert.

Tucker's voice. Evidently her father was searching for her across the meadow or in the next section of the forest.

Both stalkers were fidgeting constantly. Chrissie could hear them scraping— claws?—against the concrete floor of the pipe. Both sounded panicky, too. No, not panicky, really, because no fear was audible in their voices. Frantic. Frenzied. It was as if an engine in each of them was racing faster, faster, almost out of control.

"Chrissie there, she there, she?" Tucker asked.

The mother-thing raised its gaze from the dead raccoon and peered straight at Chrissie through the lightless tunnel.

You can't see me, Chrissie thought-prayed. I'm invisible.

The radiance of the stalker's eyes had faded to twin spots of tarnished silver. Chrissie held her breath.

Tucker said, *"Got to eat, eat, want eat."*

The creature that had been her mother said, *"Find girl, girl, find her first, then eat, then."*

They sounded as if they were wild animals magically gifted with crude speech.

"Now, now, burning it up, eat now, now, burning," Tucker said urgently, in-sistently.

Chrissie was shaking so badly that she was half afraid they would hear the shudders that rattled her.

Tucker said, *"Burning it up, little animals in meadow, bear them, smell them, track, eat, eat, now."*

Chrissie held her breath.

"Nothing here," the mother-thing said. *"Only maggots, stink, go, eat, then find her, eat, eat, then find her, go."*

Both stalkers retreated from the culvert and vanished.

Chrissie dared to breathe.

After waiting a minute to be sure they were really gone, she turned and troll-walked deeper into the upsloping culvert, blindly feeling the walls as she went, hunting a side passage. She must have gone two hundred yards before she found what she wanted: a tributary drain, half the size of the main line. She slid into it, feetfirst and on her back, then squirmed onto her belly and faced out toward the bigger tunnel. That was where she would spend the night. If they returned to the culvert to see if they could detect her scent in the cleaner air beyond the decomposing raccoon, she would be out of the downdraught that swept the main line, and they might not smell her.

She was heartened because their failure to probe deeper into the culvert was proof that they were not possessed of supernatural powers, neither all-seeing nor all-knowing. They were abnormally strong and quick, strange and terrifying, but they could make mistakes too. She began to think that when daylight came she had a fifty-fifty chance of getting out of the woods and finding help before she was caught.

14

IN THE LIGHTS OUTSIDE OF THE PEREZ FAMILY RESTAURANT, Sam Booker checked his watch. Only 7:10.

He went for a walk along Ocean Avenue, building up the courage to call Scott in Los Angeles. The prospect of that conversation with his son soon preoccupied him and drove all thoughts of the mannerless, gluttonous diners out of his mind.

At 7:30, he stopped at a telephone booth near a Shell service station at the corner of Juniper Lane and Ocean Avenue. He used his credit card to make a long-distance call to his house in Sherman Oaks.

At sixteen Scott thought he was mature enough to be home alone when his father was away on an assignment. Sam did not entirely agree and preferred that the boy stay with his Aunt Edna. But Scott won his way by making life pure hell for Edna, so Sam was reluctant to put her through that ordeal.

He had repeatedly drilled the boy in safety procedures—keep all doors and windows locked; know where the fire extinguishers are; know how to get out of the house from any room in an earthquake or other emergency—and had taught him how to use a handgun. In Sam's judgment Scott was still too immature to be home alone for days at a time; but at least the boy was well prepared for every contingency.

The number rang nine times. Sam was about to hang up, guiltily relieved that he'd failed to get through, when Scott finally answered.

"Hello."

"It's me, Scott. Dad."

"Yeah?"

Heavy-metal rock was playing at high volume in the background. He was probably in his room, his stereo cranked up so loud that the windows shook.

Sam said, "Could you turn the music down?"

"I can hear you," Scott mumbled.

"Maybe so, but I'm having trouble hearing you."

"I don't have anything to say, anyway."

"Please turn it down," Sam said, with emphasis on the "please."

Scott dropped the receiver, which clattered on his nightstand. The sharp sound hurt Sam's ear. The boy lowered the volume on the stereo but only slightly. He picked up the phone and said, "Yeah?"

"How're you doing?"

"Okay."

"Everything all right there?"

"Why shouldn't it be?"

"I just asked."

Sullenly: "If you called to see if I'm having a party, don't worry. I'm not."

Sam counted to three, giving himself time to keep his voice under control. Thickening fog swirled past the glass-walled phone booth. "How was school today?"

"You think I didn't go?"

"I know you went."

"You don't trust me."

"I trust you," Sam lied.

"You think I didn't go."

"Did you?"

"Yeah."

"So how was it?"

"Ridiculous. The same old shit."

"Scott, please, you know I've asked you not to use that kind of language when you're talking to me," Sam said, realizing that he was being forced into a confrontation against his will.

"So sorry. Same old *poop*," Scott said in such a way that he might have been referring either to the day at school or to Sam.

"It's pretty country up here," Sam said.

The boy did not reply.

"Wooded hillsides slope right down to the ocean."

"So?"

Following the advice of the family counselor whom he and Scott had been seeing both together and separately, Sam clenched his teeth, counted to three again, and tried another approach. "Did you have dinner yet?"

"Yeah."

"Do your homework?"

"Don't have any."

Sam hesitated, then decided to let it pass. The counselor, Dr. Adamski, would have been proud of such tolerance and cool self-control.

Beyond the phone booth, the Shell station's lights acquired multiple halos, and the town faded into the slowly congealing mist.

At last Sam said, "What're you doing this evening?"

"I *was* listening to music."

Sometimes it seemed to Sam that the music was part of what had turned the boy sour. That pounding, frenetic, unmelodic heavy-metal rock was a collection of monotonous chords and even more monotonous atonal riffs, so soul-less and mind-numbing that it might have been the music produced by a civilization of intelligent machines long after man had passed from the face of the earth. After a while Scott had lost interest in most heavy-metal bands and switched allegiance to U2, but their simplistic social consciousness was no match for nihilism. Soon he grew interested in heavy-metal again, but the second time around he focused on black metal, those bands espousing—or using dramatic trappings of—satanism; he became increasingly self-involved, antisocial, and somber. On more than one occasion, Sam had considered confiscating the kid's record collection, smashing it to bits, and disposing of it, but that seemed an absurd overreaction. After all, Sam himself had been sixteen when the Beatles and Rolling Stones were coming on the scene, and his parents had railed against *that* music and predicted it would lead Sam and his entire generation into perdition. He'd turned out all right in spite of John, Paul, George, Ringo, and the Stones. He was the product of an unparalleled age of tolerance, and he did not want his mind to close up as tight as his parents' minds had been.

"Well, I guess I better go," Sam said.

The boy was silent.

"If any unexpected problems come up, you call your Aunt Edna."

"There's nothing *she* could do for me that I couldn't do myself."

"She loves you, Scott."

"Yeah, sure."

"She's your mother's sister; she'd like to love you as if you were her own. All you have to do is give her the chance." After more silence, Sam took a deep breath and said, "I love you, too, Scott."

"Yeah? What's that supposed to do—turn me all gooey inside?"

"No."

" 'Cause it doesn't."

"I was just stating a fact."

Apparently quoting from one of his favorite songs, the boy said:

"Nothing lasts forever;
  even love's a lie,
  a tool for manipulation;
  there's no God beyond the sky."

Click.

Sam stood for a moment, listening to the dial tone. "Perfect." He returned the receiver to its cradle.

His frustration was exceeded only by his fury. He wanted to kick the shit out of something, anything, and pretend that he was savaging whoever or whatever had stolen his son from him.

He also had an empty, achy feeling in the pit of his stomach, because he *did* love Scott. The boy's alienation was devastating.

He knew he could not go back to the motel yet. He was not ready to sleep, and the prospect of spending a couple of hours in front of the idiot box, watching mindless sitcoms and dramas, was intolerable.

When he opened the phone-booth door, tendrils of fog slipped inside and seemed to pull him out into the night. For an hour he walked the streets of Moonlight Cove, deep into the residential neighborhoods, where there were no streetlamps and where trees and houses seemed to float within the mist, as if they were not rooted to the earth but tenuously tethered and in danger of breaking loose.

Four blocks north of Ocean Avenue, on Iceberry Way, as Sam walked briskly, letting the exertion and the chilly night air leach the anger from him, he heard hurried footsteps. Someone running. Three people, maybe four. It was an unmistakable sound, though curiously stealthy, not the straightforward slap-slap-slap of joggers' approach.

He turned and looked back along the gloom-enfolded street.

The footsteps ceased.

Because the partial moon had been engulfed by clouds, the scene was brightened mostly by light fanning from the windows of Bavarian-, Monterey-, English-, and Spanish-style houses nestled among pines and junipers on both sides of the street. The neighborhood was long-established, with great character, but the lack of big-windowed modern homes contributed to the murkiness. Two properties in that block had hooded, downcast Malibu landscape lighting, and a few had carriage lamps at the ends of front walks, but the fog damped those pockets of illumination. As far as Sam could see, he was alone on Iceberry Way.

He began to walk again but went less than half a block before he heard the hurried footfalls. He swung around, but as before saw no one. This time the sound faded, as though the runners had moved off a paved surface onto soft earth, then between two of the houses.

Perhaps they were on another street. Cold air and fog could play tricks with sound.

He was cautious and intrigued, however, and he quietly stepped off the cracked and root-canted sidewalk, onto someone's front lawn, into the smooth blackness beneath an immense cypress. He studied the neighborhood, and within half a minute he saw furtive movement on the west side of the street. Four shadowy figures appeared at the corner of a house, running low, in a crouch. When they crossed a lawn that was patchily illuminated by a pair of hurricane lamps on iron poles, their freakishly distorted shadows leaped wildly over the front of a white stucco house. They went to ground again in dense shrubbery before he could ascertain their size or anything else about them.

Kids, Sam thought, and they're up to no good.

He didn't know why he was so sure they were kids, perhaps because neither their quickness nor behavior was that of adults. They were either engaged on some prank against a disliked neighbor—or they were after Sam. Instinct told him that he was being stalked.

Were juvenile delinquents a problem in a community as small and closely knit as Moonlight Cove?

Every town had a few bad kids. But in the semirural atmosphere of a place like this, juvenile crime rarely included gang activities like assault and battery, armed robbery, mugging, or thrill killing. In the country, kids got into trouble with fast cars, booze, girls, and a little unsophisticated theft, but they did not prowl the streets in packs the way their counterparts did in the inner cities.

Nevertheless, Sam was suspicious of the quartet that crouched, invisible, among shadow-draped ferns and azaleas, across the street and three houses west of him. After all, something was wrong in Moonlight Cove, and conceivably the trouble was related to juvenile delinquents. The police were concealing the truth about several deaths in the past couple of months, and perhaps they were protecting someone; as unlikely as it seemed, maybe they were covering for a few kids from prominent families, kids who had taken the privileges of class too far and had gone beyond permissible, civilized behavior.

Sam was not afraid of them. He knew how to handle himself, and he was carrying a .38. Actually he would have enjoyed teaching the brats a lesson. But a confrontation with a group of teenage hoods would mean a subsequent scene with the local police, and he preferred not to bring himself to the attention of the authorities, for fear of jeopardizing his investigation.

He thought it peculiar that they would consider assaulting him in a residential neighborhood like this. One shout of alarm from him would bring people to their front porches to see what was happening. Of course, because he wanted to avoid calling even that much notice to himself, he would not cry out.

The old adage about discretion being the better part of valor was in no circumstance more applicable than in his. He moved back from the cypress under which he had taken shelter, away from the street and toward the lightless house behind him. Confident that those kids were not sure where he had gone, he planned to slip out of the neighborhood and lose them altogether.

He reached the house, hurried alongside it, and entered a rear yard, where a looming swing set was so distorted by shadows and mist that it looked like a giant spider stilting toward him through the gloom. At the end of the yard he vaulted a rail fence, beyond which was a narrow alley that serviced the block's detached garages. He intended to go south, back toward Ocean Avenue and the heart of town, but a shiver of prescience shook him toward another route. Stepping straight across the narrow back street, past a row of metal garbage cans, he vaulted another low fence, landing on the back lawn of another house that faced out on the street parallel to Iceberry Way.

No sooner had he left the alley than he heard soft, running footsteps on that hard surface. The juvies—if that's what they were—sounded as swift but not quite as stealthy as they had been.

They were coming in Sam's direction from the end of the block. He had the odd feeling that with some sixth sense they would be able to determine which yard he had gone into and that they would be on him before he could reach the next street. Instinct told him to stop running and go to ground. He was in good shape, yes, but he was forty-two, and they were no doubt seventeen or younger, and any middle-aged man who believed he could outrun kids was a fool.

Instead of sprinting across the new yard, he moved swiftly to a side door on the nearby clapboard garage, hoping it would be unlocked. It was. He stepped into total darkness and pulled the door shut, just as he heard four pursuers halt in the alleyway in front of the big roll-up door at the other end of the building. They had stopped there not because they knew where he was, but probably because they were trying to decide which way he might have gone.

In tomblike blackness Sam fumbled for a lock button or dead-bolt latch to secure the door by which he had entered. He found nothing.

He heard the four kids murmuring to one another, but he could not make out what they were saying. Their voices sounded strange: whispery and urgent.

Sam remained at the smaller door. He gripped the knob with both hands to keep it from turning, in case the kids searched around the garage and gave it a try.

They fell silent.

He listened intently.

Nothing.

The cold air smelled of grease and dust. He could see nothing, but he assumed a car or two occupied that space.

Although he was not afraid, he was beginning to feel foolish. How had he gotten himself into this predicament? He was a grown man, an FBI agent trained in a variety of self-defense techniques, carrying a revolver with which he possessed considerable expertise, yet he was hiding in a garage from four kids. He had gotten there because he had acted instinctively, and he usually trusted instinct implicitly but this was—

He heard furtive movement along the outer wall of the garage. He tensed. Scraping footsteps. Approaching the small door at which he stood. As far as Sam could tell, he was hearing only one of the kids.

Leaning back, holding the knob in both hands, Sam pulled the door tight against the jamb.

The footsteps stopped in front of him.

He held his breath.

A second ticked by, two seconds, three.

Try the damn lock and move on, Sam thought irritably.

He was feeling more foolish by the second and was on the verge of confronting the kid. He could pop out of the garage as if he were a jack-in-the-box, probably scare the hell out of the punk, and send him screaming into the night.

Then he heard a voice on the other side of the door, inches from him, and although he did not know what in God's name he was hearing, he knew at once that he had been wise to trust to instinct, wise to go to ground and hide. The voice was thin, raspy, utterly chilling, and the urgent cadences of the speech were those of a frenzied psychotic or a junkie long overdue for a fix:

"Burning, need, need . . . "

He seemed to be talking to himself and was perhaps unconscious of speaking, as a man in a fever might babble deliriously.

A hard object scraped down the outside of the wooden door. Sam tried to imagine what it was.

"Feed the fire, fire, feed it, feed," the kid said in a thin, frantic voice that was

partly a whisper and partly a whine and partly a low and menacing growl. It was not much like the voice of any teenager Sam had ever heard—or any adult, for that matter.

In spite of the cold air, his brow was covered with sweat.

The unknown object scraped down the door again.

Was the kid armed? Was it a gun barrel being drawn along the wood? The blade of a knife? Just a stick?

"*. . . burning, burning . . .*"

A claw?

That was a crazy idea. Yet he could not shake it. In his mind was the clear image of a sharp and hornlike claw—a talon—gouging splinters from the door as it carved a line in the wood.

Sam held tightly to the knob. Sweat trickled down his temples.

At last the kid tried the door. The knob twisted in Sam's grip, but he would not let it move much.

"*. . . oh, God, it burns, hurts, oh God . . .*"

Sam was finally afraid. The kid sounded so damned weird. Like a PCP junkie flying out past the orbit of Mars somewhere, only worse than that, far stranger and more dangerous than any angel-dust freak. Sam was scared because he didn't know what the hell he was up against.

The kid tried to pull the door open.

Sam held it tight against the jamb.

Quick, frenetic words: "*. . . feed the fire, feed the fire . . .*"

I wonder if he can smell me in here? Sam thought, and under the circumstances that bizarre idea seemed no crazier than the image of the kid with claws.

Sam's heart was hammering. Stinging perspiration seeped into the corners of his eyes. The muscles in his neck, shoulders, and arms ached fiercely; he was straining much harder than necessary to keep the door shut.

After a moment, apparently deciding that his quarry was not in the garage after all, the kid gave up. He ran along the side of the building, back toward the alley. As he hurried away, a barely audible keening issued from him; it was a sound of pain, need . . . and animal excitement. He was struggling to contain that low cry, but it escaped him anyway.

Sam heard cat-soft footsteps approaching from several directions. The other three would-be muggers rejoined the kid in the alley, and their whispery voices were filled with the same frenzy that had marked his, though they were too far away now for Sam to hear what they were saying. Abruptly, they fell silent and, a moment later, as if they were members of a wolfpack responding instinctively to the scent of game or danger, they ran as one along the alleyway, heading north. Soon their sly footsteps faded, and again the night was grave-still.

For several minutes after the pack left, Sam stood in the dark garage, holding fast to the doorknob.

15

THE DEAD BOY WAS SPRAWLED IN AN OPEN DRAINAGE DITCH along the county road on the southeast side of Moonlight Cove. His frost-white face was spotted with blood. In the glare of the two tripod-mounted police lamps flanking the ditch, his wide eyes stared unblinkingly at a shore immeasurably more distant than the nearby Pacific.

Standing by one of the hooded lamps, Loman Watkins looked down at the small corpse, forcing himself to bear witness to the death of Eddie Valdoski because Eddie, only eight years old, was his godson. Loman had gone to high school with Eddie's father, George, and in a strictly platonic sense he had been in love with Eddie's mother, Nella, for almost twenty years. Eddie had been a great kid, bright and inquisitive and well behaved. Had been. But now . . . Hideously bruised, savagely bitten, scratched and torn, neck broken, the boy was little more than a pile of decomposing trash, his promising potential destroyed, his flame snuffed, deprived of life—and life of him.

Of the innumerable terrible things Loman had encountered in twenty-one years of police work, this was perhaps the worst. And because of his personal relationship with the victim, he should have been deeply shaken if not devastated. Yet he was barely affected by the sight of the small, battered body. Sadness, regret, anger, and a flurry of other emotions touched him, but only lightly and briefly, the way unseen fish might brush past a swimmer in a dark sea. Of grief, which should have pierced him like nails, he felt nothing.

Barry Sholnick, one of the new officers on the recently expanded Moonlight Cove police force, straddled the ditch, one foot on each bank, and took a photograph of Eddie Valdoski. For an instant the boy's glazed eyes were silvery with a reflection of the flash.

Loman's growing inability to *feel* was, strangely, the one thing that evoked strong feelings: It scared the shit out of him. Lately he was increasingly frightened by his emotional detachment, an unwanted but apparently irreversible hardening of the heart that would soon leave him with auricles of marble and ventricles of common stone.

He was one of the New People now, different in many ways from the man he had once been. He still looked the same—five-ten, squarely built, with a broad and remarkably innocent face for a man in his line of work—but he wasn't only what he appeared to be. Perhaps a greater control of emotions, a more stable and analytical outlook, was an unanticipated benefit of the Change. But was that really beneficial? Not to feel? Not to grieve?

Though the night was chilly, sour sweat broke out on his face, the back of his neck, and under his arms.

Dr. Ian Fitzgerald, the coroner, was busy elsewhere, but Victor Callan, owner of Callan's Funeral Home and the assistant coroner, was helping another officer, Jules Timmerman, scour the ground between the ditch and the nearby woods. They were looking for clues that the killer might have left behind.

Actually they were just putting on a show for the benefit of the score of area residents who had gathered on the far side of the road. Even if clues were found, no one would be arrested for the crime. No trial would ever take place. If they found Eddie's killer, they would cover for him and deal with him in their own way, in order to conceal the existence of the New People from those who had not yet undergone the Change. Because without doubt the killer was what Thomas Shaddack called a "regressive," one of the New People gone bad. Very bad.

Loman turned away from the dead boy. He walked back along the county road, toward the Valdoski house, which was a few hundred yards north and veiled in mist.

He ignored the onlookers, although one of them called to him: "Chief? What the hell's going on, Chief?"

This was a semirural area barely within the town limits. The houses were widely separated, and their scattered lights did little to hold back the night. Before he was halfway to the Valdoski place, though he was within hailing distance of the men at the crime scene, he felt isolated. Trees, tortured by ages of sea wind on nights far less calm than this one, bent toward the two-lane road, their scraggly branches overhanging the gravel shoulder on which he walked. He kept imagining movement in the dark boughs above him, and in the blackness and fog between the twisted trunks of the trees.

He put his hand on the butt of the revolver that was holstered at his side.

Loman Watkins had been the chief of police in Moonlight Cove for nine years, and in the past month more blood had been spilled in his jurisdiction than in the entire preceding eight years and eleven months. He was convinced that worse was coming. He had a hunch that the regressives were more numerous and more of a problem than Shaddack realized—or was willing to admit.

He feared the regressives almost as much as he feared his own new, cool, dispassionate perspective.

Unlike happiness and grief and joy and sorrow, stark fear was a survival mechanism, so perhaps he would not lose touch with it as thoroughly as he was losing touch with other emotions. That thought made him as uneasy as did the phantom movement in the trees.

Is fear, he wondered, the only emotion that will thrive in this brave new world we're making?

16

AFTER A GREASY CHEESEBURGER, SOGGY FRIES, AND AN ICY bottle of Dos Equis in the deserted coffee shop at Cove Lodge, Tessa Lockland returned to her room, propped herself up in bed with pillows, and called her mother in San Diego. Marion answered the phone on the first ring, and Tessa said, "Hi, Mom."

"Where are you, Teejay?" As a kid, Tessa could never decide whether she wanted to be called by her first name or her middle, Jane, so her mother always called her by her initials, as if that were a name in itself.

"Cove Lodge," Tessa said.

"Is it nice?"

"It's the best I could find. This isn't a town that worries about having first-rate tourist facilities. If it didn't have such a spectacular view, Cove Lodge is one of those places that would be able to survive only by showing closed-circuit porn movies on the TV and renting rooms by the hour."

"Is it clean?"

"Reasonably."

"If it wasn't clean, I'd insist you move out right now."

"Mom, when I'm on location, shooting a film, I don't always have luxury accommodations, you know. When I did that documentary on the Miskito Indians in Central America, I went on hunts with them and slept in the mud."

"Teejay, dear, you must never tell people that you slept in the mud. Pigs sleep in the mud. You must say you roughed it or camped out, but never that you slept in the mud. Even unpleasant experiences can be worthwhile if one keeps one's sense of dignity and style."

"Yes, Mom, I know. My point was that Cove Lodge isn't great, but it's better than sleeping in the mud."

"Camping out."

"Better than camping out," Tessa said.

Both were silent a moment. Then Marion said, "Dammit, I should be there with you."

"Mom, you've got a broken leg."

"I should have gone to Moonlight Cove as soon as I heard they'd found poor Janice. If I'd been there, they wouldn't have cremated the body. By God, they wouldn't! I'd have stopped that, and I'd have arranged another autopsy by *trustworthy* authorities, and now there'd be no need for you to get involved. I'm so angry with myself."

Tessa slumped back in the pillows and sighed. "Mom, don't do this to yourself. You broke your leg three days before Janice's body was even found. You can't travel easily now, and you couldn't travel easily then, either. It's not your fault."

"There was a time when a broken leg couldn't have stopped me."

"You're not twenty any more, Mom."

"Yes, I know, I'm old," Marion said miserably. "Sometimes I think about how old I am, and it's scary."

"You're only sixty-four, you look not a day past fifty, and you broke your leg skydiving, for God's sake, so you're not going to get any pity from me."

"Comfort and pity is what an elderly parent expects from a good daughter."

"If you caught me calling you elderly or treating you with pity, you'd kick my ass halfway to China."

"The chance to kick a daughter's ass now and then is one of the pleasures of a mother's later life, Teejay. Damn, where did that tree come from, anyway? I've been skydiving for thirty years, and I've never landed in a tree before, and I swear it wasn't there when I looked down on the final approach to pick my drop spot."

Though a certain amount of the Lockland family's unshakable optimism and spirited approach to life came from Tessa's late father, Bernard, a large measure of it—with a full measure of indomitability as well—flowed from Marion's gene pool.

Tessa said, "Tonight, just after I got here, I went down to the beach where they found her."

"This must be awful for you, Teejay."

"I can handle it."

When Janice died, Tessa had been traveling in rural regions of Afghanistan, researching the effects of genocidal war on the Afghan people and culture, intending to script a documentary on that subject. Her mother had been unable to get word of Janice's death to Tessa until two weeks after the body washed up on the shore of Moonlight Cove. Five days ago, on October 8, she had flown out of Afghanistan with a sense of having failed her sister somehow. Her load of guilt was at least as heavy as her mother's, but what she said was true: She *could* handle it.

"You were right, Mom. The official version stinks."

"What've you learned?"

"Nothing yet. But I stood right there on the sand, where she was supposed to have taken the Valium, where she set out on her last swim, where they found her two days later, and I knew their whole story was garbage. I feel it in my guts, Mom. And one way or another, I'm going to find out what really happened."

"You've got to be careful, dear."

"I will."

"If Janice was . . . murdered . . . "

"I'll be okay."

"And if, as we suspect, the police up there can't be trusted . . . "

"Mom, I'm five feet four, blond, blue-eyed, perky, and about as dangerous-looking as a Disney chipmunk. All my life I've had to work against my looks to be taken seriously. Women all want to mother me or be my big sister, and men either want to be my father or get me in the sack, but darned few can see immediately through the exterior and realize I've got a brain that is, I strongly believe, bigger than that of a gnat; usually they have to know me a while. So I'll just use my appearance instead of struggling against it. No one here will see me as a threat."

"You'll stay in touch?"

"Of course."

"If you feel you're in danger, just leave, get out."

"I'll be all right."

"Promise you won't stay if it's dangerous," Marion persisted.

"I promise. But you have to promise *me* that you won't jump out of any more airplanes for a while."

"I'm too old for that, dear. I'm elderly now. Ancient. I'm going to have to pursue interests suitable to my age. I've always wanted to learn to water-ski, for instance, and that documentary you did on dirt-bike racing made those little motorcycles look like so much fun."

"I love you to pieces, Mom."

"I love you, Teejay. More than life itself."

"I'll make them pay for Janice."

"If there's anyone who deserves to pay. Just remember, Teejay, that our Janice is gone, but you're still here, and your *first* allegiance should never be to the dead."

17

GEORGE VALDOSKI SAT AT THE FORMICA-TOPPED KITCHEN table. Though his work-scarred hands were clasped tightly around a glass of whiskey, he could not prevent them from trembling; the surface of the amber bourbon shivered constantly.

When Loman Watkins entered and closed the door behind him, George didn't even look up. Eddie had been his only child.

George was tall, solid in the chest and shoulders. Thanks to deeply and closely set eyes, a thin-lipped mouth, and sharp features, he had a hard, mean look in spite of his general handsomeness. His forbidding appearance was deceptive, however, for he was a sensitive man, soft-spoken and kind.

"How you doin'?" Loman asked.

George bit his lower lip and nodded as if to say that he would get through this nightmare, but he did not meet Loman's eyes.

"I'll look in on Nella," Loman said.

This time George didn't even nod.

As Loman crossed the too-bright kitchen, his hard-soled shoes squeaked on the linoleum floor. He paused at the doorway to the small dining room and looked back at his friend. "We'll find the bastard, George. I swear we will."

At last George looked up from the whiskey. Tears shimmered in his eyes, but he would not let them flow. He was a proud, hardheaded Pole, determined to be strong. He said, "Eddie was playin' in the backyard toward dusk, just right out there in the backyard, where you could see him if you looked out any window, right in his *own* yard. When Nella called him for supper just after dark, when he didn't come or answer, we thought he'd gone to one of the neighbors' to play with some other kids, without asking like he should've." He had related all of this before, more than once, but he seemed to need to go over it again and again, as if repetition would wear down the ugly reality and thereby change it as surely as ten thousand playings of a tape cassette would eventually scrape away the music and leave a hiss of white noise. "We started lookin' for him, couldn't find him, wasn't scared at first; in fact we were a little angry with him; but then we got worried and then scared, and I was just about to call you for help when we found him there in the ditch, sweet Jesus, all torn up in the ditch." He took a deep breath and another, and the pent-up tears glistened brightly in his eyes. "What kind of monster would do that to a child, take him away somewhere and do that, and *then* be cruel enough to bring him back here and drop him where we'd find him? Had to've been that way, 'cause we'd have heard . . . heard the screaming if the bastard had done all that to Eddie right here somewheres. *Had* to've taken him away, done all that, then brought him back so we'd find him. What kind of man, Loman? For God's sake, what kind of man?"

"Psychotic," Loman said, as he had said before, and that much was true. The regressives were psychotic. Shaddack had coined a term for their condition: metamorphic-related psychosis. "Probably on drugs," he added, and he was lying now. Drugs—at least the conventional illegal pharmacopoeia—had nothing to do with Eddie's death. Loman was still surprised at how easy it was for him to lie to a close friend, something that he had once been unable to do. The immorality of lying was a concept more suited to the Old People and their turbulently emotional world. Old-fashioned concepts of what was immoral might ultimately have no meaning to the New People, for if they changed as Shaddack believed they would, efficiency and expediency and maximum performance would be the only moral absolutes. "The country's rotten with drug freaks these days. Burnt-out brains. No morals, no goals but cheap thrills. They're our inheritance from the recent Age of Do Your Own Thing. This guy was a drug-disoriented freak, George, and I swear we'll get him."

George looked down at his whiskey again. He drank some.

Then to himself more than to Loman, he said, "Eddie was playin' in the back-yard toward dusk, just right out there in the backyard, where you could see him if you looked out any window. . . ." His voice trailed away.

Reluctantly Loman went upstairs to the master bedroom to see how Nella was coping.

She was lying on the bed, propped up a bit with pillows, and Dr. Jim Worthy was sitting in a chair that he had moved to her side. He was the youngest of Moonlight Cove's three doctors, thirty-eight, an earnest man with a neatly trimmed mustache, wire-rimmed glasses, and a proclivity for bow ties.

The physician's bag was on the floor at his feet. A stethoscope hung around his neck. He was filling an unusually large syringe from a six-ounce bottle of golden fluid.

Worthy turned to look at Loman, and their eyes met, and they did not need to say anything.

Either having heard Loman's soft footsteps or having sensed him by some sub-tler means, Nella Valdoski opened her eyes, which were red and swollen from crying. She was still a lovely woman with flaxen hair and features that seemed too delicate to be the work of nature, more like the finely honed art of a master sculptor. Her mouth softened and trembled when she spoke his name: "Oh, Lo-man."

He went around the bed, to the side opposite Dr. Worthy, and took hold of the hand that Nella held out to him. It was clammy, cold, and trembling.

"I'm giving her a tranquilizer," Worthy said. "She needs to relax, even sleep if she can."

"I don't want to sleep," Nella said. "I *can't* sleep. Not after . . . not after this . . . not ever again after this."

"Easy," Loman said, gently rubbing her hand. He sat on the edge of the bed. "Just let Dr. Worthy take care of you. This is for the best, Nella."

For half his life, Loman had loved this woman, his best friend's wife, though he had never acted upon his feelings. He had always told himself that it was a strictly platonic attraction. Looking at her now, however, he knew passion had been a part of it.

The disturbing thing was . . . well, though he *knew* what he had felt for her all these years, though he remembered it, he could not feel it any longer. His love, his passion, his pleasant yet melancholy longing had faded as had most of his other emotional responses; he was still aware of his previous feelings for her, but they were like another aspect of him that had split off and drifted away like a ghost departing a corpse.

Worthy set the filled syringe on the nightstand. He unbuttoned and pushed up the loose sleeve on Nella's blouse, then tied a length of rubber tubing around her arm, tight enough to make a vein more evident.

As the physician swabbed Nella's arm with an alcohol-soaked cottonball, she said, "Loman, what are we going to do?"

"Everything will be fine," he said, stroking her hand.

"No. How can you say that? Eddie's dead. He was so sweet, so small and sweet, and now he's gone. Nothing will be fine again."

"Very soon you'll feel better," Loman assured her. "Before you know it the hurt will be gone. It won't matter as much as it does now. I promise it won't."

She blinked and stared at him as if he were talking nonsense, but then she did not know what was about to happen to her.

Worthy slipped the needle into her arm.

She twitched.

The golden fluid flowed out of the syringe, into her bloodstream.

She closed her eyes and began to cry softly again, not at the pain of the needle but at the loss of her son.

Maybe it *is* better not to care so much, not to love so much, Loman thought.

The syringe was empty.

Worthy withdrew the needle from her vein.

Again Loman met the doctor's gaze.

Nella shuddered.

The Change would require two more injections, and someone would have to stay with Nella for the next four or five hours, not only to administer the drugs but to make sure that she did not hurt herself during the conversion. Becoming a New Person was not a painless process.

Nella shuddered again.

Worthy tilted his head, and the lamplight struck his wire-rimmed glasses at a new angle, transforming the lenses into mirrors that for a moment hid his eyes, giving him an uncharacteristically menacing appearance.

Shudders, more violent and protracted this time, swept through Nella.

From the doorway George Valdoski said, "What's going on here?"

Loman had been so focused on Nella that he had not heard George coming. He got up at once and let go of Nella's hand. "The doctor thought she needed—"

"What's that horse needle for?" George said, referring to the huge syringe. The needle itself was no larger than an ordinary hypodermic.

"Tranquilizer," Dr. Worthy said. "She needs to—"

"Tranquilizer?" George interrupted. "Looks like you gave her enough to knock down a bull."

Loman said, "Now, George, the doctor knows what he's—"

On the bed Nella fell under the thrall of the injection. Her body suddenly stiffened, her hands curled into tight fists, her teeth clenched, and her jaw muscles bulged. In her throat and temples, the arteries swelled and throbbed visibly as her heartbeat drastically accelerated. Her eyes glazed over, and she passed into the peculiar twilight that was the Change, neither conscious nor unconscious.

"What's wrong with her?" George demanded.

Between clenched teeth, lips peeled back in a grimace of pain, Nella let out a strange, low groan. She arched her back until only her shoulders and heels were in contact with the bed. She appeared to be full of violent energy, as if she were a boiler straining with excess steam pressure, and for a moment she seemed about to explode. Then she collapsed back onto the mattress, shuddered more violently than ever, and broke out in a copious sweat.

George looked at Worthy, at Loman. He clearly realized that something was very wrong, though he could not begin to understand the nature of that wrongness.

"Stop." Loman drew his revolver as George stepped backward toward the second-floor hall. "Come all the way in here, George, and lie down on the bed beside Nella."

In the doorway George Valdoski froze, staring in disbelief and dismay at the revolver.

"If you try to leave," Loman said, "I'll have to shoot you, and I don't really want to do that."

"You wouldn't," George said, counting on decades of friendship to protect him.

"Yes, I would," Loman said coldly. "I'd kill you if I had to, and we'd cover it with a story you wouldn't like. We'd say that we caught you in a contradiction, that we found some evidence that *you* were the one who killed Eddie, killed your own boy, some twisted sex thing, and that when we confronted you with proof, you grabbed my revolver out of my holster. There was a struggle. You were shot. Case closed."

Coming from someone who was supposed to be a close and treasured friend, Loman's threat was so monstrous that at first George was speechless. Then, as he stepped back into the room, he said, "You'd let everyone think . . . think I did those terrible things to Eddie? Why? What're you doing, Loman? What the hell are you doing? Who . . . who are you protecting?"

"Lie down on the bed," Loman said.

Dr. Worthy was preparing another syringe for George.

On the bed Nella was shivering ceaselessly, twitching, writhing. Sweat trickled down her face; her hair was damp and tangled. Her eyes were open, but she seemed unaware that others were in the room. Maybe she was not even conscious of·her whereabouts. She was seeing a place beyond this room or looking within herself; Loman didn't know which and could remember nothing of his own conversion except that the pain had been excruciating.

Reluctantly approaching the bed, George Valdoski said, "What's happening, Loman? Christ, what is this? What's wrong?"

"Everything'll be fine," Loman assured him. "It's for the best, George. It's really for the best."

"What's for the best? What in God's name—"

"Lie down, George. Everything'll be fine."

"What's happening to Nella?"

"Lie down, George. It's for the best," Loman said.

"It's for the best," Dr. Worthy agreed as he finished filling the syringe from a new bottle of the golden fluid.

"It's really for the best," Loman said. "Trust me." With the revolver he waved George toward the bed and smiled reassuringly.

18

HARRY TALBOT'S HOUSE WAS BAUHAUS-INSPIRED REDWOOD, with a wealth of big windows. It was three blocks south of the heart of Moonlight Cove, on the east side of Conquistador Avenue, a street named for the fact that Spanish conquerors had bivouacked in that area centuries earlier, when accompanying the Catholic clergy along the California coast to establish missions. On rare occasions Harry dreamed of being one of those ancient soldiers, marching northward into unexplored territory, and it was always a nice dream because, in that adventure fantasy, he was never wheelchair-bound.

Most of Moonlight Cove was built on wooded hillsides facing the sea, and Harry's lot sloped down to Conquistador, providing a perfect perch for a man whose main activity in life was spying on his fellow townsmen. From his third-floor bedroom at the northwest corner of the house, he could see at least portions of all the streets between Conquistador and the cove—Juniper Lane, Serra Street, Roshmore Way, and Cypress Lane—as well as the intersecting streets which ran east-west. To the north, he could glimpse pieces of Ocean Avenue and even beyond. Of course the breadth and depth of his field of vision would have been drastically limited if his house hadn't been one story higher than most of those around it and if he hadn't been equipped with a 60mm f/8 refractor telescope and a good pair of binoculars.

At 9:30 Monday night, October 13, Harry was in his custom-made stool, between the enormous west and north windows, bent to the eyepiece of the telescope. The high stool had arms and a backrest like a chair, four wide-spread sturdy legs for maximum balance, and a weighted base to prevent it from tipping over easily when he was levering himself into it from the wheelchair. It also had a harness, something like that in an automobile, allowing him to lean forward to the telescope without slipping off the stool and falling to the floor.

Because he had no use whatsoever of his left leg and left arm, because his right leg was too weak to support him, because he could rely only on his right arm—which, thank God, the Viet Cong had spared—even transferring from the battery-powered wheelchair to a custom-made stool was a torturous undertaking. But the effort was worthwhile because every year Harry Talbot lived more through his binoculars and telescope than he had the year before. Perched on his special stool, he sometimes almost forgot his handicaps, for in his own way he was participating in life.

His favorite movie was *Rear Window* with Jimmy Stewart. He had watched it probably a hundred times.

At the moment the telescope was focused on the back of Callan's Funeral Home, the only mortuary in Moonlight Cove, on the east side of Juniper Lane, which ran parallel to Conquistador but was one block closer to the sea. He was able to see the place by focusing between two houses on the opposite side of his own street, past the thick trunk of a Big Cone pine, and across the service alley that ran between Juniper and Conquistador. The funeral home backed up to that alley, and Harry had a view that included a corner of the garage in which the hearse was parked, the rear entrance to the house itself, and the entrance to the new wing in which the corpses were embalmed and prepared for viewing, or cremated.

During the past two months he had seen some strange things at Callan's. To-night, however, no unusual activity enlivened Harry's patient watch over the place.

"Moose?"

The dog rose from his resting place in the corner and padded across the un-lighted bedroom to Harry's side. He was a full-grown black Labrador, virtually invisible in the darkness. He nuzzled Harry's leg: the right one, in which Harry still had some feeling.

Reaching down, Harry petted Moose. "Get me a beer, old fella."

Moose was a service dog raised and trained by Canine Companions for Inde-pendence, and he was always happy to be needed. He hurried to the small re-frigerator in the corner, which was designed for under-the-counter use in restaurants and could be opened with a foot pedal.

"None there," Harry said. "I forgot to bring a six-pack up from the kitchen this afternoon."

The dog had already discovered that the bedroom fridge contained no Coors. He padded into the hallway, his claws clicking softly on the polished wood floor. No room had carpets, for the wheelchair rolled more efficiently on hard surfaces. In the hall the dog leaped and hit the elevator button with one paw, and immedi-ately the purr and whine of the lift machinery filled the house.

Harry returned his attention to the telescope and to the rear of Callan's Funeral Home. Fog drifted through town in waves, some thick and blinding, some wispy. But lights brightened the rear of the mortuary, giving him a clear view; through the telescope, he seemed to be standing between the twin brick pilasters flanking the driveway that served the back of the property. If the night had been fogless, he would have been able to count the rivets in the metal door of the embalmery-crematorium.

Behind him the elevator doors rolled open. He heard Moose enter the lift. Then it started down to the first floor.

Bored with Callan's, Harry slowly swiveled the scope to the left, moving the field of vision southward to the large vacant lot adjacent to the funeral home. Adjusting the focus, he looked across that empty property and across the street to the Gosdale house on the west side of Juniper, drawing in on the dining-room window.

With his good hand, he unscrewed the eyepiece and put it on a high metal table beside his stool, quickly and deftly replacing it with one of several other eyepieces, thus allowing a clearer focus on the Gosdales. Because the fog was at that moment in a thinning phase, he could see into the Gosdale dining room almost as well as if he had been crouched on their porch with his face to the window. Herman and Louise Gosdale were playing pinochle with their neighbors, Dan and Vera Kaiser, as they did every Monday night and on some Fridays.

The elevator reached the ground floor; the motor stopped whining, and silence returned to the house. Moose was now two floors below, hurrying along the hallway to the kitchen.

On an unusually clear night, when Dan Kaiser was sitting with his back to the window and at the correct angle, Harry occasionally could see the man's pinochle hand. A few times he had been tempted to call Herman Gosdale and describe his adversary's cards to him, with some advice on how to play out the trick.

But he dared not let people know he spent much of his day in his bedroom—darkened at night to avoid being silhouetted at the window—vicariously participating in their lives. They would not understand. Those whole of limb were uneasy about a handicapped person from the start, for they found it too easy to believe that the crippling twist of legs and arms extended to the mind. They would think he was nosy; worse, they might mark him as a Peeping Tom, a degenerate voyeur.

That was not the case. Harry Talbot had set down strict rules governing his use of the telescope and binoculars, and he faithfully abided by them. For one thing, he would never try to get a glimpse of a woman undressed.

Arnella Scarlatti lived across the street from him and three doors north, and he once discovered, by accident, that she spent some evenings in her bedroom, listening to music or reading in the nude. She turned on only a small bedside lamp, and gauzy sheers hung between the drapes, and she always stayed away from the windows, so she saw no need to draw the drapes on every occasion. In fact she could not be seen by anyone less prepared to see her than Harry was. Arnella was lovely. Even through the sheers and in the dim lamplight, her exquisite body had been revealed to Harry in detail. Astonished by her nakedness, riveted by surprise and by the sensuous concavities and convexities of her full-breasted, long-legged body, he had stared for perhaps a minute. Then, as hot with embarrassment as with desire, he had turned the scope from her. Though Harry had not been with a woman in more than twenty years, he never invaded Arnella's bedroom again. On many mornings he looked at an angle into the side window of her tidy first-floor kitchen and watched her at breakfast, studying her perfect face as she had her juice and muffin or toast and eggs. She was beautiful beyond his abilities of description, and from what he knew of her life, she seemed to be a nice person, as well. In a way he supposed he was in love with her, as a boy could love a teacher who was forever beyond his reach, but he never used unrequited love as an excuse to caress her unclothed body with his gaze.

Likewise, if he caught one of his neighbors in another kind of embarrassing situation, he looked away. He watched them fight with one another, yes, and he watched them laugh together, eat, play cards, cheat on their diets, wash dishes, and perform the countless other acts of daily life, but not because he wanted to get any dirt on them or find reason to feel superior to them. He got no cheap thrill from his observations of them. What he wanted was to be a part of their lives, to reach out to them—even if one-sidedly—and make of them an extended family; he wanted to have reason to *care* about them and, through that caring, to experience a fuller emotional life.

The elevator motor hummed again. Moose evidently had gone into the kitchen, opened one of the four doors of the under-the-counter refrigerator, and fetched a cold can of Coors. Now he was returning with the brew.

Harry Talbot was a gregarious man, and on coming home from the war with only one useful limb, he was advised to move into a group home for the disabled, where he might have a social life in a caring atmosphere. The counselors warned him that he would not be accepted if he tried to live in the world of the whole and healthy; they said he would encounter unconscious yet hurtful cruelty from most people he met, especially the cruelty of thoughtless exclusion, and would finally fall into the grip of a deep and terrible loneliness. But Harry was as stubbornly independent as he was gregarious, and the prospect of living in a group home, with only the companionship of disabled people and caretakers, seemed worse than no companionship at all. Now he lived alone, but for Moose, with few visitors other than his once-a-week housekeeper, Mrs. Hunsbok (from whom he hid the telescope and binoculars in a bedroom closet). Much of what the counselors warned him about was proved true daily; however, they had not imagined Harry's ability to find solace and a sufficient sense of family through surreptitious but benign observation of his neighbors.

The elevator reached the third floor. The door slid open, and Moose padded into the bedroom, straight to Harry's high stool.

The telescope was on a wheeled platform, and Harry pushed it aside. He reached down and patted the dog's head. He took the cold can from the Labrador's mouth. Moose had held it by the bottom for maximum cleanliness. Harry put the can between his limp legs, plucked a penlight off the table on the other side of his stool, and directed the beam on the can to be sure it was Coors and not Diet Coke.

Those were the two beverages that the dog had been taught to fetch, and for the most part the good pooch recognized the difference between the words "beer" and "Coke," and was able to keep the command in mind all the way to the kitchen. On rare occasions he forgot along the way and returned with the wrong drink. Rarer still, he brought odd items that had nothing to do with the command he'd been given: a slipper; a newspaper; twice, an unopened bag of dog biscuits; once, a hardboiled egg, carried so gently that the shell was not cracked between his teeth; strangest of all, a toilet-bowl brush from the housekeeper's supplies. When he brought the wrong item, Moose always proved successful on second try.

Long ago Harry had decided that the pooch often was not mistaken but only having fun with him. His close association with Moose had convinced him that dogs were gifted with a sense of humor.

This time, neither mistaken nor joking, Moose had brought what he'd been asked to bring. Harry grew thirstier at the sight of the can of Coors.

Switching off the penlight, he said, "Good boy. Good, good, *gooood* dog."

Moose whined happily. He sat at attention in the darkness at the foot of the stool, waiting to be sent on another errand.

"Go, Moose. Lie down. That's a good dog."

Disappointed, the Lab moseyed into the corner and curled up on the floor, while his master popped the tab on the beer and took a long swallow.

Harry set the Coors aside and pulled the telescope in front of him. He returned to his scrutiny of the night, the neighborhood, and his extended family.

The Gosdales and Kaisers were still playing cards.

Nothing but eddying fog moved at Callan's Funeral Home.

One block south on Conquistador, at the moment illuminated by the walkway lamps at the Sternback house, Ray Chang, the owner of the town's only television and electronics store, was coming this way. He was walking his dog, Jack, a golden retriever. They moved at a leisurely pace, as Jack sniffed each tree along the sidewalk, searching for just the right one on which to relieve himself.

The tranquillity and familiarity of those scenes pleased Harry, but the mood was shattered abruptly when he shifted his attention through his north window to the Simpson place. Ella and Denver Simpson lived in a cream-colored, tile-roofed Spanish house on the other side of Conquistador and two blocks north, just beyond the old Catholic cemetery and one block this side of Ocean Avenue. Because nothing in the graveyard—except part of one tree—obstructed Harry's view of the Simpsons' property, he was able to get an angled but tight focus on all the windows on two sides of the house. He drew in on the lighted kitchen. Just as the image in the eyepiece resolved from a blur to a sharp-lined picture, he saw Ella Simpson struggling with her husband, who was pressing her against the refrigerator; she was twisting in his grasp, clawing at his face, screaming.

A shiver sputtered the length of Harry's shrapnel-damaged spine.

He knew at once that what was happening at the Simpsons' house was connected with other disturbing things he had seen lately. Denver was Moonlight Cove's postmaster, and Ella operated a successful beauty parlor. They were in their mid-thirties, one of the few local black couples, and as far as Harry knew, they were happily married. Their physical conflict was so out of character that it had to be related to the recent inexplicable and ominous events that Harry had witnessed.

Ella wrenched free of Denver. She took only one twisting step away from him before he swung a fist at her. The blow caught her on the side of the neck. She went down. Hard.

In the corner of Harry's bedroom, Moose detected the new tension in his master. The dog raised his head and chuffed once, twice.

Bent forward on his stool, riveted to the eyepiece, Harry saw two men step forward from a part of the Simpson kitchen that was out of line with the window. Though they were not in uniform, he recognized them as Moonlight Cove police officers: Paul Hawthorne and Reese Dorn. Their presence confirmed Harry's intuitive sense that this incident was part of the bizarre pattern of violence and conspiracy of which he had become increasingly aware during the past several weeks. Not for the first time, he wished to God he could figure out what was going on in his once serene little town. Hawthorne and Dorn plucked Ella off the floor and held her firmly between them. She appeared to be only half conscious, dazed by the punch her husband had thrown.

Denver was speaking to Hawthorne, Dorn, or his wife. Impossible to tell which. His face was contorted with rage of such intensity that Harry was chilled by it.

A third man stepped into sight, moving straight to the windows to close the Levolor blinds. A thicker vein of fog flowed eastward from the sea, clouding the view, but Harry recognized this man too: Dr. Ian Fitzgerald, the oldest of Moonlight Cove's three physicians. He had maintained a family practice in town for almost thirty years and had long been known affectionately as Doc Fitz. He was Harry's own doctor, an unfailingly warm and concerned man, but at the moment he looked colder than an iceberg. As the slats of the Levolor blind came together, Harry stared into Doc Fitz's face and saw a hardness of features and a fierceness in the eyes that weren't characteristic of the man; thanks to the telescope, Harry seemed to be only a foot from the old physician, and what he saw was a familiar face but, simultaneously, that of a total stranger.

Unable to peer into the kitchen any longer, he pulled back for a wider view of the house. He was pressing too hard against the eyepiece; dull pain radiated outward from the socket, across his face. He cursed the curdling fog but tried to relax.

Moose whined inquisitively.

After a minute, a light came on in the room at the southeast corner of the second floor of the Simpson house. Harry immediately zoomed in on a window. The master bedroom. In spite of the occluding fog, he saw Hawthorne and Dorn bring Ella in from the upstairs hall. They threw her onto the quilted blue spread on the queen-size bed.

Denver and Doc Fitz entered the room behind them. The doctor put his black leather bag on a nightstand. Denver drew the drapes at the front window that looked out on Conquistador Avenue, then came to the graveyard-side window on which Harry was focused. For a moment Denver stared out into the night, and Harry had the eerie feeling that the man saw him, though they were two blocks away, as if Denver had the vision of Superman, a built-in biological telescope of his own. The same sensation had gripped Harry on other occasions, when he was "eye-to-eye" with people this way, long before odd things had begun to happen in Moonlight Cove, so he knew that Denver was not actually aware of him. He was spooked nonetheless. Then the postmaster pulled those curtains shut, as well, though not as tightly as he should have done, leaving a two-inch gap between the panels.

Trembling now, damp with cold perspiration, Harry worked with a series of eyepieces, adjusting the power on the scope and trying to sharpen the focus, until he had pulled in so close to the window that the lens was filled by the narrow slot between the drapes. He seemed to be not merely *at* the window but beyond it, standing in that master bedroom, behind the drapes.

The denser scarves of fog slipped eastward, and a thinner veil floated in from the sea, further improving Harry's view. Hawthorne and Dorn were holding Ella Simpson on the bed. She was thrashing, but they had her by the legs and arms, and she was no match for them.

Denver held his wife's face by the chin and stuffed a wadded handkerchief or piece of white clothing into her mouth, gagging her.

Harry had a brief glimpse of the woman's face as she struggled with her assailants. Her eyes were wide with terror.

"Oh, shit."

Moose got up and came to him.

In the Simpsons' house, Ella's valiant struggle had caused her skirt to ride up. Her pale yellow panties were exposed. Buttons had popped open on her green blouse. In spite of that, the scene conveyed no feeling that rape was imminent, not even a hint of sexual tension. Whatever they were doing to her was perhaps even more menacing and cruel—and certainly stranger—than rape.

Doc Fitz stepped to the foot of the bed, blocking Harry's view of Ella and her oppressors. The physician held a bottle of amber fluid, from which he was filling a hypodermic syringe.

The were giving Ella an injection.

But of what?

And why?

19

AFTER TALKING WITH HER MOTHER IN SAN DIEGO, TESSA LOCK-
land sat on her motel bed and watched a nature documentary on PBS. Aloud, she
critiqued the camerawork, the composition of shots, lighting, editing techniques,
scripted narration, and other aspects of the production, until she abruptly realized
she sounded foolish talking to herself. Then she mocked herself by imitating various television movie critics, commenting on the documentary in each of their
styles, which turned out to be fun because most TV critics were pompous in one
way or another, with the exception of Roger Ebert. Nevertheless, although having
fun, Tessa *was* talking to herself, which was too eccentric even for a nonconformist
who had reached the age of thirty-three without ever having to take a nine-to-five
job. Visiting the scene of her sister's "suicide" had made her edgy. She was seeking
comic relief from that grim pilgrimage. But at certain times, in certain places, even
the irrepressible Lockland buoyancy was inappropriate.

She clicked off the television and retrieved the empty plastic ice bucket from
the bureau. Leaving the door to her room ajar, taking only some coins, she headed
toward the south end of the second floor to the ice-maker and soda-vending
machine.

Tessa had always prided herself on avoiding the nine-to-five grind. Absurdly
proud, actually, considering that she often put in twelve and fourteen hours a day
instead of eight, and was a tougher boss than any she could have worked for in
a routine job. Her income was nothing to preen about, either. She had enjoyed a
few flush years, when she could not have stopped making money if she'd tried,
but they were far outnumbered by the years in which she had earned little more
than a subsistence living. Averaging her income for the twelve years since she had
finished film school, she'd recently calculated that her annual earnings were
around twenty-one thousand, though that figure would be drastically readjusted
downward if she did not have another boom year soon.

Though she was not rich, though free-lance documentary filmmaking offered
no security to speak of, she *felt* like a success, and not just because her work
generally had been well received by the critics and not only because she was
blessed with the Lockland disposition toward optimism. She felt successful because she had always been resistant to authority and had found, in her work, a
way to be the master of her own destiny.

At the end of the long corridor, she pushed through a heavy fire door and
stepped onto a landing, where the ice-maker and soda cooler stood to the left of
the head of the stairs. Well stocked with cola, root beer, Orange Crush, and 7-Up,
the tall vending machine was humming softly, but the ice-maker was broken and
empty. She would have to fill up her bucket at the machine on the ground floor.
She descended the stairs, her footsteps echoing off the concrete-block walls. The
sound was so hollow and cold that she might have been in a vast pyramid or
some other ancient structure, alone but for the companionship of unseen spirits.

At the foot of the stairs, she found no soda or ice machines, but a sign on the
wall indicated that the ground-floor refreshment center was at the north end of

the motel. By the time she got her ice and Coke, she would have walked off enough calories to deserve a regular, sugar-packed cola instead of a diet drink.

As she reached for the handle of the fire door that led to the ground-floor corridor, she thought she heard the upper door open at the head of the stairs. If so, it was the first indication she'd had, since checking in, that she was not the only guest in the motel. The place had an abandoned air.

She went through the fire door and found that the lower corridor was carpeted in the same hideous orange nylon as was the upper hall. The decorator had a clown's taste for bright colors. It made her squint.

She would have preferred to be a more successful filmmaker, if only because she could have afforded lodgings that did not assault the senses. Of course, this was the only motel in Moonlight Cove, so even wealth could not have saved her from that eye-blistering orange glare. By the time she walked to the end of the hall, pushed through another fire door, and stepped into the bottom of the north stairwell, the sight of gray concrete-block walls and concrete steps was positively restful and appealing.

There, the ice-maker was working. She slid open the top of the chest and dipped the plastic bucket into the deep bin, filling it with half-moon pieces of ice. She set the full bucket atop the machine. As she closed the chest, she heard the door at the head of the stairs open with a faint but protracted squeak of hinges.

She stepped to the soda vendor to get her Coke, expecting someone to descend from the second floor. Only as she dropped a third quarter into the slot did she realize something was *sneaky* about the way the overhead door opened: the long, slow squeak . . . as if someone knew the hinges were unoiled, and was trying to minimize the noise.

With one finger poised over the Diet Coke selection button, Tessa hesitated, listening.

Nothing.

Cool concrete silence.

She felt exactly as she had felt on the beach earlier in the evening, when she had heard that strange and distant cry. Now, as then, her flesh prickled.

She had the crazy notion that someone was on the landing above, holding the fire door open now that he had come through it. He was waiting for her to push the button, so the squeak of the upper door's hinges would be covered by the clatter-thump of the can rolling into the dispensing trough.

Many modern women, conscious of the need to be tough in a tough world, would have been embarrassed by such apprehension and would have shrugged off the intuitive chill. But Tessa knew herself well. She was not given to hysteria or paranoia, so she did not wonder for a moment if Janice's death had left her overly sensitive, did not doubt her mental image of a hostile presence at the upper landing, out of sight around the turn.

Three doors led from the bottom of that concrete shaft. The first was in the south wall, through which she had come and through which she could return to the ground-floor corridor. The second was in the west wall, which opened to the back of the motel, where a narrow walk or service passage evidently lay between the building and the edge of the sea-facing bluff, and the third was in the east wall, through which she probably could reach the parking lot in front of the motel.

Instead of pushing the vendor button to get her Coke, leaving her full ice bucket as well, she stepped quickly and quietly to the south door and pulled it open.

She glimpsed movement at the distant end of the ground-floor hall. Someone ducked back through that other fire door into the south stairwell. She didn't see much of him, only his shadowy form, for he had not been on the orange carpet in the corridor itself but at the far threshold, and therefore able to slip out of sight in a second. The door eased shut in his wake.

At least two men—she presumed they were men, not women—were stalking her.

Overhead, in her own stairwell, the unoiled hinges of that door produced a barely audible, protracted rasp and squeal. The other man evidently had tired of waiting for her to make a covering noise.

She could not go into the hallway. They'd trap her between them.

Though she could scream in the hope of calling forth other guests and frightening these men away, she hesitated because she was afraid the motel might be as deserted as it seemed. Her scream might elicit no help, while letting the stalkers know that she was aware of them and that they no longer had to be cautious.

Someone was stealthily descending the stairs above her.

Tessa turned away from the corridor, stepped to the east door, and ran out into the foggy night, along the side of the building, into the parking lot beyond which lay Cypress Lane. Gasping, she sprinted past the front of Cove Lodge to the motel office, which was adjacent to the now closed coffee shop.

The office was open, the doorstep was bathed in a mist-diffused glow of pink and yellow neon, and the man behind the counter was the same one who had registered her hours ago. He was tall and slightly plump, in his fifties, clean-shaven and neatly barbered if a little rumpled looking in brown corduroy slacks and a green and red flannel shirt. He put down a magazine, lowered the volume of the country music on the radio, got up from his spring-backed desk chair, and stood at the counter, frowning at her while she told him, a bit too breathlessly, what had happened.

"Well, this isn't the big city, ma'am," he said when she had finished. "It's a peaceful place, Moonlight Cove. You don't have to worry about that sort of thing here."

"But it happened," she insisted, nervously glancing out at the neon-painted mist that drifted through the darkness beyond the office door and window.

"Oh, I'm sure you saw and heard someone, but you put the wrong spin on it. We *do* have a couple other guests. That's who you saw and heard, and they were probably just getting a Coke or some ice, like you." He had a warm, grandfatherly demeanor when he smiled. "This place can seem a little spooky when there aren't many guests."

"Listen, mister . . . "

"Quinn. Gordon Quinn."

"Listen, Mr. Quinn, it wasn't that way at all." She felt like a skittish and foolish female, though she knew she was no such thing. "I didn't mistake innocent guests for muggers and rapists. I'm not an hysterical woman. These guys were up to no damn good."

"Well . . . all right. I think you're wrong, but let's have a look." Quinn came through the gate in the counter, to her side of the office.

"Are you just going like that?" she asked.

"Like what?"

"Unarmed?"

He smiled again. As before, she felt foolish.

"Ma'am," he said, "in twenty-five years of motel management, I haven't yet met a guest I couldn't handle."

Though Quinn's smug, patronizing tone angered Tessa, she did not argue with him but followed him out of the office and through the eddying fog to the far end of the building. He was big, and she was petite, so she felt somewhat like a little kid being escorted back to her room by a father determined to show her that no monster was hiding either under the bed or in the closet.

He opened the metal door through which she had fled the north service stairs, and they went inside. No one waited there.

The soda-vending machine purred, and a faint clinking arose from the ice-maker's laboring mechanism. Her plastic bucket still stood atop the chest, filled with half-moon chips.

Quinn crossed the small space to the door that led to the ground-floor hall, pulled it open. "Nobody there," he said, nodding toward the silent corridor. He opened the door in the west wall, as well, and looked outside, left and right. He motioned her to the threshold and insisted that she look too.

She saw a narrow, railing-flanked serviceway that paralleled the back of the lodge, between the building and the edge of the bluff, illuminated by a yellowish night-light at each end. Deserted.

"You said you'd already put your money in the vendor but hadn't got your soda?" Quinn asked, as he let the door swing shut.

"That's right."

"What did you want?"

"Well . . . Diet Coke."

At the vending machine, he pushed the correct button, and a can rolled into the trough. He handed it to her, pointed at the plastic container that she had brought from her room, and said, "Don't forget your ice."

Carrying the ice bucket and Coke, a hot blush on her cheeks and cold anger in her heart, Tessa followed him up the north stairs. No one lurked there. The unoiled hinges of the upper door squeaked as they went into the second-floor hallway, which was also deserted.

The door to her room was ajar, which was how she left it. She was hesitant to enter.

"Let's check it out," Quinn said.

The small room, closet, and adjoining bath were untenanted.

"Feel better?" he asked.

"I wasn't imagining things."

"I'm sure you weren't," he said, still patronizing her.

As Quinn returned to the hallway, Tessa said, "They were there, and they were real, but I guess they've gone now. Probably ran away when they realized I was aware of them and that I went for help."

"Well, all's well then," he said. "You're safe. If they're gone, that's almost as good as if they'd never existed in the first place."

Tessa required all of her restraint to avoid saying more than, "Thank you," then she closed the door. On the knob was a lock button, which she depressed. Above the knob was a dead-bolt lock, which she engaged. A brass security chain was also provided; she used it.

She went to the window and examined it to satisfy herself that it couldn't be opened easily by a would-be assailant. Half of it slid to the left when she applied pressure to a latch and pulled, but it could not be opened from outside unless someone broke it and reached through to disengage the lock. Besides, as she was on the second floor, an intruder would need a ladder.

For a while she sat in bed, listening to distant noises in the motel. Now every sound seemed strange and menacing. She wondered what, if any, connection her unsettling experience had with Janice's death more than three weeks ago.

20

AFTER A COUPLE OF HOURS IN THE STORM DRAIN UNDER THE sloping meadow, Chrissie Foster was troubled by claustrophobia. She had been locked in the kitchen pantry a great deal longer than she had been in the drain, and the pantry had been smaller, yet the grave-black concrete culvert was by far the worse of the two. Maybe she began to feel caged and smothered because of the cumulative effect of spending all day and most of the evening in cramped places.

From the superhighway far above, where the drainage system began, the heavy roar of trucks echoed down through the tunnels, giving rise in her mind to images of growling dragons. She put her hands over her ears to block out the noise. Sometimes the trucks were widely spaced, but on occasion they came in trains of six or eight or a dozen, and the continuous rumble became oppressive, maddening.

Or maybe her desire to get out of the culvert had something to do with the fact that she was underground. Lying in the dark, listening to the trucks, searching the intervening silences for the return of her parents and Tucker, Chrissie began to feel she was in a concrete coffin, a victim of premature burial.

Reading aloud from the imaginary book of her own adventures, she said, "Little did young Chrissie know that the culvert was about to collapse and fill with earth, squishing her as if she were a bug and trapping her forever."

She knew she should stay where she was. They might still be prowling the meadow and woods in search of her. She was safer in the culvert than out of it.

But she was cursed with a vivid imagination. Although she was no doubt the only occupant of the lightless passageway in which she sprawled, she envisioned unwanted company in countless grisly forms: slithering snakes; spiders by the hundreds; cockroaches; rats; colonies of blood-drinking bats. Eventually she began to wonder if over the years a child might have crawled into the tunnels to play and, getting lost in the branching culverts, might have died there, undiscovered. His soul, of course, would have remained restless and earthbound, for his death had been unjustly premature and there had been no proper burial service to free his spirit. Now perhaps that ghost, sensing her presence, was animating those hideous skeletal remains, dragging the decomposed and age-dried corpse toward her, scraping off pieces of leathery and half-petrified flesh as it came. Chrissie was eleven years old and levelheaded for her age, and she repeatedly told herself that there were no such things as ghosts, but then she thought of her parents and Tucker, who seemed to be some kind of *werewolves,* for God's sake, and when the big trucks passed on the interstate, she was afraid to cover her ears with her hands for fear that the dead child was using the cover of that noise to creep closer, closer.

She had to get out.

21

WHEN HE LEFT THE DARK GARAGE WHERE HE HAD TAKEN refuge from the pack of drugged-out delinquents (which is what he had to believe they were; he knew no other way to explain them), Sam Booker went straight to Ocean Avenue and stopped in Knight's Bridge Tavern just long enough to buy a six-pack of Guinness Stout to go.

Later, in his room at Cove Lodge, he sat at the small table and drank beer while he pored over the facts of the case. On September 5, three National Farmworkers Union organizers—Julio Bustamante, his sister Maria Bustamante, and Maria's fiancé, Ramon Sanchez—were driving south from the wine country, where they had been conducting discussions with vineyard owners about the upcoming harvest. They were in a four-year-old, tan Chevy van. They stopped for dinner in Moonlight Cove. They'd eaten at the Perez Family Restaurant and had drunk too many margaritas (according to witnesses among the waiters and customers at Perez's that night), and on their way back to the interstate, they'd taken a dangerous curve too fast; their van had rolled and caught fire. None of the three had survived.

That story might have held up and the FBI might never have been drawn into the case, but for a few inconsistencies. For one thing, according to the Moonlight Cove police department's official report, Julio Bustamante had been driving. But Julio had never driven a car in his life; furthermore, he was unlikely to do so after dark, for he suffered from a form of night blindness. Furthermore, according to witnesses quoted in the police report, Julio and Maria and Ramon were *all* intoxicated, but no one who knew Julio or Ramon had ever seen them drunk before; Maria was a lifelong teetotaler.

The Sanchez and Bustamante families, of San Francisco, also were made suspicious by the behavior of the Moonlight Cove authorities. None of them were told of the three deaths until September 10, five days after the accident. Police chief Loman Watkins had explained that Julio's, Maria's, and Ramon's paper IDs had been destroyed in the intense fire and that their bodies had been too completely burned to allow swift identification by fingerprints. What of the van's license plates? Curiously, Loman had not found any on the vehicle or torn loose and lying in the vicinity of the crash. Therefore, with three badly mangled and burned bodies to deal with and no way to locate next of kin on a timely basis, he had authorized the coroner, Dr. Ian Fitzgerald, to fill out death certificates and thereafter dispose of the bodies by cremation. "We don't have the facilities of a big-city morgue, you understand," Watkins had explained. "We just can't keep cadavers long term, and we had no way of knowing how much time we'd need to identify these people. We thought they might be itinerants or even illegals, in which case we might never be able to ID them."

Neat, Sam thought grimly, as he leaned back in his chair and took a long swallow of Guinness.

Three people had died violent deaths, been certified victims of an accident, and cremated before their relatives were notified, before any other authorities could step in to verify, through the application of modern forensic medicine, whether the death certificates and police report in fact contained the whole story.

The Bustamantes and Sanchezes were suspicious of foul play, but the National Farmworkers Union was convinced of it. On September 12, the union's president sought the intervention of the Federal Bureau of Investigation on the grounds that antiunion forces were responsible for the deaths of Bustamante, Bustamante, and Sanchez. Generally, the crime of murder fell into the FBI's jurisdiction only if the suspected killer had crossed state borders either to commit the act, or during its commission, or to escape retribution subsequent to the act; or, as in this case, if federal authorities had reason to believe that murder had been committed as a consequence of the willful violation of the victims' civil rights.

On September 26, after the absurd if standard delays associated with government bureaucracy and the federal judiciary, a team of six FBI agents—including three men from the Scientific Investigation Division—moved into picturesque Moonlight Cove for ten days. They interviewed police officers, examined police and coroner files, took statements from witnesses who were at the Perez Family Restaurant on the night of September 5, sifted through the wreckage of the Chevy van at the junkyard, and sought whatever meager clues might remain at the accident site itself. Because Moonlight Cove had no agricultural industry, they could find no one interested in the farm-union issue let alone angered by it, which left them short of people motivated to kill union organizers.

Throughout their investigation, they received the full and cordial cooperation of the local police and coroner. Loman Watkins and his men went so far as to volunteer to submit to lie-detector tests, which subsequently were administered, and all of them passed without a hint of deception. The coroner also took the tests and proved to be a man of unfailing honesty.

Nevertheless, something about it reeked.

The local officials were almost too eager to cooperate. And all six of the FBI agents came to feel that they were objects of scorn and derision when their backs were turned—though they never saw any of the police so much as raise an eyebrow or smirk or share a knowing look with another local. Call it Bureau Instinct, which Sam knew was at least as reliable as that of any creature in the wild.

Then the *other* deaths had to be considered.

While investigating the Sanchez-Bustamante case, the agents had reviewed police and coroner records for the past couple of years to ascertain the usual routine with which sudden deaths—accidental and otherwise—were handled in Moonlight Cove, in order to determine if local authorities had dealt with this recent case differently from previous ones, which would be an indication of police complicity in a cover-up. What they discovered was puzzling and disturbing—but not like anything they had *expected* to find. Except for one spectacular car crash involving a teenage boy in an extensively souped-up Dodge, Moonlight Cove had been a singularly safe place to live. During that time, its residents were untroubled by violent death—until August 28, eight days before the deaths of Sanchez and the Bustamantes, when an unusual series of mortalities began to show up on the public records.

In the pre-dawn hours of August 28, the four members of the Mayser family were the first victims: Melinda, John, and their two children, Carrie and Billy. They had perished in a house fire, which the authorities later attributed to Billy playing with matches. The four bodies were so badly burned that identification could be made only from dental records.

Having finished his first bottle of Guinness, Sam reached for a second but hesitated. He had work to do yet tonight. Sometimes, when he was in a particularly dour mood and started drinking stout, he had trouble stopping short of unconsciousness.

Holding the empty bottle for comfort, Sam wondered why a boy, having started a fire, would not cry out for help and wake his parents when he saw the blaze was beyond control. Why would the boy not run before being overcome with smoke? And just what kind of fire, except one fueled by gasoline or another volatile fluid (of which there was no indication in official reports), would spread so fast that none of the family could escape and would reduce the house—and the bodies therein—to heaps of ashes before firemen could arrive and quench it?

Neat again. The bodies were so consumed by flames that autopsies would be of little use in determining if the blaze had been started not by Billy but by someone who wanted to conceal the true causes of death. At the suggestion of the funeral director—who was the owner of Callan's Funeral Home and also the assistant coroner, therefore a suspect in any official cover-up—the Maysers' next of kin, Melinda Mayser's mother, authorized cremation of the remains. Potential evidence not destroyed by the original fire was thus obliterated.

"How tidy," Sam said aloud, putting his feet up on the other straight-backed chair. "How splendidly clean and tidy."

Body count: four.

Then the Bustamantes and Sanchez on September 5. Another fire. Followed by more speedy cremations.

Body count: seven.

On September 7, while trace vapors of the Bustamante and Sanchez remains might still have lingered in the air above Moonlight Cove, a twenty-year resident of the town, Jim Armes, put to sea in his thirty-foot boat, the *Mary Leandra*, for an early-morning sail—and was never seen again. Though he was an experienced seaman, though the day was clear and the ocean calm, he'd apparently gone down in an outbound tide, for no identifiable wreckage had washed up on local beaches.

Body count: eight.

On September 9, while fish presumably were nibbling on Armes's drowned body, Paula Parkins was torn apart by five Dobermans. She was a twenty-nine-year-old woman living alone, raising and training guard dogs, on a two-acre property near the edge of town. Evidently one of her Dobermans turned against her, and the others flew into a frenzy at the scent of her blood. Paula's savaged remains, unfit for viewing, had been sent in a sealed casket to her family in Denver. The dogs were shot, tested for rabies, and cremated.

Body count: nine.

Six days after entering the Bustamante-Sanchez case, on October 2, the FBI had exhumed Paula Parkins's body from a grave in Denver. An autopsy revealed that the woman indeed had been bitten and clawed to death by multiple animal assailants.

Sam remembered the most interesting part of that autopsy report word for word: *. . . however, bite marks, lacerations, tears in the body cavity, and specific damage to breasts and sex organs are not entirely consistent with canine attack. The teeth pattern and size of bite do not fit the dental profile of the average Doberman or other animals known to be aggressive and capable of successfully attacking an adult.* And later in the same report, when referring to the specific nature of Parkins's assailants: *Species unknown.*

How had Paula Parkins really died?

What terror and agony had she known?

Who was trying to blame it on the Dobermans?

And in fact what evidence might the Dobermans' bodies have provided about the nature of their own deaths and, therefore, the truthfulness of the police story?

Sam thought of the strange, distant cry he had heard tonight—like that of a coyote but not a coyote, like that of a cat but not a cat. And he thought also of the eerie, frantic voices of the kids who had pursued him. Somehow it all fit. Bureau Instinct.

Species unknown.

Unsettled, Sam tried to soothe his nerves with Guinness. The bottle was still empty. He clinked it thoughtfully against his teeth.

Six days after Parkins's death and long before the exhumation of her body in Denver, two more people met untimely ends in Moonlight Cove. Steve Heinz and Laura Dalcoe, unmarried but living together, were found dead in their house on Iceberry Way. Heinz left a typed, incoherent, unsigned suicide note, then killed Laura with a shotgun while she slept, and took his own life. Dr. Ian Fitzgerald's report was murder-suicide, case closed. At the coroner's suggestion, the Dalcoe and Heinz families authorized cremation of the grisly remains.

Body count: eleven.

"There's an ungodly amount of cremation going on in this town," Sam said aloud, and turned the empty beer bottle around in his hands.

Most people still preferred to have themselves and their loved ones embalmed and buried in a casket, regardless of the condition of the body. In most towns cremations accounted for perhaps one in four or one in five dispositions of cadavers.

Finally, while investigating the Bustamante-Sanchez case, the FBI team from San Francisco found that Janice Capshaw was listed as a Valium suicide. Her sea-ravaged body had washed up on the beach two days after she disappeared, three days before the agents arrived to launch their investigation into the deaths of the union organizers.

Julio Bustamante, Maria Bustamante, Ramon Sanchez, the four Maysers, Jim Armes, Paula Parkins, Steven Heinz, Laura Dalcoe, Janice Capshaw: a body count of twelve in less than a month—exactly twelve times the number of violent deaths that had occurred in Moonlight Cove during the previous *twenty-three months*. Out of a population of just three thousand, twelve violent deaths in little more than three weeks was one hell of a mortality rate.

Queried about his reaction to this astonishing chain of deadly events, Chief Loman Watkins had said, "It's horrible, yes. And it's sort of frightening. Things were so calm for so long that I guess, statistically, we were just overdue."

But in a town that size, even spread over two years, twelve such violent deaths went off the top of the statisticians' charts.

The six-man Bureau team was unable to find one shred of evidence of any local authorities' complicity in those cases. And although a polygraph was not an entirely dependable determiner of truth, the technology was not so unreliable that Loman Watkins, his officers, the coroner, and the coroner's assistant could all pass the examination without a single indication of deception if in fact they were guilty.

Yet . . .

Twelve deaths. Four cremated in a house fire. Three cremated in a demolished Chevy van. Three suicides, two by shotgun and one by Valium, all subsequently cremated at Callan's Funeral Home. One lost at sea—no body at all. And the only victim available for autopsy appeared not to have been killed by dogs, as the coroner's report claimed, though she had been bitten and clawed by something, dammit.

It was enough to keep the Bureau's file open. By the ninth of October, four days after the San Francisco team departed Moonlight Cove, a decision was made to send in an undercover operative to have a look at certain aspects of the case that might be more fruitfully explored by a man who was not being watched.

One day after that decision, on October 10, a letter arrived in the San Francisco office that clinched the Bureau's determination to maintain involvement. Sam had that note committed to memory as well:

Gentlemen:

I have information pertinent to a recent series of deaths in the town of Moon-light Cove. I have reason to believe local authorities are involved in a conspiracy to conceal murder.

I would prefer you contact me in person, as I do not trust the privacy of our telephone here. I must insist on absolute discretion because I am a disabled Viet-nam veteran with severe physical limitations, and I am naturally concerned about my ability to protect myself.

It was signed, Harold G. Talbot.

United States Army records confirmed that Talbot was indeed a disabled Viet-nam vet. He had been repeatedly cited for bravery in combat. Tomorrow, Sam would discreetly visit him.

Meanwhile, considering the work he had to do tonight, he wondered if he could risk a second bottle of stout on top of what he'd drunk at dinner. The six-pack was on the table in front of him. He stared at it for a long time. Guinness, good Mexican food, Goldie Hawn, and fear of death. The Mexican food was in his belly, but the taste of it was forgotten. Goldie Hawn was living on a ranch somewhere with Kurt Russell, whom she had the bad sense to prefer to one ordinary-looking, scarred, and hope-deserted federal agent. He thought of twelve dead men and women, of bodies roasting in a crematorium until they were reduced to bone splinters and ashes, and he thought of shotgun murder and shotgun suicide and fish-gnawed corpses and a badly bitten woman, and all those thoughts led him to morbid philosophizing about the way of all flesh. He thought of his wife, lost to cancer, and he thought of Scott and their long-distance telephone conversation, too, and that was when he finally opened a second beer.

22

CHASED BY IMAGINARY SPIDERS, SNAKES, BEETLES, RATS, bats, and by the *possibly* imaginary reanimated body of a dead child, and by the real if dragonlike roar of distant trucks, Chrissie crawled out of the tributary drain in which she had taken refuge, troll-walked down the main culvert, stepped again in the slippery remains of the decomposing raccoon, and plunged out into the silt-floored drainage channel. The air was clean and sweet. In spite of the eight-foot-high walls of the ditch, fog-filtered moonlight, and fog-hidden stars, Chrissie's claustrophobia abated. She drew deep lungsful of cool, moist air, but tried to breathe with as little noise as possible.

She listened to the night, and before long she was rewarded by those alien cries, echoing faintly across the meadow from the woods to the south. As before, she was sure that she heard three distinct voices. If her mother, father, and Tucker were off to the south, looking for her in the forest that eventually led to the edge of New Wave Microtech's property, she might be able to head back the way she had come, through the northern woods, into the meadow where Godiva had thrown her, then east toward the county road and into Moonlight Cove by that route, leaving them searching fruitlessly in the wrong place.

For sure, she could not stay where she was.

And she could not head south, straight toward *them*.

She clambered out of the ditch and ran north across the meadow, retracing the route she had taken earlier in the evening, and as she went she counted her miseries. She was hungry because she'd had no dinner, and she was tired. The muscles in her shoulders and back were cramped from the time she had spent in the tight, cold concrete tributary drain. Her legs ached.

So what's your problem? she asked herself as she reached the trees at the edge of the meadow. Would you rather have been dragged down by Tucker and "converted" into one of them?

23

LOMAN WATKINS LEFT THE VALDOSKI HOUSE, WHERE DR. Worthy was overseeing the conversion of Ella and George. Farther down the county road, his officers and the coroner were loading the dead boy into the hearse. The crowd of onlookers was entranced by the scene.

Loman got into his cruiser and switched on the engine. The compact video-display lit at once, a soft green. The computer link was mounted on the console between the front seats. It began to flash, indicating that HQ had a message for him—one that they chose not to broadcast on the more easily intercepted police-band radio.

Though he had been working with microwave-linked mobile computers for a few years, he was still sometimes surprised upon first getting into a cruiser and seeing the VDT light up. In major cities like Los Angeles, for the better part of the past decade, most patrol cars had been equipped with computer links to central police data banks, but such electronic wonders were still rare in smaller cities and unheard of in jurisdictions as comparatively minuscule as Moonlight Cove. His department boasted state-of-the-art technology not because the town's treasury was overflowing but because New Wave—a leader in mobile microwave-linked data systems, among other things—had equipped his office and cars with their in-development hardware and software, updating the system constantly, using the Moonlight Cove police force as something of a proving ground for every advance-ment that they hoped ultimately to integrate into their line of products.

That was one of the many ways Thomas Shaddack had insinuated himself into the power structure of the community even before he had reached for *total* power through the Moonhawk Project. At the time Loman had been thickheaded enough to think New Wave's largesse was a blessing. Now he knew better.

From his mobile VDT, Loman could access the central computer in the de-partment's headquarters on Jacobi Street, one block south of Ocean Avenue, to obtain any information in the data banks or to "speak" with the on-duty dispatcher who could communicate with him almost as easily by computer as by police-band radio. Furthermore, he could sit comfortably in his car and, through the HQ com-puter, reach out to the Department of Motor Vehicles computer in Sacramento to get a make on a license plate, or the Department of Prisons data banks in the same city to call up information on a particular felon, or any other computer tied in to the nationwide law-enforcement electronic network.

He adjusted his holster because he was sitting on his revolver.

Using the keyboard under the display terminal, he entered his ID number, accessing the system.

The days when *all* fact-gathering required police legwork had begun to pass in the mid-eighties. Now only TV cops like Hunter were forced to rush hither and yon to turn up the smallest details because that was more dramatic than a depiction of the high-tech reality. In time, Watkins thought, the gumshoe might be in danger of becoming the gumbutt, with his ass parked for hours in front of either a mobile VDT or one on a desk at HQ.

The computer accepted his number.

The VDT stopped flashing.

Of course, if all the people of the world were New People, and if the problem of the regressives were solved, ultimately there would be no more crime and no need of policemen. Some criminals were spawned by social injustice, but all men would be equal in the new world that was coming, as equal as one machine to another, with the same goals and desires, with no competitive or conflicting needs. Most criminals were genetic defectives, their sociopathic behavior virtually encoded in their chromosomes; however, except for the regressive element among them, the New People would be in perfect genetic repair. That was Shaddack's vision, anyway.

Sometimes Loman Watkins wondered where free will fit into the plan. Maybe it didn't. Sometimes he didn't seem to care if it fit in or not. At other times his inability to care . . . well, it scared the hell out of him.

Lines of words began to appear from left to right on the screen, one line at a time, in soft green letters on the dark background:

FOR: LOMAN WATKINS
SOURCE: SHADDACK
JACK TUCKER HAS NOT REPORTED IN FROM THE FOSTER PLACE.
NO ONE ANSWERS PHONE THERE. URGENT THAT SITUATION BE
CLARIFIED. AWAIT YOUR REPORT.

Shaddack had direct entry to the police-department computer from his own computer in his house out on the north point of the cove. He could leave messages for Watkins or any of the other men, and no one could call them up except the intended recipient.

The screen went blank.

Loman Watkins popped the hand brake, put the patrol car in gear, and set out for Foster Stables, though the place was actually outside the city limits and beyond his bailiwick. He no longer cared about such things as jurisdictional boundaries and legal procedures. He was still a cop only because it was the role he had to play until all of the town had undergone the Change. None of the old rules applied to him any more because he was a New Man. Such disregard for the law would have appalled him only a few months ago, but now his arrogance and his disdain for the rules of the Old People's society did not move him in the least.

Most of the time nothing moved him any more. Day by day, hour by hour, he was less emotional.

Except for fear, which his new elevated state of consciousness still allowed: fear because it was a survival mechanism, useful in a way that love and joy and hope and affection were not. He was afraid right now, in fact. Afraid of the regressives. Afraid that the Moonhawk Project would somehow be revealed to the outside world and crushed—and him with it. Afraid of his only master, Shaddack. Sometimes, in fleeting bleak moments, he was afraid of himself, too, and of the new world coming.

24

MOOSE DOZED IN A CORNER OF THE UNLIGHTED BEDROOM.
He chuffed in his sleep, perhaps chasing bushy-tailed rabbits in a dream—although, being the good service dog that he was, even in his dreams he probably ran errands for his master.

Belted in his stool at the window, Harry leaned to the eyepiece of the telescope and studied the back of Callan's Funeral Home over on Juniper Lane, where the hearse had just pulled into the service drive. He watched Victor Callan and the mortician's assistant, Ned Ryedock, as they used a wheeled gurney to transfer a body from the black Cadillac hearse into the embalming and cremation wing. Zippered inside a half-collapsed, black plastic body bag, the corpse was so small that it must have been that of a child. Then they closed the door behind them, and Harry could see no more.

Sometimes they left the blinds raised at the two high, narrow windows, and from his elevated position Harry was able to peer down into that room, to the tilted and guttered table on which the dead were embalmed and prepared for viewing. On those occasions he could see much more than he *wanted* to see. Tonight, however, the blinds were lowered all the way to the windowsills.

He gradually shifted his field of vision southward along the fog-swaddled alley that served Callan's and ran between Conquistador and Juniper. He was not looking for anything in particular, just slowly scanning, when he saw a pair of grotesque figures. They were swift and dark, sprinting along the alley and into the large vacant lot adjacent to the funeral home, running neither on all fours nor erect, though closer to the former than the latter.

Boogeymen.

Harry's heart began to race.

He'd seen their like before, three times in the past four weeks, though the first time he had not believed what he had seen. They had been so shadowy and strange, so briefly glimpsed, that they seemed like phantoms of the imagination; therefore he named them Boogeymen.

They were quicker than cats. They slipped through his field of vision and vanished into the dark, vacant lot before he could overcome his surprise and follow them.

Now he searched that property end to end, back to front, seeking them in the three- to four-foot grass. Bushes offered concealment too. Wild holly and a couple of clumps of chaparral snagged and held the fog as if it were cotton.

He found them. Two hunched forms. Man-size. Only slightly less black than the night. Featureless. They crouched together in the dry grass in the middle of the lot, just to the north of the immense fir that spread its branches (all high ones) like a canopy over half the property.

Trembling, Harry pulled in even tighter on that section of the lot and adjusted the focus. The Boogeymen's outlines sharpened. Their bodies grew paler in contrast to the night around them. He still could not see any details of them because of the darkness and eddying mist.

Although it was quite expensive and tricky to obtain, he wished that through his military contacts he had acquired a Tele-Tron, which was a new version of the Star Tron night-vision device that had been used by most armed services for years. A Star Tron took available light—moonlight, starlight, meager electric light if any, the vague natural radiance of certain minerals in soil and rocks—and amplified it eighty-five thousand times. With that single-lens gadget, an impenetrable night-scape was transformed into a dim twilight or even late-afternoon grayness. The Tele-Tron employed the same technology as the Star Tron, but it was designed to be fitted to a telescope. Ordinarily, available light was sufficient to Harry's purposes, and most of the time he was looking through windows into well-lighted rooms; but to study the quick and furtive Boogeymen, he needed some high-tech assistance.

The shadowy figures looked west toward Juniper Lane, then north toward Callan's, then south toward the house that, with the funeral home, flanked that open piece of land. Their heads turned with a quick, fluid movement that made Harry think of cats, although they were definitely not feline.

One of them glanced back to the east. Because the telescope put Harry right in the lot with the Boogeymen, he saw the thing's eyes—soft gold, palely radiant. He had never seen their eyes before. He shivered, but not just because they were so uncanny. Something was familiar about those eyes, something that reached deeper than Harry's conscious or subconscious mind to stir dim recognition, activating primitive racial memories carried in his genes.

He was suddenly cold to the marrow and overcome by fear more intense than anything he had known since Nam.

Dozing, Moose was attuned nonetheless to his master's mood. The Labrador got up, shook himself as if to cast off sleep, and came to the stool. He made a low, mewling, inquisitive sound.

Through the telescope Harry glimpsed the nightmare face of one of the Boogeymen. He had no more than the briefest flash of it, at most two seconds, and the malformed visage was limned only by an ethereal spray of moonlight, so he saw little; in fact the inadequate lunar glow did less to reveal the thing than to deepen the mystery of it.

But he was gripped by it, stunned, frozen.

Moose issued an interrogatory *"Woof?"*

For an instant, unable to look up from the eyepiece if his life had depended on it, Harry stared at an apelike countenance, though it was leaner and uglier and more fierce and infinitely stranger than the face of an ape. He was reminded, as well, of wolves, and in the gloom the thing even seemed to have something of a reptilian aspect. He thought he saw the enameled gleam of wickedly sharp teeth, gaping jaws. But the light was poor, and he could not be certain how much of what he saw was a trick of shadow or a distortion of fog. Part of this hideous vision had to be attributed to his fevered imagination. A man with a pair of useless legs and one dead arm *had* to have a vivid imagination if he was to make the most of life.

As suddenly as the Boogeyman looked toward him, it looked away. At the same time both creatures moved with an animal fluidity and quickness that startled Harry. They were nearly the size of big jungle cats and as fast. He turned the scope to follow them, and they virtually flew through the darkness, south across the vacant lot, disappearing over a split-rail fence into the backyard of the Claymore house, up and gone with such alacrity that he could not hold them in his field of view.

He continued to search for them, as far as the junior-senior high school on Roshmore, but he found only night and fog and the familiar buildings of his neighborhood. The Boogeymen had vanished as abruptly as they always did in a small boy's bedroom the moment the lights were turned on.

At last he lifted his head from the eyepiece and slumped back in his stool.

Moose immediately stood up with his forepaws on the arm of the stool, begging to be petted, as if he had seen what his master had seen and needed to be reassured that malign spirits did not actually run loose in the world.

With his good right hand, which at first trembled violently, Harry stroked the Labrador's head. In a while the petting calmed him almost as much as it calmed the dog.

If the FBI eventually responded to the letter he had sent over a week ago, he did not know if he would tell them about the Boogeymen. He would tell them everything else he had seen, and a lot of it might be useful to them. But this . . . On the one hand, he was sure that the beasts he had glimpsed so fleetingly on three occasions—four now—were somehow related to all the other curious events of recent weeks. They were a different magnitude of strangeness, however, and in speaking of them he might appear addled, even crazed, causing the Bureau agents to discount everything else he said.

Am I addled? he wondered as he petted Moose. Am I crazed?

After twenty years of confinement to a wheelchair, housebound, living vicariously through his telescope and binoculars, perhaps he had become so desperate to be more involved with the world and so starved for excitement that he had evolved an elaborate fantasy of conspiracy and the uncanny, putting himself at the center of it as The One Man Who Knew, convinced that his delusions were real. But that was highly unlikely. The war had left his body pathetically damaged and weak, but his mind was as strong and clear as it had ever been, perhaps even tempered and made stronger by adversity. *That*, not madness, was his curse.

"Boogeymen," he said to Moose.

The dog chuffed.

"What next? Will I look up at the moon some night and see the silhouette of a witch on a broomstick?"

25

CHRISSIE CAME OUT OF THE WOODS BY PYRAMID ROCK, which once had inspired her fantasies of inch-high Egyptians. She looked west toward the house and Foster Stables, where lights now wore rainbow-hued halos in the fog. For a moment she entertained the idea of going back for Godiva or another horse. Maybe she could even slip into the house to grab a jacket. But she decided that she would be less conspicuous and safer on foot. Besides, she was not as dumb as movie heroines who repeatedly returned to the Bad House, knowing the Bad Thing was likely to find them there. She turned east-northeast and headed up through the meadow toward the county road.

Exhibiting her usual cleverness (she thought, as if reading a line from an adventure novel), *Chrissie wisely turned away from the cursed house and set off into the night, wondering if she would ever again see that place of her youth or find solace in the arms of her now alienated family.*

Tall, autumn-dry grass lashed at her legs, as she angled out toward the middle of the field. Instead of staying near the tree line, she wanted to be in the open in case something leaped at her from the forest. She didn't think she could outrun them once they spotted her, not even if she had a minute's head start, but at least she intended to give herself a chance to try.

The night chill had deepened during the time she'd taken refuge in the culvert. Her flannel shirt seemed hardly more warming than a short-sleeved summer blouse. If she were an adventurer-heroine of the breed that Ms. Andre Norton created, she would know how to weave a coat out of available grass and other plants, with a high insulation factor. Or she would know how to trap, painlessly kill, and skin fur-bearing animals, how to tan their hides and stitch them together, clothing herself in garments as astonishingly stylish as they were practical.

She simply had to stop thinking about the heroines of those books. Her comparative ineptitude depressed her.

She already had enough to be depressed about. She'd been driven from her home. She was alone, hungry, cold, confused, afraid—and stalked by weird and dangerous creatures. But more to the point . . . though her mother and father always had been a bit distant, not given to easy displays of affection, Chrissie had loved them, and now they were gone, perhaps gone forever, changed in some way she did not understand, alive but soulless and, therefore, as good as dead.

When she was less than a hundred feet from the two-lane county route, paralleling the long driveway at about the same distance, she heard a car engine. She saw headlights on the road, coming from the south. Then she saw the car itself, for the fog was thinner in that direction than toward the sea, and visibility was reasonably good. Even at that distance she identified it as a police cruiser; though no siren wailed, blue and red lights were revolving on its roof. The patrol car slowed and turned in the driveway by the sign for Foster Stables.

Chrissie almost shouted, almost ran toward the car, because she always had been taught that policemen were her friends. She actually raised one hand and waved, but then realized that in a world where she could not trust her own parents, she certainly could not expect all policemen to have her best interests in mind.

Spooked by the thought that the cops might have been "converted" the way Tucker had intended to convert her, the way her parents had been converted, she dropped down, crouching in the tall grass. The headlights had not come anywhere near her when the car had turned into the driveway. The darkness on the meadow and the fog no doubt made her invisible to the occupants of the cruiser, and she was not exactly so tremendously tall that she stood out on the flat land. But she did not want to take any chances.

She watched the car dwindle down the long driveway. It paused briefly beside Tucker's car, which was abandoned halfway along the lane, then drove on. The thicker fog in the west swallowed it.

She rose from the grass and hurried eastward again, toward the county route.

She intended to follow that road south, all the way into Moonlight Cove. If she remained watchful and alert, she could scramble off the pavement into a ditch or behind a patch of weeds each time she heard approaching traffic.

She would not reveal herself to anyone she did not know. Once she reached town, she could go to Our Lady of Mercy and seek help from Father Castelli. (He said he was a modern priest and preferred to be called Father Jim, but Chrissie had *never* been able to address him so casually.) Chrissie had been an indefatigable worker at the church's summer festival and had expressed a desire to be an altar girl next year, much to Father Castelli's delight. She was sure he liked her and would believe her story, no matter how wild it was. If he didn't believe her . . . well, then she would try Mrs. Tokawa, her sixth-grade teacher.

She reached the county road, paused, and looked back toward the distant house, which was only a collection of glowing points in the fog. Shivering, she turned south toward Moonlight Cove.

26

THE FRONT DOOR OF THE FOSTER HOUSE STOOD OPEN TO the night.

Loman Watkins went through the place from bottom to top and down again. The only odd things he found were an overturned chair in the kitchen and Jack Tucker's abandoned black bag filled with syringes and doses of the drug with which the Change was effected—and a spray-can of WD-40 on the floor of the downstairs hall.

Closing the front door behind him, he went out onto the porch, stood at the steps that led down to the front yard, and listened to the ethereally still night. A sluggish breeze had risen and fallen fitfully during the evening, but now it had abated entirely. The air was uncannily still. The fog seemed to dampen all sounds, leaving a world as silent as if it had been one vast graveyard.

Looking toward the stables, Loman called out: "Tucker! Foster! Is anyone here?"

An echo of his voice rolled back to him. It was a cold and lonely sound.

No one answered him.

"Tucker? Foster?"

Lights were on at one of the long stables, and a door was open at the nearest end. He supposed he should go have a look.

Loman was halfway to that building when an ululant cry, like the wavering note of a distant horn, came from far to the south, faint but unmistakable. It was shrill yet guttural, filled with anger, longing, excitement, and need. The shriek of a regressive in mid-hunt.

He stopped and listened, hoping that he had misheard.

The sound came again. This time he could discern at least two voices, perhaps three. They were a long way off, more than a mile, so their eerie keening could not be in reply to Loman's shouts.

Their cries chilled him.

And filled him with a strange yearning.

No.

He made such tight fists of his hands that his fingernails dug into his palms, and he fought back the darkness that threatened to well up within him. He tried to concentrate on police work, the problem at hand.

If those cries came from Alex Foster, Sharon Foster, and Jack Tucker—as was most likely the case—where was the girl, Christine?

Maybe she escaped as they were preparing her for conversion. The overturned kitchen chair, Tucker's abandoned black bag, and the open front door seemed to support that unsettling explanation. In pursuit of the girl, caught up in the excitement of the chase, the Fosters and Tucker might have surrendered to a latent urge to regress. Perhaps not so latent. They might have regressed on other occasions, so this time they had slipped quickly and eagerly into that altered state. And now they were stalking her in the wildlands to the south—or had long ago run her down, torn her to pieces, and were still regressed because they got a dark thrill from being in that debased condition.

The night was cool, but suddenly Loman was sweating.

He wanted . . . needed. . . .

No!

Earlier in the day, Shaddack had told Loman that the Foster girl had missed her school bus and, returning home from the bus stop at the county road, had walked in on her parents as they were experimenting with their new abilities. So the girl had to be conducted through the Change slightly sooner than planned, the first child to be elevated. But maybe "experimenting" was a lie that the Fosters had used to cover their asses. Maybe they had been in deep regression when the girl had come upon them, which they could not reveal to Shaddack without marking themselves as degenerates among the New People.

The Change was meant to elevate mankind; it was forced evolution.

Willful regression, however, was a sick perversion of the power bestowed by the Change. Those who regressed were outcasts. And those regressives who killed for the primal thrill of blood sport were the worst of all: psychotics who had chosen devolution over evolution.

The distant cries came again.

A shiver crackled the length of Loman's spine. It was a pleasant shiver. He was seized by a powerful longing to shed his clothes, drop closer to the ground, and race nude and unrestrained through the night in long, graceful strides, across the broad meadow and into the woods, where all was wild and beautiful, where prey waited to be found and run down and broken and torn . . .

No.

Control.

Self-control.

The faraway cries pierced him.

He must exhibit self-control.

His heart pounded.

The cries. The sweet, eager, wild cries . . .

Loman began to tremble, then to shake violently, as in his mind's eye he saw himself freed from the rigid posture of *Homo erectus* freed from the constraints of civilized form and behavior. If the primal man within him could be set loose at long last and allowed to live in a natural state—

No. Unthinkable.

His legs became weak, and he fell to the ground, though not onto all fours, no, because that posture would encourage him to surrender to these unspeakable urges; instead he curled into the fetal position, on his side, knees drawn up to his chest, and struggled against the swelling desire to regress. His flesh grew as hot as if he had been lying for hours in midday summer sun, but he realized that the heat was coming not from any external source but from deep within him; the fire arose not merely from vital organs or the marrow of his bones, but from the material within the walls of his cells, from the billions of nuclei that harbored the genetic material that made him what he was. Alone in the dark and fog in front of the Foster house, seduced by the echoey cry of the regressives, he longed to exercise the control of his physical being that the Change had granted him. But he knew if once he succumbed to that temptation, he would never be Loman Watkins again; he would be a degenerate masquerading as Loman Watkins, Mr. Hyde in a body from which he had banished Dr. Jekyll forever.

With his head tucked down, he was looking at his hands, which were curled against his chest, and in the dim light from the windows of the Foster house, he thought he saw several of his fingers begin to change. Pain flashed through his right hand. He *felt* the bones crunching and re-forming, knuckles swelling, digits lengthening, the pads of his fingers growing broader, sinews and tendons thickening, nails hardening and sharpening into talonlike points.

He screamed in stark terror and denial, and he *willed* himself to hold fast to his born identity, to what remained of his humanity. He resisted the lavalike movement of his living tissue. Through clenched teeth he repeated his name—"Loman Watkins, Loman Watkins, Loman Watkins"—as if that were a spell that would prevent this evil transformation.

Time passed. Perhaps a minute. Perhaps ten. An hour. He didn't know. His struggle to retain his identity had conveyed him into a state of consciousness beyond time.

Slowly, he returned to awareness. With relief he found himself still on the ground in front of the house, unchanged. He was drenched in sweat. But the white-hot fire in his flesh had subsided. His hands were as they'd always been, with no freakish elongation of the fingers.

For a while he listened to the night. He heard no more of the distant cries, and he was grateful for that silence.

Fear, the only emotion that had not daily lost vividness and power since he had become one of the New People, was now as sharp as knives within him, causing him to cry out. For some time he had been afraid that he was one of those with the potential to become a regressive, and now that dark speculation was proven true. But if he had surrendered to the yearning, he would have lost both the old world he had known before he'd been converted *and* the brave new world Shaddack was making; he would belong in neither.

Worse: He was beginning to suspect that he was not unique, that in fact *all* of the New People had within them the seeds of devolution. Night by night, the regressives seemed to be increasing in number.

Shakily, he got to his feet.

The film of sweat was like a crust of ice on his skin now that his inner fires had been banked.

Moving dazedly toward his patrol car, Loman Watkins wondered if Shaddack's research—and the technological application of it—was so fundamentally flawed that there was no benefit whatsoever in the Change. Maybe it was an unalloyed curse. If the regressives were not a statistically insignificant percentage of the New People, if instead they were *all* doomed to drift toward regression sooner or later. . . .

He thought of Thomas Shaddack out there in the big house on the north point of the cove, overlooking the town where beasts of his creation roamed the shadows, and a terrible bleakness overcame him. Because reading for pleasure had been his favorite pastime since he was a boy, he thought of H. G. Wells's Dr. Moreau, and he wondered if that was who Shaddack had become. Moreau reincarnate. Shaddack might be a Moreau for the age of microtechnology, obsessed with an insane vision of transcendence through the forced melding of man and machine. Certainly he suffered from delusions of grandeur, and had the hubris to believe that he could lift mankind to a higher state, just as the original Moreau had believed he could make men from savage animals and beat God at His game. If Shaddack was not *the* genius of his century, if he was an overreacher like Moreau, then they were all damned.

Loman got in the car and pulled the door shut. He started the engine and turned on the heater to warm his sweat-chilled body.

The computer screen lit, awaiting use.

For the sake of protecting the Moonhawk Project—which, flawed or not, represented the only future open to him—he had to assume the girl, Christine, had escaped, and that the Fosters and Tucker hadn't caught her. He must arrange for men to stand watch surreptitiously along the county road and on the streets entering the north end of Moonlight Cove. If the girl came into town seeking help, they could intercept her. More likely than not, she would unknowingly approach one of the New People with her tale of possessed parents, and that would be the end of her. Even if she got to people not yet converted, they weren't likely to believe her wild story. But he could take no chances.

He had to talk to Shaddack about a number of things, and attend to several pieces of police business.

He also had to get something to eat.

He was inhumanly hungry.

27

SOMETHING WAS WRONG, SOMETHING WAS WRONG, SOMEthing, something.

Mike Peyser had slipped through the dark woods to his house on the southeast edge of town, down through the wild hills and trees, stealthy and alert, slinking and quick, naked and quick, returning from a hunt, blood in his mouth, still excited but tired after two hours of playing games with his prey, cautiously bypassing the homes of his neighbors, some of whom were his kind and some of whom were not. The houses in that area were widely separated, so he found it relatively easy to creep from shadow to shadow, tree to tree, through tall grass, low to the ground, cloaked in the night, swift and sleek, silent and swift, naked and silent, powerful and swift, straight to the porch of the single-story house where he lived alone, through the unlocked door, into the kitchen, still tasting the blood in his mouth, blood, the lovely blood, exhilarated by the hunt though also glad to be home, but then—

Something was wrong.

Wrong, wrong, God, he was burning up, full of fire, hot, burning up, in need of food, nourishment, fuel, fuel, and that was normal, that was to be expected—the demands on his metabolism were tremendous when he was in his altered state—but the fire was not wrong, not the inner fire, not the frantic and consuming need for nourishment. What was wrong was that he could not, he could not, he could not—

He could not change back.

Thrilled by the exquisitely fluid movement of his body, by the way his muscles flexed and stretched, flexed and stretched, he came into the darkened house, seeing well enough without lights, not as well as a cat might but better than a man, because he was more than just a man now, and he roamed for a couple of minutes through the rooms, silent and swift, almost hoping he would find an intruder, someone to savage, someone to savage, savage, someone to savage, bite and tear, but the house was deserted. In his bedroom, he settled to the floor, curled on his side, and called his body back to the form that had been his birthright, to the familiar form of Mike Peyser, to the shape of a man who walked erect and looked like a man, and within himself he felt a surge toward normalcy, a *shift* in the tissues, but not *enough* of a shift, and then a sliding away, away, like an outgoing tide pulling back from a beach, away, away from normalcy, so he tried again, but this time there was no shift at all, not even a partial return to what he had been. He was stuck, trapped, locked in, locked, locked in a form that earlier had seemed the essence of freedom and inexpressibly desirable, but now it was not a desirable form at all because he could not forsake it at will, was trapped in it, trapped, and he panicked.

He sprang up and hurried out of the room. Although he could see fairly well in the darkness, he brushed a floor lamp, and it fell with a crash, the brittle sound of shattering glass, but he kept going into the short hall, the living room. A rag rug spun out from under him. He felt that he was in a prison; his body, his own transformed body, had become his prison, prison, metamorphosed bones serving as the bars of a cell, bars holding him captive from within; he was restrained by his own reconfigured flesh. He circled the room, scrambled this way and that, circled, circled, frenzied, frantic. The curtains fluttered in the wind of his passage. He weaved among the furniture. An end table toppled over in his wake. He could run but not escape. He carried his prison with him. No escape. No escape. Never. That realization made his heart thump more wildly. Terrified, frustrated, he knocked over a magazine rack, spilling its contents, swept a heavy glass ashtray and two pieces of decorative pottery off the cocktail table, tore at the sofa cushions until he had shredded both the fabric and the foam padding within, whereupon a terrible pressure filled his skull, pain, such pain, and he wanted to scream but he was afraid to scream, afraid that he would not be able to stop.

Food.

Fuel.

Feed the fire, feed the fire.

He suddenly realized that his inability to return to his natural form might be related to a severe shortage of energy reserves needed to fuel the tremendous acceleration of his metabolism associated with a transformation. To do what he was demanding, his body must produce enormous quantities of enzymes, hormones, and complex biologically active chemicals; in mere minutes the body must undergo a forced degeneration and rebuilding of tissues equal in energy requirements to years of ordinary growth, and for that it needed fuel, material to convert, proteins and minerals, carbohydrates in quantity.

Hungry, starving, starving, Peyser hurried into the lightless kitchen, clutched the handle on the refrigerator door, pulled himself up, tore the door open, hissed as the light stung his eyes, saw two-thirds of a three-pound canned ham, solid ham, good ham, sealed in Saran Wrap on a blue plate, so he seized it, ripped away the plastic, threw the plate aside, where it smashed against a cabinet door, and he dropped back to the floor, bit into the hunk of meat, bit and bit into it, bit deep, ripped, chewed feverishly, bit deep.

He loved to strip out of his clothes and seek another form as soon after nightfall as possible, sprinting into the woods behind his house, up into the hills, where he chased down rabbits and raccoons, foxes and ground squirrels, tore them apart in his hands, with his teeth, fed the fire, the deep inner burning, and he loved it, loved it, not merely because he felt such freedom in that incarnation but because it gave him an overwhelming sense of power, godlike power, more intensely erotic than sex, more satisfying than anything he had experienced before, power, savage power, raw power, the power of a man who had tamed nature, transcended his genetic limits, the power of the wind and the storm, freed of all human limitations, set loose, liberated. He had fed tonight, sweeping through the woods with the confidence of an inescapable predator, as irresistible as the darkness itself, but whatever he had consumed must have been insufficient to empower his return to the form of Michael Peyser, software designer, bachelor, Porsche-owner, ardent collector of movies on video disk, marathon runner, Perrier-drinker.

So now he ate the ham, all two pounds of it, and he snatched other items out of the refrigerator and ate them as well, stuffing them into his mouth with both tine-fingered hands: a bowlful of cold, leftover rigatoni and one meatball; half of an apple pie that he'd bought yesterday at the bakery in town; a stick of butter, an entire quarter of a pound, greasy and cloying but good food, good fuel, just the thing to feed the fire; four raw eggs; and more, more. This was a fire that, when fed, did not burn brighter but cooled, subsided, for it was not a real fire at all but a physical symptom of the desperate need for fuel to keep the metabolic processes running smoothly. Now the fire began to lose some of its heat, shrinking from a roaring blaze to sputtering flames to little more than the glow of hot coals.

Sated, Mike Peyser collapsed to the floor in front of the open refrigerator, in a litter of broken dishes and food and Saran Wrap and eggshells and Tupperware containers. He curled up again and willed himself toward that form in which the world would recognize him, and once more he felt a *shift* taking place in his marrow and bones, in his blood and organs, in sinews and cartilage and muscles and skin, as tides of hormones and enzymes and other biological chemicals were produced by his body and washed through it, but as before the change was arrested with transformation woefully incomplete, and his body eased toward its more savage state, inevitably regressing though he strained with all his will, all his will, strained and struggled to seek the higher form.

The refrigerator door had swung shut. The kitchen was in the grasp of shadows again, and Mike Peyser felt as if that darkness was not merely all around him but also within him.

At last he screamed. As he had feared, once he began to scream, he could not stop.

28

SHORTLY BEFORE MIDNIGHT SAM BOOKER LEFT COVE LODGE. He wore a brown leather jacket, blue sweater, jeans, and blue running shoes—an outfit that allowed him to blend effectively with the night but that didn't look suspicious, though perhaps slightly too youthful for a man of his relentlessly melancholy demeanor. Ordinary as it looked, the jacket had several unusually deep and capacious inner pockets, in which he was carrying a few basic burglary and auto-theft tools. He descended the south stairs, went out the rear door at the bottom, and stood for a moment on the walkway behind the lodge.

Thick fog poured up the face of the bluff and through the open railing, driven by a sudden sea breeze that finally had disturbed the night's calm. In a few hours the breeze would harry the fog inland and leave the coast in relative clarity. By then Sam would have finished the task ahead of him and, no longer needing the cover that the mist provided, would be at last asleep—or more likely fighting insomnia—in his motel-room bed.

He was uneasy. He had not forgotten the pack of kids from whom he'd run on Iceberry Way, earlier in the evening. Because their true nature remained a mystery, he continued to think of them as punks, but he knew they were more than just juvenile delinquents. Strangely, he had the feeling that he *did* know what they were, but the knowledge stirred in him far below even a subconscious plain, in realms of primitive consciousness.

He rounded the south end of the building, walked past the back of the coffee shop, which was now closed, and ten minutes later, by a roundabout route, he arrived at the Moonlight Cove Municipal Building on Jacobi Street. It was exactly as the Bureau's San Francisco agents had described it: a two-story structure—weathered brick on the lower floor, white siding on the upper—with a slate roof, forest-green storm shutters flanking the windows, and large iron carriage lamps at the main entrance. The municipal building and the property on which it stood occupied half a block on the north side of the street, but its anti-institutional architecture was in harmony with the otherwise residential neighborhood. Exterior and interior ground-floor lights were on even at that hour because in addition to the city-government offices and water authority, the municipal building housed the police department, which of course never closed.

From across the street, pretending to be out for a late-night constitutional, Sam studied the place as he passed it. He saw no unusual activity. The sidewalk in front of the main entrance was deserted. Through the glass doors he saw a brightly lighted foyer.

At the next corner he went north and into the alley in the middle of the block. That unlighted serviceway was bracketed by trees and shrubbery and fences that marked the rear property lines of the houses on Jacobi Street and Pacific Drive, by some garages and outbuildings, by groups of garbage cans, and by the large unfenced parking area behind the municipal building.

Sam stepped into a niche in an eight-foot-tall evergreen hedge at the corner of the yard that adjoined the public property. Though the alley was very dark, two sodium-vapor lamps cast a jaundiced glow over the city lot, revealing twelve vehicles: four late-model Fords of the stripped-down, puke-green variety that was produced for federal, state, and local government purchase; a pickup and van both bearing the seal of the city and the legend WATER AUTHORITY; a hulking street-sweeping machine; a large truck with wooden sides and tailgate; and four police cars, all Chevy sedans.

The quartet of black-and-whites were what interested Sam because they were equipped with VDTs linking them to the police department's central computer. Moonlight Cove owned eight patrol cars, a large number for a sleepy coastal town, five more than other communities of similar size could afford and surely in excess of need.

But everything about this police department was bigger and better than necessary, which was one of the things that had triggered silent alarms in the minds of the Bureau agents who'd come to investigate the deaths of Sanchez and the Bustamantes. Moonlight Cove had twelve full-time and three part-time officers, plus four full-time office support personnel. A lot of manpower. Furthermore, they were all receiving salaries competitive with law-enforcement pay scales in major West Coast cities, therefore excessive for a town as small as this. They had the finest uniforms, the finest office furniture, a small armory of handguns and riot guns and tear gas, and—most astonishing of all—they were computerized to an extent that would have been the envy of the boys manning the end-of-the-world bunkers at the Strategic Air Command in Colorado.

From his bristly nook in the fragrant evergreen hedge, Sam studied the lot for a couple of minutes to be sure no one was sitting in any of the vehicles or standing in deep shadows along the back of the building. Levolor blinds were closed at the lighted windows on the ground floor, so no one inside had a view of the parking area.

He took a pair of soft, supple goatskin gloves from a jacket pocket and pulled them on.

He was ready to move when he heard something in the alley behind him. A scraping noise. Back the way he'd come.

Pressing deeper into the hedge, he turned his head to search for the source of the sound. A pale, crumpled cardboard box, twice the size of a shoebox, slid along the blacktop, propelled by the breeze that was increasingly rustling the leaves of the shrubs and trees. The carton met a garbage can, wedged against it, and fell silent.

Streaming across the alley, flowing eastward on the breeze, the fog now looked like smoke, as if the whole town were afire. Squinting back through that churning vapor, he satisfied himself that he was alone, then turned and sprinted to the nearest of the four patrol cars in the unfenced lot.

It was locked.

From an inner jacket pocket, he withdrew a Police Automobile-Lock Release Gun, which could instantly open any lock without damaging the mechanism. He cracked the car, slipped in behind the steering wheel, and closed the door as quickly and quietly as possible.

Enough light from the sodium-vapor lamps penetrated the car for him to see what he was doing, though he was experienced enough to work virtually in the dark. He put the lock gun away and took an ignition-socket wrench from another pocket. In seconds he popped the ignition-switch cylinder from the steering column, exposing the wires.

He hated this part. To click on the video-display mounted on the car's console, he had to start the engine; the computer was more powerful than a lap-top model and communicated with its base data center by energy-intensive microwave transmissions, drawing too much power to run off the battery. The fog would cover the exhaust fumes but not the sound of the engine. The black-and-white was parked eighty feet from the building, so no one inside was likely to hear it. But if someone stepped out of the back door for some fresh air or to take one of the off-duty cruisers out on a call, the idling engine would not escape notice. Then Sam would be in a confrontation that—given the frequency of violent death in this town—he might not survive.

Sighing softly, lightly depressing the accelerator with his right foot, he separated the ignition wires with one gloved hand and twisted the bare contact points together. The engine turned over immediately, without any harsh grinding.

The computer screen blinked on.

The police department's elaborate computerization was provided free by New Wave Microtechnology because they were supposedly using Moonlight Cove as a sort of testing ground for their own systems and software. The source of the excess funds so evident in every other aspect of the department was not easy to pin down, but the suspicion was that it came from New Wave or from New Wave's majority stockholder and chief executive officer, Thomas Shaddack. Any citizen was free to support his local police or other arms of government in excess of his taxes, of course, but if that was what Shaddack was doing, why wasn't it a matter of public record? No innocent man gives large sums of money to a civic cause with *complete* self-effacement. If Shaddack was being secretive about supporting the local authorities with private funds, then the possibility of bought cops and in-the-pocket officials could not be discounted. And if the Moonlight Cove police were virtually soldiers in Thomas Shaddack's private army, it followed that the suspicious number of violent deaths in recent weeks could be related to that unholy alliance.

Now the VDT in the car displayed the New Wave logo in the bottom righthand corner, just as the IBM logo would have been featured if this had been one of their machines.

During the San Francisco office's investigation of the Sanchez-Bustamante case, one of the Bureau's better agents, Morrie Stein, had been in a patrol car with one of Watkins's officers, Reese Dorn, when Dorn accessed the central computer for information in departmental files. By then Morrie had suspected that the computer was even more sophisticated than Watkins or his men had revealed, serving them in some way that exceeded the legal limits of police authority and that they were not willing to discuss, so he had memorized the code number with which Reese had tapped into the system. When he had flown to the Los Angeles office to brief Sam, Morrie had said, "I think every cop in that twisted little town has his own computer-access number, but Dorn's ought to work as well as any. Sam, you've got to get into their computer and let it throw some menus at you, see what it offers, play around with it when Watkins and his men aren't looking over your shoulder. Yeah, I sound paranoid, but there's too much high-tech for their size and needs, unless they're up to something dirty. At first it seems like any town, even more pleasant than most, rather pretty . . . but, dammit, after a while you get the feeling the whole burg is wired, that you're watched everywhere you go, that Big Brother is looking over your shoulder every damn minute. Honest to God, after a few days you're gut-sure you're in a miniature police state, where the control is so subtle you can hardly see it but still complete, iron-fisted. Those cops are bent, Sam; they're deep into something—maybe drug traffic, who knows— and the computer is part of it."

Reese Dorn's number was 262699, and Sam tapped it out on the VDT keyboard. The New Wave logo disappeared. The screen was blank for a second. Then a menu appeared.

> **CHOOSE ONE:**
> **A. DISPATCHER**
> **B. CENTRAL FILES**
> **C. BULLETIN BOARD**
> **D. OUTSYSTEM MODEM**

To Sam, the first item on the menu indicated that a cruising officer could communicate with the dispatcher at headquarters not only by means of the police-band radio with which the car was equipped but also through the computer link. But why would he want to go to all the trouble of typing in questions to the dispatcher and reading the transmitted replies off the VDT when the information could be gotten so much easier and quicker on the radio? Unless . . . there were some things that these cops did not want to talk about on radio frequencies that could be monitored by anyone with a police-band receiver.

He did not open the link to the dispatcher because then he would have to begin a dialogue, posing as Reese Dorn, and that would be like shouting, *Hey, I'm out here in one of your cruisers, poking my nose in just where you don't want, so why don't you come and chop it off.*

Instead, he tapped **B** and entered it. Another menu appeared.

> **CHOOSE ONE:**
> **A. STATUS—CURRENT ARRESTEES**
> **B. STATUS—CURRENT COURT CASES**
> **C. STATUS—PENDING COURT CASES**
> **D. PAST ARREST RECORDS—COUNTY**
> **E. PAST ARREST RECORDS—CITY**

F. CONVICTED CRIMINALS LIVING IN COUNTY
G. CONVICTED CRIMINALS LIVING IN CITY

Just to satisfy himself that the offerings on the menu were what they appeared to be and not code for other information, he punched in selection **F**, to obtain data on convicted criminals living in the county. Another menu appeared, offering him ten choices:

MURDER
MANSLAUGHTER
RAPE
SEX OFFENSES
ASSAULT AND BATTERY
ARMED ROBBERY
BURGLARY
BREAKING AND ENTERING
OTHER THEFT
MISCELLANEOUS LESSER OFFENSES

He called forth the file on murder and discovered three convicted killers—all guilty of murder in either the first or second degree—were now living as free men in the county after having served anywhere from twelve to forty years for their crimes before being released on parole. Their names, addresses, and telephone numbers appeared on the screen with the names of their victims, economically summarized details of their crimes, and the dates of their imprisonment; none lived in the city limits of Moonlight Cove.

Sam looked up from the screen and scanned the parking lot. It remained deserted. The omnipresent mist was filled with thicker veins of fog that rippled bannerlike as they flowed past the car, and he felt almost as if he were under the sea in a bathyscaphe, peering out at long ribbons of kelp fluttering in marine currents.

He returned to the main menu and asked for item **C, BULLETIN BOARD**. That proved to be a collection of messages that Watkins and his officers had left for one another regarding matters that seemed sometimes related to police work and sometimes private. Most were in such cryptic shorthand that Sam didn't feel he could puzzle them out or that they would be worth the effort to decipher.

He tried item **D** on the main menu, **OUTSYSTEM MODEM**, and was shown a list of computers nationwide with which he could link through the telephone modem in the nearby municipal building. The department's possible connections were astonishing: **LOS ANGELES PD, SAN FRANCISCO PD, SAN DIEGO PD, DENVER PD, HOUSTON PD, DALLAS PD, PHOENIX PD, CHICAGO PD, MIAMI PD, NEW YORK CITY PD,** and a score of other major cities; **CALIFORNIA DEPARTMENT OF MOTOR VEHICLES, DEPARTMENT OF PRISONS, HIGHWAY PATROL,** and many other state agencies with less obvious connections to police work; **U.S. ARMY PERSONNEL FILES, NAVY PERSONNEL FILES, AIR FORCE; FBI CRIMINAL RECORDS, FBI LLEAS** (Local Law-Enforcement Assistance System, a relatively new Bureau program); even

INTERPOL's New York office, through which the international organization could access its central files in Europe.

What in the hell would a small police force in rural California need with all those sources of information?

And there was more: data to which even fully computerized police agencies in cities like Los Angeles would not have easy access. By law, some of it was stuff that police could not obtain without a court order, such as the files at TRW, the nation's premier credit-reporting firm. The Moonlight Cove Police Department's ability to access TRW's data base at will had to be a secret kept from TRW itself, for the company would not have cooperated in a wholesale disgorgement of its files without a subpoena. The system also offered entrance to CIA data bases in Virginia, which were supposedly secured against access from any computer beyond the Agency's walls, and to certain FBI files which were likewise believed to be inviolate.

Shaken, Sam retreated from the **OUTSYSTEM MODEM** options and returned to the main menu.

He stared out at the parking lot, thinking.

When briefing Sam a few days ago, Morrie Stein had suggested that Moonlight Cove's police might somehow be trafficking in drugs, and that New Wave's generosity with computer systems might indicate complicity on the part of certain unidentified officers of that firm. But the Bureau was also interested in the possibility that New Wave was illegally selling sensitive high technology to the Soviets and that it had bought the Moonlight Cove police because, through these law-enforcement contacts, the company would be alerted at the earliest possible moment to a nascent federal probe into its activities. They had no explanation of how either of those crimes accounted for all the recent deaths, but they had to start with *some* theory.

Now Sam was ready to discount both the idea that New Wave was selling to the Soviets and that some executives of the firm were in the drug trade. The far-reaching web of data bases that the police had made available to themselves through their modem—one hundred and twelve were listed on that menu!—was greatly in excess of anything they would require for either drug trafficking or sniffing out federal suspicions of possible Soviet connections at New Wave.

They had created an informational network more suitable to the operational necessities of an entire state government—or, even more accurately, a small nation. A small, *hostile* nation. This data web was designed to provide its owner with enormous power. It was as if this picturesque little town suffered under the governing hand of a megalomaniac whose central delusion was that he could create a tiny kingdom from which he would eventually conquer vast territory.

Today, Moonlight Cove; tomorrow, the world.

"What the fuck are they doing?" Sam wondered aloud.

29

SAFELY LOCKED IN HER ROOM AT COVE LODGE—DRESSED for bed in pale yellow panties and a white T-shirt emblazoned with Kermit the Frog's smiling face—Tessa drank Diet Coke and tried to watch a repeat of the *Tonight* show, but she couldn't get interested in the conversations that Johnny Carson conducted with a witless actress, a witless singer, and a witless comedian. Diet thought to accompany Diet Coke.

The more time that passed after her unsettling experience in the motel's halls and stairwells, the more she wondered if indeed she had imagined being stalked. She was distraught about Janice's death, after all, preoccupied by the thought that it was murder rather than suicide. And she was still dyspeptic from the cheeseburger she'd eaten for dinner, which had been so greasy that it might have been deep-fried, bun and all, in impure yak lard. As Scrooge had first believed of Marley's ghost, so Tessa now began to view the phantoms that had frightened her earlier: Perhaps they'd been nothing more than an undigested bit of beef, a blot of mustard, a crumb of cheese, a fragment of an underdone potato.

As Carson's current guest talked about a weekend he'd spent at an arts festival in Havana with Fidel Castro—"a great guy, a funny guy, a compassionate guy"—Tessa got up from the bed and went to the bathroom to wash her face and brush her teeth. As she was squeezing Crest onto the brush, she heard someone try the door to her room.

The small bath was off the smaller foyer. When she stepped to the threshold, she was within a couple of feet of the door to the hall, close enough to see the knob twisting back and forth as someone tested the lock. They weren't even being subtle about it. The knob clicked and rattled, and the door clattered against the frame.

She dropped her toothbrush and hurried to the telephone that stood on the nightstand.

No dial tone.

She jiggled the cutoff buttons, pressed O for operator, but nothing worked. The motel switchboard was shut down. The phone was dead.

30

SEVERAL TIMES CHRISSIE HAD TO SCURRY OFF THE ROAD, taking cover in the brush along the verge, until an approaching car or truck went past. One of them was a Moonlight Cove police car, heading toward town, and she was pretty sure it was the one that had come out to the house. She hunkered down in tall grass and milkweed stalks, and remained there until the black-and-white's taillights dwindled to tiny red dots and finally vanished around a turn.

A few houses were built along the first mile and a half of that two-lane blacktop. Chrissie knew some of the people who lived in them: the Thomases, the Stones, the Elswicks. She was tempted to go to one of those places, knock on the door, and ask for help. But she couldn't be sure that those people were still the nice folks they had once been. They might have changed, too, like her parents. Either something supernatural or from outer space was taking possession of people in and around Moonlight Cove, and she had seen enough scary movies and read enough scary books to know that when *those* kind of forces were at work, you could no longer trust anyone.

She was betting nearly everything on Father Castelli at Our Lady of Mercy because he was a holy man, and no demons from hell would be able to get a grip on him. Of course, if the problem was aliens from another world, Father Castelli would not be protected just because he was a man of God.

In that case, if the priest had been taken over, and if Chrissie managed to get away from him after she discovered he was one of the enemy, she'd go straight to Mrs. Irene Tokawa, her teacher. Mrs. Tokawa was the smartest person Chrissie knew. If aliens were taking over Moonlight Cove, Mrs. Tokawa would have realized something was wrong before it was too late. She would have taken steps to protect herself, and she would be one of the last that the monsters would get their hooks into. Hooks or tentacles or claws or pincers or whatever.

So Chrissie hid from passing traffic, sneaked past the houses scattered along the county road, and proceeded haltingly but steadily toward town. The horned moon, sometimes revealed above the fog, had traversed most of the sky; it would soon be gone. A stiff breeze had swept in from the west, marked by periodic gusts strong enough to whip her hair straight up in the air as if it were a blond flame leaping from her head. Although the temperature had fallen to only about fifty degrees, the night felt much colder during those turbulent moments when the breeze temporarily became a blustering wind. The positive side was that the more miserable the cold and wind made her, the less aware she was of that other discomfort—hunger.

"Waif Found Wandering Hungry and Dazed After Encounter with Space Aliens," she said, reading that imagined headline from an issue of the *National Enquirer* that existed only in her mind.

She was approaching the intersection of the county route and Holliwell Road, feeling good about the progress she was making, when she nearly walked into the arms of those she was trying to avoid.

To the east of the county route, Holliwell was a dirt road leading up into the hills, under the interstate, and all the way to the old, abandoned Icarus Colony— a dilapidated twelve-room house, barn, and collapsing outbuildings—where a group of artists had tried to establish an ideal communal society back in the 1950s. Since then it had been a horse-breeding facility (failed), the site of a weekly flea market and auction (failed), a natural-food restaurant (failed), and had long ago settled into ruin. Kids knew all about it because it was a spooky place and thus the site of many tests of courage. To the west, Holliwell Road was paved and led along the edge of the town limits, past some of the newer homes in the area, past New Wave Microtech, and eventually out to the north point of the cove, where Thomas Shaddack, the computer genius, lived in a huge, weird-looking house. Chrissie didn't intend to go either east or west on Holliwell; it was just a milestone on her trek, and when she crossed it she would be at the northeast corner of the Moonlight Cove city limits.

She was within a hundred feet of Holliwell when she heard the low but swiftly swelling sound of a racing engine. She stepped away from the road, over a narrow ditch at the verge, waded through weeds, and took cover against the thick trunk of an ancient pine. Even as she hunkered down by the tree, she got a fix on the direction from which the vehicle was approaching—west—and then she saw its headlights spearing into the intersection just south of her. A truck pulled into view on Holliwell, ignoring the stop sign, and braked in the middle of the intersection. Fog whirled and plumed around it.

Chrissie could see that heavy-duty, black, extended-bed pickup fairly well because, as the junction of Holliwell and the county road was the site of frequent accidents, a single streetlight had been installed on the northeast corner for better visibility and as a warning to drivers. The truck bore the distinctive New Wave insignia on the door, which she could recognize even at a distance because she had seen it maybe a thousand times before: a white and blue circle the size of a dinner plate, the bottom half of which was a cresting blue wave. The truck had a large bed, and at the moment its cargo was men; six or eight were sitting in the back.

The instant that the pickup halted in the intersection, two men vaulted over the tailgate. One of them went to the wooded point at the northwest corner of the intersection and slipped into the trees, no more than a hundred feet south of the pine from which Chrissie was watching him. The other crossed to the southeast corner of the junction and took up a position in weeds and chaparral.

The pickup turned south on the county road and sped away.

Chrissie suspected that the remaining men in the truck would be let off at other points along the eastern perimeter of Moonlight Cove, where they would take up watch positions. Furthermore, the truck had been big enough to carry at least twenty men, and no doubt others had been dropped off as it had come eastward along Holliwell from the New Wave building in the west. They were surrounding Moonlight Cove with sentries. She was quite sure they were looking for her. She had seen something she had not been meant to see—her parents in the act of a hideous transformation, shucking off their human disguise—and now she had to be found and "converted"—as Tucker had put it—before she had a chance to warn the world.

The sound of the black truck receded.

Silence settled in like a damp blanket.

Fog swirled and churned and eddied in countless currents, but the overriding tidal forces in the air pushed it relentlessly toward the dark and serried hills.

Then the breeze abruptly ratcheted up until it became a real wind again, whispering in the tall weeds, soughing through the evergreens. It produced a soft and strangely forlorn thrumming from a nearby road sign.

Though Chrissie knew where the two men had gone to ground, she could not see them. They were well hidden.

31

FOG FLEW PAST THE PATROL CAR AND EASTWARD THROUGH the night, driven by a breeze that was swiftly becoming a full wind, and ideas flew through Sam's mind with the same fluidity. His thoughts were so disturbing that he would have preferred to have sat in mindless stupefaction.

From considerable prior computer experience, he knew that part of a system's capabilities could be hidden if the program designer simply deleted some choices from the task menus that appeared on the screen. He stared at the primary menu on the car's display—**A, DISPATCHER; B, CENTRAL FILES; C, BULLETIN BOARD; D, OUTSYSTEM MODEM**—and he pressed **E**, though no **E** task was offered.

Words appeared on the terminal: **HELLO, OFFICER DORN.**

There *was* an **E**. He'd entered either a secret data base requiring ritual responses for access or an interactive information system that would respond to questions he typed on the keyboard. If the former was the case, if passwords or phrases were required, and if he typed the wrong response, he was in trouble; the computer would shut him out and sound an alarm in police headquarters to warn them that an impersonator was using Dorn's number.

Proceeding with caution, he typed: **HELLO.**

MAY I BE OF ASSISTANCE?

Sam decided to proceed as if this was just what it seemed to be—a straightforward, question-and-answer program. He tapped the keyboard: **MENU.**

The screen blanked for a moment, then the same words reappeared: **MAY I BE OF ASSISTANCE?**

He tried again: **PRIMARY MENU.**

MAY I BE OF ASSISTANCE?

MAIN MENU.

MAY I BE OF ASSISTANCE?

Using a system accessed by question and response, with which one was unfamiliar, meant finding the proper commands more or less by trial and error. Sam tried again: **FIRST MENU.**

At last he was rewarded.

CHOOSE ONE:

A. NEW WAVE PERSONNEL

B. PROJECT MOONHAWK

C. SHADDACK

He had found a secret connection between New Wave, its founder Thomas Shaddack, and the Moonlight Cove police. But he didn't know yet what the connection was or what it meant.

He suspected that choice **C** might link him to Shaddack's personal computer terminal, allowing him to have a dialogue with Shaddack that would be more private than a conversation conducted on police-band radio. If that was the case, then Shaddack and the local cops were indeed involved in a conspiracy so criminal that it required a very high degree of security. He did not punch **C** because, if he called up Shaddack's computer and got Mr. Big himself on the other end, there was no way he could successfully pretend to be Reese Dorn.

Choice **A** probably would provide him with a roster of New Wave's executives and department heads, and maybe with codes that would allow him to link up with their personal terminals as well. He didn't want to talk with any of them either.

Besides, he felt that he was on borrowed time. He surveyed the parking lot again and peered especially hard at the deeper pools of shadow beyond the reach of the sodium-vapor lamps. He'd been in the patrol car for fifteen minutes, and no one had come or gone from the municipal-building lot in that time. He doubted his luck would hold much longer, and he wanted to learn as much as possible in whatever minutes remained before he was interrupted.

PROJECT MOONHAWK was the most mysterious and interesting of the three choices, so he pushed **B**, and another menu appeared.

CHOOSE ONE:
A. CONVERTED
B. PENDING CONVERSION
C. SCHEDULE OF CONVERSION—LOCAL
D. SCHEDULE OF CONVERSION—SECOND STAGE

He punched choice **A,** and a column of names and addresses appeared on the screen. They were people in Moonlight Cove, and at the head of the column was the notation **1967 NOW CONVERTED.**

Converted? From what? To what? Was there something religious about this conspiracy? Some strange cult? Or maybe "converted" was used in some euphemistic sense or as a code.

The word gave him the creeps.

Sam discovered that he could either scroll through the list or access it in alphabetized chunks. He looked up the names of residents whom he either knew of or had met. Loman Watkins was on the converted list. So was Reese Dorn. Burt Peckham, the owner of Knight's Bridge Tavern, was not among the converted, but the entire Perez family, surely the same that operated the restaurant, was on that roster.

He checked Harold Talbot, the disabled vet with whom he intended to make contact in the morning. Talbot was not on the converted list.

Puzzled as to the meaning of it all, Sam closed out that file, returned to the main menu, and punched **B, PENDING CONVERSION.** This brought another list of names and addresses to the VDT, and the column was headed by the **1104 PENDING CONVERSION.** On this roster he found Burt Peckham and Harold Talbot.

He tried **C, SCHEDULE OF CONVERSION—LOCAL**, and a submenu of three headings appeared:

A. MONDAY, OCTOBER 13, 6:00 P.M.
    THROUGH
    TUESDAY, OCTOBER 14, 6:00 A.M.

   B. **TUESDAY, OCTOBER 14, 6:00 A.M.**
      THROUGH
      TUESDAY, OCTOBER 14, 6:00 P.M.

   C. **TUESDAY, OCTOBER 14, 6:00 P.M.**
      THROUGH
      MIDNIGHT

It was now 12:39 A.M., Tuesday, about halfway between the times noted in choice **A,** so he punched that one first. It was another list of names headed by the notation **380 CONVERSIONS SCHEDULED.**

The fine hairs were bristling on the back of Sam's neck, and he didn't know why except that the word "conversions" unsettled him. It made him think of that old movie with Kevin McCarthy, *Invasion of the Body Snatchers.*

He also thought of the pack that had pursued him earlier in the night. Had they been . . . converted?

When he looked up Burt Peckham, he found the tavern owner on the schedule for conversion before 6:00 A.M. However, Harry Talbot was not listed.

The car shook.

Sam snapped his head up and reached for the revolver holstered under his jacket.

Wind. It was only wind. A series of hard gusts shredded holes in the fog and lightly rocked the car. After a moment the wind died to a strong breeze again, and the torn fabric of fog mended itself, but Sam's heart was still thudding painfully.

32

AS TESSA PUT DOWN THE USELESS TELEPHONE, THE DOOR-knob stopped rattling. She stood by the bed for a while, listening, then ventured warily into the foyer to press her ear against the door.

She heard voices but not immediately beyond that portal. They were farther down the hallway, peculiar voices that spoke in urgent, raspy whispers. She could not make out anything they said.

She was sure they were the same ones who had stalked her, unseen, when she had gone for ice and a Diet Coke. Now they were back. And somehow they had knocked out the phones, so she couldn't call for help. It was crazy, but it was happening.

Such persistence on their part indicated to Tessa that they were not ordinary rapists or muggers, that they had focused on her because she was Janice's sister, because she was there to look into Janice's death. However, she wondered how they had become aware of her arrival in town and why they had chosen to move against her so precipitously, without even waiting to see if she was just going to settle Janice's affairs and leave. Only she and her mother knew that she intended to attempt a murder investigation of her own.

Gooseflesh prickled her bare legs, and she felt vulnerable in just a T-shirt and panties. She went quickly to the closet, pulled on jeans and a sweater.

She wasn't alone in the motel. There were other guests. Mr. Quinn had said so. Maybe not many, perhaps only another two or three. But if worse came to worst, she could scream, and the other guests would hear her, and her would-be assailants would have to flee.

She picked up her Rockports, in which she had stuffed the white athletic socks she'd been wearing, and returned to the door.

Low, hoarse voices hissed and muttered at the far end of the hall—then a bone-jarring crash slammed through the lodge, making her cry out and twitch in surprise. Another crash followed at once. She heard a door give way at another room.

A woman screamed, and a man shouted, but the *other* voices were what brought a chill of horror to Tessa. There were several of them, three or even four, and they were eerie and shockingly savage. The public corridor beyond her door was filled with harsh wolflike growls, murderous snarls, shrill and excited squeals, an icy keening that was the essence of blood hunger, and other less describable sounds, but worst of all was that those same inhuman voices, clearly belonging to beasts not men, nevertheless also spat out a few recognizable words: " . . . *need, need . . . get her, get . . . get, get . . . blood, bitch, blood . . .* "

Leaning against the door, holding on to it for support, Tessa tried to tell herself that the words she heard were from the man and woman whose room had been broken into, but she knew that was not true, because she also heard both a man and woman screaming. Their screams were horrible, almost unbearable, full of terror and agony, as if they were being beaten to death or worse, much worse, being torn apart, ripped limb from limb and gutted.

A couple of years ago Tessa had been in Northern Ireland, making a documentary about the pointlessness of the needless violence there, and she'd been unfortunate enough to be at a cemetery, at the funeral of one of the endless series of "martyrs"—Catholic or Protestant, it didn't matter any more, both had a surfeit of them—when the crowd of mourners had metamorphosed into a pack of savages. They had streamed from the churchyard into nearby streets, looking for those of a different faith, and soon they'd come across two British plainclothes army officers patrolling the area in an unmarked car. By its sheer size, the mob blocked the car's advance, encircled it, smashed in the windows, and dragged the would-be peacekeepers out onto the pavement. Tessa's two technical assistants had fled, but she had waded into the melee with her shoulder-mounted videotape camera, and through the lens she had seemed to be looking beyond the reality of this world into hell itself. Eyes wild, faces distorted with hatred and rage, grief forgotten and bloodlust embraced, the mourners had tirelessly kicked the fallen Britons, then pulled them to their feet only to pummel and stab them, slammed them repeatedly against the car until their spines broke and their skulls cracked, then dropped them and stomped them and tore at them and stabbed them again, though by that time they were both dead. Howling and shrieking, cursing, chanting slogans that degenerated into meaningless chains of sounds, mindless rhythms, like a flock of carrion-eating birds, they plucked at the shattered bodies, though they weren't like earthly birds, neither buzzards nor vultures, but like demons that had flown up from the pit, tearing at the dead men not only with the intention of consuming their flesh but with the hot desire to rip out and steal their souls. Two of those frenzied men had noticed Tessa, had seized her camera and smashed it, and had thrown her to the ground. For one terrible moment she was sure that they would dismember her in their frenzy. Two of them leaned down, grabbing at her clothes. Their faces were so wrenched with hatred that they no longer looked human, but like gargoyles that had come to life and had climbed down from the roofs of cathedrals. They had surrendered all that was human in themselves and let loose the gene-encoded ghosts of the primitives from whom they were descended. "For God's sake, no!" she had cried. "For God's sake, please!" Perhaps it was the mention of God or just the sound of a human voice that had *not* devolved into the hoarse gnarl of a beast, but for some reason they let go and hesitated. She seized that reprieve to scramble away from them, through the churning, blood-crazed mob to safety.

What she heard now, at the other end of the motel corridor, was just like that. Or worse.

33

BEGINNING TO SWEAT EVEN THOUGH THE PATROL CAR'S heater was not on, still spooked by every sudden gust of wind, Sam called up submenu item **B**, which showed the conversions scheduled from 6:00 this coming morning until 6:00 P.M. that evening. Those names were preceded by the heading **450 CONVERSIONS SCHEDULED**. Harry Talbot's name was not on that list either.

Choice **C**, six o'clock Tuesday evening through midnight the same day, indicated that 274 conversions were scheduled. Harry Talbot's name and address were on that third and final list.

Sam mentally added the numbers mentioned in each of the three conversion periods—380, 450, and 274—and realized they totaled 1104, which was the same number that headed the list of pending conversions. Add that number to 1967, the total listed as already converted, and the grand total, 3071, was probably the population of Moonlight Cove. By the next time the clock struck midnight, a little less than twenty-three hours from now, the entire town would be converted—whatever the hell *that* meant.

He keyed out of the submenu and was about to switch off the car's engine and get out of there when the word **ALERT** appeared on the VDT and began to flash. Fear thrilled through him because he was sure they had discovered an intruder poking around in their system; he must have tripped some subtle alarm in the program.

Instead of opening the door and making a run for it, however, he watched the screen for a few more seconds, held by curiosity.

TELEPHONE SWEEP INDICATES FBI AGENT IN MOONLIGHT COVE.
POINT OF CALL:
PAY PHONE, SHELL STATION,
OCEAN AVENUE.

The alert *was* related to him, though not because they knew he was currently
sitting in one of their patrol cars and probing the New Wave/Moonhawk
conspiracy. Evidently the bastards were tied into the phone company's data banks
and periodically swept those records to see who had made calls from what numbers to what numbers—even from all of the town's pay telephones, which in
ordinary circumstances could have been counted on to provide secure communications for a field agent. They were paranoid and security conscious and electronically connected to an extent and degree that proved increasingly astounding
with each revelation.

TIME OF CALL:
7:31 P.M., MONDAY,
OCTOBER 13.

At least they didn't keep a minute-by-minute or even hour-by-hour link with
the telephone company. Their computer obviously swept those records on a programmed schedule, perhaps every four or six or eight hours. Otherwise they
would have been on the lookout for him shortly after he had made the call to
Scott earlier in the evening.

After the legend **CALL PLACED TO**, his home phone number appeared, then
his name and his address in Sherman Oaks. Followed by:

CALL PLACED BY:
SAMUEL H. BOOKER.

MEANS OF PAYMENT:
TELEPHONE CREDIT CARD.

TYPE OF CARD:
EMPLOYER-BILLED.

BILLING ADDRESS:
FEDERAL BUREAU OF INVESTIGATION,
WASHINGTON, D.C.

They would start checking motels in the entire county, but as he was staying
in Moonlight Cove's only lodgings, the search would be a short one. He wondered
if he had time to sprint back to Cove Lodge, get his car, and drive to the next
town, Aberdeen Wells, where he could call the Bureau office in San Francisco
from an unmonitored phone. He had learned enough to know that something
damned strange was going on in this town, enough to justify an imposition of
federal authority and a far-reaching investigation.

But the very next words that appeared on the VDT convinced him that if he
went back to Cove Lodge to get his car, he would be caught before he could get
out of town. And if they got their hands on him, he might be just one more nasty
accidental-death statistic.

They knew his home address, so Scott might be in danger too—not right now, not down there in Los Angeles, but maybe by tomorrow.

DIALOGUE INVOKED
WATKINS: SHOLNICK, ARE YOU LINKED IN?
SHOLNICK: HERE.
WATKINS: TRY COVE LODGE.
SHOLNICK: ON MY WAY.

Already an officer, Sholnick, was on his way to see if Sam was a registered guest at Cove Lodge. And the cover story that Sam had established with the desk clerk—that he was a successful stockbroker from Los Angeles, contemplating early retirement in one coastal town or another—was blown.

WATKINS: PETERSON?
PETERSON: HERE.

They probably didn't have to type in their names. Each man's link would identify him to the main computer, and his name would be automatically printed in front of the brief input that he typed. Clean, swift, easy to use.

WATKINS: BACK UP SHOLNICK.
PETERSON: DONE.
WATKINS: DON'T KILL HIM UNTIL WE CAN QUESTION.

All over Moonlight Cove, cops in patrol cars were talking to one another by computer, off the public airwaves, where they could not be easily overheard. Even though Sam was eavesdropping on them without their knowledge, he felt that he was up against a formidable enemy nearly as omniscient as God.

WATKINS: DANBERRY?
DANBERRY: HERE. HQ.
WATKINS: BLOCK OCEAN AVENUE TO INTERSTATE.
DANBERRY: DONE.
SHADDACK: WHAT ABOUT THE FOSTER GIRL?

Sam was startled to see Shaddack's name appear on the screen. The alert apparently had flashed on his computer at home, perhaps also sounding an audible alarm and waking him.

WATKINS: STILL LOOSE.
SHADDACK: CAN'T RISK BOOKER STUMBLING ACROSS HER.
WATKINS: TOWN'S RINGED WITH SENTRIES. THEY'LL CATCH
           HER COMING IN.
SHADDACK: SHE'S SEEN TOO MUCH.

Sam had read about Thomas Shaddack in magazines, newspapers. The guy was a celebrity of sorts, the computer genius of the age, and somewhat geeky looking besides.

Fascinated by this revealing dialogue, which incriminated the famous man and his bought police force, Sam had not immediately picked up on the meaning of the exchanges between Chief Watkins and Danberry: *Danberry . . . Here. HQ . . . Block Ocean Avenue to interstate . . . Done.* He realized that Officer Danberry was at headquarters, HQ, which was the municipal building, and that any moment he was going to come out the back door and rush to one of the four patrol cars in the parking lot.

"Oh, shit." Sam grabbed the ignition wires, tearing them apart.

The engine coughed and died, and the video-display went dark.

A fraction of a second later, Danberry threw open the rear door of the municipal building and ran into the parking lot.

34

WHEN THE SCREAMING STOPPED, TESSA BROKE OUT OF A trance of terror and went straight to the phone again. The line was still dead.

Where was Quinn? The motel office was closed at this hour, but didn't the manager have an adjacent apartment? He would respond to the ruckus. Or was he one of the savage pack in the corridor?

They had broken down one door. They could break down hers too.

She grabbed one of the straight-backed chairs from the table by the window, hurried to the door with it, tilted it back, and wedged it under the knob.

She no longer thought they were after her just because she was Janice's sister and bent on uncovering the truth. That explanation didn't account for their attack on the other guests, who had nothing to do with Janice. It was nuts. She didn't understand what was happening, but she clearly understood the implications of what she had heard: a psychotic killer—no, several psychotics, judging by the noise they had made, some bizarre cult like the Manson family maybe, or worse— were loose in the motel. They had already killed two people, and they could kill her, too, evidently for the sheer pleasure of it. She felt as if she were in a bad dream.

She expected the walls to bulge and flow in that amorphous fashion of nightmare places, but they remained solid, fixed, and the colors of things were too sharp and clear for this to be a dreamscape.

Frantically she pulled on her socks and shoes, unnerved by being barefoot, as earlier her near nakedness had made her feel vulnerable—as if death could be foiled by an adequate wardrobe.

She heard those voices again. Not at the end of the hallway any more. Near her own door. Approaching. She wished the door featured one of those one-way, fisheye lenses that allowed a wide-angled view, but there was none.

At the sill was a half-inch crack, however, so Tessa dropped to the floor, pressed one side of her face against the carpet, and squinted out at the corridor. From that limited perspective, she saw something move past her room so quickly that her eyes could not quite track it, though she caught a glimpse of its feet, which was enough to alter dramatically her perception of what was happening. This was not an incidence of human savagery akin to the bloodbath she had witnessed—and to which she nearly had succumbed—in Northern Ireland. This was, instead, an encounter with the unknown, a breach of reality, a sudden sideslip out of the normal world into the uncanny. They were leathery, hairy, dark-skinned feet, broad and flat and surprisingly long, with toes so extrusile and multiple jointed that they almost seemed to have the function of fingers.

Something hit the door. Hard.

Tessa scrambled to her feet and out of the foyer.

Crazed voices filled the hall: that same weird mix of harsh animal sounds punctuated by bursts of breathlessly spoken but for the most part disconnected words.

She went around the bed to the window, disengaged the pressure latch, and slid the movable pane aside.

Again the door shook. The boom was so loud that Tessa felt as if she were inside a drum. It would not collapse as easily as the other guests' door, thanks to the chair, but it would not hold for more than a few additional blows.

She sat on the sill, swung her legs out, looked down. The fog-dampened walk glistened in the dim yellow glow of the serviceway lamps about twelve feet below the window. An easy jump.

They hit the door again, harder. Wood splintered.

Tessa pushed off the windowsill. She landed on the wet walkway and, because of her rubber-soled shoes, skidded but did not fall.

Overhead, in the room she had left, wood splintered more noisily than before, and tortured metal screeched as the lock on the door began to disintegrate.

She was near the north end of the building. She thought she saw something moving in the darkness in that direction. It might have been nothing more than a clotting of fog churning eastward on the wind, but she didn't want to take a chance, so she ran south, with the vast black sea beyond the railing at her right side. By the time she reached the end of the building, a crash echoed through the night— the sound of the door to her room going down—which was followed by the howling of the pack as it entered that place in search of her.

35

SAM COULD NOT HAVE SLIPPED OUT OF THE PATROL CAR without drawing Danberry's attention. Four cruisers awaited the cop's use, so there was a seventy-five-percent chance that Sam would be undetected if he stayed in the car. He slid down in the driver's seat as far as he could and leaned to his right, across the computer keyboard on the console.

Danberry went to the next car in line.

With his head on the console, his neck twisted so he could look up through the window on the passenger's side, Sam watched as Danberry unlocked the door of that other cruiser. He prayed that the cop would keep his back turned, because the interior of the car in which Sam slouched was revealed by the sulfurous glow of the parking-lot lights. If Danberry even glanced his way, Sam would be seen.

The cop got into the other black-and-white and slammed the door, and Sam sighed with relief. The engine turned over. Danberry pulled out of the municipal lot. When he hit the alley he gunned the engine, and his tires spun and squealed for a moment before they bit in, and then he was gone.

Though Sam wanted to hot-wire the car and switch on the computer again to find out whether Watkins and Shaddack were still conversing, he knew he dared not stay any longer. As the manhunt escalated, the police department's offices in the municipal building were sure to become busy.

Because he didn't want them to know that he had been probing in their computer or that he had eavesdropped on their VDT conversation—the greater they assumed his ignorance to be, the less effective they would be in their search for him—Sam used his tools to replace the ignition core in the steering column. He got out, pushed the lock button down, and closed the door.

He didn't want to leave the area by the alleyway because a patrol car might turn in from one end or the other, capturing him in its headlights. Instead he dashed straight across that narrow back street from the parking lot and opened a gate in a simple wrought-iron fence. He entered the rear yard of a slightly decrepit Victorian-style house whose owners had let the shrubbery run so wild that it looked as if a macabre cartoon family from the pen of Gahan Wilson might live in the place. He walked quietly past the side of the house, across the front lawn, to Pacific Drive, one block south of Ocean Avenue.

The night calm was not split by sirens. He heard no shouts, no running footsteps, no cries of alarm. But he knew he had awakened a many-headed beast and that this singularly dangerous Hydra was looking for him all over town.

36

MIKE PEYSER DIDN'T KNOW WHAT TO DO, DIDN'T KNOW, HE was scared, confused and scared, so he could not think clearly, though he *needed* to think sharp and clear like a man, except the wild part of him kept intruding; his mind worked quickly, and it was sharp, but he could not hold to a single train of thought for more than a couple of minutes. Quick thinking, rapid-fire thinking, was not good enough to solve a problem like this; he had to think quick *and* deep. But his attention span was not what it should have been.

When he finally was able to stop screaming and get up from the kitchen floor, he hurried into the dark dining room, through the unlighted living room, down the short hall to the bedroom, then into the master bath, going on all fours part of the way, rising onto his hind feet as he crossed the bedroom threshold, unable to rise all the way up and stand entirely straight, but flexible enough to get more than halfway erect. In the bathroom, which was lit only by the vague and somewhat scintillant moonglow that penetrated the small window above the shower stall, he gripped the edge of the sink and stared into the mirrored front of the medicine cabinet, where he could see only a shadowy reflection of himself, without detail.

He wanted to believe that in fact he had returned to his natural form, that his feeling of being trapped in the altered state was pure hallucination, yes, yes, he wanted to believe that, badly needed to believe, believe, even though he could not stand fully erect, even though he could feel the difference in his impossibly long-fingered hands and in the queer set of his head on his shoulders and in the way his back joined his hips. He needed to believe.

Turn on the light, he told himself.

He could not do it.

Turn on the light.

He was afraid.

He had to turn on the light and look at himself.

But he gripped the sink and could not move.

Turn on the light.

Instead he leaned toward the tenebrous mirror, peering intently at the indistinct reflection, seeing little more than the pale amber radiance of strange eyes.

Turn on the light.

He let out a thin mewl of anguish and terror.

Shaddack, he thought suddenly. Shaddack, he must tell Shaddack, Tom Shaddack would know what to do, Shaddack was his best hope, maybe his only hope, Shaddack.

He let go of the sink, dropped to the floor, hurried out of the bathroom, into the bedroom, toward the telephone on the nightstand. As he went, in a voice alternately shrill and guttural, piercing and whispery, he repeated the name as if it were a word with magic power: *"Shaddack, Shaddack, Shaddack, Shaddack . . ."*

37

TESSA LOCKLAND TOOK REFUGE IN A TWENTY-FOUR-HOUR coin-operated laundry four blocks east of Cove Lodge and half a block off Ocean Avenue. She wanted to be someplace bright, and the banks of overhead fluorescents allowed no shadows. Alone in the laundry, she sat in a badly scarred, yellow plastic chair, staring at rows of clothes-dryer portals, as if understanding would be visited upon her from some cosmic source communicating on those circles of glass.

As a documentarist, she had to have a keen eye for the patterns in life that would give coherence to a film narratively and visually, so she had no trouble seeing patterns of darkness, death, and unknown forces in this deeply troubled town. The fantastic creatures in the motel surely had been the source of the cries she'd heard on the beach earlier that night, and her sister had no doubt been killed by those same beings, whatever the hell they were. Which sort of explained why the authorities had been so insistent that Marion okay the cremation of Janice's body—not because the remains were corroded by seawater and half-devoured by fish, but because cremation would cover wounds that would raise unanswerable questions in an unbiased autopsy. She also saw reflections of the corruption of local authorities in the physical appearance of Ocean Avenue, where too many storefronts were empty and too many businesses were suffering, which was in-explicable for a town in which unemployment was virtually nil. She had noted an air of solemnity about the people she had seen on the streets, as well as a briskness and purposefulness that seemed odd in a laid-back northern coastal town where the hurly-burly of modern life hardly intruded.

However, her awareness of the patterns included no explanation of *why* the police would want to conceal the true nature of Janice's killing. Or why the town seemed in an economic depression in spite of its prosperity. Or what in the name of God those nightmare things in the motel had been. Patterns were clues to underlying truths, but her ability to recognize them did not mean she could find the answers and reveal the truths at which the patterns hinted.

She sat, shivering, in the fluorescent glare and breathed trace fumes of deter-gents, bleaches, fabric softeners, and the lingering staleness of the cigarette butts in the two free-standing sand-filled ashtrays, while she tried to figure what to do next. She had not lost her determination to probe into Janice's death. But she no longer had the audacity to think she could play detective all by herself. She was going to need help and would probably have to obtain it from county or state authorities.

The first thing she had to do was get out of Moonlight Cove in one piece.

Her car was at Cove Lodge, but she did not want to go back there for it. Those . . . creatures might still be in the motel or watching it from the dense shrubs and trees and omnipresent shadows that were an integral part of the town. Like Carmel, California, elsewhere along the coast, Moonlight Cove was a town virtually built in a seaside forest. Tessa loved Carmel for its splendid integration of the works of man and nature, where geography and architecture often appeared to be the product of the same sculptor's hand. Right now, however, Moonlight Cove did not draw style and grace from its verdant lushness and artful night shadows, as did Carmel; rather, this town seemed to be dressed in the thinnest veneer of civilization, beneath which something savage—even primal—watched and waited. Every grove of trees and every dark street was not the home of beauty but of the uncanny and of death. She would have found Moonlight Cove far more attractive if every street and alley and lawn and park had been lit with the same plenitude of fluorescent bulbs as the Laundromat in which she had taken refuge.

Maybe the police had shown up at Cove Lodge by now in response to the screams and commotion. But she would not feel any safer returning there just because cops were around. Cops were part of the problem. They would want to question her about the murders of the other guests. They would find out that Janice had been her sister, and though she might not tell them she was in town to poke into the circumstances of Janice's death, they would suspect as much. If they *had* participated in a conspiracy to conceal the true nature of Janice's death, they probably wouldn't hesitate to deal with Tessa in a firm and final way.

She had to abandon the car.

But damned if she was going to walk out of town at night. She might be able to hitch a ride on the interstate—perhaps even from an honest trucker instead of a mobile psychopath—but between Moonlight Cove and the freeway, she would have to walk through a dark and semirural landscape, where surely she would be at even greater risk of encountering more of those mysterious beasts that had broken down her motel-room door.

Of course, they had come after her in a relatively public and well-lighted place. She had no real reason to assume that she was safer in this coin-operated laundry than in the middle of the woods. When the membrane of civilization ruptured and the primordial terror burst through, you weren't safe anywhere, not even on the steps of a church, as she had learned in Northern Ireland and elsewhere.

Nevertheless, she would cling to the light and shun the darkness. She had stepped through an invisible wall between the reality she had always known and a different, more hostile world. As long as she remained in that Twilight Zone, it seemed wise to assume that shadows offered even less comfort and security than did bright places.

Which left her with no plan of action. Except to sit in the Laundromat and wait for morning. In daylight she might risk a long walk to the freeway.

The blank glass of the dryer windows returned her stare.

An autumn moth thumped softly against the frosted plastic panels that were suspended under the fluorescent bulbs.

38

UNABLE TO WALK BOLDLY INTO MOONLIGHT COVE AS SHE had planned, Chrissie retreated from Holliwell Road, heading back the way she had come. She stayed in the woods, moving slowly and cautiously from tree to tree, trying to avoid making a sound that might carry to the nearer of the sentries who had been posted at the intersection.

In a couple of hundred yards, when she was beyond those men's sight and hearing, she moved more aggressively. Eventually she came to one of the houses that lay along the county route. The single-story ranch home was set behind a large front lawn and sheltered by several pines and firs, barely visible now that the moon was waning. No lights were on inside or out, and all was silent.

She needed time to think, and she wanted to get out of the cold, dampish night. Hoping there were no dogs at the house, she hurried to the garage, staying off the gravel driveway to keep from making a lot of noise. As she expected, in addition to the large front door through which the cars entered and exited, there was a smaller side entrance. It was unlocked. She stepped into the garage and closed the door behind her.

"Chrissie Foster, secret agent, penetrated the enemy facility by the bold and clever use of a side door," she said softly.

The secondhand radiance of the sinking moon penetrated the panes in the door and two high, narrow windows on the west wall, but it was insufficient to reveal anything. She could see only a few darkly gleaming curves of chrome and windshield glass, just enough to suggest the presence of two cars.

She edged toward the first of those vehicles with the caution of a blind girl, hands out in front of her, afraid of knocking something over. The car was unlocked. She slipped inside behind the wheel, leaving the door open for the welcome glow of the interior lamp. She supposed a trace of that light might be visible at the garage windows if anyone in the house woke up and looked out, but she had to risk it.

She searched the glove compartment, the map-storage panels on the doors, and under the seats, hoping to find food, because most people kept candy bars or bags of nuts or crackers or *something* to snack on in their cars. Though she had eaten midafternoon, while locked in the pantry, she'd had nothing for ten hours. Her stomach growled. She wasn't expecting to find a hot fudge sundae or the fixings for a jelly sandwich, but she certainly hoped to do better than a single stick of chewing gum and one green Lifesaver that, retrieved from beneath the seat, was furry with dirt, lint, and carpet fuzz.

As if reading tabloid headlines, she said, "Starvation in the Land of Plenty, A Modern Tragedy, Young Girl Found Dead in Garage, 'I Only Wanted a Few Peanuts' Written in Her Own Blood."

In the other car she found two Hershey's bars with almonds.

"Thank you, God. Your friend, Chrissie."

She hogged down the first bar but savored the second one in small bites, letting it melt on her tongue.

While she ate, she thought about ways to get into Moonlight Cove. By the time she finished the chocolate—

CHOCOHOLIC YOUNG GIRL FOUND DEAD IN GARAGE FROM TERMINAL CASE OF GIANT ZITS

—she had devised a plan.

Her usual bedtime had passed hours ago, and she was exhausted from all the physical activity with which the night had been filled, so she just wanted to stay there in the car, her belly full of milk chocolate and almonds, and sleep for a couple of hours before putting her plan into effect. She yawned and slumped down in the seat. She ached all over, and her eyes were as heavy as if some overanxious mortician had weighted them with coins.

That image of herself as a corpse was so unsettling that she immediately got out of the car and closed the door. If she dozed off in the car, she most likely wouldn't wake until someone found her in the morning. Maybe the people who kept their cars in this garage were converted, like her own parents, in which case she'd be doomed.

Outside, shivering as the wind nipped at her, she headed back to the county road and turned north. She passed two more dark and silent houses, another stretch of woods, and came to a fourth house, another single-story ranch-style place with shake-shingle roof and redwood siding.

She knew the people who lived there, Mr. and Mrs. Eulane. Mrs. Eulane managed the cafeteria at school. Mr. Eulane was a gardener with many accounts in Moonlight Cove. Early every morning, Mr. Eulane drove into town in his white truck, the back of which was loaded with lawnmowers and hedge clippers and rakes and shovels and bags of mulch and fertilizer and everything else a gardener might need; only a few students had arrived by the time he dropped Mrs. Eulane off at school, then went about his own work. Chrissie figured she could find a place to hide in the back of the truck—which had board sides—among Mr. Eulane's gardening supplies and equipment.

The truck was in the Eulanes' garage, which was unlocked, just as the other one had been. But this was the country, after all, where people still trusted one another—which was good except that it gave invading aliens an extra edge.

The only window was small and in the wall that could not be seen from the house, so Chrissie risked turning on the overhead light when she stepped inside. She quietly scaled the side of the truck and made her way in among the gardening equipment, which was stored in the rear two-thirds of the cargo bed, nearest the tailgate. Toward the front, against the back wall of the truck cab, flanked by fifty-pound bags of fertilizer, snail bait, and potting soil, was a three-foot-high stack of folded burlap tarps in which Mr. Eulane bundled grass clippings that had to be hauled to the dump. She could use some tarps as a mattress, others as blankets, and bed down until morning, remaining hidden in the burlap and between the piles of fifty-pound bags all the way to Moonlight Cove.

She climbed out of the truck, switched off the garage lights, then returned in the dark and carefully climbed aboard once more. She made a nest for herself in the tarps. The burlap was a little scratchy. After years of use it was permeated with the scent of new-mown grass, which was nice at first but quickly palled. At least a few layers of tarps trapped her body heat, and in minutes she was warm for the first time all night.

And as the night deepened (she thought), *young Chrissie, masking her telltale human odors in the scent of grass that saturated the burlap, cleverly concealed herself from the pursuing aliens—or maybe werewolves—whose sense of smell was almost as good as that of hounds.*

39

SAM TOOK TEMPORARY REFUGE ON THE UNLIGHTED PLAYground of Thomas Jefferson Elementary School on Palomino Street on the south side of town. He sat on one of the swings, holding the suspension chains with both hands, actually swinging a bit, while he considered his options.

He could not leave Moonlight Cove by car. His rental was back at the motel, where he'd be apprehended if he showed his face. He could steal a car, but he remembered the exchange on the computer when Loman Watkins had ordered Danberry to establish a blockade on Ocean Avenue, between town and the interstate. They'd have sealed off every exit.

He could go overland, sneaking from street to street, to the edge of the town limits, then through the woods and fields to the freeway. But Watkins had also said something about having ringed the entire community with sentries, to intercept the "Foster girl." Although Sam was confident of his instincts and survival abilities, he had not had experience in taking evasive action over open territory since his service in the war more than twenty years ago. If men were stationed around the town, waiting to intercept the girl, Sam was likely to walk straight into one or more of them.

Though he was willing to risk getting caught, he must not fall into their hands until he had placed a call to the Bureau to report and to ask for emergency backup.

If he became a statistic in this accidental-death capital of the world, the Bureau would send new men in his place, and ultimately the truth could come out—but perhaps too late.

As he swung gently back and forth through the rapidly thinning fog, pushed mostly by the wind, he thought about those schedules he had seen on the VDT. Everyone in town would be "converted" in the next twenty-three hours. Although he had no idea what the hell people were being converted *to*, he didn't like the sound of it. And he sensed that once those schedules had been met, once everyone in town was converted, getting to the truth in Moonlight Cove would be no easier than cracking open an infinite series of laser-welded, titanium boxes nested in Chinese-puzzle fashion.

Okay, so the first thing he had to do was get to a phone and call the Bureau. The phones in Moonlight Cove were compromised, but he did not care if the call was noted in a computer sweep or even recorded word for word. He just needed thirty seconds or a minute on the line with the office, and massive reinforcements would be on the way. Then he'd have to keep moving around, dodging cops for a couple of hours, until other agents arrived.

He couldn't just walk up to a house and ask to use their phone because he didn't know whom he could trust. Morrie Stein had said that after being in town a day or two, you were overcome with the paranoid feeling that eyes were on you wherever you went and that Big Brother was always just an arm's reach away. Sam had attained that stage of paranoia in only a few hours and was rapidly moving beyond it to a state of constant tension and suspicion unlike anything he'd known since those jungle battlegrounds two decades ago.

A pay phone. But not the one at the Shell station that he had used earlier. A wanted man was foolish to return to a place he was known to have frequented before.

From his walks around town, he remembered one or maybe two other pay phones. He got up from the swing, slipped his hands in his jacket pockets, hunched his shoulders against the chilling wind, and started across the schoolyard toward the street beyond.

He wondered about the Foster girl to whom Shaddack and Watkins referred on the computer link. Who was she? What had she seen? He suspected she was a key to understanding this conspiracy. Whatever she had witnessed might explain what they meant by "conversion."

40

THE WALLS APPEARED TO BE BLEEDING. RED OOZE, AS IF SEEP-ing from the Sheetrock, tracked down the pale yellow paint in many rivulets.

Standing in that second-floor room at Cove Lodge, Loman Watkins was repelled by the carnage . . . but also strangely excited.

The male guest's body was sprawled near the disarranged bed, hideously bitten and torn. In worse condition, the dead woman lay outside the room, in the second-floor hall, a scarlet heap on the orange carpet.

The air reeked of blood, bile, feces, urine—a melange of odors with which Loman was becoming increasingly familiar, as the victims of the regressives turned up more frequently week by week and day by day. This time, however, as never before, an alluring sweetness lay under the acrid surface of the stench. He drew deep breaths, unsure why that terrible redolence should have any appeal whatsoever. But he was unable to deny—or resist—its attraction any more than a hound could resist the fox's scent. Though he could not withstand the tempting fragrance, he was frightened by his response to it, and the blood in his veins seemed to grow colder as his pleasure in the biological stink grew more intense.

Barry Sholnick, the officer Loman had dispatched to Cove Lodge via computer link to apprehend Samuel Booker, and who had found this death and destruction instead of the Bureau agent, now stood in the corner by the window, staring intently at the dead man. He had been at the motel longer than anyone, almost half an hour, long enough to have begun to regard the victims with the detachment that police had to cultivate, as if dead and ravaged bodies were no more remarkable a part of the scene than the furniture. Yet Sholnick could not shift his gaze from the eviscerated corpse, the gore-spattered wreckage, and the blood-streaked walls. He was clearly electrified by that horrendous detritus and the violence of which it was a remembrance.

We hate what the regressives have become and what they do, Loman thought, but in some sick way we're also envious of them, of their ultimate freedom.

Something within him—and, he suspected, in all of the New People—cried out to join the regressives. As at the Foster place, Loman felt the urge to employ his newfound bodily control not to elevate himself, as Shaddack had intended, but to devolve into a wild state. He yearned to descend to a level of consciousness in which thoughts of the purpose and meaning of life would not trouble him, in which intellectual challenge would be nonexistent, in which he would be a creature whose existence was defined almost entirely by *sensation*, in which every decision was made solely on the basis of what would give him pleasure, a condition untroubled by complex thought. Oh, God, to be freed from the burdens of civilization and higher intelligence!

Sholnick made a low sound in the back of his throat.

Loman looked up from the dead man.

In Sholnick's brown eyes a wild light burned.

Am I as pale as he? Loman wondered. As sunken-eyed and strange?

For a moment Sholnick met the chief's gaze, then looked away as if he had been caught in a shameful act.

Loman's heart was pounding.

Sholnick went to the window. He stared out at the lightless sea. His hands were fisted at his sides.

Loman was trembling.

The smell, darkly sweet. The smell of the hunt, the kill.

He turned away from the corpse and walked out of the room, into the hallway, where the sight of the dead woman—half naked, gouged, lacerated—was no relief. Bob Trott, one of several recent additions to the force when it expanded to twelve men last week, stood over the battered body. He was a big man, four inches taller and thirty pounds heavier than Loman, with a face of hard planes and chiseled edges. He looked down at the cadaver with a faint, unholy smile.

Flushed, his vision beginning to blur, his eyes smarting in the harsh fluorescent glare, Loman spoke sharply: "Trott, come with me." He set off along the hall to the other room that had been broken into. With evident reluctance, Trott finally followed him.

By the time Loman reached the shattered door of that unit, Paul Amberlay, another of his officers, appeared at the head of the north stairs, returning from the motel office where Loman had sent him to check the register. "The couple in room twenty-four were named Jenks, Sarah and Charles," Amberlay reported. He was twenty-five, lean and sinewy, intelligent. Perhaps because the young officer's face was slightly pointed, with deep-set eyes, he had always reminded Loman of a fox. "They're from Portland."

"And in thirty-six here?"

"Tessa Lockland from San Diego."

Loman blinked. "Lockland?"

Amberlay spelled it.

"When did she check in?"

"Just tonight."

"The minister's widow, Janice Capshaw," Loman said. "Her maiden name was Lockland. I had to deal with her mother by phone, and she was in San Diego. Persistent old broad. A million questions. Had some trouble getting her to consent to cremation. She said her other daughter was out of the country, somewhere really remote, couldn't be reached quickly, but would come around within a month to empty the house and settle Mrs. Capshaw's affairs. So this is her, I guess."

Loman led them into Tessa Lockland's room, two doors down from unit forty, in which Booker was registered. Wind huffed at the open window. The place was littered with broken furniture, torn bedding, and the glass from a shattered TV set, but unmarked by blood. Earlier they had checked the room for a body and found none; the open window indicated that the occupant fled before the regressives had managed to smash through the door.

"So Booker's out there," Loman said, "and we've got to assume he saw the regressives or heard the killing. He knows something's wrong here. He doesn't understand it, but he knows enough . . . too much."

"You can bet he's busting his ass to get a call out to the damn Bureau," Trott said.

Loman agreed. "And now we've also got this Lockland bitch, and she's got to be thinking her sister never committed suicide, that she was killed by the same things that killed the couple from Portland—"

"Most logical thing for her to do," Amberlay said, "is come straight to us—to the police. She'll walk right into our arms."

"Maybe," Loman said, unconvinced. He began to pick through the rubble. "Help me find her purse. With them bashing down the door, she'd have gone out the window without pausing to grab her purse."

Trott found it wedged between the bed and one of the nightstands.

Loman emptied the contents onto the mattress. He snatched up the wallet, flipped through the plastic windows full of credit cards and photographs, until he found her driver's license. According to the license data, she was five-four, one hundred and four pounds, blond, blue-eyed. Loman held up the ID so Trott and Amberlay could see the photograph.

"She's a looker," Amberlay said.

"I'd like to get a bite of that," Trott said.

His officer's choice of words gave Loman a chill. He couldn't help wondering whether Trott meant "bite" as a euphemism for sex or whether he was expressing a very real subconscious desire to savage the woman as the regressives had torn apart the couple from Portland.

"We know what she looks like," Loman said. "That helps."

Trott's hard, sharp features were inadequate for the expression of gentler emotions like affection and delight, but they perfectly conveyed the animal hunger and urge to violence that seethed deep within him. "You want us to bring her in?"

"Yes. She doesn't know anything, really, but on the other hand she knows too much. She knows the couple down the hall were killed, and she probably saw a regressive."

"Maybe the regressives followed her through the window and got her," Amberlay suggested. "We might find her body somewhere outside, on the grounds of the lodge."

"Could be," Loman said. "But if not, we have to find her and bring her in. You called Callan?"

"Yeah," Amberlay said.

"We've got to get this place cleaned up," Loman said. "We've got to keep a lid on until midnight, until everyone in town's been put through the Change. Then, when Moonlight Cove's secure, we can concentrate on finding the regressives and eliminating them."

Trott and Amberlay met Loman's eyes, then looked at each other. In the glances they exchanged, Loman saw the dark knowledge that they all were potential regressives, that they, too, felt the call toward that unburdened, primitive state. It was an awareness of which none of them dared speak, for to give it voice was to admit that Moonhawk was a deeply flawed project and that they might all be damned.

41

MIKE PEYSER HEARD THE DIAL TONE AND FUMBLED WITH THE buttons, which were too small and closely set for his long, tinelike fingers. Abruptly he realized that he could not call Shaddack, *dared* not call Shaddack, though they had known each other for more than twenty years, since their days together at Stanford, could not call Shaddack even though it was Shaddack who had made him what he was, because Shaddack would consider him an outlaw now, a regressive, and Shaddack would have him restrained in a laboratory and either treat him with all the tenderness that a vivisectionist bestowed upon a white rat or destroy him because of the threat he posed to the ongoing conversion of Moonlight Cove. Peyser shrieked in frustration. He tore the telephone out of the wall and threw it across the bedroom, where it hit the dresser mirror, shattering the glass.

His sudden perception of Shaddack as a powerful enemy rather than a friend and mentor was the last entirely clear and rational thought that Peyser had for a while. His fear was a trapdoor that opened under him, casting him down into the darkness of the primeval mind that he had unleashed for the pleasure of a night hunt. He moved back and forth through the house, sometimes in a frenzy, sometimes in a sullen slouch, not sure why he was alternately excited, depressed, or smoldering with savage needs, driven more by feelings than intellect.

He relieved himself in a corner of the living room, sniffed his own urine, then went into the kitchen in search of more food. Now and then his mind cleared, and he tried to call his body back to its more civilized form, but when his tissues would not respond to his will, he cycled down into the darkness of animal thought again. Several times he was clearheaded enough to appreciate the irony of having been reduced to savagery by a process—the Change—meant to elevate him to superhuman status, but that line of thought was too bleak to be endured, and a new descent into the savage mind was almost welcome.

Repeatedly, both when in the grip of a primitive consciousness and when the clouds lifted from his mind, he thought of the boy, Eddie Valdoski, the boy, the tender boy, and he thrilled to the memory of blood, sweet blood, fresh blood steaming in the cold night air.

42

PHYSICALLY AND MENTALLY EXHAUSTED, CHRISSIE NEVER-theless was not able to sleep. In the burlap tarps in the back of Mr. Eulane's truck, she hung from the thin line of wakefulness, wanting nothing more than to let go and fall into unconsciousness.

She felt incomplete, as though something had been left undone—and suddenly she was crying. Burying her face in the fragrant and slightly scratchy burlap, she bawled as she'd not done in years, with the abandon of a baby. She wept for her mother and father, perhaps lost forever, not taken cleanly by death but by something foul, dirty, inhuman, satanic. She wept for the adolescence that would have been hers—horses and seaside pastures and books read on the beach—but that had been shattered beyond repair. She wept, as well, over some loss she felt but could not quite identify, though she suspected it was innocence or maybe faith in the triumph of good over evil.

None of the fictional heroines she admired would have indulged in uncontrolled weeping, and Chrissie was embarrassed by her torrent of tears. But to weep was as human as to err, and perhaps she needed to cry, in part, to prove to herself that no monstrous seed had been planted in her of the sort that had germinated and spread tendrils through her parents. Crying, she was still Chrissie. Crying was proof that no one had stolen her soul.

She slept.

43

SAM HAD SEEN ANOTHER PAY PHONE AT A UNION 76 SERVICE station one block north of Ocean. The station was out of business. The windows were filmed with gray dust, and a hastily lettered FOR SALE sign hung in one of them, as if the owner actually didn't care whether the place was sold or not and had made the sign only because it was expected of him. Crisp, dead leaves and dry pine needles from surrounding trees had blown against the gasoline pumps and lay in snowlike drifts.

The phone booth was against the south wall of the building and visible from the street. Sam stepped through the open door but did not pull it shut, for fear of completing a circuit that would turn on the overhead bulb and draw him to the attention of any cops who happened by.

The line was dead. He deposited a coin, hoping that would activate the dial tone. The line was still dead.

He jiggled the hook from which the handset hung. His coin was returned.

He tried again but to no avail.

He believed that pay phones in or adjacent to a service station or privately owned store were sometimes joint operations, the income shared between the telephone company and the businessman who allowed the phone to be installed. Perhaps they had turned off the phone when the Union 76 had closed.

However, he suspected the police had used their access to the telephone-company's computer to disable all coin-operated phones in Moonlight Cove. The moment they had learned an undercover federal agent was in town, they could have taken extreme measures to prevent him from contacting the world outside.

Of course he might be overestimating their capabilities. He had to try another phone before giving up hope of contacting the Bureau.

On his walk after dinner, he had passed a coin laundry half a block north of Ocean Avenue and two blocks west of this Union 76. He was pretty sure that when glancing through the plate-glass window, he had seen a telephone on the rear wall, at the end of a row of industrial-size dryers with stainless-steel fronts.

He left the Union 76. As much as possible staying away from the streetlamps—which illuminated side streets only in the first block north and south of Ocean—using alleyways where he could, he slipped through the silent town, toward where he remembered having seen the laundry. He wished the wind would die and leave some of the rapidly dissipating fog.

At an intersection one block north of Ocean and half a block from the laundry, he almost walked into plain sight of a cop driving south toward the center of town. The patrolman was half a block from the intersection, coming slowly, surveying both sides of the street. Fortunately he was looking the other way when Sam hurried into the unavoidable fall of lamplight at the corner.

Sam scrambled backward and pressed into a deep entranceway on the side of a three-story brick building that housed some of the town's professionals: A plaque in the recess, to the left of the door, listed a dentist, two lawyers, a doctor, and a chiropractor. If the patrol turned left at the corner and came past him, he'd probably be spotted. But if it either went straight on toward Ocean or turned right and headed west, he would not be seen.

Leaning against the locked door and as far back in the shadows as he could go, waiting for the infuriatingly slow car to reach the intersection, Sam had a moment for reflection and realized that even for one-thirty in the morning, Moonlight Cove was peculiarly quiet and the streets unusually deserted. Small towns had night owls as surely as did cities; there should have been a pedestrian or two, a car now and then, *some* signs of life other than police patrols.

The black-and-white turned right at the corner, heading west and away from him.

Although the danger had passed, Sam remained in the unlighted entranceway, mentally retracing his journey from Cove Lodge to the municipal building, from there to the Union 76, and finally to his current position. He could not recall passing a house where music was playing, where a television blared, or where the laughter of late revelers indicated a party in progress. He had seen no young couples sharing a last kiss in parked cars. The few restaurants and taverns were apparently closed, and the movie theater was out of business, and except for his movements and those of the police, Moonlight Cove might have been a ghost town. Its living rooms, bedrooms, and kitchens might have been peopled only by moldering corpses—or by robots that posed as people during the day and were turned off at night to save energy when it was not as essential to maintain the illusion of life.

Increasingly worried by the word "conversion" and its mysterious meaning in the context of this thing they called the Moonhawk Project, he left the entranceway, turned the corner, and ran along the brightly lighted street to the laundry. He saw the phone as he was pushing open the glass door.

He hurried halfway through the long room—dryers on the right, a double row of washers back-to-back in the middle, some chairs at the end of the washers, more chairs along the left wall with the candy and detergent machines and the laundry-folding counter—before he realized the place was not deserted. A petite blonde in faded jeans and a blue pullover sweater sat on one of the yellow plastic chairs. None of the washers or dryers was running, and the woman did not seem to have a basket of clothes with her.

He was so startled by her—a live person, a live *civilian*, in this sepulchral night—that he stopped and blinked.

She was perched on the edge of the chair, visibly tense. Her eyes were wide. Her hands were clenched in her lap. She seemed to be holding her breath.

Realizing that he had frightened her, Sam said, "Sorry."

She stared at him as if she were a rabbit facing down a fox.

Aware that he must look wild-eyed, even frantic, he added, "I'm not dangerous."

"They all say that."

"They do?"

"But I *am*."

Confused, he said, "You are what?"

"Dangerous."

"Really?"

She stood up. "I'm a black belt."

For the first time in days, a genuine smile pulled at Sam's face. "Can you kill with your hands?"

She stared at him for a moment, pale and shaking. When she spoke, her defensive anger was excessive. "Hey, don't laugh at me, asshole, or I'll bust you up so bad that when you walk, you'll clink like a bag of broken glass."

At last, astonished by her vehemency, Sam began to assimilate the observations he'd made on entering. No washers or dryers in operation. No clothes basket. No box of detergent or bottle of fabric softener.

"What's wrong?" he asked, suddenly suspicious.

"Nothing, if you keep your distance."

He wondered if she knew somehow that the local cops were eager to get hold of him. But that seemed nuts. How could she know? "What're you doing here if you don't have clothes to wash?"

"What's it your business? You own this dump?" she demanded.

"No. And don't tell me you own it, either."

She glared at him.

He studied her, gradually absorbing how attractive she was. She had eyes as piercingly blue as a June sky and skin as clear as summer air, and she seemed radically out of place along this dark, October coast, let alone in a grungy Laundromat at one-thirty in the morning. When her beauty finally, fully registered with him, so did other things about her, including the intensity of her fear, which was revealed in her eyes and in the lines around them and in the set of her mouth. It was fear far out of proportion to any threat he could pose. If he had been a six-foot-six, three-hundred-pound, tattooed biker with a revolver in one hand and a ten-inch knife in the other, and if he had burst into the laundry chanting paeans to Satan, the utterly bloodless paleness of her face and the hard edge of terror in her eyes would have been understandable. But he was only Sam Booker, whose greatest attribute as an agent was his guy-next-door ordinariness and an aura of harmlessness.

Unsettled by *her* unsettledness, he said, "The phone."

"What?"

He pointed at the pay phone.

"Yes," she said, as if confirming it was indeed a phone.

"Just came in to make a call."

"Oh."

Keeping one eye on her, he went to the phone, fed it his quarter, but got no dial tone. He retrieved his coin, tried again. No luck.

"Damn!" he said.

The blonde had edged toward the door. She halted, as though she thought he might rush at her and drag her down if she attempted to leave the Laundromat.

The Cove engendered in Sam a powerful paranoia. Increasingly over the past few hours he had come to think of everyone in town as a potential enemy. And suddenly he perceived that this woman's peculiar behavior resulted from a state of mind precisely like his. "Yes, of course—you're not *from* here, are you, from Moonlight Cove?"

"So?"

"Neither am I."

"So?"

"And you've seen something."

She stared at him.

He said, "Something's happened, you've seen something, and you're scared, and I'll bet you've got damned good reason to be."

She looked as if she'd sprint for the door.

"Wait," he said quickly. "I'm with the FBI." His voice cracked slightly. "I really am."

44

BECAUSE HE WAS A NIGHT PERSON WHO HAD ALWAYS preferred to sleep during the day, Thomas Shaddack was in his teak-paneled study, dressed in a gray sweat suit, working on an aspect of Moonhawk at a computer terminal, when Evan, his night servant, rang through to tell him that Loman Watkins was at the front door.

"Send him to the tower," Shaddack said. "I'll join him shortly."

He seldom wore anything but sweat suits these days. He had more than twenty in the closet—ten black, ten gray, and a couple navy blue. They were more comfortable than other clothes, and by limiting his choices, he saved time that otherwise would be wasted coordinating each day's wardrobe, a task at which he was not skilled. Fashion was of no interest to him. Besides, he was gawky—big feet, lanky legs, knobby knees, long arms, bony shoulders—and too thin to look good even in finely tailored suits. Clothes either hung strangely on him or emphasized his thinness to such a degree that he appeared to be Death personified, an unfortunate image reinforced by his flour-white skin, nearly black hair, sharp features, and yellowish eyes.

He even wore sweat suits to New Wave board meetings. If you were a genius in your field, people expected you to be eccentric. And if your personal fortune was in the hundreds of millions, they accepted all eccentricities without comment.

His ultramodern, reinforced-concrete house at cliff's edge near the north point of the cove was another expression of his calculated nonconformity. The three stories were like three layers of a cake, though each layer was of a different size than the others—the largest on top, the smallest in the middle—and they were not concentric but misaligned, creating a profile that in daylight lent the house the appearance of an enormous piece of avant-garde sculpture. At night, its myriad windows aglow, it looked less like sculpture than like the star-traveling mothership of an invading alien force.

The tower was eccentricity piled on eccentricity, rising off-center from the third level, soaring an additional forty feet into the air. It was not round but oval, not anything like a tower in which a princess might pine for a crusade-bound prince or in which a king might have his enemies imprisoned and tortured, but reminiscent of the conning tower of a submarine. The large, glass-walled room at the top could be reached by elevator or by stairs that spiraled around the inside of the tower wall, circling the metal core in which the elevator was housed.

Shaddack kept Watkins waiting for ten minutes, just for the hell of it, then chose
to take the lift to meet him. The interior of the cab was paneled with burnished
brass, so although the mechanism was slow, he seemed to be ascending inside a
rifle cartridge.

He had added the tower to the architect's designs almost as an afterthought,
but it had become his favorite part of the huge house. That high place offered
endless vistas of calm (or wind-chopped), sun-spangled (or night-shrouded) sea
to the west. To the east and south, he looked out and *down* on the whole town
of Moonlight Cove; his sense of superiority was comfortably reinforced by that
lofty perspective on the only other visible works of man. From that room, only
four months ago, he had seen the moonhawk for the third time in his life, a sight
that few men were privileged to see even once—which he took to be a sign that
he was destined to become the most influential man ever to walk the earth.

The elevator stopped. The doors opened.

When Shaddack entered the dimly lighted room that encircled the elevator,
Loman Watkins rose quickly from an armchair and respectfully said, "Good evening, sir."

"Please be seated, chief," he said graciously, even affably, but with a subtle
note in his voice that reinforced their mutual understanding that it was Shaddack,
not Watkins, who decided how formal or casual the meeting would be.

Shaddack was the only child of James Randolph Shaddack, a former circuit-
court judge in Phoenix, now deceased. The family had not been wealthy, though
solidly upper middle-class, and that position on the economic ladder, combined
with the prestige of a judgeship, gave James considerable stature in his community.
And power. Throughout his childhood and adolescence, Tom had been fascinated
by how his father, a political activist as well as a judge, had used that power not
only to acquire material benefits but to control others. The control—the exercise
of power for power's sake—was what had most appealed to James, and that was
what had deeply excited his son, too, from an early age.

Now Tom Shaddack held power over Loman Watkins and Moonlight Cove by
reason of his wealth, because he was the primary employer in town, because he
gripped the reins of the political system, and because of the Moonhawk Project,
named after the thrice-received vision. But his ability to manipulate them was more
extensive than anything old James had enjoyed as a judge and canny politico. He
possessed the power of life and death over them—literally. If an hour from now
he decided they all must die, they would be dead before midnight. Furthermore
he could condemn them to the grave with no more chance of being punished
than a god risked when raining fire on his creations.

The only lights in the tower room were concealed in a recess under the immense windows, which extended from the ceiling to within ten inches of the floor.
The hidden lamps ringed the chamber, subtly illuminating the plush carpet but
casting no glare on the huge panes. Nevertheless, if the night had been clear,
Shaddack would have flicked the switch next to the elevator button, plunging the
room into near darkness, so his ghostly reflection and those of the starkly modern
furnishings would not fall on the glass between him and his view of the world
over which he held dominion. He left the lights on, however, because some milky
fog still churned past glass walls, and little could be seen now that the horned
moon had found the horizon.

Barefoot, Shaddack crossed the charcoal-gray carpet. He settled into a second armchair, facing Loman Watkins across a low, white-marble cocktail table.

The policeman was forty-four, less than three years older than Shaddack, but he was Shaddack's complete physical opposite: five-ten, a hundred and eighty pounds, large-boned, broad in the shoulders and chest, thick-necked. His face was broad, too, as open and guileless as Shaddack's was closed and cunning. His blue eyes met Shaddack's yellow-brown gaze, held it only for a moment, then lowered to stare at his strong hands, which were clasped so rigidly in his lap that the sharp knuckles seemed in danger of piercing the taut skin. His darkly tanned scalp showed through brush-cut brown hair.

Watkins's obvious subservience pleased Shaddack, but he was even more grati-fied by the chief's fear, which was evident in the tremors that the man was strug-gling—with some success—to repress and in the haunted expression that deepened the color of his eyes. Because of the Moonhawk Project, because of what had been done to him, Loman Watkins was in many ways superior to most men, but he was also now and forever in Shaddack's thrall as surely as a laboratory mouse, clamped down and attached to electrodes, was at the mercy of the scientist who conducted experiments on him. In a manner of speaking, Shaddack was Watkins's maker, and he possessed, in Watkins's eyes, the position and power of a god.

Leaning back in his chair, folding his pale, long-fingered hands on his chest, Shaddack felt his manhood swelling, hardening. He was not aroused by Loman Watkins, because he had no tendency whatsoever toward homosexuality; he was aroused not by anything in Watkins's physical appearance but by the awareness of the tremendous authority he wielded over the man. Power aroused Shaddack more fully and easily than sexual stimuli. Even as an adolescent, when he saw pictures of naked women in erotic magazines, he was turned on not by the sight of bared breasts, not by the curve of a female bottom or the elegant line of long legs, but by the thought of *dominating* such women, totally controlling them, holding their very lives in his hands. If a woman looked at him with undisguised fear, he found her infinitely more appealing than if she regarded him with desire. And since he reacted more strongly to terror than to lust, his arousal was not dependent upon the sex or age or physical attractiveness of the person who trem-bled in his presence.

Enjoying the policeman's submissiveness, Shaddack said, "You've got Booker?"

"No, sir."

"Why not?"

"He wasn't at Cove Lodge when Sholnick got there."

"He's got to be found."

"We'll find him."

"And converted. Not just to prevent him from telling anyone what he's seen . . . but to give us one of our own *inside* the Bureau. That'd be a coup. His being here could turn out to be an incredible plus for the project."

"Well, whether Booker's a plus or not, there's worse than him. Regressives attacked some of the guests at the lodge. Quinn himself was either carried off, killed, and left where we haven't found him yet . . . or he was one of the regres-sives himself and is off now . . . doing whatever they do after a kill, maybe baying at the goddamn moon."

With growing dismay and agitation, Shaddack listened to the report.

Perched on the edge of his chair, Watkins finished, blinked, and said, "These regressives scare the hell out of me."

"They're disturbing," Shaddack agreed.

On the night of September fourth, they had cornered a regressive, Jordan Coombs, in the movie theater on main street. Coombs had been a maintenance man at New Wave. That night, however, he had been more ape than man, although actually neither, but something so strange and savage that no single word could describe him. The term "regressive" was only adequate, Shaddack had discovered, if you never came face to face with one of the beasts. Because once you'd seen one close up, "regressive" insufficiently conveyed the horror of the thing, and in fact all words failed. Their attempt to take Coombs alive had failed, too, for he had proved too aggressive and powerful to be subdued; to save themselves, they'd had to blow his head off.

Now Watkins said, "They're more than disturbing. Much more than just that. They're . . . psychotic."

"I know they're psychotic," Shaddack said impatiently. "I've named their condition myself: metamorphic-related psychosis."

"They *enjoy* killing."

Thomas Shaddack frowned. He had not foreseen the problem of the regressives, and he refused to believe that they constituted more than a minor anomaly in the otherwise beneficial conversion of the people of Moonlight Cove. "Yes, all right, they enjoy killing, and in their regressed state they're designed for it, but we've only a few of them to identify and eliminate. Statistically, they're an insignificant percentage of those we've put through the Change."

"Maybe not so insignificant," Watkins said hesitantly, unable to meet Shaddack's eyes, a reluctant bearer of bad tidings. "Judging by all the bloody wreckage lately, I'd guess that among those nineteen hundred converted as of this morning, there were fifty or sixty of these regressives out there."

"Ridiculous!"

To admit regressives existed in large numbers, Shaddack would have to consider the possibility that his research was flawed, that he had rushed his discoveries out of the laboratory and into the field with too little consideration of the potential for disaster, and that his enthusiastic application of the Moonhawk Project's revolutionary discoveries to the people of Moonlight Cove was a tragic mistake. He could admit nothing of the sort.

He had yearned all his life for the nth degree of power that was now nearly within his reach, and he was psychologically incapable of retreating from the course he had set. Since puberty he had denied himself certain pleasures because, had he acted upon those needs, he would have been hunted down by the law and made to pay a heavy price. All those years of denial had created a tremendous internal pressure that he desperately needed to relieve. He had sublimated his antisocial desires in his work, focused his energies into socially acceptable endeavors—which had, ironically, resulted in discoveries that would make him immune to authority and therefore free to indulge his long-suppressed urges without fear of censure or punishment.

Besides, not just psychologically but also in practical terms, he had gone too far to turn back. He had brought something revolutionary into the world. Because of him, nineteen hundred New People walked the earth, as different from other men and women as Cro-Magnons had been different from their more primitive Neanderthal ancestors. He did not have the ability to undo what he had done any more than other scientists and technicians could *un*invent the wheel or atomic bomb.

Watkins shook his head. "I'm sorry . . . but I don't think it's ridiculous at all. Fifty or sixty regressives. Or more. Maybe a lot more."

"You'll need proof to convince me of that. You'll have to name them for me. Are you any closer to identifying even *one* of them—other than Quinn?"

"Alex and Sharon Foster, I think. And maybe even your own man, Tucker."

"Impossible."

Watkins described what he had found at the Foster place—and the cries he had heard in the distant woods.

Reluctantly Shaddack considered the possibility that Tucker was one of those degenerates. He was disturbed by the likelihood that his control among his inner circle was not as absolute as he had thought. If he could not be sure of those men closest to him, how could he be certain of his ability to control the masses? "Maybe the Fosters are regressives, though I doubt it's true of Tucker. But even if Tucker's one of them, that means you've found four. Not fifty or sixty. Just *four*. Who're all these others you imagine are out there?"

Loman Watkins stared at the fog, which pressed in ever-changing patterns against the glass walls of the tower room. "Sir, I'm afraid it isn't easy. I mean . . . think about it. If the state or federal authorities learned what you've done, if they could *understand* what you've done and really believe it, and if then they wanted to prevent us from bringing the Change to everyone beyond Moonlight Cove, they'd have one hell of a time stopping us, wouldn't they? After all, those of us who've been converted . . . we walk undetected among ordinary people. We seem like them, no different, unchanged."

"So?"

"Well . . . that's the same problem *we* have with the regressives. They're New People like us, but the thing that makes them different from us, the rottenness in them, is impossible to see; they're as indistinguishable from us as we are from the unchanged population of Old People."

Shaddack's iron erection had softened. Impatient with Watkins's negativism, he rose from his armchair and moved to the nearest of the big windows. Standing with his hands fisted in the pockets of his sweat-suit jacket, he stared at the vague reflection of his own long, lupine face, which was ghostlike in its transparency. He met his own gaze, as well, then quickly looked through the reflection of his eye sockets and past the glass into the darkness beyond, where vagrant sea breezes worked the loom of night to bring forth a fragile fabric of fog. He kept his back to Watkins, for he did not want the man to see that he was concerned, and he avoided the glass-caught image of his own eyes because he did not want to admit to himself that his concern might be marbled with veins of fear.

45

HE INSISTED ON MOVING TO THE CHAIRS, SO THEY COULD not be seen as easily from the street. Tessa was leery about sitting beside him. He said that he was operating undercover and therefore carried no Bureau ID, but he showed her everything else in his wallet: driver's license, credit cards, library card, video rental card, photos of his son and his late wife, a coupon for a free chocolate-chip cookie at any Mrs. Fields store, a picture of Goldie Hawn torn from a magazine. Would a homicidal maniac carry a cookie coupon? In a while, as he took her back through her story of the massacre at Cove Lodge and picked relentlessly at the details, making sure that she told him everything and that he understood all of it, she began to trust him. If he was only pretending to be an agent, his pretense would not have been so elaborate or sustained.

"You didn't actually *see* anybody murdered?"

"They were killed," she insisted. "You wouldn't have any doubt if you'd heard their screams. I've stood in a mob of human monsters in Northern Ireland and seen them beat men to death. I was filming an industrial in a steel mill once, when there was a spill of molten metal that splattered all over workers' bodies, their faces. I've been with Miskito Indians in the Central American jungles when they were hit with antipersonnel bombs—millions of little bits of sharp steel, bodies pierced by a thousand needles—and I've heard *their* screams. I know what death sounds like. And this was the worst I've ever heard."

He stared at her for a long time. Then he said, "You look deceptively . . . "

"Cute?"

"Yes."

"Therefore innocent? Therefore naive?"

"Yes."

"My curse."

"And an advantage sometimes?"

"Sometimes," she acknowledged. "Listen, you know something, so tell me: What's going on in this town?"

"Something's happening to the people here."

"What?"

"I don't know. They're not interested in movies, for one thing. The theater closed. And they're not interested in luxury goods, fine gifts, that sort of thing, because those stores have all closed too. They no longer get a kick from champagne . . . " He smiled thinly. "The barrooms are all going out of business. The only thing they seem to be interested in is food. And killing."

46

STILL STANDING AT A TOWER-ROOM WINDOW, TOM SHAD-dack said, "All right, Loman, here's what we'll do. Everyone at New Wave has been converted, so I'll assign a hundred of them to you, to augment the police force. You can use them to help in your investigation in any way you see fit—starting now. With that many at your command, you'll catch one of the regressives in the act, surely . . . and you'll be more likely to find this man Booker too."

The New People did not require sleep. The additional deputies could be brought into the field immediately.

Shaddack said, "They can patrol the streets on foot and in their cars—quietly, without drawing attention. And with that assistance, you'll grab at least one of the regressives, maybe all of them. If we can catch one in a devolved state, if I've a chance to *examine* one of them, I might be able to develop a test—physical or psychological—with which we can screen the New People for degenerates."

"I don't feel adequate to deal with this."

"It's a police matter."

"No, it isn't, really."

"It's no different than if you were tracking down an ordinary killer," Shaddack said irritably. "You'll apply the same techniques."

"But . . . "

"What is it?"

"Regressives could be among the men you assign me."

"There won't be any."

"But . . . how can you be sure?"

"I told you there won't be," Shaddack said sharply, still facing the window, the fog, the night.

They were both silent a moment.

Then Shaddack said, "You've got to put everything into finding these damned deviants. Everything, you hear me? I want at least one of them to examine by the time we've taken all of Moonlight Cove through the Change."

"I thought . . . "

"Yes?"

"Well, I thought . . . "

"Come on, come on. You thought what?"

"Well . . . just that maybe you'd suspend the conversions until we understand what's happening here."

"Hell, no!" Shaddack turned from the window and glared at the police chief, who flinched satisfactorily. "These regressives are a minor problem, very minor. What the shit do you know about it? You're not the one who designed a new race, a new world. *I* am. The dream was mine, the vision mine. I had the brains and nerve to make the dream real. And I *know* this is an anomaly indicative of nothing. So the Change will take place according to schedule."

Watkins looked down at his white-knuckled hands.

As he spoke, Shaddack paced barefoot along the curved glass wall, then back again. "We now have more than enough doses to deal with the remaining townspeople. In fact, we've initiated a new round of conversions this evening. Hundreds will be brought into the fold by dawn, the rest by midnight. Until everyone in town is with us, there's a chance we'll be found out, a risk of someone carrying a warning to the outside world. Now that we've overcome the problems with the production of the biochips, we've got to take Moonlight Cove quickly, so we can proceed with the confidence that comes from having a secure home base. Understand?"

Watkins nodded.

"Understand?" Shaddack repeated.

"Yes. Yes, sir."

Shaddack returned to his chair and sat down. "Now what's this other thing you called me about earlier, this Valdoski business?"

"Eddie Valdoski, eight years old," Watkins said, looking at his hands, which he was now virtually wringing, as if trying to squeeze something from them in the way he might have squeezed water from a rag. "He was found dead a few minutes past eight. In a ditch along the country road. He'd been . . . tortured . . . bitten, gutted."

"You think one of the regressives did it?"

"Definitely."

"Who found the body?"

"Eddie's folks. His dad. The boy had been playing in the backyard, and then he . . . disappeared near sunset. They started searching, couldn't find him, got scared, called us, continued to search while we were on our way . . . and found the body just before my men got there."

"Evidently the Valdoskis aren't converted?"

"They weren't. But they are now."

Shaddack sighed. "There won't be any trouble about the boy if they've been brought into the fold."

The police chief raised his head and found the courage to look directly at Shaddack again. "But the boy's still dead." His voice was rough.

Shaddack said, "That's a tragedy, of course. This regressive element among the New People could not have been foreseen. But no great advancement in human history has been without its victims."

"He was a fine boy," the policeman said.

"You knew him?"

Watkins blinked. "I went to high school with his father, George Valdoski. I was Eddie's godfather."

Considering his words carefully, Shaddack said, "It's a terrible thing. And we'll find the regressive who did it. We'll find all of them and eliminate them. Meanwhile, we can take some comfort in the fact that Eddie died in a great cause."

Watkins regarded Shaddack with unconcealed astonishment. "Great cause? What did Eddie know of a great cause? He was eight years old."

"Nevertheless," Shaddack said, hardening his voice, "Eddie was caught up in an unexpected side effect of the conversion of Moonlight Cove, which makes him part of this wonderful, historical event." He knew that Watkins had been a patriot, absurdly proud of his flag and country, and he supposed that some of that sentiment still reposed in the man, even subsequent to conversion, so he said: "Listen to me, Loman. During the Revolutionary War, when the colonists were fighting for independence, some innocent bystanders died, women and children, not just combatants, and those people did not die in vain. They were martyrs every bit as much as the soldiers who perished in the field. It's the same in any revolution. The important thing is that justice prevail and that those who die can be said to have given their lives for a noble purpose."

Watkins looked away from him.

Rising from his armchair again, Shaddack rounded the low cocktail table to stand beside the policeman. Looking down at Watkins's bowed head, he put one hand on the man's shoulder.

Watkins cringed from the touch.

Shaddack did not move his hand, and he spoke with the fervor of an evangelist. He was a cool evangelist, however, whose message did not involve the hot passion of religious conviction but the icy power of logic, reason. "You're one of the New People now, and that does not just mean that you're stronger and quicker than ordinary men, and it doesn't just mean you're virtually invulnerable to disease and have a greater power to mend your injuries than anything any faith healer ever dreamed of. It *also* means you're clearer of mind, more rational than the Old People—so if you consider Eddie's death carefully and in the context of the miracle we're working here, you'll see that the price he paid was not too great. Don't deal with this situation emotionally, Loman; that's definitely not the way of New People. We're making a world that'll be more efficient, more ordered, and infinitely more stable precisely because men and women will have the power to control their emotions, to view every problem and event with the analytical coolness of a computer. Look at Eddie Valdoski's death as but another datum in the great flow of data that is the birth of the New People. You've got the power in you now to transcend human emotional limitations, and when you *do* transcend them, you'll know true peace and happiness for the first time in your life."

After a while Loman Watkins raised his head. He turned to look up at Shaddack. "Will this really lead to peace?"

"Yes."

"When there's no one left unconverted, will there be brotherhood at last?"

"Yes."

"Tranquillity?"

"Eternal."

47

THE TALBOT HOUSE ON CONQUISTADOR WAS A THREE-STORY redwood with lots of big windows. The property was sloped, and steep stone steps led up from the sidewalk to a shallow porch. No streetlamps lit that block, and there were no walkway or landscape lights at Talbot's, for which Sam was grateful.

Tessa Lockland stood close to him on the porch as he pressed the buzzer, just as she had stayed close all the way from the laundry. Above the noisy rustle of the wind in the trees, he could hear the doorbell ring inside.

Looking back toward Conquistador, Tessa said, "Sometimes it seems more like a morgue than a town, peopled by the dead, but then . . . "

"Then?"

" . . . in spite of the silence and the stillness, you can feel the energy of the place, tremendous pent-up energy, as if there's a huge hidden machine just beneath the streets, beneath the ground . . . and as if the houses are filled with machinery, too, all of it powered up and straining at cogs and gears, just waiting for someone to engage a clutch and set it all in motion."

That was *exactly* Moonlight Cove, but Sam had not been able to put the feeling of the place into words. He rang the bell again and said, "I thought filmmakers were required to be borderline illiterates."

"Most Hollywood filmmakers are, but I'm an outcast documentarian, so I'm permitted to think—as long as I don't do too much of it."

"Who's there?" said a tinny voice, startling Sam. It came from an intercom speaker that he'd not noticed. "Who's there, please?"

Sam leaned close to the intercom. "Mr. Talbot? Harold Talbot?"

"Yes. Who're you?"

"Sam Booker," he said quietly, so his voice would not carry past the perimeter of Talbot's porch. "Sorry to wake you, but I've come in response to your letter of October eighth."

Talbot was silent. Then the intercom clicked, and he said, "I'm on the third floor. I'll need time to get down there. Meanwhile I'll send Moose. Please give him your ID so he can bring it to me."

"I have no Bureau ID," Sam whispered. "I'm undercover here."

"Driver's license?" Talbot asked.

"Yes."

"That's enough." He clicked off.

"Moose?" Tessa asked.

"Damned if I know," Sam said.

They waited almost a minute, feeling vulnerable on the exposed porch, and they were both startled again when a dog pushed out through a pet door they had not seen, brushing between their legs. For an instant Sam didn't realize what it was, and he stumbled backward in surprise, nearly losing his balance.

Stooping to pet the dog, Tessa whispered, "Moose?"

A flicker of light had come through the small swinging door with the dog; but that was gone now that the door was closed. The dog was black and hardly visible in the night.

Squatting beside it, letting it lick his hand, Sam said, "I'm supposed to give my ID to you?"

The dog wuffed softly, as if answering in the affirmative.

"You'll eat it," Sam said.

Tessa said, "He won't."

"How do you know?"

"He's a good dog."

"I don't trust him."

"I guess that's your job."

"Huh?"

"Not to trust anyone."

"And my nature."

"Trust him," she insisted.

He offered his wallet. The dog plucked it from Sam's hand, held it in his teeth, and went back into the house through the pet door.

They stood on the dark porch for another few minutes, while Sam tried to stifle his yawns. It was after two in the morning, and he was considering adding a fifth item to his list of reasons for living: good Mexican food, Guinness Stout, Goldie Hawn, fear of death, and *sleep*. Blissful sleep. Then he heard the clack and rattle of locks being laboriously disengaged, and the door finally opened inward on a dimly lighted hallway.

Harry Talbot waited in his motorized wheelchair, dressed in blue pajamas and a green robe. His head was tilted slightly to the left in a permanently quizzical angle that was part of his Vietnam legacy. He was a handsome man, though his face was prematurely aged, too deeply lined for that of a forty-year-old. His thick hair was half white, and his eyes were ancient. Sam could see that Talbot had once been a strapping young man, though he was now soft from years of paralysis. One hand lay in his lap, the palm up, fingers half curled, useless. He was a living monument to what might have been, to hopes destroyed, to dreams incinerated, a grim remembrance of war pressed between the pages of time.

As Tessa and Sam entered and closed the door behind them, Harry Talbot extended his good hand and said, "God, am I glad to see you!" His smile transformed him astonishingly. It was the bright, broad, warm, and genuine smile of a man who believed he was perched in the lap of the gods, with too many blessings to count.

Moose returned Sam's wallet, uneaten.

48

AFTER LEAVING SHADDACK'S HOUSE ON THE NORTH POINT, but before returning to headquarters to coordinate the assignments of the hundred men who were being sent to him from New Wave, Loman Watkins stopped at his home on Iceberry Way, on the north side of town. It was a modest, two-story, three-bedroom, Monterey-style house, white with pale-blue trim, nestled among conifers.

He stood for a moment in the driveway beside his patrol car, studying the place. He had loved it as if it were a castle, but he could not find that love in himself now. He remembered much happiness related to the house, to his family, but he could not *feel* the memory of that happiness. A lot of laughter had graced life in that dwelling, but now the laughter had faded until recollection of it was too faint even to induce a smile in remembrance. Besides, these days, his smiles were all counterfeit, with no humor behind them.

The odd thing was that laughter and joy had been a part of his life as late as this past August. It had all seeped away only within the past couple of months, after the Change. Yet it seemed an ancient memory.

Funny.

Actually, not so funny at all.

When he went inside he found the first floor dark and silent. A vague, stale odor lingered in the deserted rooms.

He climbed the stairs. In the unlighted, second-floor hallway he saw a soft glow along the bottom of the closed door to Denny's bedroom. He went in and found the boy sitting at his desk, in front of the computer. The PC had an oversize screen, and currently that was the only light in the room.

Denny did not look up from the terminal.

The boy was eighteen years old, no longer a child; therefore, he had been converted with his mother, shortly after Loman himself had been put through the Change. He was two inches taller than his dad and better looking. He'd always done well in school, and on IQ tests he'd scored so high it spooked Loman a bit to think his kid was *that* smart. He had always been proud of Denny. Now, at his son's side, staring down at him, Loman tried to resurrect that pride but could not find it. Denny had not fallen from favor; he had done nothing to earn his father's disapproval. But pride, like so many other emotions, seemed an encumbrance to the higher consciousness of the New People and interfered with their more efficient thought patterns.

Even before the Change, Denny had been a computer fanatic, one of those kids who called themselves hackers, to whom computers were not only tools, not only fun and games, but a way of life. After the conversion, his intelligence and high-tech expertise were put to use by New Wave. He was provided with a more powerful home terminal and a modem link to the supercomputer at New Wave headquarters—a behemoth that, according to Denny's description, incorporated four thousand miles of wiring and thirty-three thousand high-speed processing units—which, for reasons Loman didn't understand, they called Sun, though perhaps that was its name because all research at New Wave made heavy use of the machine and therefore revolved around it.

As Loman stood beside his son, voluminous data flickered across the terminal screen. Words, numbers, graphs, and charts appeared and disappeared at such speed that only one of the New People, with somewhat heightened senses and powerfully heightened concentration, could extract meaning from them.

In fact Loman could not read them because he had not undergone the training that Denny had received from New Wave. Besides, he'd had neither the time nor the need to learn to fully focus his new powers of concentration.

But Denny absorbed the rushing waves of data, staring blankly at the screen, no frown lines in his brow, his face completely relaxed. Since being converted, the boy was as much a solid-state electronic entity as he was flesh and blood, and that new part of him related to the computer with an intimacy that exceeded any man-machine relationship any of the Old People had ever known.

Loman knew that his son was learning about the Moonhawk Project. Ultimately he would join the task group at New Wave that was endlessly refining the software and hardware related to the project, working to make each generation of New People superior to—and more efficient than—the one before it.

An endless river of data washed across the screen.

Denny stared unblinkingly for so long that tears would have formed in his eyes if he had been one of the Old People.

The light of the ever-moving data danced on the walls and sent a continuous blur of shadows chasing around the room.

Loman put one hand on the boy's shoulder.

Denny did not look up or in any way respond. His lips began to move, as if he were talking, but he made no sound. He was speaking to himself, oblivious of his father.

In a garrulous, evangelistic moment, Thomas Shaddack had spoken of one day developing a link that would connect a computer directly to a surgically implanted socket in the base of the human spine, thereby merging real and artificial intelligence. Loman had not understood why such a thing was either wise or desirable, and Shaddack had said, "The New People are a bridge between man and machine, Loman. But one day our species will entirely cross that bridge, become *one* with the machines, because only then will mankind be *completely* efficient, *completely* in control."

"Denny," Loman said softly.

The boy did not respond.

At last Loman left the room.

Across the hall and at the end of it was the master bedroom. Grace was lying on the bed, in the dark.

Of course, since the Change, she could never be entirely blinded by a mere insufficiency of light, for her eyesight had improved. Even in this lightless room, she could see—as Loman could—the shapes of the furniture and some textures, though few details. For them, the night world was no longer black but darkish gray.

He sat on the edge of the mattress. "Hello."

She said nothing.

He put one hand on her head and stroked her long auburn hair. He touched her face and found her cheeks wet with tears, a detail that even his improved eyes could not discern.

Crying. She was crying, and that jolted him because he had never seen one of the New People cry.

His heartbeat accelerated, and a brief but wonderful thrill of hope throbbed through him. Perhaps the deadening of emotions was a transient condition.

"What is it?" he asked. "What're you crying about?"

"I'm afraid."

The pulse of hope swiftly faded. Fear had brought her to tears, fear and the desolation associated with it, and he already knew those feelings were a part of this brave new world, those and no other.

"Afraid of what?"

"I can't sleep," Grace said.

"But you don't need to sleep."

"Don't I?"

"None of us needs to sleep any more."

Prior to the Change, men and women had needed to sleep because the human body, being strictly a biological mechanism, was terribly inefficient. Downtime was required to rest and repair the damage of the day, to deal with the toxic substances absorbed from the external world and the toxics created internally. But in the New People, every bodily process and function was superbly regulated. Nature's work had been highly refined. Every organ, every system, every cell operated at a far higher efficiency, producing less waste, casting off waste faster than before, cleansing and rejuvenating itself every hour of the day. Grace knew that as well as he did.

"I long for sleep," she said.

"All you're feeling is the pull of habit."

"Too many hours in the day now."

"We'll fill up the time. The new world will be a busy one."

"What're we going to do in this new world when it comes?"

"Shaddack will tell us."

"Meanwhile . . . "

"Patience," he said.

"I'm afraid."

"Patience."

"I yearn for sleep, hunger for it."

"We don't need to sleep," he said, exhibiting the patience that he had encouraged in her.

"We don't need sleep," she said cryptically, "but we *need* to sleep."

They were both silent a while.

Then she took his hand in hers, and moved it to her breasts. She was nude.

He tried to pull away from her, for he was afraid of what might happen, of what had happened before, since the Change, when they had made love. No. Not love. They didn't make love any more. They had sex. There was no feeling beyond physical sensation, no tenderness or affection. They thrust hard and fast at each other, pushed and pulled, flexed and writhed against each other, striving to maximize the excitation of nerve endings. Neither of them cared for or about the other, only about himself, his own satisfaction. Now that their emotional life was no longer rich, they tried to compensate for that loss with pleasures of the senses, primarily food and sex. However, without the emotional factor, every experience was . . . hollow, and they tried to fill that emptiness by overindulgence: A simple meal became a feast; a feast became an unrestrained indulgence in gluttony. And sex degenerated into a frenzied, bestial coupling.

Grace pulled him onto the bed.

He did not want to go. He could not refuse. Literally *could not* refuse.

Breathing hard, shuddering with excitement, she tore at his clothes and mounted him. She was making strange wordless sounds.

Loman's excitement matched hers and swelled, and he thrust at her, into her, into, losing all sense of time and place, existing only to stoke the fire in his loins, stoke it relentlessly until it was an unbearable heat, heat, friction and heat, wet and hot, heat, stoking the heat to a flashpoint at which his entire body would be consumed in the flames. He shifted positions, pinning her down, hammering himself into her, into her, into, into, pulling her against him so roughly that he must be bruising her, but he didn't care. She reached back and clawed at him, her fingernails digging into his arm, drawing blood, and he tore at her, too, because the blood was exciting, the smell of the blood, the sweet smell, so exciting, blood, and it didn't matter that they wounded each other, for these were superficial wounds and would heal within seconds, because they were New People; their bodies were efficient; blood flowed briefly, and then the wounds closed, and they clawed again, again. What he really wanted—what they both wanted—was to let go, indulge the wild spirit within, cast off all the inhibitions of civilization, including the inhibition of higher human form, go wild, go savage, regress, surrender, because then sex would have an even greater thrill, a purer thrill; surrender, and the emptiness would be filled; they would be fulfilled, and when the sex was done they could hunt together, hunt and kill, swift and silent, sleek and swift, bite and tear, bite deep and hard, hunt and kill, sperm and then blood, sweet fragrant blood. . . .

For a while Loman was disoriented.

When a sense of time and place returned to him, he first glanced at the door, realizing that it was ajar. Denny could have seen them if he'd come down the hall—surely *had* heard them—but Loman couldn't make himself care whether they had been seen or heard. Shame and modesty were two more casualties of the Change.

As he became fully oriented to the world around him, fear slipped into his heart, and he quickly touched himself—his face, arms, chest, legs—to be sure that he was in no way less than he ought to be. In the midst of sex, the wildness in him grew, and sometimes he thought that approaching orgasm he *did* change, regress, if only slightly. But upon regaining awareness, he never found evidence of backsliding.

He was, however, sticky with blood.

He switched on the bedside lamp.

"Turn it off," Grace said at once.

But he was not satisfied with even his enhanced night vision. He wanted to look at her closely to determine if she was in any way . . . different.

She had not regressed. Or, if she *had* regressed, she had already returned to the higher form. Her body was smeared with blood, and a few welts showed on her flesh, where he had gouged her and where she had not finished healing.

He turned the light off and sat on the edge of the bed.

Because the recuperative powers of their bodies had been vastly improved by the Change, superficial cuts and scrapes healed in only minutes; you could actually watch your flesh knit its wounds. They were impervious to disease now, their immune systems too aggressive for the most infectious virus or bacterium to survive long enough to replicate. Shaddack believed that their life spans would prove to be of great duration, as well, perhaps hundreds of years.

They could be killed, of course, but only by a wound that tore and stopped the heart or shattered the brain or destroyed their lungs and prevented a flow of oxygen to the blood. If a vein or artery was severed, the blood supply was drastically reduced to that vessel for the few minutes required to heal it. If a vital organ other than the heart or lungs or brain was damaged, the body could limp along for hours while accelerated repairs were under way. They were not yet as fully reliable as machines, for machines could not die; with the right spare parts, a machine could be rebuilt even from rubble and could work again; but they were closer to that degree of corporeal endurance than anyone outside Moonlight Cove would have believed.

To live for hundreds of years . . .

Sometimes Loman brooded about that.

To live for hundreds of years, knowing only fear and physical sensation . . .

He rose from the bed, went into the adjacent bathroom, and took a quick shower to sluice off the blood.

He could not meet his eyes in the bathroom mirror.

In the bedroom again, without turning on a light, he pulled on a fresh uniform that he took from his closet.

Grace was still lying on the bed.

She said, "I wish I could sleep."

He sensed that she was still crying silently.

When he left the room, he closed the door behind him.

49

THEY GATHERED IN THE KITCHEN, WHICH TESSA LIKED BE-cause some of her happiest memories of childhood and adolescence involved family conferences and impromptu chats in the kitchen of their house in San Diego. The kitchen was the heart of a home and in a way the heart of a family. Somehow the worst problems became insignificant when you discussed them in a warm kitchen redolent of coffee and hot cocoa, nibbling on home-baked cake or pastry. In a kitchen she felt secure.

Harry Talbot's kitchen was large, for it had been remodeled to suit a man in a wheelchair, with lots of clearance around the central cooking island, which was built low—as were the counters along the walls—to be accessible from a sitting position. Otherwise it was a kitchen like many others: cabinets painted a pleasant creamy shade; pale yellow ceramic tile; a quietly purring refrigerator. The Levolor blinds at the windows were electrically operated by a button on one of the counters, and Harry put them down.

After trying the phone and discovering that the line was dead, that not just the pay phones but the town's entire phone system had been interdicted, Sam and Tessa sat at a round table in one corner, at Harry's insistence, while he made a pot of good Colombian in a Mr. Coffee machine. "You look cold," he said. "This'll do you good."

Chilled and tired, in need of the caffeine, Tessa did not decline the offer. Indeed, she was fascinated that Harry, with such severe disabilities, could function well enough to play the gracious host to unexpected visitors.

With his one good hand and some tricky moves, he got a package of apple-cinnamon muffins from the bread box, part of a chocolate cake from the refrig-erator, plates and forks, and paper napkins. When Sam and Tessa offered to help, he gently declined their assistance with a smile.

She sensed that he was not trying to prove anything either to them or to himself. He was simply enjoying having company, even at this hour and under these bi-zarre circumstances. Perhaps it was a rare pleasure.

"No cream," he said. "Just a carton of milk."

"That's fine," Sam said.

"And no elegant porcelain cream pitcher, I'm afraid," said Harry, putting the milk carton on the table.

Tessa began to consider shooting a documentary about Harry, about the courage required to remain independent in his circumstances: She was drawn by the siren call of her art in spite of what had transpired in the past few hours. Long ago, however, she had learned that an artist's creativity could not be turned off; the eye of a filmmaker could not be capped as easily as the lens of her camera. In the midst of grief over her sister's death, ideas for projects had continued to come to her, narrative concepts, interesting shots, angles. Even in the terror of war, running with Afghan rebels as Soviet planes strafed the ground at their heels, she'd been excited by what she was getting on film and by what she would be able to make of it when she got into an editing room—and her three-man crew had reacted much the same. So she no longer felt awkward or guilty about being an artist on the make, even in times of tragedy; for her, that was just natural, a part of being creative and *alive*.

Customized to his needs, Harry's wheelchair included a hydraulic lift that raised the seat a few inches, bringing him nearly to normal chair height, so he could sit at an ordinary table or writing desk. He took a place beside Tessa and across from Sam.

Moose was lying in the corner, watching, occasionally raising his head as if interested in their conversation—though more likely drawn by the smell of chocolate cake. The Labrador did not come sniffing and pawing around, whining for handouts, and Tessa was impressed by his discipline.

As they passed the coffee pot and carved up the cake and muffins, Harry said, "You've told me what brings you here, Sam—not just my letter but all these so-called accidents." He looked at Tessa, and because she was on his right side, the permanent cock of his head to the left made it seem as if he were leaning back from her, regarding her with suspicion or at least skepticism, though his true attitude was belied by his warm smile. "But just where do you fit in, Miss Lockland?"

"Call me Tessa, please. Well . . . my sister was Janice Capshaw—"

"Richard Capshaw's wife, the Lutheran minister's wife?" he said, surprised.

"That's right."

"Why, they used to come to visit me. I wasn't a member of their congregation, but that's how they were. We became friends. And after he died, she still stopped by now and then. Your sister was a dear and wonderful person, Tessa." He put down his coffee cup and reached out to her with his good hand. "She was my friend."

Tessa held his hand. It was leathery and calloused from use, and very strong, as if all the frustrated power of his paralyzed body found expression through that single extremity.

"I watched them take her into the crematorium at Callan's Funeral Home," Harry said. "Through my telescope. I'm a watcher. That's what I do with my life, for the most part. I watch." He blushed slightly. He held Tessa's hand a bit tighter. "It's not just snooping. In fact it isn't snooping at all. It's . . . participating. Oh, I like to read, too, and I've got a lot of books, and I do a heavy load of thinking, for sure, but it's watching, mainly, that gets me through. We'll go upstairs later. I'll show you the telescope, the whole setup. I think maybe you'll understand. I hope you will. Anyway, I saw them take Janice into Callan's that night . . . though I didn't know who it was until two days later, when the story of her death was in the county paper. I couldn't believe she died the way they said she did. Still don't believe it."

"Neither do I," Tessa said. "And that's why I'm here."

Reluctantly, with a final squeeze, Harry let go of Tessa's hand. "So many bodies lately, most of them hauled into Callan's at night, and more than a few times with cops hanging around, overseeing things—it's strange as hell for a quiet little town like this."

From across the table, Sam said, "Twelve accidental deaths or suicides in less than two months."

"Twelve?" Harry said.

"Didn't you realize it was that many?" Sam asked.

"Oh, it's more than that."

Sam blinked.

Harry said, "Twenty, by my count."

50

AFTER WATKINS LEFT, SHADDACK RETURNED TO THE COMputer terminal in his study, reopened his link to Sun, the supercomputer at New Wave, and set to work again on a problematic aspect of the current project. Though it was two-thirty in the morning, he would put in a few more hours, for the earliest he went to bed was dawn.

He had been at the terminal a few minutes when his most private phone line rang.

Until Booker was apprehended, the telephone company computer was allowing service only among those who had been converted, *from* one of their numbers *to* one of their numbers. Other lines were cut off, and calls to the outside world were interrupted before being completed. Incoming calls to Moonlight Cove were answered by a recording that pleaded equipment failure, promised a return to full service within twenty-four hours, and expressed regret at the inconvenience.

Therefore, Shaddack knew the caller must be among the converted and, because it was his most private line, must also be one of his closest associates at New Wave. A LED readout on the base of the phone displayed the number from which the call was being placed, which he recognized as that of Mike Peyser. He picked up the receiver and said, "Shaddack here."

The caller breathed heavily, raggedly into the phone but said nothing.

Frowning, Shaddack said, "Hello?"

Just the breathing.

Shaddack said, "Mike, is that you?"

The voice that finally responded to him was hoarse, guttural, but with a shrill edge, whispery yet forceful, Peyser's voice yet not his, strange: "*. . . something wrong, wrong, something wrong, can't change, can't . . . wrong . . . wrong . . .*"

Shaddack was reluctant to admit that he recognized Mike Peyser's voice in those queer inflections and eerie cadences. He said, "Who is this?"

"*. . . need, need . . . need, want, I need . . .* "

"Who is this?" Shaddack demanded angrily, but in his mind was another question: *What* is this?

The caller issued a sound that was a groan of pain, a mewl of deepest anguish, a thin cry of frustration, and a snarl, all twisted into one rolling bleat. The receiver dropped from his hand with a hard clatter.

Shaddack put his own phone down, turned back to the VDT, tapped into the police data system, and sent an urgent message to Loman Watkins.

51

SITTING ON THE STOOL IN THE DARK THIRD-FLOOR BED-room, bent to the eyepiece, Sam Booker studied the rear of Callan's Funeral Home. All but scattered scrims of fog had blown away on the wind, which still blustered at the window and shook the trees all along the hillsides on which most of Moonlight Cove was built. The serviceway lamps were extinguished now, and the rear of Callan's lay in darkness but for the thin light radiating from the blind-covered windows of the crematorium wing. No doubt they were busily feeding the flames with the bodies of the couple who had been murdered at Cove Lodge.

Tessa sat on the edge of the bed behind Sam, petting Moose, who was lying with his head in her lap.

Harry was in his wheelchair nearby. He used a penlight to study a spiral-bound notebook in which he had kept a record of the unusual activities at the mortuary.

"First one—at least the first unusual one I noticed—was on the night of August twenty-eighth," Harry said. "Twenty minutes to midnight. They brought four bodies at once, using the hearse and the city ambulance. Police accompanied them. The corpses were in body bags, so I couldn't see anything about them, but the cops and the ambulance attendants and the people at Callan's were visibly . . . well . . . upset. I saw it in their faces. Fear. They kept looking around at the neighboring houses and the alleyway, as if they were afraid someone was going to see what they were up to, which seemed peculiar because they were only doing their jobs. Right? Anyway, later, in the county paper, I read about the Mayser family dying in a fire, and I knew that was who'd been brought to Callan's that night. I supposed they didn't die in a fire any more than your sister killed herself."

"Probably not," Tessa said.

Still watching the back of the funeral home, Sam said, "I have the Maysers on my list. They were turned up in the investigation of the Sanchez-Bustamante case."

Harry cleared his throat and said, "Six days later, September third, two bodies were brought to Callan's shortly after midnight. And this was even weirder because they didn't come in a hearse or an ambulance. Two police cars pulled in at the back of Callan's, and they unloaded a body from the rear seat of each of them, wrapped in blood-streaked sheets."

"September third?" Sam said. "There's no one on my list for that date. Sanchez and the Bustamantes were on the fifth. No death certificates were issued on the third. They kept those two off the official records."

"Nothing in the county paper about anyone dying then, either," Harry said.

Tessa said, "So who were those two people?"

"Maybe they were out-of-towners who were unlucky enough to stop in Moonlight Cove and stumble into something dangerous," Sam said. "People whose deaths could be completely covered up, so no one would know *where* they'd died. As far as anyone knows, they just vanished on the road somewhere."

"Sanchez and the Bustamantes were on the night of the fifth," Harry said, "and then Jim Armes on the night of the seventh."

"Armes disappeared at sea," Sam said, looking up from the telescope and frowning at the man in the wheelchair.

"They brought the body to Callan's at eleven o'clock at night," Harry said, consulting his notebook for details. "The blinds weren't drawn at the crematorium windows, so I could see straight in there, almost as good as if I'd been right there in that room. I saw the body . . . the mess it was in. And the face. Couple of days later, when the paper ran a story about Armes's disappearance, I recognized him as the guy they'd fed to the furnace."

The large bedroom was dressed in cloaks of shadow except for the narrow beam of the penlight, which was half shielded by Harry's hand and confined to the open notebook. Those white pages seemed to glow with light of their own, as if they were the leaves of a magic or holy—or unholy—book.

Harry Talbot's careworn countenance was more dimly illuminated by the backsplash from those pages, and the peculiar light emphasized the lines in his face, making him appear older than he was. Each line, Sam knew, had its provenance in tragic experience and pain. Profound sympathy stirred in him. Not pity. He could never pity anyone as determined as Talbot. But Sam appreciated the sorrow and loneliness of Harry's restricted life. Watching the wheelchair-bound man, Sam grew angry with the neighbors. Why hadn't they done more to bring Harry into their lives? Why hadn't they invited him to dinner more often, drawn him into their holiday celebrations? Why had they left him so much on his own that his primary means of participating in the life of his community was through a telescope and binoculars? Sam was cut by a pang of despair at people's reluctance to reach out to one another, at the way they isolated themselves and one another. With a jolt, he thought of his inability to communicate with his own son, which only left him feeling bleaker still.

To Harry, he said, "What do you mean when you say Armes's body was a mess?"

"Cut. Slashed."

"He didn't drown?"

"Didn't look it."

"Slashed . . . Exactly what do you mean?" Tessa asked.

Sam knew that she was thinking about the people whose screams she had heard at the motel—and about her own sister.

Harry hesitated, then said: "Well, I saw him on the table in the crematorium, just before they slipped him into the furnace. He'd been . . . disemboweled. Nearly decapitated. Horribly . . . *torn*. He looked as bad as if he'd been standing on an antipersonnel mine when it went off and been riddled by shrapnel."

They sat in mutual silence, considering that description.

Only Moose seemed unperturbed. He made a soft, contented sound as Tessa gently scratched behind his ears.

Sam thought it might not be so bad to be one of the lower beasts, a creature mostly of feelings, untroubled by a complex intellect. Or at the other extreme . . . a genuinely intelligent computer, all intellect and no feelings whatsoever. The great dual burden of emotion and high intelligence was singular to humankind, and it was what made life so hard; you were always thinking about what you were feeling instead of just going with the moment, or you were always trying to feel what you thought you *should* feel in a given situation. Thoughts and judgment were inevitably colored by emotions—some of them on a subconscious level, so you didn't even entirely understand *why* you made certain decisions, acted in certain ways. Emotions clouded your thinking; but thinking too hard about your feelings took the edge off them. Trying to feel deeply and think perfectly clearly at the same time was like simultaneously juggling six Indian clubs while riding a unicycle backward along a high wire.

"After the story in the paper about Armes disappearing," Harry said, "I kept waiting for a correction, but none was printed, and that's when I began to realize that the odd goings-on at Callan's weren't *just* odd but probably criminal, as well— and that the cops were part of it."

"Paula Parkins was torn apart too," Sam said.

Harry nodded. "Supposedly by her Dobermans."

"Dobermans?" Tessa asked.

At the laundry Sam had told her that her sister was one of many curious suicides and accidental deaths, but he had not gone into any details about the others. Now he quickly told her about Parkins.

"Not her own dogs," Tessa agreed. "She was savaged by whatever killed Armes. And the people tonight at Cove Lodge."

This was the first that Harry Talbot had heard about the murders at Cove Lodge. Sam had to explain about that and about how he and Tessa had met at the laundry.

A strange expression settled on Harry's prematurely aged face. To Tessa, he said, "Uh . . . you didn't see these things at the motel? Not even a glimpse?"

"Only the foot of one of them, through the crack under the door."

Harry started to speak, stopped, and sat in thoughtful silence.

He knows something, Sam thought. More than we do.

For some reason Harry was not ready to share what he knew, for he returned his scrutiny to the notebook on his lap and said, "Two days after Paula Parkins died, there was one body taken to Callan's, around nine-thirty at night."

"That would be September eleventh?" Sam asked.

"Yes."

"There's no record of a death certificate issued that day."

"Nothing about it in the paper, either."

"Go on."

Harry said, "September fifteenth—"

"Steve Heinz, Laura Dalcoe. He supposedly killed her, then took his own life," Sam said. "Lovers' quarrel, we're to believe."

"Another quick cremation," Harry noted. "And three nights later, on the eighteenth, two more bodies delivered to Callan's shortly after one in the morning, just as I was about to go to bed."

"No public record of those, either," Sam said.

"Two more out-of-towners who drove off the interstate for a visit or just dinner?" Tessa wondered. "Or maybe someone from another part of the county, passing on the county road along the edge of town?"

"Could even have been locals," Harry said. "I mean, there're always a few people around who haven't lived here a long time, newcomers who rent instead of own their houses, don't have many ties to the community, so if you wanted to cover their murders, you could maybe concoct an acceptable story about them moving away suddenly, for a new job, whatever, and their neighbors might buy it."

If their neighbors weren't already "converted" and participating in the cover-up, Sam thought.

"Then September twenty-third," Harry said. "That would have been your sister's body, Tessa."

"Yes."

"By then I knew I had to tell someone what I'd seen. Someone in authority. But who? I didn't trust anyone local because I'd watched the cops bring in some of those bodies that were never reported in the newspaper. County Sheriff? He'd believe Watkins before he'd believe me, wouldn't he? Hell, everyone thinks a cripple is a little strange anyway—strange in the head, I mean—they equate physical disabilities with mental disabilities at least a little, at least subconsciously. So they'd be predisposed not to believe me. And admittedly it *is* a wild story, all these bodies, secret cremations. . . ." He paused. His face clouded. "The fact that I'm a decorated veteran wouldn't have made me any more believable. That was a long time ago, ancient history for some of them. In fact . . . no doubt they'd hold the war against me in a way. Post-Vietnam stress syndrome, they'd call it. Poor old Harry finally went crackers—don't you see?—from the war."

Thus far Harry had been speaking matter-of-factly, without much emotion. But the words he had just spoken were like a piece of glass held against the surface of a rippled pool, revealing realms below—in his case, realms of pain, loneliness, and alienation.

Now emotion not only entered his voice but, a few times, made it crack: "And I've got to say, part of the reason I didn't try to tell anyone what I'd seen was because . . . I was afraid. I didn't know what the hell was going on. I couldn't be sure how big the stakes were. I didn't know if they'd silence me, feed *me* to the furnace at Callan's one night. You'd think that having lost so much I'd be reckless now, unconcerned about losing more, about dying, but that's not the way it is, not at all. Life's probably more precious to me than to men who're whole and healthy. This broken body slowed me down so much that I've spent the last twenty years out of the whirl of activity in which most of you exist, and I've had time to really *see* the world, the beauty and intricacy of it. In the end my disabilities have led me to appreciate and love life more. So I was afraid they'd come for me, kill me, and I hesitated to tell anyone what I'd seen. God help me, if I'd spoken out, if I'd gotten in touch with the Bureau sooner, maybe some people might have been saved. Maybe . . . your sister would've been saved."

"Don't even think of that," Tessa said at once. "If you'd done anything differently, no doubt you'd be ashes now, scraped out of the bottom of Callan's furnace and thrown in the sea. My sister's fate was sealed. You couldn't unseal it."

Harry nodded, then switched off the penlight, plunging the room into deeper darkness, though he had not yet finished going through the information in his notebook. Sam suspected that Tessa's unhesitating generosity of spirit had brought tears to Harry's eyes and that he did not want them to see.

"On the twenty-fifth," he continued, not needing to consult the notebook for details, "one body was brought to Callan's at ten-fifteen at night. Weird, too, because it didn't come in either an ambulance or hearse or police car. It was brought by Loman Watkins—"

"Chief of police," Sam said for Tessa's benefit.

"—but he was in his private car, out of uniform," Harry said. "They took the body out of his trunk. It was wrapped in a blanket. The blinds weren't shut at their windows that night, either, and I was able to get in tight with the scope. I didn't recognize the body, but I did recognize the condition of it—the same as Armes."

"Torn?" Sam asked.

"Yes. Then the Bureau *did* come to town on the Sanchez-Bustamante thing, and when I read about it in the newspaper, I was so relieved because I thought it was all going to come out in the open at last, that we'd have revelations, explanations. But then there were two more bodies disposed of at Callan's on the night of October fourth—"

"Our team was in town then," Sam said, "in the middle of their investigation. They didn't realize any death certificates were filed during that time. You're saying this happened under their noses?"

"Yeah. I don't have to look in the notebook; I remember it clearly. The bodies were brought around in Reese Dorn's camper truck. He's a local cop, but he was out of uniform that night. They hauled the stiffs into Callan's, and the blind at one window was open, so I saw them shove both bodies into the crematorium together, as if they were in a real sweat to dispose of them. And there was more activity at Callan's late on the night of the seventh, but the fog was so thick, I can't swear that it was more bodies being taken in. And finally . . . earlier tonight. A child's body. A small child."

"Plus the two who were killed at Cove Lodge," Tessa said. "That makes twenty-two victims, not the twelve that brought Sam here. This town's become a slaughterhouse."

"Could be even more than we think," Harry said.

"How so?"

"Well, after all, I don't watch the place every evening, all evening long. And I go to bed by one-thirty, no later than two. Who's to say there weren't visits I missed, that more bodies weren't brought in during the dead hours of the night?"

Brooding about that, Sam looked through the eyepiece again. The rear of Callan's remained dark and still. He slowly moved the scope to the right, shifting the field of vision northward through the neighborhood.

Tessa said, "But *why* were they killed?"

No one had an answer.

"And by what?" she asked.

Sam studied a cemetery farther north on Conquistador, then sighed and looked up and told them about his experience earlier in the night, on Iceberry Way. "I thought they were kids, delinquents, but now what I think is that they were the same things that killed the people at Cove Lodge, the same as the one whose foot you saw through the crack under the door."

He could almost feel Tessa frowning with frustration in the darkness when she said, "But what *are* they?"

Harry Talbot hesitated. Then: "Boogeymen."

52

NOT DARING TO USE SIRENS, DOUSING HEADLIGHTS ON THE last quarter mile of the approach, Loman came down on Mike Peyser's place at three-ten in the morning, with two cars, five deputies, and shotguns. Loman hoped they did not have to use the guns for more than intimidation. In their only previous encounter with a regressive—Jordan Coombs on the fourth of September—they had not been prepared for its ferocity and had been forced to blow its head off to save their own lives. Shaddack had been left with only a carcass to examine. He'd been furious at the lost chance to delve into the psychology—and the functioning physiology—of one of these metamorphic psychopaths. A tranquilizer gun would be of little use, unfortunately, because regressives were New People gone bad, and all New People, regressive or not, had radically altered metabolisms that not only allowed for magically fast healing but for the rapid absorption, breakdown, and rejection of toxic substances like poison or tranquilizers. The only way to sedate a regressive would be to get him to agree to be put on a continuous IV drip, which wasn't very damn likely.

Mike Peyser's house was a one-story bungalow with front and rear porches on the west and east sides respectively, nicely maintained, on an acre and a half, sheltered by a few huge sweet gums that had not yet lost their leaves. No lights shone at the windows.

Loman sent one man to watch the north side, another the south, to prevent Peyser from escaping through a window. He stationed a third man at the foot of the front porch to cover that door. With the other two men—Sholnick and Penniworth—he circled to the rear of the place and quietly climbed the steps to the back porch.

Now that the fog had been blown away, visibility was good. But the huffing and skirling wind was a white noise that blocked out other sounds they might need to hear while stalking Peyser.

Penniworth stood against the wall of the house to the left of the door, and Sholnick stood to the right. Both carried semiautomatic 20-gauge shotguns.

Loman tried the door. It was unlocked. He pushed it open and stepped back.

His deputies entered the dark kitchen, one after the other, their shotguns lowered and ready to fire, though they were aware that the objective was to take Peyser alive if at all possible. But they were not going to sacrifice themselves just to bring the living beast to Shaddack. A moment later one of them found a light switch.

Carrying a 12-gauge of his own, Loman went into the house after them. Empty bowls, broken dishes, and dirty Tupperware containers were scattered on the floor, as were a few rigatoni red with tomato sauce, half of a meatball, eggshells, a chunk of pie crust, and other bits of food. One of the four wooden chairs from the breakfast set was lying on its side; another had been hammered to pieces against a counter top, cracking some of the ceramic tiles.

Straight ahead, an archway led into a dining room. Some of the spill-through light from the kitchen vaguely illuminated the table and chairs in there.

To the left, beside the refrigerator, was a door. Barry Sholnick opened it defensively. Shelves of canned goods flanked a landing. Stairs led down to the basement.

"We'll check that later," Loman said softly. "After we've gone through the house."

Sholnick soundlessly snatched a chair from the breakfast set and braced the door shut so nothing could come up from the cellar and creep in behind them after they went into other rooms.

They stood for a moment, listening.

Gusting wind slammed against the house. A window rattled. From the attic above came the creaking of rafters, and from higher still the muffled clatter of a loose cedar shingle on the roof.

His deputies looked at Loman for guidance. Penniworth was only twenty-five, could pass for eighteen, and had a face so fresh and guileless that he looked more like a door-to-door peddler of religious tracts than a cop. Sholnick was ten years older and had a harder edge to him.

Loman motioned them toward the dining room.

They entered, turning the lights on as they went. The dining room was deserted, so they moved cautiously into the living room.

Penniworth clicked a wall switch that turned on a chrome and brass lamp, which was one of the few items not broken or torn apart. The cushions on the sofa and chairs had been slashed; wads of foam padding, like clumps of a poisonous fungus, lay everywhere. Books had been pulled from shelves and ripped to pieces. A ceramic lamp, a couple of vases, and the glass top of a coffee table were shattered. The doors had been torn off the cabinet-style television set, and the screen had been smashed. Blind rage and savage strength had been at work here.

The room smelled strongly of urine . . . and of something else less pungent and less familiar. It was, perhaps, the scent of the creature responsible for the wreckage. Part of that subtler stink was the sour odor of perspiration, but something stranger was in it, too, something that simultaneously turned Loman's stomach and tightened it with fear.

To the left, a hallway led back to the bedrooms and baths. Loman kept it covered with his shotgun.

The deputies went into the foyer, which was connected to the living room by a wide archway. A closet was on the right, just inside the front door. Sholnick stood in front of it, his 20-gauge lowered. From the side Penniworth jerked open the door. The closet contained only coats.

The easy part of the search was behind them. Ahead lay the narrow hall with three doors off it, one half open and two ajar, dark rooms beyond. There was less space in which to maneuver, more places from which an assailant might attack.

Night wind soughed in the eaves. It fluted across a rain gutter, producing a low, mournful note.

Loman had never been the kind of leader who sent his men ahead into danger while he stayed back in a position of safety. Although he had shed pride and self-respect and a sense of duty along with most other Old People attitudes and emotions, duty was still a habit with him—in fact, less conscious than a habit, more like a reflex—and he operated as he would have done before the Change. He entered the hall first, where two doors waited on the left and one on the right. He moved swiftly to the end, to the second door on the left, which was half open; he kicked it inward, and in the light from the hall he saw a small, deserted bathroom before the door bounced off the wall and swung shut again.

Penniworth took the first room on the left. He went in and found the light switch by the time Loman reached that threshold. It was a study with a desk, worktable, two chairs, cabinets, tall bookshelves crammed full of volumes with brightly colored spines, two computers. Loman moved in and covered the closet, where Penniworth warily rolled aside first one and then the other of two mirrored doors.

Nothing.

Barry Sholnick remained in the hallway, his 20-gauge leveled at the room they hadn't investigated. When Loman and Penniworth rejoined him, Sholnick shoved that door all the way open with the barrel of his shotgun. As it swung wide, he jerked back, certain that something would fly at him from the darkness, though nothing did. He hesitated, then stepped into the doorway, fumbled with one hand for the light switch, found it, said, "Oh, my God," and stepped quickly back into the hall.

Looking past his deputy into a large bedroom, Loman saw a hellish thing crouched on the floor and huddled against the far wall. It was a regressive, no doubt Peyser, but it did not look as much like the regressed Jordan Coombs as Loman expected. There were similarities, yes, but not many.

Easing by Sholnick, Loman crossed the threshold. "Peyser?"

The thing at the other end of the room blinked at him, moved its twisted mouth. In a voice that was whispery yet guttural, savage yet tortured as only the voice of an at least halfway intelligent creature could be, it said, " . . . *Peyser, Peyser, Peyser, me, Peyser, me, me . . .* "

The odor of urine was here, too, but that other scent was now the dominant one—sharp, musky.

Loman moved farther into the room. Penniworth followed. Sholnick stayed at the doorway. Loman stopped twelve feet from Peyser, and Penniworth moved off to one side, his 20-gauge held ready.

When they'd cornered Jordan Coombs in the shuttered movie theater back on September fourth, he had been in an altered state somewhat resembling a gorilla with a squat and powerful body. Mike Peyser, however, had a far leaner appearance, and as he crouched against the bedroom wall, his body looked more lupine than apelike. His hips were set at an angle to his spine, preventing him from standing or sitting completely erect, and his legs seemed too short in the thighs, too long in the calves. He was covered in thick hair but not so thick that it could be called a pelt.

"Peyser, me, me, me . . . "

Coombs's face had been partly human, though mostly that of a higher primate, with a bony brow, flattened nose, and thrusting jaw to accommodate large, wickedly sharp teeth like those of a baboon. Mike Peyser's hideously transformed countenance had, instead, a hint of the wolf in it, or dog; his mouth and nose were drawn forward into a deformed snout. His massive brow *was* like that of an ape, though exaggerated, and in his bloodshot eyes, set in shadowy sockets deep beneath that bony ridge, was a look of anguish and terror that was entirely human.

Raising one hand and pointing at Loman, Peyser said, *" . . . help me, me, help, something wrong, wrong, wrong, help . . . "*

Loman stared at that mutated hand with both fear and amazement, remembering how his own hand had begun to change when he had felt the call of regression at the Fosters' place earlier in the night. Elongated fingers. Large, rough knuckles. Fierce claws instead of fingernails. Human hands in shape and degree of dexterity, they were otherwise utterly alien.

Shit, Loman thought, those hands, those *hands.* I've seen them in the movies, or at least on the TV, when we rented the cassette of *The Howling.* Rob Bottin. That was the name of the special-effects artist who created the werewolf. He remembered it because Denny had been a nut about special effects before the Change. More than anything else these looked like the goddamn hands of the werewolf in *The Howling!*

Which was too crazy to contemplate. Life imitating fantasy. The fantastic made flesh. As the twentieth century rushed into its last decade, scientific and technological progress had reached some divide, where mankind's dream of a better life often could be fulfilled but also where nightmares could be made real. Peyser was a bad, bad dream that had crawled out of the subconscious and become flesh, and now there was no escaping him by waking up; he would not disappear as did the monsters that haunted sleep.

"How can I help you?" Loman asked warily.

"Shoot him," Penniworth said.

Loman responded sharply: "No!"

Peyser raised both of his tine-fingered hands and looked at them for a moment, as if seeing them for the first time. A groan issued from him, then a thin and miserable wail. *" . . . change, can't change, can't, tried, want, need, want, want, can't, tried, can't . . . "*

From the doorway Sholnick said, "My God, he's stuck like that—he's trapped. I thought the regressives could change back at will."

"They can," Loman said.

"*He* can't," Sholnick said.

"That's what he said," Penniworth agreed, his voice quick and nervous. "He said he can't change."

Loman said, "Maybe, maybe not. But the other regressives can change, because if they *couldn't,* then we'd have found all of them by now. They retreat from their altered state and then walk among us."

Peyser seemed oblivious of them. He was staring at his hands, mewling in the back of his throat as if what he saw terrified him.

Then the hands began to change.

"You see," Loman said.

Loman had never witnessed such a transformation; he was gripped by curiosity, wonder, and terror. The claws receded. The flesh was suddenly as malleable as soft wax: It bulged, blistered, pulsed not with the rhythmic flow of blood in arteries but strangely, obscenely; it assumed new form, as if an invisible sculptor were at work on it. Loman heard bones crunching, splintering, as they were broken down and remade; the flesh melted and resolidified with a sickening, wet sound. The hands became nearly human. Then the wrists and forearms began to lose some of their rawboned lupine quality. In Peyser's face were indications that the human spirit was struggling to banish the savage that was now in control; the features of a predator began to give way to a gentler and more civilized mien. It was as if the monstrous Peyser was only a beast's reflection in a pool of water out of which the real and human Peyser was now rising.

Though he was no scientist, no genius of microtechnology, only a policeman with a high-school education, Loman knew that this profound and rapid transformation could not be attributed solely to the New People's drastically improved metabolic processes and ability to heal themselves. No matter what great tides of hormones, enzymes, and other biological chemicals Peyser's body could now produce at will, there was no way that bone and flesh could be re-formed so dramatically in such a brief period of time. Over days or weeks, yes, but not in *seconds*. Surely it was physically impossible. Yet it was happening. Which meant that another force was at work in Mike Peyser, something more than biological processes, something mysterious and frightening.

Suddenly the transformation halted. Loman could see that Peyser was straining toward full humanity, clenching his half-human yet still wolflike jaws together and grinding his teeth, a look of desperation and iron determination in his strange eyes, but to no avail. For a moment he trembled on the edge of human form. It seemed that if he could just push the transformation one step farther, just one small step, then he would cross a watershed after which the rest of the metamorphosis would take place almost automatically, without the strenuous exertion of will, as easily as a stream flowing downhill. But he could not reach that divide.

Penniworth made a low, strangled sound, as if he were sharing Peyser's anguish.

Loman glanced at his deputy. Penniworth's face glistened with a thin film of perspiration.

Loman realized he was perspiring too; he felt a bead trickle down his left temple. The bungalow was warm—an oil furnace kept clicking on and off—but not warm enough to wring moisture from them. This was a cold sweat of fear, but more than that. He also felt a tightness in his chest, a thickening in his throat that made it hard to swallow, and he was breathing fast, as if he'd sprinted up a hundred steps—

Letting out a thin, agonized cry, Peyser began to regress again. With the brittle splintering noise of bones being remade, the oily-wet sound of flesh being rent and re-knit, the savage creature reasserted itself, and in moments Peyser was as he had been when they had first seen him: a hellish beast.

Hellish, yes, and a beast, but enviably powerful and with an odd, terrible beauty of its own. The forward carriage of the large head was awkward by comparison to the set of the human head, and the thing lacked the sinuous inward curve of the human spine, yet it had a dark grace of its own.

They stood in silence for a moment.

Peyser huddled on the floor, head bowed.

From the doorway, Sholnick finally said, "My God, he *is* trapped."

Although Mike Peyser's problem could have been related to some glitch in the technology on which conversion from Old to New Person was based, Loman suspected that Peyser still possessed the power to reshape himself, that he could become a man if he wanted to badly enough, but that he lacked the desire to be fully human again. He had become a regressive because he found that altered state appealing, so maybe he found it so much more exciting and satisfying than the human condition that now he did not truly *want* to return to a higher state.

Peyser raised his head and looked at Loman, then at Penniworth, then at Sholnick, and finally at Loman again. His horror at his condition was no longer apparent. The anguish and terror were gone from his eyes. With his twisted muzzle he seemed to smile at them, and a new wildness—both disturbing and appealing—appeared in his eyes. He raised his hands before his face again and flexed the long fingers, clicked the claws together, studying himself with what might have been wonder.

"*. . . hunt, hunt, chase, hunt, kill, blood, blood, need, need . . .*"

"How the hell can we take him alive if he doesn't want to be taken?" Penniworth's voice was peculiar, thick and slightly slurred.

Peyser dropped one hand to his genitals and scratched lightly, absentmindedly. He looked at Loman again, then at the night pressing against the windows.

"I feel . . ." Sholnick left the sentence unfinished.

Penniworth was no more articulate: "If we . . . well, we could . . ."

The pressure in Loman's chest had grown greater. His throat was tighter, too, and he was still sweating.

Peyser let out a soft, ululant cry as eerie as any sound Loman had ever heard, an expression of longing, yet also an animal challenge to the night, a statement of his power and his confidence in his own strength and cunning. The wail should have been harsh and unpleasant in the confines of that bedroom, but instead it stirred in Loman the same unspeakable yearning that had gripped him outside of the Fosters' house when he had heard the trio of regressives calling to one another far away in the darkness.

Clenching his teeth so hard that his jaws ached, Loman strove to resist that unholy urge.

Peyser loosed another cry, then said, "*Run, hunt, free, free, need, free, need, come with me, come, come, need, need . . .*"

Loman realized that he was relaxing his grip on the 12-gauge. The barrel was tilting down. The muzzle was pointing at the floor instead of at Peyser.

"*. . . run, free, free, need . . .*"

From behind Loman came an unnerving, orgasmic cry of release.

He glanced back at the bedroom doorway in time to see Sholnick drop his shotgun. Subtle transformations had occurred in the deputy's hands and face. He pulled off his quilted, black uniform jacket, cast it aside, and tore open his shirt. His cheekbones and jaws dissolved and flowed forward, and his brow retreated as he sought an altered state.

53

WHEN HARRY TALBOT FINISHED TELLING THEM ABOUT THE Boogeymen, Sam leaned forward on the high stool to the telescope eyepiece. He swung the instrument to the left, until he focused on the vacant lot beside Callan's, where the creatures had most recently put in an appearance.

He was not sure what he was looking for. He didn't believe that the Boogeymen would have returned to that same place at precisely this time to give him a convenient look at them. And there were no clues in the shadows and trampled grass and shrubs, where they had crouched only a few hours ago, to tell him what they might have been or on what mission they had been embarked. Maybe he was just trying to anchor the fantastic image of ape-dog-reptilian Boogeymen in the real world, tie them in his mind to that vacant lot, and thereby make them more concrete, so he could deal with them.

In any event Harry had another story besides that one. As they sat in the darkened room, as if listening to ghost stories around a burnt-out campfire, he told them how he'd seen Denver Simpson, Doc Fitz, Reese Dorn, and Paul Hawthorne overpower Ella Simpson, take her upstairs to the bedroom, and prepare to inject her with an enormous syringeful of some golden fluid.

Operating the telescope at Harry's direction, Sam was able to find and draw in tight on the Simpsons' house, on the other side of Conquistador and just north of the Catholic cemetery. All was dark and motionless.

From the bed where she still had the dog's head in her lap, Tessa said, "All of it's got to be connected somehow: these 'accidental' deaths, whatever those men were doing to Ella Simpson, and these . . . Boogeymen."

"Yes, it's tied together," Sam agreed. "And the knot is New Wave Microtechnology."

He told them what he had uncovered while working with the VDT in the patrol car behind the municipal building.

"Moonhawk?" Tessa wondered. "Conversions? What on earth are they converting people into?"

"I don't know."

"Surely not into . . . these Boogeymen?"

"No, I don't see the purpose of *that*, and besides, from what I turned up, I gather almost two thousand people in town have been . . . given this treatment, put through this change, whatever the hell it is. If there were that many of Harry's Boogeymen running loose, they'd be everywhere; the town would be crawling with them, like a zoo in the Twilight Zone."

"Two thousand," Harry said. "That's two-thirds of the town."

"And the rest by midnight," Sam said. "Just under twenty-one hours from now."

"Me, too, I guess?" Harry asked.

"Yeah. I looked you up on their lists. You're scheduled for conversion in the final stage, between six o'clock this coming evening and midnight. So we've got about fourteen and a half hours before they come looking for you."

"This is nuts," Tessa said.

"Yeah," Sam agreed. "Totally nuts."

"It can't be happening," Harry said. "But if it isn't happening, then why's the hair standing up on the back of my neck?"

54

"SHOLNICK!"

Throwing aside his uniform shirt, kicking off his shoes, frantic to strip out of all his clothes and complete his regression, Barry Sholnick ignored Loman.

"Barry, stop, for God's sake, don't let this happen," Penniworth said urgently. He was pale and shaking. He glanced from Sholnick to Peyser and back again, and Loman suspected that Penniworth felt the same degenerate urge to which Sholnick had surrendered himself.

"*. . . run free, hunt, blood, blood, need . . .*"

Peyser's insidious chant was like a spike through Loman's head, and he wanted it to stop. No, truthfully, it wasn't like a spike splitting his skull, because it wasn't at all painful and was, in fact, thrilling and strangely melodic, reaching deep into him, piercing him not like a shaft of steel but like music. *That* was why he wanted it to stop: because it appealed to him, enticed him; it made him want to shed his responsibilities and concerns, retreat from the too-complex life of the intellect to an existence based strictly on feelings, on physical pleasures, a world whose boundaries were defined by sex and food and the thrill of the hunt, a world where disputes were settled and needs were met strictly by the application of muscle, where he'd never have to think again or worry or care.

"*. . . need, need, need, need, need, kill . . .*"

Sholnick's body bent forward as his spine re-formed. His back lost the concave curvature distinctive of the human form. His skin appeared to be giving way to scales—

"*come, quick, quick, the hunt, blood, blood . . .*"

—and as Sholnick's face was reshaped, his mouth split impossibly wide, opening nearly to each ear, like the mouth of some ever-grinning reptile.

The pressure in Loman's chest was growing greater by the second. He was hot, sweltering, but the heat came from within him, as if his metabolism was racing at a thousand times ordinary speed, readying him for transformation. "No." Sweat streamed from him. "No!" He felt as if the room were a cauldron in which he would be reduced to his essence; he could almost feel his flesh beginning to melt.

Penniworth was saying, "I want, I want, I want, want," but he was vigorously shaking his head, trying to deny what he wanted. He was crying and trembling and sheet-white.

Peyser rose from his crouch and stepped away from the wall. He moved sinuously, swiftly, and although he could not stand entirely erect in his altered state, he was taller than Loman, simultaneously a frightening and seductive figure.

Sholnick shrieked.

Peyser bared his fierce teeth and hissed at Loman as if to say, *Either join us or die.*

With a cry composed partly of despair and partly of joy, Neil Penniworth dropped his 20-gauge and put his hands to his face. As if that contact had exerted an alchemical reaction, both his hands and face began to change.

Heat *exploded* in Loman, and he shouted wordlessly, but without the joy that Penniworth had expressed and without Sholnick's orgasmic cry. While he still had control of himself, he raised the shotgun and squeezed off a round point-blank at Peyser.

The blast took the regressive in the chest, blowing him backward against the bedroom wall in a tremendous spray of blood. Peyser went down, squealing, gasping for breath, wriggling on the floor like a half-stomped bug, but he was not dead. Maybe his heart and lungs had not sustained sufficient damage. If oxygen was still being conveyed to his blood and if blood was still being pumped through-out his body, he was already repairing the damage; his invulnerability was in some ways even greater than the supernatural imperviousness of a werewolf, for he could not be easily killed even with a *silver* bullet; in a moment he would be up, strong as ever.

Wave after wave of heat, each markedly hotter than the one before it washed through Loman. He felt pressure from within, not only in his chest but in every part of his body now. He had only seconds left in which his mind would be clear enough for him to act and his will strong enough to resist. He scuttled to Peyser, shoved the muzzle of the shotgun against the writhing regressive's chest, and pumped another round into him.

The heart *had* to have been pulverized by that round. The body leaped off the floor as the load tore through it. Peyser's monstrous face contorted, then froze with his eyes open and sightless, his lips peeled back from his inhumanly large, sharp, hooked teeth.

Someone screamed behind Loman.

Turning, he saw the Sholnick-thing coming for him. He fired a third round, then a fourth, hitting Sholnick in the chest and stomach.

The deputy went down hard, and began to crawl toward the hall, away from Loman.

Neil Penniworth was curled in the fetal position on the floor by the foot of the bed. He was chanting but not about blood and needs and being free; he was chanting his mother's name, over and over, as if it were a verbal talisman to protect him from the evil that wanted to claim him.

Loman's heart was pounding so hard that the sound of it seemed to have an external source, as if someone were thumping timpani in another room of the house. He was half-convinced that he could feel his entire body throbbing with his pulse, and that with each throb he was changing in some subtle yet hideous way.

Stepping in behind Sholnick, standing over him, Loman rammed the muzzle of the shotgun against the regressive's back, about where he thought the heart would be, and pulled the trigger. Sholnick let out a shrill scream when he felt the muzzle touch him, but he was too weak to roll over and grab the gun away from Loman. The scream was cut off forever by the blast.

The room steamed with blood. That complex scent was so sweet and compelling that it took the place of Peyser's seductive chanting, inducing Loman to regress.

He leaned against the dresser and squeezed his eyes shut, trying to establish a firmer grip on himself. He clung to the shotgun with both hands, clasping it tightly, not for its defensive value—it held no more rounds—but because it was an expertly crafted weapon, which was to say that it was a *tool,* an artifact of civilization, a reminder that he was a man, at the pinnacle of evolution, and that he must not succumb to the temptation to cast away all his tools and knowledge in exchange for the more primal pleasures and satisfactions of a beast.

But the blood smell was strong and so alluring. . . .

Desperately trying to impress himself with all that would be lost in this surrender, he thought of Grace, his wife, and remembered how much he once had loved her. But he was beyond love now, as were all of the New People. Thoughts of Grace could not save him. Indeed, images of their recent, bestial rutting flashed through his mind, and she was not Grace to him any more; she was simply *female,* and the recollection of their savage coupling excited him and drew him closer to the vortex of regression.

The intense desire to degenerate made him feel as though he were in a whirlpool, being sucked down, down, and he thought that this was how the nascent werewolf was supposed to feel when he looked up into the night sky and saw, ascending at the horizon, a full moon. The conflict raged within him:

. . . blood . . .
. . . freedom . . .
—no. *Mind, knowledge*—
. . . hunt . . .
. . . kill . . .
—no. *Explore, learn*—
. . . eat . . .
. . . run . . .
. . . hunt . . .
. . . fuck . . .
. . . kill . . .
—*no, no! Music, art, language*—

His turmoil grew.

He was trying to resist the siren call of savagery with reason, but that did not seem to be working, so he thought of Denny, his son. He must hold fast to his humanity if only for Denny's sake. He tried to summon the love he had once known for his boy, tried to let that love rebuild in him until he could shout of it, but there was only a whisper of remembered emotion deep in the darkness of his mind. His ability to love had receded from him in much the way that matter had receded from the center of existence following the Big Bang that created the universe; his love for Denny was now so far away and long ago that it was like a star at the outer edge of the universe, its light only dimly perceived, with little power to illuminate and no power to warm. Yet even that glimmer of feeling was something around which to build an image of himself as human, human, first and always a man, not some thing that ran on all fours or with its knuckles dragging on the ground, but a man, a man.

His stentorian breathing slowed a little. His heartbeat fell from an impossibly rapid *dubdubdubdubdubdubdub* to perhaps a hundred or a hundred and twenty beats a minute, still fast, as if he were running, but better. His head cleared, too, though not entirely, because the scent of blood was an inescapable perfume.

He pushed away from the dresser and staggered to Penniworth.

The deputy was still curled in the tightest fetal position that a grown man could achieve. Traces of the beast were in his hands and face, but he was considerably more human than not. The chanting of his mother's name seemed to be working nearly as well as the thread-thin lifeline of love had worked for Loman.

Letting go of his shotgun with one cramped hand, Loman reached down to Penniworth and took him by the arm. "Come on, let's get out of here, boy, let's get away from this smell."

Penniworth understood and got laboriously to his feet. He leaned against Loman and allowed himself to be led out of the room, away from the two dead regressives, along the hallway into the living room.

Here, the stink of urine completely smothered what trace of the blood scent might have ridden the currents of air outward from the bedroom. That was better. It was not a foul odor at all, as it had seemed previously, but acidic and cleansing.

Loman settled Penniworth in an armchair, the only upholstered item in the room that had not been torn to pieces.

"You going to be okay?"

Penniworth looked up at him, hesitated, then nodded. All signs of the beast had vanished from his hands and countenance, though his flesh was strangely lumpy, still in transition. His face appeared to be swollen with a disabling case of the hives, large round lumps from forehead to chin and ear to ear, and there were long, diagonal welts, too, that burned an angry red against his pale skin. However, even as Loman watched, those phenomena faded, and Neil Penniworth laid full claim to his humanity. To his *physical* humanity, at least.

"You sure?" Loman asked.

"Yes."

"Stay right there."

"Yes."

Loman went into the foyer and opened the front door. The deputy standing guard outside was so tense because of all the shooting and screaming in the house that he almost fired on his chief before he realized who it was.

"What the hell?" the deputy said.

"Get on the computer link to Shaddack," Loman said. "He has to come out here now. Right now. I have to see him *now*."

55

SAM DREW THE HEAVY BLUE DRAPES, AND HARRY TURNED ON one bedside lamp. Soft as it was, too dim to chase away more than half the shadows, the light nevertheless stung Tessa's eyes, which were already tired and bloodshot.

For the first time she actually saw the room. It was sparely furnished: the stool; the tall table beside the stool; the telescope; a long, modern-oriental, black lacquered dresser; a pair of matching nightstands; a small refrigerator in one corner; and an adjustable hospital-type bed, queen-size, without a spread but with plenty of pillows and brightly colored sheets patterned with splashes and streaks and spots of red, orange, purple, green, yellow, blue, and black, like a giant canvas painted by a demented and color-blind abstract artist.

Harry saw her and Sam's reaction to the sheets and said, "Now, *that's* a story, but first you've got to know the background. My housekeeper, Mrs. Hunsbok, comes in once a week, and she does most of my shopping for me. But I send Moose on errands every day, if only to pick up a newspaper. He wears this set of . . . well, sort of saddlebags strapped around him, one hanging on each side. I put a note and some money in the bags, and he goes to the local convenience store— it's the only place he'll go when he's wearing the bags, unless I'm with him. The clerk at the little grocery, Jimmy Ramis, knows me real well. Jimmy reads the note, puts a quart of milk or some candy bars or whatever I want in the saddlebags, puts the change in there, too, and Moose brings it all back to me. He's a good, reliable service dog, the best. They train them real well at Canine Companions for Independence. Moose never chases after a cat with my newspaper and fresh milk in his backpack."

The dog raised his head off Tessa's lap, panted and grinned, as if acknowledging the praise.

"One day he came home with a few items I'd sent him for, and he also had a set of these sheets and pillow cases. I call up Jimmy Ramis, see, and ask him what's the idea, and Jimmy says he doesn't know what I'm talking about, says he never saw any such sheets. Now, Jimmy's dad owns the convenience store, and he also owns Surplus Outlet, out on the county road. He gets all kinds of discontinued merchandise and stuff that didn't sell as well as the manufacturers expected, picks it up at ten cents on the dollar sometimes, and I figure these sheets were something he was having trouble unloading even at Surplus Outlet. Jimmy no doubt saw them, thought they were pretty silly, and decided to have some fun with me. But on the phone Jimmy says, 'Harry, if I knew anything about the sheets, I'd tell you, but I don't.' And I says, 'You trying to make me believe Moose went and bought them all on his own, with his own money?' And Jimmy says, 'Well, no, I'd guess he shoplifted them somewhere,' and I says, 'And just how did he manage to stuff them in his own backpack so neat,' and Jimmy says, 'I don't know, Harry, but that there is one hell of a clever dog—though it sounds like he doesn't have good taste.'"

Tessa saw how Harry relished the story, and she also saw why he was so pleased by it. For one thing the dog was child and brother and friend, all rolled into one, and Harry was proud that people thought of Moose as clever. More important, Jimmy's little joke made Harry a part of his community, not just a homebound invalid but a participant in the life of his town. His lonely days were marked by too few such incidents.

"And you *are* a clever dog," Tessa told Moose.

Harry said, "Anyway, I decided to have Mrs. Hunsbok put them on the bed next time she came, as a joke, but then I sort of liked them."

After drawing the drapes at the second window, Sam returned to the stool, sat down, swiveled to face Harry, and said, "They're the loudest sheets I've ever seen. Don't they keep you awake at night?"

Harry smiled. "Nothing can keep me awake. I sleep like a baby. What keeps people awake is worry about the future, about what might happen to them. But the worst has *already* happened to me. Or they lie awake thinking about the past, about what might have been, but I don't do that because I just don't dare." His smile faded as he spoke. "So now what? What do we do next?"

Gently removing Moose's head from her lap, standing, and brushing a few dog hairs from her jeans, Tessa said, "Well, the phones aren't working, so Sam can't call the Bureau, and if we walk out of town we risk an encounter with Watkins's patrols or these Boogeymen. Unless you know a ham radio enthusiast who'd let us use his set to get a message relayed, then so as far as I can see, we've got to drive out."

"Roadblocks, remember," Harry said.

She said, "Well, I figure we'll have to drive out in a truck, something big and mean, ram straight through the damn roadblock, make it to the highway, then out of their jurisdiction. Even if we do get chased down by county cops, that's fine, because Sam can get them to call the Bureau, verify his assignment, then they'll be on our side."

"Who's the federal agent here, anyway?" Sam asked.

Tessa felt herself blush. "Sorry. See, a documentary filmmaker is almost always her own producer, sometimes producer and director and writer too. That means if the art part of it is going to work, the business part of it has to work first, so I'm used to doing a lot of planning, logistics. Didn't mean to step on your toes."

"Step on them any time."

Sam smiled, and she liked him when he smiled. She realized she was even attracted to him a little. He was neither handsome nor ugly, and not what most people meant by "plain," either. He was rather . . . nondescript but pleasant-looking. She sensed a darkness in him, something deeper than his current worries about events in Moonlight Cove—maybe sadness at some loss, maybe long-repressed anger related to some injustice he had suffered, maybe a general pessimism arising from too much contact in his work with the worst elements of society. But when he smiled he was transformed.

"You really going to smash out in a truck?" Harry asked.

"Maybe as a last resort," Sam said. "But we'd have to find a rig big enough and then steal it, and that's an operation in itself. Besides, they might have riot guns at the roadblock, loaded with magnum rounds, maybe automatic weapons. I wouldn't want to run that kind of flak even in a Mack truck. You can ride into hell in a tank, but the devil will get his hands on you anyway, so it's best not to go there in the first place."

"So where *do* we go?" Tessa asked.

"To sleep," Sam said. "There's a way out of this, a way to get through to the Bureau. I can sort of see it out of the corner of my eye, but when I try to look directly at it, it goes away, and that's because I'm tired. I need a couple of hours in the sack to get fresh and think straight."

Tessa was exhausted, too, though after what had happened at Cove Lodge, she was somewhat surprised that she not only could sleep but wanted to. As she'd stood in her motel room, listening to the screams of the dying and the savage shrieks of the killers, she wouldn't have thought she'd ever sleep again.

56

SHADDACK ARRIVED AT PEYSER'S AT FIVE MINUTES TILL FOUR in the morning. He drove his charcoal-gray van with heavily tinted windows, rather than his Mercedes, because a computer terminal was mounted on the console of the van, between the seats, where the manufacturer had originally intended to provide a built-in cooler. As eventful as the night had been thus far, it seemed a good idea to stay within reach of the data link that, like a spider, spun a silken web enmeshing all of Moonlight Cove. He parked on the wide shoulder of the two-lane rural blacktop, directly in front of the house.

As Shaddack walked across the yard to the front porch, distant rumbling rolled along the Pacific horizon. The hard wind that had harried the fog eastward had also brought a storm in from the west. During the past couple of hours, churning clouds had clothed the heavens, shrouding the naked stars that had burned briefly between the passing of the mist and the coming of the thunderheads. Now the night was very dark and deep. He shivered inside his cashmere topcoat, under which he still wore a sweat suit.

A couple of deputies were sitting in black-and-whites in the driveway. They watched him, pale faces beyond dusty car windows, and he liked to think they regarded him with fear and reverence, for he was in a sense their maker.

Loman Watkins was waiting for him in the front room. The place had been wrecked. Neil Penniworth sat on the only undamaged piece of furniture; he looked badly shaken and could not meet Shaddack's gaze. Watkins was pacing. A few spatters of blood marked his uniform, but he looked unhurt; if he'd sustained injuries, they had been minor and had already healed. More likely, the blood belonged to someone else.

"What happened here?" Shaddack asked.

Ignoring the question, Watkins spoke to his officer: "Go out to the car, Neil. Stay close to the other men."

"Yes, sir," Penniworth said. He was huddled in his chair, bent forward, looking down at his shoes.

"You'll be okay, Neil."

"I think so."

"It wasn't a question. It was a statement: You'll be okay. You have enough strength to resist. You've proven that already."

Penniworth nodded, got up, and headed for the door.

Shaddack said, "What's this all about?"

Turning toward the hallway at the other end of the room, Watkins said, "Come with me." His voice was as cold and hard as ice, informed by fear and anger, but noticeably devoid of the grudging respect with which he had spoken to Shaddack ever since he had been converted in August.

Displeased by that change in Watkins, uneasy, Shaddack frowned and followed him back down the hall.

The cop stopped at a closed door, turned to Shaddack. "You told me that what you've done to us is improve our biological efficiency by injecting us with these . . . these biochips."

"A misnomer, really. They're not chips at all, but incredibly small micro-spheres."

In spite of the regressives and a few other problems that had developed with the Moonhawk Project, Shaddack's pride of achievement was undiminished. Glitches could be fixed. Bugs could be worked out of the system. He was still *the* genius of his age; he not only felt this to be true, but knew it as well as he knew in which direction to look for the rising sun each morning.

Genius . . .

The ordinary silicon microchip that made possible the computer revolution had been the size of a fingernail, and had contained one million circuits etched onto it by photo lithography. The smallest circuit on the chip had been one-hundredth as wide as a human hair. Breakthroughs in X-ray lithography, using giant particle accelerators called synchrotrons, eventually made possible the imprinting of one *billion* circuits on a chip, with features as small as one-thousandth the width of a human hair. Shrinking dimensions was the primary way to gain computer speed, improving both function and capabilities.

The microspheres developed by New Wave were one four-thousandth the size of a microchip. Each was imprinted with a quarter-million circuits. This had been achieved by the application of a radically new form of X-ray lithography that made it possible to etch circuits on amazingly small surfaces *and* without having to hold those surfaces perfectly still.

Conversion of Old People into New People began with the injection of hun-dreds of thousands of these microspheres, in solution, into the bloodstream. They were biologically interactive in function, but the material itself was biologically inert, so the immune system wasn't triggered. There were different kinds of mi-crospheres. Some were heart-tropic, meaning they moved through the veins to the heart and took up residence there, attaching themselves to the walls of the blood vessels that serviced the cardiac muscle. Some spheres were liver-tropic, lung-tropic, kidney-tropic, bowel-tropic, brain-tropic, and so on. They settled in clusters at those sites and were designed in such a way that, when touching, their circuits linked.

Those clusters, spread throughout the body, eventually provided about fifty billion usable circuits that had the potential for data processing, considerably more than in the largest supercomputers of the 1980s. In a sense, by injection, a super-supercomputer had been put inside the human body.

Moonlight Cove and the surrounding area were constantly bathed in microwave transmissions from dishes on top of the main building at New Wave. A fraction of those transmissions involved the police computer system, and another fraction could be drawn upon to power-up the microspheres inside each of the New People.

A small number of spheres were of a different material and served as transducers and power distributors. When one of the Old People received his third injection of microspheres, the power spheres at once drew on those microwave transmissions, converting them into electrical current and distributing it throughout the network. The amount of current needed to operate the system was exceedingly small.

Other specialized spheres in each cluster were memory units. Some of those carried the program that would operate the system; that program was loaded the moment power entered the network.

To Watkins, Shaddack said, "Long ago I became convinced that the basic problem with the human animal is its extremely emotional nature. I've freed you from that burden. In so doing, I've made you not only mentally healthier but physically healthier as well."

"How? I know so little of how the Change is effected."

"You're a cybernetic organism now—that is, part man and part machine—but you don't *need* to understand it, Loman. You use a telephone, yet you've no idea of how to build a phone system from scratch. You don't know how a computer works, yet you can use one. And you don't have to know how the computer *in* you works in order to use it, either."

Watkins's eyes were clouded with fear. "Do I use it . . . or does it use me?"

"Of course, it doesn't use you."

"Of course . . . "

Shaddack wondered what had happened here tonight to have put Watkins in such a state of extreme anxiety. He was more curious than ever to see what was in the bedroom at the threshold of which they had halted. But he was acutely aware that Watkins was in a dangerously excited state and that it was necessary, if frustrating, to take the time to calm his fears.

"Loman, the clustered microspheres within you don't constitute a *mind*. The system's not in any way truly intelligent. It's a servant, your servant. It frees you from toxic emotions."

Strong emotions—hatred, love, envy, jealousy, the whole long list of human sensibilities—regularly destabilized the biological functions of the body. Medical researchers had proved that different emotions stimulated the production of different brain chemicals, and that those chemicals in turn induced the various organs and tissues of the body to either increase or reduce or alter their function in a less than productive fashion. Shaddack was convinced that a man whose body was ruled by his emotions could not be a totally healthy man and *never* entirely clear-thinking.

The microsphere computer within each of the New People monitored every organ in the body. When it detected the production of various amino-acid compounds and other chemical substances that were produced in response to strong emotion, it used electrical stimuli to override the brain and other organs, shutting off the flow, thus eliminating the physical consequences of an emotion if not the emotion itself. At the same time the microsphere computer stimulated the copious production of other compounds known to repress those same emotions, thereby treating not only the cause but the effect.

"I've released you from all emotions but fear," Shaddack said, "which is necessary for self-preservation. Now that the chemistry of your body is no longer undergoing wild swings, you'll think more clearly."

"So far as I've noticed, I've not suddenly become a genius."

"Well, you might not notice a greater mental acuity yet, but in time you will."

"When?"

"When your body is fully purged of the residue of a lifetime of emotional pollution. Meanwhile, your interior computer"—he lightly tapped Watkins's chest—"is also programmed to use complex electrical stimuli to induce the body to create wholly new amino-acid compounds that keep your blood vessels scoured and free of plaque and clots, kill cancerous cells the moment they appear, and perform a double score of other chores, keeping you far healthier than ordinary men, no doubt dramatically lengthening your life-span."

Shaddack had expected the healing process to be accelerated in New People, but he had been surprised at the almost miraculous speed with which their wounds closed. He still could not entirely understand how new tissue could be formed so quickly, and his current work on Moonhawk was focused on discovering an explanation for that effect. The healing was not accomplished without a price, for the metabolism was fantastically accelerated; stored body fat was burned prodigiously in order to close a wound in seconds or minutes, leaving the healed man pounds lighter, sweat-drenched, and fiercely hungry.

Watkins frowned and wiped one shaky hand across his sweaty face. "I can maybe see that healing would be speeded up, but what gives us the ability to so completely reshape ourselves, to regress to another form? Surely not even buckets of these biological chemicals could tear down our bodies and rebuild them in just a minute or two. How can that be?"

For a moment Shaddack met the other man's gaze, then looked away, coughed, and said, "Listen, I can explain all of this to you later. Right now I want to see Peyser. I hope you were able to restrain him without doing much damage."

As Shaddack reached toward the door to push it open, Watkins seized his wrist, staying his hand. Shaddack was shocked. He did not allow himself to be touched.

"Take your hand off me."

"How can the body be so suddenly reshaped?"

"I told you, we'll discuss it later."

"Now." Watkins's determination was so strong that it carved deep lines in his face. "Now. I'm so scared I can't think straight. I can't function at this level of fear, Shaddack. Look at me. I'm shaking. I feel like I'm going to blow apart. A million pieces. You don't know what happened here tonight, or you'd feel the same way. I've got to know: How can our bodies change so suddenly?"

Shaddack hesitated. "I'm working on that."

Surprised, Watkins let go of his wrist and said, "You . . . you mean you don't know?"

"It's an unexpected effect. I'm beginning to understand it"—which was a lie—"but I've got a lot more work to do." First he had to understand the New People's phenomenal healing powers, which were no doubt an aspect of the same process that allowed them to completely metamorphose into subhuman forms.

"You subjected us to this without knowing what all it might do to us?"

"I knew it would be a benefit, a great gift," Shaddack said impatiently. "No scientist can ever predict all the side effects. He has to proceed with the confidence that whatever side effects arise will not outweigh the benefits."

"But they *do* outweigh the benefits," Watkins said, as close to anger as a New Man could get. "My God, how could you have done this to us?"

"I did this *for* you."

Watkins stared at him, then pushed open the bedroom door and said, "Have a look."

Shaddack stepped into the room, where the carpet was damp—and some of the walls festooned—with blood. He grimaced at the stink. He found all biological odors unusually repellent, perhaps because they were a reminder that human beings were far less efficient and clean than machines. After stopping at the first corpse—which lay facedown near the door—and studying it, he looked across the room at the second body. "Two of them? Two regressives, and you killed *both?* Two chances to study the psychology of these degenerates, and you threw away both opportunities?"

Watkins was unbowed by the criticism. "It was a life-or-death situation here. It couldn't have been handled differently."

He seemed angry to a degree inconsistent with the personality of a New Man, though perhaps the emotion sustaining his icy demeanor was less rage than fear. Fear was acceptable.

"Peyser was regressed when we got here," Watkins continued. "We searched the house, confronted him in this room."

As Watkins described that confrontation in detail, Shaddack was gripped by an apprehension that he tried not to reveal and to which he did not even want to admit. When he spoke he let only anger touch his voice, not fear: "You're telling me that your men, both Sholnick and Penniworth, are regressives, that even *you* are a regressive?"

"Sholnick was a regressive, yes. In my book Penniworth isn't—not yet any-way—because he successfully resisted the urge. Just as I resisted it." Watkins boldly maintained eye contact, not once glancing away, which further disturbed Shaddack. "What I'm telling you is the same thing I told you in so many words a few hours ago at your place: Each of us, every damned one of us, is potentially a regressive. It's not a rare sickness among the New People. It's in all of us. You've not created new and better men any more than Hitler's policies of genetic breeding could've created a master race. You're not God; you're Dr. Moreau."

"You will not speak to me like this," Shaddack said, wondering who this Moreau was. The name was vaguely familiar, but he could not place it. "When you talk to me, I'd suggest you remember who I am."

Watkins lowered his voice, perhaps realizing anew that Shaddack could extinguish the New People almost as easily as snuffing out a candle. But he continued to speak forcefully and with too little respect. "You still haven't responded to the worst of this news."

"And what's that?"

"Didn't you hear me? I said that Peyser was *stuck*. He couldn't remake himself."

"I doubt very much that he was trapped in an altered state. New Men have complete control of their bodies, more control than I ever anticipated. If he could not return to human form, that was strictly a psychological block. He didn't really want to return."

For a moment Watkins stared at him, then shook his head and said, "You aren't really that dense, are you? *It's the same thing.* Hell, it doesn't matter whether something went wrong with the microsphere network inside him or whether it was strictly psychological. Either way, the effect was the same, the result was the same: He was stuck, trapped, locked into that degenerate form."

"You will not speak to me like this," Shaddack repeated firmly, as if repetition of the command would work the same way it did when training a dog.

For all their physiological superiority and potential for mental superiority, New People were still dismayingly *people*, and to the degree they were people, they were that much less effective machines. With a computer, you only had to program a command once. The computer retained it and acted upon it always. Shaddack wondered if he would ever be able to perfect the New People to the point at which future generations functioned as smoothly and reliably as the average IBM PC.

Damp with sweat, pale, his eyes strange and haunted, Watkins was an intimidating figure. When the cop took two steps to reduce the gap between them, Shaddack was afraid and wanted to retreat, but he held his ground and continued to meet Watkins's eyes the way he would have defiantly met those of a dangerous German shepherd if he had been cornered by one.

"Look at Sholnick," Watkins said, indicating the corpse at their feet. He used the toe of his shoe to turn the dead man over.

Even riddled with shotgun pellets and soaked in blood, Sholnick's bizarre mutation was unmistakable. His sightlessly staring eyes were perhaps the most frightful thing about him: yellow with black irises, not the round irises of the human eye but elongated ovals as in the eyes of a snake.

Outside, thunder rolled across the night, a louder peal than the one Shaddack had heard when he'd been crossing Peyser's front lawn.

Watkins said, "The way you explained it to me—these degenerates undergo willful devolution."

"That's right."

"You said the whole history of human evolution is carried in our genes, that we still have in us traces of what the species once was, and that the regressives somehow tap that genetic material and devolve into creatures somewhere farther back on the evolutionary ladder."

"What's your point?"

"That explanation made some sort of crazy sense when we trapped Coombs in the theater and got a good look at him back in September. He was more ape than man, something in between."

"It doesn't make crazy sense; it makes perfect sense."

"But, Jesus, look at Sholnick. *Look* at him! When I gunned him down, he'd halfway transformed himself into some goddamned creature that's part man, part . . . hell, I don't know, part lizard or snake. You telling me that we evolved from reptiles, we're carrying lizard genes from ten million years ago?"

Shaddack thrust both hands in his coat pockets, lest they betray his apprehension with a nervous gesture or tremble. "The first life on earth was in the sea, then something crawled onto the land—a fish with rudimentary legs—and the fish evolved into the early reptiles, and along the way mammals split off. If we don't contain actual fragments of the genetic material of those very early reptiles—and I believe we do—then at least we have racial memory of that stage of evolution encoded in us in some other way we don't really understand."

"You're jiving me, Shaddack."

"And you're *irritating* me."

"I don't give a damn. Come here, come with me, take a closer look at Peyser. He was a friend of yours from way back, wasn't he? Take a good, long look at what he was when he died."

Peyser was flat on his back, naked, right leg straight in front of him, left leg bent under him at an angle, one arm flung out at his side, the other across his chest, which had been shattered by a couple of shotgun blasts. The body and the face—with its inhuman muzzle and teeth, yet vaguely recognizable as Mike Peyser—were those of a shockingly horrific freak, a dog-man, a werewolf, something that belonged in either a carnival sideshow or an old horror movie. The skin was coarse. The patchy coat of hair was wiry. The hands looked powerful, the claws sharp.

Because his fascination exceeded his disgust and fear, Shaddack pulled up his topcoat to keep the hem of it from brushing the bloody corpse, and stooped beside Peyser's body for a closer look.

Watkins hunkered down on the other side of the cadaver.

While another avalanche of thunder rumbled down the night sky, the dead man stared at the bedroom ceiling with eyes that were too human for the rest of his twisted countenance.

"You going to tell me that somewhere along the way we evolved from dogs, wolves?" Watkins asked.

Shaddack did not reply.

Watkins pressed the issue. "You going to tell me that we've got dog genes in us that we can tap when we want to transform ourselves? Am I supposed to believe God took a rib from some prehistoric Lassie and made man from it before he took man's rib to make a woman?"

Curiously Shaddack touched one of Mike Peyser's hands, which was designed for killing as surely as was a soldier's bayonet. It felt like flesh, just cooler than that of a living man.

"This can't be explained biologically," Watkins said, glaring at Shaddack across the corpse. "This wolf form isn't something Peyser could dredge up from racial memory stored in his genes. So how could he change like this? It's not just your biochips at work here. It's something else . . . something stranger."

Shaddack nodded. "Yes." An explanation had occurred to him, and he was excited by it. "Something a great deal stranger . . . but perhaps I understand it."

"So tell me. *I'd* like to understand it. Damned if I wouldn't. I'd like to understand it real well. Before it happens to me."

"There's a theory that form is a function of consciousness."

"Huh?"

"It holds that we are what we think we are. I'm not talking pop psychology here, that you can be what you want to be if you'll only like yourself, nothing of that sort. I mean *physically*, we may have the potential to be whatever we think we are, to override the morphic stasis dictated by our genetic heritage."

"Gobbledegook," Watkins said impatiently.

Shaddack stood. He put his hands in his pockets again. "Let me put it this way: The theory says that consciousness is the greatest power in the universe, that it can bend the physical world to its desire."

"Mind over matter."

"Right."

"Like some talk-show psychic bending a spoon or stopping a watch," Watkins said.

"Those people are usually fakes, I suspect. But, yes, maybe that power is really in us. We just don't know how to tap it because for millions of years we've allowed the physical world to dominate us. By habit, by stasis, and by preference for order over chaos, we remain at the mercy of the physical world. But what we're talking about here," he said, pointing to Sholnick and Peyser, "is a lot more complex and exciting than bending a spoon with the mind. Peyser felt the urge to regress, for reasons I don't understand, perhaps for the sheer thrill of it—"

"For the thrill." Watkins's voice lowered, became quiet, almost hushed, and was filled with such intense fear and mental anguish that it deepened Shaddack's chill. "Animal power is thrilling. Animal need. You feel animal hunger, animal lust, bloodthirst—and you're drawn toward that because it seems so . . . so simple and powerful, so natural. It's freedom."

"Freedom?"

"Freedom from responsibility, from worry, from the pressure of the civilized world, from having to *think* too much. The temptation to regress is tremendously powerful because you feel life will be so much easier and exciting then," Watkins said, evidently speaking about what he had felt when drawn toward an altered state. "When you become a beast, life is all sensation, just pain and pleasure, with no need to intellectualize anything. That's part of it, anyway."

Shaddack was silent, unsettled by the passion with which Watkins—not ordinarily an expressive man—had spoken of the urge to regress.

Another detonation rocked the sky, more powerful than any before it. The first hard crack of thunder reverberated in the bedroom windows.

Mind racing, Shaddack said, "Anyway, the important thing is that when Peyser felt this urge to become a beast, a hunter, he didn't regress along the human genetic line. Evidently, in his opinion, a wolf is the greatest of all hunters, the most desirable form for a predatory beast, so he *willed* himself to become wolflike."

"Just like that," Watkins said skeptically.

"Yes, just like that. Mind over matter. The metamorphosis is mostly a *mental* process. Oh, certainly, there are physical changes. But we might not be talking complete alteration of matter . . . only of biological structures. The basic nucleotides remain the same, but the sequence in which they're read changes drastically. Structural genes are transformed into operator genes by a force of will. . . ."

Shaddack's voice trailed off as his excitement rose to match his fear and left him breathless. He'd done far more than he'd hoped to do with the Moonhawk Project. The stunning accomplishment was the source of both his sudden joy and escalating fear: joy, because he had given men the ability to control their physical form and, eventually, perhaps all matter, simply by the exercise of will; fear, because he was not sure that the New People could learn to control and properly use their power . . . or that he could continue to control them.

"The gift I've given to you—computer-assisted physiology and release from emotion—unleashes the mind's power over matter. It allows consciousness to dictate form."

Watkins shook his head, clearly appalled by what Shaddack was suggesting. "Maybe Peyser willed himself to become what he did. Maybe Sholnick willed it too. But I'll be damned if I did. When I was overcome by the desire to change, I fought it like an ex-addict sweating out a craving for heroin. I didn't want it. It came over me . . . the way the force of the full moon comes over a werewolf."

"No," Shaddack said. "Subconsciously, you *did* want to change, Loman, and you no doubt partially wanted it even on a conscious level. You *must* have wanted it to some extent because you spoke so forcefully about how attractive regression was. You resisted using your power of mind over body only because you found metamorphosis marginally more frightening than appealing. If you lose some of your fear of it . . . or if an altered state becomes just a little more appealing . . . well, then your psychological balance will shift, and you'll remake yourself. But it won't be some outside force at work. It'll be your own mind."

"Then why couldn't Peyser come back?"

"As I said, and as *you* suggested, he didn't want to."

"He was trapped."

"Only by his own desire."

Watkins looked down at the grotesque corpse of the regressive. "What have you done to us, Shaddack?"

"Haven't you grasped what I've said?"

"What have you done to us?"

"This is a great gift!"

"To have no emotions but fear?"

"That's what frees your mind and gives you the power to control your very form," Shaddack said excitedly. "What I don't understand is why the regressives have all chosen a subhuman condition. Surely you have the power within you to undergo evolution rather than devolution, to lift yourself up from mere humanity to something higher, cleaner, purer. Perhaps you even have the power to become a being of pure consciousness, intellect without *any* physical form. Why have all these New People chosen to regress instead?"

Watkins raised his head, and his eyes had a half-dead look, as if they had absorbed death from the very sight of the corpse. "What good is it to have the power of a god if you can't also experience the simple pleasures of a man?"

"But you can do and experience anything you want," Shaddack said exasperatedly.

"Not love."

"What?"

"Not love or hate or joy or any emotion but fear."

"But you don't *need* them. Not having them has freed you."

"You're not thickheaded," Watkins said, "so I guess you don't understand because you're psychologically . . . twisted, warped."

"You must not speak to me like—"

"I'm trying to tell you why they all choose a subhuman form over a superhuman form. It's because, for a thinking creature of high intellect, there can be no pleasure separate from emotion. If you deny men emotions, you deny them pleasure, so they seek an altered state in which complex emotions and pleasure *aren't* linked— the life of an unthinking beast."

"Nonsense. You are—"

Watkins interrupted him again, sharply. "Listen to me, for God's sake! If I remember, even Moreau listened to his creatures."

His face was flushed now instead of pale. His eyes no longer looked half dead; a certain wildness had returned to them. He was only a step or two from Shaddack and seemed to loom over him, though he was the shorter of the two. He looked scared, badly scared—and dangerous.

He said, "Consider sex—a basic human pleasure. For sex to be *fully* satisfying, it has to be accompanied by love or at least some affection. To a psychologically damaged man, sex can still be good if it's linked to hate or pride of domination; even negative emotions can make the act pleasurable for a twisted man. But done with *no emotion at all*, it's pointless, stupid, just the breeding impulse of an animal, just the rhythmic function of a machine."

A flash of lightning burned the night and blazed briefly on the bedroom windows, followed by a crash of thunder that seemed to shake the house. That celestial flicker was, for an instant, brighter than the soft glow of the single bedroom lamp.

In that queer light Shaddack thought he saw something happen to Loman Watkins's face . . . a *shift* in the relationship of the features. But when the lightning passed, Watkins looked quite like himself, so it must have been Shaddack's imagination.

Continuing to speak with great force, with the passion of stark fear, Watkins said, "It's not just sex, either. The same goes for other physical pleasures. Eating, for example. Yeah, I still taste a piece of chocolate when I eat it. But the taste gives me only a tiny fraction of the satisfaction that it did before I was converted. Haven't you noticed?"

Shaddack did not reply, and he hoped that nothing in his demeanor would reveal that he had not undergone conversion himself. He was, of course, waiting until the process had been more highly refined through additional generations of the New People. But he suspected Watkins would not react well to the discovery that their maker had not chosen to submit himself to the blessing that he had bestowed on them.

Watkins said, "And do you know why there's less satisfaction? Before conversion, when we ate chocolate, the taste had thousands of associations for us. When we ate it, we subconsciously remembered the first time we ate it and all the times in between, and subconsciously we remembered how often that taste was associated with holidays and celebrations of all kinds, and because of all that the taste made us *feel good*. But now when I eat chocolate, it's just a taste, a good taste, but it doesn't make me feel good any more. I know it should; I remember that such a thing as 'feeling good' was part of it once, but not now. The taste of chocolate doesn't generate emotional echoes any more. It's an empty sensation, its richness has been stolen from me. The richness of everything but fear has been stolen from me, and everything is gray now—strange, gray, drab—as if I'm half dead."

The left side of Watkins's head bulged. His cheekbone enlarged. That ear began to change shape and draw toward a point.

Stunned, Shaddack backed away from him.

Watkins followed, raising his voice, speaking with a slight slur but with no less force, not with real anger but with fear and an unsettling touch of savagery: "Why the hell would any of us want to evolve to some higher form with even fewer pleasures of the body and the heart? Intellectual pleasures aren't enough, Shaddack. Life is more than that. A life that's *only* intellectual isn't tolerable."

As Watkins's brow gradually sloped backward, slowly melting away like a wall of snow in the sun, heavier accretions of bone began to build up around his eyes.

Shaddack backed into the dresser.

Still approaching, Watkins said, "Jesus! Don't you see yet? Even a man confined to a hospital bed, paralyzed from the neck down, has more in his life than intellectual interests; no one's stolen his emotions from him; no one's reduced him to fear and pure intellect. We need pleasure, Shaddack, pleasure, pleasure. Life without it is terrifying. Pleasure makes life worth living."

"Stop."

"You've made it impossible for us to experience the pleasurable release of emotion, so we can't fully experience pleasures of the flesh, either, because we're creatures of a high order and need the emotional aspect to truly enjoy physical pleasure. It's both or neither in human beings."

Watkins's hands, fisted at his sides, were becoming larger, with swollen knuckles and tobacco-brown, pointed nails.

"You're transforming," Shaddack said.

Ignoring him, speaking more thickly as the shape of his mouth began to change subtly, Watkins said, "So we revert to a savage, altered state. We retreat from our intellect. In the cloak of the beast, our *only* pleasure is the pleasure of the flesh, the flesh, flesh . . . but at least we're no longer aware of what we've lost, so the pleasure remains intense, so intense, deep and sweet, sweet, so sweet. You've made . . . made our lives intolerable, gray and dead, dead, all dead, dead . . . so we have to devolve in mind and in body . . . to find a worthwhile existence. We . . . we have to flee . . . from the horrible restrictions of this narrowed life . . . this very narrowed life you've given us. Men aren't machines. Men . . . men . . . men are not *machines*!"

"You're regressing. For God's sake, Loman!"

Watkins halted and seemed disoriented. Then he shook his head, as if to cast off his confusion as he might a veil. He raised his hands, looked at them, and cried out in terror. He glanced past Shaddack, at the dresser mirror, and his cry grew louder, shriller.

Abruptly Shaddack was acutely aware of the stench of blood, to which he had somewhat accustomed himself. Watkins must be even more affected by it, though not repulsed, no, not in the least repulsed, but excited.

Lightning flashed and thunder shook the night again, and rain suddenly came down in torrents, beating on the windows and drumming on the roof.

Watkins looked from the mirror to Shaddack, raised a hand as if to strike him, then turned and staggered out of the room, into the hall, away from the ripe stink of blood. Out there he dropped to his knees, then onto his side. He curled into a ball, shaking violently, gagging, whimpering, snarling, and intermittently chanting, "No, no, no, no."

57

WHEN HE PULLED BACK FROM THE BRINK AND FELT IN control of himself once more, Loman sat up and leaned against the wall. He was wet with perspiration again, and shaky with hunger. The partial transformation and the energy expended to keep it from going all the way had left him drained. He was relieved but also felt unfulfilled, as if some great prize had been within his reach but then had been snatched away just as he had touched it.

A hollow, somewhat susurrant sound surrounded him. At first he thought it was an internal noise, all in his head, perhaps the soft boom and sizzle of brain cells flaring and dying from the strain of thwarting the regressive urge. Then he realized it was rain hammering on the roof of the bungalow.

When he opened his eyes, his vision was blurred. It cleared, and he was staring at Shaddack, who stood on the other side of the hall, just beyond the open bedroom door. Gaunt, long-faced, pale enough to pass for an albino, with those yellowish eyes, in his dark topcoat, the man looked like a visitation, perhaps Death himself.

If this *had* been Death, Loman might well have stood up and warmly embraced him.

Instead, while he waited for the strength to get up, he said, "No more conversions. You've got to stop the conversions."

Shaddack said nothing.

"You're not going to stop, are you?"

Shaddack merely stared at him.

"You're mad," Loman said. "You're stark, raving mad, yet I've no choice but to do what you want . . . or kill myself."

"Never talk to me like that again. Never. Remember who I am."

"I remember who you are," Loman said. He struggled to his feet at last, dizzy, weak. "You did this to me without my consent. And if the time comes when I can no longer resist the urge to regress, when I sink down into savagery, when I'm no longer scared shitless of you, I'll somehow hold on to enough of my mind to remember *where* you are, too, and I'll come for you."

"You threaten me?" Shaddack said, clearly amazed.

"No," Loman said. "Threat isn't the right word."

"It better not be. Because if anything happens to me, Sun is programmed to broadcast a command that'll be received by the clusters of microspheres inside you and—"

"—will instantly kill us all," Loman finished. "Yeah, I know. You've told me. If you go, we all go with you, just like people down there at Jonestown years ago, drinking their poisoned Kool-Aid and biting the big one right along with Reverend

Jim. You're our Reverend Jim Jones, a Jim Jones for the high-tech age, Jim Jones with a silicon heart and tightly packed semiconductors between the ears. No, I'm not threatening you, Reverend Jim, because 'threat' is too dramatic a word for it. A man making a threat has to be feeling something powerful, has to be hot with anger. I'm a New Person. I'm only afraid. That's all I can be. Afraid. So it's not a threat. No such a thing. It's a *promise*."

Shaddack stepped through the bedroom doorway, into the hall. A draught of cold air seemed to come with him. Maybe it was Loman's imagination, but the hall seemed chillier with Shaddack in it.

They stared at each other for a long moment.

At last Shaddack said, "You'll continue to do what I say."

"I don't have a choice," Loman noted. "That's the way you made me—without a choice. I'm right there in the palm of your hand, Lord, but it isn't love that keeps me there—it's fear."

"Better," Shaddack said.

He turned his back on Loman and walked down the hall, into the living room, out of the house, and into the night, the rain.

DAYBREAK IN HADES

I could not stop something I knew was wrong and terrible. I had an
awful sense of powerlessness.

—ANDREI SAKHAROV

Power dements even more than it corrupts, lowering the guard of
foresight and raising the haste of action.

—WILL AND ARIEL DURANT

1

BEFORE DAWN, HAVING SLEPT LESS THAN AN HOUR, TESSA LOCK-
land was awakened by a coldness in her right hand and then the quick, hot licking
of a tongue. Her arm was draped over the edge of the mattress, hand trailing just
above the carpet, and something down there was taking a taste of her.

She sat straight up in bed, unable to breathe.

She had been dreaming of the carnage at Cove Lodge, of half-seen beasts,
shambling and swift, with menacing teeth and claws like curved and well-honed
blades. Now she thought that the nightmare had become real, that Harry's house
had been invaded by those creatures, and that the questing tongue was but the
prelude to a sudden, savage bite.

But it was only Moose. She could see him vaguely in the dim glow that came
through the doorway from the night-light in the second-floor hall, and at last she
was able to draw breath. He put his forepaws on the mattress, too well trained to
climb all the way onto the bed. Whining softly, he seemed only to want affection.

She was sure that she had closed the door before retiring. But she had seen
enough examples of Moose's cleverness to suppose that he was able to open a
door if he was determined. In fact she suddenly realized that the interior doors of
the Talbot house were fitted with hardware that made the task easier for Moose:
not knobs but lever-action handles that would release the latch when depressed
either by a hand or a paw.

"Lonely?" she asked, gently rubbing the Labrador behind the ears.

The dog whined again and submitted to her petting.

Fat drops of rain rattled against the window. It was falling with such force that
she could hear it slashing through the trees outside. Wind pressed insistently
against the house.

"Well, as lonely as you are, fella, I'm a thousand times that sleepy, so you're
going to have to scoot."

When she stopped petting him, he understood. Reluctantly he dropped to the floor, padded to the door, looked back at her for a moment, then went into the hall, glanced both ways, and turned left.

The light from the hall was minimal, but it bothered her. She got up and closed the door, and by the time she returned to bed in the dark, she knew she would not be able to go back to sleep right away.

For one thing, she was wearing all her clothes—jeans and T-shirt and sweater—having taken off only her shoes, and she was not entirely comfortable. But she hadn't the nerve to undress, for that would make her feel so vulnerable that she wouldn't sleep at all. After what had happened at Cove Lodge, Tessa wanted to be prepared to move fast.

Furthermore, she was in the only spare bedroom—there was another, but unfurnished—and the mattress and quilted spread had a musty odor from years of disuse. It had once been Harry's father's room, as the house had once been Harry's father's house, but the elder Talbot had died seventeen years ago, three years after Harry had been brought home from the war. Tessa had insisted she could do without sheets and just sleep on top of the spread or, if cold, slip under the spread and sleep on the bare mattress. After shooing Moose out and closing the door, she felt chilled, and when she got under the spread, the musty odor seemed to carry a new scent of mildew, faint but unpleasant.

Above the background patter and hiss of the rain, she heard the hum of the elevator ascending. Moose probably had called it. Was he usually so peripatetic at night?

Though she was grindingly weary, she was now too awake to shut her mind off easily. Her thoughts were deeply troubling.

Not the massacre at Cove Lodge. Not the grisly stories of dead bodies being shoveled like so much refuse into crematoriums. Not the Parkins woman being torn to pieces by some species unknown. Not the monstrous night stalkers. All of those macabre images no doubt helped determine the channel into which her thoughts flowed, but for the most part they were only a somber background for more personal ruminations about her life and its direction.

Having recently brushed against death, she was more aware than usual of her mortality. Life was finite. In the business and the busyness of daily life, that truth was often forgotten.

Now she was unable to escape thinking about it, and she wondered if she was playing too loose with life, wasting too many years. Her work was satisfying. She was a happy woman; it was damned hard for a Lockland to be unhappy, predisposed as they were to good humor. But in all honesty she had to admit she was not getting what she truly wanted. If she remained on her current course, she'd never get it.

What she wanted was a family, a place to belong. That came, of course, from her childhood and adolescence in San Diego, where she had idolized her big sister, Janice, and had basked in the love of her mother and father. The tremendous amount of happiness and security she'd known in her youth was what allowed her to deal with the misery, despair, and terror that she sometimes encountered when working on one of her more ambitious documentaries. The first two decades of her life had been so full of joy, they balanced anything that followed.

The elevator had arrived on the second floor, and now, with a soft thump and a renewed hum, it descended. She was intrigued that Moose, so accustomed to using the elevator for and with his master, used it himself at night, though the stairs would have been quicker. Dogs, too, could be creatures of habit.

They'd had dogs at home when she was a kid, first a great golden retriever named Barney, then an Irish Setter named Mickey Finn. . . .

Janice had married and moved away from home sixteen years ago, when Tessa was eighteen, and thereafter entropy, the blind force of dissolution, had pulled apart that cozy life in San Diego. Tessa's dad died three years later, and soon after his funeral Tessa hit the road to make her industrials and documentaries and travel films, and although she had remained in touch with her mother and sister on a regular basis, that golden time had passed.

Janice was gone now. And Marion wouldn't live forever, not even if she actually gave up skydiving.

More than anything, Tessa wanted to re-create that home life with a husband of her own and children. She had been married, at twenty-three, to a man who wanted kids more than he wanted her, and when they had learned that she could never have children, he had left. Adoption wasn't enough for him. He wanted children that were biologically his. Fourteen months from wedding day to divorce. She had been badly hurt.

Thereafter she had thrown herself into her work with a passion she'd not shown previously. She was insightful enough to know that through her art she was trying to reach out to all the world as if it were one big extended family. By boiling down complex stories and issues to thirty, sixty, or ninety minutes of film, she was trying to pull the world in, reduce it to essences, to the size of one family.

But, lying awake in Harry Talbot's spare bedroom, Tessa knew she was never going to be fully satisfied if she didn't radically shake up her life and more directly seek the thing she so much wanted. It was impossible to be a person of depth if you lacked a love for humankind, but that generalized love could swiftly become airy and meaningless if you didn't have a particular family close to you; for in your family you saw, day to day, those specific things in specific people that justified, by extension, a broader love of fellow men and women. She was a stickler for specificity in her art, but she lacked it in her emotional life.

Breathing dust and the faint odor of mildew, she felt as if her potential as a person had long been lying as unused as that bedroom. But not having dated for years, having sought refuge from heartbreak in hard work, how did a woman of thirty-four begin to open herself to that part of life she had so purposefully sealed off? Just then she felt more barren than at any time since first learning that she would never have children of her own. And at the moment, finding a way to remake her life seemed a more important issue than learning where the Boog-eymen came from and what they were.

A brush with death could stir up peculiar thoughts.

In a while her weariness overcame her inner turmoil, and she drifted into sleep again. Just as she dropped off, she realized that Moose might have come to her room because he sensed something wrong in the house. Perhaps he had been trying to alert her. But surely he would have been more agitated and would have barked if there was danger.

Then she slept.

2

FROM PEYSER'S, SHADDACK RETURNED TO HIS ULTRAMODERN house on the north point of the cove, but he didn't stay long. He made three ham sandwiches, wrapped them, and put them in a cooler with several cans of Coke. He put the cooler in the van along with a couple of blankets and a pillow. From the gun cabinet in his study he fetched a Smith & Wesson .357 Magnum, a Remington 12-gauge semiautomatic pistol-grip shotgun, and plenty of ammunition for both. Thus equipped, he set out in the storm to cruise Moonlight Cove and immediate outlying areas, intending to keep on the move, monitoring the situation by computer until the first phase of Moonhawk was concluded at midnight, in less than nineteen hours.

Watkins's threat unnerved him. Staying mobile, he wouldn't be easy to find if Watkins regressed and, true to his promise, came after him. By midnight, when the last conversions were performed, Shaddack would have consolidated his power. Then he could deal with the cop.

Watkins would be seized and shackled before he transformed. Then Shaddack could strap him down in a lab and study his psychology and physiology to find an explanation for this plague of regression.

He did not accept Watkins's explanation. They weren't regressing to escape life as New People. To accept that theory, he would have to admit that the Moonhawk Project was an unmitigated disaster, that the Change was not a boon to mankind but a curse, and that all his work was not only misguided but calamitous in its effect. He could admit no such thing.

As maker and master of the New People, he had tasted godlike power. He was unwilling to relinquish it.

The rainswept, pre-dawn streets were deserted except for cars—some police cruisers, some not—in which pairs of men patrolled in the hope of spotting either Booker, Tessa Lockland, the Foster girl, or regressives on the prowl. Though they could not see through his van's heavily smoked windows, they surely knew to whom the vehicle belonged.

Shaddack recognized many of them, for they worked at New Wave and were among the contingent of one hundred that he had put on loan to the police department only a few hours ago. Beyond the rain-washed windshields, their pale faces floated like disembodied spheres in the dark interiors of their cars, so expressionless that they might have been mannequins or robots.

Others were patrolling the town on foot but were circumspect, keeping to the deeper shadows and alleyways. He saw none of them.

Shaddack also passed two conversion teams as they went quietly and briskly from one house to another. Each time a conversion was completed, the team keyed in that data on one of their car VDTs so the central system at New Wave could keep track of their progress.

When he paused at an intersection and used his own VDT to call the current roster onto the screen, he saw that only five people remained to be dealt with in the midnight-to-six-o'clock batch of conversions. They were slightly ahead of schedule.

Hard rain slanted in from the west, silvery as ice in his headlights. Trees shook as if in fear. And Shaddack kept on the move, circling through the night as if he were some strange bird of prey that preferred to hunt on storm winds.

3

WITH TUCKER LEADING, THEY HAD HUNTED AND KILLED, BIT-ten and torn, clawed and bitten, hunted and killed and eaten the prey, drunk blood, blood, warm and sweet, thick and warm, sweet and thick, blood, feeding the fire in their flesh, cooling the fire with food. Blood.

Gradually Tucker had discovered that the longer they stayed in their altered state, the less intensely the fire burned and the easier it was to *remain* in subhuman form. Something told him that he should be worried that it was increasingly easy to cling to the shape of a beast, but he could not raise much concern about it, partly because his mind no longer seemed able to focus on complex thoughts for more than a few seconds.

So they had raced over the fields and hills in the moonlight, raced and roamed, free, so free in moonlight and fog, in fog and wind, and Tucker had led them, pausing only to kill and eat, or to couple with the female, who took her own pleasure with an aggressiveness that was exciting, savage and exciting.

Then the rains came.

Cold.

Slashing.

Thunder, too, and blazing light in the sky.

Part of Tucker seemed to know what the long, jagged bolts of sky-ripping light were. But he could not quite remember, and he was frightened, dashing for the cover of trees when the light caught him in the open, huddling with the other male and the female until the sky went dark again and stayed that way for a while.

Tucker began to look for a place to take shelter from the storm. He knew that they should go back to where they had started from, to a place of light and dry rooms, but he could not remember where that had been exactly. Besides, going back would mean surrendering freedom and assuming their born identities. He did not want to do that. Neither did the other male and the female. They wanted to race and roam and kill and rut and be free, free. If they went back they could not be free, so they went ahead, crossing a hard-surface road, slinking up into higher hills, staying away from the few houses in the area.

Dawn was coming, not yet on the eastern horizon but coming, and Tucker knew that they had to find a haven, a den, before daylight, a place where they could curl up around one another, down in darkness, sharing warmth, darkness and warmth, safely curled up with memories of blood and rutting, darkness and warmth and blood and rutting. They would be out of danger there, safe from a world in which they were still alien, safe also from the necessity to return to human form. When night fell again, they could venture forth to roam and kill, kill, bite and kill, and maybe the day would come when there were so many of their kind in the world that they would no longer be outnumbered and could venture forth in bright daylight as well, but not now, not yet.

They came to a dirt road, and Tucker had a dim memory of where he was, a sense that the road would quickly lead him to a place that could provide the shelter that he and his pack needed. He followed it farther into the hills, encouraging his companions with low growls of reassurance. In a couple of minutes they came to a building, a huge old house fallen to ruin, with the windows smashed in and the front door hanging open on half-broken hinges. Other gray structures loomed out of the rain: a barn in worse shape than the house, several outbuildings that had mostly collapsed.

Large, hand-painted signs were nailed to the house, between two of the second-floor windows, one sign above the other, in different styles of lettering, as though a lot of time had passed between the hanging of the first and the second. He knew they had meaning, but he couldn't read them, though he strained to recall the lost language used by the species to which he had once belonged.

The two members of his pack flanked him. They, too, stared up at the dark letters on the white background. Murky symbols in the rain and gloom. Eerily mysterious runes.

ICARUS COLONY

And under that:

THE OLD ICARUS COLONY RESTAURANT
NATURAL FOODS

On the dilapidated barn was another sign—FLEA MARKET—but that meant nothing more to Tucker than the signs on the house, and after a while he decided it didn't matter if he understood them. The important thing was that no people were nearby, no fresh scent or vibration of human beings, so the refuge that he sought might be found here, a burrow, a den, a warm and dark place, warm and dark, safe and dark.

4

WITH ONE BLANKET AND PILLOW, SAM HAD MADE HIS BED ON a long sofa in the living room, just off the front hall downstairs. He wanted to sleep on the ground floor so he might be awakened by the sound of an intruder. According to the schedule that Sam had seen on the VDT in the patrol car, Harry Talbot wouldn't be converted until the following evening. He doubted that they would accelerate their schedule simply because they knew an FBI man was in Moonlight Cove. But he was taking no unnecessary chances.

Sam often suffered from insomnia, but it did not trouble him that night. After he took off his shoes and stretched out on the sofa, he listened to the rain for a couple of minutes, trying not to think. Soon he slept.

His was not a dreamless sleep. It seldom was.

He dreamed of Karen, his lost wife, and as always in nightmares, she was spitting up blood and emaciated, in the final stages of her cancer, after the chemotherapy had failed. He knew that he must save her. He could not. He felt small, powerless, and terribly afraid.

But that nightmare did not wake him.

Eventually the dream shifted from the hospital to a dark and crumbling building. It was rather like a hotel designed by Salvador Dali: The corridors branched off randomly; some were very short and some were so long that the ends of them could not be seen; the walls and floors were at surreal angles to one another, and the doors to the rooms were of different sizes, some so small that only a mouse could have passed through, others large enough for a man, and still others on a scale suitable to a thirty-foot giant.

He was drawn to certain rooms. When he entered them he found in each a person from his past or current life.

He encountered Scott in several rooms and had unsatisfactory, disjointed conversations with him, all ending in unreasoning hostility on Scott's part. The nightmare was made worse by the variation in Scott's age: Sometimes he was a sullen sixteen-year-old and sometimes ten or just four or five. But in every incarnation he was alienated, cold, quick to anger, and seething with hatred. "This isn't right, this isn't true, you weren't like this when you were younger," Sam told a seven-year-old Scott, and the boy made an obscene reply.

In every room and regardless of his age, Scott was surrounded by huge posters of black-metal rockers dressed in leather and chains, displaying satanic symbols on their foreheads and in the palms of their hands. The light was flickering and strange. In a dark corner Sam saw something lurking, a creature of which Scott was aware, something the boy did not fear but which scared the hell out of Sam.

But that nightmare did not wake him, either.

In other chambers of that surreal hotel, he found dying men, the same ones every time—Arnie Taft and Carl Sorbino. They were two agents with whom he had worked and whom he had seen gunned down.

The entrance to one room was a car door—the gleaming door of a blue '54 Buick, to be exact. Inside he found an enormous, gray-walled chamber in which was the front seat, dashboard, and steering wheel, nothing else of the car, like parts of a prehistoric skeleton lying on a vast expanse of barren sand. A woman in a green dress sat behind the wheel, her head turned away from him. Of course, he knew who she was, and he wanted to leave the room at once, but he could not. In fact he was drawn to her. He sat beside her, and suddenly he was seven years old, as he had been on the day of the accident, though he spoke with his grown-up voice: "Hello, Mom." She turned to him, revealing that the right side of her face was caved in, the eye gone from the socket, bone punching through torn flesh. Broken teeth were exposed in her cheek, so she favored him with half of a hideous grin.

Abruptly they were in the *real* car, cast back in time. Ahead of them on the highway, coming toward them, was the drunk in the white pickup truck, weaving across the double yellow line, bearing down on them at high speed. Sam cried out—"Mom!"—but she couldn't evade the pickup this time any more than she had been able to avoid it thirty-five years ago. It came at them as if they were a magnet and slammed into them head-on. He thought it must be like that at the center of a bomb blast: a great roar pierced by the shriek of shredding metal. Everything went black. Then, when he swam up from that gloom, he found himself pinned in the wreckage. He was face to face with his dead mother, peering into her empty eye socket. He began to scream.

That nightmare also failed to wake him.

Now he was in a hospital, as he'd been after the accident, for that had been the first of the six times he'd nearly died. He was no longer a boy, however, but a grown man, and he was on the operating table, undergoing emergency surgery because he had been shot in the chest during the same gun battle in which Carl Sorbino had died. As the surgical team labored over him, he rose out of his body and watched them at work on his carcass. He was amazed but not afraid, which was just how he had felt when it had *not* been a dream.

Next he was in a tunnel, rushing toward dazzling light, toward the Other Side. This time he knew what he would find at the other end because he had been there before, in real life instead of in a dream. He was terrified of it, didn't want to face it again, didn't want to look Beyond. But he moved faster, faster, faster through the tunnel, *bulleted* through it, his terror escalating with his speed. Having to look again at what lay on the Other Side was worse than his dream confrontations with Scott, worse than the battered and one-eyed face of his mother, infinitely worse (faster, faster), intolerable, so he began to scream (faster) and scream (faster) and scream—

That one woke him.

He sat straight up on the sofa and pinched off the cry before it left his throat.

An instant later he became aware that he was not alone in the unlighted living room. He heard something move in front of him, and he moved simultaneously, snatching his .38 revolver from the holster, which he had taken off and laid beside the sofa.

It was Moose.

"Hey, boy."

The dog chuffed softly.

Sam reached out to pat the dark head, but already the Labrador was moving away. Because the night outside was marginally less black than the interior of the house, the windows were visible as fuzzy-gray rectangles. Moose went to one at the side of the house, putting his paws on the sill and his nose to the glass.

"Need to go out?" Sam asked, though they had let him out for ten minutes just before they'd gone to bed.

The dog made no response but stood at the window with a peculiar rigidity.

"Something out there?" Sam wondered, and even as he asked the question, he knew the answer.

Quickly and gingerly he crossed the dark room. He bumped into furniture but didn't knock anything down, and joined the dog at the window.

The rain-battered night seemed at its blackest in this last hour before dawn, but Sam's eyes were adjusted to darkness. He could see the side of the neighboring house, just thirty feet away. The steeply sloping property between the two structures was not planted with grass but with a variety of shrubs and several starburst pines, all of which swayed and shuddered in the gusty wind.

He quickly spotted the two Boogeymen because their movement was in opposition to the direction of the wind and therefore in sharp contrast to the storm dance of the vegetation. They were about fifteen feet from the window, heading downslope toward Conquistador. Though Sam could discern no details of them, he could see by their hunchbacked movement and shambling yet queerly graceful gait that they were not ordinary men.

As they paused beside one of the larger pines, one of them looked toward the Talbot house, and Sam saw its softly radiant, utterly alien amber eyes. For a moment he was transfixed, frozen not by fear so much as by amazement. Then he realized that the creature seemed to be staring straight at the window, as if it could see him, and suddenly it loped straight toward him.

Sam dropped below the sill, pressing against the wall under the window, and pulled Moose down with him. The dog must have had some sense of the danger, for he didn't bark or whine or resist in any way, but lay with his belly to the floor and allowed himself to be held there, still and silent.

A fraction of a second later, over the sounds of wind and rain, Sam heard furtive movement on the other side of the wall against which he crouched. A soft scuttling sound. Scratching.

He held his .38 in his right hand, ready in case the thing was bold enough to smash through the window.

A few seconds passed in silence. A few more.

Sam kept his left hand on Moose's back. He could feel the dog shivering.

Tick-tick-tick.

After long seconds of silence, the sudden ticking startled Sam, for he had just about decided that the creature had gone away.

Tick-tick-tick-tick.

It was tapping the glass, as if testing the solidity of the pane or calling to the man it had seen standing there.

Tick-tick. Pause. *Tick-tick-tick.*

5

TUCKER LED HIS PACK OUT OF THE MUD AND RAIN, ONTO THE sagging porch of the decrepit house. The boards creaked under their weight. One loose shutter was banging in the wind; all the others had rotted and torn off long ago.

He struggled to speak of his intentions, but he found it very difficult to remember or produce the necessary words. Midst snarls and growls and low brute mutterings, he only managed to say, " *. . . here . . . hide . . . here . . . safe . . .* "

The other male seemed to have lost his speech entirely, for he could produce no words at all.

With considerable difficulty, the female said, " *. . . safe . . . here . . . home. . . .* "

Tucker studied his two companions for a moment and realized they had changed during their night adventures. Earlier, the female had possessed a feline quality—sleek, sinuous, with cat ears and sharply pointed teeth that she revealed when she hissed either in fear, anger, or sexual desire. Though something of the cat was still in her, she had become more like Tucker, wolfish, with a large head drawn forward into a muzzle more canine than feline. She had lupine haunches, as well, and feet that appeared to have resulted from the crossbreeding of man and wolf, not paws but not hands either, tipped with claws longer and more murderous than those of a real wolf. The other male, once unique in appearance, combining a few insectile features with the general form of a hyena, had now largely conformed to Tucker's appearance.

By unspoken mutual agreement, Tucker had become the leader of the pack. Upon submitting to his rule, his followers evidently had used his appearance as a model for their own. He realized that this was an important turn of events, maybe even an ominous one.

He did not know why it should spook him, and he no longer had the mental clarity to concentrate on it until understanding came to him. The more pressing concern of shelter demanded his attention.

"... here ... safe ... here ..."

He led them through the broken, half-open door, into the front hall of the moldering house. The plaster was pocked and cracked, and in some places missing altogether, with lath showing through like the rib cage of a half-decomposed corpse. In the empty living room, long strips of wallpaper were peeling off, as if the place was shedding its skin in the process of a metamorphosis as dramatic as any that Tucker and his pack had undergone.

He followed scents through the house, and that was interesting, not exciting but definitely interesting. His companions followed as he investigated patches of mildew, toadstools growing in a dank corner of the dining room, colonies of vaguely luminescent fungus in a room on the other side of the hall, several deposits of rat feces, the mummified remains of a bird that had flown in through one of the glassless windows and broken a wing against a wall, and the still ripe carcass of a diseased coyote that had crawled into the kitchen to die.

During the course of that inspection, Tucker realized the house did not offer ideal shelter. The rooms were too large and drafty, especially with windows broken out. Though no human scent lingered on the air, he sensed that people still came here, not frequently but often enough to be troublesome.

In the kitchen, however, he found the entrance to the cellar, and he was excited by that subterranean retreat. He led the others down the creaking stairs into that deeper darkness, where cold drafts could not reach them, where the floor and walls were dry, and where the air had a clean, lime smell that came off the concrete-block walls.

He suspected that trespassers seldom ventured into the basement. And if they did ... they would be walking into a lair from which they could not possibly escape.

It was a perfect, windowless den. Tucker prowled the perimeter of the room, his claws ticking and scraping on the floor. He sniffed in corners and examined the rusted furnace. He was satisfied they'd be safe. They could curl up secure in the knowledge that they would not be found and if, by some chance, they were found, they could cut off the only exit and dispense with an intruder quickly.

In such a deep, dark, secret place, they could become anything they wanted, and no one would see them.

That last thought startled Tucker. Become anything they wanted?

He was not sure where that thought originated or what it meant. He suddenly sensed that by regressing he had initiated some process that was now beyond his conscious control, that some more primitive part of his mind was permanently in charge. Panic seized him. He had shifted to an altered state many times before and had always been able to shift back again. But now . . . His fear was sharp only for a moment, because he could not concentrate on the problem, didn't even remember what he meant by "regressing," and was soon distracted by the female, who wanted to couple with him.

Soon the three of them were in a tangle, pawing at one another, thrusting and thrashing. Their shrill, excited cries rose through the abandoned house, like ghost voices in a haunted place.

6

TICK-TICK-TICK.

Sam was tempted to rise, look through the window, and confront the creature face to face, for he was eager to see what one of them looked like close-up.

But as violent as these beings evidently were, a confrontation was certain to result in an attack and gunfire, which would draw the attention of the neighbors and then the police. He couldn't risk his current hiding place, for at the moment he had nowhere else to go.

He clutched his revolver and kept one hand on Moose and remained below the windowsill, listening. He heard voices, either wordless or so muffled that the words did not come clearly through the glass above his head. The second creature had joined the first at the side of the house. Their grumbling sounded like a low-key argument.

Silence followed.

Sam crouched there for a while, waiting for the voices to resume or for the amber-eyed beast to tap once more—*tick-tick*—but nothing happened. At last, as the muscles in his thighs and calves began to cramp, he took his hand off Moose and eased up to the window. He half expected the Boogeyman to be there, malformed face pressed to the glass, but it was gone.

With the dog accompanying him, he went from room to room on the ground floor, looking out all the windows on four sides of the house. He would not have been surprised to find those creatures trying to force entry somewhere.

But for the sound of rain drumming on the roof and gurgling in the downspouts, the house was silent.

He decided they were gone and that their interest in the house had been coincidental. They weren't looking for him in particular, just for prey. They very likely had glimpsed him at the window, and they didn't want to let him go if he had seen them. But if they had come to deal with him, they apparently had decided that they could no more risk the sound of breaking glass and a noisy confrontation than he could, not in the heart of town. They were secretive creatures. They might rarely cut loose with an eerie cry that would echo across Moonlight Cove, but only when in the grip of some strange passion. And thus far, for the most part, they had limited their attacks to people who had been relatively isolated.

Back in the living room he slipped the revolver into the holster again and stretched out on the sofa.

Moose sat watching him for a while, as if unable to believe that he could calmly lie down and sleep again after seeing what had been on the prowl in the rain.

"Some of my dreams are worse than what's out there tonight," he told the dog. "So if I spooked easily, I'd probably never want to go to sleep again."

The dog yawned and got up and went out into the dark hall, where he boarded the elevator. The motor hummed as the lift carried the Labrador upstairs.

As he waited for sleep to steal over him again, Sam attempted to shape his dreams into a more appealing pattern by concentrating on a few images he would not mind dreaming about: good Mexican food, barely chilled Guinness Stout, and Goldie Hawn. Ideally, he'd dream about being in a great Mexican restaurant with Goldie Hawn, who'd look even more radiant than usual, and they'd be eating and drinking Guinness and laughing.

Instead, when he did fall asleep, he dreamed about his father, a mean-tempered alcoholic, into whose hands he had fallen at the age of seven, after his mother had died in the car crash.

7

NESTLED IN THE STACK OF GRASS-SCENTED BURLAP TARPS IN THE back of the gardener's truck, Chrissie woke when the automatic garage door ascended with a groan and clatter. She almost sat up in surprise, revealing herself. But remembering where she was, she pulled her head under the top half-dozen tarps, which she was using as blankets. She tried to shrink into the pile of burlap.

She heard rain striking the roof. It sliced into the gravel driveway just beyond the open door, making a sizzling noise like a thousand strips of bacon on an immense griddle. Chrissie was hungry. That sound made her hungrier.

"You got my lunch box, Sarah?"

Chrissie didn't know Mr. Eulane well enough to recognize his voice, but she supposed that was him, for Sarah Eulane, whose voice Chrissie did recognize, answered at once:

"Ed, I wish you'd just come back home after you drop me at the school. Take the day off. You shouldn't work in such foul weather."

"Well, I can't cut grass in this downpour," he said. "But I can do some other chores. I'll just pull on my vinyl anorak. Keeps me dry as bone. Moses could've walked through the Red Sea in that anorak and wouldn't have needed God's miracle to help him."

Breathing air filtered through the coarse, grass-stained cloth, Chrissie was troubled by a tickling sensation in her nose, all the way into her sinuses. She was afraid that she was going to sneeze.

STUPID YOUNG GIRL SNEEZES, REVEALING HERSELF TO RAVENOUS ALIENS; EATEN ALIVE;

"SHE WAS A TASTY LITTLE MORSEL," SAYS ALIEN NEST QUEEN. "BRING US MORE OF YOUR ELEVEN-YEAR-OLD BLOND FEMALES."

Opening the passenger door of the truck, a couple of feet from Chrissie's hiding place, Sarah said, "You'll catch your death, Ed."

"You think I'm some delicate violet?" he asked playfully as he opened the driver's door and got into the truck.

"I think you're a withered old dandelion."

He laughed. "You didn't think so last night."

"Yes, I did. But you're *my* withered old dandelion, and I don't want you to just blow away on the wind."

One door slammed shut, then the other.

Certain that they could not see her, Chrissie pulled back the burlap, exposing her head. She pinched her nose and breathed through her mouth until the tickling in her sinuses subsided.

As Ed Eulane started the truck, let the engine idle a moment, then reversed out of the garage, Chrissie could hear them talking in the cab at her back. She couldn't make out everything they were saying, but they still seemed to be bantering with each other.

Cold rain struck her face, and she immediately pulled her head under the tarps again, leaving just a narrow opening by which a little fresh air might reach her. If she sneezed while in transit, the sound of the rain and the rumble of the truck's engine would cover it.

Thinking about the conversation she had overheard in the garage and listening to Mr. Eulane laughing now in the cab, Chrissie thought she could trust them. If they were aliens, they wouldn't be making dumb jokes and lovey talk. Maybe they would if they were putting on a show for non-aliens, trying to convince the world that they were still Ed and Sarah Eulane, but not when they were in private. When aliens were together without unconverted humans nearby, they probably talked about . . . well, planets they had sacked, the weather on Mars, the price of flying-saucer fuel, and recipes for serving human beings. Who knew? But surely they didn't talk as the Eulanes were talking.

On the other hand . . .

Maybe these aliens had only taken control of Ed and Sarah Eulane during the night, and maybe they were not yet comfortable in their human roles. Maybe they were practicing being human in private so they could pass for human in public. Sure as the devil, if Chrissie revealed herself, they'd probably sprout tentacles and lobster pincers from their chests and either eat her alive, without condiments, or freeze-dry her and mount her on a plaque and take her to their home world to hang on their den wall, or pop her brain out of her skull and plug it into their spaceship and use it as a cheap control mechanism for their in-flight coffeemaker.

In the middle of an alien invasion, you could give your trust only with reluctance and considerable deliberation. She decided to stick to her original plan.

The fifty-pound, plastic sacks of fertilizer and mulch and snail bait, piled on both sides of her burlap niche, protected her from some rain, but enough reached her to soak the upper layers of tarps. She was relatively dry and toasty warm when they set out, but soon she was saturated with grass-scented rainwater, cold to the bone.

She peeked out repeatedly to determine where they were. When she saw that they were turning off the county route onto Ocean Avenue, she peeled back the soggy burlap and crawled out of her hiding place.

The wall of the truck cab featured a window, so the Eulanes would see her if they turned and looked back. Mr. Eulane might even see her in the rearview mirror if she didn't keep very low. But she had to get to the rear of the truck and be ready to jump off when they passed Our Lady of Mercy.

On her hands and knees, she moved between—and over—the supplies and gardening equipment. When she reached the tailgate, she huddled there, head down, shivering and miserable in the rain.

They crossed Shasta Way, the first intersection at the edge of town, and headed down through the business district of Ocean Avenue. They were only about four blocks from the church.

Chrissie was surprised that no people were on the sidewalks and that no cars traveled the streets. It was early—she checked her watch, 7:03—but not so early that everyone would still be home in bed. She supposed the weather also had something to do with the town's deserted look; no one was going to be out and about in that mess unless he absolutely had to be.

There was another possibility: Maybe the aliens had taken over such a large percentage of the people in Moonlight Cove that they no longer felt it necessary to enact the charade of daily life; with complete conquest only hours away, all their efforts were bent on seeking the last of the unpossessed. *That* was too unsettling to think about.

When they were one block from Our Lady of Mercy, Chrissie climbed onto the white-board tailgate. She swung one leg over the top, then the other leg, and clung to the outside of the gate with both hands, her feet on the rear bumper. She could see the backs of the Eulanes' heads through the rear window of the cab, and if they turned her way—or if Mr. Eulane glanced at his rearview mirror—she'd be seen.

She kept expecting to be spotted by a pedestrian who would yell, "Hey, you, hanging on that truck, are you nuts?" But there were no pedestrians, and they reached the next intersection without incident.

The brakes squealed as Mr. Eulane slowed for the stop sign.

As the truck came to a stop, Chrissie dropped off the tailgate.

Mr. Eulane turned left on the cross street. He was heading toward Thomas Jefferson Elementary School on Palomino, a few blocks south, where Mrs. Eulane worked and where, on an ordinary Tuesday morning, Chrissie would soon be going to her sixth-grade classroom.

She sprinted across the intersection, splashed through the dirty streaming water in the gutter, and ran up the steps to the front doors of Our Lady of Mercy. A flush of triumph warmed her, for she felt that she had reached sanctuary against all odds.

With one hand on the ornate brass handle of the carved-oak door, she paused to look uphill and down. The windows of shops, offices, and apartments were as frost-blank as cataracted eyes. Smaller trees leaned with the stiff wind, and larger trees shuddered, which was the only movement other than the driving rain. The wind was inconstant, blustery; sometimes it stopped pushing the rain relentlessly eastward and gathered it into funnels, whirling them up Ocean Avenue, so if she squinted her eyes and ignored the chill in the air, she could almost believe that she was standing in a desert ghost town, watching dust devils whirl along its haunted streets.

At the corner beside the church, a police car pulled up to the stop sign. Two men were in it. Neither was looking toward her.

She already suspected that the police were not to be trusted. Pulling open the church door, she quickly slipped inside before they glanced her way.

The moment she stepped into the oak-paneled narthex and drew in a deep breath of the myrrh- and spikenard-scented air, Chrissie felt safe. She stepped through the archway to the nave, dipped her fingers in the holy water that filled the marble font on the right, crossed herself, and moved down the center aisle to the fourth pew from the rear. She genuflected, crossed herself again, and took a seat.

She was concerned about getting water all over the polished oak pew, but there was nothing she could do about that. She was dripping.

Mass was under way. Besides herself, only two of the faithful were present, which seemed to be a scandalously poor turnout. Of course, to the best of her memory, though her folks always attended Sunday Mass, they had brought her to a weekday service only once in her life, many years ago, and she could not be sure that weekday Masses ever drew more worshipers. She suspected, however, that the alien presence—or demons, whatever—in Moonlight Cove was responsible for the low attendance. No doubt space aliens were godless or, worse yet, bowed to some dark deity with a name like Yahgag or Scogblatt.

She was surprised to see that the priest celebrating Mass, with the assistance of one altarboy, was not Father Castelli. It was the young priest—the curate, they called him—whom the archdiocese had assigned to Father Castelli in August. His name was Father O'Brien. His first name was Tom, and following his rector's lead, he sometimes insisted that parishioners call him Father Tom. He was nice—though not as nice or as wise or as amusing as Father Castelli—but she could no more bring herself to call him Father Tom than she could call the older priest Father Jim. Might as well call the Pope Johnny. Her parents sometimes talked about how much the church had changed, how less formal it had become over the years, and they spoke approvingly of those changes. In her conservative heart, Chrissie wished that she had been born and raised in a time when the Mass had been in Latin, elegant and mysterious, and when the service had not included the downright silly ritual of "giving peace" to worshipers around you. She had gone to Mass at a cathedral in San Francisco once, when they were on vacation, and the service had been a special one, in Latin, conducted according to the old liturgy, and she had *loved* it. Making ever faster airplanes, improving television from black and white to color, saving lives with better medical technology, junking those clumsy old records for compact discs—all those changes were desirable and good. But there were some things in life that shouldn't change, because it was their changelessness that you loved about them. If you lived in a world of constant, rapid change in *all* things, where did you turn for stability, for a place of peace and calm and quiet in the middle of all that buzz and clatter? That truth was so evident to Chrissie that she could not understand why grown-ups were not aware of it. Sometimes adults were thickheaded.

She sat through only a couple of minutes of the Mass, just long enough to say a prayer and beseech the Blessed Virgin to intercede on her behalf, and to be sure that Father Castelli was not somewhere in the nave—sitting in a pew like an ordinary worshiper, which he did sometimes—or perhaps at one of the confessionals. Then she got up, genuflected, crossed herself, and went back into the narthex, where candle-shaped electric bulbs flickered softly behind the amber-glass panes of two wall-mounted lamps. She opened the front door a crack, peeking out at the rain-washed street.

Just then a police car came down Ocean Avenue. It was not the same one she'd seen when she had gone into the church. It was newer, and only one officer was in it. He was driving slowly, scanning the streets as if looking for someone.

As the police cruiser reached the corner on which Our Lady of Mercy stood, another car passed it, coming uphill from the sea. That one wasn't a patrol car but a blue Chevy. Two men were in it, giving everything a slow looking over, peering left and right through the rain, as the policeman was doing. And though the men in the Chevy and the policeman did not wave to each other or signal in any way, Chrissie sensed that they were involved in the same pursuit. The cops had linked up with a civilian posse to search for something, someone.

Me, she thought.

They were looking for her because she knew too much. Because yesterday morning, in the upstairs hall, she had seen the aliens in her parents. Because she was the only obstacle to their conquest of the human race. And maybe because she would taste good if they cooked her up with some Martian potatoes.

Thus far, although she had learned that aliens were taking possession of some people, she had seen no evidence that they were actually eating others, yet she continued to believe that somewhere, right now, they were snacking on body parts. It just *felt* right.

When the patrol car and the blue Chevy passed, she pushed the heavy door open another few inches and stuck her head out in the rain. She looked left and right, then again, to be very sure that no one was in sight either in a car or on foot. Satisfied, she stepped outside and dashed east to the corner of the church. After looking both ways on the cross street, she turned the corner and hurried along the side of the church toward the rectory behind it.

The two-story house was all brick with carved granite lintels and a white-painted front porch with scalloped eaves, respectable-looking enough to be the perfect residence for a priest. The old plane trees along the front walk protected her from the rain, but she was already sodden. When she reached the porch and approached the front door, her tennis shoes made squelching-squeaking noises.

As she was about to put her finger on the doorbell button, she hesitated. She was concerned that she might be walking into an alien lair—an unlikely possibility but one which could not be lightly dismissed. She also realized that Father O'Brien might be saying Mass in order that Father Castelli, a hard worker by nature, could enjoy a rare sleep-in, and she was loath to disturb him if that was the case.

Young Chrissie, she thought, *undeniably courageous and clever, was nonetheless too polite for her own good. While standing on the priest's porch, debating the proper etiquette of an early-morning visit, she suddenly was snatched up by slavering, nine-eyed aliens and eaten on the spot. Fortunately she was too dead to hear the way they belched and farted after eating her, for surely her refined sensibilities would have been gravely offended.*

She rang the bell. Twice.

A moment later a shadowy and strangely lumpish figure appeared beyond the crackle-finished, diamond-shaped panes in the top half of the door. She almost turned and ran but told herself that the glass was distorting the image and that the figure beyond was not actually grotesque.

Father Castelli opened the door and blinked in surprise when he saw her. He was wearing black slacks, a black shirt, a Roman collar, and a tattered gray cardigan, so he hadn't been fast asleep, thank God. He was a shortish man, about five feet seven, and round but not really fat, with black hair going gray at the temples. Even his proud beak of a nose was not enough to dilute the effect of his otherwise soft features, which gave him a gentle and compassionate appearance.

He blinked again—this was the first time Chrissie had seen him without his glasses—and said, "Chrissie?" He smiled, and she knew that she had done the right thing by coming to him, because his smile was warm and open and loving. "Whatever brings you here at this hour, in this weather?" He looked past her to the rest of the porch and the walkway beyond. "Where're your parents?"

"Father," she said, not altogether surprised to hear her voice crack, "I have to see you."

His smile wavered. "Is something wrong?"

"Yes, Father. Very wrong. Terribly, awfully wrong."

"Come in, then, come in. You're soaked!" He ushered her into the foyer and closed the door. "Dear girl, what *is* this all about?"

"Aliens, F–f–father," she said, as a chill made her stutter.

"Come on back to the kitchen," he said. "It's the warmest room in the house. I was just fixing breakfast."

"I'll ruin the carpet," she said, indicating the oriental runner that lay the length of the hallway, with oak flooring on both sides.

"Oh, don't worry about that. It's an old thing, but it stands up well to abuse. Sort of like me! Would you like some hot cocoa? I was making breakfast, including a big pot of piping hot cocoa."

She followed him gratefully back down the dimly lighted hall, which smelled of lemon oil and pine disinfectant and vaguely of incense.

The kitchen was homey. A well-worn, yellow linoleum floor. Pale yellow walls. Dark wood cabinets with white porcelain handles. Gray and yellow Formica counter tops. There were appliances—refrigerator, oven, microwave oven, toaster, electric can opener—as in any kitchen, which surprised her, though when she thought about it, she didn't know why she would have expected it to be any different. Priests needed appliances too. They couldn't just summon up a fiery angel to toast some bread or work a miracle to brew a pot of hot cocoa.

The place smelled wonderful. Cocoa was brewing. Toast was toasting. Sausages were sizzling over a low flame on the gas stove.

Father Castelli showed her to one of the four padded vinyl chairs at the chrome and Formica breakfast set, then scurried about, taking care of her as if she were a chick and he a mother hen. He rushed upstairs, returned with two clean, fluffy bath towels, and said, "Dry your hair and blot your damp clothes with one of them, then wrap the other one around you like a shawl. It'll help you get warm." While she was following his instructions, he went to the bathroom off the downstairs hall and fetched two aspirins. He put those on the table in front of her and said, "I'll get you some orange juice to take them with. Lots of vitamin C in orange juice. Aspirin and vitamin C are like a one-two punch; they'll knock a cold right out of you before it can take up residence." When he returned with the juice, he stood for a moment looking down at her, shaking his head, and she figured she must look bedraggled and pitiful. "Dear girl, what on *earth* have you been up to?" He seemed not to have heard what she'd said about aliens when she'd first crossed his threshold. "No, wait. You can tell me over breakfast. Would you like some breakfast?"

"Yes, please, Father. I'm starved. The only thing I've eaten since yesterday afternoon was a couple of Hershey bars."

"Nothing but Hershey bars?" He sighed. "Chocolate is one of God's graces, but it's also a tool the devil uses to lead us into temptation—the temptation of gluttony." He patted his round belly. "I, myself, have often partaken of this particular grace, but I would *never*"—he exaggerated the word "never" and winked at her— "never, not ever, heed the devil's call to overindulge! But, see here, if you've been eating only chocolate, your teeth will fall out. So . . . I've got plenty of sausages, plenty to share. I was about to cook a couple of eggs for myself too. Would you like a couple of eggs?"

"Yes, please."

"And toast?"

"Yes."

"We've got some wonderful cinnamon sweetrolls there on the table. And the hot chocolate, of course."

Chrissie washed down the two aspirins with orange juice.

As he carefully cracked eggs into the hot frying pan, Father Castelli glanced at her again. "Are you all right?"

"Yes, Father."

"Are you sure?"

"Yes. Now. I'm all right now."

"It'll be nice having company for breakfast," he said.

Chrissie drank the rest of her juice.

He said, "When Father O'Brien finishes saying Mass, he never wants to eat. Nervous stomach." He chuckled. "They all have bad stomachs when they're new. For the first few months they're scared to death up there on the altar. It's such a sacred duty, you see, offering the Mass, and the young priests are always afraid of flubbing up in some way that'll be . . . oh, I don't know . . . that'll be an insult to God, I guess. But God doesn't insult very easily. If He did, He'd have washed His hands of the human race a long time ago! All young priests come to that realization eventually, and then they're fine. Then they come back from saying Mass, and they're ready to run through the entire week's food budget in one breakfast."

She knew that he was talking just to soothe her. He had noticed how distraught she was. He wanted to settle her down so they could discuss it in a calm, reasonable manner. She didn't mind. She *needed* to be soothed.

Having cracked all four eggs, he turned the sausages with a fork, then opened a drawer and took out a spatula, which he placed on the counter near the egg pan. As he got plates, knives, and forks for the table, he said, "You look more than a little scared, Chrissie, like you'd just seen a ghost. You can calm down now. After so many years of schooling and training, if a young priest can be afraid of making a mistake at Mass, then anyone can be afraid of anything. Most fears are things we create in our own minds, and we can banish them as easily as we called them forth."

"Maybe not this one," she said.

"We'll see."

He transferred eggs and sausages from frying pans to plates.

For the first time in twenty-four hours, the world seemed *right*. As Father Castelli put the food on the table and encouraged her to dig in, Chrissie sighed with relief and hunger.

8

SHADDACK USUALLY WENT TO BED AFTER DAWN, SO BY seven o'clock Tuesday morning he was yawning and rubbing at his eyes as he cruised through Moonlight Cove, looking for a place to hide the van and sleep for a few hours safely beyond Loman Watkins's reach. The day was overcast, gray and dim, yet the sunlight seared his eyes.

He remembered Paula Parkins, who'd been torn apart by regressives back in September. Her 1.5-acre property was secluded, at the most rural end of town. Though the dead woman's family—in Colorado—had put it up for sale through a local real-estate agent, it had not sold. He drove out there, parked in the empty garage, cut the engine, and pulled the big door down behind him.

He ate a ham sandwich and drank a Coke. Brushing crumbs from his fingers, he curled up on the blankets in the back of the van and drifted toward sleep.

He never suffered insomnia, perhaps because he was so sure of his role in life, his destiny, and he had no concern about tomorrow. He was absolutely convinced he would bend the future to his agenda.

All of his life Shaddack had seen signs of his uniqueness, omens that foretold his ultimate triumph in any pursuit he undertook.

Initially he had noticed those signs only because Don Runningdeer had pointed them out to him. Runningdeer had been an Indian—of what tribe, Shaddack had never been able to learn—who had worked for the judge, Shaddack's father, back in Phoenix, as a full-time gardener and all-around handyman. Runningdeer was lean and quick, with a weathered face, ropy muscles, and calloused hands; his eyes were bright and as black as oil, singularly powerful eyes from which you sometimes had to look away . . . and from which you sometimes could *not* look away, no matter how much you might want to. The Indian took an interest in young Tommy Shaddack, occasionally letting him help with some yard chores and household repairs, when neither the judge nor Tommy's mother was around to disapprove of their boy doing common labor or associating with "social inferiors." Which meant he hung out with Runningdeer almost constantly between the ages of five and twelve, the period during which the Indian had worked for the judge, because his parents were hardly ever there to see and object.

One of the earliest detailed memories he had was of Runningdeer and the sign of the self-devouring snake. . . .

He had been five years old, sprawled on the rear patio of the big house in Phoenix, among a collection of Tonka Toys, but he'd been more interested in Runningdeer than in the miniature trucks and cars. The Indian was wearing jeans and boots, shirtless in the bright desert sun, trimming shrubs with a large pair of wood-handled shears. The muscles in Runningdeer's back, shoulders, and arms worked fluidly, stretching and flexing, and Tommy was fascinated by the man's physical power. The judge, Tommy's father, was thin, bony, and pale. Tommy himself, at five, was already visibly his father's son, fair and tall for his age and painfully thin. By the day he showed Tommy the self-devouring snake, Running-deer had been working for the Shaddacks two weeks, and Tommy had been increasingly drawn to him without fully understanding why. Runningdeer often had a smile for him and told funny stories about talking coyotes and rattlesnakes and other desert animals. Sometimes he called Tommy "Little Chief," which was the first nickname anyone had given him. His mother always called him Tommy or Tom; the judge called him Thomas. So he sprawled among his Tonka Toys, playing with them less and less, until at last he stopped playing altogether and simply watched Runningdeer, as if mesmerized.

He was not sure how long he lay entranced in the patio shade, in the hot dry air of the desert day, but after a while he was surprised to hear Runningdeer call to him.

"Little Chief, come look at this."

He was in such a daze that at first he could not respond. His arms and legs would not work. He seemed to have been turned to stone.

"Come on, come on, Little Chief. You've *got* to see this."

At last Tommy sprang up and ran out onto the lawn, to the hedges surrounding the swimming pool, where Runningdeer had been trimming.

"This is a rare thing," Runningdeer said in a somber voice, and he pointed to a green snake that lay at his feet on the sun-warmed decking around the pool.

Tommy began to pull back in fear.

But the Indian seized him by the arm, held him close, and said, "Don't be afraid. It's only a harmless garden snake. It's not going to hurt you. In fact it's been sent here as a sign to you."

Tommy stared wide-eyed at the eighteen-inch reptile, which was curled to form an O, its own tail in its mouth, as if eating itself. The serpent was motionless, glassy eyes unblinking. Tommy thought it was dead, but the Indian assured him that it was alive.

"This is a great and powerful sign that all Indians know," said Runningdeer. He squatted in front of the snake and pulled the boy down beside him. "It is a sign," he whispered, "a supernatural sign, sent from the great spirits, and it's always meant for a young boy, so it must have been meant for you. A very powerful sign."

Staring wonderingly at the snake, Tommy said, "Sign? What do you mean? It's not a sign. It's a snake."

"An omen. A presentiment. A sacred sign," Runningdeer said.

As they hunkered before the snake, he explained such things to Tommy in an intense, whispery voice, all the while holding him by one arm. Sun glare bounced off the concrete decking. Shimmering waves of heat rose from it too. The snake lay so motionless that it might have been an incredibly detailed jeweled choker rather than a real snake—each scale a chip of emerald, twin rubies for the eyes. After a while Tommy drifted back into the queer trance that he'd been in while lying on the patio, and Runningdeer's voice slithered serpentlike into his head, deep inside his skull, curling and sliding through his brain.

Stranger still, it began to seem that the voice was not really Runningdeer's at all, but the snake's. He stared unwaveringly at the viper and almost forgot that Runningdeer was there, for what the snake said to him was so compelling and exciting that it filled Tommy's senses, demanded his entire attention, even though he did not fully understand what he was hearing. This is a sign of destiny, the snake said, a sign of power and destiny, and you will be a man of great power, far greater than your father, a man to whom others will bow down, a man who will be obeyed, a man who will never fear the future because he will *make* the future, and you will have anything you want, anything in the world. But for now, said the snake, this is to be our secret. No one must know that I've brought this message to you, that the sign has been delivered, for if they know that you are destined to hold power over them, they will surely kill you, slit your throat in the night, tear out your heart, and bury you in a deep grave. They must not know that you are the king-to-be, a god-on-earth, or they will smash you before your strength has fully flowered. Secret. This is our secret. I am the self-devouring snake, and I will eat myself and vanish now that I've delivered this message, and no one will know I've been here. Trust the Indian but no one else.

No one. Ever.

Tommy fainted on the pool decking and was ill for two days. The doctor was baffled. The boy had no fever, no detectable swelling of lymph glands, no nausea, no soreness in the joints or muscles, no pain whatsoever. He was merely gripped by a profound malaise, so lethargic that he did not even want to bother holding a comic book; watching TV was too much effort. He had no appetite. He slept fourteen hours a day and lay in a daze most of the rest of the time. "Perhaps mild sunstroke," the doctor said, "and if he doesn't snap out of it in a couple of days, we'll put him in the hospital for tests."

During the day, when the judge was in court or meeting with his investment associates, and when Tommy's mother was at the country club or at one of her charity luncheons, Runningdeer slipped into the house now and then to sit by the boy's bed for ten minutes. He told Tommy stories, speaking in that soft and strangely rhythmic voice.

Miss Karval, their live-in housekeeper and part-time nanny, knew that neither the judge nor Mrs. Shaddack would approve of the Indian's sickbed visits or any of his other associations with Tommy. But Miss Karval was kindhearted, and she disapproved of the lack of attention that the Shaddacks gave to their offspring. And she liked the Indian. She turned her head because she saw no harm in it—if Tommy promised not to tell his folks how much time he spent with Runningdeer.

Just when they decided to admit the boy to a hospital for tests, he recovered, and the doctor's diagnosis of sunstroke was accepted. Thereafter, Tommy tagged along with Runningdeer most days from the time his father and mother left the house until one of them returned. When he started going to school, he came right home after classes; he was never interested when other kids invited him to their houses to play, for he was eager to spend a couple of hours with Runningdeer before his mother or father appeared in the late afternoon.

And week by week, month by month, year by year, the Indian made Tommy acutely aware of signs that foretold his great—though as yet unspecified—destiny. A patch of four-leaf clovers under the boy's bedroom window. A dead rat floating in the swimming pool. A score of chirruping crickets in one of the boy's bureau drawers when he came home from school one afternoon. Occasionally coins appeared where he had not left them—a penny in every shoe in his closet; a month later, a nickel in every pocket of every pair of his pants; later still, a shiny silver dollar *inside* an apple that Runningdeer was peeling for him—and the Indian regarded the coins with awe, explaining that they were some of the most powerful signs of all.

"Secret," Runningdeer whispered portentously on the day after Tommy's ninth birthday, when the boy reported hearing soft bells ringing under his window in the middle of the night.

On arising, he had seen nothing but a candle burning on the lawn. Careful not to wake his parents, he sneaked outside to take a closer look at the candle, but it was gone.

"Always keep these signs secret, or they'll realize that you're a child of destiny, that one day you'll have tremendous power over them, and they'll kill you now, while you're still a boy, and weak."

"Who's 'they'?" Tommy asked.

"They, them, everyone," the Indian said mysteriously.

"But who?"

"Your father, for one."

"Not him."

"Him especially," Runningdeer whispered. "He's a man of power. He enjoys having power over others, intimidating, arm-twisting to get his way. You've seen how people bow and scrape to him."

Indeed, Tommy had noticed the respect with which everyone spoke to his father—especially his many friends in politics—and a couple of times had glimpsed the unsettling and perhaps more honest looks they gave the judge behind his back. They appeared to admire and even revere him to his face, but when he was not looking they seemed not only to fear but loathe him.

"He is satisfied only when he has all the power, and he won't let go of it easily, not for anyone, not even for his son. If he finds out that you're destined to be greater and more powerful than he is . . . no one can save you then. Not even me."

Perhaps if their family life had been marked by more affection, Tommy would have found the Indian's warning difficult to accept. But his father seldom spoke to him in more than a perfunctory way, and even more seldom touched him—never a real hug and *never* a kiss.

Sometimes Runningdeer brought a gift of homemade candy for the boy. "Cactus candy," he called it. There was always just one piece for each of them, and they always ate it together, either sitting on the patio when the Indian was on his lunch break, or as Tommy followed his mentor around the two-acre property on a series of chores. Soon after eating the cactus candy, the boy was overcome by a curious mood. He felt euphoric. When he moved, he seemed to float. Colors were brighter, prettier. The most vivid thing of all was Runningdeer: His hair was impossibly black, his skin a beautiful bronze, his teeth radiantly white, his eyes as dark as the end of the universe. Every sound—even the crisp *snick-snick-snick* of hedge clippers, the roar of a plane passing overhead on its way to Phoenix airport, the insect-hum of the pool motor—became music; the world was full of music, though the most musical of all things was Runningdeer's voice. Odors also became sharper: flowers, cut grass, the oil with which the Indian lubricated his tools. Even the stink of perspiration was pleasant. Runningdeer smelled like fresh-baked bread and hay and copper pennies.

Tommy seldom remembered what Runningdeer talked about after they ate their cactus candy, but he did recall that the Indian spoke to him with a special intensity. A lot of it had to do with the sign of the moonhawk. "If the great spirits send the sign of the moonhawk, you'll know you're to have tremendous power and be invincible. Invincible! But if you *do* see the moonhawk, it'll mean the great spirits want something from you in return, an act that will truly prove your worthiness." That much stuck with Tommy, but he remembered little else. Usually, after an hour, he grew weary and went to his room to nap; his dreams then were particularly vivid, more real than waking life, and always involved the Indian. They were simultaneously frightening and comforting dreams.

On a rainy Saturday in November, when Tommy was ten, he sat on a stool by the workbench at one end of the four-car garage, watching as Runningdeer repaired an electric carving knife that the judge always used to slice the turkey on Thanksgiving and Christmas. The air was pleasantly cool and unusually humid for Phoenix. Runningdeer and Tommy were talking about the rain, the upcoming holiday, and things that had happened at school recently. They didn't always talk about signs and destiny, or otherwise Tommy might not have liked the Indian so much; Runningdeer was a great listener.

When the Indian finished repairing the electric knife, he plugged it in and switched it on. The blade shivered back and forth so fast that the cutting edge was a blur.

Tommy applauded.

"You see this?" Runningdeer asked, raising the knife higher and squinting at it in the glow from the fluorescent bulbs overhead.

Bright glints flew from the shuttling blade, as if it were busily slicing up the light itself.

"What?" Tommy asked.

"This knife, Little Chief. It's a machine. A frivolous machine, not a really important machine like a car or airplane or electric wheelchair. My brother is . . . crippled . . . and must get around in an electric wheelchair. Did you know that, Little Chief?"

"No."

"One of my brothers is dead, the other crippled."

"I'm sorry."

"They are my half-brothers, really, but the only ones I have."

"How did it happen? Why?"

Runningdeer ignored the questions. "Even if this knife's purpose is just to carve a turkey that could be carved as well by hand, it's still efficient and clever. Most machines are much more efficient and clever than people."

The Indian lowered the cutting instrument slightly and turned to face Tommy. He held the purring knife between them and looked past the shuttling blade into Tommy's eyes.

The boy felt himself slipping into a spell similar to that he'd experienced after eating cactus candy, though they had eaten none.

"The white man puts great faith in machines," Runningdeer said. "He thinks machines are ever so much more reliable and clever than people. If you want to be truly great in the white man's world, Little Chief, you must make yourself as much like a machine as you can. You must be efficient. You must be relentless like a machine. You must be determined in your goals, allowing no desires or emotions to distract you."

He moved the purring blade slowly toward Tommy's face, until the boy's eyes crossed in an attempt to focus on the cutting edge.

"With this I could lop away your nose, slice off your lips, carve away your cheeks and ears . . . "

Tommy wanted to slip off the workbench stool and run.

But he could not move.

He realized that the Indian was holding him by one wrist.

Even if he had not been held, he would have been unable to flee. He was paralyzed. Not entirely by fear, either. There was something seductive about the moment; the potential for violence was in an odd way . . . exciting.

" . . . cut off the round ball of your chin, scalp you, lay bare the bone, and you'd bleed to death or die of one cause or another but . . . "

The blade was no more than two inches from his nose.

" . . . *but* the machine would go on . . . "

One inch.

" . . . the knife would still purr and slice, purr and slice . . . "

Half an inch.

" . . . because machines don't die . . . "

Tommy could feel the faint, faint breeze stirred by the continuously moving electric blade.

" . . . machines are efficient and reliable. If you want to do well in the white man's world, Little Chief, you must be like a machine."

Runningdeer switched off the knife. He put it down.

He did not let go of Tommy.

Leaning close, he said, "If you wish to be great, if you wish to please the spirits and do what they ask of you when they send you the sign of the moonhawk, then you must be determined, relentless, cold, single-minded, uncaring of consequences, just *like a machine*."

Thereafter, especially when they ate cactus candy together, they often talked of being as dedicated to a purpose and as reliable as a machine. As he approached puberty, Tommy's dreams were less often filled with sexual references than with images of the moonhawk and with visions of people who looked normal on the outside but who were all wires and transistors and clicking metal switches on the inside.

In the summer of his twelfth year, after seven years in the Indian's company, the boy learned what had happened to Runningdeer's half-brothers. At least he learned some of it. He surmised the rest.

He and the Indian were sitting on the patio, having lunch and watching the rainbows that appeared and faded in the mist thrown up by the lawn sprinklers. He had asked about Runningdeer's brothers a few times since that day at the workbench, more than a year and a half earlier, but the Indian had never answered him. This time, however, Runningdeer stared off toward the distant, hazy mountains and said, "This is a secret I tell you."

"All right."

"As secret as all the signs you've been given."

"Sure."

"Some white men, just college boys, got drunk and were cruising around, maybe looking for women, certainly looking for trouble. They met my brothers by accident, in a restaurant parking lot. One of my brothers was married, and his wife was with him, and the college boys started playing tease-the-Indians, but they also really liked the look of my brother's wife. They wanted her and were drunk enough to think they could just take her. There was a fight. Five against my two brothers, they beat one to death with a tire iron. The other will never walk again. They took my brother's wife with them, used her."

Tommy was stunned by this revelation.

At last the boy said, "I *hate* white men."

Runningdeer laughed.

"I really do," Tommy said. "What happened to those guys who did it? Are they in prison now?"

"No prison." Runningdeer smiled at the boy. A fierce, humorless smile. "Their fathers were powerful men. Money. Influence. So the judge let them off for 'insufficient evidence.' "

"My father should've been the judge. He wouldn't let them off."

"Wouldn't he?" the Indian said.

"Never."

"Are you so sure?"

Uneasily, Tommy said, "Well . . . sure I'm sure."

The Indian was silent.

"I hate white men," Tommy repeated, this time motivated more by a desire to curry favor with the Indian than by conviction.

Runningdeer laughed again and patted Tommy's hand.

Near the end of that same summer, Runningdeer came to Tommy late on a blazing August day and, in a portentous and ominous voice, said, "There will be a full moon tonight, Little Chief. Go into the backyard and watch it for a while. I believe that tonight the sign will finally come, the most important sign of all."

After moonrise, which came shortly after nightfall, Tommy went out and stood on the pool apron, where Runningdeer had shown him the self-devouring snake seven years earlier. He stared up at the lunar sphere for a long time, while an elongated reflection of it shimmered on the surface of the water in the swimming pool. It was a swollen yellow moon, still low in the sky and immense.

Soon the judge came out onto the patio, calling to him, and Tommy said, "Here."

The judge joined him by the pool. "What're you doing, Thomas?"

"Watching for . . . "

"For what?"

Just then Tommy saw the hawk silhouetted by the moon. For years he had been told he would see it one day, had been prepared for it and all that it would mean, and suddenly there it was, frozen for a moment in midflight against the round lunar lamp.

"There!" he said, for the moment having forgotten that he could trust no one but the Indian.

"There what?" the judge asked.

"Didn't you see it?"

"Just the moon."

"You weren't looking or you'd have seen it."

"Seen what?"

His father's blindness to the sign only proved to Tommy that he was, indeed, special and that the portent had been meant for his eyes only—which reminded him that he could not trust his own father. He said, "Uh . . . a shooting star."

"You're standing out here watching for shooting stars?"

"They're actually meteors," Tommy said, talking too fast. "See, tonight the earth's supposed to be passing through a meteor belt, so there'll be lots of them."

"Since when are you interested in astronomy?"

"I'm not." Tommy shrugged. "Just wondered what it'd look like. Pretty boring." He turned away from the pool and started back toward the house, and after a moment the judge accompanied him.

The next day, Wednesday, the boy told Runningdeer about the moonhawk. "But I didn't get any messages from it. I don't know what the great spirits want me to do to prove myself."

The Indian smiled and stared at him in silence for what began to be an uncomfortably long time. Then he said, "Little Chief, we'll talk about that at lunch."

Miss Karval had Wednesdays off, and Runningdeer and Tommy were at home alone. They sat side by side on patio chairs for lunch. The Indian seemed to have brought nothing but cactus candy, and Tommy had no appetite for anything else.

Long ago the boy had ceased to eat the candy for its flavor but devoured it eagerly for its effect. And over the years its impact on him had grown constantly more profound.

Soon the boy was in that much-desired dreamlike plane, where colors were bright and sounds were loud and odors were sharp and all things were comforting and appealing. He and the Indian talked for nearly an hour, and at the end of that time Tommy came to understand that the great spirits expected him to kill his father four days hence, Sunday morning. "That's my day off," said Runningdeer, "so I will not be here to offer you support. But in fact that's probably the spirits' intention—that you should have to prove yourself all on your own. At least we'll have the next few days to plan it together, so that when Sunday comes you'll be prepared."

"Yes," the boy said dreamily. "Yes. We'll plan it together."

Later that afternoon, the judge came home from a business meeting that had followed his court session. Complaining of the heat, he went straight upstairs to take a shower. Tommy's mother had come home half an hour earlier. She was in an armchair in the living room, feet on a low upholstered stool, reading the latest

issue of *Town & Country* and sipping at what she called a "precocktail-hour cocktail." She barely looked up when the judge leaned in from the hall to announce
his intention of showering.

As soon as his father went upstairs, Tommy went to the kitchen and got a
butcher's knife from the rack by the stove.

Runningdeer was outside, mowing the lawn.

Tommy went into the living room, walked up to his mother, and kissed her on
the cheek. She was surprised by the kiss but more surprised by the knife, which
he rammed into her chest three times. He carried the same knife upstairs and
buried it in the judge's stomach as he stepped out of the shower.

He went to his room and took off his clothes. There was no blood on his shoes,
little on his jeans, but a lot on his shirt. After he quickly washed up in his bathroom
sink and sluiced all traces of blood down the drain, he dressed in fresh jeans and
shirt. He carefully bundled his bloody clothes in an old towel and carried them
into the attic, where he hid them in a corner behind a seaman's trunk. He could
dispose of them later.

Downstairs he passed the living room without looking in at his dead mother.
He went straight to the desk in the judge's study and opened the right bottom
drawer. From behind a stack of files, he withdrew the judge's revolver.

In the kitchen he turned off the overhead fluorescents, so the only light was
what came through the windows, which was bright enough but left some parts of
the room in cool shadows. He put the butcher's knife on the counter by the
refrigerator, squarely in some of those shadows. He put the revolver on one of
the chairs at the table, and pulled the chair only partway out, so the gun could be
reached but not easily seen.

He went out through the French doors that connected the kitchen to the patio,
and yelled for Runningdeer. The Indian did not hear the boy over the roar of the
lawnmower, but happened to look up and see him waving. Frowning, he shut off
the mower and crossed the half-cut lawn to the patio. "Yes, Thomas?" he said,
because he knew that the judge and Mrs. Shaddack were at home.

"My mother needs your help with something," Tommy said. "She asked me to
fetch you."

"My help?"

"Yeah. In the living room."

"What's she want?"

"She needs some help with . . . well, it's easier to show you than to talk about
it."

The Indian followed him through the French doors, into the large kitchen, past
the refrigerator, toward the hall door.

Tommy halted abruptly, turned, and said, "Oh, yeah, Mother says you'll need
that knife, that one there behind you on the counter, by the refrigerator."

Runningdeer turned, saw the knife lying on the shadowed tile top of the
counter, and picked it up. His eyes went very wide. "Little Chief, there's blood on
this knife. There's blood—"

Tommy had already plucked the revolver off the kitchen chair. As the Indian
turned toward him in surprise, Tommy held the gun in both hands and fired until
he emptied the cylinder, though the recoil slammed painfully through his arm and

shoulders, nearly knocking him off his feet. At least two of the rounds hit Runningdeer, and one of them tore out his throat.

The Indian went down hard. The knife clattered out of his hand and spun across the floor.

With one shoe, Tommy kicked the knife closer to the corpse, so it would definitely look as if the dying man had been wielding it.

The boy's understanding of the great spirits' message had been clearer than his mentor's. They wanted him to free himself at once from *everyone* who had more than a little power over him: the judge, his mother, and Runningdeer. Only then could he achieve his own lofty destiny of power.

He had planned the three murders with the coolness of a computer and had executed them with machinelike determination and efficiency. He felt nothing. Emotions had not interfered with his actions. Well, in truth, he was scared and a little excited—even exhilarated—but those feelings had not distracted him.

After staring for a moment at Runningdeer's body, Tommy went to the kitchen phone, dialed the police, and hysterically reported that the Indian, shouting of revenge, had killed his parents and that he, Tommy, had killed the Indian with his father's gun. But he didn't put it so succinctly. He was so hysterical, they had to pry it from him. In fact he was so shattered and disoriented by what had happened that they had to work patiently with him for three or four tedious minutes to get him to stop babbling and give them his name and address. In his mind he had practiced hysteria all afternoon, since lunch with the Indian. Now he was pleased that he sounded so convincing.

He walked out to the front of the house and sat in the driveway and wept until the police arrived. His tears were more genuine than his hysteria. He was crying with relief.

He'd seen the moonhawk twice again, later in life. He saw it when he needed to see it, when he wanted to be reassured that some course of action he wished to follow was correct.

But he never killed anyone again—because he never needed to.

His maternal grandparents took him into their home and raised him in another part of Phoenix. Because he had endured such tragedy, they more or less gave him everything that he wanted, as if to deny him anything would be unbearably cruel and, just possibly, might be the additional straw of burden that would break him at last. He was the sole heir of his father's estate, which was fattened by large life-insurance policies; therefore he was guaranteed a first-rate education and plenty of capital with which to start out in life after graduation from the university. The world lay before him, filled with opportunity. And thanks to Runningdeer, he had the additional advantage of knowing beyond a doubt that he had a great destiny and that the forces of fate and heaven wanted him to achieve tremendous power over other men.

Only a madman killed without a compelling need.

With but rare exception, murder simply was not an *efficient* method of solving problems.

Now, curled up in the back of the van in Paula Parkins's dark garage, Shaddack reminded himself that he was destiny's child, that he had seen the moonhawk three times. He put all fear of Loman Watkins and of failure out of his mind. He sighed and slipped over the edge of sleep.

He dreamed the familiar dream. The vast machine. Half metal and half flesh. Steel pistons stroking. Human hearts dependably pumping lubricants of all kinds. Blood and oil, iron and bone, plastic and tendon, wires and nerves.

9

CHRISSIE WAS AMAZED THAT PRIESTS ATE SO WELL. THE TABLE in the rectory kitchen was heavily laden with food: an immense plateful of sausages, eggs, a stack of toast, a package of sweetrolls, another of blueberry muffins, a bowl of hash-brown potatoes that had been warming in the oven, fresh fruit, and a bag of marshmallows for the hot cocoa. Father Castelli was pudgy, sure, but Chrissie had always thought of priests as abstemious in all things, denying themselves at least some of the pleasures of food and drink just as they denied themselves marriage. If Father Castelli consumed as much at every meal, he ought to weigh twice what he did. No, three times as much!

As they ate, she told him about the aliens taking over her folks. In deference to Father Castelli's predisposition toward spiritual answers, and as a means of keeping him hooked, she left the door open on demonic possession, though personally she much favored the alien-invasion explanation. She told him what she'd seen in the upstairs hall yesterday, how she'd been locked in the pantry and, later, had been pursued by her parents and Tucker in their strange new shapes.

The priest expressed astonishment and concern, and several times he demanded more details, but he did not once pause significantly in his eating. In fact he ate with such tremendous gusto that his table manners suffered. Chrissie was as surprised by his sloppiness as she was by the size of his appetite. A couple of times he had egg yolk on his chin, and when she got up the nerve to point it out to him, he made a joke about it and immediately wiped it off. But a moment later she looked up, and there was more egg yolk. He dropped a few miniature marshmallows and didn't seem to care. The front of his black shirt was speckled with toast crumbs, a couple of tiny pieces of sausage, flecks of potatoes, sweetroll crumbs, muffin crumbs. . . .

Really, she was beginning to think that Father Castelli was as guilty as any man had ever been of the sin of gluttony.

But she loved him in spite of his eating habits because he never once doubted her sanity or expressed a lack of belief in her wild story. He listened with interest and utmost seriousness, and seemed genuinely concerned, even frightened, by what she told him. "Well, Chrissie, they've made maybe a thousand movies about alien invasions, hostile creatures from other worlds, and they've written maybe ten thousand books about it, and I've always said that man's mind can't imagine anything that isn't possible in God's world. So who knows, hmmmm? Who's to say they might *not* have landed here in Moonlight Cove? I'm a film buff, and I've always liked scary movies best, but I never imagined that I'd find myself in the middle of a *real-life* scary movie." He was sincere. He never patronized her.

Although Father Castelli continued to eat with undiminished appetite, Chrissie finished breakfast and her story at the same time. Because the kitchen was warm, she was rapidly drying out, and only the seat of her pants and her running shoes were still really wet. She felt sufficiently reinvigorated to consider what lay ahead of her now that she had reached help. "What next? We've got to call in the Army, don't you think, Father?"

"Perhaps the Army *and* the Marines," he said after a moment of deliberation. "The Marines might be better at this sort of thing."

"Do you think . . . "

"What is it, dear girl?"

"Do you think there's any chance . . . well, any chance of getting my folks back? The way they were, I mean?"

He put down a muffin that he had been raising to his mouth, and he reached across the table, between the plates and tins of food, to take her hand. His fingers were slightly greasy with butter, but she did not mind, for he was so reassuring and comforting; right now she needed a lot of reassuring and comforting.

"You'll be reunited with your parents," Father Castelli said with great sympathy. "I absolutely guarantee that you will."

She bit her lower lip, trying to hold back her tears.

"I guarantee it," he repeated.

Abruptly his face *bulged*. Not evenly like an inflating balloon. Rather, it bulged in some places and not others, rippled and pulsed, as if his skull had turned to mush and as if balls of worms were writhing and squirming just under the skin.

"I guarantee it!"

Chrissie was too terrified to scream. For a moment she could not move. She was paralyzed by fear, frozen in her chair, unable to summon even enough motor control to blink or draw a breath.

She could hear his bones loudly crackling-crunching-popping as they splintered and dissolved and reshaped themselves with impossible speed. His flesh made a disgusting, wet, oozing sound as it flowed into new forms almost with the ease of hot wax.

The priest's skull swelled upward and swept back in a bony crest, and his face was hardly human at all now but partly crustacean, partly insectile, vaguely wasp-like, with something of the jackal in it, too, and with fiery hateful eyes.

At last Chrissie cried out explosively, "No!" Her heart was pounding so hard that each beat was painful. "No, go away, let me alone, let me go!"

His jaws lengthened, then split back nearly to his ears in a menacing grin defined by double rows of immense sharp teeth.

"No, no!"

She tried to get up.

She realized that he was still holding her left hand.

He spoke in a voice eerily reminiscent of those of her mother and Tucker when they had stalked her as far as the mouth of the culvert last night:

" . . . need, need . . . want . . . give me . . . give me . . . need . . . "

He didn't look like her parents had looked when transformed. Why wouldn't all the aliens look the same?

He opened his mouth wide and hissed at her, and thick yellowish saliva was strung like threads of taffy from his upper to his lower teeth. Something stirred inside his mouth, a strange-looking tongue; it thrust out at her like a jack-in-the-box popping forth on its spring, and it proved to be a mouth *within* his mouth, another set of smaller and even sharper teeth on a stalk, designed to get into tight places and bite prey that took refuge there.

Father Castelli was becoming something startlingly familiar: the creature from the movie *Alien*. Not exactly that monster in every detail but uncannily similar to it.

She was trapped in a movie, just as the priest had said, a real-life horror flick: no doubt one of his favorites. Was Father Castelli able to assume whatever shape he wanted, and was he becoming this beast only because it pleased him to do so and because it would best fulfill Chrissie's expectations of alien invaders?

This was crazy.

Beneath his clothes, the priest's body was changing too. His shirt sagged on him in some places, as if the substance of him had melted away beneath it, but in other places it strained at the seams as his body acquired new bony extrusions and inhuman excrescences. Shirt buttons popped. Fabric tore. His Roman collar came apart and fell askew on his hideously resculpted neck.

Gasping, making a curious *uh-uh-uh-uh-uh* sound in the back of her throat but unable to stop, she tried to pull free of him. She stood up, knocking her chair over, but she was still held fast. He was very strong. She could not tear loose.

His hands also had begun to change. His fingers had lengthened. They were plated with a hornlike substance—smooth, hard, and shiny black—more like pincers with digits than like human hands.

"... need ... want, want ... need ..."

She plucked up her breakfast knife, swung it high over her head, and drove it down with all her might, stabbing him in the forearm, just above the wrist, where his flesh still looked more human than not. She had hoped that the blade would pin him to the table, but she didn't feel it bite all the way through him to the wood beneath.

His shriek was so shrill and piercing that it seemed to vibrate through Chrissie's bones.

His armored, demonic hand spasmed open. She yanked free of him. Fortunately she was quick, for his hand clamped shut again a fraction of a second later, pinching her fingertips but unable to hold her.

The kitchen door was on the priest's side of the table. She could not reach it without exposing her back to him.

With a cry that was half scream and half roar, he tore the knife from his arm and threw it aside. He knocked the dishes and food from the table with one sweep of his bizarrely mutated arm, which was now eight or ten inches longer than it had been. It protruded from the cuff of his black shirt in nightmarish gnarls and planes and hooks of the dark, chitinous stuff that had replaced his flesh.

Mary, Mother of God, pray for me; Mother most pure, pray for me; Mother most chaste, pray for me. *Please,* Chrissie thought.

The priest grabbed hold of the table and threw it aside, too, as if it weighed only ounces. It crashed into the refrigerator.

Now nothing separated her from him.

From *it*.

She feinted toward the kitchen door, taking a couple of steps in that direction.

The priest—not really a priest any more; a *thing* that sometimes masqueraded as a priest—swung to his right, intending to cut her off and snare her.

Immediately she turned, as she'd always intended, and ran in the opposite direction, toward the open door that led to the downstairs hall, leaping over scattered toast and links of sausage. The trick worked. Wet shoes squishing and squeaking on the linoleum, she was past him before he realized she actually was going to his left.

She suspected that he was quick as well as strong. Quicker than she, no doubt. She could hear him coming behind her.

If she could only reach the front door, get out onto the porch and into the yard, she would probably be safe. She suspected that he would not follow her beyond the house, into the street, where others might see him. Surely not everyone in Moonlight Cove had already been possessed by these aliens, and until the last real person in town was taken over, they could not strut around in a transformed state, eating young girls with impunity.

Not far. Just the front door and a few steps beyond.

She had covered two-thirds of the distance, expecting to feel a claw snag her shirt from behind, when the door opened ahead of her. The other priest, Father O'Brien, stepped across the threshold and blinked in surprise.

At once she knew that she couldn't trust him, either. He could not have lived in the same house as Father Castelli without the alien seed having been planted in him. Seed, spoor, slimy parasite, spirit—whatever was used to effect possession, Father O'Brien undoubtedly had had it rammed or injected into him.

Unable to go forward or back, unwilling to swerve through the archway on her right and into the living room because that was a dead end—in every sense of the word—she grabbed hold of the newel post, which she was just passing, and swung herself onto the stairs. She ran pell-mell for the second floor.

The front door slammed below her.

By the time she turned at the landing and started up the second flight of stairs, she heard both of them climbing behind her.

The upper hall had white plaster walls, a dark wood floor, and a wood ceiling. Rooms lay on both sides.

She sprinted to the end of the hall and into a bedroom furnished only with a simple dresser, one nightstand, a double bed with a white chenille spread, a bookcase full of paperbacks, and a crucifix on the wall. She threw the door shut after her but didn't bother trying to lock or brace it. There was no time. They'd smash through it in seconds, anyway.

Repeating, ''MarymotherofGod, MarymotherofGod,'' in a breathless and desperate whisper, she rushed across the room to the window that was framed by emerald-green drapes. Rain washed down the glass.

Her pursuers were in the upstairs hall. Their footsteps boomed through the house.

She grabbed the handles on the sash and tried to pull the window up. It would not budge. She fumbled with the latch, but it already was disengaged.

Farther back the hall toward the head of the stairs, they were throwing open doors, looking for her.

The window was either painted shut or perhaps swollen tight because of the high humidity. She stepped back from it.

The door behind her crashed inward, and something snarled.

Without glancing behind her, she tucked her head down and crossed her arms over her face and threw herself through the window, wondering if she could kill herself by jumping from the second story, figuring it depended where she landed. Grass would be good. Sidewalk would be bad. The pointed spires of a wrought-iron fence would be *real* bad.

The sound of shattering glass was still in the air when she hit a porch roof two feet below the window, which was virtually a miracle—she was uncut too—so she kept saying *MarymotherofGod* as she did a controlled roll through hammering rain toward the edge of the shingled expanse. When she reached the brink, she clung there for a moment, her left side on the roof, right side supported by a creaking and rapidly sagging rain gutter, and she looked back at the window.

Something wolfish and grotesque was coming after her.

She dropped. She landed on a walkway, on her left side, jarring her bones, clacking her teeth together so hard that she feared they'd fall out in pieces, and scraping one hand badly on the concrete.

But she didn't lie there pitying herself. She scrambled up and, huddled around her pain, turned from the house to run into the street.

Unfortunately she wasn't in front of the rectory. She was behind it, in the rear yard. The back wall of Our Lady of Mercy bordered the lawn on her right, and a seven-foot-high brick wall encircled the rest of the property.

Because of the wall and the trees on both sides of it, she could not see either the neighboring house to the south or the one to the west, on the other side of the alley that ran behind the property. If she couldn't see the rectory's neighbors, they couldn't see her, either, even if they happened to be looking out a window.

That privacy explained why the wolf-thing dared to come onto the roof, pursuing her in broad—if rather gray and dismal—daylight.

She briefly considered going into the house, through the kitchen, down the hall, out the front door, into the street, because that was the last thing they'd expect. But then she thought: Are you *insane?*

She did not bother to scream for help. Her thudding heart seemed to have swollen until her lungs had too little room to expand, so she could barely get enough air to remain conscious, on her feet, and moving. No breath was left for a scream. Besides, even if people heard her call for help, they wouldn't necessarily be able to tell where she was; by the time they tracked her down, she would be either torn apart or possessed, because the scream would have slowed her by a fateful second or two.

Instead, limping slightly to favor a pulled muscle in her left leg but losing no time, she hurried across the expansive rear lawn. She knew she could not scale a blank seven-foot wall fast enough to save herself, especially not with one stingingly abraded hand, so she studied the trees as she ran. She needed one close to the wall; maybe she could climb into it, crawl out on a branch, and drop into the alleyway or into the neighbor's yard.

Above the slosh and patter of the rain, she heard a low growl behind her, and she dared to glance over her shoulder. Wearing only tatters of a shirt, freed entirely from shoes and trousers, the wolf-thing that had been Father O'Brien leaped from the edge of the porch roof in pursuit.

She finally saw a suitable tree—but an instant later noticed a gate in the wall at the southwest corner. She hadn't seen it sooner because it had been screened from her by some shrubbery that she had just passed.

Gasping for air, she put her head down, tucked her arms against her sides, and ran to the gate. She hit the bar latch with her hand, popping it out of the slot in which it had been cradled, and burst through into the alley. Turning left, away from Ocean Avenue toward Jacobi Street, she ran through deep puddles nearly to the end of the block before risking a glance behind her.

Nothing had followed her out of the rectory gate.

Twice she had been in the hands of the aliens, and twice she had escaped. She knew she would not be so lucky if she were captured a third time.

10

SHORTLY BEFORE NINE O'CLOCK, AFTER LESS THAN FOUR hours of sleep altogether, Sam Booker woke to the quiet clink and clatter of someone at work in the kitchen. He sat up on the living-room sofa, wiped at his matted eyes, put on his shoes and shoulder holster, and went down the hall.

Tessa Lockland was humming softly as she lined up pans, bowls, and food on the wheelchair-low counter near the stove, preparing to make breakfast.

"Good morning," she said brightly when Sam came into the kitchen.

"What's good about it?" he asked.

"Just listen to that rain," she said. "Rain always makes me feel clean and fresh."

"Always depresses me."

"And it's nice to be in a warm, dry kitchen, listening to the storm but cozy."

He scratched at the stubble of beard on his unshaven cheeks. "Seems a little stuffy in here to me."

"Well, anyway, we're still alive, and *that's* good."

"I guess so."

"God in heaven!" She banged an empty frying pan down on the stove and scowled at him. "Are all FBI agents like you?"

"In what way?"

"Are they all sourpusses?"

"I'm not a sourpuss."

"You're a classic Gloomy Gus."

"Well, life isn't a carnival."

"It isn't?"

"Life is hard and mean."

"Maybe. But isn't it a carnival too?"

"Are all documentary filmmakers like you?"

"In what way?"

"Pollyannas?"

"That's ridiculous. I'm no Pollyanna."

"Oh, no?"

"No."

"Here we are trapped in a town where reality seems to have been temporarily suspended, where people are being torn apart by species unknown, where Boogeymen roam the streets at night, where some mad computer genius seems to have turned human biology inside out, where we're all likely to be killed or 'converted' before midnight tonight, and when I come in here you're grinning and sprightly and humming a Beatles tune."

"It wasn't the Beatles."

"Huh?"

"Rolling Stones."

"And that makes a difference?"

She sighed. "Listen, if you're going to help eat this breakfast, you're going to help make it, so don't just stand there glowering."

"All right, okay, what can I do?"

"First, get on the intercom there and call Harry, make sure he's awake. Tell him breakfast in . . . ummmm . . . forty minutes. Pancakes and eggs and shaved, fried ham."

Sam pressed the intercom button and said, "Hello, Harry," and Harry answered at once, already awake. He said he'd be down in about half an hour.

"Now what?" Sam asked Tessa.

"Get the eggs and milk from the refrigerator—but for God's sake don't look in the cartons."

"Why not?"

She grinned. "You'll spoil the eggs and curdle the milk."

"Very funny."

"I thought so."

While making pancake mix from scratch, cracking six eggs into glass dishes and preparing them so they could be quickly slipped into the frying pans when she needed them, directing Sam to set the table and help her with other small chores, chopping onions, and shaving ham, Tessa alternately hummed and sang songs by Patti La Belle and the Pointer Sisters. Sam knew whose music it was because she told him, announcing each song as if she were a disc jockey or as if she hoped to educate him and loosen him up. While she worked and sang, she danced in place, shaking her bottom, swiveling her hips, rolling her shoulders, sometimes snapping her fingers, really getting into it.

She was genuinely enjoying herself, but he knew that she was also needling him a little and getting a kick out of that too. He tried to hold fast to his gloom, and when she smiled at him, he did not return her smile, but *damn* she was cute. Her hair was tousled, and she wasn't wearing any makeup, and her clothes were wrinkled from having been slept in, but her slightly disheveled look only added to her allure.

Sometimes she paused in her soft singing and humming to ask him questions, but she continued to sing and dance in place even while he answered her. "You figured what we're going to do yet to get out of this corner we're in?"

"I have an idea."

"Patti La Belle, 'New Attitude,' " she said, identifying the song she was singing. "Is this idea of yours a deep, dark secret?"

"No. But I have to go over it with Harry, get some information from him, so I'll tell you both at breakfast."

At her direction he was hunched over the low counter, cutting thin slices of cheese from a block of Cheddar when she broke into her song long enough to ask, "Why did you say life is hard and mean?"

"Because it is."

"But it's also full of fun—"

"No."

"—and beauty—"

"No."

"—and hope—"

"Bullshit."

"It is."

"It isn't."

"Yes, it is."

"It isn't."

"Why are you so negative?"

"Because I want to be."

"But why do you want to be?"

"Jesus, you're relentless."

"Pointer Sisters, 'Neutron Dance.' " She sang a bit, dancing in place as she put eggshells and other scraps down the garbage disposal. Then she interrupted her tune to say, "What could've happened to you to make you feel that life's only mean and hard?"

"You don't want to know."

"Yes, I do."

He finished with the cheese and put down the slicer. "You really want to know?"

"I really do."

"My mother was killed in a traffic accident when I was just seven. I was in the car with her, nearly died, was actually trapped in the wreckage with her for more than an hour, face to face, staring into her eyeless socket, one whole side of her head bashed in. After that I had to go live with my dad, whom she'd divorced, and he was a mean-tempered son of a bitch, an alcoholic, and I can't tell you how many times he beat me or threatened to beat me or tied me to a chair in the kitchen and left me there for hours at a time, until I couldn't hold myself any more and peed in my pants, and then he'd finally come to untie me and he'd see what I'd done and he'd beat me for *that*."

He was surprised by how it all spilled from him, as if the floodgates of his subconscious had been opened, pouring forth all the sludge that had been pent up through long years of stoic self-control.

"So as soon as I graduated from high school, I got out of that house, worked my way through junior college, living in cheap rented rooms, shared my bed with armies of cockroaches every night, then applied to the Bureau as soon as I could, because I wanted to see justice in the world, be a part of *bringing* justice to the world, maybe because there'd been so little fairness or justice in my life. But I discovered that more than half the time justice doesn't triumph. The bad guys get away with it, no matter how hard you work to bring them down, because the bad guys are often pretty damned clever, and the good guys never allow themselves to be as mean as they have to be to get the job done. But at the same time, when you're an agent, mainly what you see is the sick underbelly of society, you deal with the scum, one kind of scum or another, and day by day it makes you more cynical, more disgusted with people and sick of them."

He was talking so fast that he was almost breathless.

She had stopped singing.

He continued with an uncharacteristic lack of emotional control, speaking so fast that his sentences sometimes ran together: "And my wife died, Karen, she was wonderful, you'd have liked her, everybody liked her, but she got cancer and she died, painfully, horribly, with a lot of suffering, not easy like Ali McGraw in the movies, not with just a sigh and a smile and a quiet goodbye, but in agony. And then I lost my son too. Oh, he's alive, sixteen, nine when his mother died and sixteen now, physically alive and mentally alive, but he's emotionally dead, burnt out in his heart, cold inside, so damned cold inside. He likes computers and computer games and television, and he listens to black metal. You know what black metal is? It's heavy-metal music with a twist of satanism, which he likes because it tells him there are no moral values, that everything is relative, that his alienation is right, that his coldness inside is *right*, it tells him that whatever feels good *is* good. You know what he said once?"

She shook her head.

"He said to me, 'People aren't important. People don't count. Only *things* are important. Money is important, liquor is important, my stereo is important, anything that makes me *feel* good is important, but I'm not important.' He tells me that nuclear bombs are important because they'll blow up all those nice things some day, not because they'll blow up people—after all, people are nothing, just polluting animals that spoil the world. That's what he says. That's what he tells me he believes. He says he can prove it's all true. He says that next time you see a bunch of people standing around a Porsche, admiring the car, look real hard at their faces and you'll see that they care more about that car than about each other. They're not admiring the workmanship, either, not in the sense that they're thinking about the people who *made* the car. It's as if the Porsche was organic, as if it grew or somehow made itself. They admire it for itself, not for what it represents of human engineering skills and craftsmanship. The car is more *alive* than they are. They draw energy from the car, from the sleek lines of it, from the thrill of imagining its power under their hands, so the car becomes more real and far more important than any of the people admiring it."

"That's bullshit," Tessa said with conviction.

"But that's what he tells me, and I know it's crap, and I try to reason with him, but he's got all the answers—or thinks he has. And sometimes I wonder . . . if I wasn't so soured on life myself, so sick of so many people, would I be able to argue with him more persuasively? If I wasn't who I am, would I be more able to save my son?"

He stopped.

He realized he was trembling.

They were both silent for a moment.

Then he said, "*That's* why I say life is hard and mean."

"I'm sorry, Sam."

"Not your fault."

"Not yours either."

He sealed the Cheddar in a piece of Saran Wrap and returned it to the refrigerator while she returned to the pancake mix she was making.

"But you had Karen," she said. "There's been love and beauty in your life."

"Sure."

"Well, then—"

"But it doesn't last."

"Nothing lasts forever."

"Exactly my point," he said.

"But that doesn't mean we can't enjoy a blessing while we have it. If you're always looking ahead, wondering when this moment of joy is going to end, you can never know any real pleasure in life."

"Exactly my point," he repeated.

She left the wooden mixing spoon in the big metal bowl and turned to face him. "But that's *wrong*. I mean, life is filled with moments of wonder, pleasure, joy . . . and if we don't seize the moment, if we don't sometimes turn off thoughts of the future and relish the moment, then we'll have no memory of joy to carry us through the bad times—and no hope."

He stared at her, admiring her beauty and vitality. But then he began to think about how she would age, grow infirm, and die just as everything died, and he could no longer bear to look at her. Instead he turned his gaze to the rain-washed window above the sink. "Well, I'm sorry if I've upset you, but you'll have to admit you asked for it. You insisted on knowing how I could be such a Gloomy Gus."

"Oh, you're no Gloomy Gus," she said. "You go way beyond that. You're a regular Dr. Doom."

He shrugged.

They returned to their culinary labors.

11

AFTER ESCAPING THROUGH THE GATE AT THE REAR OF THE REC-tory yard, Chrissie stayed on the move for more than an hour while she tried to decide what to do next. She had planned to go to school and tell her story to Mrs. Tokawa if Father Castelli proved unhelpful. But now she was no longer willing to trust even Mrs. Tokawa. After her experience with the priests, she realized the aliens would probably have taken possession of all the authority figures in Moon-light Cove as a first step toward conquest. She already knew the priests were possessed. She was certain that the police had been taken over as well, so it was logical to assume that teachers also had been among the early victims.

As she moved from neighborhood to neighborhood, she alternately cursed the rain and was grateful for it. Her shoes and jeans and flannel shirt were sodden again, and she was chilled through and through. But the darkish-gray daylight and the rain kept people indoors and provided her with some cover. In addition, as the wind subsided, a thin cold fog drifted in from the sea, not a fraction as dense as it had been last night, just a beardlike mist that clung to the trees, but enough to further obscure the passage of one small girl through those unfriendly streets.

Last night's thunder and lightning were gone too. She was no longer in danger of being flash-roasted by a sudden bolt, which was at least some comfort.

YOUNG GIRL FRIED TO A CRISP BY LIGHTNING THEN EATEN BY ALIENS; SPACE CREATURES

ENJOY HUMAN POTATO CHIPS; "IF WE CAN MAKE THEM WITH RUFFLES," SAYS ALIEN NEST QUEEN, "THEY'LL BE PERFECT WITH ONION DIP."

She moved as much as possible through alleyways and backyards, crossing streets only when necessary and always quickly, for out there she saw too many pairs of somber-faced, sharp-eyed men in slow-moving cars, obvious patrols. Twice she almost ran into them in alleys, too, and had to dive for cover before they spotted her. About a quarter of an hour after she fled through the rectory gate, she noticed more patrols in the area, a sudden influx of cars and men on foot. Foot patrols scared her the most. Pairs of men in rain slickers were better able to conduct a search and were more difficult to escape from than men in cars. She was terrified of walking into them unexpectedly.

Actually she spent more time in hiding than on the move. Once she huddled for a while behind a cluster of garbage cans in an alley. She took refuge under a brewer's spruce, the lower branches of which nearly touched the ground, like a skirt, providing a dark and mostly dry retreat. Twice she crawled under cars and lay for a while.

She never stayed in one place for more than five or ten minutes. She was afraid that some alien-possessed busybody would see her as she crawled into her hiding place and would call the police to report her, and that she would be trapped.

By the time she reached the vacant lot on Juniper Lane, beside Callan's Funeral Home, and curled up in the deepest brush—dry grass and bristly chaparral—she was beginning to wonder if she would ever think of someone to turn to for help. For the first time since her ordeal had begun, she was losing hope.

A huge fir spread its branches across part of the lot, and her clump of brush was within its domain, so she was sheltered from the worst of the rain. More important, in the deep grass, curled on her side, she could not be seen from the street or from the windows of nearby houses.

Nevertheless, every minute or so, she cautiously raised her head far enough to look quickly around, to be sure that no one was creeping up on her. During that reconnoitering, looking east past the alleyway at the back of the lot, toward Conquistador, she saw a part of the big redwood-and-glass house on the east side of that street. The Talbot place. At once she remembered the man in the wheelchair.

He had come to Thomas Jefferson to speak to the fifth- and sixth-grade students last year, during Awareness Days, a week-long program of studies that was for the most part wasted time, though *he* had been interesting. He had talked to them about the difficulties and the amazing abilities of disabled people.

At first Chrissie had felt so sorry for him, had just pitied him half to death, because he'd looked so pathetic, sitting there in his wheelchair, his body half wasted away, able to use only one hand, his head slightly twisted and tilted permanently to one side. But then as she listened to him she realized that he had a wonderful sense of humor and did not feel sorry for himself, so it seemed more and more absurd to pity him. They had an opportunity to ask him questions, and he had been so willing to discuss the intimate details of his life, the sorrows and joys of it, that she had finally come to admire him a whole lot.

And his dog Moose had been terrific.

Now, looking at the redwood-and-glass house through the tips of the rain-shiny stalks of high grass, thinking about Harry Talbot and Moose, Chrissie wondered if *that* was a place she could go for help.

She dropped back down in the brush and thought about it for a couple of minutes.

Surely a wheelchair-bound cripple was one of the last people the aliens would bother to possess—if they wanted him at all.

She immediately was ashamed of herself for thinking such a thing. A wheelchair-bound cripple was not a second-class human being. He had just as much to offer the aliens as anyone else.

On the other hand . . . would a bunch of aliens have an enlightened view of disabled people? Wasn't that a bit much to expect? After all, they were *aliens*. Their values weren't supposed to be the same as those of human beings. If they went around planting seeds—or spoors or slimy baby slugs or whatever—in people, and if they ate people, surely they couldn't be expected to treat disabled people with the proper respect any more than they would help old ladies to cross the street.

Harry Talbot.

The more she thought about him, the more certain Chrissie became that he had thus far been spared the horrible attention of the aliens.

12

AFTER SHE CALLED HIM DR. DOOM, HE SPRAYED THE JENN-AIR griddle with Pam, so the pancakes wouldn't stick.

She turned on the oven and put a plate in there, to which she could transfer the cakes to keep them warm as she made them.

Then, in a tone of voice that immediately clued him to the fact that she was bent on persuading him to reconsider his bleak assessment of life, she said, "Tell me—"

"Can't you leave it alone *yet?*"

"No."

He sighed.

She said, "If you're this damned glum, why not . . . "

"Kill myself?"

"Why not?"

He laughed bitterly. "On the drive up here from San Francisco, I played a little game with myself—counted the reasons that life was worth living. I came up with just four, but I guess they're enough, because I'm still hanging around."

"What were they?"

"One—good Mexican food."

"I'll go along with that."

"Two—Guinness Stout."

"I like Heineken Dark myself."

"It's okay, but it's not a reason to live. *Guinness* is a reason to live."

"What's number three?"

"Goldie Hawn."

"You know Goldie Hawn?"

"Nope. Maybe I don't want to, 'cause maybe I'd be disappointed. I'm talking about her screen image, the idealized Goldie Hawn."

"She's your dream girl, huh?"

"More than that. She . . . hell, I don't know . . . she seems untouched by life, undamaged, vital and happy and innocent and . . . *fun*."

"Think you'll ever meet her?"

"You've got to be kidding."

She said, "You know what?"

"What?"

"If you *did* meet Goldie Hawn, if she walked up to you at a party and said something funny, something cute, and giggled in that way she has, you wouldn't even recognize her."

"Oh, I'd recognize her, all right."

"No, you wouldn't. You'd be so busy brooding about how unfair, unjust, hard, cruel, bleak, dismal, and stupid life is that you would not seize the moment. You wouldn't even *recognize* the moment. You'd be too shrouded in a haze of gloom to see who she was. Now, what's your fourth reason for living?"

He hesitated. "Fear of death."

She blinked at him. "I don't understand. If life's so awful, why is death to be feared?"

"I underwent a near-death experience. I was in surgery, having a bullet taken out of my chest, and I almost bought the farm. Rose out of my body, drifted up to the ceiling, watched the surgeons for a while, then found myself rushing faster and faster down a dark tunnel toward this dazzling light—the whole screwy scenario."

She was impressed and intrigued. Her clear blue eyes were wide with interest. "And?"

"I saw what lies beyond."

"You're serious, aren't you?"

"Damned serious."

"You're telling me that you *know* there's an afterlife?"

"Yes."

"A God?"

"Yes."

Astonished, she said, "But if you *know* there's a God and that we move on from this world, then you know life has purpose, meaning."

"So?"

"Well, it's doubt about the purpose of life that lies at the root of most people's spells of gloom and depression. Most of us, if we'd experienced what you'd experienced . . . well, we'd never worry again. We'd have the strength to deal with any adversity, knowing there was meaning to it and a life beyond. So what's wrong with you, mister? Why didn't you lighten up after that? Are you just a bullheaded dweeb or what?"

"Dweeb?"

"Answer the question."

The elevator kicked in and ascended from the first-floor hall.

"Harry's coming," Sam said.

"Answer the question," she repeated.

"Let's just say that what I saw didn't give me hope. It scared the hell out of me."

"Well? Don't keep me hanging. What'd you see on the Other Side?"

"If I tell you, you'll think I'm crazy."

"You've got nothing to lose. I already think you're crazy."

He sighed and shook his head and wished that he'd never brought it up. How had she gotten him to open himself so completely?

The elevator reached the third floor and halted.

Tessa stepped away from the kitchen counter, moving closer to him, and said, "Tell me what you saw, dammit."

"You won't understand."

"What am I—a moron?"

"Oh, you'd understand what I saw, but you wouldn't understand what it meant to me."

"Do *you* understand what it meant to you?"

"Oh, yes," he said solemnly.

"Are you going to tell me willingly, or do I have to take a meat fork from that rack and torture it out of you?"

The elevator had started down from the third floor.

He glanced toward the hall. "I really don't want to discuss it."

"You don't, huh?"

"No."

"You saw God but you don't want to discuss it."

"That's right."

"Most guys who see God—that's the *only* thing they ever want to discuss. Most guys who see God—they form whole religions based on the one meeting with Him, and they tell *millions* of people about it."

"But I—"

"Fact is, according to what I've read, most people who undergo a near-death experience are changed forever by it. And always for the better. If they were pessimists, they become optimists. If they were atheists, they become believers. Their values change, they learn to love life for itself, they're goddamned *radiant*! But not you. Oh, no, you become even more dour, even more grim, even more bleak."

The elevator reached the ground floor and fell silent.

"Harry's coming," Sam said.

"Tell me what you saw."

"Maybe I can tell *you*," he said, surprised to find that he was actually willing to discuss it with her at the right time, in the right place. "Maybe you. But later."

Moose padded into the kitchen, panting and grinning at them, and Harry rolled through the doorway a moment later.

"Good morning," Harry said chipperly.

"Did you sleep well?" Tessa asked, favoring him with a genuine smile of affection that Sam envied.

Harry said, "Soundly, but not as soundly as the dead—thank God."

"Pancakes?" Tessa asked him.

"Stacks, please."

"Eggs?"

"Dozens."

"Toast?"

"Loaves."

"I like a man with an appetite."

Harry said, "I was running all night, so I'm famished."

"Running?"

"In my dreams. Chased by Boogeymen."

While Harry got a package of dog food from under one of the counters and filled Moose's dish in the corner, Tessa went to the griddle, sprayed it with Pam again, told Sam that he was in charge of the eggs, and started to ladle out the first of the pancakes from the bowl of batter. After a moment she said, "Patti La Belle, 'Stir It Up,' " and began to sing and dance in place again.

"Hey," Harry said, "I can give you music if you want music."

He rolled to a compact under-the-counter-mounted radio that neither Tessa nor Sam had noticed, clicked it on, and moved the tuner across the dial until he came to a station playing "I Heard It Through the Grapevine" by Gladys Knight and the Pips.

"All *right*," Tessa said, and she began to sway and pump and grind with such enthusiasm that Sam couldn't figure out how she poured the pancake batter onto the griddle in such neat puddles.

Harry laughed and turned his motorized wheelchair in circles, as if dancing with her.

Sam said, "Don't you people know that the world is coming to an end around us?"

They ignored him, which he supposed was what he deserved.

13

BY A ROUNDABOUT ROUTE, CLOAKING HERSELF IN THE RAIN and mist and whatever shadows she could find, Chrissie reached the alley to the east of Conquistador. She entered Talbot's backyard through a gate in a redwood fence and scurried from one clump of shrubbery to another, twice nearly stepping in dog poop—Moose was an amazing dog, but not without faults—until she reached the steps to the back porch.

She heard music playing inside. It was an oldie, from the days when her parents had been teenagers. And in fact it had been one of their favorites. Though Chrissie didn't remember the title, she did recall the name of the group—Junior Walker and the All-Stars.

Figuring that the music, combined with the drumming rain, would cover any sounds she made, she crept up the steps onto the redwood porch and, in a crouch, moved to the nearest window. She hunkered below the sill for a while, listening to them in there. They were talking, often laughing, sometimes singing along with the songs on the radio.

They didn't sound like aliens. They sounded pretty much like ordinary people.

Were aliens likely to enjoy the music of Stevie Wonder and the Four Tops and the Pointer Sisters? Hardly. To human ears, alien music probably sounded like knights in armor playing bagpipes while simultaneously falling down a long set of stairs amidst a pack of baying hounds. More like Twisted Sister than like the Pointer Sisters.

Eventually she rose up just far enough to peer over the sill, through a gap in the curtains. She saw Mr. Talbot in his wheelchair, Moose, and a strange man and woman. Mr. Talbot was beating time with his good hand on the arm of his wheelchair, and Moose was wagging his tail vigorously if out of synch with the music. The other man was using a spatula to scoop eggs out of a couple of frying pans and shift them onto plates, glowering at the woman now and then as he did so, maybe not approving of the way she abandoned herself to the song, but still tapping his right foot to the music. The woman was making flapjacks and transferring them to a warming platter in the oven, and as she worked she shimmied and swayed and dipped; she had good moves.

Chrissie crouched down again and thought about what she had seen. Nothing about their behavior was particularly odd if they were people, but if they were aliens they surely wouldn't be bopping to the radio while they made breakfast. Chrissie had a real hard time believing that aliens—like the thing masquerading as Father Castelli—could have either a sense of humor or rhythm. Surely, all that aliens cared about was taking possession of new hosts and finding new recipes for cooking tender children.

Nevertheless she decided to wait until she had a chance to watch them eating. From what she'd heard her mother and Tucker say in the meadow last night, and from what she had seen at breakfast with the Father Castelli creature, she believed that aliens were ravenous, each with the appetite of half a dozen men. If Harry Talbot and his guests didn't make absolute hogs of themselves when they sat down to eat, she could probably trust them.

14

LOMAN HAD STAYED AT PEYSER'S HOUSE, SUPERVISING THE cleanup and overseeing the transfer of the regressives' bodies to Callan's hearse. He was afraid to let his men handle it alone, for fear that the sight of the mutated bodies or the smell of blood would induce them to seek altered states of their own. He knew that all of them—not least of all himself—were walking a taut wire over an abyss. For the same reason, he followed the hearse to the funeral home and stayed with Callan and his assistant until Peyser's and Sholnick's bodies were fed into the white-hot flames of the crematorium.

He checked on the progress of the search for Booker, the Lockland woman, and Chrissie Foster, and he made a few changes in the pattern of the patrols. He was in the office when the report came in from Castelli, and he went directly to the rectory at Our Lady of Mercy to hear firsthand how the girl could have slipped away from them. They were full of excuses, mostly lame. He suspected they had regressed in order to toy with the girl, just for the thrill of it, and while playing with her had unintentionally given her a chance to escape. Of course they would not admit to regression.

Loman increased the patrols in the immediate area, but there was no sign of the girl. She had gone to ground. Still, if she had come into town instead of heading out to the freeway, they were more likely to catch her and convert her before the day was done.

At nine o'clock he returned to his house on Iceberry Way to get breakfast. Since he'd nearly degenerated in Peyser's blood-spattered bedroom, his clothes had felt loose on him. He had lost a few pounds as his catabolic processes had consumed his own flesh to generate the tremendous energy needed to regress—and to *resist* regression.

The house was dark and silent. Denny was no doubt upstairs, in front of his computer, where he had been last night. Grace had left for work at Thomas Jefferson, where she was a teacher; she had to keep up the pretense of an ordinary life until everyone in Moonlight Cove had been converted.

At the moment no children under twelve had been put through the Change, partly because of difficulties New Wave technicians had had in determining the correct dosage for younger converts. Those problems had been solved, and tonight the kids would be brought into the fold.

In the kitchen Loman stood for a moment, listening to the rain on the windows and the ticking of the clock.

At the sink he drew a glass of water. He drank it, another, then two more. He was dehydrated after the ordeal at Peyser's.

The refrigerator was chock full of five-pound hams, roast beef, a half-eaten turkey, a plate of porkchops, chicken breasts, sausages, and packages of bologna and dried beef. The accelerated metabolisms of the New People required a diet high in protein. Besides, they had a craving for meat.

He took a loaf of pumpernickel from the breadbox and sat down with that, the roast beef, the ham, and a jar of mustard. He stayed at the table for a while, cutting or ripping thick hunks of meat, wrapping them in mustard-slathered bread, and tearing off large bites with his teeth. Food offered him less subtle pleasure than when he'd been an Old Person; now the smell and taste of it raised in him an animal excitement, a thrill of greed and gluttony. He was to some degree repelled by the way he tore at his food and swallowed before he'd finished chewing it properly, but every effort that he made to restrain himself soon gave way to even more feverish consumption. He slipped into a half-trance, hypnotized by the rhythm of chewing and swallowing. At one point he became clearheaded enough to realize he had gotten the chicken breasts from the refrigerator and was eating them with enthusiasm, though they were uncooked. He let himself slip mercifully back into the half-trance again.

Finished eating, he went upstairs to look in on Denny.

When he opened the door to the boy's room, everything at first seemed to be just as it had been the last time he'd seen it, during the previous night. The shades were lowered, the curtains drawn, the room dark except for the greenish light from the VDT. Denny sat in front of the computer, engrossed in the data that flickered across the screen.

Then Loman saw something that made his skin prickle.

He closed his eyes.

Waited.

Opened them.

It was not an illusion.

He felt sick. He wanted to step back into the hall and close the door, forget what he'd seen, go away. But he could not move and could not avert his eyes.

Denny had unplugged the computer keyboard and put it on the floor beside his chair. He'd unscrewed the front cover plate from the data-processing unit. His hands were in his lap, but they weren't exactly hands any more. His fingers were wildly elongated, tapering not to points and fingernails but to metallic-looking wires, as thick as lamp cords, that snaked into the guts of the computer, vanishing there.

Denny no longer needed the keyboard.

He had become part of the system. Through the computer and its modem link to New Wave, Denny had become one with Sun.

"Denny?"

He had assumed an altered state, but nothing like that sought by the regressives.

"Denny?"

The boy did not answer.

"Denny!"

An odd, soft clicking and electronic pulsing sounds came from the computer.

Reluctantly, Loman entered the room and walked to the desk. He looked down at his son and shuddered.

Denny's mouth hung open. Saliva drooled down his chin. He had become so enraptured by his contact with the computer that he had not bothered to get up and eat or go to the bathroom; he had urinated in his pants.

His eyes were gone. In their place were what appeared to be twin spheres of molten silver as shiny as mirrors. They reflected the data that swarmed across the screen in front of them.

The pulsing sounds, soft electronic oscillations, were not coming from the computer but from Denny.

15

THE EGGS WERE GOOD, THE PANCAKES WERE BETTER, AND the coffee was strong enough to endanger the porcelain finish of the cups but not so strong that it had to be chewed. As they ate, Sam outlined the method he had devised for getting a message out of town to the Bureau.

"Your phone's still dead, Harry. I tried it this morning. And I don't think we can risk heading out to the interstate on foot or by car, not with the patrols and roadblocks they've established; that'll have to be a last resort. After all, as far as we know, we're the only people who realize that something truly . . . twisted is happening here and that the need to stop it is urgent. Us and maybe the Foster girl, the one the cops talked about in their VDT conversation last night."

"If she's literally a girl," Tessa said, "just a child, even if she's a teenager, she won't have much of a chance against them. We've got to figure they'll catch her if they haven't already."

Sam nodded. "And if they nail us, too, while we're trying to get out of town, there'll be no one left to do the job. So first we've got to try a low-risk course of action."

"Is *any* option low risk?" Harry wondered as he mopped up some egg yolk with a piece of toast, eating slowly and with a touching precision necessitated by his having only one useful hand.

Pouring a little more maple syrup over his pancakes, surprised by how much he was eating, attributing his appetite to the possibility that this was his last meal, Sam said, "See . . . this is a wired town."

"Wired?"

"Computer-linked. New Wave gave computers to the police, so they'd be tied into the web—"

"And the schools," Harry said. "I remember reading about it in the paper last spring or early summer. They gave a lot of computers and software to both the elementary and the high schools. A gesture of civic involvement, they called it."

"Seems more ominous than that now, doesn't it?" Tessa said.

"Sure as hell does."

Tessa said, "Seems now like maybe they wanted their computers in the schools for the same reason they wanted the cops computerized—to tie them all in tightly with New Wave, to monitor and control."

Sam put down his fork. "New Wave employs, what, about a third of the people in town?"

"Probably that," Harry said. "Moonlight Cove really grew after New Wave moved in ten years ago. In some ways it's an old-fashioned company town—life here isn't just dependent upon the main employer but pretty much socially centered around it too."

After sipping some coffee so strong it was nearly as bracing as brandy, Sam said, "A third of the people . . . which works out to maybe forty percent or so of the adults."

Harry said, "I guess so."

"And you've got to figure everyone at New Wave is part of the conspiracy, that they were among the first to be . . . converted."

Tessa nodded. "I'd say that's a given."

"And they're even more than usually interested in computers, of course, because they're working in that industry, so it's a good bet most or all of them have computers in their homes."

Harry agreed.

"And no doubt many if not all of their home computers can be tied by modem directly to New Wave, so they can work at home in the evening or on weekends if they have to. And now, with this conversion scheme nearing a conclusion, I'll bet they're working round the clock; data must be flying back and forth over their phone lines half the night. If Harry can tell me of someone within a block of here who works for New Wave—"

"There're several," Harry said.

"—then I could slip out in the rain, try their house, see if anyone's home. At this hour they'll probably be at work. If no one's there, maybe I can get a call out on their phone."

"Wait, wait," Tessa said. "What's all this about phones? The phones don't work."

Sam shook his head. "All we know is that the public phones are out of service, as is Harry's. But remember: New Wave controls the telephone-company computer, so they can probably be selective about what lines they shut down. I'll bet they haven't cut off the service of those who've already undergone this . . . conversion. They wouldn't deny *themselves* communication. Especially not now, in a crisis, and with this scheme of theirs nearly accomplished. There's a better than fifty-percent chance that the only lines they've shut down are the ones they figure we might get to—pay phones, phones in public places—like the motel—and the phones in the homes of people who haven't yet been converted."

16

FEAR PERMEATED LOMAN WATKINS, SATURATED HIM SO completely that if it had possessed substance, it could have been wrung from his flesh in quantities to rival the rivers currently pouring forth from the storm-racked sky outside. He was afraid for himself, for what he might yet become. He was afraid for his son, too, who sat at the computer in an utterly alien guise. And he was also afraid *of* his son, no use denying that, scared half to death of him and unable to touch him.

A flood of data coruscated across the screen in blurred green waves. Denny's glistening, liquid, silvery eyes—like puddles of mercury in his sockets—reflected the luminescent tides of letters, numbers, graphs, and charts. Unblinkingly.

Loman remembered what Shaddack had said at Peyser's house when he had seen that the man had regressed to a lupine form that could not have been a part of human genetic history. Regression was not merely—or even primarily—a physical process. It was an example of mind over matter, of consciousness dictating form. Because they could no longer be ordinary people, and because they simply could not tolerate life as emotionless New People, they were seeking altered states in which existence was more endurable. And the boy had sought *this* state, had willed himself to become this grotesque thing.

"Denny?"

No response.

The boy had fallen entirely silent. Not even electronic noises issued from him any longer.

The metallic cords, in which the boy's fingers ended, vibrated continuously and sometimes throbbed as if irregular pulses of thick, inhuman blood were passing through them, cycling between organic and inorganic portions of the mechanism.

Loman's heart was pounding as fast as his running footsteps would have been if he could have fled. But he was held there by the weight of his fear. He had broken out in a sweat. He struggled to keep from throwing up the enormous meal he had just eaten.

Desperately he considered what he must do, and the first thing that occurred to him was to call Shaddack and seek his help. Surely Shaddack would understand what was happening and would know how to reverse this hideous metamorphosis and restore Denny to human form.

But that was wishful thinking. The Moonhawk Project was now out of control, following dark routes down into midnight horrors that Tom Shaddack had never foreseen and could not avert.

Besides, Shaddack would not be frightened by what was happening to Denny. He would be delighted, exuberant. Shaddack would view the boy's transformation as an *elevated* altered state, as much to be desired as the degeneration of the regressives was to be avoided and scorned. Here was what Shaddack truly sought, the forced evolution of man into machine.

In memory even now, Loman could hear Shaddack talking agitatedly in Peyser's blood-spattered bedroom: *". . . what I don't understand is why the regressives have all chosen a subhuman condition. Surely you have the power within you to undergo evolution rather than devolution, to lift yourself up from mere humanity to something higher, cleaner, purer . . . "*

Loman was certain that Denny's drooling, silver-eyed incarnation was not a higher form than ordinary human existence, neither cleaner nor purer. In its way it was as much a degeneration as Mike Peyser's regression to a lupine shape or Coombs's descent into apelike primitiveness. Like Peyser, Denny had surrendered intellectual individuality to escape awareness of the emotionless life of a New Person; instead of becoming just one of a pack of subhuman beasts, he had become one of many data-processing units in a complex supercomputer network. He had relinquished the last of what was human in him—his mind—and had become something simpler than a gloriously complex human being.

A bead of drool fell from Denny's chin, leaving a wet circle on his denim-clad thigh.

Do you know fear now? Loman wondered. You can't love. Not any more than I can. But do you fear anything now?

Surely not. Machines could not feel terror.

Though Loman's conversion had left him unable to experience any emotion but fear, and though his days and nights had become one long ordeal of anxiety of varying intensity, he had in a perverse way come to love fear, to cherish it, for it was the only feeling that kept him in touch with the unconverted man he had once been. If his fear were taken from him, too, he would be only a machine of flesh. His life would have no human dimension whatsoever.

Denny had surrendered that last precious emotion. All he had left to fill his gray days were logic, reason, endless chains of calculations, the never-ending absorption and interpolation of facts. And if Shaddack was correct about the longevity of the New People, those days would mount into centuries.

Suddenly eerie electronic noises came from the boy again. They echoed off the walls.

Those sounds were as strange as the cold, mournful songs and cries of some species dwelling in the deepest reaches of the sea.

To call Shaddack and reveal Denny to him in this condition would be to encourage the madman in his insane and unholy pursuits. Once he saw what Denny had become, Shaddack might find a way to induce or force all of the New People to transform themselves into identical, thoroughgoing cybernetic entities. That prospect boosted Loman's fear to new heights.

The boy-thing fell silent again.

Loman drew his revolver from its holster. His hand was shaking badly.

Data rushed ever more frantically across the screen and swam simultaneously across the surface of Denny's molten eyes.

Staring at the creature that had once been his son, Loman dragged memories from the trunk of his pre-Change life, desperately trying to recall something of what he'd once felt for Denny—the love of father for son, the sweet ache of pride, hope for the boy's future. He remembered fishing trips they had taken together, evenings spent in front of the TV, favorite books shared and discussed, long hours during which they'd worked happily together on science projects for school, the Christmas that Denny had gotten his first bicycle, the kid's first date when he had nervously brought the Talmadge girl home to meet his folks. . . . Loman could summon forth images of those times, quite detailed memory-pictures, but they had no power to warm him. He knew he should *feel* something if he was going to kill his only child, something more than fear, but he no longer had that capacity. To hold fast to whatever remained of the human being in him, he ought to be able to squeeze out one tear, at least one, as he squeezed off the shot from the Smith & Wesson, but he remained dry-eyed.

Without warning something erupted from Denny's forehead.

Loman cried out and stumbled backward two steps in surprise.

At first he thought the thing was a worm, for it was shiny-oily and segmented, as thick as a pencil. But as it continued to extrude, he saw that it was more metallic than organic, terminating in a fish-mouth plug three times the diameter of the "worm" itself. Like the feeler of a singularly repulsive insect, it weaved back and forth in front of Denny's face, growing longer and longer, until it touched the computer.

He is *willing* this to happen, Loman reminded himself.

This was mind over matter, not short-circuited genetics. Mental power made concrete, not merely biology run amok. This was what the boy wanted to become, and if this was the only life he could tolerate now, the only existence he desired, then why shouldn't he be allowed to have it?

The hideous wormlike extrusion probed the exposed mechanism, where the cover plate had once been. It disappeared inside, making some linkage that helped the boy achieve a more intimate bond with Sun than could be had solely through his mutated hands and mercuric eyes.

A hollow, electronic, blood-freezing wail came from the boy's mouth, though neither his lips nor tongue moved.

Loman's fear of taking action was at last outweighed by his fear of *not* acting. He stepped forward, put the muzzle of the revolver against the boy's right temple, and fired two rounds.

17

CROUCHING ON THE BACK PORCH, LEANING AGAINST THE wall of the house, rising up now and then to look cautiously through the window at the three people gathered around the kitchen table, Chrissie grew slowly more confident that they could be trusted. Above the dull roar and sizzle of the rain, through the closed window, she could hear only snatches of their conversation. After a while, however, she determined that they knew something was terribly wrong in Moonlight Cove. The two strangers seemed to be hiding out in Mr. Talbot's house and were on the run as much as she was. Apparently they were working on a plan to get help from authorities outside of town.

She decided against knocking on the door. It was solid wood, with no panes in the upper half, so they would not be able to see who was knocking. She had heard enough to know they were tense, maybe not as completely frazzle-nerved as she was herself, but definitely on edge. An unexpected knock at the door would give them all massive heart attacks—or maybe they'd pick up guns and blast the door to smithereens, and her with it.

Instead she rose up in plain sight and rapped on the window.

Mr. Talbot jerked his head in surprise and pointed, but even as he was pointing, the other man and the woman flew to their feet with the suddenness of marionettes snapped upright on strings. Moose barked once, twice. The three people—and the dog—stared in surprise at Chrissie. From the expression on their faces, she might have been not a bedraggled eleven-year-old girl but a chainsaw-wielding maniac wearing a leather hood to conceal a deformed face.

She supposed that right now, in alien-infested Moonlight Cove, even a pathetic, rain-soaked, exhausted little girl could be an object of terror to those who didn't know that she was still human. In hope of allaying their fear, she spoke through the windowpane:

"Help me. Please, help me."

18

THE MACHINE SCREAMED. ITS SKULL SHATTERED UNDER THE impact of the two slugs, and it was blown out of its seat, toppling to the floor of the bedroom and pulling the chair with it. The elongated fingers tore loose of the computer on the desk. The segmented wormlike probe snapped in two, halfway between the computer and the forehead from which it had sprung. The thing lay on the floor, twitching, spasming.

Loman had to think of it as a machine. He could not think of it as his son. That was too terrifying.

The face was misshapen, wrenched into an asymmetrical, surreal mask by the impact of the bullets as they'd torn through the cranium.

The silvery eyes had gone black. Now it appeared as if puddles of oil, not mercury, were pooled in the sockets in the thing's skull.

Between plates of shattered bone, Loman saw not merely the gray matter he had expected but what appeared to be coiled wire, glinting shards that looked almost ceramic, odd geometrical shapes. The blood that seeped from the wounds was accompanied by wisps of blue smoke.

Still, the machine screamed.

The electronic shrieks no longer came from the boy-thing but from the computer on the desk. Those sounds were so bizarre that they were as out of place in the machine half of the organism as they had been in the boy half.

Loman realized these were not entirely electronic wails. They also had a tonal quality and character that were unnervingly human.

The waves of data ceased flowing across the screen. One word was repeated hundreds of times, filling line after line on the display:

NO NO NO NO NO NO NO NO NO NO NO NO NO NO NO NO NO NO NO NO NO NO NO NO NO NO NO NO NO NO NO NO NO NO . . .

He suddenly knew that Denny was only half dead. The part of the boy's mind that had inhabited his body was extinguished, but another fragment of his consciousness still lived somehow within the computer, kept alive in silicon instead of brain tissue. *That* part of him was screaming in this machine-cold voice.

On the screen:

WHERE'S THE REST OF ME WHERE'S THE REST OF ME WHERE'S THE REST OF ME NO NO NO NO NO NO NO NO NO NO NO NO . . .

Loman felt as if his blood was icy sludge pumped by a heart as jellid as the meat in the freezer downstairs. He had never known a chill that penetrated as deep as this one.

He stepped away from the crumpled body, which at last stopped twitching, and turned his revolver on the computer. He emptied the gun into the machine, first blowing out the screen. Because the blinds and drapes were closed, the room was nearly dark. He blasted the circuitry to pieces. Thousands of sparks flared in the blackness, spraying out of the data-processing unit. But with a final sputter and crackle, the machine died, and the gloom closed in again.

The air stank of scorched insulation. And worse.

Loman left the room and walked to the head of the stairs. He stood there a moment, leaning against the railing. Then he descended to the front hall.

He reloaded his revolver, holstered it.

He went out into the rain.

He got in his car and started the engine.

"Shaddack," he said aloud.

19

TESSA IMMEDIATELY TOOK CHARGE OF THE GIRL. SHE LED HER upstairs, leaving Harry and Sam and Moose in the kitchen, and got her out of her wet clothes.

"Your teeth are chattering, honey."

"I'm lucky to have any teeth to chatter."

"Your skin's positively blue."

"I'm lucky to have skin," the girl said.

"I noticed you're limping too."

"Yeah. I twisted an ankle."

"Sure it's just sprained?"

"Yeah. Nothing serious. Besides—"

"I know," Tessa said, "you're lucky to *have* ankles."

"Right. For all I know, aliens find ankles particularly tasty, the same way some people like pig's feet. Yuch."

She sat on the edge of the bed in the guest room, a wool blanket pulled around her nakedness, and waited while Tessa got a sheet from the linen supplies and several safety pins from a sewing box that she noticed in the same closet.

Tessa said, "Harry's clothes are much too big for you, so we'll wrap you in a sheet temporarily. While your clothes are in the dryer, you can come downstairs and tell Harry and Sam and me all about it."

"It's been quite an adventure," the girl said.

"Yes, you look as if you've been through a lot."

"It'd make a great book."

"You like books?"

"Oh, yes, I love books."

Blushing but evidently determined to be sophisticated, she threw back the blanket and stood and allowed Tessa to drape the sheet around her. Tessa pinned it in place, fashioning a toga of sorts.

As Tessa worked, Chrissie said, "I think I'll write a book about all of this one day. I'll call it *The Alien Scourge* or maybe *Nest Queen*, although naturally I won't title it *Nest Queen* unless it turns out there really is a nest queen somewhere. Maybe they don't reproduce like insects or even like animals. Maybe they're basically a vegetable lifeform. Who knows? If they're basically a vegetable lifeform, then I'd have to call the book something like *Space Seeds* or *Vegetables of the Void* or maybe *Murderous Martian Mushrooms*. It's sometimes good to use alliteration in titles. Alliteration. Don't you like that word? It sounds so nice. I like words. Of course, you could always go with a more poetic title, haunting, like *Alien Roots, Alien Leaves*. Hey, if they're vegetables, we may be in luck, because maybe they'll eventually be killed off by aphids or tomato worms, since they won't have developed protection against earth pests, just like a few tiny germs killed off the mighty Martians in *War of the Worlds*."

Tessa was reluctant to disclose that their enemies were not from the stars, for she was enjoying the girl's precocious chatter. Then she noticed that Chrissie's left hand was injured. The palm had been badly abraded; the center of it looked raw.

"I did that when I fell off the porch roof at the rectory," the girl said.

"You fell off a roof?"

"Yeah. Boy, *that* was exciting. See, the wolf-thing was coming through the window after me, and I didn't have anywhere else to go. Twisted my ankle in the same fall and then had to run across the yard to the back gate before he caught me. You know, Miss Lockland—"

"Please call me Tessa."

Apparently Chrissie was unaccustomed to addressing adults by their Christian names. She frowned and was silent for a moment, struggling with the invitation to informality. Evidently she decided it would be rude not to use first names when asked to do so. "Okay . . . Tessa. Well, anyway, I can't decide what the aliens are most likely to do if they catch us. Maybe eat our kidneys? Or don't they eat us at all? Maybe they just shove alien pill bugs in our ears, and the bugs crawl into our brains and take over. Either way, I figure it's worth falling off a roof to avoid them."

Having finished pinning the toga, Tessa led Chrissie down the hall to the bathroom and looked in the medicine cabinet for something with which to treat the scraped palm. She found a bottle of iodine with a faded label, a half-empty roll of adhesive tape, and a package of gauze pads so old that the paper wrapper around each bandage square was yellow with age. The gauze itself looked fresh and white, and the iodine was undiluted by time, still strong enough to sting.

Barefoot, toga-clad, with her blond hair frizzing and curling as it dried, Chrissie sat on the lowered lid of the toilet seat and submitted stoically to the treatment of her wound. She didn't protest in any way, didn't cry out—or even hiss—in pain.

But she *did* talk: "That's the second time I've fallen off a roof, so I guess I must have a guardian angel looking over me. About a year and a half ago, in the spring, these birds—starlings, I think they were—built a nest on the roof of one of our stables at home, and I just *had* to see what baby birds looked like in the nest, so when my folks weren't around, I got a ladder and waited for the mama bird to fly off for more food, and then I real quick climbed up there to have a peek. Let me tell you, before they get their feathers, baby birds are just about the ugliest things you'd want to see—except for aliens, of course. They're withered little wrinkled things, all beaks and eyes, and stumpy little wings like deformed arms. If human babies looked that bad when they were born, the first people back a few million years ago would've flushed their newborns down the toilet—if they'd *had* toilets— and wouldn't have *dared* have any more of them, and the whole race would've died out before it even really got started."

Still painting the wound with iodine, trying without success to repress a grin, Tessa looked up and saw that Chrissie was squeezing her eyes tightly shut, wrinkling her nose, struggling very hard to be brave.

"Then the mama and papa bird came back," the girl said, "and saw me at the nest and flew at my face, shrieking. I was so startled that I slipped and fell off the roof. Didn't hurt myself at all that time—though I did land in some horse manure. Which isn't a thrill, let me tell you. I love horses, but they'd be ever so much more lovable if you could teach them to use a litterbox like a cat."

Tessa was crazy about this kid.

20

SAM LEANED FORWARD WITH HIS ELBOWS ON THE KITCHEN table and listened attentively to Chrissie Foster. Though Tessa had heard the Boogeymen in the middle of a kill at Cove Lodge and had glimpsed one of them under the door of her room, and though Harry had watched them at a distance in night and fog, and though Sam had spied two of them last night through a window in Harry's living room, the girl was the only one present who had seen them close up and more than once.

But it was not solely her singular experience that held Sam's attention. He also was captivated by her sprightly manner, good humor, and articulateness. She obviously had considerable inner strength, real toughness, for otherwise she would not have survived the previous night and the events of this morning. Yet she remained charmingly innocent, tough but not hard. She was one of those kids who gave you hope for the whole damn human race.

A kid like Scott used to be.

And that was why Sam was fascinated by Chrissie Foster. He saw in her the child that Scott had been. Before he . . . changed. With regret so poignant that it manifested itself as a dull ache in his chest and a tightness in his throat, he watched the girl and listened to her, not only to hear what information she had to impart but with the unrealistic expectation that by studying her he would at last understand why his own son had lost both innocence and hope.

21

DOWN IN THE DARKNESS OF THE ICARUS COLONY CELLAR, Tucker and his pack did not sleep, for they did not require it. They lay curled in the deep blackness. From time to time, he and the other male coupled with the female, and they tore at one another in savage frenzy, gashing flesh that began to heal at once, drawing one another's blood simply for the pleasure of the scent— immortal freaks at play.

The darkness and the barren confines of their concrete-walled burrow contributed to Tucker's growing disorientation. By the hour he remembered less of his existence prior to the past night's exciting hunt. He ceased to have much sense of self. Individuality was not to be encouraged in the pack when hunting, and in the burrow it was even a less desirable trait; harmony in that windowless, claustrophobic space required the relinquishment of self to group.

His waking dreams were filled with images of dark, wild shapes creeping through night-clad forests and across moon-washed meadows. When occasionally a memory of human form flickered through his mind, its origins were a mystery to him; more than that, he was frightened by it and quickly shifted his fantasies back to running-hunting-killing-coupling scenes in which he was just a part of the pack, one aspect of a single shadow, one extension of a larger organism, free from the need to think, having no desire but to *be*.

At one point he became aware that he had slipped out of his wolflike form, which had become too confining. He no longer wanted to be the leader of a pack, for that position carried with it too much responsibility. He didn't want to think at all. Just be. *Be*. The limitations of all rigid physical forms seemed insufferable.

He sensed that the other male and the female were aware of his degeneration and were following his example.

He felt his flesh flowing, bones dissolving, organs and vessels surrendering form and function. He devolved beyond the primal ape, far beyond the four-legged thing that laboriously had crawled out of the ancient sea millennia ago, beyond, beyond, until he was but a mass of pulsing tissue, protoplasmic soup, throbbing in the darkness of the Icarus Colony cellar.

22

LOMAN RANG THE DOORBELL AT SHADDACK'S HOUSE ON THE north point, and Evan, the manservant, answered.

"I'm sorry, Chief Watkins, but Mr. Shaddack isn't here."

"Where's he gone?"

"I don't know."

Evan was one of the New People. To be sure of dispatching him, Loman shot him twice in the head and then twice in the chest while he lay on the foyer floor, shattering both brain and heart. Or data-processor and pump. Which was needed now—biological or mechanical terminology? How far had they progressed toward becoming machines?

Loman closed the door behind him and stepped over Evan's body. After replenishing the expended rounds in the revolver's cylinder, he searched the huge house room by room, floor by floor, looking for Shaddack.

Though he wished that he could be driven by a hunger for revenge, could be consumed by anger, and could take satisfaction in bludgeoning Shaddack to death, that depth of feeling was denied him. His son's death had not melted the ice in his heart. He couldn't feel grief or rage.

Instead he was driven by fear. He wanted to kill Shaddack before the madman made them into something worse than they'd already become.

By killing Shaddack—who was always linked to the supercomputer at New Wave by a simple cardiac telemetry device—Loman would activate a program in Sun that would broadcast a microwave death order. That transmission would be received by all the microsphere computers wedded to the innermost tissues of the New People. Upon receiving the death order, each biologically interactive computer in each New Person would instantly still the heart of its host. Every one of the converted in Moonlight Cove would die. He too would die.

But he no longer cared. His fear of death was outweighed by his fear of living, especially if he had to live either as a regressive or as that more hideous thing that Denny had become.

In his mind he could see himself in that wretched condition—gleaming mercurial eyes, a wormlike probe bursting bloodlessly from his forehead to seek obscene conjugation with the computer. If skin actually could crawl, his own would have crept off his body.

When he could not find Shaddack at home, he set out for New Wave, where the maker of the new world was no doubt in his office busily designing neighborhoods for this hell that he called paradise.

23

SHORTLY AFTER ELEVEN O'CLOCK, AS SAM WAS LEAVING, Tessa stepped out onto the back porch with him and closed the door, leaving Harry and Chrissie in the kitchen. The trees at the rear of the property were just tall enough to prevent neighbors, even those uphill, from looking into the yard. She was sure they could not be seen in the deeper shadows of the porch.

"Listen," she said, "it makes no sense for you to go alone."

"It makes perfect sense."

The air was chilly and damp. She hugged herself.

She said, "I could ring the front doorbell, distract anyone inside, while you went in the back."

"I don't want to have to worry about you."

"I can take take of myself."

"Yeah, I believe you can," he said.

"Well?"

"But I work alone."

"You seem to do everything alone."

He smiled thinly. "Are we going to get into another argument about whether life is a tea party or hell on earth?"

"That wasn't an argument we had. It was a discussion."

"Well, anyway, I've shifted to undercover assignments for the very reason that I can pretty much work alone. I don't want a partner any more, Tessa, because I don't want to see any more of them die."

She knew he was referring not only to the other agents who had been killed in the line of duty with him but also to his late wife.

"Stay with the girl," he said. "Take care of her if anything happens. She's like you, after all."

"What?"

"She's one of those who knows how to love life. How to really, deeply love it, no matter what happens. It's a rare and precious talent."

"You know too," she said.

"No. I've never known."

"Dammit, everyone is born with a love of life. You still have it, Sam. You've just lost touch with it, but you can find it again."

"Take care of her," he said, turning away and descending the porch steps into the rain.

"You better come back, damn you. You promised to tell me what you saw at the other end of that tunnel, on the Other Side. You just better come back."

Sam departed through silver rain and thin patches of gray fog.

As she watched him go, Tessa realized that even if he never told her about the Other Side, she wanted him to come back for many other reasons both complex and surprising.

24

THE COLTRANE HOUSE WAS TWO DOORS SOUTH OF THE Talbot place, on Conquistador. Two stories. Weathered cedar siding. A covered patio instead of a rear porch.

Moving quickly along the back of the house, where rain drizzled off the patio cover with a sound inaptly like crackling fire, Sam peered through sliding glass doors into a gloomy family room and then through French windows into an unlighted kitchen. When he reached the kitchen door, he withdrew his revolver from the holster under his leather jacket and held it down at his side, against his thigh.

He could have walked around front and rung the bell, which might have seemed less suspicious to the people inside. But that would mean going out to the street, where he was more likely to be seen not only by neighbors but by the men Chrissie said were patrolling the town.

He knocked on the door, four quick raps. When no one responded, he knocked again, louder, and then a third time, louder still. If anyone was home, the knock would have been answered.

Harley and Sue Coltrane must be at New Wave, where they worked.

The door was locked. He hoped it had no dead bolt.

Though he had left his other tools at Harry's, he had brought a thin, flexible metal loid. Television dramas had popularized the notion that any credit card made a convenient and unincriminating loid, but those plastic rectangles too often got wedged in the crack or snapped before the latch bolt was slipped. He preferred time-proven tools. He worked the loid between the door and frame, below the lock, and slid it up, applying pressure when he met resistance. The lock popped. He tried the door, and there was no dead bolt; it opened with a soft creak.

He stepped inside and quietly closed the door, making sure that the lock did not engage. If he had to get out fast, he did not want to fumble with a latch.

The kitchen was illuminated only by the dismal light of the rain-darkened day that barely penetrated the windows. Evidently the vinyl flooring, wall-covering, and tile were of the palest hues, for in that dimness everything seemed to be one shade of gray or another.

He stood for almost a minute, listening intently.

A kitchen clock ticked.

Rain drummed on the patio cover.

His soaked hair was pasted to his forehead. He pushed it aside, out of his eyes. When he moved, his wet shoes squished.

He went directly to the phone, which was mounted on the wall above a corner secretary. When he picked it up, he got no dial tone, but the line was not dead, either. It was filled with strange sounds: clicking, low beeping, soft oscillations—all of which blended into mournful and alien music, an electronic threnody.

The back of Sam's neck went cold.

Carefully, silently, he returned the handset to its cradle.

He wondered what sounds could be heard on a telephone that was being used as a link between two computers, with a modem. Was one of the Coltranes at work elsewhere in the house, tied in by a home computer to New Wave?

Somehow he sensed that what he had heard on the line was not as simply explained as that. It had been damned eerie.

A dining room lay beyond the kitchen. The two large windows were covered with gauzy sheers, which further filtered the ashen daylight. A hutch, buffet, table, and chairs were revealed as blocks of black and slate-gray shadows.

Again he stopped to listen. Again he heard nothing unusual.

The house was laid out in a classic California design, with no downstairs hall. Each room led directly to the next in an open and airy floorplan. Through an archway he entered the large living room, grateful that the house had wall-to-wall carpeting, on which his wet shoes made no sound.

The living room was less shadowy than any other part of the house that he had seen thus far, yet the brightest color was a pearly gray. The west windows were sheltered by the front porch, but rain streamed over those facing north. Leaden daylight, passing through the panes, speckled the room with the watery-gray shadows of the hundreds of beads that tracked down the glass, and Sam was so edgy that he could almost feel those small ameboid phantoms crawling over him.

Between the lighting and his mood, he felt as if he were in an old black-and-white movie. One of those bleak exercises in *film noir*.

The living room was deserted, but abruptly a sound came from the last room downstairs. At the southwest corner. Beyond the foyer. The den, most likely. It was a piercing trill that made his teeth ache, followed by a forlorn cry that was neither the voice of a man nor that of a machine but something in between, a semi-metallic voice wrenched by fear and twisted with despair. That was followed by low electronic pulsing, like a massive heartbeat.

Then silence.

He had brought up his revolver, holding it straight out in front of him, ready to shoot anything that moved. But everything was as still as it was silent.

The trill, the eerie cry, and the base throbbing surely could not be associated with the Boogeymen that he'd seen last night outside of Harry's house, or with the other shape-changers Chrissie described. Until now, an encounter with one of them had been the thing he feared most. But suddenly the unknown entity in the den was more frightening.

Sam waited.

Nothing more.

He had the queer feeling that something was listening for his movements as tensely as he was listening for it.

He considered returning to Harry's to think of some other way to send a message to the Bureau, because Mexican food and Guinness Stout and Goldie Hawn movies—even *Swing Shift*—now seemed precious beyond value, not pathetic reasons to live but pleasures so exquisite that no words existed to adequately describe them.

The only thing that kept him from getting the hell out of there was Chrissie Foster. The memory of her bright eyes. Her innocent face. The enthusiasm and animation with which she had recounted her adventures. Perhaps he had failed Scott, and perhaps it was too late for the boy to be hauled back from the brink. But Chrissie was still alive in every vital sense of the word—physically, intellectually, emotionally—and she was dependent on him. No one else could save her from conversion.

Midnight was little more than twelve hours away.

He edged through the living room and quietly crossed the foyer. He stood with his back against the wall beside the half-open door to the room from which the weird sounds had come.

Something clicked in there.

He stiffened.

Low, soft clicks. Not the *tick-tick-tick* of claws like those he had heard tapping on the window last night. More like a long series of relays being tripped, scores of switches being closed, dominoes falling against one another: *click-click-click-clickety-clickety-click-click-clickety*. . . .

Silence once more.

Holding the revolver in both hands, Sam stepped in front of the door and pushed it open with one foot. He crossed the threshold and assumed a shooter's stance just inside the room.

The windows were covered by interior shutters, and the only light was from two computer screens. Both were fitted with filters that resulted in black text on an amber background. Everything in the room not wrapped in shadows was touched by that golden radiance.

Two people sat before the terminals, one on the right side of the room, the other on the left, their backs to each other.

"Don't move," Sam said sharply.

They neither moved nor spoke. They were so still that at first he thought they were dead.

The peculiar light was brighter yet curiously less revealing than the half-burnt-out daylight that vaguely illuminated the other rooms. As his eyes adjusted, Sam saw that the two people at the computers were not only unnaturally still but were not really people any more. He was drawn forward by the icy grip of horror.

Oblivious of Sam, a naked man, probably Harley Coltrane, sat in a wheeled, swivel-based chair at the computer to the right of the door, against the west wall. He was connected to the VDT by a pair of inch-thick cables that looked less metallic than organic, glistening wetly in the amber glow. They extended from within the bowels of the data-processing unit—from which the cover plate had been removed—and into the man's bare torso below his rib cage, melding bloodlessly with the flesh. They throbbed.

"Dear God," Sam whispered.

Coltrane's lower arms were utterly fleshless, just golden bones. The meat of his upper arms ended smoothly two inches above the elbows; from those stumps, bones thrust out as cleanly as robotic extrusions from a metal casing. The skeletal hands were locked tightly around the cables, as if they were merely a pair of clamps.

When Sam stepped nearer to Coltrane and looked closer, he saw the bones were not as well differentiated as they should have been but had half melted together. Furthermore, they were veined with metal. As he watched, the cables pulsed with such vigor that they began to vibrate wildly. If not held fast by the clamping hands, they might have torn loose either from the man or the machine.

Get out.

A voice spoke within him, telling him to flee, and it was his own voice, though not that of the adult Sam Booker. It was the voice of the child he had once been and to which his fear was encouraging him to revert. Extreme terror is a time machine a thousand times more efficient than nostalgia, hurtling us backward through the years, into that forgotten and intolerable condition of helplessness in which so much of childhood is spent.

Get out, run, run, get out!

Sam resisted the urge to bolt.

He wanted to understand. What was happening? What had these people become? *Why?* What did this have to do with the Boogeymen who prowled the night? Evidently through microtechnology Thomas Shaddack had found a way to alter, radically and forever, human biology. That much was clear to Sam, but knowing just that and nothing else was like sensing that something lived within the sea without ever having seen a fish. So much more lay beneath the surface, mysterious.

Get out.

Neither the man before him nor the woman across the room seemed remotely aware of him. Apparently he was in no imminent danger.

Run, said the frightened boy within.

Rivers of data—words, numbers, charts and graphs of myriad types—flowed in a floodlike rampage across the amber screen, while Harley Coltrane stared unwaveringly at that darkly flickering display. He could not have seen it as an ordinary man would have, for he had no eyes. They'd been torn from his sockets and replaced by a cluster of other sensors: tiny beads of ruby glass, small knots of wire, waffle-surfaced chips of some ceramic material, all bristling and slightly recessed in the deep black holes in his skull.

Sam was holding the revolver in only one hand now. He kept his finger on the trigger guard rather than on the trigger itself, for he was shaking so badly that he might unintentionally let off a shot.

The man-machine's chest rose and fell. His mouth hung open, and bitterly foul breath rushed from him in rhythmic waves.

A rapid pulse was visible in his temples and in the gruesomely swollen arteries in his neck. But other pulses throbbed where none should have been: in the center of his forehead; along each jawline; at four places in his chest and belly; in his upper arms, where dark ropy vessels had thickened and risen above subcutaneous fat, sheathed now only by his skin. His circulatory system seemed to have been redesigned and augmented to assist new functions that his body was being called upon to perform. Worse yet, those pulses beat in a strange syncopation, as if at least two hearts pounded within him.

A shriek erupted from the thing's gaping mouth, and Sam twitched and cried out in surprise. This was akin to the unearthly sounds that he had heard while in the living room, that had drawn him here, but he had thought they'd come from the computer.

Grimacing as the electronic wail spiraled higher and swelled into painful decibels, Sam let his gaze rise from the manmachine's open mouth to its "eyes." The sensors still bristled in the sockets. The beads of ruby glass glowed with inner light, and Sam wondered if they registered him on the infrared spectrum or by some other means. Did Coltrane see him at all? Perhaps the man-machine had traded the human world for a different reality, moving from this physical plane to another level, and perhaps Sam was an irrelevancy to him, unnoticed.

The shriek began to fade, then cut off abruptly.

Without realizing what he'd done, Sam had raised his revolver and, from a distance of about eighteen inches, pointed it at Harley Coltrane's face. He was startled to discover that he also had slipped his finger off the guard and onto the trigger itself and that he was going to destroy this thing.

He hesitated. Coltrane was, after all, still a man—at least to some extent. Who was to say that he didn't desire his current state more than life as an ordinary human being? Who was to say that he was not happy like this? Sam was uneasy in the role of judge, but an even uneasier executioner. As a man who believed that life was hell on earth, he had to consider the possibility that Coltrane's condition was an improvement, an escape.

Between man and computer, the glistening, semiorganic cables *thrummed*. They rattled against the skeletal hands in which they were clamped.

Coltrane's rank breath was redolent with both the stench of rotting meat and overheated electronic components.

Sensors glistened and moved within the lidless eye sockets.

Tinted gold by the light from the screen, Coltrane's face seemed to be frozen in a perpetual scream. The vessels pulsing in his jaws and temples looked less like reflections of his own heartbeat than like parasites squirming under his skin.

With a shudder of revulsion, Sam squeezed the trigger. The blast was thunderous in that confined space.

Coltrane's head snapped back with the impact of the point-blank shot, then dropped forward, chin on his chest, smoking and bleeding.

The repulsive cables continued to swell and shrink and swell as if with the rhythmic passage of inner fluid.

Sam sensed that the man was not entirely dead. He turned the gun on the computer screen.

One of Coltrane's skeletal hands released the cable around which it had been firmly clamped. With a *click-snick-snack* of bare bones, it whipped up and seized Sam's wrist.

Sam cried out.

The room filled with electronic clicks and snaps and beeps and warblings.

The hellish hand held him fast and with such tremendous strength that the bony fingers pinched his flesh, then began to cut through it. He felt warm blood trickle down his arm, under his shirt sleeve. With a flash of panic he realized that the unhuman power of the man-machine was ultimately sufficient to crush his wrist and leave him crippled. At best his hand would swiftly go numb from lack of circulation, and the revolver would drop from his grasp.

Coltrane was struggling to raise his half-shattered head.

Sam thought of his mother in the wreckage of the car, face torn open, grinning at him, grinning, silent and unmoving but grinning. . . .

Frantically he kicked at Coltrane's chair, hoping to send it rolling and spinning away. The wheels had been locked.

The bony hand squeezed tighter, and Sam screamed. His vision blurred.

Still, he saw that Coltrane's head was coming up slowly, slowly.

Jesus, I don't want to see that ruined face!

With his right foot, putting everything he had into the kick, Sam struck once, twice, three times at the cables between Coltrane and the computer. They tore loose from Coltrane, popping out of his flesh with a hideous sound, and the man slumped in his chair. Simultaneously the skeletal hand opened and fell away from Sam's wrist. With a cold rattle it struck the hard plastic mat under the chair.

Bass electronic pulses thumped like soft drumbeats and echoed off the walls, while under them a thin bleat wavered continuously through three notes.

Gasping and half in shock, Sam clamped his left hand around his bleeding wrist, as if that would still the stinging pain.

Something brushed against his leg.

He looked down and saw the semiorganic cables, like pale headless snakes, still attached to the computer and full of malevolent life. They seemed to have grown, as well, until they were twice the length they had been when linking Coltrane to the machine. One snared his left ankle, and the other curled sinuously around his right calf.

He tried to tear loose.

They held him fast.

They twined up his legs.

Instinctively he knew they were seeking bare flesh on the upper half of his body, and that upon contact they would burrow into him and make him part of the system.

He was still holding the revolver in his blood-slicked right hand. He aimed at the screen.

Data was no longer flowing across that amber field. Instead, Coltrane's face looked out from the display. His eyes had been restored, and it seemed as if he could see Sam, for he was looking directly at him and speaking to him:

"*. . . need . . . need . . . want, need. . . .*"

Without understanding a damned thing about it, Sam knew Coltrane was still alive. He had not died—or at least not all of him had perished—with his body. He was there, in the machine somehow.

As if to confirm that insight, Coltrane influenced the glass screen of the VDT to relinquish the convex plane of its surface and adapt to the contours of his face. The glass became as flexible as gelatin, thrusting outward, as if Coltrane actually existed within the machine, physically, and was now pushing his face out of it.

This was impossible. Yet it was happening. Harley Coltrane seemed to be controlling matter with the power of his mind, a mind not even any longer linked to a human body.

Sam was mesmerized by fear, frozen, paralyzed. His finger lay immovable against the trigger.

Reality had been ripped, and through that tear a nightmare world of infinite malign possibilities seemed to be rushing into the world that Sam knew and— suddenly—loved.

One of the snakelike cables had reached his chest and found its way under his sweater to bare skin. He felt as if he'd been touched by a white-hot brand, and the pain broke his trance.

He fired two rounds into the computer, shattering the screen first, which was the second face of Coltrane's into which he'd pumped a .38 slug. Though Sam half expected it to absorb the bullet without effect, the cathode-ray tube imploded as if still made of glass. The other round scrambled the guts of the data-processing unit, at last finishing off the thing that Coltrane had become.

The pale, oily tentacles fell away from him. They blistered, began to bubble, and seemed to be putrefying before his eyes.

Eerie electronic beeps, crackles, and oscillations, not ear-torturingly loud but uncannily piercing, still filled the room.

When Sam looked toward the woman who had been seated at the other computer, against the east wall, he saw that the mucus-slick cables between her and the machine had lengthened, allowing her to turn in her chair to face him. Aside from those semiorganic connections and her nakedness, she was in a different but no less hideous condition from her husband. Her eyes were gone, but her sockets did not bristle with a host of sensors. Rather, two reddish orbs, three times the size of ordinary eyes, filled enlarged sockets in a face redesigned to accommodate them; they were less eyes than eye-shaped receptors, no doubt designed to see in many spectrums of light, and in fact Sam became aware of an image of himself in each red lens, reversed. Her legs, belly, breasts, arms, throat, and face were heavily patterned with swollen blood vessels that lay just beneath her skin and that seemed to stretch it to the breaking point, so she looked as if she were a design board for branch-pattern circuitry. Some of those vessels might, indeed, have carried blood, but some of them throbbed with waves of radiumlike illumination, some green and some sulfurous yellow.

A segmented, wormlike probe, the diameter of a pencil, erupted from her forehead, as if shot from a gun, and streaked toward Sam, closing the ten feet between them in a split second, striking him above the right eye before he could duck. The tip bit into his skin on contact. He heard a whirring sound, as of tiny blades spinning at maybe a thousand revolutions a minute. Blood ran down his brow and along the side of his nose. But he was squeezing off the last two rounds in his gun even as the probe came at him. Both shots found their mark. One slammed into the woman's upper body, and one took out the computer behind her in a blaze of sparks and crackling electrical bolts that jumped to the ceiling and snaked briefly across the plaster before dissipating. The probe went limp and fell away from him before it could link his brain to hers, which evidently had been its intention.

Except for gray daylight that entered through the paper-thin cracks between the slats of the shutters, the room was dark.

Crazily, Sam remembered something a computer specialist had said at a seminar for agents, when explaining how the Bureau's new system worked: *"Computers can perform more effectively when linked, allowing parallel processing of data."*

Bleeding from the forehead and the right wrist, he stumbled backward to the door and flicked the light switch, turning on a floor lamp. He stood there—as far as he could get from the two grotesque corpses and still see them—while he began to reload the revolver with rounds he dug out of the pockets of his jacket.

The room was preternaturally silent.

Nothing moved.

Sam's heart was hammering with such force that his chest ached dully with each blow.

Twice he dropped cartridges because his hands were shaking. He didn't stoop to retrieve them. He was half convinced that the moment he wasn't in a position to fire with accuracy or to run, one of the dead creatures would prove not to be dead, after all, and like a flash would come at him, spitting sparks, and would seize him before he could rise and scramble out of its way.

Gradually he became aware of the sound of rain. After losing half of its force during the morning, it was now falling harder than at any time since the storm had first broken the previous night. No thunder shook the day, but the furious drumming of the rain itself—and the insulated walls of the house—had probably muffled the gunfire enough to prevent it being heard by neighbors. He hoped to God that was the case. Otherwise, they were coming even now to investigate, and they would prevent his escape.

Blood continued to trickle down from the wound on his forehead, and some of it got into his right eye. It stung. He wiped at his eye with his sleeve and blinked away the tears as best he could.

His wrist hurt like hell. But if he had to, he could hold the revolver with his left hand and shoot well enough in close quarters.

When the .38 was reloaded, Sam edged back into the room, to the smoking computer on the worktable along the west wall, where Harley Coltrane's mutated body was slumped in a chair, trailing its bone-metal arms. Keeping one eye on the dead man-machine, he took the phone off the modem and hung it up. Then he lifted the receiver and was relieved to hear a dial tone.

His mouth was so dry that he wasn't sure he'd be able to speak clearly when his call got through.

He punched out the number of the Bureau office in Los Angeles.

The line clicked.

A pause.

A recording came on: "We are sorry that we are unable to complete your call at this time."

He hung up, then tried again.

"We are sorry that we are unable to complete—"

He slammed the phone down.

Not all of the telephones in Moonlight Cove were operable. And evidently, even from those in service, calls could be placed only to certain numbers. Approved numbers. The local phone company had been reduced to an elaborate intercom to serve the converted.

As he turned away from the phone, he heard something move behind him. Stealthy and quick.

He swung around, and the woman was three feet away. She was no longer connected to the ruined computer, but one of those organic-looking cables trailed across the floor from the base of her spine and into an electrical socket.

Free-associating in his terror, Sam thought: So much for your clumsy kites, Dr. Frankenstein, so much for the need for storms and lightning; these days we just plug the monsters into the wall, give them a jolt of the juice direct, courtesy of Pacific Power & Light.

A reptilian hiss issued from her, and she reached for him. Instead of fingers, her hand had three multiple-pronged plugs similar to the couplings with which the elements of a home computer were joined, though these prongs were as sharp as nails.

Sam dodged to the side, colliding with the chair in which Harley Coltrane still slumped, and nearly fell, firing at the woman-thing as he went. He emptied the five-round .38.

The first three shots knocked her backward and down. The other two tore through vacant air and punched chunks of plaster out of the walls because he was too panicked to stop pulling the trigger when she fell out of his line of fire.

She was trying to get up.

Like a goddamn vampire, he thought.

He needed the high-tech equivalent of a wooden stake, a cross, a silver bullet.

The artery-circuits that webbed her naked body were still pulsing with light, although in places she was sparking, just as the computers themselves had done when he had pumped a couple of slugs into them.

No rounds were left in the revolver.

He searched his pockets for cartridges.

He had none.

Get out.

An electronic wail, not deafening but more nerve-splintering than a thousand sharp fingernails scraped simultaneously down a chalkboard, shrilled from her.

Two segmented, wormlike probes burst from her face and flew straight at him. Both fell inches short of him—perhaps a sign of her waning energy—and returned to her like splashes of quicksilver streaming back into the mother mass.

But she *was* getting up.

Sam scrambled to the doorway, stooped, and snatched up the two cartridges he had dropped when he had reloaded the gun. He broke open the cylinder, shook out the empty brass casings, jammed in the last two rounds.

" . . . *neeeeeeeeeeeeeeeed . . . neeeeeeeeeeeeeeeeed . . .* "

She was on her feet, coming toward him.

This time he held the Smith & Wesson in both hands, aimed carefully, and shot her in the head.

Take out the data processor, he thought with a flash of black humor. Only way to stop a determined machine. Take out its data processor, and it's nothing but a tangle of junk.

She crumpled to the floor. The red light went out of her unhuman eyes; they were black now. She was perfectly still.

Suddenly flames erupted from her bullet-cracked skull, spurting from the wound, from her eyes, nostrils, and gaping mouth.

He moved quickly to the socket to which she was still tethered, and he kicked at the semiorganic plug that she had extruded from her body, knocking it loose.

The flames still leaped from her.

He could not afford a house fire. The bodies would be found, and the neighborhood, Harry's house included, would be searched door-to-door. He looked around for something to throw over her to smother the flames, but already the blaze within her skull was subsiding. In a moment it burned itself out.

The air reeked of a dozen foul odors, some of which did not bear contemplation.

He was mildly dizzy. Nausea stole over him. He gagged, clenched his teeth, and forced back his gorge.

Though he wanted desperately to get out of there, he took time to unplug both computers. They were inoperable and damaged beyond repair, but he was irrationally afraid that, like Dr. Frankenstein's homebuilt man in movie sequel after sequel, they would somehow come to life if exposed to electricity.

He hesitated at the doorway, leaned against the jamb to take some of the weight off his weak and trembling legs, and studied the strange corpses. He had expected them to revert to their normal appearance when they were dead, the way werewolves in the movies, upon taking a silver bullet in the heart or being beaten with a silver-headed cane, always metamorphosed one last time, becoming their tortured, too-human selves, finally released from the curse. Unfortunately this was not lycanthropy. This was not a supernatural affliction, but something worse that men had brought upon themselves with no help from demons or spirits or other things that went bump in the night. The Coltranes remained as they had been, monstrous half-breeds of flesh and metal, blood and silicon—human and machine.

He could not comprehend *how* they had become what they had become, but he half remembered that a word existed for them, and in a moment he recalled it. *Cyborg*: a person whose physiological functioning was aided by or dependent on a mechanical or electronic device. People wearing pacemakers to regulate arrhythmic hearts were cyborgs, and that was a good thing. Those whose kidneys had both failed—and who received dialysis on a regular basis—were cyborgs, and that was good too. But with the Coltranes the concept had been carried to extremes. They were the nightmare side of advanced cybernetics, in whom not merely physiological but mental function had become aided by and almost certainly dependent on a machine.

Sam began to gag again. He turned quickly away from the smoke-hazed den and backtracked through the house to the kitchen door, by which he had entered.

Every step of the way, he was certain that he would hear a voice behind him, half human and half electronic—"*neeeeeeeeeeeed*"—and would look back to see one of the Coltranes lumbering toward him, reanimated by a last small supply of current stored in battery cells.

25

AT THE MAIN GATE OF NEW WAVE MICROTECHNOLOGY, ON the highlands along the northern perimeter of Moonlight Cove, the guard, wearing a black rain slicker with the corporate logo on the breast, squinted at the oncoming police cruiser. When he recognized Loman, he waved him through without stopping him. Loman had been well known there even before he and they had become New People.

New Wave power, prestige, and profitability were not hidden in an unassuming corporate headquarters. The place had been designed by a leading architect who favored rounded corners, gentle angles, and the interesting juxtaposition of curved walls—some concave, some convex. The two large three-story buildings—one erected four years after the other—were faced with buff-colored stone, had huge tinted windows, and blended well with the landscape.

Of the fourteen hundred people employed there, nearly a thousand lived in Moonlight Cove. The rest resided in outlying communities elsewhere in the county. All of them, of course, lived within the effective reach of the microwave broadcasting dish on the roof of the main structure.

As he followed the entrance road around the big buildings toward the parking area behind, Loman thought: Sure as hell, Shaddack's our very own Reverend Jim Jones. Needs to be sure he can take every last one of his devoted followers with him any time he wants. A modern pharaoh. When he dies, those attending him die, too, as if he expects them to continue to attend him in the next world. Shit. Do we even believe in a next world any more?

No. Religious faith was akin to hope, and it required emotional commitment.

New People did not believe in God any more than they believed in Santa Claus. The only thing they believed in was the power of the machine and the cybernetic destiny of humanity.

Maybe some of them didn't even believe in that.

Loman didn't. He no longer believed in anything at all—which scared him because he had once believed in so many things.

The ratio of New Wave's gross sales and profits to its number of employees was high even for the microtechnology industry, and its ability to pay for the best talent in its field was reflected in the percentage of high-ticket cars in the two enormous lots. Mercedes. BMW. Porsche. Corvette. Cadillac Seville. Jaguar. High-end Japanese imports with every bell and whistle.

Only half the usual number of cars were in the lot. It looked as if a high percentage of the staff was at home, working by modem. How many were already like Denny?

Side by side on the rainswept macadam, those cars reminded Loman of the orderly ranks of tombstones in a cemetery. All those quiescent engines, all that cold metal, all those hundreds of wet windshields reflecting the flat gray autumn sky, suddenly seemed a presentiment of death. To Loman, that parking lot represented the future of the entire town: silence, stillness, the terrible eternal peace of the graveyard.

If the authorities outside of Moonlight Cove tumbled to what was happening there, or if it turned out that virtually every one of the New People *was* a regressive—or worse—and the Moonhawk Project was a disaster, the remedy would not be poisoned Kool-Aid this time, like Reverend Jim Jones used down there in Jonestown, but lethal commands broadcast in bursts of microwaves, received by microsphere computers inside the New People, instantly translated into the language of the governing program, and acted upon. Thousands of hearts would stop as one. The New People would fall, as one, and Moonlight Cove would in an instant become a graveyard of the unburied.

Loman drove through the first parking lot, into the second, and headed toward the row of spaces reserved for the top executives.

If I wait for Shaddack to see that Moonhawk's gone bad and to take us with him, Loman thought, he won't be doing it because he cares about cleaning up the messes he makes, not that damn albino-spider-of-a-man. He'll take us with him just for the bloody hell of it, just so he can go out with a big bang, so the world will stand in awe of his power, a man of such incredible power that he could command thousands to die simultaneously with him.

More than a few sickos would see him as a hero, idolize him. Some budding young genius might want to emulate him. That was no doubt what Shaddack had in mind. At best, if Moonhawk succeeded and all of mankind was eventually converted, Shaddack literally would be master of his world. At worst, if it all went bad and he had to kill himself to avoid falling into the hands of the authorities, he would become a nearly mythic figure of dark inspiration, whose malign legend would encourage legions of the mad and power-mad, a Hitler for the silicon age.

Loman braked at the end of the row of cars.

He wiped at his greasy face. His hand was shaking.

He was filled with a longing to abandon this responsibility and seek the pressure-free existence of the regressive.

But he resisted.

If Loman killed Shaddack first, before Shaddack had a chance to kill himself, the legend would be tarnished. Loman would die a few seconds after Shaddack died, as would all the New People, but at least the legend would have to incorporate the fact that this high-tech Jim Jones had perished at the hands of one of the creatures he'd created. His power would be shown to be finite; he would be seen as clever but not clever enough, a flawed god, sharing both the hubris and the fate of Wells's Moreau, and his work more universally would be viewed as folly.

Loman turned right, drove to the row of executive parking spaces, and was disappointed to see that neither Shaddack's Mercedes nor his charcoal-gray van was in his reserved slot. He might still be there. He could have been driven to the office by someone else or could have parked elsewhere.

Loman swung his cruiser into Shaddack's reserved space. He cut the engine.

He was carrying his revolver in a hip holster. He had checked twice before to be sure it was fully loaded. He checked again.

Between Shaddack's house and New Wave, Loman had parked along the road to write a note, which he would leave on Shaddack's body, clearly explaining that he had killed his maker. When authorities entered Moonlight Cove from the unconverted world beyond, they would find the note and know.

He would execute Shaddack not because he was motivated by noble purpose.

Such high-minded self-sacrifice required a depth of feeling he could no longer achieve. He would murder Shaddack strictly because he was terrified that Shaddack would learn about Denny, or would discover that others had become what Denny had become, and would find a way to make *all* of them enter into an unholy union with machines.

Molten silver eyes . . .

Drool spilling from the gaping mouth . . .

The segmented probe bursting from the boy's forehead and seeking the vaginal heat of the computer . . .

Those blood-freezing images, and others, played through Loman's mind on an endless loop of memory.

He'd kill Shaddack to save himself from being forced to become what Denny had become, and the destruction of Shaddack's legend would just be a beneficial side-effect.

He holstered his gun and got out of the car. He hurried through the rain to the main entrance, pushed through the etched-glass doors into the marble-floored lobby, turned right, away from the elevators, and approached the main reception desk. In corporate luxury, the place rivaled the most elaborate headquarters of high-tech companies in the more famous Silicon Valley, farther south. Detailed marble moldings, polished brass trim, fine crystal sconces, and modernistic crystal chandeliers were testament to New Wave's success.

The woman on duty was Dora Hankins. He had known her all of his life. She was a year older than he. In high school he had dated her sister a couple of times.

She looked up as he approached, said nothing.

"Shaddack?" he said.

"Not in."

"You sure?"

"Yes."

"When's he due?"

"His secretary will know."

"I'll go up."

"Fine."

As he boarded an elevator and pushed the 3 on the control board, Loman reflected on the small talk in which he and Dora Hankins would have engaged in the days before they had been put through the Change. They would have bantered with each other, exchanged news about their families, and commented on the weather. Not now. Small talk was a pleasure of their former world. Converted, they had no use for it. In fact, though he recalled that small talk had once been a part of civilized life, Loman could no longer quite remember why he ever had found it worthwhile or what kind of pleasure it had given him.

Shaddack's office suite was on the northwest corner of the third floor. The first room off the hall was the reception lounge, plushly carpeted in beige Edward Fields originals, impressively furnished in plump Roche-Bobois leather couches and brass tables with inch-thick glass tops. The single piece of art was a painting by Jasper Johns—an original, not a print.

What happens to artists in the new world coming? Loman wondered.

But he knew the answer. There would be none. Art was emotion embodied in paint on a canvas, words on a page, music in a symphony hall. There would be no art in the new world. And if there was, it would be the art of fear. The writer's most frequently used words would all be synonyms of darkness. The musician would write dirges of one form or another. The painter's most used pigment would be black.

Vicky Lanardo, Shaddack's executive secretary, was at her desk. She said, "He's not in."

Behind her the door to Shaddack's enormous private office stood open. No lights were on in there. It was illuminated only by the light of the storm-torn day, which came through the blinds in ash-gray bands.

"When will he be in?" Loman asked.

"I don't know."

"No appointments?"

"None."

"Do you know where he is?"

"No."

Loman walked out. For a while he prowled the half-deserted corridors, offices, labs, and tech rooms, hoping to spot Shaddack.

Before long, however, he decided that Shaddack was not lurking about the premises. Evidently the great man was staying mobile on this last day of Moonlight Cove's conversion.

Because of me, Loman thought. Because of what I said to him last night at Peyser's. He's afraid of me, and he's either staying mobile or gone to ground somewhere, making himself difficult to find.

Loman left the building, returned to his patrol car, and set out in search of his maker.

26

IN THE DOWNSTAIRS HALF-BATH OFF THE KITCHEN, NAKED from the waist up, Sam sat on the closed lid of the commode, and Tessa performed the same kind of nursely duties she'd performed earlier for Chrissie. But Sam's wounds were more serious than the girl's.

In a dime-size circle on his forehead, above his right eye, the skin had been flensed off, and in the center of the circle the flesh had been entirely eaten away, revealing a speck of bared bone about an eighth of an inch in diameter. Stanching the flow of blood from those tiny, severed capillaries required a few minutes of continuous pressure, followed by the application of iodine, a liberal coating of NuSkin, and a tightly taped gauze bandage. But even after all these efforts, the gauze slowly darkened with red stain.

As Tessa worked on him, Sam told them what had happened:

" . . . so if I hadn't shot her in the head, just then . . . if I'd been a second or two slower, I think that damn thing, that probe, whatever it was, it would have bored right through my skull and sunk into my brain, and she'd have connected with me the way she was connected with that computer."

Her toga forsaken in favor of dry jeans and blouse, Chrissie stood just inside the bathroom, white-faced but wanting to hear all.

Harry had pulled his wheelchair into the doorway.

Moose was lying at Sam's feet, rather than at Harry's. The dog seemed to realize that at the moment the visitor needed comforting more than Harry did.

Sam was colder to the touch than could be explained by his time in the chilly rain. He was trembling, and periodically the shivers that passed through him were so powerful that his teeth chattered.

The more Sam talked, the colder Tessa became, too, and in time his shivers were communicated to her.

His right wrist had been cut on both sides, when Harley Coltrane had gripped him with a powerful bony hand. No major blood vessels had been severed; neither gash required stitches, and Tessa quickly stopped the bleeding there. The bruises, which had barely begun to appear and would not fully flower for hours yet, were going to be worse than the cuts. He complained of pain in the joint, and his hand was weak, but she did not think that any bones had been broken or crushed.

" . . . as if they'd somehow been given the ability to control their physical form," Sam said shakily, "to make anything they wanted of themselves, mind over matter, just like Chrissie said when she told us about the priest, the one who started to become the creature from that movie. . . ."

The girl nodded.

"I mean, they changed *before my eyes*, grew these probes, tried to spear me. Yet with this incredible control of their bodies, of their physical substance, all they apparently wanted to make of themselves was . . . something out of a bad dream."

The wound on his abdomen was the least of the three. As on his forehead, the skin was stripped away in a dime-sized circle, though the probe that had struck him there seemed to have been meant to burn rather than cut its way into him. His flesh was scorched, and the wound itself was pretty much cauterized.

From his wheelchair Harry said, "Sam, do you think they're really people who control themselves, who have *chosen* to become machinelike, or are they people who've somehow been taken over by machines, against their will?"

"I don't know," Sam said. "It could be either, I guess."

"But how could they be taken over, how could this happen, how could such a change in the human body be accomplished? And how does what's happened to the Coltranes tie in with the Boogeymen?"

"Damned if I know," Sam said. "Somehow it's all related to New Wave. Got to be. And none of us here knows anything much about the cutting edge of that kind of technology, so we don't even have the basic knowledge required to speculate intelligently. It might as well be magic to us, supernatural. The only way we'll ever really understand what's happened is to get help from outside, quarantine Moonlight Cove, seize New Wave's labs and records, and reconstruct it the way fire marshals reconstruct the history of a fire from what they sift out of the ashes."

"Ashes?" Tessa asked as Sam stood up and as she helped him into his shirt. "This talk about fires and ashes—and other things you've said—make it sound as if you think whatever's going on in Moonlight Cove is building real fast toward an explosion or something."

"It is," he said.

At first he tried to button his shirt with one hand, but then he allowed Tessa to do it for him. She noticed that his skin was still cold and that his shivers were not subsiding with time.

· He said, "All these murders they've got to cover up, these things that stalk the night . . . there's a sense that a collapse has begun, that whatever they tried to do here isn't turning out like they expected, and that the collapse is accelerating." He was breathing too quickly, too shallowly. He paused, took a deeper breath. "What I saw in the Coltranes' house . . . that didn't look like anything anyone could have planned, not something you'd *want* to do to people or that they'd want for themselves. It looked like an experiment out of control, biology run amok, reality turned inside out, and I swear to God that if *those* kinds of secrets are hidden in the houses of this town, then the whole project has to be collapsing on New Wave right now, coming down fast and hard on their heads, whether they want to admit it or not. It's all blowing up now, right now, one hell of an explosion, and we're in the middle of it."

From the moment he'd stumbled through the kitchen door, dripping rain and blood, throughout the time Tessa had cleaned and bandaged his wounds, she had noticed something that frightened her more than his paleness and shivering. He kept touching them. He had embraced Tessa in the kitchen when she gasped at the sight of the bleeding hole in his forehead; he'd held her and leaned against her and assured her that he was okay. Primarily he seemed to be reassuring himself that she and Harry and Chrissie were okay, as if he had expected to come back and find them . . . changed. He hugged Chrissie, too, as if she were his own daughter, and he said, "It'll be all right, everything'll be all right," when he saw how frightened she was. Harry held out a hand in concern, and Sam grasped it and was reluctant to let go. In the bathroom, while Tessa dressed his wounds, he had repeatedly touched her hands, her arms, and had once put a hand against her cheek as if wondering at the softness and warmth of her skin. He reached out to touch Chrissie, too, where she stood inside the bathroom door, patting her shoulder, holding her hand for a moment and giving it a reassuring squeeze. Until now he had not been a toucher. He had been reserved, self-contained, cool, even distant. But during the quarter of an hour he'd spent in the Coltrane house, he had been so profoundly shaken by what he had seen that his shell of self-imposed isolation had cracked wide open; he had come to want and need the human contact that, only a short while ago, he had not even ranked as desirable as good Mexican food, Guinness Stout, and Goldie Hawn films.

When she contemplated the intensity of the horror necessary to transform him so completely and abruptly, Tessa was more frightened than ever because Sam Booker's redemption seemed akin to that of a sinner who, on his deathbed, glimpsing hell, turns desperately to the god he once shunned, seeking comfort and reassurance. Was he less sure now of their chances of escaping? Perhaps he was seeking human contact because, having denied it to himself for so many years, he believed that only hours remained in which to experience the communion of his own kind before the great, deep endless darkness settled over them.

27

SHADDACK AWOKE FROM HIS FAMILIAR AND COMFORTING dream of human and machine parts combined in a world-spanning engine of incalculable power and mysterious purpose. He was, as always, refreshed as much by the dream as by sleep itself.

He got out of the van and stretched. Using tools he found in the garage, he forced open the connecting door to the late Paula Parkins's house. He used her bathroom, then washed his hands and face.

Upon returning to the garage, he raised the big door. He pulled the van out into the driveway, where it could better transmit and receive data by microwave.

Rain was still falling, and depressions in the lawn were filled with water. Already wisps of fog stirred in the windless air, which probably meant the banks that rolled in from the sea later in the day would be even denser than those last night.

He took another ham sandwich and a Coke from the cooler and ate while using the van's VDT to check on the progress of Moonhawk. The 6:00 A.M. to 6:00 P.M. schedule for four hundred and fifty conversions was still under way. Already, at 12:50, slightly less than seven hours into the twelve-hour program, three hundred and nine had been injected with full-spectrum microspheres. The conversion teams were well ahead of schedule.

He checked on the progress of the search for Samuel Booker and the Lockland woman. Neither had been found.

Shaddack should have been worried about their disappearance. But he was unconcerned. He had seen the moonhawk, after all, not once but three times, and he had no doubt that ultimately he would achieve all of his goals.

The Foster girl was still missing too. He didn't trouble himself about her either. She had probably encountered something deadly in the night. At times regressives could be useful.

Perhaps Booker and the Lockland woman had fallen victim to those same creatures. It would be ironic if the regressives—the only flaw in the project, and a potentially serious one—should prove to have preserved the secret of Moonhawk.

Through the VDT, he tried to reach Tucker at New Wave, then at his home, but the man was at neither place. Could Watkins be correct? Was Tucker a regressive and, like Peyser, unable to find his way back to human form? Was he out there in the woods right now, trapped in an altered state?

Clicking off the computer, Shaddack sighed. After everyone had been converted at midnight, this first phase of Moonhawk would not be finished. Not quite. They'd evidently have a few messes to mop up.

28

IN THE CELLAR OF THE ICARUS COLONY, THREE BODIES HAD become one. The resultant entity was without rigid shape, boneless, featureless, a mass of pulsing tissue that lived in spite of lacking a brain and heart and blood vessels, without organs of any kind. It was primal, a thick protein soup, brainless but aware, eyeless but seeing, earless but hearing, without a gut but hungry.

The agglomerations of silicon microspheres had dissolved within it. That inner computer could no longer function in the radically altered substance of the creature, and in turn the beast had no use any more for the biological assistance that the microspheres had been designed to provide. Now it was not linked to Sun, the computer at New Wave. If the microwave transmitter there sent a death order, it would not receive the command—and would live.

It had become the master of its physiology by reducing itself to the uncomplicated essence of physical existence.

Their three minds also had become one. The consciousness now dwelling in that darkness was as lacking in complex form as the amorphous, jellid body it inhabited.

It had relinquished its memory because memories were inevitably of events and relationships that had consequences, and consequences—good or bad—implied that one was responsible for one's actions. Flight from responsibility had driven the creature to regression in the first place. Pain was another reason for shedding memory—the pain of recalling what had been lost.

Likewise, it had surrendered the capacity to consider the future, to plan, to dream.

Now it had no past of which it was aware, and the concept of a future was beyond its ken. It lived only for the moment, unthinking, unfeeling, uncaring.

It had one need. To survive.

And to survive, it needed only one thing. To feed.

29

THE BREAKFAST DISHES HAD BEEN CLEARED FROM THE TABLE while Sam was at the Coltranes' house, battling monsters that apparently had been part human and part computer and part zombies—and maybe, for all they knew, part toaster oven. After Sam was bandaged, Chrissie gathered with him and Tessa and Harry around the kitchen table again, to listen to them discuss what action to take next.

Moose stayed at Chrissie's side, regarding her with soulful brown eyes, as if he adored her more than life itself. She couldn't resist giving him all the petting and scratching-behind-the-ears that he wanted.

"The greatest problem of our age," Sam said, "is how to keep technological progress accelerating, how to use it to improve the quality of life—without being overwhelmed by it. Can we employ the computer to redesign our world, to remake our lives, without one day coming to worship it?" He blinked at Tessa and said, "It's not a silly question."

Tessa frowned. "I didn't say it was. Sometimes we have a blind trust in machines, a tendency to believe that whatever a computer tells us is gospel—"

"To forget the old maxim," Harry injected, "which says—'garbage in, garbage out.' "

"Exactly," Tessa agreed. "Sometimes, when we get data or analyses from computers, we treat it as if the machines were all infallible. Which is dangerous because a computer application can be conceived, designed, and implemented by a madman, perhaps not as easily as by a benign genius but certainly as effectively."

Sam said, "Yet people have a tendency—no, even a deep desire—to *want* to depend on the machines."

"Yeah," Harry said, "that's our sorry damn need to shift responsibility whenever we possibly can. A spineless desire to get out from under responsibility is in our genes, I swear it is, and the only way we get anywhere in this world is by constantly fighting our natural inclination to be utterly irresponsible. Sometimes I wonder if *that's* what we got from the devil when Eve listened to the serpent and ate the apple—this aversion to responsibility. Most evil has it roots there."

Chrissie noticed this subject energized Harry. With his one good arm and a little help from his half-good leg, he levered himself higher in his wheelchair. Color seeped into his previously pale face. He made a fist of one hand and stared at it intently, as if holding something precious in that tight grip, as if he held the idea there and didn't want to let go of it until he had fully explored it.

He said, "Men steal and kill and lie and cheat because they feel no responsibility for others. Politicians want power, and they want acclaim when their policies succeed, but they seldom stand up and take the responsibility for failure. The world's full of people who want to tell you how to live your life, how to make heaven right here on earth, but when their ideas turn out half-baked, when it ends in Dachau or the Gulag or the mass murders that followed our departure from Southeast Asia, they turn their heads, avert their eyes, and pretend they had no responsibility for the slaughter."

He shuddered, and Chrissie shuddered too, though she was not entirely sure that she entirely understood everything he was saying.

"Jesus," he continued, "if I've thought about this once, I've thought about it a thousand times, ten thousand, maybe because of the war."

"Vietnam, you mean?" Tessa said.

Harry nodded. He was still staring at his fist. "In the war, to survive, you had to be responsible every minute of every day, unhesitatingly responsible for yourself, for your every action. You had to be responsible for your buddies, too, because survival wasn't something that could be achieved alone. That's maybe the one positive thing about fighting in a war—it clarifies your thinking and makes you realize that a sense of responsibility is what separates good men from the damned. I don't regret the war, not even considering what happened to me there. I learned that great lesson, learned to be responsible in all things, and I still feel responsible to the people we were fighting for, always will, and sometimes when I think of how we abandoned them to the killing fields, the mass graves, I lay awake at night and cry because they depended on me, and to the extent that I was a part of the process, I'm responsible for failing them."

They were all silent.

Chrissie felt a peculiar pressure in her chest, the same feeling she always got in school when a teacher—any teacher, any subject—began to talk about something which had been previously unknown to her and which so impressed her that it changed the way she looked at the world. It didn't happen often, but it was always both a scary and wonderful sensation. She felt it now, because of what Harry had said, but the sensation was ten times or a hundred times stronger than it had ever been when some new insight or idea had been passed to her in geography or math or science.

Tessa said, "Harry, I think your sense of responsibility in this case is excessive."

He finally looked up from his fist. "No. It can never be. Your sense of responsibility to others can never be excessive." He smiled at her. "But I know you just well enough to suspect you're already aware of that, Tessa, whether you realize it or not." He looked at Sam and said, "Some of those who came out of the war saw no good at all in it. When I meet up with them, I always suspect they were the ones who never learned the lesson, and I avoid them—though I suppose that's unfair. Can't help it. But when I meet a man from the war and see he learned the lesson, then I'd trust him with my life. Hell, I'd trust him with my soul, which in this case seems to be what they want to steal. You'll get us out of this, Sam." At last he opened his fist. "I've no doubt of that."

Tessa seemed surprised. To Sam she said, "You were in Vietnam?"

Sam nodded. "Between junior college and the Bureau."

"But you never mentioned it. This morning, when we were making breakfast, when you told me all the reasons you saw the world so differently from the way I saw it, you mentioned your wife's death, the murder of your partners, your situation with your son, but not that."

Sam stared at his bandaged wrist for a while and finally said, "The war is the most personal experience of my life."

"What an odd thing to say."

"Not odd at all," Harry said. "The most intense and the most personal."

Sam said, "If I'd not come to terms with it, I'd probably still talk about it, probably run on about it all the time. But I *have* come to terms with it. I've understood. And now to talk about it casually with someone I've just met would . . . well, cheapen it, I guess."

Tessa looked at Harry and said, "But you knew he was in Vietnam?"

"Yes."

"Just *knew* it somehow."

"Yes."

Sam had been leaning over the table. Now he settled back in his chair. "Harry, I swear I'll do my best to get us out of this. But I wish I had a better grasp of what we're up against. It all comes from New Wave. But exactly what have they done, and how can it be stopped? And how can I hope to deal with it when I don't even *understand* it?"

To that point Chrissie had felt that the conversation had been way over her head, even though all of it had been fascinating and though some of it had stirred the learning feeling in her. But now she felt that she had to contribute: "Are you really *sure* it's not aliens?"

"We're sure," Tessa said, smiling at her, and Sam ruffled her hair.

"Well," Chrissie said, "what I mean is, maybe what went wrong at New Wave is that aliens landed *there* and used it as a base, and maybe they want to turn us all into machines, like the Coltranes, so we can serve them as slaves—which, when you think about it, is more sensible than wanting to eat us. They're aliens, after all, which means they have alien stomachs and alien digestive juices, and we'd probably be real hard to digest, give them heartburn, maybe even diarrhea."

Sam, who was sitting in the chair beside Chrissie, took both her hands and held them gently in his, as aware of her abraded palm as he was aware of his own injured wrist. "Chrissie, I don't know if you've been paying too much attention to what Harry's been saying—"

"Oh, yes," she said at once. "All of it."

"Well, then you'll understand when I tell you that wanting to blame all these horrors on aliens is yet another way of shifting the responsibility from where it really belongs—on us, on people, on our very real and very great capacity to do harm to one another. It's hard to believe that anybody, even crazy men, would want to make the Coltranes into what they became, but somebody evidently did want just that. If we try to blame it on aliens—or the devil or God or trolls or whatever—we won't be likely to see the situation clearly enough to figure out how to save ourselves. You understand?"

"Sort of."

He smiled at her. He had a very nice smile, though he didn't flash it much. "I think you understand it more than sort of."

"More than sort of," Chrissie agreed. "It'd sure be nice if it was aliens, because we'd just have to find their nest or their hive or whatever, burn them out real good, maybe blow up their spaceship, and it would be over and done with. But if it's not aliens, if it's us—people like us—who did all this, then maybe it's never quite over and done with."

30

WITH INCREASING FRUSTRATION, LOMAN WATKINS CRUISED from one end of Moonlight Cove to the other, back and forth, around and around in the rain, seeking Shaddack. He had revisited the house on the north point to be sure Shaddack had not returned there, and also to check the garage to see which vehicle was missing. Now he was looking for Shaddack's charcoal-gray van with tinted windows, but he was unable to locate it.

Wherever he went, conversion teams and search parties were at work. Though the unconverted were not likely to notice anything too unusual about those men's passage through town, Loman was constantly aware of them.

At the north and south roadblocks on the county route and at the main blockade on the eastern end of Ocean Avenue, out toward the interstate, Loman's officers were continuing to deal with outsiders wanting to enter Moonlight Cove. Exhaust plumes rose from the idling patrol cars, mingling with the wisps of fog that had begun to slither through the rain. The red and blue emergency beacons were reflected in the wet macadam, so it seemed as if streams of blood, oxygenated and oxygen-depleted, flowed along the pavement.

There weren't many would-be visitors because the town was neither the county seat nor a primary shopping center for people in outlying communities. Furthermore, it was close to the end of the county road, and there were no destinations beyond it, so no one wanted to pass through on the way to somewhere else. Those who did want to come into town were turned away, if at all possible, with a story about a toxic spill at New Wave. Those who seemed at all skeptical were arrested, conveyed to the jail, and locked in cells until a decision could be made either to kill or convert them. Since the establishment of the quarantine in the early hours of the morning, only a score of people had been stopped at the blockades, and only six had been jailed.

Shaddack had chosen his proving ground well. Moonlight Cove was relatively isolated and therefore easier to control.

Loman was of a mind to order the roadblocks dismantled, and to drive over to Aberdeen Wells, where he could spill the whole story to the county sheriff. He wanted to blow the Moonhawk Project wide open.

He was no longer afraid of Shaddack's rage or of dying. Well . . . not true. He was afraid of Shaddack and of death, but they held less fear for him than the prospect of becoming something like Denny had become. He would have as soon entrusted himself to the mercies of the sheriff in Aberdeen and the federal authorities—even scientists who, cleaning up the mess in Moonlight Cove, might be sorely tempted to dissect him—than stay in town and inevitably surrender the last few fragments of his humanity either to regression or to some nightmare wedding of his body and mind with a computer.

But if he ordered his officers to stand down, they would be suspicious, and their loyalty lay more with Shaddack than with him, for they were bound to Shaddack by terror. They were still more frightened of their New Wave master than of anything else, for they had not seen what Denny had become and did not yet realize that their future might hold in store something even worse than regression to a savage state. Like Moreau's beastmen, they kept The Law as best they could, not daring—at least for now—to betray their maker. They would probably try to stop Loman from sabotaging the Moonhawk Project, and he might wind up dead or, worse, locked in a jail cell.

He couldn't risk revealing his counterrevolutionary commitment, for then he might never have a chance to deal with Shaddack. In his mind's eye he saw himself caged at the jail, with Shaddack smiling coldly at him through the bars, as they wheeled in a computer with which they somehow intended to fuse him.

Molten silver eyes . . .

He kept on the move in the rain-hammered day, squinting through the streaked windshield. The wipers thumped steadily, as though ticking off time. He was acutely aware that midnight was drawing nearer.

He was the puma-man, on the prowl, and Moreau was out there in the island jungle that was Moonlight Cove.

31

INITIALLY THE PROTEAN CREATURE WAS CONTENT TO FEED on the things it found when it extended thin tendrils of itself down the drain in the cellar floor or through fine cracks in the walls and into the moist surrounding earth. Beetles. Grubs. Earthworms. It no longer knew the names of those things, but it avidly consumed them.

Soon, however, it depleted the supply of insects and worms within ten yards of the house. It needed a more substantial meal.

It churned, seethed, perhaps striving to marshal its amorphous tissues into a shape in which it could leave the cellar and seek prey. But it had no memory of previous forms and no desire whatsoever to impose structural order on itself.

The consciousness which inhabited that jellid mass no longer had more than the dimmest sense of self-awareness, yet it was still able to remake itself to an extent that would satisfy its needs. Suddenly a score of lipless, toothless mouths opened in that fluid form. A blast of sound, mostly beyond the range of human hearing, erupted from it.

Throughout the moldering structure above the shapeless beast, dozens of mice were scurrying, nibbling at food, nest-building, and grooming themselves. They stopped, as one, when the call blared up from the cellar.

The creature could sense them above, in the crumbling walls, though it thought of them not as mice but as small warm masses of living flesh. Food. Fuel. It wanted them. It *needed* them.

It attempted to express that need in the form of a wordless but compelling summons.

In every corner of the house, mice twitched. They brushed at their faces with forepaws, as if they'd scurried through cobwebs and were trying to scrape those clingy, gossamer strands out of their fur.

A small colony of eight bats lived in the attic, and they also reacted to the urgent call. They dropped from the rafters on which they hung, and flew in frenzied, random patterns in the long upper room, repeatedly swooping within a fraction of an inch of the walls and one another.

But nothing came to the creature in the basement. Though the call had reached the small animals for which it had been intended, it did not have the desired effect.

The shapeless thing fell silent.

Its many mouths closed.

One by one the bats returned to their perches in the attic.

The mice sat as if in shock for a moment, then resumed their usual activities.

A couple of minutes later, the protean beast tried again with a different pattern of sounds, still pitched beyond human hearing but more alluring than before.

The bats flung themselves from their perches and roiled through the attic in such turmoil that an observer might have thought they numbered a hundred instead of only eight. The beating of their wings was louder than the rush of rain on the leaky roof.

Everywhere, mice rose on their hind feet, sitting at attention, ears pricked.

Those in the lower reaches of the house, nearer the source of the summons, shivered violently, as though they saw before them a crouched and grinning cat.

Screeching, the bats swooped through a hole in the attic floor, into an empty room on the second story, where they circled and soared and dove ceaselessly.

Two mice on the ground floor began to creep toward the kitchen, where the door to the basement stood open. But both stopped on the threshold of that room, frightened and confused.

Below, the shapeless entity tripled the power of its call.

One of the mice in the kitchen suddenly bled from the ears and fell dead.

Upstairs, the bats began to bounce off walls, their radar shot.

The cellar dweller cut back somewhat on the force of its summons.

The bats immediately swooped out of the upstairs room, into the hallway, down the stairwell, and along the ground-floor hall. As they went, they flew over a double score of scurrying mice.

Below, the creature's many mouths had connected, forming one large orifice in the center of the pulsing mass.

In swift succession the bats flew straight into that gaping maw like black playing cards being tossed one at a time into a waste can. They embedded themselves in the oozing protoplasm and were swiftly dissolved by powerful digestive acids.

An army of mice and four rats—even two chipmunks that eagerly abandoned their nest inside the dining-room wall—swarmed down the steep cellar steps, falling over one another, squeaking excitedly. They fed themselves to the waiting entity.

After that flurry of movement, the house was still.

The creature stopped its siren song. For the moment.

32

OFFICER NEIL PENNIWORTH WAS ASSIGNED TO PATROL THE northwest quadrant of Moonlight Cove. He was alone in the car because even with the hundred New Wave employees detailed to the police department during the night, their manpower was stretched thin.

Right now, he preferred to work without a partner. Since the episode at Peyser's house, when the smell of blood and the sight of Peyser's altered form had enticed Penniworth to regress, he had been afraid to be around other people. He had avoided total degeneration last night . . . but only by the thinnest of margins. If he witnessed someone else in the act of regression, the urge might stir within him, too, and this time he was not sure that he could successfully repress that dark yearning.

He was equally afraid to be alone. The struggle to hold fast to his remaining shreds of humanity, to resist chaos, to be responsible, was wearying, and he longed to escape this new, hard life. Alone, with no one to see him if he began to surrender the very form and substance of himself, with no one to talk him out of it or even to protest his degeneration, he would be lost.

The weight of his fear was as real as a slab of iron, crushing the life out of him. At times he had difficulty drawing breath, as though his lungs were banded by steel and restricted from full expansion.

The dimensions of the black-and-white seemed to shrink, until he felt almost as confined as he would have been in a straitjacket. The metronomic thump of the windshield wipers grew louder, at least to his ears, until the volume was as thunderous as an endless series of cannon volleys. Repeatedly during the morning and early afternoon, he pulled off the road, flung open the door, and scrambled out into the rain, drawing deep breaths of the cool air.

As the day progressed, however, even the world outside of the car began to seem smaller than it had been. He stopped on Holliwell Road, half a mile west of New Wave's headquarters, and got out of the cruiser, but he felt no better. The low roof of gray clouds denied him the sight of the limitless sky. Like semitransparent curtains of tinsel and thinnest silk, the rain and fog hung between him and the rest of the world. The humidity was cloying, stifling. Rain overflowed gutters, churned in muddy torrents through roadside ditches, dripped from every branch and leaf of every tree, pattered on the macadam pavement, tapped hollowly on the patrol car, sizzled, gurgled, chuckled, snapped against his face, beat upon him with such force that it seemed he was being driven to his knees by thousands of tiny hammers, each too small to be effective in itself but with brutal cumulative effect.

Neil clambered back into the car with as much eagerness as he had scrambled out of it.

He understood that it was neither the claustrophobic interior of the cruiser nor the enervating enwrapment of the rain that he was desperately trying to escape. The actual oppressor was his life as a New Person. Able to feel only fear, he was locked in an emotional closet of such unendurably narrow dimensions that he could not move at all. He was not suffocating because of external entanglements and constrictions; rather, he was bound from within, because of what Shaddack had made of him.

Which meant there was no escape.

Except, perhaps, by regression.

Neil could not bear life as he must now live it. On the other hand he was repelled and terrified by the thought of devolution into some subhuman form.

His dilemma appeared irresoluble.

He was as distressed by his inability to stop thinking about his predicament as he was by the predicament itself. It pried constantly at his mind. He could find no surcease.

The closest he came to being able to put his worry—and some of his fear— out of mind was when he was working with the mobile VDT in the patrol car. When he checked the computer bulletin board to see if messages awaited him, when he accessed the Moonhawk schedule to learn how conversions were progressing, or undertook any other task with the computer, his attention became so focused on the interaction with the machine that briefly his anxiety subsided and his nagging claustrophobia faded.

From adolescence, Neil had been interested in computers, though he had never become a hacker. His interest was less obsessive than that. He'd started with computer games, of course, but later had been given an inexpensive PC. Later still he had bought a modem with some of the money earned at a summer job. Though he could not afford much long-distance telephone time and never spent leisurely hours using the modem to reach far from the backwaters of Moonlight Cove into the fascinating data nets available in the outside world, he found his forays into on-line systems engrossing and fun.

Now, as he sat in the parked car along Holliwell Road, using the VDT, he thought that the inner world of the computer was admirably clean, comparatively simple, predictable, and sane. So unlike human existence—whether that of New People or Old. In there, logic and reason ruled. Cause and effect and side-effect were always analyzed and made perfectly clear. In there, all was black and white—or, when gray, the gray was carefully measured, quantified and qualified. Cold facts were easier to deal with than feelings. A universe formed purely of data, abstracted from matter and event, seemed so much more desirable than the real universe of cold and heat, sharp and blunt, smooth and rough, blood and death, pain and fear.

Calling up menu after menu, Neil probed ever deeper into the Moonhawk research files within Sun. He needed none of the data that he summoned forth but found solace in the process of obtaining it.

He began to see the terminal screen not as a cathode-ray tube on which information was displayed, but as a window into another world. A world of facts. A world free of troubling contradictions . . . and responsibility. In there, nothing could be felt; there was only the known and the unknown, either an abundance of facts about a particular subject or a dearth of them, but not *feeling*; never feeling; feeling was the curse of those whose existence was dependent upon flesh and bone.

A window into another world.

Neil touched the screen.

He wished the window could be opened and that he could climb through it to that place of reason, order, peace.

With the fingertips of his right hand, he traced circles across the warm glass screen.

Strangely, he thought of Dorothy, swept up from the plains of Kansas with her dog Toto, spun high into the tornado, and dropped out of that depression-era grayness into a world far more intriguing. If only some electronic tornado could erupt from the VDT and carry him to a better place . . .

His fingers passed through the screen.

He snatched his hand back in astonishment.

The glass had not ruptured. Chains of words and numbers glowed on the tube, as before.

At first he tried to convince himself that what he had seen had been a hallucination. But he did not believe that.

He flexed his fingers. They appeared unhurt.

He looked out at the storm-swept day. The windshield wipers were not switched on. Rain rippled down the glass, distorting the world beyond; everything out there looked twisted, mutated, strange. There could never be order, sanity, and peace in such a place as that.

Tentatively he touched the computer screen once more. It felt solid.

Again, he thought of how desirable the clean, predictable world of the computer would be—and as before his hand slipped through the glass, up to the wrist this time. The screen had opened around him and sealed tight to him, as if it were an organic membrane. The data continued to blaze on the tube, the words and numbers forming lines around his intruding hand.

His heart was racing. He was afraid but also excited.

He tried to wiggle his fingers in that mysterious, inner warmth. He could not feel them. He began to think they had dissolved or been cut off, and that when he withdrew his hand from the machine, the stump of his wrist would spout blood.

He withdrew it anyway.

His hand was whole.

But it was not quite a hand any more. The flesh on the upper side, from the tips of his fingernails to his wrist, appeared to be veined with copper and threads of glass. In those glass filaments beat a steady and luminous pulse.

He turned his hand over. The undersides of his fingers and his palm resembled the surface of a cathode-ray tube. Data burned there, green letters on a background glassy and dark. When he compared the words and numbers on his hand to those on the car's VDT, he saw they were identical. The information on the VDT changed; simultaneously, so did that on his hand.

Abruptly, he understood that regression into bestial form was not the only avenue of escape open to him, that he could enter into the world of electronic thought and magnetic memory, of knowledge without fleshly desire, of awareness without feeling. This was not an insight strictly—or even primarily—intellectual in nature. It wasn't just instinctive understanding, either. On some level more profound than either intellect or instinct, he knew that he could remake himself more thoroughly than even Shaddack had remade him.

He lowered his hand from the tilted computer screen to the data-processing unit in the console between the seats. As easily as he had penetrated the glass, he let his hand slide through the keyboard and cover plate, into the guts of the machine.

He was like a ghost, able to pass through walls, ectoplasmic.

A coldness crept up his arm.

The data on the screen were replaced by cryptic patterns of light.

He leaned back in his seat.

The coldness had reached his shoulder. It flowed into his neck.

He sighed.

He felt something happening to his eyes. He wasn't sure what. He could have looked at the rearview mirror. He didn't care. He decided to close his eyes and let them become whatever was necessary as part of this second and more complete conversion.

This altered state was infinitely more appealing than that of the regressive. Irresistible.

The coldness was in his face now. His mouth was numb.

Something also was happening inside his head. He was becoming as aware of the inner geography of his brain circuits and synapses as he was of the exterior world. His body was not as much a part of him as it had once been; he sensed less through it, as if his nerves had been mostly abraded away; he could not even tell if it was warm or chilly in the car unless he concentrated on accumulating that data. His body was just a machine casing, after all, and a rack for sensors, designed to protect and serve the inner him, the calculating mind.

The coldness was inside his skull.

It felt like scores, then hundreds, then thousands of ice-cold spiders scurrying over the surface of his brain, burrowing into it.

Suddenly he remembered that Dorothy had found Oz to be a living nightmare and ultimately had wanted desperately to find her way back to Kansas. Alice, too, had found madness and terror down the rabbit hole, beyond the looking-glass. . . .

A million cold spiders.

Inside his skull.

A billion.

Cold, cold.

Scurrying.

33

STILL CIRCLING THROUGH MOONLIGHT COVE, SEEKING SHAD-dack, Loman saw two regressives sprint across the street.

He was on Paddock Lane, at the southern end of town, where the properties were big enough for people to keep horses. Ranch houses lay on both sides, with small private stables beside or behind them. The homes set back from the street, behind split-rail or white ranch fencing, beyond deep and lushly landscaped lawns.

The pair of regressives erupted from a dense row of mature three-foot-high azaleas that were still bushy but flowerless this late in the season. They streaked on all fours across the roadway, leaped a ditch, and crashed through a hedgerow, vanishing behind it.

Although immense pines were lined up along both sides of Paddock Lane, adding their shadows to the already darkish day, Loman was sure of what he had seen. They had been modeled after dream creatures rather than any single animal of the real world: part wolf, perhaps, part cat, part reptile. They were swift and looked powerful. One of them had turned its head toward him, and in the shadows its eyes had glowed as pink-red as those of a rat.

He slowed but did not stop. He no longer cared about identifying and apprehending regressives. For one thing, he'd already identified them to his satisfaction: all of the converted. He knew that stopping them could be accomplished only by stopping Shaddack. He was after much bigger game.

However, he was unnerved to see them brazenly on the prowl in daylight, at two-thirty in the afternoon. Heretofore, they had been secretive creatures of the night, hiding the shame of their regression by seeking their altered states only well after sunset. If they were prepared to venture forth before nightfall, the Moonhawk Project was disintegrating into chaos even faster than he had expected. Moonlight Cove was not merely teetering on the brink of hell but had already tipped over the edge and into the pit.

34

THEY WERE IN HARRY'S THIRD-FLOOR BEDROOM AGAIN, where they had passed the last hour and a half, brainstorming and urgently discussing their options. No lamps were on. Watery afternoon light washed the room, contributing to the somber mood.

"So we're agreed there are two ways we might send a message out of town," Sam said.

"But in either case," Tessa said uneasily, "you have to go out there and cover a lot of ground to get where you need to go."

Sam shrugged.

Tessa and Chrissie had taken off their shoes and sat on the bed, their backs against the headboard. The girl clearly intended to stay close to Tessa; she seemed to have imprinted on her the way a baby chick, freshly hatched from the egg, imprints on the nearest adult bird, whether it's the mother or not.

Tessa said, "It's not going to be as easy as slipping two doors south to the Coltrane house. Not in daylight."

"You think I ought to wait until it gets dark?" Sam asked.

"Yes. The fog will come in more heavily, too, as the afternoon fades."

She meant what she said, though she was worried about the delay. During the hours that they bided their time, more people would be converted. Moonlight Cove would become an increasingly alien, dangerous, and surprise-filled environment.

Turning to Harry, Sam said, "What time's it get dark?"

Harry was in his wheelchair. Moose had returned to his master, thrusting his burly head under the arm of the chair and onto Harry's lap, content to sit for long stretches in that awkward posture in return for just a little petting and scratching and an occasional reassuring word.

Harry said, "These days, twilight comes before six o'clock."

Sam was sitting at the telescope, though at the moment he was not using it. A few minutes ago he had surveyed the streets and reported seeing more activity than earlier—plenty of car and foot patrols. As steadily fewer local residents remained unconverted, the conspirators behind Moonhawk were growing bolder in their policing actions, less concerned than they'd once been about calling attention to themselves.

Glancing at his watch, Sam said, "I can't say I like the idea of wasting three hours or more. The sooner we get the word out, the more people we'll save from . . . from whatever's being done to them."

"But if you get caught because you didn't wait for nightfall," Tessa said, "then the chances of saving *anyone* become a hell of a lot slimmer."

"The lady has a point," Harry said.

"A good one," Chrissie said. "Just because they're not aliens doesn't mean they're going to be any easier to deal with."

Because even the working telephones would allow a caller to dial only approved numbers within town, they'd given up on that hope. But Sam had realized that any PC connected by modem with the supercomputer at New Wave—Harry said they called it Sun—might provide a way out of town, an electronic highway on which they could circumvent the current restrictions on the phone lines and the roadblocks.

As Sam had noted last night while using the VDT in the police car, Sun maintained direct contacts with scores of other computers—including several FBI data banks, both those approved for wide access and those supposedly sealed to all but Bureau agents. If he could sit at a VDT, link in to Sun, and through Sun link to a Bureau computer, then he could transmit a call for help that would appear on Bureau computer screens and spew out in hard copy from the laser printers in their offices.

They were assuming, of course, that the restrictions on outside contact that applied to all other phone lines in town did *not* apply to the lines by which Sun maintained its linkages with the broader world. If Sun's routes out of Moonlight Cove were clipped off, too, they were utterly without hope.

Understandably, Sam was reluctant to enter the houses of those who worked for New Wave, afraid that he would encounter more people like the Coltranes. That left only two ways to attain access to a PC that could be linked to Sun.

First, he could try to get into a black-and-white and use one of their mobile terminals, as he'd done last night. But they were alert to his presence now, making it harder to sneak into an unused patrol car. Furthermore, all of the cars were probably now in use, as the cops searched diligently for him and, no doubt, for Tessa as well. And even if a cruiser were parked behind the municipal building, that area was at the moment bound to be a lot busier than the last time he had been there.

Second, they could use the computers at the high school on Roshmore Way. New Wave had donated them not out of a noble concern for the educational quality of local schools but as one more means of tying the community to it. Sam believed, and Tessa agreed, that the school's terminals probably had the capacity to link with Sun.

But Moonlight Cove Central, as the combination junior-senior high was called, stood on the west side of Roshmore Way, two blocks west of Harry's house and a full block south. In ordinary times it was a pleasant five-minute walk. But with the streets under surveillance and every house potentially a watchtower occupied by enemies, reaching Central School now without being seen was about as easy as crossing a minefield.

"Besides," Chrissie said, "they're still in class at Central. You couldn't just walk in there and use a computer."

"Especially," Tessa said, "since you can figure the teachers were among the first converted."

"What time are classes over?" Sam asked.

"Well, at Thomas Jefferson we get out at three o'clock, but they go an extra half hour at Central."

"Three-thirty," Sam said.

Checking his watch, Harry said, "Forty-seven minutes yet. But even then, there'll be after-school activities, won't there?"

"Sure," Chrissie said. "Band, probably football practice, a few other clubs that don't meet during regular activity period."

"What time would all that be done with?"

"I know band practice is from a quarter to four till a quarter to five," Chrissie said, "because I'm friends with a kid one year older than me who's in the band. I play a clarinet. I want to be in the band, too, next year. If there is a band. If there is a next year."

"So, say . . . by five o'clock the place is cleared out."

"Football practice runs later than that."

"Would they practice today, in pouring rain?"

"I guess not."

"If you're going to wait until five or five-thirty," Tessa said, "then you might as well wait just a little while longer and head down there after dark."

Sam nodded. "I guess so."

"Sam, you're forgetting," Harry said.

"What?"

"Sometime shortly after you leave here, maybe as early as six o'clock sharp, they'll be coming to convert me."

"Jesus, that's right!" Sam said.

Moose slipped his head off his master's lap and from beneath the arm of the wheelchair. He sat erect, black ears pricked, as if he understood what had been said and was already anticipating the doorbell or listening for a knock downstairs.

"I believe you *do* have to wait for nightfall before you go, to have a better chance," Harry said, "but then you'll have to take Tessa and Chrissie with you. It won't be safe to leave them here."

"We'll have to take you too," Chrissie said at once. "You and Moose. I don't know if they convert dogs, but we have to take Moose just to be sure. We wouldn't want to have to worry about him being turned into a machine or something."

Moose chuffed.

"Can he be trusted not to bark?" Chrissie asked. "We wouldn't want him to yap at something at a crucial moment. I guess we could always wind a long strip of gauze bandage around his snout, muzzle him, which is sort of cruel and would probably hurt his feelings, since muzzling him would mean we don't entirely trust him, but it wouldn't hurt him physically, of course, and I'm sure we could make it up to him later with a juicy steak or—"

Suddenly recognizing an unusual solemnity in the silence of her companions, the girl fell silent too. She blinked at Harry, at Sam, and frowned at Tessa, who still sat on the bed beside her.

Darker clouds had begun to plate the sky since they had come upstairs, and the room was receding deeper into shadows. But at the moment Tessa could see Harry Talbot's face almost too clearly in the gray dimness. She was aware of how he was striving to conceal his fear, succeeding for the most part, managing a genuine smile and an unruffled tone of voice, betrayed only by his expressive eyes.

To Chrissie, Harry said, "I won't be going with you, honey."

"Oh," the girl said. She looked at him again, her gaze slipping down from Harry to the wheelchair on which he sat. "But you came to our school that day to talk to us. You leave the house sometimes. You must have a way to get out."

Harry smiled. "The elevator goes down to the garage on the cellar level. I don't drive any more, so there's no car down there, and I can easily roll out into the driveway, to the sidewalk."

"Well, then!" Chrissie said.

Harry looked at Sam and said, "But I can't go anywhere on these streets, steep as they are in some places, without someone along. The chair has brakes, and the motor has quite a lot of pull, but half the time not enough for these slopes."

"We'll be with you," Chrissie said earnestly. "We can help."

"Dear girl, you can't sneak quickly through three blocks of occupied territory and drag me with you at the same time," Harry said firmly. "For one thing, you'll have to stay off the streets as much as possible, move from yard to yard and between houses as much as you can, while I can only roll on pavement, especially in this weather, with the ground so soggy."

"We can carry you."

"No," Sam said. "We can't. Not if we hope to get to the school and get a message out to the Bureau. It's a short distance but full of danger, and we've got to travel light. Sorry, Harry."

"No need to apologize," Harry said. "I wouldn't have it any other way. You think I want to be dragged or shoulder-carried like a bag of cement across half the town?"

In obvious distress, Chrissie got off the bed and stood with her small hands fisted at her sides. She looked from Tessa to Sam to Tessa again, silently pleading with them to think of a way to save Harry.

Outside the gray sky was mottled now with ugly clouds that were nearly black. The rain eased up, but Tessa sensed that they were entering a brief lull, after which the downpour would continue with greater force than ever.

Both the spiritual and the physical gloom deepened.

Moose whined softly.

Tears shimmered in Chrissie's eyes, and she seemed unable to bear looking at Harry. She went to a north window and stared down at the house next door and at the street beyond—staying just far enough back from the glass to avoid being spotted by anyone outside.

Tessa wanted to comfort her.

She wanted to comfort Harry too.

More than that . . . she wanted to make everything *right*.

As writer-producer-director, she was a mover and shaker, good at taking charge, making things happen. She always knew how to solve a problem, what to do in a crisis, how to keep the cameras rolling once a project had begun. But now she was at a loss. She could not always script reality with the assurance she brought to the writing of her films; sometimes the real world resisted conforming to her demands. Maybe that was why she had chosen a career over a family, even after having enjoyed a wonderful family atmosphere as a child. The real world of daily life and struggle was sloppy, unpredictable, full of loose ends; she couldn't count on being able to tie it all up the way she could when she took aspects of it and reduced them to a neatly structured film. Life was life, broad and rich . . . but film was only essences. Maybe she dealt better with essences than with life in all its gaudy detail.

Her genetically received Lockland optimism, previously as bright as a spotlight, had not deserted her, though it definitely had dimmed for the time being.

Harry said, "It's going to be all right."

"How?" Sam asked.

"I'm probably last on their list," Harry said. "They wouldn't be worried about cripples and blind people. Even if we learn something's up, we can't try to get out of town and get help. Mrs. Sagerian—she lives over on Pinecrest—she's blind, and I'll bet she and I are the last two on the schedule. They'll wait to do us until near midnight. You see if they don't. Bet on it. So what you've got to do is go to the high school and get through to the Bureau, bring help in here pronto, before midnight comes, and then I'll be all right."

Chrissie turned away from the window, her cheeks wet with tears. "You really think so, Mr. Talbot? You really, honestly think they won't come here until midnight?"

With his head tilted to one side in a perpetual twist that was, depending on how you looked at it, either jaunty or heart-wrenching, Harry winked at the girl, though she was farther away from him than Tessa and probably didn't see the wink. "If I'm jiving you, honey, may God strike me with lightning this instant."

Rain fell but no lightning struck.

"See?" Harry said, grinning.

Though the girl clearly wanted to believe the scenario that Harry had painted for her, Tessa knew that they could not count on his being the last or next to last on the final conversion schedule. What he'd said made a little sense, actually, but it was just too neat. Like a narrative development in a film script. Real life, as she had just reminded herself, was sloppy, unpredictable. She desperately wanted to believe that Harry would be safe until a few minutes till midnight, but the reality was that he would be at extreme risk as soon as the clock struck six and the final series of conversions was under way.

35

SHADDACK REMAINED IN PAULA PARKINS'S GARAGE THROUGH most of the afternoon.

Twice he put up the big door, switched on the van's engine, and pulled into the driveway to better monitor Moonhawk's progress on the VDT. Both times, satisfied with the data, he rolled back into the garage and lowered the door again.

The mechanism was clicking away. He had designed it, built it, wound it up, and pushed the start button. Now it could go through its paces without him.

He passed the hours sitting behind the wheel, daydreaming about the time when the final stage of Moonhawk would be completed and all the world would be brought into the fold. When no Old People existed, he would have redefined the word "power," for no man before him in all of history would have known such total control. Having remade the species, he could then program its destiny to his own desires. All of humankind would be one great hive, buzzing industriously, serving his vision. As he daydreamed, his erection grew so hard that it began to ache dully.

Shaddack knew many scientists who genuinely seemed to believe that the purpose of technological progress was to improve the lot of humanity, lift the species up from the mud and carry it, eventually, to the stars. He saw things differently.

To his way of thinking, the sole purpose of technology was to concentrate power in his hands. Previous would-be remakers of the world had relied on political power, which always ultimately meant the power of the legal gun. Hitler, Stalin, Mao, Pol Pot, and others had sought power through intimidation and mass murder, wading to the throne through lakes of blood, and all of them had ultimately failed to achieve what silicon circuitry was in the process of bestowing upon Shaddack. The pen was not mightier than the sword, but the microprocessor was mightier than vast armies.

If they knew what he had undertaken and what dreams of conquest still preoccupied him, virtually all other men of science would say that he was bent, sick, deranged. He didn't care. They were wrong, of course. Because they didn't realize who he was. The child of the moonhawk. He had destroyed those who had posed as his parents, and he had not been discovered or punished, which was proof that the rules and laws governing other men were not meant to apply to him. His *true* mother and father were spirit forces, disembodied, powerful. They had protected him from punishment because the murders that he'd committed in Phoenix so long ago were a sacred offering to his real progenitors, a statement of his faith and trust in them. Other scientists would misunderstand him because they could not know that all of existence centered around him, that the universe itself existed only because *he* existed, and that if he ever died—which was unlikely—then the universe would simultaneously cease to exist. He was the center of creation. He was the only man who mattered. The great spirits had told him this. The great spirits had whispered these truths in his ear, waking and sleeping, for more than thirty years.

Child of the moonhawk . . .

As the afternoon waned, he became ever more excited about the approaching completion of the first stage of the project, and he could no longer endure temporary exile in the Parkins garage. Though it had seemed wise to absent himself from places in which Loman Watkins might find him, he was having increasing difficulty justifying the need to hide out. Events at Mike Peyser's house last night no longer seemed so catastrophic to him, merely a minor setback; he was confident that the problem of the regressives would eventually be solved. His genius resulted from the direct line between him and higher spiritual forces, and no difficulty was beyond resolution when the great spirits desired his success. The threat he'd felt from Watkins steadily diminished in his memory, too, until the police chief's promise to find him seemed empty, even pathetic.

He was the child of the moonhawk. He was surprised that he had forgotten such an important truth and had run scared. Of course, even Jesus had spent his time in the garden, briefly frightened, and had wrestled with his demons. The Parkins garage was, Shaddack saw, his own Gethsemane, where he had taken refuge to cast out those last doubts that plagued him.

He was the child of the moonhawk.

At four-thirty he put up the garage door.

He started the van and pulled down the driveway.

He was the child of the moonhawk.

He turned onto the county road and headed toward town.

He was the child of the moonhawk, heir to the crown of light, and at midnight he would ascend the throne.

36

PACK MARTIN—HIS NAME WAS ACTUALLY PACKARD BECAUSE his mother named him after a car that had been her father's pride—lived in a house trailer on the southeast edge of town. It was an old trailer, its enameled finish faded and crackled like the glaze on an ancient vase. It was rusted in a few spots, dented, and set on a concrete-block foundation in a lot that was mostly weeds. Pack knew that many people in Moonlight Cove thought his place was an eyesore, but he just plain did not give a damn.

The trailer had electrical hookup, an oil furnace, and plumbing, which was enough to meet his needs. He was warm, dry, and had a place to keep his beer. It was a veritable palace.

Best of all, the trailer had been paid for twenty-five years ago, with money he had inherited from his mother, so no mortgage hung over him. He had a little of the inheritance left, too, and rarely touched the principal. The interest amounted to nearly three hundred dollars a month, and he also had his disability check, earned by virtue of a fall he had taken three weeks after being inducted into the Army. The only real work in which Pack had ever engaged was all the reading and studying he had done to learn and memorize all of the subtlest and most complex symptoms of serious back injury, before reporting per the instructions on his draft notice.

He was born to be a man of leisure. He had known that much about himself from a young age. Work and him had nothing for each other. He figured he'd been scheduled to be born into a wealthy family, but something had gotten screwed up and he'd wound up as the son of a waitress who'd been just sufficiently industrious to provide him with a minimum inheritance.

But he envied no one. Every month he bought twelve or fourteen cases of cheap beer at the discount store out on the highway, and he had his TV, and with a bologna and mustard sandwich now and then, maybe some Fritos, he was happy enough.

By four o'clock that Tuesday afternoon, Pack was well into his second six-pack of the day, slumped in his tattered armchair, watching a game show on which the prize girl's prime hooters, always revealed in low-cut dresses, were a lot more interesting than the MC, the contestants, or the questions.

The MC said, "So what's your choice? Do you want what's behind screen number one, screen number two, or screen number three?"

Talking back to the tube, Pack said, "I'll take what's in that cutie's Maidenform, thank you very much," and he swigged more beer.

Just then someone knocked on the door.

Pack did not get up or in any way acknowledge the knock. He had no friends, so visitors were of no interest to him. They were always either community do-gooders bringing him a box of food that he didn't want, or offering to cut down his weeds and clean up his property, which he didn't want, either, because he liked his weeds.

They knocked again.

Pack responded by turning up the volume on the TV.

They knocked harder.

"Go away," Pack said.

They really *pounded* on the door, shaking the whole damn trailer.

"What the hell?" Pack said. He clicked off the TV and got up.

The pounding was not repeated, but Pack heard a strange scraping noise against the side of the trailer.

And the place creaked on its foundation, which it sometimes did when the wind was blowing hard. Today, there was no wind.

"Kids," Pack decided.

The Aikhorn family, which lived on the other side of the county road and two hundred yards to the south, had kids so ornery they ought to have been put to sleep with injections, pickled in formaldehyde, and displayed in some museum of criminal behavior. Those brats got a kick out of pushing cherry bombs through chinks in the foundation blocks, under the trailer, waking him with a bang in the middle of the night.

The scraping at the side of the trailer stopped, but now a couple of kids were walking around on the roof.

That was too much. The metal roof didn't leak, but it had seen better days, and it was liable to bend or even separate at the seams under the weight of a couple of kids.

Pack opened the door and stepped out into the rain, shouting obscenities at them. But when he looked up he didn't see any kids on the roof. What he saw, instead, was something out of a fifties bug movie, big as a man, with clacking mandibles and multifaceted eyes, and a mouth framed by small pincers. The weird thing was that he also saw a few features of a human face in that monstrous countenance, just enough so he thought he recognized Daryl Aikhorn, father of the brats. *"Neeeeeeeeeeeed,"* it said, in a voice half Aikhorn's and half an insectile keening. It leaped at him, and as it came, a wickedly sharp stinger telescoped from its repulsive body. Even before that yard-long, serrated spear skewered his belly and thrust all the way through him, Pack knew that the days of beer and bologna sandwiches and Fritos and disability checks and game-show girls with perfect hooters were over.

■   Randy Hapgood, fourteen, sloshed through the dirty calf-deep water in an overflowing gutter and sneered contemptuously, as if to say that nature would have to come up with an obstacle a thousand times more formidable than that if she hoped to daunt him. He refused to wear a raincoat and galoshes because such gear was not fashionably cool. You didn't see rad blondes hanging on the arms of nerds who carried umbrellas, either. There were no rad girls hanging on Randy, as far as that went, but he figured they just hadn't yet noticed how cool he was, how indifferent to weather and everything else that humbled other guys.

He was soaked and miserable—but whistling jauntily to conceal it—when he got home from Central at twenty minutes till five, after band practice, which had been cut short because of the bad weather. He stripped out of his wet denim jacket and hung it on the back of the pantry door. He slipped out of his soggy tennis shoes, as well.

"I'm *heeeeerrreeeee,"* he shouted, parodying the little girl in *Poltergeist*.

No one answered him.

He knew his parents were home, because lights were on, and the door was unlocked. Lately they'd been working at home more and more. They were in some sort of product research at New Wave, and they were able to put in a full day on their dual terminals upstairs, in the back room, without actually going in to the office.

Randy got a Coke out of the refrigerator, popped the tab, took a swig, and headed upstairs to dry out while he told Pete and Marsha about his day. He didn't call them mom and dad, and that was all right with them; they were cool. Sometimes he thought they were even too cool. They drove a Porsche, and their clothes were always six months ahead of what everyone else was wearing, and they'd talk about anything with him, *anything,* including sex, as frankly as if they were his pals. If he ever *did* find a rad blonde who wanted to hang on him, he'd be afraid to bring her home to meet his folks, for fear she'd think his dad was infinitely cooler than he was. Sometimes he wished Pete and Marsha were fat, frumpy, dressed out of date, and stuffily insisted on being called mom and dad. Competition in school for grades and popularity was fierce enough without having to feel that he was also in competition at home with his parents.

As he reached the top of the stairs, he called out again, "In the immortal words of the modern American intellectual, John Rambo: 'Yo!' "

They still didn't answer him.

Just as Randy reached the open door to the workroom at the back of the hall, a case of the creeps hit him. He shivered and frowned but didn't stop, however, because his self-image of ultimate coolth did not allow him to be spooked.

He stepped across the threshold, ready with a wisecrack about their failure to respond to his calls. Too late, he was flash-frozen in place by fear.

Pete and Marsha were sitting on opposite sides of the large worktable, where their computer terminals stood back to back. No, they were not exactly sitting there; they were wired into the chairs and the computers by scores of hideous, segmented cables that grew out of them—or out of the machine; it was hard to tell which—and not only anchored them to their computers but to their chairs and, finally, to the floor, into which the cables disappeared. Their faces were still vaguely recognizable, though wildly altered, half pale flesh and half metal, with a slightly melted look.

Randy could not breathe.

But abruptly he could move, and he scrambled backward.

The door slammed behind him.

He whirled.

Tentacles—half organic, half metallic—erupted from the wall. The entire room seemed weirdly, malevolently alive, or maybe the walls were filled with alien machinery. The tentacles were quick. They lashed around him, pinned his arms, thoroughly snared him, and turned him toward his parents.

They were still in their chairs but were no longer facing their computers. They stared at him with radiant green eyes that appeared to be boiling in their sockets, bubbling and churning.

Randy screamed. He thrashed, but the tentacles held him.

Pete opened his mouth, and half a dozen silvery spheres, like large ball bearings, shot from him and struck Randy in the chest.

Pain exploded through the boy. But it didn't last more than a couple of seconds. Instead, the hot pain became an icy-cold, crawling sensation that worked through his entire body and up into his face.

He tried to scream again. No sound escaped him.

The tentacles shrank back into the wall, pulling him with them, until his back was pinned tightly against the plaster.

The coldness was in his head now. Crawling, crawling.

Again, he tried to scream. This time a sound came from him. A thin, electronic oscillation.

■   Tuesday afternoon, wearing warm wool slacks and a sweatshirt and a cardigan over the sweatshirt because she found it hard to stay warm these days, Meg Henderson sat at the kitchen table by the window, with a glass of chenin blanc, a plate of onion crackers, a wedge of Gouda, and a Nero Wolfe novel by Rex Stout. She had read all of the Wolfe novels ages ago, but she was rereading them. Returning to old novels was comforting because the people in them never changed. Wolfe was still a genius and gourmet. Archie was still a man of action. Fritz still ran the best private kitchen in the world.' None of them had aged since last she'd met them, either, which was a trick she wished she had learned.

Meg was eighty years old, and she looked eighty, every minute of it; she didn't kid herself. Occasionally, when she saw herself in a mirror, she stared in amazement, as if she had not lived with that face for the better part of a century and was looking at a stranger. Somehow she expected to see a reflection of her youth because inside she was still that girl. Fortunately she didn't *feel* eighty. Her bones were creaky, and her muscles had about as much tone as those of Jabba the Hut in the third *Star Wars* movie she'd watched on the VCR last week, but she was free of arthritis and other major complaints, thank God. She still lived in her bungalow on Concord Circle, an odd little half-moon street that began and ended from Serra Avenue on the east end of town. She and Frank had bought the place forty years ago, when they had both been teachers at Thomas Jefferson School, in the days when it had been a combined school for all grades. Moonlight Cove had been much smaller then. For fourteen years, since Frank died, she had lived in the bungalow alone. She could get around, clean, and cook for herself, for which she was grateful.

She was even more grateful for her mental acuity. More than physical infirmity, she dreaded senility or a stroke that, while leaving her physically functional, would steal her memory and alter her personality. She tried to keep her mind flexible by reading a lot of books of all different kinds, by renting a variety of videos for her VCR, and by avoiding at all costs the mind-numbing slop that passed for entertainment on television.

By four-thirty Tuesday afternoon, she was halfway through the novel, though she paused at the end of each chapter to look out at the rain. She liked rain. She liked whatever weather God chose to throw at the world—storms, hail, wind, cold, heat—because the variety and extremes of creation were what made it so beautiful.

While looking at the rain, which earlier had declined from a fierce downpour to a drizzle but was once more falling furiously, she saw three large, dark, and

utterly fantastic creatures appear out of the stand of trees at the rear of her property, fifty feet from the window at which she sat. They halted for a moment as a
thin mist eddied around their feet, as if they were dream monsters that had taken
shape from those scraps of fog and might melt away as suddenly as they had
arisen. But then they raced toward her back porch.

As they drew swiftly nearer, Meg's first impression of them was reinforced. They
were like nothing on this earth . . . unless perhaps gargoyles could come alive and
climb down from cathedral roofs.

She knew at once that she must be in the early stages of a truly massive stroke,
because that was what she had always feared would at last claim her. But she was
surprised that it would begin like this, with such a weird hallucination.

That was all it could be, of course—hallucination preceding the bursting of a
cerebral blood vessel that must be already swelling and pressing on her brain. She
waited for a painful exploding sensation inside her head, waited for her face and
body to twist to the left or right as one side or the other was paralyzed.

Even when the first of the gargoyles crashed through the window, showering
the table with glass, spilling the chenin blanc, knocking Meg off her chair, and
falling to the floor atop her, all teeth and claws, she marveled that a stroke could
produce such vivid, convincing illusions, though she was not surprised by the
intensity of the pain. She'd always known that death would hurt.

■ Dora Hankins, the receptionist in the main lobby at New Wave, was accustomed to seeing people leave work as early as four-thirty. Though the official
quitting time was five o'clock, a lot of workers put in hours at home, on their own
PCs, so no one strictly enforced the eight-hour office day. Since they'd been converted, there had been no need for rules, anyway, because they were all working
for the same goal, for the new world that was coming, and the only discipline
they needed was their fear of Shaddack, of which they had plenty.

By 4:55, when no one at all had passed through the lobby, Dora was appre-
hensive. The building was oddly silent, though hundreds of people were working
there in offices and labs farther back on the ground floor and in the two floors
overhead. In fact the place seemed deserted.

At five o'clock no one had yet left for the day, and Dora had decided to see
what was going on. She abandoned her post at the main reception desk, walked
to the end of the large marble lobby, through a brass door, into a less grand
corridor floored with vinyl tile. Offices lay on both sides. She went into the first
room on the left, where eight women served as a secretarial pool for minor department heads who had no personal secretaries of their own.

The eight were at their VDTs. In the fluorescent light, Dora had no trouble
seeing how intimately flesh and machine had joined.

Fear was the only emotion Dora had felt in weeks. She thought she had known
it in all its shades and degrees. But now it fell over her with greater force, darker
and more intense, than anything she had experienced before.

A glistening probe erupted from the wall to Dora's right. It was more metallic
than not, yet it dripped what appeared to be yellowish mucus. The thing shot
straight to one of the secretaries and bloodlessly pierced the back of her head.
From the top of one of the other women's heads, another probe erupted, rose like
a snake to the music of a charmer's flute, hesitated, then with tremendous speed

snapped to the ceiling, piercing the acoustic tile without disturbing it, and vanished toward rooms above.

Dora sensed that all of the computers and people of New Wave had somehow linked into a single entity and that the building itself was swiftly being incorporated into it. She wanted to run but couldn't move—maybe because she knew any escape attempt would prove futile.

A moment later they plugged her into the network.

■ Betsy Soldonna was carefully taping up a sign on the wall behind the front desk at the Moonlight Cove Town Library. It was part of Fascinating Fiction Week, a campaign to get kids to read more fiction.

She was the assistant librarian, but on Tuesdays, when her boss, Cora Danker, was off, Betsy worked alone. She liked Cora, but Betsy also liked being by herself. Cora was a talker, filling every free minute with gossip or her boring observations on the characters and plots of her favorite TV programs. Betsy, a lifelong biblio-phile obsessed with books, would have been delighted to talk endlessly about what she'd read, but Cora, though head librarian, hardly read at all.

Betsy tore a fourth piece of Scotch tape off the dispenser and fixed the last corner of the poster to the wall. She stepped back to admire her work.

She had made the poster herself. She was proud of her modest artistic talent. In the drawing, a boy and a girl were holding books and staring bug-eyed at the open pages before them. Their hair was standing on end. The girl's eyebrows appeared to have jumped off her face, as had the boy's ears. Above them was the legend BOOKS ARE PORTABLE FUNHOUSES, FILLED WITH THRILLS AND SURPRISES.

From back in the stacks at the other end of the library came a curious sound—a grunt, a choking cough, and then what might have been a snarl. Next came the unmistakable clatter of a row of books falling from a shelf to the floor.

The only person in the library, other than Betsy, was Dale Foy, a retiree who'd been a cashier at Lucky's supermarket until three years ago when he'd turned sixty-five. He was always searching for thriller writers he had never read before and complaining that none of them was as good as the really old-time tale-spinners, by which he meant John Buchan rather than Robert Louis Stevenson.

Betsy suddenly had the terrible feeling that Mr. Foy had suffered a heart attack in one of the aisles, that she had heard him gurgling for help, and that he had pulled the books to the floor when he'd grabbed at a shelf. In her mind she could see him writhing in agony, unable to breathe, his face turning blue and his eyes bulging, a bloody foam bubbling at his lips. . . .

Years of heavy reading had stropped Betsy's imagination until it was as sharp as a straight razor made from fine German steel.

She hurried around the desk and along the head of the aisles, looking into each of the narrow corridors, which were flanked by nine-foot-high shelves. "Mr. Foy? Mr. Foy, are you all right?"

In the last aisle she found the fallen books but no sign of Dale Foy. Puzzled, she turned to go back the way she had come, and *there* was Foy behind her. But changed. And even Betsy Soldonna's sharp imagination could not have conceived of the thing that Foy had become—or of the things that he was about to do to her. The next few minutes were as filled with surprises as any hundred books she had ever read, though there was not a happy ending.

■ Because of the dark storm clouds that clotted the sky, an early twilight crept
over Moonlight Cove, and the entire town seemed to be celebrating Fascinating Fiction Week at the library. The dying day was, for many, filled with thrills
and surprises, just like a funhouse in the most macabre carnival that had ever
pitched its tents.

37

SAM SWEPT THE BEAM OF THE FLASHLIGHT AROUND THE
attic. It had a rough board floor but no light fixture. Nothing was stored there
except dust, spider webs, and a multitude of dead, dry bees that had built nests
in the rafters during the summer and had died either due to the work of an ex-
terminator or at the end of their span.

Satisfied, he returned to the trapdoor and went backward down the wooden
rungs, into the closet of Harry's third-floor bedroom. They had removed many of
the hanging clothes to be able to open the trap and draw down the collapsible
ladder.

Tessa, Chrissie, Harry, and Moose were waiting for him just outside the closet
door, in the steadily darkening bedroom.

Sam said, "Yeah, it'll do."

"I haven't been up there since before the war," Harry said.

"A little dirty, a few spiders, but you'll be safe. If you're not at the end of their
list, if they *do* come for you early, they'll find the house empty, and they'll never
think of the attic. Because how could a man with two bad legs and one bad arm
drag himself up there?"

Sam was not sure that he believed what he was saying. But for his own peace
of mind as well as Harry's, he wanted to believe.

"Can I take Moose up there with me?"

"Take that handgun you mentioned," Tessa said, "but not Moose. Well-behaved
as he is, he might bark at just the wrong moment."

"Will Moose be safe down here . . . when *they* come?" Chrissie wondered.

"I'm sure he will be," Sam said. "They don't want dogs. Only people."

"We better get you up there, Harry," Tessa said. "It's twenty past five. We've
got to be out of here soon."

The bedroom was filling with shadows almost as rapidly as a glass filling with
blood-dark wine.

THE NIGHT
BELONGS TO THEM

Montgomery told me that the Law . . . became oddly weakened about

nightfall; that then the animal was at its strongest; a spirit of

adventure sprang up in them at the dusk; they would dare things

they never seemed to dream about by day.

—H. G. WELLS,

THE ISLAND OF DR. MOREAU

1

IN THE SCRUB-COVERED HILLS THAT SURROUNDED THE ABAN-
doned Icarus Colony, gophers and field mice and rabbits and a few foxes scrambled out of their burrows and shivered in the rain, listening. In the two nearest
stands of pine, sweet gum, and autumn-stripped birch, one just to the south and
one immediately east of the old colony, squirrels and raccoons stood to attention.

The birds were the first to respond. In spite of the rain, they flew from their
sheltered nests in the trees, in the dilapidated old barn, and in the crumbling eaves
of the main building itself. Cawing and screeching, they spiraled into the sky,
darted and swooped, then streaked directly to the house. Starlings, wrens, crows,
owls, and hawks all came in shrill and flapping profusion. Some flew against the
walls, as if struck blind, battering insistently until they broke their necks, or until
they snapped their wings and fell to the ground where they fluttered and squeaked
until they were exhausted or had perished. Others, equally frenzied, found open
doorways and windows through which they entered without damaging themselves.

Though wildlife within a two-hundred-yard radius had heard the call, only the
nearer animals responded obediently. Rabbits leaped, squirrels scurried, coyotes
loped, foxes dashed, and raccoons waddled in that curious way of theirs, through
wet grass and rain-bent weeds and mud, toward the source of the siren song.
Some were predators and some, by nature, were timid prey, but they moved side
by side without conflict. It might have been a scene from an animated Disney
film—the neighborly and harmonious folk of field and forest responding to the
sweet guitar or harmonica music of some elderly black man who, when they
gathered around him, would tell them stories of magic and great adventure. But
there was no kindly, tale-spinning Negro where they were going, and the music
that drew them was dark, cold, and without melody.

2

WHILE SAM STRUGGLED TO LIFT HARRY UP THE LADDER AND into the attic, Tessa and Chrissie took the wheelchair to the basement garage. It was a heavy-duty motorized model, not a light collapsible chair, and would not fit through the trap. Tessa and Chrissie parked it just inside the big garage door, so it looked as if Harry had gotten this far in his chair and had left the house, perhaps in a friend's car.

"You think they'll fall for it?" Chrissie asked worriedly.

"There's a chance," Tessa said.

"Maybe they'll even think Harry left town yesterday before the roadblocks went up."

Tessa agreed, but she knew—and suspected Chrissie knew—that the chance of the ruse working was slim. If Sam and Harry really had been as confident in the attic trick as they pretended, they would have wanted Chrissie to be tucked up there, too, instead of sent out into the storm-lashed, nightmare world of Moonlight Cove.

They rode the elevator back to the third floor, where Sam was just folding the ladder and pushing the trapdoor into place. Moose watched him curiously.

"Five forty-two," Tessa said, checking her watch.

Sam snatched up the closet pole, which he'd had to remove to pull down the trap, and he reinserted it into its braces. "Help me put the clothes back."

Shirts and slacks, still on hangers, had been transferred to the bed. Working together, passing the garments like amateur firemen relaying pails of water, they quickly restored the closet to its former appearance.

Tessa noticed that traces of fresh blood were soaking through the thick gauze bandage on Sam's right wrist. His wounds were pulling open from the exertion. Although they weren't mortal injuries, they must hurt a lot, and anything that weakened or distracted him during the ordeal ahead decreased their chances of success.

Closing the door, Sam said, "God, I hate to leave him there."

"Five forty-six," Tessa reminded him.

While Tessa pulled on a leather jacket, and while Chrissie slipped into a too-large but waterproof blue nylon windbreaker that belonged to Harry, Sam reloaded his revolver. He had used up all the rounds in his pockets while at the Coltranes'. But Harry owned a .45 revolver and a .38 pistol, both of which he had taken with him into the attic, and he had a box of ammunition for each, so Sam had taken a score or so of the .38 cartridges.

Holstering the gun, he went to the telescope and studied the streets that lay west and south toward Central School. "Still lots of activity," he reported.

"Patrols?" Tessa asked.

"But also lots of rain. And fog's coming in faster, thicker."

Thanks to the storm, an early twilight was upon them and already fading. Although some bleak light still burned above the churning clouds, night might as well have fallen, for cloaks of gloom lay over the wet and huddled town.

"Five fifty," Tessa said.

Chrissie said, "If Mr. Talbot's at the top of their list, they could be here any minute."

Turning from the telescope, Sam said, "All right. Let's go."

Tessa and Chrissie followed him out of the bedroom. They took the stairs down to the first floor.

Moose used the elevator.

3

SHADDACK WAS A CHILD TONIGHT.

Circling repeatedly through Moonlight Cove, from the sea to the hills, from Holliwell Road on the north to Paddock Lane on the south, he could not remember ever having been in a better mood. He altered the patterns of his patrol, largely to be sure that eventually he would cover every block of every street in town; the sight of each house and every citizen on foot in the storm affected him in a way they never had previously, because soon they would be his to do with as he pleased.

He was filled with excitement and anticipation, the likes of which he had not felt since Christmas Eve when he was a young boy. Moonlight Cove was a huge toy, and in a few hours, when midnight struck, when this dark eve ticked over into the holiday, he would be able to have so much fun with his marvelous toy. He would indulge in games which he had long wanted to play but which he had denied himself. Henceforth, no urge or desire would be denied, for despite the bloodiness or outrageousness of whatever game he chose, there would be no referees, no authorities, to penalize him.

And like a child sneaking into a closet to filch coins from his father's coat to buy ice cream, he was so completely transported by contemplation of the rewards that he had virtually forgotten there was a potential for disaster. Minute by minute, the threat of the regressives faded from his awareness. He did not entirely forget about Loman Watkins, but he no longer was able to remember exactly why he had spent the day hiding from the police chief in the garage at the Parkins house.

More than thirty years of unrelenting self-control, strenuous and undeviating application of his mental and physical resources, beginning with the day he had murdered his parents and Runningdeer, thirty years of repressing his needs and desires and of sublimating them in his work, had at last led him to the brink of his dream's realization. *He could not doubt.* To doubt his mission or worry about its outcome would be to question his sacred destiny and insult the great spirits who had favored him. He was now incapable of even seeing a downside; he turned his mind away from any incipient thought of disaster.

He sensed the great spirits in the storm.

He sensed them moving secretly through his town.

They were there to witness and approve his ascension to the throne of destiny.

He had eaten no cactus candy since the day he had killed his mother, father, and the Indian, but over the years he had been subject to vivid flashbacks. They came upon him unexpectedly. One moment he would be in this world, and the next instant he would be in that other place, the eerie world parallel to this one, where the cactus candy had always conveyed him, a reality in which colors were simultaneously more vivid and more subtle, where every object seemed to have more angles and dimensions than in the ordinary world, where he seemed to be strangely weightless—buoyant as a helium-filled balloon—and where the voices of spirits spoke to him. The flashbacks had been frequent during the year following the murders, striking him about twice a week, then had gradually declined in number—though not in intensity—through his teenage years. Those dreamy, fuguelike spells, which usually lasted an hour or two but could occasionally last half a day, were responsible in part for his reputation, with family and teachers, of being a somewhat detached child. They all had sympathy for him, naturally, because they assumed that whatever detachment he displayed was a result of the shattering trauma that he had endured.

Now, cruising in his van, he was phasing slowly into that cactus-candy condition. This flashback was unexpected, too, but it didn't *snap* upon him as all the others had. He sort of . . . drifted into it, deeper, deeper. And the further he went, the more he suspected that this time he would not be pulled rudely back from that realm of higher consciousness. From now on he would be a resident of both worlds, which was how the great spirits themselves lived, with awareness of both the higher and the lower states of existence. He even began to think that what he was undergoing now, spiritually, was a conversion of his own, a thousand times more profound than that the citizens of Moonlight Cove had undergone.

In this exalted state, everything was special and wondrous to Shaddack. The twinkling lights of the rainswept town seemed like jewels sprinkled through the descending darkness. The molten, silvery beauty of the rain itself astonished him, as did the swiftly dimming, gorgeously turbulent gray sky.

As he braked at the intersection of Paddock Lane and Saddleback Drive, he touched his breast, feeling the telemetry device he wore from a chain around his neck, unable for a moment to remember what it was, and *that* seemed mysterious and wonderful, as well. Then he recalled that the device monitored and broadcast his heartbeat, which was received by a unit at New Wave. It was effective over a distance of five miles, and worked even when he was indoors. If the reception of his heartbeat was interrupted for more than one minute, Sun was programmed to feed a destruct order, via microwave, to the microsphere computers in all of the New People.

A few minutes later, on Bastenchurry Road, when he touched the device, the memory of its purpose again proved elusive. He sensed that it was a powerful object, that whoever wore it held the lives of others in his hands, and the fantasy-tripping child in him decided that it must be an amulet, bestowed upon him by the great spirits, one more sign that he stood astride the two worlds, one foot in the ordinary plane of ordinary men and one foot in the higher realm of the great spirits, the gods of the cactus candy.

His slowly phased-in flashback, like time-released medication, had carried him back into the condition of his youth, at least to those seven years when he'd been in the thrall of Runningdeer. He was a child. And he was a demigod. He was the favored child of the moonhawk, so he could do anything he wanted to anyone,

anyone, and as he continued to drive, he fantasized about just what he might want to do . . . and to whom.

Now and then he laughed softly and slightly shrilly, and his eyes gleamed like those of a cruel and twisted boy studying the effects of fire on captive ants.

4

AS MOOSE PADDED AROUND THEM AND WAGGED HIS TAIL SO hard it seemed in danger of flying off, Chrissie waited in the kitchen with Tessa and Sam until more light bled out of the dying day.

At last Sam said, "All right. Stay close. Do what I say every step of the way."

He looked at Chrissie and Tessa for a long moment before actually opening the door; without any of them speaking a word, they hugged one another. Tessa kissed Chrissie on the cheek, then Sam kissed her, and Chrissie returned their kisses. She didn't have to be told why they all suddenly felt so affectionate. They were people, *real* people, and expressing their feelings was important, because before the night was out they might not be real people any more. Maybe they wouldn't ever again feel the kinds of things real people felt, so those feelings were more precious by the second.

Who knew what those weird shape-changers felt? Who would *want* to know?

Besides, if they didn't reach Central, it would be because one of the search parties or a couple of the Boogeymen nailed them along the way. In that case this might be their last chance to say goodbye to one another.

Finally Sam led them onto the porch.

Carefully, Chrissie closed the door behind them. Moose didn't try to get out. He was too good and noble a dog for such cheap stunts. But he did stick his snout in the narrowing crack, sniffing at her and trying to lick her hand, so she was afraid she was going to pinch his nose. He pulled back at the last moment, and the door clicked shut.

Sam led them down the steps and across the yard toward the house to the south of Harry's. No lights were on there. Chrissie hoped no one was home, but she figured some monstrous creature was at one of the dark windows right now, peering out at them and licking its chops.

The rain seemed colder than when she'd been on the run last night, but that might have been because she had just come out of the warm, dry house. Only the palest gray glow still illuminated the sky to the west. The icy, slashing droplets seemed to be tearing the last of that light out of the clouds and driving it into the earth, pulling down a deep, damp darkness. Before they had even reached the fence separating Harry's property from the next, Chrissie was grateful for the hooded nylon windbreaker, even though it was so big on her that it made her feel as if she was a little kid playing dress-up in her parents' clothes.

It was a picket fence, easy to clamber over. They followed Sam across the neighbor's backyard to another fence. Chrissie was over that one, too, and into yet another yard, with Tessa close behind her, before she realized they had reached the Coltranes' place.

She looked at the blank windows. No lights on here, either, which was a good thing, because if there *had* been lights, that would mean someone had found what was left of the Coltranes after their battle with Sam.

Crossing the yard toward the next fence, Chrissie was overcome by the fear that the Coltranes had somehow reanimated themselves after Sam had fired all of those bullets into them, that they were standing in the kitchen and looking out the windows right this minute, that they had seen their nemesis and his two companions, and that they were even now opening the back door. She expected two robot-things to come clanking out with metal arms and working massive metal hands, sort of like tin versions of the walking dead in old zombie movies, miniature radar-dish antennae whirling around and around on their heads, steam hissing from body vents.

Her fear must have slowed her, because Tessa almost stumbled into her from behind and gave her a gentle push to urge her along. Chrissie crouched and hurried to the south side of the yard.

Sam helped her over a wrought-iron fence with spearlike points on the staves. She would probably have gored herself if she'd had to scale it alone. Chrissie shishkebab.

People were home at the next house, and Sam took refuge behind some shrubbery to study the lay of things before continuing. Chrissie and Tessa quickly joined him there.

While clambering over the last fence, she'd rubbed the abraded palm of her left hand, even though it was bandaged. It hurt, but she gritted her teeth and made no complaint.

Parting the branches of what appeared to be a mulberry bush, Chrissie peered at the house, which was only twenty feet away. She saw four people through the kitchen windows. They were preparing dinner together. A middle-aged couple, a gray-haired man, and a teenage girl.

She wondered if they had been converted yet. She suspected not, but there was no way to be sure. And since the robots and Boogeymen sometimes hid in clever human disguises, you couldn't trust anyone, not even your best friend . . . or your parents. Pretty much the same as when aliens were taking over.

"Even if they look out, they won't see us," Sam said. "Come on."

Chrissie followed him from the cover of the mulberry bush and across the open lawn toward the next property line, thanking God for the fog, which was getting denser by the minute.

Eventually they reached the house at the end of the block. The south side of that lawn fronted the cross street, Bergenwood Way, which led down to Conquistador.

When they were two-thirds of the way across the lawn, less than twenty feet from the street, a car turned the corner a block and a half uphill and started down. Following Sam's lead, Chrissie threw herself flat on the soggy lawn because there was no nearby shrubbery behind which to take refuge. If they tried to scramble too far, the driver of the approaching car might get close enough to spot them while they were still scuttling for cover.

No streetlamps flanked Bergenwood, which was in their favor. The last of the ashen light was gone from the western sky—another boon.

As the car drew nearer, moving slowly either because of the bad weather or because its occupants were part of a patrol, its headlights were diffused by the fog, which seemed not to be reflecting that light but glowing with a radiance of its own. Objects in the night for yards on both sides of the car were half revealed and weirdly distorted by those slowly churning, ground-hugging, luminous clouds.

When the car was less than a block away, someone riding in the back seat switched on a handheld spotlight. He directed it out his side window, playing it over the front lawns of the houses that faced on Bergenwood and the side lawns of houses facing the cross streets. At the moment the beam was pointed in the opposite direction, south, toward the other side of Bergenwood. But by the time they had driven this far, they might decide to spotlight the properties to the north of Bergenwood.

"Backtrack," Sam said fiercely. "But stay down and crawl, *crawl.*"

The car reached the intersection, half a block uphill.

Chrissie crawled after Sam, not straight back the way they had come but toward the nearby house. She didn't see anywhere he could hide, because the back-porch railing was pretty open and there were no large shrubs. Maybe he figured to slip around the side of the house until the patrol passed, but she didn't think she and Tessa would make it to the corner in time.

When she glanced over her shoulder, she saw that the spotlight was still sweeping the front lawns and between the houses on the south flank of the street. However, there was also the side-glow effect of the headlights to worry about, and that was going to wash across *this* lawn in a few seconds.

She was half crawling and half slithering on her belly, moving fast, though no doubt squashing lots of snails and earthworms that had come out to bask on the wet grass, which didn't bear thinking about. She came to a concrete walkway close to the house—and realized that Sam had disappeared.

She halted on her hands and knees, looking left and right.

Tessa appeared at her side. "Cellar steps, honey. Hurry!"

Scrambling forward, she discovered a set of exterior concrete steps leading down to a cellar entrance. Sam was crouched at the bottom, where collected rainwater gurgled softly as it trickled into a drain in front of the closed cellar door. Chrissie joined him in that haven, slipping below ground level, and Tessa followed. About four seconds later a spotlight swept across the wall of the house and even played for a moment inches above their heads, on the concrete lip of the stairwell.

They huddled in silence, unmoving, for a minute or so after the spotlight swung away from them and the car passed. Chrissie was sure that something inside the house had heard them, that the door at Sam's back would fly open at any second, that something would leap at them, a creature part werewolf and part computer, snarling and beeping, its mouth bristling with both teeth and programming keys, saying something like, "To be killed, please press Enter and proceed."

She was relieved when at last Sam whispered, "Go."

They recrossed the lawn toward Bergenwood Way. This time the street remained conveniently deserted.

As Harry promised, a stone-lined drainage channel ran alongside Bergenwood. According to Harry, who had played in it when he was a kid, the channel was about three feet wide and maybe five feet deep. Judging by those dimensions, a foot or more of runoff surged through it at the moment. Those currents were swift, almost black, revealed at the bottom of the shadow-pooled trench only by an occasional dark glint and chuckle of roiling water.

The channel offered a considerably less conspicuous route than the open street. They moved uphill a few yards until they found the mortared, iron handholds that Harry had promised they'd find every hundred feet along the open sections of the channel. Sam climbed down first, Chrissie went second, and Tessa brought up the rear.

Sam hunched over to keep his head below street level, and Tessa hunched a bit less than he did. But Chrissie didn't have to hunch at all. Being eleven had its advantages, especially when you were on the run from werewolves or ravenous aliens or robots or Nazis, and at one time or another during the past twenty-four hours, she had been on the run from the first three, but not from Nazis, too, thank God, though who knew what might happen next.

The churning water was cold around her feet and calves. She was surprised to discover that although it only reached her knees it had considerable force. It pushed and tugged relentlessly, as if it were a living thing with a mean desire to topple her. She was not in any danger of falling as long as she stood in one place with feet widely planted, but she was not sure how long she could maintain her balance while walking. The watercourse sloped steeply downhill. The old stone floor, after several decades of rainy seasons, was well polished by runoff. Because of that combination of factors, the channel was the next best thing to an amusement-park flume ride.

If she fell, she'd be swept all the way downhill, to within half a block of the bluff, where the channel widened and dropped straight down into the earth. Harry had said something about safety bars dividing the passage into narrow slots just before the downspout, but she figured that if she were swept down there and had to rely on those bars, they would prove to be missing or rusted out, leaving a straight shot to the bottom. The system came out again at the base of the cliffs, then led part of the way across the beach, discharging the runoff onto the sand or, at high tide, into the sea.

She had no difficulty picturing herself tumbling and twisting helplessly, choking on filthy water, desperately but unsuccessfully grabbing at the stone channel for purchase, suddenly plummeting a couple of hundred feet straight down, banging against the walls of the shaft when it went vertical, breaking bones, smashing her head to bits, hitting the bottom with . . .

Well, yes, she *could* easily picture it, but suddenly she didn't see any wisdom in doing so.

Fortunately Harry had warned them of this problem, so Sam had come prepared. From under his jacket and around his waist, he unwound a length of rope that he had removed from a long-unused pulley system in Harry's garage. Though the rope was old, Sam said it was still strong, and Chrissie hoped he was right. He had tied one end around his waist before leaving the house. Now he looped the other end through Chrissie's belt and finally tied it around Tessa's waist, leaving approximately eight feet of play between each of them. If one of them fell—well, face it, Chrissie was far and away the one most likely to fall and most likely to be swept to a wet and bloody death—the others could stand fast until she had time to regain her footing.

That was the plan, anyway.

Securely linked, they started down the channel. Sam and Tessa hunched over so no one in a passing car would see their heads bobbling above the stone rim of the watercourse, and Chrissie hunched over a bit, too, keeping her feet wide apart, sort of troll-walking as she had done last night in the tunnel under the meadow.

Per Sam's instructions, she held on to the line in front of her with both hands, taking up the slack when she drew close to him, to avoid tripping on it, then paying it out again when she fell back a couple of feet. Behind her, Tessa was doing the same thing; Chrissie felt the subtle tug of the rope on her belt.

They were heading toward a culvert half a block downhill. The channel went underground at Conquistador and stayed subterranean not just through the intersection but for two entire blocks, surfacing again at Roshmore.

Chrissie kept glancing up, past Sam at the mouth of the pipe, not liking what she saw. It was round, concrete rather than stone. It was wider than the rectangular channel, about five feet in diameter, no doubt so workmen could get into it easily and clean it out if it became choked with debris. However, neither the shape nor the size of the culvert made her uneasy; it was the absolute blackness of it that prickled the nape of her neck, for it was darker even than the essence of night at the bottom of the drainage channel itself—absolutely, absolutely black, and it seemed as if they were marching into the gaping mouth of some prehistoric behemoth.

A car cruised by slowly on Bergenwood, another on Conquistador. Their headlights were refracted by the incoming bank of fog, so the night itself seemed to glow, but little of that queer luminosity reached down into the watercourse, and none of it penetrated the mouth of the culvert.

When Sam crossed the threshold of that tunnel and, within two steps, disappeared entirely from sight, Chrissie followed without hesitation, although not without trepidation. They proceeded at a slower pace, for the floor of the culvert was not merely steeply sloped but curved, as well, and even more treacherous than the stone drainage channel.

Sam had a flashlight, but Chrissie knew he didn't want to use it near either end of the tunnel. The backsplash of the beam might be visible from outside and draw the attention of one of the patrols.

The culvert was as utterly lightless as the inside of a whale's belly. Not that she knew what a whale's belly was like, inside, but she doubted it was equipped with a lamp or even a Donald Duck night-light, like the one she'd had when she was years younger. The whale's belly image seemed fitting because she had the creepy feeling that the pipe was really a stomach and that the rushing water was digestive juice, and that already her tennis shoes and the legs of her jeans were dissolving in that corrosive flood.

Then she fell. Her feet slipped on something, perhaps a fungus that was growing on the floor and attached so tightly to the concrete that the runoff had not torn it away. She let go of the line and windmilled her arms, trying to keep her balance, but she went down with a tremendous splash, and instantly found herself borne away by the water.

She had enough presence of mind not to scream. A scream would draw one of the search teams—or worse.

Gasping for breath, spluttering as water slopped into her mouth, she collided with Sam's legs, knocking him off balance. She felt him falling. She wondered how long they'd all lie, dead and decomposing, at the bottom of the long vertical drain, out at the foot of the bluff, before their bloated, purple remains were found.

5

IN THE TOMB-PERFECT DARKNESS, TESSA HEARD THE GIRL fall, and she immediately halted, planting her legs as wide and firm as she could on that sloped and curved floor, keeping both hands on the security line. Within a second that rope pulled taut as Chrissie was swept away by the water.

Sam grunted, and Tessa realized that the girl had been carried into him. Slack developed on the line for an instant, but then it went taut again, pulling her forward, which she took to mean that Sam was staggering ahead, trying to stay on his feet, with the girl pressing against his lower legs and threatening to knock them out from under him. If Sam had been brought down, too, and seized by tumultuous currents, the line would not have been merely taut; the drag would have been great enough to wrench Tessa off her feet.

She heard a lot of splashing ahead. A soft curse from Sam.

The water was creeping higher. At first she thought she was imagining it, but then she realized the torrent had risen to above her knees.

The damned darkness was the worst of it, not being able to see anything, virtually blind, unable to be sure what was happening.

Abruptly she was jerked forward again. Two, three—oh, God—half a dozen steps.

Sam, don't fall!

Stumbling, almost losing her balance, realizing that they were on the edge of disaster, Tessa leaned backward on the line, using its tautness to steady herself instead of rushing forward with the hope of developing slack again. She hoped to God she didn't resist too much and get yanked off her feet.

She swayed. The line pulled hard at her waist. Without slack to loop through her hands, she was unable to take most of the strain with her arms.

The pressure of water against the back of her legs was growing.

Her feet skidded.

Like videotape fast-forwarded through an editing machine, strange thoughts flew through her mind, scores of them in a few seconds, all unbidden, and some of them surprised her. She thought about living, surviving, about not wanting to die, and that wasn't so surprising, but then she thought about Chrissie, about not wanting to fail the girl, and in her mind she saw a detailed image of her and Chrissie together, in a cozy house somewhere, living as mother and daughter, and she was surprised at how much she *wanted* that, which seemed wrong because Chrissie's parents were not dead, as far as anyone knew, and might not even be hopelessly changed, because the conversion—whatever it was—just might be reversible. Chrissie's family might be put back together again. Tessa couldn't see a picture of that in her mind. It didn't seem as much a possibility as she and Chrissie together. But it might happen. Then she thought of Sam, of never having a chance to make love to him, and *that* startled her, because although he was sort of attractive, she truly hadn't realized she was drawn to him in any romantic way. Of course his grit in the face of spiritual despair was appealing, and his perfectly serious four-reasons-for-living shtick made him an intriguing challenge. Could she give him a fifth? Or supplant Goldie Hawn as the fourth? But until she found herself tottering on the brink of a watery death, she didn't realize how very much he had attracted her in such a short time.

Her feet skidded again. Beneath the surging water, the floor was much more slippery than it had been in the stone channel, as if moss grew on the concrete. Tessa tried to dig in her heels.

Sam cursed under his breath. Chrissie made a coughing-choking sound.

The depth of water in the center of the tunnel had risen to about eighteen or twenty inches.

A moment later the line jerked hard, then went completely slack.

The rope had snapped. Sam and Chrissie had been swept down into the tunnel.

The gurgle-slosh-slap of gushing water echoed off the walls, and echoes of the echoes overlaid previous echoes, and Tessa's heart was pounding so loud she could hear it, but still she should have heard their cries, too, as they were carried away. Yet for one awful moment they were silent.

Then Chrissie coughed again. Only a few feet away.

A flashlight snapped on. Sam was hooding most of the lens with his hand.

Chrissie was sideways in the passage, pressed up out of the worst of the flow, her back and the palms of both hands braced against the side of the tunnel.

Sam stood with his feet planted wide apart. Water churned and foamed around his legs. He had gotten turned around. He was facing uphill now.

The rope hadn't snapped, after all; the tension had been released because both Sam and Chrissie had regained their equilibrium.

"You all right?" Sam whispered to the girl.

She nodded, still gagging on the dirty water she had swallowed. She wrinkled her face in distaste, spat once, twice, and said, "Yuch."

Looking at Tessa, Sam said, "Okay?"

She couldn't speak. A rock-hard lump had formed in her throat. She swallowed a few times, blinked. A delayed wave of relief passed through her, reducing the almost unbearable pressure in her chest, and at last she said, "Okay. Yeah. Okay."

6

SAM WAS RELIEVED WHEN THEY GOT TO THE END OF THE CULvert without another fall. He stood for a moment, just outside the lower mouth of the drain, happily looking up at the sky. Because of the thick fog, he couldn't actually see the sky, but that was a technicality; he still felt relieved to be out in the open air again, if still knee-deep in muddy water.

They were virtually in a river now. Either the rain was falling harder in the hills, at the far east end of town, or some breakwater in the system had collapsed. The level had swiftly risen well past midthigh on Sam and nearly to Chrissie's waist, and the deluge poured from the conduit at their back with impressive power. Keeping their footing in those cataracts was getting more difficult by the second.

He turned, reached for the girl, drew her close, and said, "I'm going to hold tight to your arm from here on."

She nodded.

The night was grave-deep, and even inches from her face, he could see only a shadowy impression of her features. When he looked up at Tessa, who stood a few feet behind the girl, she was little more than a black shape and might not have been Tessa at all.

Holding fast to the girl, he turned and looked again at the way ahead.

The tunnel had extended for two blocks before pouring the flood forth into another one-block length of open drainage channel, just as Harry had remembered from the days when he had been a kid and, against every admonition of his parents, had played in the drainage system. Thank God for disobedient children.

One block ahead of them, this new section of stone watercourse fed into another concrete culvert. *That* pipe, according to Harry, terminated at the mouth of the long vertical drain at the west end of town. Supposedly, in the last ten feet of the main sloping line, a row of sturdy, vertical iron bars was set twelve inches apart and extended floor to ceiling, creating a barrier through which only water and smaller objects could pass. There was virtually no chance of being carried all the way into that two-hundred-foot drop.

But Sam didn't want to risk it. There must be no more falls. After being washed to the end and crashing against the safety barrier, if they were not suffering from myriad broken bones, if they were able to get to their feet and move, climbing back up that long culvert, on a steep slope, against the onrushing force of the water, was not an ordeal he was willing to contemplate, let alone endure.

All of his life he had felt he'd failed people. Though he had been only seven when his mother had died in the accident, he'd always been eaten by guilt related to her death, as if he ought to have been able to save her in spite of his tender age and in spite of having been pinned in the wreckage of the car with her. Later, Sam had never been able to please his drunken, mean, sorry son-of-a-bitch of a father—and had suffered grievously for that failure. Like Harry, he felt that he had failed the people of Vietnam, though the decision to abandon them had been made by authorities who far outranked him and with whom he could have had no influence. Neither of the Bureau agents who had died with him had died *because* of him, yet he felt he had failed them too. He had failed Karen, somehow, though people told him he was mad to think that he had any responsibility for her cancer; it was just that he couldn't help thinking that if he had loved her more, loved her harder, she would have found the strength and will to pull through. God knew, he had failed his own son, Scott.

Chrissie squeezed his hand.

He returned the squeeze.

She seemed so small.

Earlier in the day, gathered in Harry's kitchen, they'd had a conversation about responsibility. Now, suddenly, he realized that his sense of responsibility was so highly developed that it bordered on obsession, but he still agreed with what Harry had said: A man's commitment to others, especially to friends and family, could never be excessive. He had never imagined that one of the key insights of his life would come to him while he was standing nearly waist-deep in muddy water in a drainage canal, on the run from enemies both human and inhuman, but that was where he received it. He realized that his problem was not the alacrity with which he shouldered responsibility or the unusual weight of it that he was willing to carry. No, hell no, his problem was that he had allowed his sense of responsibility to obstruct his ability to cope with failure. All men failed from time to time, and often the fault lay not in the man himself but in the role of fate. When he failed, he had to learn not only to go on but to *enjoy* going on. Failure could not be allowed to bleed him of the very pleasure of life. Such a turning away from life was blasphemous, if you believed in God—and just plain stupid if you didn't. It was like saying, "Men fail, but *I* shouldn't fail, because I'm more than just a man, I'm somewhere up there between the angels and God." He saw why he had lost Scott: because he had lost his own love of life, his sense of fun, and had ceased to be able to share anything meaningful with the boy—or to halt Scott's own descent into nihilism when it had begun.

At the moment, if he had tried to count his reasons for living, the list would have had more than four items. It would have had hundreds. *Thousands.*

All of this understanding came to him in an instant, while he was holding Chrissie's hand, as if the flow of time had been stretched by some quirk of relativity. He realized that if he failed to save the girl or Tessa, but got out of this mess himself, he would nevertheless have to rejoice at his own salvation and get *on* with life. Although their situation was dark and their hope slim, his spirits soared, and he almost laughed aloud. The living nightmare they were enduring in Moonlight Cove had profoundly shaken him, rattling important truths into him, truths which were simple and should have been easy to see during his long years of torment, but which he received gratefully in spite of their simplicity and his own previous thickheadedness. Maybe the truth was always simple when you found it.

Yeah, okay, maybe he could go on now even if he failed in his responsibilities to others, even if he lost Chrissie and Tessa—but, shit, he wasn't *going* to lose them. Damned if he was.

Damned if he was.

He held Chrissie's hand and cautiously edged along the stone channel, grateful for the comparative unevenness of that pavement and the moss-free traction it provided. The water was just deep enough to give him a slight buoyant feeling, which made it harder to put each foot down after he lifted it, so instead of walking, he dragged his feet along the bottom.

In less than a minute they reached a set of iron rungs mortared into the masonry of the channel wall. Tessa moved in, and for a while they all just hung there, gripping iron, grateful for the solid feel of it and the anchor it provided.

A couple of minutes later, when the rain abruptly slacked off, Sam was ready to move again. Being careful not to step on Tessa's and Chrissie's hands, he climbed a couple of rungs and looked out at the street.

Nothing moved but the fog.

This section of open watercourse flanked Moonlight Cove Central School. The athletic field was just a few feet from him, and, sitting beyond that open space, barely visible in the darkness and mist, was the school itself, illuminated only by a couple of dim security lamps.

The property was encircled by a nine-foot-high chain-link fence. But Sam wasn't daunted by that. Fences always had gates.

7

HARRY WAITED IN THE ATTIC, HOPING FOR THE BEST, EX-pecting the worst.

He was propped against the outer wall of the long, unlighted chamber, tucked in the corner at the extreme far end from the trapdoor through which he had been lifted. There was nothing in that upper room behind which he could hide.

But if someone went so far as to empty out the master-bedroom closet, pull down the trap, open the folding stairs, and poke his head up to look around, maybe he wouldn't be diligent about probing every corner of the place. When he saw bare boards and a flurry of spiders on his first sweep of the flash, maybe he would click off the beam and retreat.

Absurd, of course. Anyone who went to the trouble to look into the attic at all would look into it properly, exploring every corner. But whether that hope was absurd or not, Harry clung to it; he was good at nurturing hope, making hearty stew from the thinnest broth of it, because for half his life, hope was mostly what had sustained him.

He was not uncomfortable. As preparation for the unheated attic, with Sam's help to speed the dressing process, he had put on wool socks, warmer pants than what he had been wearing, and two sweaters.

Funny, how a lot of people seemed to think that a paralyzed man could feel nothing in his unresponsive extremities. In some cases, that was true; all nerves were blunted, all feeling lost. But spinal injuries came in myriad types; short of a total severing of the cord, the range of sensations left to the victim varied widely.

In Harry's case, though he had lost all use of one arm and one leg and nearly all use of the other leg, he could still feel heat and cold. When something pricked him he was aware—if not of pain—at least of a blunt pressure.

Physically, he felt much less than when he'd been a whole man; no argument about that. But all feelings were not physical. Though he was sure that few people would believe him, his handicap actually had enriched his emotional life. Though by necessity something of a recluse, he had learned to compensate for a dearth of human contact. Books had helped. Books opened the world to him. And the telescope. But mostly his unwavering will to lead as full a life as possible was what had kept him whole in mind and heart.

If these were his final hours, he would blow out the candle with no bitterness when the time came to extinguish it. He regretted what he had lost, but more important, he treasured what he had kept. In the last analysis, he felt that he had lived a life that was in the balance good, worthwhile, precious.

He had two guns with him. A .45 revolver. A .38 pistol. If they came into the attic after him, he would use the pistol on them until it was empty. Then he would make them eat all but one of the rounds in the revolver. That last cartridge would be for himself.

He had brought no extra bullets. In a crisis, a man with one good hand could not reload fast enough to make the effort more than a comic finale.

The drumming of rain on the roof had subsided. He wondered if this was just another lull in the storm or if it was finally ending.

It would be nice to see the sun again.

He worried more about Moose than about himself. The poor damn dog was down there alone. When the Boogeymen or their makers came at last, he hoped they wouldn't harm old Moose. And if they came into the attic and forced him to kill himself, he hoped that Moose would not be long without a good home.

8

TO LOMAN, AS HE CRUISED, MOONLIGHT COVE SEEMED BOTH dead and teeming with life.

Judged by the usual signs of life in a small town, the burg was an empty husk, as defunct as any sun-dried ghost town in the heart of the Mohave. The shops, bars, and restaurants were closed. Even the usually crowded Perez Family Restaurant was shuttered, dark; no one had showed up to open for business. The only pedestrians out walking in the aftermath of the storm were foot patrols or conversion teams. Likewise, the police units and two-man patrols in private cars had the streets to themselves.

However, the town seethed with perverse life. Several times he saw strange, swift figures moving through the darkness and fog, still secretive but far bolder than they had been on other nights. When he stopped or slowed to study those marauders, some of them paused in deep shadows to gaze at him with baleful yellow or green or smoldering red eyes, as if they were contemplating their chances of attacking his black-and-white and pulling him out of it before he could take his foot off the brake pedal and get out of there. Watching them, he was filled with a longing to abandon his car, his clothes, and the rigidity of his human form, to join them in their simpler world of hunting, feeding, and rutting. Each time he quickly turned away from them and drove on before they—or he—could act upon such impulses. Here and there he passed houses in which eerie lights glowed, and against the windows of which moved shadows so grotesque and unearthly that his heart quickened and his palms went damp, though he was well removed from them and probably beyond their reach. He did not stop to investigate what creatures might inhabit those places or what tasks they were engaged upon, for he sensed that they were kin to the thing Denny had become and that they were more dangerous, in many ways, than the prowling regressives.

He now lived in a Lovecraftian world of primal and cosmic forces, of monstrous entities stalking the night, where human beings were reduced to little more than cattle, where the Judeo-Christian universe of a love-motivated God had been replaced by the creation of the old gods who were driven by dark lusts, a taste for cruelty, and a never-satisfied thirst for power. In the air, in the eddying fog, in the shadowed and dripping trees, in the unlighted streets, and even in the sodium-yellow glare of the lamps on the main streets, there was the pervasive sense that nothing good could happen that night . . . but that anything *else* could happen, no matter how fantastical or bizarre.

Having read uncounted paperbacks over the years, he was familiar with Lovecraft. He had not liked him a hundredth as much as Louis L'Amour, largely because L'Amour had dealt with reality, while H.P. Lovecraft had traded in the impossible. Or so it had seemed to Loman at the time. Now he knew that men could create, in the real world, hells equal to any that the most imaginative writer could dream up.

Lovecraftian despair and terror flooded through Moonlight Cove in greater quantities than those in which the recent rain had fallen. As he drove through those transmuted streets, Loman kept his service revolver on the car seat beside him, within easy reach.

Shaddack.

He must find Shaddack.

Going south on Juniper, he stopped at the intersection with Ocean Avenue. At the same time another black-and-white braked at the stop sign directly opposite Loman, headed north.

No traffic was moving on Ocean. Rolling his window down, Loman pulled slowly across the intersection and braked beside the other cruiser, with no more than a foot separating them.

From the number on the door, above the police-department shield, Loman knew it was Neil Penniworth's patrol car. But when he looked through the side window, he did not see the young officer. He saw something that might once have been Penniworth, still vaguely human, illuminated by the gauge and speedometer lights but more directly by the glow of the mobile VDT in there. Twin cables, like the one that had erupted from Denny's forehead to join him more intimately with his PC, had sprouted from Penniworth's skull; and although the light was poor, it appeared as if one of those extrusions snaked through the steering wheel and into the dashboard, while the other looped down toward the console-mounted computer. The shape of Penniworth's skull had changed dramatically, too, drawing forward, bristling with spiky features that must have been sensors of some kind and that gleamed softly like burnished metal in the light of the VDT; his shoulders were larger, queerly scalloped and pointed; he appeared earnestly to have sought the form of a baroque robot. His hands were not on the steering wheel, but perhaps he did not even have hands any more; Loman suspected that Penniworth had not just become one with his mobile computer terminal but with the patrol car itself.

Penniworth slowly turned his head to face Loman.

In his eyeless sockets, crackling white fingers of electricity wiggled and jittered ceaselessly.

Shaddack had said that the New People's freedom from emotion had given them the ability to make far greater use of their innate brain power, even to the extent of exerting mental control over the form and function of matter. Their consciousness now dictated their form; to escape a world in which they were not permitted emotion, they could become whatever they chose—though they could not return to the Old People they had been. Evidently life as a cyborg was free of angst, for Penniworth had sought release from fear and longing—perhaps some kind of obliteration, as well—in this monstrous incarnation.

But what did he feel now? What purpose did he have? And did he remain in that altered state because he truly preferred it? Or was he like Peyser—trapped either for physical reasons or because an aberrant aspect of his own psychology would not permit him to reassume the human form to which, otherwise, he desired to return?

Loman reached for the revolver on the seat beside him.

A segmented cable burst from the driver's door of Penniworth's car, without shredding metal, extruding as if a part of the door had melted and re-formed to produce it—except that it looked at least semiorganic. The probe struck Loman's side window with a snap.

The revolver eluded Loman's sweaty hand, for he could not take his eyes off the probe to look for the gun.

The glass did not crack, but a quarter-size patch bubbled and melted in an instant, and the probe weaved into the car, straight at Loman's face. It had a fleshy sucker mouth, like an eel, but the tiny, sharply pointed teeth within it looked like steel.

He ducked his head, forgot about the revolver, and tramped the accelerator to the floor. The Chevy almost seemed to rear back for a fraction of a second; then with a surge of power that pressed Loman into the seat, it shot forward, south on Juniper.

For a moment the probe between the cars stretched to maintain contact, brushed the bridge of Loman's nose—and abruptly was gone, reeled back into the vehicle from which it had come.

He drove fast all the way to the end of Juniper before slowing down to make a turn. The wind of his passage whistled at the hole that the probe had melted in his window.

Loman's worst fear seemed to be unfolding. Those New People who didn't choose regression were going to transform themselves—or be transformed at the demand of Shaddack—into hellish hybrids of man and machine.

Find Shaddack. Murder the maker and release the anguished monsters he had made.

9

PRECEDED BY SAM AND FOLLOWED BY TESSA, CHRISSIE squelched through the mushy turf of the athletic field. In places the soggy grass gave way to gluey mud, which pulled noisily at her shoes, and she thought she sounded like a sort of goofy alien herself, plodding along on big, sucker-equipped feet. Then it occurred to her that in a way she *was* an alien in Moonlight Cove tonight, a different sort of creature from what the majority of the citizens had become.

They were two-thirds of the way across the field when they were halted by a shrill cry that split the night as cleanly as a sharp ax would split a dry cord of wood. That unhuman voice rose and fell and rose again, savage and uncanny but familiar, the call of one of those beasts that she'd thought were invading aliens. Though the rain had stopped, the air was laden with moisture, and in that humidity, the unearthly shriek carried well, like the bell-clear notes of a distant trumpet.

Worse, the call at once was answered by the beast's excited kin. At least half a dozen equally chilling shrieks arose from perhaps as far south as Paddock Lane and as far north as Holliwell Road, from the high hills in the east end of town and from the beach-facing bluffs only a couple of blocks to the west.

All of a sudden Chrissie longed for the cold, lightless culvert churning with waist-deep water so filthy that it might have come from the devil's own bathtub. This open ground seemed wildly dangerous by comparison.

A new cry arose as the others faded, and it was closer than any that had come before it. Too close.

"Let's get inside," Sam said urgently.

Chrissie was beginning to admit to herself that she might not make a good Andre Norton heroine, after all. She was scared, cold, grainy-eyed with exhaustion, starting to feel sorry for herself, and hungry again. She was sick and tired of adventure. She yearned for warm rooms and lazy days with good books and trips to movie theaters and wedges of double-fudge cake. By this time a true adventure-story heroine would have worked out a series of brilliant stratagems that would have brought the beasts in Moonlight Cove to ruin, would have found a way to turn the robot-people into harmless car-washing machines, and would be well on her way to being crowned princess of the kingdom by acclamation of the respect-ful and grateful citizenry.

They hurried to the end of the field, rounded the bleachers, and crossed the deserted parking lot to the back of the school.

Nothing attacked them.

Thank you, God. Your friend, Chrissie.

Something howled again.

Sometimes even God seemed to have a perverse streak.

There were six doors at different places along the back of the school. They moved from one to another, as Sam tried them all and examined the locks in the hand-hooded beam of his flashlight. He apparently couldn't pick any of them, which disappointed her, because she'd imagined FBI men were so well trained that in an emergency they could open a bank vault with spit and a hairpin.

He also tried a few windows and spent what seemed a long time peering through the panes with his flashlight. He was examining not the rooms beyond but the inner sills and frames of the windows.

At the last door—which was the only one that had glass in the top of it, the others being blank rectangles of metal—Sam clicked off the flashlight, looked solemnly at Tessa, and spoke to her in a low voice. "I don't think there's an alarm system here. Could be wrong. But there's no alarm tape on the glass and, as far as I can see, no hard-wired contacts along the frames or at the window latches."

"Are those the only two kinds of alarms they might have?" Tessa whispered.

"Well, there're motion-detection systems, either employing sonic transmitters or electric eyes. But they'd be too elaborate for just a school, and probably too sensitive for a building like this."

"So now what?"

"Now I break a window."

Chrissie expected him to withdraw a roll of masking tape from a pocket of his coat and tape one of the panes to soften the sound of shattering glass and to prevent the shards from falling noisily to the floor inside. That was how they usually did it in books. But he just turned sideways to the door, drew his arm forward, then rammed it back and drove his elbow through the eight-inch-square pane in the lower-right corner of the window grid. Glass broke and clattered to the floor with an awful racket. Maybe he had forgotten to bring his tape.

He reached through the empty pane, felt for the locks, disengaged them, and went inside first. Chrissie followed him, trying not to step on the broken glass.

Sam switched on the flashlight. He didn't hood it quite so much as he had done outside, though he was obviously trying to keep the backwash of the beam off the windows.

They were in a long hallway. It was full of the cedar-pine smell that came from the crumbly green disinfectant and dust-attractor that for years the janitors had sprinkled on the floors and then swept up, until the tiles and walls had become impregnated with the scent. The aroma was familiar to her from Thomas Jefferson Elementary, and she was disappointed to find it here. She had thought of high school as a special, mysterious place, but how special or mysterious could it be if they used the same disinfectant as at the grade school?

Tessa quietly closed the outside door behind them.

They stood listening for a moment.

The school was silent.

They moved down the hall, looking into classrooms and lavatories and supply closets on both sides, searching for the computer lab. In a hundred and fifty feet they reached a junction with another hall. They stood in the intersection for a moment, heads cocked, listening again.

The school was still silent.

And dark. The only light in any direction was the flashlight, which Sam still held in his left hand but which he no longer hooded with his right. He had withdrawn his revolver from his holster and needed his right hand for that.

After a long wait, Sam said, "Nobody's here."

Which did seem to be the case.

Briefly Chrissie felt better, safer.

On the other hand, if he really believed they were the only people in the school, why didn't he put his gun away?

10

AS HE DROVE THROUGH HIS DOMAIN, IMPATIENT FOR MID-night, which was still five hours away, Thomas Shaddack had largely regressed to a childlike condition. Now that his triumph was at hand, he could cast off the masquerade of a grown man, which he had so long sustained, and he was relieved to do so. He had never been an adult, really, but a boy whose emotional development had been forever arrested at the age of twelve, when the message of the moonhawk had not only come to him but been *imbedded* in him; he had thereafter faked emotional ascension into adulthood to match his physical growth.

But it was no longer necessary to pretend.

On one level, he had always known this about himself, and had considered it to be his great strength, an advantage over those who had put childhood behind them. A boy of twelve could harbor and nurture a dream with more determination than could an adult, for adults were constantly distracted by conflicting needs and desires. A boy on the edge of puberty, however, had the single-mindedness to focus on and dedicate himself unswervingly to a single Big Dream. Properly bent, a twelve-year-old boy was the perfect monomaniac.

The Moonhawk Project, his Big Dream of godlike power, would not have reached fruition if he had matured in the usual way. He owed his impending triumph to arrested development.

He was a boy again, not secretly any more but openly, eager to satisfy his every whim, to take whatever he wanted, to do anything that broke the rules. Twelve-year-old boys reveled in breaking the rules, challenging authority. At their worst, twelve-year-old boys were naturally lawless, on the verge of hormonal-induced rebellion.

But he was more than lawless. He was a boy flying on cactus candy that had been eaten long ago but that had left a psychic if not a physical residue. He was a boy who knew that he was a god. *Any* boy's potential for cruelty paled in comparison to the cruelty of gods.

To pass the time until midnight, he imagined what he would do with his power when the last of Moonlight Cove had fallen under his command. Some of his ideas made him shiver with a strange mixture of excitement and disgust.

He was on Iceberry Way when he realized the Indian was with him. He was surprised when he turned his head and saw Runningdeer sitting in the passenger seat. Indeed he stopped the van in the middle of the street and stared in disbelief, shocked and afraid.

But Runningdeer did not menace him. In fact the Indian didn't even speak to him or look at him, but stared straight ahead, through the windshield.

Slowly understanding came to Shaddack. The Indian's spirit was his now, his possession as surely as was the van. The great spirits had given him the Indian as an advisor, as a reward for having made a success of Moonhawk. But *he*, not Runningdeer, was in control this time, and the Indian would speak only when spoken to.

"Hello, Runningdeer," he said.

The Indian looked at him. "Hello, Little Chief."

"You're mine now."

"Yes, Little Chief."

For just a brief flicker of time, it occurred to Shaddack that he was mad and that Runningdeer was an illusion coughed up by a sick mind. But monomaniacal boys do not have the capacity for an extended examination of their mental condition, and the thought passed out of his mind as quickly as it had entered.

To Runningdeer, he said, "You'll do what I say."

"Always."

Immensely pleased, Shaddack let up on the brake pedal and drove on. The headlights revealed an amber-eyed thing of fantastic shape, drinking from a puddle on the pavement. He refused to regard it as a thing of consequence, and when it loped away, he let it vanish from his memory as swiftly as it disappeared from the night-mantled street.

Casting a sly glance at the Indian, he said, "You know one thing I'm going to do some day?"

"What's that, Little Chief?"

"When I've converted everyone, not just the people in Moonlight Cove but everyone in the world, when no one stands against me, then I'll spend some time tracking down your family, all of your remaining brothers, sisters, even your cousins, and I'll find all of *their* children, and all their wives and husbands, and all their *children's* wives and husbands . . . and I'll make them pay for your crimes, I'll really, really make them pay." A whining petulance had entered his voice. He disapproved of the tone he heard himself using, but he could not lose it. "I'll kill all the men, hack them to bloody bits and pieces, do it myself. I'll let them know that it's because of their relation to you that they've got to suffer, and they'll despise you and curse your name, they'll be sorry you ever existed. And I'll rape all the women and hurt them, hurt them all, really bad, and then I'll kill them too. What do you think of that? Huh?"

"If it's what you want, Little Chief."

"Damn right it's what I want."

"Then you may have it."

"Damn right I may have it."

Shaddack was surprised when tears came to his eyes. He stopped at an intersection and didn't move on. "It wasn't right what you did to me."

The Indian said nothing.

"Say it wasn't right!"

"It wasn't right, Little Chief."

"It wasn't right at all."

"It wasn't right."

Shaddack pulled a handkerchief from his pocket and blew his nose. He blotted his eyes. Soon his tears dried up.

He smiled at the nightscape revealed through the windshield. He sighed. He glanced at Runningdeer.

The Indian was staring forward, silent.

Shaddack said, "Of course, without you, I might never have been a child of the moonhawk."

11

THE COMPUTER LAB WAS ON THE GROUND FLOOR, IN THE center of the building, near a confluence of corridors. Windows looked out on a courtyard but could not be seen from any street, which allowed Sam to switch on the overhead lights.

It was a large chamber, laid out like a language lab, with each VDT in its own three-sided cubicle. Thirty computers—upper end, hard-disk systems—were lined up along three walls and in a back-to-back row down the middle of the room.

Looking around at the wealth of hardware, Tessa said, "New Wave sure was generous, huh?"

"Maybe 'thorough' is a better word," Sam said.

He walked along a row of VDTs, looking for telephone lines and modems, but he found none.

Tessa and Chrissie stayed back by the open lab door, peering out at the dark hallway.

Sam sat down at one of the machines and switched it on. The New Wave logo appeared in the center of the screen.

With no telephones, no modems, maybe the computers really had been given to the school for student training, without the additional intention of tying the kids to New Wave during some stage of the Moonhawk Project.

The logo blinked off, and a menu appeared on the screen. Because they were hard-disk machines with tremendous capacity, their programs were already loaded and ready to go as soon as the system was powered up. The menu offered him five choices:

A. TRAINING 1
B. TRAINING 2
C. WORD PROCESSING
D. ACCOUNTING
E. OTHER

He hesitated, not because he couldn't decide what letter to push but because he was suddenly afraid of using the machine. He vividly remembered the Coltranes. Though it had seemed to him that they had elected to meld with their computers, that their transformation began within them, he had no way of knowing for sure that it had not been the other way around. Maybe the computers had somehow reached out and *seized* them. That seemed impossible. Besides, thanks to Harry's observations, they knew that people in Moonlight Cove were being converted by an injection, not by some insidious force that passed semimagically through computer keys into the pads of their fingers. He was hesitant nevertheless.

Finally he pressed **E** and got a list of school subjects:

A. ALL LANGUAGES
B. MATH

C. ALL SCIENCES
D. HISTORY
E. ENGLISH
F. OTHER

He pressed F. A Third menu appeared, and the process continued until he finally got a menu on which the final selection was **NEW WAVE.** When he keyed in that choice, words began to march across the screen.

HELLO, STUDENT.
YOU ARE NOW IN CONTACT WITH THE SUPERCOMPUTER AT NEW
WAVE MICROTECHNOLOGY.
MY NAME IS SUN.
I AM HERE TO SERVE YOU.

The school machines were wired directly to New Wave. Modems were unnecessary.

WOULD YOU LIKE TO SEE MENUS?
OR WILL YOU SPECIFY INTEREST?

Considering the wealth of menus in the police department's system alone, which he had reviewed last night in the patrol car, he figured he could sit here all evening just looking at menu after menu after submenu before he found what he wanted. He typed in: **MOONLIGHT COVE POLICE DEPARTMENT.**

THIS FILE RESTRICTED.
PLEASE DO NOT ATTEMPT TO PROCEED WITHOUT
THE ASSISTANCE OF YOUR TEACHER.

He supposed that the teachers had individual code numbers that, depending on whether or not they were converted, would allow them to access otherwise restricted data. The only way to hit on one of their codes was to begin trying random combinations of digits, but since he didn't even know how many numbers were in a code, there were millions if not billions of possibilities. He could sit there until his hair turned white and his teeth fell out, and not luck into a good number.

Last night he had used Officer Reese Dorn's personal computer-access code, and he wondered whether it worked only on a designated police-department VDT or whether any computer tied to Sun would accept it. Nothing lost for trying. He typed in **262699.**

The screen cleared. Then: **HELLO, OFFICER DORN.**

Again he requested the police-department data system.

This time it was given to him.

CHOOSE ONE:
A. DISPATCHER

B. CENTRAL FILES
C. BULLETIN BOARD
D. OUTSYSTEM MODEM

He pressed **D.**

He was shown a list of computers nationwide with which he could link through the police-department's modem.

His hands were suddenly damp with sweat. He was sure something was going to go wrong, if only because nothing had been easy thus far, not from the minute he had driven into town.

He glanced at Tessa. "Everything okay?"

She squinted at the dark hallway, then blinked at him. "Seems to be. Any luck?"

"Yeah . . . maybe." He turned to the computer again and said softly, "Please. . . . "

He scanned the long roster of possible outsystem links. He found **FBI KEY,** which was the name of the latest and most sophisticated of the Bureau's computer networks—a highly secure, interoffice data-storage, -retrieval, and -transmission system housed at headquarters in Washington, which had been installed only within the past year. Supposedly no one but approved agents at the home office and in the Bureau's field offices, accessing with their own special codes, were able to use **FBI KEY.**

So much for high security.

Still expecting trouble, Sam selected **FBI KEY.** The menu disappeared. The screen remained blank for a moment. Then, on the display, which proved to be a full-color monitor, the FBI shield appeared in blue and gold. The word **KEY** appeared below it.

Next, a series of questions was flashed on the screen—**WHAT IS YOUR BU-REAU ID NUMBER? NAME? DATE OF BIRTH? DATE OF BUREAU INDUC-TION? MOTHER'S MAIDEN NAME?**—and when he answered those, he was rewarded with access.

"Bingo!" he said, daring to be optimistic.

Tessa said, "What's happened?"

"I'm in the Bureau's main system in D.C."

"You're a hacker," Chrissie said.

"I'm a fumbler. But I'm in."

"Now what?" Tessa asked.

"I'll ask for the current operator in a minute. But first I want to send greetings to every damned office in the country, make them all sit up and take notice."

"Greetings?"

From the extensive **FBI KEY** menu, Sam called up item **G—IMMEDIATE IN-TEROFFICE TRANSMISSION**. He intended to send a message to every Bureau field office in the country, not just to San Francisco, which was the closest and the one from which he hoped to obtain help. There was one chance in a million that the night operator in San Francisco would overlook the message among reams of other transmissions, in spite of the **ACTION ALERT** heading he would tag on to it. If that happened, if someone was asleep at the wheel at this most inopportune of moments, they wouldn't be asleep for long, because every office in the country would be asking HQ for more details about the Moonlight Cove bulletin and requesting an explanation of why they had been fed an alert about a situation outside their regions.

He did not understand half of what was happening in this town. He could not have explained, in the shorthand of a Bureau bulletin, even as much as he *did* understand. But he quickly crafted a summary which he believed was as accurate as it had to be—and which he hoped would get them off their duffs and running.

ACTION ALERT
MOONLIGHT COVE, CALIFORNIA

* SCORES DEAD. CONDITION DETERIORATING. HUNDREDS MORE COULD DIE WITHIN HOURS.
* NEW WAVE MICROTECHNOLOGY ENGAGED IN ILLICIT EXPERI- MENTS ON HUMAN SUBJECTS, WITHOUT THEIR KNOWLEDGE. CONSPIRACY OF WIDEST SCOPE.
* THOUSANDS OF PEOPLE CONTAMINATED.
* REPEAT, ENTIRE POPULATION OF TOWN CONTAMINATED.
* SITUATION EXTREMELY DANGEROUS.
* CONTAMINATED CITIZENS SUFFER LOSS OF FACULTIES, EXHIBIT TENDENCY TO EXTREME VIOLENCE.
* REPEAT, EXTREME VIOLENCE.
* REQUEST IMMEDIATE QUARANTINE BY ARMY SPECIAL FORCES. ALSO REQUEST IMMEDIATE, MASSIVE, ARMED BACKUP BY BUREAU PERSONNEL.

He gave his position at the high school on roshmore, so incoming support would have a place to start looking for him, though he was not certain that he, Tessa, and Chrissie could safely continue to take refuge there until reinforcements arrived. He signed off with his name and Bureau ID number.

That message was not going to prepare them for the shock of what they would find in Moonlight Cove, but at least it would get them on the move and encourage them to come prepared for anything.

He typed **TRANSMIT**, but then he had a thought and wiped the word from the screen. He typed **REPEAT TRANSMISSION**.

The computer asked **NUMBER OF REPEATS?**

He typed **99**.

The computer acknowledged the order.

Then he typed **TRANSMIT** again and pressed the **ENTER** button.

WHAT OFFICES?

He typed **ALL**.

The screen went blank. Then: **TRANSMITTING**.

At the moment every **KEY** laser printer in every Bureau field office in the country was printing out the first of ninety-nine repeats of his message. Night staffers everywhere soon would be climbing the walls.

He almost whooped with delight.

But there was more to be done. They were not out of this mess yet.

Sam quickly returned to the **KEY** menu and tapped selection **A—NIGHT OP-ERATOR**. Five seconds later he was in touch with the agent manning the **KEY** post at the Bureau's central communications room in Washington. A number flashed on the screen—the operator's ID—followed by a name, **ANNE DEN-TON**.Taking immense satisfaction in using high technology to bring the downfall of Thomas Shaddack, New Wave, and the Moonhawk Project, Sam entered into a long-distance, unspoken, electronic conversation with Anne Denton, intending to spell out the horrors of Moonlight Cove in more detail.

12

THOUGH LOMAN NO LONGER WAS INTERESTED IN THE activities of the police department, he switched on the VDT in his car every ten minutes or so to see if anything was happening. He expected Shaddack to be in touch with members of the department from time to time. If he was lucky enough to catch a VDT dialogue between Shaddack and other cops, he might be able to pinpoint the bastard's location from something that was said.

He didn't leave the computer on all the time because he was afraid of it. He didn't think it would jump at him and suck out his brains or anything, but he did recognize that working with it too long might induce in him a temptation to become what Neil Penniworth and Denny had become—in the same way that being around the regressives had given rise to a powerful urge to devolve.

He had just pulled to the side of Holliwell Road, where his restless cruising had taken him, had switched on the machine, and was about to call up the dialogue channel to see if anyone was engaged in conversation, when the word **ALERT** appeared in large letters on the screen. He pulled his hand back from the keyboard as if something had nipped at him.

The computer said, **SUN REQUESTS DIALOGUE**.

Sun? The supercomputer at New Wave? Why would it be accessing the police department's system?

Before another officer at headquarters or in another car could query the machine, Loman took charge and typed **DIALOGUE APPROVED**.

REQUEST CLARIFICATION, Sun said.

Loman typed **YES**, which could mean **GO AHEAD**.

Structuring its questions from its own self-assessment program, which allowed it to monitor its own workings as if it were an outside observer, Sun said, **ARE TELEPHONE CALLS TO AND FROM UNAPPROVED NUMBERS IN MOONLIGHT COVE AND ALL NUMBERS OUTSIDE STILL RESTRICTED?**

YES.

ARE SUN'S RESERVED TELEPHONE LINES INCLUDED IN AFORE-MENTIONED PROHIBITION? the New Wave computer asked, speaking of itself in third person.

Confused, Loman typed **UNCLEAR**.

Patiently leading him through it step by step, Sun explained that it had its own dedicated phone lines, outside the main directory, by which its users could call other computers all over the country and access them.

He already knew this, so he typed **YES.**

ARE SUN'S RESERVED TELEPHONE LINES INCLUDED IN AFORE-MENTIONED PROHIBITION? it repeated.

If he'd had Denny's interest in computers, he might have tumbled immediately to what was happening, but he was still confused. So he typed **WHY?**—meaning **WHY DO YOU ASK?**

OUTSYSTEM MODEM NOW IN USE.

BY WHOM?

SAMUEL BOOKER.

Loman would have laughed if he had been capable of glee. The agent had found a way out of Moonlight Cove, and now the shit was going to hit the fan at last.

Before he could query Sun as to Booker's activities and whereabouts, another name appeared on the upper left corner of the screen—**SHADDACK**—indicating that New Wave's own Moreau was watching the dialogue on his VDT and was cutting in. Loman was content to let his maker and Sun converse uninterrupted.

Shaddack asked for more details.

Sun responded: **FBI KEY SYSTEM ACCESSED.**

Loman could imagine Shaddack's shock. The beast master's demand appeared on the screen: **OPTIONS.** Which meant he desperately wanted a menu of options from Sun to deal with the situation.

Sun presented him with five choices, the fifth of which was **SHUT DOWN**, and Shaddack chose that one.

A moment later Sun reported: **FBI KEY SYSTEM LINK SHUT DOWN.**

Loman hoped that Booker had gotten enough of a message out to blow Shaddack and Moonhawk out of the water.

On the screen, from Shaddack to Sun: **BOOKER'S TERMINAL?**

YOU REQUIRE LOCATION?

YES.

MOONLIGHT COVE CENTRAL SCHOOL, COMPUTER LAB.

Loman was three minutes from Central.

He wondered how close Shaddack was to the school. It didn't matter. Near or far, Shaddack would bust his ass to get there and prevent Booker from compromising the Moonhawk Project—or to take vengeance if it had already been compromised.

At last Loman knew where he could find his maker.

13

WHEN SAM WAS ONLY SIX EXCHANGES INTO HIS DIALOGUE with Anne Denton in Washington, the link was cut off. The screen went blank.

He wanted to believe that he had been disconnected by ordinary line problems somewhere along the way. But he knew that wasn't the case.

He got up from his chair so fast that he knocked it over.

Chrissie jumped up in surprise, and Tessa said, "What is it? What's wrong?"

"They know we're here," Sam said. "They're coming."

14

HARRY HEARD THE DOORBELL RING DOWN IN THE HOUSE below him.

His stomach twisted. He felt as if he were in a roller coaster, just pulling away from the boarding ramp.

The bell rang again.

A long silence followed. They knew he was crippled. They would give him time to answer.

Finally it rang again.

He looked at his watch. Only 7:24. He took no comfort in the fact that they had not put him at the end of their schedule.

The bell rang again. Then again. Then insistently.

In the distance, muffled by the two intervening floors, Moose began barking.

15

TESSA GRABBED CHRISSIE'S HAND. WITH SAM, THEY HURRIED out of the computer lab. The batteries in the flashlight must not have been fresh, for the beam was growing dimmer. She hoped it would last long enough for them to find their way out. Suddenly the school's layout—which had been uncomplicated when they had not been in a life-or-death rush to negotiate its byways—seemed like a maze.

They crossed a junction of four halls, entered another corridor, and went about twenty yards before Tessa realized they were going the wrong direction. "This isn't how we came in."

"Doesn't matter," Sam said. "Any door out will do."

They had to go another ten yards before the failing flashlight beam was able to reach all the way to the end of the hall, revealing that it was a dead end.

"This way," Chrissie said, pulling loose of Tessa and turning back into the darkness from which they'd come, forcing them either to follow or abandon her.

16

SHADDACK FIGURED THEY WOULDN'T HAVE TRIED TO BREAK into Central on any side that faced a street, where they might be seen—and the Indian agreed—so he drove around to the back. He passed metal doors that would have provided too formidable a barrier, and studied the windows, trying to spot a broken pane.

The last rear door, the only one with glass in the top, was in an angled extension of the building. He was driving toward it for a moment, just before the service road swung to the left to go around that wing, and from a distance of only a few yards, with all the other panes reflecting the glare of his headlights, his attention was caught by the missing glass at the bottom right.

"There," he told Runningdeer.

"Yes, Little Chief."

He parked near the door and grabbed the loaded Remington 12-gauge semi-automatic pistol-grip shotgun from the van's floor behind him. The box of extra shells was on the passenger seat. He opened it, grabbed four or five, stuffed them in a coat pocket, grabbed four or five more, then got out of the van and headed toward the door with the broken window.

17

FOUR SOFT THUDS REVERBERATED THROUGH THE HOUSE, EVEN into the attic, and Harry thought he heard glass breaking far away.

Moose barked furiously. He sounded like the most vicious attack dog ever bred, not a sweet black Lab. Maybe he would prove willing to defend home and master in spite of his naturally good temperament.

Don't do it, boy, Harry thought. Don't try to be a hero. Just crawl away in a corner somewhere and let them pass, lick their hands if they offer them, and don't—

The dog squealed and fell silent.

No, Harry thought, and a pang of grief tore through him. He had lost not just a dog but his best friend.

Moose, too, had a sense of duty.

Silence settled over the house. They would be searching the ground floor now.

Harry's grief and fear receded as his anger grew. Moose. Dammit, poor harmless Moose. He could feel the flush of rage in his face. He wanted to kill them all.

He picked up the .38 pistol in his one good hand and held it on his lap. They wouldn't find him for a while, but he felt better with the gun in his hand.

In the service he had won competition medals for both rifle sharpshooting and performance with a handgun. That had been a long time ago. He had not fired a gun, even in practice, for more than twenty years, since that faraway and beautiful Asian land, where on a morning of exceptionally lovely blue skies, he had been crippled for life. He kept the .38 and the .45 cleaned and oiled, mostly out of habit; a soldier's lessons and routines were learned for life—and now he was glad of that.

A clank.

A rumble-purr of machinery.

The elevator.

18

HALFWAY DOWN THE CORRECT HALLWAY, HOLDING THE dimming flashlight in his left hand and the revolver in his other, just as he caught up with Chrissie, Sam heard a siren approaching outside. It was not on top of them, but it was too close. He couldn't tell if the patrol car was actually closing in on the back of the school, toward which they were headed, or coming to the front entrance.

Apparently Chrissie was uncertain too. She stopped running and said, "Where, Sam? Where?"

From behind them Tessa said, "Sam, the doorway!"

For an instant he didn't understand what she meant. Then he saw the door swinging open at the end of the hall, about thirty yards away, the same door by which they had entered. A man stepped inside. The siren was still wailing, drawing nearer, so there were more of them on the way, a whole platoon of them. The guy who'd come through the door was just the first—tall, six feet five if he was one inch, but otherwise only a shadow, minimally backlighted by the security lamp outside and to the right of the door.

Sam squeezed off a shot with his .38, not bothering to determine if this man was an enemy, because they were all enemies, every last one of them—their name was legion—and he knew the shot was wide. His marksmanship was lousy because of his injured wrist, which hurt like hell after their misadventures in the culvert. With the recoil, pain burst out of that joint and all the way back to his shoulder, then back again, Jesus, pain sloshing around like acid inside him, from shoulder to fingertips. Half the strength went out of his hand. He almost dropped the gun.

As the roar of Sam's shot slammed back to him from the walls of the corridor, the guy at the far end opened fire with a weapon of his own, but he had heavy artillery. A shotgun. Fortunately he was not good with it. He was aiming too high, not aware of how the kick would throw the muzzle up. Consequently the first blast went into the ceiling only ten yards ahead of him, tearing out one of the unlit fluorescent fixtures and a bunch of acoustic tiles. His reaction confirmed his lack of experience with guns; he overcompensated for the kick, swinging the muzzle too far down as he pulled the trigger a second time, so the follow-up round struck the floor far short of target.

Sam did not remain an idle observer of the misdirected gunfire. He seized Chrissie and pushed her to the left, across the corridor and through a door into a dark room, even as the second flock of buckshot gouged chunks out of the vinyl flooring. Tessa was right behind them. She threw the door shut and leaned against it, as if she thought that she was Superwoman and that any pellets penetrating the door would bounce harmlessly from her back.

Sam shoved the woefully dim flashlight at her. "With my wrist, I'm going to need both hands to manage the gun."

Tessa swept the weak yellow beam around the chamber. They were in the band room. To the right of the door, tiered platforms—full of chairs and music stands—rose up to the back wall. To the left was a large open area, the band director's podium, a blond-wood and metal desk. And two doors. Both standing open, leading to adjoining rooms.

Chrissie needed no urging to follow Tessa toward the nearer of those doors, and Sam brought up the rear, moving backward, covering the hall door through which they had come.

Outside, the siren had died. Now there would be more than one man with a shotgun.

19

THEY HAD SEARCHED THE FIRST TWO FLOORS. THEY WERE IN the third-floor bedroom.

Harry could hear them talking. Their voices rose to him through their ceiling, his floor. But he couldn't quite make out what they were saying.

He almost hoped they would spot the attic trap in the closet and would decide to come up. He wanted a chance to blow a couple of them away. For Moose. After twenty long years of being a victim, he was sick to death of it; he wanted a chance to let them know that Harry Talbot was still a man to be reckoned with—and that although Moose was only a dog, his was nevertheless a life taken only with serious consequences.

20

IN THE EDDYING FOG, LOMAN SAW THE SINGLE PATROL CAR parked beside Shaddack's van. He braked next to it just as Paul Amberlay got out from behind the wheel. Amberlay was lean and sinewy and very bright, one of Loman's best young officers, but he looked like a high-school boy now, too small to be a cop—and scared.

When Loman got out of his car, Amberlay came to him, gun in hand, visibly shaking. "Only you and me? Where the hell's everybody else? This is a major alert."

"Where's everybody else?" Loman asked. "Just listen, Paul. Just listen."

From every part of town, scores of wild voices were lifted in eerie song, either calling to one another or challenging the unseen moon that floated above the wrung-out clouds.

Loman hurried to the back of the patrol car and opened the trunk. His unit, like every other, carried a 20-gauge riot gun for which he'd never had use in peaceable Moonlight Cove. But New Wave, which had generously equipped the force, did not stint on equipment even if it was perceived as unnecessary. He pulled the shotgun from its clip mounting on the back wall of the trunk.

Joining him, Amberlay said, "You telling me they've regressed, all of them, everyone on the force, except you and me?"

"Just listen," Loman repeated as he leaned the 20-gauge against the bumper.

"But that's crazy!" Amberlay insisted. "Jesus, God, you mean this whole thing is coming down on us, the whole damn thing?"

Loman grabbed a box of shells that was in the right wheel-well of the trunk, tore off the lid. "Don't *you* feel the yearning, Paul?"

"No!" Amberlay said too quickly. "No, I don't feel it, I don't feel anything."

"I feel it," Loman said, putting five rounds in the 20-gauge—one in the chamber, four in the magazine. "Oh, Paul, I sure as hell feel it. I want to tear off my clothes and change, *change*, and just run, be free, go with them, hunt and kill and run with them."

"Not me, no, never," Amberlay said.

"Liar," Loman said. He brought up the loaded gun and fired at Amberlay point-blank, blowing his head off.

He couldn't have trusted the young officer, couldn't have turned his back on him, not with the urge to regress so strong in him, and those voices in the night singing their siren songs.

As he stuffed more shells into his pockets, he heard a shotgun blast from inside the school.

He wondered if that gun was in the hands of Booker or Shaddack. Struggling to control his raging terror, fighting off the hideous and powerful urge to shed his human form, Loman went inside to find out.

21

TOMMY SHADDACK HEARD ANOTHER SHOTGUN, BUT HE didn't think much about that because, after all, they were in a war now. You could hear what a war it was by just stepping out in the night and listening to the shrieks of the combatants echoing down through the hills to the sea. He was more focused on getting Booker, the woman, and the girl he'd seen in the hall, because he knew the woman must be the Lockland bitch and the girl must be Chrissie Foster, though he couldn't figure how they had joined up.

War. So he handled it the way soldiers did in the good movies, kicking the door open, firing a round into the room before entering. No one screamed. He guessed he hadn't hit anyone, so he fired again, and still no one screamed, so he figured they were already gone from there. He crossed the threshold, fumbled for the light switch, found it, and discovered he was in the deserted band room.

Evidently they had left by one of the two other doors, and when he saw that, he was angry, really angry. The only time in his life that he had fired a gun was in Phoenix, when he had shot the Indian with his father's revolver, and that had been close-up, where he could not miss. But still he had expected that he would be *good* with a gun. After all, Jeez, he had watched a lot of war movies, cowboy movies, cop shows on television, and it didn't look hard, not hard at all, you just pointed the muzzle and pulled the trigger. But it hadn't been that easy, after all, and Tommy was angry, furious, because they shouldn't make it look so easy in the movies and on the boob tube when, in fact, the gun jumped in your hands as if it was alive.

He knew better now, and he was going to brace himself when he fired, spread his legs and brace himself, so his shots wouldn't be blowing holes in the ceiling or bouncing off the floor any more. He would nail them cold the next time he got a whack at them, and they'd be sorry for making him chase them, for not just lying down and being dead when he *wanted* them to be dead.

22

THE DOOR OUT OF THE BAND ROOM HAD LED INTO A HALL that served ten soundproofed practice rooms, where student musicians could mutilate fine music for hours at a time without disturbing anyone. At the end of that narrow corridor, Tessa pushed through another door and coaxed just enough out of the flashlight to see that they were in a chamber as large as the band room. It also featured tiered platforms rising to the back. A student-drawn sign on one wall, complete with winged angels singing, proclaimed this the home of The World's Best Chorus.

As Chrissie and Sam followed her into the room, a shotgun roared in the distance. It sounded as if it was outside. But even as the door to the corridor of practice rooms swung shut behind them, another shotgun discharged, closer than the first, probably back at the door to the band room. Then a second blast from the same location.

Just like in the band room, two more doors led out of the choral chamber, but the first one she tried was a dead end; it went into the chorus director's office.

They dashed to the other exit, beyond which they found a corridor illuminated only by a red, twenty-four-hour-a-day emergency sign—STAIRS—immediately to their right. Not EXIT, just STAIRS, which meant this was an interior well with no access to the outside. "Take her up," Sam urged Tessa.

"But—"

"Up! They're probably coming in the ground floor by every entrance, anyway."

"What're you—"

"Gonna make a little stand here," he said.

A door crashed open and a shotgun exploded back in the chorus room.

"Go!" Sam whispered.

23

HARRY HEARD THE CLOSET DOOR OPEN IN THE BEDROOM below.

The attic was cold, but he was streaming sweat as if in a sauna. Maybe he hadn't needed the second sweater.

Go away, he thought. Go away.

Then he thought, Hell, no, come on, come and get it. You think I want to live forever?

24

SAM WENT DOWN ON ONE KNEE IN THE HALL OUTSIDE THE chorus room, taking a stable position to compensate somewhat for his weak right wrist. He held the swinging door open six inches, both arms thrust through the gap, the .38 gripped in his right hand, his left hand clamped around his right wrist.

He could see the guy across the room, silhouetted in the lights of the band-room corridor behind him. Tall. Couldn't see his face. But something about him struck a chord of familiarity.

The gunman didn't see Sam. He was only being cautious, laying down a spray of pellets before he entered. He pulled the trigger. The click was loud in the silent room. He pumped the shotgun. *Clackety-clack.* No ammo.

That meant a change in Sam's plans. He surged to his feet and through the swinging door, back into the chorus room, no longer able to wait for the guy to switch on the overhead lights or step farther across the threshold, because now was the time to take him, before he reloaded. Firing as he went, Sam squeezed off the four remaining rounds in the .38, trying his damnedest to make every slug count. On the second or third shot, the guy in the doorway squealed, God, he squealed like a kid, his voice high-pitched and quaverous, as he threw himself back into the practice-room corridor, out of sight.

Sam kept moving, fumbling in his jacket pocket with his left hand, grabbing at the spare cartridges, while with his right hand he snapped open the revolver's cylinder and shook out the expended brass casings. When he reached the closed door to the narrow hall that connected chorus room to band room, the door through which the tall man had vanished, he pressed his back to the wall and jammed fresh rounds into the Smith & Wesson, snapped the cylinder shut.

He kicked the door open and looked into the hall, where the overhead fluorescents were lit.

It was deserted.

No blood on the floor.

Damn. His right hand was half numb. He could feel his wrist swelling tight under the bandage, which was now soaked with fresh blood. At the rate his shooting was deteriorating, he was going to have to walk right up to the bastard and ask him to bite on the muzzle in order to make the shot count.

The doors to the ten practice rooms, five on each side, were closed. The door at the far end, where the hall led into the band room, was open, and the lights were on there. The tall guy could be there or in any of the ten practice rooms. But wherever he was, he had probably slipped at least a couple of shells into that shotgun, so the moment to pursue him had passed.

Sam backed up, letting the door between the hall and the chorus room slip shut. Even as he let go of it, as it was swinging back into place, he glimpsed the tall man stepping through the open door of the band room about forty feet away.

It was Shaddack himself.

The shotgun boomed.

The soundproofed door, gliding shut at the crucial moment, was thick enough to stop the pellets.

Sam turned and ran across the chorus room, into the hall, and up the stairs, where he had sent Tessa and Chrissie.

When he reached the top flight, he found them waiting for him in the upper hall, in the soft red glow of another STAIRS sign.

Below, Shaddack entered the stairwell.

Sam turned, stepped back onto the landing and descended the first step. He leaned over the railing, looked down, glimpsed part of his pursuer, and squeezed off two shots.

Shaddack squealed like a boy again. He ducked back against the wall, away from the open center of the well, where he could not be seen.

Sam didn't know whether he'd scored a hit or not. Maybe. What he *did* know was that Shaddack wasn't mortally wounded; he was still coming, easing up step by step, staying against the outer wall. And when that geek reached the lower landing, he would take the turn suddenly, firing the shotgun repeatedly at whoever waited above.

Silently Sam retreated from the upper landing, into the hall once more. The scarlet light of the STAIRS sign fell on Chrissie's and Tessa's faces . . . an illusion of blood.

25

A CLINK. A SCRAPING SOUND.

Clink-scrape. Clink-scrape.

Harry knew what he was hearing. Clothes hangers sliding on a metal rod.

How could they have known? Hell, maybe they had smelled him up here. He was sweating like a horse, after all. Maybe the conversion improved their senses.

The clinking and scraping stopped.

A moment later he heard them lifting the closet rod out of its braces so they could lower the trap.

26

THE FADING FLASHLIGHT KEPT WINKING OUT, AND TESSA had to shake it, jarring the batteries together, to get a few more seconds of weak and fluttery light from it.

They had stepped out of the hall, into what proved to be a chemistry lab with black marble lab tables and steel sinks and high wooden stools. Nowhere to hide.

They checked the windows, hoping there might be a roof just under them. No. A two-story drop to a concrete walk.

At the end of the chemistry lab was a door, through which they passed into a ten-foot-square storage room full of chemicals in sealed tins and bottles, some labeled with skulls and crossbones, some with DANGER in bright red letters. She supposed there were ways to use the contents of that closet as a weapon, but they didn't have time to inventory the contents, looking for interesting substances to mix together. Besides, she'd never been a great science student, recalled nothing whatsoever of her chemistry classes, and would probably blow herself up with the first bottle she opened. From the expression on Sam's face, she knew that he saw no more hope there than she did.

A rear door in the storage closet opened into a second lab that seemed to double as a biology classroom. Anatomy charts hung on one wall. The room offered no better place to hide than had the previous lab.

Holding Chrissie close against her side, Tessa looked at Sam and whispered, "Now what? Wait here and hope he can't find us . . . or keep moving?"

"I think it's safer to keep moving," Sam said. "Easier to be cornered if we sit still."

She nodded agreement.

He eased past her and Chrissie, leading the way between the lab benches, toward the door to the hall.

From behind them, either in the dark chemical-storage room or in the unlighted chemistry lab beyond it, came a soft but distinct *clink*.

Sam halted, motioned Tessa and Chrissie ahead of him, and turned to cover the exit from the storage room.

With Chrissie at her side, Tessa stepped to the hall door, turned the knob slowly, quietly, and eased the door outward.

Shaddack came from the darkness in the corridor, into the pale and inconstant pulse of light from her flash, and rammed the barrel of his shotgun into her stomach. "You're gonna be sorry now," he said excitedly.

27

THEY PULLED THE TRAPDOOR DOWN. A SHAFT OF LIGHT from the closet shot up to the rafters, but it didn't illuminate the far corner in which Harry sat with his useless legs splayed out in front of him.

His bad hand was curled in his lap, while his good hand fiercely clasped the pistol.

His heart was hammering harder and faster than it had in twenty years, since the battlefields of Southeast Asia. His stomach was churning. His throat was so tight he could barely breathe. He was dizzy with fear. But, God in heaven, he sure felt *alive*.

With a squeak and clatter, they unfolded the ladder.

28

TOMMY SHADDACK SHOVED THE MUZZLE INTO HER BELLY and almost blew her guts out, almost wasted her, before he realized how *pretty* she was, and then he didn't want to kill her any more, at least not right away, not until he'd made her do some things with him, do some things *to* him. She'd have to do whatever he wanted, anything, whatever he told her to do, or he could just smear her across the wall, yeah, she was his, and she better realize that, or she'd be sorry, he'd make her sorry.

Then he saw the girl beside her, a pretty *little* girl, only ten or twelve, and she excited him even more. He could have her first, and then the older one, have them any which way he wanted them, make them *do* things, all sorts of things, and then hurt them, that was his right, they couldn't deny him, not him, because all the power was in his hands now, he had seen the moonhawk *three* times.

He pushed through the open door, into the room, keeping the gun in the woman's belly, and she backed up to accommodate him, pulling the girl with her. Booker was behind them, a startled expression on his face. Tommy Shaddack said, "Drop your gun and back away from it, or I'll make raspberry jelly out of this bitch, I swear I will, you can't move fast enough to stop me."

Booker hesitated.

"Drop it!" Tommy Shaddack insisted.

The agent let go of the revolver and sidestepped away from it.

Keeping the muzzle of the Remington hard against the woman's belly, he made her edge around until she could reach the light switch and click on the fluorescents. The room leaped out of shadows.

"Okay, now, all of you," Tommy Shaddack said, "sit down on those three stools, by that lab bench, yeah, there, and don't do anything funny."

He stepped back from the woman and covered them all with the shotgun. They looked scared, and that made him laugh.

Tommy was getting excited now, really excited, because he had decided he would kill Booker in front of the woman and the girl, not swift and clean but slowly, the first shot in the legs, let him lie on the floor and wriggle a while, the second shot in the gut but not from such a close range that it finished him instantly, make him hurt, make the woman and the girl watch, show them what a customer they had in Tommy Shaddack, what a damned tough customer, make them grateful for being spared, so grateful they'd get on their knees and let him *do* things to them, do all the things he had wanted to do for thirty years but which he had denied himself, let off thirty years of steam right here, right now, tonight. . . .

29

BEYOND THE HOUSE, FILTERING INTO THE ATTIC THROUGH vents in the eaves, came eerie howling, point and counterpoint, first solo and then chorus. It sounded as if the gates of hell had been thrown open, letting denizens of the pit pour forth into Moonlight Cove.

Harry worried about Sam, Tessa, and Chrissie.

Below him, the unseen conversion team locked the collapsible ladder in place. One of them began to climb into the attic.

Harry wondered what they would look like. Would they be just ordinary men— old Doc Fitz with a syringe and a couple of deputies to assist him? Or would they be Boogeymen? Or some of the machine-men Sam had talked about?

The first one ascended through the open trap. It was Dr. Worthy, the town's youngest physician.

Harry considered shooting him while he was still on the ladder. But he hadn't fired a gun in twenty years, and he didn't want to waste his limited ammunition. Better to wait for a closer shot.

Worthy didn't have a flashlight. Didn't seem to need one. He looked straight toward the darkest corner, where Harry was propped, and said, "How did you know we were coming, Harry?"

"Cripple's intuition," Harry said sarcastically.

Along the center of the attic, there was plenty of headroom to allow Worthy to walk upright. He rose from a crouch as he came out from under the sloping rafters near the trap, and when he had taken four steps forward, Harry fired twice at him.

The first shot missed, but the second hit low in the chest.

Worthy was flung backward, went down hard on the bare boards of the attic floor. He lay there for a moment, twitching, then sat up, coughed once, and got to his feet.

Blood glistened all over the front of his torn white shirt. He had been hit hard, yet he had recovered in seconds.

Harry remembered what Sam had said about how the Coltranes had refused to stay dead. *Go for the data processor.*

He aimed for Worthy's head and fired twice again, but at that distance—about twenty-five feet—and at that angle, shooting up from the floor, he couldn't hit anything. He hesitated with only four rounds left in the pistol's clip.

Another man was climbing through the trap.

Harry shot at him, trying to drive him back down.

He came on, unperturbed.

Three rounds in the pistol.

Keeping his distance, Dr. Worthy said, "Harry, we're not here to harm you. I don't know what you've heard or *how* you've heard about the project, but it isn't a bad thing. . . ."

His voice trailed off, and he cocked his head as if to listen to the unhuman cries that filled the night outside. A peculiar look of longing, visible even in the dim wash of light from the open trap, crossed Worthy's face.

He shook himself, blinked, and remembered that he had been trying to sell his elixir to a reluctant customer. "Not a bad thing at all, Harry. Especially for you. You'll walk again, Harry, walk as well as anyone. You'll be whole again. Because after the Change, you'll be able to heal yourself. You'll be free of paralysis."

"No, thanks. Not at that price."

"What price, Harry?" Worthy asked, spreading his arms, palms up. "Look at me. What price have I paid?"

"Your soul?" Harry said.

A third man was coming up the ladder.

The second man was listening to the ululant cries that came in through the attic vents. He gritted his teeth, ground them together forcefully, and blinked very fast. He raised his hands and covered his face with them, as if he were suddenly anguished.

Worthy noticed his companion's situation. "Vanner, are you all right?"

Vanner's hands . . . *changed*. His wrists swelled and grew gnarly with bone, and his fingers lengthened, all in a couple of seconds. When he took his hands from his face, his jaw was thrusting forward like that of a werewolf in midtransformation. His shirt tore at the seams as his body reconfigured itself. He snarled, and teeth flashed.

" . . . *need,*" Vanner said, " . . . *need, need, want, need* . . . "

"No!" Worthy shouted.

The third man, who had just come out of the trap, rolled onto the floor, changing as he did so, flowing into a vaguely insectile but thoroughly repulsive form.

Before he quite knew what he was doing, Harry emptied the .38 at the insect-thing, pitched it away, snatched the .45 revolver off the board floor beside him, also fired three rounds from that, evidently striking the thing's brain at least once. It kicked, twitched, fell back down through the trap, and did not clamber upward again.

Vanner had undergone a complete lupine metamorphosis and seemed to have patterned himself after something that he had seen in a movie, because he looked familiar to Harry, as if Harry had seen that same movie, though he could not quite remember it. Vanner shrieked in answer to the creatures whose cries pealed through the night outside.

Tearing frantically at his clothes, as if the pressure of them against his skin was driving him mad, Worthy was changing into a beast quite different from either Vanner or the third man. Some grotesque physical incarnation of his own mad desires.

Harry had only three rounds left, and he had to save the last one for himself.

30

EARLIER, AFTER SURVIVING THE ORDEAL IN THE CULVERT, SAM had promised himself that he would learn to accept failure, which had been all well and good until now, when failure was again at hand.

He could *not* fail, not with both Chrissie and Tessa depending on him. If no other opportunity presented itself, he would at least leap at Shaddack the moment before he believed the man was ready to pull the trigger.

Judging that moment might be difficult. Shaddack looked and sounded insane. The way his mind was short-circuiting, he might pull the trigger in the middle of one of those high, quick, nervous, boyish laughs, without any indication that the moment had come.

"Get off your stool," he said to Sam.

"What?"

"You heard me, dammit, get off your stool. Lay on the floor, over there, or I'll make you sorry, I sure will, I'll make you very sorry." He gestured with the muzzle of the shotgun. "Get off your stool and lay on the floor *now.*"

Sam didn't want to do it because he knew Shaddack was separating him from Chrissie and Tessa only to shoot him.

He hesitated, then slid off the stool because there was nothing else he could do. He moved between two lab benches, to the open area that Shaddack had indicated.

"Down," Shaddack said. "I want to see you down there on the floor, groveling."

Dropping to one knee, Sam slipped a hand into an inner pocket of his leather jack, fished out the metal loid that he had used to pop the lock at the Coltranes' house, and flicked it away from himself, with the same snap of his wrist that he would have used to toss a playing card at a hat.

The loid sailed low across the floor, toward the windows, until it clattered through the rungs of a stool and clinked off the base of a marble lab bench.

The madman swung the Remington toward the sound.

With a shout of rage and determination, Sam came up fast and threw himself at Shaddack.

31

TESSA GRABBED CHRISSIE AND HUSTLED HER AWAY FROM THE struggling men, to the wall beside the hall door. They crouched there, where she hoped they would be out of the line of fire.

Sam had come up under the shotgun before Shaddack could swing back from the distraction. He grabbed the barrel with his left hand and Shaddack's wrist with his weakened right hand, and pressed him backward, pushing him off balance, slamming him against another lab bench.

When Shaddack cried out, Sam snarled with satisfaction, as if *he* might turn into something that howled in the night.

Tessa saw him ram a knee up between Shaddack's legs, hard into his crotch. The tall man screamed.

"All *right*, Sam!" Chrissie said approvingly.

As Shaddack gagged and spluttered and tried to double over in an involuntary reaction to the pain in his damaged privates, Sam tore the shotgun out of his hands and stepped back—

—and a man in a police uniform came into the room from the chemistry storage closet, carrying a shotgun of his own. "No! Drop your weapon. Shaddack is *mine.*"

32

THE THING THAT HAD BEEN VANNER MOVED TOWARD HARRY, growling low in its throat, drooling yellowish saliva. Harry fired twice, struck it both times, but failed to kill it. The gaping wounds seemed to close up before his eyes.

One round left.

"*. . . need, need . . .* "

Harry put the barrel of the .45 in his mouth, pressed the muzzle against his palate, gagging on the hot steel.

The hideous, wolfish thing loomed over him. The swollen head was three times as big as it ought to have been, out of proportion to its body. Most of the head was mouth, and most of the mouth was teeth, not even the teeth of a wolf but the inward-curving teeth of a shark. Vanner had not been satisfied to model himself entirely after just one of nature's predators, but wanted to make himself something more murderous and efficiently destructive than anything nature had contemplated.

When Vanner was only three feet from him, leaning in to bite, Harry pulled the gun out of his own mouth, said, "Hell, no," and shot the damn thing in the head. It toppled back, landed with a crash, and stayed down.

Go for the data-processor.

Elation swept through Harry, but it was short-lived. Worthy had completed his transformation and seemed to have been thrown into a frenzy by the carnage in the room and the escalating shrieks that came through the attic vents from the world beyond. He turned his lantern eyes on Harry, and in them was a look of unhuman hunger.

No more bullets.

33

SAM WAS SQUARELY UNDER THE COP'S GUN, WITH NO ROOM to maneuver. He had to drop the Remington that he'd taken off Shaddack.

"I'm on your side," the cop repeated.

"No one's on our side," Sam said.

Shaddack was gasping for breath and trying to stand up straight. He regarded the officer with abject terror.

With the coldest premeditation Sam had ever seen, with no hint of emotion whatsoever, not even anger, the cop turned his 20-gauge shotgun on Shaddack, who was no longer a threat to anyone, and fired four rounds. As if punched by a giant, Shaddack flew backward over two stools and into the wall.

The cop threw the gun aside and moved quickly to the dead man. He tore open the sweat-suit jacket that Shaddack wore under his coat and ripped loose a strange object, a largish rectangular medallion, that had hung from a gold chain around the man's neck.

Holding up that curious artifact, he said, "Shaddack's dead. His heartbeat isn't being broadcast any more, so Sun is even now putting the final program into effect. In half a minute or so we'll all know peace. Peace at last."

At first Sam thought the cop was saying they were all going to die, that the thing in his hand was going to kill them, that it was a bomb or something. He backed quickly toward the door and saw that Tessa evidently had the same expectation. She had pulled Chrissie up from where they'd been crouching, and had opened the door.

But if there was a bomb, it was a silent one, and the radius of its small explosion remained within the police officer. Suddenly his face contorted. Between clenched teeth, he said, "God." It was not an exclamation but a plea or perhaps an inadequate description of something he had just seen, for in that moment he fell down dead from no cause that Sam could see.

34

WHEN THEY STEPPED OUT THROUGH THE BACK DOOR BY
which they had entered, the first thing Sam noticed was that the night had fallen
silent. The shrill cries of the shape-changers no longer echoed across the fogbound
town.

The keys were in the van's ignition.

"You drive," he told Tessa.

His wrist was swollen worse than ever. It was throbbing so hard that each pulse
of pain reverberated through every fiber of him.

He settled in the passenger seat.

Chrissie curled in his lap, and he wrapped his arms around her. She was uncharacteristically silent. She was exhausted, on the verge of collapse, but Sam
knew the cause of her silence was more profound than weariness.

Tessa slammed her door and started the engine. She didn't have to be told
where to go.

On the drive to Harry's place, they discovered that the streets were littered with
the dead, not the corpses of ordinary men and women but—as their headlights
revealed beyond a doubt—of creatures out of a painting by Hieronymus Bosch,
twisted and phantasmagorical forms. She drove slowly, maneuvering around
them, and a couple of times she had to pull up on the sidewalk to get past a pack
of them that had gone down together, apparently felled by the same unseen force
that had dropped the policeman back at Central.

*Shaddack's dead. His heartbeat isn't being broadcast any more, so Sun is even
now putting the final program into effect. . . .*

After a while Chrissie lowered her head against Sam's chest and would not look
out the windshield.

Sam kept telling himself that the fallen creatures were phantoms, that no such
things could have actually come into existence, either by the application of the
highest of high technology or by sorcery. He expected them to vanish every time
a shroud of fog briefly obscured them, but when the fog moved off again, they
were still huddled on the pavement, sidewalks, and lawns.

Immersed in all that horror and ugliness, he could not believe that he had been
so foolish as to pass years of precious life in gloom, unwilling to see the beauty
of the world. He'd been a singular fool. When the dawn came he would never
thereafter fail to look upon a flower and appreciate the wonder of it, the beauty
that was beyond man's abilities of creation.

"Tell me now?" Tessa asked as they pulled within a block of Harry's redwood
house.

"Tell you what?"

"What you saw. Your near-death experience. What did you see on the Other
Side that scared you so?"

He laughed shakily. "I was an idiot."

"Probably," she said. "Tell me and let me judge."

"Well, I can't tell you exactly. It was more an *understanding* than a seeing, a
spiritual rather than visual perception."

"So what did you understand?"

"That we go on from this world," he said. "That there's either life for us on another plane, one life after another on an endless series of planes . . . or that we live again on this plane, reincarnate. I'm not sure which, but I felt it deeply, *knew* it when I reached the end of that tunnel and saw the light, that brilliant light."

She glanced at him. "And *that's* what terrified you?"

"Yes."

"That we live again?"

"Yes. Because I found life so bleak, you see, just a series of tragedies, just pain. I'd lost the ability to appreciate the beauty of life, the joy, so I didn't want to die and have to start in all over again, not any sooner than absolutely necessary. At least in *this* life I'd become hardened, inured to the pain, which gave me an advantage over starting out as a child again in some new incarnation."

"So your fourth reason for living wasn't technically a fear of death," she said.

"I guess not."

"It was a fear of having to live again."

"Yes."

"And now?"

He thought a moment. Chrissie stirred in his lap. He stroked her damp hair. At last he said, "Now, I'm *eager* to live again."

35

HARRY HEARD NOISES DOWNSTAIRS—THE ELEVATOR, THEN someone in the third-floor bedroom. He tensed, figuring two miracles were one too many to hope for, but then he heard Sam calling to him from the bottom of the ladder.

"Here, Sam! Safe! I'm okay."

A moment later Sam climbed into the attic.

"Tessa? Chrissie?" Harry asked anxiously.

"They're downstairs. They're both all right."

"Thank God." Harry let out a long breath, as if it had been pent up in him for hours. "Look at these brutes, Sam."

"Rather not."

"Maybe Chrissie was right about alien invaders after all."

"Something stranger," Sam said.

"What?" Harry said as Sam knelt beside him and gingerly pushed Worthy's mutated body off his legs.

"Damned if I know," Sam said. "Not even sure I want to know."

"We're entering an age when we make our own reality, aren't we? Science is giving us that ability, bit by bit. Used to be only madmen could do that."

Sam said nothing.

Harry said, "Maybe making our own reality isn't wise. Maybe the natural order is the best one."

"Maybe. On the other hand, the natural order could do with some perfecting here and there. I guess we've got to try. We just have to hope to God that the men who do the tinkering aren't like Shaddack. You okay, Harry?"

"Pretty good, thanks." He smiled. "Except, of course, I'm still a cripple. See this hulking thing that was Worthy? He was leaning in to rip my throat out, I had no more bullets, he had his claws at my neck, and then he just fell dead, bang. Is that a miracle or what?"

"Been a miracle all over town," Sam said. "They all seemed to have died when Shaddack died . . . linked somehow. Come on, let's get you down from here, out of this mess."

"They killed Moose, Sam."

"The hell they did. Who do you think Chrissie and Tessa are fussing over downstairs?"

Harry was stunned. "But I heard—"

"Looks like maybe somebody kicked him in the head. He's got this bloody, skinned-up spot along one side of his skull. Might've been knocked unconscious, but he doesn't seem to've suffered a concussion."

36

CHRISSIE RODE IN THE BACK OF THE VAN WITH HARRY AND Moose, with Harry's good arm around her and Moose's head in her lap. Slowly she began to feel better. She was not herself, no, and maybe she never would feel like her old self again, but she was better.

They went to the park at the head of Ocean Avenue, at the east end of town. Tessa drove right up over the curb, bouncing them around, and parked on the grass.

Sam opened the rear doors of the van so Chrissie and Harry could sit side by side in their blankets and watch him and Tessa at work.

Braver than Chrissie would have been, Sam went into the nearby residential areas, stepping over and around the dead things, and jump-started cars that were parked along the streets. One by one, he and Tessa drove them into the park and arranged them in a huge ring, with the engines running and the headlights pointing in toward the middle of the circle.

Sam said that people would be coming in helicopters, even in the fog, and that the circle of light would mark a proper landing pad for them. With twenty cars, their headlights all blazing on high beam, the inside of that ring was as bright as noon.

Chrissie liked the brightness.

Even before the landing pad was fully outlined, a few people began to appear in the streets, live people, and not weird looking at all, without fangs and stingers and claws, standing fully erect—altogether normal, judging by appearances. Of course, Chrissie had learned that you could never confidently judge anyone by appearances because they could be anything inside; they could be something inside that would astonish even the editors of the *National Enquirer*. You couldn't even be sure of your own parents.

But she couldn't think about that.

She didn't *dare* think about what had happened to her folks. She knew that what little hope she still held for their salvation was probably false hope, but she wanted to hold on to it for just a while longer, anyway.

The few people who appeared in the streets began to gravitate toward the park while Tessa and Sam finished pulling the last few cars into the ring. They all looked dazed. The closer they approached, the more uneasy Chrissie became.

"They're all right," Harry assured her, cuddling her with his one good arm.

"How can you be sure?"

"You can see they're scared shitless. Oops. Maybe I shouldn't say 'shitless,' teach you bad language."

" 'Shitless' is okay," she said.

Moose made a mewling sound and shifted in her lap. He probably had the kind of headache that only karate experts usually got from smashing bricks with their heads.

"Well," Harry said, "look at them—they're scared plenty bad, which probably tags them as our kind. You never saw one of those others acting scared, did you?"

She thought about it a moment. "Yeah. I did. That cop who shot Mr. Shaddack at the school. He was scared. He had more fear in his eyes, a lot more, than I've ever seen in anybody else's."

"Well, these people are all right, anyway," Harry told her as the dazed stragglers approached the van. "They're some of the ones who were scheduled to be converted before midnight, but nobody got around to them. Must be others in their houses, barricaded in there, afraid to come out, think the whole world's gone crazy, probably think aliens are on the loose, like you thought. Besides, if these people were more of those shapechangers, they wouldn't be staggering up to us so hesitantly. They'd have loped right up the hill, leaped in here, and eaten our noses, plus whatever other parts of us they consider to be delicacies."

That explanation appealed to her, even made her smile thinly, and she relaxed a little.

But just a second later, Moose jerked his burly head off her lap, yipped, and scrambled to his feet.

Outside, the people approaching the van cried out in surprise and fear, and Chrissie heard Sam say, "What the blazing *hell*? "

She threw aside her warm blankets and scrambled out of the back of the van to see what was happening.

Behind her, alarmed in spite of the reassurances that he had just given her, Harry said, "What is it? What's wrong?"

For a moment she wasn't sure what had startled everyone, but then she saw the animals. They swarmed through the park—scores of mice, a few grungy rats, cats of all descriptions, half a dozen dogs, and maybe a couple of dozen squirrels that had scampered down from the trees. More mice and rats and cats were racing out of the mouths of the streets that intersected Ocean Avenue, pouring up that main drag, running pell-mell, frenzied, cutting through the park and angling over to the county road. They reminded her of something she'd read about once, and she only had to stand there for a few seconds, watching them pour by her, before she remembered: lemmings. Periodically, when the lemming population became too great in a particular area, the little creatures ran and ran, straight toward the sea, into the surf, and drowned themselves. All these animals were acting like lemmings, tearing off in the same direction, letting nothing stand in their way, drawn by nothing apparent and therefore evidently following an inner compulsion.

Moose jumped out of the van and joined the fleeing multitudes.

"Moose, no!" she shouted.

He stumbled, as if he had tripped over the cry that she had flung after him. He looked back, then snapped his head toward the county road again, as if he had been jerked by an invisible chain. He took off at top speed.

"Moose!"

He stumbled once more and actually fell this time, rolled, and scrambled onto his feet.

Somehow Chrissie knew that the image of lemmings was apt, that these animals were rushing to their graves, though away from the sea, toward some other and more hideous death that was part of all the rest that had happened in Moonlight Cove. If she did not stop Moose, they would never see him again.

The dog ran.

She sprinted after him.

She was bone weary, burnt out, aching in every muscle and joint, and afraid, but she found the strength and will to pursue the Labrador because no one else seemed to understand that he and the other animals were running toward death. Tessa and Sam, smart as they were, didn't get it. They were just standing, gaping at the spectacle. So Chrissie tucked her arms against her sides, pumped her legs, and ran for all she was worth, picturing herself as Chrissie Foster, World's Youngest Olympic Marathon Champion, pounding around the course, with thousands cheering her from the sidelines. (*"Chrissie, Chrissie, Chrissie, Chrissie . . . "*) And as she ran, she screamed at Moose to stop, because every time he heard his name, he faltered, hesitated, and she gained a little ground on him. Then they were through the park, and she nearly fell in the deep ditch alongside the county road, leaped it at the last instant, not because she saw it in time but because she had her eye on Moose and saw *him* leap something. She landed perfectly, not losing a stride. The next time Moose faltered in response to his name, she was on him, grabbing at him, seizing his collar. He growled and nipped at her, and she said, "Moose," in such a way as to shame him. That was the only time he tried to bite her but, Lord, he strained mightily to pull loose. Hanging on to him took everything she had, and he even dragged her, big as she was, about fifty or sixty feet along the road. His big paws scrabbled at the blacktop as he struggled to follow the wave of small animals that was receding into the night and fog.

By the time the dog calmed down enough to be willing to go back toward the park, Tessa and Sam joined Chrissie. "What's happening?" Sam asked.

"They're all running to their deaths," Chrissie said. "I just couldn't let Moose go with them."

"To their deaths? How do you know?"

"I don't know. But . . . what else?"

They stood on the dark and foggy road for a moment, looking after the animals, which had vanished into the blackness.

Tessa said, "What else indeed?"

37

THE FOG WAS THINNING, BUT VISIBILITY WAS STILL NO MORE than about a quarter of a mile.

Standing with Tessa in the middle of the circle of cars, Sam heard the choppers shortly after ten o'clock, before he saw their lights. Because the mist distorted sound, he could not tell from which direction they were approaching, but he figured they were coming in from the south, along the coast, staying a couple of hundred yards out to sea, where there were no hills to worry about in the fog. Packed with the most sophisticated instruments, they could virtually fly blind. The pilots would be wearing night-vision goggles, coming in under five hundred feet in respect of the poor weather.

Because the FBI maintained tight relationships with the armed services, especially the Marines, Sam pretty much knew what to expect. This would be a Marine Reconnaissance force composed of the standard elements required by such a situation: one CH-46 helicopter carrying the recon team itself—probably twelve men detached from a Marine Assault Unit—accompanied by two Cobra gunships.

Turning around, looking in every direction, Tessa said, "I don't see them."

"You won't," Sam said. "Not until they're almost on top of us."

"They fly without lights?"

"No. They're equipped with blue lights, which can't be seen well from the ground, but which give them a damned good view through their night-vision goggles."

Ordinarily, when responding to a terrorist threat, the CH-46—called the "Sea Knight," officially, but referred to as "The Frog" by grunts—would have gone, with its Cobra escorts, to the north end of town. Three fire teams, composed of four men each, would have disembarked and swept through Moonlight Cove from north to south, checking out the situation, rendezvousing at the other end for evacuation as necessary.

But because of the message Sam had sent to the Bureau before Sun's links to the outside world had been cut off, and because the situation did not involve terrorists and was, in fact, singularly strange, SOP was discarded for a bolder approach. The choppers overflew the town repeatedly, descending to within twenty or thirty feet of the treetops. At times their strange bluish-green lights were visible, but nothing whatsoever could be seen of their shape or size; because of their Fiberglas blades, which were much quieter than the old metal blades that once had been used, the choppers at times seemed to glide silently in the distance and might have been alien craft from a far world even stranger than this one.

At last they hovered near the circle of light in the park.

They did not put down at once. With the powerful rotors flinging the fog away, they played a searchlight over the people in the park who stood outside the illuminated landing pad, and they spent minutes examining the grotesque bodies in the street.

Finally, while the Cobras remained aloft, the CH-46 gentled down almost reluctantly in the ring of cars. The men who poured from the chopper were toting automatic weapons, but otherwise they didn't look like soldiers because, thanks to Sam's message, they were dressed in biologically secure white suits, carrying their own air-supply tanks on their backs. They might have been astronauts instead of Marines.

Lieutenant Ross Dalgood, who looked baby-faced behind the faceplate of his helmet, came straight to Sam and Tessa, gave his name and rank, and greeted Sam by name, evidently because he'd been shown a photograph before his mission had gotten off the ground. "Biological hazard, Agent Booker?"

"I don't think so," Sam said, as the chopper blades cycled down from a hard rhythmic cracking to a softer, wheezing chug.

"But you don't know?"

"I don't know," he admitted.

"We're the advance," Dalgood said. "Lots more on the way—regular Army and your Bureau people are coming in by highway. Be here soon."

The three of them—Dalgood, Sam, and Tessa—moved between two of the encircling cars, to one of the dead things that lay on a sidewalk bordering the park.

"I didn't believe what I saw from the air," Dalgood said.

"Believe it," Tessa said.

"What the hell?" Dalgood said.

Sam said, "Boogeymen."

38

TESSA WORRIED ABOUT SAM. SHE AND CHRISSIE AND HARRY returned to Harry's house at one in the morning, after being debriefed three times by men in decontamination suits. Although they had terrible nightmares, they managed to get a few hours' sleep. But Sam was gone all night. He had not returned by the time they finished breakfast at eleven o'clock Wednesday morning.

"He may think he's indestructible," she said, "but he's not."

"You care about him," Harry said.

"Of course I care about him."

"I mean *care* about him."

"Well . . . I don't know."

"I know."

"I know too," Chrissie said.

Sam returned at one o'clock, grimy and gray-faced. She'd made up the spare bed with fresh sheets, and he tumbled into it still half dressed.

She sat in a chair by the bed, watching him sleep. Occasionally he groaned and thrashed. He called her name and Chrissie's—and sometimes Scott's—as if he had lost them and was wandering in search of them through a dangerous and desolate place.

Bureau men in decontamination suits came for him at six o'clock, Wednesday evening, after he'd slept less than five hours. He went away for the rest of that night.

By then all the bodies, in their multitudinous biologies, had been collected from where they had fallen, tagged, sealed in plastic bags, and put into cold storage for the attention of the pathologists.

That night Tessa and Chrissie shared the same bed. Lying in the half-dark room, where a towel had been thrown over a lamp to make a night-light, the girl said, "They're gone."

"Who?"

"My mom and dad."

"I think they are."

"Dead."

"I'm sorry, Chrissie."

"Oh, I know. I know you are. You're very nice." Then for a while she cried in Tessa's arms.

Much later, nearer sleep, she said, "You talked to Sam a little. Did he say if they figured out . . . about those animals last night . . . where they were all running to?"

"No," Tessa said. "They haven't got a clue yet."

"That spooks me."

"Me too."

"I mean, that they haven't got a clue."

"I know," Tessa said. "That's what I mean too."

39

BY THURSDAY MORNING, TEAMS OF BUREAU TECHNICIANS and outside consultants from the private sector had pored through enough of the Moonhawk data in Sun to determine that the project had dealt strictly with the implantation of a nonbiological control mechanism that had resulted in profound physiological changes in the victims. No one yet had the glimmer of an idea as to how it worked, as to how the microspheres could have resulted in such radical metamorphoses, but they were certain no bacterium, virus, or other engineered organism had been involved. It was purely a matter of machines.

The Army troops, enforcing the quarantine against newsmedia interlopers and civilian curiosity-seekers, still had their work to do, but they were grateful to be able to strip out of their hot and clumsy decon suits. So were the hundreds of scientists and Bureau agents who were bivouacked throughout town.

Although Sam would surely be returning in the days ahead, he and Tessa and Chrissie were cleared for evacuation early Friday morning. A sympathetic court, with the counsel of a host of federal and state officials, had already granted Tessa temporary custody of the girl. The three of them said see-you-soon to Harry, not goodbye, and were lifted out by one of the Bureau's Bell JetRanger executive helicopters.

To keep onsite researchers from having their views colored by sensationalistic and inaccurate news accounts, a media blackout was in force in Moonlight Cove, and Sam did not fully realize the impact of the Moonhawk story until they flew over the Army roadblock near the interstate. Hundreds of press vehicles were strewn along the road and parked in fields. The pilot flew low enough for Sam to see all the cameras turned upward to shoot them as they passed over the mob.

"It's almost as bad on the county route, north of Holliwell Road," the chopper pilot said, "where they set up the other block. Reporters from all over the world, sleeping on the ground 'cause they don't want to go away to some motel and wake up to find that Moonlight Cove was opened to the press while they were snoozing."

"They don't have to worry," Sam said. "It's not going to be opened to the press—or to anyone but researchers—for weeks."

The JetRanger transported them to San Francisco International Airport, where they had reservations for three seats on a PSA flight south to Los Angeles. In the terminal, scanning the news racks, Sam read a couple of headlines:

ARTIFICIAL INTELLIGENCE BEHIND COVE TRAGEDY
SUPERCOMPUTER RUNS AMOK

That was nonsense, of course. New Wave's supercomputer, Sun, was not an artificial intelligence. No such thing had yet been built anywhere on earth, though legions of scientists were racing to be the first to father a true, thinking, electronic mind. Sun had not run amok; it had only served, as all computers do.

Paraphrasing Shakespeare, Sam thought: the fault lies not in our technology but in ourselves.

These days, however, people blamed screwups in the system on computers—just as, centuries ago, members of less sophisticated cultures had blamed the alignment of celestial bodies.

Tessa quietly pointed out another headline:

SECRET PENTAGON EXPERIMENT
BEHIND MYSTERIOUS DISASTER

The pentagon was a favorite boogeyman in some circles, almost beloved for its real and imagined evils because believing it was the root of all malevolence made life simpler and easier to understand. To those who felt that way, the Pentagon was almost the bumbling old Frankenstein monster in his clodhopper shoes and too-small black suit, scary but understandable, perverse and to be shunned yet comfortably predictable and preferable to consideration of worse and more complex villains.

Chrissie pulled from the rack a rare special edition of a major national tabloid, filled with stories about Moonlight Cove. She showed them the main headline:

ALIENS LAND ON CALIFORNIA COAST
RAVENOUS FLESH-EATERS SACK TOWN

They looked at one another solemnly for a moment, then smiled. For the first time in a couple of days, Chrissie laughed. It was not a hearty laugh, just a chuckle, and there might have been a touch of irony in it that was too sharp for an eleven-year-old girl, not to mention a trace of melancholy, but it *was* a laugh. Hearing her laugh, Sam felt better.

40

JOEL GANOWICZ, OF UNITED PRESS INTERNATIONAL, HAD been on the perimeter of Moonlight Cove, at one roadblock or another, since early Wednesday morning. He bunked in a sleeping bag on the ground, used the woods as a toilet, and paid an unemployed carpenter from Aberdeen Wells to bring meals to him. Never in his career had he been so committed to a story, willing to rough it to this extent. And he was not sure why. Yes, certainly, it was the biggest story of the decade, maybe bigger than that. But why did he feel this need to hang in there, to learn every scrap of the truth? Why was he obsessed? His behavior was a puzzle to him.

He wasn't the only one obsessed.

Though the story of Moonlight Cove had been leaked to the media in piecemeal fashion over three days and had been explored in detail during a four-hour press conference on Thursday evening, and though reporters had exhaustively inter-viewed many of the two hundred survivors, no one had had enough. The singular horror of the deaths of the victims—and the number, nearly three thousand, many times the number at Jonestown—stunned newspaper and TV audiences no matter how often they heard the specifics. By Friday morning the story was hotter than ever.

Yet Joel sensed that it wasn't even the grisliness of the facts or the spectacular statistics that gripped the public interest. It was something deeper than that.

At ten o'clock Friday morning, Joel was sitting on his bedroll in a field alongside the county route, just ten yards away from the police checkpoint north of Holliwell, basking in a surprisingly warm October morning and thinking about that very thing. He was starting to believe that maybe this news hit home hard because it was about not just the relatively modern conflict of man and machine but about the eternal human conflict, since time immemorial, between responsibility and irresponsibility, between civilization and savagery, between contradictory human impulses toward faith and nihilism.

Joel was still thinking about that when he got up and started to walk. Somewhere along the way he stopped thinking about much of anything, but he started walking more briskly.

He was not alone. Others at the roadblock, fully half the two hundred who had been waiting there, turned almost as one and walked east into the fields with sudden deliberation, neither hesitating along the way nor wandering in parabolic paths, but cutting straight up across a sloped meadow, over scrub-covered hills, and through a stand of trees.

The walkers startled those who had not felt the abrupt call to go for a stroll, and some reporters tagged along for a while, asking questions, then shouting questions. None of the walkers answered.

Joel was possessed by a feeling that there was a place he must go to, a special place, where he would never again have to worry about anything, a place where all would be provided, where he would have no need to worry about the future. He didn't know what that magic place looked like, but he knew he'd recognize it when he saw it. He hurried forward excitedly, compelled, *drawn*.

■ *Need*.

The protean thing in the basement of the Icarus Colony was in the grip of need. It had not died when the other children of Moonhawk had perished, for the microsphere computer within it had dissolved when it had first sought the freedom of utter shapelessness; it had not been able to receive the microwave-transmitted death order from Sun. Even if the command had been received, it would not have been acted upon, for the cellar-dwelling creature had no heart to stop.

Need.

Its need was so intense that it pulsed and writhed. This need was more profound than mere desire, more terrible than any pain.

Need.

Mouths had opened all over its surface. The thing called out to the world around it in a voice that seemed silent but was not, a voice that spoke not to the ears of its prey but to their minds.

And they were coming.

Its needs would soon be fulfilled.

■ Colonel Lewis Tarker, Commanding Officer at the Army field headquarters in the park at the eastern end of Ocean Avenue, received an urgent call from Sergeant Sperlmont, who was in charge of the county-route roadblock. Sperlmont reported losing six of his twelve men when they just walked off like zombies, with maybe a hundred reporters who were in the same strange condition.

"Something's up," he told Tarker. "This isn't over yet, sir."

■ Tarker immediately got hold of Oren Westrom, the Bureau man who was heading the investigation into Moonhawk and with whom all of the military aspects of the operation had to be coordinated.

"It isn't over," Tarker told Westrom. "I think those walkers are even weirder than Sperlmont described them, weird in some way he can't quite convey. I know him, and he's more spooked than he thinks he is."

■ Westrom in turn, ordered the Bureau's Jetranger into the air. He explained the situation to the pilot, Jim Lobbow, and said, "Sperlmont's going to have some of his men track them on the ground, see where the hell they're going—and why. But in case that gets difficult, I want you spotting from the air."

"On my way," Lobbow said.

"You filled up on fuel recently?"

"Tanks are brimming."

"Good."

■   Nothing worked for Jim Lobbow but flying a chopper.

He had been married three times, and every marriage had ended in divorce. He'd lived with more women than he could count; even without the pressure of marriage weighing him down, he could not sustain a relationship. He had one child, a son, by his second marriage, but he saw the boy no more than three times a year, never for longer than a day at a time. Though he'd been brought up in the Catholic Church, and though all his brothers and sisters were regulars at Mass, that did not work for Jim. Sunday always seemed to be the only morning he could sleep in, and when he considered going to a weekday service it seemed like too much trouble. Though he dreamed of being an entrepreneur, every small business he started seemed doomed to failure; he was repeatedly startled to find how much work went into a business, even one that seemed designed for absentee management, and sooner or later it always became too much trouble.

But nobody was a better chopper pilot than Jim Lobbow. He could take one up in weather that grounded everyone else, and he could set down or pick up in any terrain, any conditions.

He took the JetRanger up at Westrom's orders and swung out over the county-route roadblock, getting there in no time because the day was blue and clear, and the roadblock was just a mile and a quarter from the park where he kept the chopper. On the ground, a handful of regular Army troops, still at the barricade, were waving him due east, up into the hills.

Lobbow went where they told him, and in less than a minute he found the walkers toiling busily up scrub-covered hills, scuffing their shoes, tearing their clothes, but scrambling forward in a frenzy. It was definitely weird.

A funny buzzing filled his head. He thought something was wrong with his radio headphones, and he pulled them off for a moment, but that wasn't it. The buzzing didn't stop. Actually it wasn't a buzzing at all, not a sound, but a *feeling*.

And what do I mean by that? he wondered.

He tried to shrug it off.

The walkers were circling east-southeast as they went, and he flew ahead of them, looking for some landmark, anything unusual toward which they might be headed. He came almost at once to the decaying Victorian house, the tumbledown barn, and the collapsed outbuildings.

Something about the place drew him.

He circled it once, twice.

Though it was a complete dump, he suddenly had the crazy idea that he would be happy there, free, with no worries any more, no ex-wives nagging at him, no child-support to pay.

Over the hills to the northwest, the walkers were coming, all hundred or more of them, not walking any more but running. They stumbled and fell but got up and ran again.

And Jim knew why they were coming. He circled over the house again, and it was the most appealing place he had ever seen, a source of surcease. He wanted that freedom, that release, more than he had ever wanted anything in his life. He took the JetRanger up in a steep climb, leveled out, swooped south, then west, then north, then east, coming all the way around again, back toward the house, the wonderful house, he had to be there, had to go there, had to go, and he took the chopper straight in through the front porch, directly at the door that hung open and half off its hinges, through the wall, plowing straight into the heart of the house, burying the chopper in the heart—

■ *Need.*
The creature's many mouths sang of its need, and it knew that momentarily its needs would be met. It throbbed with excitement.

Then vibrations. Hard vibrations. Then heat.

It did not recoil from the heat, for it had surrendered all the nerves and complex biological structures required to register pain.

The heat had no meaning for the beast—except that heat was not food and therefore did not fulfill its needs.

Burning, dwindling, it tried to sing the song that would draw what it required, but the roaring flames filled its mouths and soon silenced it.

■ Joel Ganowicz found himself standing two hundred feet from a ramshackle house that had exploded in flames. It was a tremendous blaze, fire shooting a hundred feet into the clear sky, black smoke beginning to billow up, the old walls of the place collapsing in upon themselves with alacrity, as if eager to give up the pretense of usefulness. The heat washed over him, forcing him to squint and back away, even though he was not particularly close to it. He couldn't understand how a little dry wood could burn that intensely.

He realized that he could not remember how the fire had started. He was just suddenly *there,* in front of it.

He looked at his hands. They were abraded and filthy.

The right knee was torn out of his corduroys, and his Rockports were badly scuffed.

He looked around and was startled to see scores of people in his same condition, tattered and dirty and dazed. He couldn't remember how he had gotten there, and he definitely didn't recall setting out on a group hike.

The house sure was burning, though. Wouldn't be a stick of it left, just a cellarful of ashes and hot coals.

He frowned and rubbed his forehead.

Something had happened to him. Something . . . He was a reporter, and his curiosity was gradually reasserting itself. Something had happened, and he ought to find out what. Something disturbing. *Very* disturbing. But at least it was over now.

He shivered.

41

WHEN THEY ENTERED THE HOUSE IN SHERMAN OAKS, THE music on Scott's stereo, upstairs, was turned so loud that the windows were vibrating.

Sam climbed the steps to the second floor, motioning for Tessa and Chrissie to follow. They were reluctant, probably embarrassed, feeling out of place, but he was not certain he could do what had to be done if he went up there alone.

The door to Scott's room was open.

The boy was lying on his bed, wearing black jeans and a black denim shirt. His feet were toward the headboard, his head at the foot of the mattress, propped up on pillows, so he could stare at all of the posters on the wall behind the bed: black-metal rockers wearing leather and chains, some of them with bloody hands, some with bloody lips as if they were vampires who had just fed, others holding skulls, one of them french-kissing a skull, another holding out cupped hands filled with glistening maggots.

Scott didn't hear Sam enter. With the music at that volume, he wouldn't have heard a thermonuclear blast in the adjacent bathroom.

At the stereo Sam hesitated, wondering if he was doing the right thing. Then he listened to the bellowed words of the number on the machine, backed up by iron slabs of guitar chords. It was a song about killing your parents, about drinking their blood, then "taking the gas-pipe escape." Nice. Oh, very nice stuff. That decided him. He punched a button and cut off the CD in midplay.

Startled, Scott sat straight up in bed. "Hey!"

Sam took the CD out of the player, dropped it on the floor, and ground it under his heel.

"Hey, Christ, what the hell are you doing?"

Forty or fifty CDs, mostly black-metal albums, were stored in open-front cases on a shelf above the stereo. Sam swept them to the floor.

"Hey, come on," Scott said, "what're you, nuts?"

"Something I should've done long ago."

Noticing Tessa and Chrissie, who stood just outside the door, Scott said, "Who the hell are they?"

Sam said, "They the hell are friends."

Really working himself into a rage, all lathered up, the boy said, "What the fuck are they doing here, man?"

Sam laughed. He was feeling almost giddy. He wasn't sure why. Maybe because he was finally doing something about this situation, assuming responsibility for it. He said, "They the fuck are with me." And he laughed again.

He felt sorry that he had exposed Chrissie to this, but then he looked at her and saw that she was not only unshaken but giggling. He realized that all the angry and bad words in the world couldn't hurt her, not after what she had endured. In fact, after what they'd all seen in Moonlight Cove, Scott's teenage nihilism *was* funny and even sort of innocent, altogether ridiculous.

Sam stood on the bed and began to tear the posters off the wall, and Scott started screaming at him, opening up full volume, a real tantrum this time. Sam finished with those posters he could reach only from the bed, got down, and turned toward those on another wall.

Scott grabbed him.

Gently, Sam pushed the boy aside and clawed at the other posters.

Scott struck him.

Sam took the blow, then looked at him.

Scott's face was brilliant red, his nostrils dilated, his eyes bulging with hatred.

Smiling, Sam embraced him in a bear hug.

At first Scott clearly didn't understand what was happening. He thought his father was just making a grab for him, going to punish him, so he tried to pull away. But suddenly it dawned on him—Sam could *see* it dawn on him—he was being hugged, his old man was for God's sake embracing him, and in front of people—strangers. When that realization hit him, the boy *really* began to struggle, twisting and thrashing, pushing hard against Sam, desperate to escape, because this didn't fit into his belief in a loveless world, especially if he started to respond.

That was it, yes, damn, Sam understood now. That was the reason behind Scott's alienation. A fear that he'd respond to love, respond and be spurned . . . or find the responsibility of commitment too much to bear.

In fact, for a moment, the boy met his father's love with love of his own, hugged him tight. It was as if the real Scott, the kid hidden under the layers of hipness and cynicism, had peeked through and smiled. Something good remained in him, good and pure, something that could be salvaged.

But then the boy began to curse Sam in more explicit and colorful terms than he had used previously. Sam only hugged him harder, closer, and now Sam began to tell him that he loved him, desperately loved him, told him not the way that he had told him he loved him on the telephone when he had called him from Moonlight Cove on Monday night, not with any degree of reservation occasioned by his own sense of hopelessness, because he *had* no sense of hopelessness any more. This time, when he told Scott that he loved him, he spoke in a voice cracking with emotion, told him again and again, demanded that his love be heard.

Scott was crying now, and Sam was not surprised to find that he was crying, too, but he didn't think they were crying for the same reason yet, because the boy was still struggling to get away, his energy depleted, but still struggling. So Sam held on to him and talked to him: "Listen, kid, you're going to care about me, one way or the other, sooner or later. Oh, yes. You're going to know that I care about you, and then you're going to care about me, and not just me, no, you're going to care about yourself, too, and it's not going to stop there, either, hell, no, you're going to find out you can care about a lot of people, that it feels good to care. You're going to care about that woman standing there in the doorway, and you're going to care about that little girl, you're going to care about her like you'd care about a sister, you're going to *learn,* you're going to get the damn machine out of you and learn to be loved and to love. There's a guy going to come visit us, a guy who's got one good hand and no good legs, and *he* believes life is worth living. Maybe he's going to stay a while, see how he likes it, see how he feels about it, 'cause maybe he can show you what I was too slow to show you—that it's good, life's good. And this guy's got a dog, what a dog, you're going to love that dog, probably the dog first." Sam laughed and held fast to Scott. "You can't say 'Get outta my face' to a dog and expect him to listen or care, he won't get out of your face, so you'll have to love him first. But then you'll get around to loving me, because that's what I'm going to be—a dog, just a smiling old dog, padding around the place, hanging on, impervious to insult, an old dog."

Scott had stopped struggling. He was probably just exhausted. Sam was sure that he had not really gotten through the boy's rage. Hadn't more than scratched the surface. Sam had let an evil into their lives, the evil of self-indulgent despair, which he transmitted to the boy, and now rooting it out would be a hard job. They had a long way to go, months of struggle, maybe even years, lots of hugging, lots of holding on tight and not letting go.

Looking over Scott's shoulder, he saw that Tessa and Chrissie had stepped into the room. They were crying too. In their eyes he saw an awareness that matched his, a recognition that the battle for Scott had only begun.

But it *had* begun. That was the wonderful thing. It *had* begun.

A NOTE TO
MY READERS

MOOSE, THE LABRADOR WHO SO ABLY SERVES HARRY TALBOT IN
Midnight, is based upon actual service dogs trained by Canine Companions for
Independence, a non-profit organization that provides its furry assistants at nom-
inal cost to those who need them. All dogs give us love and loyalty, but *these*
splendid animals give even more than usual; they literally transform the lives of
the disabled people with whom they are paired, serving as their arms or legs or
eyes or ears, and allowing them to venture into the world with confidence. The
bond that exists between these service dogs and their masters is inspiring, enno-
bling, and deeply moving to anyone who loves humanity or dogs—or both. If you
set aside part of your income for charity, I urge you to consider a donation to
Canine Companions for Independence:

> 4350 Occidental Road
> P.O. Box 446
> Santa Rosa, California 95402-0446

This is a rare opportunity to make a *real* difference in the world.

—Dean Koontz